DUST
of the
EARTH

Also by Tim Murgatroyd:

THE CHINA TRILOGY:
Taming Poison Dragons
Breaking Bamboo
The Mandate of Heaven

The Nazi's Daughter

THE PILGRIM TRILOGY:
Pilgrim Tale
Pilgrim Lost
Pilgrim City

The Electric

PLAYS:
Sea Stories
Rip Tides

DUST
of the
EARTH

Tim Murgatroyd

MYRMIDON

Myrmidon
Rotterdam House
116 Quayside
Newcastle upon Tyne
NE1 3DY

www.myrmidonbooks.com
First published in the United Kingdom by Myrmidon 2024

Set in Bembo MT Std by Ellipsis, Glasgow

Printed in the UK by CPI Group (UK) Ltd, Croydon, CRO 4YY

ISBN 978-1-910183-35-9

A catalogue record for this book is available from the British Library.

1 3 5 7 9 10 8 6 4 2

For Dori and Jim Murgatroyd

Contents

Author's Note

Writing historical fiction can often involve walking a tightrope between the sensibilities of past times and our own. When writing and editing *Dust of the Earth*, I thought long and hard about including words that, freighted with racism as they are, would inevitably chafe contemporary sensitivities. To take one example, Chinese males in 1870s California would be, at best, referred to as 'Chinamen', and too often in far more abusive terms. Californian Native Americans were usually called Diggers, African-Americans were called Negroes (both by more enlightened sections of the white population and reform-seeking African-Americans themselves) or just routinely abused with the altogether more egregious term also beginning with 'n'. There were disparaging epithets for other groups too, such as the English, Italians, Irish, Scots, Polish, Jews and Hispanics.

Faced with that reality, what is a writer to do? Censor past ignorance or let the world being depicted speak with its own harsh, misguided and iniquitous tongue? I opted for the latter, hopeful that readers would recognise *Dust of the Earth* is a novel that not only opposes, but ridicules and defies racism in all its forms, a call for unity between all human beings and peoples with a message that love is always bigger and finer than prejudice.

I started writing the novel over a decade ago, before the term *cultural appropriation* had entered my consciousness. At the time, I firmly believed there is one race on this earth, the human race. It seemed to me then that people in all places and times are driven by similar essential imperatives – love, belonging, children, status, the need for philosophy, religion, family loyalties, moral codes and beliefs, the desire for security and prosperity – and that what differs from age to age, and society to society, are the cultural forms those imperatives take. Nothing in the intervening years has persuaded me otherwise.

So, to anyone who may feel offended that I, a white Englishman, should write from the character perspective of a mixed-race Chinese man or, as a male, a Frenchwoman, I urge them to consider these points. Firstly, that every human being has the capacity to access the inner lives of their fellow humans to some degree, not exactly or completely – how can we, when it is so hard to know our own contradictory and multi-layered selves truly? Secondly, that without the greatest forms of inner 'cultural appropriation' granted to us – namely, empathy, sympathy, instincts of loving kindness, tolerance, acceptance and the celebration of differences yet connections between people – there can be no hope for lasting peace in the world.

Which brings me to the Heavenly Kingdom of Great Peace. This is not the place to discuss the Taiping Revolution's complex genesis and history. For those wishing to learn more about this genuinely astonishing period of history, can I suggest they begin with Jonathon Spence's classic, *God's Chinese Son*, and then seek out primary sources and accounts of that tumultuous era. Millenarian movements are not restricted to history. Our troubled, divided world can learn much from appreciating how belief systems of all kinds – including the apparently 'moderate' – can be twisted by ambitious, greedy men and women to secure power before their rule blows away like all dust, scattered by winds of time.

Historical Note

Between 1850 and 1864 the Taiping ('Great Peace') Rebellion tore China apart. Inspired by the self-styled Heavenly King, Hong Xiuquan, a humble village schoolmaster who believed himself to be Jesus's younger brother, the Taiping rebels almost toppled the ruling Ching Dynasty. Their aim: to establish a Heavenly Kingdom on earth where land was shared among the poor, opium banned, women freed from foot-binding and China modernised. Millions believed the Taiping Heavenly Kingdom would arise from the ashes of civil war . . . A holy war that claimed twenty to thirty million lives.

And the Lord said . . . I will make thy seed as the dust of the earth.

Genesis, 13

SEED

San Francisco, California
September 1877

Where Chinatown's frontier grated against white Frisco stood two crooked, soot-stained buildings. The first, a cigar factory, the other a Chinese warehouse stacked with exports for Canton. Between these buildings lay an alley whose best light was shadow. A hand-painted sign in Chinese and English hung beside the entrance:

CHI-EN SHAMBLES

TRANSLATOR OF NINE LANGUAGES ANCIENT AND MODERN

LEGAL COUNSEL OFFERED AT GENEROUS RATES

Anyone tempted to consult Mr Shambles had to brave the alley and its carpet of crunching cinders. At the end was an airshaft between the sweatshop and warehouse. There, another hand-painted sign hung above a fog-blistered door: *Shambles*.

He sat at a writing table beneath a barred window providing the apartment's only light. Though he could not settle, his high cheek-boned face appeared calm. An unlit cigarette dangled between delicate fingers that

3

had known rough work before the calluses softened. He glanced frequently at a tin pocket watch open on the table.

At the age of thirty, Chi-en Shambles was either unusually tall or merely of good height — depending which half of his parentage you considered decisive. His complexion and curved eyes suggested a Chinaman, as did his thick black hair. The square jaw implied English forebears.

He reached for a match to light the cigarette. The flame revealed a room clean but bare, the home of someone who invested little faith in the future. Only his bookshelves showed signs of love. Yet he had lived there for two years, fortunate to rent such large quarters. Countless families in San Francisco shared single rooms.

He glanced at the watch. An hour to go before the *California Star* reached newsboys in his neighbourhood.

For a moment he considered the fate awaiting this evening's *California Star*. Some might consider his arguments and be swayed. Libraries all over America would preserve the newspaper within leather ledgers and future scholars might ask: *Who was this Shambles fellow?* He ground out the cigarette. Far, far better men than him were forgotten sooner than last year's rain . . .

He took out a thick, clothbound notebook from a drawer. Its title page was inscribed in intricate, hand-drawn letters: *A Modest Memoir of Prince Hong*. The loving script was his own. Yet the rest of the notebook was empty, waiting to be filled. Cinders crunched outside and he hid it away.

Opening the door, he was confronted by cold, almond eyes. His visitor wore a Chinese embroidered silk tunic, whereas Chi-en's shirt and waistcoat were European. His caller's hair, too, conformed to the laws of the Manchu Emperor in their distant homeland: a shaved forehead and long braided pigtail. By contrast Chi-en's hung loose to his shoulders.

'Secretary Ah Ling,' said Chi-en in flawless Cantonese dialect. 'Please honour my home.'

Ah Ling examined him warily. Perhaps he feared the half *fan gui* or foreign devil before him employed dark magic to recreate the exact accent of his home village. After all, the secretary must have heard him apply the same magic to others, white and Chinese.

'Mister Sha-bells,' replied Ah Ling in haughty Mandarin, 'I come from the Presidents of the Six Companies. They require you at Hang Far Low Restaurant.'

'*Require?*'

'At once.'

'I would be honoured,' said Chi-en. 'Perhaps I should dress for dinner?'

'No.'

'Then I take it you are here on business?'

'We go at once.'

'*You* shall go,' said Chi-en. 'First, there is something I must do.'

Ah Ling stiffened. 'The Presidents will be displeased.'

'Please tender my apologies.'

Ah Ling crunched back across the cinders in sabots and thick white socks. A young Chinese man waited in the airshaft, cradling something in his open tunic: a blackjack or knife. Maybe, given the danger in venturing out of Chinatown since last month's riots, a revolver.

Chi-en donned a black frock coat and plain bow tie, concealing his face below a broad-brimmed hat. Then he locked his room and left the relative safety of Portsmouth Square.

It took longer than usual to locate a newsboy selling the *California Star*. The paper was in demand that twilight, on account of a long speech denouncing the Coolie Threat delivered by a popular demagogue in the city, Denis Kearney. Back in Portsmouth Square, Chi-en chose an empty bench.

He soon found the article bearing his name. At once he stiffened. His palms began to sweat. Only then, heart thumping, did he comprehend the danger he had blundered into – and why the Six Presidents *required* him.

Yesterday there had been no question of fear. His mood had been triumphant. Hired by the Six Companies to compose a letter to the President of the United States himself, Ulysses S. Grant. The intention: to frustrate the Mayor of San Francisco's campaign to halt further Chinese immigration. The Six Companies' leaders, all wealthy businessmen, had listened in respectful silence as he read aloud the completed document.

'Mr Sha-bells has done the Six Companies a great service!' declared his friend and patron, Lu Kan of the Kong Chow Company.

Emboldened, Chi-en asked, 'Sirs, can it be you do not intend to publish this letter in the press? Are you really sending it in secret? That is not how one gains influence in this country. I urge you to reconsider.' His answer had been six suspicious faces. Only Lu Kan saw some merit in his suggestion.

That night Chi-en had celebrated with a large jug of Californian claret. How, he asked himself, could his compatriots be so blind? Their hope lay in swaying fellow Americans. To do that one must use newspapers. Drunk, he composed his own letter for the press.

Dear Fellow Human Beings, he had begun, chuckling at his own wit. *It is a scarcely acknowledged truth that everyone dwelling between New York and San Francisco is descended from immigrants – unless, of course, you are an Indian.* And so it had run on: four neatly written pages proving the benefits of Chinese immigration and condemning the angry mob that murdered four Chinese and burned down a dozen buildings in Chinatown a month earlier. His favourite part had been an extended allusion to Shakespeare.

It had been with pride that he signed the letter: *Most sincerely, Mr Chi-en Shambles of Portsmouth Square, San Francisco.*

How he had paced with delight at his cleverness! How sure he had been of success. Perhaps the wine was to blame, unless years of anger made him reckless. Whatever the reason, Chi-en had donned his best European clothes and delivered his appeal to the offices of the *California Star*. Returning to his room, he drank yet more wine and smoked cigarette after cigarette, too excited for sleep.

But in the hands of the *California Star* his heartfelt arguments suffered a grotesque change. The letter assigned to 'Mr Chi-en Shambles' ran thus:

Lookee here Whiteman! You and Diggers and Greasers all same numbah one bad fellow! We wan' votee bad so Whiteman Pres'dent we choose! Then you not waste so much water washin' but use to boil lice! We wan' nice big numbah one b'som White Woman for two or three nice Wifee. Ha! Then we send she back to spez'l bizness in Peking owned by Uncle M'ngol Woo Woo! We Chinaman jus' like you white fella on'y smell differen'! You get to likee me smellee lots when we take over Californee! Then you come to Chinatown look sharp an' give us plenee dollar to sen' back Chinee! An' don' forget bring White Wifee with big b'som! Signee: Mistah Chi-en Shambles of Portsmouth Square, Chinatown.

He closed the newspaper. Struggled to roll a cigarette. In the tinderbox of San Francisco, here was a spark to re-ignite the mob that had burned and lynched in Chinatown. Worst of all, they had printed his address.

Hang Far Low Restaurant was on Dupont Street in the heart of Chinatown, a few minutes' walk from Portsmouth Square. Chi-en loitered on the wooden sidewalk opposite.

Hang Far Low rose in three broad storeys, the top two marked by ornate wooden balconies where globe lanterns hung beside dwarf trees in splendid pots. Chi-en knew from leaner days the basement would be full of labourers and unemployed men dining on rice or noodles. The top floor – it was here Chi-en expected to be led – contained the Grand Dining Room, a place he had visited just once, as the guest of Lu Kan. In the vestibule he found Secretary Ah Ling.

'Secretary!' exclaimed Chi-en, adopting the man's Cantonese dialect. As usual, Ah Ling looked uneasy.

'You are very late, Mister Sha-bells,' he said, in Mandarin.

'I came as soon as I could.'

'You will be sorry. Follow me.'

At first, Chi-en felt inclined to refuse. Allowing yourself to be addressed as an underling was the first step to becoming one. But he followed the bustling little man up the stairs to the Grand Dining Room.

It was an island of splendour in Chinatown. Proof of fortunes to be made. Panels inlaid with mother-of-pearl and exquisite lacquers hung beside carved teak screens. Lanterns created a cheerful glow. A dozen waiters lined the walls, ready to scurry forward.

Ah Ling led him to the very back of the banqueting hall. A private salon had been set up behind thick silk drapes and two burly men guarded the entrance.

'In there,' said Ah Ling. Then he leaned forward and Chi-en at last understood the man's animosity. 'Longhair scum!' he hissed. 'Taiping rebel! Your Heavenly Army killed my brother. Where is your Heavenly King now?'

Chi-en met the man's eyes. 'Many fine men perished in that rebellion. On both sides. I am sorry to hear your brother was among them.'

Within the private salon, two round tables had been placed together. Dozens of porcelain dishes were arranged across the red and gold tablecloth. At each table sat three soft-bellied men in late middle age, their turquoise, yellow and pink silk robes glinting in the candlelight. All wore black silk pillbox caps over a shaved forehead and dangling pigtail. The corners of their mouths drooped with stern authority.

'Mister Sha-bells,' began the eldest of the Presidents, Zhi Tong. 'You have many charges to answer.'

Chi-en looked around for a chair. There was none.

'Secretary Ah Ling has been discourteous to me,' he said. 'And now I am expected to stand before you like a criminal. How is this, Honoured Sirs?'

Zhi Tong smiled thinly. 'Perhaps you are a kind of criminal.'

At this Lu Kan stirred. He had been Chi-en's regular employer for over a year. 'We run ahead of ourselves,' he warned. 'We must hear all sides of this story.'

'Perhaps,' said Zhi Tong. 'Mister Sha-bells, I see you carry a copy of the *California Star*. We have found out you sent a long letter to the editor, based upon our private communication to President Grant.'

'That is true.' Chi-en realised he was sweating. 'I take it you have read the forgery? My original bears no resemblance to it.'

'Your work as translator for the Six Companies means you are closely associated with us,' continued Zhi Tong. His voice rose in angry accusation, a tone Chi-en remembered from mandarins in the old country. 'Your *letter*, as you call it, shames us and weakens our position in San Francisco!'

Chi-en laughed hollowly. 'The *California Star* should blush, not I.'

'Mister Sha-bells,' said another President, sporting a walrus moustache. 'Do you not know our great enemy, the trouble-maker Denis Kearney, has read out your letter in a speech to his followers tonight? Our spy at the meeting tells us he called for vengeance against its author on behalf of all white women. Here are his exact words.'

Chi-en took the paper and read: *Any Chinese slave wanting to fawn before his masters on Nob Hill should take heed! Judge Lynch is a close ally of the workingmen in this city*! There was more concerning Judge Lynch's habit of dangling Mongolian savages with lustful designs on white women from the first convenient lamppost.

Chi-en bowed stiffly. 'Hateful nonsense! Thank you for bringing it to my attention.' No one replied. His temper flickered. 'You are afraid there will be another riot against our people. Sirs, I also think you believe President Grant will reply to your appeal as an Emperor might, issuing a great edict all Americans will obey. Sirs, only by making the laws just and equal shall we have freedom in America. We must not be silenced by threats or forgeries. Put our case before the American people. Persuade them to change their laws!'

Zhi Tong's chopsticks pointed straight at Chi-en's face. 'For all your scholarship and cleverness, it is *you* who is wrong! The only Americans who help us are those who wish to exploit us.'

He did not speak without reason. Each day the press circulated cartoons depicting Johnny Chink as a heathen devil, a locust ravaging fields of corn and stealing jobs from hapless white boys.

'Sirs,' said Chi-en, 'though a just cause may be unpopular, one is bound by honour to espouse it, whatever the danger. Did not Confucius teach us that? Every drip of truth wears down our opponents' lies.'

Lu Kan coughed and turned to his fellows. 'See! It is as I said. Mister Sha-bells' motives are noble. He is full of ideals. A scholar.'

Hostile faces met this plea.

'Consider also,' continued Lu Kan, 'the many services Mister Sha-bells performs for the poorest of our people in Chinatown. I believe dozens have benefited in the matter of legal advice and certificates from the city authorities. Think how he helps them for little or no charge.'

'No, my friend,' interrupted Zhi Tong, 'I beg to remind you we have already decided. Mister Sha-bells, listen and listen well. As Presidents of the Six Companies, it is our duty to protect this community. Your reckless ways put us all in danger. Who knows if a mob has not gathered to punish you – and us – even as we speak. Henceforth, you are forbidden to remain in Chinatown. Go! *Go!*'

Chi-en listened in amazement. 'But where? For how long?'

'Until it is safe for you to return,' broke in Lu Kan.

'That will be a long time,' muttered Zhi Tong.

Chi-en recovered his voice. 'You are not the law! You are not a jury. Only a court may banish a man . . .' Before he could say more, strong hands pinioned his arms.

'Do not be found in Chinatown at dawn,' warned Zhi Tong, taking up his ivory chopsticks and extracting a cube of chicken from a porcelain bowl. With a grunt, he popped it in his mouth and chewed.

Chi-en knew that men banished by the Six Companies generally found themselves savagely beaten if caught in Chinatown. Some ended up floating in the Bay.

He was hustled down a narrow flight of stairs at the back of the restaurant and shoved through a rear entrance into a courtyard. Rats scuttled into shadows and the door slammed behind him.

As Chi-en entered the dark streets it seemed Zhi Tong's fears were justified. A dozen Chinamen outside a butcher's store discussed how a compatriot had been attacked near the docks, his body tossed off a pier. Soon afterwards he encountered an acquaintance who called out: 'Take care . . . a mob left a meeting . . . Denis Kearney . . . they want trouble.' Shutters were going up on the borders of Chinatown.

Yet Portsmouth Square was quiet. Still he hesitated in a doorway, examining shadows that might conceal enemies, before strolling down the tarred boards of the sidewalk. Danger prickled his gut, even as he entered the alley between the sweatshop and warehouse. No unwanted visitors were apparent.

Locking his door behind him, he secured the bolts before lighting a lamp. Never had the simple apartment seemed so welcoming. The airshaft had been his most permanent home since fleeing China fifteen years before.

His purse contained a handful of silver dollars and loose change: ten dollars or so. He had earned a large fee for the letter to President Ulysses S. Grant but also spent recklessly – some given to beggars, far more on respectable clothes. Above all, on a three volume Californian Legal Code and Constitution bound in leather. This costly purchase had been an attempt to find a new purpose in life. He believed the books might help him secure justice for his abused countrymen. That noble intention mocked Chi-en now. Those same compatriots had expelled him from Chinatown without recourse to any law except naked power.

He dragged out a dusty carpetbag from a corner near the low, back door of the apartment, an exit he never used, hastily thrusting in spare clothes, a writing case, his precious notebook, *A Modest Memoir of Prince Hong*. Finally, he tied the heavy volumes of the Californian Legal Code in a bundle with sturdy leather straps. Only then did he become aware of whispers in the airshaft. Boots crunching cinders.

'Is this the one? We've got the sonofabitch, boys! Tight as a cunny hole!'

The voices grew loud, careless. Shadowy faces peered in through the grimy, barred window. A speculative rattle shook the door.

'Git that Celestial son o' bitch righ' now, boys!'

Chi-en had seen enough war and massacre in his youth to know when to flee. Blowing out the lamp, he seized his stick, hat and coat, grabbed the bag and bundle of law books. In a moment he was at the backdoor.

'Hey! The light's gone out! Heave that door!'

A jarring crash. Feverishly, Chi-en yanked the stiff metal bar of the backdoor. It moved a fraction.

'Nearly through! More shoulder!'

He tore at the bar so hard it cut his fingers. At last, the metal rose. Realising the door opened outward rather than inward, he booted. A loud crack and the fog-swollen wood parted from the frame. He dived into an alley, a narrow crevasse between buildings.

'It's a-going, me boyos! Let's see how he likes his white women then!'

Chi-en slammed shut the back door just as the front burst open. From within came inarticulate bellows, furniture smashing. Bracing his stick against the brick wall, he jammed it hard against the back door. The stick was stout and lead-knobbed, meant for defence in the harsh streets. It would hold the door a good while.

He crept down the alley, drawn by a tiny glow. The passage turned at an angle so acute that Chi-en struggled to squeeze through. At the end, blocking his escape, stood a towering, bowler-hatted man in a worn brown suit. A pickaxe handle dangled from his meaty fist. A band played lustily in the adjacent Bella Union Theater.

Ducking low, Chi-en advanced until the alley widened. If he could only get past, he might disappear into the bustle of Market Street. The man in the brown suit yawned, then Chi-en stepped on a bottle and it skittered away. At once the big man turned. His eyes were blue and unflinching.

'Why, goodness, excuse me, sir!' cried Chi-en in a fussy Boston accent, pulling his hat low to conceal his face. 'I'd appreciate it mightily if you stepped aside.'

'Now then, me fellah,' replied the other. 'Where might you be goin'?'

The pickaxe handle rose to bar his way. With a lunge, Chi-en leapt at him, carpetbag and law books thrust out as a battering ram.

'Ya' divil!' roared the man. The pickaxe handle bounced harmlessly off the books. Chi-en paused long enough to drop his carpetbag and smash the heavy volumes into his opponent's face with all his strength.

There was a spurt of blood. Then Chi-en swung the books hard into the side of the Irishman's head. His opponent staggered back. Dropping the law books, Chi-en scooped up the carpetbag and was free, running down cobbles, dodging a hack pulled by two trotting horses, until he veered into a side road leading back to Chinatown.

Moments later men emerged from the narrow alley to find their comrade on his knees, blood running down his face. While they eagerly questioned him, lighting matches to examine his injuries, no one saw an arm reach out from behind a stack of old wooden crates and drag the law books out of sight.

Chi-en knew Californian justice well enough to anticipate the penalty for a Chinaman injuring a white man. Attempted murder was the probable charge. If Judge Lynch did not get him first, any court would find a single verdict. Self-defence could not apply: a Chinaman was virtually barred from acting as a witness against anyone of the white race. Assuming Chi-en did not hang, mercy might consist of a lifetime in a State penitentiary – a lifetime that would prove painfully short.

Back in Chinatown, Chi-en squeezed his purse and considered Lu Kan. Not only did the President of the Kong Chow Company owe him money, he had spoken out in his defence. And he had always proved honourable in the past.

Lu Kan's principal business address and home lay on Sacramento Street. Carpetbag in hand, Chi-en entered the large store. He had been here many times as a respected business associate; though Lu Kan spoke excellent English, he fared less well when it came to drawing up contracts.

The bazaar was lined with shiny wooden shelves containing imports from the home country: opium, silk, lacquered boxes and statuettes, bronze ornaments, precious teas. Hissing gaslights illuminated the long room.

'Young Master Lu,' said Chi-en in Cantonese, nodding to a youth in silks stood uneasily before the till. 'Delighted to see you again.'

The young man was Lu Kan's eldest son. Chi-en glanced to the side. Secretary Ah Ling perched stiffly on a high-backed chair. Behind him were the same two bravos who had ejected Chi-en from Hang Far Low Restaurant. Lu Kan's son scowled.

'You're not welcome here,' said Ah Ling. His normally bland features contorted: 'Longhair rebel devil! Your Taiping magic is broken!'

Chi-en ignored him. 'Master Lu, may I see your honoured father?'

The young man looked to Ah Ling. 'You will get nothing here,' warned the Secretary. 'It is time for you to vanish.'

At this the bravos stirred.

'Yes!' cried Lu Kan's son, shrilly. 'You think you are clever not shaving your forehead as the Emperor commands. My father does not need you!'

'Show Mister Sha-bells the street,' Ah Ling ordered the bravos.

One withdrew a revolver from his tunic so the barrel rested across his stomach.

Chi-en raised a hand. 'Please, gentlemen, that will not be necessary.' He turned to Lu Kan's son. 'One day you will need to explain this dishonourable action to your father. It is for him to decide who he sees, not you. Then Secretary Ah Ling will seem a false counsellor.'

Ah Ling leapt to his feet. 'Escort this Taiping devil-magician to the borders of Chinatown! If he tries to come back, take him to an alley and shoot him.'

The two men bowed. Chi-en anticipated them by striding out of the bazaar so briskly that they trotted to keep up. For the first time he felt defiance drain away. Passersby stepped aside, eyeing his escort nervously.

'Hey, Mister Sha-bells!' Chi-en recognised a pigtailed fortune-teller from Portsmouth Square. 'I have . . .'

Chi-en dared not pause to listen. His heart hammered painfully. At the corner of Sacramento Street, he bowed to his escort and hurried into the Saturday night crowds.

Twelve hours later, Chi-en loitered on the waterfront seeking a ferry to anywhere – so long as it was away from San Francisco. Longshoremen came and went amidst shouts, rumbling wheels, clattering hooves on cobblestones and the stench of horse manure and burning coals.

He found himself beside a wooden jetty where a narrow, single-funnelled river steamer loaded crates and passengers. A chalked blackboard indicated the boat was bound for Napa City.

His heart quickened. Two policemen approached, swinging their billy clubs nonchalantly. He had to decide. And at once. All he knew about Napa Valley was that wine came from there.

Drawing himself up, Chi-en walked as Chinamen never dared walk outside the safety of Dupont Street, his shoulders back, head held high. In European clothes, hat brim low over his face, no one paid him attention. On the jetty a steward sold tickets from a roll. The man barely glanced at Chi-en, too busy eyeing a group of Chinese labourers waiting to board the steamer.

'Lots of 'em going over to Napa for the harvest,' said the steward. 'There's a big warren o' rice bunnies up in Perryville. Second biggest Chinatown in the State.'

'That so?' asked Chi-en, in a perfect Galway accent. 'Who'd o' thought such a thing?'

'They're cheap.' The man tore off a ticket. 'Poor bastards.'

Chi-en took a seat facing the Bay, away from the waterfront. Out of the corner of his eye he watched the policemen saunter past, still swinging their clubs. Soon the boat cast off. Warehouses and wharfs, tenements and millionaire palaces on Nob Hill, his hopes and fears in that city, shrank and dwindled. He would have wept — longed to weep — but tears could only draw dangerous attention. So he blinked furiously, breathing deeply to soothe losses murky and thick as the sea fret rolling over the Bay.

Napa Valley, California
Autumn 1877

'Madame Brann'gan, do not leave us please!'

Widow Brannigan, a stout woman of fifty, perched beside the drayman as the cart jolted away. She stared implacably at the horse's backside. Behind her was a pile of suitcases, including a hatbox containing her Sunday bonnet. It had been stuffed with horse manure the previous night and left at the foot of her bed. At dawn her screams had woken the household.

Catherine Bourchier did not care to think how the stout lady's fellow Congregationalists in Perryville would wrinkle their noses that Sunday. How stories would circulate of the wicked French boy and young widow who seldom wore black – a Catholic, to boot.

Mrs Brannigan had been hired as housekeeper and tutor. Neither role delivered satisfaction. Meals lacking the slightest pretence of flavour, dangerously insipid coffee, lessons with Catherine's only son consisting of interminable Bible readings. Emile had regarded Mrs Brannigan with horrified curiosity. It took three weeks before his *petites blagues*, as he called them, sent her packing. Her predecessor hadn't lasted that long.

Catherine watched the cart disappear into the woods and turned to find Emile sneaking behind her. His grubby face wore a rare smile.

For a long moment mother and son regarded one another. Clouds of outrage condensed into a feeble cuff aimed at his head. He dodged, halting a few feet away, his grin wider than ever.

'My God! How Grandpère would weep to see you like this! I will tell you why you refuse to learn English. It is because you cannot!' She tapped her forehead. 'Hollow! Nothing there!'

His grin hardened.

'I send you to school when we cannot afford it. You fight with the other boys and insult the teacher. You never speak to me except to spit!'

The corners of his grin drooped.

In triumphant fury she pressed on, 'If your father was here . . .'

She gasped, realising what she had said. An unbidden image of Antoine looming over her, riding crop raised, made her turn fearfully. Emile's tears began to flow – not from remorse as she had hoped. For the first time in days he found a voice, bitter and cold.

'With Papa I lived in a château . . .' He glanced at the mountains, woods and shabby buildings around them. 'Now I live *here*! You know why Papa is not here? Papa did not love you. That is why he died. I hate you more than anything!'

Catherine's hand swung. The slap on his cheek sent him reeling. Then he was away, running up the hillside through rows of vines, past stooping lines of Chinese labourers gathering grapes, away across dry, dusty earth into shadowy woods and rocky mountain slopes.

Tears trickled down her cheeks and her lungs and chest hurt. *Oh, Emile, come back.* He was too far away to hear her voice, let alone thoughts. Why could she not be gentler? More patient? It was just the piles of chores and negotiations and decisions, all pressing down upon her, all vital if the farm was to avoid bankruptcy.

For the thousandth time she feared Emile would have fared better back in France with his father. After all, Antoine's family might have ensured an education, of sorts. Her hopes for Emile mocked her now. If she weakened, hope for herself would perish, too.

Catherine shielded her eyes and gazed up the hillside. Emile had disappeared. It might take a whole day to find him – even then, only hunger would flush him out. Too dispirited to begin the tasks goading her, she retreated to the porch of the two-storey wooden farmhouse. The varnished oak floorboards creaked beneath her boots as she slumped on a bench, smoothing folds of skirt over her thighs.

Long evaded memories returned of nights after Emile's birth when she barely persuaded him to feed at her breast. Was there ever a child that cried so long and loud? And she, too, had cried – constantly tearful, restless, unable to eat. In the dark of night she dreamed of killing herself, so worthless had the baby made her feel; so confused, so tired, always tired. And then, after months of misery, her mood lifted like clouds blown away. Yet, ever since, she had never felt Emile quite belonged to her, that he was somehow to be feared, distrusted more than loved. Feelings she knew were unnatural.

She picked at a loose thread of her skirt. No doubt she was a bad mother. And, given the slim wad of dollar bills left in her iron strong box, she was leading to penury those foolish enough to trust her judgement.

Still, she did not seek out old Jean-Pierre, her steward, or help him with the next, vital stage of the *vendange*, the harvest that must justify or confound her gambles. As though to recover the excitement of arriving in Napa, a time when barely-defined success beckoned like sunlight on a dark, moving stream, she stared across the valley.

Her vineyard was called *Royaume Céleste*, or 'Heavenly Kingdom'. She had purchased the auspicious name along with thirty-six acres, two thirds planted to grapes; along with a house, barns, a never-failing well and a convenient creek; with a three-storey winery constructed of soft, porous local lava stone and built into the contours of the hill; together with an open-sided bunkhouse for migrant workers and a wine tunnel dug into the hillside to age bottles and barrels of claret. A wilderness of pine, Californian oak and a few giant redwoods surrounded this Heavenly Kingdom. Above rose low mountains and bluffs, forming the rugged walls of a corridor marching up Napa Valley to Mount St Helena and the Lake Country.

Buying Royaumd Céleste had been no easy decision. First there had been the little matter of finding it.

The Atlantic passage to America had been deceptively pleasant as the steamship dipped and rose through placid summer seas. Upon arrival in New York a storm of bustle convulsed them: hotels, railroad tickets to California, new clothes. By then Emile had commenced an epic silence of unrelenting ferocity, one he maintained all the way out West.

Emile was not the only travelling companion to cause concern. From the moment they left Marseille, Catherine struggled to find the right tone with Jean-Pierre, her father's loyal steward, a man who had tended Bourchier family vines in Languedoc for five decades. The old steward insisted on treating her with the deference he felt was owed to Monsieur Bourchier's daughter. In fact, the slightest hint of equality in Catherine's manner made him uncomfortable and she learned to address him with polite, yet firm, condescension. That, and Emile's obdurate silence, made for a lonely journey across the ocean and then the prairies. She spent it devouring English books and practising her accent with fellow passengers. Most of all, forcing herself to forget Languedoc and the grief threatening to overwhelm her. To forget the nagging fear they would be pursued, dragged back to France.

Then came California. To Catherine, everything in this young land inspired her. By stages, however, Jean-Pierre grew morose, except for conversations concerning when and where they would buy a vineyard.

Even then, fate had guided her. After San Francisco the next place they visited was Napa. As the steam ferry chugged up the Napa River she had turned to Jean-Pierre.

'Have you noticed the wind from the Bay? It is like the Marin wind at home, blowing in sea mists to cool the grapes. And those mountains! The hot wind coming from them blows like the Tramontane.'

Jean-Pierre had tugged his walrus moustache. 'One must live a long while in a place to learn its winds,' he said.

Napa's closeness to San Francisco, a mere day's ferry ride, also drew her to the long valley. How easy it would be to bring grapes and wine to market! And when she saw the low mountain ranges flanking the valley, she had visions of vineyards on their slopes. Her own might become the foremost.

'Red wine country over there,' Jean-Pierre opined, sniffing and pointing.

'I sense it also!' she cried.

But Catherine knew he did not believe her. She longed to win Jean-Pierre's respect, prove herself equal to Papa Bourchier in the old steward's estimation.

They had arrived in Napa City at the end of 1875, dazed by travel. Drought, distress, dreams winnowed into dust were everywhere in California. Thousands of unemployed labourers walked the roads, begging at every ranch and town, only to be turned away or driven on by lawmen with guns.

Catherine had wasted no time in drawing up a list of available farms and vineyards for sale in Napa. Given the harsh times, land was advertised at knockdown prices, but she refused to rush. Leaving Emile in the care of a Swiss restaurant owner's wife who provided lodgings, she and Jean-Pierre drove up and down the valley seeking a suitable *terroir*. At last, half way between Napa City and the County's second town,

Perryville, they found it. Royaume Céleste had been built by a French-man who succumbed to a brain tumour, leaving a widow only too pleased to accept the insulting price Catherine offered.

The widow would have sold her soul to return to Gascony: an irony not lost on Catherine Bourchier, even as she rejoiced at paying $2,000, a quarter of the vineyard's true value. Of course, there had been guilt. But why should she care? Nobody cared for her. Or Emile. Or all they had sacrificed and lost. Why should she care?

'Madame,' the widow had said after the cash and deeds changed hands, 'my husband killed himself trying to make this vineyard pay.' Her face contorted. 'Can you succeed when my husband did not?'

The widow's question had shaken her until Jean-Pierre whispered: 'They're just Gascons.'

Back then how sure they had been! How secure in their superior knowledge of the vine. For they had discovered a vineyard already mature, its rootstock thick and knotty – twenty thousand native Califor-nian plants, many bearing grafts of sophisticated European vines that must have cost the previous owner a year's profit.

'The winery roof leaks and the press is rusty,' said Jean-Pierre. 'Most of all we must graft noble French vines onto the rest of these *Yankee* ones.'

Yet in far off Languedoc those wonderful French plants Jean-Pierre so honoured had shrivelled and returned to the earth like all empires.

A year and a half later, Catherine rubbed an itchy corner of one eye as she examined Napa Valley. In the flat valley bottom, steam-driven threshing machines and gangs of labourers, tiny dots on the brown earth, harvested fields of anaemic wheat. The drought bleaching California filled the roads with dust clouds whenever a wind rose. Only damp sea fogs rolling in from San Francisco Bay prevented a universal withering of crops.

On the far side of the valley, two miles away, a second mountain chain stretched from north to south. Upon its green foothills, another vineyard faced Catherine's, a constant reminder how her family had diminished. For the estate was ten times the size of Royaume Céleste. In the midst stood a white mansion and ornate gardens. Its name was Trubody Nook, the holiday retreat of a San Francisco railroad millionaire.

She sighed and, being a practical woman, turned back to examine her own vines. Although her harvest had been absurdly fruitful compared to most winegrowers in Napa, it came at a cost. While she and Jean-Pierre worked tirelessly, Emile had played alone, his long silences and desperate bursts of chatter too often ignored. Yet when she tried to talk with him, he refused to reply. She was unforgiven, would always be unforgiven.

She examined the woods for her son. How small he was, despite his grand rages, small and helpless as her own dead little brothers, who she barely remembered.

She had decided to spend the day coaxing him from wherever he was hiding in the woods when a commotion arose at the winery. Reluctantly, she hurried down the wooden steps of the porch.

Jean-Pierre stood outside the tall stone building, hands on hips. With the help of Chinese labourers hired from the nearby town of Perryville, he had assembled crate after crate of plump purple grapes. The barns were crammed. Before him stood the labourers' gangmaster and spokesman, Sam Yip. Behind Sam Yip, twenty Chinese crowded in their conical straw hats, loose tunics without lapels, baggy blue canvas trousers and sandals.

'You no' pay men direc'!' shouted Sam Yip, gesturing at the labourers. 'I pay men! Tha' is contrac'. You no' pay men!'

Jean-Pierre, perhaps envious of the Chinaman's English, maintained an aura of unshakeable dignity. At the sight of Catherine he smoothed his large moustache.

'Madame, you must ask this little monkey what the matter is,' he said in French. 'I paid the men their daily wage this morning and – pouf! – he becomes deranged.'

She nodded, stepped round him. 'Please leave this to me, Jean-Pierre.'

Catherine went over to the winery's tall wooden doors, where Sam Yip was addressing the labourers in Chinese. Many appeared frightened.

'Sam Yip,' she said, 'what is this?'

The Chinaman turned to her. He squinted against the sun, detecting only a soft-spoken young woman, one he took to be the fat old farmer's wife.

'No talk with wifee!'

Catherine flushed. 'I am not *wifee*,' she said. 'I own this land. I am Madame Bourchier. I pay your wages. Now explain why you are not pressing the grapes.'

This was the crucial thing. The only thing that mattered. The ripe, sweet grapes in their wooden boxes would last another day without starting to spoil or rot – assuming the weather stayed cool. If the crush did not proceed from this very hour she might as well forget a profitable vintage.

'I wan' one dollar fifty cent day! You pay to my Uncle Sam Wah in Pellyville. Tha' is our contrac'! You no' pay men direc'.'

Catherine's breath quickened. 'My contract with your uncle, Mr Sam Wah, was for *one* dollar a day only.'

'Tha' was then. No' now,' said Sam Yip. 'B'cause you pay my men direc', now we wan' one dollar fifty cent or we go back to Pellyville.'

She turned to Jean-Pierre and said in French: 'Do you understand what he is saying, Jean-Pierre? He wants more money or they will leave.

If that happens, we have lost everything. But I cannot afford extra. What am I to do?'

It was the steward's turn to redden. He shook an angry fist at Sam Yip.

'Thieves!' he bellowed in French. 'If you pay them, Madame . . . Robbers! By my honour, if you pay . . . Scoundrel! I regret to inform you, Madame, for my honour's sake, I must find a new employer!'

With that he stomped into the winery. She knew these moods of old. It would pass in an hour, especially if doused with brandy. By then Sam Yip would have taken his gang of labourers away.

Catherine became aware the little Chinaman was watching avidly, a growing assurance in his eyes. Had she, also, watched the widow from Gascony sign away her precious home for a quarter its worth with the same silent gloating? Like a cat with an injured bird?

Her will to fight wavered. Then Sam Yip frowned and Catherine followed his gaze. A little way off stood a tall man in respectable city clothes so white with dust he resembled a ghost. The stranger had been listening for some time.

'Who on earth are you?' she asked.

An hour earlier, Chi-en Shambles had toiled up the dusty highway. His lips were cracked, tongue parched, but he feared drinking ditch water. Falling sick again, lying down in a bed of dust, to never rise, never reach the mountain that rose to the north, never stare out across the kingdoms of the world like Prometheus. If it hadn't been for the fever that struck as he left Napa City — so sudden and hot he staggered from the road into a ruined stone barn on a hill overlooking a broad sweep of valley — if not for the restless sweats and nausea of a day and night when he had been too weak to move, he would already be on the mountain at the valley's end, already perched on the high throne of the world. Sickness would not trouble him there. Nor time. Nor men's envy or spite. Nor ignorance, senseless hatred. Nor power, nor greed. All scattered by the wind, far away, to the Earth's wide corners . . . First, he must get there.

Chi-en lifted one weary foot after another. How full of visions he had been in the ruined barn overlooking Napa River! He had glimpsed the Yangtze, a hundred times as wide . . . But he shrank from memories. All reverted to sorrow in the end – and Prince Hong.

That night in the barn he had woken with nostrils full of acrid smoke, coughing and wheezing like a starved beggar he once saw in Guangzhou. Summoning an improbable strength, he had crawled to the doorway of the barn and wondered if God, as he had to Dante, was granting a glimpse of hell.

The Napa River ablaze! Smoke, flames roaring. A great city wall blown apart, rubble and dust forming a cloud. Smoke and billowing fire as wooden palaces and houses and temples burned. Thousands of demon-soldiers dancing, looting, dragging people from their homes, especially women and girls. Over the roar of the flames a constant, high-pitched wailing. Now the sound resolved itself into boys' voices. 'No,' he murmured, 'why do we not fight?' A house for orphans appeared through the smoke. Soldiers roasting alive the boys trapped inside. Tiny fists pounding iron bars meant to protect them. 'We must save these at least!' he cried. 'Hong, why not these?'

At last, his fevered brain comprehended: farmers were burning tall reeds alongside the creeks and rivers and ponds of Napa Valley, stems ten or twelve feet high, dried out by summer. Waves of flame lit the night; pillars of smoke obscured his view. The earth was alight. But it was time. He had been shown a sign of the Heavenly Capital. Time itself burned!

Chi-en had crawled back to his carpetbag, shivering convulsively, and thus the long night passed. Often his spirit returned to the Heavenly Capital and a face he both dreaded and longed to see. 'Tell the world about me, Chi-en,' whispered the face. 'Do not let me be forgotten.' Then the fever abated, replaced by hunger and thirst. A bemused cow watched as he lapped and scooped from a filthy pond with trembling hands. No water ever tasted sweeter.

Chi-en plodded. Farms, vineyards, all passed without incident. Sometimes he examined the low mountain ranges on either side that defined the valley's shape and width. Its flat bottom was given over to wheat fields and pasture, ancient oak trees like guardians, dried out ponds. Side roads led from the highway to farms nestling on spurs of hillside. At one such tributary of the road he sank to his knees.

The nearest farmhouse was a mile or so away in the flat centre of the valley. He needed food and rest. He fumbled in his pocket for coins. Nothing. A gust of hot wind rose, whirling up a cloud of white dust from the road.

On the far side of the valley a train clanked by, huffing clouds of steam. He watched curiously. Then he glanced at the side road and noticed an old hand-painted sign streaked with the same white dust as himself: *Royaume Céleste*. The name startled him. Heavenly Kingdom!

He left the highway and took the side road. What he sought was unclear. At the very least, fresh water unspoiled by animal droppings and duckweed.

The track climbed through ancient groves of Californian oak and fir, brambles and shrubs, grotesque, tortured outcrops of volcanic rock. Woodpeckers and nuthatch flickered in the canopy. At several places he found tall cairns of stones, as though countless travellers had paused to add one more pebble as they passed. Proof that Indians had used this way. At each cairn he offered a stone of his own.

Beyond the trees, a farm and vineyard occupied a large bowl of land cleared from wooded hillsides. Half a dozen buildings clustered: a farmhouse, two barns, an impressive three-storey stone winery set into a contour of the hill. Rows and rows of ochre, purple and green vines climbed slopes at the back of the buildings. Down the centre of the vineyard ran a small, winding creek overhung by willows.

Chi-en squinted at the winery. A group had gathered outside: a woman, a fat man and twenty Chinese. He trudged over in time to witness Catherine's confrontation with Sam Yip.

At last, the pair fell silent. The woman and gangmaster noticed him beside the well, drinking deeply from a bucket of fresh water.

'Who on earth are you?' asked the woman in heavily accented English.

'No Chinese work here unless I say so!' called out Sam Yip in Cantonese. 'No work for you, mister. Go to Pellyville and register with my uncle, Sam Wah.'

Chi-en looked from one to the other. He understood Sam Yip's game: squeeze the stupid *fan gui* woman out of a few more dollars while he had her – literally in this case – over a wine barrel. Not a cent of that extra money would go to the labourers, a hungry-looking bunch, no doubt loyal to the Sam clan because of obligations back in Guangzhou. Such was the way for poor Chinese in California.

Chi-en removed his hat and unwittingly worsened matters. His unshaved forehead and long, pigtail-less hair provoked a collective intake of Chinese breath.

'Can you not afford a barber?' demanded Sam Yip. He shot a glance at his followers to indicate a witticism. 'Or are you a filthy rebel, Mister Longhair?'

Silence except for birdsong in the woods, a rustle of dry leaves from the vines. Chi-en met the gangmaster's eye. 'You decide.'

Sam Yip's amusement ceased.

'*Who . . . are . . . you?*' repeated the woman, as though addressing a halfwit.

With an ironic flourish, Chi-en bowed. The sweet, cool water had given him strength. He felt giddy, elated.

'Madame, forgive me for not replying,' he said in best Parisian French. Her own French, he noted, possessed the vulgar vowels of Languedoc. 'I was distracted by this fellow before you, Monsieur Sam Yip.'

The Chinese muttered amongst themselves, observing Chi-en with new interest. Sam Yip had clearly caught his own name amidst the babble. The young woman's hazel-green eyes opened wide. Her plump lips pursed. She turned imploringly to Chi-en.

'Monsieur,' she said in French, 'please explain to me the real reason they won't work. I have always tried to be fair with them!'

'You be careful, Longhair!' warned Sam Yip in Cantonese, stepping forward.

This tipped Chi-en. He replied in her language. 'Madame, this fellow hopes to profit from you and the men under him. I gather he is in the employ of his uncle, a Sam Wah of Pellyville . . .'

'Perryville,' corrected the grave woman.

'Of course,' said Chi-en, thoughtfully. 'It is a peculiarity of the Southern Han dialect that *r* is rendered as *l*. I was using Mr Sam's pronunciation.'

Her expression indicated a complete lack of interest in consonants. 'How do I persuade them to work?'

He hesitated. Why help her or anyone else? But then Sam Yip made a big show of removing his coat, the traditional Chinese sign for a fight, and shouted out: 'Watch you don't pay for this, Longhair!'

Chi-en grew haughty. 'Offer one dollar and ten cents,' he said in French, 'then ask him to go back to his uncle, Sam Wah, to ascertain whether your revised offer is acceptable. Our friend is unlikely to refuse. It might look like he's dishonouring his uncle. Everything should revert to its former state until he returns.'

The young woman watched him. 'Can you be sure?'

'I know how my people conduct business,' he said. 'If you have a better plan, follow it.'

'What do you get out of this, Monsieur?'

'A meal. A bed. Some days' food for my journey.'

'Agreed,' she said. 'And I shall add a dollar if it works. As well as my thanks. Now tell Monsieur Yip what you have proposed.'

Chi-en bowed. Naturally an argument followed. It ended exactly as he predicted, for Yip dared not supersede his uncle's authority. Within minutes the Chinese labourers were back at work. Crate after crate of grapes cascaded into the wine press. Under Jean-Pierre's supervision, the levers of the press were lowered. A cloud of fruit aromas gathered. Chi-en turned to the young woman, who was dabbing the corners of her eyes. She laughed with relief.

'Follow me,' she said in English. 'You pop out of the earth like a ghost but I am obliged. I will show you where to sleep. What is your name?'

He hesitated. For all he knew, a warrant was out for Chi-en Shambles.

'Madame, my name is Humble.' Using the English translation of *Chi-en* was unplanned but prudent. He added with gentle mockery. 'That is *H*umble not '*U*mble. Just as *Perry*ville is not *Pe*llyville.'

She smiled. 'Of course, Monsieur 'Umble.'

Napa Valley, California
Autumn 1877

Catherine Bourchier led Chi-en to the farmhouse kitchen, where a bedroll awaited in an adjoining storeroom. He found himself hired to prepare dinner.

'We did have a Mrs Bran'gan as *chef d'hôtel*,' she intimated, darkly, 'until my son persuaded her to leave.'

By dusk, a cauldron of fresh tomato and salt pork stew, seasoned with red wine, garlic, chervil, parsley, yellow peppers and courgettes, released flavoursome bubbles. Round loaves cooled. A pharaoh's pyramid of rice steamed on a platter, courtesy of Sam Yip, who had left behind a small sack when he hurried off to consult his uncle. Chi-en cooked the lot, thereby tripling the labourers' usual ration.

Madame Bourchier and Jean-Pierre were served their stew and bread in the farmhouse's dining room. The Frenchman sniffed suspiciously, raised an eyebrow then set to with a grunt. She ate more delicately – but as heartily.

'My goodness, 'Umble,' she said, wiping her lips with a napkin, 'you are a chef as well!'

He glanced out of the window.

'If you see a small boy,' she said, 'about this high, send him to me. He will be very hungry.'

Taking the dishes, he returned to the kitchen. A thief lurked there, younger than your usual bandit. A boy of ten stuffed handfuls of warm bread into his mouth. At the sight of Chi-en he sidled to the back door.

'Ah!' Chi-en laid down the dirty crocks. 'I see you are not shy about helping yourself. I detect a certain resemblance to Madame Bourchier. She said you would be hungry.'

Chi-en frowned. Was the child simple? Or deaf? Then he understood, and repeated what he had said in French. The boy looked at him warily. Chi-en could hear Madame Bourchier instructing the labourers down at the winery.

'Eat at the kitchen table,' he said. 'Then go see your Maman.'

One, two, a third bowl vanished, along with slices of bread sticky with molasses. Chi-en washed the dishes in a wooden bucket while the boy ate. When he looked up the child had gone. Scrabbling noises followed as a drainpipe was scaled. Feet scurried across the steep kitchen roof. A window slammed somewhere in the house.

Darkness brought a clear, cloudless night lit by more stars than Chi-en ever glimpsed above smoky, foggy San Francisco. He sat on the raised porch of a narrow store attached to the house. The room contained barrels and kegs, a blanket and sweat-stained mattress stuffed with straw – a city of fleas.

He walked round the farmhouse for clear views of the valley. A sliver of moon rose from behind the mountain, casting a faint light on wooded slopes and bare peaks. Scents of fruit from the winery distracted him. He listened to the night and heard the wine press grating. Jean-Pierre's deep voice rolled round the farm, urging on the Chinese labourers. He and his mistress would supervise the crush all night, dividing the task into watches like sailors traversing a jagged coast.

Another noise penetrated the night: Madame Bourchier scolding her wayward son in a voice wobbly with tears. Angry accusations answered her.

Chi-en felt a stab of sympathy for the half-wild boy — fatherless, so far as he could tell. Oh, he knew about that. He himself had come to America to find a father. A quest abandoned — painfully, reluctantly — as hopeless when he settled in San Francisco.

Exhausted, he sought his bed.

The tide of darkness washing over the earth retreated west. In Royaume Céleste sleepers created shifting worlds of dream: men from Guangzhou sighed as half-forgotten faces welcomed them home; Emile searched and searched the empty corridors of a grand château for something or someone he could not name except as fear; and Chi-en Shambles curled on his bedroll in the store room, each breath granting a little more strength to a body weakened by sickness and a mind wounded by rejection and loss.

All slept soundly, wearied by honest labour, except for Catherine Bourchier. She sweated on an iron bedstead formerly belonging to the widow from Gascony. Just as the grape crush bubbled and fermented in the winery, so did her soul.

Her dreams were almost memories, none welcome . . .

In her dream she waited for her husband on the cracked marble steps of Château de Chauveterre.

Even at dusk the long day's heat shimmered. Drowsy wasps, midges, a relentless creak of cicadas. A familiar wind, the Tramontane, blew from the north but it brought no comfort. Far to the west, the blue peaks of the Pyrenees blushed as though anticipating darkness.

From its vantage point in the hills, Château de Chauveterre overlooked a vine-clad plain running down to the Mediterranean, the ancient towers of distant Cathar strongholds and spires like dark, up-raised fingers of warning. Catherine sweated as she waited. The château's housekeeper, maids, grooms and footmen stood in rows behind her.

'He comes,' muttered the estate steward, old Jean-Pierre Leclos.

Le Comte's barouche, drawn by two dappled horses, climbed like a black beetle through a lattice of tree-shadow and fading light. Behind came a smaller carriage crammed with baggage and valets.

Catherine folded her arms and adjusted her elegant cream gown. Her eyes sought out Jean-Pierre. He seemed oblivious to the heat in his woollen Sunday suit, waistcoat and black hat. Some of the other servants shuffled and, with a thin smile of encouragement, she positioned herself between them and the approaching carriage.

But when Monsieur le Comte Antoine de Rivac de Chauveterre descended from the barouche, barely acknowledging his wife, she understood this visit would go no better than the last. Her one hope was that it might be as short.

'I'm thirsty,' declared her husband.

She noticed more grey in his curly hair than seven months before. He stalked past, tapping his stovepipe hat against a thigh.

Before she could follow, a second gentleman emerged from the carriage. He, too, sported a waxed, upward-pointing moustache in best Paris style. Where Antoine's handsome face projected stubborn, ingrained wilfulness, this man's dreamy smile suggested a fluttering aesthete in a vulgar world. He flapped his top hat at the wasps and midges.

'Ah, la comtesse!' he cried, stepping forward to kiss her hand. 'Seeing our dear Antoine has neglected to introduce me, I shall undertake that office myself. Baron Cesar Foche! At your *every* service!'

He kissed her hand a second time, peering up through a monocle to note her reaction. For all his gallantry, Foche's eyes were intent as a hungry bird's. Then Catherine knew this visit would be far worse than the last.

The dining room of Château de Chauveterre was a long, elm-panelled hall. Portraits of the Comte's ancestors watched them eat in silence; even Baron Foche abandoned his forays of wit halfway through the cold meats. As for husband and wife, not a crumb of conversation existed between them.

A dozen candelabras cast a softening glow over the long, white-linened table and monogrammed dinner service. At last, the dinner ended and Comte de Rivac de Chauveterre looked up from a barely touched apricot sorbet. He had already downed half a bottle of champagne and several glasses of Domaine Bourchier claret. Catherine had learned to anticipate him through liquid measurements. With luck, given the heat, sufficient wine would enter his bloodstream to make him neglect his rights and duties as a husband. She rose with a stiff smile to leave the gentlemen to their cigars when he noticed her.

'Wait,' he said, with a lazy gesture.

His impassive gaze was upon her, the same look as on the first day they met. Seven years of marriage had neither softened nor hardened it.

'You ought to know I've arranged for some companions of mine to come down from Paris as my guests for a little country amusement.'

Baron Foche dabbed his wet, rosebud mouth with a napkin. 'A pleasant company!' he cried. 'Including some delightful ladies to entertain la comtesse! Such a gay party!'

Perhaps Catherine's speculations concerning these ladies showed in her face, for Antoine frowned.

'How many *companions* must we expect?' she asked.

'That does not concern you.'

'If I am to make the necessary preparations . . .'

'At least twelve, wasn't it, Antoine?' offered Baron Foche. 'Such rustic fun, I'm sure you'll agree.'

'And their servants?' She was unable to conceal her dismay. 'That makes twenty – no, more than thirty mouths to feed. And their horses and lapdogs . . .'

'Enough!' Her husband's frown had become a fierce scowl.

'Antoine, can't you understand? We do not have enough money for extravagance. Have you not received my letters? You must send a telegram. Put them off . . .'

'Enough! Go to your room. You forget yourself.'

As great revolutions of the soul will sometimes occur in a moment, her habitual fear of him vanished. Instead of the object of awe accepted by her father as the best means to save their family, she saw a feckless, wearisome fool. A charmless bully. A man ruined by privilege. In the angry jut of his jaw she saw the future face of her son – and knew she could defer to Antoine no longer.

'I will not be silent,' she said. 'This cannot continue . . .'

A fist swept the table, shattering crystal glasses on the flagstones of the ancient hall. Catherine became aware of servants listening from the shadows.

'My wife,' drawled Antoine to Baron Foche, 'suffers from a nervous malady. Whenever she is in the company of her betters she acts as though the devil has a grip on her. I really must send her to a sanatorium for a long stay. Go to your room, Madame! I shall visit you later and ensure you are feeling better.'

Shaking, Catherine rose. Baron Foche's eyes followed her from the room. Now her boldness seemed a pit of stupidity. Antoine would not neglect his honour as a husband now. He might even decide honour required a riding crop.

He came at midnight. By then she calculated his intake of wine must have doubled. But rage always had a sobering effect on him, allowing the worst of his faculties full rein. As she hid in her bedchamber, the door firmly locked, Catherine heard snatches of an old monarchist song from the *salle de diner* below:

Jusqu'à ce qu'on prenne La lune avec les dents . . .

Could he truly have ignored her warnings they were down to the last *franc*? No, the last *sou*! Perhaps he did not believe her. Or held his bourgeois wife in such contempt her warnings could be dismissed as parsimony. Above all, Antoine despised parsimony.

The hand that shook the door handle was clumsy. Catherine froze on the bed, hugging her drawn up knees. The lock had been changed since his last visit. There existed only two keys: one on the inside of the lock, the other entrusted to her maid, Clotille, a tight-breasted girl from the village who cultivated an expression of perpetual surprise. Again the door shook, more urgently now. Within moments there came loud, rhythmic bangs, followed by a drunken hiss: 'Open that door, damn you!'

She stayed motionless, hardly daring to breathe.

'Open it, you little slut!'

A kick shook the door. It was murky in the large bedchamber though moon and starlight filtered through open stone casements. Clumsy footsteps receded down the corridor and her heartbeat slowed. As minutes passed, she relaxed. Of course, every servant in the château would have heard his outburst. She released her knees from their tight hug and lay back on the bed. Even with the windows open the chamber was breathlessly close. She removed a heavy dressing gown worn as a layer of protection, so that she rested on the four-poster bed in her cotton nightgown. A nervous giggle escaped. Oh, he had not expected her to change the lock! Though he was sure to punish her tomorrow, tonight she was secure.

She stretched with wary pleasure. If only she had the courage to put her plans into action, there would be no more locks, no fear. She listened to the familiar screech of an owl hunting round one of the towers. Sounds learned by heart since girlhood. Dare she really leave all that was known? The cicadas that stopped their song only at night? The *garrigue* above Château de Chauveterre, oak and olive and oleander-studded hills where she had watched sprays of constellations cross an azure-black sky, mirrored by star patterns of glow worms in the vineyards below. Even at night the baked earth released its warmth, jasmine and honeysuckle scenting the darkness, reminding her that she was a woman still, with a woman's needs . . .

Abruptly a noise disturbed her reverie. The key in the bedroom door had been pushed from the outside. It tinkled as it struck the floor. Too late she remembered Clotille. But no, the girl would not betray . . . Instantly her fear was realised. The lock clicked and the door opened. A familiar shape stepped inside.

No banging now. No anger. He walked straight to the bed where she lay. Half his moustachioed face was grey with moonlight, the other concealed. He stood looking down at her. The scents of pomade, cigars, Eau de Cologne and brandy reached out.

'Antoine,' she whispered, drawing herself deeper into the pillows, 'I did not mean . . .'

He stepped forward. She caught a strange flash of eyes.

'If I want my wife, why should I not have her? You seem determined to disobey even your dear Papa's wishes.'

'No, not tonight,' she pleaded. 'I am so tired . . . the heat.'

'You thought to embarrass me, eh?' he said. 'With my friend Foche, eh?'

'Please, Antoine, tomorrow . . .'

'You must be reminded who now owns Domaine Bourchier.'

She heard him fumbling with his breeches. A faint rattle from the corridor outside reached the four-poster bed. Could someone be listening? Clotille? The unspeakable possibility of Baron Foche? Then in the quarter-light of the moon he was upon her, his breath acrid on her face. For the first time in seven years she kicked and scratched. He froze in surprise. A blow to the side of her head sent her reeling deeper into the coverlet, moaning with panic. Another slap, harder than before, to her upper arm. Another blow – a punch this time. Her nightgown was open. It seemed to embolden him.

'I made a bargain with your dear papa,' he said, positioning her to his taste. He was panting now. 'I, at least, am . . . That's better . . . Honourable enough to . . . Wider! . . . Fulfil my bargain.'

He said nothing more. His language was brute body. Forced to kneel on the side of the bed, pain tore her open from behind, Antoine grunting as he laboured until she cried out pleasurelessly like a trapped she-cat. Afterwards she heard him mutter through her sobs as she pressed her face into the quilt.

'Do not misunderstand your position in my household again.'

That night, a heavy, desolate resolve hardened in her soul. She barely slept, weighing every detail of her plan. A desperate, crazy plan to retrieve plain Mademoiselle Catherine Bourchier from Comtesse de Rivac de Chauveterre. To undo their losses by losing everything – far, far away . . .

Catherine woke in her small bedroom, nine thousand kilometres from Languedoc. She blinked stupidly at light penetrating the thick drapes. For a moment she could not comprehend the strange room with its cheap chest of drawers and mildewed, peeling wallpaper. Her hair was matted with dried sweat. She felt unclean. Sniffing her armpits, she wrinkled her nose. She had always been particular about her toilette, but without a maid to fetch warm water and towels she was descending to the standards of a peasant woman.

Throwing off the coarse blankets, she perched on the edge of the bed in her nightgown. Her breath slowed. *The past is dead,* she told herself, over and over. *The past is dead.* What were the hours of her life but ghosts only she might summon if she chose? Could not a will that had proved strong enough to drag servant and defiant son halfway across the world make that choice? If the past was dead, every moment she called *now* was fading even as it unfurled. And yet, for all her strong will, she felt dirty, bedraggled.

After a long scrub and rinse with sponge and cold water, she dripped on towels laid out across the varnished floorboards of her bedroom. Then she dressed in clean, simple clothes. Today must see the end of the crush and the beginning of fermentation in the vats.

Outside she encountered an unfamiliar sight. At first, she thought it must be another boy, for Emile never undertook chores. But no, her son was staggering towards the kitchen with an armful of logs, his ingrained scowl replaced by a resolute expression. Too intent on his work to notice his own mother, he vanished into the kitchen. She followed and watched from the doorway.

Monsieur Humble was feeding a blaze in the cast iron range, taking logs from the pile Emile had brought. Like her, the Chinaman had bathed and wore clean clothes. His brown eyes and golden complexion marked him as a Celestial, a perpetual foreigner, but the rest was deceptively European. It took little imagination to deduce his status: a white sailor or merchant's bastard. His mother must have been a lovely woman;

41

his father handsome. She grew uneasy. Had she reduced her only son to little more than a bastard by denying him a father?

Emile finally noticed her standing at the door.

'Why are you carrying wood?' she asked. 'Did I not tell you to begin your English studies today?' She added in that same tongue. '*Without fail?*'

His shoulders hunched. He looked past her at the sunlight outside.

'Madame Bourchier,' said the half-Chinaman, 'Emile is not to blame. I persuaded him that we would have no breakfast until he fetched wood. He was obliging enough to delay his studies.'

Emile cast Monsieur Humble a grateful look. She narrowed her eyes but before she could gain the last word, Catherine heard Jean-Pierre's heavy stride.

'More trouble, Madame,' he said, his clothes flecked with scraps of fruit flesh, seeds, purple grape skins. 'Sam Wah has come with that little yellow rat, Sam Yip. They've ordered the men to stop working.'

Catherine found them gathering bedrolls and bags outside the winery, marshalled by a short Chinaman with a freshly shaved forehead and neatly tied grey pigtail. Though she guessed he was around sixty years of age, Sam Wah possessed still the squat, broad-shouldered physique of a wrestler. Everyone paused. Sam Wah bowed, his grin revealing two blackened front teeth.

'Mrs Borsh,' he said. 'Very honoured.'

Her glance flickered to Sam Yip, back to the older man. Yip had started whispering in his uncle's ear.

'Jean-Pierre,' she said, in French, 'please ask Monsieur 'Umble to come here. Straight away.'

As Chi-en stepped from the kitchen he spied a large group outside the winery. Madame Bourchier's expression suggested relief at his arrival, even hope. A fine, tall woman, her hourglass figure showing through clothes made shapeless by work, he could not suppress dangerous pity for her situation. One look at the Chinese gangmaster, who reminded Chi-en of a river pirate he once met in Nanking, confirmed the feeling.

'Monsieur 'Umble,' she said in French, 'that pair of rogues mean to strip me bare, do they not?' Catherine nodded at Sam Wah and Sam Yip; both were listening darkly.

'If you let them.'

'Will you act as an interpreter for me again, Monsieur 'Umble, before you go? You see, I am pretending I cannot understand their English. It would help me a great deal.'

She had put herself in his power. He became aware of intense, hostile scrutiny from the two Sams.

'What do you wish to say?' he asked.

The young woman drew breath then emitted a stream of angry French at Sam Wah. After a while, Chi-en held up a hand.

'Mister Sam,' said Chi-en in Cantonese, 'the lady says you are breaking your deal. One dollar a day, she says, was agreed. She is very angry. She says that asking for one dollar fifty while her harvest is at so critical a stage is not honourable.'

Sam Wah smiled. 'Is that what she really said, Foreign Devil?' he replied in Cantonese.

Chi-en bowed. 'Mister Sam, we are all foreigners here.'

'You play a dangerous game, Longhair,' spluttered the nephew, Sam Yip. 'We Sams are bosses in Pellyville Chinatown.'

'What is your answer for Madame Bourchier?' asked Chi-en.

'Tell her,' said Sam Wah, 'I am surprised how quickly her understanding of English has deteriorated since our last meeting in Perryville.'

Chi-en obliged.

'Tell Sam Wah,' she said, 'if he breaks the terms of our contract I shall personally ride to every farm in this valley and inform its owner how I was cheated by his family. Tell him, if he ruins me, I'll ruin him. I insist on one dollar a day.'

Chi-en nodded thoughtfully. 'The problem with your position,' he said in French, 'is that it diminishes Sam Wah in the eyes of his followers. Especially as you sent his nephew as go-between last night with an offer of one dollar *ten* cents. Losing so much face will certainly make him obdurate. Might I suggest a compromise? Begin with one dollar ten cents. Finally, after much haggling, settle for one dollar fifteen. After all, one dollar fifteen is very little for labouring in the hot sun from daybreak to dusk. *N'est-ce pas?*'

'As you suggest, Monsieur 'Umble,' she sighed. 'Start with a dollar ten cents.'

Negotiating for Lu Kan in Chinatown had taught Chi-en how to find points of mutual profit with Chinese merchants. As predicted, the haggling ended at one dollar fifteen and a commitment that the labourers would make up for lost time.

When the terms were settled, he realised that at no point had the men been consulted. He recollected the taunt in the *California Star* that Chinamen were natural slaves and wondered why he had helped this young woman. Turning to leave, he found his way blocked by the squat, powerful form of Sam Wah.

'I have seen you someplace before,' he said. 'A long time ago, I think. A long way from here.'

He stared back at Sam Wah. 'I do not recognise you.'

'We're going to find out all about you, *fan gui*!' crowed Sam Yip, as Chi-en walked away. 'We don't like Longhair rebels in Pellyville!'

Back in the kitchen, the Frenchwoman waited at the kitchen table. 'Monsieur 'Umble, sit down for a moment.'

Perhaps he should feel flattered a white woman wished to share a table with a Celestial. Except several had granted him more intimate favours. As for this one, he wasn't sure he trusted her.

'Thanks to you, 'Umble, that went well.' She seemed elated by victory. The brittle, nervous elation of someone at the very edge of their inner resources.

Chi-en remained standing. Pouring from the water jug, he filled a clay cup and drank.

'It went well for you, Madame,' he grunted, 'not me. Nor, I fear, for the labourers.'

Her glee subsided. 'When I can afford to pay more, I will be more generous. If you please . . .' She fumbled in her apron pocket for a coin. 'I wish to honour my promise and pay you a dollar.'

Exhaustion made him unsteady. The fever was still in him. If it struck on the road, he might never reach the mountain. Not that he knew what to do when he got there. Suddenly the room swirled. He became aware of a scent, warm and musky, and turned to discover her face close to his own. Her hand propped his arm as she steered him to a chair.

'You almost fainted!' she cried. 'Please sit. Are you sick?'

'No, no.' He shook himself free, forced down more water. 'Keep your dollar.'

She smiled uncertainly. 'I have another offer. Will you stay for a day or so as our cook? Longer if you wish.'

Chi-en's instinct was to say no, that he should get to the mountain, but he knew the fever must be settled first.

'Very well,' he said. 'But my wage . . .' He met her eye. 'Must be one dollar fifty cents a day.'

She frowned, as if deciding whether he was mocking her.

'The extra fifty cents is to buy rice for the labourers. They look very thin, *n'est-ce pas?*'

Her blush of discomfort gave him a curious satisfaction.

'How generous of you,' she muttered in English. 'We have a deal, 'Umble.'

Twilight drew Chi-en from the kitchen, his chores and duties fulfilled. Evening air was the cordial he sought by walking the long, silent rows of vines. Between finger and thumb, he rubbed dusty autumn leaves waiting to be discarded by the mother plant. The events of the day played through his mind.

He drifted down the hillside, back to the house and kitchen table. There he extracted the clothbound notebook from his carpetbag. For a long time, he gazed at the title page, *A Modest Memoir of Prince Hong*. Moths flapped helplessly around the paraffin lamp. Often in San Francisco he had tried to begin his memoir, always lacking courage. But his vision of the Heavenly Capital amidst the burning reeds and the auspicious name of this farm, Royaume Céleste, were signs, perhaps, the time had come to discharge the debt weighing his spirit. Here, of all places on earth.

The plaintive voice of an oboe flowed from the Frenchwoman's salon, a melancholy folksong. Startled, he listened intently, clouded by emotion.

Then he opened the thick, empty notebook. Blank pages stretched like doors to the past.

Mixing ink on a saucer, he gently loaded his writing brush and began, at last, with a tentative joy, to form neat, precise columns of Chinese characters. So intent he was, so lost to the people who formed him, that he did not notice Emile Bourchier watching through the open doorway.

Chapter the First: *The Tower of Babel*

I

When I imagine Canton in 1854, I am always running. Not *from* but *to*. Who I ran to is the subject of this humble memoir.

For now I am skipping along the crowded dockside. On one side, the glinting Pearl River choked with a second city of boats. On the other, European factories, warehouses and, behind them, a maze of Chinese houses, shanties, temples. My entire horizon overlooked by ancient ramparts, huge bastion gates. Behind those walls lies the Chinese city proper, where people of our kind are beaten if recognised. Sometimes *unto death*, like the holy martyrs among whom Aunty-Mother says all should aspire to follow.

On I run, to a small chapel with a bell tower between the Chinese and European quarters. Locals call it Clear Bell Temple. My special duty and joy is tugging the bell-rope until a sweet, pure chime sounds out. Behind our church is a tiny wooden house of two storeys.

'Aunty-Mother!' I cry, bursting through the door, knowing she will be in the kitchen. 'What's to eat?'

Though she may be cooking or cleaning or mending Spiritual Uncle Father's clothes, she will sigh, set aside her chore.

'First you must study, Little Humble,' she will say. 'An hour's writing before you eat and an hour's reading after.'

I never argue, for I am proud to be true to my name. Besides, it's safer that way.

Though small, our church was a world in itself. Nearly twenty Christians worshipped there, all Chinese except for Spiritual Uncle Father who was American. We gladly adopted the surname of the man who had saved our eternal souls.

Reverend Ezekiel Shambles was a giant. Often, I hid beneath the kitchen table, watching his tree-trunk legs pace up and down as he complained to Aunty-Mother about ignorance and wickedness. She rarely replied, except with low sighs.

To me, Spiritual Uncle Father was a far more important person than Jesus. For one thing, he had named me, inspired by his favourite hymn:

> *He that is down need fear no fall,*
> *He that is low no Pride,*
> *He that is Humble ever shall*
> *Have God to be his guide.*

For all his kindness, Spiritual Uncle Father was a stern shepherd. His tantrums made Aunty-Mother flinch; fits of temper that erupted in a moment. Then his followers grew nervous. Several had been expelled from Clear Bell Temple for contradicting God's word. Eternal torture would surely be their punishment. As Aunty-Mother whispered to me fearfully, 'That is why all his followers add Shambles to their own names. Lest we seem ungrateful.' A lesson I took to heart.

As for me, I had another, special reason to be careful. As soon as

I was old enough to understand, Aunty-Mother informed me with tears in her eyes, 'You are a child of shame, Chi-en!' In that, and so many other things, I differed from the other children around me.

At the age of four I was speaking English, Cantonese, a little Mandarin, and gaining swift ground in the diverse dialects of Reverend Shambles's flock – Hakka, in particular. 'Lo, the Tower of Babel!' cried Spiritual Uncle Father, gesticulating at the walls of Canton. 'Where every language except God's own is spoken!' I cowered in the congregation, guilty of understanding more and more of those evil tongues with every month that passed. Yet I could not help my precocious gift for languages.

Our failings were not the only reason for Spiritual Uncle Father's righteous anger. Sometimes he quarrelled with other European missionaries. These false priests, inspired by Satan, withheld funds vital to his work. Yet woe betide any of us who were disrespectful to them when they visited. After they had gone, he withdrew to his private chamber. Then his flock gathered outside, waiting for him to emerge. Spiritual Uncle Father's quarrel with the missionaries meant short rations until fresh funds arrived from America.

Though far away in time, Aunty-Mother's earnest face fills my mind. She was young, beautiful, her complexion smooth as chrysanthemum petals. Yet she never laughed: her mirth was a slight, sad smile. Indeed, she often had cause to rebuke me for laughing too much. For she, too, was tainted by shame. And I was the outcome of that sin.

'I fell from grace with a foreigner.' She glanced nervously to Reverend Shambles who watched, grim-faced. 'That is why you are half-European. Your father was a sailor, Humble, who traded in jade and ivory with my family. They are big merchants in Hong

Kong. Both of us would have perished on the streets if Spiritual Uncle Father had not found us there and pitied us . . .' She fell silent, dabbing a tear. I glanced at the Reverend Shambles but he, if anything, looked grimmer than before.

'Your natural father, Humble, was a damnable sinner!' he declared. 'We want none of him! None of that sinner, I say!'

I cowered, as did Aunty-Mother, terrified he would cast us back on the streets where beggars were starved, beaten and abused by petty tyrants.

'Oh, Humble, you and I can never be like others,' she blurted. 'My sin spoiled us forever!'

Thankfully, Spiritual Uncle Father's expression softened. He assured her even Jezebel the Temptress could find forgiveness if truly repentant, citing that Mary Magdalene washed Jesus's feet. But I did not believe Aunty-Mother was convinced. Nor do I believe it now.

Only two things made her wide eyes brighten. The first was teaching me to read and write both English and Chinese. She was a remarkably educated woman, a natural teacher, and once let slip that her own father had been a Confucian scholar. The second was when Reverend Shambles granted her the smallest word or gesture of approval. I understood, as only a jealous son can, how she worshipped him for saving us both.

Sometimes I went to the docks for an hour or two, finding a corner to watch the hundreds of foreign sailors and merchants parade outside the factories, stores and exchanges. 'Is *he* my father?' I asked myself, picking a handsome one. 'Or him?' But that one's face had a wart and he swigged from a bottle of neat grog. In my secret heart, I refused to believe my father was a *damnable sinner* as Reverend Shambles claimed. Sometimes I imagined my father on the ocean, prevented from returning to claim his son by terrible storms and sea monsters. But I'd never seen the open ocean; everything was surmise.

Back home, Aunty-Mother would notice my dejection and sing our favourite hymn to cheer me up while she cooked supper: *He that is down need fear no fall . . .*

II

As I grew older, the docks where tea, opium and bales of cloth were traded no longer marked the frontier of my world. I found myself drawn to Guangzhou, to use Canton's true name, the city of a million souls. I would climb a wobbly ladder into the bell tower and survey the city ramparts. At last, I understood my position. I was between two worlds, unnoticed by either.

Half of me – the white sailor part – was fascinated by the foreigners and their ceaseless trade. Steamships arrived regularly from across the globe, flying the flags of many nations. Of course, hordes of Chinese tried to profit from the strangers. Most popular were brothels, drinking and opium dens for sailors.

A thousand babbles and aromas swirled round the Foreign Concession of Canton. Endless loading and unloading of crates, casks, barrels. I flitted like a ghost, listening until patterns of speech made magical sense to me. Patterns that imprinted themselves on my brain so I have never forgotten them.

The other world was close and distant: Guangzhou, City of Bulls, a place where foreigners entered with an armed escort and their revolvers handy.

As a missionary with a reputation for snaring gullible Chinese, it was particularly dangerous for Reverend Shambles to step inside the city gates. His broad, towering physique made him instantly recognisable. In those days, before the Second Opium War, the authorities regularly diverted the people's hatred of their own corrupt rule by blaming the *fan gui*.

The problem was that Spiritual Uncle Father's divine mission demanded secret forays into the city. Aunty-Mother could not go, of course, for reasons never fully explained. I suspect my status as a child of shame was to blame. She once told me her family had threatened dire punishments when driving her from their door. Whatever the reason, it was decided I would attract the least attention.

Every month I took a large empty sack, shaded my half-sailor features and cherub mouth beneath a peasant's conical hat, and trotted past the bored soldiers at the gates. My mission, though not strictly illegal, would have cost me a flaying.

Through narrow streets I plodded, past shop fronts and banners painted with the Chinese characters Aunty-Mother taught me. Past temples where idols and devils grinned, bells and gongs clanging, incense drifting into the street. Fear contended with curiosity and another feeling, a desire to win Spiritual Uncle Father's praise at any cost.

Bored gangs of Manchu soldiers and Chinese militia loitered on corners, eager to supplement their unpaid wages or simply have a little cruel fun. I witnessed searches of houses where rebels against the Ching Emperor were thought to hide: men and women beaten mercilessly while neighbours carried on their business as though nothing was happening. The casual viciousness of the Manchu had brutalised the people, forcing them to rely on the usual resources of the weak and exploited: passivity, cunning, deceit. Did I feel the first stirrings of hatred for injustice? Probably. I longed to understand this dangerous Chinese world further – it was half of me, after all.

My destination was a print shop near the Rice Controller's *yamen*. Its owner was either brave or avaricious to risk commissions from a foreign missionary. His workshop and precious wood printing blocks could easily have been torched by Triad gangs dedicated to purging China of foreigners – including the hated Manchu. He would load my sack with tracts proclaiming the way to salvation through Jesus. These exhortations had been dictated by Spiritual Uncle Father then translated by Aunty-Mother into Chinese characters.

The printer always examined me and shook his head. 'Wife!' he would call, 'They say that a lean dog shames its master! Give this poor boy food.' Sometimes it was dumplings or rice balls or sugar cakes. These I gulped before re-tracing my steps to Clear Bell Temple. Strangely, I was never once accosted by soldiers or brigands (they amounted to the same thing). As I laid my bounty of God's word at Spiritual Uncle Father's feet he chuckled, patted my head. Then I felt joy and safety. Even now it makes me tearful. Aunty-Mother's relief to see me home was expressed in rare, uncertain hugs that I treasured beyond pearls.

III

On my eighth birthday I returned home to find an unexpected present. Not for me, of course. Aunty-Mother could hardly celebrate an event that damned us both to eternal shame.

Reverend Shambles paced round the kitchen that doubled as my bedroom. A thick sheet of parchment crackled in his hand.

'Praise the Lord of Hosts!' he declared, staring ecstatically at the ceiling. I followed his gaze: just the usual cobwebs and rat droppings.

'Chi-en! On your knees in prayer!' whispered Aunty-Mother in Mandarin to show the gravity of the situation. She switched to English so that no Chinese might eavesdrop, though we were quite alone. 'A letter sent in secret from Nanking! Spiritual Uncle Father's old pupil has written to him! Just think!'

Whether a letter from an old student excites a teacher depends upon the student. This particular pupil had joined Spiritual Uncle Father for Christian instruction in 1847, a year before my birth. He had worshipped at Clear Bell Temple for nearly three months, studying Mr Gutzlaff's Chinese translation of the Bible and learning Christian ritual. A misunderstanding had led him to join a rival missionary's flock in the Canton area. After that, Reverend Shambles lost contact with him.

Not that one didn't hear the pupil's name on every tongue. For he was none other than Hong Xiuquan, who later gained great fame as the Divine Prophet of the Taiping Heavenly Kingdom. In short, this Hong became its Heavenly King, appointed by God (or so he claimed), to rule from the ancient Imperial capital of Nanking, which the Taipings had captured to the amazement of the world in 1853.

At the time we received this letter, the Taiping Heavenly Kingdom was an area of vast extent, threatening to bring down the Ching Emperor himself. Little wonder it excited consternation in our modest kitchen. As Aunty-Mother translated the characters for the tenth time (Spiritual Uncle Father read no Chinese and spoke only a smattering), I learned Hong Xiuquan was inviting his old teacher to visit the Taipings' splendid new Heavenly Capital.

'Praise the Lord's doings! The Good Book is full of instances where righteous priests succour rulers new to the Faith! Thank Jesus!'

We promptly did, kneeling and beseeching His blessed guidance.

Reverend Shambles did not choose to visit his old pupil in the Heavenly Capital at Nanking. Events in Canton were offering splendid opportunities to harvest souls far closer to home. He contented himself with writing letters to English language journals and periodicals in Shanghai, Hong Kong, Macao and Canton, sharing his knowledge of the Heavenly King and hinting – humbly, I have no doubt – that any Christian virtues flowering amongst the Taiping had been planted by Reverend Ezekiel Shambles, DD (Massachusetts), in his role as sower of the Lord's seed.

IV

A boy needs a wise, kindly model to become a proper man – father, uncle, friend or teacher. Women cannot answer. Such is obvious. Perhaps that is why I begged to accompany Spiritual Uncle Father on his missionary expeditions beyond the relative safety of Canton city.

These 'nettings of lost souls' had been made possible by the Manchu authorities' crushing defeat of an interminable rebellion in the rural districts that had nothing to do with the Taipings. Half of China was in revolt against the Ching Emperor at that time. Some say a million were executed in Canton Province, rebel and innocent alike, an atrocity we called the White Terror. In Canton city alone, seventy thousand were decapitated, their bodies thrown into the

Pearl River to prevent a decent burial. Years later, I read a historian who wrote of a vanquished enemy of the ancient Romans lamenting: 'They make a desert and call it peace'. Just so in Canton.

Spiritual Uncle Father found himself able to journey unmolested through the countryside. It was an eerie, uncomfortably silent place. Survivors maintained high walls round their villages to prevent the incursions of bandits. We passed creeks choked with rotting, headless corpses, the water covered by dense clouds of flies and swarming maggots. The smell alone made one retch. Most villages were deserted, others burned.

'Perhaps it's the End of Days, Humble,' mused Reverend Shambles, turning my face away. 'The Book of Revelations speaks of such a time. No wonder millions have joined the Heavenly King in Nanking. Now is the time for true men of God to take their place as leaders.' It was obvious Spiritual Uncle Father craved to be such a leader.

I said earlier a boy needs good models. Certainly I learned courage and persistence from Spiritual Uncle Father. Anti-foreign feeling remained strong and I translated many placards threatening revenge against foreign devils. Each time he would smile or ask: 'How can I be a foreigner when we're all children of the Lord?' So we marched to the next village. There he attempted to preach and distribute Bible tracts. At some villages we were merely abused as he ranted in smatterings of dreadful Cantonese. Once we were robbed until the thieves realised our wealth was a large bag of tracts. These they politely handed back. The bag they kept. Twice we were driven off with stones. Each reverse made Reverend Shambles more determined.

'You see, Humble,' he said, wiping an eyebrow split open by a rock, 'the Lord said: *Let he without sin cast the first stone*. One day I hope they'll learn the beauty in that.'

As he spoke, that feeling of joyous safety was again mine. I gazed up at his bearded, sincere face, longing to be just like him. Yet at Clear Bell Temple another letter had arrived, this time from America. One might say it ended my childhood.

V

The letter came from someone we always knew existed but never expected to see. When summoned by the Lord to garner heathens in China, Reverend Shambles had left an older wife in Salem, Massachusetts. That was fifteen years earlier. During that time, he had returned to America on several occasions to extol his mission and raise funds. He had also sired a son, Corey, by his wife.

All this – except for the fundraising – barely affected us in Canton. Spiritual Uncle Father never spoke of his family. Many realities are best ignored. Yet the letter awaiting him when we returned from the countryside changed everything.

Over ten closely written pages, Mrs Martha Shambles threatened to join her husband in Canton *as soon as practable*. Indeed, she might arrive *at any instants* and anticipated *respictable acomoddattions* for herself and Corey not too near *the Chinee heathens* who, she had heard, were prone to infectious diseases – *a very reel mortication* to little Corey given his *delicate constitutionals*.

Spiritual Uncle Father's reaction to this announcement was extreme, even by his mercurial standards. He went white as a flag of surrender then blood crimson. The sequel was predictable. He stormed to his chamber, Aunty-Mother in pursuit with doses of neat brandy to doctor his trembling fit. This time, however, even her influence was ineffectual. The next day I was ringing the bell at the usual hour, its pure peal rolling over filthy rooftops and alleys, when a cruel grip dragged me backwards. Squirming, I met a pair of bloodshot, glittering eyes. Brandy fumes engulfed me. Even in my terror I was aware of Aunty-Mother plucking at him as he bellowed: 'Ye bastard child of sin! How dare ye ring forth the Lord's bell unto the Temple!' There was more, mainly incoherent. He concluded with a cuff that sent me reeling.

I ran. This time *from* not *to*. Deep into the maze of Guangzhou where I knew he could not follow. Anger mingled with self-pity. How had I deserved his blame? He had betrayed my deepest trust. I hated and worshipped him.

At last, I found myself on a bare, stony hill north of the city where ancient forts squatted. There I gazed down upon teeming streets: pagodas and ramparts, the river clogged with boats and foreign ships, including European merchantmen spewing smoke and steam. In such a vessel Mrs Shambles might already be arriving. I thought she must be a terrible demon indeed to mortify Spiritual Uncle Father! This realisation softened my anger. Yet I sat on until dark. By then I was hungry, cold, thirsty, and missed Aunty-Mother. I discovered all kinds of excuses for Reverend Shambles's behaviour. As stars rose over Canton and the Pearl River, I trailed back miserably to Clear Bell Temple.

VI

I shall spare you my recollections of the Second Opium War. How the Ching Emperor was utterly humbled and Canton occupied by foreign troops; how the chaos in the Empire deepened, to the great advantage of the Taiping rebels. There are far better historians than myself.

Needless to say, we fled Canton during the fighting. For many weeks we ended up in a houseboat, hidden from government troops and pirates by Spiritual Uncle Father's loyal followers. After that came months in Macao, Hong Kong, Shanghai, always relying on charity. Thus, my ninth year passed. For all its tedium and dangers, the war had one positive effect: we heard no more from Mrs Shambles.

By 1858, Canton belonged to British and French troops; trade in opium was resuming. Why not then in souls?

We arrived home that autumn to find home no longer existed. I shall never forget searching the burned rectangle of the chapel and finding, amidst the rubble and charred roof beams, the blackened, cracked bell I had loved to peal. Reverend Shambles at once petitioned the British authorities to secure compensation, or 'war indemnities', from the defeated Chinese governor. 'The Lord will provide,' he informed us. 'Besides, everyone else is getting *demnities*.' Though we all prayed fervently for *demnities*, I could imagine no recompense worthy of our lovely kitchen and bell. In the end, the Lord sent us something, or someone, far less welcome.

We had been barely a month in Canton when a coolie banged on the door of our tiny house near the old Russian Factory. Spiritual Uncle Father had established an outdoors chapel in the backyard, using a water trough for baptisms. The coolie was followed by half-a-dozen others, led by two sullen American sailors escorting a sedan chair of the kind one hired for a few coppers. Perched within was a corpulent white woman so ugly she possessed a kind of distinction. Nevertheless, her clothes were those of a lady; the sort of respectable, wealthy European woman who never frequented Spiritual Uncle Father's acts of worship. Mrs Martha Shambles, accompanied by a small, ill-favoured boy, had tracked down her husband.

Once she was installed in the house, Aunty-Mother and me were ejected to a miserable lean-to behind the baptismal water trough. This precaution was intended to safeguard little Corey's *constitutionals*. Certainly, Reverend Shambles's heir was sickly. When I tried to befriend him, I was rebuffed as a 'slit-eyed heathen'. An understandable mistake, I thought.

'No,' I said, solemnly, 'I am a Christian just like you. And Jesus loves us both.'

Corey's lower lip trembled and he ran off to his mama, crying, 'He says he's jus' like me an' Jesus loves him!'

After this, Mrs Shambles conceived a loathing for myself and Aunty-Mother that exceeded my understanding. I heard her arguing for hours with her husband, who alternated between a feeble, whining defence aimed at placating her temper and a deep-throated roar. My own name and a stranger called *That Temptress Whore of Babylon* frequently entered their quarrels. One thing was certain, Mrs Shambles possessed a power over Spiritual Uncle Father that frightened his followers.

One morning, when Reverend Shambles was out seeking *demnities*, she advanced to where Aunty-Mother mournfully chopped vegetables. The contrast between the two women was stark: one resembling a sullen toad, fierce as a poison dragon; the other meek, willow-like, lovely. Beauty seemed a terrible affront to Mrs Shambles that day.

'Whore!' she shrieked. 'Painted Jezebel! I know your game!' Aunty-Mother wept, bowing low before her tormentor, and raising a submissive cheek as Our Saviour taught.

'Madame,' she begged, 'please consider! Even Mary Magdalene was allowed to wash Jesus's feet.'

Slap. First one cheek. Aunty-Mother meekly offered the other. *Slap*. Back to the first. *Slap*. Like a game of cruel tennis. Mrs Shambles wept as she struck. All the while Aunty-Mother neither flinched nor moved.

I stared in horror then could endure no more. Yes, we were children of shame, unlike Mrs Shambles or Corey, but this was a different kind of shame.

'No!' I rushed forward. 'Hit me instead!'

'What is this?' demanded a deep, familiar voice. 'Martha! Are you gone mad? This fallen woman and her poor child have suffered enough, I say!'

We turned in relief to see Spiritual Uncle Father striding towards us, waving a piece of paper.

'Thank the Lord!' he cried. 'They've paid the *demnities*.'

This news calmed his wife instantly. 'How much?' she sniffed.

'Six thousand dollars! Enough for us to return to Salem and start again.'

We were forgotten as Reverend Shambles bustled his wife indoors. On the way he glanced down at me. I could have sworn he winked.

A few days later, Mrs Shambles and her husband took passage on the good steamship *Lucretia*, bound directly for Boston with a cargo of tea. The vessel was already waiting in the centre of the Pearl River for the tide to turn. Reverend Shambles's tiny flock wept as he was rowed out to the long vessel, its funnels issuing smoke and steam. All but a large chest of his Chinese clothes and religious books had been loaded on board. Mrs Shambles surveyed us triumphantly from the poop deck, Corey by her side. I had expected Spiritual Uncle Father to wave to us, those faithful souls who had risked their lives for him, but he was nowhere to be seen. Perhaps he was overcome by the same miserable feelings as ourselves.

The ship's whistle sounded. Great paddlewheels on the sides of the vessel churned white water. Slowly the *Lucretia* headed for the Pacific. Then I felt a tight grip on my arm. Heard a gasp of joy.

'Humble!' cried Aunty-Mother. 'Look! Look!'

A small rowing boat had appeared in the wake of the steamship. There, his top hat at a jaunty angle, sat Spiritual Uncle Father, while a boatman ferried him back to shore.

At that moment Mrs Shambles spied him. As the vessel drew away, she gesticulated wildly. Above the threshing of the paddle wheels, we heard not a single word of her frenzied cries.

As soon as he was back on Chinese soil, Reverend Shambles urged us to our knees in prayer, where he joined us.

'Dearly beloved,' he intoned, 'the Lord has vouchsafed to me that my work in this land is not complete. I have therefore sent my wife and son to the safety of home. They shall find their baggage contains half the demnities for my lost chapel, a tidy sum. In the meantime, I'm bidden by the Lord to undertake a journey of the *uttermost* importance to the Christian faith in this heathen land. Praise Jesus for it!'

Tears of joy streamed down our cheeks.

'Where is our journey taking us?' I asked, as we rose. He ruffled my hair in a way that delighted me.

'To visit my old pupil in Nanking, Humble,' he said. 'We're going to visit the Heavenly King in his palace and teach him the true scriptures of Our Lord.'

'Amen!' choked Aunty-Mother, clutching her bosom. 'Amen!'

Napa Valley, California
Autumn 1877

The next morning brought a new stranger to Royaume Céleste. He rode a white horse up the steep dirt track from the valley bottom. His straight back rose and fell in rhythm to the horse's movements with the stiff grace of a cavalryman. He wore tight riding breeches and a well-tailored blue frock coat. The leather band round his Stetson caught the sun.

Catherine, who was conferring with Jean-Pierre in the vines, watched him trot up to the winery. One of the Chinese pointed in her direction. The rider urged his mount into a canter, forcing his informant to jump aside. Catherine smoothed her skirt and patted her hair as he approached. Closer up, she caught a glimpse of neat moustaches, a trim goatee beard and the long flowing locks of a Southern gentleman. Reining his horse, he dismounted nimbly, simultaneously removing his hat. With a sweeping bow, he said, 'I assume the pleasure of speaking to Mrs Catherine Bourchier?'

He was older than she had expected from his masterful control of the horse, and no less handsome for grey hairs or having evidently passed his fortieth year.

'I am Catherine Bourchier,' she said.

'Then let me introduce myself.' He had a deep, booming voice softened by a self-deprecating glint in his brown eyes. 'Colonel Hercules Smithson-Mackay, at your service, Ma'am.'

'Delighted,' she said. It did not surprise her so confident a man was a colonel.

Patting the neck of his horse, he looked around. 'Nice little spread you've got yourself here, Mrs Bourchier. Always a pleasure to meet a fellow devotee of the grape. That's why I've ridden over, Ma'am, to cordially (he pronounced the word with four distinct syllables) invite you to the next meeting of the Perryville Viniculturalist Club. We'd be highly esteemed to welcome you.'

She smiled. Boyish charm lurked in his bluff manner.

'So you are a . . .' she pouted slightly, as though struggling over the word, '*viniculturalist* yourself, Colonel?'

He laughed. 'Most surely! Two hundred acres dedicated to the fruit of Bacchus, Ma'am! If that don't make me a viniculturalist, then I'm a chicken farmer.'

Jean-Pierre, summoned by tasks in the winery, left them standing together.

'Perhaps you'd be so kind as to walk your vines with me, Ma'am? So I can get a clearer idea of this fine spread.'

Catherine could hardly refuse. Nor did she wish to. Here was a chance to show off the fruit of her courage: except, she hoped, for Emile. She had little doubt how a manly gentleman like the Colonel would regard her surly, gawky son. As they walked, he asked few questions, preferring to explain his own situation in the world.

'Now I don't want you to think I'm just some kind of farmer, Mrs Bourchier. My little spread north of Perryville is a sort of country retreat. My main business is in Frisco. I own the *California Star*, you see. That, and whole parcels of property here and there.' For a moment, she felt disappointed, but why shouldn't he boast? Unlike Antoine, he was a self-made man. As he spoke his sharp brown eyes observed restlessly and, despite his sweeping gestures, Catherine sensed a more intriguing interior.

'Whoa there!' he said with a gentle touch on her arm. 'That slope should be cleared of chaparral and set to the vine, Ma'am! I've rarely seen a more promising prospect.'

The small slope in question was periodically flooded by the creek, as was obvious from the nature of the willows covering it. Vines prefer to keep their feet dry. Tree frogs croaked, competing with songbirds tardy in their migration.

'I shall consider your advice carefully, Colonel,' she said.

'You'll find yourself mighty glad to have settled in California,' he declared as they walked amiably towards the winery, leading his horse. He gestured at the horizon. 'God's own land! There's no better country on the face of this whole damn earth!'

Catherine was about to speak but he ploughed on: 'I was sure disappointed to see you using Chinese labour. You see, that's one of the items at the Viniculturalist Club meeting. I don't mind telling you, Ma'am, I insist, positively *insist*, the editor of my *California Star* shows no quarter to the Mongolian plague. And I sure am concerned to see a highly attractive white woman – forgive me, Ma'am, I mean no harm by pointing out the obvious – at the mercy of a dozen, no, two dozen Celestials.'

She looked over at the busy group of Chinese labourers singing in unison as they gathered the last few spoilt grapes. Others sorted the bunches on long trestles with patient industry.

'I never feel afraid of them,' she said. 'They are a gentle people.'

'Ma'am, you should! That's exactly why good, law-abiding folk were driven to riot in Frisco . . .' He stopped himself and grinned broadly. 'There I go again! It's just that concern for your welfare riled me. I'll say no more.'

Catherine flushed. Despite his gaucheries, it felt comforting to have a successful, powerful man like the Colonel concerned for her.

'I am not afraid in the least . . .' she began.

'Then you'll come to our meeting next week,' he said. 'I'll look out for you specially and consider it a great honour for our little club.'

With that he bowed and mounted the horse, revealing strong legs and thighs above his high polished boots. Catherine glanced away. Nevertheless, she watched until he cantered into the wooded bank that divided her farm from the placid valley bottom, hoping he might turn to wave. He did not. And, somehow, she liked him more for it.

After he had gone, Catherine drifted upstairs. She felt restless and slightly ashamed of her relief that the Colonel had not met Emile. An impulse drew her to a dusty lumber-room full of half-empty trunks and boxes. Unlatching a valise, she removed a small, framed watercolour that depicted Château de Chauveterre on its hillside, surrounded by abundant vines and fruit trees. For a long while she traced the familiar shapes of the buildings, recollecting small events that had taken place in their rooms and the gravel-walked garden, the orchards of apple and apricot trees. What would Colonel Smithson-Mackay think, she wondered, if he knew of her lost wealth, that her family had been respected for generations?

Then her eye fell on a neat pile of clothes in the trunk. At once she set the painting aside. Emile's baby clothes, packed even as she crammed her own garments into the valise before their flight to America.

Here was a miniature sailor suit. And a white linen baptism robe that she'd sewed herself. She traced with her finger a blue heart stitched in silk near the hem. And here, yes, delightfully small woollen bootees! She placed them on her forefingers like puppet gloves, imagining his little legs and feet, his tiny, pink hands. Yet the clothes, once sweet with the perfume of his warmth, reeked of mothballs and camphor.

But that sailor suit! She remembered him wearing it when he was two – no, maybe just three. She had fed him grapes after carefully removing the bitter seeds. 'More,' he'd cried, 'Maman more!' Strange to remember so small a thing. Catherine searched for other instances of closeness. None came.

Sadness of the quiet kind that lingers longest, filtering like winter rain down to the deep earth of one's soul, settled within her. Taking up the sailor suit, she hurried downstairs. Emile was carving his initials into the wooden porch with a penknife.

'Don't do that!' she said, irritably. Then she recollected the clothes in her hand. 'Look, Emile, look what I have found! You wore this when you were only two. Do you remember?'

She knew it was dangerous to remind him of France. But it seemed to her the baby clothes might unlock the closeness they had never properly found. He glanced haughtily at the outfit.

'I don't remember,' he said. A sly expression crossed his face as he recognised her eagerness. 'But I must have been happy when I wore them. I was happy in France.'

Tears of frustration touched her eyes. 'What would make you happy here?' She was afraid of his answer. 'Tell, Maman!'

She leaned forward to embrace him, to show how dearly she loved him. He pulled away.

'I'll never be happy *here*!' he said, savagely. 'With just *you*!'

He stalked off. Catherine could tell the boy believed he had won a victory. Perhaps he had, for she was wounded into silence. The little sailor suit mocked her. Without thinking, she used it to wipe her eyes.

She became aware of someone outside the kitchen holding a bucket of slops: Monsieur Humble, his face unreadable. No doubt he had witnessed her humiliation, found it entertaining. She glared at him; the baby clothes twisted in her hands. With quiet dignity, he emptied his bucket. The kitchen door closed tactfully behind him.

Catherine dressed for the Perryville Viniculturalist Club with particular care. Old hoops were found for her skirt in the Parisian style, as well as an embroidered and fur-hemmed jacket. Her best bonnet received a careful dusting and she picked loose threads from her shawl.

Standing before the mirror revealed a woman she had almost forsaken, stylish with gracefully-figured clothes. Yet the face in the glass was harder than the one she remembered, its green eyes watchful, mouth unyielding. A face like a closed bud.

Jean-Pierre drove her flatback wagon to Perryville. She would have preferred a more elegant carriage. Antoine had taught by example that gaining credit was merely a question of appearances. Given Royaume Céleste's tottering finances, a need for loans might arise any moment. Never mind that she had crossed the world precisely to escape debt: Papa Bourchier had been too proud to owe a single *franc* in his life. Yet Catherine no longer possessed the luxury of believing only wastrels relied upon credit.

Perryville came into view towards late afternoon, a stripling kind of town, twenty years old. A rich diet of dollars provided by wealthy San Franciscans seeking a country idyll had forced its rapid growth. Neat wooden buildings of all shapes and sizes spread from the central navel of the railroad station. Several banks lined Main Street, along with saloons and hotels, fancy goods stores and glass-fronted emporiums catering for rich and poor. Blacksmiths' forges scented the air with charcoal. Elsewhere, wineries built of stone, brick and wood nestled amidst ancient Californian oaks.

Perryville possessed many of the awkward humours associated with youth: intolerance, a tendency to get drunk whenever possible, a desire to look well at all costs – especially if someone else bore those costs – ignorance, boastfulness and lurking insecurity.

As Catherine rattled into town that October dusk, her thoughts fluttered around the prospect of meeting Colonel Smithson-Mackay. A meal at a local hotel restaurant was followed by the commencement of the Vinicultural Club meeting in a splendid new wooden hall. The streets round the building were littered with carriages, buggies, horses tethered to posts. Dozens of farmers in Sunday best suits and hats smoked near the front porch. Many fell silent as Catherine approached. One man coarse enough to emit a stream of tobacco juice onto the dirt road was swiftly rebuked by his companions.

Staring straight forward, she entered the large meeting room. Benches and chairs had been set out in rows before a long table where six gentlemen sat in state. Amongst them, Colonel Smithson-Mackay, conferring with an elderly, whiskered man of German appearance. Catherine stood uncertainly. Rather than the small club she had anticipated, scores of farmers and prosperous vintners were gathered. For the first time she realised how large a quantity of wine was produced in Napa – and how small a proportion by Royaume Céleste. When her family owned Domaine Bourchier they had been amongst the foremost growers and sellers in the whole of Languedoc. Now she was a nobody, a nothing, just a woman.

Colonel Smithson-Mackay caught sight of her. Rising rapidly, he pushed through the growing crowd. 'Why, Ma-am! Delighted you could honour us! Let me show you to a seat near the front. I noticed Widow Tychson earlier and I'm sure she'd be mighty pleased to have you alongside her. Mrs Tychson inherited a fine spread from her husband . . .'

Speaking in a soft, confidential tone he conducted her to a seat of honour with a few other ladies near the front. All were respectably dressed and in late middle age. They nodded with polite appraisal. Catherine shot him a grateful glance. Even though *the flower of our gathering*, as he referred to the ladies, ignored her, she was no longer conspicuous. One lady, who he had introduced with perceptible froideur as Mrs Trubody, whispered, 'I do believe we are neighbours, my dear.' Before Catherine could reply, the chairman's gavel banged.

Catherine sensed growing tension in the room. Voices broke into an argument at the back. Even on the high table a heated debate began sotto voce. From her front seat Catherine caught snatches: *Damn it, Smithson, you can't expect us to pass a resolution like that . . . Trubody, these men are here precisely to . . .* But she never heard what they were precisely there for. The stout, whiskered German gentleman, who she later learned was Mr Charles Krug, again banged his gavel.

'Good evening,' he said in a thick accent. 'Let our proceedings begin.'

Item One was the adverse effects of frost on this year's crop; then good news on tariffs for foreign wine imports; next, the woeful lack of a market for Californian wine given the universal trade depression . . . Catherine realised someone had mentioned her name. It was Mr Krug. 'Madame,' he said, stiffly, 'it has come to my attention you are related to the famous Bourchier Domaine. A most noble heritage of the vine!'

Catherine felt all eyes upon her. Heat rose up her neck.

'Mr Krug is wondering whether you have a view on how we Californians might improve the sales of our wine,' added Smithson-Mackay, helpfully.

For a moment she was tempted to claim ignorance. A memory of Papa addressing a respectful crowd of vintners at the annual sales in Paris made her stubborn. 'I have tasted many wines from this valley,' she said. 'Some are very good. Many are not vintages of the best.'

Murmurs rose from winemakers sensing a foreign slight.

'It is my belief,' she said, echoing Papa Bourchier's favourite sentiment when it came to wine. 'Subtlety is all. Learn quality then the selling happens of itself. Also, do not be afraid to blend wines, sirs,' she advised. 'It is my intention that Royaume Céleste Vineyard shall lead in the matters of quality and blending.'

Now the room listened with respect. This style of talk went down well in Perryville. All those on the high table nodded vigorously.

'We owe thanks for that, Madame,' said Smithson-Mackay, glancing round the hall with a faintly proprietorial air.

The next item was announced, leaving Catherine crimson and elated. But hers was a flimsy confidence. She had no more buyers for her wine, however superior or subtle, than neighbours brewing swill fit for pig feed. Mrs Trubody leaned across to pat her hand. 'Well done, my dear,' she whispered. 'It takes a woman to talk a little sense round here.'

By the time Catherine regained her composure, the tension she detected earlier had returned. Colonel Smithson-Mackay was on his feet, denouncing Chinese labour: 'Mongolians are as common as rats in a sewer throughout this fair valley of Napa! I insist this club sends a resolution to the Governor of California condemning the presence of Chinamen in our glorious State as an unpatriotic abomination!' Others, eager for cheap labour, bellowed back at him. Pounding his gavel, the chairman restored order by declaring the meeting over.

While Jean-Pierre fetched their horse and wagon for the journey home, Hercules Smithson-Mackay appeared by her elbow. His eyes were bright.

'Mrs Bourchier! I hope our little disputation will not deter you from our next meeting!'

She caught a warm, musky odour masked by soap. It seemed a long time since she had smelt a man in that way.

'No,' she said. 'Even if I had been deterred, I suspect you would have done what you liked anyway.'

He chuckled. 'You speak the truth there, Ma-am,' he began, then voices and congratulatory pats on the shoulder summoned him and he bowed farewell.

It was growing dark as they left Perryville. Jean-Pierre's breath was sweet with brandy and he seemed unusually cheerful.

The night was clear, whorls of bright stars lit their way along the flat valley bottom. Dark silhouettes of mountain ranges on either side seemed comforting and solid, like views of the Pyrenees she remembered as a girl. Night-scents drifted – plants earthy and medicinal, rich manure, traces of honeysuckle – but still she smelt Hercules Smithson-Mackay as he bowed to her outside the Vinicultural Club Hall.

'Madame,' said Jean-Pierre, suspiciously, 'someone is coming up behind us quickly.'

Catherine had heard rumours of a notorious road agent holding up stagecoaches higher up the valley. She stared back down the road. A brougham was trotting along the dusty highway at some speed. Soon enough, it caught up.

Lamps hung from ornate bronze fittings on either side of the hood. By their light Catherine recognised Mrs Trubody, the lady who had introduced herself as a neighbour. Beside her was one of the men from the high table – indeed, the gentleman who had opposed Colonel Smithson-Mackay's thunder about Mongolian pests. Both vehicles halted, their horses snorting in the cool night air.

'Madame Bourchier!' called Mrs Trubody. 'So glad we caught up with you! Did you know about the highwayman in this valley? Mr Trubody here – please let me introduce my husband – was concerned to see you riding home alone.'

The gentleman wore a smart overcoat and top hat of the highest quality. His face was notable only for its ordinariness – yet Catherine detected a strong, calm resolve.

'But Mr Trubody, I am not alone.' She introduced Jean-Pierre as her trusted steward. 'So you see, I have a gallant chaperone.'

Trubody touched his hat to the Frenchman. 'Relieved to know it!' he declared. 'I was surely interested to hear your comments about quality blends tonight, Ma-am. If you'd be so kind as to pay us a visit, we could discuss it further.'

Catherine's pulse quickened. Was this the stroke of good fortune she needed? Trubody's white mansion on the opposite side of the valley spoke of vast resources.

'You must visit us soon, my dear,' urged Mrs Trubody. 'If only so I can ask where you French ladies find so much *style* in a place like Napa!'

With that, despite their earlier concerns about the road agent, the Trubodys rattled off, their well-sprung brougham propelled by a stately pacer.

While Catherine spoke of blends and quality at Perryville Viniculturalist Club, a different debate took place in the kitchen of Royaume Céleste. Emile had just finished his stew, scraping the bowl clean with bread. Chi-en stood with his back to the boy, observing twilight through the open kitchen door.

'Put your plate in the tub,' he said, over his shoulder, 'and make sure no crumbs go on the floor.'

A stuck-out tongue was aimed at the Chinaman's back.

'In the tub,' repeated Chi-en, absent-mindedly, still watching the dusk.

'That's your job! You're my servant.'

Now he had Chi-en's full attention. 'Is that so?'

'Yes.'

'I suppose everyone serves something or someone,' mused Chi-en. 'What do you serve?'

The child looked at him uncomprehendingly.

'How odd,' remarked Chi-en, 'you cannot understand a stupid servant's question.'

'Oh, I can! Now collect my plate.'

'First answer my question, *grand seigneur.*'

Emile looked round, cornered. 'I serve myself. No one else.'

'No one?'

'No.'

'Then you are selfish?'

'Yes.'

'And proud of it?'

The boy hesitated. 'Yes.'

'Leave the plate,' said Chi-en, 'then go to your room. I'll clear up later.'

The child, confused by his dismissal, did not move. 'Don't want to,' he said.

'As you like.'

A long silence followed while Chi-en smoked a cigarette, leaning against the frame of the open back door. Sunset softened obdurate mountains and hardy pines. The autumn winds blew a little colder each day.

'What do you write in your notebook?' asked the boy. 'I . . . I looked when you weren't there but the letters are queer. Just squiggles and shapes.'

'Firstly, never read another person's private writing without an invitation,' said Chi-en. 'Secondly, it is written in Chinese. As I expect you cannot read English, Chinese is out of the question.'

'No,' said the boy, crestfallen, 'I can read English a little. What are you writing about?'

'About China,' said Chi-en, 'and a great man. A king, no less. How he turned China upside down when I was a boy. Most of all, a wonderful friend I met in those days called Prince Hong.'

Emile leaned forward curiously. 'Who was this king?'

Chi-en hesitated then, to his wonder, found himself answering, 'Once there was a humble schoolteacher in Canton Province who dreamed of going to Heaven. When he got there, God said to him: "You are my youngest son, second only to your eldest brother, Jesus. You shall be the Heavenly King on Earth and establish my Kingdom of Great Peace."'

Emile giggled. 'A schoolteacher? Like Mr Crane in Perryville?'

Chi-en wasn't listening. Gripped by a forgotten fervour, he recited a poem in Chinese, *Zhan yao jian*, he began. When he had finished the boy was grinning.

'What does *that* mean?'

'It is a poem written by the Heavenly King, the schoolmaster you find so amusing. It means, roughly, let me think . . .

With our swords we bring order to mountains and valleys,

All people between the seas shall live as one family.

Tigers and dragons roar. Light covers the earth.

Our joy shall be boundless when the Great Peace comes.'

'Do you believe in the poem?' asked Emile.

Chi-en felt uneasy. 'Once I did. When everyone around me did. I was young and knew no better.'

Emile answered with a snort. 'I'm young and I don't believe in it!'

'Then I congratulate you.'

The boy thought for a moment. To Chi-en's surprise, he picked up the dirty stew bowl and spoon, dropping them in the tub used for washing dishes. 'I might be interested in hearing more about this Heavenly King,' he announced, 'but now I'm going to bed.'

'Sleep well, *grand seigneur*. And remember, only a fool serves just himself.'

Napa Valley, California
Autumn 1877

The next dawn, Chi-en woke early and decided to walk the boundaries of Royaume Céleste before his chores began. Three pheasants rose from the vines with loud, beating wings. Tendrils of mist rose with them, stirred by the sun climbing over eastern hills. Inspired by his conversation with ten-year-old Emile, each step drew him back to another Heavenly Kingdom where, as a youth, he had served a cause hoping to liberate all China. *Taiping. The Great Peace.* Ruefully, he recollected his own advice: only a fool serves just himself. Truly his service had diminished.

Mid-morning found Chi-en in the farmhouse of Royaume Céleste removing chamber pots. Their contents joined a heap of horse manure at the rear of the stable before the pots were washed and hidden beneath their owners' beds – just one of his many household duties. Days had assumed a routine: light fires, prepare breakfast, wash dishes, clean, dust, sweep, prepare lunch, wash dishes, prepare dinner, wash dishes, until – as darkness fell – the starlit autumn evenings with their silences and scents and night noises, their drone of insects around lamps, became his own.

Chi-en suspected Jean-Pierre considered a male housekeeper comical but valued his cookery too much to show it. Madame Bourchier was less easily satisfied. Chi-en knew she believed that he saw more than any servant should – as was probably true. Glimpses of her private papers had revealed letters from tradesmen demanding overdue payments. Her worried expression when she bent over Royaume Céleste's account book almost made him regret asking for an extra fifty cents a day.

He also saw her watching when the other Chinese ignored him or muttered insults. Not that he blamed them. The Sam clan had ordered that no one – on pain of losing his livelihood – should associate with the Taiping Longhair. One day Catherine asked him bluntly if the Chinamen hated him because his forehead was unshaved. Chi-en paused in his work of carrying out potato peelings to the sow and her litter.

'Madame,' he said, 'I believe they do not hate me, so much as fear me.'

She seemed to consider the idea for a moment. 'Fear grows to feel like hate until one can hardly tell them apart.'

It surprised him that she could be wise.

Two weeks passed and Chi-en's health improved. Each evening he listened to Madame's oboe sing jigs and etudes, folksongs and wistful adagios. The latter seemed her favourites. Often he stared at the mountain, speculating whether he was strong enough to move on. Lingering in Royaume Céleste, though comfortable, was a betrayal of the good he felt compelled to attempt in this world. At least he was adding more pages to *A Memoir of Prince Hong*.

For all that, Chi-en judged it dangerous to stay. Even now the Sam clan might have used their contacts in Chinatown to discover his true name – and status as a wanted man.

One afternoon, his chores completed early, Chi-en wandered to the winery where wooden vats jostled for space on the second floor. It was a large, high-ceilinged room heady with aromas of fruit. The cobbled floors and smooth walls were kept scrupulously clean to avoid tainting the fermentation.

He found Catherine Bourchier holding a glass flask of purple liquid to the light. The constant buzz and hum from the *chapeau* or cap of fermenting grape skins and stalks masked his footsteps.

After tasting from the flask, she frowned. Taking out a stoppered jar of white crystals from a pocket in her apron, she spooned careful measurements into the vat. Candles had been spread round the winery floor. Some flickered, others burned brightly.

'Does Madame need a lamp?' His voice echoed in the long room.

She looked up with a start. 'My goodness, 'Umble! You arrive as quietly as a cat.'

He repeated his question.

'Ah, you mean the candles,' she said. 'No, I am merely measuring the gas from each vat. If the candle goes out I need to add more of this sulphur.' She held up the jar of white crystals. 'But see! All are alight, a good sign.'

'Is not sulphur the substance of hell?' he asked, wryly. 'Or am I thinking of brimstone?'

'I have no idea what you are thinking. Anyway, I'm glad you found me. This afternoon I will be away, visiting our neighbours, Mr and Mrs Trubody. Please look out for Emile. I worry he spends too much time by himself.'

An awkward silence settled.

'May I ask, Madame, why you are rubbing grape skins between your fingers?'

All her attention was on the fruit, looking, sniffing, feeling, even nibbling shreds of grape. When she ignored him, he said, 'Never mind.'

She glanced up. 'Please, what was your question?'

After he repeated it, she scattered the handful of fleshy seeds and stalks and skin back over the bubbling *chapeau*.

'Because, Monsieur 'Umble, I prefer red wine to white. Just as I prefer warm-blooded people to cold fish who listen to other people's private conversations with their sons.'

She drew breath. Chi-en understood she was referring to her argument with Emile over the sailor suit. He was about to retort that at least some cold fish possess manners, *Madame*, when she continued, 'But to answer your question, the exact colour of the wine can be determined if one is attentive. Even its precise shade and lustre if one watches and guides. You see, the colour comes from the grape skins. I must find a balance between the tartness of the skins and stalks and the sweetness of the juice.'

Again, she tasted from the flask. 'This wine will need a little more tartness,' she said, 'the yeast is stimulated by tartness. Only in six months' time, when I hold a full glass to the sun and glints catch the light, will I know for sure.'

Chi-en suspected this demonstration of her mastery of the winemaker's art was meant to compensate for her lack of authority over Emile.

'I see.'

'My apologies if I am confusing you.'

He smiled blandly. As did she.

'Interesting,' he said.

'I'm glad you find it so, Monsieur 'Umble.'

After blowing out the candles, she left him among the vats. He listened to the turbulent liquid's buzz and whisper: a living process. Time was fermenting through the young wine, breathing out and in, seething and relaxing. Yet he knew that in a few weeks the wine would calm itself, the hum become stray pops, murmurs, then silence. Always, in the end, silence. For no clear reason he thought of Aunty-Mother and sighed.

Leaning over a vat, he watched the floating crust shiver as bubbles rose and he listened hard for patterns. Thus Chi-en became aware of surreptitious movements behind the vat.

'Either that's Emile Bourchier or the largest rat I ever heard,' he announced in French. A suppressed snigger settled the question.

After a pause, the boy emerged. Even by country standards he cut a wild figure, hair half-clipped on one side after he broke free from his mother's grip while she sheared him. His clothes were filthy, too, on account of refusing to wear anything other than the threadbare French suit he had outgrown within six months of arriving in America.

'Well, Emile,' he said, 'your Maman has gone to visit your neighbours in the white mansion across the valley. What will you do that is useful until she returns?'

At the mention of his mother, Emile's scowl resumed.

'Papa's house is bigger than that white *hut*,' he muttered. 'Maman says we had to leave France because Papa died and we had no money. But I don't believe her. Papa is still alive! When I'm a man I shall go home and find him.'

Chi-en stared at Emile. He had never heard him speak so frankly. And he understood the boy's quest only too well – it could never be reasoned away.

'Then ask yourself, Emile . . . would your Papa be proud of a boy dressed like you?' he asked, softly. 'Proud of a son who cannot read or write properly?'

Emile reddened in a manner uncannily like his mother's. 'I can write!' he cried, shrilly. '*And* read!'

'Then show me. Prove it to the world. Go to school.'

Instead, the boy spat into the nearest vat and fled. Chi-en sighed.

An hour later, he was idly stirring a stew of rabbits shot by Jean-Pierre when Emile appeared in the doorway. A piece of paper flapped tentatively in his hand.

'See!' he said. 'I can write.'

Chi-en continued stirring. 'I shall look in a moment. Meanwhile, sit down and read out exactly what you have written. The exact words.'

Scowling, Emile took a seat. 'It is a letter to Papa.'

'Read it out.'

'Dear Monsieur,' began the boy in an expressionless voice. 'I hope and trust you are in good health. We are all in good health in America. I do not like America. It is a bad place. Please come and fetch me home. Very soon. Your loving son, Emile.'

Chi-en continued to stir. 'A promising letter,' he conceded. 'If you went to school you would learn an even better style. Why do you refuse to go to school?'

'I hate it here. *That's* why.'

'Why won't you learn English?'

'Because I hate it here.' A cunning expression flickered across his face. 'Besides, I know more than Maman guesses. A *lot* more.'

Spoon circled pot then stopped.

'Make yourself proud by going back to school,' said Chi-en. 'Everyone must find some worthwhile duty to follow. A purpose that is honourable and good. It is what separates good men from bad. Never mind *hate*. I cannot begin to tell you all the things I hate in this world.'

'What do you hate?' Emile asked, hesitantly.

Chi-en's expression grew blank. 'I hate to see anyone make an imbecile of himself, that is all.'

For a long while Emile sat at the table, the letter to his father clutched tightly in a grubby hand. Chi-en removed three golden loaves from the oven, tapped their bases and put them aside to cool. The kitchen filled with a warm, yeasty smell. At last Emile looked up. 'I've discovered ghosts in the woods,' he whispered. 'There! You didn't know that.'

Laying a palm across the hot crusts of the loaves, Chi-en said, 'Ghosts are everywhere.'

'Do you want me to show you where they go?' asked Emile.

Chi-en stifled the word *non*. The boy, certainly an unpleasant child, was taking a risk. He was offering his trust.

'Is it far?' Madame Bourchier's dinner was due in an hour or so.

'Just in the woods above the vineyard.'

'Show me these ghosts.'

They walked uphill through rows of vines stripped bare by patient hands and winter's shadow. It was late afternoon, thin, wispy clouds over the distant mountain. Neither spoke as they crushed dusty earth and stones beneath their booted feet. Yet when they reached the line of trees surrounding the vineyard, Emile paused.

'No one goes further into the woods than me,' he whispered, 'except the ghosts.'

Chi-en glanced up the steep hillside dark with thickets, pines and ancient redwoods. At his feet he noticed a worked piece of flint and stooped.

'An arrowhead,' he muttered.

The boy grew uneasy. 'We should have brought something to give them.'

Chi-en held up the flint. 'Let's give them this.'

Emile led him onto a faint trail. At first Chi-en thought it had been made by deer, even bears, but soon they encountered conical piles of small stones, several higher than a man, way-markers up the hillside. His grip on the arrowhead tightened. Here was a world far removed from the pastoral quiet of the valley bottom; wild, heedless woods clinging to inhospitable slopes and bare, pockmarked volcanic rocks. Below, the land had been measured and divided into squares, rectangles, straight lines. This wild place defied ownership.

The trail passed glens and side valleys dense with chaparral. They followed the course of the stream that flowed through Royaume Céleste, brushing against plants which, for all the words heaped in his brain, Chi-en had no name: madrona, manzanita, buckeye, as well as the more familiar maples, ponderosa pines, oaks and redwoods. And amidst the life-giving plants: poison oak, poison ivy. Finally, Emile squatted on the track. 'Once I heard the ghosts singing,' he whispered. 'I didn't dare go near. It was a sad singing.'

Despite himself, Chi-en felt oddly unnerved. He listened carefully. Wind in the trees, a flutter of discarded autumn leaves. Somewhere in the valley below, the faint echo of a gunshot.

'They are not singing now,' he reassured the crouching boy.

'Shhh! Listen.'

Was that a strange echo at the edge of hearing? Emile nodded decisively. 'They don't mind me showing you their place.'

Once more Chi-en followed the path upwards. Quite suddenly, they arrived.

'This is where the singing came from,' said Emile.

Volcanic boulders formed an oval area seventy feet across. Chi-en noticed a faint circle of ash near the centre. He examined the arrowhead in his hand, glanced at the earnest boy.

'You are right,' he said, 'ghosts visit here. We should not be afraid of them – they have more reason to fear us. Thank you for showing me this place.'

They climbed back down the hillside to the vineyard in silence, Chi-en aware the expedition had taken longer than expected. Madame's dinner would be late. So be it. For all her bourgeois manners, Madame had aristocratic pretensions. Waiting would do her good.

As they entered the vineyard, Emile halted, staring straight ahead, his fists clenched. Clearly the child had worked himself up to something momentous.

''Umble . . .' he said. It was the first time he had addressed Chi-en by name. 'I have decided. Papa will not be proud of me if I cannot read and write well. Tell Maman, I will go back to school.'

'Will you change your mind?'

'Never!' Emile's eyes flashed angrily. '*Never!*'

There's the father, thought Chi-en, dead or alive.

They found Catherine Bourchier waiting on the farmhouse porch. Emile marched straight past, head held upright.

'Where have you been with my son?'

Chi-en examined her frankly. 'In the woods.'

'I called on my neighbours but they were not at home. Then I visited Perryville to buy supplies. And when I return, no one!'

'Emile wished to show me somewhere important to him. By the way, Madame, I believe Indians visit ancient places up there. If you see them, there is no need for alarm.'

'My son showed you that?' Jealousy and distrust made her tone harsh. 'It is me he should show!'

Abruptly, Chi-en tired of Catherine Bourchier – if that was her real name. 'Madame, your son has agreed to return to school. May I respectfully suggest you meet his teacher. I believe the boy will try his best from now on.'

'Why? I wish to believe you, Monsieur 'Umble. You have no idea how badly. But Emile is incorrigible. Did he say why he wishes to go back?'

'Ask him yourself,' he said in English. There was a dozen, no, a hundred things he would have liked to add. 'Ask him and then you might learn.'

After dinner, Emile sought out Chi-en in the kitchen. The Chinaman had his notebook ready on the table and, at the sight of the boy, instinctively closed it. The child stood awkwardly, shoulders hunched.

'I told Maman,' he said, 'that I will return to school.'

'You did well.'

'She was cross because I showed you where the ghosts live,' explained the boy. 'I told her it wasn't your fault.'

'No one is at fault,' said Chi-en. 'Your mother is busy with running the vineyard. And she is naturally concerned that you do not have more companions of your own age. A boy needs friends to share his adventures. Have you any nearby?'

'No.'

'Do something about that,' advised Chi-en, 'when you return to Mr Crane's school.'

'Maybe.' The child screwed up his face. 'Did *you* have many friends as a boy?'

Now Chi-en felt less assured.

'Not many. In fact, I had just one. But he was a great, great friend. A Prince of the Heavenly Kingdom! Prince Hong was his name. He saved my life when I was just two years older than you.'

'That sounds like a fairy story Maman used to tell me,' said Emile, doubtfully. 'It had a prince and a pauper in it as well. But why would a prince want a cook for a friend?'

The boy's question fanned ever-smouldering doubts.

'Because,' Chi-en said, 'a prince is only as powerful as his followers. Prince Hong found me useful in many ways, not least because I made him laugh.'

'Were you a jester?' asked Emile, puzzled. 'Or a clown?'

Chi-en decided the boy had no conception of his rudeness.

'Not exactly a jester.'

'Then how were you useful?'

'I forget. Enough talk, Emile Bourchier! Back to your English or *you* will be laughed at like a jester at Mr Crane's school.'

The dead Gascon's winery exploited the contours of Royaume Céleste. Built into a cutaway section of the hill, three storeys high; walls of pink lava stone thick as a cathedral's ensured coolness during the hot Napa summer and warmth when cold winds blew from the north. Catherine had every reason to thank her predecessor. His design made gravity work harder than muscle.

First, wagons carried freshly-picked grapes up the hillside to the topmost storey, a long room containing wine presses. From there, crushed juices flowed down channels into fermentation vats on the second storey below. In due course, that same gravity would decant her wine into barrels for aging on the ground floor.

Catherine stood among the vats of fermenting grapes and juice. Tasting had confirmed her suspicion: this *vendange* promised an exceptional vintage. The Gascon's vines had surpassed his frailty.

Often when she came here alone, she sensed someone watching. Inexplicable noises: a scrape, footstep. Nonsense, of course, rats, mice . . . Unless the disappointed Gascon haunted his winery, hating her for fleecing his desperate widow.

But he hardly needed to curse her. Even if the fermentation bore out its promise, how could she sell what no one was buying? And she could scarcely afford casks and bottles for half the wine she had produced that year. The rest might end up in the creek. Otherwise there would be no precious barrels for next year's *vendange*. The Gascon widow's voice echoed in Catherine's mind: *My husband killed himself trying to make this vineyard pay. Can you succeed when my husband did not?* Except now the widow gloated rather than moaned with despair.

Catherine went to a wooden door and winch built into the side of the winery. From this vantage she observed the remaining Chinese workers scrubbing out containers and baskets used during the crush, their arms and hands blood red. Monsieur Humble watched from the kitchen doorway, a peculiar expression on his face. This intrigued her. She sometimes caught herself wondering what he was thinking.

Jean-Pierre joined her. Following her gaze, he said, 'Last night's *cassoulet* needed more salt.'

'On Saturday,' she said, 'we will go to the Harvest Fiesta in Perryville. I will speak to Emile's old teacher, Mr Crane, and arrange for him to resume his lessons.'

She knew who to thank for Emile's decision to walk miles each day to Perryville and back for dull lessons in a language he barely comprehended.

'Madame . . .' Jean-Pierre disturbed her thoughts. 'Do you mean to approach Monsieur Trubody with your plan today?'

She hesitated. She could not explain how it hurt her pride to woo strangers.

'The last time I called on them, they were away from home. Jean-Pierre, whatever happens, I want you to know how I marvel at the vintage you are producing from an unfamiliar *terroir*.'

Perhaps she also hoped for a little appreciation of her own contribution to the new wine.

Jean-Pierre frowned. 'It is incredible there are no buyers. Monsieur Bourchier would have found buyers by now. "Leclos," he used to say to me, "make the finest wine and I will find the finest customers!" Ah, if only he were here!'

'That would be difficult,' she snapped, 'this side of the Resurrection.'

He smoothed the tips of his moustache. 'Convince Monsieur Trubody of your plan,' he said, gravely. 'Great wine turns to piss if no one buys it.'

Catherine had dressed with particular care for the Vinicultural Club; today she did the same, but with greater calculation. She must look respectable – clean, competent, confident. Anything flattering was to be avoided. Nature had blessed Mrs Trubody more in her choice of husband than beauty. Essential that the older woman felt no rivalry.

She chose a plain, dark green gown and a modest silver crucifix once inseparable from her mother's neck. This last item caused much indecision – would the Trubodys condemn her as a Papist? No matter. Some things were too much her own to be discarded.

Finally, the question of transport. It was an unseasonably warm afternoon, perhaps the last before autumn banished summer. She could easily walk the two or three miles across the valley, but that would make her look *trop paysanne*. Instead, using a side saddle, she trotted her faithful mare down the steep track from Royaume Céleste to the highway. Thence she took a series of faint, dusty paths through stubble-fields shorn of wheat, round ponds and groves of majestic oaks until another road appeared on the opposite side of the valley. Here an imposing stone gateway proclaimed *Trubody Nook*. A road screened by rhododendrons led her to the front entrance of the mansion.

Trubody Nook blended the architectural styles of a dozen lands and centuries: mock Tudor beams and plasterwork studded with Greek masks hung below roofs reminiscent of Gothic cathedrals; chimneypots that would have smoked quite contentedly above an eighteenth century English gentleman's residence gazed down upon modern glass cupolas; there were faux-Medieval turrets, hothouses and modern cast iron railings.

As Catherine swung from the side saddle, a large, leisurely man in a butler's uniform emerged from the imposing front entrance. He bowed with studied solemnity, muttering to someone behind him. A young footman with powdered hair and extraordinarily tight breeches trotted from the house and took the horse's reins with a bow. Catherine had been in California long enough to know that obsequious servants came at a very high price. The butler examined her with quiet appraisal. 'Whom may I have the pleasure of announcing, Ma'am?'

'Mrs Trubody is at home?' She felt ashamed of her nervousness.

'Indeed, Ma-am. Whether she is disposed to receive visitors I cannot say.'

Catherine had an anxious wait in an oak-panelled hall decorated with baronial pretensions – swords, maces, coats of arms and two gleaming suits of armour. If Mrs Trubody declined to receive her, the hope that had brought her to America might fail. And her fallen status in the world would be confirmed. The butler returned.

'Madame Bourchier,' he said, 'Mrs Trubody requests that you join her in the garden for afternoon tea.'

She followed him through long corridors decorated as expensively – and in the same hotch-potch of styles – as the exterior of Trubody Nook. It felt as though the paint had not quite dried. Her confidence dwindled like the echo of the butler's hard soles on the parquet floor.

They passed through a pair of open glass doors, emerging onto a terraced, south-facing garden. Rows of vines scaled gentle slopes near the house, just as at Royaume Céleste. There, however, comparisons ended. Catherine remembered Emile's taunt that they had traded a castle for a hovel.

Then she was smiling as Mrs Trubody advanced towards her with a cry of pleasure.

Nancy Trubody was a well-preserved woman in her fifties, hair tied back in a neat bun. Everything about her appearance suggested a reassuring neatness: white dress and perfectly straight cuffs, diamond and gold jewellery worn at regular intervals around her person. Even her cheeks were neatly plump and rosy.

'Madame Bourchier!' she said. 'How clever of you to appear just when I needed some interesting company. You will take a cup of tea with me?'

'With great pleasure.'

Soon a procession of servants carried trays and trundled laden trolleys to a linen-covered table in the middle of the lawn. Silver cutlery twinkled in the autumn sunshine.

'I am quite determined that, as close neighbours, we should know each other better,' declared Mrs Trubody. 'Napa can be such a dreadfully dull place, though my husband thinks it's a kind of heaven. *The New Eden* is what he calls it.'

Catherine detected an intelligent scrutiny and awaited awkward questions. Yet the older woman seemed content to utter ten words for every one of her guest's. Catherine soon learned Mr Trubody had made his fortune building railroads and their great regret was a lack of children. Trubody Nook, it seemed, was no more than a 'country cottage'. Their main residence being a 'little enough place compared to Stanford's' on Nob Hill in San Francisco.

Catherine also discovered wine was a recent passion of Mr Trubody's, partly, confessed his wife, because of an absurd wager with some gentlemen at the Viniculturalist Club over who could produce the best vintage. 'Especially Colonel Smithson-Mackay,' added Mrs Trubody. 'But I believe you are acquainted with the Colonel?'

'Very little,' she replied. Indeed, he had occupied more time in her imagination than real life.

'It's just men and their foolish top-doggery,' sighed Mrs Trubody. 'Colonel Smithson-Mackay has an eye on the Senate and my husband favours the other fellow. Silly *men*-politics, my dear. The Colonel fought for the Confederacy during the war. But we're all friends now, thank the Good Lord above!' She examined her guest with a slight smile.

While they talked Chinese gardeners snipped silently and re-arranged the dry earth of the flowerbeds. A shadow fell across the tea table. Catherine looked up to find a sharp-chinned, long face looking down at her, hat in hand. Although Mr Trubody wore bushy side-whiskers the rest of his head was bald except for thin white locks at the very crown.

'What's this? A visitor!' said Mr Trubody, glancing at his wife with the barest flicker of raised eyebrows. 'Now, before we commence the pleasantries, let me say straight off that I hope your visit isn't of an entirely social nature. You'll not escape without discussing that little piece of business I mentioned the other night!'

Mrs Trubody laughed with embarrassment. Or its semblance.

'Why, Nathaniel, dear! There you go again! Straight for the bullseye!'

'No point shilly-shallying with a practical lady like Madame Bourchier.'

'There are *decencies*, my love,' reproved Mrs Trubody, fondly. 'I do declare, Madame Bourchier! What am I to do with such a man?'

The answer, it transpired, was to suggest Mr Trubody drive their guest around the vineyard in a small buggy to discuss 'that piece of business'. Catherine tried to conceal her enthusiasm for the proposal but caught a twinkle of complicity between the pair.

'Mr Trubody,' she confessed, 'you are right to say my motive for coming here was not entirely one of pleasure.'

'Good.' He rubbed his hands together. 'I like people to talk plain.'

Soon they were trotting in a two-seat buggy behind a magnificent palfrey with ribbons in its mane. As they passed through rows of stripped vines, Mr Trubody explained his situation. Although his scores of acres produced many tons of fruit, the resulting wine was vinegary – poorer, indeed, than that of his neighbours, a disparity he found 'most grievous'. Catherine could not help wondering if those neighbours included Colonel Smithson-Mackay.

'You see,' he said, 'I have bottles of Domaine Bourchier in my cellars. No need to look surprised, my dear! California is no stranger to the good things of this earth. I have also discovered a certain pest has laid waste to the ancient Bourchier vineyards. Forgive me for presuming, but I suspect that's why you're here.'

Catherine's heart beat swiftly. What else did he know? That she was not a real widow? She must be bold. Papa Bourchier always said ripeness is when one reaps.

'You are right again,' she sighed. 'I have come here to start afresh. Here the earth is clean.'

As the wheels of the buggy turned his questions revolved round Catherine's knowledge of the vine. She explained how she had assisted her father with blending, on account of her fine palate, and that she was fermenting a superb crop at Royaume Céleste. He led her through his enormous winery, asking her to test his own fermenting wine.

Using a dipper, she filled a glass and held it to the light. Even before tasting its bitter tannins made her sniff. The new wine had not spoiled but time was against it. Catherine let the juice linger on her tongue. If the tartness could be softened, it might become respectable, a harmless base one might transform with a judicious blend. But only if it was properly *fined* – and very soon.

'Mr Trubody,' she said, 'you must first remove the *chapeau* of skins and stalks. At once, sir! Let your men be instructed today if possible.'

He squinted at her. 'How d'you know?'

Catherine felt her cheeks redden. 'Because I do. More importantly, you must add . . . Let me see.' She tasted again. 'Yes, bull's blood and egg whites to each vat.' A memory of a particularly bad harvest at Château de Chauveterre made her eyes brighten. 'Oh, and you must use fish glue, Mr Trubody, what we call isinglass. Its preparation is slow and patient but it will work.'

'Will it, young lady?'

'Yes, it will. And as for that faint smell of rotten eggs.' She held out the glass to him and he sniffed suspiciously. 'If you tie a silver spoon to a piece of string and lower it into each of these vats, the smell will vanish after a few weeks.' She laughed. 'Of course, the spoon will turn black as tar but I'm sure your butler has silver polish!'

'Oh, we can be sure of that,' he said.

She dared herself to go further. 'I could help you with this.' She tore a page from her pocketbook and scribbled with a small pencil. 'Here are the correct proportions of blood and egg white and fish glue for each gallon of wine.'

'My, you are a practical lady!' he said, pocketing the piece of paper. 'Obliged, Ma-am, I'm sure.'

Though Catherine suspected his pride was working against her, such an opportunity might never come again. Boldly, she made her proposal, one that might save Royaume Céleste from ruin when spring came. Did he sense her desperation? Still she tried, stating that she wished to bottle half of the exceptional vintage she anticipated and sell it under her own label. As for the other half, if they blended her fine wine with his inferior wine, a very respectable claret would result. 'We could split the profits,' she concluded.

He looked at her sharply; dipped a finger into the vat of fermenting grapes and tasted the mixture. A vexed expression stole across his hawk-like face. Evidently, he thought her impertinent.

'I shall consider your proposal,' he said.

As Catherine bade farewell to Mr and Mrs Trubody on the stone steps of Trubody Nook, she felt all the discomfort of wounded hope and pride. Perhaps Nancy Trubody sensed her guest's feelings, for the older lady called out, 'Madame Bourchier, I'm counting on you to help with our charity table at the Harvest Fiesta on Saturday! I'd love to introduce you to the other ladies in the valley. We did enjoy your visit today!'

With a wave, Catherine set her horse in motion, wondering if Mrs Trubody's parting *we* included her husband.

On the far side of the valley, Chi-en Shambles stared ruefully at the notebook containing *A Memoir of Prince Hong*. Its dull cover seemed a mirror for his own failures. Yet once the future had seemed glorious and endless. Sighing, he took up brush and ink.

Chapter the Second: *The Heavenly Capital*

I

We left Canton the next day and sailed to Shanghai. There we joined a party of merchants hoping to sell rifles and percussion caps to the Taiping rebels at ten times their true value. Our route west to Nanking followed rivers, lakes, canals, across a vast watery plain given over to rice and swamp. An uneasy peace lay across the region, both sides having exhausted themselves by war. Though we passed numerous towns and villages I remember none distinctly. All I possess are crumbs of memory: a watchman's wooden clapper at night, customs men demanding their usual squeeze from the merchants, a woman wringing out a wet sheet and draping it across a stand of bamboo to dry.

When we entered Taiping territory, Reverend Shambles grew enthusiastic. Smashed idols and Buddhist temples became common, their heathen texts rotting amidst the rubble. Aunty-Mother shared his excitement. 'Spiritual Uncle Father will convert the rebels into orthodox Christians,' she whispered to me. 'It is his divine mission.'

But I noticed heathen temples were not the only casualties of war. Houses and villages stood in ruins amidst the waterways. Quails and pheasants rose in huge flocks from untilled paddy fields choked by reeds.

White bones lay beside the roadside, puzzles no one could reassemble or solve. Likewise, abandoned fortifications were still besieged by mounds of graves.

As we approached Nanking – or the Heavenly Capital, as the rebels called it – Spiritual Uncle Father boasted to Aunty-Mother of his influence over his former pupil, Hong Xiuquan, the Heavenly King. 'I tell ye, he learned everything from me. Hymns, prayers, sermons, Holy Scripture . . . I've sent a letter to the Baptist Council in Boston. Think of it! Thirty million souls currently under Taiping rule. I purpose to win the consternation and admiration of all Christendom by correcting their doctrine. Thank Jesus, I say!'

Even at ten years old I detected the deadly sin of pride.

II

Nanking, China's second greatest city, had fallen to the rebels five years earlier. It possessed thirty-three miles of high, thick stone ramparts surrounding a huge area of broad streets, hills, temples, palaces, woods and uncultivated ground. The Golden Pearl Mountain gazed down at the city and all around were ranges of stony hills.

As we approached the Heavenly Capital, differences with the China I had always known became evident. First, the rebels' appearance: they wore bright colours and embroidered shoes rather than the dull slavish robes of Manchu decree. No one shaved their foreheads or sported pigtails. Instead, their hair grew free, healthy, unfettered.

Then there was the atmosphere of calm compared to squalid, brutish Canton. Everyone carried brass badges stating their name and place of residence. In some districts of the city, men and women resided in separate barracks to avoid temptation and sin. Yet women were everywhere, their feet unbound, with not a chaperone in sight, and Aunty-Mother delighted in being addressed as *Sister*, just as a man was *Brother*.

Most of all, our entry into the city excited none of the usual curses and threats accorded to foreigners. We were viewed as fellow God-worshippers, Jesus-followers. Curious crowds of children surrounded us: and I threw back my head with pride to walk behind the giant, ambling form of Spiritual Uncle Father.

I did not attend Reverend Shambles's reception by the Heavenly King in his golden palace. As servants, myself and Aunty-Mother squatted in the street amidst our meagre baggage. Crowds were celebrating outside the palace with prayers, joyful hymns, fire crackers.

'The Heavenly King has been granted a vision of slaying demon tigers,' a man explained. 'A great, great victory over the devil-dog Manchus!'

It occurred to me that the victory had only taken place in a dream, but I said nothing. Strangers embraced and congratulated each other, crying out that the Heavenly King and his son, the Young King, would rule for a thousand years.

When Reverend Shambles emerged from the Holy Palace, we rose excitedly. Gone were his shabby European clothes. He was resplendent in a bright blue satin gown lined with fur, a marvellously embroidered yellow jacket with a red hood and silk boots. Servants followed with boxes of presents. We soon learned Jesus had personally informed the Heavenly King that his old teacher was a good man and that he should be rewarded with a title. Thus, modest Reverend Ezekiel Shambles had become Minister of Justice for All Cases Involving Foreigners.

'Of course,' he chuckled, 'I told him I'm a Minister of Religion, not a Minister of State, but he would hear none of it!'

Part of his duties involved assessing the spiritual worthiness of foreign merchants trading with the Taipings. 'It may well be they choose to make a small donation to support our missionary work here,' predicted Spiritual Uncle Father. This prophecy came true. Over thirty foreign ships arrived to trade at the Heavenly Capital each day: most thought it prudent to donate a few dollars to Spiritual Uncle Father's mission fund. Only a small grasp of mathematics is needed to calculate the result.

We were assigned quarters above a bureau for the translation of holy texts into Chinese. This was an office of special importance to the Heavenly King. Runners were kept busy all day carrying his instructions to the printers and translators.

Finally, we mattered a little in the world. The Reverend Shambles delivered daily sermons in stumbling Cantonese on street corners — though the vast majority of his curious audience spoke Mandarin and did not understand a word. And I, to my indescribable pleasure, acted as interpreter when Reverend Shambles met with high Taiping officials and princes, or *Wangs*, as they were known.

III

Our suite of rooms was near the Heavenly King's palace, an enormous compound surrounded by thick, high walls painted red and yellow. One might pass through gates and over ornate stone bridges to a huge square where God-worshipping took place on a broad, ornate platform. At the end of this square the Inner Palace began — a place utterly forbidden to males, for all the Heavenly King's hundreds of palace servants and officials were women. Here stood a long wall painted with phoenixes and dragons where the Heavenly King posted his mandates and decrees. It was my habit to stand before the painted yellow silk proclamations, deciphering the characters.

One morning I was passing an idle hour in this fashion when I became aware of a figure beside me. Turning, I saw a boy of fourteen or so, wearing the rich yellow and red silks of Taiping nobility. Silver and gold bangles jangled at his wrist. Despite his seniority, he was far shorter than me. Perhaps that explains why I failed to bow, a presumption that didn't seem to offend my new neighbour.

'Do the edicts interest you?' he asked.

I shrugged. 'I have few books to read. I like reading things.'

He considered this idea. 'I have thousands of books! My tutor, Ren Xudong, says I should know the obscurest characters but I do struggle. What does that edict say?'

I peered at it closely: '*The New Jerusalem is the Heavenly Capital. Its King shall succour virtuous men everywhere.*'

My new friend seemed delighted. 'Where did you learn to read so well?'

'From my Aunty-Mother.' I chose not to add more in case he guessed I was a child of shame.

'I see you can be very useful to me,' he mused. 'What are you called?' When I replied *Chi-en*, he laughed, though not scornfully. 'I'm not sure you are at all humble, Humble! Really you should bow to me. Did you not guess I'm the Heavenly King's favourite nephew, Fourth Prince Hong?'

Now I did bow, and deeply.

'Don't worry,' he said, still amused. 'It is my wish that you accompany me round the city. Do you ride?'

Of course, I had never ridden a horse in my life. But soon enough my new friend summoned a horse so placid I need only keep my feet in the stirrups to remain seated. In addition, he provided a groom to ride alongside and steady me. Half a dozen other servants followed at a polite distance.

As we trotted from the palace, Fourth Prince Hong pointed out objects of interest. 'See that dragon boat? Our family rode in it to Nanking, surrounded by thousands of smaller boats. A hundred thousand Holy Soldiers greeted us at the city gates. Ah, what a procession as we entered! You see, the Heavenly Kingdom of Great Peace had commenced . . . You are smiling, Chi-en? Why?'

I did not know why. Perhaps because it sounded like a fairytale. I said, 'I wish I had been there!'

Fourth Prince Hong regarded me with a smile of his own. 'That is all right then,' he said. 'Come, Chi-en! I'll show you the Manchu city where our enemies took their last stand.'

Here was a ruined and burned city within the city. Flowers and coarse plants grew between tumbled bricks and tiles. As our horses picked a way over rubble-strewn streets, I was amazed by tall pyramids of bleached bones. First on our journey, now here, it seemed China was littered with bones like fallen leaves in autumn.

Glancing at me, Prince Hong sighed regretfully. 'My cousin, the Young King, calls these bones Manna from Heaven. But I believe some of the killing here was not needful.'

He told me how every Manchu defender, thirty thousand or more, perished in the final battle. Thousands of women were herded like cattle to a wide moat and either drowned, stabbed or burned in oil. Again, he shook his head. 'Our destiny is to unite all Earth's people as God-worshippers,' he said. 'Even the Manchu one day.'

My companion's demeanour, wise and noble, made me long for his approval. I stooped to touch a splintered skull, wondering what thoughts and feelings once resided within it.

'Prince Hong! Your Highness!' We turned to find several youths in gaudy Taiping robes racing up on ponies. 'A foreign warship is approaching!'

A canter commenced to the Yangtze shore, several miles distant. How I kept my seat on my pony was a matter of wonder – and great pride.

Once there, we took up position on the fortifications while Prince Hong produced a telescope from his saddlebags. By now twenty Taiping youths, all highborn, surrounded my new friend. Naturally I felt clumsy and stupid. I wished myself back with Aunty-Mother. But Hong beckoned me over, pointing across the mile-wide Yangtze at a British steamship, its churning paddles, numerous cannon.

'Chi-en,' he said, 'one day our Holy Navy will have ships bigger and more powerful than that! I promise you! After all, the foreigners are Christians like ourselves.'

The British ship trailed steam and smoke then headed west where the Manchu Emperor had granted them trading concessions after the recent opium war.

'We must have cannon like those,' said Prince Hong, softly. 'We must learn everything the foreigners know.' He appraised me, his brass telescope dangling from one hand like a club. 'I'm sure you can be of use to me,' he said. 'One day you must teach me the foreigners' language. I have heard that you speak it.' As we returned to the horses he said casually: 'Few know this, but Imperialist armies are closing in on the Heavenly Capital. Soon they will be here.'

I searched the horizon for hordes of merciless, vengeful soldiers. My new friend smiled. 'Don't worry, Chi-en. My uncle is God's Youngest Son! Besides, if we were ever in *real* trouble, Jesus would lead an army from Heaven to help us. It has all been foretold in the Heavenly King's visions. You see, we're quite safe.'

IV

As I write, impressions and images of the Heavenly Capital rise like mist from a lake. There is no logic, no order. Yet it was a secure, orderly place compared to Canton – if you obeyed its harsh rules.

The birthday of the Heavenly King . . . People gay as spring flowers fill the streets with dragon processions, firecrackers, hundreds of thousands rejoicing. We walk through the city like guests at a wedding – Reverend Shambles five paces ahead of Aunty-Mother and me. He is exultant, calling out in garbled Cantonese: *Praise the Lord! Praise Jesus!* Earlier I smelt brandy on his breath and trembled to recollect how drinking is punished under the Taiping laws. Luckily, the whole world is drunk that day. Tipsy with faith.

Another time I explore the city. Older now, hair grown long, my clothes the harlequin of a Taiping youth. Slogans on banners hang from every gate and street corner: *Everybody worships God! Everybody goes up to Heaven! Come quickly! Come quickly to worship God!* Twice a day, cannon shots echo from the palace, proclaiming the Heavenly King is at prayer, beseeching Heaven's goodwill. There seems no shortage of goodwill in this little heaven. One might see thousands of destitute left to die in the streets of Canton or other Imperialist cities. Not here. I pass an 'Institute for the Sick', even one for cripples. Others house women in dormitories and assign them useful labour. Orphanages. Hospitals. Houses for the aged who lack relatives. On I walk. Gigantic barracks full of Holy Soldiers echo with the sound of ceaseless drilling. For the Imperialists draw nearer to the Heavenly Capital, mile by mile, town by town.

✵

Some evenings, Spiritual Uncle Father reads out letters he has composed for the foreign press. Each praises Taiping devotion and energy. Though he concedes the 'Christian rebels' are misguided on many points of theology, they are wholly sincere.

'You'll like this,' he chuckles. '*With the patient admonitions of Reverend Ezekiel Shambles, DD (Massachusetts), they are slowly perfecting the errors in their doctrine.*' He glances at Aunty-Mother for admiration. '*It is my unquenchable belief,*' he continues, '*that inscrutable Providence has decreed the Taipings will vanquish their heathen foes, the Manchu.*'

Aunty-Mother, pale from confinement in our modest quarters, applauds Spiritual Uncle Father like a conquering hero. 'Clap, Humble!' she urges. 'Clap!' And I do, secretly praying his 'unquenchable belief' is correct.

A final memory rises like mist . . . The devil-demon siege forts are now only five miles from the ramparts. Supplies of food are dwindling in the city. Soon there will be hunger. Every day a great gong sounds in the Heavenly King's palace. Similar bells and gongs spread like fire-seeds from house to house, street to street. Tens of thousands kneel in prayer, beseeching divine aid in their Holy War. The city fills with a humming noise like an enormous nest of bees or wasps.

That evening a messenger arrives and Aunty-Mother hurries to conceal herself while I translate for Spiritual Uncle Father. Our visitor introduces himself as Tutor Ren Xudong – Prince Hong's tutor. A notable invitation follows: for Reverend Shambles to attend the children of the royal family *so they might meet a real foreigner*. Likewise, *the half-foreign boy with the gift of tongues*.

V

Cavalry escorted us to the Heavenly King's eldest son and heir, the Young King, and the other royal children. We were taken by sedan chair to an ancient pagoda on a hill in the centre of the Heavenly Capital.

From this high point, the city seemed a place of deep, contented peace. Yet as we approached the pagoda a peevish shriek broke the calm. 'If you don't do what I say I'll order to you to pray *all* day!'

Within, we found an unexpected battle. The Young King, a puny boy around my own age, recognisable by his regalia and golden crown, stood shaking with rage. His face was purple, fists clenched. Before him, Prince Hong, hands on hips. A dozen other children knelt fearfully.

'Prayer is a blessing not a punishment,' replied Prince Hong. 'Why should I play every game you want?'

The future monarch's lower lip trembled. He seemed far younger than his years. Then he caught sight of Reverend Shambles and stared – quite insolently, it seemed to me.

'Tutor Ren Xudong!' he cried. 'You did not tell me the foreigners are giants! Look at his funny beard! Are they all so ugly?'

Luckily, Spiritual Uncle Father's poor Mandarin saved him from embarrassment. While he addressed the younger children in stumbling Cantonese, I was summoned by Tutor Ren Xudong.

'Prince Hong has asked me to explain our faith,' he said. 'He believes it will be important for your future.'

How or why, I did not comprehend, yet I listened carefully. Questions filled my mind. However, my lesson in God-worshipping was interrupted by the children chanting Taiping holy verses like a line of fledglings with upturned beaks.

So far all had gone well. Then the Young King took his seat on an ivory throne that dwarfed him. A swift glance at Reverend Shambles made me tremble. Along with everyone else, he was being commanded to kneel before the child. Even Prince Hong had knelt, though with an air of amusement.

'Reverend!' urged several important Wangs. 'Kneel! It is God's will!'

Spiritual Uncle Father's smile was ghastly. Yet he managed a low bow, his face bright with anger.

When we reached our quarters he raged at Aunty-Mother until she clutched his knees, tears trickling down her smooth cheeks. I sensed how brittle and unstable Spiritual Uncle Father had grown – and feared the consequences for us all.

VI

It was Spiritual Uncle Father who taught me the hymn:

He that is down need fear no fall,
He that is low no Pride . . .

Alas, he should have remembered his own words! For I believe pride brought about the end of our honoured position in the Heavenly Capital.

For two years he had refused to acknowledge a painful truth – that the Heavenly King had no intention of being converted to Baptist orthodoxies. By 1860 Reverend Shambles was little better than a dogsbody. He wrote endless articles for the English and American press, urging the virtues of the Taipings. He even set up a Committee of Brotherhood in America to promote the rebel cause, an organisation requiring large sums from the Heavenly Kingdom's treasury. In the end, his hosts refused to pay a dollar more, for the Committee achieved nothing. Needless to say, Reverend Shambles viewed this as a betrayal worthy of Judas himself.

Perhaps his subsequent behaviour was inspired by the daily tightening of the siege. The banners of Imperial troops were clearly visible on hills round the city, along with earthworks and trenches. It seemed only a matter of time before their trap snapped shut, bringing famine then defeat. Perhaps he concluded Providence was guiding him to act while he still could.

But I believe the true cause was pride. Articles mocking his self-appointed mission appeared in the China press and several rival missionaries wrote of him as *His Shabby Grace the Archbishop of Nanking*. Others jibed that he had allowed himself to become a coolie for men of inferior race and that the Taipings considered him a clown. Spiritual Uncle Father's spirit crawled with revulsion at such injuries.

Maybe there was another reason. He had amassed a sizable fortune in donations from European merchants trading with the rebels. I firmly believe he hoped to use this money to further God's work in America.

Shortly after our visit to the pagoda, he was summoned to an audience with the Prime Minister of the Heavenly Kingdom. At this Taiping chief's palace a terrible quarrel occurred. What about, or why, Spiritual Uncle Father would not explain when he returned to our quarters.

One thing I do know: while Aunty-Mother and I cowered in an adjoining room, his bedchamber rang with curses, threats, crashes. Furniture was thrown to the floor. Rapid footsteps descended the stairs and I rushed to the window, in time to see him emerge onto the street with a large bag.

Gone were the extravagant Taiping robes he had delighted in for over two years. Now he wore his old black suit and top hat from Canton days. For a moment he stared up at the window, meeting my startled gaze. Was he leaving us? We, who had served him so faithfully? And Aunty-Mother especially, who worshipped him with such quiet devotion? Dear, kind Spiritual Uncle Father could never do such a thing.

But he turned and walked briskly towards the Yangtze. Tears blinded my eyes. And I remember thinking that, with his black suit and heavy black bag, he resembled a hunched, clumsy bear scurrying away to find fresh shelter.

VII

The rest is soon told. Aunty-Mother ventured into Spiritual Uncle Father's room and discovered his Chinese clothes strewn across the floor. A brief search revealed he had left nothing valuable.

I shall never forget the hurt in her pure, lovely face. Yet she dried her eyes and smiled bravely. 'Stop crying, Chi-en!' she commanded. 'He will return soon. Spiritual Uncle Father's rages never last long. He would never simply abandon us.'

All night we waited until her brave smile became strained. Early next morning a harsh knocking made us clutch one another. Outside, thick mist swirled, obscuring the sun. Lifting a corner of a bamboo blind, I saw Taiping soldiers.

Their search of our rooms was brutal. We soon found ourselves kneeling in the street. I do not care to speculate what would have happened to us. Beheading was the standard fate for traitors in the Heavenly Kingdom. At the very least, both of us would have been conscripted: Aunty-Mother to a women's labour battalion, myself as a boy soldier. Instead, a loud, commanding voice called out. A diminutive figure wearing a golden crown strode from the mist. Prince Hong! Behind him were bodyguards from his personal retinue. The men sent to arrest us fell to their knees.

'Take this Sister to the Palace,' he ordered his men. 'Treat her honourably.'

The soldiers bowed and prepared to lead Aunty-Mother in the direction of the Heavenly King's Palace. I clutched her arm with all a twelve-year-old boy's fierce love. For I knew well that no male other than the Heavenly King himself was permitted entry into the Palace.

'No!' I cried. 'I will protect her until our master returns!'

Prince Hong turned to me. 'Your master has boarded a British warship and is now heading down the Yangtze to Shanghai.'

I moaned. 'That cannot be true!'

'It is true,' he said, gently. 'You must be strong, Chi-en. I had to argue with the Prime Minister himself to prevent both of you being beheaded as traitors. I have arranged for your mother to become a servant of the Heavenly King. She will be safe in his palace. Yet it is her fate to never leave without royal permission. Likewise, it is forbidden for you to see her again.'

'No!' I cried once more, gripping Aunty-Mother yet tighter. 'We shall return to Canton!' I would have fought an entire army to defend her.

But her hand gently loosened my own. Though tears glittered dully on her pure, chrysanthemum cheeks, her expression was proud. I have never forgotten it.

'You must obey Prince Hong,' she said. 'He is your master now. Remember, I shall always love my dear, brave, clever Chi-en. My dear, brave boy.'

With that she kissed me once on the forehead and walked stiffly to the waiting soldiers, who led her away into the thick fog. Away forever to the Heavenly King's maze-like corridors and painted halls. How I have reproached myself for not chasing after her. At the very least I should have escorted her, as a loyal son should, to her new and final home. But I was paralysed.

The early morning mist swirled around me. Prince Hong smiled the sad, kindly smile I came to rely upon. 'I told you once, Chi-en, your fate is to be of use to me. Now Heaven has arranged matters. Come with me and I'll explain.'

Trailing after him with a bundle of shabby clothes, I left the rooms where two years had passed; and only entered them again in dreams.

Napa Valley, California
Autumn 1877

Wraiths of mist crept between dew-soaked vines on the morning of the Harvest Fiesta. Clouds louring over Mount St Helena threatened to roll south and spoil the fun. All over the valley people converged – by locomotive, wagon, horse, foot – on a field near the outskirts of Perryville. Of the Wappo Indians who once hunted there, or the Mexicans who had fattened cattle on this same land, no trace remained. They had blown away in a breeze of time.

Temporary plots were roped out across the meadow for animal competitions, horse races, mountebank tents and a small fun fair. In the centre stood a dancing and dining area sheltered by gigantic canvas awnings, ready for the evening's festivities.

Catherine wandered through the crowds with Emile and Jean-Pierre while Chi-en stayed with the horse and wagon. They passed boys dressed as pantomime vaqueros in mother-of-pearl studded leather chaps, sombreros and plum-coloured breeches. Elsewhere, genuine cowboys from local cattle ranches staged a rodeo to the applause of onlookers. A whole ox roasted on a gigantic spit, presided over by a saloon-keeper in a long white apron and two Italians to crank the handle.

Soon they reached the amusements. Here Emile begged to enter a tent containing a real native Indian chief wearing an eagle-feathered war bonnet. Catherine paid and waited outside until he returned, not scared or excited, but thoughtful.

'What did you see?' she asked.

He shook his head. 'A drunk old man pretending to be proud.'

The boy cheered up when a fairground geek, huge, fat and evidently a simpleton, roared as he bit the heads off live chickens. Then came a shooting gallery with air rifles, a real roundabout and swinging gondola. Though Catherine could ill-afford the slightest luxury, she paid whatever Emile asked. He was growing so big she feared the day he wouldn't need her for anything; least of all, love.

Everywhere farmers, labourers, idlers from the town drank cheap wine so coarse her sensitive nose wrinkled. 'No wonder these people cannot sell their vintage,' she said to Jean-Pierre. 'When our own is ready we shall soon find buyers.'

Yet the old Bourchier confidence tasted bitter, for Royaume Céleste was no better placed than the most inept winery in the valley.

'Let us hope so, Madame,' he said, well aware her offer to Mr Trubody had received no response.

They reached a more refined area of the fiesta and Catherine's step slowed to a lady-like stroll. It was easy to nurse lost superiority among bumpkins, however sparse the dollars in one's purse, but here a different quality was on display. Gentlemen in frock coats escorted ladies in long, lacy cream gowns. Elegant bonnets and feathers bobbed as they paraded, serenaded by the town band.

The previous day Catherine had received a note on absurdly thick paper from Nancy Trubody, saying how much she had enjoyed 'their little tea party' and asking her to 'help out' at the Perryville Ladies' Society 'lumber stall'. Still smarting from Mr Trubody's lack of interest in her proposal, she had been inclined to refuse. But Catherine was more given to rapprochement than reproach – except when standing in judgement upon herself. Besides, she liked Nancy. The benefits of any friend where she had none outweighed a little hurt pride.

'Jean-Pierre,' she said, 'please show Emile the rest of the fiesta. I shall join you later.'

The Perryville Ladies' Society stall was littered with objects donated by Napa's 'chivalry': Morocco-bound volumes of sermons and morally improving works no one had ever opened; vases and chinaware of all kinds; home-stitched exhortations to *Love Thy Neighbour*. Nancy Trubody stood at one end, apart from the other ladies. Most were younger, more fashionable and chatting gaily. A relieved smile appeared on her rosy face.

'More help is at hand, ladies!' she declared. 'Here is the lovely Madame Bourchier I told you about.'

Six pairs of eyes traversed Catherine's figure, face, hair, hat, jewellery and apparel in a collective glance. A lady at the centre of the group smiled sweetly. She wore diamonds and a white silk gown too perfect and sumptuous for a humble fiesta. Aged between thirty-five and forty, her narrow features retained youthful beauty. Catherine glanced down at her own sober blue dress, smoothing the material. The lady's smile grew sweeter still.

'Why, *enchanté*,' she said, sleepily, to the delight of her companions. 'I'm sure!'

Catherine smiled. 'Likewise,' she said, adding in French. 'A pleasure to be greeted in my own language! You have visited France, perhaps?'

A slight narrowing of the lady's eyelids taught Catherine her mistake. 'Delighted!' she added, hastily, in English.

'Madame Bourchier, let me introduce you to Mrs Lydia Smithson-Mackay,' broke in Mrs Trubody. 'She's the general of our little army. So be prepared to take orders, my dear!'

Mrs Smithson-Mackay's smile broadened. 'Why, Nancy,' she said in her soft, languid voice, 'how dull it would be without you.'

Catherine found herself ignored by everyone except Nancy Trubody. Meanwhile Napa Valley's 'chivalry' bought small items at large prices. Her glance often strayed to Lydia Smithson-Mackay. Of course, she should have expected a man like the Colonel to be married to quality. How could it be otherwise? Yet a secret part of her felt disappointed.

At last, Mrs Trubody whispered in her ear, 'I think we've suffered enough for a good cause. Let's find my husband and badger him into a little refreshment.'

Before they could leave, a visitor arrived.

'Ladies!' declared Colonel Smithson-Mackay, every inch the fine, prosperous gentleman. He noticed Catherine and chuckled in surprise.

'Madame Bourchier! So they press-ganged you as well.' He shot a look at his wife. 'Hello, my dear. Business good?'

'Very good,' she murmured, her glance straying over the crowded field.

Colonel Smithson-Mackay frowned then grinned at Catherine. 'Well, a good day to you, Mrs Bourchier. Perhaps you'll grace us with your presence at tonight's dancing?'

As he left, Catherine became aware the other ladies were watching her closely, while appearing to rearrange unsold lumber.

Chi-en lay in the back of the high-sided wagon, concealed from passers-by. Above, clouds parted, drifted, merged. It was pleasant to lie on the grape-scented boards of the wagon, his wakefulness a dream. He interpreted the aromas of the fiesta: roasting meat, horse manure, sulphurous gunpowder from fire-crackers. Then an excited voice speaking Italian scattered his thoughts.

'So, I said to Guiseppe, "Hey, you want fun? Even with no dollars you think we can have fun?" And he said to me, "I want to collect a scalp like Big Chief Buffalo in the tent." And I said, "You're a crazy fellow!" And he told me, "No, I'm going to collect one of those Chinese pigtails and hang it from my door like a rabbit's foot."'

A cheer followed. Chi-en estimated half a dozen Italian youths. Their accents reminded him of a precious month spent exploring the antiquities of Rome. He remained motionless in the bottom of the wagon.

'I want a pigtail, too!' cried another boy.

'Let's get the fellows together,' resumed the first speaker, 'go to Chinatown when it gets dark and scalp a few pigtails.'

Chi-en listened as a rendezvous was agreed near the outskirts of Perryville's Chinatown. When the voices faded, he sat up in the wagon.

Most white folks considered snipping a Chink's pigtail harmless fiesta fun. For the Chinaman concerned it had grave consequences. Strict Manchu laws forbade his re-entry into the Empire and he would certainly lose great face among his countrymen. Chi-en knew too well how Longhairs were despised.

It seemed prudent to keep quiet. After all, he owed the unfriendly Chinese of Perryville nothing. Except Chi-en had never been prudent.

To reach Perryville's Chinatown he was obliged to walk the length of town. A few white folks loitering on the dusty street and wooden sidewalks watched the half-Chinaman pass.

A buffer of poor houses lay between Main Street and Chinatown. Here was the Italian neighbourhood: laundry-tangled yards surrounded low clapboard houses; barefoot, grimy children played in the street. Chi-en observed a few throwing stones at a bean-skinny Chinaman who scurried past, head shielded by bony hands, afraid to admonish his attackers.

Chinatown was a warren of miserable wooden shacks. Here Orientals paid twice the rent a poor white paid for the same floorspace of hovel. So lowly-regarded were Perryville's Celestials, the town's only Negro-owned business advertised itself as 'white-owned' and no one demurred.

Faces peeped out of doorways and windows. Hundreds were crammed in there. Chi-en's nose wrinkled at open cesspits, rubbish tips, mounds of cinders. Opium and gambling dens spilled customers onto the street. He passed a shabby, two-storey Daoist temple, herbalists, merchants selling cheap, imported reminders of home, cobblers, tailors, brokers and pimps. Pigs, ducks and chickens were guarded like precious heirlooms.

At the centre stood a tall, whitewashed building with an English sign: *Sam Wah General Store and Laundry*. A smaller notice in Chinese warned: *All labour contracts in Perryville to be conducted through Sam Wah without exception. Register within.*

For a moment Chi-en hung back. He had visited a number of Chinatowns in California and the Eastern states. This one made him uneasy. Its residents seemed fearful. And he had witnessed how the Sam clan's rule was less than benign.

Sam Wah's store was lined with shelves of cans, packages, rolls of cloth, sacks of rice and beans, boxes of vegetables. In the centre stood a table where several men in silk outfits played *fantan*. Cups of imported rice wine waited at their elbows and cigarettes curled. Chi-en looked from face to face until he located Sam Wah. Beside the older man sat Sam Yip, flushed with alcohol and counting a stack of coins.

Chi-en waited. Gradually the *fantan* ceased. Silence lengthened like a shadow. When Chi-en met Sam Yip's eye, the young man rose, rolling up his sleeves, until restrained by his uncle.

'Mr Longhair,' said Sam Wah.

'A pleasure and honour,' said Chi-en.

They inspected one another.

'Sam Wah, because you are the foremost man in this place, I wish to warn you of a plot against our people.'

The word *plot* set off a general murmur. Chi-en related all he had heard, word for word.

Sam Yip, no longer able to restrain himself, leapt to his feet.

'Taiping demon!' he cried. 'We know these Italians. How can you speak their language unless you are in league with them?'

All eyes were upon Chi-en.

'Enough!' commanded Sam Wah. 'You speak their tongue?' he asked in Cantonese. 'Truly? As well as the foreign woman's? And English?'

'Yes, among other languages.'

'You say they plan to steal the pigtails of our people for a joke?'

'I only tell you what I overheard.'

Sam Wah nodded. 'The white people will all be drunk tonight. It has happened before.' He turned to his fellow gamblers. 'Friends, spread the word.'

The *fantan* players departed, one by one, leaving Chi-en alone with Sam Wah.

'Only magicians speak every tongue,' pointed out the older man.

Faint peals reached them – the station clock chiming the hour. Chi-en checked his tin pocket watch.

'I must go, Mr Sam.'

'Why did you put yourself at risk by coming here? I could easily arrange that you never leave Chinatown. Can it really be for men's pigtails when you don't wear one yourself?'

Chi-en drew breath to explain then realised he couldn't. Nor did he care for the labour contractor's threats. His fear was letting down a boy too used to neglect, a boy familiar from his own childhood.

'I have another appointment,' he said, bowing slightly.

★

Chi-en had promised to escort Emile to Perryville Grammar School and kept his word, loitering outside the gate. Catherine, however, was half an hour late for her meeting with the schoolmaster. She arrived just as Mr Crane was showing Emile out.

'Ah, Mrs Bourchier,' declared the schoolmaster, 'I am mightily gratified by the alteration in your son's attitude and demeanour. We shall be happy to clasp him back into the ample bosom of our *alma mater*. On consideration of his half semester fees, of course, *ahem*, in advance.'

Back on the street, she hugged her son with unusual warmth. He remained stiff and unyielding. 'I am so proud of you, Emile!' she cried. 'So proud! But you should have waited for me.'

The boy shook her off brusquely. 'I am not doing this for you.' He stalked away with awkward strides.

Catherine's elation faded. She turned wearily to Chi-en. 'Well, Monsieur 'Umble, you, too, I perceive, consider me a bad mother for arriving late. No doubt you think me indifferent to my own son's education. Thank you for helping him. You seem to understand him better than . . . well, never mind. Please look after Emile until we return home. Here is money for his dinner and, of course, your own.'

Chi-en took the proffered coins. 'Does not Madame dine with her son?'

She shrugged helplessly. 'Tell him, I must take supper with Mr and Mrs Trubody.' She threw up her hands in despair. 'Tell him I'm trying so very hard to look after him! After us all!'

Catherine hurried away in the direction of the fiesta, angry with herself for displaying weakness.

Of course, Humble lacked the deference proper in a servant — especially a Chinese one. Yet she detected sympathy behind his guarded face, a handsome face, by some standards . . . Confusion quickened her step as she re-entered the fiesta field. Chi-en's cleverness and ability to mimic every language alarmed her. Wasn't that an attribute of Satan? Though Humble seemed kind, she dared not rely on anyone except Jean-Pierre.

She made her way to a central dance floor marked out by hay bales. Here the town band, mostly of German stock, consumed beer and sausages before the dancing. This would follow a Charity Harvest Supper served to scores of ladies and gentlemen. A waiter stopped her at the entrance.

'I am the guest of Mr and Mrs Trubody,' she said, looking round.

She became aware of a waving hand amidst a crowd of people seated at long trestle tables covered with checked cloths.

The waiter led her to the Trubodys, who were engaged in small talk with other well-dressed couples. One place remained empty. Among Napa's moneyed gentry she felt uncomfortably singular. But Papa Bourchier had never been ashamed that their forebears were peasants. And in the New World such distinctions were said to be unimportant. So she smiled boldly as Mr Trubody summoned a waiter with a tray of Napa Valley champagne.

'My dear!' exclaimed Nancy Trubody. 'We'd almost given up on you.'

'Forgive me if I seem rude,' she said, 'I had the most important of reasons.'

In a quiet voice she explained Emile's dismal career as a scholar and his amazing transformation. Somehow it seemed natural to leave out her lateness and Monsieur Humble's role.

Nancy squeezed Catherine's hand. 'Why, my dear, how wonderful.'

A misty look crossed her pink face and Catherine knew she was contemplating her own lack of a child.

Sandwiches, cold roast beef, pork, legs and breast of duck and chicken, English-style pastries and pickles, seeded and unseeded white rolls with Napa butter, German-style salads and preserves were served up. Catherine ate hungrily, aware that the Trubodys had paid a ludicrous ten dollars for her Charity Supper meal. They seemed to approve of her appetite. She began to suspect they had taken some kind of pity on her.

Few of Napa's elite greeted the Trubodys. On the opposite side of the roped off dining area, however, another table attracted a stream of gentlemen and ladies. There sat Colonel Smithson-Mackay and his ever-smiling wife, along with leading viniculturalists from the valley and a rowdy party up from Frisco.

Bang!

The first firework of the evening exploded high above the dance floor. Petals of light flashed then faded. Other explosions followed, making a few veterans of the Civil War flinch involuntarily. *Ooohs*, *aaahs* and gasps rippled through the tipsy crowd of genteel folk. Amongst the common people out on the Fiesta field, a loud cheer rose. Catherine became aware that Nancy's kindly face had been replaced by Mr Trubody's. He leaned forward confidentially.

'My dear,' he said, slightly drunk, 'I have something important to say. I have considered your proposal.'

Catherine waited, her fingers closing round the stem of her glass.

'Now let me say at once,' he continued, 'I wavered long and hard whether to follow your advice concerning my wine. Long and hard! Fish glue and egg white indeed! Nancy approved because she said it sounded like nursery medicine. Darn it, I even used the silver spoons. And the result?'

Now her heart fluttered with hope. For she was confident of the result.

'Vinegar into wine!' He seemed to like the phrase. 'Vin-e-gar into wine! Miraculous!'

A fountain of fizzing sparks in the night sky accompanied by a loud crack made him pause. He chuckled and sipped his champagne.

'I have considered and I agree,' he continued. 'Let us blend our vintages! We'll show 'em! However, there's one condition. The claret we produce must be labelled *Chateau Trubody Nook*. Will you shake on it?'

Catherine stifled a cry of delight and held out her hand. His own grasped hers firmly.

'Of course,' he added, pleasantly, 'if your wine isn't as fine as you promised, the whole deal falls flat. I'll not be made a fool of. Not with my name and reputation plum on the label for all to read.'

'It shall be a fine wine that I blend with yours,' she promised, too elated by champagne for doubt. She sensed that must come later — along with sleepless nights. For now, the rest of the evening passed in a haze.

The town band played waltz after waltz. Although she sat with the Trubodys and some older gentlefolks, Colonel Smithson-Mackay sought her out with a request to dance. It took great presence of mind to refuse, her face flushed in the light of the glowing, coloured lanterns. He met the rejection with a mischievous grin, murmuring that, as an old soldier, he knew losing a battle wasn't the same as losing the campaign.

She watched him waltz less fastidious ladies round the straw-covered dance floor and noted their stimulation in his arms. A memory of the Colonel's manly smell as he stood outside the Vinicultural Club meeting could not be suppressed — or ignored in warm, ready places of her body. She noticed, too, Mrs Smithson-Mackay's glances in her direction.

While Catherine ate and declined to dance, Chi-en perched upon the seat of the Bourchier wagon, smoking a cigarette and gazing at the mountain that first summoned him to Napa. In the pale light of a fat, blushing harvest moon, Mount St Helena's unflinching outline reproached his idleness.

Images of the past found his troubled mind. How few people were willing to sacrifice themselves for a just cause – their only cause being self-interest. Was he no better?

He looked out across the Fiesta. It had entered an indecorous phase with the coming of darkness. Several different dances were taking place to the light of bonfires and lanterns on poles. The strains of clashing melodies and instruments created a babble of music.

One dance seemed to be for Perryville's poorest whites, capering with wine keg in hand to the strains of fiddle and accordion. In dark corners of the field, people gathered in furtive or jocose groups for gambling around fires. At the centre was a splash of light where Perryville's 'chivalry' waltzed. All of them, rich and poor, gaining or wasting, their lives weighed by dollars, badges, temporary stances.

Chi-en felt the burned down cigarette scorch his hand and tossed away the butt. Licking the sore patch of skin, he tasted tobacco, ash, something unique to himself. In his pocket were new ink cakes and writing brushes bought in Perryville Chinatown, sufficient to finish his *Modest Memoir of Prince Hong*.

A murmur in the back of the wagon made him look round. The boy was asleep, wrapped in horse blankets and Chi-en's jacket. If ever a child needed encouragement, it was Emile Bourchier. Not that he was a likeable boy – arrogant, angry, self-absorbed, shot through with doubt. The good in him had yet to be teased out.

They arrived back at Royaume Céleste as clouds obscured the harvest moon over Napa Valley. At first, they didn't hear the pattering rain – Jean-Pierre and Catherine were singing a Languedoc folk tune about an amorous shepherdess and a fickle chevalier – but all felt it soon enough. The dusty, thirsty earth darkened as rain fell in gusts, breaking the long drought.

While Catherine hustled a sleepwalking Emile to bed, Chi-en stood in the kitchen doorway, listening to a language as ancient as the world, a language of drips, trickles, whispers, splashes. With it came new scents of soil and damp wood and plants. Seeds of elation and hope revived in his soul. He added glistening eyes to the general wetness of the night. A glow appeared in the corridor leading from house to kitchen. Catherine entered, lantern in hand, her long, dark hair disordered by the rain.

'Monsieur 'Umble,' she said, slurring from champagne. She giggled and added in English, 'I mean Monsieur *H*umble!'

He said without thinking, 'Of course, Madame knows I'm not really called that.'

Catherine laughed, threw out her arms. 'I'm not as stupid as you think, Monsieur 'Umble-*H*umble.'

'I do not consider you stupid.'

'Perhaps not.' She swayed, seemed to gather her thoughts. 'There is something,' she muttered, as if to herself. 'You see, I want you to stay on as our cook and housekeeper. But most of all – no, especially – because of Emile.' She laughed a little nervously. 'You are a good influence on him.'

Chi-en shrugged. 'Not as good as his mother.'

She waved away the idea. 'Pooh, Monsieur 'Umble! How kind of you to say so!' Then she slapped the table. 'Do you accept?'

For a long moment he studied her in the lamplight. Her shapely face and figure confused him. He didn't trust her, that much he knew, and perhaps didn't like her worldliness. But he had nowhere else to go. And she left him to his duties without interference or nagging. Yet working as a humble cook betrayed ideals once shared with Prince Hong, larger than either of them, ideals to set humanity ablaze. Hopes he dared not forsake; without them the earth would seem barren.

'I don't know,' he said.

Was that a flicker of disappointment? Surprise?

'Jean-Pierre will miss your cassoulets,' she said, 'as will I. They put him in a good mood for a change.'

Now he chuckled. 'Very well, Madame, just until spring. After that I must be away, though I do not know where. Not yet. Until then, a dollar a day. Plus food and board.'

To his surprise she stepped forward and held out her right hand. 'This is the second time I have shaken hands on a deal tonight.'

His smile vanished as he took her warm fingers. Few white women dared risk a Chinese hand. There was an awkward pause.

'What *is* your real name?' she asked, quietly.

He told her. She repeated the strange syllables twice.

'Chi-en. *Chi-en.*'

Napa Valley, California
Autumn 1877

It was not just Chi-en who brooded on the future as autumn settled across the valley. Hope is the headiest and hardiest of wines yet Mr Trubody's offer to blend his vintage provoked more fears in Catherine than pleasant expectations.

Several times a day she visited the winery to test the fermentation: examining, tasting, stirring the *chapeau* of grape skins, seeds and stalks. Eavesdropping as the growing wine whispered its secrets.

Yet at night her dreams were drawn across time and leagues of ocean, back to France. Often she moaned in her sleep, haunted by tiny yellow lice gnawing at vine roots she could not save. And sometimes, through that alchemy which salvages truth from impossible dreams, the lice wore human faces: her faithless maid, Clotille, her husband, Antoine, and all too often his insinuating companion who loved *such fun*, Baron Cesar Foche, *at your every service* . . .

In Languedoc the Bourchier family had been no strangers to pests in their *domaine*. For generations they tended their vineyards, coaxed, garnered, protected. Catherine had learned all the potential plagues before she knew how to read. Cicadelles, tiny green grasshoppers that turned juicy leaves the colour of bronze. Dust mites painting ochre spots on the summer canopy of a row. The grape worm's dotted, translucent slimy circle of eggs. She knew how to save the harvest, or some of it, for Papa Bourchier had taught her.

The Bourchiers were also no strangers to tragedy. Though the family vineyards stretched in all directions, a model of prosperity, the juice pressed from its owners' loins was less fecund. Two sons preceded Catherine, both living long enough to establish a bond with her then die before their tenth birthday. Another two brothers went the same way.

Small surprise then, perhaps, that her mother, a sickly, irritable woman, withdrew into piety and gloom, rarely showing affection for her daughter. Little wonder, too, Papa Bourchier selected their only surviving child – though undeniably female – to bear the family's harvest into the future. For Comte Antoine de Rivac de Chauveterre had condescended to hint through intermediaries that he would consider an alliance with the wealthy yet common Bourchiers – if the terms of the dowry proved agreeable.

'We Bourchiers need new blood,' Papa advised Catherine after church one Sunday. 'Blood one can trust. And pedigrees come at a price.'

Papa had chuckled. 'Healthy seed, healthy plant. Imagine being a comtesse, Catherine! You'll see how well I provide for you.'

Her duty was to trust his judgement. So when Papa appeared with a man ten years her senior, she curtsied and blushed.

'Catherine,' said Father, 'let me introduce Monsieur le Comte Antoine de Rivac de Chauveterre. He is eager to know you better.'

Even at their first meeting, she grew uncomfortable under Antoine's distant, appraising glance. Yet he was handsome in a way Catherine knew girls admired, tall and slim with long curly hair and an elegant little beard. Certainly girls noticed him, though less for his looks than the way he moved, smiled, watched a woman enter and leave the room. His effortless self-assurance posed a challenge.

'Enchanted to meet Mademoiselle at last!' he said. 'And delighted to discover that reports do her little justice. As do reports of this fine estate and château.'

How Papa had beamed at the compliment! Here was the healthy grafting he craved. Catherine, though only eighteen, remembered whispered talk of le Comte's predilection for cards and horse-flesh. She also remembered the Bourchier family had purchased their own estate from one of de Rivac de Chauveterre's profligate ancestors after the Revolution.

'Comte,' she said, cautiously, 'I believe this château once belonged to your family?'

His smile had been more of mouth than eyes.

'We made a great error in allowing it to leave our possession.'

A month later, Catherine bound herself to Antoine until death parted them. Appropriately, it proved a widow-like marriage. He rarely returned to Languedoc, being pressed by tiresome affairs in Paris requiring large loans from his new father-in-law. On one visit he did his duty so thoroughly Catherine bore him a son, Emile. She had been nineteen. It frightened her that the baby was male. Boys were weak. Had not her brothers died young?

Papa Bourchier ordered a *fête* amongst the estate workers to celebrate his grandson's birth. At last, he congratulated himself, the Bourchier line was secure.

'Catherine,' he said, drunk on his own wine. She lay in bed, exhausted by the ordeal of birth. Outside, fireworks lit the darkness, followed by cheering. 'Catherine, I know your marriage is not easy. Monsieur le Comte is a difficult man. But think, one day my grandson will be Comte de Rivac de Chauveterre himself! Surely that is worth a little sacrifice?'

She had watched him through red-rimmed eyes. Was her loveless marriage the little sacrifice required by her brothers' failure to live?

'I will make sure Antoine is pruned back where necessary,' he had promised, stoutly. 'Papa always knows what to do.'

But when the phylloxera came, the hordes of tiny yellow aphids, first to neighbouring vineyards then to Domaine Bourchier, not even Papa knew what to do.

'This pest will not last,' he declared, as ancient rootstock wasted away, woody stems that once produced vintages so exquisite the nobility of Paris uncorked nothing else – and at such prices! 'Never fear, Catherine, ours are aristocrats of vines.'

The newspapers said phylloxera lice came from America where native vines were immune. Priests blamed the people's sins for the plague; politicians blamed their laziness. She and Papa inspected the roots of stricken plants under a magnifying glass. Hundreds of crawling, devouring creatures on just a few centimetres of root. How might one destroy so many?

'If the roots are sick, *patron*,' said Jean-Pierre Leclos, the domaine's chief winemaker, 'how may we save the fruit?'

Catherine had longed to answer that question, to win Papa's gratitude. The pests were destroying the work of generations . . .

Thus, the green land of Languedoc, sticky with sap, had concealed legions of lice. At night in California, they stole into Catherine's dreams like pinching fingers, spiteful words, all teeth and appetite. Sucking, gnawing her roots and loves. No one knew how to vanquish them, neither wise man nor fool. They were *le peche originale*, the original sin, taught by the white-cowled nuns when she was a girl . . .

Three days after her husband's return with Baron Cesar Foche, Catherine had hurried out of the ancient stone gatehouse of Château de Chauveterre, pulling her shawl tight. A dry, itchy wind blew down the valley.

'Jean-Pierre!' she called. 'Wait for me, please!'

The sow-bellied man halted on the dusty road. As usual he wore his lumpy three-piece suit and shapeless black hat. He seemed reluctant to face her, staring across the valley at hillsides covered with gnarled, leafless vines. One hand concealed his left cheek. Walls and towers, gabled roofs and mullioned windows cast long shadows.

'Jean-Pierre, what did he . . . Oh!'

A bloody weal lay across his coarse, grey-stubbled cheek: the welt of Antoine's riding crop.

'I tell you . . .' Her voice was steady and earnest. 'You must inform the magistrate. Though it means speaking against my husband, I'll act as your witness.'

Jean-Pierre's eyes were bloodshot, his nose bulbous, red-veined. He replied in a Languedoc accent clotted by decades of wine and coarse tobacco. 'The magistrate is Monsieur le Comte's uncle. There will be no justice. Ah, if only your father was alive!'

But both Father and Mother had lain for two years in the cemetery at the foot of the hill.

With that, Jean-Pierre hurried away, down a path white with dust, through *parcelles* of vines, tamarisks and wisteria, over cloddy earth. Languedoc shimmered – ancient walled towns and villages, parched hills and valleys – and vines, always rows of bare, leafless vines that could never again flower.

Catherine had watched him go and the last thread of obedience to Papa Bourchier's master plan for her life snapped. She walked slowly back to the gatehouse.

★

Luncheon in Château de Chauveterre that day had been a long, thirsty affair. Noise echoed round the courtyard from the dining room. Cries of mirth were punctuated by popping corks and girlish squeals of mock outrage, quarrels dissolving into oily fellowship.

By three o'clock, all was silent. Peacocks trod with careful dignity around empty gardens, their gorgeous tail feathers furled. Antoine's guests had retired to snore away the hot afternoon, preferably in the arms of a companion. Monsieur le Comte also vanished. Since returning he had seduced Catherine's maid, Clotille.

This last betrayal hurt more than Catherine expected. As mistress of the château, she had given Clotille's family winter clothes and halted Jean-Pierre's attempts to evict them when they fell behind with the rent. Perhaps Antoine was right to say people only cared for themselves. Yet her heart revolted against such a world.

An eight-year-old boy with curly auburn hair marched across the stone-flagged floor of the hall. Ignoring his mother, he stamped past.

'Emile! Come here!'

He pouted. 'Where's Papa?'

The boy prepared to climb a grand staircase that led to the bed-rooms.

'Come here at once! You must not go upstairs. There are unpleasant people up there.'

'Won't!'

The boy mounted the first stair. Three swift paces and she was shaking him.

'Never speak to Maman like that again!'

He did not seem daunted.

'Papa talks to you that way!' he whined. 'Let me go! I want Papa! Papa promised me he'd come home more often if you were more *gentille* to him. Where's Papa?'

Tightening her grip on his arm, she dragged him, kicking and writhing across the hall. Unexpectedly his defiance collapsed. He allowed himself to be led across the courtyard and through the shadowy gatehouse.

'You are a naughty, naughty child! I do not know why I bother with you.'

Through tear-swollen lids he peered up at her. She propelled him from the château, towards the church at the foot of the valley. On the way they found Jean-Pierre Leclos instructing a group of labourers. The domain's steward had doused the humiliation of Antoine's riding crop with glasses of *calva*.

'There must be a can of oil in every row,' he told the men. 'Your job is to make plenty of smoke. That's all.'

The labourers exchanged sullen glances. Leclos had never been popular among the servants of Château de Chauveterre due to his gruff, high-handed manner. Luckily for him, the Bourchiers found his dogged loyalty and skill as a winemaker more palatable.

'Why so much smoke?' asked an old peasant, genuinely puzzled. 'I have heard of smoking sausages, even cheese. Never vines!'

The men laughed but Jean-Pierre did not answer. That morning Baron Foche had suggested cleansing the entire domaine, vineyards of huge extent, with oil and paraffin fumes. This, Antoine had been assured, would suffocate the phylloxera. Of course, Jean-Pierre had protested. Such waste, monsieur! And astonishing expense! The lice were in the roots not the stems. Monsieur Bourchier would never, never have allowed so foolish a thing . . .

'Ah, Madame,' said Jean-Pierre. He was about to say more then noticed Emile.

'Do you feel better?' asked Catherine, drawing him aside.

'I thank you for asking, Madame.' He touched the cut on his cheek made by Antoine's riding crop. 'I take it you are aware that Monsieur le

Comte has given me a week's notice. A week! After forty-five years' service to your family! And Monsieur le Comte has told me to leave my cottage at once. He said he needs it for his new steward. I laughed and said – straight to his face for I have nothing to lose – "There will be no grapes this year for you to make wines." And he said: "Ah, but after tonight my domaine will be free of pests. And that includes you, Leclos!" That is what he said to me. Forty-five years serving this domaine, only to be dismissed as a pest.'

'He cannot! I . . . I did not know.'

An insolent, childish voice addressed the peasants handing out small metal drums of paraffin. 'I'm thirsty! Fetch me water!'

The labourers stirred uneasily.

'This is paraffin, young master.' The old peasant winked at his friends. 'You wouldn't like that. It burns the tongue.'

'Emile, come away!' called Catherine. 'Jean-Pierre, find me in the château when you are finished here. I want you to come directly to my bedchamber . . .'

He stepped back in surprise. 'Madame, that is not possible. What are you thinking of?'

'Listen, Jean-Pierre,' she pleaded, 'you must come in secret because Monsieur Bourchier would have wished you to help me.'

'But to your chamber!'

'Please help me. I have a plan that . . .'

'What *plan*?' demanded a triumphant voice. 'What *plan*?'

Catherine and Jean-Pierre examined the boy. His smirk was disconcerting.

'As you say,' muttered the old winemaker, 'I'll be along.'

Catherine realised the labourers, many of whom she had known since childhood, were whispering excitedly. Easy to guess why. Responsibility for them weighed heavy on her.

'Messieurs! If le Comte wishes to smoke the vines we may be sure he'll get his way.'

They listened, hat in hand. The domaine's servants had learned who to turn to when their families fell on hard times.

'Messieurs, regard the vines! You have wives, children, grandparents. I would not think less of you for seeking work away from Domaine Bourchier, much as it grieves me to say so.'

They exchanged looks. Here was confirmation of rumoured bankruptcy. A chance to flee before the ship dragged them down as it went under.

'Can it be so?' asked the old peasant in wonder. 'Generations of my family have worked for a Bourchier.'

His question wounded Catherine into silence. Finally, she said, 'All must rise and fall, monsieur. Look to your loved ones.'

Serenaded by cicadas, mother and son walked through the heat of the afternoon, past fields of stunted vines and drab green olive groves to the cemetery where her parents and four brothers lay. As she walked, she recalled a curious visitor to Château de Chauveterre. He had arrived in a one-horse gig during the February rains, several months before Antoine's recent return from Paris . . .

The old man was a *notaire*, her father's solicitor. His name was Monsieur Delon and he had driven over from Carcassonne, a sticky, muddy journey. Languedoc was as wet in winter as it was parched in summer.

'Madame,' he said, after a cognac to warm himself, 'for once I bear good tidings. You are the sole beneficiary of an unexpected legacy . . .'

A decrepit aunt of her father's, herself a childless widow, had left a handsome property in Normandy that reverted to his only child, Catherine.

'Does my husband know of this?'

'Why no, unless you tell him.'

'*Must* he know of it?'

Monsieur Delon observed her shrewdly. 'Of course, word of Monsieur le Comte's exploits reach Carcassone. Forgive me, but I know he has mortgaged all the lands inherited from your father. How hard your Papa worked to build his fortune!'

'Everything has been mortgaged or sold,' said Catherine, dully. 'Everything except the contents of the chamber pots.' Tears welled in her eyes. 'Monsieur, please arrange for my great aunt's property to be turned into ready cash. Keep it safe on my behalf until I need it. But I do not wish my husband to know.'

Monsieur Delon had nodded. 'It will take a little time.'

'Do it as quickly as possible, I urge you, even if it means selling cheaply.'

'As you say, madame. I will contact you when the transactions are complete.'

'I rely on your discretion, monsieur,' said Catherine, with quiet dignity.

'Madame is my principal in this matter,' he said, 'not Comte Antoine de Rivac de Chauveterre. I am pleased to perform this service for Monsieur Bourchier's only child.'

In the cemetery, shadows lengthened, cast by the church tower and cypress trees bordering the road. Swallows flitted and wheeled. Insects chirruped. Clearing dead leaves and twigs from her parents' grave, Catherine finally understood the impulse that drove her here. She must bid *adieu*. The unexpected legacy was a rope thrown by destiny and Emile would drown alongside her if she failed to seize it. A bulging wallet of thousand franc notes lay hidden in a hatbox in her bedchamber.

'I'm bored,' protested Emile. 'Can we find Papa now!'

Catherine recollected how she had smelled brandy on her little boy's breath the day before. How his words had slurred like a drunken sot's. How Antoine had insisted the child watch as two cocks tore themselves apart with razors tied to their legs. With no money for a good school, Emile would be condemned to the education of a swineherd.

She traced the name *Bourchier* on her father's headstone.

'Forgive me, Papa,' she murmured.

But his judgements had failed. Every one of them. She had to rely on her own.

'I said I'm bored!' Emile stamped his foot. 'I'm going to tell Papa. What is this *plan*?'

Catherine rose, brushing dust from her long skirt.

'Hush,' she said. 'We will go home now. Maman has a surprise to arrange.'

Her first dilemma had been how much luggage to risk. How could she know? Then there were hatboxes, valises, Papa's old attaché case of legal papers . . .

It took little effort to drag the empty trunks across the corridor. No one disturbed her. The château had lapsed into torpor. One of her husband's more bibulous guests snored fitfully in a nearby bedchamber. Her heart pounded as though she was a thief in her own home.

If Antoine discovered her preparations he would question, probe, bully until she revealed her great aunt's legacy, anything to be left in peace. Perhaps Clotille would catch her packing dresses, stockings, shoes, cramming them into the trunks so roughly she was forced to remove the contents and start again. How clumsy she felt, how ill-equipped to flee one life for another.

Catherine had started re-packing the second small trunk when she heard a knock on the bedroom door. Her instinct was to freeze. Pray she had turned the key in its lock.

For a moment her visitor made no sound.

'Madame! I know you are within. It is I, your friend, Cesar Foche.'

Her insides twisted with anguish. Foche's attentions over the last few days had been so pointed she did not doubt Antoine's guests were in on the joke. Perhaps they viewed his public displays of gallantry as *such fun*. Worse, she once caught Foche exchanging an amused glance with her husband after a particularly impudent kiss on her hand. The possibility of some arrangement between the two men made her fists clench.

Her gaze remained on the doorknob. If she had not locked it . . . But the knob turned fruitlessly. Catherine exhaled with relief. Baron Foche, at least, could not procure a spare key from Clotille.

'There is no need to be shy, my dear,' cooed her visitor. 'Do be nice and open the door. I only want to help you.'

Silence was her sole weapon. She used it.

'I have important information, Madame. Things you should know about Antoine's intentions towards you. Please let me help you.'

For a moment she wavered.

'What a shame,' he said, carelessly, though she detected pique. Again, the doorknob rattled. 'Au revoir, my dear!'

She remained motionless until a woman's bustling skirts in the corridor persuaded her that he had gone.

The château clock struck four. At five everyone would stir, dress for dinner, servants hurrying up and down stairs with pitchers of water. Quickly! Thank God she had already gathered the papers she must take, the copies of deeds and Papa's will, the certificates. Above all, the miniature portraits in silver frames of Maman and Papa. All she retained to remember their faces.

She was closing a valise when another knock rattled the bedroom door. She stiffened. A firm knock, not like Clotille's.

'Who is it?' she asked, softly. 'Jean-Pierre, is that you?'

'Yes, Madame.'

She unlocked the door. A quick glance confirmed the corridor was empty.

Once he was safely inside, she turned the key. Tested the lock thoroughly. The old winemaker examined her through bloodshot eyes. Fresh wine was on his breath. Oh, he must not get drunk! Even Papa had grown exasperated with his fondness for the vintages they created. Lacking wife or children, Jean-Pierre had many thirsts to drown.

He nodded at the trunks. 'You are going somewhere?'

'Yes.'

'Does Monsieur le Comte know?'

'He does not.'

There were two things she needed from him, the first being the easiest.

'Jean-Pierre, you know my husband has mortgaged all the Bourchier lands, don't you? He cannot repay a single *sou* of his debts. All, all will be lost.'

'It is a blessing Monsieur Bourchier did not live to see it.' He shook his head. 'This estate was his life. And mine, too. Those dead vines out there were my family.'

'For me, also,' she said, quietly. 'But I do not intend to witness the sale of our home. Tonight, I am going to Carcassone and from there I will take a train to Marseilles. That is why these trunks are packed. Will you help me, Jean-Pierre? Will you bring the trap to the back servants' entrance while my husband is dining? I can do the rest.'

The bleary-eyed man laughed. 'My God, I will! And with pleasure!'

'Good.'

Now the second thing. Yet she hesitated. Despite the excellence of his wine-making skills, his ability to finger a leaf and sense its season, his proven loyalty to her family and his physical endurance, Jean-Pierre Leclos was less than reliable. Neither was he young. Could she risk another dependent, slowing her flight? But he had always accompanied Papa on his trips to sell wines. He was no fool. She took a deep breath.

'I have another proposition. You have, of course, heard of California?'

'I am not an imbecile.'

'Jean-Pierre, I must go somewhere Monsieur le Comte cannot find us! According to the law every *franc* I possess is his property. And he may steal my Emile!'

The way Jean-Pierre pursed his lips suggested the latter would be no grave loss.

'I will take my son away from this place forever,' she added, firmly. 'All across Europe the old vineyards are dying. Only in California is there no plague. The phylloxera is harmless there. Can't you see? People like us, who know the vine, will be valued. And do you remember Sister Perpetua from the convent school in Carcassone? She was born in America. So *gentille*, so kind! It was she who taught me English to help Papa sell his wine in London. I have never forgotten her. And look, I have proof right here. California is a land of gold!'

They bent over a coarsely-printed pamphlet in French entitled: *All About California and the Wondrous Inducements to Settle There*, translated and published by the Immigrant Association of California. Inside were pictures of fields heavy with vines and corn; maps depicting swathes of land awaiting those bold enough – or desperate enough – to arrive first. Tables of numbers proved with scientific precision how anyone could double or triple their wealth within twelve months. For those with higher ambitions, vast fortunes awaited.

'What of money for travel, Madame?' he said. 'To buy land one needs
. . . *Mon Dieu!*'

Catherine had produced the thick wad of thousand-franc notes.

'Have you stolen it?' he whispered.

'It is mine,' she said, quietly. 'My last inheritance as a Bourchier. That
is why I need a trustworthy steward where I am going. I offer you the
same wage my father paid you. In addition, I will meet all your travelling
expenses.'

Jean-Pierre's bloodshot eyes filled with tears, so that she glanced away to
spare him. Besides, her own were brimming: to leave all sense of belonging, all she had ever known for the most dubious of futures. But she must
be strong. Papa Bourchier had hated weakness. Perhaps that was why he
relinquished her to Antoine, because he despised his own blood's frailty.

'Ah, Madame,' said Jean-Pierre, 'you know that I was an orphan.
Monsieur Bourchier saved me from the gutter when I was just a boy. He
treated me with honour and I was glad to serve him. Now is my chance
to pay back his kindness.'

'Are you sure?' she asked, dabbing her eyes. 'You must be completely
sure.'

'I am sure.'

Perhaps he should have hesitated longer. After all, the other side of the
world wasn't next door.

'Yes,' he said, 'I will go. I have nothing left here. After forty-five
years!'

Arrangements were soon made. Catherine was left to finish packing
Emile's clothes. As for the boy himself, she could not find him when she
searched the quiet château.

The tower clock chimed rhythmically. Five o'clock! Catherine
strapped in her sole luxury, an oboe given to her as a girl – her faithful
friend during lonely evenings. Antoine always mocked her precious

hautbois, calling it a peasant's instrument, so that she feared playing it in his presence lest he throw it on the fire. She had just closed the final trunk when the doorknob turned and rattled.

'Madame!' cooed a low voice. Clotille, evidently pleased with herself. 'May I enter?'

'No, not now. Tell Monsieur I am indisposed. I cannot take my place at dinner.'

A pause. The girl was considering how the news affected her own comfort.

'Should I bring you something, Madame?'

'Nothing. Do not bother me again. Make sure Emile has a large dinner. Then you are free to do as you please.'

Catherine sat on the bed while the château stirred. Through the window she could see labourers preparing cans of paraffin, piles of dead leaves and wet wood to make smoke. Clouds and clouds of purifying smoke.

At seven o'clock that evening Catherine had buttoned up a plain brown travelling dress and laced her boots. The roll of banknotes hung from her girdle in a silk bag, drawstring tied tight. She listened at the door. No movement in the corridor. That was to be expected: not only were the guests starting a prolonged dinner but every servant in the château would be busy. Now was the time to make sure of Emile.

She climbed a narrow, uncarpeted staircase to the nursery. Twilight thickened shadows in corners. A few hours would bring darkness.

At the top of the stairs, she paused. Sobbing came from Emile's nursery, the deep, reckless sob of a small child that shakes his entire being. Tears found her own eyes. She brushed at them. No time for that. He must co-operate.

Inside the attic room, Emile lay face down on the carpet, curly hair over his face. Catherine watched, aware he was returning her inspection through his fringe and fingers.

She knelt on the carpet and stroked the small head.

'You are sad,' she whispered. 'Tell Maman why you are sad?'

Still he sniffled. Catherine felt a flash of irritation and guilty, furtive dislike. 'Won't you tell Maman?'

'I don't want to tell you! Papa was angry with me!' cried Emile. 'He said I was naughty for coming into the room when Clotille was helping him put on his trousers. I didn't know it was naughty!'

A sickening image silenced Catherine. She glared at the boy. Papa this! Papa that! Always Papa! Then she saw what to say.

'It was because you almost spoiled his surprise. You need to get dressed. We're going to play hide and seek with Papa. Think of it! Papa wants us to get on a train. A real locomotive!'

Emile had seen the puffing, clanking iron monsters at Carcassone.

'Papa wants that?' he asked, doubtfully.

'You must be very quiet and good. The game is to entertain his guests. Will you do that for Papa, Emile?'

A haughty expression crossed the child's face, one of his father's. 'Of course!'

Catherine's smile was fixed as he gathered toys and followed her back to her bedchamber.

By eight-thirty Emile had fallen asleep on her bed, clutching a wooden train he needed to show Papa. Whenever Catherine poked her head into the corridor the voices rising from the dining room were more raucous. She went to the window. Dusk deepening, the labourers at their assigned positions, ready to begin. No sign of Jean-Pierre, yet he had agreed to be here by eight. He must be drunk. Stupid to expect more of him! Struck with a whip by his employer and dismissed, all in the same day. Where else would he turn for comfort but a bottle?

Eight forty-five and Catherine had almost resolved to bribe a stable lad into harnessing a horse and trap. Then came a knock.

'Madame! It's me!'

She glanced at Emile. The boy had not woken. Jean-Pierre wore his best frock coat and bow tie as though attending a wedding. Or funeral.

'You are so late,' she moaned. 'They will be out of dinner soon.'

He shrugged, as if to say it happens.

'Is the wagon ready?'

'Of course.'

Together they carried the largest trunk down a steep, lightless back staircase intended for servants. Catherine felt her way by hand and foot. At last, they reached the waiting trap. The horse snorted. It scented paraffin in the night air, unfamiliar, unsettling.

'The other bags!' urged Catherine. 'Perhaps Emile has woken. We must be gone before they light the fires.'

If Jean-Pierre sensed the precariousness of their position, he gave no sign. At least he was strong, carrying trunks and valises down the dark stairwell. Catherine followed when he was done, Emile clutched to her chest, wrapped in his favourite blanket. He had grown so big she staggered under his weight. The steep stairs and darkness yawned like a pit. Somehow, they reached the carriage.

'The attaché case,' she moaned. 'I forgot it. Oh, I shall go!'

Up the stairs, down again. She was trembling with fatigue and tension. Finally they were seated in the trap. Now it was Catherine who hesitated. The high walls of Château de Chauveterre rose solid and secure, the only home she had ever known. Once abandoned, it could never be reclaimed. Excited voices reached them from the front of the château.

'Idiots!' muttered Jean-Pierre. 'They are lighting the fires.'

With a flick of reins, he urged the horse forward. Iron-shod hooves clattered on cobblestones. Then they were through a low arch and onto a rutted, dusty road. At once Catherine became aware something was missing. The wind! People thereabouts said one noticed it more when it did not blow, and the Tramontane had blown without cease for weeks, bringing heat and dust; now the wind was finding new directions. Soon pine trees hid them and Jean-Pierre let the horse pick its own way. The stench of ash and burning oil grew stronger. Abruptly, they emerged from the wood into the valley and Catherine cried out.

On the hillside, fire cans were belching smoke into the night sky. Antoine and his friends were small figures at the front of the château, lit by torches and lanterns. It seemed they did not trust the labourers – or were too drunk to miss out on such novel fun – for they streamed into the rows of vines and began thrusting torches into oilcans. Cheers and shouts reached Catherine above the clop of the horse's hooves and rattle of the trap. Then came the strains of a familiar song:

> *'Jusqu'à ce qu'on prenne*
> *La lune avec les dents!'*

'My God!' she muttered, clutching Emile closer. The sleeping boy groaned. 'They have gone mad!'

Rank fumes billowed into the air and swirled over the vines. Antoine's companions were capering and waltzing to the music of the flames. Chief among the dancers, waving his arms like a conductor, Baron Cesar Foche.

Heat made the air shimmer over Domaine Bourchier. A dull glow lit the valley, visible for kilometres. Sparks of burning straw and leaves ascended, drifting over lifeless vines. Through the murk Catherine glimpsed the silhouettes of Papa Bourchier's noble plants like contorted sufferers in paintings of hell, a tangle of distorted limbs and poses.

Jean-Pierre doggedly urged on the trotting horse.

'Imbeciles!' He spat into the road. 'The smoke hides us.'

The horse shied, its heavy hooves stamping the ground. A family of wild boars, squealing in terror, charged across the road before disappearing into the smoke. Tears trickled down Catherine's cheeks. Was it a sin to abandon *le terroir* that had nourished and raised her? Could California, utterly unknown, deserve such a sacrifice? Emile woke with a start, almost slipping from her arms.

'Papa!' he shrieked, choking on a cloud of fumes engulfing the road. 'Papa! Where do you want us to hide?'

Napa Valley, California
Winter 1877

A month passed. Winter in the New Eden began with steady rain. For a year every cloud above California had inspired speculation and hope. Farmers prayed a land withered by drought would renew its promise in the spring. A thousand businesses where dollars are the sap prayed alongside the farmers.

Frosty winds, countered by a feeble sun, drove the clouds. The valley grassland filled with grey metallic pools reflecting the sky's moods. Thick beds of parched dirt transformed into bogs. Easy to forget then, squelching through quagmire Main Streets in Perryville or Napa City, how dust outstayed water.

Their larder was almost bare yet Chi-en hesitated to ask for more supplies, aware that Catherine Bourchier's pool of dollars was drying up. Instead, he eked out their stores until all the salt and oil had nearly gone.

He found her in the second storey of the winery where huge, round vats stood in rows, and sensed she was troubled. The fermenting wine no longer bubbled or hissed and a deep, lifeless silence filled the long, high-vaulted room.

'All is well, Madame?'

She turned. It surprised him to see her close to tears.

'I am alarmed,' she said. 'Despite starting well, the wine I must blend with Mr Trubody's may yet turn out to be *vin ordinaire*. I assured him it would be superior. If it is not, our whole deal falls through. But it is cloudy in ways I did not expect.'

Chi-en stepped further into the winery and looked around. 'I have noticed each vat is slightly different,' he said. 'The aroma and colour, the cap of grape skins on the surface.'

'Then you are observant,' she said. 'These vats are Merlot and those Pinot Noir. Over here, Gamay. But most are plain, ordinary Petite Syrah, the base on which I must blend.' Her forehead furrowed. 'You see, I must find the right balance to turn my cloudy wine bright so that it welcomes sunlight. Yet I must leave a little bitterness, a firmness on the tongue.'

'Is that no longer possible?'

'It is a delicate matter. It shall be settled soon, when we rack the wine into casks.'

'You seem to have the matter in hand.'

Her eyes flashed with unexpected emotion. 'I fear not! One mistake and everything will be ruined. Jean-Pierre counsels that we should settle for *ordinaire* rather than take risks. Why? Because I am not my father, not the great Monsieur Bourchier, therefore my judgement is suspect. Always! But my heart tells me he is wrong.'

'Perhaps you should follow your nose,' said Chi-en. 'Maybe it is more reliable than your heart.'

Her gaze returned moodily to the vats. 'I regret my heart has always been directed by others at the expense of my nose.'

'Perhaps those *others* are not here to direct you.'

She brightened. 'You are more philosopher than chef! Yes, I will teach myself the secrets of this blend. And I shall trust my nose.'

Catherine Bourchier glanced up at him, pursing the plump mouth that often seemed to draw his attention. 'Tell me,' she asked with sudden seriousness, 'how did you learn to blend so much? China, Europe, America. You are educated, cultured. How did *your* blend occur, Monsieur Chi-en?'

His instinct was to view the question as impertinence. Maybe mockery. After all, he was just the Chinaman who emptied Royaume Céleste's chamber pots.

'Oh, some have called me a curiosity,' he said. 'Even a cold fish. Madame will excuse me.' He turned to leave, though he had meant to discuss their need for oil and salt.

'Monsieur Chi-en!'

Her tone stopped him. It was oddly unsure.

'I did not mean to offend you.'

'Of course.'

'Thank you for listening to my troubles.' She smiled ironically. 'A dollar a day seems little recompense.'

'It is what we agreed. Excuse me, Madame.'

He felt her eyes upon him as he left the long room full of contending processes, diverse fruits.

Three mud-caked men took up position in the vineyard of Royaume Céleste, directed by Jean-Pierre. They stood beside rows of vines, their breath steaming. The cold earth likewise released misty tendrils. The workers were Chinese hired through Sam Wah in Perryville.

'*Maintenant, mes petits amis jaunes,*' began Jean-Pierre. 'I mean, now my friends yellow. Listen *particularement . . .*'

They did so without a flicker of comprehension.

'Talk English!' urged one.

His companions nodded.

Jean-Pierre rolled his eyes.

'Imbeciles! *Fieulles mortes!*' he cried. 'Dead! Brown! No want!'

'You mean clear old leaves and branches?' asked the senior of the Chinese. 'We know that work.'

Again, his companions nodded.

'Speak English!' commanded Jean-Pierre. '*Mon Dieu!*'

It soon became clear the labourers were adept at clearing vines. At a signal from the corpulent Frenchman, they advanced up different rows, discarding dead twigs and leaves. Jean-Pierre followed with a pair of secateurs, engaged in the precise task of pruning to ensure the maximum yield of grape clusters next spring.

Dry leaves rustling, the click of snapped wood, chuckling music from the swollen creek in the arroyo, sometimes the caw of crows, always the enveloping scent of wet earth.

When the men had advanced halfway up the hillside, Catherine arrived from the winery to inspect.

She found Jean-Pierre tugging at his walrus moustache, always a bad sign. For weeks she had tiptoed round his moods.

'Ah, Mademoiselle,' he grumbled, as though she was still Monsieur Bourchier's precocious slip of a daughter, 'there is a matter of grave concern I wish to discuss.'

'Yes.'

'It is impossible for me to continue sleeping down the corridor from you. If Monsieur Bourchier could see . . . But, of course, he would never have allowed such impropriety. Madame, as steward of Royaume Céleste, I require my own small cottage and garden with a fence. Nothing else would be proper.'

Catherine understood his real concern: Jean-Pierre Leclos needed a private domain, however small, to feel at ease. Even in Languedoc he had discouraged visitors to his cottage. Not that there were many. As one soon discovered, a little of his company went a long way.

'Please, Monsieur,' she said, 'I have explained this! When I have the money, a cabin shall be built for you.'

He quivered with annoyance. 'That could be years, Madame.'

'Not if we blend a *vin supérieur* with Mr Trubody's *ordinaire*.'

'Ah! Then I fear my wait shall be long indeed.'

'I am more confident. Very confident! And if my Royaume Céleste vintage is fine, perhaps I may take a little credit? Do you not think so, Jean-Pierre?'

He sniffed. 'It is not *vin supérieur* yet, Madame, and one cannot cook an egg until it is laid.'

With that, he resumed pruning, his eye and steady hand maddeningly exact. Defeated, Catherine returned to the winery. Scents from the fermenting vats distracted her angry thoughts. Recently odours of wine had begun to drift through her dreams. Even during the day her imagination was laced with aromas – blackberry, raspberry, citrus – heady in the fermenting vats. She bubbled with calculations: when to transfer the wine to barrels for aging, how many to use, who would buy – always, who would buy. Yet as she glanced beyond her vines, up towards the pine-clad slopes above Royaume Céleste, towards crags and tortured behemoths of volcanic rock, she grew pensive. The woods were dark, brooding. Unexpectedly she thought of Hansel and Gretel. Obdurate stone gazed down upon all their toil, not caring if she and Emile and faithful Jean-Pierre were pruned along with the vines.

She suddenly pictured Emile plodding home from school through the mud. Panic seized her that he would catch a fever and die like her little brothers.

Half an hour later, Chi-en perched on the driver's bench of a mud-spattered wagon, urging on their mare, Jeanne d'Arc. His orders were to pick up the boy from school, rather than let him walk the usual three miles of country road.

A cloud rolled up the valley as though pursuing the wagon. Glancing back, Chi-en detected slanting veils of rain, a shimmer between reality and fancy.

'Hey ya!' he commanded Jeanne d'Arc. The old mare's steady plod barely gained pace.

In the two months since arriving at Royaume Céleste, Chi-en's appearance had changed. Most obviously he was well fed and sleek; as for sickness, no visible trace remained. Perhaps the main alteration was one of mood. Haunted shadows behind his brown eyes came less frequently. Humour conveyed through laconic asides, raised eyebrows and slight smiles filled the vacancy.

Soon the pursuing rain became spatters, gusts and splashes. Unfurling a large, tasselled pink umbrella, Chi-en flicked the reins. In this stately manner, umbrella held aloft, he entered Perryville.

It was a dreary little town without the sun to lend it lustre. Wide-spreading Californian oaks and neat wooden houses, wineries and small manufactories, all looked grey that sodden afternoon. Water noises from gutters and dripping roofs merged with stray voices: a blacksmith's dull hammer blows, an angry shout, the whistle of an approaching locomotive.

'Hey ya, Jeanne d'Arc!' urged Chi-en, approaching the whitewashed wooden buildings of Perryville Grammar School. A horde of chattering, leaping, wrestling young scholars was being discharged.

Chi-en waited beneath his pink umbrella. After an interval, Emile emerged in the company of his teacher, Mr Crane. The boy stood with head bowed for a character-forming harangue. A knot of pupils listened, nudging each other delightedly.

Finally, Mr Crane stepped back inside. Hands deep in pockets, Emile walked through the yard. Chi-en remembered that kind of invisibility from his own boyhood, where everyone notices and ignores all you do and say – or so it feels.

'*Mon brave!*' he called. 'Jeanne d'Arc has come to say hello!'

The boy halted. 'Why are *you* here?'

'Sent by your mother,' said Chi-en. 'She's afraid you'll catch cold.'

'Not likely,' grunted Emile, kicking a stone towards Main Street, shoulders hunched against the rain so that Chi-en was forced to urge the mare into motion. 'Climb aboard,' he called down. Emile ignored him. 'Do you want to catch cold?'

'Yes. Go away.'

'Your mother–'

'Go away! You're embarrassing me! Tomorrow they'll say I have a Mongol nanny and I'll be forced to fight.'

For a while the wagon kept pace with the boy, Chi-en's pink umbrella angled against the rain.

'Of course, neither proposition is true,' he called down.

'Yes, it is!' replied Emile. 'You are a Mongol! *And* Mr Crane mocked me in front of the class because I couldn't read out a speech by Abraham Lincoln properly. Albert Krug called me a French fool and everyone laughed.'

'Then they're the fools,' said Chi-en. 'Prove them wrong. But first get in the wagon.'

Reluctantly, Emile climbed aboard. 'They will still call you a Mongol nanny,' he predicted.

Chi-en yanked at the reins. With a whinny, Jeanne d'Arc shied, stamping the muddy road with iron-shod hooves. She had grown accustomed to Chi-en's gentleness as a driver.

'Chalk and slate,' he commanded. As surprised as the mare, Emile rummaged in his satchel. 'Hold the umbrella.'

Emile watched a neat map appear on the slate.

'See!' commanded Chi-en. 'Mongolia. That is a land, like France. Here is the Middle Kingdom, China. That is another land. I am not a Mongol. I belong to China.'

Passing back the slate, he urged Jeanne d'Arc forward. The boy slumped. 'How can I pay back Albert Krug without fighting?' he asked, in despair.

'Work! Be cleverer than he is. I will help you. When I was young my mother beat me if I did not learn my lessons. Beat yourself if necessary.'

After a long silence Emile said in English: 'I am sick of being called a fool. I can speak and understand much more than I let them see. Much more!'

'Display your knowledge. Practise! But forget my help if you are not willing to work hard. Why pour clean water into dirty?'

The boy was left to ponder the ambiguities of this question all the way home through the mud and rain.

Later the rain cleared and Chi-en was treated to a display of martial prowess as he emptied peelings into the sow's sty. Emile had found an old scarecrow and was attacking it with a stick. *Thwack! Thwack!* Between blows he grunted inarticulate curses and threats.

'What are you doing?' he asked the boy.

'I'm . . . *Thwack!* . . . Going to do this to . . . *Thwack!* . . . Albert Krug! I'm practising like you told me!'

'I see.'

'You don't believe me, do you? But I will. And when I'm older I'm going . . . *Thwack!* . . . to be a soldier. Then *no one* will dare mock me. *Thwack!* Especially Albert Krug. But you wouldn't know about that.'

'Why wouldn't I?'

'You're only a cook.'

Chi-en went very still and gazed into the sty where the sow snuffled at cabbage stalks.

'I was a soldier when I was just fifteen,' he said, quietly. 'I can assure you there are better ways to settle disputes than war.'

Pictures flashed across his inward eye. Wounded men pleading for their mothers to help. A waist-deep swamp where a Manchu brave — little more than a youth — held Prince Hong's head beneath the foul water, Chi-en yanking back the surprised Manchu's head by his pigtail, screaming, sawing at the exposed throat with a rusty knife, screaming and sawing, until Prince Hong, half-drowned, rose gasping and coughing and the Manchu floated face down amidst a scum of weed and frothy blood . . .

Thwack! Thwack! Blinking, Chi-en registered the sow's snuffle and Emile's querulous voice. His heart beat too fast. He gulped back memories like a man trying not to retch.

'I bet you never fought in a *real* battle,' Emile was saying. 'I'm not afraid to fight!'

Chi-en rubbed his forehead. 'You should be.'

'I'm *still* going to be a soldier,' said Emile with a sly grin, '*and* beat up Albert Krug. So there!'

Chi-en's patience expired. 'Good! Then I'm happy for you both. Now I must work.'

As he left, Emile raised his weapon to finish off the scarecrow with a savage blow. Through narrow eyes he watched Chi-en disappear into the kitchen and, reluctantly, lowered the weapon. He tossed it aside and stalked, scowling, to his bedroom.

In the weeks leading to Christmas, Emile was often found in the warm kitchen that was the Chinaman's kingdom. The boy's allotted estate was a small corner of the table where he toiled over exercises, copied lists of words and recited them aloud while Chi-en corrected his pronunciation, teaching American English with a hint of high-class Boston. He knew how ephemeral scales weigh a man's worth.

In late December the rains slackened and frost set in. At times, shouts of pettish rage escaped from the kitchen, followed by a sullen boy. Yet always he returned, resuming his corner at the table, its wood stained with nib marks, spilt ink and frustrated tears.

On Christmas Eve, Catherine entered the kitchen to issue instructions for dinner the next day. She found Emile bent over an exercise book. Chi-en was plucking a hen, handfuls of feathers scattering.

'Emile,' she said, ignoring the servant, 'why do you spend so much time in here? What on earth do you write about? Did you not know there is a fine bureau for you to use in the salon?'

Emile's pen continued to loop and advance. He did not look up.

'Answer your mother!' commanded Chi-en.

Still the pen dipped in the inkbottle and scratched.

'He does not listen to me at all,' said Catherine. 'This is your doing, Monsieur 'Umble.'

'That is hardly fair.'

'No, it is not fair. I am not fair. How can I be fair when I am neglected by my own–'

'Maman! Please!'

Both fell silent. The boy stared between them. Then he said in clear, measured English with a hint of Boston round the vowels: 'Mother, I have written a letter to myself, saying what I wish to become in life. Do you wish to hear it?'

Catherine laughed nervously. '*Mon Dieu*! I mean, of course.'

He smiled thinly. 'Dear Emile,' he began, staring closely at the notebook. 'Are you surprised to receive a letter from yourself?' He glanced up to establish whether anyone had noticed the cleverness of this question. Chi-en nodded his approval. 'But I say to you, all our thoughts and ideas are letters to ourselves, so do not be surprised.'

The sentences flowed on for several long paragraphs. Catherine watched, a finger laid upon the corner of her lower lip. When Emile had finished she raised a sceptical eyebrow.

'Did you write this for him?' she asked Chi-en.

A small, angry shape pushed past. A door slammed. Catherine's eyes opened wide as she realised the truth. 'My God!' she cried, rushing after him. 'Of course you wrote it by yourself! And you read it aloud so well. You clever boy!'

The kitchen door rattled. Chi-en listened for a moment, sighed, plucked the chicken. For all its gay plumage, a scrawny bird. Feathers flew a-flutter. *Until spring*, he thought, *just until spring*. Where he would go then was uncertain; it shocked him to realise that, somehow, through carelessness or folly, he had misplaced his own future.

Catherine was relieved a bitter argument did not immediately follow her blunder over Emile's letter. She found him in his room, sat on the bed, writing on note paper evidently taken from her bureau. He put it away hurriedly and stared at the wall. When she apologised for doubting his authorship a scornful smile appeared. But he did not shift his gaze.

'We all make mistakes, after all,' she concluded.

Still no reply. At last, he yawned, or pretended to. 'I accept your apology,' he said. 'Will you leave now?'

Catherine retreated to her salon and lifted the lid of her bureau. As ever, Royaume Céleste's account book drew her eye. She knew what lay between the black leather covers down to the last cent: barely enough to make it through to spring. If Mr Trubody refused to blend their wines there would be nothing to maintain them over the summer. She would be forced to sell Royaume Céleste at a knockdown price, just like the Gascon's widow. And so everything would turn full circle.

Her glance fell on a pigeonhole in the bureau containing a thick envelope. Curiously, she pulled it out, surprised by its weight. Then she remembered. It contained a tin photograph brought from France.

She pulled out the rectangular plate and held it to the lamplight. Emile stared back at her, four years old, dressed in a stiff, high-collared new suit, puffy knickerbockers and lace up boots. The tintype had been taken at the fair in Carcassone. Of course, there was no Antoine – away in Paris, as usual.

She peered closely at the lost boy. He stood before a crudely painted backdrop of a ruined Greek temple, his expression sad, or perhaps strained, though that could be the photographer's insistence on him staying perfectly still for three whole minutes.

His curly hair, even after combing, had been as unruly as his father's. But the mouth! That rosebud mouth made her blink back tears. And the boots seemed so big on such a little body, his limbs out of proportion until, one day, age would stretch and shape him like clay.

She recollected the photographer pressing her to stand beside her son, so their joint image, side by side, would imprint itself on the metal plate forever. Somehow, she had not wanted to. Why? She could not say, just wished it was otherwise with all her heart. That way a trace or shadow might have been preserved of something they had shared – amidst all the things they never shared.

Upstairs in his room, Emile resumed the letter interrupted by his mother. Defiantly, he wrote in French: *Dear Papa, I trust this letter finds you in good health. I have written letters to you before but never sent them. Maman and Jean-Pierre both tell me you are dead and that is why we have come to America. But, Papa, I do not believe them. That is why I wish to tell you where you can find and collect me . . .* Pent up words guided Emile's pen. Finally, he folded an envelope stolen from his mother's bureau along with a nub of red sealing wax, and wrote: *Château de Chauveterre, near Carcassone, Languedoc, France* and its recipient, *Le Comte Antoine de Rivac de Chauveterre.*

As Emile pondered how to find or steal the postage, a half-remembered song came to his lips:

> *Jusqu'à ce qu'on prenne*
> *La lune avec les dents!*

Downstairs another inmate of Royaume Céleste wrote to recover the past. Chi-en trimmed an oil lamp and opened *A Memoir of Prince Hong*. Blending water and shavings from a new ink cake, he dipped his writing brush. Long, flowing columns of Chinese characters streamed like lost swans or messenger-geese into the night, their wings beating hard as his heart.

Chapter the Third: *The Rider on the White Horse*

I

Just as every litter includes a runt, so Nature delivers master-spirits to each generation, people born to command and inspire. Such was Fourth Prince Hong.

His person was light, well proportioned, wiry. Yet he was short. Indeed, I towered over him like a clumsy bear. His features were restless and he had a habit of fidgeting – crossing and re-crossing his legs, tapping his feet. By contrast, his voice was low and soft.

Tutor Ren Xudong told me Prince Hong was close in character to the Heavenly King: both were instinctive leaders, ablaze with a self-confidence that is instantly attractive to weaker souls, just as pale flowers are drawn to the sun.

Despite inner chafing that I should rescue Aunty-Mother and escape the Heavenly Capital, I longed to establish myself as more than one of Prince Hong's numerous servants. The Taipings often swore oaths of brotherhood with trusted fellow-believers. Such a bond had to be earned. It might also preserve one's life, for the Heavenly Kingdom was always threatened, never truly secure.

Fourth Prince Hong not only won respect for his personal qualities.

Even at a young age he had developed a plan – albeit copied from his uncle, the Prime Minister – to solve the miseries of the Chinese people. First, to establish an empire truly for the Chinese, no longer ruled by the corrupt Manchu. Secondly, destroy all false idols and propagate the Bible. Thirdly, distribute land and wealth more fairly. Above all, seek alliances with fellow Christian nations. 'I shall be our ambassador,' he told me. 'I shall persuade them to share their science and marvellous inventions.'

One day I found him examining a pile of European revolvers, clocks, compasses, tinned foodstuffs and Manchester fabrics imported at considerable expense.

'Ah, Chi-en, perhaps you can help me make sense of this lot. You are half-foreign, after all.'

I blushed at this allusion to my perpetual shame. Prince Hong smiled to set me at ease: he was always quick to understand another's discomfort. We walked to the garden and paused to listen. Amidst the birdsong, the echo of cannonades indicated another foray by the Imperialist forces surrounding us.

'Never mind them,' said Hong, 'let's make a few bangs of our own.'

For an hour we practised with the revolvers. Prince Hong's aim was variable, but I held the pistol steady in two hands and shattered the clay pots set as our targets. Afterwards he regarded me with new respect.

'Keep the Colt,' he said. 'You'll be a formidable bodyguard.'

Our hands reeking of gunpowder, we listened once again to the cannonade.

'I do not fear them,' he said. 'Only that I will never get my chance to save the people. One day the Young King will inherit the throne and nothing will improve. I am only Fourth Prince, not First. It is folly for one like me to possess such dreams.'

A lump formed in my throat. How I admired his selfless ideals! In a rush, I repeated an old proverb learned from Aunty-Mother.

'Why should not sparrows have the dreams of swans?' I asked. 'It is your destiny to save China!'

He looked at me steadily. The cloud on his face lifted.

'We *shall* win through,' he said with quiet dignity. 'Now teach me some of the foreigners' strange language, Chi-en.'

I thought for a moment then found the expression that summed up my estimation of him. '*Numbah one*,' I said, using the Pidgin English popular in Shanghai. 'It means *the best*.'

'*Numbah one*! Yes, I like that.'

It became his standard response whenever pleased or impressed. Naturally, all his followers took it up. That hour in the garden marked a change in his regard for me, so that I found less leisure to fret about Aunty-Mother.

II

All noble spirits contend with their opposites; thus, progress occurs. In the case of Prince Hong that opposite had a name: the Young King.

Even in appearance they were opposed. The Young King was soft-bellied, passive, with an air of the palace eunuch about him. Indulged since birth so not a single fear troubled his childhood other than not getting his way, he was impractical, naïve, impressionable. At the age of nine he had been given his own palace and banned from meeting his mother except on the Heavenly King's birthday. One consolation for this loss was that Jesus officially appointed him His adopted son.

The question of palaces brought my master and the Young King into open conflict. Prince Hong's was ancient and full of wonderful paintings stolen during the Taiping army's bloody march through China to the Heavenly Capital. He also possessed an immense library. He often asked me to read aloud poems by classical authors. 'I'd do it myself,' he'd say, 'except you do it in a tenth of the time.'

From morning until night, a full orchestra played in my master's central courtyard, for he could not bear silence or a sense that nothing was afoot. He needed bustle and noise as some require solitude. Yet his palace possessed gardens where I sat for hours contemplating pools of golden carp, drooping willows, rustling bamboo.

Although far smaller than the Young King's palace, such was the elegance of Prince Hong's establishment that word soon reached his jealous cousin.

Even when the Imperialists were pressing close to the Heavenly Capital and all seemed lost, the Young King persuaded his father to write an edict condemning Fourth Prince Hong. The reprimand concerned the decorations on my master's ceremonial crown. This marvellous golden headpiece was, at Prince Hong's insistence, identical to the Young King's own, namely, *A Lone Phoenix Perching in Clouds*. Armed with his edict, the Young King commanded that he should be carried in a sedan chair to Prince Hong's palace, escorted by a hundred Holy Soldiers and high officials.

When he arrived, my master's entire household and followers were drilling with muskets, bamboo spears and rifles he had acquired from foreign merchants. With the Imperialist forces so near, he deemed it essential that every man capable of fighting should be properly trained. Although I was just twelve, I stood proudly beside him with a long-barrelled Colt revolver and a carbine that bruised my shoulder each time I fired. We exchanged puzzled glances and ceased drilling as the Young King's entourage jogged into the courtyard.

Upon stepping from his sedan chair, our future monarch commanded us all – five hundred men, including Prince Hong – to kneel before him. We watched through downcast eyes as, waving the edict, the Young King motioned for my master to come over.

I shall not recount his exact words. Suffice to say they were wholly critical and delivered in a high-pitched, dreary voice. At the end, Prince Hong was ordered to produce his ceremonial crown for confiscation. 'You can only have *A Heron Flourishing Its Wings* on yours!' concluded the Young King, triumphantly.

Emotions contended on Prince Hong's face. I longed to whisper a warning not to allow himself to be provoked. Finally, he turned to a servant. 'Fetch my crown as the Heavenly King commands.'

We all sighed with relief. But the Young King wasn't done yet.

'When I was born,' he boasted, 'thousands of birds settled round our family home in Canton. They stayed a whole month, paying homage to my cradle. I bet such miracles didn't happen at *your* birth.'

Hundreds of eyes were upon my master. There was no doubt now the Young King wished to trick him into a blasphemous reply. But Prince Hong smiled his usual quiet smile.

'I believe God is saving my miracles for later,' he said.

No one dared applaud his wit except in their hearts.

After the Young King had gone, Prince Hong resumed drilling the troops as though no interruption had occurred. Later, over dinner, he chuckled. 'Thousands of birds! Imagine the squawking. All that tweeting and whistling! Not to mention the bird shit.'

He made flapping actions with his arms. Though he roared with laughter, I could tell he was angry. His was a cold, controlled anger one does not wish to provoke.

III

Then a great miracle occurred. Just as the devil-demons seemed ready to triumph in a siege that had lasted years, a long-prepared stratagem by the

Prime Minister opened like a tiger's jaws. As if from nowhere, two hundred thousand Holy Soldiers recalled from the Heavenly Kingdom's far-flung provinces, descended on the besiegers, effectively reversing their position. For days both sides hacked at each other in torrential rain. Prince Hong added to his honour by leading a sortie of his household battalion against a siege work near the walls.

At last the Imperialist ranks broke, leaving a quarter of their army to be buried by as many prisoners. The noose around the Heavenly City had been severed. For weeks no one quite believed it. Except, that is, for the Heavenly King, who proclaimed Jesus's wife, his sister-in-law, had told him in a dream to expect the victory long before it happened.

IV

I was twelve years old when the siege was lifted. It ushered in a time of joy. For that, along with so many blessings, I had reason to thank Fourth Prince Hong.

Within its thirty-three miles of walls, the Heavenly Capital comprised a world in itself. For us, and it should be noted that Prince Hong could only leave the city with royal permission, it was our entire world.

What a noble, gay sight we made! There were twenty young men of good family in Prince Hong's entourage, each talented in different ways, for he considered mediocrity a catching disease. How we galloped over hills and down long boulevards! We raced through copses, uncultivated wasteland, paddy fields and market gardens, all within the safety of the ramparts. What excitable, thoughtless conversation passed between us! Yet we had contemplative moods, too, sometimes visiting a particular sunlit pool to examine our reflections until the jump of a tiny fish obscured us with ripples.

During those bright, happy years the Heavenly Capital vibrated with youthful energy. Perhaps, being young ourselves, we noticed only our own kind. Child-soldiers thronged the streets along with attractive young women saved from lives of degradation and sin. Prince Hong counselled us to beware these sirens. He need hardly have bothered; everyday a few more hapless sinners were beheaded for fornication. At night I dreamt of these forbidden girls with a fascination intensified by danger. In that, I am sure, I was far from alone.

Indeed, to live in the Heavenly Capital was to be rarely alone. Wherever we roamed, walls and gates hemmed us in. Troops patrolled ceaselessly; the city was a vast military camp with food doled out to fighting men and labourers from government warehouses. Shops and markets had been banished beyond the city walls, not because the Taipings despised trade, but to ensure better defence. The absence of frantic buying and selling made the city eerily quiet.

Sometimes Prince Hong and I would leave the other boys and go hunting. We both carried English shotguns and became pretty fair marksmen.

One morning, a year or so after the siege ended, Prince Hong took it into his head to visit the ancient tombs of the Ming Emperors, a few miles beyond the ramparts. Boldly, he did not seek permission, thereby risking the Heavenly King's displeasure. For this reason – and a youthful desire for adventure – we dressed in plain Taiping outfits with borrowed identity tags and left the palace through a side gate in the hour before dawn.

First, we hired a rowboat from the South Gate, following a wide moat beneath the high walls for several miles, the boatman propelling us with sideways movements of his rudder-oar. The sun rose to a strangely still world. No human voices disturbed the drip and plop of water, the gentle plash of the oar. Birds cheeped and fluttered. Leaves hung limp in the breezeless air.

We passed an ancient gate and bridge blockaded with rubble during the long siege. After another hour, the boatman guided us to a jetty and moored his craft.

Shotguns slung over our shoulders, we trudged a mile or so, passing through the remains of Imperialist siege trenches full of mottled water.

By now the sun was high enough to leach sweat from every pore. The unnatural silence when sailing up the moat followed us to a hill of limestone and bare, dry earth: we had reached the Ming Emperors' Tombs.

Prince Hong laughed, leaning on his shotgun as he mopped his brow. 'Is this all?' he asked. 'I expected more.'

Indeed, the ancient tombs had collapsed in upon themselves. Here and there, walls stood intact amidst broken arches and filthy, mildew-stained frescoes depicting the great deeds of the Ming. Though I stared hard at these fragments, their message eluded me: time had rendered them forever dumb. Meanwhile, Prince Hong was examining stone camels, elephants, horses, dogs – some twice as tall as him – lining the road as eternal guardians. All were falling apart.

Eventually we found the tomb of the first Ming Emperor, a tyrant who drove out a barbarian dynasty just as Prince Hong hoped to scatter the Manchu and their Ching Emperor. Fallen masonry lay amidst bright, yellow-glazed tiles decorated with five-claw Imperial dragons.

'Look at this!' I said, rushing to the improbable hump of an ornate stone bridge. The joke was that the pond it once crossed had long dried out and become tawny grass.

We sat in silence on this absurd bridge for a while. I believe a sense of our own littleness made us reluctant to step from it. Suddenly Prince Hong leapt up and ascended to the apex of the bridge.

'I will conquer the Manchu!' he shouted. 'See that city!' He waved at the Heavenly Capital. 'It shall have factories! Steam trains! Steamboats! Everything that will make us strong again!'

He fell silent. A strange trick of the hillsides made his shout echo from bare limestone crag to crag: *strong again . . . strong again . . . strong again . . .* until it faded. We were shaken and I saw him reach for his shotgun. Then a pheasant flapped up from the First Ming Emperor's tomb. Its wings beat noisily, echoing just as Prince Hong's shouts had done. He turned to me. 'Let us go,' he said. 'There is nothing to see here.'

We left quietly, afraid of stirring the dead with our noise. Fourth Prince Hong never again expressed a desire to visit the Ming Tombs.

V

During those years of youthful excitement, a ghost surveyed all my actions. Sad as trampled flowers, she was no angry spirit. In my imagination she never aged. Never has done. I refer, of course, to Aunty-Mother.

The one thing I knew for sure was that she continued to serve in the Heavenly King's palace. Once a woman entered the Holy Court (and only women dwelt there to avoid the manifold evils to good government caused by palace eunuchs) she never came out again, except to escort our Holy Ruler. Given that he was a recluse, pre-occupied with correcting errors of doctrine in the Bible, such excursions never took place. One came to the Heavenly King, not the other way round. So I held no hope of seeing her that way.

Most days I found an opportunity to loiter outside the palace walls where edicts and proclamations painted on yellow silk hung until they faded. A new one appeared each afternoon, sometimes several. Every facet of human conduct was thereby improved. One edict abolished laziness. Another did away with lustful speculations.

No one stopped me reading the columns of divinely-inspired red ink. And I never glimpsed the faintest trace of Aunty-Mother.

Could her life in the palace be so horrible? I consoled myself with thoughts that the Taipings treated women unusually well. Purchasing a wife, foot-binding, prostitution, all were strictly forbidden. Women wandered freely, addressed by strangers as *Sister*. Yet rumour had it the Heavenly King was harsh and unrelenting to his female servants, that beheading for a second offence of displeasing His Highness was customary. First offences were merely punished with a severe beating.

Despite Taiping laws forbidding more than one wife, the Heavenly King had received personal dispensations from God allowing him to marry one hundred and twenty. Given Aunty-Mother's natural grace and beauty, I worried constantly she would become a lesser wife and somehow displease her husband twice. Even when being beaten, the palace women were obliged to smile and laugh after each stroke of the bamboo cane and call out: 'Thank you for your blessings, Heavenly King!' They were also said to cruelly slander and bully each other.

Finally, when I was fourteen years old, I could stand uncertainty no longer. Though such questions were strictly forbidden, I resolved to press Prince Hong for news of Aunty-Mother. Indeed, I was pacing before my favourite fishpond, watching builders repair a low wall, when his voice startled me.

'Chi-en! By yourself again? I came to find you.'

I bowed, sighed. A thoughtful look crossed his young face.

'Come back in an hour!' he ordered the labourers. 'Ask for rice at the kitchens.'

They gladly obliged. I felt his cool, appraising glance as I stared at the pile of bricks, tubs of mortar and abandoned tools.

'One may not fix a gap in one's heart as easily as a wall,' he said. 'I believe you are thinking of your Aunty-Mother again.'

When I confirmed his guess, Prince Hong rubbed his hands with delight. 'You see!' he chuckled. 'I understand you exactly. Come, sit down, Chi-en. Tell me what troubles you.'

We perched on a bench near the broken wall and watched the fish circle lazily. They, at least, seemed content with the confines of a palace.

'Can I not meet her?' I asked. 'At least once?'

He shook his head while waving off midges that danced near the water. 'You must dismiss such a hope.'

'What is life like for her?' I whispered.

He clapped me on the shoulder. 'Better than it would be otherwise.' But I sensed evasion. You can imagine how intently I had studied his moods, expressions, hesitations over the years.

'It would be better not to draw too much attention to her,' he said. 'I must tell you, Chi-en, our spies in Shanghai report that your old master, Reverend Shambles, regularly slanders the Heavenly Kingdom in newspapers. He claims the reason he fled the Heavenly Capital was because my uncle, the Prime Minister, beat a boy servant to death with a club. He refers to you, Chi-en. Did my uncle ever beat you?'

'Never!'

Prince Hong's news astounded me. But I knew he would not lie. Hurtful, too, was the revelation that Reverend Shambles lived a wealthy man, having crammed his pockets whilst under the protection of those he now abused.

'So, you see,' said Prince Hong, 'it is dangerous to make enquiries.'

Prudence could not stop me grieving. All too often I pictured Aunty-Mother frightened and alone in halls decorated with gold and jewels and silver but lacking precious kindness. Did she think about me? About her Little Humble, her Chi-en? Asking that question was enough to start my tears. Then I would roar inside with anger against Spiritual Uncle Father, the master she had trusted and idealised. Anger, too, that my father, that mysterious sailor characterised by Reverend Shambles as a 'damnable sinner', had floated away, forcing her to rely on a stranger's fickle charity. *I will find you, Father*, I promised myself. *One day I will find you and tell you what your thoughtlessness has done!*

VI

For all my hidden grief over Aunty-Mother, those were days of excitement and hope. I cannot return to them. Cannot gallop once more with my dear, carefree brothers in Prince Hong's retinue. Most, I know, are dead. The youth I was then died long ago.

We called the ancient city of Nanking our *Little Heaven*, a glimpse of paradise on earth. Even then I dared to doubt. For as the years of youth ran through me, so did veins of corruption in the Taipings' noble ideals.

The fault was by no means restricted to the Heavenly Kingdom. Afraid of treachery, the Heavenly King appointed family members and lickspittles to powerful positions rather than men of talent and ability. The result was predictable. Decisions mired in squabbling, incompetence, venality and self-interest. Meanwhile, the Imperialists waged ceaseless war on us.

For years I was kept busy translating articles from the foreign press for Prince Hong or providing summaries of foreign books he acquired. My uncanny ability to speak, read and write languages gained me the nickname 'Hong's Sorceror'.

Events in the Heavenly Capital made me question whether we indeed dwelt in Paradise. As news from the Taiping provinces deteriorated, executions became common. The Young King took a keen interest in these proceedings. Yet I grew weary of seeing men flogged insensible for drinking a little wine or smoking tobacco. Especially as I knew full well members of the Heavenly Family indulged both vices with impunity. Worse was the fate accorded to fornicators and opium smokers. Each month dozens were soaked in oil and set ablaze as 'Lighted Heavenly Lanterns'.

Prince Hong always averted his eyes from these scenes and urged me to take care. 'Treason trials will come next,' he predicted. So, I doubted in silence. If God is pure Love and Forgiveness, I wondered, can He not pardon those so unhappy they seek an oblivion that poisons them? In the depths of night, I had fearful thoughts: that God was a tyrant no better than the Manchu Emperor. What then, I wondered, was the Heavenly King? Torments of guilt followed, torments I tried to counter with faith in man's essential goodness.

During my fourteenth and fifteenth years, the Heavenly Kingdom shrank. One by one Taiping cities that cost thousands of lives to liberate fell to the enemy. Rumours of cruel massacres cast shadows even in the happy, purposeful world of Prince Hong's palace.

Still the foreign merchants came with their cargoes of imported goods: cloth that had travelled half way round the world, weapons, munitions. I often accompanied Prince Hong to the port. It was then I was most useful to him, acting as a faithful, incorruptible interpreter. He understood the Heavenly Kingdom had been inspired by foreign missionaries. The merchants were another kind of missionary, their creed being earthly power through trade.

'Would you have it that way in China?' I asked.

'Do we have a choice?' he said.

Whenever I could speak to foreigners in private, I enquired after Reverend Shambles in Shanghai. Only a few had heard of him. Those who knew his name knew little else. I often considered sending a message concerning Aunty-Mother's plight. But what good would it do? Most likely it would join his other condemnations of the Taipings in the *North China Herald*. Besides, I remembered Prince Hong's warning about treason charges. Even then we suspected the Young King's spies reported our every move.

VII

Prince Hong regularly sat in a particular tower of the fortifications to drink tea and watch the mile-wide Yangtze flow past. Examining foreign steamers through his telescope was a special pleasure.

In winter the river was at its lowest ebb. Cold mists swirled round shivering reeds and bamboo. But in summer the Yangtze's waters rushed and bubbled, yellowy-brown with earth gathered en route to the sea. Then it frequently flooded the countryside in a surging, boiling tide. We observed the tops of trees bent by the rushing stream, temporary home to flocks of squabbling white herons and other waterfowl. In the distance hung the purple, ghostly shapes of mountains.

At times of flood the Heavenly Capital seemed an island in a floating world, circled by stiff-sailed junks and vast flocks of birds.

'Where does the sea go?' Prince Hong asked me eagerly. 'What is the sea like?'

And I, who had sailed upon the sea only a few years earlier, could find nothing to say except: 'The sea is big as dreams.'

Napa Valley, California
Winter 1877

After Christmas the earth hardened with frost. No longer a quagmire, soil nurtured crystal-seeds of ice. Slender plants and stems grew stiff as wires, casting strange shadows.

One forenoon a horseman emerged from the steep wood dividing Royaume Céleste and the valley lowlands. Returning to the farmhouse from the winery, Catherine shielded her eyes against the low sun. The horseman's seat rose and fell rhythmically as he urged his fine white Spanish stallion into a canter.

Conscious of her unflattering, practical dress and shawl, she hurried into the farmhouse and up to her bedroom. It was a surprise – half pleasant – to feel her heart beat fast. She fumbled with blouse and skirt, aware of Colonel Smithson-Mackay's deep voice outside and Jean-Pierre's respectful reply. Finally, Catherine examined her face in the oval mirror above the dressing table.

It was a face strangely unfamiliar. Contending selves within her stared back. Why should she not provoke admiration? Her high cheekbones and neat nose were not ugly. Likewise, the full mouth above a chin – too pointy for beauty, true – but not hideous.

These reflections absorbed her as she descended the stairs. In the hall,

Colonel Smithson-Mackay was addressing Chi-en Shambles. Her servant's folded arms and slightly tilted head lacked a proper deference. Catherine hastened her step.

'Don't like your manners, boy,' warned Smithson-Mackay. 'You some kind of half-breed? From those slitty eyes of yours I do believe you are.' The colonel's face reddened. 'I'd wipe that grin off of your yeller face, if I were you.'

'I am too old to be called a boy,' said Chi-en. 'Would you like me to take your hat?'

Smithson-Mackay twitched his riding crop as though tempted to flick Chi-en across the face.

Catherine cried from the stairs, 'Colonel! How delightful!'

The riding crop lowered, swishing near Smithson-Mackay's tight breeches.

'Greetings, Ma-am!' he drawled, after a final glance at Chi-en. 'Peculiar kind of servant you keep, if you'll forgive me saying. Not quite your reg'lar Mongol. A mighty curious specimen. And damned insolent with it.'

To a stranger, Chi-en's expression might have contained hurt. Catherine, who knew him better, recognised contempt. She saw, too, his carapace of irony hid something inward and smouldering. Something she recognised from memories of Antoine as shame – bitter, untellable shame.

'Forget my servant, Colonel.' She advanced to shake his hand. 'He is a little odd, as you say. But you may be sure he works hard. Please go back to the kitchen, 'Umble!'

With the slightest of bows, Chi-en withdrew and Catherine felt somehow at fault.

'Perhaps you will take some refreshment, Colonel?' she said.

The riding crop continued to tap Smithson-Mackay's outer thigh.

'Truth is, Ma-am,' he said, 'I wondered if you might join me for a little ride, seeing the ground is so firm and all. You see, I heard you helped out Trubody with his wine. And I thought to myself, "Heck! I could use a little of that French magic myself!" I'd sure value your opinion about my grapes.'

She felt warmth on her cheeks. 'I would be honoured, Colonel.'

Her horse was soon saddled by Jean-Pierre, who received a shiny dollar from the Colonel for his pains. While they waited, Smithson-Mackay produced a silver flask etched with the Confederate battle flag. Catherine gulped a mouthful of aqua vitae. Though it burned she did not cough and he toasted her fortitude. The neat spirits made her giddy.

With the breath of both mounts and riders visible in the cold air, they trotted between rows of wizened, leafless vines. At first neither spoke. Halfway up the hillside he reined his horse and gazed across the valley at Trubody Nook.

'I hear you and Old Trubody are partners,' he remarked, casually.

Jeanne d'Arc let out a long, complex emission of wind, followed by a self-satisfied whinny. 'Indeed we are.' Catherine patted the mare's neck.

'I sure hope his terms are straight,' said Smithson-Mackay. 'Trubody's famous for dealing a crooked hand.'

She felt a stab of anxiety. Had she been cheated? Her knowledge of American prices was incomplete, but surely Nancy would never let her husband cheat her. 'In France we are accustomed to say nothing of business arrangements. They are, as we say, *in confidence*.'

'Oh ho! Gracefully put, Ma-am! Rest assured I'll hush my mouth. Only, as a sincere friend, if I was you I'd not put too much trust in our friend yonder.' He nodded at the fabulous towers and turrets of Trubody Nook. 'In particular, I'd advise you not to mention that I'm a good friend of yours.'

Catherine found herself saying, 'I shall not mention it,' and wondered whether they were indeed good friends, based on so limited an acquaintance. What kind of friendship must be kept secret from the world?

They rode round the vineyard at a steady trot, skirting dark thickets of woodland. She became aware of her shyness in his company. After all, she was more than capable of knowing – and speaking – her own mind. Papa Bourchier had encouraged her to have opinions so she might be useful to her future husband. Ironic then that Antoine had never consulted her on anything.

'Tell me, Catherine,' he said. 'Do you enjoy California?'

She narrowed her eyes. Again, warmth stole over her face. Had she encouraged the intimacy of her first name? Yet there it was.

'Now I fear I've displayed our rough frontier manners, Madame Bourchier, by taking the liberty of your Christian name?'

'Why, I . . .'

'You must forgive our American style of politeness between friends. I guess we're straight to the point, without meaning harm by it.'

'Still,' she said, her throat tightening, 'perhaps I would prefer you to . . .'

'Address you as Madame Bourchier? Why, sure!' His wolfish grin returned. 'But only if you forgive any impertinence on my part.'

'I'm sure none was intended.'

'Then we're still friends!' he declared, his horse drifting closer to her own, so that he patted Jeanne d'Arc's broad rump. 'Giddy up, you slow old mare!' he said, breaking into a canter that Catherine felt obliged to copy, lest she look feeble. She followed him to the edge of the arroyo, where he gazed down at the creek swollen with rain. Unaccountably his playful mood had darkened.

'Though I am a Californian through and through, Ma-am,' he said, 'I hail from Georgia's fine cradle.'

She waited: evidently, he had something to share.

'I guess my father liked the bottle so much he died when I was a boy. Even though my mother and sisters doted on me, a man with no father must find his own fortune in the world. I make no apologies for working hard and being smart, unlike some of the fancy, so-called *chivalry* in the State of Georgia! Or for gathering my own pile during the war.'

She leaned forward curiously. 'You were a colonel in the Confederate Army, I believe?'

'I was proud to bear that honourable rank. They nicknamed my regiment the Georgia Raiders. And by God when we got behind enemy lines, we stuck it to them Yankees! A man had to do what he must. I make no apology for lovin' my state and my country.' His expression lightened as he stared into the creek. 'After the war I found myself in Frisco with a handy pile to invest. The rest, I guess, is history.'

Catherine realised Lydia Smithson-Mackay had played no part in his story.

'And now you have a lovely wife and family,' she said, with false brightness. 'A son and two daughters, is it not?'

He shot her a sharp glance. 'I see you've found out all about me, Madame Bourchier,' he chuckled. 'I'm flattered.' The dark shadow returned. 'Let me tell you about those children you mentioned. I paid for them to go to Europe with their mother for a tour and vacation. A year they spent there, then another, despite me writing to my wife that I wanted 'em home. It pains me to tell you, as a friend, the only reason they came is that I refused to wire another cent!'

Catherine thought of her own ill-matched marriage. 'It is hard for a child to be separated from his father.'

'I don't mind saying those children of mine feel like strangers since they returned.'

'Perhaps that is natural after a long separation.'

The Colonel seemed too engrossed by his own story to hear her. 'I guess my wife doesn't understand me,' he declared. 'Oh, I don't ask for sympathy from any man or woman on this earth! But it makes a fellah lonely as hell.'

With a flick of his riding crop, he wheeled his horse. Once more Catherine was forced to follow. Back at the winery he reined the stallion and simultaneously touched his hat.

'Well, I guess I've made a tomfool of myself,' he said without any sign of embarrassment. 'I'm just thankful I can rely on your discretion.'

'You can rely on it, Colonel,' she said with feeling.

His glance took in Emile who was watching from the farmhouse porch.

'I saw your boy in the Post Office in Perryville last week. Guess you sent him with a letter.'

Catherine looked at him blankly. 'I do not think so.'

'Must've mistook him for another boy.'

Another thought seemed to strike him. 'I wanted to warn you . . . hunters have seen redskins skulking in the hills above the valley. A whole posse of Diggers left my ranchero a few days ago. If you see any savages, let me know. Two of my men, Parker and Temple, will sort 'em out for you. They were with me back in Georgia, so you can trust those boys.'

Still, he seemed reluctant to go, a delay Catherine both desired and feared.

'So long, Madame Bourchier.'

As he turned his horse, the stallion snorted impatiently. Smithson-Mackay met her eye and she felt a pleasurable weakness flood her body. Perhaps he sensed or shared it, for he reached out and rubbed Jeanne d'Arc's perspiring head.

'*Au revoir*, Monsieur,' said Catherine, pulling back the rein after an inner struggle.

Once more he grinned. 'Obliged, Ma-am! I'll be in Frisco on business until the spring. Perhaps I'll have the pleasure to meet you when I return.'

As he cantered away, Catherine realised he had forgotten to ask her advice concerning his grapes.

She retreated to her bedroom, led by unwelcome, enticing images. That he held her waist tightly, filling her nostrils with a mingled scent of soap and perspiration. Of lying on the bed while he lifted her layers of skirts without restraint, her head pressed back against the pillow.

The ghosts arrived an hour after Smithson-Mackay left Royaume Céleste. No one saw them trek through gloomy, silent woods overlooking the vineyard. On their backs were bundles of rags; rusty, discarded tools; cracked iron pots. One young man carried a large, painted rocking chair. No one heard their whispered talk.

They came from the direction of Perryville and would have muttered fearfully to learn who had just visited Royaume Céleste. Had the names Parker and Temple been mentioned, a swift departure would have ensued.

As it was, the ghosts climbed to the large oval clearing concealed by looming volcanic boulders and ancient redwoods. Here they looked around, a dozen people of all ages dressed in a haphazard blend of native and white man's clothes. Their long black hair was matted, lousy, cut in a fringe over thick bushy eyebrows. Half were pureblood Wappo, most obviously the big old woman. The rest formed a complex medley of races.

At the matriarch's instigation, they paced out a circle twenty steps across and began to erect a crude hut, guided by her memories of a village ploughed under the vines, so its very name fluttered like the last leaf of autumn, before it falls and melts into dust.

A fire blazed, built high by the clan's small children. With its heat came bolder talk, tentative song, laughter.

Down below, on the porch of the farmhouse, Jean-Pierre summoned Catherine and pointed out a reddish glow, high on the dark hillside.

'Hunters?' he suggested.

'Perhaps.'

She watched for a while, remembering Smithson-Mackay's warning about savages.

'Let them be,' she said. 'They do us no harm. Who knows, if they are Indians, we might be less obliged to Sam Wah for our hired hands.'

Outside the kitchen, Emile also noted the distant, flickering glow. 'Chi-en!' he cried, rushing inside, 'the ghosts are back!'

Chi-en's first warning was a word. An unfamiliar word he rolled round mouth and mind: *kanamoto*. Emile was staring out of the kitchen window at Mount St Helena, distracted from a dull comprehension exercise about George Washington and his father's cherry tree.

'Kanamoto,' the boy announced.

'What does *kanamoto* mean?' asked Chi-en.

A grin overspread Emile's face. 'Don't know. Made it up.'

'Did you?'

'Unless I know something you don't.'

'It would be strange if you didn't,' said Chi-en, sternly. 'Go ask your mother for chores!'

After the boy left, still grinning, Chi-en went over to the flour bin. Filled yesterday, it was almost empty.

'*Kanamoto*,' he said to himself, trying out the vowels and syllables in different ways.

The New Year's ice melted, banished by a dull winter sun warm enough to hearten the weeds. Again, the earth grew sticky: wet enough for footprints.

Chi-en noticed a clear trail from the house to the Indian path into the hills. More food went missing and he suspected the reason, a situation that could not continue. The cent-pinching household accounts of Catherine Bourchier were sure to uncover the theft and he wished to avoid yet another rift between mother and son.

The next Saturday, when Catherine and Jean-Pierre had driven to Napa City to order oak barrels, Chi-en's chance came. As expected, Emile sneaked away, a school satchel heavy around his shoulders. After an interval to allow the boy to reach the woods, Chi-en put on his coat and followed. It occurred to him Jean-Pierre's shotgun might prove useful, but the thought of holding a gun opened raw, unhealed places in his heart.

The path was exactly as it had been when he last came: the same man-high piles of small stones; the same unvisited glens and canyons; and always, the bubbling song of the creek as it flowed down to Royaume Céleste. Near the clearing he smelled smoke. Children's voices squealed in excited play. Stooping, he examined Emile's boot prints in the mud. Walking unannounced into an Indian squatter camp might be dangerous. He did not even possess the protection of a white skin.

Chi-en resumed his climb, emerging to find the ghosts' clearing transformed. A large domed hut made of reeds, mud and branches stood in the shelter of a towering volcanic outcrop. Smoke rose from a hole at its apex. A group of men sat on logs, weaving baskets and talking quietly.

A separate circle of women pounded acorns into meal on a large flat rock.

His eye passed to a battered wooden rocking chair near the hut entrance. On it was enthroned a large, copper-skinned old woman with lank grey hair. A corncob pipe protruded from her wrinkled lips as the chair rocked back and forth. Emile, accompanied by three other children, was pouring out potatoes from his satchel. Chi-en could not doubt the food's provenance and understood the Indian clan's danger. Squatting on useless land was one thing: stealing from white folks would result in punishments far in excess of the stolen food's value.

The men noticed him first, rising one by one. Chi-en stepped forward. For no logical reason, he called out in a clear, commanding voice: '*Kanamoto*!'

The Indians glanced at Mount St Helena. Finding it no different from usual, they turned to face him. He advanced with palms held open, nodding politely to the shabby men and women he passed.

Reaching the matriarch, who was trying to hide potatoes beneath her voluminous skirts, Chi-en bowed. Then he waited. One of them was sure to speak English. A tall young man came over. Chi-en noted the large knife in a decorated sheath at his belt – and that his hand rested on the hilt.

'What you want?' demanded the youth.

'Is this woman the chief?' asked Chi-en.

The old hag rocked back and forth.

'I am the chief,' declared the young man, striking his chest, but it was obvious where the real authority lay. The Old Mother folded her arms over a huge bosom.

'Emile,' said Chi-en, 'stand beside me.'

'Why are you here?'

'This is not a time to argue,' said Chi-en, quietly in French.

Tears filled the boy's eyes. 'They are my *friends*.' He pointed at the ragamuffin children. 'You said I should make more friends. I've done nothing wrong!'

Chi-en turned back to the 'chief'. 'Does the Old Mother speak English?'

'Why should we answer a Chinaman?' he countered.

It was a good question. To most Californians, a Chink was lower than a Digger, just as Diggers were lower than Niggers and Italians lower than nearly every other kind of White. 'You should answer a Chinaman because the boy's visits could bring big trouble. He has been stealing food.'

'I haven't!' Emile seemed aware suddenly of the consequences of his actions. 'It's my fault, not theirs! I should be blamed!'

'Most people would not see it that way,' said Chi-en, 'including your mother.'

He turned back to the chief. 'Ask the Old Mother why she has brought her people here. I mean you no harm – just like the boy.'

This motive proved decisive. Emile had clearly found, or purchased, a position where he was well regarded.

A curious tale followed, narrated by the matriarch in a style emphasised by cutting hand gestures. Her grandson acted as interpreter. Chi-en learned her clan of Wappo had been press-ganged from their village near Mount St Helena by men with guns – the names Parker and Temple were accompanied by fierce curses – then marched to the ranch of a man called Colmackay. There they had been forced to sign crosses on paper and work every hour, every day, and given scraps of food in return. If they did not work hard enough, Temple and Parker beat them. The matriarch insisted her grandson, the chief, show the weals of recent whip marks on his back. These indignities, it seemed, had been too much for

181

the Old Mother. Remembering her village as a girl – a village currently beneath the vineyard of Royaume Céleste – she had brought her clan where their ancestors' ghosts could offer protection. Already these spirits had brought the white boy with food. In the spring they would begin a dance strong enough to return the valley to the Wappo and their dead relatives.

'Let us stay in peace,' she concluded. 'We are here for peace.'

Chi-en's extraordinary ear for languages – and vanity – strained for meaning during this long story. Finally, a smile crossed his face.

'*Ah ono . . . si . . .*yes, that's right . . . *ah ono si okel hati . . . khi,*' he tried, tentatively. 'I know that you, yes, *ha'goosha,* hungry, but no more taking food from the boy.'

The effect of this statement in their language was general consternation. Even the indomitable matriarch examined him nervously. Then she understood. 'The ancestors' spirits speak through him,' she declared, her words hurriedly translated by the chief.

'At dusk,' said Chi-en, 'go to the farm below and ask the woman for permission to stay on her land. She is a strong mother like you. Say you will work for fifty cents a day before and during the harvest. If that doesn't persuade her to let you stay, nothing will. Oh, and call her *big white princess.* She'll like that.'

So, it was arranged. Before they left, Chi-en turned to his interpreter, the chief. 'What does *kanamoto* mean in your language?'

'People Mountain,' came the reply.

'All people or just Wappo people?'

'All people.'

'I see. Come, Emile! We must get home. Never lie to your mother, for that is a sin, but perhaps don't mention your visits here. Or your gifts to our new friends.'

With a reluctant farewell, the excited boy followed Chi-en down the muddy paths back to Royaume Céleste.

'Where did you learn to speak their language?' asked Emile.

Chi-en stooped to pick up an acorn on the path and, without warning, tossed it to Emile. The boy caught it in one hand.

'Where did you learn to catch acorns?' asked Chi-en.

The boy laughed. 'Everyone can.'

'Can they? How did you learn to catch things?'

'That's easy. Because I've caught them before.'

'Now you've answered your own question,' said Chi-en. 'That's how I can speak their language.'

Still Emile was unsatisfied. As they entered the first row of vines, he asked, 'If I wanted to learn their language, how could I?'

'Find the logic of their tongue. If need be, write down their words and what they mean. Make your own dictionary. By and by, you'll learn.'

The boy's head lowered. His customary surliness returned. 'Maman says I must learn how to make wine. But peasants make wine and gentlemen drink it. That's what . . . what someone once told me.' He squeezed the acorn and muttered, 'Maybe I'll see that someone soon.'

'Obey your Maman,' said Chi-en. 'Besides, you can learn more than one thing at once.'

With a flick, Emile tossed the acorn back to him. It bounced off his nose onto the muddy ground before he could react. The boy chuckled. 'You don't know everything!' he taunted.

Chi-en rubbed his nose. 'I'd be a fool to think I did.'

Towards dusk, a small procession left the shelter of the woods. A young chief wearing yellow-hammer feathers round his forehead led the way, followed by a large, huffing old woman with long braided hair.

Emile, who had been playing with a hoop outside the kitchen door, called into the farmhouse: '*Maman! Maman!* People are coming!'

A minute later, Catherine Bourchier appeared on the wooden porch, wiping her hands on a cloth. Emile was about to rush up to her when Chi-en whispered, 'Let your mother speak with them. There is nothing you can do to help.'

'Will she let them stay?'

'It is for her to decide.'

They watched the procession shuffle on bare feet and crude moccasins across the clammy mud. Catherine waited on the porch without moving, shoulders drawn back, shawl neatly arranged. At last, the group stood before her, a wretched collection of scarecrows.

Her dignity attracted Chi-en's full attention. He had expected her to summon Jean-Pierre when faced by a band of savages. Instead, she looked from face to face, undaunted.

As before, the Old Mother told their story, using her grandson as interpreter. It was a long story, involving many gestures in the direction of Perryville and Mount St Helena. At one point, the young chief's whip weals were displayed in the light of the fading sun. One of the grimy children was pushed forward to offer a heavy necklace of polished abalone shells. Catherine accepted it with a slight nod.

For a long moment everyone waited. Crows cawed in the woods. Then Catherine Bourchier hung the necklace of shells from an old nail on the wooden porch. Again, she spoke quietly, accompanying her words with an expansive wave at the hills where the Wappo had built their camp. Chi-en felt a tug on his arm and looked down. The boy was grinning. 'She said they can stay! I know she has!'

Sure enough, the Wappo nodded to the young woman who stood like a proud chatelaine before her ancestral château. Forming another file, they retraced their steps.

Chi-en wondered if she understood their true motive in coming here: to dance the white men from their lives forever. As for Catherine's motives, labourers willing to work for fifty cents a day were rare even in times like these. He felt ashamed for suggesting such a paltry wage.

That night the glow re-appeared on the hillside, bolder than before. As Chi-en watched the Wappo's fire, he heard Catherine singing in French then rare laughter from her son.

Later, there was a knock on the kitchen door. He looked up from *A Modest Memoir of Prince Hong*. Perhaps his morose expression made Catherine uneasy for her smile was uncertain. She carried an earthenware jug emitting the aroma of wine. It came not just from the jug, but her breath.

'Do not rise,' she said. 'I have brought something for you.'

He closed the thick notebook.

'It is a small gift to show our family's gratitude for your work these last few months.'

Awkwardly she came over to the table and set down the jug.

'You see,' she said, 'you have helped Emile so much.'

She gestured at the jug.

'Drink to the good health of my family! The fermented wine is ready to go into the barrels. It was always our custom in Domaine Bourchier to share the new wine with the servants.'

Was that her motive for seeking him out? To boast about her splendid new wine and re-live the pleasure of largesse? Next, she would congratulate herself for hiring the Wappo at fifty cents a day.

'Do you know about good wine as well as books and languages?' she asked, filling the silence.

'When I was younger,' he said, cautiously, 'I served a wealthy man kind enough to treat me as a companion and friend. I tasted some very fine wines indeed.'

He sensed she did not believe him and regretted revealing so much. But the hopeful, elated expression on her face softened Chi-en. A desire to test her made him add, 'Shall I fetch two glasses or one?'

'Two,' she said, occupying the very edge of a seat at the kitchen table. 'I have had too much already. Just a drop.' He poured the wine into chunky glass tumblers and raised it to the lamp. Inner glints refracted and shone.

'You will notice it is gaining a true character,' she said. 'I believe it shall be a splendid vintage. Then *Royaume Céleste* will be on everyone's lips!'

He swirled the blood red liquid. Did its fine promise justify the sacrifices she made – and must yet make – to establish a new Domaine Bourchier in this half-tamed land?

'*Santé!*' he said, taking a swallow.

The new wine was indeed excellent. Better than he'd thought possible. 'How is new wine different from old?'

For a moment she weighed her answer, swirling the bright liquid in the tumbler. 'Wine is a living thing. Therefore, it must perish. Some wines are sturdy, some feeble, and from birth they risk disease, accidents . . . but that does not answer your question.'

'Not really.'

'Old age brings infirmity to every wine then it dies,' she said. 'All this my Papa told me. One may only avoid a wine's dotage by enjoying it when it is healthy. I must tell you, Chi-en, a hundred-year-old bottle gone bad is just a full coffin.'

She snorted and sipped deeply.

'My Papa once said that to me and now I say it to you. As for a sick wine . . . one pours it away. It is seldom worth the effort of rescue. In any case, one may rarely revive its health.'

He took a pull at his glass.

'But you saved this vintage when you thought it was sick,' he reminded her.

'True, and even now we have much left to do. We shall rack the wine at least three times, pouring it from one cask to another, each time adding sulphur, a little bull's blood and egg white, making it brighter, more perfect. But it will still be a young wine and that is what I want. California is a young country, after all.'

'Can a young wine really be great?' he asked, provoked by her confidence. Her ambition affronted him: his own had perished like one of the feeble, unhealthy wines she deplored.

She sipped thoughtfully. 'Of course, where I spent my childhood wine was part of every family, quite ordinary. We celebrated the best as one might a rare, clever child. And this year's vintage shall be such a child.'

'You are very sure,' he said. 'You remind me of someone I came to know better than myself.'

But she was drunk on her new wine, hardly listening.

'I will test and cherish this vintage at every stage from its first fruit to bottle,' she said. 'You shall see, Monsieur Chi-en. The world shall see!'

He listened curiously. Did she remember Emile when she spoke of cherishing? Yet he said nothing. Again, he sipped, seeking flaws, traces of bitterness. No mistake, the new wine's edges were smooth, subtle, delectable.

'You see?' Catherine smiled, her green eyes shining in the lamplight. 'Am I not right?' She raised her glass in a toast. 'To Royaume Céleste! To our Heavenly Kingdom!'

That name was too sad, burdened, raw with memories of loss. '*Santé!*' he mumbled.

Quite unreasonably, he resented the pain she had unwittingly caused. Resented that she would never understand if he explained a thousand times. That he would be alone when she left the room. That she possessed a future, whereas he had none.

'What did you tell the Indians?' he asked, adding harshly, 'I fear they will fare no better here than with their former employer.'

'I told them they might camp in the woods above the vineyard. My Papa always allowed gipsies to stay on our land. He said God placed them on the earth for a reason. All creatures deserve a means to live.'

'Your father was wise.'

'Oh, he was. The Indians told me a bad story about someone I know. They showed me . . . but perhaps it is not true. And imagine! They offered to work for just fifty cents a day.'

Chi-en looked at the table. His own fault.

'I told them that a dollar a day is what we pay at Royaume Céleste. And that they need not call me *big white princess* – just work hard.'

Chi-en was taken aback. 'I see.'

With that, she left him to finish the jug alone. Soon afterwards, the voice of the oboe parted night's shadows, jollier than usual, even frisky.

Blending water and shavings of a new ink cake on a saucer, Chi-en dipped his writing brush. Flowing columns of precise Chinese characters marched like a lost army into the night.

Chapter the Fourth: *The Armies of Heaven*

I

Now this modest history must discharge a solemn promise.

By the commencement of 1863, Imperialist armies were again closing in on the Heavenly Capital. It was the Prime Minister's idea to dispatch a huge expedition north, towards the Manchu capital of Peking, in order to draw away the Imperialist forces. This expeditionary force fought itself to a standstill some three hundred miles short of its objective. At this critical moment it was decided — as if on a whim — to send a small relief force to help the expedition return to the capital, abandoning any gains that had been made.

Prince Hong never complained at being assigned this perilous mission, though we heard rumours the Young King's malicious scheming lay behind the appointment.

'Take your Colt,' Prince Hong warned me, restless with excitement. 'I'll need a good shot like you by my side.'

The Thrice-Blessed Relief Army consisted of thirteen thousand men. Our banners dazzled the crowds that came from all over the Heavenly City to watch us drill. Disabled veterans of the Taiping rebellion's early days declared it was like seeing the first Holy Army. Indeed, Prince Hong announced we were to be a righteous force, kind to the people. Looting or rape would lead to beheading by one's own comrades.

With a Colt in his belt, he rode up and down the lines of silent Holy Soldiers. Then he halted and raised his hand. '*Sha yao!*' he cried in his thin reedy voice. His call to arms echoed back from the army with one voice, one beating heart, '*Sha yao!* Kill the demons!' Amidst our pride, I remembered how his voice had echoed off the Ming Tombs, and grew uneasy.

We departed on a chilly dawn in May, riding through long, tunnel-like city gates lit by red torches and lanterns. Rain fell continuously. Trees and houses were distorted by the sodden mist. Hooves and bare toes splashed up flecks of mud. The very earth seemed intent on slowing our progress. So miserable a start filled the army with foreboding. Prince Hong, however, was far from downhearted.

'See!' he cried, galloping down the ranks. 'See!'

As the sun rose, the rain stopped suddenly. Before us a rainbow arched over the road we must take. At this sign, men fell on their knees and praised God. Prince Hong smiled at me and muttered, 'We should get moving before it melts away.' But he shouted out, 'Worship God! Worship God! He blesses our enterprise!'

II

Once we had crossed the Yangtze, our route led through contested territory. Now we advanced warily, for hereabouts the enemy were aided by British mercenaries and steamboats led by General Gordon.

Our instructions were to avoid all engagements and sweep north without delay to join the beleaguered Northern Expedition. To do so, we approached the ancient city of Quin-san. Our scouts reported it was being besieged by a large Imperialist force, supported by foreign artillery and armoured steamboats.

Imagine a maze of creeks, lakes, canals stretching for fifty square miles and at its centre a fairytale city on low hills, surrounded by ornate ramparts and towers: thus we spied Quin-san in the distance.

Fourth Prince Hong paced up and down. It was his first chance to alleviate the sufferings of the common people. Tens of thousands were trapped in Quin-san, waiting for the deadly British artillery to demolish their ancient defences and allow the Manchu to pour in. Senseless and complete slaughter was inevitable, for it was the Imperialist policy to punish with death all who joined the Taipings.

'We must do something, Chi-en,' he said, gazing at distant puffs of smoke through a long, brass telescope resting on a coolie's shoulder. Prince Hong loved telescopes.

'Are not our orders to avoid engagements?' I offered, uncertainly.

How little I understood the instinctive fearlessness of that great leader, just eighteen years old!

'Of course,' he said, grinning. 'With regard to our *main force*. I shall lead three hundred picked men into Quin-san and organise an evacuation of civilians.'

We were horrified at this suggestion. His duty was to lead, not put himself in danger. Prince Hong laughed at our fears. 'Bah!' he cried. 'It is not my destiny to die here. I was born for greater things than that.'

That evening, we crept along a road raised upon an embankment running through flooded, swollen watercourses to the city. I shall not detail Prince Hong's brilliant, decisive leadership that night. Suffice to say, by dawn the causeway we had secured was a flowing stream of men, women and children, heading for the safety of the Taiping-held Yangtze ports. The entire civilian population of Quin-san was on that road, while Holy Soldiers prepared to fight a rearguard action in case of pursuit.

The morning was well advanced when a line of black shapes came into view, following a broad canal that lay alongside our causeway road. Soon they resembled dragons, spewing out smoke and steam – for the British gunboats, protected by steel armour, were in close pursuit, their paddle-wheels churning. We increased our pace. Still they drew closer, finally coming within cannon shot of the densely packed people.

One endures many hard sights in a lifetime: cruelty, indifference, barbarity. Sometimes betrayal by a beloved friend. What we saw that day – perpetrated by fellow Christians against defenceless civilians – even now makes my fists clench with helpless rage. For the British gunboats commenced with shelling at a distance, mowing down a dozen with each shot, and progressed to canister as they drew near. A continuous roar of Armstrong guns and rifles filled the air, interspersed with the triumphant shriek of steam whistles. I witnessed one woman cut in half by a shell fragment, her tiny children rushing back to embrace her lifeless, upper torso. Screams, wails, curses and a continual moaning provided a background to the crash of the guns. My one satisfaction was that I shot a British officer in the head with my carbine as he leaned out of his steel turret to empty a shotgun into a crouching family. For hours the British gunboats pursued the hapless people of Quin-san, killing thousands.

When they finally halted, turning back to rejoin their Manchu employers, Prince Hong seized my arm. His usual confidence was gone. One could not call it fear: more astonishment and simmering rage.

'Why?' he gasped. 'Why should the British hate us, Chi-en?'

I read the *North China Herald* on a regular basis and so could answer: 'There is no opium trade in Taiping territories. They kill us to sell opium.'

Deep frown-lines appeared on his hitherto carefree face. Marks that never quite left him. The events at Quin-san carved fissures into his soul.

'I tell you, Chi-en Shambles,' he said, 'we will have guns like theirs! And steamships like theirs! I promise my poor people that much. I pledge it to them with my life! And the foreigners, oh yes, they shall learn the true price of opium.'

III

Prince Hong's failure at Quin-san cast him into a dark, brooding humour I dared not disturb. Failure had rarely fallen his way, now it menaced him on every side.

North we were bound – a grim march. The first province we traversed had been fought over several times, tides of war flowing back and forth like vast, destructive floods. Nearly every house had been torched by one army or another, all available timber stolen to form earthworks or bridges. It was standard for both sides to conscript men and boys before carrying off the women as booty.

I had seen cities teeming with life. Could a land teem with death? The dead are silent witnesses one consults through memories. Death made the corpses we encountered oddly alike, void of personality. So what was personality, character? Speculations impossible to resolve at fifteen. Twice as hard when twice that age.

Not everyone perished. Now and then we encountered groups of refugees, lame or strong, all ages, carrying a few possessions. Some erected feeble shelters of reeds or bamboo with their last dregs of strength. There they curled up in heaps and expired, one by one, unmourned and unnoticed. The world cares only for victors, seldom victims.

Yet such is the human spirit, I remember a village freshly torched by Manchu river pirates, its houses still smouldering, where we discovered a family brewing tea. To my astonishment, laughter reached us as we trudged doggedly past. 'See!' said Prince Hong. 'Hope will outlive this war.'

I felt proud to share a thought with so remarkable a mind.

Our route took us through a barren, waterlogged country. A strange silence lay over this region. We saw hardly a single human being, just birds and animals. Not a scrap of food was available for purchase – and Prince Hong had brought plenty of cash for that purpose. This was clearly the Imperialists' intention. Fortunately, our noble general's foresight meant we carried large supplies of grain. Yet it was a fearful journey. Our one hope lay in constant progress. No one hindered our way, as though the enemy wished to draw us north, always north, each step taking us further from the Heavenly Capital.

IV

We caught up with the Northern Expedition three hundred miles from the Yangtze. For us – and them – it had been a terrible journey.

A large force awaited us, quartered in a sizable town whose name I forget. Fifty thousand of the Heavenly Kingdom's best soldiers, veterans who had never known defeat since taking up arms against the Manchu. In addition, twice as many refugees, prisoners, coolies who had attached themselves to the fighting men. All were tired and hungry. Little enough food existed for the civilian population, let alone our combined armies. Gaunt faces peeped from windows as we marched through the city gate.

Fourth Prince Hong immediately held a lengthy council of war with the Northern Expedition's redoubtable leader, General Li, better known as the Loyal Wang. When he emerged, his expression was sombre.

'Well, Chi-en,' he told me. 'I have placed myself and the Thrice-Blessed Relief Army under Loyal Wang's direct command. He is a far more capable general than I. If anyone can get us home, it is him.'

'Must we retrace our route?' I asked.

'Loyal Wang considers it the safest way,' said Prince Hong.

To me, it seemed madness. We knew for a fact that not a peck of rice or other food was available for three hundred miles. Besides, I had noticed water levels rising as the monsoon rolled west.

'I can read your thoughts,' said Prince Hong. 'Believe me the alternatives are worse. Besides, Loyal Wang has received fresh intelligence concerning the Heavenly Capital. The devil-demons are approaching the same siege positions they fled three years ago.' He stared into the distance. 'Loyal Wang expressed sorrow and amazement to see me here. I mentioned the Young King's vision of Jesus commanding I should be assigned this mission. He understood at once what mischief is afoot. That the Young King hopes I will not return.'

'How little he knows your true destiny!' I cried.

Prince Hong smiled sadly. 'We shall see, Chi-en. Stay close to me. I need loyal friends.'

I cannot express how the word *friends* rather than *servants* delighted me. Inwardly, I swore to lay down my life to preserve him at the first opportunity.

V

So began a month-long nightmare.

For the first two weeks the Northern Expedition maintained good order. Our rations, though meagre, were sufficient to sustain us over weary forced marches through a blighted countryside. From the start, Prince Hong insisted on sharing the men's privations, despite passionate entreaties from his retinue. I saw him frequently allow a footsore, limping Taiping veteran the use of his horse. Naturally, we of the royal party followed suit.

By now, we were within a hundred miles of the Yangtze, two thirds of our return journey complete. Here our troubles began in earnest.

First, we were exhausted, with not a single means of sustenance for a hundred miles. Moreover, we still faced a vast territory of marshy, swampy ground choked with tangled bamboo and reeds. Heavy rains had raised water levels everywhere, as had seasonal floods flowing inland from the Yangtze. In addition, we endured itchy, unbearable heat during the day and bitter cold at night. As for the swarms of mosquitoes and blood-sucking creatures, our skin was soon a mass of sores.

'Only one direction is available,' counselled Prince Hong. 'And that is forward. A way we shall pursue on foot, for I have decided to slaughter our horses and share the flesh amongst the men.'

One may read of starvation's physical effects – wasting muscles, cramps, sickness, constant fatigue. I soon learned its mental effects were as harsh: I spied the Reverend Shambles's florid, bearded face peeping between stands of bamboo like a vulture waiting to dine on my soul; the Young King, pointing at Prince Hong and gloating; even dear Aunty-Mother's lovely features contorted by malicious glee.

Wherever we encountered higher ground amidst the bamboo wetlands, Manchu troops had set up forts and stockades, provisioned by fleets of small, oar-propelled gunboats. Well fed, armed with muskets (our own powder was long since soaked), they resisted our assaults until superior numbers forced them back onto their boats. Each small battle cost absurdly large casualties before we could resume our retreat.

To truly appreciate our plight, one would have had to be a bird circling high overhead. From that vantage, our straggling army formed a column a dozen miles long amidst the green swamps and morasses. Surrounding us, were countless dark larvae swimming in the water: small gunboats that refrained from coming close as we toiled forward, mile after mile, but picked away with muskets and miniature cannons. Any group separated from the main column soon found itself encircled and shot down, drowned or butchered mercilessly.

A month into our march, we drew close to the Yangtze. Our diet had been reduced to grass, the green tops of bamboo, insects and snails. A few desperate souls furtively devoured raw meat carved from corpses.

The flooding worsened as we approached the river and some crossings became possible only by swimming. All too often we used our own dead as makeshift bridges. Gunboats poured fire on us whenever space allowed them to manoeuvre close. Fortunately, the dense bamboo jungles, latticed by muddy channels, frustrated their assaults. At last, however, we found ourselves separated from the main column and in terrible danger. Prince Hong's instinctive valour and selflessness were to blame.

How altered we were from the gay, silk-uniformed nobles who had left the Heavenly Capital three months before! We had long ago lost our revolvers and were reduced to bamboo spears. Our clothes were filthy, torn rags. Dirt and lice encrusted our long Taiping hair. Shivering constantly from river fever, our bodies bore countless scars, scratches and pus-oozing hives from insect bites.

But I digress. At Prince Hong's insistence, our company of twenty or so men left the safety of the main column to help a group of stragglers return to the fold. Just as we succeeded in gathering them together, the air filled with the crash of muskets and light cannons. Several Imperialist gunboats had paddled between us and the main column. Within moments our men, up to their waists in water, were ducking to avoid the singing lead balls.

'Back to the column!' shouted Prince Hong. 'Back!'

We lost all cohesion. I found myself with Prince Hong and a few others wading across a muddy channel when a devil-demon boat appeared nearby. The air filled with the sharp reports of gunfire. Instinctively, I placed myself between the enemy and my master.

'Back to the column!' he shouted, still seeking to save our men.

I have no doubt we would have fallen had not a reckless idea occurred to me. I lunged forward to reach the boat, bullets whistling past – thankfully it had drifted close – and then dived beneath the hull. It had a shallow draft and was unevenly laden. With my last remaining strength I heaved until, with unexpected ease, the boat rolled over and capsized, casting its crew into the swamp.

I need hardly describe how we grappled our frantic enemies. Prince Hong was held beneath the water and would have drowned had I not surprised his assailant from behind with my knife.

'I shall not forget this, Chi-en!' gasped Prince Hong, as we rejoined the main column. 'You have won great honour!'

But cutting a terrified man's throat (I say *man*, he was little more than a youth like myself) while we both screamed and wept in a swamp felt, alas, a muddy kind of honour. And does to this very day.

VI

Finally, the northern bank of the Yangtze! Through Loyal Wang's foresight we arrived at Kufu-chu, a fortress held by Taiping forces on the opposite side of the river to our Heavenly Capital. We were safe! Or almost. For the raggedy survivors of the Northern Expedition must somehow cross more than a mile of water to attain the security of our ramparts and towers.

My relief can hardly be expressed. The Heavenly Capital dominated the plain. Beyond lay mountains, cloud-capped and mysterious in the haze.

Yet we were not to be allowed a peaceful crossing. Lines of Imperialist warships sailed downstream to bombard the fort of Kufu-chu, then tacked round to batter the Taiping forts on the city side of the river. An indescribable noise arose. Thousands upon thousands of voices – urging, shrieking, bellowing commands. Cannons roared, smoke rolling from their hungry jaws. Everywhere flags fluttered. Oars churned. Sails billowed. Great plumes of water rose and fell as cannonballs skipped or sank.

I watched the Taiping navy (far inferior in numbers to the Imperialist fleet) ferry our weary, desolate troops to the safety of the Heavenly Capital. For two miles on the northern shore our troops waited, thousands huddled together, incapable of further resistance. Soon enough the Imperialists were pouring whatever fire they could into this tempting target.

'I cannot allow this!' cried Prince Hong.

'Stay under cover,' I begged.

'Have the men suffered so grievously to be abandoned now?'

I shall never forget how he requisitioned a horse from the fortress and rode among those living skeletons, encouraging order and discipline. Nor shall I forget the appalling thud of cannonballs smashing into human flesh. How starving, exhausted men slowly extricated themselves from the heaped corpses of their comrades.

It was through Prince Hong's intervention that thousands near the fort were kept back from the water and so did not drown, forced into the flood by those pushing and milling behind. All the while, the Heavenly

Capital's batteries blazed, creating a corridor for our vessels to ferry troops.

It took several days for the pitiful remnant of our great army to cross – less than twenty thousand men. To his eternal fame, Prince Hong was among the very last to leave the thousands of piled bodies in their grave-yard of mud, filthy water and splintered bamboo. As he scrambled ashore, Hong took my arm and wept. I felt no shame in adding to his tears.

'Of those who perished,' he said, 'only a handful will be remembered. Promise you will not allow their memory to perish. Or their sacrifice to be forgotten. Promise me, Chi-en!'

I promised with all my soul.

San Francisco, California
Spring 1878

The mind cannot measure what a blue sky brings to the heart. There were skies of surpassing clarity over Napa that spring. Country folks accustomed to live by the seasons found reasons to work outdoors.

Sodden ground gave moisture back to air. Week by week, ponds and pools shrank. Spring was a precious between-time more pleasant than its destination. For summer's dust would soon loosen and blow.

Sea breezes flowed inland or crept round the flanks of Mount St Helena. Sometimes the mountain's summit, bald of trees and shrubs, appeared stark. Other times it brooded beneath a mask of clouds.

Down in the valley, bright yellow mustard grew between vines, field boundaries, roadsides, anywhere promiscuous seed found root. Purple hyacinth and orange Californian poppies took their chance amidst the green grass, on hillsides that would shortly turn tawny with summer. Oak savannahs filled with wildflowers – maroonspots, tidytips, lupine, goldfields – scenting the air so bees came calling. Sap flowed tentatively through the canes and spurs of pruned vines, swelling a light green fluff of leaves fed by the sun.

By the end of March, buds broke from knotty stems into clusters of furled flags. A late frost now would be ruinous to the grape harvest. But that year, as though to balance the previous year's losses, no killing frost came. Just more clear skies during the day and hazy clouds at night to trap the day's heat.

On the first day of April, Catherine travelled to Napa City to arrange her first prolonged absence from Royaume Céleste in over two years. Chi-en took the wagon's reins beside her, charged with buying groceries and other supplies. She had come to trust his knack for running the household cheaply.

Despite the new life around them, her thoughts reverted to old memories. In Languedoc spring had been her favourite season, a time of scents on the breeze when she seemed to see through her nose: lilac and rosemary, fennel, mint and wild parsley, muddy stream-scents and sharp, medicinal pine resin. At Easter they had attended Mass in Carcassone amidst painted martyrs and bittersweet incense, a city where history was written in gables and walls. There she smelt yeasty bread and truffles and cheeses with tangs unique to the farms that churned them; and spicy sausages and pork bubbling in a *pot-au-feu*, the salty-milkiness of flaking fish . . .

A peculiar moaning, part wail, part music, disturbed her memories. It came from the back of the wagon. Chi-en Shambles was singing softly in Chinese.

'An interesting melody,' she remarked.

It promptly stopped. Birdsong and hoof-plod and the rumble of wheels filled the vacancy.

'It is a song from Guangzhou,' he said, 'for welcoming the spring. My mother taught it to me.'

She glanced at his face. 'I was also reminiscing!'

He seemed quite at ease, his head moving in time to the jolt of the wagon.

'Spring always reminds me of special places near my old home,' she said. 'The fields and trees and vineyards.'

For a while neither spoke, just the clip-clop of Jeanne d'Arc's hooves and the rattle of the wagon. He disapproved of her, she felt sure. But his was a quiet, flexible disapproval. And he was not easily provoked. She admired his self-control without wishing to resemble a passionless fish herself; and Emile seemed calmer under the Chinaman's influence. Yet there was no denying his oddities. A curious fish indeed.

'Places soon forget us,' he said. 'Then we re-invent them in our minds.'

Such thoughts were too gloomy for a spring morning. Catherine was determined to be gay and had every reason for happiness. Half her new wine had been blended with Mr Trubody's and a large down payment received. Yet the Chinaman did intrigue her. His conversation was a mix of the surprising and the familiar. He gave Jeanne d'Arc's reins a flick.

'How old were you when you left China?'

'I was sixteen, so nearly half my life has passed away from there.' He hesitated before adding, 'Still, I once read a poet — a Chinaman, by the way — who said the first rings of a tree shape its trunk.'

She laughed. 'Not with vines! You can take a vine with deep roots and graft on an entirely different variety of grape. One year Grenache, two or three later, Pinot Noir. Tell me, why did you leave China?'

Perhaps he chose not to hear. He sang the Chinese song again in a low, wistful voice, staring sightlessly ahead. For a moment she was tempted to repeat her question. But doing so would show too much interest, give the wrong impression — both to him and, she acknowledged reluctantly, to herself.

Blue skies over Sonoma County and Napa. Over the glittering expanse of San Francisco Bay. Over green islands and white sails and slug trails of billowing steam from ships' boilers. One such plume rose from the daily paddle steamer between Napa City and San Francisco. Standing at the stern was a boy, intrigued as a gull by the ferryboat's wake. Nearby sat a handsome woman examining a small black account book and jotting down calculations. For once, she was smiling.

At dusk the steamboat docked in San Francisco. The waterfront was gloomy, shadowed by towering warehouses, masts and cranes. Catherine and Emile Bourchier were among the first off the ferry, followed by Chi-en Shambles struggling with cases and hatboxes.

The baggage and several wooden cases of Royaume Céleste claret were loaded on a gaily-painted, four-wheel hack. The driver assigned Chi-en a precarious perch on the outside of his vehicle. Catherine and Emile took padded leather seats inside. A flick of the whip and they were away. The hack's lowered hood allowed idlers to notice the elegant young widow's profile.

Catherine Bourchier's heart fluttered when she caught sight of the What Cheer Hotel. The wide, tram-lined boulevard of Market Street climbed towards stone mansions and a high-steepled church. Townhouses sported pillars, balconies, elegant facades. What Cheer Hotel, six storeys high and crowned by turrets, reminded her of hotels described by Papa Bourchier when he returned from his annual trips to Paris. Now she could afford her own luxuries.

The transformation in her affairs had occurred courtesy of Nathaniel Trubody. Just as her vintage had made good, so had their deal. Hundreds of wooden crates containing fancy green bottles with gilded labels filled San Francisco's best wine merchants. Other cases were rushing east on express locomotives to slake discerning palates in New York, Boston, Chicago. In short, *Chateau Trubody Nook* was being toasted as definitive proof, if any were needed, that Californian claret could out-taste, out-match, out-class the best French burgundy. Mr Trubody had scored a hit, never mind that *Chateau Trubody Nook* was no more than a respectable wine.

In his enthusiasm, he had badgered her to blend her entire vintage with his, including the half she purposefully kept back. When she refused, the millionaire grew suspicious then resentful. Even Nancy Trubody failed to thaw her husband's coolness. Now Catherine had come to San Francisco seeking buyers for her own wine.

There were other reasons for the visit. Catherine's role as supervisor of the crucial blending that created *Chateau Trubody Nook* had multiplied her neglect of Emile. At last she had a chance to pamper him and demonstrate, by living in a little style, that her sacrifices were for his benefit.

So it was that Catherine climbed the magnificent sweeping staircase of the hotel to her private suite. The manager hovered, wringing his hands. 'Madam will be delighted,' he predicted. 'A splendid prospect of Market Street. Just as you wired. Two *boudoirs* and a large *salon*.'

Catherine became aware of Chi-en puffing along behind, tottering beneath the weight of her baggage. The hotel porter had restricted his own burdens to a hatbox as soon as he realised a Chinaman was available.

'What of my manservant?' she asked. 'He will be chaperoning my son.'

At this the manager's hand-wringing became distressed. 'We don't accommodate Mongolian servants, Madam, I'm sure you understand.' He leaned forward so a lady and gentleman passing on the way down might not be offended. 'Our guests *will* worry about disease.'

Catherine halted. 'What a nuisance! Now I must move to another hotel.'

The manager looked at her and realised she was serious. 'Perhaps a *corner* with good ventilation can be found for him. I'm sure it might.'

Once Chi-en had carried the baggage, the porter pocketed a tip and led him to his quarters.

'Up here,' ordered the young man – less than sixteen from the fluff on his chin. 'You understandee?' The youth muttered '*Dumb chink*' under his breath then tried again. 'Understandee? Up the stairs! Uppee! Up!'

The stairs were at the end of Madame Bourchier's corridor, behind a plain door.

'Thank you,' said Chi-en in his best Bostonian, holding out a quarter as a tip, 'I'll find my own way from here.'

The youth almost refused the money – until old habits asserted themselves. 'Don't you go nowhere else!' he ordered, angrily. 'Hear me?'

The narrow staircase led up to the roof. Here another low door opened onto the slates. Beside it was a recess large enough for a mattress sprouting horsehair. No other furniture was provided, not even a blanket.

Chi-en unbolted the door onto the flat roof and stepped outside. Smoking chimney pots rose like monoliths. Several gulls took wing, shrieking their eternal, mournful cry of the sea. His fears at returning to San Francisco stirred. Yet he must test his status in the world as a free man and, above all, collect the unpaid wages Lu Kan owed. If no warrant was out for his arrest, Chi-en had decided to resume the search for his father that brought him to America. A search so costly he hardly dared count his losses.

Lighting a cigarette, he walked over to the parapet and glanced down at Market Street, six storeys below. From here people were tiny heads and shoulders. He lifted his gaze to the horizon.

Above Market Street were the millionaires' mansions of Nob Hill. In another direction stretched a smoky warren: seedy, begrimed, turbulent, rancid tenements known collectively as South of Market. Beyond the city he glimpsed hills, glinting blue water, islands and miles of dunes.

One by one the gulls returned and regarded him with pitiless yellow eyes.

The invitation was printed on pasteboard in ornate gilt lettering. Tasteful depictions of comic and tragic masks bordered the text. The pleasure of Madame Catherine Bourchier's company was requested at the residence of Mr and Mrs Nathaniel Trubody of Nob Hill, San Francisco, for a charity auction and garden party in aid of the city's new Grand Opera House.

She chose to ride there upon her feet. Nob Hill was not far from the What Cheer Hotel and, more importantly, a perverse corner of Bourchier pride refused to be seen in the cheapest carriage at any gathering. On Market Street she took a wrong turn. Within a few blocks, fancy brick and pillared porches grew shabby, petering into wooden tenements and streets littered with every kind of waste – human and animal. Grimed children played with anything inedible or unsellable. She halted, examining boarding houses where families shared single rooms with other families, trapped in lightless courtyards and garrets and daily struggles for work.

She became conscious of her spotless white muslin dress, elegant parasol and bonnet, her lack of a chaperone, and hurried back the way she'd come. Youths hung round a corner, jobless, without a possibility of school, shouting bored obscenities at passers-by. Her pace quickened. Next, she came upon a drunk accosting two working girls, arm-in-arm for protection, their faces pasty from a long shift in some lightless den of manufacture.

Then she was back in prosperous, confident Market Street, where the miseries of South of Market could be dismissed as self-inflicted.

★

Half an hour later, Catherine climbed a broad sidewalk near the top of California Street. From Nob Hill everything lay downhill. It was a district of mansions surrounded by high, granite walls to exclude gawping eyes. Other great houses, less shy, preferred solid brass railings polished daily by men on ladders until the metal glowed. Within these boundaries towered residences so extravagant that visitors thought of fairy tales. But on Nob Hill fairy tales came true, sprouting forests of turrets and steeples and crystal-roofed cupolas – all that unimaginable wealth could conceive and construct within a few short years. For Nob Hill was home to stockjobber bankers and sandlot millionaires, silver and railroad kings. Among them, further down the hill, dwelt Nathaniel Trubody.

That sunny afternoon the Trubody residence attracted dozens of splendid carriages. Catherine soon realised the naivety of joining such well-heeled company on foot. But Royaume Céleste's winery was crammed with claret she must bottle and sell. Papa Bourchier's fierceness when faced with an obstacle gave her courage.

Straightening her clothes and swinging her parasol, she strolled gracefully through the iron gates into the front courtyard, where magnificent horses and glossy equipages were tended by liveried servants. A circular entrance hall at the front admitted guests, overseen by footmen and charitable ladies. These worthies assessed her invitation before directing her to a hall bathed in amber light from a coloured glass dome high above the parquet floor.

Then she was through to the garden and could survey the company. Polite chatter filled gaps between ornamental hedgerows and gravel walks. At one end, an auctioneer's table was laden with items donated by culture-loving San Franciscans.

Catherine descended stone steps to find Mr Trubody greeting guests. Ahead of her, hands in pockets, lounged a tall man in a spotless burgundy frockcoat. Her heart beat uncomfortably. Unaccompanied by his wife and looking around with a provocative grin was Hercules Smithson-Mackay.

'Why, Trubody,' drawled the Colonel. 'I'm surprised you forgot to send me an invitation to your little fiesta. You know how my wife dotes on opera.'

His reluctant host's scowl deepened. 'And *I'm* surprised to see you here, Smithson.'

'It's Smithson-Mackay,' said the Colonel, acidly.

An elderly gentleman beside Mr Trubody stepped forward, rubbing his hands. Now it was the Colonel's turn to look displeased. 'Senator Collis,' he said, 'I guess you're here for the election?'

'That's my privilege, sir,' said the Senator.

'Well, well.' Smithson-Mackay turned to Trubody. 'I guess I'll see who's here this afternoon and . . .' He coughed significantly. 'Who isn't. Good afternoon to you both, gentlemen!'

The handsome Colonel strode into the crowd, touching his hat to acquaintances. Catherine considered making her presence known to Trubody, but the intensity of his whispered conversation with Senator Collis encouraged her to seek the refreshments table.

She found herself alone with a glass of *Chateau Trubody Nook* in her hand, wondering where Nancy Trubody was hiding, when a presence loomed behind her.

'I was hoping to find you here.'

Catherine turned quickly. Hercules Smithson-Mackay smiled down at her, one hand respectfully touching the brim of his top hat.

'Indeed?' she said, annoyed by the feebleness of her reply.

He, too, held a glass in his hand – French champagne rather than *Chateau Trubody*. Noticing a passing waiter he drained it, exchanging empty for full. 'You see,' he said, leaning forward confidentially. 'I've been sent here by my wife's family to settle a little wager. I mean, what kind of folks Trubody can manage to muster.'

'Are you disappointed?' she asked. 'Have you won your bet?'

He chuckled. 'I usually do. You see, my wager was that no San Franciscan of *real* quality would be here. I mean the quality that matters. And, apart from your charming self, I guess I've been proved just about right.'

Catherine abruptly recollected the whip-marks on a starved Indian's back. It seemed impossible to connect this genial man to such cruelty. Yet she drew back from further intimacy until that question was settled. Her tête-à-tête with Colonel Smithson-Mackay was attracting attention. Nathaniel Trubody stared from his station by the steps, then glanced away with a frown.

'Colonel,' she said, hurriedly, 'forgive me, but I really must greet our host.'

Once more Smithson-Mackay chuckled. She realised he had observed Trubody's reaction.

'Au revoir, Ma-am!' he said, so loudly a few guests turned and whispered to each other.

Her blush deepening, Catherine made her way over to Trubody.

'I was just telling Senator Collis,' he said, pitching straight in, 'how you're looking for investors a little more *chivalrous* than me.'

Catherine's embarrassment hardened. 'You are very mistaken, sir,' she said. 'I am not seeking investors.'

'Well, Madame, you'll find plenty of dollars here today, if that's what you're after,' said Trubody, as though not hearing her comment. 'I see you've already tried our friend Smithson-Mackay.'

'You are mistaken, sir,' she repeated. Her mouth twitched and she turned to Senator Collis. 'Sir, I have noticed since my arrival in your beautiful country how the word *dollars* appears in every conversation. Indeed, I have heard it said that the proper duty of mankind is to amass more and more dollars. That to have dollars makes a person *somebody*, and that to have none makes one *nobody*. Indeed, that having dollars is proof of goodness. Even a moral duty, like possessing kindness or a loving heart. What is your opinion, sir?'

Her passionate voice fell silent and she became aware a curious circle was listening.

'Well, my dear,' said Senator Collis. 'How could there be charity without dollars to pay for it? Besides, without an accumulation of dollars how will the State of California develop and take its rightful place in the Union? I believe the good book tells us *a love of money is the root of all evil.* Not money itself.'

'Alas, sir, I fear that all too often the tail, as you say, is wagging the dog.'

Trubody, who seemed surprised by her ideas, or perhaps that a woman should possess any at all, leaned forward irritably. 'Dollars may not make a man good,' he said, 'but dollars sure mark out the sheep from the goats. How else do you test a man's worth? And they sure help a man judge other folk's gratitude. Oh yes, they make *that* clear.'

'Goodbye, Mr Trubody,' she said. 'Thank you for your kind invitation today. I will make a donation to the opera, you may be sure.'

With that, Catherine walked away, feeling a prickle of eyes on her back. Finding a secluded corner of the garden she stared angrily at the smoky city below Nob Hill and, in the distance, the green rectangle of Golden Gate Park. As she prepared to leave, a servant in livery came over.

'Excuse me, Madam,' he said. 'Mrs Trubody requests your company. She wishes to speak to you on a most particular matter.'

He led her through the outskirts of the fashionable crowd. The auctioneer's voice floated above packed rows of chairs and tables: 'What am I bid? Ladies and gentlemen, what am I bid for this case of the finest Californian claret, courtesy of Mr Trubody himself?' The eager voice faded. Catherine found herself at the entrance to a long glass hothouse attached to the mansion. Here, the butler bowed. 'Mrs Trubody is within.'

A wave of heat engulfed her as she stepped inside. Exotic orchids grew in long lines, petals and stamens grotesque, oddly alluring. Moist air circulated, sickly with musk. Condensation dripped from the painted metal frame of the glass roof.

'Catherine! How good of you to come.'

She followed Nancy's voice to a large flowering bush. Behind it was an area of ornately-tiled floor. A small table and two comfortable chairs had been set up, along with a stand of tiny cakes, a carafe of iced lemonade and two glasses.

It was a month since they had last met. In that time a change had occurred. Nancy Trubody looked puffy and bloated. Despite the heat she wore a crocheted shawl. Catherine realised why Nancy was absent from so important a social event for her husband – and the reason for his tension.

'My dear,' said Nancy, 'take a seat and pour yourself a drink. I'd apologise about the heat if I didn't fear a chill so much. Now, before you say a word, Senator Collis came to me just now and mentioned – he's such an old friend, Catherine, a dear friend to Mr Trubody – he said my naughty husband had "Let off a little steam" in your direction. Those were his words.'

Catherine, who was already perspiring, poured out two glasses of lemonade.

'First, Nancy,' she said, 'have you been unwell?'

The older woman shrugged. 'Time of life, my dear,' she said, stoutly. 'Less said the better. It doesn't change anything however often you say it.'

'Of course,' said Catherine. 'As you wish.'

Nancy sipped her lemonade and smiled. 'But don't distract me. I want to straighten out any quarrel between you and Mr Trubody right away.'

'There is no quarrel,' said Catherine. 'Except . . .'

'Except what, my dear? I do hate being left in suspense.'

'Only, I fear he feels aggrieved. He believes I have used him badly by not wishing to blend all my wine with his. That I have used him for his money. But you must understand that I came to California to give my family's vineyard a new life. How can I do it without a *Vin de Domaine Bourchier*? A wine with our family name on its label? So that two hundred years of tradition is not lost like dust that blows away.'

Nancy nodded decisively. 'I see. It would have saved us all a heap of trouble and obfuscation if you'd explained that to him yourself. Before you leave Frisco, I'll make sure you get a chance to do exactly that.'

'It would make me happy,' said Catherine. 'I am grateful to Mr Trubody, though he may not see it.'

Nancy smiled sadly. 'Then you're one of few. Recently two – not one, but two – old business associates and friends of Mr Trubody tried to swindle him out of a considerable sum. It feels to him the whole world is after his money.'

'I am not,' said Catherine. 'That is all.'

'Of course! But you must understand how strange it is for Mr Trubody. Only fifteen years ago we had nothing. And now! You have no idea how few of our old friends remain. Why it makes me quite agitated to think of it.'

Nancy dabbed tears and Catherine leaned forward to touch her arm.

'To top it all, despite the fact that Mr Trubody acts as benefactor to a number of very respectable churches and a school for the deserving poor, he is snubbed by what is known as *society* in this city. Yet he could buy the lot of 'em with change to spare! Senator Collis told me that damned Dixie rebel and swindling rogue Smithson-Mackay was snooping, no doubt trying to find out if people of influence had come today. His wife is an Atherton, you see, and *they're* thick with Memlo Park . . .'

Catherine barely heard, enervated by the heat and irrelevance of rich men's feuds. She poured another glass of tart lemonade. A bluebottle landed on her hand and she brushed it away.

'Anyway,' concluded Nancy, more coolly, 'you can expect an invitation to our box in the opera as soon as I'm on my feet. Which, I may say, despite all appearances, will be sooner than some people expect.'

'I would enjoy that immensely,' said Catherine.

'So will I,' said Nancy, her tired face brightening. 'So will I.'

Catherine no longer felt awkward for entering the Trubody residence on foot. She was glad to be able to escape without waiting at the front porch for a carriage. She simply left the hothouse, walked round the mansion and, in a minute, was out on California Street, her parasol's iron tip clicking on the pavement.

Liberation sped her down Nob Hill. The sea breeze cooled her damp forehead after the confinement of the orchid-filled room. With physical relief came a realisation: she could never now ask for Mr Trubody's help to sell her wine.

'Whoa there!'

Catherine glanced up, startled. A fashionable two seat, four-wheel gig had halted in the road beside her. A familiar figure leaned down, reins in hand.

'Madame Bourchier! I can't have you walking with so many scoundrels on the streets.' Colonel Smithson-Mackay climbed nimbly from the gig and beckoned her to take a seat. 'Let me drive you to your hotel.'

Catherine's instinct was to refuse. But here was a chance to confirm her new freedom from Mr Trubody. More importantly, to find out whether the Colonel had mistreated the Wappo Indians. And it would shorten her journey to the What Cheer Hotel, from where she planned to take Emile somewhere pleasant for a change.

So, she took the hand that helped her onto the high leather seats of the gig. A moment later, Colonel Smithson-Mackay took up his whip and they were in motion.

Hooves clattering on the cobbled road, they left California Street. Neither spoke. The Colonel was intent on safely traversing the steep hillsides; Catherine, still flustered by Mr Trubody's rudeness, sank back in her seat. At a crossroads, he slowed the carriage.

'Can I persuade you to take a scenic drive, Ma-am?' he asked. 'It's the great pleasure of us San Franciscans.'

Catherine had arranged to collect Emile from the hotel to buy toys at a nearby department store, followed by an English high tea.

'If it is a very short drive, I may,' she said.

He touched his hat. 'Ma-am, I am entirely at your disposal.'

He guided the gig from Market Street to a broad boulevard heading west. Houses lining the road became rare. They passed vacant lots where weeds clung to sand hills over which San Francisco would inexorably expand.

'Where are we going?' she asked.

'Golden Gate Park. You won't be disappointed.'

She looked at him. Now was the time, before they went further, to discover the truth about the Wappo. 'Colonel, do you ever employ Indians on your ranchero?'

He glanced at her in surprise. 'You mean, redskins? Diggers?'

'Yes,' she said.

'I surely do. Or used to. Why do you ask?'

An inner warning urged her to say nothing that might betray the

Wappo's presence on her land. 'I wondered,' she said, 'if they do not work hard . . . how do you *make* them?'

He chuckled. 'There's a puzzler. You see, savages are like hogs. When you herd 'em, always use a firm stick.'

'Do you use a firm stick?'

He looked across at her sharply. 'I declare, Ma-am, you're cross-examining me.'

'I saw some of the unfortunate creatures in Napa recently,' she said. 'I would like to know.'

'Then I'll tell you the best way to manage a redskin. The firmest stick you can use on a Digger is to take away his whiskey bottle. That's all those savages live for. No other stick is necessary, and I practise no other.'

She digested his words. Had the Wappo lied? Perhaps she should order them off her land. Her thoughts were diverted by the gigantic gates of the park, painted silver rather than gold.

The park was truly a marvel of man's ingenuity. Though only a few years old, a landscape of windswept, rolling sand dunes several miles long was already settled and green – pines, eucalyptus, cyprus binding the unstable sands. Yellow lupis grew where saplings and trees did not. Scores of carriages bearing sightseers or clandestine couples rattled along the winding roadways.

'My goodness,' she said, 'half of San Francisco is driving here!'

'Only the better half,' he said. 'There's talk of running a streetcar out here so workingmen can take a lungful of clean air. Damn radicals want to ruin everything!'

As he described his investments in sandlots bordering the park and the tidy profits to be made, they circled a man-made hill surrounded by a lake. Again, she became aware of his musky odour. She heard herself laughing at his gallant asides. The park was full of spring. Distant views of the ocean contrasted the blues of sea and sky. A good hour passed before she realised the time.

'My goodness! We should be going back!' she cried, 'Emile will think I have forgotten him.'

He grinned his empty grin. 'As I said, Ma-am, you decide on the ride.'

During the drive back, Catherine's admiration of the park faded. She suppressed a growing sense of – not irritation, exactly – but relief that soon she could step out of Colonel Smithson-Mackay's shadow. He demanded constant attention. At the hotel he insisted on tipping the concierge and escorting her up to her suite. There, Catherine expected the polite parting that had eluded her downstairs. Emile would be waiting, no doubt in a foul mood because of her lateness.

When she opened the door of the salon between her own and Emile's bedrooms, an odd silence prevailed. 'Emile!' she called. 'Emile!'

No one answered. A sudden fear Antoine had stolen her son hurried her to the open door of his bedroom. He was not there. Hercules Smithson-Mackay entered behind her and closed the door.

'How strange!' she said. 'Emile should be here.'

'There's a note on this sideboard,' he pointed out, laying his hat on the marble surface. Catherine took a sheet of paper from his outstretched hand. It read:

Madame,

I regret to inform you that Emile became excessively restless and hungry. Assuming you are unavoidably delayed, I have taken the liberty of conducting him to a nearby park for exercise and refreshments.

Trusting this meets your approval.

Chi-en Shambles

'Good Lord!' she exclaimed. 'Could they not have waited a couple of hours?'

'Let me see that, Catherine,' said Smithson-Mackay with a voice of concern. She felt the note removed from her hand. He swiftly perused the contents and looked up thoughtfully: 'Chi-en Shambles,' he said. 'Now that name rings a bell . . . Can't think where. Never mind. We're alone together at last!'

He began to pace the small area of carpet before the fireplace, evidently seeking the right words. 'I guess you know my wife doesn't appreciate me,' he said, belligerently, as though that fact explained and justified anything. 'Hell, what can a man do, if he's a man? And, by God, no one can accuse me of being anything less!'

She shrank a little closer to the marble mantle of the fireplace and the large, ornately framed mirror above it.

'Catherine.' His glance strayed momentarily to his reflection. 'I expect you've realised I'm a man who gets what he wants.'

'Colonel . . .' she began.

'No, Catherine, I want you to call me Hercules from now on.' He smiled. 'I guess you'll find out why soon enough.'

'Please,' she said, 'I did not expect . . .'

'Neither of us expected this,' he said, drawing closer. 'But you can't fight nature. And I'm a force of nature in my own way. I believe you are, too.'

By now he stood close to her in front of the fireplace. Again, his glance strayed to the mirror. This time it remained there and, reluctantly, she looked the same way. Their reflections, side by side, were clear in the glass.

'By God, we look fine together!' he said. 'Damn fine!'

Yet Catherine perceived him as looming over her; too large; too masterful; he would overshadow all she was, all she might become.

'Colonel,' she said, desperately, 'I really do not . . .'

Perhaps he did not hear. Or decided not to hear. For his muscular arms were round her, tipping her face to his. She felt the coarse brush of his moustache, smelled sharp, acidic breath. His eyes remained open as he tried to kiss her. With a sudden jerk she pulled away.

'No!' she cried. 'That is enough!'

He took hold of an arm. Her free arm swung, slapping his face. For a moment he stood still, one hand gripping her wrist, the other rubbing his cheek. Then, effortlessly, Smithson-Mackay manoeuvred her, step by step, towards the sofa.

'No need to pretend,' he murmured, breathing heavily, 'I know what you want. I want the same thing. It's just nature. You can't fight it.'

'Get off me!' she cried.

Then she was on her back, his heavy bulk on top of her, hands lifting her long skirts to uncover what lay beneath. She sobbed, aware that he was too strong. Perhaps she should scream. Gasping for breath, there seemed not enough air to scream.

'Please,' she whispered.

He did not hear, would not hear. His impatient hands were pulling at ribbons, buttons, layers of cloth. Soon she would be exposed to whatever he desired. Helpless tears trickled down her cheeks.

Abruptly he stopped. Swore. She followed his gaze. The door to the suite had opened. A tall figure dressed in a battered yet respectable suit filled the doorway: Chi-en Shambles.

The Chinaman rapidly took in the scene. Instantly he turned and called into the corridor: 'Emile! Do not come any further! Return to the stairs!'

He glanced at the couple on the sofa, then addressed his remarks to the wall. 'Madame, I shall be back with your son shortly.' His voice expressed a contempt she had never imagined possible from him. The door closed gently. The weight on her chest lifted, allowing her to breathe.

'Get away from me!' she cried. 'I hate you!'

Smithson-Mackay stood up, fumbling with his trousers. Angry, red streaks discoloured his face. Snatching his hat from the marble sideboard, he turned. 'So, you hate me now? Damn your French whore tricks! Leading a man on!' He barged to the door and opened it. Once more Chi-en filled the space, ensuring Emile did not enter.

'I see you've got your own entertainment.' He gave a savage, sideways leer at Chi-en. 'Fancy goods shipped all the way from Chinee!'

Chi-en stepped aside to allow the big man through. His heavy footfall thumped down the hotel carpet. Emile's voice reached them from the far end of the corridor. 'Why must I wait here?' he wailed in French. 'What is wrong with Maman?'

'Your maman and the Colonel have had an argument about the price of wine,' called out Chi-en.

Turning to Catherine he said quietly. 'I will show Emile the view from the roof. When I return, I expect you will no longer be in a state of . . .' His lips puckered as he prepared the French word: '*Deshabille*.'

Indeed, when they came downstairs again, having surveyed the whole panorama of San Francisco with the help of a map, and frightened the seagulls resident amongst the chimney pots, Emile found his mother on the sofa. Her arms seemed to be hurting for she rubbed them compulsively and her face was strangely pale.

After dinner, Emile crept to the servants' staircase and climbed through the darkness to Chi-en's attic quarters. He found him out on the roof, examining the jumbled skyline and hills of San Francisco. Wisps of smoke from thousands of fires drifted. Carriage wheels and voices and bustle hummed in the dusk. Though a parody of great capitals in Europe, Frisco seemed an indomitable city.

Catherine Bourchier's liaison with the boorish, bigoted Colonel was much in Chi-en's thoughts. Part of him sought to excuse her. After all, a powerful businessman like Smithson-Mackay was bound to appeal to a woman bent on worldly success. And why should it matter to him? Soon she would be outside his life. In fact, Chi-en felt glad to have discovered her *in flagrante* with a bully who used whips against Wappo labourers and owned the vile, Chinese-baiting *California Star* – the same rag that had exiled him from Chinatown through a shameful forgery. One might judge her perfectly by such friends.

A noise disturbed him. He wondered if it was Catherine. Then Emile stepped onto the slates. 'Careful!' warned Chi-en. 'Come no nearer to the edge! Why are you not with your maman?'

The boy shrugged. 'She went to her room. I think her quarrel with the Colonel made her sad. What *did* they quarrel about?'

'The cost of wine,' said Chi-en, 'I told you.'

'Oh.' The boy stared moodily across the rooftops. 'You never told me more about the Heavenly King and Prince Hong.'

'I didn't?' Chi-en considered for a moment. 'One day I shall. Now, Emile, go back down before your mother misses you. Remember she loves you and it is getting late.'

The boy paused at the door. 'I bet Prince Hong was lucky to have a friend like you.'

Unexpected tears pricked Chi-en's eyes. 'Go to bed,' he said, 'your mother will be anxious.'

That night, the What Cheer Hotel's seagulls were disturbed by lamplight spilling from Chi-en's garret. He had borrowed a chair and card table and the memoir of Prince Hong lay ready beside his ink and writing brush.

Sometimes he glanced through the open doorway at the dark, angular shapes of buildings and hills, candles winking in windows, yellow globes of gaslight. Chi-en wrote deep into the darkness, pursuing the destruction of a city lost in time and place – losses too dear to account.

Chapter the Fifth: *Gog and Magog*

I

Winters in the Heavenly Capital were cold and gaunt. Icy winds scoured the plains, ruffled the waters of grey lakes, made the shrunken Yangtze shiver.

Throughout that winter terrible news arrived at regular intervals: Soochow's fall and the infamous massacre that followed; the loss of Hangchow and inordinate slaughter round the picturesque West Lake. The erosion of the Taiping provinces, one by one, partly due to collusion between the Manchu Court and 'neutral' foreign powers.

Noticeable, too, was how our Holy Soldiers fought with less zeal than previously. Many of the bravest were dead or grown soft, drifting from their initial enthusiasm as God Worshippers. I shared their silent doubts. Our hellish march through the bamboo swamps had drowned my faith a thousand times over.

Prince Hong, however, was undaunted. 'To win ten thousand battles we must unite ten thousand spirits into one spirit,' was the slogan he taught his much-reduced household. Before the New Year, Imperialist siege works were only half a mile from the city walls, a calamitous proximity: near enough to dig tunnels beneath the more exposed ramparts and destroy them with mines.

As food supplies dwindled, so did hope. Not long after New Year, the city was encircled completely; no new supplies could be expected. Bombardments occurred daily. I accompanied Prince Hong as he inspected the city's valiant defenders and we invariably returned in a sombre mood.

'The time has come to set in motion some preparations,' he said, after one such visit. What preparations exactly, he declined to explain.

By the beginning of March all but the most fanatical God Worshippers understood the Heavenly Capital was lost. I must confess that craven voices – exacerbated by short rations – tormented me as I lay in bed at night. *Flee now*, urged one, *even if it means deserting Prince Hong. Why throw your life away?* Of course, oaths of loyalty and obligations too deep for words argued against such a betrayal. And what of Aunty-Mother? I had heard nothing of her for so long. One night, curled beneath my blanket, listening to the bangs of artillery and stray gunshots, I wept to think of her as a prisoner in that doomed, gilded palace. *Prince Hong is the one who banished her there*, urged my inner voice. *It is he who betrayed you. Aunty-Mother would want you to escape and find the sailor, your father* . . . Oh, treacherous voice! Urgings that made me despise myself.

II

So much had changed since my arrival in the Heavenly Capital. Then I had walked streets calm and orderly. It was strange how easily the opposite became natural.

As spring advanced, public order fell apart. One might blame the grain supplies for running out or the steady stream of contradictory orders flowing from the Heavenly King's palace. Whatever the reason, the first to lose control were those who claimed the right to wield it. A reign of terror commenced, led by the extended family of the Heavenly King and their numerous followers. House to house searches for grain and valuables filled the streets with wailing. Arrests emptied whole households, piling their corpses in the marketplaces.

Prince Hong tried to restrain his relatives. He urged them to hand over the most valuable of the spoils for transfer to the public treasury. We witnessed gruesome spectacles intended to awe the people: convicted traitors ripped apart by four straining horses.

Despite these displays of justice, chaos reigned at night. The city swarmed with bandits and thieves – mostly our own soldiers seeking to supplement their meagre rations. Darkness triggered steady shooting as the Heavenly Capital's people were robbed, raped, murdered. Rumours became a general certainty that God intended to bring about the end of the world.

It amazed me the Imperialist armies did not press home a final attack. Spies informed Prince Hong that our enemies contented themselves with gambling, smoking opium, drinking rice spirits and acts of sodomy, too indigent or drunk to risk their own lives. Instead, they waited for starvation to force our surrender.

For me, the end – or beginning of the end – was a rude, impatient shake of my shoulder. I woke with a cry of alarm, imagining the devil-demons had surprised us. In the sickly light of dawn, I stared up at Prince Hong's anxious face.

'Chi-en!' he said. 'Quickly! Dress! We must go!' No more would he say except that I should conceal a revolver beneath my coat.

Half a dozen of his most trusted bodyguards waited by the gate, armed with British rifles. We jogged through the streets, wary of looters, but as day approached most had returned to their lairs with whatever booty they had managed to gather.

'Where are we going?' I whispered.

'The Heavenly King's palace,' he replied.

At once I thought of Aunty-Mother. 'Why? Has something happened?'

His laugh was hoarse. 'I shall tell you a great secret. A few hours ago my uncle ascended to Heaven.'

His words made no sense. Did not the Heavenly King visit his Father regularly in visions? Then my heart lifted with hope. 'God has assured him of our salvation!'

Again, he laughed. 'Ah, Chi-en, how your innocence refreshes my soul! Do you not understand? The Heavenly King is dead.'

I halted. Somewhere in the city a cock crowed.

'How?'

'He has been ill for weeks,' said Hong, 'but refused to see a doctor. He told the palace women he would return to visit his Father and Brother Jesus in Heaven when fate decreed. All he ate for a month was manna – boiled weeds and grass. But listen, that is not important . . .'

'Not important!'

'Listen. We must save something very few know about. I fear the Young King will get there first! Chi-en, I need your help to carry it. You are such a tall, strong fellow, after all.'

I asked no more. Is it not a follower's duty to risk terrible danger without question?

Prince Hong was well known to the Heavenly Guards at the palace, for he had made it his business to win their loyalty with gifts. We easily gained admittance, though his bodyguard were required to wait outside.

Female voices formed a fog of mourning throughout the palace. We hurried down gilded corridors, Prince Hong scarcely able to stop himself breaking into a run. As for me, I felt only excitement. At last, I had a chance to save Aunty-Mother!

More corridors. Painted doors. Ancient vases. Frescoes. All passed in a blur. I slowed to examine the face of each woman we encountered, holding up a silver lantern acquired from a niche beside a chapel. Up-turned, panic-stricken eyes met my own then looked away. None belonged to Aunty-Mother. Wherever women gathered I sensed competition over who moaned and wailed the loudest. We passed one group beating and kicking a sobbing Sister as she lay on the ground.

'This way!' whispered Hong, ignoring them. 'I fear we will be too . . . Ah!'

He pulled me into a shadowy doorway. By now watery daylight filtered through silk-draped windows. Beyond an archway, a bizarre four-wheeled carriage trundled across one of the numerous inner court-yards. Its badly-oiled wheels squeaked. 'Do not move,' murmured Hong in my ear. 'He has not seen us.'

He being none other than the heir to the Heavenly Kingdom — or what remained of it — the Young King. A team of four women with bullish physiques pulled the carriage. Upon it, our future ruler reclined. Then the carriage was gone.

A small patch of shadow shifted opposite our doorway. Laying a hand on my concealed revolver, I stepped smartly across, surprising a short girl in the drab uniform of a housemaid.

'Are you spying on us?' I asked. Prince Hong brushed past me. He showed her the Taiping golden seal of a Wang and she cowered before him.

'I need your help, Sister,' he said, gently. 'Take us by the most direct route to the Heavenly King's private chambers. Quickly now! It is the Young King's command after a vision from Uncle Jesus!'

For a moment she digested this nonsense. But habits of obedience and fear stain humble spirits deepest.

'Hurry!' he urged. And she was off, scurrying with a lowered head back the way we had come.

Prince Hong, perceptive as ever, had fixed upon the best possible guide. No one learns the hidden corners and passageways of a palace better than a housemaid. The route she chose was grimmer than I imagined possible. She led us across a weed-choked courtyard with small, rapid steps.

I called out in alarm. A scarred executioner's block had been set up in the yard. Nearby lay a pile of ghastly white female heads and no sign of the bodies to which they belonged. 'Stop!' I cried. Could Aunty-Mother's dear face be one of those on the ground?

'We cannot stop,' said Prince Hong. 'I assure you she is not among them.' How did he read my thought so clearly? I found myself hurrying behind him, dragged by the force of his will.

One thing is certain, we did beat the Young King to his father's death chamber. God's youngest son lay in golden robes upon a bed draped with yellow silk. Here, strangely, no one wailed or wept. A few of his closest female relatives knelt in silence beside braziers where incense curled listlessly upward. Their eyes registered surprise at the arrival of Prince Hong but no one spoke.

'Stay here,' he whispered, disappearing into a side chamber. The door closed behind him and I waited. The women stared at the corpse with blank expressions. Incense snaked towards the ceiling. I examined the man whose visions had torn apart a whole Empire, costing millions upon millions their lives. Was this thin, emaciated strip of inert flesh and bone God's progeny? One could not disprove unreasoning faith.

Prince Hong lurched out of the side chamber, dragging a brass-bound ebony chest and two weighty bags. He beckoned me over. 'Carry this!'

When I took the chest from him I literally reeled. Despite being only two feet long and one wide, it weighed half as much as my master.

Wiping his forehead, Prince Hong knelt before the corpse and stared at the ceiling in mute appeal to Heaven. Then he rose hurriedly and slung the bags upon his shoulder. The squeak of wheels became audible. The Young King was almost upon us.

'This way,' murmured Prince Hong, shoving me through a side exit, just as the main door to the royal bedchamber swung open. We escaped detection by an instant.

'Fast as you can, Chi-en,' whispered Hong, bolting the door so we could not be pursued. 'This way.'

'Won't the women tell the Young King we were there?' I panted, stumbling beneath the weight of my burden.

'Maybe. It doesn't matter. He's too stupid and lazy to understand.'

An exhausting journey to the palace gates. Incredibly, amidst the confusion and mourning, no one stopped or questioned us. Back at his own palace, Prince Hong ordered me to deposit the heavy chest in a private chamber.

'What does it contain?' I asked, rubbing an aching back.

He chuckled.

'The salvation of China.'

III

For days after the Heavenly King's ascent to Heaven the besieged city waited. Everywhere one heard the prayer he had taught his people to guarantee victory. Ardent God Worshippers did not consider his death a disaster at all, having persuaded themselves his ascent was proof of imminent salvation. Such is the ingenuity of hope.

Thousands gathered outside his palace to stare up at the sky for the Heavenly King's air-borne chariot. Jesus would ride beside his Little Brother, magical demon-slaying swords in their hands. Meanwhile, angel battalions would sweep together the sinful hordes outside the Heavenly Capital's ramparts like rice husks, before herding them to eternal torment in hell. What was foretold must fulfil itself. The Heavenly Kingdom of Great Peace would end human history, so I heard them say. Their fervour shook my scepticism.

As days passed and the Imperialists brought up more reserves, the God Worshippers' brittle certainty dissolved by slow degrees into dismay, fear, panic. Understanding spread that their faith was misplaced. Hope no longer staved off hunger. Thousands of starving people pleaded for help outside the palaces of the Wangs, including Prince Hong's own. He had nothing to give them. Nothing at all.

The people's misery, caused by the ignorance of corrupted men, was a terrible sight. I shall never forget the skeletal forms and empty eyes we rode through on our way to inspect the defences. Or the swollen, distended bellies of stick-limbed children.

At last, fully assured his father wasn't coming back to chastise him, the Young King found the courage to declare the commencement of his own Holy Reign. For five more dreadful weeks he ruled a Heavenly Capital collapsing inwards. No one saw him, not even his ministers, for he imitated his father's disregard for worldly affairs – other than managing his young wives.

All the while, Prince Hong was busy with arrangements so secret even I had no idea of his plans. Neither could I discover what lay within the brass-bound ebony chest I had lugged from the Heavenly King's apartments.

IV

Then, like a long-awaited storm, the end came.

For weeks, the Imperialists had dug tunnels to undermine our walls, so many that we struggled to prevent them. Our bravest Heavenly Soldiers fought their miners with sharpened shovels in underground battles. Counterattacks were to no avail; starved men make feeble warriors.

Day and night a hundred cannons poured their fire on the Taiping Gate until we were tricked into believing the final assault would come there. The continual noise of the cannonade sapped one's spirit but it was a mere whisper compared to the explosion that tore a large stretch of the city wall apart, hurling dust and stone high into the air – for the Imperialists had dug a secret tunnel and crammed it with gunpowder.

I tremble to tell the tale of that day. How a merciless battle in the rubble cost both sides hundreds of lives before twenty thousand devil-demons poured into the city. Fighting raged in the streets and round the city gates for hours. Prince Hong watched with Tutor Ren Xudong and his bodyguard from a ruined pagoda on a hill, away from the city defences. Towards dusk, Taiping resistance collapsed and, with it, all discipline among the Imperialists. Destroying the fleeing remnants of our forces no longer interested them; all their efforts concentrated on looting and rape. Soon enough the streets filled with corpses. People were dragged out of their homes and beheaded or mutilated in staggering numbers. Neither extreme youth nor age inspired the slightest mercy. Children and the old were considered worthless, whereas young women were rounded up for sale or debauch. Later reports speak of a hundred thousand perishing in the rampage, many burned to death.

'Why do we not fight?' I cried to Prince Hong. 'Let me ride to the Palace and save Aunty-Mother!'

'Not yet,' commanded Prince Hong. 'Trust me! Your death would be for no purpose.'

At last, Prince Hong commanded us to join the Royal Party gathered on a ridge near the breached ramparts. Several thousand officials, soldiers and their families huddled together for mutual protection, including hundreds of cavalry. The Imperialists, intent on loot, avoided engaging so large a force and we found it relatively easy to ride over to them.

Once there, Prince Hong ordered us to shoot anyone who touched our horses while he sought out the Young King. It was hard to hear much above the weeping and bellowed appeals to an indifferent God. The general hysteria unnerved us all. It seemed to portend dreadful tragedy.

I broke ranks to see if any of the Heavenly King's female servants were amongst the crowd. Even then I hoped to find Aunty-Mother. But it seemed all had chosen – or been forced – to remain in his Palace.

When Prince Hong returned, he looked relieved rather than infected by despair. 'They are going to charge through the breach in the city ramparts and take their chances,' he said. 'It will provide a diversion for us.'

'Are we to join them?' I asked, quite as frantic as those around me to leave the city. By now fires were lighting the dusk. You will recall the Heavenly Capital occupied an area of wide extent, pooled with shadows when night fell, yet already a hellish, dancing red glow was spreading along with the flames. 'May I seek Aunty-Mother now?'

'No, we will return to the ruined pagoda,' he said. 'We will be safe there for a while. It is time for the plan I prepared. Do not lose heart, Chi-en!'

Before we rode away, I witnessed thousands of Royal family members and their retainers streaming like lost souls towards the breach in the walls, trampling each other in their eagerness to escape. The few Imperialist troops in their way were scattered easily. Later, I heard those who reached the countryside were hunted mercilessly for days afterwards, the most important Wangs facing prolonged torture before their executions.

Perhaps God favoured our own small band. Perhaps Fourth Prince Hong anticipated everything. Whatever the reason, we found our place of refuge, the ruined pagoda, still ignored by looters. Our gallop there through streets littered with corpses took little time and the few Imperialist soldiers we encountered fled at our approach or let off wild, ineffective musket shots. By now it was late evening.

An hour later we emerged from that tower as men transformed. Prince Hong and his bodyguard wore the blue, brass-buttoned uniforms of British-sponsored Chinese mercenaries. They had shaved their foreheads and tied back their hair into pigtails in accordance with Manchu laws. I had been permitted to retain my long hair and don a European officer's splendid frock coat and cocked hat. With the aid of this disguise, we hoped to flee the city.

My last impressions of the Heavenly Capital were in horrible variance to my first. We passed palaces already on fire to cover up the looting that had occurred. A crimson, sickly glow illuminated unspeakable sights. At one crossroads, a dozen maidens were on their backs, stripped naked, soldiers grunting on top of them while scores more queued or scuffled with each other for a turn.

For a third time I begged, 'Let me seek Aunty-Mother! Let me find her!' But Prince Hong seemed not to hear.

In another street, an old man was being tortured to reveal hidden gold he did not possess, burning torches applied to the soles of his feet. We passed numberless carts full of valuables guarded by Imperialist officers and their men — loot that should rightly have been tendered to the Manchu Emperor. Sickening and senseless injustices. We could do nothing.

I say that. And I believe we were powerless in most cases. But now my racing pen slows. For at the very edge of the suburbs where Imperialist soldiers were few, we encountered a house for the orphaned sons of veterans. A small party of Manchu braves, crazed by brandy and opium, had set light to the wooden building, trapping dozens of fatherless boys inside. The roof was starting to blaze as we rode by. What motivated their cruelty? Fear? Revenge? Inebriation? It could be any. Or none. Yet the pleading, screaming voices reached out above the roar of the flames. Tiny fists pounded against metal bars once intended to protect them. Their shrieks made me rein in my horse. In a flash, I had drawn my revolver.

'We must save them!' I shouted. 'Why do we not save them?'

An iron hand gripped my arm, forcing down the revolver before I could fire.

'Keep riding, Chi-en!' urged Prince Hong. 'We are not safe!'

Of course, I obeyed. But often the image of those beseeching children wakes me in the dead of night. One cannot reproach Prince Hong. His duty was to save a whole nation, not a few unfortunates. It is lesser men like myself who wonder if the ends justify the means.

On we galloped through uncultivated areas within the city walls we had explored in happier days. Dawn was still distant when we escaped through a gate Prince Hong remembered from our trip to the Ming Tombs. Needless to say no Imperialist troops molested us. All had deserted their posts to enter the city and claim a slice of the loot.

Amidst the ruined mausoleums of the Ming Emperors we rested our horses. The Heavenly City boiled with flames like a sunset. Somewhere, abandoned in that hell, was Aunty-Mother.

'What is the point of escaping?' I wept. 'Where in the world can we go? Oh, Aunty-Mother forgive me!'

'Look in your saddlebags!' commanded Prince Hong.

Each contained many small leather sacks sealed by drawstrings. The first I opened made me gasp: it was crammed with emeralds, diamonds, pearls, gems, precious gold trinkets.

'You see,' he murmured, lest the bodyguards hear us, 'with this we can go anywhere. On your horse and mine and Tutor Ren Xudong's, we carry the heart of the Taiping treasury. With such wealth our cause shall be renewed. Your Aunty-Mother and countless others will be revenged. *That* is the point of escaping.'

When the horses were sufficiently rested, we galloped west, heading for a rendezvous on the Yangtze where a chartered vessel awaited us. As I said, Prince Hong considered everything – except the wounds to a man's soul that never quite heal.

San Francisco, California
Spring 1878

The morning after Smithson-Mackay's tête-à-tête with Catherine, a thick mist rolled over San Francisco. Chi-en woke to find his rooftop nest in the What Cheer Hotel afloat on a sea of grey. He hovered at the very edge of the slates, peering into canyons hidden by fog rolling in from the Bay.

When he descended to the Bourchiers' suite, a different fog filled the room. Madame was agitated, her son surly. It became clear she had no intention of going anywhere without Emile on a tight leash. Her indiscretion on the sofa evidently tickled her conscience as a mother. Well it might.

Chi-en's thoughts were interrupted by her warm scent. She had sidled over while Emile was out of the room. 'About yesterday afternoon,' she began, softly.

Stepping back, he held up a palm. 'No, Madame, say no more.'

'It is just that—'

'I insist.'

She bit her lower lip and glanced aside. 'As you like.'

After a pause, she added, coldly, 'I wish to allow you the next few days off. It was always my intention to spend this time with Emile.'

'As *you* like, Madame.'

Was she examining him for irony? For scorn? Neither would be hard to find. A disappointed part of him wished to punish her indiscretion.

'Of course, your wages will be paid as usual,' she said.

His bow of acknowledgement was slight, stiff. More nod than bow.

Chi-en retrieved a respectable suit from a case kept with Emile's luggage. He dared not leave anything of value where the hotel staff might find it. The police would probably view robbing a Chinaman as a public-spirited act.

Once changed, he surveyed himself in a full-length mirror used by the hotel servants. A rangy, handsome man in a well-brushed black frockcoat returned his gaze; the expression of the brown eyes perhaps a little too grave, the smile too cautious. Two chambermaids bustled past with armloads of sheets. They giggled, casting back-glances. He watched their swaying rumps and sighed.

Soon he was out in the fog, joining ghostly clerks and factory hands hurrying to toil. Carriages appeared and vanished. Noises were distorted by echoes. Everything he passed was less than thirty years old – streets, hotels, stores – and he recollected ancient cities in China explored as a youth.

It seemed that nation clung to him. In the six months he had spent in Napa, antipathy for Celestials had increased in Frisco. Random beatings, even knifings, were common for Chinamen caught alone at night, though there was no more rioting. Newspapers canvassed new laws to exclude Mongolians from California and guarantee jobs for whites.

As he entered Chinatown, conflicting emotions made Chi-en dawdle: relief, recognition of old haunts, fear of the Six Companies after his banishment. Murk-shrouded streets swallowed him. Crowds of Chinese were in Frisco for the great spring hiring by labour contractors. Spectres, some loitering, others carrying fish, fruit, chickens. Street barbers shaved foreheads alongside cobblers and sweet sellers. Fog swirled in alleys and courtyards where tiny rooms sheltered a dozen men.

Buildings rose from basements given over to gambling or opium. Rooftops hung with a bunting of dank laundry above painted verandas, paper lanterns, miniature trees and flowers beaded with moisture. Gaudy signs of red, gold, gloss black, were drained of spirit by the fog.

Essences combined to create an aroma unique to this one place on earth, this one ghetto on earth. Though surely other ghettos smelled of sewers, spices, woodsmoke, tobacco, opium, meat fried and boiled, the exact combination was special to Chinatown that morning. Chi-en passed through the fog like a dream-walker, down muddy streets lined with handwritten Chinese posters, notices, announcements pasted on dripping walls. At last, a voice woke him from his reverie. 'Mr Sha-bells!'

He realised the voice belonged to a fortune-teller behind a portable card table covered with green baize. A box of writing equipment lay on the table, along with tools for divination. A hand-painted sign read: *Divine your life.*

This particular fortune-teller, one of dozens in Chinatown, usually frequented Portsmouth Square to attract white tourists. Chi-en had sometimes talked with him about the world's changes and moods.

The man's face was wrinkled by five decades of contemplating fate. He waved at the customer's stool. 'Please!' he urged. 'Prepare yourself for what lies ahead.'

Chi-en obliged and the fortune-teller shook a cylindrical wooden box until an ivory stick marked with ancient characters and symbols spilled out. 'Yes, yes, you will live long but not too long,' he intoned. 'You will love and be loved but not as you expect. You will never be rich and never be poor. Yes, yes, you will go on a journey that will kill you and give you birth.'

'I would like a prediction on something more pressing,' said Chi-en. 'Whether I'm likely to be troubled by the Six Companies if recognised here.'

The fortune-teller smiled thinly. 'I need no divination for that. Last autumn, I heard you were not welcome in Chinatown. But I have not heard it since.'

'And the police?' asked Chi-en, remembering the Irishman in the alley he had struck down with his heavy law books.

'No police.'

'Are you sure?'

'If the police were involved, there would be a reward offered and lots of posters. No reward, no police.'

'I understand.' Chi-en passed over two dollars, an extravagant fee for such a short divination. 'Perhaps you will also take a note to Lu Kan for me?'

The fortune-teller looked round the street. The concealing fog was thick. 'Gladly,' he said. 'But you must watch my stall.'

Minutes passed as Chi-en stood beside the green card table. Chinese labourers, singly or in groups, weaved through the fog. Some cast sideways glances, for in his American clothes he resembled a *fan gui*, but no one troubled him.

At last the fortune-teller returned. 'Mr Lu will see you at once,' he said.

'I thank you.'

'It is my pleasure, Mr Sha-bells. By the way, I have something that belongs to you in my home. Return to this table after seeing Mr Lu and I shall return your property.'

'I am grateful,' said Chi-en.

Lu Kan's bazaar on Sacramento Street had not changed since Chi-en's last visit except in one particular. Instead of a hostile Secretary Ah Ling and two bravos, Lu Kan waited by the till. His son, Lu Bing, hovered nearby.

For a moment Chi-en and Lu Kan examined each other. Both bowed solemnly, followed by a reluctant Lu Bing.

'Come to my private room,' said Lu Kan.

Lu Bing waited anxiously to see if he, too, was wanted. 'Order the servants to bring refreshments,' Lu Kan told his son. 'And take my place here while I discuss business with Mr Sha-bells.'

Lu Kan's private room was above the store, its window consisting of high, narrow glass doors opening onto a balcony overlooking Sacramento Street. Right now the door was closed to keep out the chilly fog.

Lu Kan pointed to a silk-covered sofa. 'Be seated, please.' An exquisite bronze statue of the Buddha stared at them from a carved ebony table. Both waited while an ugly girl with bound feet shuffled in, arranging tea and *dim sum*.

'Please smoke,' said Lu Kan, holding out an ivory box.

Once they were settled, cigars in hand, Chi-en asked, 'How is business, Mr Lu?'

'Not exceptional, but good enough,' said the merchant. 'And do you prosper, Mr Sha-bells?'

'I am as you see.'

Lu Kan chuckled. 'With you, appearances are seldom the whole story. I suppose you have come to ask about your banishment?'

Chi-en nodded. 'I hope it does not inconvenience you.'

'It does not. I will explain the situation.'

The mood among the Presidents of the Six Companies had grown defiant since the autumn, less willing to appease their enemies. No reply had been received from President Ulysses S. Grant in response to their memorandum. Closer to home, the demagogue Kearney and his party were gaining offices and influence throughout California, so much so that a private message had been sent from the Six Companies to the State Governor, pointing out that it was an inalienable right of all human beings to defend themselves. Any mob invading Chinatown would be met with armed force.

'In short,' said Lu Kan, 'I believe it will not be hard to reconcile the Presidents. Even so, until I can confirm it, I would avoid Chinatown, Mr Sha-bells.' He smiled politely. 'If you value your health.'

'I am grateful for your advice,' said Chi-en.

He noticed a collection of different wine bottles on the sideboard. Each had been uncorked and a small amount consumed.

'You are extending your range of business.' He nodded at the bottles.

'Rich white people in Shanghai and Hong Kong,' explained Lu Kan. 'Potentially very profitable. But the wine I am offered here is poor. Not worth the price of shipment and insurance.'

Chi-en recollected the many gallons of high-quality claret needing to be sold back in Royaume Céleste. He might have mentioned his employer, if it weren't for her liaison with the Chinese-baiting Colonel.

'There is one other matter,' said Chi-en.

Lu Kan flapped a hand. 'Forgive me if I anticipate you. You refer, perhaps, to dollars I owe you? I believe you had trouble claiming that sum, ahem, on the night you left Chinatown?'

'You are well informed.'

'I am. I regret to say that I do not have the necessary cash with me.'

Chi-en frowned. It was impossible that a wealthy man like Lu Kan did not keep a few hundred dollars on his premises.

'You must trust me, Mr Sha-bells,' said Lu Kan, smoothly. 'Would it be inconvenient for you to collect what you are owed in a couple of days? Not all debts require payment in cash, as I'm sure you understand.'

Chi-en was unsure that he did. But he could wait. The Bourchiers were not due to return to Napa for days. He was not even certain he would accompany them.

'Until then, Mr Lu.' Chi-en gave him the address of the What Cheer Hotel so a message might be sent.

The fog was clearing as Chi-en left the bazaar. Time to be gone from Chinatown. Nevertheless, he chose a route that passed the fortune-teller's table. As before, the older man waited for customers. At the sight of Chi-en he reached beneath the table and lifted a heavy parcel wrapped in brown paper.

Chi-en's breath caught. It was his package of expensive law books, the brown wrapping paper stained with an Irishman's blood.

'How did you get this?' he asked.

'I was hiding behind a crate in an alley, trying to avoid some *fan gui* out to beat our people with clubs. It was dark in the alley. After you struck down one of them and fled, I pulled the parcel out of sight and waited until they had taken their injured friend away. You see, Mr Sha-bells, even in the dark I recognised you.'

'Did you not know how valuable these books are?' he asked, in wonder. 'Why did you not sell them?'

'Because I am not a thief,' replied the man, clearly offended.

Why did you not sell them? The question lingered in Chi-en's mind as he sat in Portsmouth Square, looking at the new Hall of Justice. Lawyers in sharp suits came and went, along with plaintiffs, defendants, clerks and reporters. *Why did you not sell them?* He wondered whether those attorneys on the Hall of Justice's granite steps were somehow more eloquent than he was. Or more intelligent. Or loved justice more passionately. After all, he had studied legal codes and systems in London at the behest of Prince Hong – a man of greater integrity than any shyster politician or lawyer in this boomtown clinging to mounds of sand.

Chi-en Shambles knew only too well why the question haunted him. He had sold the destiny for which he had been prepared, a noble destiny in the service of mankind. Sold it for regret.

A San Francisco day passed. An evening. Another day. For Catherine Bourchier the time was slow; and she blamed her son.

The first argument started as soon as Chi-en departed into foggy streets for destinations unknown. By evening, Emile had hurled a pack of cards round their little *salon*, accused his mother of hating him, stormed to his bedroom then refused to emerge. So much for yesterday.

Today had offered a new chance. Certainly, Catherine had meant to be patient. But when she found him making up his own silly language in one of the innumerable notebooks he loved filling, bafflement turned to irritation.

'What is this?' she demanded, peering at the page. 'I cannot believe this is schoolwork . . . *Mena-tee-meta: river crab*. My God! You have made up dozens of words! *Pee-pee: quail*.' She laughed coarsely. '*Pee-pee* means something else.'

He had snatched back the notebook, resisting her incursions into his room all morning. Relief came around teatime, in the form of visitors.

'Mr and Mrs Trubody of Nob Hill are waiting in the lobby,' announced the porter, new respect in his voice. 'They wish to know if it is convenient for Madam to receive them.'

Catherine looked hastily round the small salon. Scraps of a sketch Emile had torn to shreds after she pointed out the rules of perspective littered the floor, along with last night's flying cards.

'I shall receive them in the lobby,' she said. 'Tell them I will be down very shortly.'

Hair and clothes set in order, she descended the grand staircase to find the Trubodys stiff on a sofa, behind a silver-plated teapot, china teacups and a laden cake stand. Crustless, triangular sandwiches completed the refreshments.

Nancy's puffy complexion had gone and she smiled warmly. Mr Trubody adopted a hawkish expression. He rose, almost upsetting the teapot. 'Madame Bourchier! Much obliged . . . Please sit down! Waiter! Set another place!'

Catherine took the offered seat, unsure of the alteration in his manner.

'Before we go any further . . .' He fixed her with his steely grey eyes. 'It seems I owe you an apology. Both my friend Senator Collis and Nancy think so, and I guess they're right. If I seemed rude at our garden party the other day . . . Well, all I can say is that my temper sometimes gets the better of me.'

Nancy leaned forward confidentially. 'I fear Mr Trubody's temper was affected by a certain *Southern* gentleman's discourtesy.'

'Damned insolent, Greyback bushwhacker!' muttered Trubody. 'He's a big supporter of Senator Collis's main rival in the upcoming election and is scheming to stand as Senator for this State.'

Catherine grimaced. 'A small misunderstanding between friends. But since you mention a *certain gentleman*, I can assure you he is no friend of mine. Appearances may sometimes deceive, Mr Trubody.'

Trubody met his wife's eye with a look of surprise that became calculating. 'Well, that settles that,' he declared. 'But there's another matter. I know you need help to sell your wine – no, please don't interrupt me – well, I intend to use my contacts on your behalf for that very purpose, in recompense for past misunderstandings.'

For a moment, Catherine hesitated. Here was everything she needed to make Royaume Céleste secure. Then she recollected Nancy saying how old friends used Mr Trubody for his money; she understood, too, the pride his apology had cost.

'No. I thank you deeply, but no. You have already been so kind. If I am, as you Americans say, *to make it* in California, I must do it myself.'

Nancy watched her with open delight. 'Well, I declare! And people say ladies have no backbone in matters of business! Let *that* be a warning to you obdurate males and your bullish ways!'

'Now, now, Nancy,' chuckled Trubody. 'But I like your spirit, Madame Bourchier. Like it a great deal.'

Perhaps that was why he insisted she accompany them to the Opera House that evening, to enjoy a gala performance in their private box.

'Alas,' she sighed, 'I cannot leave my son alone.' Although she might have added the prospect appealed greatly. But Mrs Trubody offered to send round their housekeeper to watch over him and Catherine's resistance proved flimsy. She hurried upstairs to inspect her best evening gown, carried all the way from France and not worn since the night she fled Château de Chauveterre.

She arrived like Cinderella in a coach pulled by four piebald, high-stepping horses. A liveried footman with a grave demeanour perched beside the driver. As they entered Mission Street, Catherine examined the crowds drifting to the Opera House. Blue-uniformed police twirled batons to deter pickpockets. Hawkers with trays hung round their necks offered matches, candy, nuts and fruit.

The grandeur of the Opera House surprised her. Lofty arches propped by Greek columns lined the façade, crested by a triangular cornice fit for a Roman Emperor's palace. Hundreds queued and gathered on the steps; many more had already flowed into the building. Their carriage joined a line pausing at the front entrance to discharge its occupants.

The Trubody party's arrival was anticipated, for the manager waited on the steps with flunkeys to clear a passageway. 'Nathaniel is a very valued patron of the opera,' whispered Nancy.

The lobby, watched over by statues of Greek gods and goddesses, shone with black and white marble. On one wall a crystal fountain sprayed tiny jets of cologne water into a basin modelled on Venus's giant oyster shell.

Gentlemen and ladies stepped aside to allow the Trubody party through. Nancy glittered with gold and pearls; Senator Collis and Trubody walked with the self-assurance of men who have gone beyond the vagaries of vulgar fortune. With these titans, wearing a silk dress already démodé after three short years, stepped Catherine Bourchier. The few diamonds she possessed, though real, were specks of dew compared to Nancy Trubody's. But her complexion glowed from fresh air and busy, active days. Her bearing expressed an innate, sensual pride. Whispered enquiries followed her progress.

Murmuring pleasantries, the manager led them to a wide corridor round the auditorium and an area guarded by yet more ushers. From here they were conducted up plush steps to a short passage with four leather-covered doors.

'Ladies! Sirs!' simpered the manager. 'Please!'

Catherine could hear a great buzz of voices beyond the door. Nodding to their guide, Trubody led the way inside. At once the noise increased.

They had stepped into a magnificent proscenium box directly above the stage. The interior of the box was painted with frescoes, columns, fake drapery matched by real satin. Most astonishing was the box's position: fully exposed to the horseshoe tiers of the auditorium, three layers high to accommodate over two thousand people.

Catherine was shown to a chair beside Senator Collis and his wife. Meanwhile Trubody issued instructions concerning refreshments.

'Well, Madame Bourchier,' said Senator Collis, 'how does our little opera house compare with your French ones?'

She flapped an excited hand. 'Comparisons are meaningless. What matters is one's impressions. Certainly, this is a fine, no, magnificent sight. It thrills me.'

Collis nodded and leaned forward conspiratorially. 'It's here because of the dollars we talked about at Trubody's little party, my dear.'

Yet it occurred to her, of all the tens of thousands in San Francisco that night, only a small proportion could afford a seat in the auditorium.

Catherine glanced across the large, empty stage where less grand proscenium boxes faced their own. In one, she recognised Colonel Smithson-Mackay and his statuesque wife. It was impossible that he did not see Catherine. Certainly, he noticed Trubody and bowed coldly, before turning back to his companions.

Catherine's heart beat too fast – and not pleasantly. But it was over. It was done. She had encountered him. Now she could begin ignoring the Colonel as he deserved, and evidently desired. Yet she feared he would brood upon his rejection in the What Cheer Hotel and seek a spiteful revenge.

'My dear,' said Trubody, 'you'll find something unexpected in the program.'

Obediently she flicked through page after page of small advertisements until a picture of a bottle in three different colours made her blink. It filled a whole page and read:

CHATEAU TRUBODY NOOK

FOR TRULY DISCERNING PALATES, NOBODY CAN DENY!

THE NEW CLARET OF THE CONNOISSEUR THIS SEASON.

MAKE SURE YOU GET THE GENUINE ARTICLE AND BEWARE IMITATION LABELS. OUR VIGNIER'S LABEL GUARANTEES THE QUALITY.

'That's one in the eye for our friend in the box yonder,' chuckled Trubody.

Now Catherine was glad of Smithson-Mackay's earlier snub. Had he greeted her, it would have been noticed – and unfavourably.

'It is a very clever advertisement,' she said. 'Let us hope the people here like wine as well as music.'

Taking up a pair of powerful opera glasses – absurd in a box directly overlooking the stage – Catherine examined the ornate ceiling high above, painted with nymphs, naiads and dryads being accosted by muscular heroes. A huge gas-lit chandelier lit the auditorium and Trubody proudly pointed it out as the biggest in America.

Although most of the opera house was in shadow from where Catherine sat, one section, being nearest to the level of the chandelier, was clearly visible. Catherine adjusted the lenses. Up there, cramped against the ceiling were a few rows of hard wooden benches occupied by men and women in shabby clothes. At one end, set aside from the poor white folks, sat a man she recognised instantly.

Focusing the powerful glasses to their full extent, she magnified Chi-en Shambles's face. He was looking round with undisguised fascination. Was he spying on her? Why else would he come here? Perhaps he had noticed her looking.

Catherine struggled to be sensible. Ever since he discovered her on the sofa with Colonel Smithson-Mackay, she had avoided the Chinaman's company. No great challenge, seeing he was obviously playing the same game.

After all, why should he not enjoy music? Although Chinese, he was a man of culture. He had already read every book in her small library and often wrote for hours in his notebook. Yet she could not deny an interest in his motives for being at the Opera House, motives connected to a history hard to imagine. Clues, it was true, had been revealed, some inadvertently, others deliberately. Perhaps she flattered herself to say *deliberately*. Finding Smithson-Mackay with his hands up her skirts gave him every reason to dismiss her as a whore . . . Further speculation was cut short by the overture.

The curtain rose to reveal a quaint taverna. The opera, *Carmen*, had begun.

Hours later, after wine and intermissions and charming visitors to their box and music that would cling to Catherine's soul all her life, the last bouquet was tossed and the applause subsided.

'Do all bad women deserve such an end?' she asked Nancy, tears in her eyes. 'Is it so very wrong for a woman to be free?'

Nancy, too, seemed thrilled. 'Was she not magnificent?'

Catherine could only agree.

As the Trubody party left their splendid box they joined streams flowing towards lives where uncongenial work must be confronted in the morning. Many were affected by the drama they had witnessed, shuffling between art's dream and the one called reality.

Perhaps that was why, still transported, Catherine did not anticipate the meeting that followed in the lobby.

The Trubody party awaited their carriage beside a stained-glass door leading onto the street. Nearby stood the party of Colonel Smithson-Mackay about the same business. Both groups ignored one another with unimpeachable politeness.

The usher assigned to call them stepped outside. A moment later, the glass door opened and a tall, stovepipe hat poked in.

Time halted for Catherine Bourchier. She was provided dreadful leisure to take in every detail of the man's face: his slightly bilious complexion and nose, the mottled skin of a heavy drinker. His waxed, upward-pointing moustache. Three years had not been kind to that face.

Yet it retained all the characteristics she remembered when its owner was her husband's bosom companion. Monstrous, unjust and inconceivable as it seemed to her, none other than Baron Cesar Foche was poking his head into the lobby. At the sight of Catherine, he smiled in quiet triumph and she sensed he had been seeking her — hungrily, eagerly — before she vanished into the night.

Slowly, though in reality the action took no longer than the step of a cat, his thin body followed the stovepipe hat inside.

Catherine looked for somewhere to hide, an excuse to flee, but he was upon her, bowing, smirking, just as he had on the day that she escaped Château de Chauveterre.

'Comtesse!' He spoke with the same drawled lisp that had so amused Antoine and persuaded him Baron Foche was a gentleman of style. 'Enchanted! Such a delight to recognise you in your box above the stage! Here, of all places. The performance was marvellous, was it not? But so very tragic. Why, you look pale, Comtesse!'

Indeed, she was trembling. 'Baron Foche, I am no longer . . . that name. As you know.'

He smiled once again then bowed to Catherine's companions who were bemused by the rapid French. The Smithson-Mackay party had also fallen silent.

'Well, well, Madame,' he said, 'I see we have much to *share*.' He laid peculiar emphasis on the word. '*N'est pas*?'

Removing a monocle attached to a ribbon from his waistcoat, he played with it between finger and thumb.

'Of course,' she said, hurriedly.

'And where is *la Comtesse* staying . . .'

Before he could finish his question, the street door opened. 'Trubody carriage!' bellowed the usher. 'Carriage for Mr Trubody!'

Trubody hurried Catherine through the door and towards the carriage, murmuring, 'I guess that fellow was bothering you.'

'Comtesse, wait!' But her friends were around her. In a moment she was safe, rattling through the streets of San Francisco.

While Trubody and Senator Collis talked in low tones about a rival Congressman, Nancy leaned close, watching her expression whenever they passed a gas lamp.

If Catherine noticed, she gave no sign; her mind was feverish with possibilities. What if Baron Foche, abandoned in the lobby, fell into conversation with Colonel Smithson-Mackay? Would Foche write to Antoine – or even telegram – to reveal her whereabouts? For all she knew, Antoine was also in San Francisco. She feared returning to the hotel and finding Emile gone. And what if Napa society discovered she was no widow, but an impostor, a fraud? Despair clutched grasping fingers round her heart: fingers that would never be satisfied until they despoiled all she possessed, all she had won, not least the future.

Meanwhile, Nancy's animated voice described her impressions of the opera. Sixteen high-stepping legs and hooves clattered. Iron-shod wheels ground against flinty cobblestones like fate.

San Francisco, California
Spring 1878

The next day, Chi-en Shambles left the What Cheer Hotel by the trades-man's entrance. Melodies and emotions from the opera still resonated in his spirit.

On Market Street, he strolled in his brushed black frockcoat, ignoring curious or hostile glances. Most people were pre-occupied by their own affairs. One mother, recognising the Mongol taint in his face, beckoned her daughters to the protective circle of her hooped skirts.

He turned a corner and was surprised by a crowd, perhaps two hundred strong. Banners proclaimed: *JUSTICE AND JOBS FOR WORKING-MEN . . . THE CHINESE MUST GO! VOTE KEARNEY FOR A NEW CONSTITUTION.* A shabby gathering, in the main, labourers cast out of work by the Great Panic. Their leaders wore smart suits and fashionable hats: riding the poor like jockeys in an electoral race.

He had a few seconds to decide. Flee or try to slip through this thicket of fists and boots. The men were handing out leaflets about the state-wide elections only a few weeks off – elections to appoint a Convention that would re-write the constitution of California. Noticing a book store he had frequented when he dwelt in Portsmouth Square, Chi-en hurried across the street and entered just in time.

'Hey, Mister!' an Irishman called out after him. 'Here's a bill for ya!'

The shop bell jangled, dimming sounds from outside. He looked round but there were no other customers. The bookseller peered through rimless glasses from behind the counter. Then the small man's round, whiskered face broke into a genuine smile.

'*Guten tag! Wie gehts, Herr Shambles?*'

Chi-en's reply came in faultless German with a Hamburg twang suspiciously like the bookseller's. Over the years they had confided a little of their respective histories. The man was a disappointed socialist forced from his homeland.

When Catherine Bourchier entered the shop two minutes later, she found Chi-en deep in conversation with the bookseller, dissecting the motives of Denis Kearney and his supporters. As soon as they noticed her, both sidled apart. Chi-en bowed stiffly to his employer, before taking up a thick volume of Thomas Paine.

'May I assist?' asked the diminutive German.

Catherine glanced defiantly at Chi-en. 'I am seeking good books for a boy of eleven,' she said. 'A fairly intelligent boy for his age.'

'I discern Madame is French,' said the bookseller. 'Books in French?'

Chi-en closed the heavy volume with a decisive thump. 'In *English*,' he said at exactly the moment Catherine uttered the same words. They knitted their brows at one another. Then both laughed: Chi-en's a hoarse bark, Catherine's more mellifluous and arch.

Two hundred lusty voices broke into song outside:

> '*For our sons and daughters*
> *We'll fight till we're free,*
> *For we're bound to be rid*
> *Of the Heathen Chinee!*'

Chi-en and the bookseller exchanged looks.

'Perhaps Herr Shambles might find it more convenient to leave by the back door on this occasion?' suggested the German, nervously. 'And return when our friends have moved on?'

Chi-en nodded to the bookseller, who locked the front door of his store. Wasting no more time, Chi-en hurried down a short passageway behind the counter to a back door that he quickly unbolted. Outside lay an alley full of trash. He realised Catherine Bourchier had accompanied him. On all sides grimy windows stared down.

Still flustered, Chi-en took off his hat and tossed it derisively at a wall. With clumsy fingers, he rolled a cigarette, aware she was watching.

'Madame need not leave by the back door,' he pointed out. 'That privilege is reserved for *the Heathen Chinee*.'

The first match he struck broke, his hands were trembling.

'I know,' she said.

The second match caught and he drew in a big lungful of smoke. Breathing it out, he coughed, 'Filthy habit.'

'I would not know. I have never smoked.'

He glanced at her sharply. 'I have known a few women who do.'

She seemed about to retort concerning such women but bit her lip. 'I'm sure you have.'

Unexpectedly, he felt wrong-footed. Tossing aside the cigarette, he picked up his hat. 'Where is Emile?'

'I have granted him a break from his *chére Maman*. You will not be surprised that he is rather pleased. He is visiting Mr and Mrs Trubody in Nob Hill and, in particular, their housekeeper, who my son has taken a liking to – rather as he did with you, Monsieur 'Umble.'

It was a while since she had called him that. 'I see,' he said.

'No doubt you will also see why *chére Maman* wants to buy him expensive books he will enjoy. Who knows, perhaps even treasure. I'm sure you see my motives. You see so much, after all.'

He shrugged. 'Given the position I find some people in, I get little choice.'

They looked round the alleyway. A cat padded along a wall.

'Let me conduct you to the hotel,' he offered.

Her smile confused him, for it was small and sad. He found her easier to deal with when she was distant or offended.

'I am in no hurry, Monsieur Chi-en. Actually, I wish to explain something. Something I believe even you do not see. So perhaps it is a good thing we meet as we do.'

They sat on a bench among the beady-eyed pigeons in Portsmouth Square. In the distance rose the imposing façade of the Halls of Justice. It was mid-morning and the young city surged with life. Everywhere people. Everywhere desire in a hundred thousand forms. San Francisco's nature was to lust for more – more swagger, dollars, wagers.

They sat side by side. Though voluble, opinionated people, neither had a clue what to say. A glance in the direction of Chi-en's old home provided a topic. He pointed at an alleyway drab as a pit.

'I once lived down there,' he remarked. 'A whole large room to myself! A small library, furniture, all the things we use to judge that a man is indeed a man. Just down that alley, over there.'

She followed his gaze. 'What happened?'

'Ah! What indeed?' He fell silent.

'If I knew the answer I would not ask.'

'Madame, I will tell you. I placed too much faith in the American Constitution. As a result, books, furniture, clothes and a little enamel coffee pot I was rather fond of were confiscated, and no doubt ended up in a pawnshop to pay for a damn good night's whiskey at *the Heathen Chinee*'s expense.'

Her eyelids fluttered – another of those mannerisms he had begun to notice.

'You have a habit of speaking in riddles,' she pointed out.

Chi-en considered her comment. Perhaps she was right. 'Read this.' He withdrew a pocket book from his jacket. In it was a bruised, yet neatly folded newspaper article. While she read, he examined the pecking, strutting pigeons.

'Did you really write *this*?' she asked, incredulously.

'Of course not.'

'Then how?'

'It is a forgery. A disgrace to the free press! That is why I was forced to flee to Napa Valley and ended in Royaume Céleste. My original letter was distorted horribly.'

She read the article again. Coughed. 'Then you made no reference to . . . *White wifee with big b'som*?'

He glanced sharply at her. 'None.'

'Or a *spez'l bizness in Peking owned by Uncle M'ngol Woo Woo*?'

'No.'

'I see this forgery was published in the *California Star*.' Unease crossed her face. 'That newspaper is owned by Colonel Smithson-Mackay.'

'I know.'

They sat in silence for a while.

'Please smoke, if you wish,' she said. 'My father smoked. Perhaps that is why he died younger than most and in great pain.'

Chi-en reached for his tobacco pouch then put it back.

'Monsieur Shambles,' she said, suddenly agitated, 'I am sitting here with you for a reason!'

He waited.

'In short,' she continued in a rush, 'I wish you to know that the gentleman you saw . . . I mean, on the sofa. In short, he was forcing himself upon me.' She wiped her eyes. 'His attentions were never welcome.'

This came as such a surprise that he did roll and light a cigarette. The only reply he could manage was so fatuous he cringed inwardly as soon as it was uttered. 'So, your trip here has not been a success.'

'Ha! A success! Monsieur Chi-en, you cannot *know*.'

He listened as she hinted at being recognised by someone that she had travelled halfway across the world to escape. So that now she hardly dared wait in the What Cheer Hotel in case he tracked her there. How she had failed to find a buyer for her wine and refused Trubody's help out of stupid pride.

'But everyone needs a little pride, don't you think?' she said. 'And if one sells it?'

'I know about selling one's pride,' he said.

With that, Chi-en flicked the cigarette butt at a pair of courting pigeons. Both pecked in fierce competition before resuming their courtship. He spied his friend the fortune-teller.

'Come with me,' he said, on impulse. 'Perhaps you shall receive guidance on how to sell your wine.'

The two strolled over to the wrinkled soothsayer and Chi-en insisted on paying the fee before wandering off. A person's future was, after all, a private thing until it had occurred for all to comment upon.

After the divination, she came over to where he sat. 'It seems I must avoid naughty companions,' she said, with a slight smile, 'and never forget the numbers nineteen and twenty-six as long as I live. Oh, and fires. None of which will sell my wine.'

Chi-en looked at her closely. Green eyes were hard to read. In China only demons possessed green eyes. Her handsome face touched him with a pleasant, impossible confusion.

'But your wine is good,' he said, 'how can it not sell?'

'What is good does not always attract. You see, a new wine cannot sell itself. Before someone pulls a cork of Royaume Céleste they must first pay another someone for it. And that someone must have bought it off me in the knowledge someone else wants it. In France the name Domaine Bourchier was sufficient to sell our wine. Here, we have no name, no respectability, no persuasion. That is yet to be won.'

For all the pride he had vowed to never sell again he found himself saying, 'Perhaps I know a man who may be interested in your wine.'

She looked at him sceptically. Then her face cleared and the melodious, arch laugh returned. 'You are so full of surprises that I would be foolish to doubt it. Now I wish to fetch Emile. Really, I must go.'

That night Chi-en again perched on the roof of the What Cheer Hotel, restless after his conversation with Catherine. Her words and expressions, the play of her eyes, even her scent, seemed dangerous. Yet Chi-en could not help imagining her hourglass figure and smile, just two storeys below. Doggedly, he sipped cheap Californian claret from a cracked teacup. He had even agreed to introduce her to Lu Kan, thereby allowing her deeper into his life. And for what? A demeaning itch that must end in frustration – or worse.

So, it was a relief to work through the jug of wine and recollect happier days, when he had been the one staying in a luxurious hotel room, when the world had doffed its cap to Prince Hong's fabulous wealth.

It was midnight when Chi-en retired to his cot beneath the slates. He was drunk. Sleep brought jagged, discordant dreams. Englishmen in expensive cravats guffawed and congratulated one another by the bar of a Piccadilly public house. Chinese peasants queued outside, whispering, staring up at a vast, dark tower that filled the horizon. A voice entered his dream, deep and sonorous, intoning, 'Lo, the Tower of Babel, where every language is spoken except God's own!' Chi-en murmured in his sleep, 'We shall be free of the tower! We shall yet be free!' Then the tower's red, hellish flames faded and Chi-en dreamt of a glowing waterfall of sweet moonlight.

The next morning, a meeting occurred in Lu Kan's office. It was a carefully furnished room, every waxed surface and lacquered ornament denoting prosperity.

Lu Kan sat on one side of a low table, his son Lu Bing standing behind. On the other side sat Catherine Bourchier, accompanied by Chi-en Shambles, also standing. On the table was a corked bottle of Royaume Céleste claret and examples of possible labels to be pasted across it. There was also a new glass decanter Catherine had brought for Lu Kan on Chi-en's advice – thereby wrong-footing him before any negotiations began, as the Chinese merchant had no immediate gift in return.

Lu Kan leaned forward with a polite smile. 'Madame Bourchier,' he began in heavily accented English, 'we have agreed there is a great demand for wine of quality among the foreigners in Shanghai, Ningpo and Hong Kong – places known to Mr Sha-bells, if not yourself. Perhaps even Guangzhou. And you tell me your wine is as good as any French?'

'Mr Lu,' she said, 'perhaps one should taste it?'

Here was the critical test. For Chi-en had told her the suave merchant had already tried a dozen Californian clarets and rejected them as too coarse or ordinary to justify the expense of packing, shipping and insurance.

Lu Kan nodded to Lu Bing, who produced a corkscrew from his

pocket like a waiter. However, the cork proved obdurate and though Lu Bing tugged it would not pop free.

'Please, sir,' said Chi-en, to the sweating youth, 'if I might undertake this service for you.'

He felt Catherine's eyes upon him as he took the bottle and, with a smooth motion practised a thousand times in the service of one who would never taste another drop, pulled the cork. He was about to pour it into the decanter when Catherine stopped him.

'Perhaps Mr Lu wishes to smell the cork and bottle?' she suggested.

Lu Kan did so. 'A very pleasing aroma,' he conceded.

'Now one may decant the wine, perhaps?' suggested Catherine.

The three men examined this authoritative female suspiciously. Lu Kan shrugged and Chi-en poured a ruby, bubbling cascade into the decanter.

More sniffing followed, with Lu Kan issuing instructions to his son to do the same in rapid Cantonese. Catherine sensed a tension between parent and child, one she knew well. She saw, also, that Lu Bing cast furtive glances at Chi-en whenever he thought his father would not notice.

'May I?' asked Lu Kan, pouring out a glass of wine.

He examined. Swirled. Smelled again. Then the merchant sipped slowly, so the wine lingered on lips, palate and tongue. Lu Kan's caution in the matter of quality intrigued Catherine. Clearly there was a great deal of profit – and potential loss – at stake.

A look of surprise betrayed itself on the Chinaman's face, vanishing as soon as it came. He tasted again, rolling the wine round his mouth. Time passed slowly in the room, though it was merely a few seconds. Lu Kan set down the glass on the table.

'How many bottles of this . . .' He struggled with the words. 'Roy-ame Seel-ist-ee have you?'

Catherine mentioned a number in thousands.

'All as good as this?'

'Of course, quality will vary a small amount between bottles,' she said. 'And the quality of wine depends on how one cherishes it, Mr Lu. Wine is like a woman.'

Lu Kan took another sip and ordered his son to fetch three more glasses.

'I believe we should toast this new business arrangement with your own excellent wine,' he said. 'I am sure you will find my offer reasonable.'

When he explained, Catherine's mind whirled, adding noughts and multiplying.

'You wish to purchase it all?'

'If you are willing to sell.'

'I am very willing.'

Then Catherine Bourchier committed an act that would have appalled many in Napa. She shook the Celestial's hand, finding it much like any other man's, except cleaner, for Lu Kan was particular about his toilette.

It was agreed that Chi-en would draw up contracts and bring them the next day with her signature for Lu Kan to add his own.

'How would Madame like to be paid the first instalment?' Lu Kan asked, casually, as Lu Bing poured out the rest of the wine to toast their deal. 'Cash or draft?'

The following afternoon, Chi-en returned to Lu Kan's store with signed copies of the contract. His volumes of the Californian legal code proved a useful reference point for ensuring the terms were equally binding upon both parties. Above all, that the agreement was fair.

No fog hid him as he walked through Chinatown that early May afternoon, his face warmed by the lazy confidence of a summer sun. It felt no little thing to smell frying ginger and pork, the starchy steam of rice; to hear voices conversing in the language of his childhood, a tongue inscribed across every lineament of his skin, eyes, hair, face.

At Lu Kan's store he was ushered by a clerk to the back office, where he expected to find the merchant alone. Three pairs of watchful eyes awaited him. One belonged to Lu Kan, as anticipated, the others to Lu Bing and Secretary Ah Ling. The merchant rose politely, forcing his companions to do likewise.

'Please enter, Mr Sha-bells,' he said. 'Chi-en, take a seat beside me, I insist.'

This act of condescension was accomplished with bows on all sides. The contracts were duly tendered up, including American and Chinese versions. Secretary Ah Ling read the latter carefully, while Lu Kan studied both. He grunted with satisfaction.

'Exactly what was agreed with Madame Bourchier,' he said. 'I congratulate you, Chi-en. Yet again you prove your diligence. You shall be rewarded for it.' He cast a cold eye upon his son, who was looking through the contracts without any sign of interest or understanding. 'The box, Lu Bing.'

The youth brought forth a carved hardwood box that his father unlocked. Inside, were stacks of coins and dollar bills.

'Of course, I do not just owe you for the contract with Madame Bourchier,' said Lu Kan, 'I owe you for previous services dating back nearly, oh, half a year.'

Chi-en nodded, glancing at Secretary Ah Ling. The latter met his eye with a faint sneer.

'I have discovered,' continued Lu Kan, 'you tried to claim these unpaid fees on a night when you needed the money badly. I mean, the night you received the Six Companies' unfortunate banishment.'

Again Chi-en examined Lu Bing and the Secretary. Now they seemed less assured.

'I would be honoured if you accepted this money and my personal apology for late payment,' said Lu Kan.

Three hundred dollars were meticulously counted and passed over.

'Now to another matter,' said the merchant. 'Last night I met with the Presidents of the Six Companies and argued that, in your case, we acted hastily last October. Moreover, I pointed out you now represent an important business associate of mine and that I need you to act as a go-between. As a result, your previous exclusion from Chinatown is fully lifted and forgotten.'

Not by Ah Ling, thought Chi-en, the Secretary would never forget.

'I am grateful and relieved,' he said.

'Now to the matter of my son,' said Lu Kan. 'He wishes to apologise for preventing you from speaking to me and thereby putting you in a dangerous position. It is no easy thing to be a Chinaman without dollars in America.'

Flushing deeply, Lu Bing stammered out a brief apology.

'I am doubly honoured by Mr Lu Bing's words,' said Chi-en.

'But, of course,' said Ah Ling, no longer able to contain himself, 'Mr Sha-bells is not a real Chinaman. He is a *fan gui* and rebel who dabbles in demonic arts. How else do you explain his ability to speak and write every language! It is . . .'

'Enough! You insult a guest in *my* house!' Lu Kan shook his fist at the Secretary. Chi-en had never seen the affable merchant so angry. Ah Ling licked dry lips. It was plain he would never bring himself to apologise to the Longhair Demon.

Chi-en observed the man's inner struggle – one that might easily cost his lucrative position as Secretary. He also recollected Ah Ling saying his brother had died in battle against the Heavenly Army. Before Lu Kan could intervene further, he held up a hand. 'Please! I will be content if, rather than apologising, the Secretary acknowledges a simple truth.'

He paused. The three men waited expectantly.

'A truth I mentioned once before to Secretary Ah Ling. Namely, good men fought on both sides in that terrible war. Many were conscripted against their will. I am sorry his brother was among the fallen.'

Ah Ling started with surprise. His eyes hardened.

'I know the Secretary's feelings,' said Chi-en. 'Yet I would remind him the war ended fifteen years ago. It is time, perhaps, to mourn with something other than hatred, anger and vengeance. And,' he added, more forcefully, 'the Secretary should know that I, too, have cause to mourn. My own mother was lost in terrible circumstances . . . I do not like to say more.'

Lu Kan looked between the two men, awaiting Ah Ling's reply. When it came his voice was clutched by emotion. 'Not just my brother,' he said, 'my mother, father, grandparents, uncles, cousins, aunts, sisters — all. *All!* So that I was driven to this improper country to find a living. But I, I will consider your ideas, Mr Sha-bells, I will consider your simple truth.'

Chi-en bowed. Then, to his relief, Ah Ling bowed, too. When his head rose, light from the window caught a glitter of tears in the Secretary's eyes.

Lu Kan grunted. 'That's better. Always better to live as friends, eh?'

At the merchant's request, Chi-en waited while the others left. Once they were gone, he was offered a cigar and the two men smoked silently.

'Will you be re-joining us in Chinatown?' asked Lu Kan.

'Perhaps. But I do not find my life in the countryside unpleasant. It gives me time to undertake a duty to one passed from this earth.' Chi-en hesitated, then said, 'Mr Lu Kan, I have never asked you for a favour before.'

The merchant nodded.

'Sir, you have contacts in every Chinatown in the West, is that not true?'

'In one way or another, the Six Companies have numerous contacts. So do I.'

'Then I will ask my favour.'

The merchant listened impassively as the younger man requested information concerning the whereabouts, or history, or any information at all, concerning a Reverend Ezekiel Shambles, formerly a Baptist missionary to China.

Lu Kan blew out smoke. '*Shambles?*'

'My mother and about two dozen of her fellow Christians – all Chinese converts – adopted his surname out of respect. And fear for their souls, I dare say. He was our master and protector when I was young. More importantly, he is the only man alive with information of great significance to me.'

Lu Kan stubbed out his cigar. 'Very well. I will try my best. But may I remind you of the proverb . . . *Do not climb a tree to look for fish*. Who knows what you will find.'

'I have another proverb,' said Chi-en. '*One cannot clap with one hand*. I shall await news from you in Madame Bourchier's farm in Napa Valley.'

One late afternoon in early May, a locomotive from Napa City puffed and clanked and chuffed into Perryville Station. The railroad clerk in his bright blue frockcoat paced self-importantly, a flag on a small pole tucked under his arm. A small group of country people waited on the duckboard platform for strangers and loved ones to disembark. Among them, wearing his Sunday best suit, was Jean-Pierre.

He ambled forward as three figures emerged from a cloud of billowing steam. 'Madame! Over here!' he cried in French.

When the steam blew away, he could see clearly.

'My God! What is this?' he demanded, jovially. 'Have you robbed a bank in San Francisco? Look at you! New clothes, hats, shoes . . . Why, even you, Monsieur 'Umble! You look like a . . .' he hesitated to use the word *gentleman*, but Chi-en Shambles in a smart new suit and necktie was as far removed from Sam Wah's pigtailed Chinamen as Jean-Pierre could imagine. 'And little Emile! Why are your clothes not torn and filthy? Could you not find another boy to fight?'

Emile shot Jean-Pierre a mocking glance. 'Maman will kill me if I ruin my new suit,' he said in English.

'It speaks!' cried Jean-Pierre, throwing up his arms in mock horror. 'We must send you to San Francisco more often. And for much longer.'

Six months earlier such a *blague* would have provoked a storm of sulking. Now Emile shrugged.

'How are you, Jean-Pierre?' asked Catherine. 'You look well.'

In fact, streaks on the steward's face suggested he had monitored the progress of the maturing wine all too closely.

'It is dull on the farm without you both,' he admitted. 'But, Madame, perhaps they heard you were returning. There is quite a party in Main Street. Lots of flags! How these Americans love a *fête*.'

'It's the election,' muttered Emile, as though to an idiot.

'There he goes again!' said Jean-Pierre in French. 'I shall need ear-plugs soon.'

It took longer than expected to load the wagon. Catherine – flush with Lu Kan's dollars – had bought outfits, ornaments, all manner of luxuries from the stores of San Francisco: most especially, risqué novels and collections of oboe music to fill empty evenings.

Happy with her purchases and smart apparel, excited, too, to be almost home and free from the possibility of encountering Baron Foche in San Francisco, Catherine had no expectation of what awaited on Main

Street. Crowds of dispossessed and angry men existed in the New Eden as surely as in Frisco.

A political meeting was taking place outside the Grand Hotel. As Jean-Pierre had hinted, patriotic bunting of red, white and blue draped the street. Crimson and white Bear Flags of California waved in the crowd. It was a plain, no nonsense, no nigger, no Chinee, folksy kind of assemblage on Main Street that day.

A wooden platform had been erected before the hotel bar, surrounded by a hundred of Perryville's male – and enfranchised – citizens. From this elevated position a candidate for the new Constitutional Convention addressed the crowd.

As the Bourchier wagon rattled closer, Catherine heard snatches of his angry harangue: '. . . enemies in our midst, spreading disease and moral contagion . . . cleanse Perryville and all California of the abomination known as *Chinatowns* . . . I say, employ no Mongolians! Buy from White-labour-only businesses!'

By now they were level with the platform, their progress slowed by the crowd. She shot a glance at the speakers. In his role as Senatorial candidate, Hercules Smithson-Mackay sat with his wife, Lydia, glaring down at their wagon. Just as the orator concluded, Lydia called out in a shrill voice, pointing at Chi-en who perched prominently upon the shiny new baggage.

'My goodness! Look! There's one of them! Over there!'

Heads turned obediently and took in the Chinaman wearing fancy city clothes. Clothes poor farmers bled by drought and failure could only dream of owning.

'Shame!' came the cry. More voices joined the chorus. 'Shame on you!' 'Shame! Goddamn shame!' 'Mongols stealing our goddamn suits now!'

'Quickly,' Catherine whispered to Jean-Pierre. 'Can you not drive on?'

But people were in the way. Some pushed closer to stare and gesticulate at the dandy-pandy Celestial, as though preparing to drag him off the wagon into the dust where he belonged. Drag him down for a taste of swift justice. So it might have turned out. But just then the town band beside the platform broke into a fanfare of brass and clashing cymbals. Encouraged by *um-pahs* from the tuba, a patriotic air burst forth. Perhaps their old mare, Jeanne d'Arc, had an aversion to German bands. With a whinny, she broke into a brisk trot and clattered through the crowd. Catherine and the others hung onto their hats. Abuse and jeering trailed after them until they were on the Napa Road, bound for Royaume Céleste.

'A bad business,' muttered Jean-Pierre, casting an angry glance at Chi-en, who he obviously blamed. 'I have heard of arson against farmers not using white labour. Madame should be careful, as Monsieur Bourchier would have been. A barn burned down last week further up the valley.'

Catherine frowned at Jean-Pierre's words, aware Chi-en was listening. She could guess how the winegrowers of Napa would react to the news a French comer-in had sold all her wine to filthy Chinese merchants.

'We shall never be intimidated!' she declared, hoping it was true. 'All the world's honest people are welcome to labour at Royaume Céleste!'

Whether Chi-en's eyebrows rose through irony or a painful jolt of the wagon, she could not determine.

That evening he stared at the distant mass of Mount St Helena, smoking a cigarette. The memoir of Prince Hong lay abandoned on the kitchen table, along with ink and writing brush. A new fear haunted Chi-en: that rather than elevating Prince Hong, preserving his lost friend for the admiration of history, his account demeaned him. That betrayal, on top of the others, was unbearable. Nor dared he betray the truth. Tossing aside his cigarette, Chi-en returned warily to the table.

A HUMBLE MEMOIR

OF

HIS MOST NOBLE HIGHNESS, FOURTH PRINCE HONG

Chapter the Sixth: *The River of Life*

I

Two years after the Heavenly Capital was consumed by flame, greed, wicked lust and anguish, a paddlewheel steam packet from Calcutta nosed through fog to enter the English Channel. At regular intervals its shrill whistle warned approaching ships. Three passengers stood at the prow. Two wore splendid Chinese silks protected by oilskins. The third — myself — wore a smart woollen suit of European cut.

My companions on this alien ocean thousands of miles from China? Fourth Prince Hong and Tutor Ren Xudong.

The river of life flows many ways. Yet always, in the end, to the same lifeless sea. Fate rushed us in that direction and we called it choice — or Prince Hong's choice, for he decided everything of importance.

The intervening two years had passed in a blur of constant danger. I shall not report the perilous regions we crossed to reach the relative safety of Hong Kong. There we posed as refugee merchants before rumours of Prince Hong's true identity drove us to Shanghai then Macao — anywhere communities of Europeans provided shelter. It was a great irony that foreigners who had helped defeat the Heavenly Kingdom were now our unwitting protectors, though we hid behind aliases at all times. Meanwhile, the last smouldering of the Taiping rebellion was doused with the blood of our few remaining Holy Armies.

It has been said that Fourth Prince Hong played a coward's part by not joining the doomed armies in Chekiang. Of course, that is nonsense. His destiny was to found a new Righteous Kingdom, not perish with the failed Heavenly one. Hence his brave decision that China was too dangerous at this time, especially as we carried with us unimaginable wealth in the form of the Heavenly Kingdom's treasury. The loss of those riches to the Manchu would have been our ultimate defeat. Therefore, he resolved on a sacrifice that shall enter the annals of the long-suffering Chinese nation.

His plan was exceptionally bold, proof of an extraordinary understanding and vision. Namely, to take ship to India and study how the invincible British ruled their Empire. From there, Europe itself beckoned. His aim: discover what China must become in order to gain equality with the great foreign powers. Commerce, justice, education, industry and manufacture, above all, transport and modern armaments would be his study.

In addition, he would persuade influential men to assist his cause – no less than the establishment of a wholly Chinese-ruled state to be known as the Righteous Kingdom. With their help, we would return to China in two or three years (earlier if opportunities proved favourable) and lead a great rebellion to drive out the Manchu and their hangers-on forever.

Thus, we found ourselves entering the English Channel after a long voyage in the SS *Britannic Enterprise*. It had been a gratifying journey. Prince Hong was feted as the wealthiest person aboard. Besides, many passengers approved of our Christianity.

My own excitement at sailing upon a sea without discernible shores or limits was boundless. I had escaped the confinement of China! My lost father, the sailor, might be captaining any of the larger vessels we passed.

Even in heavy seas I promenaded eagerly, relishing the wind's buffet, the complex bitterness of salt on my lips.

Prince Hong and Tutor Ren Xudong kept to their cabins except in calm weather, both suffering dreadful seasickness. I tried to teach my master the rudiments of polite, conversational English but – surprisingly for so intelligent and remarkable a man – found him a slow student. My own peculiar gift for languages became crucial to Prince Hong at this time. It is no exaggeration to say I enabled him to communicate with a world of utter strangers. Tutor Ren Xudong made no effort at all to learn 'barbarian tongues', preferring to lecture us for hours each day on the finer points of Taiping theology and Prince Hong's destiny.

Meanwhile, our leviathan powered through the roughest waves, a great marvel to us. Indeed, Prince Hong summoned the captain and insisted on inspecting the engine room. After clambering down narrow stairs we entered a hell of incessant clanking, steam, smoke, sickly red illumination from the boilers. The stench of coal was undiluted by any access to fresh air. While Prince Hong pretended to understand the Chief Engineer's explanations of the boiler, deep satisfaction on his face as though this fearsome machinery was already serving the Righteous Kingdom, I discovered we were not the only Chinese on board. Dozens of dog-thin, emaciated coolies fed the monster in which we sailed, shovelling dusty coal from vast bunkers. I am not sure whether I felt guilty to sleep in a luxurious cabin while my fellow countrymen toiled like slaves. I do remember fearing that one day I might join them.

II

My eighteenth year offered me a new continent to explore, courtesy of Prince Hong's limitless wealth. All I need do was serve him faithfully.

Yet we lived in constant dread of Imperialist assassins and I routinely carried a small revolver. Often, we grew dispirited and anxious.

The first stage of his mission was visiting the main European capitals to seek support. Now my ability to devour and regurgitate languages became invaluable, especially as Prince Hong hired tutors of French, German and Italian for me. Though it may sound immodest, I must truthfully record that all my professors regarded me as a prodigy.

London, Paris, Rome, Vienna, Berlin, St Petersburg . . . over the next few years we travelled to each, cities that filled us with awe. Yet I was the only one to truly appreciate their delights – opera, theatre, libraries, galleries, parks. Prince Hong and Tutor Ren Xudong schemed constantly to win over influential supporters for our Righteous Kingdom, meeting with almost no success. One might accuse them of poor judgement in the choice of men they approached – some have done so – but I believe it demonstrated Prince Hong's ever-hopeful sense of patriotic duty. His favourite sightseeing involved fortifications and armament manufactures rather than museums. All that interested him was the future, not the past. Truly he was a forward thinker.

I must relate our travels were not without humorous episodes. Our first encounter with telegrams convinced Tutor Ren Xudong that captive ghosts travelled up and down the wires, bearing messages for mortals who used this infernal device. Upon realising his Tutor's mistake, Prince Hong sent him a telegram purportedly from the first Ming Emperor, encouraging our efforts to create a Righteous Kingdom. The joke backfired badly. Ren Xudong took the prophecy so seriously he treasured the thin yellow paper as a kind of talisman. He also prayed to God to release the Ming Emperor's soul from the wire. In the end, neither of us dared explain the truth of the matter.

For years our ignorance meant we routinely misplaced people's status. Especially when it came to fancy railway or postal uniforms. As for the quality of the tea, Prince Hong was convinced the Manchu were plotting to sap European morale by exporting third-rate leaves. It became a source of great debate between my companions why foreigners smelled so peculiar. After much deliberation, an excess of butter and cow's milk was found to be the cause, along with unnaturally close cohabitation with unworthy animals like dogs and cats.

Some misunderstandings offered insights. When we first arrived in London, Prince Hong assumed advertisements were official edicts commanding the populace to buy things. A quite natural mistake, considering he read no English. When I explained the true situation, he purchased five different brands of chocolate, soap and coffee.

'There is hardly any difference between them,' announced Tutor Ren Xudong, after testing each. 'Only the paper flags in which they are wrapped differ.'

'Indeed,' said Prince Hong. 'In my Righteous Kingdom such attempts to deceive the people will be punished by flogging.'

Mostly, we admired the modern innovations surrounding us. Gas lights. Railways and timetables. Factories producing a hundred thousand kinds of object. Newspapers. Periodicals. Department stores overflowing. Horse-drawn double-decker trams. I could provide an endless list. Enough to say those giddy years were rich with discovery. Still our hearts, tied to China by invisible cords, were divided. Mine, being half-European, tangled itself beyond unravelling.

III

At last Tutor Ren Xudong called a council to debate Prince Hong's duty. Although various Chinese had tried to gain the Fourth Prince's ear, we had kept them at a distance, afraid of spies or Manchu assassins. So the council consisted of Ren Xudong and our master: my own role was to act as secretary.

After an interminable Taiping service involving three bowls of tea and a sermon read aloud then burned, the Holy Tutor decided God was sufficiently alerted to our need for Divine Guidance.

'Prince! It is four years since the Heavenly Capital fell,' began Ren Xudong. 'Now I must ask your intentions. When will you return to China? How else will the Heavenly Kingdom be renewed?'

We waited expectantly. I dreaded the thought of attempting a fruitless rebellion. Tutor Ren Xudong desired nothing more than martyrdom. After a long silence, Prince Hong sighed.

'Old friend,' he said, addressing his Tutor. 'My loyal friend. And you, no less, Chi-en. Much as we all long to strike a blow that will send the Manchu devil-dogs reeling, we lack an army. Even a small force, armed with modern Western rifles and artillery would be sufficient. But we have no such army ready. And I spurn the idea of mercenaries. We need volunteers loyal to the new Righteous Kingdom.'

I nodded gladly. The opera and pleasure trips would continue. Tutor Ren Xudong was not so easily appeased.

'Then you must become a scholar,' he said, 'while you wait to regain your rightful throne! You must study Confucius and the Five Classics. As well as all the Taiping books we can find, especially the corrected Bible . . .' For a long while he expounded the benefits to China of its future ruler undertaking such studies. Prince Hong listened impatiently then rose in a state of agitation.

'No!' he cried. 'Did I journey here to learn the Chinese classics? Of course not. I must study Engineering or Science, not Confucius!'

Such a notion appalled Ren Xudong, though I doubt he even knew what Engineering or Science might be. Back and forth they argued.

Finally, I cleared my throat loudly enough to catch their attention. Or perhaps they were just pausing for breath.

'When I think of China,' I said, 'I recollect cruelties beyond calculation. Injustices without recompense. Prince, if you must become a scholar, let your study be Law. How else will the people gain justice? How else will the endless killing stop?'

He looked at me closely then clapped me on the shoulder.

'You are my conscience, Chi-en. Centuries hence, historians will record your words and say you commenced a new, brighter epoch for the people. I shall study Law!'

Even Tutor Ren Xudong seemed pleased. Perhaps he thought *Law* meant the Ten Commandments, for I am sure he could not conceive of the labyrinths of a European legal system, its avaricious gatekeepers and guides through the maze.

Prince Hong was admitted as a student to London University rather than a solicitor's chambers. A large donation was needed to secure his place. I sat the entrance examination on his behalf and no one quibbled. Though we congratulated ourselves on this ruse, it was plain the Professors did not take him at all seriously. In retrospect, they were right. Prince Hong's English was always painful and meandering. I accompanied him to lectures as a translator but he was too proud to acknowledge his ignorance. After a few weeks it was agreed I should attend on his behalf, taking notes in Chinese.

How his loss was my gain! Yet again I must thank that gracious, generous nature for allowing me access to knowledge. It was during these studies I glimpsed how mankind must not rely on physical coercion to regulate its affairs. At night, having cooked my master's meal, for increasingly I played the role of chef, I would strive to comprehend the human propensity for evil. How, I wondered, would it ever be cured?

Such thoughts obsessed me. I secured volumes by Kant, Schopenhauer, Marx and read them in German. Likewise, Voltaire, Montaigne and Rousseau in French. Once, as I read and took notes in a corner of the London apartment we occupied, Prince Hong watched me and smiled sadly.

'You shall be Minister of Justice in my Righteous Kingdom,' he said. 'How I long to witness the good you would do! But I fear that day will never come.'

As another year passed, Prince Hong's indolence grew. How could a master-spirit like his, created for decisive leadership and action, bear to wait passively for the Chinese people to summon him as their saviour? It grieved and frustrated me in equal measure.

One of my duties was to scour the English and French press for news relating to China. This I would translate to Prince Hong as he sat on his sofa before the fire. The slightest hint of weakness amongst the Manchu seeded hours of feverish speculation. Tutor Ren Xudong invariably cried out: 'Finish your uncle's divine mission, Prince! Save your people! God will grant you visions that point the way.' But talk changed nothing. The call from a desperate people never came. Neither did the visions Tutor Ren Xudong craved.

Now I must address a libellous slur against Prince Hong's character circulated in China by the Manchu government press, whose agents in London kept a close eye on our activities. Namely, that he entertained ladies of ill-repute in his London apartments on a regular basis. Indeed that, as a result, he was syphilitic.

One might recall the Heavenly King taking one hundred and twenty wives. One might argue such tendencies were Prince Hong's birthright. I can assert with complete truth that at no time was he adulterous or depraved, as has been suggested by malicious pens. It is true that I was required to accompany him as his translator on trips to 'houses of fashion'. One needed no English for the *conversations* he conducted in such places; and I was allowed to engage the young ladies there in conversations of my own. Yet I fear we practised the mechanics of love rather than its essence. In that, we were like many another dissatisfied gentleman. I need hardly add such excursions were kept secret from Tutor Ren Xudong at all costs.

IV

One proof of Prince Hong's extraordinary foresight and genius was his abiding interest in the steam locomotive. It astounded me how completely he grasped the potential of these amazing machines.

When bored – sadly all too often – he loved to take a hackney cab to Victoria Station and watch the trains' arrivals and departures. Each week he made at least one substantial train journey, if he was melancholy, two or three. Watching the world fly past calmed his restless spirit for a few hours.

He would ask me to translate timetables and maps, instructing me to ascertain how many Chinese miles per hour the trains could travel, taking into account stops. Such calculations did not interest me. In fact, I was fairly certain my mathematics was faulty. But I was delighted to distract my friend and master in any way I could.

One gloomy winter's evening, after reading reports in a newspaper that the Manchu had finally suppressed a long-standing rebellion in Szechuan, Prince Hong paced like a caged lion around our apartment. At last, an agitated notion took hold of him. Ordering me to take out a large map of China bought from a naval stationer's, he laid it across our extended dining table. For a long while he circled round it, examining rivers and major cities, muttering to himself: *Ah* or *I see.* Then he took up pencil and ruler to mark out rail routes for the whole of China, from the Mongolian Provinces down to jungles in the South; from populous Chekiang to the Western Mountains of Nepal. At their hub lay Nanking, Heavenly Capital of our youth, soon to become the Righteous Capital of Great Peace.

All the while, Tutor Ren Xudong watched in puzzled delight, thinking the lines represented routes Taiping armies would follow.

With my help, Prince Hong ran train lines through impassable mountains ('We shall dig tunnels, Chi-en! Tunnels to amaze the world!'), over swamps and rivers and lakes miles wide ('Viaducts and bridges on high embankments, Chi-en!'). Once the Righteous Kingdom's railway web was spun, he rubbed his hands together in glee. 'Think how our armies could travel by train! A thousand men transported in an hour over territory that would have taken a miserable day's march. No more struggling through swamps and mosquitoes as we did, Chi-en. Everything neat and efficient!'

He even asked me to draft out a timetable for the major routes, dictating while I took hurried notes. Finally dawn peered through the curtain at our efforts and we collapsed in armchairs, exhausted. Tutor Ren Xudong had long been asleep on the sofa, covered by blankets at my master's command. Prince Hong clutched the papers of the 'All China Timetable' he had created. Silent tears ran down his cheeks so that I, too, felt my eyes fill.

'We have lost so much,' he said, dully. 'So very much.'

I threw open the curtains, hoping dawn would teach him fresh heart. He looked at me bitterly. 'I am weary,' he said. 'I am unwell.' With that, he withdrew to his bedchamber, tossing our timetable into the fire so that it flared in the grey light.

I wept to see my friend and dear master hurt by fate. More than that, I wept because I knew that one day, perhaps a hundred years hence, someone would build for real the railways we had constructed as dreams. And it would not be us. Not us.

V

I have mentioned that when we first arrived in Europe, Prince Hong visited munitions factories as though preparing to equip an army. As years passed such visits dwindled then ceased.

One day in spring, however, he joined a gentleman's club that welcomed foreign members. It had been recommended by a Chinese acquaintance with unfortunate links to the opium trade, who claimed men of high influence belonged to it. I shall never forget how Prince Hong smiled his sad smile as he asked me to wait for him outside. 'No doubt I am wasting my time,' he said. 'But I must try. It is my duty.'

'Do not try too hard,' I said, as though touched by a premonition. He had already entered and did not hear.

I expected he would receive snubs and petty humiliations because his English almost always provoked mirth. It is a testament to his force of character that only the most depraved of men dared mock him to his face.

The sky turned from pale blue to inky black before he emerged from the club. I waited on a vacant doorstep, smoking and reading a book of law in order to impersonate him for an examination at London University. Not only did the late hour surprise me: he was beaming!

'It went well?' I asked, delighted.

Close up, I smelt a strong aroma of wine and spirits. As a good Taiping, Prince Hong had little taste for alcohol and only drank a glass of fine wine with each meal to prepare himself for dining with the Queen of England and other foreign heads of state. As a bad Taiping, I would finish off the bottle in my room and sometimes open another, developing a taste for inebriation that would have cost my head in the Heavenly Capital. But I digress.

'Oh, it went very well,' he said. 'At last things are moving! Think of it, I have met a nobleman – Lord Cadogan – who is completely sympathetic to our cause. And he knows China very well, having been stationed in Canton and Shanghai. You must pack my finest clothes. Tomorrow, we take a train north!'

That unfortunate journey and its aftermath, ruinous in every way imaginable, shall occupy the last chapter of this humble memoir.

Napa Valley, California
Summer 1878

In the woods surrounding Royaume Céleste, heat made pinecones hiss, sigh, click on their branches. Coastal breezes dropped. Without wind, the Valley hushed and a little birdsong or cricket creak or the huff of a distant locomotive travelled far.

Far travellers, too, were covered wagons trundling up dusty roads, bearing settlers to the Lake Country and Northern California. Despite the trade depression and Great Panic, perhaps because of them, the Golden State retained its draw.

When wind did rise, the woods mimicked the sea. Threshing, restless oaks filled the air with a roar of headstrong, leafy branches.

True relief from the heat came only with the sea fogs, ground-hugging clouds sucked up from San Pablo Bay to roll remorselessly inland. Then the air cooled and silence returned, more complete because the crickets and birds went still. In Royaume Céleste the most common fog-sound became Emile's stubborn, asthmatic cough.

One evening, Catherine glanced out of her bedroom window to see Chi-en Shambles by the well. Heat lay across the valley like a haze. He had stripped off his cotton shirt and stood, barefoot, wearing just trousers. Half against her will she watched as he cranked the pump to fill a wooden bucket with cool water. Midges danced round him, tiny specks of silver light.

He was pale, thin, hardened by physical work. Scars on his back spoke of old struggles, wounds she could only surmise. His chest and shoulders and arms were broad for a Chinaman. No doubt his white father had been of burly physique.

Then it occurred to her – a shocking thought – that perhaps, perhaps his father had been Chinese and his mother white.

As she watched, he poured water from the bucket over his head, grunting with pleasure, splashing his arms then pouring out more. She should not watch. A forbidden warmth and restlessness stirred. She closed the curtains hastily and sat on the bed, glancing at herself in the mirror until her breath slowed.

In Languedoc the only way a girl learned a man's body was by dancing at balls or harvest fêtes. Here, she had no dancing; neither was she a girl. Catherine descended to her salon and played an old folk dance on her oboe, the instrument jigging up and down as she tapped her foot and blew.

June advanced and the state-wide Constitutional Elections passed with great dismay for all Chinese – and a matching hope for pinched, hungry Californians who blamed Mongols for their sufferings. As though mirroring human politics, the fogs thickened.

When winds returned, Royaume Céleste's moat of woods and brambles swayed to their ancient rhythms. Those walking the rows of vines discovered a full canopy of leaves concealing clusters of hard, young green grapes. Filtered sunlight reached through, prompting each separate vine to concentrate a mindless will.

Lines of Wappo, clothes caked with white dust, raked and weeded the gaps between rows. The soil was as dry as their ancestors' bones. No need to irrigate, for the vines possessed roots deeper than the remains of Indian roundhouses.

Farmers in the valley bottom squinted up at the dark figures amongst the grapes of Royaume Céleste. Later they gossiped in Perryville saloons that Diggers were labouring in the Frenchie widow's place – she sure was a lady who knew how to hire cheap.

One Sunday afternoon when even the flies drowsed, two horsemen rode out of the woods leading from the valley bottom to Royaume Céleste and reined in their horses. They sat very still, surveying the barns and winery, the farmhouse and rows of vines climbing up to shady crags and forest. Exchanging blank looks, they urged their mounts forward into a thudding canter.

Chi-en watched their approach through the kitchen window and walked quickly round the outside of the house to warn his mistress. She was on a rocking chair, reading a novel.

'Madame,' said Chi-en, 'visitors . . .'

Before he could say more a rattle of hooves made his warning irrelevant. Catherine rose from her chair as the two riders approached the porch, reining in with practised ease. Both wore grimy shirts and once-fancy waistcoats. The first was short-legged on his high cavalry horse, barrel-chested, a natural brawler. His flushed face would have appeared angry except it lacked visible emotion. A low, dented black top hat added a little respectability.

Where the first was squat, the second man's limbs gangled. Despite being nearer forty than thirty, he retained the petulant frown of an adolescent boy. An impression deepened by darting, empty eyes and a wet, crooked mouth. His cap was just about recognisable as a Confederate States Army kepi, its original shape distorted and yellow trim bleached by thirteen years of unprofitable peace.

Both carried revolvers in open holsters, though such a frontier custom was discouraged in Napa Valley.

Chi-en anticipated their names and business before either spoke. He glanced anxiously up at the hillside where the Wappo encampment lay hidden amongst the trees. Fortunately, there was no trace of smoke or drumbeat from their mournful ghost dance.

'You the Frenchie widow?' demanded the first rider.

Catherine laid her open book on the chair and rose to her full height. 'I am afraid we need no labourers here, gentlemen. So sorry.'

Neither man spoke. The lanky one looked round like a hungry bird.

'We ain't here for that kind of work,' explained the first rider, evidently the spokesman. 'You see, we kinda heard talk of redskins being seen on your land. Injuns should rightly be in the Mendocino Res'vation. That's why me and my partner here, Mr Temple, thought we'd ride over.'

'And your name, sir?'

'Parker.'

She was careful to give no sign the names were known to her.

'Well, Parker, I have no Indians on my land who need to go to a reservation.'

Again, the visitors fell silent. Mr Temple's glance ceased darting and fixed itself on Catherine Bourchier, travelling over her breasts, waist, back to her breasts.

'Ma-am,' continued Parker, 'you'll appreciate there's a twenty-five-dollar bounty for every savage brought alive to the Mendocino Res'vation. Now, we both purpose to be claiming that bounty.'

'Perhaps so, gentleman,' said Catherine. 'In the meantime, I would be glad if you left my land. I do not like guns here, except for hunting.'

Mr Temple laughed. A high snort that abruptly cut itself short. He added no further comment. Mr Parker nodded. 'We sure will be keeping an eye out for them redskins.'

With that, he cast a curious glance at Chi-en then spurred his horse. Catherine watched them ride into the trees.

'Do you think they believed me?' she said, turning to Chi-en.

'That kind of man believes in nothing,' he said, 'except his purse.'

That evening Chi-en resorted to his law books. The guns hanging from Parker and Temple's belts told him some greater force was needed to counteract their claims on the Wappo.

The thick, costly volumes were kept on a clean shelf along with the breadbin. Both were stored high to frustrate rats. Sometimes, when he fingered the books' embossed spines, he glanced at the breadbin and remembered Reverend Shambles intoning in his tiny chapel outside the walls of Guangzhou: *Man cannot live by bread alone.*

Insects flapped round the lamp. He read, taking notes on a sheet of blank paper that became ten closely written pages. Afterwards, he sat back and considered his discovery, smoking a cigarette in the breathless midnight air.

Terrible things were said of the Indian reservations by men returning to Chinatown, always with the unspoken fear that similar treatment might come their way: toil without a single dollar's recompense; fists and clubs amidst disease-ridden squalor; missionaries who reached for whips as often as their Bibles; tales of kidnapped children sold to ranchers as indentured slaves by Reservation Agents. Yet that fact, Chi-en had discovered, offered the Wappo above Royaume Céleste some protection. If Catherine Bourchier formally indentured them – man, woman and child – the law was plain: bonded natives could not be forcibly reserved unless and until their indenture expired. Nor could the indenture be repudiated, save by its owner.

Pouring out a glass of claret to accompany his smoke, Chi-en contemplated Parker and Temple. Defying such men was a dangerous game indeed.

The next morning, Chi-en walked the rows of vines to the ancient Indian track Emile had shown him. This time he had a more talkative companion.

'Are you sure they will be there?' asked Catherine.

'I would imagine so.'

She wore plain clothes. An emerald green headscarf accentuated the paler green of her eyes. 'And you are sure that – how did you call it? – *indenturing* will give them lawful protection?'

'Their labour would, in effect, become your property.' He added wryly, 'Like slaves of old.'

Catherine retained her thoughts. All morning she had given no sign of her intentions towards the Wappo. A little breathless from the climb, she said, 'I never told you how we chose Royaume Céleste, did I?'

'No, Madame.' Nor did he see why she should want to now – except, perhaps, to make sense of her own story, an impulse he understood well. Why else did he fret over his memoir of Prince Hong?

'It was a question of finding our ideal *terroir*,' she began, 'the most important question if one wishes to make good wine.'

They were some way up the slope and she paused beside a volcanic boulder. A fine view of Royaume Céleste stretched out.

'From the first, I sensed that here was a place I could labour for – and expect a return. Do you see that slope?'

Her enthusiasm made him curious. 'Evidently not as you do,' he said.

'Of course not, such a way of seeing comes from knowledge, Monsieur Chi-en. But look, good drainage and yet water in winter from the creek. A south-facing slope protected from frost by the curve of the hills. A steady breeze to dry the grapes and prevent mould. Oh, there must be no compromise in one's choice of *terroir*!' She smiled a little sadly and added, 'Like one's choice of husband.'

'Perhaps you can only discover a land's true worth through trial and error,' he suggested.

'Why no! There are always signs to read. Look over there. No shade from the trees and hills? Good! Shade shrinks the grapes. And the soil? Fertile, yes, but not too rich. One needs good drainage. A little grit and sand does no harm. When we first came here, we dug holes four feet deep in different parts of the vineyard. You will laugh, but I even tasted the earth, as Papa did when he chose where to plant.'

'So is Royaume Céleste truly perfect?' Perfection was an idea he had learned to distrust. It connected him to disappointed hopes for a better world.

'Of course not. These woods have wild vines that are a home to pests: insects, deer, birds, heaven know what else. Besides, Royaume Céleste is not one *terroir* but many.' She pointed at the northern curve of the hills. 'There the soil will sustain a plainer grape and, over there, yes, to the left, a more delicate kind. It is not perfect yet I still intend to give what is left of my life to this vineyard, to restore what my family lost.'

'Why are you telling me this? I cannot believe it is because you wish to turn me into a winemaker.'

She glanced at him sharply. 'I tell you because I know you will understand. Above all, so you will see that Royaume Céleste must always be my first concern, not the welfare of the Wappo. Now I would like to carry on.'

After a hot ascent through the woods, both were soon perspiring. As he helped her over a mossy log, Chi-en detected her musk amidst the scents of earth and coarse vegetation.

'What do you wish to learn from them?' he asked, hurriedly.

Catherine stretched and breathed out. 'My own mind.'

He led her the last quarter mile until they arrived at the Wappo dancing ground. The settlement had grown a new hut since his last visit. Several chickens – whose relatives dwelt in the barns of Royaume Céleste – pecked the earth. Naked children splashed and played in the creek. Men lolled under the shade of a huge, overhanging rock while the women husked acorns. A couple of older uncles were drunk, bottles of cheap brandy beside them. Flies buzzed everywhere.

At the sight of Catherine, a general flurry to cover nakedness set in. The ancient matriarch rose from her rocking chair and shuffled over, accompanied by her grandson, the young chief, as interpreter.

'Do you want us to work?' asked the chief.

Catherine looked round, counting heads. Their numbers had increased.

'I come with bad news,' she said. 'Yesterday two men called at my house.'

Consternation greeted the names of Parker and Temple. One young woman nursing a half-white baby wailed and beat her breasts. Only the old woman remained impassive.

'We have nowhere to go,' she told Catherine through the young chief. 'Here is our home. Here our ancestors live amongst us. Here I was born.'

'They are dangerous men,' warned Catherine. 'They carried guns.'

'We have nowhere to go,' repeated the woman. 'You promised we could stay and work the harvest.'

Chi-en watched Catherine, awaiting her decision. He almost spoke but thought better of it. The choice – and danger – must be hers alone. Perhaps it was a kind of test, set by whom and to what purpose, he could not say. Virtue seemed as great an enigma as evil.

'I will think what is best,' said Catherine. 'Meantime, you may stay as before. When I have decided, I shall return.'

As they turned to go one of the drunk men burst out laughing, calling out in his language. Catherine, to whom the words were mere sounds, frowned. Chi-en, however, understood: a coarse joke about the shaman and the white woman.

A careless, wilful sense of freedom grew in Catherine Bourchier. Perhaps it was her power over the respectful savages. She preferred not to think so. It was just that, among wild pines and mossy, lichen-clad boulders, she could breathe more easily than down in the dusty farm. And Chi-en's company was not obtrusive – or unpleasant. Sometimes she caught herself wanting to seek him out, an unsettling urge, given their mutual positions.

Halfway down the hillside, they reached a shady waterfall dappled with sunlight filtering through branches. A large, flat rock lay beside the trickling stream.

Catherine knelt on the sun-bleached rock to drink, cupping cool water with two hands. She sat on the ledge and sighed, her legs dangling over the edge. The creek formed a small pool below. The Chinaman bathed his face and hair.

'Monsieur Chi-en,' she said, 'I noticed your surprise as we left our Indian friends. It had something to do with that drunken man calling out.'

He smoothed back wet, black hair. It turned silver in the sun.

'Madame is observant.' He fanned himself with his wide-brimmed hat.

'You understand their language. What did he say?'

He smiled thinly. 'He called me a shaman because, I expect, I've learned the basics of their tongue. Yet there's no sorcery to it.'

'It seems magical.'

'Is it magical to blend wines so Mr Trubody throws dollars your way? Or that you taste the wine and identify the source of each separate flavour?'

She stretched, wriggled, leant back on flat palms. The stone beneath her was warm. 'That is different. I learned the skill as a girl from my Papa. Now it is an instinct. Sometimes I have to concentrate when tasting. Not often.'

'Then we are alike, except I taste words.' He stared up at Mount St Helena. 'I like the fact it gives me a kind of distinction in the world.'

They sat in silence, listening to the waterfall and stillness of the woods. She looked at him then away.

Catherine realised she would like to strip off her long skirt and respectable layers of clothes and bathe in the cool, murmuring stream. If she asked Chi-en to return alone to Royaume Céleste she might do so. Except the Wappo were likely to spy. Unexpectedly, she thought of Baron Foche in the San Francisco opera house. When she looked up, Chi-en was examining her. 'You seem troubled,' he said.

She laughed bitterly. 'Do you ask in order to learn my secrets? So you can use them against me? As others wish to do?'

He did not seem offended. 'Your secrets are more obvious than you imagine. You need not fear me.'

'Indeed?'

'I don't want your money. Forgive me for my indiscreet question. We should return now.'

Shadows that had parted between them rushed back. Perhaps through loneliness, or because she sensed that, truly, he did not mean Emile or her harm, she said quickly: 'I will tell you why I frowned, Monsieur Chi-en, though I shouldn't.'

It trickled out like the waterfall beside them, only unclean, not pure, a dirty story – and far more of it than she had intended. One explanation demanded another: Antoine's expensive vices and cruelty; the phylloxera and their ruin; and now, Baron Foche's appearance in California like a taunting devil, ready to inform Antoine of her whereabouts so he might steal Emile, ready to fetch the bankrupt nobleman here like a new plague of lice.

'So you see,' she concluded, 'I am afraid. Not just for my own sake, but Emile's. Though I may not be the best of mothers, it is impossible to imagine a more uncaring father.'

Chi-en had listened without speaking during her long account. 'You have trusted me, Madame,' he said. 'I promise to help you and your son if I can. For as long as I remain here.'

'You intend to leave Royaume Céleste?'

'It depends when, or whether, I receive a certain piece of information.'

His revelation was more unwelcome than she expected. Catherine watched the water flow over the lip of the stone and splash into the small pool.

'Would American law allow my husband to take Emile?' she asked, at last.

'I could find out, but a father's claims are likely to take precedence over a mere woman's.'

'Thank you.'

He stepped over, offering a hand to help her rise with dignity from the flat rock where her legs dangled. The arm that pulled her up was steady, strong.

He led the way down the hillside. Having said so much, far too much for prudence, Catherine was reluctant to betray the most unexpected secret of all: she did not wish this stranger – a man from the most despised of races, a man who treated all he met, high or low, powerful or weak, with the same respect and dignity – to leave Royaume Céleste.

That dusk, anyone looking across the Napa Valley at Royaume Céleste might have thought dozens of stars had drifted down to surround the tall stone winery. They glowed and twinkled on the hillside.

Close up, an acrid reek like rotten eggs dispelled romantic notions. The lights were sulphur candles burning in barrels to purge them of mould or anything that might infect the wine. Near the well, cleanliness was also the aim as Chinese labourers scrubbed wooden pails and tubs, rubbing in paraffin wax to seal purity into the wood. Catherine knew it was never too late for a wine to spoil. Only when her first Royaume Céleste vintage was safe in the bottles would she lower her guard.

Inside the winery, Jean-Pierre Leclos siphoned wine into purged barrels, the final racking before bottling. Each was carefully topped up to avoid a taint of air. Then Catherine tasted the wine and added a last, medicinal dose of sulphur crystals before tapping the lid into place. Though they worked well together, neither spoke. She could tell he was building up to an outburst.

When the last barrel had been racked, he smoothed his walrus moustache in readiness.

'Tell me, Jean-Pierre,' said Catherine, with a sigh, 'what is wrong?'

He spluttered. 'Wrong? It is more a question of *surprise*. On several grave matters, Madame.'

'I believe you are going to mention the fact you still lack a steward's cottage and that Monsieur Bourchier would never have allowed his steward to sleep on the same corridor as his daughter?'

'Yes, that is precisely—'

'And you will point out that I have now received a large payment from Mr Trubody and can afford to construct a cabin, at the very least.'

'Of course—'

'And I shall reply that all the money has been invested in bottles and other necessary costs so that we can sell our wine to Mr Lu Kan in Chinatown.'

Now he was glaring, arms folded across his chest. 'Do you mock me, Madame?'

'No, Jean-Pierre, I do not. But we have had this same conversation many times.'

'You exaggerate, Madame!'

'Perhaps it just feels that way.'

They lapsed into silence. 'I believe,' he said, with strained dignity, 'that without my skill and hard work your Chinese merchant fellow would not have a drop of excellent wine to buy!'

'Yes,' retorted Catherine, 'and I have thanked you. But what of *my* hard work? *My* skill? Has that had no effect?'

'Monsieur Bourchier would never have . . .'

She stopped listening, for the old steward was reminiscing how Monsieur Bourchier taught him everything he knew, a story she could almost recite by heart.

'And what of this Monsieur 'Umble?' he demanded.

Now Catherine paid attention. 'What of him?'

'You speak to those savages in the hills with him as your chaperone. But I am steward here! It is I, Jean-Pierre Leclos, who should address the hired hands. Not our chef and housemaid.'

'Chi-en speaks the Wappo language. Besides, he has made an important discovery about the laws concerning Indians.'

'Laws! Pfoo! What can a Chinaman chef know about laws?'

'Please do not talk about him like that,' she said, unhappily. 'Without Monsieur Shambles we would not have sold our wine in San Francisco. Where would your steward's cottage be then?'

But now Jean-Pierre wasn't listening. 'I tell you, Madame,' he sighed, 'Monsieur Bourchier would never . . .'

Catherine retreated to the house with a jug of new wine as soon as she was able.

In her salon, she poured out a glass and admired its soft clarity in the lamplight. The time had come to decide upon a label for the new vintage.

A tap on the door. Chi-en Shambles appeared, candle in hand, his expression guarded. 'Madame, a word if I may.'

'Very well,' she sighed, 'come in.'

He closed the door behind him. 'Madame, I heard your conversation with Monsieur Leclos tonight. Indeed, he spoke so loudly only a deaf man could not hear. I wish to say that, if I am a source of discord here, I would not be offended to return to San Francisco. Nor would I blame you.'

Her eyebrows shot upwards. 'I am sorry you overheard his . . . his words. But no more of that, please, it is all nonsense and it has given me a headache. Perhaps you can help me. For I must decide on a label for my new wine.'

Before he could reply she passed him examples of old Domaine Bourchier labels brought from France. They were plain and without images. Then she explained her idea: *Domaine Bourchier Claret* in red with *Napa Valley, California, 1878* printed beneath. 'I am thinking,' she said, 'of a picture on the label that will make my wine stand out and represent our vineyard, so that people learn to recognise it more easily.'

He thought for a moment. 'Pass me that pencil, madame.' He began a rapid sketch on the paper she offered. The words she wanted appeared in the middle of an upright rectangle, flanked by trellises of vines laden with fruit. At the top, the silhouette of a mountain.

'Mount St Helena!' she exclaimed. 'You capture it well, Chi-en.'

'The Wappo call it *People Mountain*,' he said. 'Perhaps it will draw people to your wine.'

Catherine declared the suggestion was so good she would be ungrateful not to share a glass with him. He accepted warily. It was a crystal glass bought in San Francisco, the first he had drunk from since his days with Prince Hong.

'To our new label!' she said, hoping Jean-Pierre did not walk in.

They both sipped.

'Do you know,' she said, 'a wine's label is like a person's passport. It tells you who they are, their age, where they are from.'

'But not their true character,' he said.

'Perhaps. For that there are other tests. My father always said one may approach a bottle of wine two ways. From the outside in or from the inside out.'

Chi-en sipped again. 'One may also say that about people. Please explain what your father meant.'

'Ah, that is simple. I shall start with the outside in. Take the label, the quality of the bottle, the wine's colour through the glass. All may dissuade or persuade.'

'And inside out?'

'More complex. Through one's senses – scent, texture and taste on the tongue, colour in the glass. Even one's ears. You look amused, Monsieur Chi-en, but think of the music of wine as it froths and cascades into a carafe, releasing an opera of aromas!'

He shook his head, smiled. 'Ears are going too far. You are fanciful.'

'Hear me out, for that is not all. One tastes for balance, virtues and weaknesses, unique qualities, rolling the wine round one's palate, like so. And you should never rush to judgement.'

'I might reply that it's no more than a matter of opinion. If you think a wine is great, it becomes great.'

She sensed he was provoking her, that he enjoyed clever arguments as a lawyer might, and allowed herself to be provoked. 'I cannot agree with you! I am surprised to hear you say such things. There has to be ways of measuring the good from the bad. If I play a false note on my oboe you call it out of tune.'

'An ordinary wine is still a pleasure,' he countered.

'Nevertheless, I want my new Domaine Bourchier Claret to be a *vin supérieur*. Or do you disapprove of ambition?'

'That depends on the ambition.'

Catherine realised she was leaning towards him, that she was more intent upon him than was proper. A faint flush had touched her cheeks and neck. Perhaps he shared her confusion, for he drained his glass.

'An interesting debate, Madame,' he said, rising. 'I enjoyed it. Thank you for the wine.'

Catherine was left alone to examine his sketch of laden vines and Mount St Helena, aware she would have liked to pour him another glass and continue their conversation to wherever it might lead – until the carafe was empty.

Napa Valley, California
Summer 1878

There should have been no reason for Chi-en to collect Emile from school each afternoon. First the weather: long, sunshine days of the kind that paint a wash over childhood memories, littering the mind with lost summers. As importantly, the boy needed independence.

And there were prudent reasons to avoid Perryville. The election of the Californian Convention had stirred a renewed fury in the press against Chinamen. An Exclusion Act preventing further immigration seemed inevitable – sentiments by no means restricted to California. Reports circulated of a Chinatown looted and burned by a mob of silver miners, the blaze festooned with dangling 'Mongols'. Similar rampages in South Dakota, Wyoming, Denver.

For all these dangers – and Chi-en was conscious sleepy, prosperous Perryville was unlikely to copy the frenzies of frontier Nebraska – he did not forget Catherine Bourchier's troubles. Or that Emile might find himself accosted by Baron Foche in a secluded place, perhaps even by his errant Papa. If either event occurred, Chi-en had no idea how to act.

He rode Royaume Céleste's wagon through a heat haze into dusty Perryville. Jeanne d'Arc's flanks reeked of sweat as he halted outside

Bell's Grocery and Dry Goods Store on Main Street, his first chore being to collect supplies.

It was a large, brick building of some pretension. Though hundreds regularly went hungry in Napa County, more possessed spare cash beyond the basic demands of roof and dinner. Such folks insisted on respectable destinations for their dollars.

Perhaps that was why a small group of ladies near the counter fell silent as he entered. Chi-en instantly recognised a tall blonde in a neat riding dress as the woman who pointed him out to the angry crowd when they returned from Frisco. His shiny new boots sounded loud on the varnished floorboards. The store's owner, Mr Bell, cast a wary eye in his direction then chose to ignore him. 'That'll be eight dollars and fifty-five cents, Mrs Smithson-Mackay.' He wiped damp palms on his white apron. 'I thank you kindly.'

The slender lady reached into her reticule for a purse then hesitated.

'Mr Bell,' she said with wide-eyed innocence. Her voice was pitched high, like a girl's. 'Had I known the *sort* of customers you keep . . .' She glanced significantly in Chi-en's direction.

For a moment, Mr Bell seemed confused. He had dealt with Chi-en on several occasions, always treating him decently; and Royaume Céleste's large monthly order would be waiting in boxes and sacks in the stock room. Yet the ladies' eyes were upon the storekeeper and in response he scowled masterfully. 'Use backee dooree! Next time, backee dooree!'

The ladies near the till tittered and Mr Bell's face reddened. Chi-en usually responded to such affronts with his best Bostonian diction. Today his courage failed. The mood against Chinese in Perryville was too heated to risk the magnifying glass of irony.

He strode over to the pile of sacks and crates, taking up a load. As he carried them out, he heard one of Mrs Smithson-Mackay's friends murmur in a Southern drawl: 'I've seen a buck nigger, my dear, but never a buck Mongolian before.' Her companion's eyes rolled significantly. 'I'd *heard* the French woman likes to do herself well.'

Ashamed, he hurried back and forth under the ladies' appraising eyes until the groceries were loaded and Jeanne d'Arc was plodding onwards.

A short, frail Chinese man appeared from a gap between two buildings and ran over. Chi-en had the unsettling impression he was anticipated. 'Sam Wah wants to speak to you!' cried the old fellow in Cantonese. 'Follow me please!'

Chi-en considered refusal. He had every reason to distrust Sam Wah. But his humiliation in Bell's Store made the prospect of being among his own people – even Sam Wah and his clan – suddenly attractive.

'Climb up beside me, old father,' he said. The man scrambled up and lolled with the dignity of a Mandarin in a thousand-tasselled carriage as they rolled through the Italians' laundry-strewn slum into Chinatown.

Sam Wah's store was unchanged since Chi-en's last visit, still displaying the sign in Chinese: *All labour contracts in Perryville to be conducted through Sam Wah without exception.*

The prospect of early harvest work had swollen the population of Perryville's Chinatown. By autumn, hundreds more would have been summoned to gather grapes and other crops.

Chi-en followed the old man inside. Sam Wah, his nephew, Sam Yip, and several cronies sat round a table to fritter the afternoon on *fantan*. Cigar smoke drifted round the store.

'You wish to speak with me, Mr Sam,' said Chi-en, by way of greeting.

Sam Wah rose instantly to his feet, followed by Sam Yip. Their friends rose, too.

'Mr Sha-bells!' cried Sam Wah, as though genuinely delighted. 'You honour my house! Enter, please! Wine for Mr Sha-bells! A seat! I beg you, be seated!'

Chi-en looked round warily. No one lurked behind the piles of sacks and canned beans.

'Ah!' declared Sam Wah, at a loss for further words. 'Delighted!'

'As am I,' said Chi-en.

At that moment Sam Yip bustled over with a lacquered tray of rice wine. It seemed churlish to refuse. The warm liquor burned Chi-en's throat.

'I have a letter, Mr Sha-bells,' said Sam Wah. 'A most important letter composed by the President of the Kong Chow Company himself.'

'You mean my friend Lu Kan?' asked Chi-en, innocently.

'Yes. He is a gentleman with whom we do important business in Perryville. Much business!' Sam Wah examined Chi-en coolly. 'You have many dealings with Mr Lu Kan? Perhaps you are related to him?'

Chi-en held out his empty porcelain cup and was rewarded with more wine from the grinning Sam Yip.

'We have profitable dealings,' he said.

'Ah! Delighted!'

Again, they fell silent. Chi-en emptied his cup.

'Here is the letter, Mr Sha-bells.' Sam Wah handed over a packet secured with red wax and an ornate, hand-carved seal denoting the sacred characters of the Honourable Kong Chow Company. To a Chinaman in California, such a letter was like a private memorandum from the Son of Heaven's Chief Minister in Beijing.

Chi-en, warmed by the wine, fanned himself with the package and smiled. 'Another hot day, gentlemen!'

Now Sam Wah's delight grew brittle. 'So, Mr Sha-bells, you are still in Napa.' He offered a cigarette.

'For now,' said Chi-en. 'Tell me, have there been threats to Perryville Chinatown?'

The topic made Sam Wah uncomfortable.

'Of course, from drunken men. Stones are thrown. Beatings occur. What do you expect?'

'You are not alarmed?'

'Why should I be? They need us, Mr Sha-bells! Who else will gather their harvests for a dollar a day?'

Chi-en glanced round the circle of businessmen who exploited their own people as surely as any white man. Because of Lu Kan's letter they regarded him as one of their own. He stubbed out the cigarette Sam Wah had given him.

'Thank you for the letter, Mr Sam.'

The labour boss grunted. 'There are many Americans in this town who hate us,' he conceded. 'Sometimes I feel anxious travelling alone.'

'In that, at least,' said Chi-en, 'we are alike.'

It was dusk before Chi-en opened Lu Kan's letter. He sat on the back step of the kitchen and glanced over the twilit valley. Blooming orchards and extravagant Californian oaks, dusk-softened hillsides and placid farmhouses eased a vale in his soul.

Chi-en picked at the wax seal. Surely the letter contained news of Reverend Shambles. Why else would Lu Kan write?

With stiff, awkward fingers he tore open the seal. Setting the oil lamp, he scanned columns of Chinese characters:

To Mr Chi-en Shambles,

 First, every felicitation in your country retreat.

 I have heard news sooner than expected. I refer, of course, to Reverend Ezekiel Shambles. A certain Sin Goon is one of our Company's agents in a laundry business at a place called North Platte, Nebraska. He wrote to me and I copy here his exact words. The style will tell you much of the man. 'President! Our Noble Company! May the Emperor live a thousand years! I know the man you ask about. He is a big man here. Send my reward by next post or I may be in a different town.'

Now you know everything I do. Yet I ask you, Chi-en, is there truly a reward at the end of your search? Consider these things before rushing to North Platte, a place of which I hear nothing good.

Your patron and friend, Lu Kan.

Chi-en folded the letter carefully and put it in his pocket. Then he paced outside the kitchen door. Emile's ticklish cough reached through chirruping cicadas. A darkening sky revealed its first stars.

North Platte, Nebraska. The name was familiar. But how?

With a chuckle he recollected. On his way out West from New York, the emigrant train stopped there on its seemingly endless voyage across the prairie. Perhaps he had walked within a mile of Reverend Shambles and never realised!

Chi-en rolled a cigarette. Tonight, he would open some of Catherine Bourchier's excellent claret and toast that excellent little town. Had he not stayed in America to find this man? To answer questions haunting his dreams and unguarded thoughts?

His pacing slowed. Of course, Sin Goon might simply point him in a fresh direction or possess false information. Doubts rose like a cloud of wasps. Faces circled, some changed beyond recognition, others turned to dust. So many years had passed since the Reverend Shambles fled the Heavenly Capital. What would he remember of a bastard servant boy's father? But all Chi-en required was a name to start his trail. A simple name.

Chi-en rubbed upper arms that were not cold. Would Spiritual Uncle Father greet his old servant warmly? Would he show him the door? The

Reverend was a man of God, a good man. One might rely on a good man. The guiltiest of creatures relied on that – even children born of shame.

Chi-en's fears had no resolution other than a journey and a meeting. Rather than opening a bottle in celebration, he sat for a long while, hugging himself on the doorstep.

Bottles were very much on Catherine's mind. Most wine in California was sold by the jug and glass bottles were a risky investment; only a valuable wine repaid such expense. Crates were also on her mind; and packing straw; and extra labour; and reliable teamsters; schedules; locomotives; wagons . . . the lists in her bureau stretched for pages.

First, in every sense, came the bottling. And she knew the exact time had arrived. No more fermentation in the casks – the new wine was of brilliant clarity with not a hint of haze or sediment. Her nose confirmed the judgements of her eyes and palate, a perfectly clean aroma. Most of all, the summer heat had slackened and she needed to use the cool spell.

Every clean hand in Royaume Céleste – and she insisted they were very clean indeed – was recruited for the bottling. A production line commenced at midnight, when temperatures were lowest, and worked until morning.

First a Chinaman rinsed and wire-brushed the bottles with elaborate care, before Jean-Pierre siphoned wine from the cask to fill them, ensuring that he left a tiny gap at the top for the wine to grow. Next, more Chinese labourers took corks soaking in a vat and slotted them into a lever-driven corker. Once the corks were driven home, a third dipped their ends in red wax melted in a tin cup suspended over a candle. The wax soon hardened, whereupon Chi-en and Emile (who had been allowed time off school for the bottling) pasted on Domaine Bourchier labels fresh from the printer, depicting Mount St Helena and extravagant vines. Last of all, Catherine sat on an adjoining bench to inspect each and every bottle, sixteen thousand in total, before a fourth Chinese labourer placed them in straw-stuffed cases and tacked on their wooden lids. Several nights passed in this manner before the work was complete.

Catherine wept with relief and tiredness as the last lid sealed the final case. It was dawn and Chi-en handed round bitter coffee to the labourers. All were exhausted. He brought a cup over to Catherine, who was wiping her eyes.

'So, it is done,' he said. 'Your wine is fixed and preserved for a hundred years. An offering to the future, you might say.'

She cradled her hot coffee cup in two hands and grew tearful again. 'Do not make me cry.'

'Still, you should be proud. Especially as a woman, for business is naturally a man's domain.'

'I am proud,' she sniffed, 'I am!'

'As I believe your father and ancestors would be.'

'Now I *will* cry,' she protested.

Chi-en's mouth tasted dry as he watched her dab red-rimmed eyes. She met his glance. For a reckless moment, a flash of longing, he wanted to reach out, take her hand, squeeze her fingers tight. Then he understood – with a shock of clarity – she shared his impulse.

'I must prepare breakfast,' he said, stepping back. 'Everyone is hungry.'

She nodded, her eyes filling. 'Thank you,' she whispered.

He left her to discreet tears. Finches flitted and twittered over the vines; and the woods surrounding Royaume Céleste were carolled by a dawn chorus of birds waking to another spin round the sun. For Catherine it was the sweetest choir she ever heard.

Napa was a sociable valley: San Francisco's best families summered there. Both facts posed dilemmas for Catherine Bourchier, not least when she received an invitation to the Jockey Club Gymkhana.

The Smithson-Mackays were conspicuous patrons of the Jockey Club and any possibility of meeting them was unwelcome. Yet fear would make her a prisoner in Royaume Céleste and it was essential to spread the reputation of her wine by mingling with other vintners. So she decided to go – devil take the consequences.

On the morning of the Gymkhana, Catherine rose before dawn to find a dozen deep-bellied wagons hauled by teams of dray horses beside the winery. She had overslept. Fortunately, Jean-Pierre was already supervising the loading of the wagons. Chi-en Shambles had set up a field kitchen outside the rear of the house for the teamsters.

Straw-stuffed wooden cases, each containing twelve bottles of best Domaine Bourchier Claret were stacked onto the wagons for transportation to the railhead on the opposite side of the valley and thence to Napa City.

One by one, wagons were filled and departed. At the railhead more teamsters waited, ready to fasten the cases onto pallets in open freight cars specially hired from the Southern Pacific Railroad Company with Mr Trubody's assistance.

Catherine watched the last wagon depart and looked round for Emile. He was to accompany her on their chartered locomotive, puffing fifteen miles to the freight warehouse in Napa City.

'Emile! Emile!' Her voice echoed in the empty winery. When she looked across the rows of vines a strange manhunt was underway. Her son waved a defiant stick decorated with feathers like an Indian spear, pursued by Wappo children wearing absurdly large white men's hats. Around them, grapes blushed a first shade of crimson as they plumped. A steady wind made the woods above Royaume Céleste whisper like the sea. The wind swirled up dust so that Catherine blinked, tasting grit on her lips as she watched him run through the rows, and a memory blew upon her like the hot breeze . . .

Outside the gatehouse of Château de Chauveterre, Emile beside her, as the Tramontane, the wind from the north, rustled olive trees and ancient vines. Together they watched Comte Antoine de Rivac de Chauveterre's carriage rattle away after another brief visit. Catherine knew her six-year-old son blamed Maman for Papa's departure. 'Never mind,' she told little Emile as he sobbed. His reply was a scowl ugly upon a face so young.

'Papa gave me an iron hoop and stick!' he had declared, as though it proved his father's love. 'When is Papa coming back?'

'I do not know,' she said. 'Show me your hoop! I bet you can make it go faster than a carriage!'

The iron hoop merely wobbled and fell and would not roll, though he struck it over and over.

'Let me show you how,' she said. 'You must be gentler.'

'No!' Emile had been crimson with failure. 'Only Papa knows how!'

'But he is not here. If you let me show you, think how happy he will be when he returns.'

So, Emile reluctantly agreed and all that afternoon they made the hoop bounce and roll between rows of vines, Emile squealing with proud glee, and she, running breathlessly to keep up, for that hour or so, at least, close as mother and son should be, the Tramontane blowing dust onto their clothes. Dust neither brushed off . . .

As the Napa Valley breeze blew more grit in Catherine's face she felt barbs of anti-climax, even failure. Never mind that sixteen thousand bottles of superior claret were being loaded onto railroad trucks across the valley. Watching Emile in the vines with his Wappo friends reminded her how few afternoons of intimacy and fun, yes, simple fun, had been shared with her son. A futile sorrow for them both. An unbridgeable sorrow that time lost could not be re-travelled. It had rolled away from them like Emile's hoop, always ahead or alongside, until it wobbled, lost momentum, toppled over.

A steam whistle sounded from the far side of the valley and Catherine struggled to compose herself. A train to their future awaited them at the railhead below Trubody Nook.

'Emile!' she called. If he heard, the boy gave no indication. 'Emile! What are you doing?'

Still the children dodged and weaved, her son so absorbed by the game he did not notice until she was upon him.

'Emile! Look at your clothes! Covered in dust. Did you not remember we must go to Napa City and the Gymkhana today?'

He watched ruefully as his friends melted into the leaves.

'Why do you spend so much time with the Indians?' she asked. 'I think they are not fitting companions. Besides, it might be dangerous – in ways you cannot understand. Remember they are savages.'

She expected him to be angry, perhaps wanted him to be, to stir a reaction.

'They are savage compared to us,' he conceded, 'but are not we savage, only with more clothes on?'

Hearing her son speak so wisely surprised her. She glimpsed a man, authoritative and daunting, who might emerge from his habitual defiance. Her impatience faded. It would take hours to load the train, time to listen and talk.

'Maman,' he said, waving at Royaume Céleste, 'do you want to know this place's real name? It is *Tse-ma-noma*. Ear Town.'

She laughed uneasily. 'What nonsense! It is our home, our property, *Royaume Céleste*. Not some silly See-me-meena.'

'*Tse-ma-noma*.' His correction was firm. 'Look how the crags and shape of the hills bend round. The land forms the shape of an ear.'

She had to admit it did.

'The Wappo are very angry with us white people,' he said with a boy's solemnity. 'But they think you will help them. Will you, Maman?'

The train's whistle drifted from the other side of the valley. Taking his reluctant hand – a hand that liberated itself from her own with a fierce jerk – she marched him back to the farmhouse.

'I help everyone,' she said. 'Now I need you to help me.'

Nib into inkwell. With a scratch and flourish, she wrote *Catherine Antoinette Bourchier*. The shipping clerk took up the paper, examined her signature through half-moon spectacles and blotted it. Behind him, thirteen hundred wooden crates branded with the name *Royaume Céleste, Napa* filled half the warehouse. Catherine almost hugged the clerk, then wiped her eyes with a lacy handkerchief. She gripped Jean-Pierre's arm tightly while Emile watched from the doorway. The old steward nodded. 'Monsieur Bourchier would be pleased with this wine,' he declared.

'Would he, Jean-Pierre?'

'I believe so.'

'Would he be proud of me?'

Maybe Jean-Pierre did not hear the yearning in her voice. He sniffed, considered. Outside the warehouse, groups of people strolled towards the Gymkhana at the edge of town, parasols and hats angled against the sun. She waited, her grip still tight on his arm.

'Monsieur Bourchier always approved of good wine,' he said, finally.

'You have not answered my question!'

For a moment he seemed about to speak directly, just a moment. Then he shrugged and said, 'You are the son denied to him by God.' With that, the faithful steward patted a case of Royaume Céleste claret three times for luck and stepped outside to fill his pipe.

An hour later, they strolled through a crowded meadow outside Napa City. At the centre of the field, a racecourse had been marked out by rope fences. Ponies and thoroughbreds were competing, cheered on by farmers and townsfolk. In the centre of the course a special ladies' event was underway, involving low jumps and sharp turns around barrels. Catherine watched Lydia Smithson-Mackay complete the challenges in a graceful canter, displaying both fine horsemanship and a neat bust.

The Bourchiers approached an enclosure shaded by red and white awnings where Napa's 'chivalry' circulated. For all the modesty of her estate, Catherine felt no hesitation in entering the roped off enclosure. Roars filled the field as a dozen stallions galloped past, kicking up clods. Jean-Pierre wandered off to seek his own amusement at the betting and wine stalls.

Plump matrons chaperoned prim daughters in the great game of catching a rich, respectable husband, a game Catherine had lost beyond retrieval. What was a husband anyway? One joined the world alone and rejoined the earth alone. She had proved that a woman could establish herself in a man's world. In any case, what man would want her with a boy in tow and bigamy all too real. Unless that man was after her money . . . Her reflections were cut short by the approach of Lydia Smithson-Mackay in her tight-waisted, elegant riding dress, accompanied by three other ladies. The stately blonde seemed inclined to snub Catherine by strolling past; at the last moment she frowned lazily.

'My! And I was told the stewards were being *very* particular about who they let in today.'

The other ladies adjusted their parasols and scanned every inch of Catherine's attire. Though her dress was elegant, it was hardy and practical, as befitted someone who had just supervised the transportation of sixteen thousand wine bottles.

'My husband tells me you've sold all your wine to a Chinaman,' sniffed one of Lydia's companions. 'Are honest Americans not good enough for you?'

'I am more than willing to sell my wine to Americans,' replied Catherine, 'if they wish to buy.'

Lydia Smithson-Mackay hid a lady-like yawn behind a gloved hand. 'I wouldn't mention your husband if I were you,' she advised her friend, 'Madame Bourchier likes husbands. Or should I say *Le Comtesse*.'

Though her expression was dreamy, even distracted, Lydia Smithson-Mackay's blue eyes never left Catherine's blushing face.

So the Colonel was spreading a slander that she had tried to seduce him, in case the truth came out. More disturbing was a title unheard for years: *Comtesse*. Perhaps Lydia had merely overheard Baron Foche address her that way in the Opera. Perhaps it meant nothing. She must not lose her nerve.

'Good luck in the competition,' she said. 'Come Emile! Let us look at those lovely horses.'

'Maman,' he muttered as they walked away, 'those ladies do not like us, do they?'

'Me,' she corrected, in a tight voice, 'they do not like me.'

She found Jean-Pierre drinking brandy with a crowd of men she recognised as grape growers. He was holding forth in comical English. Among the circle of listeners were Parker and Temple.

'Hey, Frenchie!' Parker called out to Jean-Pierre. 'I was out hunting the other day and I'm damn sure I saw some redskins up at your spread.'

Jean-Pierre looked puzzled. 'Redskins?'

'Indians. Diggers. Get me?'

'Ah! Of course. Why not? They work 'ard. And very cheap!'

Catherine felt Emile's tug on her arm. 'Maman,' he whispered in French. 'Jean-Pierre should not tell them! The Wappo told me it is not safe.'

She glanced down at her son's brown eyes. A jolt of recognition struck her. Those eyes reminded her of Papa Bourchier, not Antoine. Her lower lip jutted.

'Jean-Pierre! We must go now!' she called in the obscure dialect of Languedoc.

'I am happy with my new friends,' he replied in the same language. 'I shall join you later, Madame.'

'Please. They are bad men. I will explain later.'

'Oh la la!' he cried, as though at the endless demands of women. But he was cut short by Mr Parker.

'Why, Mrs Bourchier, I hear some damn redskins are camped on your land. That's a matter of abidin' int'rest to Mr Temple and myself.'

'There are Indians on my land,' she said, aware Emile was watching. 'All are in my employ. They shall stay on my land, gentlemen, until I give them notice to leave. Jean-Pierre!'

Squinting suspiciously at Parker and Temple, the lumbering steward followed. They picked a way through the crowd, in the direction of Napa Station. Yet it seemed her discomforts were to have no end, despite the triumph of gaining financial security by shipping the wine. In the distance she recognised Baron Foche's absurdly tall stovepipe hat beside Colonel Smithson-Mackay and his fair lady. All three seemed to be staring in her direction.

Napa Valley, California
Summer 1878

Two drowsy summer days passed. Days where Catherine withdrew into fears over the presence of Baron Foche in Napa.

Chi-en was the first to rise that morning. He hummed a wistful aria from the San Francisco Opera as he mixed pancake batter. Only when the thud of iron-shod hooves grew loud did he drop the long wooden spoon and hurry outside.

Seven men were riding into Royaume Céleste, their horses' nostrils flaring from a hard canter. The riders wore civilian clothing except for Mr Temple, who sported his stained Confederate States Army kepi at a jaunty angle. All were armed with pistols or shotguns.

Chi-en instinctively glanced at the woods above Royaume Céleste. A single plume of smoke betrayed the Wappo encampment. The purposeful way the riders ignored the farmhouse, fanning out into the vines, revealed they already knew the location of their quarry.

As the riders passed, one reined his magnificent stallion. The beast reared slightly, dancing on its hind legs. Chi-en recognised the exhilarated face of Colonel Smithson-Mackay.

'Tell Madame Bourchier we're mighty obliged for her permission to collect our friends from her land,' he said. 'I've got a dozen witnesses who heard her say it at the Napa Jockey Club.' With a *gee-aah!* the Colonel spurred after his comrades.

Chi-en hesitated. Should he fetch Jean-Pierre's shotgun? Let off a warning shot? But it was the steward's habit to hunt rabbits and pheasants around this time of day: no one would notice a few shots. Besides, he dared not. Once men like Parker and Temple started shooting it was unlikely to be in the air. His gaze took in Trubody Nook on the far side of the valley, its white walls and towers.

'Chi-en! What is happening? Tell me!'

Catherine emerged onto the porch, still hooking her blouse. Behind came Emile and Jean-Pierre, the latter in flannel underwear. They stared up the sloping vines where a dismounted man was picketing the horses while his comrades entered the woods.

'We must warn them!' cried Catherine. 'Jean-Pierre, what are we to do?'

One person knew. Emile sprinted from the house, raising spurts of dirt.

'Come back!' screeched Catherine.

He did not listen. Soon his small shape was lost amidst foliage. For a moment Chi-en considered chasing after him but knew it would be pointless.

'Madame,' he said, 'gallop over to your friend, Mr Trubody. Fetch him here!' Then he remembered he was Chinese. 'No,' he said, 'instead, dress respectably – you also, Monsieur Jean-Pierre – and walk in a dignified way to the man waiting with the horses. They are less likely to harm you. I will ride to Mr Trubody and tell him what is happening.'

She raised a clenched knuckle to her mouth. 'I must go after Emile!'

'No, Madame. Join the man on guard and wait for Emile to show himself. It is the best you can do.'

Precious minutes were wasted persuading her. But saddling the old mare with Jean-Pierre's assistance took little time. All the while, smoke from the Wappo encampment rose. The woods maintained their leafy summer silence. By now the Indian-takers would be well advanced up the hill.

Chi-en pulled himself into the saddle and almost slipped over the other side. It was a long time since he had ridden. An unbidden image gave him confidence: of young men laughing wildly as they galloped along the wide boulevards of the lost Heavenly Capital, hair streaming behind them . . . With a harsh heel and hand, he urged the old mare into motion and they cantered down the hillside towards the valley bottom. Then he was crossing flat, open country.

At last, he reined up outside the stately front porch of Trubody Nook and called for help. Servants appeared, holding the horse's bridle as he jumped down.

'I must see Mr Trubody,' he gasped, as winded and dust-smeared as Jeanne d'Arc. 'A child's life depends on it!'

Chi-en was led to a splendid morning room where three gentlemen sat at a breakfast of eggs, coffee, hot and cold meats and fresh breads. Later he would learn their names: Mr Trubody, who he recognised, his friend Senator Collis, as well as Judge Dawson of the California Supreme Court. For now, he saw three men in late middle age, bewhiskered and respectably attired.

'Mr Trubody!' he cried, before calming himself and speaking in his most refined English accent. 'Forgive this intrusion! You may rest assured only the gravest of circumstances would warrant it!'

They stared in amazement at the dust-covered Chinaman speaking like an English milord.

'This some kind of prank?' asked Judge Dawson.

'Please,' urged Chi-en less grandly. 'Hear me out!'

After he had explained the situation in Royaume Céleste, silence settled on the breakfast table.

'It sounds very regrettable,' said Senator Collis. 'Anyone who follows my speeches and letters in the press will know I have long been a proponent of milder treatment for our native breeds. Assuming they abandon their Godless, savage ways, of course. But I don't see how we might help. Between you and me, your mistress will be better off without a pack of redskins on her land.'

Mr Trubody shot him an irritated look.

'Gentlemen,' said Chi-en, 'I merely ask that you help Madame Bourchier protect her rights under the law.'

Now Judge Dawson seemed more interested, especially when Chi-en mentioned the statute ensuring indentured Indians could not be forcibly removed to government reservations.

'Hear him, Collis!' said Judge Dawson. 'A subtle point. Our oriental friend has the right of the law.'

Mr Trubody pushed back his chair. 'So that Jonny Reb rogue, Smithson-Mackay, is setting himself against the law?'

'Might be seen that way,' conceded Judge Dawson. 'Civil rather than felony.'

'There is another matter,' said Chi-en. 'Madame Bourchier's son – I believe you entertained the child recently, Mr Trubody, in San Francisco – has put himself in grave danger to defend the Indians. I fear a tragedy will occur.'

Now Trubody rose to his full height. 'That settles it,' he said. 'I'm going right over there with some of my men to see what's happening. There is, I believe, a sacred Constitution in this Republic. And no damnable Dixie rebel is going to trample it!'

Such a declaration left Senator Collis and Judge Dawson, both vocal advocates of the Constitution, little choice but to accompany their host.

The saddling of horses took an absurdly long time. At least, for Chi-en. In truth, every available servant was put to the task and only ten minutes elapsed. Throughout, Chi-en stood beside Jeanne d'Arc, monitoring the distant buildings of Royaume Céleste. Nancy Trubody pleaded with her husband to let her join the rescue party but his refusal was too curt to allow a second attempt. Finally, eight mounted men gathered. None carried firearms at Judge Dawson's insistence.

'I don't fancy a gun fight,' he said, dryly. 'I rather fancy we'd come off badly.'

So the posse galloped out of Trubody Nook, retracing Chi-en's route across the valley bottom. As they rode, distant gunshots startled them. They paused to decide whether men should be sent back for rifles. Perhaps they would have done just that, had not Chi-en urged them to follow Judge Dawson's earlier advice.

'With respect,' he said, 'Parker and Temple are former military men. One may fight them with words more powerfully than swords.'

Senator Collis seemed inclined to disagree until Judge Dawson declared, 'Hear him, Collis! Our celestial friend has the right side of licking this kind of ruffian!'

Nevertheless, it was a surly, anxious group of balding men and their followers who galloped out of the trees and up to the farmhouse of Royaume Céleste. It became clear they had arrived just in time.

Over twenty Wappo stood miserably in front of the porch, hands tied by ropes. Some of the younger, stronger men wore iron manacles, relics from pre-Civil War days. Catherine was trying to drag Emile away from a crumpled body in the dust. Crimson patches from gaping shotgun wounds spread across the baked earth. Chi-en, who had seen too many of such injuries in his youth, realised the dead man had been shot at close range. The face stared blindly upward and belonged to the young Chief, the matriarch's grandson. A rope was tied round his chest and, given the dirt and dead leaves on his body, he had been dragged through the vineyard to the house behind a horse.

The armed men sat on their mounts round the herded Wappo, no doubt calculating the bounty if all twenty-two savages could be got to the Mendocino Reservation alive. At twenty-five dollars a head, five hundred and fifty dollars, minus transportation expenses. A tidy recompense, though the Indian Agent would make much more, especially from the children. Mr Parker was grumbling about this injustice as the Trubody party arrived, their horses snorting.

Heads turned. For long seconds both sides assessed each other. Smithson-Mackay's cheeks were red with excitement as he drank deeply from a hip flask. Parker and Temple remained expressionless.

'Morning, Trubody,' called the Colonel. 'Out for an early ride? I see from your friends you don't want to risk getting lonesome.'

His eyes flicked towards Parker and Temple for appreciation of the joke. Neither showed the slightest amusement.

'What do you mean by this outrage?' spluttered Trubody. 'A dead man lying here! Do you mean to just leave him in the dust?'

A faint smile touched Mr Temple's lips. It soon vanished and he murmured gently into his restless horse's ear.

'Damn digger took a shot at us,' said Smithson-Mackay. 'Self-defence, Trubody! I've half-a-dozen witnesses to prove it.'

'You shot him, sir?' asked Judge Dawson, his bushy grey eyebrows bunching. 'Where's the gun he used?'

'I didn't pull the trigger,' said Smithson-Mackay. 'Can't say I saw who did. I'm only along for the ride. But, say, are you holding a trial, Judge? Where's your jurisdiction in this matter?'

'Be careful,' warned Dawson, 'I see a man shot to death. That gives me more jurisdiction than you can imagine.'

'Maybe,' said Smithson-Mackay. 'But as these redskins here can't testify in a court of law, I guess the whole matter is exactly as I call it.'

Judge Dawson exchanged looks with Trubody and Collis. 'God forgive us,' he muttered. 'Or teach us better ways. The fellow's pretty much in the right.'

'So I guess we'll just be getting on our way,' said Colonel Smithson-Mackay. 'Mr Parker! Mr Temple! If you could prevail on those savages I'd sure be grateful.'

Several of the Indian-takers whooped with delight.

Mr Trubody had climbed from his horse and was trying to persuade Catherine and Emile to return to the farmhouse. Now he glanced up at Smithson-Mackay.

'I'll pray to the Good Lord you come to regret this,' he said, 'but slaughtering an innocent man is nothing new to you. Not if what they say about your bushwhacking in the war holds true. We fought your kind for four long years so there would be no slaves in this Republic. Today it feels we fought in vain.' He glanced bitterly at the huddled Wappo, many of whom moaned or sobbed.

Senator Collis looked away. Judge Dawson pursed his lips.

Now was the time! Chi-en could not believe they had forgotten his words concerning the law. Dismounting, he strode over to the group of Wappo and called out to Mr Trubody.

'Sir!' he cried. 'Wait! The law of your Republic does not allow the Colonel to drive off these people. They are not ownerless cattle. Let me remind you . . .'

Then Chi-en stated the exact statutes and terms learned from his precious law books while Smithson-Mackay peered down at him in astonishment.

'So, you see,' he concluded, 'until their indenture expires, only Madame Bourchier may release these Indians from her service.'

'Sweet Lawd!' declared the Colonel. 'Now I have seen it all! A

Mongolian Chinee law-wrangler! Seems you've got competition, Dawson.'

Judge Dawson's pursed mouth resolved into a thin, inflexible line. 'Slow down, Mister,' he said. 'I believe we should ask the lady's opinion. Ma-am,' he said, solemnly, 'do you freely, and without constraint, release these Indians from your indenture and into Colonel Smithson-Mackay's, hmm, legal protection?'

Catherine paused at the door of the house, her body stiff. She stared through red-rimmed eyes at Smithson-Mackay. 'I would sooner hand them to the devil.'

If the Colonel was offended, he gave no sign.

'Well then,' continued Judge Dawson, 'I suggest you men throw down those ropes fixed to them squaws and braves. There's been a mighty big mistake about Mrs Bourchier's intentions concerning her indentured field hands.'

'God damn you!' cried Colonel Smithson-Mackay, his horse starting.

'That's the law you're damning and cussing!' intoned Judge Dawson. 'And woe betide anything happens to these Indians or Mrs Bourchier or her property as a result!'

It seemed Colonel Smithson-Mackay would ignore the judge. His hand rested on the butt of his revolver. Around him, men's grips tightened on weapons. There were two sharp clicks as Mr Temple's shotgun cocked.

'Remember we're unarmed!' cried Senator Collis.

'You can't shoot us all, Smithson-Mackay,' pointed out the Judge, coolly. 'Even if these Indians are forbidden to stand witness in court, we sure as hell can.'

The Colonel's hand lifted from the revolver. His eyes narrowed. He nodded.

'As you say . . . *Judge*. But you'll hear of this scandal in the pages of the

California Star! And you shall hear of it when the next election arises! Long and hard, sir! As for you . . .' He glared down at Chi-en. 'I'm not sure I like me a Mongol lawman. Not sure I like me a Chinee lawman. And neither do these gentlemen here!'

One by one, the armed riders threw down the ropes attached to the Wappo's bindings and trotted away, led by the blank-faced Parker and Temple, who never ceased looking this way and that as though impressing upon their memories the faces, layout, entrances, exits and combustibles of Royaume Céleste.

Mr Trubody suggested two of his burliest men stay for a day or two in case Parker and Temple returned. The Bourchiers did indeed face a fresh assault late in the afternoon: Nancy Trubody rattled up the track in a gig driven across the valley by herself. The drama of the occasion required such a heroic — and unladylike — response. Mr Trubody rode alongside, trying to look as though he approved. She came armed with baskets of food, bandages and other needful supplies, not least an arsenal of goodwill.

Chi-en watched her disappear into the farmhouse with her husband and went over to inspect the Wappo. It had been agreed they could camp beside the barn that night as a precautionary measure. The young chief lay wrapped in an old horse blanket, awaiting removal to their ancient spirit ground for cremation. Chi-en's nose wrinkled as he approached the corpse: flies rose in clouds then settled again. The silence of the mourners was unnerving. Even the Old Mother, normally voluble, stared mutely at the bundle of her grandson.

Chi-en was about to return to his kitchen when he noticed a hunched figure among the restless children ordered to sit in gloomy, dignified silence. Emile's forehead was pinched with concentration.

'*Mon petit brave*,' said Chi-en, softly in his ear, 'come and speak with me. There is something I must explain.'

Reluctantly, Emile rose and followed the Chinaman back to the kitchen. Ten minutes later, the door swung open with a bang and the boy emerged, his eyes full of tears.

'You are a coward!' he cried, in a Boston accent Chi-en had taught him. The boy rushed off to his room, wiping furiously at his eyes with a sleeve.

By the time darkness settled over Royaume Céleste, the Wappo had built a large fire and were dancing a slow circular shuffle to the beat of a woodblock drum and bone flute. The two men assigned by Trubody were already deep into their second jug of Royaume Céleste claret. Chi-en could only hope Parker and Temple returned before Catherine's protectors toppled over.

Little time was needed to pack the old carpetbag: his smart suit, changes of linen, writing materials. For a while he hesitated over *A Memoir of Prince Hong*. The bulky, closely written notebook was dense with more than words, too precious to risk losing on his journey. So Chi-en took up a second valise purchased in San Francisco and filled it with the remainder of his possessions – a small enough pile – before adding the *Memoir* for safekeeping at Royaume Céleste while he travelled. Chi-en Shambles had reached the end of Prince Hong's memoir. That debt, so long owed and contemplated and mourned, was paid.

Catherine sat on the edge of Emile's bed. He lay beneath woollen blankets in a white cotton nightshirt, the top half of his face poking out. Rare tears wetted the edge of his blanket.

It seemed a long time since she had occupied this position, a hand smoothing her son's forehead. When he was very small, she had told him stories to help him sleep, enjoying the warmth of his breath and sweet childish smell, his little body against her own. Fairy tales and folktales of Languedoc learned from her nurse as a girl; sometimes stories of the Bourchier family's history and exploits. Those spells of time before his exhausted eyelids fluttered then closed had been when she felt nearest to him.

But after they left France, Emile would hear no more of her stories. Acknowledging it stirred a many-layered grief.

'Tell Chi-en he is not allowed to go!' he commanded, his voice muffled by the covers. 'Not after what the bad men did!'

'I am certain that Chi-en is wise to leave us for a while,' she said. 'Those wicked men will want to punish someone. Remember, Chi-en is Chinese. Though they may fear the consequences of troubling us again, especially after Judge Dawson's warning, they will feel no hesitations about him.'

Emile peered miserably over the edge of the blanket. 'He is a coward to run away! I told him so!'

'Then you should apologise. The only reason your Wappo friends were not taken is his courage. And your own, Emile, I am very proud of my brave boy. But you must never, ever take such risks again. Will you promise me that?'

He turned to face the wall, yet more tears forming. She tutted and stroked his hair, afraid that the image of the young chief's wounds as he lay in the dust would haunt Emile, bringing bad dreams to many, many nights.

'I'm sure the young man they killed is in heaven,' she said.

'Are you sure?'

'Oh yes. He'll be with his Wappo ancestors and the angels, all together, all happy! Fishing and shooting arrows at elk. Singing and dancing.'

A sob escaped from him, one he fought hard to suppress. She stroked his soft, curly hair as she used to do and tears found her own eyes. 'I'll tell a story to help you sleep,' she said, with false brightness. 'Shall Maman do that?'

His face pressed against the pillow and she took it for assent. But what story? What story for such an occasion? For no logical reason she thought of Bluebeard and his locked, secret chamber full of murdered wives. In a quiet voice she explained his new, young bride's greed for Bluebeard's wealth and how she married him for money and her burning curiosity to open the forbidden chamber. All the while, Emile scarcely moved but she could tell he was listening. Then she told how Bluebeard found blood on the magic key he had lent his bride. 'And he shouted, "Oh, I shall cut off your head, for you are wicked and ungrateful!" And Bluebeard raised his long, curved sword over her head to sweep it off. "Help me," she cried, "or am I all alone?" Three times she cried, "Help me!" Then, just when she had lost all hope, two men galloped up to Bluebeard's château. "Help me!" cried the foolish bride yet again. And do you know what,' said Catherine, 'those two gallant men heard her. They were the silly girl's brother and his brave friend. They drew their swords and a terrible fight commenced, up and down the stairs, along battlements and corridors. At last, when both of the brave men were wounded, they struck off Bluebeard's head and that was the end of him! Good riddance, too.'

She paused, stirred by her own story. Emile lay quite still, snoring gently. 'And do you know,' she whispered, 'the foolish bride's saviours were really her father's old servant and a poor Chinaman.' Emile murmured in his sleep then relaxed. The distant bark of a coyote drifted through the open window from the mountains above Royaume Céleste. Somewhere in the darkness an owl hooted. 'And do you know,' she whispered, hoping it might come true despite all likelihood, 'they lived happily in Bluebeard's château without a care in the world, for ever and ever.'

A noise at the kitchen door made Chi-en look up. Catherine was watching, her arms folded.

'You appear to be leaving us,' she said. 'At least, Emile thinks so.'

Chi-en carried on adjusting the strap of his carpetbag. It was stubborn and would not fasten. 'I have no choice. The gallant Colonel was hardly subtle in his threats. I fear Emile believes I am running away. He feels betrayed.'

'Is that so surprising?'

'Perhaps not.'

'You became, dare I say it, a kind of father to one who has none.'

He looked up. 'It troubles me to leave suddenly. He is a fine boy who shows the promise of a finer man. But I have no choice – not just because I am afraid, though that is true. There is someone I must find. Someone important to me.'

He tugged at the strap, buckling it finally. When he looked up, she was still watching, her eyes softened by lamplight.

'It might be sensible to walk around Royaume Céleste tonight,' she said. 'Will you join me?'

They left the buildings and went among shadowy vines. The mournful voices of the Wappo's drum and flute crept through the night air. An azure sky spun nets of constellations round a delicate quarter-moon. Cicadas sang. Their boots crunched gritty, clumpy earth.

'You were brave today,' she said 'And resourceful. I wish to thank you.'

He grimaced. 'Let us not talk of it.'

'Perhaps I embarrass you?'

'No, it is not that.'

'Then what is it, Chi-en? I find you hard to anticipate. I ask myself why and the answer is simple: I know so little about you.'

He met her eye, glanced aside. 'Maybe you would not like what you learned,' he said, 'I have not always been brave and resourceful.'

'You are too harsh on yourself!'

'I fear you cannot understand,' he said, stiffly, 'what it is to betray someone in their most helpless hour. Someone who is utterly reliant upon you. No, I believe you can never understand. It is a burden I must carry alone.'

They walked side by side in the darkness. Chi-en found himself longing to reach out for her warmth. How easy it would be to touch her arm and put his own round her waist. Easy to find her soft face with his lips.

'Madame,' he began. The cold title seemed a secure toehold. 'Madame, while I am gone, will you . . . No, it is more than that . . . I wish to tell you, since you trusted me with the story of your errant husband . . . I wish to explain, though it is no easy thing to say, about the former master I hope to find. And who I hope he will lead me to.'

A passing cloud obscured the slender moon, dimming gaps between the vines. They halted in the darkness and she listened carefully. In his agitation, he did not notice how she drew close. Finally, he fell silent and was surprised by the flash of her white eyes near his own. Then the cloud that had obscured the moon blew on, its soft light resuming. Both recollected themselves. Chi-en was the first to step back.

'You see,' he said, 'tomorrow I must set out on my journey. It is one I can no longer avoid. It might tell me who I am. Where and how I began.'

Was she disappointed in him? Her face showed no sign. Yet there was a catch in her voice when she asked, 'Will you return soon?'

'I do not know. I will leave the remainder of my possessions here, if I may, until that time.'

'When will that be?'

'I do not know, Madame. How can I?'

He waited for her to speak.

'Do not call me that!' she exclaimed, with sudden passion. 'Not after what happened today!'

'Call you what?'

'*Madame*. Do not call me that ever again! It is no longer necessary between us.'

'What am I to call you?'

'Catherine,' she said, 'as I call you by your name. Come back from finding who you are, Chi-en. We will be here, Emile and I. We have nowhere else to go. Perhaps, at the end of your journey, you will find the same thing.'

She left him in the vines and returned to the house. Chi-en reached out, brushing a cluster of grapes. They were hard, unripe. He almost called out after her, *I will return in time for the harvest, Catherine*. Somehow, he dared not use that intimate name. For her sake. Most of all, his own.

Chapter the Seventh: *Alpha and Omega*

I

Now this humble memoir must reach its sad end.

When Prince Hong ordered me to pack his finest clothes, I naturally prepared a modest valise of my own. For the last eleven years, since I was twelve, we had barely spent a day apart. Was I not his interpreter, confidant, valet, friend, personal chef — and a hundred other roles? Yet as I informed him of our readiness to leave for the station, he seemed surprised.

'*We*, my dear Chi-en,' he tried to drawl in English (I say *tried* because everything he said in that tongue came out slightly wrong). I suspected his new acquaintance, Lord Cadogan, lay behind this affectation. Fortunately, he shifted back to Mandarin. 'This time I will travel alone. No need to look astonished! My noble friend Lord Cadogan has promised me the use of his own valet.'

'Why do you not want me?' I blurted.

He rose and paced restlessly. 'Most men have one shadow, I have two. You with your perpetual cleverness and Tutor Ren Xudong with his endless disappointment in me.'

'Where are you going?' I asked.

'To see factories and iron works in the north. Really there is no call for such a long face.'

Prince Hong explained that he had revealed to Lord Cadogan – after several 'stiff whisky and sodas', his phrase not mine, and one entirely new to him – his longheld plan to arm a legion of Chinese patriots with the latest British rifles so they might spark a general uprising against the Manchu. To his surprise, Lord Cadogan had immediately expressed enthusiasm for such a coup, the first European of influence to entertain the slightest sympathy for our cause.

'When I described how the Righteous Kingdom would end the injustices and abuses in China, Lord Cadogan declared himself *the very chap for that* and offered to help in any way possible.' That was why he arranged for Prince Hong to accompany him when he visited his uncle, a great landowner and manufacturer of armaments, who resided near Newcastle. 'So, you see, Chi-en,' said Prince Hong, 'I am in very safe hands and you must not worry about a thing.'

I need hardly describe my feelings as I watched his train depart. I lingered on the platform until it passed out of sight. For the next few days, I could not concentrate on my studies. Contradictory emotions raged within me. Anger that he had discarded me so casually – it seemed a dreadful punishment for faults I had never committed. Then a strange relief to be away from him. I had been dependent on Prince Hong half my life. The merest sign of his approval lifted my mood. By the same logic, his disapproval made me anxious and eager for praise.

Those days of waiting were grey and long. I reproached myself constantly for bitterness against him while stoking it continuously. Between extra prayers at his homemade altar, Tutor Ren Xudong stared listlessly at the wall.

When Prince Hong returned to London, he was pale, tense, and again smelled of alcohol. He went straight to bed and did not emerge until the next morning. Over breakfast he told me with forced casualness: 'A most successful trip, Chi-en. I ordered a thousand rifles. Very successful.'

My astonishment must have been evident for he slurped his tea angrily.

'Who is to carry these rifles?' I asked. 'Who will load and fire them?'

At this, Prince Hong's bluff manner melted into uneasiness: '*My dear friend Cadogan* (he always used this badly pronounced English phrase when referring to his *dear friend*) says I can hardly expect recruits without weapons to give them.'

There were so many arguments against such a position I did not deign to utter them.

'Were the rifles expensive?' I asked.

When Prince Hong named the sum, I gasped. The price was four times that of other manufacturers we had canvassed in the early days of our stay in Europe.

'Is it too late to cancel the order?' I asked, anxiously.

Prince Hong rose and began to pace. 'I will not lose face before *my dear friend Cadogan*,' he said. 'Besides, his uncle explained how payment is made in advance in such cases and I signed a banker's draft.'

Not long afterwards, Lord Cadogan visited our apartment with a few young men oddly like himself – raffish, moustachioed, well-tailored and with loud, barking voices. All smelled of tobacco and strong spirits. All grunted in a manly way when Lord Cadogan announced they were 'game' in the matter of helping out 'those wretched Chinese'. I felt sure ironic glances passed between them when Prince Hong wasn't looking.

My master evidently considered his visitors wonderful fellows. Flushed and excited, he left with them for a gentleman's club where they wished to have further discussions about 'settling Johnny Manchu once and for all'.

He arrived home in the early hours to find me waiting up for him.

Once more he was drunk. As I helped him undress, I noticed his purse was empty except for a single roulette chip.

The next morning Prince Hong did not appear for breakfast and Tutor Ren Xudong took me to one side. 'Those Englishmen are not to be trusted, are they, Chi-en?'

'I fear not,' I replied. 'I fear not.'

II

I defy anyone to say it was not natural for me to feel jealous. Weeks of late nights followed, engagements at gentleman's clubs where cards, roulette, spirits, tobacco and brittle good cheer contended for mastery. Of course, my friend and master was flattered to have gained his new companions. He had been slighted by men of position for years, his dream of saving China restricted to two servants.

One thing was certain: excessive drinking did not agree with the balance of Prince Hong's constitution. Mornings found him pale, peevish, afflicted by sudden bouts of perspiration and shivering. Neither did it agree with the balance of his bank account. I grew alarmed by how often Prince Hong sent me to draw fresh funds. His new friends requested loans he thought it would be dishonourable and mean-spirited to refuse. This was money intended to finance a government free of corruption in our homeland, not pay for debauches.

When I tentatively mentioned my worries, the savagery of Prince Hong's response took me by surprise. He had always been so calm, controlled. Perhaps he was especially delicate that morning, I do not know. Even now I remember the insults he cast at me: 'Who is the master here!' he roared, shaking with passion. 'My dear friend Cadogan warned me I was too ruled by old Ren Xudong. It seems *you*, a mere servant, must be added to the list! How dare *you*, a bastard child, question *me*?' There was more. Finally came a threat to dismiss me from his service.

The following hour was among the lowest I have known. Something profound changed in me during that short time: one might even call it the end of innocence.

Of course, the greatness of my master's spirit soon reasserted itself. I heard a cautious tap on my door and found him there, pale and shaking despite his thick dressing gown.

'*My dear fr . . .*' he began in English before turning to Mandarin. 'Good Chi-en. My old friend. Forgive my outburst. You see, I am not well. These London fogs! I can see no further than my nose! And so much is at stake right now. We are close to our goal!'

I took his hand. It was unnaturally hot. 'Prince, you must get away from London and its fogs! Let us take the train to Hastings.'

I should explain Hastings was a favourite resort of my master's. He loved to breathe the sea air there each summer and would often pace on the high cliffs with his telescope, staring out to sea as though for a glimpse of our lost homeland.

'It shall be so,' he said, heavily. 'I am strangely tired. In spirit as much as body. Yes, Hastings might revive me.'

I believe it was the last time he allowed himself to be influenced by me. Until, that is, a friend's influence was past repairing the damage he had done.

Still, a day later we found ourselves on the shingle beach of Hastings. It was late August and already I detected autumn in the softening sky. Feeble waves lapped on the beach, for the tide was turning. Gulls shrieked and dipped as fishing boats returned.

Back at the hotel, I was amazed to find a letter from Lord Cadogan. The fact he had tracked Prince Hong there should have taught us the truth. Written in a careless scrawl — everything he did *appeared* careless — he invited Prince Hong to a *conspirators' supper* when back in town, for he had *important developments* to share concerning *your plan to put a decent fellow on the throne of China for a change.* Prince Hong clapped his hands with pleasure at so bluff and manly a tone. We returned to London the next day by an early morning train.

It was indeed a conspirator's supper that Lord Cadogan organised. I accompanied Prince Hong to the restaurant where he met his wine-flushed and effortlessly confident host. He was seven years older than my master, the youngest son of an aristocratic family with a long tradition of horse racing. Prince Hong once called him 'the brother I should have had', a statement that troubled me deeply.

It was a fashionable restaurant and, as a servant, I was not welcome beyond the lobby, but I had time to witness Lord Cadogan leading Prince Hong to a private dining salon where a dozen of his cronies were already at champagne and oysters. All wished to join the 'Righteous Legion' and save the Chinese from themselves as only foreigners know how. Prince Hong insisted on paying the restaurant's substantial bill when the company dispersed at midnight.

He returned to our apartment drunk. I listened as he related the plan that had been settled over cheese. First, raise a legion of British volunteers. Many were sure to be ex-military. Better still, Lord Cadogan was assured thousands would wish to serve the noble cause of patriotism and Christianity in China. 'We'll have the pick of 'em!' repeated Prince Hong, chuckling as he used Lord Cadogan's phrase. While we talked, Tutor Ren Xudong entered the room in plain silk robes and listened. His presence emboldened me.

'What connection with China do these *patriots* have?' I enquired.

None, it seemed, except for Lord Cadogan, who had served as a junior officer in Shanghai.

'With Butcher Gordon?' I asked, shrilly. 'The man whose steamships killed so many at Quin-san! Have you forgotten? For all we know, Lord Cadogan was on one of those boats!'

Prince Hong examined me unsteadily. Perhaps, after so much wine, he saw two of me.

'Why do these strangers wish to risk their lives for us?' I pressed, exasperated beyond caution. 'Look at the history of the British in China – opium, war, looting, every kind of greed and cruelty. Why are these young men different? And how will their imaginary legion even get to China? Will it fly?'

'Ah!' replied Prince Hong, triumphantly. 'You don't understand, Chi-en! My dear friend Cadogan has offered to personally meet all the expenses of transportation.'

This set me back a little. But I was furious enough to press my point.

'Will the people really rise just because a thousand *fan gui* (I must confess I used that term) wade ashore with British rifles?'

Again, Prince Hong laughed. 'I can't fault your questions, Chi-en! The Righteous Legion will act as elite troops during the initial landing. After that, they shall train native Chinese to fight like modern soldiers. We shall be invincible!'

Finally, I asked the question that burned in my mind. 'How much money do they want to organise this Righteous Legion?'

Now Prince Hong wagged his finger reprovingly. 'It is not about money! We need articles in the press, advertisements, hand bills. Equipment for our men. Setting free a whole nation costs money. Besides, my dear friend Cadogan says that after the initial expenses we will be flooded with donations from the public. All shall be recouped within a month or so.'

I listened, horribly afraid for my friend and master. The sum he mentioned would drain the last of the Taiping Heavenly Kingdom's treasury. It seemed like betting one's entire fortune on an unknown horse.

'Think, Chi-en!' said Prince Hong. 'By spring we will be back in China. We will land near Canton, gathering recruits as we march north just as my uncle did twenty years ago! Except, this time, we shall not fail.'

I begged him to wait at least a week before paying out so large a sum to Lord Cadogan's Committee of Righteous Chinese Patriots.

'They toasted me as the new Garibaldi!' said Prince Hong, blissfully. 'They called me the Chinese Garibaldi! Things are moving, Chi-en. Things are moving at last!'

The next morning Tutor Ren Xudong summoned Prince Hong to a full Taiping God Worshipping ceremony in our living room. Three bowls of tea were set out to refresh the Trinity: God, Elder Brother Jesus and his Younger Brother, the Heavenly King. Together we chanted, my dear friend sick from his hangover. During a lengthy sermon, Tutor Ren Xudong begged God to proffer guidance.

For a long while we knelt together, rain spattering against the window. Prince Hong looked up. I had rarely seen him so pale. He looked younger than his twenty-six years so that I felt like his older brother.

'God expects me to decide,' he mumbled. 'If I am to be the Righteous King, I must decide. I shall tell my dear friend Cadogan he shall have his answer in three days' time.'

III

Days of waiting. It was made clear to me Fourth Prince Hong did not require my advice. He wished to ponder the destiny of the Chinese nation alone. I, too, pondered. Except my thoughts rarely strayed to that faraway land, likewise my feelings, blinded by hurt. Guilt comes all too easily to a child of shame. Guilt that brought helpless anger then more guilt, spinning coins tossed into a well.

As I waited for Prince Hong to emerge from his bedchamber with a decision I could neither challenge nor debate, uncomfortable realisations took shape. I had no one to rely upon in this world. Family had been denied to me. A loyal, loving wife was inconceivable in my present situation. I was burdened with the constant itch of self-disgust all bastards endure. Aunty-Mother's loss meant the only person on earth who knew my sailor-father's identity was Reverend Ezekiel Shambles. This thought became an obsession. From it grew another obsession, one I dared only acknowledge in troubled dreams: that I should quit Prince Hong's company and seek my father's name.

With this in mind, I hurried to the British Museum reading room. Consulting volumes of American Baptist periodicals and newspapers from the United States and the *North China Herald* from 1862 onwards, I spent long hours looking for references to the Reverend E. Shambles. At last, I spotted a brief notice in the *Baptist Bugle* for 17th July 1864 (the very day the Heavenly Capital burned), celebrating the return of an American missionary with his wife and son to Boston. It read: *The well-known Reverend Shambles, formerly of Shanghai, Canton, Hong Kong etc, hopes by the grace of God to save sinners in his native land as he has in China.* This was the only mention of him I discovered, yet it sufficed. *Boston!* Feverish examination of the atlas fuelled my imagination. I pictured him in a clean, homely chapel with a single clear bell: wise, patient, kindly, ready to welcome his lost servant and share all he knew.

Time ran away with me and it was nearly ten in the evening when I returned to our hotel. I found Tutor Ren Xudong sitting before a cold grate, sorrow upon his tired, drawn old face.

'Where is the prince?' I asked.

Tutor Ren Xudong shook his head. 'Prince Hong has allowed his desires to shape reality,' he said. 'He has fallen prey to despair.'

'What has happened? Tell me!'

'While you were out, Lord Cadogan came here with a few of his friends. He implored Prince Hong to commence his righteous campaign at once.'

A few more questions revealed the truth. Lord Cadogan had shown Prince Hong a tawdry flag (I later discovered it was of a kind used for signalling between ships that a surgeon was required), claiming it was to be the standard of their Righteous Legion. Elated beyond caution, Prince Hong left with them to celebrate the founding of their Committee of Righteous Chinese Patriots.

When he returned, long after midnight, he was incoherent with drink and vomited beside his bed. I cleaned up the mess by candlelight while my friend lay insensible and snoring. My fear and humiliation can scarcely be expressed: for the last of the Taiping treasure was to be passed over to Lord Cadogan.

As I dabbed the stinking carpet with a wet towel, I almost decided to take ship to America the next morning. I would land in New York, find the Reverend Shambles and learn my lost father's identity. Of course, I did no such thing. Not then. But those ideas came to haunt me.

IV

The rest, I suppose, was inevitable. Only the speed of events might cause surprise. Lord Cadogan arranged matters so that he was not only President but Chairman and Treasurer of the 'Righteous Committee'. Within a month of us paying over the money to a special fund he became hard to locate. I picked up a rumour that, suddenly flush with cash, he had indulged in gambling of the most reckless kind. His London apartment acquired a new tenant and I learned from his former landlady the rent had long been in arrears. A single, small advertisement calling for volunteers to take up the cause of a just, free China appeared in the press. Hordes of volunteers failed to rush forward.

Committee meetings supposedly took place, but were so artfully arranged that we only got to attend one of them. By now it was October 1871. Prince Hong should have been confined to bed with a fever in his lungs but refused to heed the doctor's advice.

'I must hear what my dear friend Cadogan has achieved on our behalf,' he said. 'I expect the best of news.' Yet his voice was bleached, oddly lifeless. I believe the killing despair Tutor Ren Xudong had mentioned already lay in the roots of his soul.

I went along as a loyal helper. Prince Hong's main intention was to organise a viewing of the rifles, uniforms, boots, backpacks, hats, blankets, ammunition, bayonets and other military paraphernalia Lord Cadogan claimed were awaiting 'the cause' in a secret warehouse.

The Committee meeting was held in a room above a public house in Piccadilly. As soon as we arrived, I sensed trouble. Lord Cadagon, more red-faced than ever, looked defiantly nervous. Half a dozen of his cronies sat round the long table. I counted three toughs guarding the door and stairs.

Prince Hong, forehead shiny with sweat from his fever, tried to shake his *dear friend Cadogan*'s hand but was rebuffed. Instead, the Committee of Righteous Chinese Patriots' President, Chairman and Treasurer delivered a short, inelegant speech in which he proposed that the Committee vote to dissolve itself. Whereupon, his six friends (all of whom were drunk) banged the table to demonstrate their approval. All our funds were gone, he said; and the warehouse full of military supplies and weapons had been looted by unknown thieves. He went so far as blaming Prince Hong for inadvertently revealing this secret arsenal's whereabouts to Manchu agents. So absurd were his claims they do not deserve repetition. The way he avoided my master's eye revealed that even he was ashamed.

When the truth dawned on Prince Hong, he watched in his quiet way as Lord Cadogan blustered improbable replies to each of his courteous enquiries. Finally, the latter gentleman rose angrily, accompanied by his cronies, who were in high spirits. A hubbub ensued and the three toughs broke into the committee room ready for violence. Quite abruptly, Prince Hong's customary calm dissolved. Sick as he was, he bellowed accusations in nonsensical English so offensive to Lord Cadogan's honour that the latter took a swing. I leapt between them, taking a heavy blow to the shoulder. My one consolation was that I ground my fist into Lord Cadogan's nose before being dragged off. As soon as I broke free, we left in a hurry.

Naturally, I tried to interest the police. But there were no receipts, not even a written constitution we could use as evidence. Prince Hong's faith in *my dear Cadogan* meant the entire project had been based on honour.

In fairness to Scotland Yard, I believe they did interview Lord Cadogan in the comfort of his new, plush lodgings. Our whole complaint boiled down to one man's word against another; a Chinaman's against the youngest son of an aristocratic family. When I next saw the detective, he spoke gravely of slandering an honest gentleman and criminal proceedings against us for false accusations.

My studies in the law encouraged me to pay far too large a proportion of the money left in our account to a solicitor. He was honest enough to counsel against a lengthy civil action we would surely lose. It seemed that justice, like everything else in Britain, was a commodity to be bought and sold. And Prince Hong was no longer wealthy.

V

Oh, we learned how quickly a man can descend from a position of high regard. The ladder he travels down is measured, rung by rung, in gold and silver. Beyond a certain point respectability has gone. Only luck, talent or hard work push you back up.

Prince Hong had never known poverty in all his twenty-six years. Perhaps that is why he found it easy to deny that hardship might afflict his own comfort. After the disastrous committee meeting, we should have left our costly rooms in the Ambassador Hotel for cheap lodgings in the suburbs. By selling clothes and other personal effects we could have eaten well and stayed warm for years. No stranger to poverty in my early childhood, I urged such a move. As ever, Prince Hong did not listen. Any form of ordinariness was alien to his noble nature.

Soon we were selling valuables to pay large hotel and dining bills. My master's extravagant tips to flunkies filled me with dismay. By December, I was forced to pawn items of apparel. Even then, though I begged, he would not move to cheaper quarters. It was not through denial of reality – I am sure he understood our situation. No, it was despair. It is no exaggeration to say Lord Cadogan's betrayal was the final, fatal blow to his strength. He had been sickly, before. Now, days passed when he could not stir from his bed. The knowledge that he had squandered much of the Taiping treasure before he even met *my dear Cadogan* tormented him. Wealth meant to liberate China had financed the role of Eastern Prince in a comic opera of our own composition. I'm sure that's how he came to view himself, forgetting all his talents, all his gifts.

By February 1872, we had been evicted from our hotel and resided in an attic garret overlooking the London Docks. A small room, whitewashed with soot, ash, grease. A cracked window gave a view of wharves lined with the ocean-going steamships we had admired as boys, convinced that one day Prince Hong would command a navy.

Our tiny grate lacked even a candle flame – we had long run out of money for fuel or light. Ten days of snow driven by harsh winds turned our refuge into an icehouse with ourselves the ice. For days we had nothing to eat, nothing to pawn except the clothes we shivered in.

No one would lend to us or give us charity, as I learned when I went to Prince Hong's old club to beg from Lord Cadogan. Such was our desperation. Of course, Prince Hong refused to allow my mission out of sheer pride. I went in direct defiance of him. Lord Cadogan happened to be dining there and returned my note promptly, with particular instructions to the uniformed porters. After they had kicked me up the backside, I toiled miserably back to our garret.

I returned to find Prince Hong and Tutor Ren Xudong in a state of wretched health. Both had been coughing blood for weeks, the treatment for which had cost the last of our resources. All to no avail. Their condition worsened by the day.

Darkness came early to our room, partly because the feeble afternoon light could not penetrate thick patterns of frost on the window. I laid my coat over Prince Hong and went to examine Tutor Ren Xudong, who had been given our only blanket. Little good it did him. He shivered and sweated between hacking coughs that gurgled from somewhere deep within his breast. A voice disturbed me as I knelt by the kindly old man who had been so loyal to the cause of decency and a free China.

'Chi-en? Are you there?'

It was Hong. He sounded afraid, almost like a boy. 'Chi-en?'

'I am here,' I said, stepping over.

His forehead burned beneath my hand. While my breath steamed in the grey air his own created a wisp.

'Don't worry, dear Hong,' I said, sitting on the narrow cot beside him.

How I longed to transfer my health and strength to him! He coughed into his threadbare mattress.

'Do not sit near,' he whispered. 'You might catch my sickness.'

'Good,' I said. 'If you have it, then so should I. We always did everything together. You and I.'

'We did,' he said. 'We did.'

'And so we shall again! Do not lose heart.'

For a long while I sat beside him. At last he stirred.

'Chi-en, are you still there?'

'I am here. I will always be here.'

'When I am gone, do not forget the work I failed to do, Chi-en. You must finish what I started. What we dreamt of as boys. Do you remember those days, Chi-en? How fine we were! How fine!'

'And shall be again,' I said. 'You shall soon be strong.'

He did not reply to that.

'Can it be I dreamt the Heavenly Kingdom all along?' he asked, afraid once more.

'No, it was real! And you shall return there.'

His eyes seemed to glaze. 'Do you remember the railways, Chi-en? We must plan railways for China. All China!'

'We shall! We shall build them!' I promised with all my soul.

But he had fallen asleep. Insensibility seemed a great blessing. How acutely we needed food. A hot meal seemed beyond human expectation, a kind of paradise.

Night filled the attic room with freezing darkness. I sat on beside my friend. Even as I drowsed, emotions blended and broke within me, one minute dulled then the next exacerbated by famine. Oh, there was anger at Prince Hong for his foolishness and my own folly for allowing it – guilt for simply being what I am – then fear and deep pity for my beloved companion. I cannot truly describe the tumult of my feelings.

Dawn brought a terrible revelation. When I tried to stir Tutor Ren Xudong, I found him stiff and lifeless. In his fist was the crumpled telegram Hong and I had sent him as a joke, supposedly from the First Ming Emperor. Half-crazed by hunger I shook him repeatedly, crying out: 'Pray to the Heavenly King to save us! Where is your Heavenly King now?' At last, I fell silent, glancing round at Prince Hong in the brackish light. Fortunately, he had not woken. I knew then I must find my friend some food – anything, even a crust – or he would join Tutor Ren Xudong in the grave.

In a dream I trudged to the snow-covered docks. There, to my surprise, were several Chinamen gathered beside a towering steamship, bowing to a fat sailor with a peaked cap. Impoverished as myself, they were being hired to work in the ship's engine rooms. The sailor told us in a thick American accent that a dozen of their stokers had jumped ship a few hours before and that they needed instant replacements before sailing at noon. The stokers' desertion should have been a warning in itself.

'You fellers wan' three hot meals a day?' demanded the sailor. 'By God, you look like you need 'em!'

I watched from the rear as the Chinese signed up on the spot. Then it was my turn.

'Hey you, big fellah!' called out the sailor. 'You signin', too?'

Why did I sign? I was barely conscious of signing, too hungry to think, to make decisions.

'We sail in four hours' time,' said the man. 'When the tide turns. Be here an hour before that, shabbee?'

I nodded and wandered off in a daze to continue my quest for food. Two hours passed before I returned to the garret. I had found nothing.

Again, Prince Hong was asleep, his breathing a series of gasps. Flecks of foaming blood covered his lips. Tears ran down my cheeks as I stared at his grey face. The frozen corpse of Tutor Ren Xudong was already stiffening. I took my dear friend's hand and found it cold. A terrible fear gripped me. He was dead! Despite his coughing and laboured breath, Prince Hong was dead! I rose in terror. The only way I could bring him back to life was to bring him food! I must earn some money. I stumbled to the waiting steamship on the nearby dock. My mind was strangely blank, confused. Hunger made me an imbecile. Once aboard, I was hustled down to an engine room glowing red as hell. A shovel was pushed into my hand. I suppose I must have thrown coal into the boiler furnace. Certainly, I remember nothing of it. It was a dream, even to the point when a plate of hot stew and bread was placed before me, my first sustenance for four days. Only after I had eaten, gripped by wonder that here, at last, was food – *food!* – did I wake to find the dream a nightmare. As the nourishment worked through me, I became aware of clanking pistons, a slight rolling motion. I was in a ship! It was underway! Then I remembered Prince Hong on his cot in the garret, the snow outside, and struggled to my feet.

I was later told that I fought like a lunatic to escape the engine room, shoving burly men aside to reach the fresh air. I emerged on a tilting deck at twilight to find myself in the broad Thames estuary. It was too late to return. I had abandoned my friend to whatever fate awaited him.

'No!' I screamed like a madman. 'No! We must turn back!'

Of course, they did not. I vomited the stew I had just eaten and was bundled, sobbing, back to the hellish engine room where I had to stoke coal until we reached New York. I should have leaped into the freezing sea and drowned myself. I deserved nothing but drowning. Or perhaps thrown myself into the furnace until I was nothing but ash and vapour.

VI

I arrived in New York with a broken heart. The journey took three long weeks: we were delayed by a defective boiler, poor weather and unseasonable icebergs. My plan was to take ship back to London the very next day but I found myself without enough money for a steerage ticket. Likewise, I could not find employment on any London-bound vessel.

Two months passed and I was still struggling for the means to feed myself, let alone pay for an expensive sea voyage. Whenever I could, I went to the reading room of a great library, feverishly studying the London newspapers which generally arrived a fortnight after publication. There I found a small article in the *London Illustrated News*. It concerned the discovery of two dead Chinamen in an East London lodging house. The police coroner declared no foul play had occurred, for both men *starved and froze to death*. Passports on the deceased identified the younger of the pair as a former leader of the defunct Taiping Rebellion and reported that this same Prince Hong had, until quite recently, *lived the life of a highborn aristocrat*.

VII

There is little for me to add to this humble and wholly truthful memoir of Fourth Prince Hong. Some might say he was never a true prince, his title deriving from the Heavenly King who was no legitimate king at all. I say, what is legitimacy? All except the very fortunate suffer from badly used power − from superiors in places of employment, from priests and professors, officials of all kinds. I say, power is not legitimacy unless one uses it with justice and for the people's good.

By that test, Fourth Prince Hong was entirely legitimate. Despite extreme youth, he conducted himself with the utmost probity and highest sense of duty during the Taiping rebellion, aiding the poor with all his might. It grieves me to consider what he might have become if fate had been kinder.

No sane person can doubt he would have renewed China as a nation, bringing the benefits of Western science, education and manufacture to raise his oppressed brethren from Manchu misrule. No one can doubt he would have merged the benefits of Western thought with the Chinese genius to create something wonderful and new. No one can doubt he would have instituted a proper system of impartial justice and an era of Great Peace. Above all, he would have given power to those without power, by sharing out the land more equitably. Just as, through his many kindnesses, he helped even the most unworthy – including myself.

Thus, I pray this humble memoir will encourage you to remember Prince Hong and his noble example. May you be inspired by him as I must always be. As I must grieve until the day I die, or his work on Earth is complete.

(Here the handwritten manuscript breaks off.)

HARVEST

California and Nebraska
Summer 1878

An unshaded corner of the platform was reserved for travellers of inferior race. Chi-en waited for the Central Pacific emigrant train in the company of eight Chinamen, two Negroes and a dignified, olive-skinned youth wearing a grubby turban.

The platform lay in the heart of Sacramento and Chi-en had arrived there from Napa earlier that day. Time enough to wander the small city of dusty gardens amidst a plain of corn. A terrible, suffocating heat smothered the State Capital. When he visited its splendid Capitol building, neither senators nor placemen were in evidence: presumably taking extended siestas.

At Sacramento Station he sat mournfully. The past opened graves within him: Prince Hong's frozen corpse in an attic garret, remorse twisting deeper into Chi-en's soul. Tears had to be suppressed as he pictured Aunty-Mother, her terror as the Heavenly King's palace collapsed around her in flames. Yet she had honoured Reverend Shambles. And it was true that, for many years, he had been a kind master in his stern, stormy way. Unfair to judge him too harshly. Defining a man by his lapses was to distort his character – so Chi-en prayed, longed to believe true.

Eight pairs of Chinese eyes observed with mute interest as he paced. To calm himself, Chi-en rolled a cigarette. He had to be clear-headed. Dignified. Already he felt the Reverend's assessing gaze.

For the hundredth time he doubted this reckless journey. Lu Kan warned against it. So did his heart. He had too many questions – and did not doubt more must grow from whatever answers he uncovered. Questions concerning Aunty-Mother, of course, but mostly the anonymous mariner, his father.

Perhaps his old master would drive him away as a tainted thing, an odious creature of shame. But Chi-en recalled, as though it was yesterday, Reverend Shambles preaching in Clear Bell Temple how lost sheep may return to the fold. How wanderers were twice, nay, thrice welcome.

This sent him hurrying back to the stores of Sacramento. Amidst disapproving looks at so wealthy a Mongolian, he bought presents for his old master: on the assumption the Reverend still enjoyed a tipple, the finest bourbon in a shiny maple case; French eau-de-cologne; a box of fancy cuff links and tiepins.

Humming a hymn, he concealed his gifts in the dusty carpetbag. Oh, he would not arrive empty-handed! Not like some despised coolie without a cent. And he could boast about his prospects as a legal adviser in Chinatown. He need not fear the usual, tedious prejudice. Reverend Ezekiel Shambles, who had taught *let he without sin cast the first stone*, understood a Chinaman's essential humanity. 'Amen,' Chi-en whispered to himself, again blinking back tears. *Amen.*

The emigrant train bound for the east consisted of a single locomotive and two-dozen freight wagons. At the back came long wooden passenger cars: one for women and children; a second for white men travelling alone; the third, and shabbiest, for Chinese and negroes. Last of all, came the conductor's caboose.

It was early evening before the long train jolted out of Sacramento, measuring progress across the plain by small settlements, rivers, curves of the earth. Always they steamed towards the high barrier of the snow-capped Sierra Nevada. Smoke-scented steam blew through the open windows. Even with the coming of darkness the day's heat lingered and lightning flashed in the distance.

The occupants of the Chinese car soon divided: Cantonese with Cantonese, Negro with Negro. Only Chi-en and the turbaned man lacked travelling companions.

Dawn rose. They huffed across the plains of California, drawing close to the mountains. Chi-en realised the train habitually deferred to superior ones heading West, pulling into sidings to allow the other locomotives passage. Sometimes they waited hours in a stew of heat. He also realised why his fare was so low. If a ship of fools could sprout wheels, he'd joined the crew. Most passengers were failed emigrants, returning in despair to the very towns and lives they had abandoned.

When they passed an emigrant train heading West to California, those whose luck had failed in the Golden State shouted out bitter warnings: *Go back! There's nothin' but hunger in Californee! Go back, you fools!* Then the trains pulled in opposite directions and they slumped on hard wooden benches, staring forward blankly. Later, these same men would taunt the Chinese at some wayside stop, more confident with each jibe.

The slow ascent through the Sierra Nevada commenced. Now a second engine was added to the train's rear. They passed through wooden snow sheds attached to cliffs, skirted waterfalls and rivers bright with foam. Everywhere, pine forests, bluffs, ravines in a profusion of shapes.

Chi-en drowsed through much of the ascent. Watery bowels forced him to squat over a round privy hole in the wooden floor, shielded by a single, torn Civil War army blanket. Then he slaked his thirst from a rusty iron water urn and repeated the process an hour later.

At last, they descended towards high desert plateaux where thorny sagebrush made pacts of life with sand and alkali.

Snoring and groaning, the Chinese wagon endured dull hours of darkness. During the day, they stared at cliffs forming structures unimaginable to an orderly mind: contorted boulders, lone pillars of rock like fingers accusing Heaven. No tree or greenery gave hope other than spiked bushes.

In the Rockies, silver ribbons of water became scarce. The only sounds were monotonies: levers repeating their functions, engines, pistons, wheels rattling, punctuated by defiant steam whistles. Every eight hours or so they halted at an out of the way station to replenish fuel and water and also to purchase cheap, unappetising railroad company food. Chi-en kept his carpetbag with him constantly. It lay beside him even when he washed alongside the other Chinese, using water tanks intended for the locomotives.

At night, feeble oil lamps swayed on hooks, too dim for reading. He sat by the open window and smoked. Tedious hours where feverish speculations multiplied.

Then the plains of Nebraska came into view. It was dawn when word passed round the Chinese car. Many of the men were bound for Nebraskan silver mines and a dream of amassing a fortune that would make them kings in Cantonese villages.

Chi-en chose to breakfast with his eyes rather than mouth. Climbing an iron ladder beside the rear door of the car, he crawled onto its flat roof. A sea of green stretched to horizons concealing more horizons. A land of apparent sameness. Yet as Chi-en watched he noticed archipelagos of wild flowers — blue, golden-yellow, maiden pink — upon the flat oceans of green. Regularly they passed fissures in the plain scoured by floods. In the distance, vast herds of cattle, flocks of sheep. Occasionally small settlements of plank cabins came and went. When the train's noise hushed, he heard symphonies, chorales, operas of grasshoppers swelling a single, continuous song.

The train reached North Platte at the cusp between day and dusk. It was a between kind of city in many ways. A few hundred wooden buildings, mostly one storey, at the confluence of two wide, flat rivers. Just outside the town were large brick hangars for the repair of locomotives on their voyages between one shore of the continent and the other.

Using a mirror borrowed from the dandiest of the Negroes, Chi-en smoothed his suit and long hair. He felt itchy all over and was determined to bathe before meeting Reverend Shambles.

He stumbled onto the gravelly earth beside the railway track, carpet-bag gripped tight, and skirted a bedlam of panicking, lowing cattle being channelled into roofless wagons with high sides. These would transport them to the slaughterhouses and stockyards of Chicago. Behind him, bullwhips cracked.

He passed a huge dining hall intended for travellers and emigrants resting at North Platte. Dozens of Negro waiters hurried between tables, bearing tureens of steaming soup, baskets of bread, platters of tough, gristly steak and heaps of half-cold potatoes. Others carried pitchers of fresh milk and enormous coffee pots. Chi-en stared through the open window at hundreds of pink, sweating faces, jaws working tirelessly. A terrible foreboding urged him to get straight back on the train.

Instead, he hurried to the lights of North Platte and was soon among houses and yards. Saloons and brothels stood on every corner, sweating out a roar liberated by whiskey and gin.

The dusty main street had been churned by cattle, horses, donkeys, wheels and men. Deep ruts formed meaningless hieroglyphs across the earth. Chi-en paused outside one saloon to hear the tinkle of a piano – hopelessly discordant – the heedless *umpah* of a tuba and a ribald trombone. Gunshots and whooping started up in a parallel street. He did not wish to be abroad when darkness truly fell. Seeing a passerby, he asked, 'Sir! Where may I find the laundry of Sin Goon?' The man stared and snorted. 'God damn!' he muttered. 'A Chinee is it now!' With that he strolled on his way.

Chi-en ventured deeper into the town, anxious to avoid attention. His cash was hidden in a money belt beneath his trousers, but it would be no challenge to relieve him of the carpetbag.

A group of cowboys, itchy with dollars from driving their herds hundreds of miles to the railroad, staggered out of a saloon, bawling a song. Chi-en slipped into the shadow between two buildings. At his feet lay an abandoned newspaper that he pocketed out of instinct. On a wall hung a poster:

RED RIBBON CONGREGATIONAL!
COME ALL YE SOLDIERS OF TEMPERANCE AND BEAR WITNESS TO THE
REVEREND EZEKIEL SHAMBLES (FORMERLY OF NEW YORK STATE).
HEAR HIS CALL TO ARMS AS HE LOGICATES AND DELINEATES THE
RATIONALITY OF STRICTEST TEMPERANCE!

The date for the meeting was the following night. The place: Knights of Pythias Hall, North Platte. So, his journey had not been in vain. Chi-en squeezed his eyes shut in a thankful prayer.

When he glanced up, he was granted another sign, painted on crude planks above the double doors of a large wooden shed: **LAWNDRY – REEL CHEEP**. Though the sign was clearly the work of an American, Chi-en suspected its inspiration came from Sin Goon. Crossing a street littered with rocks, broken bottles and dung of dubious provenance, he reached the double doors. Now he knew for sure. Above the lintel was a crude print of an Immortal, Lu Dong-bin, slayer of demons. He had found Sin Goon as well.

Emile Bourchier's sickness began after Chi-en left Royaume Céleste. For weeks he had complained – intermittently, because bottling and shipping the wine had distracted everyone, including himself – of a painful lower molar. When Catherine pried open his reluctant mouth the tooth looked like all the others and she believed his protestations that he didn't need a dentist. Then Parker and Temple's raid on the Wappo drove the matter from her mind.

'Maman!' said Emile, unusually plaintive.

She was in the middle of a letter to Sam Wah explaining her need for a new cook in the plainest English at her disposal. A large dictionary and thesaurus rested on the bureau. It astounded Catherine how many words the English language had devised for *servant*.

'Maman!'

'You will have my entire attention in a moment,' she said, her pen scratching. 'I'm sure you are as sick of my cooking as I am.'

'I feel . . . ill.'

Her pen dipped into the inkwell. Should she offer one dollar a day, as usual? Surely Sam Wah would not delay in sending someone for the sake of a few cents? Not if he wanted her to use his men at harvest time. In fact, hints could be dropped concerning the *vendange* . . .

'Maman!'

She turned in surprise. He had pressed close and clutched her arm. The nib scored the paper, creating a blot.

'Look what you have done!' she cried, reaching for the blotter. She paused. 'Let me look at you.'

Her palm touched his forehead. It certainly seemed warm. Hot, even, but then, it was a bright day, perfect for ripening the grapes.

'Go and drink a large glass of water,' she said, turning back to the letter. 'No, drink *two* glasses. Then lie down for an hour or so. Tell me if you do not feel better after you have rested.'

For once he followed her advice and when Catherine glanced into his room she was relieved to find him asleep. Laying her hand on his forehead, she frowned. It was still hot and damp. For a moment doubt gripped her. Could the fever be serious? Memories of her little brothers made the prospect unthinkable, so she sought distraction by walking the vines.

Each afternoon, Catherine tasted the fruit in different parts of the *terroir*. Bitter grape juice lingered on her tongue, along with the texture and sourness of the berry's skin. After each tasting she swilled out her mouth from a can of water and proceeded to the next spot. She calculated ten, maybe twelve weeks before the harvest. Tiny traces of white mould on some of the hard green berries alarmed her: if the fungus spread there would be rot, and poor grapes meant poor wine. She would instruct the Wappo to thin the foliage so more wind and sun reached the young fruit.

Catherine found herself at a familiar crossroads between rows. Here, only a few days before, she had stood beside the tall Chinaman as he explained his journey to seek a father who – she sensed, perhaps thinking of Antoine – was unlikely to offer affection. A sad, intriguing story. But Chi-en Shambles, as she had witnessed with her own eyes, was brave to the point of recklessness. A man of honourable convictions. That evening, as they walked in the twilight, she had recognised feelings – sensations in dormant, fallow places of her body – feelings that troubled her. And remembering seemed only to revive them. No, she was glad he had gone for his sake, not her own.

Catherine returned to the house and found Emile slumped on the steps of the porch. His face was shiny with perspiration.

'My goodness!' she cried. 'Why are you out of bed?'

He regarded her through red-rimmed eyes.

'Straight back to bed,' she said, gently. 'I will bring food on a tray.'

Wearily, slowly, he rose. Catherine walked behind him up the stairs, taking his arm when he stumbled.

'You will feel better tomorrow,' she promised. 'And if you do not, I will send for the doctor.'

The next morning, Emile did not stir at his usual early hour. Catherine prepared porridge and took a bowl up to Emile's room on a tray. There, she threw wide the curtains and was surprised to find him still asleep. Perhaps that was a good sign. Yet his breath laboured and smelled rancid – and his face was as pale as the porridge. Again, his forehead felt moist, hot. She decided to send for the doctor if he did not convince her that he felt better.

'Emile, how are you today?'

He turned in restless sleep. Catherine watched indecisively. Soon ten Wappo labourers would arrive and Jean-Pierre needed her help to direct them – at least, until they understood the task properly.

'I will be back in a few minutes,' she whispered to the sleeping child.

Leaving the tray by the side of his bed, Catherine hurried down to the winery.

Minutes dragged into a frustrating half hour. Though the Wappo worked well in the fields, scrubbing out the winery with soapy water offended their dignity. Breezeless, shimmering heat across the valley did not help. Drawing and carrying buckets of water proceeded without urgency. As she watched, a baffled, helpless anger gripped Catherine.

For these people she had put Royaume Céleste at risk. Her own and Emile's lives at risk. Who could say when Parker and Temple might seek a drunken revenge? The Indians had, somehow, become her responsibility. Yet casting them adrift in a world that persecuted their race could only burden her with remorse. She was *obligé*, stuck with them like unwanted relatives. It was Chi-en who had taught her the old Chinese proverb: *No good deed goes unpunished.*

Catherine watched with gloomy anticipation as their ancient matriarch waddled from the shade where her rocking chair had been placed.

'Is Little Wappo not here?' asked the old woman through her new interpreter, a mop-haired granddaughter with plenty of bastard Spanish blood.

'He is in bed,' said Catherine, 'I must go back to him now.'

The Old Mother nodded with immense certainty. 'We know summer sickness. I have seen it since I was a girl,' the old woman said through her interpreter. She made a hacking, coughing noise.

Catherine frowned. 'I must send for the doctor,' she said, turning to go.

Two hours later Jean-Pierre arrived with Perryville's best practitioner – if one's measure was expense. Dr Boomer was a top-heavy man with a shiny, jovial face beneath a spotless black bowler. He joined her at Emile's bedside. Not a spoonful of the porridge had been eaten. It was black with flies.

Dr Boomer took the boy's pulse and listened to his chest through the biggest stethoscope Catherine had ever seen. Finally, he used a funnel to decant some of Emile's urine from the chamber pot to a glass flask. After much swirling, sniffing and holding the yellow liquid to the light, Dr Boomer grew thoughtful.

'Heat's got into his blood,' he explained. 'You should've called me earlier, Ma-am. But we ain't beat yet!'

Catherine hovered in the doorway as leeches were applied to Emile's chest and shoulders. The boy shivered convulsively. Afterwards, Dr Boomer produced a large, cork-stoppered bottle of bright blue liquid.

'Half a cup of this tonic, Ma-am,' he said. 'Morning, noon, night. Reg'lar though, Ma-am! It must be reg'lar. And if he'll take a full cup even better. You'll need, oh, three bottles at fifty cents a bottle. And he must drink plenty of cold water. If he don't want it, hold his nose an' make him!' Dr Boomer chuckled.

The consultation cost a ridiculous seven dollars, including thirty cents for additional horse feed because he had been forced to hurry over. Such a fee surely guaranteed a speedy recovery.

Yet when Dr Boomer had gone and she administered the tonic, Emile choked then vomited. She was forced to spoon it in tiny amounts. Meanwhile, the flies, having been robbed of their porridge, turned with relish to spilt droplets of the sugary blue medicine.

Chi-en knocked on the door of the Reel Cheep Lawndry. Muffled curses within became a scrape of harsh bolts. The double doors opened a few inches to frame a face.

Sin Goon was just beyond middle age but appeared far older. His forehead was badly shaved, nicked and scarred by blunt razors. A pigtail of grey hair hung behind his back. Steam and heat drifted through the crack in the door. Despite the late hour, the laundry was at full boil.

The Chinaman examined his visitor by the light of an upheld lamp. Chi-en's long hair and lack of a pigtail made Sin Goon cry out, 'Haah!'

Whether in fear or disgust Chi-en could not tell. The door slammed in his face. Chi-en glanced anxiously round the dark street.

'Sin Goon! I bring a message from the Kong Chow Company!' he called in Cantonese, banging on the door. He was sure the old man still hovered by the entrance. 'If you are to receive your reward you must let me in.'

A long pause: then the bolts scraped back.

'What do you want?' demanded the Chinaman. 'How do you know my name?'

Chi-en held up the letter from Lu Kan bearing the ornate wax seal of the Kong Chow Company. Sin Goon stepped aside to allow him entry then hastily barred the doors.

Within lay a long, vaulted shed lit by oil lamps and the red glow of fires. More double doors were open at the rear. A counter stood near the street entrance, otherwise the space was dominated by copper and tin vats of water bubbling over railroad coal fires and the alkaline stench of soap. Steam drifted, obscuring piles of clothes, blankets, bedding, methodically sorted into old whiskey crates marked by hand-painted Chinese characters.

As Chi-en watched, Sin Goon scurried over to a long rubber hose attached to a water tank and pump. The Chinaman pumped angrily, muttering to himself. Finally, he examined Chi-en's features minutely in the dim light. What he saw displeased him.

'No one mentioned a *fan gui*. Where is my reward? Mr Lu Kan wrote of a big reward.'

Reaching for his purse, Chi-en extracted several gold dollars. The Chinaman bit the coins, mumbling to himself as he inspected them back and front.

'Where does Reverend Ezekiel Shambles live?' asked Chi-en.

But Sin Goon had hurried into the backyard and he was forced to follow. Here, a web of clotheslines hung between high wooden fences forming a stockade. Sin Goon clearly feared the good citizens of North Platte would help themselves to his customers' laundry.

'Where does Reverend Ezekiel Shambles live?' repeated Chi-en, more firmly.

His host laughed. 'How should I know? But he's here, Mr Fan Gui! He's here!'

Another dollar persuaded his fellow-countryman to provide bed and food. After a meal of cold rice and canned beans, Chi-en lay in an exhausted daze upon a nest of unwashed sheets, trying to ignore the oily, pungent stains and rank aroma of dried sweat. Only in the middle of the night did he suspect the sheets emanated from one of North Platte's numerous whorehouses.

That night stray gunshots and wild carousing filtered into his dreams through the constant bubble of Sin Goon's vats.

California and Nebraska
Summer 1878

Chi-en woke late to find his makeshift bed being yanked from under him, sheet by sheet. 'Get up now!' chided the old man. 'Lazy *fan gui*! You leave today!'

Chi-en brushed himself down, peering at the bright rectangle of sunlight formed by the rear double doors. Night's bacchanal had been replaced by a mournful lowing of cattle. In the distance a train whistled. When he turned to address his host, Sin Goon was back at work, stirring the grey, frothy water with a large wooden paddle and chuckling to himself.

Something poked from Chi-en's pocket. He extracted the newspaper found the previous night. It was entitled *The Nebraskan Plaindealer*, above the banner *Official Organ of the Grand Lodge of Good Templars*.

Sitting on a low bench outside, Chi-en read curiously. The newspaper, a badly printed affair, wore the red ribbon of temperance with pride. Sure enough, Reverend Shambles's name appeared in a long article, describing him as *a public speaker and logician of such power the legions of rum tremble at his name*.

Praise was also accorded to Mrs Ada Van Pelt, *a widow of exceedingly large fortune and piety*, who discovered the Reverend in New York and *prevailed upon him to accompany her back to Nebraska in her capacity as Grand Chief Templar.* He learned this removal came more easily due to the sad loss of the Reverend's wife. So, Mrs Shambles was enjoying the company of her angry, spiteful God.

The Reverend had fought the good battle in Nebraska for nine months. The article concluded by welcoming him and his only son, Mr Corey Shambles, as *permanent Nebraskans* and praying that, with the Lord's assistance, the *29,142 souls he has caused to sign a pledge of utter abstinence shall double, nay, treble in number.*

Chi-en smoked a cigarette thoughtfully. Spiritual Uncle had certainly relished a drop or two in Canton. Now, it seemed, he'd gone the other way. But then, he had always revelled in enthusiasms and reinventions. Why shouldn't he have repented under the rich widow's influence?

'Sin Goon!' he called out. 'What do you know about Mrs Ada Van Pelt?'

The Chinaman stopped stirring the vat. 'Two dollars to stay another night,' he declared. 'No, *three* dollars. Having a Longhair here will bring me bad luck.'

'Sin Goon, do you know anything about the Reverend's son?'

Sin Goon regarded him coldly. 'Three dollars!' he cried. 'Or you do not spend another night under my roof.'

Later, Chi-en risked a walk round the streets of North Platte. An hour taught him all he needed to know. A tiny city struggling to shake off its lawless past like a prodigal that can't bring himself to drive away bad companions. Two camps were evident, each co-existing uneasily. The first were respectable settlers seeking a permanent stake in the new State of Nebraska. On the other side were those patronising the town's saloons and brothels, a wild, restless population of cowboys, ex-buffalo hunters, itinerant labourers, pimps, gamblers and whores.

Small wonder the decent portion welcomed a powerful advocate for temperance. Their entire future was invested in wooden buildings afloat on a sea of buffalo grass. And Chi-en sensed how sincerely his old master would respond to their need. Back at the Reel Cheep Lawndry, he took a bath and waited for evening.

The Knights of Pythias Hall was a far plainer castle than its name suggested. Instead of lofty towers it had a low wooden balcony and hard benches. Chi-en chose a seat at the very rear of the balcony. He wore his smartest clothes, long hair washed and neatly combed, swept back and tied with a red ribbon bought specially that day.

The hall soon filled: mostly with respectable women glad of an opportunity to display their finery other than in church. A few idlers and cowboys who had run through their stakes lounged with an intention to mock.

A long table had been placed at the front beside a raised pulpit. The murmured conversation increased as speakers and worthies emerged from a back door, taking places at the table.

The most prominent sat in the centre: a diminutive, elderly lady with a bird-like face and fierce blue eyes, walking with the aid of a stick. Presumably the so-called Grand Chief Templar, Mrs Ada Van Pelt. Next came a large, bumbling fellow who took up the chairman's gavel. Lastly, a man Chi-en had despaired of meeting upon earth.

All faces are partly imagined: people see features they seek or choose. As Chi-en stared down at Reverend Ezekiel Shambles's once pink, boyish face he strove to ignore time's alterations. *Just the same*, he assured himself, *just the same*. Except the genial roundness of cheek and squareness of jaw had grown pinched. Brown eyes that once twinkled no longer reflected the lamplight.

But soon, very soon, Chi-en went stiff. An outlandish notion waylaid him. A notion so sudden, so like an enemy lunging out of the darkness, his heart beat painfully. He found it hard to breathe. Sweat gathered on forehead and palms. But the appalling notion, once conceived, would not conveniently die away.

'No,' he assured himself. 'No.'

Oh, Chi-en had to marvel at the human capacity for craven, perverse, contemptible folly!

Reverend Shambles murmured to the elderly lady beside him at the speakers' table and she nodded gravely. Chi-en became aware of two men in shadows behind the lamp-lit top table.

The first inspired him to crane for a better view. Here, unless family characteristics lied, was Shambles's son, Corey. Could that young man be the whining, petulant boy who watched impassively while Mrs Shambles slapped Aunty-Mother? He had grown short and fat, his fleshy neck squeezed by a stiff, buttoned up collar.

Instinct commanded Chi-en to rise, get the hell out of the Knights of Pythias Hall before some unguessable danger consumed him. But he had come too far to retreat. He sought distraction by studying the man beside Corey, who sported an ugly, angry squint and a loud check suit. Chi-en's closest neighbour on the balcony, wearing the long black coat of an undertaker, whispered to his wife, 'See that fellah in the check suit? That's Joe Finnegan.'

'Who, dear?'

'The fellah as gunned down two men in Omaha a few years back. Self-defence his attorney called it, but he lost his place as sheriff. The Reverend persuaded him to take the pledge an' wear the ribbon.'

'Thank the Lord!' murmured his wife, admiringly.

'Finnegan guards the Reverend day an' night 'gainst the rum interest,' continued the undertaker. 'Seems they been threatening the Reverend. If it was me, I'd want guarding 'gainst Finnegan. Ha! Ha!'

Chi-en realised the Reverend Shambles was scanning the packed rows of seats. As his glance ascended to the balcony, Chi-en shrank back. Did that gaze pause at the corner where he sat? Did it move on, then back, as though to confirm something?

With a bang, the chairman, who introduced himself as Mr Augustus Keen, called the meeting to order. A long tribute to Mrs Ada Van Pelt provoked applause. At once Reverend Shambles was on his feet, striding to the raised pulpit, which he gripped like a doughty lookout in his crow's nest amidst a raging, boiling ocean of incontinence. The audience waited. Some, especially a group of spinsters near the front, did not disguise their adulation. When he spoke, his voice was sonorous with purpose and dignity. Chi-en stared. Where had Spiritual Uncle Father's chaotic, endearing way with a sermon gone?

'Let me commence my oration with a single word.' He raised his finger. 'Nay, with *two* words. And those words are addressed to the munificent lady upon my right hand. I say to Mrs Ada Van Pelt two words on behalf of us all. *Thank you.*'

Was that a blush on the widow's cheek as fresh applause rose? Chi-en heard the man in the undertaker's suit whisper to his wife, 'She owns half of Lincoln County an' whole city blocks in Omaha. Shame she's a cripple.'

Now Reverend Shambles was speaking with the fervour Chi-en recalled. 'Brothers, sisters, property-owners set upon this free land by Jesus Christ Our Risen Lord! I beg of ye! Lower your heads, pray with me before I commence my oration! Pray the Good Shepherd lends me eloquence in our sacred war against the ejaculations of Satan's juice!'

Hundreds of necks bent obediently and Chi-en was moved to join them.

For the next hour and a half, the Reverend expounded the cause of temperance without reference to notes. Words poured from him as from a divine spring. Words so charged with furious passion that Chi-en lost a grip on logic, washed away by floods of conviction.

'The liquor power! Ah yes, my friends! I tell you I was actuated by one determination . . . Is that not so? Verily I see tears in many an eye tonight! Not tears of weakness but pious resolution . . . Aye! Canst thou feel the rumbling, friends!' There were cries of agreement in the audience. 'Canst thou feel that tidal wave of temperance building, surging like a great white spume of frothy virtue to wash away the impure desires of Satan's hot lust? Forgive me for the tear in my eye, ladies. Perhaps it is unmanly. But when I behold Christian women and mothers in this State, in our blessed State of Nebraska, praying for their happy, happy home to be reclaimed from the drunkard's chains, from those Demon-tyrants, Whiskey and Gin . . . Hear our war cry ye sinners and topers! Moral 'suasion for the drunkard and legal 'suasion for the drunkard-maker!'

Chi-en assessed and re-assessed the gaunt face of the man in the pulpit. The years had changed Spiritual Uncle more than seemed possible. Something intangible had left that handsome face. Was it spirit? Inner fire? As the oration built to its climax, he realised what had departed: a redeeming softness, a gentle humour. Its absence robbed Reverend Ezekiel Shambles of his unique charm.

He could only speculate what misfortunes had caused the change. Maybe the loss of Mrs Shambles, though the Reverend had laboured mightily to maintain thousands of miles' separation from his wife when he lived in Canton. Or failed hopes and ambitions. Maybe even slander. Chi-en began to fear how this new Reverend Shambles would react when he made himself known.

'Now friends,' concluded the Reverend, 'for I believe we are friends.

Nay, not just friends but soldiers together! Comrades in the mighty army of temperance! I tell ye, we shall squeeze Satan's juice out of this state! If we are humble, if we show no pride in our good work or hope of worldly reward, if we love the work for its own holy sake . . .'

By prior arrangement an organ sounded and the small choir of ladies at the front broke into a low song:

> *'He that is down need fear no fall,*
> *He that is low no pride.*
> *He that is humble ever shall*
> *Have God to be his guide.'*

And the Reverend's triumphant voice rose in a clarion call above the hymn: 'Then, as the Good Book that never lies doth promise us, the Lord shall be exceeding glad!'

It was too much for Chi-en. Hearing the words that had inspired his own name. Hearing Spiritual Uncle Father's favourite hymn.

He left while applause still shook the hall. Though intent on escape, he noticed Mrs Ada Van Pelt dabbing her flinty blue eyes. And Reverend Shambles glancing up at the balcony as Chi-en hurried away.

Out on the dark street he wept. Inside the applause continued, accompanied by a fresh, rousing temperance battle song: *The Pledge! The Pledge! The mighty rock* . . .

Chi-en returned to the Reel Cheep Lawndry, not noticing the drunks and whorehouses he passed. Pillars of steam rose from the railroad into the cloudless, star-filled Nebraskan night. As he walked, he chuckled almost hysterically. For he was sure in his heart, quite sure. Tomorrow would settle the question that had haunted all his life.

The next morning, Catherine quarrelled with Jean-Pierre. Perhaps it was caused by the temperature inching up the thermometer; perhaps it was rising in the middle of the night to discover Emile's own wakefulness, then sitting beside him until his lids closed at the first sign of dawn; perhaps it was her son's inability to stomach the blue medicine that must cure him.

Whatever the reason, she was pointing out the deficiencies of the fermenting barrels while Jean-Pierre made barbed comparisons between how a woman runs a vineyard and how Monsieur Bourchier earned the admiration of 'all who know' about wine, when a long shadow filled the doorway. Both fell silent.

Catherine peered uncertainly, dazzled by the glare outside. The shadow's length grew from a black stovepipe hat. Closer examination revealed Baron Cesar Foche, a tiny smile upon his sallow, unshaven face.

He had found her. The only surprise was it had taken so long.

For all the scuffs on his patent leather boots and the worn patches on his long-tailed dandy's suit, the gentleman of fashion who once paraded Parisian boulevards was still evident – though far, far from home. He fixed her with a cold, aristocratic eye and bowed languidly. 'Comtesse . . . at last we can continue the *tête-à-tête* we began at l'Opera.'

She turned hurriedly to Jean-Pierre. 'I do not want you getting angry,' she whispered. 'Let me talk to him alone. Please do not get angry.'

Jean-Pierre's left cheek still bore a scar from Antoine's riding crop; a blow delivered at Baron Foche's instigation. The steward's throat worked convulsively but he steadied himself.

'They say the devil pops up when you least expect him, Madame.' Jean-Pierre's voice lowered. 'Call me if you need me to load my shotgun.'

With that, he stalked off. Foche seemed too pre-occupied with his silver-topped cane and cuffs to notice. 'By the way,' he remarked, once

Jean-Pierre had gone, 'it was I who advised dear Antoine to dismiss your oafish friend. I may be obliged to compel you to do the same. But back to our conversation . . .'

'Monsieur,' broke in Catherine, 'I believe we will not be able to continue our conversation. Or any conversation. No conversation is possible between us.'

Baron Foche's smile became regretful. 'I disagree, Comtesse.' He rolled his monocle between finger and thumb. 'I feel *assured* you will find time for an old friend.' They assessed one another. Catherine glanced away. 'And you have acquired a splendid new Bourchier *terroir*,' he remarked. 'Perhaps you could show me your vines?'

Donning a straw hat woven for her by the Wappo and decorated with concentric patterns, Catherine led him outside the winery. He was all admiration and enquired closely how much it would cost him to purchase such a vineyard. Each time he drew near, Catherine pulled away. An odd, medicinal odour clung to his coat.

'Royaume Céleste indeed!' he said. 'I congratulate you. But I must spoil our agreeable chat.'

Catherine waited. Her glance drifted to the farmhouse and Emile's open window. Half an hour had passed since she last checked whether he was awake. Yet she dared not get rid of Foche without finding out his intentions.

'I take it you are kept informed of your husband's affairs?' he began.

'I hear nothing about Antoine. Nor do I wish to hear.'

'Indeed?' This seemed to surprise and, perhaps, please him. 'Then you will be grateful for my news, Comtesse.'

A predictable tale followed. Having auctioned the last of his own property and the Bourchier estate – land, animals, chattels, furnishings – Antoine had thrown himself upon the generosity of the wider de Rivac de Chauveterre family and, in particular, his younger brothers.

Alas, they harboured old resentments occasioned by his high-handed treatment of them during better days. The result? An allowance, yes, but merely enough for the name de Rivac de Chauveterre not to be disgraced. In short, he was reduced to the level of a clerk on a miserly pension.

'Am I supposed to weep?' she said. 'Perhaps send some drinking or whoring money?'

Baron Foche ignored her outburst. 'What astonishes me, Comtesse, is dear Antoine's reaction to your dramatic departure. He is in a fury to be re-united with his son and heir.' He examined her. 'Do you think I should write and tell him where Emile may be collected?'

Catherine lowered her head so that her broad hat concealed her face.

He coughed delicately. 'Of course, his motives are not entirely paternal. I suspect – no, I *know* that he needs the son to regain the support of his family. After all, Emile is the legal heir to the title Comte de Rivac de Chauveterre. You will recollect, I'm sure, that Antoine's brothers' children are all female. So *they* don't count.'

'Comte de Nowhere!' spat Catherine. 'A title without dignity and honour! My son needs no such title to earn respect.'

'You believe so,' said Foche, mildly, 'but does Emile, as the rightful heir? And what of your American hosts? They may be surprised to discover why you have dropped the title *Comtesse*.'

Catherine retreated into sullen silence.

'Imagine my surprise at learning that you are a widow. *Madame Bourchier* of all things. Good Lord, didn't you anticipate the consequences of such deception? Society will shun you and your wines will be tainted forever. What a pity!'

She waited. It was coming. All along it had been coming. The only question was how much.

'But to business, as our American friends like to say. For a small consideration there shall be no letter to my old friend Comte Antoine de Rivac de Chauveterre. No exposure of your lies. No ruin. I shall vanish as quickly as I appeared. And never return.' He waited, apparently admiring the view of the valley.

'What is that small consideration?' asked Catherine.

'Ten thousand dollars. Cash.'

'Are you mad?'

'No, Comtesse. Are you?'

'I would be mad to pay you! Why should I?'

'Otherwise, you will be ruined. Your little Royaume Céleste will no longer live up to its name. Your son will be taken home to France where he belongs. I would be happy to act as Emile's guardian until he is re-united with his father. You may be sure the de Rivac de Chauveterre family would meet any travelling or legal expenses involved.'

'Do you think I have ten thousand dollars in cash!' exclaimed Catherine. 'I have barely half that amount. Even if I did—'

'Enough!' The sheer assurance of his command stopped her. 'I am not an unreasonable man. I shall accept five thousand dollars if the payment is made in five days.' He smoothed his mustachios. 'I know from past experience with *apparently* reluctant ladies, you will learn to find me reasonable.'

A memory of him banging on her bedroom door at Château de Chauveterre made Catherine step back. 'You are a blackmailer! A monster!'

'I consider it monstrous to deny a son his father,' he said. 'Monstrous to pretend that father is dead. Actually, we are more alike than you imagine.'

His calmness abashed her. If she had eaten that morning or slept more than an hour the night before, perhaps she would not have murmured, 'I need time to think.'

'Of course, my dear. But I require a little deposit, let us call it. A hundred dollars will suffice for now.'

Back at the house she went to her study while he prepared his hired horse outside. When she emerged, it was with fifty dollars in small bills. It seemed a small price to clear him from her land.

'It's all I have. Here, take it! And never come back.'

He plucked it from her shaking hand.

'I will return in a few days,' he said. 'In the meantime, you may find me at the Star Hotel in Perryville. *Au revoir, Comtesse*! Such a pleasure! Act wisely, my dear!'

He removed his stovepipe hat and bowed very low before mounting his horse.

Reeling, Catherine could think of nothing except Baron Foche: his smug, moustachioed face; his suave insinuations; above all, his complete self-assurance. Oh, he held all the cards! His explanation of why Antoine was searching for Emile – to win back the financial backing of his family, some of whom were ambitious enough to pay dearly for an aristocratic title – convinced her entirely. Yet she despised herself for paying him even fifty dollars. Perhaps it would keep him quiet. Perhaps he would use the money to drink and whore himself stupid, never to be seen again.

But Catherine feared she had committed a terrible, terrible error. For there were Languedoc proverbs just as wise as Chi-en's Chinese ones: *Allow a beggar into your house and he'll soon have his feet on the table.*

With a gasp, she recollected Emile. He had not eaten since . . . she could not be sure when.

She hurried to the kitchen and prepared gruel. Upon entering Emile's room the stench shocked her: a metallic stink of sweat mingled with something fetid, revolting. He had soiled himself. All the water in the carafe had gone. He lay with limbs twisted, shivering convulsively.

A realisation churned the deepest earth of her soul. Her own stupidity amazed her. How could she not have seen it before? A vision of coming to this dark room and finding his stiff body beneath the blankets made her cry out. Then she would be alone forever, alone with the creeping, engulfing vines in this strange land. And their fruit would not matter at all.

'I'm so cold, Maman,' he whispered, his red-rimmed eyes fixed on her own. 'Don't leave me by myself.'

'I won't leave you again,' she said, stroking his hair. 'First, I must wash you and change your sheets. I will be back with water and your medicine.'

He rolled over, muttering to himself.

After changing the sheets and feeding him a little gruel, Catherine was true to her promise and lit a lamp in preparation for a long watch through the night.

What should she do? What could she do? Memories of her dear younger brothers succumbing one by one to fevers like this, made her rock slightly as she sat on the bed. Boys were weak! No one had been able to keep them from the darkness.

A new thought occurred: she must tell Nancy. She would know a reputable doctor. One more skilful than that horse quack in Perryville with his sugary, absurdly blue medicine . . .

She rose and descended to her bureau. A short note was soon dispatched, Jean-Pierre beating Jeanne d'Arc's stubborn flanks as he crossed the valley to Trubody Nook.

When the old steward joined Catherine at Emile's bedside an hour later, there was bad news. The Trubodys were in San Francisco and would not return for days.

'Go to the post office!' she urged. 'Wire a telegram. We must send it to their home in Nob Hill.'

Jean-Pierre regarded her gravely. 'Is Mrs Trubody a celebrated doctor?'

'She will know a doctor.'

He leaned over the sick boy then glanced at a shadowy corner. 'I am entirely at your disposal, Madame.'

After he had gone, she took up position by Emile's pillow. Midnight was long past when she woke with a cry of alarm. She had been dreaming of the graveyard below Château de Chauveterre where generations of Bourchiers slept their last sleep. Except for the faint rasp of his breath, Emile's bedroom was silent as a crypt.

California and Nebraska
Summer 1878

The morning after the temperance congregational, Chi-en arrived outside a splendid maple and brick ranch house a mile from North Platte. Horizons of tawny plain stretched far away. In between lay a broad, shallow river bordered by dried-out shrubs and reeds; it had been a bad rain year for the whole of Nebraska.

To the east a billowing dust cloud advanced towards the river: cattle driven from Texas to the rail depot at North Platte, destined for the butchers' knives and steam saws of Chicago.

He hesitated beneath a whitewashed arch topped by a horned buffalo skull. Upon it was the legend: *Eldorado Ranch. Proprietor. Judge G. Van Pelt.*

Sturdy fences divided the land into orchards and gardens, pasture for horses, cattle, sheep. Neat wooden buildings – stables, hay stores, sheds for tools and workers – surrounded the magnificent ranch house.

Chi-en wondered if he had found the right place. He could not imagine the shabby, perpetually penniless Reverend Shambles in so large and thriving a landowner's residence. Gathering courage, Chi-en walked down the driveway, ignoring two mastiffs that barked frantically, straining their chains.

The front porch was occupied by the ex-sheriff who had served at the temperance meeting as the Reverend's bodyguard. Finnegan now protected his hearth – or Mrs Van Pelt's hearth. Hard living and drinking made it hard to assign an age to his leathery face. His eyes were disconcerting: yellow and bloodshot. Chi-en noticed the bulge of a revolver beneath his frock coat. He wore a red temperance ribbon as a veteran might a proud medal.

'What you want?' asked Finnegan.

Chi-en bowed. 'To see Reverend Shambles.'

This provoked hoarse laughter. 'An' how's I to know whether a murderin' Chinee monkey ain't been sent by them licker barons to harm the Rev'rend?' There was no humour in the flat, toneless question.

'Sir,' said Chi-en, 'I believe he will be pleased to see me.'

Finnegan laughed again. 'Like shit he will!' Rage flooded his face so that Chi-en stepped back warily. 'Like shit he'll be seein' a Chinee heathen monkey!'

'Finnegan?' A short, round figure appeared in the doorway – Corey Shambles. 'What's going on?'

'Like shit!' exclaimed Finnegan, rising dangerously.

Corey frowned and laid an uncertain hand on the other's pistol arm. Finnegan started at the touch.

'Now then, Finn, you know the Reverend don't hold with cussin'.'

This seemed enough to pacify the ex-lawman, who returned to his chair beside the door and stared at the dust cloud raised by the approaching cattle herd.

'Well, mister,' said Corey to Chi-en, 'state your business. Only I warn you now, we ain't buyin'.'

Chi-en examined the younger man expectantly, waiting for a sign of recognition. None came. 'Do you not remember me? We did meet long ago, in a faraway place.'

Corey turned to Finnegan. 'I see what you mean, fellah's crazy. Now, I don't know who put you up to this, Mr Chinee-man, but I'd sure advise you . . .' He glanced at Finnegan and tittered. '*Not* to aggravate my friend here.'

'Git!' commanded Finnegan, more succinctly.

Chi-en was about to protest when a new voice reached them from the dark interior of the house. A deep masterful voice that made Corey duck.

'Show him in, Corey! Show him to the study!'

With a suspicious glance, the young man stepped aside in time for Chi-en to glimpse the back of a large figure walking quickly into a nearby room.

'In there!' ordered Corey.

'I trust we shall speak later,' Chi-en said. 'I'm sure you will remember me. And fondly, I hope.'

Many emotions contended in Corey Shambles's expression. None were fond.

The room was a gentleman's library and study. A life-size oil portrait of a soldier in a US Army General's uniform hung over the wide fireplace. Gilt letters underneath read *General G. Van Pelt*.

A small glass case of law books stood on one side of the portrait, along with a dangling hangman's noose above a plaque bearing a list of names. On the right of the painting, a gun cabinet stored handguns, rifles and shotguns.

High south-facing windows formed a wall of brightness. Amidst the glare, Chi-en made out a large desk. A dark, motionless silhouette sat behind it. He shielded his eyes and identified Reverend Shambles. Tongue-tied, he struggled for the least foolish way to begin. Fortunately, the Reverend broke the silence. 'You look a long way from home. What's your business with me?'

'Do you really not recognise me?' Chi-en asked in wonder. 'Have I changed so much?' Again, he shielded his eyes with his hand. He could not see clearly enough to read the expression of the man framed by light.

'I do not know you,' said Reverend Shambles. 'Should I?'

Chi-en shifted uncomfortably. He must make no assumptions. Yet a gulp of emotion left him fumbling for words: 'Do you not remember your old servant, Little Humble?'

It seemed a long time before the Reverend spoke. 'My God.'

'You recognise me!'

He was answered by a violent scrape of chair legs. Then Reverend Shambles stepped from behind the desk into shadow and the sun no longer blinded Chi-en.

Close up, very close, the appalling notion that had struck him at the temperance meeting flooded back with undammable force. He stared at the face of Reverend Ezekiel Shambles. And the more he stared, the more he detected another face. One familiar from mirrors, diverse reflections. A face learned through three decades of change and growth: his own.

No, he assured himself, *no*. He didn't want this. Shrank from it. It demeaned everything – Aunty-Mother, everyone. And yet . . . *And yet* . . . Why exactly had Aunty-Mother and Reverend Shambles both refused to reveal his true father's name? Always there had been evasion, sometimes anger. Except once, in an unguarded moment, Aunty-Mother had said his father was a purer, better soul than either she or Chi-en might ever be.

Still, he gazed at the older man's face.

As a young man, his own features had changed rapidly, a square English jaw banishing the softness of boyish cheeks. A jaw suspiciously similar to the man's who stood before him.

No, he repeated, as one might to a stubborn child, *no, no, no*. Ludicrous to imagine it! Reverend Shambles had rescued Aunty-Mother from ignominy on the streets of Hong Kong. Chi-en had heard that story a dozen times. Just as often, she had refused to name her own family when Chi-en pressed for his grandfather's name, once even striking him across the face. Surely, she had important reasons for concealing his family's name. And yet, faces told stories as well as names. Sometimes truer ones.

Conviction and denial swarmed through every room of his soul like clouds of black, buzzing flies. Settling, itching, taking wing.

He became aware that Reverend Shambles was examining him with something akin to horror. The older man's first word came out as a croak, 'I . . . I saw you last night. On the balcony. But I thought . . . Good God!'

Chi-en struggled to reply.

'What brings you here, Humble?'

'I thought you might tell me that, sir.'

'I'm doing the asking here, boy, not the telling!' The Reverend's face hardened. His eyes brooded. 'I repeat, what brings you here? Now of all times? Did you think Mrs Van Pelt would be home?'

Ignoring the oddness of this last question, Chi-en began eagerly, 'I have so many things to ask, Spiritual Uncle Father!' He used the Chinese words for the title. Shambles's frown deepened. 'So many things to learn!' continued Chi-en. 'Things I *need* to learn, sir! For it was you who taught me that man cannot live by bread alone. Your lessons remain where you planted them.' Chi-en touched his breast. 'Here.'

Reverend Shambles coughed, sighed. 'Shame I have an appointment in . . .' He examined his pocket watch. 'My goodness, very soon. Damn shame. I'll be gone for weeks spreading the Lord's message of a pure breath.'

Chi-en gripped his hat brim anxiously. 'Sir,' he said with desperate gaiety, 'I have never forgotten those happy times in your chapel in Canton! People said bad things about you, sir, after you left the Heavenly Capital so suddenly. But I never believed them.'

'Long time ago.' There was a flash of his old anger. 'And don't you go calling it the *Heavenly Capital*! It was never that.' He stared at Chi-en suspiciously. 'You still haven't answered my question. Why are you here, Humble? I'm thinking Augustus Keens put you up to it. Answer me truthfully! How much did he pay you?' Bitterness entered the Reverend's voice. 'Keens hoped *she* would see us together, didn't he? That Mrs Van Pelt would see us together. Don't deny it, Humble! I could never bear a liar! Shame she decided to spend the day with her niece. Keens didn't bargain for that, damn him!'

Chi-en listened to this tirade with growing alarm. 'Who is this *Keens*?'

'Don't lie to me!'

'You mean the chairman at last night's meeting? But we have never spoken.'

Reverend Shambles subsided. 'Perhaps I misjudge you, Humble.'

They were distracted by laughter outside as two farmhands walked past. Chi-en struggled to right the conversation as one might a listing ship. 'Sir, I came here to ask something only you are left alive to answer.'

'Yes?'

'You remember Aunty-Mother, sir?'

The pause was long. 'Yes.'

Instead of asking the question that burned and tormented him, Chi-en said hurriedly, 'I'm sure you wish to hear what became of her, after you left us so suddenly in the Heavenly Capital . . .'

'No, no!' broke in Shambles, rubbing his forehead. 'I'm assured the Good Lord in His Grace supplied both manna and dew to his handmaiden!'

For the first time a bubble of anger – fetid and long-brewed – rose through the depths of Chi-en's soul. 'I'll tell you anyway,' he said, hoarsely. And he did. How she became a lowly servant in the Heavenly King's Palace. How he feared she had been beaten and abused. How they were never allowed to meet again as mother and son. How she perished in terror and agony when looters torched the Palace – at least, such a quick end was to be prayed for. Far worse endings were perpetrated that day.

Chi-en fell silent. The Reverend Shambles paced before the stern portrait of General Van Pelt.

'I never guessed . . . Damn those savages masquerading as Christians! God rest her sweet soul. Lord, rest her soul.' His voice trailed and Chi-en rubbed at tears.

'Sir,' he said, 'I came here . . . I came here to learn about my father.'

Shambles leaned against the mantelpiece, massaging his brow as though a great pain had settled there. He shot Chi-en a wary glance. 'How am I meant to know that?'

'You must know his name!'

'If I ever did, I've long forgotten. It's best that way, Humble. *Hide me from the secret counsel of the wicked*, I say!'

'You must know! You took Aunty-Mother in, fallen as she was. You told me my father was a "damnable sinner" – your exact words, sir – and that he should be forgotten, just as you do now. But she said before we were parted . . . Oh, this is so hard to say! Yet I must. She said once, when I asked her my father's name, that he was a better, purer soul than she or I could ever be.' Chi-en twisted his hat brim with sweating hands. 'Sir, when I saw you again at the temperance meeting, I marvelled at the physical likeness between us. Just as I marvel looking upon you now. Sir, I believe the purer, better soul she meant was you.'

It had been said. Could not be unsaid. Chi-en stared at the hearthrug, his heart racing. Everything depended upon the Reverend's reply. Yet it came not through words but a movement. Shambles hurried to the door and threw it open, so as to surprise anyone listening. There was no one. He closed the door carefully and went back to the chair behind the desk.

'You are saying that I . . . I am your natural father? Have I heard correctly?'

'This is not easy for me!' exclaimed Chi-en. 'Nor for you, sir! How I understand that! But I remember you telling me, teaching me, the truth will set us free. I cannot be free until I know the truth. All my life it has haunted me like a frowning ghost. So, you see, I cannot feel complete until I know the name of my father. I cannot feel whole.'

If Reverend Shambles was listening, he gave no sign. Once more he had risen from behind the desk and was pacing.

'You come here to accuse me of being your father!'

Now the lone bubble of anger bursting in Chi-en's soul became a rapid stream. '*Accuse*? Is it a crime to be my father? Am I so low? So worthy to be despised that only the *accused* can be my father? No, I don't *accuse* you. I simply want the truth.'

Shambles raised a trembling finger. 'You have no proof, Humble. Not a shred! You tell Mr Keens *that* and see if he pays your thirty pieces of silver. No bastard child can be laid at the door of Ezekiel Shambles to bring him shame. You tell Keens! He'll do anything to poison Mrs Van Pelt against me. After all my years of sacrifice for the Lord, see how I'm rewarded!'

'What is your answer?'

'Oh, I see Keens's game! And you allow yourself to be *that* man's pawn! A man who uses the sacred cause of temperance for his own worldly profit! Oh, Humble. *Humble*. You were such an earnest, sweet little boy.'

Shambles shivered, glancing at the portrait of General Van Pelt on the wall.

'I'm sure you look at this house and call it mine. No, Humble, not mine. Keens wishes to prevent a condition of holy matrimony arising between myself and Mrs Van Pelt. He knows I haven't a dime in the world. Shame on you, Humble! I taught you the Word of our Redeemer. I saved your soul from eternal damnation.'

Bile burned Chi-en's throat. He swallowed convulsively, coughed. When he fixed his eye on Reverend Shambles it did not waver. 'I see why you will not answer. After all, what would people say? The crusader with a Chinese bastard. The saint who took a Chinese girl and left her to perish alone. The sober man who drank like a sailor.' His anger faded and tears returned. Helpless as a small boy, he lowered his head. 'Forgive me!' he cried. 'Please forgive me! But I must know the truth. Please help me to learn it.'

Shambles's restless eye flicked round the room – from law books to gun case and, finally, the hangman's noose.

'I have to think, Humble. I will tell you the truth. I promise that. But I need to think. And pray. Pray for guidance. This is so sudden! Where are you staying, Humble?'

Chi-en wiped his eyes. 'The Reel Cheep Lawndry in town.'

'Good boy. Go back there, Humble. Meanwhile I will think. And I will pray. But I promise to give my answer tonight. In return, there is something you must promise. Will you do that for me?'

'Yes. Yes, I will.'

'Tell no one about your visit here. No one! Do I have your solemn word?'

'Yes.'

'Sometimes things happen to a man that do not belong with that man. Not rightly. So, he must leave them behind. Wait for my message, son.'

That last word, so casually given, provided the answer Chi-en desired. Bowing, he went to the door and left the way he had entered. Finnegan and Corey lounged at the far end of the porch, talking in low voices. Amidst the turbulence of his joy and sorrow, he felt the intensity of their eyes on his back.

He reached Sin Goon's laundry in a daze. So much emotion had drained him of the capacity for more. Yet, for the first time in his life, Chi-en Shambles walked with the assurance of a surname. One not borrowed but owned. Spiritual Uncle had been right all those years ago: the truth set him free.

For he could not doubt Reverend Shambles would confirm his paternity that evening. Whether he chose to acknowledge it publicly did not matter. Indeed, Chi-en feared so drastic a step. But the truth would help them understand the past − fully, compassionately − and each other, at last. That morning a great scrubbing had taken place and from stains must emerge . . . he could not guess what. Yet he did not doubt it would prove kind.

Even as he reassured himself, Chi-en marvelled at his boldness in marching straight to his father's house. Reverend Shambles could hardly acknowledge him in North Platte. It would compromise all his good work.

Chi-en discovered that a full spirit provoked great hunger. He needed to eat, to be strong. Once through the door of the Reel Cheep Lawndry he held up three shiny dollar coins.

'Sin Goon,' he said, 'this afternoon will see a banquet. And I will be its chef. But first you must go out and buy the necessary ingredients.'

An hour later, Chi-en busied himself at Sin Goon's fireplace, all the while waiting for shadows to creep across the laundry floor, hastening the hour he would receive Reverend Shambles's reply. In honour of the occasion, he cooked with the most Chinese flavour he could muster in such a town. Fortunately, Sin Goon had a small supply of spices and even rice wine hoarded for the New Year.

As the old Chinaman stirred his vats of boiling clothes, Chi-en made lucky dumplings of herbs and pork, steaming them in a large wicker hat laid over a pan of boiling water. He stir-fried peppery sliced beefsteak flavoured with pinches of precious five-spice. A dish of plain greens was enlivened with vinegar and sugar. Catfish from the North Platte River broiled with wine and onions. Of noodles, there was not a hope, but rice filled the gap.

At first Sin Goon said nothing, plying his chopsticks and grunting. As cup after cup of wine vanished, he grew more eloquent, listing his principle relatives in order of seniority and how he hoped to aid each of them when he made his fortune in America. Chi-en said little, too full for words.

Afternoon gathered shadows. Once the dishes were washed, Sin Goon, restless as ever, ironed a basket of linen. The boiling vats were re-charged and steam billowed round the laundry.

Chi-en took a chair near the counter, sipping tea.

While Sin Goon stoked the fire beneath a wide vat, Chi-en wondered what he expected from his father. The best he could hope for was a secret embrace, a blessing. Then he must return to San Francisco and unpick the tangled threads of his life. Perhaps they would correspond. Such a prospect offered new possibilities. He would strive to be a success in Chinatown. Who knows, he might grow rich. Then his letters would be proud yet modest affairs.

Chi-en took out his watch and went into the backyard. Hints of twilight were in the sky. Where was the message he had been promised? He must be patient, not afraid, for at last, he *knew*.

A loud knock rattled the door.

Chi-en looked up eagerly. He exchanged glances with Sin Goon. The old man, anticipating business, hurried to the front entrance. 'Comee!' he called. 'No go 'way!'

The bolt drawn, Sin Goon bowed obsequiously. A tall, thin figure pushed past into the shadowy room. He was followed by a rotund young man in a sober suit: Corey Shambles.

Chi-en started forward at the sight of his half-brother, whose very presence confirmed his dearest wish. 'Please, come in! You, too, Mr Finnegan. Has my . . . I mean, Reverend Shambles, sent a message for me?'

He examined their faces. Finnegan had a leering squint. Corey, however, seemed fearful. He carried a long, thin bundle wrapped in cloth.

'You are very welcome, sirs,' Chi-en said, puzzled.

Finnegan went back to the street door, bolting it top and bottom.

'You wan' laundry?' demanded Sin Goon. 'We ha' no dollar steal!'

'Check there ain't no more in the yard,' growled Finnegan.

Corey hurried to the rear double doors.

'No one out here, Finn.'

'Then close 'em up.'

To Chi-en's astonishment, Finnegan reached under his coat and produced a large revolver. Sin Goon began to tremble. 'We no dollar!' he cried.

'Shut it!'

'We no dollar!' repeated Sin Goon, loudly. 'We no dollar steal!'

'I said shut it!' warned Finnegan, stepping forward.

'Shut him up, Finn!' called Corey. 'The whole neighbourhood'll hear!'

Lunging forward, bloodshot eyes wide, Finnegan pistol-whipped the shaking Chinaman across the face. 'Shut up, I tell yer!'

'Please, gentlemen!' begged Chi-en.

A terrible, keening wail broke the fitful silence of the North Platte evening. Sin Goon was shrieking at the top of his voice – a high-pitched, wailing screech of primal terror that made the three men stare in surprise.

'I said shut it!' roared Finnegan.

The shrieking cut into the night like a train whistle.

'Jesus, Finn! Do something!'

'Please, gentlemen!'

Another blow from the pistol. If possible, the screaming grew louder. Now Finnegan was beyond control. 'Shut it! Yer yeller bastard!'

Crack. The shaved forehead split open, forming a bright well of blood. The screeching intensified.

'Damn ye!'

'Stop! You'll kill him!' Chi-en rushed at the man kneeling over Sin Goon, the pistol raised for another blow. A blur of motion in the corner of his eye revealed a long axe handle emerging from the cloth held by Corey Shambles. A glancing blow on the back of his head drove him to the floor. Still the wailing screech of Sin Goon continued.

'Damn ye!'

From the earthen floor, even as he grovelled and tried to rise, Chi-en saw Finnegan pick up the slender old man by the waist and lunge towards a bubbling vat of soapy, grey water, four feet wide.

'No dollar! Aieeee!'

The screeching stopped. Sin Goon had been tossed, head first into the murky, boiling liquid. For a moment his legs twitched frantically.

'My God!' cried Corey. 'My God, what have you done?'

Another ill-aimed blow struck Chi-en's head, knocking sight and sense out of him. He folded into oblivion.

California and Nebraska
Summer 1878

After Dr Boomer's second visit, Catherine remained with the sick child. Fresh rings of bruised, lacerated skin showed where the leeches had fed. Yet it seemed they drank only strong blood, not feverish blood. If anything, Emile looked paler, weaker. And the bright blue medicine seemed only to worsen the pain stabbing beneath his chest. Gasps and sobs. Coughing, coughing when there was no phlegm to retch.

Catherine glanced at her tired, lined face in the mirror. Within the glass of her soul unfamiliar feelings created new reflections.

If only Chi-en had stayed! Emile would surely get better with his encouragement. No doubt she was deceiving herself. Yet she would have given all the Dr Boomers in the world for Chi-en's steady presence now. Especially if Emile . . . No, she must not think of it! Must not! Even to consider or name it brought closer the unbearable possibility.

Emile's coughing subsided and he seemed to sleep. Catherine grew restless. Noticing toys and clutter — a boy's treasures — in corners and under the bed, she tidied listlessly. A penknife. Flints. A collection of feathers. Exercise books full of methodical columns of words: English with French translations, lists of irregular verbs and nouns. Another book bore a sketch of Mount St Helena, *Kanamoto: People Mountain* on its cover. This contained hundreds of Wappo phrases and words rendered into writing through a system of Emile's own creation.

Beneath the bed was a large compendium of boys' adventure stories bought in San Francisco. As she retrieved it, a letter sealed with red wax dropped to the floor.

The envelope was scuffed, dirty, as though carried in pocket or satchel. She turned it over and gasped. *Château de Chauveterre!* And it was addressed to *M. le Comte Antoine de Rivac de Chauveterre!*

She glanced at Emile in horror. Was this how the hideous Baron Foche had found them? Through letters sent by her son? But Foche claimed Antoine did not know her whereabouts. Indeed, that piece of information represented his power over her. Unless, of course, he was playing a double game to squeeze her dry then sell her son's whereabouts to Antoine. Being paid twice would appeal to a man without honour or scruple like Foche.

Emile murmured in his sleep. She inspected the red sealing wax. The letter did not appear to have been sent. Tearing it open, she scanned its brief contents. Dated just before Christmas. Catherine remembered Emile storming off to punish her around that time – for what? – not believing him. This letter must be his revenge. In a short, plaintive note *Cher Papa* was urged to collect Emile soon. He was lonely and had no friends. He felt lost and hopeless. He longed to return to Château de Chauveterre and prayed Papa would not be angry.

Nausea shook Catherine. How could Emile betray her? Was she so despicable a mother? She sat on the bed for a long while staring at the mould-specked wallpaper, the letter twisted in her hands.

A faint voice disturbed her reverie. Emile, pale with unnaturally bright eyes, had woken. She did not conceal the letter on her lap. Knew he had seen it.

'Maman,' he whispered, 'are you angry?'

'No,' she said, sadly. And truly she was not.

For a long minute, silence. When he spoke again it was without emotion or apology, a voice enfeebled. 'I never sent the letter, Maman. I went to the post office in Perryville. They said it would cost three dollars. I meant to steal the money. For Papa's sake.'

Catherine recollected Colonel Smithson-Mackay saying he had seen her son at the post office. A lifetime ago.

Emile sighed. 'Then the Wappo came,' he whispered. 'Somehow I forgot Papa. Any money I stole went to my new friends. So they could buy food.'

'You never sent a letter to France?'

'No.'

'Not one?'

'Never.'

Catherine tried to smile. 'I am glad, Emile. Our future belongs here now.'

He seemed to consider this. His reply came in a murmur. 'Sometimes I feel afraid. Am I going to die? I think that I shall.'

'Of course not! Dr Boomer has given you medicine and leeches to suck out the bad blood. He says you will be better soon if you drink his medicine.'

'I don't like it,' whispered Emile. 'It hurts.'

'We must trust Dr Boomer's advice.' Catherine took her son's hand, held it firmly. 'You will get better soon.'

'Maman,' he whispered, 'I don't want to die. Sometimes I lie here and think of it. Do you remember the graves in the churchyard at home?'

She squeezed his hand tight, as though his spirit and unlived life were balloons that might float away.

'Then I think of all the things I wish to do when I'm a man.'

'You will do them,' she murmured. 'You will!'

He struggled to sit up in his agitation. 'I'd like to speak languages no one else understands. Just like Chi-en does. Already I know so much of the Wappo's language! No one writes it down except me!'

'Don't distress yourself, Emile. Please, rest.'

'When I die, their language will be forgotten. Forever and ever!'

'Hush, my love. And don't be afraid. Maman will keep you safe.'

His glow of clarity, so precious after days of delirious torpor, faded. He turned wearily to face the wall and was soon asleep.

Dusk to night. No stopping that. No stopping the dawn that must follow, whether one witnessed it or not, the turmoil across the face of the earth, men and animals and plants and numberless living creatures on the dusty troughs and peaks of the earth. No stopping their rush toward replacement. One might only belong for a while.

In the dark bedroom, Catherine went to the window. Gazing up, she watched constellations blink: not for her, not for anyone. Behind her, Emile floated on the hot, surging sea of his fever. She sensed the throbbing pain in his throat, chest, the marrow of his limbs. Every hour beneath those slowly rotating patterns of stars weakened him further.

His bedroom had filled with invisible doors. His pores and mouth, burning the earth's air like precious oil in a lamp – a light that glowed and dimmed with each breath. She sensed other doors. Exits leading nowhere but infinity, where the gathered specks of his poor body would disperse across the universe. All he might become, tendrils of self, spreading across time and place, his unscattered seed and probing roots, all that made a man complete – might never be. Children tugging his sleeve, followed by grandchildren. Friends clapping his back. Lovers gazing at him with softened eyes, temporarily blind to his faults. All that might never be. And those future losses seemed bitterest of all.

Mid-morning when Catherine woke with a jolt. She remembered a dream of sitting beside Emile until dawn.

Emile! She leaned forward, dreading what she would find. But he was breathing heavily, murmuring unfamiliar words. She strained to hear, recollecting the Wappo for Royaume Céleste: *Ear Town*. A whoop from his chest became a rattle.

When would Nancy reply! She hated Dr Boomer. Indeed, she had noticed a whiskey bottle in his side pocket when he last came with his infernal leeches. No more would she allow him to apply those creatures. She would as soon let the lice, the phylloxera, gnaw and suck at Emile until her boy was shrivelled as a lifeless vine.

Aware she was feeble with hunger and developing a fever of her own, Catherine tucked him into his blanket and quietly left. In her bedroom she sat at the dressing table and opened a drawer to look for smelling salts, anything that might revive her if she grew faint. Alongside the blue glass bottle of scented ammonia, there was a small wooden box. She took it out curiously.

How strange to re-discover this now! It had come all the way from France, unopened until this moment. Within lay a dozen of Emile's baby teeth that he had proudly traded for sweets: molars, incisors, some still stained crimson-black with blood. And curls of his auburn hair tied in loops, cut from his head like talismans each birthday until he would allow it no more.

Silent tears rolled down her cheeks. 'Oh. Emile!' she whispered, touching the soft hair. 'Don't leave Maman now!'

How she longed to reclaim the little face that once contained those teeth, that was shaded by this hair, and start again, only with more love, more affection. At once the echo came back to her mind, *too late, too late*.

'No,' she whispered to herself, rising convulsively. She must eat or she would faint.

Halfway down the staircase, she grew dizzy and clutched the rail. Oh, she must not sicken as well! Who would tend Emile if she fell ill? Yet there was no denying the ache in her bones, the light-headedness. Exhaustion sapping energy and will. If only Chi-en could appear like a good genie to set everything right.

When her eyes opened a black chimney had appeared at the foot of the stairs. Beneath it, smiling with every inch of his face apart from his eyes, was Baron Cesar Foche.

'Comtesse! You are not looking your best! What is the matter?'

With as much dignity as she could manage, Catherine ignored him and walked towards the kitchen.

'You are distressed, my dear,' he murmured, gently. He supported her with his hand. 'What is the matter? Please tell me. Remember, I am your friend.'

That simple word broke all reserve. She began to cry, sniffling at first, then sobbing. He led her to a kitchen chair and leaned over her, full of concern.

'What has happened? Surely not bad news from your bank or . . . Tell me as a friend, what has brought this about?'

'Emile,' she began. Then the sorry story spilled out, interrupted by bouts of helpless weeping.

He tutted sympathetically. 'How hard it is with the young. One must not have the slightest additional worry if one has a sickly child.'

She looked up at him.

The face bent over her own hardened. 'That is why it would be better if you paid me the money you owe me. For Emile's sake. Then I can leave you to care for him without interruption.'

She stared at him, trapped. Her customary determination was broken. Too exhausted, too thirsty, too hungry to deny him anything.

'I have not been able to . . . My son!' she explained. 'I have not been able to think of anything but him.'

For a long moment, Baron Foche's eyelids fluttered. Then he paced up and down the kitchen, emphasising his words with sharp raps of his silver-knobbed cane on the floor.

'That will not *do*. It will not *do*, I say! I expressly warned you, Comtesse. Do not mistake me. I will be paid what I am owed, one way or another.'

'Monsieur, I mean, Baron . . .'

'Do not interrupt me. Can't you see he will soon recover? And then what? Either I shall return him to his father – and I have no doubt my friend Colonel Smithson-Mackay, who was enquiring about you, by the way – would assist me with the legal niceties . . . No need for fresh alarm, Comtesse! I did not reveal your secret, though you can tell he smells a rat. What exactly *did* you do to offend him and his lovely wife? They seem to positively dislike you. You do not wish to tell? Never mind. Later. Where was I? Ah yes, and what if precious Emile found out dear Papa is not dead after all? You see, it is all for his sake. Pay me everything I am owed and I will vanish forever.'

She endured his diatribe with a bowed head. A desire to punish herself grew with every word. What did money matter compared to Emile? Had not Antoine whipped her like a disobedient bitch when she did not satisfy his whims? She deserved nothing less now. One could not explain Baron Foche's presence here otherwise. And she was too tired. If she agreed to pay him, he might leave her in peace.

'I will go to the bank at Napa City when Emile's fever lessens,' she said, wretchedly. 'Return here in two days. That is all I can do.'

Again, the cane banged onto the floor and she flinched. Abruptly, he softened. He came close, so that she felt his breath on her face. 'Catherine, do not think I wish to make you suffer. But you must face reality, for dear Emile's sake and your own. You will find I can be gentle when I am happy. All you need do is keep me happy.'

She gazed up at him. 'Yes,' she said in an empty voice. 'When Emile's fever lessens, I shall go straight to the bank.'

His long-fingered hand touched her cheek. She jerked her head away. He chuckled. 'Rest, Comtesse! Rest! But first I need more money as an advance on your debt to me. Let us call it *interest*.'

She found her purse and watched him pluck it from her hand then empty it.

'Twenty dollars only?' he said, suspiciously.

'The bank,' she pleaded, 'I must go to the bank at Napa City.'

He went to a small mirror that Chi-en had attached to the kitchen wall for shaving. Observed by its rectangular eye, he preened and tugged his tuft of beard.

'Very well,' he said, languidly, 'I shall return the day after tomorrow. Do not dare play a silly game with me or I will be forced to seek recompense for my losses from Antoine, not you. Count yourself lucky that I have a pressing need for cash. *Au revoir*, Comtesse.'

When he had gone, she sank onto a divan. Silent tears trickled down her face. Would Nancy Trubody ever reply to her telegram asking for a doctor capable of curing her son? She feared Dr Boomer as much as Emile's disease. She hurried back upstairs with bread soaked in warm milk and a large pitcher of water.

A jolt woke Chi-en. Another jerked up his head. His forehead fell on something unyielding. For a long moment he grovelled, aware of lying face down. Then pain – a cannon flash – lit the back of his skull, stifling every sense.

★

396

Later, how long he could not say, Chi-en's eyes opened with a start. He was in darkness. The darkness of the earth. The grave. Terror contended with waves of pain from his skull. They had buried him alive! They had plunged Sin Goon into the boiling vat. Now they had . . .

All thought was replaced by harsh vibrations; he was being shaken like soil in a sieve as he clung to the floor of his coffin. Rattling broke through horror, then realisation: wheels. *Wheels*!

Reason returned. Not a coffin, a wagon. He lay on the wooden planks of a wagon bed crossing rough terrain. And the darkness? Gingerly, Chi-en strained to lift his arm and touched tarpaulin, no sooner felt than smelled: oily, rank. One by one, his senses resumed. He gasped, almost cried out for help until recollections of Corey and Finnegan stifled the sound.

A few experiments revealed his limbs were unbound. At first this confused him. Perhaps they did not consider him a threat, or thought Corey's blows with the axe handle had been fatal.

He lay still. Above the rattle of the wagon came a loud, discordant song, punctuated by a drunken man's laughter.

'*The Pledge! The Pledge! The mighty rock*
Whereon the temp'rance fabric's set . . .'

Another voice, scared and pleading, broke in: 'Stop it, Finn! Someone'll hear!'

'Damn ye!' roared his companion. 'Who's to hear out here? There in't no one for miles!

When diss-i-pation, fierce an' dark,
Poured on the worl' its an-gree floods . . .'

An odd gurgling noise interrupted the hymn, then a satisfied belch. Chi-en risked lifting a corner of the tarpaulin. A moment later he lowered it silently, leaving a tiny crack. His plight was now very clear.

The wagon was crossing empty prairie, using its gentle contours as a road. And he had located Corey Shambles and Finnegan. They sat, side by side, on the wagon seat, their backs to him. A large bottle of vintage bourbon – originally intended as a gift to Reverend Ezekiel Shambles – was tilted to Finnegan's mouth, his Adam's apple working. Hence the gurgling noise. Corey hugged himself, though the night was oppressively hot.

'Stop it, Finn!' he begged. 'You'll go crazy again!'

'Damn ye!' shouted his companion. 'If I do the devil's work I'll drink his juice! I tell ye! The devil! The devil's behin' all o' this!

The Pledge! The Pledge! The glorious Pledge!

Oh! Let it ne'er forsaken be . . .'

'How much further, Finn?' whined Corey. 'Why don't we dump his body here for the buzzards? Nobody'll know.'

'God damn it!' Finnegan laughed peculiarly. 'I keep tellin' ye! They've got to think our frien' in the back did for the other Chink. An' that he ran out o' town. No one mus' find that feller's body.'

'I know, Finn, but . . . I can't believe nobody heard that damn ol' Chinaman screechin' and hollerin'.'

'Someone'll have heard,' said Finnegan, grimly. 'Jus' didn't want to get dragged in for a Chinee.'

'I can't seem to get him out of my head, Finn,' said Corey, 'like a soul burnin' in hell. Screechin' and hollerin'. Why did you have to kill the old man? Pa said to just frighten 'em out of town, not boil one of 'em alive!'

Finnegan brandished the bottle without spilling a drop. 'Yer little shit! Don't ye go yeller on me now. This is war. An' we're soldiers. The Rev'rend says at every meetin' it's war! That means dead men, that means things best forgotten.' Again, the bottle tilted. 'Empty bitch!' Finnegan hurled the bottle into the darkness and sang in a bitter, low voice:

'Firm to the Pledge let's stan' till we

Through Heaven's aid the victors be!'

Chi-en let the tarpaulin fall back and lay quiet, trying to gather strength. Perhaps he should climb out of the wagon and hope they did not notice. But Finnegan had a gun and the moon gave plenty of light for shooting. Besides, he was exhausted and could not run. They'd soon turn the wagon and be upon him.

So, he stayed still, aware his carpetbag's contents were strewn around him, the valuables looted. An hour passed. Perhaps less. Hard to judge in the dark, covered hold of the wagon. At last, they halted and Corey broke out anxiously, 'We here?'

'It'll do.' Finnegan sounded weary. Drunk. Defeated. 'Damn these bitches of a Chinee!'

Chi-en lay as still as the corpse they took him for. His hearing grew acutely sensitive: running water nearby, the faint rustle of a breeze across the plains. Night insects chirruped, so that Finnegan, still on the wagon seat, slurred angrily. 'Critters never stop! Singin' every night in my head! An' now I hear tell locusts are comin'. Maybe it's the end of the world.'

'Never mind locusts!' cried Corey. 'Can't you just get rid of him?'

'Can I bury him, ye mean? Can I hide him from the eyes of God? Damn ye, I will! Not for you, boy, but the Rev'rend. No licker int'rest'll get the Rev'rend while I draw breath.'

Trickles of sweat itched on Chi-en's forehead, mingling with dried blood. His breath quickened and muscles tensed. This was his chance. His one chance. Oh, let it be Finnegan who opened the back of the wagon to drag him out!

The tarpaulin was hauled away and he heard bolts removed to allow the tailgate to drop. A rough hand grabbed his ankle. In a flash, Chi-en surged up, drew back his booted feet and kicked out at the looming figure. It gasped in surprise. Foot connected to face, crushing the man's nose. Face flew backwards. Now Chi-en scrambled in pursuit.

And his prayer was answered. The man, reeling and cursing, hands on his broken nose, was Finnegan, too drunk and astounded to resist. Chi-en dived, his eye fixed on a glint at Finnegan's belt. Before he knew what had happened the revolver butt was heavy in his hand. A tug, then it came free from the belt.

He staggered back a few steps, cocked the gun, raised it, crying out inarticulately in his fear.

The fat, lazy moon hung low as a rising or setting sun across the horizon. Otherwise, the cloudless, blue-black sky staged a mess of constellations. Far to the south there was a faint glow: North Platte, perhaps, or the moon reflected on the wide, shallow river. The hot breeze stirred then died away. Grasshoppers sang, unconscious of the gun pointed at a man's chest, of the need for two or one to leave this place. Corey was first to speak. 'Don't shoot!' he pleaded. 'It wasn't me that killed your friend! You can't blame me!'

Chi-en glanced at the younger man. As he did, there was a movement in front of him and he steadied the revolver. Finnegan had used the distraction to edge closer.

'He won't shoot,' said the drunk, leering at Chi-en, his freshly broken nose spurting blood. 'Damn Chinee's yeller inside an' out.' He took another step forward.

'I will shoot,' said Chi-en, 'if you come closer!'

Now Finnegan chuckled. 'Lookee at that feller's hand! Shakin' like a leaf!'

'Do not make me,' urged Chi-en. 'Go! Take the wagon and go!'

'Damn ye!' chuckled Finnegan, his eyes glassy. Then he raged: 'Why, he speaks like an American! I tell ye the devil's with him. Leavin' that bottle for me to fin'. The devil made me! Don' you dare tell the Rev'rend I broke the Pledge! Don' you dare!'

'Go!' commanded Chi-en. 'Do not throw your life away!'

'Please, Finn, listen to him,' begged Corey. 'He's lettin' us go!'

'Oh, I'll go . . .' Finnegan lowered his head and lumbered forward with a roar. Sped by whiskey, maybe he believed he moved quickly, that he would surprise the cowardly Mongol devil who had tempted him back to sin.

The heavy revolver bucked in Chi-en's hand. A bright flash blinded him. There was a reek of black powder then something warm splashed over his cheeks and lips. A heavy shape crashed to the ground, its chest smouldering from the gunshot so close.

For a moment Chi-en panicked. He cocked the revolver and sought out Corey Shambles, lest the shovel land on his head. But the young man stood hunched, hiding his eyes with a hand.

'What have you done?' whispered Chi-en.

He looked at the man sprawled at his feet. His throat burned with a need to retch.

'Don't shoot!' whined Corey. 'Show Christian mercy! I'm beggin' you not to shoot!'

Chi-en gasped for air, wobbled. The wound on his head throbbed with renewed vigour. He must not fall. Must not let go of the gun.

'I'm innocent!' begged Corey. 'I never wanted nothin' of this. Finn was just meant to run you out of town, I swear.' He began to snivel. 'Pa told us you were sent by the liquor interest. I ain't to blame!'

Chi-en knew he should shoot very soon. Before he fainted. If their positions were reversed, he knew Corey Shambles would, albeit reluctantly, squeeze the trigger. But executing a man in cold blood was unbearable. There was another reason. What circle of hell, Buddhist or Christian, was assigned to a man who killed his own brother? What hell of guilt and remorse would he suffer before leaving this vile, corrupted earth? Chi-en lowered the gun.

'Could he not have shown charity?' he asked. 'I would never have troubled or blackmailed him, if that was his fear. Tell him that. Tell him two men have died tonight to satisfy his fear.'

Corey sobbed, 'I'm not to blame! Pa told us to do it!'

'Go!' Chi-en commanded. 'Tell my father what his cowardice has done to us all. Say that Chi-en Shambles, for I have no other name, wants him to know what evil and sorrow his cowardice has caused.'

Corey stared at him. 'Father? What the hell?'

'Father. Yes. By his Chinese whore . . . by my mother. Tell him!'

'You're a liar!'

'You know I'm telling the truth, Corey. Take the truth with you.' He raised the pistol again. 'And take your poor friend for an honourable burial. Go!'

Corey Shambles bolted to the wagon. The horses, frightened by the gunshot, had dragged it a dozen yards. Abandoning Finnegan's corpse, he scrambled onto the bench, seized the reins and whipped the two horses into motion.

Chi-en watched the wagon jolt and bump into the moonlit night until consumed by the curve of the land. He sank to his knees beside the dead man.

California and Nebraska
Summer 1878

'Madame! Come quickly! Our friend is back!'

Catherine woke with a jolt. She was sitting beside Emile's bed. Jean-Pierre leant over her. No need to ask their *friend*'s identity. Yet Foche had agreed not to return for two days. No doubt he had grown impatient and decided to torment her some more.

Jean-Pierre looked grimmer than she had ever seen him. 'I could show Monsieur a certain way home,' he said. 'I have my shotgun. And it is loaded.'

Catherine rose with a struggle. 'Think what you are saying! Are we come to that?' But the idea, once planted, put out instant roots. 'No, Jean-Pierre. Please watch over Emile while I speak to him.'

The steward hovered uncertainly beside the sleeping boy. His was an oddly motionless sleep. Jean-Pierre made a hurried sign of the cross.

She stepped outside just as a smart four-wheel brougham whipped on by a servant in livery rattled to a halt. The horses snorted, flanks shiny with sweat. Too grand a carriage for Baron Foche, at least until he stripped her bare like a row of cabbages. The door swung open and a short, fussy-looking man in a black suit descended, bag in hand.

Removing spotless white kid gloves, the stranger examined the farm buildings and vines. A curt bow of greeting was the sole social nicety he permitted himself.

'Winkler,' he said, as though it explained everything. 'Now, the child, if you please!'

'But . . .'

'Please lead the way. And your son's exact age? General health? Commencement of this particular affliction? Symptoms observed?'

She looked at him in bewilderment.

'I divine that you have not received notice of my coming?'

'No.'

'Never mind, we shall establish the child's history by and by.' Sighing, he hustled her inside. 'I assume the boy's room is upstairs?'

'Yes.'

He marched up the stairs. 'What treatment has already been undertaken?'

Catherine produced Dr Boomer's brilliant blue medicine from a washstand in the hall. He regarded it gravely, uncorked, sniffed, tasted. 'Powdered chalk, food-colouring, tincture of opium, salt and sugar,' he declared. 'Please dispose of it somewhere safe.'

Then he stalked towards Emile's bedroom, bag in hand.

'Doctor,' said Catherine, 'you have not explained. How is it you are here?'

Once more he sighed. 'Madame Bourchier, I was told the case was urgent. It is not my habit to waste time when a case is urgent. I reside in San Francisco where I am Mrs Nancy Trubody's personal physician. She instructed me by telegram to come here without a single moment's delay.'

Catherine frowned. 'From San Francisco?

Dr Winkler nodded. 'I should add that Mrs Trubody insists – her word not mine – *insists* on meeting all, ahem, *disbursements* arising from the treatment. Now, the boy!'

Dr Winkler stayed by Emile's bed for an hour, exercising the mysteries of his craft. When he descended, his breezy confidence was replaced by a distinct caginess.

'Mrs Bourchier,' he said, shaking his head, 'I really should have been called much sooner. A serious fever has spread to your son's heart. He is truly a doughty little fellow not to have succumbed. I should most definitely have been called earlier.'

Catherine listened but scarcely heard. She rested against the top of a chair, swaying slightly.

'I knew it,' she whispered. 'Tell me, doctor, will he . . . You see, the same thing happened to my brothers . . . Is he dying?'

Dr Winkler leaned forward intently. 'Tell me about your brothers.'

Though tears welled in her eyes, Catherine's voice did not waver as she related that bitter story, how her brothers' deaths ruined her parents' happiness – and her own childhood. Every so often Dr Winkler asked one of his sharp questions.

'Heredity may be a factor,' he concluded, 'a hereditary weakness or predilection to heart failure. It carries away a great many children. But what of his father's family? Did they suffer similar . . . premature morbidities?'

'I do not know.'

She could have added, that they never talked of such things or talked of anything intimate, least of all admissions that Antoine's glorious ancestors possessed flaws. After all, her husband had nothing other than his family's past and a handsome face to lend him the slightest distinction. He knew little and had achieved far less.

'Emile's father's family was very ordinary,' she said.

'Nevertheless, if there is no hereditary frailty there, the father's blood may yet pull Emile through,' said the doctor. 'How did your husband join his Maker?'

'Drink,' said Catherine. 'Dissipation.'

Dr Winkler nodded. 'Hmm. We shall give Emile every help within our power.'

Catherine listened numbly as he prescribed a tincture of foxglove to ease the blood's flow through the heart. It surprised her that Emile should no longer be encouraged to drink large jugs of water each day to cool the fever. 'Feed him a porridge of oats and this tincture of asparagus and dandelion. The more water he passes the better.'

At twilight Emile struggled into a fitful doze that deepened into motionless sleep. A putrid aroma rose from the pores of his skin and shallow breath. He slept as though rehearsing the deepest sleep of all.

Catherine stroked his lank, damp hair. The gauntness of his body appalled her. *Should have called me earlier . . . Should have called me earlier.* The phrase revolved round her tired brain. She had to leave this suffocating room for a few minutes and breathe fresh air. She'd be no use to Emile on a sickbed.

When she walked the vines, the soil was still warm from the long day's sun. Dust scattered beneath her boots, along with snail shells and flints. She stooped, gathering up a handful. It ran through her fingers like sand. Would Emile be joining the dust soon? Blending into that dust? She glanced fearfully at the silent house.

If they had stayed in France, perhaps he would be well. Who was to say he had not caught the disease during the voyage across the ocean? Sickness could linger inside one for years.

Unless, of course, the Wappo had infected him. The Old Mother had said they knew of his illness. There would be a neat irony in that. After all, the Indians were almost extinguished by white men's diseases. Perhaps Emile's kindness and interest in the savages was to blame. The Indians were heathens and God might wish to punish her son for helping devil worshippers. A spasm of distress, almost physical, gripped her.

But that was nonsense. Easy to turn on the Wappo as scapegoats, easy to blame those the whole world despised – a stupid habit of consolation.

No, Emile's sickness was the reward for her own sins. The punishment was her own. She had been the worst of mothers, always finding reasons to criticise. She had not cherished her son. Often, very often, she had considered him a nuisance.

Up and down the row of vines she drifted, hugging breasts that had fed her infant son. She passed a particularly fat cluster of darkening grapes. Instinctively, she picked one, testing the fruit for ripeness. Since Emile's illness began the grapes had sweetened without the slightest help from her, promising another fine harvest.

She glanced up at distant Mount St Helena, trying to remember the Wappo name Emile had taught her. He was about to be picked too early. She could see what he might become if given time: his intelligence, sympathies, courage and resilience. He had nearly fought Parker and Temple with his bare fists when they shot the young chief. Perhaps the shock of that murder had triggered his illness.

Back and forth she paced, praying to St Vincent, patron saint of winemakers, as she had in the ancient church below Château de Chauve-terre in lost Domaine Bourchier. Her dear, abandoned Languedoc! Could St Vincent hear her so far away? She was not even convinced that he or God or the Blessed Virgin or the angels were real. Without pure faith, why should they heed her prayer?

Give me a second chance, she prayed, *though I do not deserve it.*

She halted, staring up at distant flashes of sunset fading behind eastern hills. Somewhere beyond them, Chi-en was seeking his father. Perhaps in danger. Yet he was not afraid to risk himself for a lost love. He was brave and strong.

St Vincent, take me instead of Emile. My life is worthless compared to his. Think of the good he could do in this world.

Her only answer was the mocking chirrup of insects. Now she despaired and prayed. *St Vincent, protector of all who tend the vine, if you let him live I shall surrender this vineyard to someone more worthy. If you are merciful you will give me a chance to know my son better. He shall be my vineyard. For I have been foolish. Oh, I see that now! I have been cold towards him!*

And, through her pain, she acknowledged without blame where that coldness began: her own maman's stiff face – never affectionate – always angry that it was she, not her adored brothers, who survived. And she acknowledged without blame her own fear of loving when all one loves dies.

There came a simple thought. At first it astounded her. As its roots pushed into her soul, hope battled despair. *I can change. I can change.* Catherine tasted the simple words. *If Emile only lives, I can change.*

She noticed a single horseman riding towards the farmhouse. It could not be Dr Winkler. He had promised to return in a couple of hours after racing to the apothecary in Perryville for a medicine he believed might help Emile see the dawn. And his mode of transport would be a shiny carriage, not a gangly, hired mare.

Slanted evening sunshine lengthened the rider's shadow. St Vincent had answered her prayer by sending Baron Foche. He was to be the first test whether she would sacrifice Royaume Céleste in exchange for her son's life. An image of Jean-Pierre's loaded shotgun flashed across her mind. She hurried through rows of vines to intercept Baron Foche before he could reach the farmhouse.

Thirst revived Chi-en. Murmurs of water drew him to investigate why Finnegan had chosen this spot amidst the apparent sameness of the prairie.

A meandering fissure had been carved into the plain by ancient floods and downpours, forming a steep-banked streambed. Shrubs and brambles lined the course of the narrow creek. Chi-en pushed through their spindly branches. There he scooped up handfuls of water until strength returned.

Now he could think of Finnegan. Should he abandon him as Corey had? He owed his failed murderer no loyalty, after all. Chi-en climbed out of the gully. The long drought had created deep clefts in the earth. He did not doubt Finnegan had intended to hide him in one; it would be easy enough.

Not so dragging the heavy corpse to a suitable cleft and rolling him in. Chi-en was already enfeebled by his wound. With a last effort, he used Corey's shovel to collapse the side of the cleft over the corpse. Then he covered the bare earth with brushwood.

Midnight had gone when he curled up beside the improvised grave, too weary to care if Corey returned with armed men.

Chi-en woke from dreamless sleep. Stumbling to his knees, he was confronted with a fiery tidal wave rising in the east. When he looked again, he recognised clouds, layers of burning light, molten gold, silver, copper, every metal considered precious by deluded men. The sunrise appeared strangely close, a place he could reach if he hastened.

A cool wind blew steadily from the west. When he turned to face it, the horizon was still dark, circled by stars.

After breakfasting on a bellyful of water, Chi-en reviewed his resources in this empty land. No habitation could be seen in any direction. A few deer grazed far away, their white rumps catching the sunlight. He possessed a shovel, a revolver with five rounds and – by some miracle – his hidden money belt containing nearly seventy dollars.

Although there was no sign of Corey, Chi-en knew he must keep moving. He tried to remember maps of Nebraska. They offered little help now. It seemed probable this creek might eventually join the wide North Platte River. On the far bank, a few miles south of the water, ran the Union Pacific Railroad. If he could reach the tracks, perhaps – perhaps – he might buy a passage back West.

Taking up the revolver, Chi-en fired a single shot at the long handle of the shovel. The sound of the shot echoed round the gully, stilling all birdsong. It was a risk he must take. Now the splintered wood could be separated from the metal head of the shovel and he had a support to lean on. He took up the revolver and threw it into another cleft in the earth. Whatever happened, he would kill no more.

In the hour before dawn, aided by his makeshift staff, Chi-en walked beside the streambed, hidden from watchers on the prairie. As the narrow gully wound gently downhill it opened into a wider valley, terraced on either side. Still, he encountered no one in the deserted land.

Fear drove him to ignore numerous aches, especially within his soul. The worst, so deep nothing might relieve it, was his own father's betrayal. Oh, he could never forget that hurt! It would never mend. Never settle. He must bury it deep forever. His own father, dear, kindly Spiritual Uncle Father, had set son against son; had sought, in his cowardice, to drive him away like an enemy. Reverend Shambles did not love his little Humble, his bastard little boy. Would never love him.

Perhaps neither father nor son was worthy of love. Tainted to the marrow, as Aunty-Mother had believed, long ago. Perhaps he, like his own father, was too cowardly to love – must always drive love away, finding new places to hide.

Chi-en might have lain down in despair had not a memory of a vineyard fat with grapes drawn him on. He recollected a promise made beneath the moon, that he would return in time for the harvest. And so, step by weary step, he followed the muttering stream as it meandered south.

His plodding march was rewarded with a distant flash of silver. Soon the creek, his sole guide through the wilderness, reached the edge of a bluff descending steeply to an area of bottom lands filled by a confusion of vegetation and swamp; above all, by the North Platte River.

Chi-en crouched on his knees and watched for signs of movement below. North Platte must be a good way to the east. He saw no tell-tale plumes of smoke. Certainly, none between his present position and the river.

Sheer will drove him to his feet. He must reach the silver ribbon of water before he rested. A few miles lay between. He would cross the swampy ground to the river.

It was a slow, dreadful few miles beneath the pitiless Nebraskan sun. Even the constant wind seemed not to cool, merely blow dust and tiny midges into his face. If the marshy ground hadn't been parched by the drought, he would never have made it through.

At last, he drew near the slowly drifting water. Without a thought for observers or hunters, he staggered to the bank and drank. The water tasted muddy, left specks of silt on his tongue.

Then he found a small, dense stand of trees and thickets on what would be a shingle island when the river rose higher. In this shelter he lay down to sleep, clutching his staff, and dreamt.

A red glow emanated from the tower that spiralled up like a miles-wide conch shell: ten, twenty, a soaring number of miles high; high as the millennia of mankind. The dungeons beneath went as deep, boring into the flame-lit centre of the Earth.

'Lo, the Tower of Babel!' cried a voice he feared, 'where every language except God's own is spoken!'

The tower stood on a dark plain, the blighted land's only source of light. Holes in its sides spewed sparks and flames. Sometimes he glimpsed tiny, blackened figures inside. Winds of sound swept the land: gales of anger, terror, sobs of unquenchable regret.

Chi-en knew he must approach the tower and stumbled forward. As he drew near to a field of bubbling, steaming cauldrons, the inhuman screeching intensified.

'Where is the gate?' he cried to a figure hurrying before him. He could not see the man's face, only the back of his head. 'Where's the gate? Stop! Tell me!'

The man turned and Chi-en stepped back in horror. Half the man's chest had burned away. It was Finnegan.

'I'm a-goin' there,' said the sorrowing man. 'Ye can't stop me now, mister!' Then he broke into a song so sweet and melancholy tears started to Chi-en's eyes.

The Pledge! The Pledge! The glorious Pledge!
Firm to the pledge let's stand till we
Through Heaven's aid the victors be!

'I know who will save you,' urged Chi-en. 'Let us find him together.'

Instantly they were outside a vast stone arch leading into the tower. There, just as Chi-en had hoped, waited a short, neat figure, his expression kindly.

'Oh, Prince!' Chi-en grasped the young man's hands. 'My dear friend! You have returned!'

Prince Hong smiled gently. 'I cannot return.'

'You must!' said Chi-en. 'You must help poor Finnegan, here. I promised you would save him from the tower.'

'I cannot save him from the tower.'

'Think of the poor souls inside! Who will save them if you do not? The abandoned souls in their misery!'

'I cannot save them,' said Prince Hong. Then a long, shining sword appeared in his hand. 'Take this. It is your turn now, Chi-en.'

Still, he would not let go of his lost prince's hand, the hand that held the sword. Sobbing helplessly, Chi-en asked, 'Have you forgiven me? Have you forgiven your old friend?'

Hong's sad smile returned. 'Take this.' He offered the sword. 'Finish my work on earth. Then, perhaps, you will find forgiveness.'

Chi-en reached for the sword with a fearful grasp. Was he to enter the tower and kill all the demons? As soon as the sword was in his hand it changed, became insubstantial. An orb of pure light like a full moon rested on his palm. He gazed into its depths.

'Hong,' he pleaded, 'show me how to use the light!'

But Prince Hong, his dear friend and guide, had vanished, leaving him alone in the black tunnel. Must he enter and fight the demons with nothing sharper than a soft, glowing light?

'Why did you not give me the sword?' he shouted. 'I am too weak to fight! Too weak to finish your crazy, stupid dreams! You always let me down in the end!'

Chi-en dropped the orb and it shattered into a thousand sparks that glowed for an instant then faded.

When he stirred it was almost noon. A few images from his dream lingered, more as a deep unease than intelligible pictures. Others jumbled: Sin Goon's legs sticking from the vat of bubbling, stewing laundry; Finnegan's chest crushed and scorched by the gunshot at point blank range. Where, he wondered was Corey Shambles? As for his father, Chi-en could not bring himself to think.

Any posse raised in North Platte should have found him by now. His trail along the gully and across the half-dried swamp would be easy enough for a bloodhound or experienced hunter to follow. Yet when he stood by the broad North Platte River no one was visible. He shielded his eyes against the sun and gazed longingly at the far bank. The river would wash away his scent. It would wash clean his own and Finnegan's blood. If he drowned in the crossing his troubles would end.

Using his makeshift staff to steady himself, Chi-en waded into shallow water. Even with the West's long drought, the river was a mile wide, divided into numerous streams and channels, islands of sand and gravel where opportunistic plants raced to erect leaves.

Soon he was gasping, struggling to lift his feet from sucking mud. Despite a blazing sun the water was icy. Using his staff for leverage, he plied himself free, pushed towards a sandbank island. There he rested, staring at the far bank. But he must risk the next channel, and the next, each current stronger as he approached the centre of the river.

A weary hour later, Chi-en crawled onto the North Platte's southern shore, collapsing on a beach of fine gravel. The sun revived his shivering limbs.

When he rose, an unexpected wonder gripped his soul. All around birds sang in shrubs and low trees that had found a home in the uncertain soil of the floodplain. He stripped off his soaking clothes until he was naked, hanging them on branches or stretching them flat on stones to dry.

He lay back against the trunk of a wild plum tree, part of a large thicket, and ate the small, ripe crimson fruit. Catbirds and bluebirds flitted. As he watched, a herd of graceful, leaping antelope trotted to the river and drank. Their patriarch, its forehead crowned with low, curved horns, regarded the bare man, sniffed, decided he was no threat.

High clouds billowed like sails across the clear blue sky and he thought of San Francisco. Maybe his luck would hold, he would make it back. Then he thought of Catherine in Royaume Céleste and wondered what she was doing. Walking the vines, perhaps, tasting the grapes' progress towards harvest. How he longed to help her and Emile's *vendange*, to give his energies and loves to an attainable warmth. Too long he had seared himself by flapping at unreachable suns, a moth drawn to pitiless candles. Too often he'd ignored affections that might make him happy. Affections within his grasp! If he had been wise enough to see what was good and what was worthless. If he could just be wise.

But some desires were without end. Or satisfaction. He did not expect to witness the harvest of the fruit in Royaume Céleste.

His clothes dried quickly in the noon sun. Towards mid-afternoon he felt strong enough to dress and resume his journey. Away to the south he saw a tiny plume of smoke above a line of trees. His prediction had been correct! To the south lay the Union Pacific Railroad – and hope of home. He also knew each step in that direction increased the danger of encountering people. Had news of Sin Goon's murder – a killing that would be attributed to his mysterious Chinese guest – already travelled along the tracks? He must hurry, board a train before Nebraskan justice found him.

The long plod to the railroad proved hardest. Weakened by hunger; his head wound aching even as it formed a fragile scab; above all, wounded in spirit, Chi-en picked a weary way south – or, at least, the direction he believed was south. Later he realised that, in fact, he turned as if by instinct to the west, away from the perils of North Platte – and straight into one unanticipated.

★

A few miles from the river he entered a bottomland of slender trees stripped by deer. He halted abruptly. Something was different, an agitation in the air. Chi-en's attention was attracted to the west, the direction from which the hot wind blew.

A low, unstable cloud rolled over the land towards him. At first, he watched with mild interest. Then the first skirmishers flitted past and he had no doubt: Finnegan's prophecy had come true.

Birds in the shrubs rose, flying off in alarm. If Chi-en had possessed wings he, too, would have taken flight. All he could do was plod forward: straight into a swarm of locusts carried by the wind.

Within moments they were colliding with his face, hands, chest. Vision blurred to a mist of flickering, fluttering specks. The noise of a million tiny wings was vast, drowning out thought. Still he plodded on, covering his head with his coat like a shawl so they could not infest his hair, his ears. Locusts bloated with vegetation crunched beneath his boots. The swarm stank: a putrid horror of decaying bodies.

Now the noise was maddening. 'Leave me in peace!' he shrieked, only to be rewarded with a vile creature in his mouth. He spat and spat shreds of papery wings, rubbing his lips with frantic fingers.

Which way? He realised that in the midst of the cloud he had no direction. Then he halted, tried to think through the constant roar of wings. They had come from the west. He must keep the stream of filthy creatures always to his right: that way he would head south and, eventually, break away from the column blown across the floodplain towards North Platte.

How long or far he walked, blinded and buffeted, Chi-en could not tell. At last, the swarm around him thinned like the borders of a snowstorm. Once more he was in scrubland. Where was the railroad? Was he lost? Perhaps he would walk and walk until an inevitable collapse: and the bones of a man joined those of the slaughtered buffalo.

He had almost begun to despair when a rattle and huff and hiss found the edge of hearing. Another swarm? But the noise was unmistakeable. A locomotive!

Twilight now, and Chi-en stumbled toward the noise, arriving at the railroad tracks in time to watch the caboose of a long train vanish in the direction he must take. This last effort broke his strength. Resting beside the still humming iron he longed for water. Another night out here seemed an impossible desert to cross. What if a fresh cloud of locusts descended?

Again, he rose, this time making for the final embers of the setting sun. When he slipped on scree, falling over backwards, his head banged against the rails, reopening the wound on his scalp. Blood dripped down his cheek. He lay, staring up at a darkening sky.

Long ago, Prince Hong had asked him. 'Is there no Providence, Chi-en? No destiny? Are we what we plant and harvest from ourselves? If so, then we are free. That is what sets us free!'

Did kindly Providence or chance place the squatters' cabin near a creek beside the Union Pacific Railroad on land owned by Mrs Ada Van Pelt? Perhaps it was irony.

Afterwards, Chi-en remembered a few facts as certain. A dog barked and rushed at him, so that he feebly waved his staff. A large, buxom woman hurried from the cabin, calling to a man named David. There was a fold of latticed coppice wood in which sheep bleated, alarmed by the dog's excitement. He had blundered upon a shepherd's hut in the wilderness.

Strange to sit on the embankment of the railroad while a concerned, half-frightened woman held back the sheepdog. Strange to see the pinched, appraising face of the shepherd, who carried a bright, round lamp.

'I guess the Lord's sent us another one, Martha,' said the shepherd. 'And, lookee, he's a Chinee!'

Strange to close his eyes and await whatever Providence visited upon him, too exhausted to resist.

California and Nebraska
Summer 1878

Catherine meant to find Jean-Pierre's shotgun, intercept Baron Foche, refuse him permission to dismount, drive him from Royaume Céleste. Yet for all her long strides, he was already tying up his horse when she reached the porch. His air was proprietorial, good-humoured. Her acute nose detected brandy and, as before, something sweet and medicinal.

'Comtesse! You look more pleasing than at our last interview.' His smile was thin as a whip. 'But I see you are in a serious humour.' He raised a long finger of command. 'You neglect a hostess's duty. After such a hot, dusty ride to visit an old friend, might I not expect something to quench my thirst?'

She glanced at the house. There was no avoiding what must follow. Her ruin was the first sacrifice Saint Vincent required to save Emile. His interests alone must guide her actions now.

He pushed past her into the salon and looked round. His eye fell on a decanter containing Royaume Céleste claret. It stood on a burnished pewter tray she had bought in San Francisco to mark the restoration of the Bourchier family fortunes, along with two crystal glasses. One had been used by Chi-en when he sketched Mount St Helena for her new wine label.

'Good!' said Foche. 'I am thirsty!'

He poured himself a measure and was about to drink when he noticed her staring.

'No need to look at me like Medusa,' he said. 'So this is the famous vintage I have heard about from Colonel Smithson-Mackay. He is quite jealous. As a gentleman of taste, let me give your Royaume Céleste my full attention.' Foche swirled and sniffed with the aplomb of a true connoisseur. 'Not bad for such a savage *terroir*.' He swallowed the wine and, with a contented sigh, poured himself another.

Still Catherine did not speak.

Laying his stovepipe hat on a cabinet by the door, Foche wandered to the largest chair in the room, one she customarily used for reading or playing her oboe during the long evenings. With a flap of his bony, white hand, she was instructed to sit upon a footstool beneath him. Catherine remained near the door.

'I see Madame is defiant,' he said. 'May one conclude it concerns Antoine's son and heir?'

Catherine's mouth twitched.

'I conclude my guess is correct,' he said. 'Why Antoine is so eager to have the boy back is a mystery to me. But there it is. Even he must work a little for his pay.' Now his good humour vanished. 'Comtesse, you recollect what I am here for? I take it you have my money?'

Her attention did not shift from his face.

'A simple *oui* or *non* will suffice,' he said. 'Do not play nursery games with me. I am far too determined for it to work.'

'You will get no money from me,' she said with icy vehemence.

He laughed. 'A little spirit, at last! You would have disappointed me otherwise. How you bourgeois hate to part with your precious cash! But this is a bargain you cannot refuse.'

'I do refuse.'

He tutted and poured himself another glass of wine.

'Then you will be exposed. Ruined. I shall summon Antoine like a hungry wolf. With financial assistance from his brothers, he could be in San Francisco within a few weeks. Once he's there, I could extract a considerable sum from him in exchange for dear Emile's whereabouts. Of course, Antoine speaks no English. That, too, will prove profitable should he need access to the law.'

'You will get no more money from me,' she said. 'I do not care if you ruin my reputation. Now go.'

Baron Foche sighed with regret. But she could tell he was calculating rapidly.

'I should have known you are too selfish to save your son.' Taking up his wineglass, he contemplated then swallowed. 'Too, too selfish!' He gently tossed the crystal glass so it smashed against the iron grate of the fire. Red wine dripped like blood. Catherine's flinch was momentary.

'Get out!' she cried, advancing towards him from the doorway. 'Do your worst to me, you pig! My son's happiness is not for sale.'

At that moment the door opened. Baron Foche and Catherine turned in surprise. When she realised who stood in the entrance, astonishment became horror.

'Emile! Why are you out of bed?'

The sick boy stood in his nightshirt, face wan as a ghost, once-muscular limbs wasting away. He looked around feverishly, crying out at the sight of Baron Foche. 'Papa? Is that you, Papa? I heard your voice!'

Catherine rushed to the door. 'It is not, Papa,' she said. 'See! It is his old friend, Baron Foche, who is just leaving.'

Emile seemed more confused than upset. 'Not Papa,' he mumbled. 'Where is Chi-en? I want Chi-en!'

'You should be in bed, my pet. You must rest now. Baron Foche is leaving and will never come back.'

Mentioning his name seemed to snap some cord of self-control within Foche. He stepped forward, blocking the way out of the room.

'No, Emile! You should learn the truth about your lovely *Maman*. Then you might persuade her to be sensible. You think your father is dead? That is what she has told you?'

'Stop it!' cried Catherine. 'Can you not see how sick he is?'

'Your father is very much alive, *mon petit brave*,' leered Foche. 'Maman lied to steal his money. Why else did she run to this horrible country? But Papa has sent me to claim what was stolen. Oh yes, and bring you back to France!'

Emile stared in confusion at the smashed glass around the fireplace; Catherine realised that if she let go of his arm he would fall. 'Get out of our way!' she said, pushing past so that the stovepipe hat was knocked to the floor and rolled in front of her like tumbleweed.

'As for you,' said Foche, in his eagerness to wound, 'Antoine despises you. Ever heard of Madame Lavier from Carcasonne? I thought you might have. A *real* lady of property and now, sadly, a widow. He's due to marr . . .' Abruptly, he fell silent.

Even in her distress, Catherine's mind seized the implication. Antoine intended to re-marry! That meant he could not wish to trace his son. Above all, trace his lawful wife. For then he would be a bigamist, no divorce or legal separation having taken place. Antoine had probably persuaded Madame Lavier that Catherine had perished in America – and Emile with her. Forging letters to prove such a thing would not be hard. A cork of hope popped in Catherine's soul. Foche's threats to take Emile away were bluster. The worst he could do was ruin her in California.

She turned to the drooping Emile. 'Never mind this nasty man. You must go back to bed and get strong.' But he could not hear. He had half-fainted and slid one foot in front of the other through instinct alone.

Foche pursued her, step by step, with a vexed sneer. 'A pity! The first person I intend to inform of your duplicity is Colonel Smithson-Mackay. I might even suggest an article in his *California Star* condemning fake Comtesses. Such an entertaining scandal!'

At the bottom of the stairs, Catherine encountered the stovepipe hat. A quick stamp flattened it into the varnished floorboards, splitting peak from crown.

Baron Foche stooped to save what remained. For once he was speechless. His face turned pale with cold, cruel rage. 'I shall take a payment for that. A payment requiring no money. And I shall enjoy every moment of it.' He lunged forward as though to drag her away.

'I would not, Monsieur, if I were you.'

Catherine and Foche froze.

'Not a single step nearer!'

The voice belonged to an old man and spoke a thick, Languedoc brogue. They glanced up. Jean-Pierre was at the top of the stairs. His shotgun pointed directly at Baron Foche. The latter seemed to weigh something, reach a conclusion, then he stepped back gingerly.

'Do not tempt me,' growled Jean-Pierre. 'My God, it would be my pleasure! Madame, please proceed.'

Catherine manoeuvred Emile up the stairs, gasping at the effort. At the top, she paused and looked down at Foche. His little smile was back.

'Do not imagine,' he said, 'you shall have the last word.'

She carried on down the hall with her precious Emile, limp and broken. As she tucked him beneath his blanket, Catherine heard a gallop of horse's hooves and Jean-Pierre's angry bellow outside.

She sat beside Emile while he slept, stroking his hot, damp forehead. Even if he lived – as Dr Wrinkler hinted was unlikely, saying she must prepare herself for the will of God – Emile would hate and distrust her forever. He would remember Foche's words: that his father was alive and that she had stolen his fortune. That she had lied and lied. Her last hope, firm as a feather, was that Dr Winkler's frantic dash to the apothecary in Perryville would secure the drugs he believed might quell the infection around Emile's heart.

The room darkened slowly as night came on. She knew, in her own heart, this night would decide Emile's sickness – and all their harvests.

Correspondence
Summer 1878

Extract from a letter. Lu Kan to Catherine Bourchier, 15th July 1878

Chinatown, San Francisco

. . . and so we look for as plenty number cases sold in Shanghai and
Hong Kong next year.

Now business very different. Two day ago a letter come to Lu Kan
Store. It was about Mr Chi-en Shambles. It was paper good quality
but yellow with ancient. Printed on top is PURE AIR HOTEL,
PROMETHEUS, CALIFORNIA.

We look very hard at map to find this Prometheus. A tiny dot
on Union Pacific Railroad high in mountains of Sierra Nevada. We
find nothing more. On the letter is following memorial I copy
exactly:

SIR or CELESTIAL MANDARIN in Chinatown (To whom this
may concern),

Our guest is one Mr Shambles, a man of ALMOST ORIENTAL
hue. He resides in our ESTABLISHMENT incapable of
MOVEMENT until his funds EXPIRE. It was HE who told me your

ADDRESS. In expectation of your remittance as
COMPENSATION.

Robert E. Phillimore Patterson (Hotel proprietor)

p.s. He has ELEVEN DOLLARS, FIFTY-INE CENTS remaining.

We know no more than this. Mr Shambles must be very sick if he cannot write.

With every respect

Lu Kan

President, Kong Chow Company

Extract from a letter. Catherine Bourchier to Lu Kan, 19th July 1878

Royaume Céleste, Napa County

. . . If this year's harvest fulfils its promise, we shall certainly satisfy all your requirements next year.

Thank you for your news concerning Mr Shambles. I was gravely concerned by his malady and the unkindly tone of Mr Phillimore Patterson's letter.

Since he joined my household, Mr Shambles has earned my gratitude many times over. For this reason, I wish to make an offer. If you can contact him, I undertake to meet all travelling expenses required for his return to San Francisco, where he may convalesce among friends. If he prefers, I would gladly welcome him as my guest at Royaume Céleste. I await your earliest reply.

Yours sincerely

Catherine Bourchier

Letter. Lu Kan to Catherine Bourchier, 31st July 1878

Chinatown, San Francisco

Dear Madam,

I inform you news concerning Mr Chi-en Shambles. After much discussion Kong Chow Company sent ambassador to bring back Mr Shambles to San Francisco at our expense. Ah Ling Company Secretary insist on that honour duty and discovered Mr Shambles about to be thrown from Pure Air Hotel, Prometheus.

Mr Chi-en Shambles is very sick. He has lodgings in Chinatown and the concern of good doctor.

With every respect
Lu Kan

Letter. Catherine Bourchier to Lu Kan, 4th August 1878

Dear Sir,

Thank you for your letter. Please pass the enclosed package to Mr Shambles.

Yours sincerely
Catherine Bourchier

Letter. Catherine Bourchier to Chi-en Shambles, 4th August 1878

My dear Chi-en,

We were very happy to hear about your return to Chinatown. I hope this finds you in better health. Emile urges me to send his good wishes and commands me (quite forcibly) to inform you he is still compiling a dictionary of Wappo words. Alas, dear Emile fell very sick after you left for Nebraska. We all feared greatly for his life. Whatever Power, divine or otherwise, determines such things decided he should live. Now I fear his least cough!

When you feel strong enough, be sure to recount your adventures.

With every good wish I sign myself

Catherine

p.s I enclose $100 unpaid wages from your employment at Royaume Céleste.

Letter. Chi-en Shambles to Catherine Bourchier, 9th August 1878

Dear Catherine, as you are generous enough to sign yourself (and so I presume to address you), I received your letter with great interest.

The news of Emile's illness was distressing both for his sake and your own. So much so – and I believe this will make you smile considering my free-thinking ways – I prevailed upon my landlord (of whom, more later) to hurry to the nearest Daoist Temple, or *Joss House* as the Americans call such places, to burn incense on Emile's behalf. It is not that I believe in the efficacy of scented smoke, but gestures relieve one's feelings.

In your kind letter you asked for an account of my 'adventures'.

What a euphemism that word seems! Suffice to say, I travelled to North Platte, Nebraska, without mishap. What occurred in that place is a subject so painful I beg you to never allude to it. I feel like a ghost who has been given a second life.

For all the sorrows of my sojourn in that cursed, locust-plagued region, I retain one comfort. No longer shall I worry about my father. Fate has decreed we are to remain severed forever, unless reconciled beyond the grave.

Enough of these morbid thoughts. They stem, I am sure, from a sickness that leaves me bedridden – hence the unevenness of my writing.

To my 'adventures'. I shall commence with fainting in a wounded state beside a section of the Union Pacific Railroad far from human habitation. My prospects were poor indeed. If I had not been discovered by a shepherd and his wife, then tended in their rustic cabin, all would have been over for me. This kindly couple went a long way to restoring my faith in humanity's goodness, a faith nigh on destroyed. Poor as famine mice, these gentle people did not steal my money, but fed me at their own expense until I was ready to resume my escape.

For days I travelled by slow emigrant train toward California. Alas, I had left my shepherd friend's care too early! As we crossed the mountains, a bad wound on my scalp re-opened and became putrid. In short, once more I was gravely ill.

Upon being informed of my condition, the Conductor decided I was infectious and ejected me at the next stop, a tiny place on the California side of the Sierra Nevada called Prometheus. This eyrie consisted of a station platform and single building clinging to a steep mountainside – a wooden hotel overlooking foothills and forests and plains. Unconscious of the fact my arrival had just doubled the population of the Pure Air Hotel, I was assigned a bed smelling of mildew by its proprietor, one Mr Phillimore Patterson, a man of dubious sanity who expects his hotel to become the hub of a great health resort. He mercilessly despoiled my modest store of dollars as I lay helpless and feverish. If Secretary Ah Ling had not appeared, I do not doubt I would have been dumped on the railroad platform to live or die as chance dictated.

The rest of my 'adventures' I believe you know.

Thank God they are over. I am recuperating in a lodging house owned by the Kong Chow Company and leased to an amiable rogue named Lee Wei. From my balcony I watch people enter the Chinese Theatre opposite and hear faint clashes of cymbals, drums and the actors' falsetto exclamations. Next door, a teahouse specialising in illegal gambling pays many a San Francisco policeman's whiskey bill. My great ambition is to hobble across the road to the theatre and enjoy someone else's drama. That, I fear, is still a way off.

With every good wish

Chi-en (Shambles)

p.s. I enclose a banker's draft arranged by Lu Kan for the $100 you sent me in error. You owe me nothing, as I believe you are aware. Yet I thank you.

Letter. Catherine Bourchier to Chi-en Shambles, 13th August 1878

Dear Chi-en,

My head buzzes with your letter! Despite your request that I never refer to North Platte, Nebraska, I shall speak once on that subject so hateful to you. Namely, I honour your courage in seeking your father and am assured that whatever occurred was no fault of your own. I shall say no more unless invited to do so.

Here in Royaume Céleste we walk the vines each day as they ripen. No rain clouds darken the horizon with a threat of mildew on the fruit. Jean-Pierre and I prepare the winery for the coming vendange with the help of the Wappo labourers. Life here is slow, predictable: comforting in its routines.

I say that, but there is a scandal in Napa County! It concerns one of my compatriots. Some weeks ago a Frenchman was shot during a card game in Perryville after accusations of cheating. The man survived but did not press charges. I hear he left for San Francisco before the County Sheriff could investigate. Of course, this compatriot was known to me and not in a pleasant way. I would rejoice he has disappeared if I did not fear time will wash him back to my door, hungrier than ever.

I shall end with news of Emile. He thanks you for burning incense in the Joss House. He especially wanted you to know his dictionary of Wappo (What should one call their language? Wappish?) advances in a way that seems far too logical for a boy of eleven. He has devised his own method of rendering their strange sounds into letters one may easily understand. His long illness, so dangerous and alarming, has made him more thoughtful than before. He is becoming a grave, serious boy. And very earnest, so that he reminds me of you.

I conclude with a proposal, though I fear it may prove unwelcome. After all, the Kong Chow Company and Lu Kan would be wise to employ your special talents when you recover. In addition, the attractions of our homely Royaume Céleste can hardly compete with the excitements and gaieties of San Francisco. Nevertheless, I shall make my proposal.

Why do you not conclude your recuperation by staying as our guest at Royaume Céleste? I emphasise the word guest. It would be pleasant for myself and Emile, at least. Perhaps it could be so for you? Besides, we have a suitcase of yours waiting to be collected.

   With every good wish

      Catherine

PS Since you returned the $100, I have instructed a vintner in San Francisco to send you a case of our Royaume Céleste claret to aid your recovery.

Letter. Chi-en Shambles to Catherine Bourchier, 18th August 1878

Dear Catherine,

   Today, accompanied by my garrulous landlord, Lee Wei, and leaning on a stick of imported bamboo (I am assured American wood will not do), I walked across the road to the Chinese Theatre. There, the performance squeezed reluctant tears from my eyes – reluctant because inspired by my childhood in far off Guangzhou. I enjoyed myself thoroughly!

   You may wonder why I write with frankness rather than politeness. It is because, after the theatre, I drank deep from a bottle of excellent Royaume Céleste claret. So, blame yourself! Your liquid gift returns as a flow of words.

   It would be easier to explain if we walked together in the vines, as once we did. Perhaps you recollect that evening? Perhaps not. Probably not. If the latter is true, I apologise for reminding you.

   As I sit on the balcony, chasing down your gift with coffee brought by Lee Wei (he disapproves by the way, for he believes a scholar should temper his wine with pure Fukkien tea not *fan gui* coffee) I feel only half at home in Chinatown. Why are some raised to belong in one place and others not? My life has been lived between destinations. That is true of all people, of course. Even those who never leave their birthplace traverse time. And nowhere stays the same.

But to practical matters. Your prediction concerning the Kong Chow Company using my talents proved correct. I am to be employed by the Presidents of the Six Companies. My role? Advising on legal matters, particularly when it comes to immigration. I shall also interpret and translate. Such a chance to use my knowledge for the benefit of my people is a great satisfaction. Yet when I walk in Chinatown some of those same compatriots abuse me as a foreign devil. Never mind. It must not discourage me from doing good in the world.

I will leave off now. From my balcony perch I see Secretary Ah Ling bustling up the street. His progress requires many bows from passersby. He comes every day to enquire decorously about my health, drink tea (he, like Lee Wei, despises coffee) and slyly test my knowledge of the Chinese classics. Oddly enough we are becoming friends.

Pass my thanks to Emile for his labours on the Wappo dictionary.

With every good wish

Chi-en

Letter. Catherine Bourchier to Chi-en Shambles, 25th August 1878

Dear Chi-en,

One frank letter deserves another, I believe. For that reason I have resorted to the same medicine as yourself, consuming an unladylike quantity of Royaume Céleste claret with my dinner, a very pleasant meal cooked by our new chef, Wong Wu.

I find myself at my bureau as twilight gathers. I have taken up my pen because I wondered, on a sudden thought, if you, too, were examining the dusk in bustling Chinatown.

Your letter set me thinking, my friend. Indeed, I have just re-read your words. For one thing, I share your sense of not quite belonging – in California or anywhere. Of course, I blame my own awkwardness for that. Nor can I return to France. As you know, my widowhood is so suspect that if my 'dead' husband discovered me I might lose Emile. That is the one prospect I cannot bear. My son is all the love I dare expect. After all, one would be selfish indeed to delude a man into bigamous matrimony. I speak far too frankly, I'm sure, but you are well aware of the truth. I am a practical woman at heart (I believe the majority of the so-called weaker sex are fiercely practical) and must not deceive myself if I am to provide for Emile.

Enough of such musings. You must find me a very dull correspondent! Indeed, I believe you only write to me out of boredom.

Here is an amusing thing to end my letter. I have taken to playing my hautbois out on the porch in the evenings, the musical score lit by a lantern that attracts moths and fruit flies. The Wappo children are fascinated by the throaty strains of my instrument and gather to listen in deep – and unnerving – silence. If you come across any oboe music in Chinatown, let me know.

Emile is calling and I shall seal this letter. I did note, however, you have not mentioned our invitation to stay here as our guest. That would please us both greatly before you begin your admirable duties with the Six Companies. Let me congratulate you on your appointment! I do so very gladly, for it is clear you are glad.

I remain your sincere friend

Catherine

Letter. Chi-en Shambles to Catherine Bourchier, 31st August 1878

Dear Catherine,

Thank you for your letter. Thank you also for your kind invitation, an offer I have decided to accept despite very real misgivings. I fear my presence at Royaume Céleste will only provoke trouble for you. Be that as it may, I hope to join you in time for the harvest. Unil then, *à bientôt*.

Your sincere friend

Chi-en

P.S. I enclose a volume of oboe music and hope the Wappo children enjoy it.

Napa Valley, California
Autumn 1878

The Great Panic deepened and no one could predict its end. Still, emigrants poured into California. Some found routes to Napa, fleeing San Francisco streets paved with dust, lured to the green wine country by unquenchable hope.

Such work as came their way traded pitiful wages for long, hard days. Easy then to blame the Chinese. Easy to stare sullenly as steam threshing machines gathered wheat along the valley bottom. Or watch huge wagons pulled by six, even ten pairs of mules, laden with grain to profit another man.

In the vineyards no helpful machines huffed and yammered. Get on your knees in the dirt. Pray with restless hands until baskets overflow with fruit that no one can sell.

In Royaume Céleste, tawny grass drooped through hazy afternoons. Only deep-rooted trees and the hardy vines showed vigour. The waiting earth's surface was grit, dried twigs, old snail shells, discarded leaves.

Unfallen vine leaves created blends of colour that changed daily. Gold to ochre, purple like a Roman Emperor's time-stained robe, every shade of green and every shade between, patterns defining light and shadow as the sun circled.

Each morning, Catherine walked the rows, tasting, deciding. Each day she delayed the *vendange*, greedy for sweeter grapes, aware that if autumn rains broke early her crop might spoil. The colours of the vines pleased and comforted her, reviving a lost girlhood. In faraway France the leaves had rustled with harvest excitement; grand *vendange* lunches where Papa went from table to table ensuring all the labourers were fed and paid before they dispersed.

Sharing her fear of rain, Jean-Pierre ordered a last thinning of the vine leaves, summoning the entire Wappo clan. Only the Old Mother stayed away, too sick to watch from her rocking chair. A gang of Italian workmen arrived, thin as greyhounds sniffing for work, and would have been taken on, except they refused to labour alongside Diggers. They left for Perryville with dark looks and mutterings: trouble plumping itself out as surely as the grapes.

When Jean-Pierre warned Catherine, she said, 'You know I must go to Napa City tomorrow to meet our guest. Be careful. If there is danger, send word at once to Mr Trubody.'

Jean-Pierre did not state his opinion of Madame's guest. His frown said it all.

Napa City styled itself the 'Oxford of the West', though its institutions generated dollars rather than knowledge. As Emile and Catherine waited outside Napa Station, she noted a very different mood from Perryville. Tall brick chimneys spewed black smoke into the clear air. The Napa River, long ago denuded of its pebbly bed to bulk up San Francisco streets, swirled with mud and waste from the tanning factories.

They dined at a French restaurant on coarse goose paté, *coq-au-vin* and a passable cheese. She should have been sleepy, contented, especially after a trip to the Napa Union Bank revealed her affluence. Deals with Lu Kan and Nathaniel Trubody were set to maintain a steady flow of dollars for years to come. Yet she was tempted to snap at Emile for fiddling constantly with his precious exercise book.

'Emile,' she said, 'go to the platform and wait there. Here is ten cents for *bons bons*.'

He rolled his eyes. 'It's called *candy*, Ma!'

'For that as well. I will guard the wagon and ensure no one steals Jeanne d'Arc.' The old mare's ears twitched, otherwise she did not stir in the heat.

Catherine watched passers-by. What would they make of a white woman riding beside a despised Chinaman? Not that Chi-en was *exactly* a Chinaman: no forehead shaving and pigtailing for him. She shifted uneasily. What *did* she hope to gain? Her motives disturbed and intrigued her. What intimacy dare any sensible woman risk with a man who stole into troubling dreams? She did not know. Wished and did not wish to know. Yet he was a friend, she felt sure of that. And both of them were far too sensible for any kind of silliness or indiscretion.

A puffing plume appeared behind rooftops and soon the train eased into Napa Station. From Catherine's seat on the wagon, she heard doors slam. A hiss of steam. Whistles. Her heart quickened to a pace she could not call sensible; likewise, her breath grew shallow, slightly uneven. She pretended to be very interested in a brewer's dray rattling up the street.

A tall, broad figure in smart city clothes emerged, Emile chattering excitedly by his elbow. Chi-en Shambles looked paler than when he had left Royaume Céleste to find his father. But she detected a new confidence in his manner as he talked to Emile. Two young ladies whispered and stared at the Chinaman. Catherine blushed and re-adjusted her hat with a slight toss of the head.

'Here he is, Ma!' cried Emile.

'So I see.'

She smiled as she climbed down from the wagon.

For a moment, both glanced aside, unsure how to act. The servant had shed his deferential, protective cocoon to reveal an equal guest. She held out a hand.

'*Bienvenue, mon ami,*' she said, wishing to set a proper tone. 'Welcome back, Monsieur 'Umble.'

A shadow stiffened his smile. 'I prefer the name Chi-en. I am determined to be Humble no more.'

'Humility is a virtue, is it not?' she said, gaily.

Emotion touched his face and she regretted her witticism.

'Sometimes,' he conceded. 'Sometimes it hides its contrary.'

'Hides what?' demanded Emile, sucking a stick of candy. 'What *contrary*?'

They looked at him in surprise. Neither answered his question.

An awkward silence settled as they trotted from the station. Catherine pretended that Jeanne d'Arc needed more attention with the reins than usual. At last, Chi-en turned to her.

'It's a long drive to Napa. Why meet me here instead of Perryville?'

She glanced back at the luggage where Emile perched, happy as any boy allowed to do something forbidden.

'I had business.'

'When I received your letter, I thought of other reasons.'

Jeanne d'Arc's hooves clip-clopped along the dusty road. Trees murmured in the hot breeze.

'There are other reasons,' she admitted.

'In San Francisco, I found a newspaper boy with copies of the Napa weeklies. The *Perryville Herald* urged its readers to hire no more "Mongol rat-eating slaves".'

Catherine affected a shudder. 'That dreadful *Herald*. One has to laugh as one might at a lunatic.'

'It said anonymous letters are being sent to winegrowers using Chinese labour. Threats of arson. Have you received such letters?'

Once more Catherine glanced back at Emile. 'Perhaps. Cowardly threats do not interest me.'

It proved a long, vexing drive for Catherine. She had imagined they would fall into the playful, bantering tone of their correspondence while he was recuperating in San Francisco. Instead, Chi-en's reserve reminded her of his early days at Royaume Céleste. The same air of being a cold fish that confused her then and did so now. She found herself prattling about the harvest and grapes and an owl nesting in the winery roof. He listened intently, occasionally replying in a grave, cautious voice. In short, he was as stiff and unyielding as his starched white collar.

As they approached Royaume Céleste, she wondered whether he regretted his decision to return. So much had changed since the previous autumn. Perhaps he shared her thought. Turning to ask him a question, she caught intent eyes upon her face. Both looked away.

'Yah!' cried Catherine, encouraging Jeanne d'Arc up the steep track from the valley bottom.

'Have you found a chance to play the oboe music I sent?' he asked, hurriedly.

Emile giggled behind them. 'Only every night,' he muttered.

Catherine squeezed the reins tightly. 'Yah! Giddy up!'

The farmhouse came into view and Emile cried out: 'Look!'

Two male Wappo wearing necklaces of polished clamshells and headbands decorated with yellow feathers talked to Jean-Pierre outside the winery. White designs were painted on their cheeks. Catherine directed the wagon to the tall building.

'Madame, you have returned just in time!' called out the steward, ignoring Chi-en. 'These savages babble at me and I at them. No one is wiser!'

Once they had all climbed down from the wagon, the Indians' message emerged from a jumble of English, Wappo and Spanish. The men were relations of the Old Mother. She had died in the night and her funeral was the next day. Until then, no Wappo could work. Before her spirit went away, the Old Mother had commanded that the Shaman, Brave Young One and his mother be invited to bear witness to her last journey. That was their message. Once it had been delivered, they tramped away through the vines. Still ignoring Chi-en, Jean-Pierre began to unbuckle Jeanne d'Arc's harness.

'Can I go to her funeral?' pleaded Emile. 'I'm old enough! Please, Maman! You must let me go!'

'We shall see.'

At the farmhouse, Wong Wu, the new young cook, came out to pay his respects. He examined his mistress's guest intently, even as he bowed to them both.

Chi-en turned to Catherine. 'If I may suggest,' he said, in French, 'can I be assigned my old quarters in the store room?'

Catherine hesitated, leaned closer. No doubt he had been building up to this rejection of her hospitality all the way from Napa.

'I did not invite you here to sleep on the floor,' she said, firmly. 'There is a bedroom prepared.'

'You mean in the house?'

'Where else?'

'Upstairs?'

'Really, Chi-en, you know we have no others.'

Quite suddenly his strained expression melted into a slight smile. He chuckled, stiffness visibly leaving his shoulders. At once she understood his awkwardness during the drive over.

'I'm afraid it is just the small lumber room next to Jean-Pierre's,' she said, returning his smile. 'And I fear that he snores.'

Wong Wu, who understood no French, watched their exchange curiously. In the distance, Jean-Pierre led Jeanne d'Arc to her stall.

'Now I understand Monsieur Leclos's long face,' said Chi-en. 'I suspect he would not relish my presence in the room next to his own.'

'That is for me to decide,' she said, 'not him.'

'True, but I do not wish to provoke gossip in Perryville – or China-town, for that matter.'

'How will you regain your strength without a comfortable bed?'

He shook his head. 'A foolish scandal would make me more uncom-fortable than a mattress on the storeroom floor. As would offending Monsieur Leclos, who I respect greatly. Besides, I am stronger than you seem to think. Therefore, I must insist on my old quarters or return to San Francisco.'

His assertiveness caused a warm flicker inside her.

'It appears I have no choice.'

'On this, at least,' he said.

He turned to Wong Wu and addressed him in Cantonese. The pigtailed cook bobbed his shaved head as he replied.

'Mister Wong says he always sleeps under the kitchen table in case of earthquakes,' translated Chi-en. 'So, it will not inconvenience him if I occupy the storeroom as before.'

Catherine had observed this to be true.

'*Comme tu veut*,' she muttered.

The *tu* did not go unnoticed by Chi-en.

Later, Catherine was secretly relieved; she admired the firmness of his discretion. Another part of her was oddly restless.

It is a long climb to the ridge-top above Tsenoma. From here gaze down on the distant vines and buildings of the white invaders. Imagine a town of forty circular thatch huts, dancing grounds, sweathouses. Oaks harvested for their acorns by uncounted generations. Raise your eyes to Kanamoto, slopes and peak looming at the great valley's end. People Mountain at the end of home.

In the cool of late afternoon climb paths steep and bare, weaving around volcanic boulders and ancient, patient pines. Carry the Old Mother's bloated body. Her meagre possessions. Three days dead, she stinks. Flies seek her sustenance; too many to brush away.

No wailing from the men, women, children of all ages making the climb. That is not the Wappo way. No wailing as they take the ghost path from Tsenoma to the funeral stone. The Old Mother's clan has new, temporary members: a few Wappo who hear of her death, she who was one of the last pure-bloods after a century of war, murder, rape, disease. A pitiful assembly for so formidable a woman, youngest daughter of the giant, Chief Colorado, who made the Spaniards flee in battle like frightened boys.

At the rear of the silent line, three strangers. For the Old Mother said she would fly more peacefully to the Happy Land across the ocean knowing the white employers of her people had witnessed her departure. Perhaps the sweating white woman in black knows the Old Mother is binding her with obligations – even from the grave.

Gather round the pyre of pine and brushwood scavenged from the slopes.

She lies face down, her head to the south. South her spirit will fly after resting four days. First light the pyre, throw on the Old Mother's clothes, pipe, tobacco, bedding, her treasured rocking chair. Watch as the flames leap, dancing to the hilltop wind. Watch until smoke billows and eyes water. Watch in resolute silence and smell her body, roasting fat, scorched meat, a long life's sacrifice.

High over the valley vultures circle, along with an eagle.

Stony silence as the white people bow to the pyre and leave, the boy's gaze darting everywhere, storing memories. Later, while flames still flare like a watch beacon on the high ridge, dance the ghost dance dreamed by Wowoka, the magic earthquake that will cleanse the land. Beseech gods soon to be forgotten: Old Man Coyote, Chicken Hawk, Kuksu.

Above hangs a bright half-moon amidst the stars, a mocking grin of light in the dark.

Night after night the moon swelled as waning summer sunshine fed the grapes. What monstrous greed to grow accounted for bunches of a hundred, two hundred berries? What self-seeking pride donned Imperial purple, what modesty softened pride with fuzz like down on youth's hot cheeks? How was it some grapes shrivelled and others did not? What selection or command made each globe of fruit-flesh unique?

All doomed to never spread their own seed, struggle for mastery of root space, found new colonies. Each orb of juice must, in time, face press, fermenting vat, barrel, bottle, tongue, belly, bladder – and so back to earth.

Catherine Bourchier was a gambler. First on Antoine, then on fleeing Antoine. On California. On Royaume Céleste. All other vintners for miles around had already gathered their crop. Still she held off, seeking a final flavour, not too sweet, not too tart on the tongue. If the rains came, so would powdery white mildew on leaves and fruit, perhaps even black rot that dried out grapes to dusky, mummified corpses. Jean-Pierre urged her to commence the *vendange*, offering a dozen sound reasons. Each time she refused. Reckless, defiant, as though black clouds over Mount St Helena dared not blow her way.

'I tell you, in a hot country like this the fruit could be over-ripe before we even notice. Ah, then comes the spoilage!' He referred to *piqûre*, the hot, sharp vinegary odour and taste that could corrupt the finest wines.

'It is a risk,' she conceded, 'it is always a risk. Yet we should wait another day, I think.'

'The wine will be *piqué*,' warned Jean-Pierre. 'I fear Monsieur Bourchier would never have—'

'There shall be no *piqûre*!' cried Catherine. 'Will you never trust my judgement?'

In the end, the pest that threatened to destroy their entire crop came from an unanticipated direction.

The next morning a swirling black cloud appeared over that portion of Napa Valley where Royaume Céleste faced Trubody Nook; it was travelling south towards San Pablo Bay. Jean-Pierre spotted it first, squinting through narrowed eyes that soon bulged with alarm.

'Madame!' he shouted. 'Mon Dieu! Madame! Come quickly!'

Soon everyone on the farm was outside, staring up as thousands of black, flitting shapes wheeled over the vineyard. A huge flock of starlings was migrating unseasonably early. Vines laden with grapes drew them: a banquet of fuel for their journey.

'Pans!' bellowed Jean-Pierre in French. 'Everyone! Noise, we must make noise!'

He rushed for his shotgun and began to fire as rapidly as he could load. The air filled with a whoosh of beating wings and constant, high-pitched, jagged tweeting that drowned out his gunshots. Over a dozen Wappo were working in the vines and all ran to and fro, clattering pans and shouting curses at the skimming birds.

'Merde!' roared Jean-Pierre, for starlings had begun to settle and feed. Once the flock settled, Royaume Céleste would be stripped of grapes within an hour. Tossing the shotgun to Chi-en, he ran into the wine cave dug into the hillside, emerging with a small wooden cask.

'Back!' he shouted, waving frantically.

'What are you doing?' cried Catherine, striking out at a flitting bird with a broom.

'Back, Madame!' urged Jean-Pierre, trotting to a bare patch of earth beside the creek, well away from the buildings.

'Emile!' cried Catherine, her voice drowned out by the whirring wings and maddening *cheep cheep cheep* of the starlings. 'Go inside!'

The boy ignored her, lunging up at the birds with a long stick.

'Jean-Pierre!' she shrieked. 'Do something!'

The old steward did not reply but poured a long, thin trail of black powder from the cask. With trembling hands, he lit a match and tossed it onto the powder. A whoosh, a race of flame, then the small cask exploded with a boom that echoed round the hills and could be heard in Perryville, three miles away, smoke and dust billowing high into the clear summer air. Emile and the Wappo threw themselves to the ground. As one, the huge stream of birds poured away from Royaume Céleste and back into the valley, whence it continued south. Soon not a single starling's cheep could be heard. Even the crickets were silent, awed by the explosion. Chi-en and Catherine, who had grabbed each other's arms, shook their heads to clear the ringing in their ears. When Catherine tried to step forward, she felt dizzy.

'Jean-Pierre!' she moaned, 'are you alright? Where are you, Jean-Pierre?'

Smoke worthy of a battlefield formed an acrid fog. Then he stumbled out of the cloud, his clothes and face streaked with soot. When he grinned, his few remaining teeth appeared as white as a shark's beneath the stiff, coal-black walrus moustache.

'Ah, if only Monsieur Bourchier could have seen *that*!' he declared, between coughs, while Catherine plied him with some of his home-brewed pear brandy.

That afternoon, Emile and Chi-en found Catherine in earnest debate with Jean-Pierre. It was obvious she was now ready to agree to anything he suggested. Sooner than interrupt, man and boy climbed up the ancient Wappo path to the ghost ground where the Old Mother's corpse had burned a few days before. Only charred, blackened sticks remained: hilltop winds had scattered the ash. They sat for a long while looking out across the broad valley at Kanamoto, content with each other's silence. When they returned to Royaume Céleste they found Catherine giving Jean-Pierre a letter for Sam Wah in Perryville. At the sight of them, she smiled excitedly. 'We are agreed, the time is ripe,' she said.

'The time is *right*, Mother.' Emile had taken to correcting her English mercilessly.

Catherine shrugged. 'Is it not the same thing? In any case, tomorrow we harvest!'

The time was ripe. Ripeness brought a dozen Chinese labourers the next morning in a hay wagon driven by Sam Wah. As many Wappo already worked the rows under Jean-Pierre's unwavering eye. He wore a purple-stained coat and carried a tally book to record the number of baskets filled by each picker. His glance lingered uneasily on black clouds above Mount St Helena.

The picking proceeded with fresh urgency. As the sun reached its zenith, tension from electric storms over the distant Lake Country travelled like an unsettling rumour. Baskets of grapes filled, to be sorted on purple-stained trestles, leaves and twigs removed. Sorting was Catherine's domain, picking belonged to Jean-Pierre. Her hands were crimson with juice as she instructed a select trio of Chinese how to sort rotten from healthy, bitter from sweet.

Every so often she stared up at Mount St Helena. Would the brooding rain clouds descend south? Perhaps her arrogant gamble would cripple what should have been a splendid *vendange*. Her rivals' fermenting vats were already bubbling.

'Jean-Pierre,' she called, 'I have decided. We will pick into the night. Let fires be lit. The men will need lanterns and torches. Tell them they will be paid extra for each basket of good grapes.'

Twilight became darkness and still busy fingers gripped wiry stems, severing with practised pulls of tiny sickles, fat bunches falling into the waiting baskets. Flaring torches cast odd glimmers amongst the vines. From the valley below, Royaume Céleste appeared to have spawned monstrous fireflies. Catherine recalled the night she had fled Domaine Bourchier, the flames and smoke . . . did Emile also remember? Guilt or fear led her to explain the night harvest to him in French. For once, he did not insist she speak English. Perhaps he sensed how the harvest, its tactics and calculations, its losses and gains, sprang from his family's deepest roots.

Towards midnight, Catherine left Jean-Pierre among the pickers and returned to the winery. Here, sorting continued: ripe, under-ripe, over-ripe, spoiled. Each was consigned a use. She discovered Chi-en in his old kitchen clothes. Several Chinese worked alongside him.

'Take a rest,' she told the labourers. 'Go to the kitchen. Ask Wong Wu for food and a drink.'

They left with deferential bows. Only Chi-en remained, sorting the purple bunches by lantern glow. Flies swarmed, attracted equally by fruit and light. Catherine came over to the long sorting table.

'I did not ask this of you,' she said. 'You are here as my guest, not as a common labourer.'

He watched as she deftly emptied a basket and sorted bunches.

'Are you a common labourer?' he asked.

'Yes,' she said, 'a greedy, ambitious woman who wants to regain her place in the world. But you, Chi-en Shambles, will only be happy with *uncommon* labour. I think you are an idealist – of a kind sometimes classified as hopeless. I must honour that.'

They worked for a while. His companionable silence provoked her into a topic long suppressed, yet considered every day since his return from Nebraska.

'Chi-en,' she began, 'I owe you an apology.'

'I do not know what for.'

'Because I prattle on about my affairs constantly and never ask about your own.'

'Then ask me.'

'It is just . . . You see, I wanted to ask what happened in Nebraska. With your father, I mean.'

His sorting did not cease. Neither did he reply.

'Perhaps it is wrong of me to mention it,' she said, hurriedly.

'No, no, your intentions are generous. I am not offended. Not by you, Catherine. But there is a man on this earth I have decided to forget entirely, if I can, both in thought and word. Henceforth, I hope to live my life more in the present than the past. Do you understand?'

Surprised by tears in her eyes, she smiled at him. 'Oh, Chi-en,' she laughed, 'that is my philosophy also!'

With that, Catherine swept a pile of ripe, swollen grapes from the table into a wooden tub. She sensed his closeness, the reassuring bulk of him. Both reached for the same bunch. By accident his fingers closed over her own and they froze. Gently he apologised, releasing her hand. Yet she noticed, as though it had found a will of its own, her juice-stained fingers lingered where they had touched. Her heart quickened, just as when they stood in the moonlit vineyard before he left for Nebraska. Surely, he meant nothing by the touch. Yet she was both relieved and disappointed when he retired to his mattress in the store-room.

Napa Valley, California
Autumn 1878

At dawn, gunshots rang out in the half-light. Those who knew firearms detected four shotgun blasts, followed by a dozen barks from at least two revolvers. The last shot rolled round the early morning stillness.

Ten minutes later an unarmed group, still wearing nightclothes beneath their coats, left the farmhouse. Dozens of labourers roused from exhausted sleep watched anxiously. The reconnaissance party consisted of Chi-en, Catherine and Jean-Pierre.

'I believe it came from this end of the vineyard,' said Chi-en.

'How do you know?' she asked.

'Because I was awake. I never sleep well.'

They discovered the victim of the shooting at the end of a long row. The wooded hillside rose nearby, hoarding night's shadows. A large, grinning pumpkin head with carved slanting eyes had been shot in the forehead at close range, so that its pulpy brains spilled out. Other bullets had smashed the vines, shredding fruit. Catherine picked up the split head and threw it into a bush.

'Why can you not leave us alone?' she shouted at the undergrowth.

Birds chorused the coming day and a few insects chirruped. Otherwise, not even a rustle.

'We must keep this secret,' she said.

Jean-Pierre met Chi-en's eye. 'No, Madame,' said the steward, 'you must tell Mr Trubody. I insist on it, for your safety and Emile's, as well as my own.'

Chi-en nodded gravely. 'Monsieur Leclos is right. You have no choice.'

'Damn you!' She called at the unheeding trees. 'We'll gather our harvest, whatever you do!'

Did a branch crack? The three exposed figures in the vines went still. No other reply came to Catherine's challenge.

'Let's go back,' said Chi-en. 'We make a tempting target out here.'

She shivered, as though waking from a dream. They retreated with twitchy backs. Once Catherine thought she heard harsh laughter. It might have been a fox signalling to its mate.

After breakfast the *vendange* resumed with fresh urgency. Catherine was relieved that none of the hired hands demanded their wages as a result of the gunshots.

Baskets of sorted grapes were loaded onto a cart pulled by Jeanne d'Arc, then dragged up an earthen ramp at the rear of the winery to the topmost storey. Here, the first pressing commenced. Streams of juice flowed into fermentation vats, followed by crushed stalks, skin, flesh, seeds to add colour, texture, balance.

When Catherine descended from supervising this operation, she found a fancy carriage outside the farmhouse.

'There you are!' cried Nancy Trubody, her eyes bright with mingled concern and excitement. 'We read your note and could scarcely credit it!'

Nathaniel Trubody joined them with questions of his own. After inspecting the bullet marks, he grew stern. 'I'll telegram Judge Dawson and the County Sheriff. I'm sure they'll nip this in the bud. Frightening a defenceless woman brings no credit to Napa.'

'I'm grateful,' she said. 'Thank you.'

His attention had wandered to the nearest row of unpicked grapes, enticingly ripe and plump, dusted with that natural white bloom known to winemakers as 'blush'. He shook his head in astonishment.

'I don't know how you do it, my dear,' he said. 'I gathered mine a fortnight ago to avoid rains that never came. Even if I hadn't, I can assure you they wouldn't be a patch on your crop! It seems there'll be no Chateau Trubody Nook this year. Damn shame. But there it is.'

She could have told him why. His wistful glance at the vines sowed an idea that soon became a firm intention. She would need to write to Lu Kan, of course, reducing her estimate of Royaume Céleste claret he could ship to Shanghai and Hong Kong this year. It would cost her several thousand dollars. Let it be so. She owed her generous neighbour too much, perhaps their entire prosperity in California. Let it be repaid.

'Mr Trubody,' she said, taking his arm and leading him into a row of unharvested fruit, 'I have a proposition concerning a new vintage of Chateau Trubody Nook.'

Half an hour later he strolled off with Jean-Pierre to inspect his newly-acquired share of the *vendange*.

'You won't regret it,' he called over his shoulder, 'and I'd darned well like to see Smithson-Mackay's face when I advertise Trubody Nook '78 in this season's opera programme! This year I'll take out a double page.'

Catherine waved him goodbye and turned to find Nancy waiting with a short, dark-eyed girl a year or so older than Emile. The girl, scarcely concealing her admiration, gazed up at the eccentric Frenchwoman who spoke and acted with the confidence of a man.

'Let me introduce a new addition to our household,' said Nancy. 'Sarah is the only daughter of a former business partner of my husband who fell on hard times. She's an orphan child. Say hello to Madame Bourchier, Sarah.'

The girl curtsied.

'Ah, you are very pretty!' said Catherine. 'And very welcome. My son, Emile, will show you Royaume Céleste . . . Emile! Come and greet our guests. Here is a new friend for you.'

After the two children had been dispatched to explore, Nancy took Catherine's elbow and said, 'We need to talk, my dear. I have unpleasant news.'

They sat in the same salon where Baron Foche had smashed a crystal glass. Perhaps that was why Catherine felt little surprise when Nancy said, 'I've hesitated long and hard about whether to say this. I've never been a one for prying. Can't abide it. But I consider you a dear friend – Nathaniel and I simply dote on that boy of yours! That's why I feel compelled to speak.'

It was soon told. The notorious Frenchman who had gotten himself shot in a gambling dispute had told many strange tales about Catherine Bourchier before fleeing Napa. That she was no widow, at all, but a comtesse and a gold digger. That she was wanted by both her husband (to reclaim his son) and the French authorities (to reclaim stolen property). In short, she was an impostor.

Catherine's gut twisted. Her mouth opened to reply but Nancy leapt in, 'No need to say a word, my dear! I insist. It's just that I believe you should know. So you can protect yourself and Emile.'

For a long moment Catherine sat with a bowed head, tears forming. When she looked up, her smile was bitter.

'Nancy,' she said, 'now it is time for me to insist that *you* listen. Though you may find me less agreeable afterwards.'

Sick of lies, she cast out the truth like a net to catch acceptance and kindness – or, more probably, outraged rejection.

'So, you see,' she concluded, 'I apologise for deceiving you, Nancy. My one justification is that I acted for Emile's sake.'

She waited bleakly. Besmirched respectability was like water mixed with ink, fine wine with coarse; it could never revert to its former state. Nancy's quick, searching glance confirmed Catherine's fears. But when the older woman spoke her tone was conciliatory.

'My dear Catherine, please credit my husband and I with *some* intelligence. We knew you weren't telling *everything*. Who does?'

Catherine's shoulders rose a little.

'Quite frankly, my dear,' continued Nancy, 'I never thought you were a widow. Half the people in California have run away from something and the other half pretend they haven't.'

Catherine dabbed the corner of her eyes. 'I do not know what to say.'

'Then don't say anything. Certainly don't repeat what you've told me to another soul. You may rely on my discretion. But I'm not finished, my dear. There is something – or someone – else.'

Catherine waited. What lay so near the surface and depths of her heart, body, the flow of her thoughts, warned what must come next. She listened numbly as Nancy enquired about the return of Chi-en Shambles to Royaume Céleste.

'It is not how it *is*, but how it *looks*,' explained Nancy. 'More importantly, how it might be *made to look*, especially by Lydia Smithson-Mackay. It seems two of the horsey gals in her set saw you with a tall, handsome Chinaman at Napa Station. You can be sure Lydia has her own explanation.'

'I must stop you now,' said Catherine, stiffly. 'Mr Shambles has been a kind and loyal friend to Emile and I. But especially to Emile. His influence persuaded my son to return to school, to take a proper pride in himself. Besides, he helped negotiate contracts with a Chinese merchant that mean I no longer worry about money. Without him, there would be no Domaine Bourchier claret. No restoration of my own and my family's pride. I will not deny such a friend to satisfy spiteful tongues.'

Nancy nodded, as though something had been confirmed. Her look of mingled concern and excitement was back.

'Thought you'd say that, my dear, it's one of the reasons I like you.' She squeezed Catherine's hand. 'Just be careful. Don't give Lydia Smithson-Mackay and her pony friends cause for gossip.'

The next morning brought trouble far worse than gunshots: more war than warning.

As flickers of sunrise showed between peaks on the eastern rim of the valley, smaller flames kindled closer to home. Catherine should have placed a guard outside the winery: without that building and its expensive equipment the *vendange* was pointless. All too easy for experienced bushwhackers to pick a route through the dark huddles of Chinese labourers asleep in their blankets beneath the stars.

At the winery, no door was locked: they walked right in, startling mice and rats about their nocturnal feeding. Now the first flaw in their plan. Instead of creeping up to the top storey where the crucial presses and fermenting barrels stood ready for the next day's work, where pipes and channels ran down to the middle storey and its barrels for maturing the fermented wine, they entered the lowest, ground floor.

A whispered conversation, a match struck to discover combustibles, revealed plenty of dry wood and stacks of empty casks. The two men, belts weighed by revolvers, had brought an oilcan as well.

The first Catherine learned of the fire was a change of mood in her dream. She sat on a large flat rock over which a stream tumbled to form a waterfall. How hot it was! She longed to step out of her clothes and stand beneath the singing, plashing, laughing water until it dripped from the ends of her long hair, her nipples and thighs. Then she sensed someone behind her. Whatever Nancy said she was not afraid! Would he reach out, help her find the cool relief of the water? Wash away the dust and mites of the harvest? She squeezed her eyes tight. Except the gentle touch was not on her hair or expectant neck, nor was it soft. Someone was shaking her arm. 'Madame! *Madame*!'

She opened her eyes to find Jean-Pierre in his woollen under-trousers and a torn vest.

'The winery is on fire!'

It took less than a minute to seize a dressing gown, snatch up a pair of boots and run barefoot into the sickly dawn. Shadow-men were drawing buckets from the well and rushing to the lowest entrance of the winery, from which smoke drifted. A red and orange glow revealed the fire was spreading.

She shrieked, 'Do something Jean-Pierre! It is still small. Stop it now!'

The old steward stepped forward. Back again. Fortunately, a body of men used to relying upon each other in a hostile land were camped in Royaume Céleste. Under orders from Sam Yip, a human chain between well and winery formed. Buckets passed at high speed, to be emptied and recharged. Chi-en Shambles and Wong Wu dashed into the building and dragged out smouldering casks with the aid of long rakes normally used to clear weeds between rows. The fires had yet to take serious hold. Within a few minutes the flames were wavering. Their end came when Jean-Pierre remembered the rubber pipes running down from the top storey, where several fermenting vats were full of watery grape juice.

This purple stream doused the smouldering fire before it could rally itself.

A smoke-blackened Chi-en appeared before Catherine. Floating sparks had burned his cheek. She felt an urge to touch the open sore.

'I shall go into the woods and see if anyone is there,' he said. 'This fire was no accident.'

She laughed in disbelief. 'By yourself? Unarmed?'

Catherine realised how often he showed little regard for his life. And wondered what *exactly* had happened in Nebraska. They were interrupted by Sam Yip, talking excitedly. Two white men had been seen hurrying into the woods when a Chinese labourer rose to relieve himself. Without his weak bladder, the fire might not have been discovered until it was out of control.

'Uncle told me there is going to be a big meeting in Perryville,' said Sam Yip. 'A few days from now. Uncle says many men who hate us are coming all the way from San Francisco.'

Chi-en translated Sam Yip's words. Amidst her anger and fear, it occurred to Catherine that all she need do to stop further attacks was dismiss the Chinese and Wappo, hire a dozen Italians or Swiss. The thought of such a submission provoked a foul word in her native patois. She realised Chi-en was watching closely.

'I shall write to Mr Trubody and ask him to send another telegram to the County Sheriff in Napa,' she said.

They stood in silence, watching wisps of smoke and steam. Hundreds of dollars' worth of casks had been lost or tainted with the stench of smoke.

'Thank you for risking the fire,' she said. 'Do not worry, I will not lose heart.'

Around mid-morning, Mr Trubody's reply came in the form of a letter:

Dear Catherine,

I have decided to inform the County Sheriff about the attack on your property in person. The Perryville Deputy Sheriff, Mr Dwyer (a man I do not trust), is employed by the County, so this seems the most expeditious course. We can be sure Mr Dwyer has an inkling who is behind this outrage and, accordingly, who should be warned to stay away from Royaume Céleste.

I will tell the County Sheriff that if your winery burns all men of property in Napa will be held to ransom over who they choose to hire, and that men of property expect the law to be maintained.

I will also tell him my own vintage this year, Chateau Trubody Nook, depends on your harvest. I might even drop a hint that if Royaume Céleste burns, so does any prospect of his re-election. Then he'll understand I'm darn serious.

Yours sincerely
Nathaniel Trubody

All day new unity and defiance drove on the labourers, for the fire had lit a blaze of energy. If nothing else, it persuaded Catherine to increase the wages for each full basket and that was motivation enough. All day the sorting and pressing continued, so that numerous fermenting tubs on the top and middle storeys of the Gascon's splendid winery were full to the brim.

The County Sheriff, accompanied by Deputy Sheriff Dwyer from Perryville, rode up the dirt track from the valley bottom, silver stars glinting in the afternoon sun.

Catherine hurried out as the leisurely horsemen approached, wiping crimson hands on a rag. They dismounted and tied up.

'Mrs Boosher?' began the shorter of the two, doffing a fine Stetson hat. 'I'm County Sheriff Smith.' He nodded at his companion. 'This here is Deputy Sheriff Dan Dwyer from Perryville.'

The latter, a minotaur of a man, scowled at his superior.

'Guess you know why we're here,' continued County Sheriff Smith. 'I'd be obliged to see any traces of the fire Mr Trubody told me about.'

It took little time to show the charred remains and tell of men running into the woods.

'Sounds like an accident to me,' said Deputy Sheriff Dwyer. 'Hell, there ain't even no proof of arson!'

County Sheriff Smith bent over a half-burned cask. 'Strong smell of oil here, Ma-am,' he said. 'You store oil in this winery of yours?'

'No, it is stored in the barn.'

'Thought so, Ma-am. Now Mr Dwyer, what were you sayin'?'

The Deputy Sheriff stiffened: 'There ain't no solid proof other than a Chinaman's word that—'

'Whoa!' cried the County Sheriff, holding up a hand. 'You going to tell that to Mr Trubody, Dan? Thought not.' He turned back to Catherine. 'Tell you what, Ma-am, we'll put the word round. No leniency will be shown to anyone setting fires in this property o' yours. Dammit, arson's a hangin' offence in this County! And while I'm County Sheriff, the law is sorely minded to let folks dangle. Ain't that exactly what we're goin' to do, Dan?'

Mr Dwyer nodded, an angry flush creeping to his ears.

'Guess not much damage has been done,' said County Sheriff Smith. 'Guess whoever did this'll back off this year. But folks hereabouts have long memories, Ma-am.'

He pushed back the Stetson to the back of his head and examined the lines of Wappo and Chinese gathering the last of the harvest. His eyebrows rose laconically.

'Next year I'd hire me some white pickers if I was you, ma-am. Could prove cheaper in the long run.'

Catherine almost delivered a tart reply. Except that, helplessly, bitterly, she knew he was right. Next year she would hire some white labourers.

After they had gone, the afternoon dwindled along with bunches still on the vines. Shadows advanced with the sun. Picking continued into twilight. By nightfall the last grapes were being sorted and pressed, skin and pulp poured into fermenting vats under Catherine's direction.

When Chi-en joined her, she made no effort to disguise her elation. 'So nearly there! We have done it, Chi-en!'

Her face shone with sweat and triumph beneath a lamp besieged by flies and moths.

'I am so proud of our Royaume Céleste! I believe Papa would be, too. He always gave the labourers a large *vendange* lunch after paying them. *Se Dius Va Vol*, it was called, or *What God Wanted*. It was to offer thanks for the harvest. Old, old ways, all eaten up at the roots by phylloxera. Well, there is no helping it.' She shook her head sadly. 'I do not even believe God *is* to be thanked. It is each other we should thank for this *vendange*.'

They regarded the labourers slumped on the ground, eating a simple meal of rice and beans ladled out by Wong Wu.

'Why not keep the old customs alive in America?' said Chi-en. 'We Chinese do, when we can. Give these men a *vendange* lunch like your father did. You have chickens, a young pig, everything you need. I believe they deserve it.'

She smiled. 'Who will cook such a feast?'

'Wong Wu and me.'

'I keep saying, you are my guest, not a servant!'

'Then you must help as well.'

461

She felt trapped — and an odd kind of joy. This was the entrapment she had craved for years. Yet part of her sensed that every time she followed one of his suggestions, she granted him a little more power, a deeper trust. And Catherine feared entrusting her happiness to any man.

'Very well,' she said, uncertainly, 'I shall help a little. But it would not do for *la patrone* to be seen doing too much. Besides, I am a terrible cook, as Emile will tell you.'

'A little would be much,' he said. 'If you are as bad a cook as you say, perhaps too much.'

Napa Valley, California
Autumn 1878

Chi-en Shambles was used to watching from the outside, between two hostile worlds, Chinese and White, never belonging to either. Today, he woke with a whole heart.

When he emerged from the storeroom to ask if Wong Wu required further help with the *vendange* lunch, morning was advanced. So was the cooking.

'No more assistance from you, Mr Sha-bells,' said Wong Wu in Cantonese. Then he grinned like a harvest moon and dropped into Pidgin he had picked up in an English tramp steamer's galley. 'All poppa! Numbah One chow-chow for fookee!'

'Belly well!' replied Chi-en to the other's amusement. 'Chin-chin!'

Despite his joke, as though he had stepped from sunlight into shadow, Chi-en's blithe mood faltered. *Numbah One* was a phrase haunted by Prince Hong.

Shaved, dressed, he left the kitchen's bustle and steam. Over twenty labourers were to be fed that noon, as well as the Bourchier party. Many had slept long after sunrise, an unexpected holiday at harvest time. A few Chinese smoked and talked; others played *fantan* while they waited for dinner.

He found Emile with the Wappo. The Indians had resumed their policy of separation from the Chinese, but Chi-en, well-known for his magical powers with words, received a guarded welcome. Several older Wappo nursed bottles of whiskey.

'They are calling today a *Big Time* in their language!' cried Emile. 'The chief has told me they will have races and wrestling.'

As if to emphasise *how* big a time, a bone pipe trilled excitedly, accompanied by a woodblock drum. Young men competed in a tug of war, hauling the ends of a long pole, cheered on by rival supporters. Whiskey-sipping uncles gambled away wages yet to be paid in a guessing game of bones wrapped in grass. Chi-en examined his companion. 'Tell me, Emile, why do the Wappo interest you so much?'

The boy shouted encouragement to one of the war-tuggers. 'Don't know,' he said.

'There must be a reason,' said Chi-en, 'people always have reasons, even if they are bad.'

'I think . . . it's because I'm the only one who *is* interested. Someone must be. Or nothing will be left. Old Mother told me only a few dozen true Wappo survive.'

'Did she ask you to help her people survive?'

The boy nodded.

'And asked you to promise?'

'Yes.'

'Then you must keep your promise if you can.' He clapped Emile on the shoulder. 'You're a very different boy from the one I caught stealing bread. Think, just a year ago! It makes me very glad.'

The boy wasn't listening. He had lunged forward to cheer on his champion in the tug of war.

Chi-en wandered to the farmhouse, where he found Jean-Pierre on a rocking chair beneath a shady porch. The last few weeks had exhausted the old steward. There would not be many more harvests in him. He nodded curtly, re-filling his glass of home-distilled pear brandy.

'Monsieur Leclos,' said Chi-en, 'are you happy with the *vendange*?'

Jean-Pierre shrugged. 'I am glad to see Monsieur Bourchier's daughter and grandson prosper,' he said. 'Monsieur Bourchier was the kindest *patron* imaginable. Ah, those were good days! But you would not understand.'

Chi-en thought of Prince Hong and felt a familiar guilt-prick. Oh, he understood. It was finding him again now: the old weariness and self-doubt.

Jean-Pierre drank gloomily, tiny beads of brandy sticking to his bushy moustache. 'I never had children. Or a wife. And after Monsieur died I did not belong at Château de Chauveterre anymore. I did not like the people there and they did not like me. Especially after the lice came and Monsieur joined the angels.' He drank again and sighed. 'The strange thing is, I travel two thousand miles and it's just the same!'

'Perhaps your heart has not left home,' said Chi-en.

Jean-Pierre looked at him blankly and nodded in the direction of the dirt track. 'Well, it is all *merde*. And look . . . even more people!'

As befitted a homely, country fiesta, Mr and Mrs Trubody arrived in their oldest carriage and outfits worn at least twice. Nancy's petite companion, Sarah, dark-haired, prim and unsmiling, sat between them. Chi-en lingered on the porch – after all, he had stood beside Mr Trubody in situations requiring equality of sorts. Then he grew uneasy. For all his Western clothes and education, he was still *fookee*, still John Chinaman.

'Adieu,' he said to Jean-Pierre, 'your loyalty does you credit.'

In the hour before the *vendange* lunch, Chi-en sat outside the winery, looking over *A Memoir of Prince Hong*. What, he wondered would Hong make of his position in Royaume Céleste? One thing was certain, he would insist on dining with the white people.

Slowly, Chi-en's mood darkened. Could the debt he owed his friend's memory ever be discharged? Perhaps he had not sacrificed enough. Until he truly aided their benighted people, it could never be settled.

His gaze drifted to the front of the farmhouse where Catherine stood with her guests, laughing gaily. She was indeed handsome – no, lovely. Yet her firm-breasted figure and piled, dark hair inspired self-contempt in Chi-en Shambles. He knew well enough what lay behind his interest. That it defied honour, wisdom, respect. He desired to unpin that hair and scoop it in his hands. To lift that cotton gown until the figure he admired was revealed. An image of white thighs, her fragrance, appalled him. Not from prudery or religion, simply because it could never be. Thus it diminished him. Still, he watched her, the *Memoir* forgotten on his knee.

Sighing, Chi-en closed the manuscript book. Three distinct dining areas were being established in Royaume Céleste. A long, chequer-clothed trestle table beneath the shade of a large oak for the white folks. On the opposite side of the winery, an area for the Wappo to squat. Besides the kitchen, Wong Wu's domain, space for the Chinese to sit with plates resting on their knees.

And he belonged to none of those groups. His position was in the centre of the triangle, perpetually alone.

Chi-en walked away from the buildings and into the vines. A hymn learned in the Heavenly Capital touched his memory, so that he sang quietly as he climbed. Soon he stood beside the creek running through Royaume Céleste. It had worn an arroyo into the earth over the centuries, fringed by shrubs and trees. In summer, only a thin trickle ran over the smooth white and grey pebbles of the streambed, but in winter it ran fast and loud, siphoning rain from the hills to flood the valley bottom.

He watched butterflies chasing one another over the water. Songbirds flitted from branch to branch.

His head lowered as the hymn died on his lips. Oh, he could not deceive himself. Despite the completed memoir and all his good intentions, the debt he owed Prince Hong for abandoning him to ice and hunger would never be discharged. He might linger in this new Eden for a while but any solace must be temporary. The lapse had occurred; with it came harsh, unforgiving knowledge. Just as for Adam and Eve, that knowledge must drive him out into the world's cruel corners. With an inward shiver, he recalled Prince Hong's wan face as he lay in the filthy London garret, starving, freezing, pleading. *Chi-en, are you still there? . . . I am here. I will always be here.*

The life-giving stream at his feet flowed on down the arroyo and through Royaume Céleste.

Then a voice startled him.

'Chi-en, why are you here alone? I came to find you.'

He turned. It was Catherine, concern on her face. The late morning sun glinted on her long hair, washed in rose-scented water that morning. How little she knew! How little! When all was measured and judged he did not deserve her friendship. It seemed essential to deceive her no longer.

'You are upset,' she said, stepping closer. 'Tell me what has happened.'

'Nothing.'

He met her troubled inspection. 'Don't waste your time here, go back to your friends.'

'Do not think for one moment that because you do not dine with Mr and Mrs Trubody . . . No, you must never imagine that I . . . You are my dear friend, Chi-en!'

'I imagine nothing.'

'What do you mean?' She stepped close to touch his arm. 'How strange your mood is today.'

He jerked away. 'If you knew about me, Catherine, you wouldn't waste time here. And yes, you shall know!'

In a harsh, painfully dignified voice he told her of his deep obligations to Prince Hong. How he abandoned him to starvation and cold by taking passage to America. It was a story he had entrusted to no one. For years it had grown and festered in his mind, a bloated toadstool of self-contempt. Guilt so spongy and dense he could not conceive its removal. Yet even as he related how the ship carried him across the icy ocean to America, a longing gripped Chi-en to kick over that poisonous spore, that fungus of shame, and stamp, stamp it into the earth.

He awaited her response. Golden-chested chats and cuckoos with yellow bills flitted over the creek, along with a hovering blue dragonfly. His passion subsided into sadness.

'Oh, Chi-en,' she murmured.

Calm now, he laughed. 'Forgive me for burdening you with this! Today of all days. *Se Dius Va Vol*! That was selfish of me. Do not worry, I am quite myself again, as you see.'

'Chi-en, please do not—'

'Madame! Are you all right here?'

They looked around. Jean-Pierre stood watching, hat in hand. His glance took in Chi-en's moist eyes, Catherine's distress. He was no fool.

'Madame,' he said, 'you must come now to pay the men's wages. All is ready.'

She glanced anxiously at Chi-en. When she spoke, Jean-Pierre listened suspiciously. 'We shall discuss this later,' she said to Chi-en. 'Thank you for informing me of . . . I must go.'

With that she followed Jean-Pierre back towards the buildings, glancing over her shoulder uneasily. A look, it seemed to him, of injured reproach.

★

Before noon, the men lined up to receive their pay in dollar bills and small coins. One of the drunker Wappo argued about his wages until the Chief intervened. The rest did not complain, for Catherine could afford to be generous: her wage bill for the entire harvest was half what it would have been if she had hired white labour.

At last, a pan was beaten with a metal ladle. *Se Dius Va Vol* began. It was a fine feast, testament to Wong Wu's skill: a spit-roasted pig provided meat in plenty, scenting the air with a sugary marinade of his own devising; salads of various greens, tomato, cucumber, all from Royaume Céleste's kitchen garden; bowls of many fruits; a mountain of coloured, flavoured rice for the Chinese; bacon and bean stew; a huge round of pungent, crumbling cheese bought from a neighbouring dairy farm; fried chicken for the white people; freshly baked bread for all; finally, tarts of molasses-sweetened apples in the French style.

Last year's red wine washed down the feast. As Chi-en ate, he remembered momentarily the famine in Nanking. But noon was bright in Napa, shadows blinded by sunlight.

'I propose a toast. To our neighbour and friend and hostess . . . Now, don't you go interruptin' me, Nancy!'

Nathaniel Trubody was drunk on Royaume Céleste claret, his wine-flush deepened by the heat.

'Our friend and business partner! Without who there'd be no Chateau Trubody Nook this year. In short, I pro-pose Madame Catherine Bourchier!'

Around the white people's table were Nancy, Sarah, Emile and Jean-Pierre, as well as Judge Dawson and his wife who had turned up unexpectedly. All solemnly raised glasses and drank. Lattices of shade and light cast by the ancient oak shifted across their laden dishes and plates. Wappo drums and chanting drifted from behind the winery. Catherine's glance strayed to the kitchen door, where Chi-en talked with Sam Wah, the latter nodding respectfully.

Surely Chi-en should be sitting at this table. He was a natural gentleman, needing no title or cashbook to assert his right. She did not care to think how he must resent being excluded. All morning they had avoided the question – and, indeed, each other.

It troubled her deeply to have left him before she could respond to his confession about the dead Chinese prince. To Catherine Bourchier, Prince Hong sounded unworthy of Chi-en's excessive respect. But she had never seen him so close to tears before. She must honour his scruples.

After all, this Prince Hong and Chi-en once shared noble hopes for their country and fought side by side. She believed that comrades in arms often established the strongest of bonds. In addition, it seemed Prince Hong had saved the life of Chi-en's mother (Catherine intended to find out more about *her* as soon as possible), as well as saving Chi-en's own life. No wonder he felt a profound obligation. And his friend's death had taken place not so many years ago. There hadn't been time for him to accept that he was not at fault.

Catherine knew with all her heart no justification for his guilt existed. He was too noble, that was all. If only she could help him see! That might be her gift to him, just as he had helped bring her closer to Emile.

Again, she sought out his face. Chi-en had stepped away from the house and was staring at Mount St Helena, lost to his thoughts. Yes, she would teach him to think kindlier about himself, she would . . . She realised Nancy had noticed her close observation of the tall Chinaman.

The older woman cleared her throat and declared, 'How clever of you to organise such a lovely harvest dinner, my dear!'

Before she could reply Emile burst out to Sarah, who sat beside him, 'They are not savages, it is just you do not *know* them!'

The adults turned to the children in surprise.

'Emile,' cautioned Catherine, 'remember, Sarah is our guest.'

'She called the Wappo heathen savages. But we were like them once, before our machines and clothes and religion.'

Judge Dawson nodded. 'Emile is right to say the revelations of Our Saviour is why Divine Providence places us over such primitives.'

'Let the boy prove his point,' said Mr Trubody, belligerent with wine. 'Sir!' He addressed Emile directly, man to man. 'I give you full permission to take my ward to observe these Indians of yours at close quarters. It does no harm to watch their dancing.'

'Now, dear,' warned Nancy.

An excited Emile led an even more excited Sarah to the back of the winery.

'A remarkable boy,' declared Judge Dawson.

'I predict a future in the scientific line for him,' said Mr Trubody. 'Indeed, I'd be happy to contribute to his education . . .'

'Nathaniel!' urged Nancy.

'Why, we've talked about it before! What's wrong with sayin' it?

Catherine examined them in surprise. Could Emile turn out a scholar, the first in her family?

'Anyway, anyway . . .' Trubody scythed the air with a flattened palm. 'There's something you must know. There's to be a big meeting in Perryville tomorrow.'

'You'll have read there's a law taking shape,' said Judge Dawson. 'To exclude further Chinese from entering California – even from entering the whole Republic.'

'Now I'm advisin' you,' said Trubody. 'Do not go to Perryville tomorrow. You are by no means the only one using Chinese labour, but there's still muttering about how you allow Diggers to squat on your land.'

Catherine's glance returned instinctively to Chi-en. If the new law excluded his people from America, perhaps he would return to his birth-place. The prospect made her impatient for a chance to speak with him.

After the harvest dinner, Royaume Céleste emptied. First the Chinese, singing as Sam Yip drove a hay wagon sent from Perryville's Chinatown. He insisted on driving because he liked flicking the whip.

The Trubody party prepared to leave next with Emile. The boy needed little persuasion to accept their invitation to spend the night at Trubody Nook. He felt instantly at home in the Trubodys' country mansion after spending the first half his life in Château de Chauveterre. The justification that Catherine needed rest was also true: even before they had gone, she retired to her room.

Emile sought out Chi-en, who stood outside the kitchen, hands in pockets.

'I won't be back here until tomorrow,' said the boy. 'I guess I'm having an adventure like you did in Nebraska.'

Chi-en smiled. 'For your sake, I sincerely hope not.'

'Oh, I'll have lots of fun.' Emile glanced furtively at the Trubodys, then back to the Chinaman. 'I was going to add some new words to my Wappo dictionary but I'm afraid they're rude.'

'What are they?'

The boy whispered and translated, then tittered.

'Yes, they are rude,' said Chi-en, 'but preserve them anyway. There can be no high without low.'

'I will. *Au revoir*, Uncle Chi-en.'

For a moment Chi-en wondered if he had misheard. 'What did you say?'

'I said *au revoir*.'

'Oh.' But he had not misheard. And because it was his curse to never miss an irony, he remembered a lost spiritual uncle, long ago in Canton.

'So long!' called the boy.

'So long, Emile.'

Chi-en smiled at his new title as the Trubodys' carriage bumped and rattled down the track.

Once the Wappo had returned to their huts in the woods, Royaume Céleste grew quiet. Jean-Pierre stumbled to his room with a fresh bottle of pear brandy, unlikely to emerge until late the next day. Wong Wu sang softly as he washed dishes then entered a deep slumber beneath the kitchen table; Chi-en also slept soundly. But Catherine's sleep wanted harmony.

She dreamt of Baron Foche knocking at her chamber door. Then of someone forbidden by every decency she had ever been taught. And that she opened the door to him eagerly. As soon as its gap widened, she was no longer in Château de Chauveterre, but upon blankets spread over a flat rock beneath a star-lit Californian sky. Nearby, a constant music of water, trees murmuring approval. The despised one knelt as she lay naked on blankets spread across the broad, sun-warmed stone. His presence excited her.

All that afternoon the best of summer skies gathered for one last blend before autumn transformed the valley. Sugars and yeast and crimson fruit fermented in the vats; bubbles and a froth formed over the juice.

Napa Valley, California
Autumn 1878

Before twilight, Catherine woke. A whinnying snore rumbled down the hallway from Jean-Pierre's room. After days of harvest bustle a pregnant stillness lay over Royaume Céleste. She peered at the familiar room through softening light. Unconscious traces of her dream lingered.

She rose, removing the last of her coverings. She emptied a large water jug into a bowl, washing breasts, armpits, the triangle between her legs. She examined her shadowy reflection in the mirror. Long, dark tresses hung over bare shoulders. From instinct she reached up to pin back her hair, then let her hands fall.

Heat had worked through the wooden floors and walls of the farmhouse. She dressed in the lightest of cotton gowns, with only a thin shift beneath. In the hallway, she paused at the open door of Jean-Pierre's room. He lay on his back, greasy moustache stirring each time he snored. A rush of loyalty and affection softened her. She closed his door so no one would disturb him.

When she descended, the silhouette of a man's head and shoulders showed through a window. She stepped outside, conscious that her hair hung loose.

Chi-en sat on the porch, watching dusk gather over Napa Valley.

'May I join you?' she asked.

He rose, bowed stiffly. 'It is your porch.'

'You are my guest.'

The realisation he had been far less than her guest at the *vendange* lunch warmed her cheeks. Perhaps the same thought occurred to him.

'I'm grateful for your kindness,' he said, 'but there is something I must tell you. My strength recovered some time ago. Really, I should be in Chinatown, winning myself an honourable position.'

'Not tonight,' she said, firmly. 'Tonight, you are welcome anywhere in Royaume Céleste. You see at lunch I had to consider—'

'Please! I am not a child, Catherine. Neither are you. We both know the world's disdain and prejudices. How often we must sacrifice our own inclinations.'

She indicated he should sit again and found a matching chair nearby. They both pretended to inspect Mount St Helena. Was there reproach in his manner? No, it was hurt. And, in a flash, she sensed the reason. That it had nothing to do with his exclusion from the white people's table.

'Chi-en, before you go anywhere, let us finish the conversation we began this morning by the creek.'

She felt him tense beside her.

'I know it is a painful topic for you,' she said, hurriedly. 'Jean-Pierre's timing could not have been worse, but I had to pay the men.'

'Of course. That was your duty.'

'This is my duty also. As your friend. To say that you are wrong about Prince Hong. I have thought about it all day, Chi-en! You did not betray your friend. Think, you were starving, about to perish, incapable of rational thought. Little wonder that—'

'No, no. You do not understand.'

'I understand this . . . it is a kind of vanity to insist you must be better than everyone on earth. There was nothing deliberate in what you did, no choice, barely a decision. It just *happened*. As soon as you realised, did you not try to return to your friend? Try to do everything in your power?'

'Yes, I tried.'

'But to no avail,' she said, softly. 'It was Prince Hong's fate, Chi-en. His and your own. That is the truth.'

For a moment they regarded each other. He found himself repeating a phrase used by Secretary Ah Ling. 'I shall consider your truth, Catherine. Thank you.'

Like children who have played a game of holding their breath until their lungs hurt, they exhaled, breathed deeply, tension resolving itself into nervous smiles, then uncertain laughter at their own absurdity, the world's.

'Why are we laughing?' She leaned forward to brush his arm.

'I don't know!'

'What do you mean, don't know? Mind you, I don't either!'

'Maybe that's the joke.'

They subsided, cleared their throats, sniffed, smiled at each other. With their smiles came awareness. They were alone together on a hot evening at the end of summer. No one was around to spy or interrupt. For once, they were at full liberty.

'Would you object if I smoked?' he asked.

Catherine remembered ladies in France, her mother amongst them, reacting with horror to females who smoked. France seemed far away.

'Make me one also.'

He chuckled at her attempt to inhale.

'Of course, a lady does not do such things in France,' she coughed.

'Women do. I've known them.'

'I'm not that kind of woman.'

A silence charged with speculation lengthened. How intimately had he known such women? She felt a perverse desire to prove herself bolder than invisible rivals.

'Your cigarette has made me thirsty,' she declared. 'Now I wish to show *you* something new. Consider it a thank you for persuading me to revive our old harvest tradition.'

'*Se Dius Va Vol*,' he said, 'though I'm not sure God wanted the Wappo to get quite as drunk as they did. Judge Dawson seemed to feel the same way.'

'I saw worse as a girl in France. Many a baby arrived nine months after the harvest dinner.'

Catherine went inside, fetching a corkscrew, glasses and a dusty bottle, its neck coated with old red wax.

'Read the label,' she said.

He wiped off a shred of cobweb. '*Domaine Bourchier*. Your family's famous vintage. And 1848. The year I was born.'

She laughed. 'Me also! Clearly the best of vintages! It is all I saved from our cellars. My dear husband sold whatever he did not guzzle.'

'Why do you wish to show me this bottle?'

'Not show, Monsieur 'Umble, but share. Imagine! The grapes in this bottle were growing on the vine while we were forming inside our mothers.'

She gripped the bottle between her thighs and pulled the cork deftly. He watched her ritual of smelling the wine, examining, swirling and, finally, tasting.

'It is your turn,' she said.

He sipped. 'Why is this so good?'

She smiled. 'One only answers that question by tasting. They say that a good tasting reveals a wine's character, its past and present, maybe its future.'

'A good tasting?'

'Yes. With one's eyes, nose, tongue.'

'Is that all you need for a good tasting?'

'Put all three together. Then you know.' She realised her voice had grown husky. 'But I am dry and must follow my own advice.' Again, she drank.

The wine on her palate lit a flash of comprehension. It was as good as running with her little brothers through ancient vines now dead – and quarrelling with them, too, for all complex flavours require contraries. Good as dull piety at church and the excitement of harvest. Good as Papa and Maman, their blessings and burdens. Good as her dreams before she married. Good as subtle strength, flexibility, warmth. Always the sun's kindly warmth.

'I don't know why it's good,' she said. 'Once I would have called it God's will. Now I think good things are drawn together naturally.'

'That rarely happens by accident,' he suggested, 'but by agreement.'

After the bottle was empty, they grew giddy, as serious people sometimes will. Both admired the emerging globe of the moon. A fat, grinning, winking harvest moon over Napa. He told how Chinese ladies went on moon-gazing parties late into the night, dining on delicacies and sipping rice wine. He even recited a moon-gazing poem by Su Tong-po and translated it. At once she proposed such a party beneath the Californian moon. Chi-en stole into the kitchen where Wong Wu slumbered, gathering bread, cheese, cold meat. She found more wine and a basket, as well as two large, thick blankets.

'Where are you taking me?' he asked, as she marched ahead between vines stripped of fruit. Night insects rehearsed songs. Even as dusk deepened into darkness the air was unseasonably warm.

'Do you remember the waterfall? How cool it was there? Why shouldn't you and I have a moon-gazing party up there? Unless I am not as beautiful as a Chinese lady, of course.'

For no clear reason he placed his wide-brimmed black hat on her head. She did not remove it.

'To shade your face from moonlight,' he said, 'in case it burns you.'

They entered the woods and followed a creekside trail. She grew aware of his legs and body moving ahead. In the distance she heard the Wappo, drunk and still busy with their hopeless Ghost Dance to turn back fate and time.

They reached the waterfall as the last sunlight vanished over hillcrests. It was just as she had imagined in her dream: the flat sun-baked stone and stream trickling into its pool below; the murmur and mutter of water familiar as an old song; a dark circle of trees surrounding them like sentinels. But Catherine did not feel watched. It was as if the trees faced outwards. In the centre of the pool hung a small, wavering moon. Chi-en stood beside her.

'Look at the stars over Mount St Helena,' he said.

Constellations formed glittering patterns across the indigo sky.

'Do you know,' he said, as though surprised, 'I feel happy. Very happy. And clear at last. I think you helped me to that, Catherine.'

She giggled, removing her shoes and his wide-brimmed hat. 'I don't want to shade my face from the moonlight,' she said.

'They say it burns one inside.'

'I don't care.'

She drew close, so that she looked up into his face. A face marked by character, the world's blows. Her heart beat too quickly for self-deception. She wanted to take his hands, draw them over her body. Guide him to the swollen feeling in her breasts, the restlessness between her unsteady legs.

'I am not a child, Chi-en,' she whispered, remembering his words earlier. 'Neither are you.'

For a long while they kissed, stood upon the flat rock. Both were unpractised, discovering their way round lip and tongue with each other's encouragement, urged on by quickening breath. Then he broke away.

'Catherine, I'll bring you trouble! I care for you too much for this. It is dangerous.'

She reached out for him and would not let go. His chest felt solid, the same chest she had glimpsed as he washed — a long time ago, it seemed — yet now she touched it with impatient hands and understood what she had wanted all along. She wished for nothing more than to pull his shirt over his head, to bare that chest.

'You must trust me,' she whispered.

He did not resist as she ruffled his cotton shirt upwards; his arms rose and she pulled it off, resting her cheek against his breast. She could hear the swift pace of his heart.

'Do as much for me,' she whispered.

And he did, struggling a little with the bone buttons, until their naked breasts pressed tight. Too late to pull back now. She closed her eyes as his hands reached to lift her skirts and murmured encouragement as his fingers brushed and explored.

Blankets were laid out across their clothes. The wide, flat rock, still warm from the day's unheeding sun, became their bed where breath and pleasure mingled with the murmur of the waterfall beside them. The hardness of their bed left nowhere soft to stray except the blankets they shared and each other's bodies.

Afterwards, as she fell asleep, Catherine had the strange thought her act of love with Chi-en was the sacrifice St Vincent required for saving Emile and no sin, no sin at all.

Later they drew close to one another again, warming each other with their limbs and long denied desires until her cries disturbed the darkness. Later still, they bathed in the pool, laughing as they shivered beneath the blankets, sharing their picnic of bread and wine. It was long after midnight when they walked back through the silent, moonlit vines, hand in hand like foolish, drowsy children.

Napa Valley, California
Autumn 1878

Chi-en stirred in his bed on the storeroom floor. Morning cast a beam of circling dust motes. After a momentary confusion, the previous night returned as images, sensations. Surely a dream.

Rubbing his unshaven chin, he froze. A lingering scent of another squeezed his eyes tight. He saw her face and pale skin in the moon's wan glow, her breasts and shape as she moved.

His head fell back on the rough pillow. He stared at a cobweb in the rafters, half-afraid of the tightening in his loins.

All true. Last night had happened. Now its consequences must be lived.

How would she greet him in the light of a new, sober day? He must find her at once – perhaps she was already up, wondering why he slept late, thinking he avoided her. Perhaps wanting him to ... He rose hurriedly. He must not encounter her like this, dishevelled and unshaven.

Wong Wu sat at the kitchen table when Chi-en entered, sipping tea, visibly hungover. They acknowledged each other, one bleary, the other afraid his tryst with Catherine was known. The younger man gave no sign. 'Do you want tea, Mr Sha-bells?'

'Yes. And heat plenty of water. It is my tenth day,' he added, alluding to the tradition that Confucian scholars should bathe every tenth day.

While Chi-en drank tea, Wong Wu set about filling a deep wooden tub used for laundry. He also produced rough towels and soap then went to smoke in front of the winery.

As Chi-en washed, last night revived. Could she love him? She had murmured so. In the fog of passion, certainly, but she had murmured it. And he had promised to stand by her forever.

Chi-en closed his eyes, splashed to cool himself. Did he deserve such a wife? Beautiful, determined, blessed with a gift for transformation.

Anxiety returned. If Royaume Céleste's neighbours found out, she would be driven from Napa, a pariah because of his race. Besides, it was a grave offence under Californian law for a white woman to marry a Chinaman.

Where in the wide world could they be accepted? Not here. Not in California. To join him she must sacrifice Royaume Céleste and all she had achieved – for a penniless man whose best prospect was an apartment in Chinatown and uncertain earnings from the Six Companies. Besides, he feared his own people's intolerance as much as the whites'.

But in his heart, despite the strictures of reason and prudence, he knew they could win a happy place in this world. How hard he would work to support her and Emile! To purchase the best of educations for that boy. To ensure her old age was secure.

Thoughts of Emile set off a fresh doubt. Could the boy accept him as a father? Certainly, there was great affection and respect between them. Trust, too.

The bitter joke was that if she was half-Chinese and he white, people would acknowledge his choice of wife. Disapprove, of course, but accept it. None of those bitter ironies could be wished away. Not a single one.

Chi-en dressed in his most gentlemanly attire and went off to test the future. Whatever she wanted, he would want. There would be no attempt to persuade or cajole. She had so much more to lose. He could demand nothing, merely hope for love freely given. For it seemed to him that love grown from obligation or coercion was a worthless plant.

He glanced at his tin pocket watch. Nine o'clock, far earlier than he had thought. An urge to rush from Royaume Céleste and make his fortune gripped Chi-en, to return when he was rich enough to support her in the grandest style. But he must be sensible. Had not Prince Hong's life revealed the folly of running away in expectation of a triumphant return? If he left now, without speaking, there could be no going back to this moment. This doorway when all lay open.

He looked for her in the winery. The ground floor was deserted but he heard movement in the middle storey. Climbing the steep stairs he discovered Jean-Pierre stirring the fermentation vats with a long wooden paddle. The frothy liquid released stray bubbles and seemed to hiss. Chi-en examined the steward's face for hostility.

'Have you seen Madame Bourchier?'

The steward yawned. 'Still asleep.'

Back outside, Chi-en looked up at the closed curtains of her room. Was she avoiding him? The arrival of a dogcart bouncing up the pot-holed track to Royaume Céleste, driven by none other than Sam Yip, halted further speculation. Chi-en hurried out to meet him.

'Mister Sha-bells!' called down Sam Yip. His horse reeked of sweat. 'I have a message from my uncle! He begs you to come. They are planning to march on Chinatown and drive us from Perryville!'

'Slow down,' said Chi-en. 'Who is planning this?'

'Men from San Francisco and local men. This afternoon! They say the Chinese must go. Uncle is afraid for our people. He says you speak the languages of all the *fan gui*. Come, so we may talk with them!'

Chi-en glanced at Catherine's window. The curtain remained closed.

'I will come,' he said. 'First I must write a short note.'

Inside the farmhouse, he went to the salon containing Catherine's bureau. There he found paper, pen and ink. With no time to perfect the letter, he wrote as his heart dictated.

My Dearest Catherine,

Do not read anything from my sudden absence. I have a duty to perform and must help my people in Perryville, if I may. For I have been told lives are at risk and cannot refuse. I will return this evening. Then I trust we shall share the wishes of our hearts. Mine is full of you. For now, I must go.

Your ever affectionate Chi-en

Blotting the ink, he folded the note and hurried upstairs, tucking it beneath her bedroom door. Was that movement within? No time to delay. Chi-en strode from the farmhouse, climbing up beside Sam Yip.

'Yaaah!' cried the pigtailed Chinaman as he whipped the horse into motion. The dogcart rattled down the track and Chi-en clung on tight. He did not look around. If he had, a sleepy Catherine opening her curtains would have been clearly visible, peering at his disappearing back.

Many in the crowd outside the Grand Hotel on the corner of Main and Spring had been drinking since before noon. Several casks of coarse Napa red lay empty. Perhaps the patriotic winemakers who donated their wares, all of whom lacked cash buyers, figured to exchange worthless goods for goodwill.

Everyone in the crowd figured to gain something, even if just a little diversion. Colonel Smithson-Mackay had hired the town band and, between tunes, speakers from the Workingmen's Party of Mr Denis Kearney thundered at the crowd. Several frock-coated gentlemen had travelled all the way from Frisco to tell stirring tales of sandlot meetings thousands strong. Their message was simple: *The Chinese Must Go!* And shame on any employers favouring Mongol labour to white.

With each hour the crowd swelled. A babble of accents filled Main Street: Irish, German, American-born settlers from back East, Swiss and Italians. Although the intention was to march on Chinatown in support of a new law to exclude the Chinese from California, the demonstration's organisers had delayed their departure.

For one thing, a hundred miners and labouring men from further up the valley were known to be tramping towards Perryville to join the party. It would be mighty uncivil to start without them. For another, the boys were having themselves a ball.

Chief among the latter was Hercules Smithson-Mackay. He, too, drank to blot out his troubles – problems the extinction of the entire Celestial race would not cure. His wife was threatening a costly divorce on the grounds of infidelity. A French opera singer had caught his fancy at the performance of *Carmen* he had attended that spring. He had used the *California Star* to promote his musical mistress so successfully that she decamped to New York in triumph, leaving Smithson-Mackay with countless unpaid bills.

The Colonel suspected his infatuation with the opera singer was the fault of another French siren. If Catherine Bourchier hadn't led him on, a whole series of blows to his pride wouldn't have occurred – not least his humiliation when Parker and Temple tried to round up the Wappo. Those two stalwarts were all that remained of a time when he had been Colonel in more than name. Their continuing respect meant more to him than any lost mistress.

Worse still, his campaign for election as Senator for the State of California was faltering, clogged by articles in the press concerning his wartime record – and California could be such a damnably Yankee state.

A cheer rose. 'The up-valley boys is comin'! Here they come!'

Smithson-Mackay looked over at Parker and Temple, lounging in the shadow of the hotel. A sudden fury made him grab the elbow of one of the demonstration's organisers.

'Tell the boys out front I'll address 'em! Dammit, *I'll* lead the way to that Mongol rat-hole.'

He shouted over to Parker and Temple, 'Hear that, boys?'

Mr Parker exchanged a glance with Mr Temple. Both nodded at their old bushwhacking, Georgia Raider colonel, though what their gesture signified Smithson-Mackay had no steady notion. He liked it enough to recharge his glass.

Chi-en Shambles had arrived at Perryville around midday. Chinatown was a crude rectangle of rotting clapboard shanties surrounding a central square, a fetid, teeming warren where human and animal shit reeked in hot weather. All year round there was a stink of smoke and carbolic steam from the laundries and a sickly-sweet aroma from an abattoir specialising in rendered meat.

Chinatown filled a muddy tongue of land liable to flooding on the south side of town, where a smaller stream joined the Napa River. Every square foot had been set to profitable use by its white landlords. Streets were narrow and gloomy. Many buildings had acquired rickety extra storeys that shook in high winds.

Nearly five hundred seasonal labourers, waiting to be hired for the harvest, had joined the existing population, and all available rooms were occupied several times over. Pressure on farmers and winegrowers to hire 'whites only' left the Chinese milling listlessly on crowded streets. The mood was of a fortress about to be overrun by barbarians. A fortress without defenders or walls.

Sam Yip drove straight to Chinatown's central market square. His uncle's store stood between a shabby Daoist temple and a gambling house. Groups of men had gathered for the Sam clan's protection. They muttered among themselves as Chi-en stepped from the dogcart in fine American clothes. On most days his attire and lack of a pigtail would have earned distrust; now he lent them courage.

Inside Sam Wah's store, nine men sat round a table, leaders of the Perryville Chinatown community, men of property. Sam Wah rose to greet him.

'Glad to see you here, Mr Sha-bells!' He clapped impatient hands. 'Refreshment for Mr Sha-bells! Please have a seat.'

Chi-en bowed and took the proffered chair.

'Mr Sha-bells speaks all the *fan gui* languages,' confided Sam Wah to the assembled worthies. 'He knows the American law.'

This news inspired general approval. They must be frightened indeed to pay a Longhair such respect.

'I will help in any way I can,' he promised.

Their debate, interrupted by his arrival, resumed. Its essence was simple: what to do when the crowd on Main Street reached Chinatown. Spies had reported growing drunkenness and angry speeches. Deputy Sheriff Dwyer had vacated Perryville. A note on the door of his office said he and his deputies would not return until midnight, at the earliest. No clue was given of his whereabouts.

It was a circular debate. One man advocated resistance; there were a few guns in Chinatown and improvised weapons could be produced. The rest talked of barricading houses until the demonstrators passed through the narrow streets. Sam Wah listened gloomily.

'Let's hear Mr Sha-bells,' he said.

All eyes turned to Chi-en. He abandoned his cigarette in a copper ashtray and sipped from a porcelain bowl of tea before speaking.

'My friends,' he began, 'let us ask ourselves why these men are on Main Street. Why they wish to frighten us. Why they hate us.'

'It is because they are barbarians!' shouted the man who wanted to fight.

'Perhaps,' conceded Chi-en. 'You might say that of any nation. All are guilty of some barbarity.'

'One may only deter force with force,' said the fighter.

'Water wears down the strongest stone,' pointed out Chi-en.

'A scholar!' groaned a second merchant. 'Are we to drive them back with words?'

Chi-en raised a disputatious finger. Anyone observing the animation in his face and voice might have concluded that he was enjoying himself. 'What other weapon do you possess?'

The worthies muttered. Sam Wah rubbed his beard. 'Return to your point,' he said to Chi-en. 'Why do they trouble us? We do them no harm!'

'Come, come,' said Chi-en. 'They travel half-way round the world to escape poverty. They risk everything. They are promised easy wealth in the Golden State. Instead? Their labour – where it is needed – is *sometimes* undercut by our people.'

'That is well-known,' said Sam Wah, impatiently, 'meanwhile, they may already be marching this way.'

'I say this . . .' said Chi-en, 'we must urge them to remember their own Holy Book. *The labourer is worthy of his hire.* If all were paid a decent wage for the same work, and the greed of rich men was controlled, all races could share California in harmony.'

Sam Wah regarded him in amazement. 'I have not heard such theories since my youth,' he said. 'Then it came from Taiping rebels who wished to turn the world on its head.' He laughed bitterly. 'If you care to reason with them in that way, Mr Sha-bells, be my guest. A fist in the ear shall be your reply. Or a noose.'

Chi-en hardly listened. His growing excitement had created an image, striding from heart to mind, of brave Prince Hong.

'I will reason with them,' he declared, 'and remind them of their own laws. It is a crime according to the Constitution of California to damage your property. Better still, your white landlords' property.'

'That is a stronger argument,' conceded Sam Wah.

Still his supporters urged a less confrontational policy: hiding in their homes until trouble passed. After all, patience was the oldest weapon of the powerless. At last Sam Wah raised his hand for silence.

'Mr Sha-bells is right,' he said. 'Our houses and stores are owned by white men who have more influence than us. Besides, we have nowhere to hide. He and I shall speak to their leaders and remind them of the law.'

With that, Sam Wah asked the worthies to return to their families. Pouring out two cups of wine imported at great expense from Guangzhou, he grunted to Chi-en. 'Drink! While we still can. Now we are alone, I have something to tell you, Mr Longhair. Something that may surprise you.'

Late afternoon, the up-valley contingent entered Main Street, led by a hand-painted banner stretched between two poles, *Californian Work for Californians*. Behind came eighty dust-covered miners and unemployed farm labourers from the foothills of Mount St Helena. Though fewer than expected, the crowd on Main Street erupted. Handbells rang, whistles blew. Drunken men rushed forward with earthenware cups of Napa wine for their thirsty comrades. The town band broke into frenzied *umpahs*.

After the commotion died down, Colonel Smithson-Mackay mounted the podium and waved for attention.

He surveyed their upturned faces with the same confidence he had enjoyed when reviewing his Georgia Raiders. The same justification for just about anything. Not for the cause of Dixie, exactly, but a new Dixie. Right here, in the Golden State.

'Fellow Californians!' he cried. A roar greeted him. Red-faced, sweating men punched the air. 'Californians! Am I the only man here who wants his country back?' More cheering. 'I say, let them Mongols know it's time to get packin'! But boys!' He stood, hands on hips. 'Boys! When we get there, watch what you touch! I'd sure hate you to catch one of their Celestial diseases!'

'Burn 'em out!' shouted a voice. 'Then there'd be no d'sease!' The uproar greeting this comment concealed the speaker's identity, none other than Mr Parker.

'We need it peaceful and orderly, boys!' shouted Smithson-Mackay, sensing control of the crowd slip away. Already a few were forming up to march the half mile to Chinatown. 'One man should do the talking!' he added, meaning himself.

It was hard to judge if anyone heard. Anxious that his authority – as had happened with that bitch of a wife – might slip away, Smithson-Mackay leapt from the podium and pushed to the front. A servant led out his magnificent white stallion and Colonel Smithson-Mackay mounted proudly, taking his place at the crowd's head. Whistles, bells and drums carried him forward like a tide.

'Let's show 'em what we're here for!' he bellowed.

As the demonstration stepped out, a select group of men drew aside. A few carried clubs and pickaxe handles. Others nursed suspicious bulges beneath their jackets. Two watchful, expressionless figures surveyed these forces. Parker and Temple knew what the Colonel wanted – or decided they did.

'Frighten 'em out of their rat-holes!' called out Mr Parker, to the approval of the small band hanging back, dollarless, rootless men who had been present at the ill-fated round up of the Wappo. 'We'll flank 'em by followin' the river. Make sure you got your matches an' pistols handy, boys!'

With that, they took a side road to a path beside the Napa River. No one in this small party blew a whistle or beat a drum. If there were two men in Perryville that day who knew how to organise a bushwhacking attack on unprotected houses and civilians, it was Parker and Temple.

Meanwhile, the main demonstration roared loud enough to scare off devils from hell – which was its intention. At the outskirts of China-town, they found the way blocked.

Two men stood in the dusty, narrow road. One short, with a shaved forehead and a long, ribboned pigtail. Beneath a wide-brimmed black hat, he wore Chinese clothes and an incongruous morning coat worthy of a mayor. The second, tall as any white man, sported a Frisco gentle-man's suit. They weren't much of a barricade, but the front rank of the demonstration came to a halt. Those behind slowed and stopped.

Colonel Smithson-Mackay stared down from his horse at the impudent John Chinamen. The stallion nickered impatiently, pawing the dirt with an iron-shod hoof. Then Smithson-Mackay recognised Chi-en Shambles. He glanced round for Parker and Temple, mindful that they could easily find a dark corner for some swift justice worthy of Judge Lynch. Worthy of a Mongol with a taste for white women.

'My! If it ain't the Mongol law-wrangler!' he exclaimed.

Chi-en and Sam Wah had been waiting at the entrance to Chinatown for two hours before the Colonel arrived, resting upon stools in the shade. Sam Wah chewed sunflower seeds while Chi-en smoked nervous cigarettes.

For the first time he had space to consider Catherine. If she could see his determination before an oncoming tide of deluded, deceived men, she might see how he would stand by her and risk his life. Another part of him knew very well she'd call him a damned fool.

The crowd on Main Street grew noisier than ever.

'What did you wish to tell me?' he asked Sam Wah. 'You spoke of surprising me.'

Sam Wah continued chewing. 'How do you think I recognised your ideas as Taiping rebel notions?'

'Such things are common knowledge.'

'Do you recollect that when I first met you, I said I'd seen you someplace before?'

'Yes.'

'It was only today, after you spoke of the rich and poor being made one, I remembered where.'

Chi-en's throat tightened. 'Where?'

A hollow laugh shook Sam Wah's barrel chest. 'In the Heavenly Capital, of course. In Nanking. I remembered a half-foreigner boy like you, a half *fan gui*, riding behind a Taiping Prince. We Holy Soldiers knelt in the mud as you trotted by. My brothers and I talked excitedly about you. We said the foreigners had sent you as a sign because they were God-worshippers, too. That they would help us destroy the Ching Emperor.' Again, he laughed, bitterly this time. 'Those same foreigners sold the Manchu cannon and guns and sent their men to loot our cities. Of all the Holy Soldiers in my regiment, a handful survived.'

Understanding connected the two men, an emptiness crowded with words.

Chi-en sighed. 'Was the Heavenly Kingdom of Great Peace not a dream worth fighting for? What if it had come true?'

Sam Wah shook out more sunflower seeds from a bag. 'It didn't.'

'But if it had!'

'The Heavenly King was a madman,' said Sam Wah, 'and I was a fool.'

They listened to the approaching commotion from Main Street.

'Whatever happened back then, our people need us here today,' said Chi-en. 'They are terribly afraid.'

'As we should be,' muttered Sam Wah. 'Or are you in the mood to become a martyr, Mr Sha-bells?'

The front rank came into view, led by a frock-coated gentleman on a magnificent horse. Sam Wah spat out half-chewed sunflower seeds and Chi-en ground out his cigarette beneath a boot heel. Side by side, arms folded across their chests, they blocked the narrow road.

Thus Colonel Smithson-Mackay discovered them, cursing Chi-en as a Mongol law-wrangler.

'You sure are swimmin' out of your depth, boy!' he warned.

His fellow leaders were more forthright.

'Git outta here!' called the first, an inverted pyramid of a man, one of Denis Kearney's strong-arm boys from Frisco. 'We ain't here to negotiate with yeller rat-eaters!'

A murmur rose from the ranks of men about to pour like a cleansing flood into the pathways and narrow streets of Perryville's pitiful Chinatown. Smithson-Mackay noted the Mongol lawyer's fancy clothes – a get-up fit for a white man, not some monkey masquerading as a better race – and he noted the Celestial was younger and handsomer than he was. Amidst so much noticing he ignored the Mongol lawyer's words.

'Sirs! There are women and children in the houses behind us. Innocent people, sirs!'

'Step aside!' roared the inverted pyramid.

'Think of your own wives and children, gentlemen!' continued the Chinaman. 'Let the law settle any grievances you have. After all, the buildings in Chinatown are white-owned.'

'Our children and wives ain't Mongols!' called out an outraged voice. 'D'ye hear that? He's sayin' our wives should be Chinee whores now!'

The angry murmur became a roar and the crowd jostled forward.

'Hold boys!' bellowed Smithson-Mackay. 'Hold, dammit!'

There remained sufficient discipline in the mob to obey. He had seen men blood-crazy in battle, how the most placid, church-fearing farm boy could shoot and burn and rape unarmed families. He had seen the panic of men gone coward-crazy, how they could trample their own brothers to escape. Foreboding made him face the pushing crowd.

'Hold, boys! I said one man should do all the talking. Hold back, boys! We keep this lawful!'

A new contender stepped into the relative hush that followed. Smithson-Mackay recognised him as the local Chinese labour contractor, a man with whom his neighbours had done business.

'Col'nel! You in charge here?' cried the Chinaman. 'You wan' bad thing happen here? No, sir! We work your harvest free! Guarantee! You take your frien's away and we work free! Guarantee!'

Colonel Smithson-Mackay had not anticipated this ingenious offer. Abruptly – with an ex-soldier's admiration for a brave opponent – he acknowledged the sheer courage of the two Chinamen. And wondered, if their positions were reversed, whether he'd dare halt a raging crowd, hundreds strong. For a long moment he considered the possibility of free labour for his own harvest. In that lapse, those without harvests to gather plucked off the final bindings of restraint.

'Damn slaves!' bellowed a drunken voice. 'Damn slaves wan' work for nothin'! Let's show 'em we mean business, boys!'

The foremost, angriest ranks surged forward, engulfing Colonel Smithson-Mackay. Passing men punched or kicked the Chinese ambassadors cowering in a doorway.

'One man should speak for all!' cried Smithson-Mackay, struggling to control his horse.

No one listened. The tide of burly muscle and frustration surged up the alleyways of Perryville Chinatown, rattling locked doors and smashing windows as they ran. Once more the drums and whistles sounded.

'Frighten 'em out of their rat-holes! Frighten 'em out!'

Soon Smithson-Mackay had been swept into a small central square. On one side towered an imposing, well-maintained wooden building, a large general store and warehouse bearing the name *Sam Wah*. Men who longed to own any structure, however humble, stared up bitterly at the Chinese merchant's property.

Screams rose on one side of the square. Stiff necks turned. Dozens of Chinese were being driven out of the Joss House where they had taken shelter. One in silks was dragged out by his pigtail, wailing pitifully. Though some in the crowd laughed, others woke to the dangers of their presence here. Outside the Joss House, fists rose and fell, men panting with exertion. Somewhere out of sight a pistol shot rang out.

'Stop! Are you mad?'

The confused crowd turned to see a bedraggled figure standing on an upturned barrel. It was the Mongol lawyer. Gone was his natty appearance. Blood poured from his nose and red patches all over his face presaged terrible bruises. His once elegant clothes were torn.

'You will murder someone!' he cried, apparently unafraid that someone might be himself. 'Where is the law here?'

A fresh tattoo of drums and whistles drowned him out. Above the commotion a new call went up: 'Smoke! Smoke! Fire! 'Ware that, boys! Fire!'

'Damn!' said a man next to Colonel Smithson-Mackay. 'This whole rat-hole'll blaze quick as black powder! I'm gittin' outta here!'

Napa Valley, California
Autumn 1878

Catherine Bourchier had woken an hour before Chi-en rattled away to Perryville.

That hour had been like the magic earthquake the Wappo prayed for during their Ghost Dance. It re-shaped her inner contours, her settlements, horizons, forming a new world from the old. The earthquake that changed her was invisible, ordinary yet tumultuous, a ripple of deep yearning. Its force would always outwear the coarse hatred brewing in Perryville that day – love seemed to her as inevitable and hardy as the seasons. She felt these truths more in her body than conscious mind.

It was a body brimming with pleasant drowsiness. A single person filled her thoughts – she thanked Heaven that person was no longer just herself or Emile.

Catherine hugged the blankets, drawn to practical considerations. If necessary, she would sell Royaume Céleste so they might be together. After all, she had promised St Vincent to sacrifice her vineyard if Emile was allowed to live. But was it necessary? Why should she throw away all she had worked so hard to build? With cleverness, a little guile, she and Chi-en might enjoy the fruits of Royaume Céleste together.

But in head and heart Catherine knew that could never be. They would be treated as lepers here — and Emile would suffer alongside them.

Catherine pulled the blankets closer. *I can change*, she had promised herself. Had she not learned that what is lost can be replaced? In part, at least? Even if just in spirit. And Royaume Céleste was now worth five times what she had paid for it, probably far more. With that money they could start again, anywhere they chose. It was clear that Emile both respected and trusted Chi-en, a true father except in blood. One who would help educate her son — guide him to become a good man.

In the winery the grapes were fermenting. Bubbles rising, slowly sweetening. As she drowsed, a dreadful uncertainty gripped her. How arrogant to assume Chi-en wished to bind himself to her! She acknowledged she was not an easy person. Perhaps he had used her for his pleasure like Antoine — and as others had tried. Seducing a white woman might be a triumph to one scorned by whites.

No. She screwed her fists tight. No, Chi-en was not such a man.

It was then, as though driven by a premonition, she rose and hurried to the window. Just in time to watch him dwindle in Sam Yip's dog-cart . . .

It took fevered minutes to dress, discover Chi-en's note and read it a dozen times. His words possessed her . . . *share the wishes of our hearts* . . . *Mine is full of you* . . . Yet to sign it so coldly! *Your ever affectionate.* Did he not love her then? If he loved her, could he who had at his disposal half the world's words not use the one word she craved instead of cold, heartless *affectionate.* Affection was for favourite cats or nephews or maiden aunts!

As she squeezed the letter, Catherine sensed his fear of unreturned love. If so, she honoured him. Except his caution seemed an affront, a challenge to overcome.

Hair still disordered, Catherine hurried down to the winery where she found Jean-Pierre treading grapes in a fermenting vat, his crimson-stained trousers rolled up to reveal old, spindly legs. He examined her hastily buttoned dress.

'Is something wrong, Madame?'

'Did Chi-en tell you where he was going? Or why? I just saw him drive away.'

Jean-Pierre picked a slow path round the circular vat, each step a tiny shuffle.

'I wonder what your father would make of Monsieur 'Umble,' he said, cautiously.

'What?'

She was staring out of the window in the direction of Perryville.

'It does not matter, Madame, except . . .' He paused in his circular walk. 'I do not think Monsieur Bourchier would approve of Monsieur 'Umble. Do you?'

Catherine regarded him sullenly. No, Papa would never see the virtues of a penniless man of no family as a suitor for his precious daughter.

'His name is Shambles,' she said, 'Chi-en Shambles.'

Jean-Pierre circled the vat. 'Of course, Monsieur Bourchier's judgement in matters other than wine was not always reliable.' He touched the scar on his cheek left by Antoine's riding crop. Such an admission of his lost patron's frailty made him uneasy. 'You see how I tread the wine, Madame,' he said, hurriedly. 'It is because, as I warned you, the grapes were almost too ripe. If we do not air the yeast there may be *piqûre* later.'

Catherine looked at him in astonishment. Could he really talk of *piqûre* at a time like this, when Chi-en was in danger? Yet his tone was anxious. She recognised it as his way of discussing Chi-en, a conversation they could no longer avoid. Faithful, resourceful Jean-Pierre Leclos deserved no less.

Hitching up her dress and tucking it into the waistband, she went to the water butt and scrubbed her bare legs.

'You should not!' he cried. 'It is not proper work for a lady!'

She clambered into the vat adjoining his own, forcing a hole through the chapeau of grape-skins and stalks and fruit-flesh. The fermenting wine buzzed like a swarm of wasps, gases tickling her legs.

'There,' she said, 'now we can talk frankly.'

He watched her, half in horror, half in admiration. 'You are as bold as your father. No, bolder!'

'Is that a good thing?'

'In this country, Madame, yes. But I have a fear. Look at this young wine, how it sings. But we both know that in a few weeks it will settle down, become something else. Is it not like love, Madame? A certain, mad kind of love?'

They circled their respective vats, passing each other then continuing round.

'Some loves mature and improve with age,' she said.

'Many do not, Madame. I am afraid you will lose everything all over again.'

'It was our skill that built Royaume Céleste so quickly. Yours and mine. That could work just as well in a more congenial place.'

'You are an excellent winemaker,' he conceded, 'for a woman.'

This praise, more than she had ever expected from him, made her flush.

'And you are undoubtedly shrewd,' he said, 'though a little *piqué* yourself, at times.'

There were a thousand things she might say to him, so many explanations and confusions – and questions, too, for she had never really understood Jean-Pierre Leclos, despite knowing him all her life. Words seemed inadequate for so huge a crossing: she must find another way.

She waded to the edge of the vat and held out a crimson-stained hand. At first he pretended not to notice. Then, uncertainly, the old man held out his own hand and their fingers met in the gulf between the wine vats.

Uncomfortable at her touch, he muttered, 'Monsieur Bourchier would never!' When he tried to pull away, she did not let go. And her grip was strong. She felt a tear drip from her cheek into the wine frothing and sloshing around her, hissing and whispering, building and transforming. It seemed right, somehow, to add droplets of salt.

'If you did leave here, Madame, would you still have a place for old Jean-Pierre Leclos?'

Catherine laughed amidst her tears. 'We would share our last crust with you! You know that!'

He nodded with a laconic peasant's acceptance of the seasons. 'In the meantime, perhaps Madame would let go of my hand? It is beginning to hurt.'

She released her grip.

Jean-Pierre smoothed his walrus moustache and continued to tread the grapes, round and round, a resigned expression on his weathered face.

A restless day followed. Catherine could not settle, always with an ear tuned for horses' hooves. But Chi-en did not return.

She recollected Trubody saying there would be a demonstration in Perryville against the Chinese in their ghetto. She had once visited Sam Wah's store to hire workers and been disgusted by the slum's open sewers. The people had grown wary at the sight of a white face.

Chi-en's letter made it clear he was putting himself in danger. Why must he play the hero? Why now, when the world's possibilities were widening? Yet that was precisely what she respected in him. Antoine never did anything except for himself. People who acted otherwise provoked his scorn. Still, Chi-en should take greater care. That was one of the things she would help him see.

When she tried to practise her oboe, nothing would agree: the twin reeds stuck together and squawked; she couldn't play in tune; the keys were sticky and stiff; above all she sensed no pulse to the meandering notes on the clef.

Around mid-afternoon she drove their new two-wheel gig to collect Emile from Trubody Nook. She wondered what Nancy would say if she knew about last night's nakedness on a flat rock beneath the moon, a nakedness still insistent in her body.

The valley was soon crossed. At Trubody Nook she found the household in a flurry. Horses were being led from the stable and saddled. Mr Trubody stood on the front steps, staring through a telescope in the direction of Perryville. Emile and his new friend, the orphan girl, Sarah, whispered nearby. As she climbed down from the gig, Judge Dawson bustled through the front door, buttoning up his coat.

'Ah, Catherine,' said Trubody, 'you've arrived just when we're leaving!'

'What is happening?' she asked, mounting the stone steps of the house.

'Look for yourself.'

She took up the heavy telescope and adjusted it until the dark blur of Perryville, three or four miles up the flat valley, came into focus.

'What is that? It looks like mist or . . . yes. A fire! There is much smoke.'

'It's coming from Chinatown,' said Judge Dawson, grimly. 'I suspect your rogue of a Deputy Sheriff, Dan Dwyer, has failed to keep the demonstration peaceful. If they burn half of Perryville there'll be hell to pay.'

'There are hundreds of the poor devils crammed into Chinatown round harvest time,' pointed out Trubody. 'Sooner we get there the better. Eh, Dawson?'

'They'll have their Chinese Exclusion Act within a few years,' predicted the Judge. 'Just wait and see. Though what possible principle of economy or law justifies the barring of law-abidin', industrious people from our state is a mystery to me.'

Once more she focussed the telescope. Chi-en should be safe if he was careful. He would not put himself in danger to fight their stupid fire. Her grip trembled. The image blurred with tears.

'Oh, Chi-en . . .' she whispered, remembering how he had dashed into the burning winery.

A clatter of hooves filled the courtyard. Trubody, Dawson and a few armed men deputised by the Judge, galloped in the direction of Perryville.

Several fires had started simultaneously, coinciding with the entry into Chinatown of Parker and Temple's 'flankers'. Whether these men breaking from the main demonstration were to blame no one ever established. Afterwards there were low conversations in Perryville saloons. Some muttered about thatched roofs stuffed with burning rags. Others, the majority, swore a lantern had been accidentally knocked off its hook in the middle of the day. As one wit observed, it must have been a hell of a magic lantern to start fires in five different places at the same time.

The press, especially the *California Star*, had no doubt about the blaze's origin. Alarmed by a demonstration of Free Americans in streets claimed as a colony of the Celestial Empire, the Chinese had set fire to their own homes in a conspiracy to harm the Lawful Marchers. Naturally, so many wooden buildings joined and jammed together made a ready bonfire – and soon the conflagration was beyond control. It said much about the generosity of spirit possessed by the Lawful Marchers that they endeavoured to put out the fire, at great risk to themselves, while the Chinese hampered their efforts by running round in a panic or simply watching honest white men risk their lives. An unexpected consequence of the conflagration was that Chinese desperadoes used the confusion to settle old scores. Two bodies were found the next day with gunshot wounds. A dozen more Chinese perished in the blaze, mainly because the stupefied denizens of an opium den could not be persuaded to leave their pipes, though the Lawful Marchers implored them to do so. The *California Star* concluded that the blaze, though unfortunate, cleared the air of Perryville to such an extent that infectious diseases decreased in the district by sixty-three percent.

As smoke drifted through Chinatown, Sam Wah appeared at the upturned barrel where Chi-en, beside himself with passion and outrage, harangued the crowd. Both were bruised and bleeding, Chi-en from the nose, Sam Wah's forehead split open.

'We must get the people away from here!' shouted Chi-en above the drums and uproar. Then he called out in Mandarin: 'They are hiding in their homes! They fear the devil-demon soldiers! I tell you, the people will burn if we do not lead them to safety!'

Sam Wah dragged him to the ground, steadying his arm. 'What soldiers? Are you mad?'

Chi-en stared at him in shock and bewilderment. Perhaps it was the blows to his head. Momentarily, Perryville had blurred with the Heavenly Capital. The mob of white men, scattering as they realised the fire's danger, had become the Manchu Emperor's looting troops. His hold on reality was loosening. Unless . . . unless it was a sign. A sign Chi-en must act as Prince Hong should have done that terrible day when the Heavenly Capital burned like the hottest corner of hell. A sign that he, the servant, must restore the honour his master lost . . .

Chi-en blinked, shook his head. All around, terrified Chinese were emerging from houses. By now most of the whites had retreated. Those that remained were looting stores and houses. As the smoke thickened, marchers carrying handfuls of clothes or stolen objects of small value, ran past in the direction of Main Street.

Sam Yip appeared at their side, waving a revolver. 'Uncle! Uncle! They are bandits! What are we to do!'

The three men ducked at the bark of gunshots. Someone in an adjoining street was steadily emptying a pistol. A slow, creaking crash followed by a whoosh indicated that, hidden by tides of rolling smoke, a building had collapsed. Coughing. Screams. Bellowed questions. Exclamations.

'Never mind the looters,' said Chi-en, 'gather the people. We must lead the people to safety.'

Sam Wah hesitated. 'What of my store?'

People were already collecting in the market square, clutching meagre possessions. Soon a hundred huddled together, including a few women and children, though the population of Chinatown was mainly bachelor. A fresh wave of smoke engulfed them with a reek of burning oil. At once a terrible, keening wail arose, the fear of people who believe themselves trapped. Sparks blew like hot sleet through the smoke. Hacking, grating coughs. Gasps for air. Chi-en looked around, his eyes smarting. When the smoke rolled away, he saw a stream of rats flowing down open sewers, seeking the safety of the Napa River. No white men were left in the small square, just a few abandoned banners bearing the slogan *The Chinese Must Go*. Advice he was eager to heed.

'Sam Wah! Follow the rats to the river and the fields south of town. We will be safe there. Sam Yip! Take these people to the river!'

The younger man looked to his uncle, but Sam Wah was staring at half a dozen men with a handcart, their faces covered by wet handkerchiefs. They vanished into a street leading to Chinatown's plushest gambling house.

'Did you see?' he cried. 'They had guns!'

'Uncle, look!'

Sam Wah wheeled. 'My store!'

A new blaze had started in houses near the back of the three-storey building. The front door of the store opened and a stream of Sam Wah's clan – uncles, nephews, wife and precious son, followed by servants – rushed out, crying that white men were breaking into the rear, looking for cash.

'I must stop them! Give me the revolver!'

Before Sam Wah could charge inside, Chi-en took him by both arms. They grappled like wrestlers while Chi-en spoke.

'They have guns! Save your family!'

The two men, momentarily engulfed by smoke, ceased to struggle. Weeping, Sam Wah spluttered. 'You are right. Sam Yip! Take these people away! We will stay to gather more.'

His nephew obeyed, leading a crowd two hundred strong down Chinatown's broadest street until they reached the highway outside town. Still, fresh refugees from the flames kept appearing in the square.

The fire spread faster than malicious rumours. A wind was up in the valley, feeding the flames. The blaze created swirling, over-heated air that fed itself. It was time to abandon Chinatown while they still could.

His arm supporting a drooping Sam Wah, Chi-en led the remainder of Chinatown's population beyond the burning hovels, over a footbridge spanning the Napa River and across a field to the highway. When he glanced back, Perryville was hidden by a haze of heat and smoke.

Hundreds of Chinese knelt or stood around the road, coughing and spluttering as men cleared sooty lungs. A few wept openly. Women lamented in Cantonese or Mandarin, prostitutes mainly, who had lost the expensive silk costumes and shoes that set their value as courtesans.

At that moment, Nathaniel Trubody and Judge Dawson galloped up the highway. Chi-en strode forward. His white linen shirt was streaked with his own blood.

'Mr Trubody!' he called. 'Over here, sir!'

It took little time to tell the story. How Colonel Smithson-Mackay had led his supporters to Chinatown and the chaos that ensued.

'Damn those fools!' cried Trubody. 'We'll need to find temporary shelter for these people.'

They watched Chinatown in its shroud of billowing smoke. Gunshots were again heard.

'They will also need food, sir,' said Chi-en. 'Perhaps you could fetch help from Trubody Nook?'

Trubody conferred with Judge Dawson. Before Chi-en learned their decision, a renewed wailing broke out.

The wail came from a round, squat woman who rushed up to Sam Wah, crying out in Hakka: 'My son! Mr Sam, my son is missing! I cannot find my son! You must find him, Mr Sam!'

'Who is this woman?' Chi-en asked Sam Yip, who stood nearby.

'A servant in my uncle's house,' said Sam Yip. 'Not important. Her son is a bastard child. Pay no heed, Mr Sha-bells.'

While she begged, men and women of the labour contractor's household tried to calm her. But her panic was infectious. Soon Sam Wah's own young son began to sob.

'I know Bai Yu will return to the store, Mr Sam!' she cried. 'It is the only place he knows.'

'Stupid woman!' said Sam Wah. The store is on fire! Look for your son among the people here. See! More are escaping all the time.'

Indeed, groups of Chinese still stumbled out of the clouds drifting from Chinatown.

'We cannot leave a child to burn in there,' said Chi-en.

Sam Wah turned to him. 'You have done enough. Leave this to me. We need you here. If need be, let another man go.'

'The boy is just a whore's bastard,' pointed out Sam Yip.

Chi-en almost struck him. Once again, his head reeled between past and present, between America and the burning Heavenly Capital.

'I am an unfortunate woman's bastard!' he cried.

He knew Catherine would clutch his arm if she were here. Do anything to hold him back. Chinatown was half way to an inferno. He picked up a blanket and, covering his face, charged back into the smoke and pulsing heat haze.

The last he heard was Sam Wah crying, 'Come back! He's . . .' Then he was passing a wooden house that cracked and roared as flames ate it up, and so did not hear them calling.

'Bai Lu is here! The boy is here! Come back!'

Terrified Bai Lu had hidden in a huddle of Chinese labourers and finally ran forward.

Chi-en plunged into Chinatown. A strange elation touched his spirit. He seemed to hear a dear, lost friend's voice urging him on. Except that Hong spoke another ghost's words. *Remember, Chi-en, remember . . . He that is down need fear no fall . . . He that is low no pride . . .'*

Chi-en rushed to the central square, his face covered by the blanket. Oddly, there was less smoke here. The fires were younger. Though he could not know it, Parker and Temple's 'flankers' had started their diversionary blazes on the outskirts of Chinatown, away from buildings they wished to loot – a tactic learned when burning out Yankees in the Civil War.

Coughing, Chi-en stared in disbelief. A Chinaman's corpse lay stretched in front of Sam Wah's store. The building itself had been systematically emptied of valuables before being set alight, no doubt to cover traces of the crime. Just like the devil-demon soldiers had done in the Heavenly Capital. Everything the same! Except this time, the orphan boy in the burning house would be saved.

In the square, too, his hat lost and hair dishevelled, was Colonel Smithson-Mackay, struggling to keep his bucking stallion under control with harsh tugs of the bridle and blows from a riding crop.

As he watched, a small iron safe was hoisted onto a handcart. Dark shapes flitted through the murk with their booty, preparing to escape as a group. Two masked men shouted commands, 'Load her, boys! Nice 'n' steady, boys!'

Chi-en hung back fearfully. The only way into the building was past the assembled looters. Oh, he must be brave! Sam Wah's store oozed smoke. Bai Lu might be watching, hiding until the men left.

Covering his nose and mouth with the wet blanket, Chi-en prepared to charge through his enemies.

Ten minutes earlier, Colonel Smithson-Mackay had been lost in a maze of wooden tenements. Every smoke-choked alley and road seemed to lead nowhere but to the central square. Few people could be seen, stray looters seeking a swift escape, flitting Chinese with armloads of possessions.

He recognised a storefront, its door broken open and goods strewn across the dirt road: spilt rice and dried peas, smashed bottles. It was here the Mongol law-wrangler had tried to stop the marchers and been beaten for his insolence. That meant the entrance to Chinatown lay nearby. With a whoop Smithson-Mackay spurred his stallion round a corner, only to haul the reins so sharply the horse reared, almost throwing him.

'Damn you!' A burning house had fallen, blocking the way. Smoke and sparks billowed: the wind in the valley was rising.

'Whoa! Steady boy!' But the stallion, a cool thousand dollars of elegant horseflesh, would not obey. Smithson-Mackay yearned for his ugly old cavalry charger during the war. Let off a cannon by that creature's head and all it did was snicker. It seemed the bucking, highly-strung mount beneath him was just another costly disappointment – like the Frenchie bitch opera singer and ungrateful bloodsucker of a wife.

Smithson-Mackay turned the horse and trotted back the way he'd come. At the looted store he found his way blocked again.

An old Chinaman, blood oozing from a gash across his shaved forehead, grovelled among split rice sacks and jagged, broken glass. His eyes rolled in terror as he gazed up at the horse's huge, looming chest and heavy, thudding hooves. With a curse, Smithson-Mackay reined up.

For a long moment he examined the old man. Despite a growing certainty of danger and his need to be gone from this place, time slowed. He thought of wounded Yankees in the war, bleeding out their guts as they gazed up at him with helpless, imploring eyes. Enemies like this dumb old man, forgotten except by their families and acquaintances. He noticed the Chinaman's legs were burned, feet bloody and black from fire. Unless someone carried him out, he wasn't going no place. He thought of dismounting, throwing the helpless old man across the back of his horse, getting them both the hell out of there.

'Mister!' moaned the Chinaman, as though reading Smithson-Mackay's doubt. A plea that put in question all his struggles to rid California of the perpetual foreigners sucking its marrow bare.

'Damn rat-eater!' cried the Colonel, suddenly afraid. 'Yaah!'

He spurred the horse over the old coolie. If a crushing hoof stumbled on something soft, Smithson-Mackay was soon away through a billow of smoke.

Then he was back in the central square. To his relief the smoke was less dense here. And there were friends! He sure as hell needed a helping hand. Two men with scarves over their faces were manhandling an iron safe onto a handcart while Parker and Temple watched, hands on holstered pistol butts. Another handcart waited nearby, laden with silks, bags, boxes.

Outside Sam Wah's store, a Chinese corpse stretched facedown, a flower of red showing where the bullet had struck his back. The scent of fresh blood made Smithson-Mackay's horse shy yet again. 'Whoa!' he cried, dragging the reins tight.

He trotted over to Parker and Temple; the two bushwhackers examined him coolly. Their old colonel felt a fierce, mastering urge to resume command. He waved at the piles of loot.

'May as well gather your property, men,' he said, liking his laconic tone, 'then let's get away from here!'

Parker spat on the floor. 'That's kindly meant, Colonel, but we purpose to search that las' house yonder before we go.'

A crash from an adjoining street made the stallion shy and whinny. Dammit, thought Smithson-Mackay, it looked like he couldn't even control his own mount!

'I said let's get outta here!' he roared. 'That's an order!'

Parker scowled, lips tightening. Temple merely grinned.

'Guess we don't purpose to take no orders we don't like no more,' said Parker. 'Meanin' no disrespect, Colonel.'

Then Smithson-Mackay understood. They blamed him for failing to profit from the Indians at the French widow's spread. After all, he had assured them his authority would answer any difficulties with the law.

The two men loading the iron safe onto the handcart shouted, 'Another one of 'em! 'Ware! Over there!'

Sure enough, a Chinaman hovered at the entrance to the square, smoke blowing round his legs. When he lowered the blanket covering his face and mouth, Smithson-Mackay gasped. The half-breed Mongol lawman! The damn Chinee law-wrangler that lost him the respect of two subordinates he never expected to doubt this side of the grave. Instantly, Smithson-Mackay knew how to win back that respect. Judge Lynch needn't rely on dangling ropes to secure justice.

'Mr Temple,' drawled the Colonel, 'I'd be mightily obliged if you loaned me your revolver. I intend to shoot me a goddamn Mongol-Nigger with an appetite for white women!'

Temple whooped as he passed up the gun. The heavy weight of the butt and solidity of the loaded weapon felt good. Smithson-Mackay urged his horse towards the Chinaman, who was peering this way and that like a startled hog. Cocking the revolver, he took careful aim. At that moment the frightened horse bucked slightly, so that its rider swore and yanked the reins. When he had regained control, the target was bolting for Sam Wah's store.

Smithson-Mackay aimed once more. Squeezed the trigger. An echoing bang and bright flash erupted inches from the horse's ears and eyes. The terrified creature reared convulsively, heavy legs flailing at the air. Smithson-Mackay felt himself fly backward. Six, seven feet he flew, landing in mud and filth. The world swirled.

With a thud of hooves, the stallion galloped off into smoke and flames.

As Smithson-Mackay spurred at him, pistol aimed, Chi-en Shambles had dashed forward. Shouts went up. A shot. He felt the bullet whistle inches from his head.

Leaping over the corpse in front of Sam Wah's store, he scrambled into swirling, poisonous clouds consuming the building. Acrid smoke blinded him.

'Bai Lu!' he called, between savage, racking coughs. 'Bai Lu!'

If the boy heard he gave no sign. Chi-en staggered as far as the stairs before the futility of his quest drove him back. The top storeys of the building were raging. Floorboards creaked amidst a shower of sparks and smoke.

'Bai Lu!' he shouted one last time.

Defeated, Chi-en turned back towards the front entrance. His lungs ached. Two or three breaths were left before he doubled up, fainted. The house creaked in its distress. At the entrance he stumbled over something. The corpse had been tossed into the fire. With it, piles of burning wood and rags.

The creak above him became a tortured groan of wood. Chi-en jerked back his neck. A smouldering roof beam rushed down at him. He did not notice the entrance darken with moving shadows. Raising soot-stained, scorched hands, he covered his head . . .

In that elongated doorway of time, a heavenly vision found Chi-en Shambles. Once more he was alone on the endless plains of the Earth. Except now, a miracle!

The dark, indestructible Tower of Babel, constructed layer upon layer of human misery and injustice, generation after generation of hapless, corrupted men, lay in ruins.

The plain itself glimmered with spring sunshine. The spoiled earth grew green. Everywhere green. Grass and trees curled heavenwards. Birds skimmed the land, pouring out mellifluous joy for all to gather freely, to seed their souls freely.

Then Chi-en cried out in wonder. Prince Hong! Beckoning from a hilltop crowned with white flowers, a broad smile on his tired face. Prince Hong motioning that Chi-en should join the people pouring out of the broken tower to walk in peace across the earth.

'You see?' called out Chi-en, hurrying to take his old place beside Hong, as when they were earnest boys who would save the world. He feared someone else would get there first, replace him. 'We found the Heavenly Kingdom in the end! We found it, Hong!' Tears started into Chi-en's eyes. 'I'm afraid we will lose what we have found!'

'My dear friend,' chided Hong, 'one never quite loses love. It's time to forget your old grief. You always lived in the past. Now we may rest forever.'

Still a terrible doubt shook Chi-en. 'Am I forgiven?' he asked. 'For betraying you? For leaving you to die alone?'

Hong nodded. 'You were always forgiven. And now we may rest forever.'

In his vision, Chi-en stepped away from his friend. 'No,' he said, 'I cannot join you. There is someone, a woman . . . Can you forgive me for deserting you again?'

But Chi-en need not have feared. Need never have feared.

'That makes me gladdest of all,' said Hong. 'Chi-en Shambles, Little Humble! Glad forever, my dear, faithful friend!'

The flowers around them were waist high, filling the plain with perfume. The sky arched, an infinite gateway one passed through simply by living. By striving to live well until your last breath, so others might do the same . . .

In Sam Wah's burning store, the beam started its descent to release him forever from the dusty earth. He glimpsed two shadows lunging through the flames. Devil-demons grasping for his soul. But no, he was forgiven. His failings forgiven. Prince Hong's firm hands dragged him back to the Heavenly Kingdom.

Epilogue

San Francisco, California
Summer 1943

It was because of the rain, that's what the old man told himself. But he was forgetting it hadn't rained yet. All day he had forgotten and remembered.

Professor Emile Bourchier stood on the steps of Chinatown Library on Powell Street, blinking up at the sky. A summer storm with all heaven's trimmings was on its way. Oily black clouds swirled between skyscrapers. Distant thunder rolled – though it might easily be his ears playing tricks again.

The librarian, a grey stick of a woman, spectacles hanging from a ribbon round her neck, peered at the automobiles and on Powell Street. She smiled uncertainly. 'I'm sure *someone* will come, Professor.' Her coo was of a type reserved for the very old or young. 'It's early, after all.' She leaned forward in conspiratorial delight. 'And why, my goodness, just think who *is* coming!'

'She certainly draws a crowd,' he conceded.

'I loved *all* her movies when I was a girl. Just imagine! Vivienne Bourchier in *my* library!' She returned happily to her date stamp and little cards.

Rows of empty chairs and a stack of slim, cloth-bound volumes waited in the library foyer. Emile wondered why he was fretting. After all, this wasn't his first published book. Professor Emile Bourchier's *History of the Indian Tribes of California* and *Lost Voices: Californian Indian Dialects* were classics of their kind. Not to mention his groundbreaking *Wappo Language and Customs*. For he had kept his promise to the Old Mother; half the labour of his life fulfilled that promise. He had helped her people survive.

Emile hadn't even written this particular book, except for a foreword. He had, however, bankrolled its printing. Enough copies to send to every major library in the world. The remaining hundred or so would clutter his book-filled house. One day soon his daughters would inherit all those words in dozens of languages. Yet he thought of the fresh-printed volumes inside the library as a legacy to the dead rather than the living.

Emile removed an ancient tin pocket watch from his waistcoat pocket.

Where were they? Of course, Vivienne would be late, the very reason he'd told her the speeches were scheduled to start an hour before the actual time. His daughters, at least, should be punctual. He'd bullied them to come along, knowing they'd bring nine rowdy grandchildren and even a couple of great-grandchildren to swell the party. The teenage boys were sure to get bored and misbehave. Sober old Professor Bourchier could forgive that. He seemed to remember another boy, long ago, who created his own slice of mischief.

There it was again! Thunder out across the Bay. Within the space of a few minutes the clouds had thickened, darkened.

Of course, there were some – more than he cared to recollect – who could never walk up Powell Street to join him on the steps of Chinatown Library. Emile's wife for forty years, Sarah, left him a widower in his sixties. He'd dearly love to see her brisk, determined bustle heading his way again. Or even Old Man Trubody and Nancy, Sarah's guardians, whose money smoothed him through college and the early years of marriage, buying an impossibly grand house for a humble Professor of Anthropology. Room enough to raise four daughters and host the suitors who came calling, one by one, to steal them away.

But surely folks would come. A decent man's work must have a little endurance. Never mind that the slender volume's author died twenty-six years before. When Emile considered what Uncle Chi-en did for the good – and bad – people of Chinatown he felt sure *someone* must remember.

After being dragged from the burning store in Perryville by Sam Wah and Sam Yip, Chi-en had returned to Chinatown a hero, his courage 'written on the body' like knights of old. Uncle Chi-en never commented on the burned, mulberry wounds on his hands and arms. He served quietly for forty years as chief legal adviser of the Chinese Consolidated Benevolent Association that grew out of the Six Companies. Though barred from pleading in court, he was able to hire and work closely with sympathetic white law firms. Many an immigration tribunal or unjust accusation in the Halls of Justice had been settled by his calm, logical, persuasive arguments. Hundreds followed his coffin down Stockton Street when he died after a swift, painful cancer in 1917. Emile had joined that parade – along with a dozen city officials and attorneys.

Before Uncle Chi-en died, Emile had called at his spacious apartment overlooking Portsmouth Square. His Chinese housekeeper, a dragon Emile never saw smile in thirty years, shooed him to the salon.

'You wait,' she whispered. 'Vis'tor already!'

Taking a seat, Emile could not help overhearing the conversation in Uncle Chi-en's bedroom next door. The other visitor being Maman.

'How can I believe you?' she sobbed.

'You must, Catherine!'

'If I had not been so greedy you could have found someone else. Had a proper family.'

'What! You know better than anyone I have a family.'

'But a proper *home*, Chi-en. I stole that from you.'

'It was stolen from us by ignorance and folly. Besides, *Nemo dat quod non habet.*'

Maman's snort mingled vexation and amusement. 'No, do not bother to translate. Ah, always so clever! It is annoying to be so clever every time!'

A pause. Bedsprings creaked.

'Was that clever?' came Uncle Chi-en's coaxing voice.

'No.'

'How about this?'

Another creak.

'Well, perhaps.'

Emile had almost melted into the chair with embarrassment. The couple creaking the bed were nearly seventy years old! He would have snuck away but feared making a noise.

Maman was crying again. 'But I did keep you to myself!'

'It was not always easy. For you as well as me.'

'Do you ever wish . . . do you regret?'

His failing, cancerous breath wheezed as he laughed. 'I regret not seeing you every day.' He coughed, gasped. 'That was the world's stupidity, not ours.'

Emile had used the cover of a loud sob from Maman to tiptoe to the stairwell outside Uncle Chi-en's apartment. Half an hour later, Maman emerged, and he pretended to have just arrived.

'Why didn't you tell me you were coming to town, Maman?' he'd said. 'Where are you staying?'

She seemed calmer now, even happy.

'Go to him,' she had murmured, pressing her son's hand. 'He always loves to see you.'

He found the old man propped up in bed. Once tall and broad-shouldered, he had shrunk to a bag of bones and skin. Ugly white mottles had spread across his face. He lay beneath a thick quilt, eyes swollen as though he, like Maman, had been weeping. At the sight of Emile he brightened, grew animated.

'Professor Bourchier! It seems I am to be spoilt in my visitors today. How is Sarah? And your lovely daughters?'

When Emile mentioned meeting Maman on the stairs, the dying old man managed a smile. 'She never really goes away,' he said, tapping his heart.

Then Uncle Chi-en had grown serious. 'Vivienne also came to see me yesterday.'

'Did she, now?' Emile tried to keep the conversation light. 'And no doubt she looked swell as ever. Sarah swears she'd give a fortune to know how Vivienne manages to look so young. We enjoyed her last motion picture a great deal. She's quite the star.'

Still Uncle Chi-en sighed. 'Never mind looking young. She is a woman full grown. But I worry about her. No husband or child. At her age! Can a woman truly be happy without those things? I worry.'

Emile placed his hand on the old man's. The skin felt soft as damp paper.

'Look after your sister,' whispered Uncle Chi-en, 'I charge you with that. She does not have someone like Sarah, someone to keep her steady and safe.'

Finally, Uncle Chi-en spoke of anything but himself: Emile's latest research on the Wappo and the terrible trench warfare in Europe.

'Will we ever learn to stop killing each other? And now so scientifically?' he asked with genuine sorrow. 'Yet I believe we will. Do you know, Emile, I'm sure of it. One day we shall tear down the Tower of Babel and set the peoples of the world free!'

Emile had marvelled that a man in constant pain, about to quit the earth, should care so sincerely about its future tenants. Now, twenty-six years later, they were in another bloody war. Contrary to Uncle Chi-en's hopes, they hadn't learned. Not yet, at least. The Tower of Babel stood secure.

He was jolted back to the present. A group of Chinese men in respectable suits mounted the library steps. Emile glanced hurriedly at his tin watch – Uncle Chi-en's old watch, given to him as a boy and repaired many times. Thirty minutes early! And there were five – no, six.

'You're very welcome, sirs!' he said. 'Come in, gentlemen. You'll find refreshments inside.'

Emile felt better in his heart as he leaned upon the stone parapet. With his family and the librarian and the dignified Chinese gentlemen he could count on twenty at the party. If Vivienne was on time, twenty-one.

Of course, the woman who would *really* have loved to be here was years too late. Like Sarah and the Trubodys, she could only walk up Powell Street in his imagination.

Maman had visited San Francisco several times a year, every year, after Perryville's Chinatown burned. She hired a mix of Chinese and white labour, expanding Royaume Céleste and avoiding the phylloxera plague of the nineties that destroyed her neighbours' vineyards.

'Don't believe in noble root stock,' she told her son. 'Judge each vine by its merits, however ugly it looks.'

Perhaps that was why she built a fine cottage for poor, wheezing Jean-Pierre and allowed him to sip his way to contented oblivion.

Her annual exports of Domaine Bourchier claret through Lu Kan made both of them wealthy, but she never recovered a position of respectability. When she gave birth to Vivienne in the summer of 1879, Catherine Bourchier's status as the scarlet Frenchie Jezebel of Napa had been confirmed for eternity. Everyone assumed Vivienne was the natural child of the French gambler, Baron Foche, who caused such a scandal by getting himself shot when cheating at cards. Maman neither confirmed nor contradicted such rumours. She told Vivienne her father had abandoned them and was dead. In short, pretty much what she'd told Emile about his own father.

Prim, proper ladies enriched their lives by snubbing Catherine Bourchier for decades – all except Nancy Trubody, who compromised her own reputation by strolling brazenly with her scandalous friend down Perryville Main Street.

'Don't mind *her*,' she whispered to Emile when Mrs Smithson-Mackay was offensive. 'She's just ornery because her husband lost half his fortune. It's dollars that make you respectable in *this* State, my dear!'

Fortunately, the Bourchiers, unlike the hollow-eyed poor who were everywhere, had more dollars than they needed or could ever justify.

Maman never seemed to care what her neighbours thought or said. Yet Emile understood why she educated him and Vivienne in fancy boarding schools back East. At least, he only had to fight Napa boys impugning the Bourchier family honour in the school holidays rather than all year round.

Twenty minutes to go. Another group of Chinese arrived; older women propped by daughters. His own were nowhere to be seen. Plenty of time . . .

As he thought back, Emile acknowledged there had been plenty of time to see Uncle Chi-en when he was young. They visited San Francisco so frequently. Christmas and Easter were relished. Uncle Chi-en dropped his legal work to spend time with Emile and, later, Vivienne. Boat trips round San Pablo Bay. Theatres and bookstores. Long walks in Golden Gate Park where they debated everything beneath the sun and beyond.

Uncle Chi-en's intelligence had been broad, informed and tolerant: infectious qualities.

Every summer he took a week's vacation in Royaume Céleste. Then Maman would flutter, tidying house and vineyard. She learned new pieces for her oboe, insisting on a concert specially for their guest. While she played, Vivienne would dance nimble, intense ballets of her own devising to entertain Uncle Chi-en. Yet he always slept in the storeroom beside the kitchen, where Maman set up a comfortable folding bed, carpet, wardrobe, bookshelves and washstand.

Vivienne doted on Uncle Chi-en from the start. Emile had guessed why. Even as a boy he had not felt shocked or jealous.

She brought a crazy joy to Royaume Céleste, creating something neither Maman nor Emile was good at – simple fun. A wild toddler: dancing, singing, crying as though her heart would break then, a moment later, chuckling in a voice far too deep for a girl no bigger than a milk churn. It came as little wonder she drifted down to Hollywood in her early twenties, enraptured by the new motion pictures. Or that she cut herself a career alongside Douglas Fairbanks, Charles Chaplin, Harold Lloyd. Her unusual beauty, described in fan magazines as 'mysterious' and 'exotic', only added to her allure. She even weathered the transition to talkies as an eccentric mom or ditsy aunt.

Uncle Chi-en studied her early, silent movies when they were shown in San Francisco and wrote long, polite essays analysing her depiction of human nature. Treasured letters that made Vivienne hoot and cry.

But after Prohibition ended, it was flighty, silly Vivienne who doggedly revived Royaume Céleste, hiring the best vintners to produce a Domaine Bourchier claret worthy of their mother's memory. She built a swimming pool and modernised the winery and house, adopting it as her country retreat.

★

Emile opened his pocket watch. Fifteen minutes to go.

Though Uncle Chi-en had been a father to him, another always haunted the backstage of his life. A father remembered as a feared and adored giant amidst fairy tale turrets and château walls. It had always been his intention to visit the grave of the ruined Comte Antoine de Rivac de Chauveterre. When, as a young man, he confided this intention to Chi-en, the Chinaman grew sombre.

'Many years ago,' he said, 'a friend advised me: *Do not climb a tree to look for fish*. I wish that I had heeded that counsel.'

'What did he mean?' Emile asked.

'That you'll never catch what isn't there.'

Then Chi-en told a long, sad story about his own search for a father. 'Besides,' he had added, 'it would distress your maman more than you can imagine.'

Perhaps that was why Emile restricted his search to a cautious examination of maps and discreet questions to people who had visited Languedoc. He assembled, over the decades, a crazed jigsaw of rumour and supposition, a puzzle with nearly all its pieces missing. He discovered that an elderly, bibulous Comte de Rivac de Chauveterre – evidently an uncle – did live in Carcassone until the early 1900s, hen-pecked by a bourgeois wife who ruled him through her purse strings. Another name he recognised from his childhood, Baron Cesar Foche, became a prominent politician in Paris, a passionate advocate of Church and family.

Perhaps he would have learned more except that when Emile married Sarah, four daughters arrived in rapid succession, fatherhood distracting him from his own father. And the years flowed by. Too late now to fish for information. Too late for anything except reeling in his line then bidding farewell to the river forever.

Another group of Chinese showed up. His daughters and grand-children had already entered Chinatown Library, stuffed with noodles, rice, fried pork and vegetables at Hang Far Low Restaurant. They were waiting inside, more interested in digestion than Uncle Chi-en's book. To them, the old, half-burned Chinaman was a far from respectable rumour. Thus, goes history.

Emile stared up at thick black clouds. The thunder was closer now. And he thought again about Chi-en Shambles and Maman. Of course, they had been discreet. Unthinkable consequences would have followed otherwise. But Emile recollected watching from his bedroom window as they crossed the vineyard at midnight during one of Uncle Chi-en's annual visits, heading for the wooded slopes above Royaume Céleste.

When Maman died in 1926, he found boxes of photographs from the eighties and nineties, before the earthquake and after. A few showed them together in Golden Gate Park or fancy Chinese restaurants or theatres. There had been faded opera programmes and ticket stubs for private boxes. In those photographs, grainy and shadowy, Maman looked happier than he remembered her. Less guarded. One had been framed at Sarah's insistence: Uncle Chi-en and Maman, together with a wrinkled fortune teller in Portsmouth Square.

'Why that one?' he asked his wife.

She had frowned. As ever, her seriousness etched with playful irony. 'I like your maman's smile. It's hopeful and grave all at the same time. And Uncle Chi-en's so much more interested in looking at her than the camera.'

He had known exactly what she meant. And loved his wife at that moment for so many separate, intricate, contradictory reasons there seemed no explaining it.

After Maman's death, he also found a small trunk undisturbed for decades. It contained musty clothes and a thick notebook filled with tiny handwritten Chinese characters. Paying for a translation and researching the Taiping rebellion took the best part of fifteen years. His legacy to the dead. *Taiping Rebel: A Modest Memoir* by Chi-en Shambles.

Emile flipped open the tin watch. Ten minutes to go. The sky was black now over San Francisco. Lightning flashed on the horizon. Thunderclaps rolled over skyscrapers built literally on sand. At that moment a gay, excited hooting filled Powell Street. For all his habitual gravity, Professor Bourchier chuckled.

A ludicrously long, lipstick-red, open-topped roadster screeched to a halt outside Chinatown Library, parking illegally beside a fire hydrant. Waving frantically, Vivienne Bourchier swung out slender legs. As ever, she looked twenty years younger than her age.

'Darling!' She hurried up the steps. 'Am I late?'

Emile grinned wolfishly. 'Bang on when I expected you.'

Then Vivienne was hugging him. Perfume like misplaced love filled his nostrils. She waved a manicured hand at the soot-stained exterior of the municipal library.

'How clever of you to pick here! Uncle Chi-en loved this library.'

'I think the librarian's pleased as well,' he said, dryly. 'Though for different reasons.'

'But Emile . . .' She took his arm. 'Who would have thought Uncle Chi-en suffered so badly when he was young. That he was so brave and self-sacrificing. I cried when I read about his poor mother and those horrible swamps and the city burning.'

'The Heavenly Capital,' corrected Emile, 'better known as Nanking or sometimes Nanjing. Though I suppose either rendering is just an approximation . . .'

'Yes! But do you know, having read Uncle Chi-en's book, I believe there is someone else we should thank for all the good he went on to do.'

'Who?'

'Why, Prince Hong!'

'Are you sure?'

'Yes.'

Her certainty and unexpected gravity made him pause. Then she was smiling again.

'But I never guessed Uncle Chi-en was so *exciting*! I always thought he was fundamentally bookish, and, well, kind-hearted and brave but *bookish*. I never dreamed he fought in battles and galloped into the night with bags of treasure. And what about those naughty *conversations* with ladies of no virtue whatsoever?'

'I think,' said Emile, 'Uncle Chi-en was always a mystery. Perhaps even to himself. So many contradictory things went into his making. But I believe he was happy in the end.'

Vivienne nodded. The playfulness left her face. An abrupt shift to eye-catching earnestness that had made her irresistible on the silent screen. She leaned close to her brother.

'Do you know what,' she whispered, 'I think Maman loved him more than anyone. Don't you?'

'I guess she did.'

'That's why I brought over a case of the new Domaine Bourchier claret. So Royaume Céleste and Maman are *right here*, in a funny kind of way, at his special party. A libation in honour of Maman and Uncle Chi-en! They did share rather a lot of the stuff together over the years.' She paused archly. 'Among other things.'

With a throaty laugh, Vivienne swept into the library for a grand entrance destined to end in autographs and flashbulbs popping. Emile was left to wonder if his cotton headed sister knew more about her parentage than he imagined. A suspicion he found oddly gratifying.

He placed the tin watch against an ear to confirm it still ticked. Two minutes to go. He need wait on the steps no longer. Everyone who mattered was here.

In a minute he would take a seat behind a table stacked with slender books and listen to the librarian's nervous, rapid speech. 'Distinguished professor from Stanford University . . . A real honour, folks . . . A bit of history I'd never heard about myself, but very special so close to China-town . . . And, my goodness, Miss Vivienne Bourchier! Here in our humble library! Miss Vivienne Bourchier, folks!' And he would deliver a lecture explaining the forgotten Taiping rebels to those with no clue such outlandish, misguided people with hearts and ideals and bodies to break ever existed on this earth. Meanwhile his grandsons would sneak off for a little rebellion of their own in the reference section. Possibly involving Domaine Bourchier claret. He might even read out a page or two of Uncle Chi-en's memoir, unsure how his audience would react.

As Emile entered the library, fat droplets spilled from a bloated sky. Rain bounced off sidewalks, trickled down drains, whispered, sang, gathered, wept, sighed, chortled in gutters — refreshing the dust of the earth.

Acknowledgements

Many thanks to Ed Handyside for his incisive editing and for making *Dust of the Earth* a reality – and for some very interesting debates over a lager or two! Thanks also to everyone at Myrmidon. A number of people have been kind enough to read and offer feedback and encouragement over the years. Could I especially thank Richard Gray and Sara Bowland, Steve Lewis, Mary Jones, Jim and Dori Murgatroyd, Bob Horne, Ian Parks and Dr Craig Smith. A special thank you to Joe Mills at Black Sheep for his wonderful cover art. Finally, as always, my biggest thank you is reserved for my wife, Ruth, for helping this beloved vineyard bear fruit at long last.

M

SenLinYu

ALCHEMISED
NO QUEDA NADIE A QUIEN SALVAR

montena

Papel certificado por el Forest Stewardship Council®

MIXTO
Papel | Apoyando la
silvicultura responsable
FSC
www.fsc.org
FSC® C117695

Penguin
Random House
Grupo Editorial

Título original: *Alchemised*

Primera edición: septiembre de 2025

© 2025, SenLinYu
Publicado originalmente por Del Rey y Penguin Random House USA
2025, Penguin Random House Grupo Editorial, S. A. U.
Travessera de Gràcia, 47-49. 08021 Barcelona
2025, Ankara Cabeza y Patricia Mora, por la traducción

Printed in Spain – Impreso en España

ISBN: 978-84-10050-07-5
Depósito legal: B-12.139-2025

Compuesto en Grafime S. L.
Rotoprint By Domingo, S. L.
Castellar del Vallès (Barcelona)

GT 50075

Para Jame, por encontrarme

Nota de le autore

Esta obra de ficción trata con profundidad temas como la guerra y la supervivencia. El contenido puede herir la sensibilidad del lector.

PARTE I

PRÓLOGO

A VECES, HELENA SE PREGUNTABA SI aún tendría ojos. La oscuridad que la rodeaba nunca acababa. Al principio pensó que, si aguardaba lo suficiente, aparecería un atisbo de luz o alguien vendría. Pero, por mucho que esperó, nunca vio nada.

Solo una oscuridad infinita.

Tenía un cuerpo que sentía como una jaula a su alrededor, pero, por más que se esforzara, no podía moverlo. Flotaba inerte e inconsciente, salvo cuando convulsionaba con violencia al recibir las descargas: unas electrocuciones que le recorrían el cuerpo desde la base del cuello y le provocaban espasmos en todos los músculos. Luego, desaparecían tan repentinamente como habían surgido. Era lo único que le indicaba el paso del tiempo.

Las recibía para que sus músculos no se deterioraran mientras permanecía inmóvil. Helena se acordaba de ese detalle. Recordaba que la habían dejado ahí prisionera, preservada, pero que algún día alguien vendría a por ella.

Al principio contaba el tiempo que pasaba entre descarga y descarga para calcular la frecuencia, segundo a segundo. Diez mil ochocientos, cada tres horas exactas. Siempre transcurría el mismo intervalo. Luego empezó a contar las descargas, pero, a medida que aumentaba el número, dejó de hacerlo. Le daba miedo saber cuántas horas habían pasado.

Se obligó a pensar en otras cosas que no fuesen la espera, el infinito o la oscuridad. No le quedaba más remedio que aguardar, así que se impuso una rutina para mantener la mente fuerte. Imaginó que paseaba, imaginó acantilados y el cielo, visitó de nuevo los lugares en los que había estado y rememoró todos los libros que había leído.

Tenía que aguantar, mantenerse alerta. Así estaría preparada. Tenía que seguir preparada.

No iba a permitir que su mente se desvaneciera.

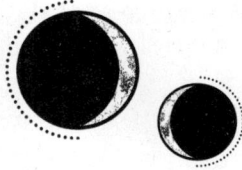

CAPÍTULO 1

CUANDO LLEGÓ LA LUZ, ESTUVO a punto de partirle el cerebro.

Se escucharon gritos.

—¡Joder! ¿Cómo es posible que esté despierta? —Una voz se abrió paso entre el tormento de los sentidos.

La luz casi la apuñalaba. Era como tener una daga clavada entre los ojos que se enterraba en su cráneo. Por Dios, sus ojos...

Se retorció mientras veía la luminosidad borrosa, descentrada. Sintió la quemazón de un líquido que le bajaba por la garganta y un rugido en los oídos.

Unos dedos hábiles se le clavaron en los brazos, contra el hueso, y la arrastraron. El aire le entró de golpe en los pulmones y empezó a toser cuando el fluido volvió a subir.

—Maldita sea con el líquido de suspensión. No hay forma de agarrarla. ¡Haz que se calle! Está a punto de ahogarse.

Cuando la soltaron, notó un golpe en la cabeza, también una piedra áspera bajo las manos. Arañó a ciegas la oscuridad para intentar incorporarse. Tenía los ojos cerrados, pero la luz seguía apuñalándole el cerebro como si fuera un cuchillo. Entonces le arrancaron un objeto duro de la nuca y sintió que algo caliente y húmedo le recorría la piel.

—¿Cómo es posible que esté despierta, joder? Está claro que alguien cometió un error con la dosis. No dejes que se vaya.

La volvieron a sujetar por los brazos y la levantaron del suelo.

Ella se zafó y se obligó a abrir los ojos, y, aunque solo veía un blanco cegador, se lanzó hacia esa dirección.

15

—¡Maldita zorra, me has cortado!

Sintió un dolor intenso en la parte de atrás de la cabeza.

———————

Todavía había luz cuando recobró la consciencia.

Fue poco a poco, como si estuviera bajo el agua nadando hacia una superficie que se extendía más allá de su alcance, hasta que la consciencia fue colándose de nuevo en su cerebro. Tenía los ojos cerrados porque la luz era muy intensa, pero aun así le dolían.

Estaba tumbada sobre algo duro. Una mesa fría, un metal inerte que podía palpar con los dedos.

Distinguía vagamente algunas voces, que sonaban amortiguadas pero próximas.

—¿Y bien? —Era la voz de una mujer—. ¿Alguno más?

—No —respondió un hombre, el que había escuchado antes—. Hemos sacado a los demás, pero esta se encontraba donde no debía.

—¿Y estaba consciente cuando abristeis el tanque?

—Claro que sí, y empezó a gritar en cuanto levantamos la tapa y la sacamos. A mí casi me da un infarto y Willems se asustó tanto que a punto estuvo de ahogarla. Cuando la tuvimos fuera, se puso como loca. Me hizo un montón de arañazos antes de que la dejáramos inconsciente. Tenía la intravenosa puesta, pero estaba sin sedación. Imagino que alguien la habrá desactivado.

—Eso no explica la ausencia de información sobre ella —dijo la mujer—. Qué extraño.

—Seguramente se hizo con prisas. No debe de llevar ahí mucho tiempo. Incluso los que se preservaron bien están casi todos muertos. La mayoría de los tanques no son más que una sopa de huesos —añadió el hombre, soltando una risilla nerviosa.

—Sabremos más cuando la llevemos a la Central —aseguró la mujer, a quien parecía que no le interesaba demasiado lo ocurrido—. Has hecho bien en avisarme porque es anómalo. Infórmame de todos los que despierten. Los cadáveres que estén intactos serán reanimados para trasladarlos a las minas y los que estén vivos irán al Reducto.

—Por supuesto. También querría saber si usted hablará bien de mí. Me serviría de mucho viniendo de su parte. —El tono del hombre era esperanzador y su risa, forzada—. Ya no soy tan joven, como bien sabe.

—El Sumo Nigromante tiene muchas peticiones que atender, pero tu trabajo no caerá en el olvido. Prepara un camión para el transporte.

Se oyeron unos pasos que se alejaban seguidos de un suspiro irritado.

—No tienes por qué fingir que estás inconsciente. Sé que has despertado, así que abre los ojos —le ordenó la mujer a Helena—. He alterado tus sentidos para que la luz no te moleste demasiado.

Helena parpadeó con cautela.

El mundo que la rodeaba estaba bañado por un crepúsculo verdoso y todo parecía una sombra. Logró atisbar la silueta de una persona moviéndose a la derecha.

Ella la siguió con la mirada lentamente.

—Bien, parece que entiendes las órdenes y captas los movimientos.

Helena intentó hablar, pero solo logró emitir un jadeo áspero. Oyó el chasquido de un bolígrafo y el roce de unas páginas al pasar.

—A ver… ¿Eres la prisionera 1273 o la prisionera 19819? Hay dos números de identificación y ninguno de ellos está registrado en esta prisión. ¿Tienes nombre, por casualidad?

Helena no dijo nada. Ahora que la sola idea de enfrentarse a la luz no le daba pavor, pensaba con más claridad. Seguía siendo una prisionera.

La mujer soltó un bufido de impaciencia.

—¿Me entiendes?

Helena no respondió.

—Bueno, supongo que era de esperar, aunque pronto lo sabremos. Tú, tráela.

La sombra se disipó frente a Helena y aparecieron otras personas. Unas manos frías le tocaron las muñecas, mientras el hedor a conservantes químicos y a carne podrida inundaba su nariz. Eran necrómatas. Helena trató de distinguir sus rostros, pero la mirada se le perdía y era incapaz de enfocar la vista.

La mesa empezó a vibrar cuando la empujaron sobre el suelo pedregoso, con un traqueteo que le retumbaba hasta en el cerebro y los dientes. Después hubo tanta luz que parecía que le hubieran clavado agujas en las retinas, y soltó un grito ahogado, cerrando de nuevo los ojos con fuerza.

Sintió una sacudida hacia delante que la mareó, y todo volvió a sumirse en la oscuridad. Un motor empezó a emitir un zumbido al encenderse por debajo de ella.

Tenía que escapar. Trató de moverse, pero sintió un chasquido metálico.

—Quédate quieta. —De pronto, volvió a oír a aquella mujer. Le pareció que estaba demasiado cerca.

Helena se resistió, respirando entre jadeos descontrolados, y retorció las manos y los pies contra las ataduras. Tenía que huir, tenía que…

—No me compliques el día —dijo la mujer con un tono glacial.

Entonces unos dedos agarraron la nuca de Helena, y sintió una descarga de energía extendiéndose por su cerebro.

Volvió la oscuridad.

———

UNA SACUDIDA AGÓNICA Y UN TERROR repentino lograron que Helena recobrara la consciencia esta vez.

Se incorporó con los ojos muy abiertos, justo a tiempo para ver cómo retiraban una jeringuilla de su brazo. Escuchó el tintineo de unas cadenas al hacerlo y volvió a tumbarse con el corazón en un puño. Cada vez que le latía, sentía una punzada de dolor, como si la hubieran apuñalado.

—Ya está —oyó el repiqueteo que produjo la jeringuilla al caer en una bandeja metálica que había a su derecha—. Con eso estarás lúcida y podrás hablar.

Era la mujer de antes.

Helena ya no estaba en la camilla ni en un camión. Debajo de su cuerpo había un colchón duro y el aire olía intensamente a antiséptico, como si todo hubiese sido recién desinfectado. Arriba, se veía un techo gris apagado.

A pesar del dolor que sentía, notaba que la energía le fluía con fuerza por las venas hasta convertirse en un calor abrasador que se expandía por sus manos cuando las flexionaba. Se percató de que iba recuperando la consciencia y de que todo se estaba volviendo más brillante, más claro. Se retorció sobre sí misma, y algo metálico se le clavó en la muñeca.

—De eso nada. Te romperías los huesos antes de partir uno de esos grilletes. Responde a mis preguntas y tal vez te permita levantarte antes de que se te pase el efecto de la medicación. Sin ella te dolería demasiado.

Como no podía moverse, Helena sintió que su mente comenzaba a activarse. Le habían puesto una inyección, seguramente con algún tipo de estimulante potente. Atrapada en su interior, la energía se concentró en su cerebro, y los pensamientos dispersos y aterrorizados empezaron a ordenarse con una claridad cristalina.

—Helena Marino. Deberías... —escuchó cómo pasaba las páginas— estar muerta, según el expediente 1273. Se te condenó a muerte, debido a «heridas graves» que no se especifican. Pero el expediente 19819 dice que fuiste condenada al tanque de suspensión. —Pasó más páginas—. Sin embargo, no hay registros de que llegaras allí o de que pasaras por algún procedimiento. —La mujer se mordió el labio inferior—. No apareces en ninguna parte en nuestros archivos desde augustus del año pasado. Es decir, desde hace catorce meses. Y ahora te encontramos en el almacén de suspensión al que nunca llegaste. ¿Cómo es eso posible?

Helena parpadeó lentamente mientras asimilaba la información. ¿Catorce meses?

—Evidentemente, nadie sobrevive tanto tiempo en ese estado. Es casi imposible aguantar seis meses en perfectas condiciones, y a ti ni siquiera te almacenaron correctamente. Así que ¿de dónde vienes? ¿Y quién te llevó allí?

Helena apartó la mirada. Se negaba a responder.

La mujer murmuró mientras se acercaba.

—No te vas a meter en ningún lío si hablas. Dime la verdad y pondremos fin a todo esto. ¿Dónde estuviste antes de que te llevaran a suspensión?

Formuló la pregunta lentamente.

Helena no respondió, aunque le ardían los músculos de su rostro de las ganas que tenía de moverlos. Empezó a temblarle el cuerpo cuando los latidos del corazón impulsaron el medicamento por sus venas.

Ya no quedaba nadie a quien proteger, pero se negaba a cooperar con sus carceleros. No quería ayudarlos en nada, ni siquiera con sus registros.

Además, en realidad ella no había estado en ningún otro sitio.

—¿Dónde. Estuviste. Antes. De. Que. Te. Llevaran. A. Suspensión? —La mujer casi estaba gritando.

Helena sintió que se le cerraba la garganta. No quería ni pensar en la respuesta, porque la destrozaban los recuerdos que le venían al hacerlo.

Antes de acabar en el almacén, la habían capturado junto con todos los demás y los habían metido en jaulas a la entrada de la Torre de Alquimia, adonde llevaron a todos los prisioneros para que fueran testigos de las «celebraciones» del fin de la guerra.

Todavía recordaba el olor a humo y a sangre en el calor del verano, todavía escuchaba los roncos vítores de sus enemigos al ver cómo morían los líderes de la Resistencia, cuyos gritos se iban desvaneciendo poco a poco. Aunque los veían morir, sabían que aquello aún no se había acabado, ni siquiera después de muertos.

Porque entonces emergía de entre la multitud algún nigromante, deseoso de alardear de sus poderes, y, en cuestión de segundos, ese cadáver volvía a levantarse. Esa persona, en la que Helena había confiado o a la que había servido, regresaba a la vida gracias a la reanimación, convertido en un necrómata, un cuerpo autómata completamente vacío. Los abrían en canal, los despellejaban, les extirpaban los órganos, los dejaban sin ojos y sin boca, y los usaban para matar al siguiente «traidor» de una forma todavía más salvaje.

Las ejecuciones no pararon hasta que el aire estuvo completamente rojo del vapor de la sangre.

Incluso usaron el cadáver del general Titus Bayard para asesinar a su mujer. Poco a poco, le hicieron comerse las partes del cuerpo que le iba cortando.

Cada muerte se llevó un trozo del alma de Helena hasta que en su pecho solo quedó un vacío doloroso. Y, cuando ya no hubo nadie a quien mereciera la pena matar públicamente, la metieron en un tanque de suspensión.

El resto de los prisioneros estaban inconscientes cuando los paralizaron, cuando les clavaron agujas en las venas, cuando les metieron tubos por la nariz, cuando les pusieron mascarillas en la cara... En cambio, Helena no.

La habían mantenido despierta, plenamente consciente de todo lo que le estaba pasando, mientras la encerraban en su propio cuerpo y la abandonaban en la oscuridad, a la espera de que alguien viniera a por ella.

Pero no vino nadie.

Al sentir el chasquido de unos dedos delante de ella, Helena despertó de sus recuerdos. La mujer que tenía delante la estaba fulminando con la mirada.

—No arriesgaré mi reputación por un error de registro. Si no me respondes, dejaré de hacer esto por las buenas.

Helena torció el gesto.

—¿Ves? Sí que me entiendes.

A Helena se le encogió el estómago, pero mantuvo la boca cerrada.

La mujer se acercó un poco más a ella. Helena aguzó la vista para verla mejor: un rostro cuadrado con unos labios fruncidos que denotaban impaciencia, una bata médica.

—Tal vez es el momento de darte un ejemplo de cómo será si no colaboras. —La mano de la mujer presionó el cuello de Helena, y esta soltó un chillido ahogado cuando notó que una energía candente pero heladora la traspasaba hasta la columna.

No era una descarga eléctrica como las que había experimentado en el tanque, sino que salía de la mano de la mujer y se clavaba en Helena como una aguja. El chorro de energía la hizo vibrar como un diapasón hasta que ambas resonaron en la misma frecuencia.

La mujer cerró entonces los dedos. Helena sintió un dolor que le atravesaba todos los nervios del cuerpo. Se le escapó un grito ahogado e incoherente, y notó que su cuerpo convulsionaba con las manos aferradas a los grilletes.

—Quédate quieta.

Con un chasquido, Helena se paralizó. No sentía nada desde el pecho hacia abajo, como si le hubieran dañado la columna, y el pánico le hacía arder la sangre.

Luego, con un simple movimiento de la mano de la mujer, el entumecimiento desapareció. Unos dedos ásperos por el excesivo uso de jabón recorrieron el brazo de Helena.

—¿Lo entiendes ahora?

La resonancia de la mujer seguía atravesándola como una corriente, como si fuera una advertencia imposible de ignorar. Helena consiguió asentir entre temblores. Debería haberse dado cuenta: la mujer era una vivemante. Es decir, lo contrario a un nigromante: los vivemantes controlaban a los vivos en vez de a los muertos.

—Sabía que lo pillarías al vuelo. Probemos de nuevo.

A Helena se le cerró aún más la garganta y también le ardían los ojos. Sentía punzadas en todos los nervios de su cuerpo y la sangre golpeándole en los oídos. ¿Qué tenía de malo responder?, se preguntó a sí misma.

—¿De dónde viniste?

—Esss-te-e-ssst... —Helena intentó que su lengua cooperara.

—Déjate de chorradas extranjeras. Habla en paladio —le instó la mujer.

No existía ningún idioma llamado paladio; en realidad, la mujer estaba hablando en el dialecto del Norte. Helena quiso explicárselo, pero supo que no serviría de nada. Tragó saliva y lo intentó de nuevo, pero su lengua arrastraba todas las palabras al pronunciarlas.

La mujer suspiró.

—¿Por qué los integrantes de la Resistencia siempre me hacéis perder el tiempo? Tal vez si te damos una descarga en el cerebro, te acuerdes de hablar como es debido.

Esta vez agarró la cabeza de Helena al hacerlo, y ella sintió que una onda de resonancia la atravesaba de lado a lado como si chocaran dos platillos.

Todo se tornó rojo y la garganta de Helena emitió un grito atroz.

La mujer retiró las manos.

—¿Pero qué sucede?

Helena no estaba segura de si la mujer estaba moviéndose en círculos o si era la habitación la que daba vueltas.

—¿Qué es esto? ¿Quién te lo ha hecho?

Helena contempló el techo mareada hasta que el color rojo desapareció de su vista. Sentía cómo le temblaban las manos, que se retorcían convulsivamente contra los grilletes. No sabía de qué estaba hablando aquella mujer.

—Te han hecho algo en la mente —explicó esta, sorprendida pero extrañamente fascinada al mismo tiempo—. Algún tipo de transmutación, nunca había visto nada igual. Voy a tener que informar de esto. Necesito un experto. Tienes… —La mujer se quedó callada—. ¡No existe un nombre para esto! Tendré que inventarlo yo…

Parecía que estaba hablando consigo misma.

—Barreras de transmutación en un cerebro. ¿Cómo es posible? Nunca he visto… Siguen… siguen un patrón.

Volvió a tocar a Helena, y ella torció el gesto, pero en esta ocasión la resonancia no le pareció una tortura; solo sintió un escalofrío que lo envolvió todo en un rojo chillón.

—Esta obra es compleja, precisa, muy profesional. Un vivemante ha reconectado manualmente la consciencia humana.

Helena permaneció quieta, sin entender nada.

La mujer se acercó tanto que Helena pudo distinguir sus ojos azules, con unas arrugas marcadas en el entrecejo y alrededor de la boca. Miró a Helena con gran fascinación.

—Si Bennet siguiera vivo, se maravillaría al ver lo preciso que es este trabajo. —La resonancia recorrió la mente de Helena de una forma tan tangible que parecía como si unos dedos estuvieran deslizándose por su cerebro. Los ojos claros de la mujer se desenfocaron mientras trabajaba—. Si hubiera cometido el más mínimo error, habrías quedado en estado vegetal, pero quien hizo esto te mantuvo casi intacta. Qué perfección.

—¿Quééé? —Helena por fin consiguió pronunciar una palabra completa.

—Me pregunto... ¿Cómo será? —La mujer se alejó y regresó un minuto después con una lámina de cristal.

Helena entrecerró los ojos y reconoció el objeto: una pantalla de resonancia. Se solía usar en presentaciones académicas y en operaciones médicas de alquimia. El gas estaba formado por partículas reactivas que reflejaban la forma y el patrón de un canal de resonancia.

La mujer sostuvo el cristal por encima de su cabeza y posó la otra mano en su frente para hacerle una resonancia cerebral. La visión de Helena se tornó roja de nuevo, pero aguzó la vista y observó cómo la tenue nube entre los paneles se transformaba en la forma difusa de un cerebro humano y, acto seguido, en una incomprensible telaraña de líneas que lo cruzaban por todas partes.

—Dudo que entiendas esto, pero imagínate que tu mente es una... una ciudad. Tus pensamientos recorren distintas calles para llegar a su destino. Esas líneas que ves son las calles que se han desviado. Hay barreras creadas por la transmutación, así que, en lugar de seguir el curso natural del cerebro, alguien ha generado rutas alternativas. Existen zonas que están fuera de alcance. No imagino cómo... Estas habilidades serían...

La mujer dejaba las frases a medias, y puso la pantalla a un lado mientras miraba detenidamente a Helena.

—¿Quién te hizo esto? —preguntó en voz alta, con lentitud y vocalizando exageradamente.

Helena solo negó con la cabeza.

El gesto de la mujer se endureció peligrosamente, pero entonces pareció reconsiderarlo.

—Supongo que es imposible que lo sepas dado el estado de tu cerebro. Seguramente tengas suerte si recuerdas cómo te llamas. Fuiste alumna de alquimia, supongo. —Tamborileó distraída el grillete de metal que Helena tenía alrededor de la muñeca.

Helena asintió con cautela.

—Y eres extranjera, evidentemente. —Miró a Helena de arriba abajo.

Esta tragó saliva.

—Etras.

—Ah, entonces estás muy lejos de casa. ¿Recuerdas tu repertorio de resonancia?

—Div... erso.

—Hum. —La mujer frunció el entrecejo y analizó a Helena con más atención—. Espera. Creo que me hablaron de ti. Eres esa chica que recibió la beca de los Holdfast, ¿verdad? Eso debió de ser hace más de una década, así que ahora tienes... ¿Cuántos? ¿Veintitantos años?

A Helena le ardían los ojos, pero asintió brevemente.

La mujer arqueó una ceja.

—¿Recuerdas qué le pasó a tu mecenas, al principado Apollo?

—Fue... asesinado.

—Hum. Y la guerra, seguro que te acuerdas de eso. ¿Ayudaste al joven Holdfast a quemar la ciudad? A vuestro querido Luc, como os gustaba llamarlo.

A Helena se le contrajo la garganta.

—Yo no... luché.

La mujer soltó un breve sonido de sorpresa y entrecerró los ojos.

—¿Y en la batalla final? Supongo que recuerdas eso, ¿no?

Helena abrió la boca varias veces, pero la lengua se le enredaba y le impedía hablar.

—Nosotros... La... la Resistencia perdió. Hubo... ejecuciones. M-Morrough vino... al final. Tenía... tenía a Luc. L-lo mató... allí. Luego... luego me... me llevaron al almacén.

—¿Quiénes?

Helena tragó con dificultad.

—L-liches.

La mujer rio por lo bajo.

—Hace mucho tiempo que no escucho a nadie atreverse a usar este insulto. Todos los inmarcesibles, independientemente de su forma, son los seguidores más allegados del Sumo Nigromante. Se les concede la inmortalidad por su excelencia. En este nuevo mundo, la muerte solo se lleva a los indignos. Da igual que los insultes, porque tus amigos no son más que cenizas olvidadas.

Palpó entonces la frente de Helena.

—Aunque tú pareces casi intacta. Así que ¿por qué se emplearon tan a fondo contigo? ¿Y quién podría haber...? —La mujer cogió la pantalla de resonancia, la observó de nuevo y luego desapareció entre las cortinas.

Helena sintió alivio al quedarse sola.

¿Habían alterado su memoria o su mente?

Si no hubiera visto la pantalla de resonancia, habría pensado que la estaba engañando. Sabía cómo era un cerebro. Quien lo hizo debió de emplear una vivemancia muy especializada y probablemente poseía extensos conocimientos para transmutar la mente de esa forma.

No era algo que alguien olvidaría con facilidad.

Aun así, Helena no sentía que hubiera olvidado nada, salvo la mención de una herida grave.

En realidad, no recordaba haber sufrido ningún daño, solo conmoción, dolor y terror.

Tragó saliva y parpadeó con fuerza para intentar no pensar en ello.

Miró a su alrededor, tratando de descubrir qué había en la habitación. El medicamento que le habían administrado era increíblemente efectivo. Justo donde la aguja se había clavado en el corazón, se le estaba formando un moratón y le dolía con cada latido.

Miró hacia abajo. La cama tenía barras a ambos lados, y los grilletes que sujetaban sus muñecas estaban encadenados a ellas. Bajo los grilletes, la piel se mostraba en carne viva, amoratada, y alrededor de cada muñeca había sendas bandas metálicas de color verdoso.

Esas sí que le resultaron familiares: las había llevado durante la celebración.

En la oscuridad, bañada en sangre, bajo la tenue luz de las antorchas y rodeada de tantos cadáveres en la jaula, no las había visto bien, pero las recordaba perfectamente.

Dentro del tanque de suspensión, siempre fue consciente de que las tenía. La existencia de esas bandas metálicas había permanecido al borde de su consciencia, una presencia ineludible que reprimía su resonancia y le impedía usar la transmutación para escapar.

Hasta en el tanque era capaz de sentir el lumitio que había en ellas.

La naturaleza del lumitio unía los cuatro elementos de aire, agua, tierra y fuego, y, mediante esa unión, se creaba la resonancia.

La Fe Sagrada consideraba que la resonancia era un regalo de Sol, la deidad de la Quintaesencia elemental, para elevar a la humanidad. La resonancia era una habilidad escasa en muchas partes del mundo, pero no en la nación elegida por Sol, Paladia. Según los censos anteriores a la guerra, se estimaba que casi un quinto de la población poseía un nivel de resonancia cuantificable. Y, además, se estimaba que ese número aumentaría en la siguiente generación.

Normalmente, la resonancia se canalizaba a través de la alquimia de metales y compuestos inorgánicos, y eso permitía la transmutación o alquimización. Sin embargo, en un alma defectuosa que se rebelaba contra las leyes naturales de Sol, la resonancia terminaba corrompiéndose, dando lugar a la vivemancia (la técnica que esa mujer había empleado contra Helena) y la nigromancia, utilizada para crear necrómatas.

Como canalizador de la resonancia, el lumitio podía aumentar o incluso crear resonancia en objetos inertes mediante la exposición, que los hacía maleables a la alquimia. Sin embargo, el lumitio puro era demasiado sagrado para los mortales; la sobreexposición provocaba enfermedades debilitantes y, en los individuos con resonancia, una exposición directa podía causarles un dolor lacerante y metálico en los nervios.

El lumitio de las esposas no parecía haber enfermado a Helena, lo que indicaba que algo lo había alterado. La energía punzante de su interior estaba sintonizada con su resonancia, y, en lugar de destruirla, le anulaba los sentidos. Helena sentía su propia resonancia, pero, cuando intentaba controlarla, las esposas le generaban una especie de energía estática en los nervios. Por mucho que lo intentara, no era capaz de deshacerse de ella.

Lo único que sabía era que, mientras llevara puestas esas esposas, no era una alquimista.

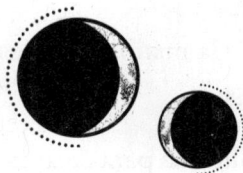

CAPÍTULO 2

Había un necrómata cerca. Sola e incapaz de enfocar la vista, Helena percibía el olor a carne podrida y a conservantes químicos. Los inmarcesibles usaban a los muertos como marionetas para realizar las tareas desagradables o de poca importancia. Mientras esperaba encadenada, se preguntó para qué estarían empleando a aquel necrómata. Echó un vistazo a su alrededor, buscando sombras más allá de las cortinas.

—¿Marino?

Alguien susurró su nombre en voz tan baja que podría haber sido tan solo la brisa.

Helena se giró y alcanzó a distinguir un rostro asomándose por la cortina que los separaba. Entrecerró los ojos y consiguió enfocarlos lo suficiente para ver una cara y un cabello de color claro.

—Marino, ¿eres tú?

Helena asintió, intentando aún descifrar quién era.

—Soy Grace. Era camillera en el hospital. —Se deslizó entre las cortinas mientras hablaba, con un marcado acento del Norte que enfatizaba las consonantes.

—Perdona, estoy… desorientada —respondió Helena.

—No esperaba verte aquí.

Grace se acercó. Al salir de entre las sombras, Helena notó que era joven, a pesar de sus rasgos hundidos. Su expresión mostraba una mezcla de miedo y curiosidad.

Helena abrió los ojos de par en par.

El rostro de Grace estaba marcado por cicatrices: unos cortes largos que le atravesaban las mejillas, la barbilla y la nariz. No eran heridas accidentales, sino intencionadas.

Helena intentó levantar la mano, pero los grilletes en sus muñecas se lo impedían.

—¿Qué te pasó? —preguntó.

Grace la observó desconcertada y, al seguir la mirada de Helena, llevó la mano a su rostro para tocarse la cara.

—Ah, ¿los cortes? Todas los tenemos.

—¿Qué? ¿Por qué los liches…?

Grace sacudió la cabeza con vehemencia.

—Baja la voz. —Grace miró a su alrededor rápidamente y olfateó el aire. Después, volvió a mirar a Helena con ojos furiosos—. A veces usan a los necrómatas para espiarnos. Hay uno aquí, ¿no lo hueles? No puedes llamar «liches» a los inmarcesibles. —La palabra era apenas un susurro—. Si nos escuchan…, habrá… consecuencias.

Helena se apresuró a asentir. Temía que Grace saliera corriendo si no tenía cuidado.

Grace se acercó a ella un poco más.

—No fueron los inmarcesibles quienes nos hicieron esto. —Se señaló la cara—. Fuimos nosotras mismas. Los inmarcesibles pueden hacer lo que quieran con nosotras, con cualquiera que pertenezca a la Resistencia. Ahora está de moda tener necrómatas en vez de contratar empleados. Pero hay veces… que solo quieren algo con lo que jugar. En una fiesta o… después de salir por la noche. —Hizo un gesto—. Nadie interviene para evitarlo. Incluso los que no son inmarcesibles o pertenecen al gremio les siguen la corriente, porque todos esperan que eso aumente sus posibilidades de ganar también la inmortalidad.

Grace se encogió de hombros de forma poco natural.

—Pero, si tienes mala pinta, no te usan mucho tiempo. —Suspiró entrecortadamente y miró a Helena con dureza—. ¿Dónde has estado?

Helena negó con la cabeza mientras intentaba asimilar todo lo que Grace le había contado.

—Me llevaron a un almacén… después de…

Grace entrecerró los ojos.

Helena la miró, vacilante.

—¿La Llama Eterna sigue…?

—No. —Grace sacudió la cabeza con vehemencia y su expresión se tornó en rabia—. Están todos muertos. Todos y cada uno de ellos.

Después de la muerte de Luc, nos enviaron a los demás a la fábrica del Reducto, bajo la presa. La mayoría de nosotros no puede marcharse. Necesitas varios meses de buen comportamiento para que te den permiso y hay que llevar esto siempre. —Levantó la mano para enseñar una banda de cobre, más brillante y mejor ajustada que la de Helena—. Tenemos que fichar por la mañana y por la noche porque hay toque de queda. Si alguien desaparece más de veinticuatro horas… —Tragó saliva—. Si no aparece, envían al Sumo Inquisidor para que le dé caza, y siempre está muerto cuando lo traen de vuelta. A la custodio le gusta colgarlos, los deja así durante días y, cuando empiezan a pudrirse, los reanima y los pone a «trabajar» para nosotros antes de mandarlos a la mina. Dice que así no se nos olvidan las reglas.

—¿Quién…? —Helena se obligó a preguntar, aunque temía saberlo.

Grace titubeó. Sus ojos se suavizaron ligeramente.

—Lila Bayard fue la primera a la que trajo de vuelta.

Grace seguía hablando, pero Helena no la escuchaba. Lo único que oía una y otra vez era «Lila Bayard fue la primera».

Lila no…

Poco a poco volvió a escuchar la voz de Grace.

—La custodio la obligó a ponerse la armadura paladina y la dejó en la puerta. Ya llevaba un tiempo fallecida. Debió de llegar bastante lejos. Le faltaba más de la mitad de la cara y ya no tenía la prótesis de la pierna, así que le soldaron una barra de hierro para mantenerla en pie. No… no puede moverse. Simplemente permanece allí. Pasamos a su lado todos los días. —Grace pareció entonces percatarse del semblante de Helena y bajó la mirada—. Ahora solo quedan sus huesos. La custodio cree que es… divertido.

Helena sacudió la cabeza, le costaba aceptarlo, pero, por supuesto, Lila estaba muerta. Para capturar y asesinar a Luc, sus paladines debían morir. Ese fue el juramento que hicieron: morir por el principado.

Helena tragó saliva con dificultad.

—Pero seguro que en algún lugar… la Resistencia…

—¡No existe la Resistencia! —exclamó Grace en un susurro—. ¿De verdad crees que íbamos a seguir luchando cuando toda la Llama Eterna murió? No sirve de nada. El Sumo Inquisidor los mata a todos. Por cualquier movimiento, incluso los susurros están penalizados con la muerte. Tiene un… un monstruo que usa para cazar. Es absurdo huir, resistir u organizarse, a menos que quieras ser el próximo cadáver.

Helena se sumió en el silencio. Grace la observaba con recelo, nerviosa. Parecía que iba a salir corriendo en cualquier momento.

—¿Quién es el Sumo Inquisidor? —preguntó Helena, rezando por ser capaz de formular esa pregunta. No recordaba el título.

Grace negó con la cabeza.

—No lo sé. Sigue llevando el yelmo que usaban los inmarcesibles durante la guerra. El Sumo Nigromante es demasiado importante para aparecer en público, así que manda al Sumo Inquisidor en su lugar. Es una especie de vivemante, pero no como los demás. Mata a la gente sin tan siquiera tocarla.

—La resonancia no funciona así —repuso Helena, corrigiéndola de forma automática—. Sin sellos, solo se puede crear un canal estable cuando se establece un contacto y luego...

—Sé cómo funciona la resonancia —la cortó Grace sin miramientos—. Pero he visto cómo lo hace. La semana pasada... —A Grace le tembló la voz; su nuez subió y bajó varias veces—. Había un grupo de contrabando... Hemos tenido escasez de grano. La mayor parte del que recibimos en el Reducto está podrido. Algunos estaban trayendo comida extra de fuera. No era mucho, pero la custodio oyó rumores de que los prisioneros se estaban organizando. Eran diez personas: ejecución pública. El Sumo Inquisidor los mató a todos a la vez. Lo hizo de forma «limpia» para que duraran más tiempo trabajando en las minas de lumitio.

Grace pareció estremecerse mientras hablaba, como si el mero recuerdo la paralizara.

—Los que quedamos estamos sobreviviendo. Eso es lo único que importa. —Las últimas palabras las susurró como si hablara más para sí misma que para Helena.

—¿Por qué estás aquí, Grace? —preguntó Helena mirando a su alrededor, aunque no veía mucho—. Esto no es... No estamos en el Reducto, ¿verdad?

Grace negó con la cabeza.

—No. Esto es ahora la Central. Es donde los inmarcesibles hacen todos sus experimentos. Yo... —Se atragantó con la palabra—. Tengo tres hermanos. Son más pequeños que yo. Ninguno de ellos era lo bastante mayor para alistarse, así que no formaron parte de la Resistencia. Mi hermano Gid tendrá edad de trabajar dentro de poco y podrá salir del Reducto. Recibirá un sueldo de verdad cuando llegue el momento. Tenemos... tenemos que resistir hasta entonces.

—Grace…

—Están ofreciendo mucho dinero por los ojos. Solo uno ya nos permite subsistir durante meses.

Helena la miró desconcertada.

—¿Para qué quieren los ojos?

Grace negó con la cabeza.

—No lo sé. A mí solo me interesa el dinero.

Si no hubiera estado encadenada a la cama, Helena se habría acercado a ella.

—Grace, si lo haces…, nunca podrás recuperarlos…

A Grace se le escapó una carcajada repentina, casi enajenada.

—Sé que los ojos no crecen. Por eso pagan tanto.

—Sí, pero…

—¿Para qué quiero quedármelos? —Grace hablaba muy nerviosa—. ¿Para tener dos ojos con los que ver morir de hambre a mis hermanos? ¡No hay comida! —Ya no estaba susurrando. En su rostro, las cicatrices se enrojecieron y crisparon—. No sabes… No tienes ni idea de cómo vivimos ahora. ¿Dónde has estado? ¿Por qué no salvaste a Luc? Deberías haberlo hecho, pero no lo hiciste. ¡Murió! Todos lo vimos. Y los Bayard están muertos también. Y todos los de la Llama Eterna están muertos…, menos tú. ¿Y crees que me preocupan mis ojos?

Antes de que Helena pudiera contestar o que Grace pudiese decir algo más, oyeron unos pasos que se acercaban.

El terror se abrió paso por el semblante de Grace, que huyó rápidamente.

Alguien apartó las cortinas de Helena hacia un lado, y aparecieron varias personas. Cuando una de ellas se acercó a la cama, Helena reconoció a la interrogadora. Las arrugas de su rostro estaban marcadas y en tensión.

Helena no distinguía a quienes estaban detrás de ella, pero tenían la piel de un color gris poco natural que le erizó el vello al instante. El espacio delimitado por las cortinas se impregnó del olor a conservantes.

—Es esta —dijo la mujer—. Está bien atada, como os aseguré. —Miró con nerviosismo a los cuerpos, que parecían moverse como si fueran uno solo.

Necrómatas, todos eran necrómatas.

La mujer miró a Helena.

—El Sumo Nigromante te ha hecho llamar. Quiere presenciar tu análisis en persona.

Helena sintió una presión en el pecho y forcejeó contra sus ataduras.

—No.

No podía hacerlo, no era capaz de verlo de nuevo. La única vez que había visto al Sumo Nigromante, Morrough, fue cuando este asesinó a Luc.

Luc, que había sido todo su mundo.

Helena se unió a la Resistencia y había jurado lealtad a la Orden de la Llama Eterna no por fe, sino por Luc Holdfast. Porque tal vez no creía en los dioses, pero sí creía en él, que era bueno y amable y se preocupaba por los demás.

Prometió que haría cualquier cosa por él.

Pero Luc murió ante sus ojos.

Se le estaba cerrando la garganta.

—No —repitió mientras la cama rebotaba al ponerse en movimiento. Sus captores no le prestaron atención.

Fue en los ascensores cuando Helena supo dónde estaba, qué era la Central. Habían quitado todos los murales y el arte de las paredes, también habían desaparecido los cuadros y las decoraciones, dejando el interior en bruto y vacío, pero reconoció la detallada ornamentación de la puerta metálica del ascensor.

Era algo que había visto a diario desde que tenía diez años.

Estaba en la Torre de Alquimia, en el corazón de la Academia de Alquimia que habían fundado los Holdfast.

Eso era la Central.

—¿Qué habéis hecho? —le temblaba la voz del horror y la pena—. ¿Qué habéis hecho?

—Tranquilízate —le dijo la mujer con los dientes apretados mientras le dirigía una mirada fulminante. No dejaba de mirar por el rabillo del ojo a los necrómatas que las rodeaban.

Helena no podía tranquilizarse. Era como haber vuelto a casa para darse cuenta de que habían destrozado todo lo que la hacía acogedora, que la habían destripado de su belleza, desollado todo cuanto le era familiar.

Helena había cruzado medio mundo para estudiar en esa Torre. Luc siempre estuvo muy orgulloso de la Academia que construyó su familia. Había sido el corazón de Paladia. Helena lo había visto con sus propios ojos: toda la historia y su significado. Ahora lo habían arrasado y destruido por completo.

Las repercusiones de la muerte de Luc eran más de lo que podía asimilar, pero, por algún motivo, aún tuvo la capacidad de llorar esta pérdida. Se le escapó un sollozo agudo.

Unos dedos agarraron la base del cráneo de Helena hasta que las uñas se clavaron en su piel.

Estaba hundiéndose hasta el fondo.

Un túnel muy largo, una oscuridad retorcida.

Unas manos frías sin vida y un olor a muerte.

Cuando se le despejó la mente, se dio cuenta de que se encontraba atada encima de una mesa. Había una luz brillante en el techo, un foco que apuntaba directamente a Helena y que hacía desaparecer la habitación que la rodeaba.

A su lado, un hombrecillo de nariz estrecha no dejaba de tocarle la cara con unos dedos sudorosos y húmedos. La palpó entre los ojos, en las sienes, y metió sus dedos en su cabello para comprobar su cráneo.

—Esto es… toda una maravilla de la transmutación humana —decía el hombre en un tono agudo y ligero. Tenía acento, pero no era un dialecto del Norte, más bien sonaba a algo occidental—. Una vivemancia de esta categoría es… milagrosa. Ha hecho bien en llamarme.

Se produjo un silencio largo y agobiante.

Tosió.

—La… la cosa es… Esto es… imposible. No… no se puede hacer.

—Es evidente que sí. La prueba la tienes aquí delante —replicó la mujer con dureza desde el lado contrario. Helena apenas lograba verla en la profunda oscuridad.

—Sí, es cierto, doctora Stroud. Por supuesto, tiene razón. Pero… aplicar la vivemancia en un cerebro siempre ha sido un procedimiento extremadamente delicado. Una transmutación de esas características y con esta complejidad va más allá de toda evidencia científica conocida. La memoria es algo misterioso, muy maleable cuando se manipula. No es un lugar, es… el viaje de la mente. Un camino. Cuanto más importante y experimentada sea la persona, más fuerte será el camino. Si se ha hecho poco en la vida —sus dedos se movieron—, entonces se desvanece.

—Ve al grano —dijo la doctora Stroud.

—Sí, sí. Hay partes del cerebro que se pueden modificar. En los laboratorios hemos hecho vivisecciones a muchos cerebros humanos para luego reconstruirlos de distintas maneras con cierto éxito y… también con fracasos. Sin embargo, esta transmutación va más allá. M-m-memoria. Lo que han hecho aquí... —Helena sintió algo húmedo en el rostro y se dio cuenta de que el hombre estaba transpirando encima de ella—. Esto es una alteración de lo inalterable. Alguien... ha desmantelado los caminos de su mente para crear rutas alternativas. ¿Cómo es posible que lo haya hecho sin saber todos sus pensamientos y recuerdos? No. No. Es científicamente imposible.

—Creía que la mente era tu especialidad.

La voz que había hablado emergía de la oscuridad, era grave y áspera.

El hombre gimoteó. Parecía a punto de echarse a llorar.

—El... cerebro, Su Eminencia. —Le hizo una reverencia a las sombras—. Pero esta obra escapa a mis conocimientos. Bennet y yo, ¿recordáis nuestros trabajos para la causa? Confío en que... Los recuerdos no pueden regenerarse sin más; son la mente y el espíritu los que deben forjarlos. Ninguna fuerza externa puede alterar el espíritu..., las... las fiebres...

—¿Hay alguna forma de descubrir lo que oculta?

El hombre abrió y cerró la boca, igual que un pez, contemplando la oscuridad, como esperando que fuese a tragárselo.

—Los Holdfast están muertos —afirmó la voz áspera—, la Llama Eterna ha sido erradicada de este mundo. ¿Por qué esconderían algo en su mente?

Solo hubo silencio como respuesta.

—¿Quién la metió en ese almacén?

Stroud dio un paso al frente.

—No hay nada que lo confirme, pero, según los informes, Mandl era la supervisora en aquella época. Fue poco antes de que ascendiera y la trasladaran al Reducto.

—Traedla.

Stroud asintió y desapareció. Al hacerlo, las sombras se movieron.

Helena solo veía por el rabillo del ojo, pero, aun así, se percató de cuando Morrough emergió de la oscuridad.

El Sumo Nigromante no se parecía en nada a como ella lo recordaba. Cuando asesinó a Luc, era humano. Ahora había mutado. Sus brazos sobresalían de las articulaciones en un ángulo imposible, y tenía casi el tamaño de dos hombres.

Al principio, pensó que llevaba una máscara. El Sumo Nigromante había acudido enmascarado a la celebración. Una medialuna enorme y dorada le había tapado la mitad de la cara como en un eclipse de sol.

Sin embargo, cuando se acercó más a ella, se dio cuenta de que no era una máscara lo que estaba viendo. La cara de Morrough parecía como una calavera de lo hundidos que estaban sus rasgos. La piel era tan translúcida y pálida que dejaba entrever hasta el hueso.

Donde antes tenía los ojos, ahora había dos cuencas vacías y negras, como si se los hubieran quemado con carbón ardiente.

Aun así, veía a Helena.

Caminó hacia ella con una mano estirada, pero algo sucedía: la piel se estiraba y plegaba de forma extraña, como si tuviera demasiados huesos dentro. Helena sintió el dolor de su resonancia atravesándole el cerebro antes de que la rozara con los dedos.

Su visión se tornó roja.

Oyó que gritaba hasta reventarse los oídos, cada vez más fuerte, mientras los recuerdos estallaban en su mente. Una cascada de imágenes se abrió paso por su consciencia.

Allá donde mirara había gente muriendo. Tenía las manos llenas de sangre y los cadáveres se amontonaban por todas partes.

Estaba arrodillada en el suelo, uniendo torsos, caras y extremidades, intentando recomponerlos, cosiéndolos para lograr completarlos. Una y otra y otra vez. Cuerpos en carne viva, llenos de quemaduras, tan consumidos por el fuego que no distinguía sus rostros.

Siempre había otro cuerpo, y otro más.

La resonancia cavó aún más profundo, y Helena gritó con más fuerza todavía.

Vio a Luc, tan vívido como si estuviera frente a ella. Su bello rostro, sus ojos tan azules como el cielo de verano, reflejando la luz dorada del sol.

Luego desapareció. Había sangre por todas partes. Lo único que veía era una luz roja, fragmentada y quebradiza, que se mecía en el techo. Y los gritos.

Sus propios gritos. Tenía las cuerdas vocales deshilachadas; un dolor desgarrador le atravesaba los pulmones y la garganta. Cada inhalación le provocaba una punzada lacerante en el pecho, como si su corazón estuviera a punto de romperse.

El hombrecillo mascullaba «No os recomiendo...» una y otra vez, cubriéndose la cabeza con los brazos como si quisiera protegerse.

Helena oyó que alguien llamaba a la puerta y Stroud volvió a aparecer, aunque apenas se fijó en Helena.

—Mandl viene de camino. Y… —vaciló al hablar—. He traído a Shiseo. Pensé que podría tener alguna información sobre la prisionera. Trabajó para la Llama Eterna. Necesita un nuevo par de anuladores y creí que podría encargarse él mismo antes de marcharse.

Helena oyó que algo se agitaba en la oscuridad y giró el cuello todo lo que pudo mientras entrecerraba los ojos para ver al traidor.

Un hombre de rostro redondeado y cabello oscuro apareció portando un pequeño maletín. Se detuvo a hacer una breve reverencia ante el Sumo Nigromante.

Morrough hizo un gesto en dirección a Helena.

—¿Qué tipo de vivemancia utilizaba la Llama Eterna?

Shiseo se acercó un poco más, y Helena se percató de que provenía del Imperio Oriental, del Lejano Oriente. Solo le dedicó un instante a la mirada acusadora de Helena antes de apartar la vista.

—Lo siento. —Volvió a hacer una breve reverencia—. Solo acudían a mí de vez en cuando por mis conocimientos metalúrgicos.

Helena dejó escapar un suspiro de alivio.

—Seguro que sabes algo… Trabajaste en sus laboratorios —insistió Stroud con impaciencia—. ¿La reconoces, al menos?

Shiseo miró a Helena de soslayo.

—Creo que era sanadora —dijo en voz baja mientras volvía a revisar su maletín.

Helena reprimió un gesto.

Stroud miró de nuevo a Helena con los ojos entrecerrados.

—¿En serio? ¿Sanadora, has dicho? —preguntó como si escupiera veneno. Se aclaró la garganta y observó a su alrededor—. Por supuesto, sabía que había vivemantes que apoyaban a la Llama Eterna. Como si martirizarse les fuera a conceder la aceptación, a pesar de que la Fe consideraba sus talentos una abominación. —Su mirada era feroz—. No me percaté de que esta era uno de ellos.

Nadie dijo nada y Stroud enrojeció.

—Me habría dado cuenta si hubiera tenido más tiempo para revisar los registros de la Resistencia. ¿Pero por qué transmutarían la mente de una sanadora?

Shiseo se inclinó ante Stroud.

—No sabría decirle.

El ambiente empezó a caldearse. Morrough suspiró como una ráfaga de viento.

—No sabe nada. Ponle la anulación y lárgate de aquí.

Shiseo hizo otra reverencia y levantó tanto como pudo la mano de Helena para inspeccionarle la muñeca y las esposas que la rodeaban. Tenía la piel suave para ser metalúrgico.

—Estas son… son un modelo muy antiguo. No suprimen del todo la resonancia —comentó. Deslizó los grilletes de Helena por el antebrazo todo lo que pudo, y esta sintió como si la estática de la supresión se desplazara hasta su cerebro.

Shiseo presionó con manos hábiles el brazo de Helena, hasta encontrar la hendidura justo debajo de la muñeca y entre los dos huesos del antebrazo.

Su latido palpitaba entre los dedos de Shiseo. Este lo sintió un instante, apretó un poco y luego se apartó para girarse hacia Stroud.

—Aquí.

Los dedos duros y secos de Stroud rodearon la muñeca de Helena. Ella sintió un breve cosquilleo de la resonancia de Stroud y, acto seguido, perdió la sensibilidad desde la mano hasta el codo y su cuerpo se quedó inerte y paralizado. Sin previo aviso ni explicación, Stroud sacó algo del maletín. Al relucir bajo la luz, Helena vislumbró el mango redondeado y la punta larga y afilada de una lezna.

Con la destreza que da la práctica, Stroud introdujo la punta en la muñeca de Helena. Esta no sintió nada, pero se le cerró la garganta y se le encogió el estómago cuando contempló a Stroud trazar lentos círculos con la lezna hasta hundirla entre los huesos. La punta salió por el otro lado.

Cuando Stroud retiró la herramienta, había una gota de sangre en la punta y un agujero atravesaba la muñeca de Helena. Era una herida limpia. La piel y el músculo desgarrados, así como las venas partidas, volvieron a cerrarse de inmediato.

Stroud dejó la lezna a un lado y manipuló la mano de Helena, doblándola hacia delante y hacia atrás para evaluar el rango de movimiento. Aunque volvió a sentirla, la parálisis persistía.

—Los nervios y las venas están intactos —dijo Stroud, y la soltó.

Helena solo pudo observar mientras Shiseo intervenía e introducía un tubito con muescas por el agujero que le atravesaba la muñeca, hasta que el extremo salió por el otro lado. Cuando el tubo estuvo en su sitio, la leve sensación de resonancia que Helena sentía en la mano izquierda desapareció por completo.

Fue como si le arrebataran uno de los sentidos.

Notaba el tubo dentro de su cuerpo, irradiando una sensación adormecida, como de inercia.

Shiseo sacó entonces una cinta de metal, suave y reluciente por un lado y con estrías por el otro. Deslizó la parte estriada por la ranura de uno de los extremos del tubo y luego envolvió la cinta alrededor de la muñeca de Helena para introducirla por el extremo contrario. Así, el tubo quedó sujeto. Después continuó envolviéndole la muñeca con la cinta de metal.

Inspeccionó la tensión y el ajuste, alineó todas las capas y, con un simple chasquido, estas se transformaron en un sólido anillo de metal que se ajustaba perfectamente a su muñeca.

No tenía cierre ni forma de abrirse sin resonancia.

Luego, Shiseo introdujo un alambre con una forma extraña en una abertura diminuta del antiguo grillete. El mecanismo interior cedió y el grillete se abrió. Shiseo lo recogió con cuidado, como si fuera una valiosa antigüedad, y lo guardó en su maletín. Después, se situó a la derecha de Helena.

Esta buscó desesperadamente algo de la resonancia que le quedaba. Intentó concentrarse para recordar la sensación de quién y qué era, sabiendo que desaparecería en cuestión de minutos.

Shiseo estaba quitándole el segundo grillete cuando se abrió la puerta y entró una vigilante.

—Custodio Mandl.

Una mujer con uniforme recorrió la habitación a zancadas; su paso rápido y decidido se detuvo al ver a Helena.

Tenía una boca enorme que se abrió de par en par por la sorpresa.

—¿Qué le hiciste a esta prisionera, Mandl? —preguntó Morrough. Había desaparecido entre las sombras, pero su voz emergió de nuevo. Ahora sonaba más amenazante.

Mandl se postró de inmediato, desapareciendo de la vista de Helena.

—Su Eminencia… —Su tono suplicante provenía del suelo.

—Te salvé de los Holdfast y de la Fe. Te salvé de todos los nigromantes y vivemantes como tú, que vivían como ratas, temiendo que la Llama Eterna os castigara por vuestros «talentos antinaturales». Te di el poder para ascender sobre aquellos que habían pretendido subyugarte. ¿Y ahora me entero de que me has traicionado?

—¡No! ¡No fue una traición! Soy leal. Leal a nuestra causa ¡y leal a vos! Solo fue un estúpido deseo de venganza, lo confieso. Quería que sufriera. Pero yo nunca os traicionaría.

—Explícate.

Mandl se incorporó, todavía de rodillas y con la cabeza agachada, pero con la voz temblorosa de la emoción.

—¡Es una traidora a los vivemantes! ¡Me atormentó! Se creía mejor que yo por formar parte de la Academia de los Holdfast; se pensaba que su vivemancia estaba bendecida por la Llama Eterna. ¡Merecía un castigo!

Helena miró a la mujer, aturdida y desconcertada.

—¿Manipulaste a una prisionera y sus informes por... envidia? —Stroud parecía atónita—. ¿Por qué no diste parte de sus habilidades?

Mandl se volvió a encoger.

—Me daba miedo que recibiera un trato de favor si se sabía la verdad. Que la encontraseis útil y no fuese castigada como se merecía.

Stroud se inclinó sobre ella.

—¿Y qué castigo pensabas que se merecía?

Mandl tragó saliva, nerviosa.

—L-la dejé consciente en el tanque de suspensión. Mi intención era volver a por ella. Quería que estuviera atrapada, que lo supiera y temiera lo que podrían hacerle, pero entonces me trasladaron al Reducto y ascendí. Tenía miedo de que ese ocasional error de juicio fuera visto como una decepción, así que no lo conté. ¡Pero jamás traicionaría nuestra gran causa!

—Ha pasado catorce meses en ese almacén desde que te transfirieron. ¿Por qué no hay registros? —Stroud sonaba muy escéptica.

—Pensaba rellenar sus informes cuando hubiera... terminado con ella. Al irme, supuse que habría muerto y que nadie se enteraría. ¡Perdonadme! No hice nada más, lo juro. —Mandl se tiró de nuevo al suelo.

—Ahora veo que he sido demasiado generoso —dijo Morrough. Su rostro espeluznante y las cuencas vacías de sus ojos emergieron de entre las sombras. Ladeó la cabeza como si mirara a Mandl—. No te mereces mi confianza.

—¡Por favor! Su Eminencia, se lo suplico... Deme...

Mandl dejó de hablar cuando una fuerza invisible la hizo ponerse en pie. La parte delantera del uniforme gris se desgarró al estallar su pecho. Las costillas se le abrieron, acompañadas de un chorro de sangre que brotaba sin cesar.

A Helena se le erizó la piel y sintió el miedo enroscándose en sus entrañas cuando el olor cálido y húmedo de la sangre fresca y los órganos descubiertos inundó la habitación. En el aire vibraba algo extraño, y ella lo notaba cada vez que introducía aire en sus pulmones.

Pero Mandl no había muerto, pese a estar abierta en canal.

Levantó las manos e intentó cerrarse las costillas con una de ellas y protegerse de Morrough con la otra. Sus pulmones expuestos palpitaban con desesperación.

—¡Deme otra oportunidad, por favor! ¡No os fallaré! Lo juro. No os arrepentiréis.

—No, no volverás a fallarme —replicó Morrough. Su voz áspera casi sonó amable cuando metió la mano en el pecho abierto de Mandl y sacó de entre sus pulmones una pieza de metal resplandeciente que había encajada en algún sitio junto a su corazón. Estaba envuelta en finos tentáculos de vísceras que se aferraron tanto al metal como a los dedos de Morrough cuando este la arrancó.

Al quitarla, el cuerpo de Mandl cayó al suelo, silencioso, muerto.

Morrough suspiró suavemente y pareció encogerse un instante antes de enderezarse con el metal en las manos. A pesar de la sangre, la pieza brillaba con un intenso resplandor propio del lumitio.

Hizo un ademán con la otra mano. Un necrómata surgió de entre las sombras como si fuera un animal acechando. Era una mujer joven en fase temprana de necrosis que todavía llevaba los harapos del uniforme del hospital de la Llama Eterna. Tenía un semblante inexpresivo y un tajo en el uniforme dejaba a la vista un pecho lleno de venas negras entrelazadas.

Cuando el cadáver llegó hasta Morrough, se estiró, y este le introdujo la pieza de metal. Helena oyó el leve crujido de un hueso fracturado y vio que se le abría un agujero morado, cubierto de sangre seca, en el centro del pecho.

La mujer cadavérica se estremeció y, acto seguido, su semblante se transformó. Dejó de mirar al vacío.

Trastabilló y soltó un gemido agudo al contemplar sus dedos negros y su cuerpo en descomposición.

—¡No! Por favor, no… No fue mi…

—No vuelvas a fallarme, Mandl —dijo Morrough—, y, con el tiempo, tal vez te permita vivir en otro cuerpo. Incluso tal vez en tu cuerpo original.

Señaló el cuerpo de Mandl, que yacía inmóvil en el suelo. El ambiente vibró de nuevo cuando curvó los dedos y las costillas se cerraron. La parte delantera del uniforme quedó abierta, dejando el pecho a la vista, totalmente cubierto de sangre. La piel volvió a coserse, pero el rostro de Mandl permanecía inexpresivo. La mujer cadavérica se desplomó en el suelo gimoteando y suplicando, aferrándose a la herida supurante que tenía en el centro del pecho como si quisiera arrancarse el metal incrustado mientras Morrough se giró hacia Helena.

Stroud le dio una patada a Mandl.

—Da gracias al Sumo Nigromante por su compasión al permitirte vivir en el cuerpo de una vivemante. Tal vez puedas ganarte el perdón en el futuro y volver al Reducto, custodio.

La mujer cadavérica emitió un último gimoteo gutural antes de incorporarse tambaleante.

—Gracias, Su Eminencia —musitó con voz ronca, y salió trastabillando de la habitación.

Stroud se colocó junto a Morrough. No parecía sorprendida por lo que habían descubierto.

—¿Es posible que alguien sobreviva catorce meses en un tanque de suspensión? —preguntó Stroud.

Morrough no respondió, pero el hombre que estaba también en la estancia, nervioso y sudoroso, dio su opinión desde donde había estado escondiéndose, junto a la pared.

—E-en realidad, esa idea puede tener algo de potencial —dijo dando un paso al frente, aunque inmediatamente se encogió al ver que los ojos vacíos de Morrough se centraban en él.

Se ajustó el cuello de la camisa varias veces.

—Nuestro buen amigo del Lejano Oriente —señaló a Shiseo, que estaba absorto limpiando la lezna— ha mencionado que la supresión que llevaba es un modelo antiguo que no bloquea la resonancia por completo. Tal vez eso explique tanto la fortaleza de su mente como que haya sobrevivido.

Stroud entrecerró los ojos.

—¿Cómo?

—La transmutación que presenta no se la pudo hacer otra persona. Esos recuerdos están demasiado enredados en su mente. Sin embargo, si fuera alguien capaz de llevar a cabo algo tan complejo, una sanadora, tal como ha dicho nuestra amiga que era, tal vez…

—¿Quieres decir que se lo hizo ella misma? —Stroud señaló a Helena con una incredulidad mordaz.

El hombre se atragantó con su propia saliva.

—Bueno…, me parece la explicación más plausible, en mi opinión. —Le brillaba la cara del sudor.

Stroud se mordió el labio.

—¿Y que sobreviviera?

—No… no se permitió morir. P-puede que unos niveles reducidos de resonancia interna, al ser una sanadora experta, le bastaran para mantenerse con vida, mientras que el resto de los cuerpos se descomponen en esas mismas circunstancias.

—¡Eso es absurdo! —estalló Stroud.

—Es irrelevante. ¿Podemos recuperar los recuerdos? —preguntó Morrough—. La Llama Eterna no se tomaría tantas molestias si la información no fuera de vital importancia.

—Su Eminencia. —La voz de Stroud era una súplica—. La Orden de la Llama Eterna no existe, solo quedan cenizas.

—No te he preguntado a ti —dijo Morrough, y miró al hombre, que ahora lucía un verde enfermizo.

—No… creo…

—Fuera. —El ambiente vibró.

El hombre palideció, hizo varias reverencias y agradeció a Morrough su compasión y paciencia mientras caminaba hacia atrás hasta salir de allí con un alivio evidente en el rostro.

—¿Qué estás escondiendo? —Morrough se cernió sobre ella.

El corazón le empezó a latir más rápido. No tenía respuesta a esa pregunta.

Stroud también se inclinó sobre ella con los ojos entrecerrados, como si estuviera pensando.

—Su Eminencia, si le extirpamos la parte delantera del cerebro, quizá podamos acceder a algunos de esos recuerdos antes de que las fiebres lo deterioren —comentó mientras pasaba el dedo por la frente de Helena—. O tal vez altere los senderos y consigamos revertir la situación. Sería un honor para mí mantener sus constantes vitales mientras vos hacéis la vivisección.

El terror atravesó a Helena al ver que Morrough asentía. Stroud se colocó a un lado y ajustó la luz desde arriba, como si estuvieran a punto de comenzar.

—Perdonad —interrumpió una voz suave, y Helena sintió un enorme alivio hasta que reconoció al traidor, Shiseo, que estaba ahí plantado con el maletín en las manos—. Me acabo de acordar de algo. Se trata del general Bayard, que sufrió una lesión cerebral durante la guerra.

—Sí —respondió Stroud, que parecía irritada por la interrupción.

—El cerebro sanó, pero —se detuvo como si le costara encontrar las palabras— olvidó quién era, su mente, su verdadero ser.

—Sí, todos sabemos lo que le pasó a Bayard. No hablaba, quedó incapacitado. Su mujer tuvo que cuidarlo como a un niño —replicó Stroud de mal humor.

—Por supuesto, mis disculpas. Seguramente no sea nada. —Shiseo se inclinó, parecía a punto de marcharse.

—Espera —dijo Stroud en tono conciliador—. Ya que has empezado, dinos adónde querías llegar.

Shiseo se detuvo.

—No conozco todos los detalles, pero creo que encontraron una cura a finales de la guerra. Fue una operación mental bastante complicada.

—¿La llevó a cabo un sanador o un cirujano? —Stroud se inclinó hacia delante, interesada.

Shiseo ladeó la cabeza como si tratara de recordar.

—Una sanadora.

Stroud frunció los labios, pensativa.

—Supongo que fue Elain Boyle.

Shiseo ladeó la cabeza, no parecía reconocer ese nombre.

—Era la sanadora personal de Luc Holdfast. La Llama Eterna no era muy hábil para guardar registros, pero el nombre de Elain Boyle aparece con frecuencia en el último año de la guerra. Al parecer, fue excepcionalmente destacada. —Stroud tamborileó los dedos sobre sus labios y volvió a morderse el labio inferior.

—¿Dónde está Boyle ahora? —preguntó Morrough.

—Murió cuando tomamos la Academia. Creo que mandaron su cuerpo a las minas. Podemos comprobar si queda algún resto. —Stroud se giró hacia Shiseo—. ¿Qué le hizo la Llama Eterna a Bayard para que creas que es relevante?

Shiseo repitió la reverencia.

—Solo lo sé porque pensaron que en el Imperio Oriental tendríamos alguna técnica parecida. Según me contaron, la sanadora tenía la habilidad especial de alterar no solo el cerebro, sino también la mente. Pretendían entrar en la mente de Bayard para curarlo desde dentro.

Los ánimos en la sala cambiaron de repente; se volvieron más estimulantes.

—Eso sería animancia, no sanación —dijo Stroud lentamente, incrédula.

—No lo sé. Antes se usaban otras... palabras —replicó Shiseo—. Por lo que me dijeron, la mente se resistía a la presencia de otra persona, pero esta sanadora creía que, mediante tratamientos poco invasivos, podía lograrse. Es como aprender a tolerar poco a poco un veneno.

—Mitridatismo —dijo Morrough pensativo, y se estiró todo lo alto que era—. Mitridatismo del alma...

Se acercó a Shiseo, como si pretendiera arrancarle las respuestas a la fuerza.

—¿La Llama Eterna encontró la forma de que personas vivas sobrevivieran a una transferencia del alma? ¿Y nunca se te ocurrió contarlo?

Helena pensó que estaba a punto de ver cómo se abría en canal otra caja torácica.

Shiseo mantuvo la calma y se inclinó de nuevo.

—Os pido disculpas. Me hicieron muchas preguntas y es difícil recordarlo todo.

Morrough pareció aceptar la excusa y se dio la vuelta. Luego miró a Helena como si quisiera hacerle una vivisección para buscar las respuestas.

—Si la Llama Eterna contaba con una animante que desarrolló un método de transferencia temporal..., ¿no explicaría eso esta pérdida de memoria? Si alguien pudiera entrar en la mente de otra persona de esta manera, podría alterar pensamientos y recuerdos, tal y como ocurre en este caso. Lo explicaría todo —planteó Stroud señalando a Helena—. Y... debo decir que me parece más plausible que esa teoría descabellada de la autotransmutación.

—Si la Llama Eterna descubrió un método viable de transferencia, eso tiene más relevancia que una simple pérdida de memoria —replicó Morrough. Helena sentía su resonancia en la médula ósea, como si estuviera escarbando en su carne para despellejarla capa a capa.

Morrough miró a Stroud.

—Toma nota de todo lo que recuerde Shiseo sobre esta operación antes de que se marche al este. Pondremos a prueba este método de transferencia gradual. Quiero que se perfeccione. Si es posible, lo usaremos para borrar la transmutación que le hicieron a ella y ver qué quería esconderme tan desesperadamente la Llama Eterna.

Morrough dio una bocanada de aire entrecortada al girarse.

—Su Eminencia —dijo Stroud con voz nerviosa—, esta operación de transferencia que deseáis poner a prueba requeriría un animante, ¿verdad? —Tosió débilmente—. Estoy segura de que a Bennet le habría entusiasmado esta oportunidad, pero, por desgracia, las almas no forman parte de mi repertorio de resonancia, y solo hay otro más. ¿Creéis que esto es algo que...? —Su voz se llenó de esperanza.

—Deja que se encargue el Sumo Inquisidor.

A Stroud se le descompuso la cara.

—Pero yo la encontr...

—Tengo otro trabajo para ti.

Stroud se enderezó, aunque seguía decepcionada.

—Después de todo, el Sumo Inquisidor era el favorito de Bennet. —Morrough hizo un gesto de desdén con la mano y luego desapareció entre las sombras—. Es hora de que se dedique a algo más que cazar.

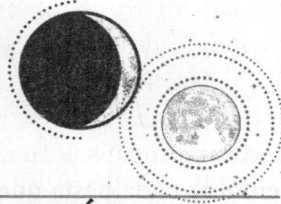

CAPÍTULO 3

Cuando volvieron a meter a Helena en el ascensor de la Central, contó los pisos de la Torre conforme bajaban.

Durante siglos, la Torre de Alquimia había sido una maravilla arquitectónica. Solo tenía cinco pisos cuando se construyó como monumento a la Primera Guerra Nigromántica. En aquel momento, la resonancia alquímica era una habilidad arcana considerada mágica. Los que la practicaban se rodeaban de mitos y misterios, como Cetus, el primer alquimista del Norte.

Los Holdfast y la Academia habían cambiado esa percepción; establecieron la alquimia como la ciencia noble, algo digno de estudio y dominio. Cuando la Academia de Alquimia amenazó con superar en altura a la Torre, usaron sistemas de poleas forjados con alquimia para añadir pisos en la base. Fue el edificio más alto del continente Norte durante casi dos siglos, alzándose por encima de la ciudad que se expandía a sus pies, y los alquimistas jamás dejaron de atravesar sus puertas.

Los estudios de alquimia que se llevaban a cabo en el Norte estaban entrelazados con la propia estructura de la Torre. Los cinco primeros pisos, los que contaban con las aulas más grandes, eran los «cimientos», llenos de iniciados que todavía estaban descubriendo su resonancia y aprendiendo los principios de transmutación más básicos. Había que pasar exámenes anuales para ir ascendiendo. Después del quinto año, la mayoría de los alumnos abandonaban la Academia con un título que les permitía unirse a los gremios, y solo los universitarios más cualificados continuaban al siguiente piso de la Torre, que se iba estrechando. Allí estudiaban temas y disciplinas más técnicas. Solo unos pocos subían a los pisos de posgrado e investigación para conseguir el rango de gran maestre.

El ascensor se detuvo en alguno de los antiguos pisos de investigación.

Helena aguzó la vista y se obligó a mirar a través de un aura de dolor que le nublaba la visión constantemente. Veía las paredes borrosas. Sus ojos fueron incapaces de enfocar nada hasta que dejaron de empujar su camilla y la colocaron en el centro de una sala vacía.

Probablemente antes habría sido un laboratorio privado.

Le desabrocharon las correas que la mantenían atada, y Stroud se detuvo a su lado para comprobar las muñecas de Helena.

Los tubos que se colaban entre su cúbito y su radio le daban náuseas y le provocaban la profunda sensación de que algo iba mal. Ni siquiera podía doblar los dedos sin sentir que los músculos, tendones, nervios y venas se veían obligados a acomodarse en aquel espacio reducido, junto a la anulación que le habían insertado.

—Muy bien —dijo Stroud para sí misma antes de girarse para marcharse. Al cerrar la puerta, Helena la escuchó añadir—: Que no entre nadie sin mi permiso.

Helena oyó un sonoro chasquido y el giro de una cerradura, y la dejaron sola.

Se incorporó, aunque el fármaco ya había desaparecido de sus venas, por lo que le dolían los músculos y sentía calambres cada vez que los estiraba. Intentó levantarse, pero se desplomó en cuanto sus pies tocaron el suelo. Cayó pesadamente.

«Huye», le repetía una voz sin cesar. Pero no podía hacerlo; no la sostenían los brazos ni las piernas. Al verse privada de sus capacidades físicas, sus pensamientos se volvieron introspectivos.

¿De verdad había olvidado algo?

Tal vez la Llama Eterna no había desaparecido, sino que resistía como unas ascuas escondidas, esperando que llegara el momento oportuno. La posibilidad encendió una chispa de esperanza en su interior. ¿Cómo le habían hecho que olvidara?

Transferencia. Animancia. Las dos palabras le resultaban desconocidas.

Las repasó mentalmente. Intentó dar contexto a los comentarios que habían hecho: almas y mentes, y ocupar el paisaje mental de otra persona para transmutarla desde dentro. ¿Y la Llama Eterna había descubierto eso?

Desde luego que no, los creyentes consideraban que las almas eran inviolables. La Llama Eterna creía incluso que las alteraciones físicas de la vivemancia y la nigromancia suponían un riesgo para un alma inmortal.

La alteración de una mente, la transferencia de un alma: ambas cosas habrían sido consideradas como algo infinitamente peor.

Aun así, Shiseo afirmaba que la Llama Eterna había desarrollado una manera de hacer esta operación de transferencia mediante la animancia. Algo que Morrough, que había desentrañado los secretos de la inmortalidad, no había logrado descubrir.

¿Quién era Elain Boyle? A Helena no le sonaba el nombre y estaba segura de que nunca habían contado con una sanadora que se ocupara exclusivamente de Luc, y mucho menos con una sanadora personal.

Luc jamás habría consentido recibir nada que no se distribuyera de forma equitativa entre toda la Resistencia, y eso incluía los cuidados médicos y la sanación. Ni siquiera le gustaba que los paladines juraran protegerlo, a pesar de que se trataba de una tradición más antigua que la propia Paladia.

Stroud tenía que estar equivocada.

Sin embargo, existía un misterio oculto. Habían cambiado algo en su interior, un secreto enterrado con tal celo que Helena no lograba imaginar de qué podía tratarse.

Sintió más calambres recorriéndole el cuerpo. Permaneció en el suelo, encogida como una araña muerta, pero sin dejar de pensar.

¿Qué habría hecho Luc si fuera el único que siguiera con vida? Si estuviese cautivo, ya tendría un plan. Habría persuadido a Grace para que enviara un mensaje de su parte, comenzando a coordinar una manera de escapar, y también a idear cómo rescatar a todos los que estaban en el Reducto.

Eso es lo que él haría, pero ahora le tocaba a Helena.

No le fallaría, esta vez no.

HELENA SUPUSO QUE LA TRANSFERENCIA empezaría de inmediato, pero, en cambio, pasaron lo que le parecieron días sin apenas moverse, mientras sus músculos se iban destensando poco a poco.

—Abstinencia —dijo Stroud con una mirada cargada de condescendencia mientras le introducía a Helena una sonda de alimentación por la nariz y le administraba suero fisiológico en el brazo para mantenerla sedada—. Da igual. Supongo que te enseñaron a disfrutar del sufrimiento. Después de todo, la vocación de una sanadora es el sacrificio, ¿no?

Stroud no escondía el desdén que sentía por Helena desde que descubrió que ambas eran vivemantes, pero en bandos opuestos de la guerra.

Stroud la consideraba una traidora.

—No me gustan esos espasmos —comentó poco después mientras la examinaba. Frunció los labios cuando Helena dejó caer una taza al sentir un calambre en los dedos—. No son causados por la anulación. ¿Sabes cuándo empezaron?

Helena negó con la cabeza y se encogió de dolor cuando notó el ardor frío que le provocó la resonancia de Stroud al deslizarse por su muñeca izquierda, serpenteando entre los huesos mientras la retorcía y manipulaba durante varios minutos.

—Por el estado en el que está, diría que te has roto esta muñeca unas cuantas veces. Hay una herida antigua en los nervios. ¿Te acuerdas de cuándo sucedió?

Helena no recordaba haberse hecho nunca un daño grave en las manos. Unas manos diestras eran vitales para canalizar y controlar la resonancia, tanto en el laboratorio de un alquimista como en la consulta de una sanadora. Siempre había tenido mucho cuidado con ellas.

—No se menciona nada en tu expediente de alumna, así que debió de ser durante la guerra, pero tampoco hay registros de ello.

Habían encontrado el expediente académico de Helena, y a Stroud le gustaba usarlo para interrogarla sobre aspectos insignificantes de su vida. Helena sospechaba que lo hacía porque tenía permiso para castigarla si se negaba a responder.

¿Dónde pusieron a prueba por primera vez su resonancia alquímica? En la embajada paladina de su hogar, las islas sureñas de Etras. ¿Qué edad tenía cuando emigró a Paladia para estudiar en la Academia de Alquimia? Diez años.

¿Cuántos cursos terminó en la Academia? Seis.

¿Recordaba la muerte del principado Apollo Holdfast? Sí, estaba en clase con Luc.

¿Cuándo se unió a la Resistencia? Cuando los gremios destituyeron al Gobierno legítimo y hubo una Resistencia a la que unirse.

A Stroud no le gustó esa respuesta.

¿Cuándo empezó a formar parte de la Orden de la Llama Eterna?

Helena no quiso responder, pero Stroud tenía el libro con los miembros de la Orden, junto con los votos y el nombre de Helena, escritos con su propia sangre.

—¿Sabía el Consejo de la Llama Eterna que eras una vivemante cuando te uniste?

Helena negó con la cabeza.

Stroud se sentó y la fulminó con la mirada, a la espera de una respuesta verbal.

—Yo no sabía que lo era —dijo Helena al cabo de un tiempo—. Y después..., cuando todo el mundo lo supo..., a Luc no le importó. Él pensaba que las habilidades de una persona no cambiaban quién era, solo lo que hacía con ellas.

—Qué magnánimo. —La voz de Stroud sonó gélida. Arrugó el documento que tenía en la mano—. Una pena que no dejase el cargo. Todavía seguiría viva mucha gente con talento.

—Su familia era la elegida —respondió Helena, aunque sabía que no tenía sentido discutir.

—Sí, por el Sol —replicó Stroud con mofa, y su tono adquirió cierta virulencia—. Sé que no enseñaban astronomía moderna en la Academia, pero ¿has estudiado alguna vez las teorías astrológicas más actuales? Provienes de las islas comerciantes, al fin y al cabo; habrás conocido todo tipo de ideas. ¿De verdad crees que el Sol, a miles de kilómetros de distancia, miró a la Tierra y eligió un favorito? ¿Que una gota de luz solar le otorgó a Orion Holdfast tal condición divina que todos sus descendientes merecían gobernar sobre Paladia como si fueran dioses?

Helena apretó la mandíbula, pero Stroud no paró de hablar.

—Según tu expediente académico, se te consideraba inteligente. Seguro que no te tragaste todas las historias que te contaron sobre los Holdfast. Mírame a los ojos y dime: ¿de verdad crees que los Holdfast tenían derecho a gobernar?

Stroud clavó los dedos bajo la barbilla de Helena para obligarla a alzar la vista. Esta fijó sus ojos en el rostro de Stroud, sintiendo la amenaza de su resonancia.

—Mejor ellos que gente como tú.

Stroud quitó la mano y su resonancia se esfumó. Acto seguido, le dio una bofetada a Helena que le cruzó la cara con tanta fuerza que se golpeó la cabeza contra la pared.

—Si te hubieras unido a nuestra causa, podrías haber sido excepcional. —Stroud respiraba con dificultad mientras se inclinaba sobre Helena—. Habrías sido alguien, pero ahora no eres nada. Desperdiciaste tu talento en el bando equivocado y nadie te recordará. Eres ceniza, como todos los demás. Y una traidora a los vivemantes.

Cuando estuvo sola, Helena se llevó la mano a la hinchazón de la cara y sintió que le palpitaba la cabeza.

La Resistencia había considerado la guerra como un acto sagrado, una batalla divina entre el bien y el mal, una prueba de la Fe. Pero los motivos de Helena habían sido una cuestión personal.

Luc no necesitaba ser divino para que ella quisiera salvarlo. Aunque hubiese sido absolutamente ordinario, ella habría tomado las mismas decisiones.

¿Podría haber hecho algo que hubiera cambiado las cosas?

Cuando llegó a Paladia, pensó que aquello era el paraíso. Etras no tenía mucho metal como recurso natural. La resonancia era poco habitual. Había algunos gremios de alquimistas, pero ninguno ofrecía una formación reglada. Al llegar a Paladia, se sintió como si por fin estuviese en su hogar, como si hubiera encontrado el sitio en el que siempre debió estar.

Fue vagamente consciente de que existía una jerarquía entre los alquimistas que dividía incluso el cuerpo estudiantil, separando a las familias devotas y allegadas de los Holdfast de los gremios, pero no conocía lo suficiente de la política de la ciudad Estado como para entender su complejidad.

Lo único que sabía era que había alumnos que no le dirigían la palabra, que se reían cuando hacía preguntas y se burlaban de su acento y de cómo gesticulaba con las manos cuando hablaba. Más tarde descubrió que se trataba de los alumnos del gremio y que debía tratarlos con recelo.

Fue Luc quien le explicó que los alumnos del gremio pensaban que la matrícula de Helena debería haberse adjudicado a los gremios, aunque Luc le aseguró que estaban equivocados. La Academia de su familia no se había fundado para los gremios, sino para gente como ella, para los que no tenían la oportunidad de estudiar alquimia por su cuenta. Los alumnos del gremio no tenían ni por qué asistir; ya tenían asegurado sus puestos y su futuro. Para ellos, obtener una plaza en la Academia era cuestión de estatus y, cuando conseguían el certificado, se marchaban.

Pero Helena era especial. Sería de las que se quedaban cuando terminara el quinto año, de las que estudiarían algo más que los principios básicos de la alquimia. Ascendería a los pisos superiores, haría descubrimientos y se dedicaría a asuntos que cambiarían el mundo. Siempre recordarían su nombre.

¿Por qué querría la familia de Luc a otro alumno del gremio en su Academia cuando podían tener a alguien como ella?

Luc siempre tuvo la habilidad de hacer sentir especial a Helena, en vez de señalar lo fuera de lugar que estaba allí. A su vez, ella siempre quiso demostrarle que tenía razón, que había algo por lo que merecía la pena creer en ella. Su familia no cometería un error apoyándola.

Helena se centró en sus estudios e ignoró la hostilidad política que la rodeaba.

En ocasiones, Luc le mencionaba que los gremios creían que su familia estaba conteniendo el avance científico de la alquimia y poniendo trabas a la industrialización, y entonces señalaba las fábricas que había bajo la presa, que inundaban el cielo de nubes de humo negro. Decían que habían acusado a su padre de permitir que el país se quedara atrasado por culpa de la negligencia de su gobierno. O que los gremios proponían limitar el poder del principado a las cuestiones religiosas, mientras que ellos debían encargarse de gestionar el país.

Parecía que nada de lo que hiciera el principado Apollo era suficiente para los gremios; siempre estaban quejándose y exigiendo más.

Cuando asesinaron al principado Apollo, los gremios no lo consideraron una tragedia, sino una oportunidad. Aprovecharon que Luc solo tenía dieciséis años para usarlo como pretexto y declarar una reforma: Paladia ya no sería gobernada por las élites religiosas y un grupo de guerreros. La ciudad Estado pasaría a estar bajo el control del recién formado Concejo de Gremios.

A la Orden de la Llama Eterna no le habría costado demasiado contener la sublevación de los gremios si no hubiera sido por Morrough. Apareció de la nada en plena revuelta y empezó a ofrecer la inmortalidad. No se refería a una vida eterna de descomposición, sino a una inmune a la edad y a las heridas, descubierta gracias a la ciencia, no al poder divino.

Los gremios aprovecharon la oportunidad, y así comenzaron a aparecer los inmarcesibles. Al principio solamente se elegía a unos pocos selectos, que no solo eran inmortales, sino también expertos en los aspectos más avanzados de la alquimia. De repente, el poder y la vida eterna estaban al alcance de cualquiera que demostrara su lealtad a Morrough. Los aspirantes acudieron en masa a unirse y aliarse con los gremios.

La concepción de la «Nueva Paladia» que prometía el Concejo de Gremios se extendió entre los habitantes como una enfermedad.

Cuando la Llama Eterna intentó restaurar el orden, los inmarcesibles revelaron una nueva habilidad: la nigromancia, y a una escala nunca vista. En vez de reclutar sin criterio entre los aspirantes, esperaban a que los soldados de la Llama Eterna fueran atacados y fallecieran para luego reanimarlos y hacerlos luchar contra sus propios compañeros. Así crearon un ejército de muertos vivientes al servicio de la Llama Eterna.

Luc, recién coronado como principado, estaba convencido de que los ciudadanos de Paladia entrarían en razón cuando comprendieran, estupefactos, que se estaban aliando con nigromantes. Durante siglos, la nigromancia se había considerado un crimen moral en todo el continente. Ni siquiera los gremios se atreverían a ir tan lejos.

Se equivocó.

———

—Si eras sanadora, ¿por qué apenas se te menciona en los archivos del hospital?

Stroud regresó furiosa, con un montón de papeles en la mano.

El nombre de Helena casi no aparecía en ninguno de ellos. Stroud solo había conseguido encontrar su firma en el inventario de suministros médicos, una solicitud para un cuchillo básico de alquimia y unas pocas peticiones de ciertos compuestos a los departamentos de química y metalurgia. Lo único interesante era una lista preliminar de bajas en la que Helena figuraba entre los presuntos fallecidos.

A pesar de todo, según esos archivos militares que abarcaban años, Helena apenas había existido. Stroud parecía tomarlo como un agravio personal.

—¿Y bien?

—La sanación es un milagro; no es algo para lo que haga falta firmar —respondió Helena, recitando lo que le habían enseñado hacía tanto tiempo—. Usamos símbolos en los expedientes médicos para indicar que se ha… intervenido.

—¿Te refieres a…? —Stroud deslizó los documentos hasta llegar a uno que giró hacia Helena. En la esquina aparecía una medialuna con un tajo en medio—. ¿Esto?

Helena apenas asintió.

Stroud se quedó mirándolo.

—¿Entonces cómo demonios se controlan los procedimientos?

La presión se extendió desde el pecho hasta la garganta de Helena, oprimiéndola.

—La sanación no es un procedimiento.

El falcón Matias, consejero espiritual del Consejo de la Llama Eterna y superior directo de Helena, siempre fue estricto a la hora de exigir que la vivemancia no se documentara de ninguna forma que pudiera glorificarla. Según él, la vivemancia solo se purificaba mediante el altruismo.

Aunque los sanadores eran una figura relativamente común en las zonas remotas de Paladia, la vivemancia resultaba tan poco habitual que existían numerosas teorías sobre las capacidades de los vivemantes: si podían hechizar a los vivos, tal y como hacían los nigromantes con los muertos, por ejemplo, o realizar transmutaciones prohibidas sobre la carne viviente.

Helena solía pensar que esta percepción de los vivemantes era irracional y severa, pero tras conocer a Stroud empezaba a entenderla.

Stroud no hechizaba, pero era experta en paralizar y manipular a Helena mediante transmutaciones al menor descuido. Y, si Helena se retorcía demasiado, Stroud le soldaba los huesos para que se mantuviera quieta. Parecía disfrutar del hecho de que, técnicamente, no la estaba torturando. A veces dejaba a Helena así, inmovilizada, durante horas.

Fue un alivio cuando, finalmente, Stroud pareció perder el interés y anunció que ya no tenía tiempo para ocuparse de Helena. Varias veces al día acudían un par de necrómatas para sacarla de la celda y hacerla caminar por el pasillo que rodeaba el ascensor.

Recuperó la vista, aunque los necrómatas eran algo horrible de ver. La adipocira les confería un brillo grasiento y viscoso a las motas moradas y grisáceas de su piel, y la esclerótica de sus pupilas nubladas era roja o de un amarillo intenso. Las puntas de sus dedos estaban negras y en descomposición. El olor a conservantes químicos y a putrefacción le daba ganas de vomitar, pero no le permitían dejar de caminar hasta que sus piernas cedían y tenían que arrastrarla de vuelta a la celda.

Las caminatas se confundieron con los días. Helena había perdido la noción del tiempo que llevaba en la Central; las luces permanecían siempre encendidas, y todas las ventanas estaban cubiertas y tapiadas.

—¿Es ella? —Un hombre con rostro pálido, casi fantasmal, y una nariz puntiaguda y fina como una aguja salió de repente de una habitación y se interpuso en el camino de Helena mientras los necrómatas la obligaban a continuar su rutina interminable.

Helena profirió un grito ahogado de sorpresa. Frente a ella, vestido con ropas de bordados intrincados y joyas, estaba Jan Crowther, uno de los cinco miembros del Consejo de la Llama Eterna.

—Crowth…

Él estiró una mano cargada de anillos, la agarró por el hombro y la atrajo hacia sí para echarle un vistazo.

—¿Lo conocías? —preguntó. Le estaba clavando los dedos y los anillos en la piel.

Helena intentó liberarse, pero los necrómatas la sujetaron cuando Crowther se inclinó cada vez más, inhaló profundamente y sacó una lengua ancha y morada, como si quisiera lamerla.

Helena se encogió, pero Crowther estaba tan cerca que pudo distinguir cada detalle. Sus escleróticas mostraban un leve tono amarillento y por sus ojos ligeramente nublados surcaban unas venas oscuras. Tenía la piel cubierta de talco y desprendía un intenso olor a lavanda.

No era Crowther. Uno de los inmarcesibles estaba usando su cadáver.

En las pocas ocasiones en que sus heridas eran tan graves que ya no podían seguir regenerándose, por ejemplo, por haber resultado tan gravemente heridos en batalla que sus cuerpos inmortales no lograban curarse, los inmarcesibles podían trasladarse a sus necrómatas. Por eso la Resistencia los llamaba «liches».

Era una solución imperfecta; a pesar de que se mantenían vivos, los cuerpos iban pudriéndose poco a poco y perdían la capacidad regenerativa de los cuerpos originales, que eran casi inmunes. Helena sospechaba que Morrough estaba tan interesado en la transferencia porque era un método que abría la puerta a que los inmarcesibles pudieran trasladarse a cuerpos vivos.

El liche que estaba usando el cuerpo de Crowther dio un paso atrás y volvió a mirarla con un gesto extraño en el rostro.

—Te conozco —dijo en voz baja.

Le agarró la cara y la hizo girar de forma que la luz le llegaba desde un ángulo diferente. Sus ojos repasaron cada centímetro de su piel, como si estuviera buscando algo. Entonces el liche le cogió una de las manos; los pesados anillos negros se le clavaron contra la piel, y manipuló el grillete, provocándole una punzada de dolor en todo el brazo. Luego le miró los dedos y volvió a observar su rostro.

Los necrómatas no hicieron nada.

¿Era este el Sumo Inquisidor?

—Sí. Es ella. —Stroud apareció entonces, con un tono mucho más amable del que empleaba con Helena. Parecía molestarle la forma en la que el liche estaba tocando a Helena, pero no dijo nada—. Pronto estará lista.

El liche agarró a Helena del pelo. Cuando volvió a acercarse a ella, esbozó una mueca retorcida, con una mirada voraz y desesperada, algo que ella jamás había percibido en el semblante impasible de Crowther.

—La he visto en alguna parte. —La agarró con más fuerza, sacudiéndola con tanto ímpetu que a Helena se le cayó la cabeza hacia atrás—. ¿Dónde ha sido?

—Era la mascota de los Holdfast, maese gremial. Seguramente la conociste en la Academia.

El rostro del liche se contrajo con desdén al oír hablar de los Holdfast y la soltó de inmediato. De repente, había perdido todo el interés. Ahora parecía enfadado y por el cuello se le estaba extendiendo una sombra de color morado oscuro que le moteaba la cara.

—Esperaba algo más. Me dijeron que este encargo era algo especial.

Stroud se mordió el labio.

—Las apariencias no lo son todo. Puedes decirle al Sumo Inquisidor que pronto estará lista. Ahora querías comprobar cómo preparaban las habitaciones, ¿no? —Stroud señaló los ascensores—. Mi intención es comenzar con una remesa de prueba muy pronto para evaluar cuándo podemos poner en marcha todo esto. El interés es abrumador. He recibido decenas de solicitudes, y aún faltan semanas para el anuncio. —A Stroud se le escapó una risa nerviosa, pero se contuvo y se aclaró la garganta mientras presionaba la mano contra el panel del ascensor—. Ha sido difícil determinar las combinaciones más prometedoras. He sacado lo máximo posible de los historiales médicos. También me han sido útiles los archivos gremiales, que estaban muy adelantados a su tiempo. Pero tú eres el único que ha producido exactamente lo que esperamos replicar aquí, así que estoy deseando escuchar tu aportación.

La expresión del liche se volvió impasible, a pesar del halago. Cuando llegó el ascensor, Stroud y él se marcharon sin decir palabra.

Los necrómatas la empujaron para que siguiera caminando. Helena exhaló lentamente. No era el Sumo Inquisidor entonces. Era un alivio que el primer cadáver reanimado que había reconocido fuera el de Crowther, uno de los miembros más indiferentes del Consejo, y no alguien que conociera de verdad.

Alzó la vista y se encogió al ver el único cuadro que había en el pasillo.

Antes, la Torre estaba muy decorada y llena de obras artísticas, con cuadros de importantes alquimistas que habían estudiado o impartido clase en la Academia. Ahora solo quedaba uno que mostraba a un hombre de piel cetrina y aspecto taciturno, con frente ancha y barbilla gruesa.

La placa que había debajo lo identificaba: ARTEMON BENNET, junto a dos fechas que abarcaban más de ochenta años.

Helena recordó con una claridad que le atravesaba las entrañas los informes relacionados con ese nombre. Cuando los inmarcesibles se hicieron fuertes en la ciudad, convocaron a todos los vivemantes y nigromantes ocultos para que se unieran a su causa. También construyeron laboratorios donde estos aliados pudieran explorar sus poderes y librarse de la opresión de la Fe.

Y, cuando los combatientes de la Resistencia no solo morían, sino que eran reanimados como necrómatas, los enviaban a estos laboratorios para estudiarlos. Artemon Bennet era el director de los departamentos de ciencia e investigación de Nueva Paladia. Según decían, tenía un interés particular en los experimentos con alquimistas.

Lo único interesante del cuadro era saber que Bennet había muerto.

La caminata estaba llegando a su fin. Helena seguía respirando profundamente; un hábito que había adoptado en el tanque de suspensión, donde el oxígeno era limitado, y que había empeorado por el hedor de los necrómatas. Sentía que empezaba a marearse, que la vista se le nublaba. Sus piernas comenzaron a flaquear.

Los necrómatas la sujetaron para que no se detuviera. Helena casi arrastraba los pies por el suelo al caminar.

Un grito ahogado la puso en alerta.

—¿Marino?

Una chica morena en una silla de ruedas pasaba a su lado. Estaba demacrada, casi encogida sobre sí misma, pero se incorporó y se inclinó hacia delante para mirarla fijamente. Tenía cicatrices similares a las de Grace y una manta cubriéndole el regazo. También llevaba los mismos grilletes que Helena alrededor de la muñeca. La estaban empujando por el pasillo, en dirección al quirófano que Helena había visto abierto unos minutos antes.

Helena tropezó y trató de recuperar el equilibrio.

—Penny.

Penny tenía un año más que ella. Había sido una de las pocas chicas de la Academia que había decidido estudiar un posgrado en alquimia. Fue también una de las primeras en alistarse a la Resistencia, decidida a ir al frente y luchar.

El camillero que empujaba a Penny apretó el paso y giró la silla para evitar que conversaran.

Helena y Penny estiraron el cuello para seguir mirándose mientras las separaban.

—Penny, ¿qué van a...? —Helena no alcanzó a terminar la pregunta porque la empujaron hacia su habitación.

Penny se inclinó sobre el brazo de la silla y miró hacia atrás con una expresión de congoja.

—Tenías razón. Lo siento mucho. Deberíamos haberte escuchado.

No hubo tiempo de preguntar a qué se refería. El camillero aligeró el paso y Penny desapareció.

—Te voy a entregar hoy —dijo Stroud al entrar, absorta en un montón de papeles que estaba revisando. Cada vez que Helena la veía, estaba más distraída—. Prepárate.

—¿Me voy?

Stroud alzó la vista y le dedicó una sonrisa a medio camino entre la irritación y los nervios.

—Sí. La Central tiene otros asuntos entre manos. El Sumo Inquisidor te está esperando. Vamos. Ahora.

Helena no tenía nada que preparar. La metieron en el ascensor con algo de ropa y un par de zapatillas de lana que le quedaban demasiado grandes.

El ascensor descendió hasta el quinto piso, donde la Torre de Alquimia conectaba con el resto de los edificios de la Academia a través de puentes colgantes. En una ciudad tan vertical como Paladia, solían usarse los puentes colgantes para unir edificios; algunos no eran más que pasajes estrechos, mientras que otros tenían el tamaño suficiente como para albergar plazas y jardines de muchos pisos por encima del nivel de las calles. Conforme la ciudad fue creciendo, las partes más bajas quedaron sumidas en la sombra, convertidas en zonas cavernosas, húmedas y oscuras, plagadas de enfermedades.

Helena distinguió los jardines más abajo: un terreno de césped dividido por caminos geométricos que conectaban los dormitorios con la Torre y el pabellón científico.

Unos escalones de mármol blanco desembocaban en las amplias puertas de la Torre. Al verlos, su memoria superpuso al instante la imagen de sangre y vísceras y cadáveres que los había cubierto la última vez que los contempló.

Apartó rápidamente la mirada. Tenía que centrarse en el presente.

OBLIGARON A HELENA A METERSE en el asiento trasero de un coche, y un necrómata la empujó hacia el centro para sentarse a su lado. El olor a putrefacción se extendió rápidamente por el espacio cerrado.

Le dieron arcadas y se llevó una mano a la nariz y la boca para taparlas e intentar no vomitar.

Stroud se colocó al otro lado. Al parecer, era inmune al hedor, porque no dejaba de hojear el montón de papeles que llevaba encima en todo momento.

El coche atravesó un largo túnel; las luces ambarinas de las farolas eléctricas se deslizaron por el regazo de Helena hasta dar paso a un gris verdoso cuando el coche salió del nivel subterráneo. Helena se inclinó un poco para ver el cielo. Estaba oscuro y nublado, de un gris que parecía privar de color al mundo. Al observar la ciudad, se sorprendió de las cicatrices tan visibles que había dejado la guerra: enormes huecos donde antes se alzaban rascacielos, edificios quemados o en ruinas. No parecía haber comenzado la reconstrucción. La carretera era lo único que parecía nuevo.

Cuando el vehículo cruzó de la isla Este a la isla Oeste, dejaron atrás casi todas las secuelas visibles de la guerra.

Paladia se había fundado sobre el delta de un río que descendía a los pies de las montañas Novis. La isla original contaba con una meseta alta en el norte que se extendía hacia el sur. La Torre de Alquimia se había construido en el punto más alto de la isla, y la Torre (y, con el paso del tiempo, la ciudad) se fue extendiendo hasta cubrir con edificios cada centímetro de tierra. En la isla de Paladia, más tarde conocida como la isla Este, se concentraban la industria, el comercio, el Gobierno, las catedrales periheliales y la Academia de Alquimia.

La isla Oeste, construida siglos más tarde, había sido diseñada para albergar a la desbordante población. Todo allí era más nuevo, de mayores dimensiones.

Durante la guerra, los inmarcesibles mantenían un control difuso sobre la isla Oeste, mientras que la Resistencia tenía sus cuarteles generales en la Academia de Alquimia, un baluarte firme de defensa en la isla Este, lo que dividió la ciudad Estado en dos zonas enfrentadas. Como la mayor parte de las infraestructuras esenciales y los puertos principales se encontraban en la isla Este, esta había sido la que se había llevado la peor parte cuando los inmarcesibles intentaron conquistarla.

En comparación con las ruinas de la isla Este, la Oeste parecía prácticamente intacta; sus enormes edificios interconectados se alzaban al cielo, relucientes e indemnes.

La primera vez que Helena llegó en barco por el río y contempló Paladia, le pareció como si alguna deidad excepcional hubiera posado su corona en la cima de las montañas; los capiteles y el resplandor de la ciudad se reflejaban en el agua. Helena pensó que no existía un lugar en el mundo más bello que aquel.

El vehículo parecía diminuto mientras aceleraba por la isla Oeste y cruzaba otro puente en dirección al continente de Paladia, que se extendía kilómetros más allá de la costa ribereña, hasta donde comenzaban los árboles en la ladera de la montaña.

El continente se dedicaba principalmente a la minería y la agricultura, y las pocas tierras no explotadas económicamente pertenecían a las familias más antiguas, las que habían acudido a la Academia desde hacía siglos, en la época de su fundación.

Si la estaban llevando al continente debía de ser porque el Sumo Inquisidor tenía una propiedad en ese territorio. Tal vez la habían conquistado y cedido después de la guerra, o quizá formaba parte de una de las familias adineradas del gremio. Algunas de ellas habían multiplicado su fortuna gracias a la industrialización del último siglo.

Helena se inclinó hacia delante buscando a través del parabrisas alguna señal que le indicara cuál era su destino.

Alejada por fin de la Central, Helena estaba empezando a vislumbrar algo parecido a un plan.

Siendo realista, sus probabilidades de escapar eran nulas. Aunque no llevara los grilletes que le impedían moverse con destreza y anulaban su resonancia, carecía de suficiente formación de combate. Su resonancia siempre había sido su mejor arma. Si consiguiese escapar, no tendría adónde ir. No sabía quién seguía con vida, en quién podría confiar ni quién estaría dispuesto, a su vez, a confiar en ella.

Sabía que, si cooperaba, existía la posibilidad de que sobreviviera a la transferencia, pero hacerlo significaba traicionar a la Llama Eterna, ya que tendría que revelar la información por la que había sacrificado su propia memoria.

Apretó las manos con fuerza, lo que le provocó una punzada de dolor en las muñecas.

En el tanque de suspensión, se repetía una y otra vez que, si sobrevivía, no podía rendirse. No sabía explicar por qué.

Al fin y al cabo, el propósito de la sanación era asegurarse de que los demás sobrevivieran, ser quien le salvara la vida a Luc. No tenía sentido ser sanadora si todos estaban muertos.

No sería una traidora. Independientemente de lo que ocultara su mente, no permitiría que los inmarcesibles lo descubrieran. Le daba igual sobrevivir o no. Se suicidaría antes de que le arrancaran algo por la fuerza.

Tal vez su agresivo captor fuera de ayuda para ese fin.

Si lo que le había dicho Grace era cierto, el Sumo Inquisidor prefería el asesinato a otras tácticas, como los interrogatorios. Los hombres propensos a la violencia solían ser impulsivos, actuaban por instinto y razonaban después.

Si conseguía provocarlo, tal vez la matara en un arrebato. Solo necesitaba que cometiera un error, y todos sus secretos desaparecerían. Ningún tipo de nigromancia podía recuperar una mente una vez muerta.

¿Qué le haría Morrough al Sumo Inquisidor en ese caso? Algo peor que lo que le hizo a Mandl, no le cabía duda.

O eso esperaba Helena.

Ya no podría vengar a Luc, pero sí podía aún hacerle justicia a Lila.

Al pensar en Lila Bayard, muerta, con la cara destrozada, cuyo cadáver ahora servía para encerrar a la gente que antes protegía, Helena sentía una presión en el pecho tan intensa que le dolía.

Lila había sido una de las pocas personas que no se inmutaron al saber que Helena era una vivemante. Durante la guerra incluso compartieron habitación. No fueron especialmente amigas (al ser paladina, Lila pasaba mucho tiempo fuera, luchando en el frente), pero jamás trató como alguien inferior a Helena por no participar en el combate.

Lila era considerada una alquimista de combate excepcional. Se unió a las cruzadas de la Llama Eterna a los quince años, viajando por el continente, e investigó los rumores sobre la nigromancia. Toda su vida había estado orientada a convertirse en paladina y servir al principado.

La gente decía que Lila era la personificación de Lumitia, la diosa guerrera de la alquimia.

Helena no podía imaginar cómo alguien logró matar a Lila, sobre todo, después de que Luc fuera asesinado. Lila habría muerto mil veces antes de permitir que capturaran a Luc. Vivía y respiraba por mantener el juramento que había hecho de protegerlo.

Helena parpadeó cuando el vehículo se detuvo en un control fronterizo.

Los árboles a ambos lados de la carretera se alzaban esqueléticos y con las ramas desnudas. El vehículo avanzó unos kilómetros más y abandonó la carretera principal.

Vio un edificio que se erguía entre los árboles cuando enfilaron por un carril largo, hacia unas verjas pesadas y ornamentadas, abiertas de par en par. El vehículo las atravesó y se dirigió en dirección a una casa de gran altura.

Era un edificio antiguo, con una fachada cubierta de parras desnudas que trepaban por las paredes como venas negras. Su estilo arquitectónico no tenía nada que ver con la elegancia moderna de la ciudad. Los detalles ornamentales, oscuros y pesados, parecían llevar al menos un siglo desgastándose. Contaba con cinco pináculos negros que se alzaban hacia el cielo: tres en la sección principal y uno en cada ala, que se extendían formando un semicírculo.

La puerta, los muros y el resto de los edificios circundantes configuraban un patio cerrado en cuyo centro había un jardín asilvestrado. El vehículo se acercó a la entrada, crujiendo sobre la gravilla blanca, y se detuvo.

En lo alto de unos amplios escalones de piedra había una mujer joven.

Helena salió a empujones del coche tras Stroud y respiró una bocanada de aire fresco, estremeciéndose. Hacía un frío penetrante; el aire húmedo del campo le caló hasta los huesos de inmediato. Había olvidado lo duros que eran los inviernos del Norte.

La mujer de las escaleras parecía apenas una niña, pero destacaba entre los tonos apagados que la rodeaban. Su cabello castaño claro le caía en perfectos bucles alrededor de su rostro pálido. Llevaba puesto un vestido de color verde veneno, ceñido por un corsé negro con la forma de una caja torácica, y un collar de plata brillante cuyo colgante, el cráneo de un pájaro de largo pico, caía entre sus pechos. Helena vio que tenía anillos de alquimia en varios dedos, que jugueteaban con un pequeño bastón. La mujer los observó mientras subían los escalones.

Miró directamente a Helena, entrecerrando sus ojos azul claro.

—Bueno —dijo cuando llegaron—, supongo que hay fanáticos de todo tipo.

Entonces se giró hacia Stroud, a quien le dedicó una frágil sonrisa.

—Bienvenida a Puntaférreo. Mi marido las está esperando.

Stroud la siguió hacia el interior de la casa y los necrómatas obligaron a Helena a avanzar a empujones.

Un mayordomo muerto les sostuvo la puerta abierta y, al verlo, a Helena se le congeló la sangre.

Al contrario que los necrómatas de la Central, el mayordomo había fallecido hacía poco y estaba vestido de forma impoluta. Por un instante, Helena pensó que estaba vivo, o que era un liche. No tenía el brillo grasiento de la adipocira y no se movía con el aletargamiento de los necrómatas. Sin embargo, su semblante y sus ojos estaban totalmente inertes.

Debían de haberlo matado recientemente. Grace le había contado que los inmarcesibles usaban necrómatas como empleados, pero una familia adinerada no soportaría ese olor, así que seguramente los sustituirían con frecuencia.

Se le hizo un nudo en el estómago cuando entró en la casa y vio los adornos.

El vestíbulo era grande y frío, y lo primero que llamó su atención fue una mancha reluciente de sangre.

Helena dejó escapar un grito ahogado y apartó de forma instintiva la mirada y la cabeza.

—¿Qué sucede? —preguntó Stroud en tono cortante.

—La sangre —se obligó a responder, incapaz de mirar de nuevo. Le vinieron a la mente todas las ejecuciones, los olores y el ambiente nauseabundo, como si se estuviera produciendo una inundación de sangre sobre el mármol blanco.

Stroud miró a su alrededor.

—¿Dónde?

Helena intentó señalar, pero Stroud parecía desconcertada. Volvió a mirar y se dio cuenta de su error: no había sangre.

Sobre una mesa en el centro de la sala, reposaba un ramo de rosas rojas. Solo con mirarlas, sintió un escalofrío.

—No he dicho nada —masculló.

La mujer vestida de verde la observaba. Sus ojos iban de Helena a las rosas y, tras esbozar una leve sonrisa, se dio la vuelta para dirigirse al par de puertas que había al otro lado del vestíbulo.

—Espera aquí —le dijo Stroud. La puerta se cerró, dejando a Helena sola con los muertos. Miró a su alrededor, tratando de asimilar cada detalle salvo las rosas.

El ambiente plomizo parecía más denso dentro del edificio que bajo el opresivo cielo gris. La casa le parecía una caverna, oscurecida con filigranas artesanales. A la derecha, una escalera enorme y ornamentada desembocaba en distintos rellanos con vistas al vestíbulo.

Los pasillos oscuros se internaban en la vivienda, apenas iluminados por unos apliques de tenue luz eléctrica que emitían un zumbido y no mantenían a raya a las sombras. Las ventanas superiores parecían diseñadas para iluminar únicamente la mesa que había en el centro. En el suelo de mármol que la rodeaba, una forma distorsionada de color negro se dibujaba, como si fuera un mosaico. Desde donde estaba, Helena no distinguía qué era.

La casa le parecía sucia. No se veía polvo, pero Helena no podía quitarse la sensación de abandono. El aire era rancio, como si el edificio fuera también un cadáver en descomposición.

De repente, la puerta de enfrente se abrió.

—Entra, Marino —dijo Stroud como si llamara a un animal.

La habitación tenía dos enormes ventanas entramadas que ofrecían vistas a los jardines y a un gran laberinto de setos verdes. Habían retirado las cortinas de invierno para que entrara la luz fría en la estancia. La chica vestida de verde dejó su bastoncito a un lado y se sentó al borde de una silla giratoria, extendiendo sus faldas alrededor como si presumiera de la riqueza de la tela. Al otro lado de la sala, junto a las ventanas, Helena distinguió una figura oculta en la penumbra.

Se le erizó el vello de los brazos.

Stroud la condujo más allá de las sillas giratorias, para encontrarse con aquella persona.

La luz invernal contorneaba su silueta, y no fue hasta que se acercó que Helena empezó a distinguir sus rasgos: piel pálida, cabello rubio plateado.

Por su aspecto, debía de tratarse de alguien mayor, uno de los patriarcas del gremio.

Había conocido a unos cuantos en la Academia. Solían ser iguales: orgullosos, obsesionados con el poder y el estatus, preocupados por las apariencias, siempre exigiendo más respeto.

Justo el tipo de persona que se dejaba manipular con facilidad. Helena sabía que solo tenía que envalentonarse un poco y entonces él le partiría el cuello.

Con suerte, estaría muerta en quince días.

Cuando se dio la vuelta, a Helena se le cerró la garganta. El mundo que la rodeaba desapareció y le fallaron las piernas.

No era mayor en absoluto.

Era el heredero del gremio del hierro: Kaine Ferron.

Lo reconoció, estupefacta. Había sido uno de los pocos alumnos del gremio que permanecieron en la Academia para seguir estudiando. Habían ido al mismo curso, compartido clases, hasta incluso trabajaron como ayudantes en los mismos pisos dedicados a la investigación.

Su mente se negaba a aceptar lo que veía, pero no podía ser otro que Kaine Ferron.

Antes tenía el pelo moreno, pero ahora solo lucía canas. Sin embargo, la palidez de su piel no era consecuencia de la edad, sino que parecía haberse bañado en luz de luna.

Al principio, Helena pensó que debía de ser un cadáver, como el cuerpo de Crowther en la Central, pero los ojos grises plateados que la miraban estaban nítidos: la esclerótica blanca, las pupilas negras, sin venas oscuras bajo la piel. No le vio ninguna vena, como si en lugar de mercurio tuviera sangre.

—Os traigo a la última miembro de la Orden de la Llama Eterna, Sumo Inquisidor —dijo Stroud como si le estuviera enseñando un trofeo—. Creo que os conocisteis en la Academia de Alquimia.

Kaine apartó de ella esos espeluznantes ojos plateados.

—De vista.

—Sé que se ha anticipado a su llegada —siguió Stroud mientras se sentaba—, pero yo no me preocuparía demasiado. No tiene formación ni experiencia de combate reseñable. Será bastante manejable.

Ferron volvió a mirar a Helena sin emoción alguna, pero había cierto cálculo depredador en sus ojos, como los de un lobo.

—Estoy seguro de ello.

Stroud se aclaró la garganta, parecía sentirse incómoda ante la sequedad de Ferron.

—Muy bien. El Sumo Nigromante desea ver resultados antes del solsticio de invierno. Tal como os ha ordenado, deberéis aplicar el método de transferencia temporal tanto como sea posible para entrar en su cerebro sin extinguir su alma. Cuando lo hayáis conseguido y la prisionera se haya acostumbrado a vuestra mente, creo que revertir las transmutaciones de su memoria será sencillo para vos. Podréis examinar lo que esconde y, cuando acabéis, vendré a recogerla. El Sumo Nigromante también quiere extraer sus recuerdos.

Ferron asintió con desdén.

—Estoy segura de que comprendéis que esto es una prioridad absoluta. El resto de las obligaciones quedan relegadas hasta que terminéis.

La chica de verde emitió un sonido repentino, y todos sus ricitos perfectos se estremecieron.

—¿Quiere decir que tenemos que quedárnosla? —espetó—. No creo que sea justo, ni siquiera es paladina. ¿Por qué no sigue en el Reducto con los demás? ¿Por qué tiene que ser aquí? Tengo varias fiestas planeadas y ya he tenido que cancelar tres cenas e inventarme excusas para todas. Nadie me ha preguntado si quería una prisionera —se quejó con un tono agudo y vano—. ¿Y qué es lo que lleva puesto? Si la ve alguien, dará que hablar.

—Cállate, Aurelia —le soltó Ferron en un tono glacial. Ni siquiera se molestó en girarse para mirarla.

—N-no estaba segura de qué ropa debía ponerle —respondió Stroud, de nuevo compungida por la vergüenza—. Evidentemente, no tiene que quedarse con eso. Es solo lo que había disponible.

Las ventanas vibraron y el viento sonó como un aullido grave y serpenteante que recorrió toda la casa. Stroud se sobresaltó, pero Ferron y Aurelia no parecieron darse cuenta.

—No hay nada de lo que preocuparse —aseguró Ferron—. Seguro que le encontramos algo adecuado que ponerse. Aurelia tiene mucha ropa.

Aurelia abrió los ojos de par en par.

—¿Pretendes que le dé mi ropa?

—No queremos que nadie la confunda con el personal. A menos que prefieras que le hagamos algo a medida.

Aurelia soltó un grito de horror, como si esa idea fuera más escandalosa que tener una prisionera o vivir en una casa con sirvientes muertos.

—Estupendo —concluyó Stroud, animada, mientras todos fingían no darse cuenta de que Aurelia estaba a punto de colapsar—. De acuerdo, sois libre de examinarla, Sumo Inquisidor. Es toda vuestra —dijo señalando a Helena.

Ferron la miró sin inmutarse.

—¿Aquí?

—Solo un análisis preliminar para ver si tenéis alguna pregunta antes de que me vaya. ¿O… preferís intimidad?

—No, eres bienvenida si quieres mirar.

Ferron se acercó a Helena. Iba vestido de negro, con ropa propia de la ciudad. El chaleco y el abrigo tenían un diseño intrincado con un bordado de hilo negro que solo se veía cuando le daba la luz. En la garganta lucía un pañuelo blanco como la nieve.

Helena nunca había visto a un alquimista del gremio con tan poco metal encima. Los alquimistas solían llevar metal en todas sus formas: joyas, bordado en la ropa, bastones de caminar, armas… Los escasos alquimistas que se dedicaban a la piromancia no se separaban de sus anillos de ignición, a menos que les obligaran a desprenderse de ellos.

Aurelia iba cubierta de metal, pero Ferron no.

Se quitó un guante negro y dejó a la vista una mano pálida con unos dedos largos.

Un vivemante, había dicho Grace. Claro, no necesitaba el metal.

Helena intentó dar un paso atrás, acostumbrada al peligro que suponían los dedos de Stroud, pero cuando quiso moverse no pudo.

Sin llegar a tocarla, Ferron había introducido en su cuerpo un escalofrío de resonancia tan fino como la seda de araña, tan sutil que apenas lo había sentido. Ahora la retenía con una fuerza invisible. Era diferente a Morrough, no embargaba el ambiente hasta que todo vibraba. Si no hubiera intentado moverse, no se habría dado cuenta de que estaba ahí.

Los ojos de Ferron centellearon, como si notara que se estaba resistiendo. Cuando le tocó suavemente la sien con el dedo índice, entonces sí que sintió su resonancia, vívida como un hilo conductor.

Se sumergió en su cerebro de una forma nítida y perfectamente pulida. La habitación, Ferron y todo lo demás desapareció cuando sus recuerdos se activaron ante sus ojos como un zoótropo.

El camino a Puntaférreo. Penny. Los interrogatorios de Stroud. El liche de la Torre que usaba el cuerpo de Crowther. Las discusiones sobre cuál era la mejor forma de extraer los recuerdos de la mente de Helena.

Shiseo emergiendo de la oscuridad con su pequeño maletín y su lezna. Conforme Ferron retrocedía en su memoria, los recuerdos se atenuaban, reproduciéndose en su cabeza como si hojeara un libro buscando algo interesante.

Retrocedió hasta el tanque de suspensión y la nada se extendió cada vez más. Luego siguió hacia atrás, hasta la Torre, la sangre y los años en el hospital.

Helena nunca se había planteado que su vida pudiera parecer repetitiva e insignificante hasta que la experimentó de esta forma.

Cuando Ferron paró, tenía la mente acelerada. El tacto de Ferron permaneció en ella un poco más, su resonancia aún recorría su cerebro, tiñéndolo todo de rojo.

Por fin, bajó la mano y se quedó ahí, mirándola.

—Bien —dijo al fin.

—Es extraordinario, ¿verdad? —afirmó Stroud desde algún lugar tras él.

—Bastante —coincidió Ferron con una mirada dura como el cristal. Arqueó una ceja sin apartar la mirada de Helena—. La guerra ha terminado. ¿Qué crees que está protegiendo tu cerebro?

La miró a los ojos sin pestañear.

A Luc. Estaba protegiendo a Luc.

—Holdfast está muerto —añadió con mordacidad, como si hubiera leído la respuesta en sus ojos—. La Llama Eterna ya no existe. No queda nadie a quien salvar.

Apartó la mirada con gesto venenoso.

—¿Algo más? —le preguntó a Stroud.

Esta negó con un gesto.

Entonces la parálisis de Helena se desvaneció de golpe. Había estado resistiéndose y, cuando desapareció tan repentinamente, se le doblaron las rodillas. Cayó al suelo y, en un intento de remediarlo, apoyó las manos con todo el peso de su cuerpo. Un dolor desgarrador le atravesó las muñecas, un ardor punzante que le ascendió hasta los hombros.

Se derrumbó completamente.

Aurelia reprimió una risa.

—Según tengo entendido, hablasteis con Shiseo y lo repasasteis todo varias veces antes de que se marchara —escuchó que decía Stroud—. Después de la primera sesión, enviaré a alguien para la evaluación y así podremos establecer un marco de tiempo para los resultados.

—Sí, me han explicado este plan hasta el más mínimo detalle —respondió Ferron sin mostrar ninguna emoción—. Me encargaré de todo. Ahora, si me disculpas.

Pasó por encima del cuerpo de Helena y salió de la habitación sin echar la vista atrás.

Helena intentó incorporarse, pero, al no poder apoyarse en las manos, tuvo que rodar lentamente y usar los codos. Se abrazó las muñecas instintivamente.

Cuando por fin alzó la vista, Stroud se había marchado, y Aurelia estaba esperando con impaciencia a unos metros de distancia. Tenía el bastoncillo aferrado entre los dedos.

—Levántate del suelo —le instó—. Voy a enseñarte tu habitación.

Helena se puso en pie y siguió con cautela a Aurelia hasta el vestíbulo. Le palpitaban dolorosamente las muñecas. El necrómata de la Central los seguía de cerca, pisándoles los talones, mientras Aurelia la guiaba por un pasillo, subía un tramo de escaleras, atravesaba varias habitaciones y doblaba en dirección a otro pasillo.

Allí la luz era más tenue. Por el ángulo en el que entraba la claridad, parecía un ala distinta de la casa. La mayoría de las ventanas estaban cubiertas con cortinas pesadas y los muebles protegidos con sábanas.

—Me gustaría que te quedara claro: que tengamos que alojarte aquí no significa que quiera verte —dijo Aurelia avanzando a paso ligero.

Helena estaba sin aliento tras subir unas escaleras y no lograba seguir el ritmo de Aurelia.

—Entiendo que esos brazaletes te impiden usar la alquimia, aunque tampoco te serviría de mucho aquí. Los Ferron construyeron esta casa con hierro puro, y no me eligieron como esposa de Kaine por casualidad.

Aurelia se detuvo y se giró para mirar a Helena con una mano levantada. Meneó la muñeca con ímpetu, y los anillos de alquimia que decoraban sus dedos se transformaron. Se alargaron, afilándose como cuchillos, haciendo que sus dedos parecieran las patas de una araña.

Helena observó la transmutación con un interés propio de una académica. La resonancia natural del hierro era un fenómeno poco común entre los alquimistas, aunque no tanto como la resonancia del oro o la piromancia. El hierro puro tenía una naturaleza intratable, hasta el punto de que se consideraba algo inerte. La mayoría de los alquimistas no lograban transmutarlo sin exponerlo continuamente a los efluvios que emanaba el lumitio en un Horno de Athanor, e incluso así les salía más rentable hacerlo con acero que con hierro.

Aurelia había realizado esa transmutación con rapidez para presumir. En clase, le habrían restado puntos por exceso de movimiento y una distribución imperfecta del hierro, pero la seguridad con la que había transformado sus anillos implicaba un alto nivel de resonancia férrea y, si la casa estaba construida con hierro, eso significaba que también podía usarla como arma.

Helena bajó la vista y se percató del hierro forjado que recorría los suelos y decoraba las paredes.

—No usamos esta ala —comentó Aurelia mientras seguía avanzando por el pasillo. Sus anillos se habían convertido de nuevo en delicadas bandas alrededor de los dedos—. No quiero verte, especialmente cuando tenga invitados. Mantente fuera de la vista, a menos que te llamemos. Los necrómatas tienen órdenes de vigilarte, así que nos enteraremos si provocas algún problema.

Aurelia se detuvo, clavó el bastoncillo en una de las barras de hierro del suelo y lo hizo girar. Con un chirrido metálico, el hierro se desplazó y una puerta ricamente decorada con adornos de hierro se abrió de par en par.

Detrás se encontraba un dormitorio amplio, con dos ventanas alargadas y una cama con dosel situada entre ellas. Había un sillón orejero junto a una ventana y una mesa tallada al lado. En la pared contraria se erguía un gran armario, y una pesada alfombra cubría casi todo el suelo.

Las paredes se encontraban desnudas, salvo por un reloj colocado demasiado alto para alcanzarlo, pero todo el espacio estaba limpio y parecía bien aireado.

Helena entró en la habitación y miró a su alrededor con cautela.

—Te traerán la comida —dijo Aurelia cerrando la puerta tras de sí.

Hasta que se quedó sola, Helena no se había dado cuenta de lo extraño que era que Aurelia la hubiese escoltado a su habitación.

Tal vez los Ferron no eran tan ricos como su hogar aparentaba.

La casa parecía contar con poco personal. El mayordomo era un cadáver, y quizá lo mismo ocurría con los demás sirvientes. Si estaban tan desesperados por el dinero, eso explicaría por qué no habían podido negarse a acoger a Helena y por qué Ferron se ganaba la vida persiguiendo a los combatientes de la Resistencia, en vez de gestionar el gremio y las fábricas de su familia.

Recordó que los Ferron pertenecían a una de las familias más poderosas y adineradas de Paladia. Habían inventado la industria del acero, lo que les permitió crear un monopolio que no solo se limitaba al comercio de Paladia. La mayoría de los países vecinos también compraban acero a los Ferron.

Era evidente que la fortuna ya no existía si tenían la casa así.

Se acercó a la ventana más cercana. Debajo había un radiador anclado al suelo, y la ventana parecía protegida con un entramado de hierro forjado. Estaba cerrada, así que no había opción de saltar entonces.

Tocó el hierro con la punta de un dedo y no sintió nada. Ninguna conexión al frío metal, solo esa sensación muerta y vacía que emanaba de su muñeca.

Presionó entonces toda la mano contra la superficie de hierro y, con amargura, echó de menos su resonancia. El mundo que había conocido estaba lleno de energía, vibrante con un poder al que se había sentido sintonizada desde que nació.

Ahora todo estaba muerto y esa sensación constante de inercia la desorientaba.

Al asomarse al cristal, vio un bosque y unas montañas a lo lejos.

Reconsideró sus planes. Si los necrómatas iban a vigilarla, lo más probable era que tuvieran la orden de impedir que se suicidara.

Tamborileó los dedos sobre el alféizar de la ventana, ignorando las leves punzadas de dolor que le atravesaban el brazo al hacerlo.

Por desgracia, Ferron no era el patriarca estúpido e iluso que ella había esperado.

Su resonancia se parecía a la de Morrough, superando cualquier límite que Helena hubiera creído posible, pero lo que más le inquietaba era cómo había penetrado en su memoria. Morrough había hecho algo parecido, pero esa violación mental había sido brutal y despiadada; la de Ferron había tenido una precisión quirúrgica.

Antes pensaba que sus matanzas rápidas eran un signo de impulsividad, pero ahora entendía que no necesitaba hacer prisioneros cuando podía acceder a sus mentes y arrebatarles todas las respuestas.

¿Cómo podía enfrentarse ella a algo así? ¿Era capaz de ver solo sus recuerdos o también sus pensamientos?

Se apartó de la ventana y observó la habitación, preguntándose si el extraño aspecto de Ferron sería una consecuencia de sus habilidades.

¿Por qué tenía ese aspecto?

Parecía… destilado. Como si lo hubieran cogido y sublimado hasta que lo único que quedó de él fue una esencia: algo letalmente frío y reluciente. El Sumo Inquisidor.

No era una persona, sino un arma, por lo que Helena tendría que asegurarse de tratarlo como tal.

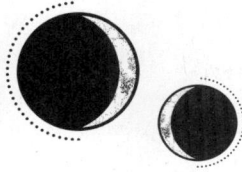

CAPÍTULO 4

HELENA TARDÓ APENAS UNOS MINUTOS en explorar hasta el último rincón de su habitación y el baño privado. Le habían proporcionado los objetos más básicos: jabón, toallas, un cepillo de dientes y un vaso metálico para el agua. Apretó el vaso para ver si se doblaba y lo logró. Si lo partía, tendría un borde afilado con el que podría abrirse las venas.

Tras varios minutos intentándolo, lo único que consiguió fue hacerse rozaduras en los pulgares y que le dolieran ambas muñecas.

Luego probó a arrancar el espejo, pero estaba tan bien anclado a la pared que ni siquiera consiguió meter los dedos por debajo. Tampoco se rompió cuando lo golpeó con el vaso.

Retrocedió, lanzó una mirada furibunda al vaso y torció el gesto al ver su reflejo.

Casi no reconocía a la persona que le devolvía la mirada con el ceño fruncido. Su piel cetrina no había visto la luz del sol en más de un año, su cabello largo y moreno estaba enredado hasta convertirse en una mata indomable. Tenía los rasgos hundidos y parecería una necrómata si no fuera por la rabia que ardía en sus ojos marrones.

Volvió al dormitorio y sintió decepción al darse cuenta de que no había cordeles en las cortinas con los que ahorcarse. Comprobó también por detrás, por si había pasado alguno por alto.

«Sigue viva, Helena», le suplicó una voz en su mente.

Se detuvo, trazando con los dedos el bordado de la cortina, tratando de sofocar aquella voz.

Luc... Oh, Luc. Cómo no iba a atormentarla negándose a aceptar una decisión tan pragmática. Si hubiera estado allí, le habría dicho que su plan era terrible. Siempre detestó este tipo de ideas, que la gente se sacrificara por él y su familia. Siempre se sentía responsable, convencido de que, si hubiera sido mejor, los habría salvado a todos.

Ahora podía oírlo insistiendo, terco, que no iba a morir. Que podía idear un plan mejor si tan solo dejaba de obsesionarse con este.

Helena negó con la cabeza.

—Lo siento, Luc. Esto es lo mejor que puedo hacer.

Se acercó a la puerta que desembocaba en el pasillo.

Las órdenes de permanecer fuera de la vista significaban que podía salir de la habitación. Al pensarlo, un temblor le recorrió el cuerpo y se le aceleró el corazón.

Agarró el pomo, que giró con facilidad. La pesada puerta se abrió sin resistencia, dejando al descubierto un largo pasillo que se adentraba en la oscuridad. Pero, en vez de emocionarse por aquella libertad, el corazón de Helena se detuvo.

Las lámparas de las paredes estaban apagadas. No se había percatado de lo siniestro que resultaba el pasillo: estrecho y retorcido, plagado de sombras acechantes, como dientes afilados, abriendo paso a unas fauces oscuras.

En la Central se había acostumbrado a tener luz constantemente.

Permaneció inmóvil. Era un sentimiento irracional, porque ahora estaba en una casa y había visto demasiadas cosas horribles en su vida como para tener miedo de sombras y pasillos oscuros, pero no logró mover las piernas. El pomo traqueteó entre sus dedos.

La penumbra era como un esófago palpitante; las sombras alargadas se mecían con el viento y amenazaban con tragarla. Si daba un paso más, caería otra vez en aquella oscuridad fría, terrible e interminable.

Nunca la encontrarían.

El terror se le clavó en el cuerpo como una lanza cuando las sombras volvieron a agitarse, arrastrándose hacia ella.

Se le contrajo el pecho y sintió una punzada de dolor en los pulmones. Sin pensarlo, Helena se metió de nuevo en la habitación y cerró la puerta, apoyando su cuerpo contra la superficie fría y sólida. Sentía los pulmones encogidos y el corazón en un puño, no podía respirar.

Sabía que el terror del tanque de suspensión la perseguiría siempre, pero no era consciente de que aquel temor se había enraizado en su interior, extendiéndose a través de los nervios y los órganos hasta paralizarla por completo.

Permaneció agachada y perdió la noción del tiempo, hasta que oyó que alguien llamaba a la puerta. Al sonido le siguió un tintineo de platos y pasos que se alejaban.

Abrió una rendija y encontró un bulto de ropa y una bandeja con comida. Los introdujo rápidamente e intentó no mirar de nuevo hacia la oscuridad acechante del pasillo.

Cuando cerró la puerta, dirigió una mirada de asco a la bandeja. La comida era una porquería, como si alguien hubiera reunido las sobras del día, las hubiera metido en una olla y las hubiera hervido. Prefería morirse de hambre.

Dejó la bandeja a un lado.

Al desplegar el bulto, encontró varios conjuntos de ropa interior, unas medias de lana y un vestido rojo, tan intenso como la sangre.

Había marcas de costura en los dobladillos, en el cuello y en el corpiño, parecía que habían arrancado los bordados y el encaje para hacer las prendas lo más sencillas posible.

Helena se arrepintió amargamente de haberse asustado al ver aquellas rosas.

Volvió a mirar la comida, recordando que debía tener cuidado con Aurelia.

En el fondo del bulto, había tres pares de zapatillas de baile: unos zapatos delicados con una suela fina y poco práctica, y con lacitos que se habían desprendido porque la tela que envolvía los dedos de los pies se estaba desgastando y había perdido el brillo satinado.

Excepto las medias, Helena guardó todo en el armario. Prefería llevar el vestido fino y áspero de la Central.

Por la mañana llegó otra bandeja, con un aspecto aún peor, si es que eso era posible. Helena tenía tanta hambre que eligió con cuidado unos cuantos trozos de comida que no estaban tan hervidos que hubieran perdido el color.

Quiso intentar salir de su habitación de nuevo, pero solo de pensarlo se le formó un nudo en el estómago.

En lugar de eso, se dedicó a hacer ejercicios de calistenia. Al menos, debía ser capaz de subir un tramo de escaleras sin que sus piernas amenazaran con ceder. También tenía los brazos débiles, pero descartó cualquier ejercicio que añadiera peso a las muñecas.

Miró con amargura los grilletes. Siempre se había sentido muy orgullosa de sus manos, de todo lo que podía hacer con ellas.

Cuanto más tiempo dedicaba a buscar excusas para no salir de la habitación, más culpable se sentía.

Cualquier miembro de la Resistencia ya habría memorizado la distribución de la casa, habría identificado posibles armas e incluso habría asesinado a los Ferron.

Lila no se habría permitido ser tan débil, sin importar a qué le tuviera miedo. Pero Helena nunca fue como ella, así que tendría que hacer las cosas a su manera. Era mejor esperar, dejar que Ferron viniera a ella.

Seguro que acudía pronto.

Helena solo podía imaginar cómo sería la transferencia.

Se acordó del cadáver de Crowther que tenía el liche dentro. Tal vez ella acabaría convertida en algo parecido, consciente de lo que le sucedía mientras Ferron la dominaba, poseyendo su mente y su cuerpo.

Al menos, si debía ver a Ferron a menudo, tendría la oportunidad de adivinar qué le sacaba de sus casillas, de encontrar una debilidad.

Se devanó los sesos tratando de recordar lo que sabía de su familia. Los Ferron habían participado en la industrialización alquímica del último siglo.

Crearon el primer gremio del hierro poco después de la fundación de Paladia. El hierro era uno de los ocho metales tradicionales que se asociaban a los ocho planetas: plomo para Saturno, estaño para Júpiter, hierro para Marte, cobre para Venus, mercurio para Mercurio, plata para la Luna, lumitio para Lumitia y oro para el Sol.

Por ser intratable y muy propenso a la corrosión, el hierro se consideraba un metal de bajo rango e innoble, sobre todo comparado con las sustancias incorruptibles, como la plata, el lumitio y el oro. Los Ferron habían sido una familia plebeya, herreros y forjadores que fabricaban arados y herramientas para la agricultura, en vez de trabajos de relumbre, como forjar armas de acero para la Llama Eterna, como hacían otros alquimistas férreos.

Conforme pasó el tiempo y se fueron descubrieron otros metales, el hierro siguió siendo un elemento difícil de tratar y básico, hasta que los Ferron desarrollaron un método para crear acero de forma eficiente mediante la alquimia. Con la precisión de su resonancia férrea, aseguraban una calidad a escala industrial que nadie podía igualar. Fue algo que cambió el mundo, a la par que a los Ferron. Pasaron de ser comerciantes a una burguesía trabajadora que albergaba mucha riqueza mientras la realidad a su alrededor se transformaba al mismo tiempo.

No importó que teológicamente el hierro estuviera clasificado como un metal celestialmente inferior; la era moderna se construyó con acero de la familia Ferron: las fábricas, las líneas de ferrocarril, los vehículos, incluso la propia Paladia, cuya arquitectura se elevaba hacia el cielo al ritmo del desarrollo industrial.

Puntaférreo, aunque ahora estuviera deteriorado, se había erigido como un monumento a esa influencia y riqueza, y al inmenso orgullo que la familia no dejaba de exhibir.

El primer recuerdo que Helena tenía de Kaine Ferron era del segundo curso, no como persona, sino como un nombre en una lista. Helena había sido la que sacó la nota más alta en el examen nacional de Alquimia ese año, desbancando a Ferron, que lo había conseguido el año anterior.

Luc se sintió muy orgulloso de ella. Siempre que tenía ocasión, repetía que el primer año no contaba, porque era la primera vez que Helena estudiaba alquimia y además lo había hecho en un idioma que no era el suyo.

Helena estuvo a punto de desmayarse de alivio. La beca de la Academia dependía de su rendimiento académico y aquel examen era una parte crucial de su evaluación. Su padre lo había dejado todo en Etras para traerla a Paladia, y habrían quedado arruinados si ella hubiera perdido la beca.

Las seis veces que Helena se presentó al examen nacional, el primer puesto osciló entre ambos como un péndulo: Helena Marino, Kaine Ferron.

Una rivalidad, aunque fuese indirecta, que jamás se reconoció en voz alta.

Él pertenecía al gremio y los alumnos del gremio no le dirigían la palabra a la «mascota de los Holdfast».

No comprendía cómo se había convertido en Sumo Inquisidor.

Había cursado una carrera académica, igual que ella. No era un alquimista especializado en combate como Lila, ni había hecho la doble vía como Luc. ¿Por qué un heredero del gremio se dedicaba a cazar y asesinar a todos los miembros que quedaban vivos de la Resistencia?

Cuanto más tiempo pensaba en ello, más le hervía la sangre al saber, aunque fuera de oídas, que existía alguien tan cruel.

De algún modo, era casi poético que fuese Helena la que había acabado cautiva en Puntaférreo.

Ya había vencido a Ferron en el pasado. Si tenía cuidado y era lista, lo haría de nuevo.

CUANDO FERRON NO APARECIÓ AL segundo día, Helena se obligó a salir al pasillo. Ignoró el temblor que le sacudía los órganos y la opresión que le cerraba la garganta. Se pegó a la pared y recorrió con los dedos el revestimiento de madera, sin reparar en el polvo que se le incrustaba en los surcos de las yemas de los dedos, oscureciéndolos como si tuviera una infección.

«Puedes hacerlo», se repetía a sí misma mientras avanzaba bordeando la oscuridad, paso a paso, e intentaba esquivar las sombras más profundas. Quiso abrir la puerta que le quedaba más cerca, pero estaba cerrada con llave, así que siguió adelante un poco más.

El viento gimió entre los corredores, retorciéndose en un grito ahogado. Las ventanas traquetearon y la casa crujió como si tuviera huesos que se resquebrajaran.

Helena intentó respirar, pero no lo logró, era incapaz de hacerlo en ese pasillo donde las sombras se estiraban como si fuesen dedos hacia ella.

Cuando llegó a la tercera puerta, el miedo la detuvo por completo. Se dio la vuelta, mareada, el pasillo giraba a su alrededor y la oscuridad se cernía sobre ella.

Antes de alcanzar la puerta abierta, le fallaron las piernas. La visión se volvió borrosa y todo se oscureció a su alrededor.

Lila Bayard emergió de la oscuridad.

No era la Lila que Helena recordaba. No se trataba de la chica preciosa y esbelta que usaba armadura y tenía el cabello claro trenzado como una corona alrededor de la cabeza, como las estatuas de Lumitia.

Ahora Lila llevaba el pelo corto, casi como un chico. Parecía pequeña, a pesar de su imponente altura.

Fijó la mirada en Helena. El lado derecho de su rostro y cuello estaba amoratado y cubierto con una cicatriz, un tajo largo y cruel que le recorría desde la mejilla hasta la garganta. Sus ojos eran rojos.

—Lila, Lila, ¿qué sucede? ¿Qué te ha pasado?

Helena sintió que tenía cada vez más frío, que los dedos se le entumecían al estirar la mano hacia ella.

Lila abrió la boca para responder, pero entonces se desvaneció.

—Lila…

Cuando Helena abrió los ojos, estaba tirada en el suelo de su habitación con el corazón desbocado.

Intentó enfocar la mirada, pero un dolor intenso y punzante le taladraba la cabeza. Aquello que había visto se desvanecía como el agua entre la arena.

Las ventanas traquetearon con un golpe seco y la casa lanzó un gemido profundo, una vibración que recorrió el suelo como si estuviera cobrando vida. Helena se levantó apoyándose en las manos y se acercó a la ventana.

Las montañas estaban ya blancas, pero la nieve aún no había alcanzado la cuenca del río. Todavía debían de quedar unas semanas para el solsticio de invierno, con el que daba comienzo el año nuevo.

Catorce meses. Helena trató de recordar el último día del que tenía recuerdos durante la guerra. La batalla final tuvo que ocurrir a finales de verano, pero no se acordaba del mes o de las fases lunares exactas. El hospital permanecía ajeno al paso de las estaciones.

Mientras contemplaba el exterior, la puerta se abrió. Un escalofrío recorrió su espalda al darse la vuelta, pensando que sería Ferron.

Pero fue Aurelia la que entró envuelta en un remolino de tela azul, de nuevo cubierta de metal como un exoesqueleto delicadamente afiligranado. Si los Ferron andaban escasos de dinero, seguramente fuese porque la falda de Aurelia estaba hecha con decenas de metros de seda importada.

Tal vez Aurelia poseía una resonancia de hierro poco común, pero parecía una recién llegada respecto al dinero. No es que Helena tuviera alguna experiencia de eso, pero era algo que había aprendido sin quererlo al codearse con las familias nobles que servían a los Holdfast y a la Llama Eterna.

La vestimenta en las fincas solía ser menos formal. Luc le habló en muchas ocasiones de la casa de campo que su familia poseía en las montañas, de que la ropa que allí usaban era mucho más cómoda. Cada año, tras los desfiles del solsticio de verano que celebraban el cumpleaños del principado, siempre la invitaba a ir, para escapar del calor de la ciudad y de las epidemias fluviales que brotaban en las épocas de calor.

Ella siempre prefirió quedarse con su padre.

Años después, sí llegó a conocer la casa de campo, pero fue sola. Luc le había dicho la verdad: era un lugar precioso y la ropa cómoda, pero ella detestó cada minuto que pasó allí.

Aurelia miraba a Helena con repulsión.

—¿Por qué sigues llevando eso? ¿No te has lavado desde que llegaste?

No lo había hecho. Le parecía más seguro estar sucia.

—Sabía que eras extranjera, pero di por hecho que en el cuchitril en el que te encontraron los Holdfast existía una higiene básica.

Helena apretó los dientes.

—Ha llamado Stroud. Se te realizará el procedimiento esta noche. Lávate y arréglate ese pelo asqueroso que tienes antes de que vuelva, o le pediré a los necrómatas que te desnuden y lo hagan ellos. Tenemos algunos que huelen de lo lindo, y los llamaré si vuelvo a verte con esta pinta.

Se dio la vuelta y se alejó mientras la falda hacía frufrú a su paso.

Helena fue al baño, se arrancó su sencillo vestido y giró los grifos de la ducha rápidamente. Las tuberías escupieron varias veces antes de que el agua fluyera entre chirridos y siseos. Se frotó de la cabeza a los pies con un paño tan deprisa como le fue posible e intentó desenredarse el pelo con los dedos. No había peines por ninguna parte.

¿Se habría imaginado Ferron que lo usaría para rajarse la garganta?

No era mala idea, la verdad.

Cuanto estuvo lo bastante aseada, se puso la ropa interior limpia y áspera que le habían dejado, y se obligó a ponerse también el vestido, con cuidado de no mirar el color rojo.

Luego se sentó en la cama y siguió peleándose con los nudos del cabello. Le dolían las manos y las muñecas, pero no estaba dispuesta a poner a prueba la amenaza de Aurelia.

Los paladinos siempre habían considerado que Helena tenía el pelo muy alborotado. El cabello norteño solía ser fino e increíblemente liso, y los rizos solo se toleraban si se moldeaban con una barra de hierro candente que dejaba los mechones con la forma de un sacacorchos.

Cuando Helena se convirtió en sanadora, aprendió a llevarlo dispuesto en dos trenzas apretadas, enroscadas en la nuca, y, aunque ahora intentó trenzárselo, no podía hacer ese movimiento con las muñecas.

La puerta se abrió de par en par con un sonoro golpe, y Aurelia apareció bajo el marco. La recorrió de arriba abajo con sus ojos azul intenso, cargados de desdén. Helena se irguió, tensa, preparándose para el veredicto.

Aurelia soltó un bufido y frunció los labios.

—Vamos.

Helena la siguió en silencio, fijándose en las enrevesadas filigranas de metal que adornaban su ropa, en vez de prestar atención a las sombras que la envolvían.

A su escolta no pareció agradarle el silencio.

—Kaine dice que lo único valioso que tienes es el cerebro. —Miró a Helena por encima del hombro, como si esperara que ese comentario la afectara de algún modo—. Supongo que eso significa que puedo hacer lo que quiera con el resto de ti.

Mientras hablaba, transmutó los dedos en los que llevaba anillos de hierro.

A pesar del poder de su resonancia férrea, los movimientos de Aurelia no eran más que para alardear. Las armas que transmutaba le partirían las falanges si trataba de usarlas de verdad.

Helena dudaba que hubiera recibido algún tipo de entrenamiento formal. Por lo general, los gremios solo enviaban a sus hijos a la Academia; las hijas estaban destinadas al matrimonio. Tal vez les enseñaban algún truco alquímico, pero casi nunca se licenciaban.

Aun así, Helena fingió encogerse y apartó la mirada con cautela, intentando que sus pensamientos críticos no la delataran.

Aurelia hinchó el pecho, apretado bajo el corsé, y volvió a transformar sus dedos.

—Seguro que ahora te arrepientes de haberte unido a los Holdfast. Los gremios siempre estuvieron destinados a ganar. Intentasteis detenernos y mira adónde os ha llevado eso.

Volvió la cabeza y siguió caminando.

El vestíbulo estaba desierto. Aurelia subió los escalones con rapidez y apretó el paso por el pasillo del segundo piso, hasta detenerse en la primera puerta que había a mano izquierda. Tocó un panel de la puerta por encima del pomo, se oyó un chasquido y se abrió la cerradura.

—Es aquí. Entra y espera —le ordenó Aurelia, que miraba a todas partes. Fue entonces cuando Helena se percató demasiado tarde de que estaba cayendo en una trampa.

—Kaine vendrá enseguida. No salgas hasta que llegue —añadió Aurelia.

Y, sin decir nada más, echó a correr por el pasillo, dejando a Helena con la certeza creciente de que no debería estar en esa habitación.

Miró a su alrededor. ¿Debería volver? ¿O había alguna posibilidad de que esto la metiera en un lío tan serio como para que Ferron la matara?

Antes de que pudiera replanteárselo, el pasillo empezó a estirarse y dilatarse hasta que todas las superficies estuvieron fuera de su alcance. El pomo se encogía, mientras las sombras acechaban a su alrededor.

Se abalanzó hacia la puerta, consiguió hacer girar el pomo y se precipitó al interior de la habitación.

Era más pequeña que el pasillo.

Se apoyó contra la puerta y palpó la veta de la madera con la mano abierta, fijándose en todo cuanto la rodeaba en aquel espacio reducido.

Helena se sorprendió al ver que la habitación era igual que la suya: dos ventanas, una cama y un armario, pero en esta había un escritorio y una silla en vez de un sillón. Era todo muy austero.

Se acercó al escritorio junto a la ventana, había un montón ordenado de papeles.

Levantó el primer folio y lo sostuvo bajo la tenue luz, buscando si la correspondencia de Ferron se había traspasado a la página de abajo, pero el papel era grueso y sin marcas visibles. Pasó los dedos por la superficie del escritorio; tenía unas filigranas de plata horizontales, y unas hojas y unas parras talladas que estaban alineadas de una manera perfecta. No había duda: era obra de un alquimista de plata con talento.

El escritorio estaba muy bien conservado, al contrario que las telarañas que cubrían las filigranas de hierro de toda la casa.

Se dio la vuelta, en tensión, atrapada en una habitación en la que, casi con certeza, no debía estar. Dudó si volver o no a la suya, porque sabía que, si Aurelia la descubría, le haría algo desagradable.

¿Pero y si era Ferron quien la encontraba? ¿Colarse en una habitación cerrada le serviría para ganarse algún castigo letal? Helena dudaba que fuera una persona impulsiva y, si Stroud conocía tal cantidad de castigos mediante la vivemancia que no contaban técnicamente como tortura, Ferron, sin duda, también.

Se le secó la boca.

Todavía no sabía cómo sería la transferencia. A pesar de lo mucho que había oído hablar del tema, nadie le explicó qué le iba a hacer Ferron. Helena solo podía suponerlo, basándose en lo que había dicho Shiseo, aunque no tenía mucho sentido, porque Helena fue la que había curado al general Bayard cuando lo hirieron. Había puesto a prueba su conocimiento y habilidad para salvarlo, regenerando poco a poco el tejido cerebral afectado. Cuando sobrevivió, todos lo consideraron un milagro; decían que las manos de Helena estaban bendecidas por Sol.

Ese halago se desvaneció en cuanto el general Bayard despertó. Se había convertido en un niño: un general poderoso con las emociones de un crío de tres años. El que había sido un militar brillante no era capaz de abrir una puerta sin ayuda.

Helena había salvado su cuerpo, pero aprendió de su error que la mente era otro asunto. Durante años intentó, sin éxito, reparar el daño que había causado. En algún rincón oculto de su memoria, se le aparecía Elain Boyle, trayendo una cura, un procedimiento que más tarde aplicaría en Helena. Y ahora los inmarcesibles se enterarían de todo.

Oyó un chasquido en la puerta que la sacó de sus pensamientos. Se giró para ver entrar a Ferron. Tenía la mano en la garganta, pues se estaba desabrochando el cuello de la camisa.

Se detuvo al verla.

—Vaya —pronunció—, esto sí que es una sorpresa.

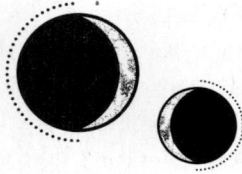

CAPÍTULO 5

HELENA NO RESPONDIÓ. No tenía ni idea de qué esperar o qué hacer, así que observó a Ferron como un animal acorralado.

Este desvió la mirada a la puerta.

—Supongo que ha sido Aurelia quien te ha traído aquí. —Suspiró—. Entiendo que ya ha llegado la hora de empezar.

Se acercó. Helena se tensó, pero Ferron pasó de largo hasta el armario y lo abrió de un tirón.

Por lo visto, no era tan ascético como sugería la habitación. Las puertas del armario ocultaban un estante repleto de decantadores. Escogió uno, vertió un par de dedos de líquido ambarino en un vaso y, tras girarse, le dio un sorbo, mirándola por encima del borde del cristal. Una mirada que empezó en el suelo y fue subiendo lentamente por su cuerpo.

Cuando alcanzó sus hombros, apartó la vista. Observó el vaso y soltó otro suspiro, como si la situación le resultara de lo más inconveniente.

—Acabemos con esto.

Helena no se movió.

Ferron levantó la vista.

—Ven aquí.

Cuando ella no obedeció, esbozó lentamente una sonrisa.

—Puedo obligarte si no lo haces.

Alzó una mano y gesticuló sin aspavientos; sus largos dedos se curvaron con una precisión impecable, nudillo a nudillo.

Las piernas de Helena comenzaron a moverse en contra de su voluntad, como una marioneta manejada desde fuera del escenario. Dobló las piernas, las levantó, cambió el peso, dio un paso y luego otro. Se resistió a ello, tensando cada músculo, pero eso solo hizo que sintiera cómo los huesos amenazaban con partirse.

La presión desapareció cuando estuvo situada a un brazo de distancia de Ferron, que le levantó la barbilla con la yema de un dedo y la miró directamente a los ojos.

—¿Ves? —dijo—. Será más fácil si obedeces.

Le hubiera gustado escupirle, si hubiera podido, pero cuando lo intentó comprobó que tenía la mandíbula apretada y los dientes encajados. Los ojos de Ferron resplandecieron.

—No me pongas a prueba; no conseguirás lo que quieres —le dijo mirándola con esos ojos espeluznantemente caídos—. Mira, esto es nuevo para mí. No suelo hacer prisioneros.

Vació el vaso y lo dejó sobre la mesa.

—Siéntate. —Señaló la silla.

Helena notó que podía mover las extremidades. Por un instante, se planteó salir corriendo, aunque solo fuera por molestarlo, pero la resonancia de Ferron seguía atravesándole los nervios como una cuerda tensa.

Se sentó y, en cuanto lo hizo, no pudo volver a moverse.

Ferron se colocó detrás de ella. Aunque no podía verlo, oía su respiración y el roce de su ropa, lo que hacía que su corazón latiese más deprisa y sus oídos se esforzaran por captar todos los sonidos.

Con una mano le sujetó la mandíbula y le echó la cabeza hacia atrás hasta que quedó mirando el techo. No le veía la cara, solo la otra mano, que llevaba un anillo oscuro que brillaba débilmente bajo la tenue luz. Colocó dos dedos contra su sien y el pulgar entre sus ojos.

Ferron se inclinó hacia delante lo justo para que ella pudiera verle el rostro.

—Ahora veamos lo que es ser tú.

Helena se puso en tensión cuando sintió que un peso le envolvía toda la parte frontal del cráneo. La presión aumentó gradualmente, hasta que algo cedió en su interior, como si los dedos de Ferron hubieran atravesado su frente y se hubiesen metido en su cerebro.

De repente, notó que se abría paso por su mente y por su cuerpo. Sabía que su cráneo seguía intacto, que Ferron aún tenía las manos sobre su piel, pero sentía como si le hubiera abierto la cabeza como quien casca un huevo, dejando su cerebro expuesto a la resonancia de Ferron.

No era un canal de energía como el que empleaba la resonancia normal, sino algo inmenso y fluido que se infiltró en cada rincón de su mente, hasta que Helena empezó a asfixiarse bajo su peso. Las fisuras y los recovecos de su consciencia se llenaron con la creciente opresión de una fuerza desconocida que trataba de ocupar el plano de su existencia cerebral. Cuando no quedaron más recovecos, aplastó su consciencia, que pareció venirse abajo.

Todo se tornó rojo.

Helena estaba gritando.

Lo oía, lo sentía. La parte física de su ser que seguía inmovilizada en la silla gritaba, pero la mente de Helena estaba en otro sitio, resquebrajándose bajo la presión cada vez mayor que Ferron ejercía contra su consciencia.

Ferron no se detuvo, aumentó la intensidad. Helena se estaba ahogando en su propio cerebro, atrapada conforme subía el nivel del agua y aumentaba la presión, sin escapatoria. Ferron la había devorado por completo.

Un zumbido sísmico resonó en sus oídos y, después, apareció una luz, como si una neblina se evaporara.

Aún miraba fijamente el techo cuando un rostro pálido se cernió sobre ella, observándola.

Helena movió los ojos de un lado a otro, sobrecogida por los rasgos crueles de Ferron, por lo extraño y antinatural que era. Con cierto sopor, se percató de que él estaba ya en su mente, mirándose a sí mismo a través de sus ojos.

Y entonces, de repente, desapareció. Arrancó su resonancia y su mente como si fueran malas hierbas.

Toda la mente de Helena se desplomó alrededor de aquel vacío y la integridad de su propia consciencia se resquebrajó.

Cayó de la silla hacia un lado mientras la habitación giraba con ella.

Los pensamientos le dieron vueltas en el cráneo, como un dado lanzado al azar.

¿Dónde estaba?

—Vete.

Reconocía las palabras, pero provenían desde muy lejos. Sonidos. No era etrasiano. El idioma etrasiano era más bello, más melódico.

Esto era…

Un dialecto.

Estaba pensando muy lentamente.

Intentó levantar la cabeza, pero la habitación seguía dando vueltas.

Debía de estar en un barco, cruzando el mar, dejando atrás los acantilados y las islas.

¿Adónde se dirigía?

Al colegio. Sí, iba a estudiar alquimia.

Tenía algo húmedo en la cara. Con esfuerzo, intentó mover la mano y consiguió limpiarlo.

Acabó con los dedos rojos. ¿Por qué estaban rojos?

—¡Vete!

La habitación tembló. Helena sintió cómo una fuerza invisible la levantaba y la empujaba hacia la puerta. Se desplomó, mareada, pero la sacudida la hizo volver en sí y recordar.

Ferron, la transferencia.

Se le encogió el estómago. Si no hubiera estado vacío, habría vomitado.

Miró hacia atrás. Ferron seguía allí, con el rostro blanco y terrorífico, retorcido por la rabia. La habitación vibraba.

—¡He dicho que te vayas! —gritó, como un animal, listo para abalanzarse sobre ella y arrancarle la garganta con sus propios dientes.

Un terror absoluto la impulsó a ponerse en movimiento. Se incorporó, abrió la puerta y huyó.

El suelo parecía hundirse bajo sus pies. Aún lo veía todo bañado en rojo, por mucho que parpadease, como si las paredes estuvieran cubiertas de sangre y las sombras hechas de entrañas. Siguió frotándose los ojos mientras buscaba desesperadamente una salida.

Lo único que oía era su respiración agitada y el sonido de sus pies contra la madera desnuda. Sentía el hierro del suelo como si fuera hielo.

Al llegar a la parte superior de las escaleras, supo que iba a sufrir una conmoción, le pesaban las extremidades como si fueran de plomo, empujándola hacia el suelo. Su cuerpo se enfriaba cada vez más conforme la consumía un escalofrío febril.

Se mareó y estuvo a punto de caer escaleras abajo, así que se agarró a la barandilla para mantenerse recta y contempló el vestíbulo inferior.

Las rosas ondeaban como si estuvieran sumergidas bajo el agua, el suelo se movía y, a su alrededor, daba vueltas un dragón negro.

Se enroscaba hacia el interior, girando en torno a la mesa, con las alas extendidas y la cabeza gacha, de forma que la cola quedaba atrapada entre los dientes, consumiéndose a sí mismo.

Era un uróboro, y en su visión teñida de rojo, parecía que estaba nadando en sangre.

¿Y si se tiraba desde la balaustrada? No había nadie que la pudiera detener. Los secretos que Luc le hubiera confiado estarían a salvo, y Ferron habría fracasado.

Se inclinó hacia delante con manos temblorosas.

Se tiraría de cabeza.

Tenía que morir al instante, o Ferron usaría la vivemancia para mantenerla con vida.

Solo un poco…

Alguien le agarró el brazo con fuerza y la echó hacia atrás un segundo antes de que se lanzara por encima de la barandilla.

Al girarse, encontró a Ferron, que la fulminaba con la mirada.

—Ni. Se. Te. Ocurra.

Trató de zafarse y salir corriendo, pero Ferron la apartó de la barandilla y la obligó a bajar las escaleras mientras Helena lo golpeaba y lo arañaba para liberarse. Pero él no se detuvo. La arrastró por toda la casa, abrió la puerta de su habitación de una patada y luego la soltó sobre la cama.

Helena cayó, respirando entrecortadamente; le dolían las manos y las muñecas.

—¿Creías que no sabría que intentarías suicidarte? —preguntó Ferron con veneno en la voz—. Como si hubiera algo que le gustase más a la Llama Eterna que morir por sus causas.

—Creía que preferías vernos muertos. —Le dolía tanto la cabeza que quería vomitar.

Ferron soltó una risotada.

—Considérate la única excepción a esa norma. El Sumo Nigromante quiere saber tus secretos y, hasta que los consiga, no vas a morir.

Miró su habitación y pareció que le brillaban los ojos. Después, los cerró y sacudió la cabeza.

—Pensé que la transferencia sería suficiente por una noche, pero parece que te has empeñado en ponértelo lo más difícil posible.

Se echó sobre ella.

Helena lo observó horrorizada.

—Veamos qué más ideas tienes. —Posó los dedos fríos en su sien.

No era una transferencia, y Helena sintió tanto alivio que estuvo a punto de relajarse. Pero entonces comprendió que estaba violando sus recuerdos.

La resonancia de Ferron se coló por su mente como una brisa, haciendo que se estremecieran todos sus pensamientos.

Se movió lento. En vez de recorrer su vida, se limitó a interesarse por los últimos acontecimientos, serpenteando entre sus recuerdos como una corriente de agua.

Pareció leer detenidamente cada detalle: cuando exploró su habitación, cómo la asustaba el pasillo, y lo que había pensado sobre él y su familia, también sus intentos de hacer ejercicio.

Cuando terminó, se le había secado la sangre que le corría por la cara, dejándole surcos en las mejillas.

—Diligente, como siempre —comentó Ferron en tono burlón, y apartó la mano.

Helena apretó la mandíbula.

Todavía estaba inclinado sobre ella, con la mano clavada en el colchón junto a su cabeza.

—¿De verdad crees que puedes engañarme para que te mate?

Helena contempló el dosel fijamente.

—Inténtalo si quieres. —Se giró para marcharse, pero se detuvo como si hubiera recordado algo—. No vuelvas a entrar en mi habitación. Si quiero saber de ti, vendré aquí.

Cuando por fin se fue, Helena no se movió.

No había depositado demasiada fe en sus planes. Siempre supo que sus probabilidades de éxito eran ínfimas, pero, aun así, había tratado de convencerse de lo contrario. Luc no se rendiría. Si él estuviera allí, lucharía hasta el último aliento. ¿Cómo iba a traicionarlo no haciendo nada?

Pero Luc estaba muerto. Independientemente de lo que hiciera, no lo traería de vuelta.

Empezó a temblar sin control. Se acurrucó, hecha una bola, y se metió entre las sábanas. La herida que sentía en la cabeza creció hasta convertirse en un hoyo que la absorbía, y la piel se tornó tirante, como si fuese un exoesqueleto membranoso.

Las sábanas se humedecieron del sudor cuando empezó a subirle la fiebre. Tenía el cuerpo helado, pero su mente estaba ardiendo.

El tiempo se deformó, retorciéndose, y Helena perdió la noción de todo lo que no fuera su miseria.

Oyó voces, muchas voces. Le vertieron por la garganta brebajes repugnantes que le hicieron dar arcadas, unos líquidos abrasadores que le calcinaron los órganos. Le aplicaron sobre la piel sustancias calientes y también otras frías y pegajosas. La levantaron y la sumergieron en un agua gélida, luego la sacaron para que respirara y la volvieron a sumergir.

Su mente ardía como unas ascuas que lo quemaban todo a su alrededor.

Hubo agujas, unos pinchazos que apenas sintió y luego unas punzadas de dolor agónico en los brazos.

La presión en su cabeza aumentó, bloqueando cualquier pensamiento que pudiera surgir.

Al cabo de un rato, desfalleció. Su mente se desconectó como si cayera en caída libre.

Había sangre por todas partes. Estaba en el hospital del Cuartel General. Sonaban unas campanas, y el personal médico y de enfermería arrastraba cuerpos cuyos rostros se emborronaban al pasar.

Helena sostenía a un chico moribundo en sus brazos. Trató de tranquilizarlo, de centrarse también ella misma, de no dejarse arrastrar por el pánico que iba adueñándose de la sala como unas garras que le oprimían los pulmones, pero él no permitía que lo curase. Cada vez que lo intentaba, el chico la rechazaba. La sangre negra brotaba de sus heridas a borbotones y su calor pegajoso se adhería a la piel de Helena. La gente la llamaba entre el caos, pero ella tenía que salvar a ese chico.

Estaba ahí mismo.

Al final, el chico dejó de resistirse. Helena lo percibió a través de su resonancia y, por un instante, sintió un atisbo de esperanza al notar la sensación vibrante de la vida. Pero entonces murió y para Helena fue como recibir un puñetazo en el pecho. Demasiado tarde.

Contempló los cadáveres que se amontonaban a su alrededor, apilados unos sobre otros, un muro que no dejaba de crecer y que amenazaba con aplastarla, ríos de sangre que serpenteaban por el suelo.

Trató de respirar. El olor a bilis, a carne quemada y sangre, a sudor, desechos y líquido antiséptico le ardió en la nariz y le quemó los pulmones hasta asfixiarla.

Allá donde mirara había más cadáveres, incluso bajo sus pies. Los pisaba cuando se movía.

Decisiones: quién vivía y quién moría. Tenía que tomar decisiones.

Debía decidirlo ella. Estiró la mano con dedos temblorosos, pero una mano tomó la suya y la detuvo.

Era Luc.

Helena emitió un grito ahogado de alivio y se aferró a él.

Estaba de pie con su armadura dorada; se había quitado el yelmo para que pudiera verle la cara. Le estaba sonriendo y, por un instante, la pesadilla desapareció.

Luego empezó a caerle sangre por la cara.

Lila se encontraba a su lado, con una aguja en la mano. Tenía el pelo claro recogido en una corona alrededor de la cabeza, pero la mitad de su rostro estaba podrido, despellejado, con el cráneo al descubierto. Había alguien más junto a ella, aunque Helena no lograba recordar su rostro.

Al otro lado vio a Titus y a Rhea y, detrás de ellos, al Consejo y a la Llama Eterna, dispuestos en círculo a su alrededor.

Todos sus rostros eran un borrón, todos excepto el de Luc.

Luc seguía vivo. Sangraba, pero Helena podría curarlo. Su mano le tembló al buscarlo, y entonces habló:

—Estoy muerto por tu culpa.

Helena sacudió la cabeza; no le salía la voz.

—Mira, Hel —dijo Luc. Se tocó la coraza y la armadura dorada se derritió, dejando a la vista su pecho desnudo. Tenía un cuchillo negro y reluciente clavado entre las costillas, una herida limpia. La incisión se extendió, abriéndole el torso hasta que el cuchillo cayó al suelo, repiqueteando, y sus órganos se derramaron, negros por la gangrena. El olor a descomposición lo inundó todo, como si llevara meses pudriéndose—. ¿Lo ves?

—No, no… —Intentó acercarse a él igualmente, pero Luc se deshizo, dejando los dedos de ella teñidos con su sangre.

Entonces apareció su madre. Helena no distinguía su rostro, pero sabía que era ella. La embriagó un aroma a hierbas secas cuando se plantó delante de Helena.

Esta quiso acercarse, pero su madre se deshizo en neblina.

Luego su padre.

Estaba junto a los norteños. Tenía los ojos negros y el cabello oscuro rizado, igual que el suyo.

Llevaba su bata médica de color blanco y, cuando lo miró a los ojos, le dedicó una sonrisa. Justo por debajo de la mandíbula lucía un tajo que imitaba la curva de su sonrisa; lo atravesaba de oreja a oreja.

—Helena —le dijo—. Estoy muerto por tu culpa.

Dio un paso hacia ella con un bisturí brillante en la mano.

Helena no se movió; esta vez no se resistió cuando la cogió entre sus brazos y le rajó la garganta.

CUANDO EL MUNDO VOLVIÓ A cobrar vida, Helena deseó estar muerta.

Le palpitaba la cabeza y tenía el pelo pegado a las mejillas y a la frente. En la habitación hacía un calor insoportable. Su boca estaba tan seca que parecía que se le iba a resquebrajar la lengua.

Con esfuerzo, logró rodar sobre un costado. En la mesita de noche había una jarra y un vaso de agua, junto a varios frascos. Cogió el vaso con torpeza y bebió el agua de un trago.

Se volvió a tumbar y retiró las sábanas con un movimiento brusco. El olor a cataplasma de mostaza le quemaba las fosas nasales. Doblando el cuello, volvió a mirar los frascos que había en la mesa: pastillas de hierro y arsénico, también sales aromáticas e ipecacuana.

Extendió el brazo para coger el arsénico, pero, al acercar la mano, la puerta se abrió y entró el hombre nervioso y tartamudo de la Central, acompañado de Ferron.

—Es poco probable que mejore de la fiebre si continúa el procedimiento —decía el hombre, que parecía tan asustado de Ferron como lo había estado de Morrough.

Sin prestar atención a sus palabras, Ferron se fijó de inmediato en la mesita de noche y en el frasco que Helena había estado a punto de agarrar. Cruzó la habitación a zancadas, cogió los tres frascos y se los metió en el bolsillo sin tan siquiera mirar a Helena.

Cabrón.

—¿Tengo que aguantar esto todas las semanas? —preguntó Ferron, que la observaba con el ceño fruncido, como si fuera un perro callejero al que preferiría ahogar.

El hombre inclinó la cabeza.

—Según tengo entendido, la asimilación del proceso de transferencia que desarrolló la Llama Eterna se diseñó para ir generando una tolerancia progresiva. Al igual que sucede con el mitridatismo tradicional, provoca efectos secundarios. La próxima vez podréis avanzar un poco más, pero, como consecuencia, ella sufrirá unas fiebres mentales de igual magnitud. Debéis entender que no es un estado natural del ser humano. Nunca se ha conseguido que un cuerpo vivo sobreviva a ninguna presencia de otra alma. Deberíais considerar un milagro que aún siga viva. Como el único propósito de todo esto es mantenerla con vida lo suficiente para revertir las transmutaciones, el deterioro a largo plazo es irrelevante.

—No tengo tiempo para hacer de niñera —replicó Ferron mirándo-lo con desdén—. Tu cura es casi tan mala como la enfermedad. A este paso, no creo que vaya a sobrevivir lo suficiente como para que pueda descubrir algo. Que tolere la transferencia y consiga revertir por comple-to todo lo que le hicieron a su memoria son solo los primeros pasos. Luego tendré que encontrar la información, y eso podría llevar meses. No pienso consentir que todo esto se vaya al traste solo porque tú has decidido que es «irrelevante».

El hombre se estremeció y encogió el cuello como si quisiera hundir-lo en la cavidad del pecho, subiendo los hombros hasta las orejas.

—Os lo aseguro, Sumo Inquisidor, es poco probable que muera por el arsénico. Puede que muestre algunos signos de envenenamiento, pero, según nuestros estudios, el procedimiento acabará antes de que desarro-lle una necrosis grave o algún daño significativo en el hígado.

—¿Cómo sabes cuánto va a durar este procedimiento? Ni siquiera sabemos lo que le hicieron a Bayard. —La voz de Ferron se había vuelto letal—. Si tan seguro estás de que no va a morir antes de que el Sumo Nigromante haya obtenido sus respuestas, y yo debo seguir tu consejo, entonces quiero que lo expliques delante de nuestro líder supremo, y le dejes claro que voy a actuar siguiendo tus consejos y teorías.

El hombre perdió el color que le quedaba.

—B-bueno, visto así, es posible que, al espaciar un poco más las se-siones, reduzcamos los efectos secundarios y las fiebres mentales. Pero yo no me atrevería a dar consejos. Veréis, no soy experto en esta nueva cien-cia. Esto debe decidirlo Stroud o el Sumo Nigromante.

—Te han mandado a ti. Así que espero que al menos sepas lo sufi-ciente como para tener una opinión —replicó Ferron.

El hombre se secó la frente.

—Os aconsejo fervientemente que Stroud la visite para que ella pue-da daros alguna recomendación —dijo evitando la mirada de Ferron.

—¡Vete!

Helena se encogió.

Ferron observó cómo el hombre desaparecía por la puerta y, acto se-guido, fulminó a Helena con la mirada, como si toda esa situación fuera culpa suya.

Se acercó, y Helena se encogió de nuevo, pero su mano pasó de largo y se deslizó por debajo de la almohada, donde rebuscó entre las sábanas para asegurarse de que no hubiera conseguido robar nada de arsénico.

Helena lo miró con odio hasta que Ferron estuvo convencido de que no tenía veneno escondido por ninguna parte y se marchó de la habitación, pegando un portazo.

Le temblaban las piernas cuando se levantó. Tuvo que sentarse en el suelo, bajo la alcachofa de la ducha, porque estar de pie le resultaba agotador, pero se sintió mejor cuando se quitó de encima todo el sudor y el olor de las cataplasmas.

El horrible vestido rojo estaba lavado, planchado y guardado en el armario junto a nuevos vestidos, todos ellos rojos. Algunos tendían más al burdeos, mientras que otros eran de un tono más vivo. Los habían teñido, todavía quedaban entre las costuras algunas trazas del verde salvia y el rosa claro originales.

Estaba claro que, cuando a Aurelia se le metía algo en la cabeza, no había quien la hiciera cambiar de opinión.

***

STROUD LLEGÓ AL DÍA SIGUIENTE, acompañada de una sirvienta muerta y de Mandl, o, mejor dicho, del cadáver que ahora ocupaba esta.

La sirvienta era una mujer mayor, vestida con el mandil típico de los empleados del hogar. Su cabello castaño claro estaba peinado cuidadosamente hacia atrás, y tenía arrugas alrededor de la boca y los ojos. Estos estaban velados por una neblina espeluznante, que contrastaba con el resentimiento que brillaba con fuerza en los ojos nuevos de Mandl.

—Levanta —le ordenó Stroud a Helena mientras dejaba un maletín médico sobre la mesa.

Helena obedeció sin pronunciar palabra y se mantuvo impasible mientras Stroud la palpaba. Notó cómo las muñecas de Helena habían encogido en el interior de los grilletes y comprobó sus constantes vitales, chasqueando la lengua con irascibilidad.

—Vaya, menuda decepción —dijo al fin—. La verdad es que esperaba que lo llevases mejor.

Helena no dijo nada, aunque notó cierto sentimiento triunfal en su pecho.

—Supongo que era demasiado esperar que tuvieras la resiliencia física de un hombre como Bayard —añadió Stroud con un resoplido, tras revisar durante un minuto sus órganos con una resonancia intrusiva.

Posó los dedos sobre la cabeza de Helena y envió un leve escalofrío de energía a su mente. Helena torció el gesto por el dolor; aún sentía la mente en carne viva.

—Este nivel de inflamación después de siete días me parece preocupante. Ninguno de los sujetos de prueba muestra estos síntomas.

Se mordió el labio y miró a Mandl con gesto grave.

—Es una pena que no nos informaras de su existencia en su momento. Esto sería ahora mucho más fácil.

Mandl inclinó la cabeza con rigidez, pero, a los ojos de Stroud, aquello no era suficiente.

—Deberías darme las gracias de que no le haya contado a Su Eminencia que, si lo hubiéramos descubierto antes, aún tendríamos el cadáver de Boyle y también a una animante para los inmarcesibles.

—Ya he pedido perdón —replicó Mandl—. No sé qué más quieres que haga o por qué me has traído aquí.

—Te concedieron la ascensión por recomendación mía. Si esto se va a convertir en una molestia para mí, también lo será para ti —dijo Stroud—. Y, si algo me cuesta a mí, me aseguraré de que a ti te cueste aún más.

Stroud se giró hacia Helena y la examinó de nuevo con una expresión cada vez más amarga.

—Tendremos que retrasar la próxima intervención hasta que recupere fuerzas. Si muere antes de tiempo, perderemos la información.

Luego volvió la mirada hacia la otra necrómata que había en la habitación.

—¡Sumo Inquisidor!

La sirvienta giró la cabeza y enfocó los ojos neblinosos en Stroud.

—Quiero hablar con vos. En privado.

La sirvienta necrómata asintió y señaló la puerta.

De todos los usos que le daban a la nigromancia, la creación de sirvientes para los Ferron le parecía uno de los más crueles. En una guerra, podía comprender los horribles razonamientos que llevaban a actuar, pero los sirvientes de Puntaférreo eran civiles, asesinados para no tener que pagar por sus servicios.

Con cada minuto que pasaba en la casa, más crecía el odio que sentía por Ferron. Conocía la historia, el lujo y los privilegios de su familia. Una vida fácil. Los Ferron no habrían llegado a nada sin los Holdfast y la Academia de Alquimia; su fortuna jamás hubiera existido sin ellos.

Deberían haber estado agradecidos, haber mostrado su lealtad a Luc por lo que su familia les había dado, pero fueron unos traidores y eligieron a Morrough.

Tal vez, el dragón uróboro no solo era un elemento de decoración pretencioso, sino algo de lo que los Ferron se sentían orgullosos: un presagio de una voracidad destructiva e insaciable que no dejaba más que ruinas a su paso.

AL DÍA SIGUIENTE, FERRON ENTRÓ en su habitación. El cuerpo de Helena se quedó rígido; el miedo la embargó como una marejada. El dolor físico de la transferencia se retorcía en su mente, como la réplica de un temblor que no cesa.

Se detuvo en la puerta y la contempló con esos ojos claros que destellaron al fijarse en los dedos de Helena, que le temblaban incontroladamente cada vez que se sobresaltaba. Los escondió entre los pliegues de la falda.

—Stroud quiere que salgas al jardín —dijo—. Cree que el aire fresco mejorará tu constitución. —Le tiró un bulto de ropa—. Póntela.

Helena lo desenrolló y descubrió que se trataba de una capa gruesa teñida de carmesí. Frunció el ceño.

—¿Pasa algo?

Lo miró.

—¿Solo tenéis tinte rojo en esta casa?

—Así te distinguen mejor los necrómatas. ¡Vamos!

Ferron salió al pasillo y Helena lo siguió con cautela. Las lámparas del corredor proyectaban una luz tenue que ahuyentaba las sombras. Ferron se dirigió al extremo de aquella ala de la casa y bajó por unas escaleras que desembocaban en unas puertas dobles que se abrían al porche del jardín.

Estaba lloviendo, y una ráfaga de viento rodeó la casa y le azotó el rostro. A Helena se le escapó un grito sobrecogido.

Ferron se giró de inmediato.

—¿Qué?

—Había… —Se le rompió la voz y tragó saliva—. Había olvidado cómo era sentir el viento.

Ferron apartó la mirada, incómodo.

—El jardín está vallado. Puedes pasear por donde quieras.

Helena miró a su alrededor y se fijó en los detalles de la casa y de los edificios circundantes. El porche donde estaban continuaba más allá de aquella ala de la casa y se transformaba en un sendero techado que conectaba la casa principal con el resto de los edificios, rodeándolo todo. Se podía recorrer el camino desde las verjas hasta la casa y los edificios, sin exponerse a la lluvia, como si formara un anillo de hierro.

—Vamos. —Ferron le hizo un ademán con la mano y se sentó a una mesa que tenía con dos sillas. Sacó un periódico del abrigo.

Los ojos de Helena leyeron los titulares sin vacilar.

«¡APRESADA TERRORISTA DE LA LLAMA ETERNA!», rezaba en la parte superior, todo en mayúsculas.

Se acercó sin pensarlo. ¿A quién habrían encontrado?

Grace le dijo que todos estaban muertos, pero eso demostraba que había supervivientes. Ferron no los había matado a todos.

Este alzó la vista y Helena se quedó paralizada, incapaz de despegar los ojos del periódico, buscando con desesperación algún nombre.

—¿Quieres verlo? —preguntó arrastrando las palabras de un modo que le erizó la piel.

Abrió el periódico de golpe y Helena contempló desconcertada una foto suya, drogada y sedada en la Central. Estaba demacrada, con el rostro contraído, agotada por la abstinencia de la droga del interrogatorio, y el pelo enmarañado.

Era evidente que querían mostrarla como una extremista sucia y salvaje.

«La última fugitiva de los terroristas de la Llama Eterna ha sido apresada e interrogada», proclamaba el subtítulo por encima del pliegue del periódico.

—Por fin eres famosa, y mira, yo también salgo. —Los ojos de Ferron relucieron con maldad al señalar la foto de sí mismo que aparecía más abajo, en la misma columna, en ese mismo jardín, con los pináculos de la casa de fondo—. Por si alguien quiere saber dónde estás o quién te mantiene cautiva.

Helena lo miró desconcertada. ¿Por qué querrían publicitar que estaba cautiva y dónde se encontraba? ¿Y por qué justo ahora? Se había pasado semanas en la Central, su detención era agua pasada.

—Pensé que sería una trampa demasiado obvia —dijo Ferron con un suspiro, pasando la página—. Pero, claro, tu Resistencia nunca fue famosa por su inteligencia. Las cosas más sutiles se escapan a su comprensión. El Sumo Nigromante confía en que, si queda alguien, se sentirá moralmente obligado a venir a rescatar a la última ascua de la Llama. —La miró de reojo—. Yo tengo mis dudas, pero supongo que no está de más intentarlo.

Se echó hacia atrás y volvió a centrarse en la siguiente columna de texto.

Helena trastabilló también hacia atrás.

¿Por eso la habían enviado a Puntaférreo en vez de dejarla en la Central, para usarla como cebo?

Un gemido estrangulado se le escapó de la garganta. Dio media vuelta y bajó los escalones hasta que estuvo bajo la lluvia. No tenía adónde ir, pero debía dirigirse a algún sitio.

La capa, anudada a su garganta, la ahogaba, la arrastraba. Tironeó de ella con los dedos hasta que la soltó y se libró de su peso. Salió corriendo al jardín.

La lluvia gélida empapó la tela fina y moderna de su vestido, pero Helena apenas la sentía. Más allá de Puntaférreo, las torres de la ciudad se alzaban oscuras. Buscó el faro, la luz que siempre había brillado en lo alto de la Torre de Alquimia y que la Llama Eterna se había encargado de mantener encendida desde la fundación de Paladia, pero no la encontró. Se había apagado.

Aun así, se movió en su dirección, aunque, cuando llegó al borde del jardín, las torres desaparecieron detrás del muro. Fue de un lado a otro en busca de alguna escapatoria, hasta que al final llegó a la verja. Sabía que sería inútil, pero no pudo evitarlo.

La puerta estaba fabricada de un hierro forjado con tantas florituras que era imposible colarse entre los barrotes, y estaba cerrada a cal y canto. Zarandeó la verja con fuerza, hasta que le dolieron las muñecas.

Intentó treparla, pero las zapatillas se le rompían, y el hierro estaba tan frío que le quemaba la piel. Cuando intentó auparse, el dolor de las muñecas le dejó las manos entumecidas.

Al otro lado del jardín, Ferron seguía leyendo el periódico, sin preocuparse de los intentos de Helena por escapar.

Quiso gritar. Agarró la verja y volvió a zarandearla.

¿Y si alguien venía sin saber que estaba cayendo en una trampa?

Alguien que hubiese conseguido sobrevivir todo este tiempo y que acabaría en prisión por su culpa.

Dio una bocanada de aire, sentía como si el pecho fuera a abrírsele en canal. Finalmente, se dejó caer, zarandeando la verja una y otra vez, como si el hierro fuera a doblarse si seguía insistiendo.

Al cabo de un rato, abatida, volvió a la casa.

Adonde quiera que mirara solo había gris: el césped muerto y deshojado, los árboles esqueléticos, la casa oscura con sus enredaderas y sus pináculos negros. Hasta la ladera erosionada de la montaña y la cima blanca estaban envueltas en la neblina del cielo encapotado.

Era como si hubieran robado el color del mundo. Nada tenía tonalidades, menos ella. Helena estaba ahí plantada, con sus ropas de color rojo sangre, contrastando con los demás tonos monocromáticos.

El viento azuzaba la lluvia, abofeteándola con gotas congeladas que la hacían estremecer. Estaba completamente empapada, y sus manos empezaban a volverse blancas; le dolían los dedos con cada ráfaga de viento. El metal de los grilletes le provocó un escalofrío que le caló hasta los huesos.

Se llevó los dedos a los ojos e intentó pensar. ¿Qué podía hacer? Seguro que era capaz de encontrar alguna solución.

No, el plan seguía siendo el mismo: morir, por mano de Ferron o por la suya propia.

La lluvia le caía por el pelo y la cara mientras caminaba forzadamente de vuelta a la casa. En el rellano de los escalones que llevaban al ala principal de la casa la esperaban dos necrómatas. Eran los mismos de la Central. Se estaban descomponiendo y parecían tan decrépitos que se mimetizaban con la fachada de piedra, pero, al acercarse Helena a Ferron, ambos la observaron.

Este levantó la vista y la miró con dureza.

—No has estado fuera el tiempo suficiente. Sigue caminando.

Volvió al jardín. Gracias a los árboles que se alzaban en el centro, desapareció de su vista cuando se acurrucó en el pasillo techado del jardín para recuperar el calor. Desde allí veía su capa sobre la gravilla, empapada de lluvia. Se cruzó de brazos para intentar conservar el calor corporal.

Poco a poco, los temblores desaparecieron. Una ráfaga de viento la arrasó de nuevo. Se sentía fina como el papel, tan cansada que podía quedarse dormida allí mismo.

Lo cual podría indicar hipotermia…

Si se lograba dormir de esa manera, sus órganos dejarían de funcionar y fallecería. Una vez leyó que era una de las formas más apacibles de morir. Así que se dejó arrastrar por la inconsciencia hasta que todo se volvió agradablemente difuso.

—Qué creativa —dijo Ferron, con una voz que sonaba más fría que el viento. Unos dedos la agarraron del brazo y sintió calor de nuevo al desbocársele el corazón, que bombeó sangre caliente por todo su cuerpo.

Helena lanzó un grito ahogado y quiso soltarse, pero ya era demasiado tarde. Ferron la miró con furia.

—Levanta.

Se puso en pie con torpeza; le dolían las muñecas. Aún estaba azulada por el frío y las extremidades seguían entumecidas debido a la congelación, pero ahora tenía demasiado calor para morir.

—No me obligues a arrastrarte —gruñó Ferron entre dientes, y se dio la vuelta y se alejó.

Helena lo siguió de mala gana. En la puerta los esperaba una sirvienta. Era la tercera que veía, pero estaba muerta, al igual que los demás. Esta era más joven y llevaba el uniforme de criada, y en la mano tenía un cepillo y un trapo. Helena intentó pasar a su lado, pero ella no la dejó avanzar.

—Aurelia se pondrá histérica si entras con barro en su casa. Siéntate.

—Sé limpiarme sola —replicó Helena con rigidez.

—Me da igual —dijo Ferron. Helena notó que empleaba la resonancia para contener sus nervios, y le cedieron las rodillas, por lo que tuvo que sentarse en una silla. La criada se arrodilló y empezó a limpiar las zapatillas mojadas de Helena, mientras esta aguardaba en tensión, debatiéndose entre el estupor y la vergüenza.

La Fe afirmaba que el alma y el cuerpo permanecían unidos únicamente hasta la cremación. Solo entonces, cuando el fuego consumía la carne, el alma etérea se desprendía de la forma terrenal que la había contenido. Una persona que hubiera vivido con devoción y sin maldad liberaba un alma pura, que ascendía a lo más alto de los reinos celestiales.

Si el cuerpo no se incineraba, entonces el alma quedaba atrapada, incapaz de ascender, y corría el peligro de contaminarse de la putrefacción del cuerpo. Además, si se abandonaba durante mucho tiempo, la impureza del cuerpo podía convertir el alma en gusanos e insectos, en enfermedades y otras formas grotescas de maldad, condenados a hundirse bajo la superficie de la tierra hasta consumirse para siempre en el fuego oscuro y líquido del Abismo.

Al reanimar un cuerpo, se corría el peligro de sufrir esa metamorfosis. Y atar tanto el cuerpo como el alma a un nigromante hacía que hasta las almas más puras se corrompieran tanto que jamás llegarían a ascender, a menos que las liberaran con fuego sagrado.

Helena no pudo evitar contemplar el rostro de la criada en busca de algún indicio que indicara que aún le quedaba alma, pudriéndose lentamente, atrapada en un estado que no era ni la vida ni la muerte. La mirada de la criada estaba vacía. Si quedaba algún vestigio de alma en ella, estaba sometida a la voluntad de Ferron.

Helena alzó la vista para mirarlo.

—Eres un monstruo.

Ferron arqueó una ceja.

—Lo sé. Te has dado cuenta, ¿verdad?

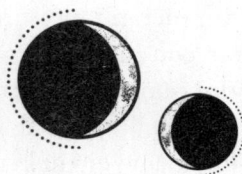

CAPÍTULO 6

FERRON SE MARCHÓ CUANDO LA criada terminó de limpiar las zapatillas de Helena, y esta se puso en pie de inmediato. No soportaba que ese cadáver siguiera tocándola.

La criada entró en la casa. En cuanto se dio la vuelta, Helena aprovechó para coger el periódico que Ferron había dejado allí y se lo escondió detrás de la espalda. Después, respiró hondo y la siguió.

Se concentró en el papel que palpaba con la mano mientras corría hacia las escaleras.

Las sombras se cernían sobre ella, pero Helena se negó a mirarlas. En su lugar, se dedicó a contar todos sus pasos, con una mano apoyada en la barandilla y, más tarde, a lo largo de la pared. Por el camino fue observando los charcos de luz ambarina que proyectaban las lámparas hasta que llegó a su habitación.

Habían aireado la habitación durante su ausencia, también habían deshecho la cama y cambiado las sábanas. El aire era casi tan frío como el del exterior, aunque las ventanas volvían a estar cerradas a cal y canto.

Helena estaba empapada y congelada, pero sabía que Ferron podía darse cuenta de que se había olvidado el periódico y vendría a por él. No tenía tiempo que perder.

Se acurrucó junto a la ventana, allí donde había más luz, y devoró las palabras con los ojos, empezando desde el principio: «NOVEMBRIS, 1788».

Contempló la fecha conmocionada. No podía ser cierto. El último recuerdo del que tenía una referencia temporal exacta era haber oído a Lila Bayard hablar de retomar sus obligaciones de paladina y regresar al combate, a principios de 1786.

Si la guerra había terminado hacía catorce meses, eso significaba que habría sucedido a finales del verano de 1787. Lo que significaba que no tenía recuerdos de casi diecinueve meses de guerra. Se le desenfocó la vista cuando trató de recordar algo más allá de los turnos del hospital. No se acordaba de nada, de ninguna conversación, ni de las estaciones, ni de las fases de sublimación y latencia de Lumitia; de nada, salvo el bucle infinito de turnos en el hospital, repitiéndose una y otra vez como un grito eterno.

Cerró con fuerza los ojos e intentó concentrarse. Debía de haber algo, no podía haber perdido tantos recuerdos, pero era inútil, como intentar atrapar el viento con los dedos. Sintió un dolor agudo que le astilló el cerebro.

Parpadeó y al abrir los ojos comprobó que lo veía todo rojo.

Tenía el periódico en las manos.

Lo aferraba con fuerza. Debía leerlo rápido, antes de que Ferron notara su ausencia. Sus ojos se movieron a toda velocidad por el primer artículo.

La última fugitiva del grupo extremista conocido como la Orden de la Llama Eterna ha sido apresada y será interrogada próximamente. La administración de la Central de Nueva Paladia ha confirmado que se trata de Helena Marino, una alumna extranjera de alquimia originaria de las islas sureñas de Etras. Por su parte, el Gobierno etrasiano niega cualquier implicación o apoyo a los actos terroristas de la Llama Eterna. Para proteger a los ciudadanos de Nueva Paladia de más violencia, Marino está detenida a las afueras de la ciudad, en Puntaférreo, donde se decidirá su destino.

Urius Ferron construyó con hierro Puntaférreo, la famosa mansión de los Ferron. Gracias a su estructura única, erigida en honor a la resonancia excepcional de esa familia, la casa constituye un enclave seguro para los prisioneros más peligrosos.

Los Ferron, una de las familias más antiguas de Nueva Paladia, han vivido en la región desde antes de los Holdfast. Fueron víctimas frecuentes de la persecución de la Orden de la Llama Eterna. Atreus Ferron, maese gremial del hierro, acabó arrestado y ejecutado por pronunciarse contra el régimen opresor de los Holdfast, y su hijo, Kaine Ferron, fue acusado sin pruebas de haber asesinado al principado Apollo Holdfast. Más tarde, se archivaron todas las denuncias contra padre e hijo...

¿Ferron había sido acusado de matar al principado? ¿Del asesinato que desencadenó la guerra?

Miró fijamente las palabras hasta que se emborronaron.

Recordaba la muerte del principado Apollo. Lo encontraron brutalmente asesinado en las zonas comunes de la Academia de Alquimia, y enseguida se abrió una investigación. No recordaba que hubieran llegado a ninguna conclusión. Aquella época estuvo marcada por muchos sucesos: el funeral, las preparaciones para la coronación de Luc... Lo que debería haber sido un momento de júbilo se transformó en dolor y conmoción. Luc estuvo en entredicho hasta cuando sus amigos juraron morir para protegerlo. La ceremonia acabó poco antes de que se produjera el alzamiento, la llegada de los inmarcesibles y la guerra que parecía no tener fin.

¿Ferron había asesinado al principado Apollo? Probablemente no, solo tenía dieciséis años entonces. Tal vez se habían inventado aquello para presentar a la familia Ferron como víctimas de los Holdfast. Eso parecía más probable.

Leyó el resto del artículo con la esperanza de encontrar más información, pero solo halló la reiteración de la narrativa de los inmarcesibles sobre la guerra: que ellos no la habían comenzado; que, en realidad, nunca hubo una guerra, solo una inquietud civil provocada por un grupo de extremistas religiosos que se negaba a aceptar al Concejo de Gremios, elegido democráticamente por los paladinos.

Retrataban a Luc como un monstruo avaricioso de poder, dispuesto a quemar la ciudad hasta los cimientos, antes de permitir que todos la disfrutaran.

Luc, que la noche previa a convertirse en principado se había subido al tejado de la Torre de Alquimia, al borde del abismo.

Helena lo había seguido, manteniéndose todo lo cerca que pudo, prometiéndole que haría lo que fuera por él si daba un paso atrás y la tomaba de la mano.

Él no le prestó atención hasta que Helena juró que, si él saltaba, ella iría detrás. Fue entonces cuando se bajó para salvarla.

Se quedaron sentados en el tejado hasta el amanecer. Helena le sostuvo la mano y hablaron toda la noche, le contó sobre Etras: los acantilados, los pueblecitos con burros que tiraban de carruajes pintados, los olivos, las granjas y el mar en los días de verano. Algún día irían allí, le prometió ella. Cuando todo se calmara, lo llevaría allí para que viera lo hermoso que era.

Luc nunca quiso ser principado. Si hubiera tenido otra opción, habría renunciado al cargo sin dudarlo.

Helena pasó la página del periódico, parpadeando lentamente.

Una columna enumeraba las ejecuciones llevadas a cabo por el Sumo Inquisidor la semana anterior. Junto al texto había una foto de hombres y mujeres con aspecto torturado, de rodillas sobre un estrado. Vestido de negro y con un yelmo intrincado que le ocultaba el rostro y el cabello, se encontraba Ferron, con una mano pálida extendida.

Sabía que se trataba de Ferron por la postura y por la manera en que tenía doblados los largos dedos, pero el artículo solo se refería a él como «el Sumo Inquisidor».

No se mencionaba por ninguna parte que Kaine Ferron fuera el Sumo Inquisidor.

¿Era un secreto?

¿Qué conseguían con eso? Los Ferron no mucho, considerando el estado deteriorado en el que se encontraba la mansión.

No. La decisión debía de haber sido de Morrough. Al fin y al cabo, mantener oculta la identidad del Sumo Inquisidor le otorgaba al Sumo Nigromante una herramienta increíblemente poderosa. Si cualquiera podía ser el Sumo Inquisidor, la gente viviría alarmada, siempre desconfiando. Además, impedía que Ferron tuviera sus propios seguidores o acumulase poder suficiente para destronar a Morrough.

Tal vez Ferron era ambicioso y Morrough lo temía por ello. Esa posibilidad resultaba tentadora, algo de lo que Helena podía aprovecharse.

También convertía Puntaférreo en una trampa perfecta. Si alguien intentaba salvar a Helena, darían por hecho que estaban atacando al heredero de un gremio, sin tener idea de quién era en realidad su carcelero.

Leyó deprisa el resto del periódico. Había ciertas alusiones a la escasez de grano. Qué extraño, pensó. Los dos países vecinos eran grandes exportadores de productos agrícolas. La monarquía Novis mantenía lazos históricos con los Holdfast, así que era predecible que interviniera el comercio, pero Hevgoss, el vecino occidental, un país especialmente belicista, llevaba décadas buscando mejorar sus acuerdos comerciales con los gremios.

Los Holdfast siempre bloquearon las negociaciones, negándose a que la alquimia se utilizara con fines bélicos. Cuando se descubría que algún gremio había violado las restricciones comerciales con Hevgoss, se le cortaba el suministro de lumitio para evitar que procesaran alquimia a escala industrial.

¿Por qué Hevgoss no estaba inundando Paladia de grano?

La sección política del periódico le pareció casi ridícula, aunque de una forma horrible. El Concejo de Gremios —cuya existencia había sido precisamente lo que desencadenó la guerra— llevaba tres semanas negociando la tarifa de transportes, como si Nueva Paladia no tuviera asuntos más importantes que tratar antes de que el solsticio de invierno diera comienzo al año nuevo.

Pero lo que más le llamó la atención fue un párrafo que mencionaba la llegada de un emisario paladino al Imperio Oriental, al que por primera vez en los últimos siglos le habían permitido la entrada. ¿Ahí era donde había ido ese traidor de Shiseo?

Helena se saltó la mayoría de las páginas de sociedad, pero no pudo evitar fijarse en que el nombre de Aurelia Ferron aparecía con mucha frecuencia. Era bastante famosa, al parecer.

Luego le llamó la atención un artículo del periódico. En un principio, no suscitó su interés, ya que se limitaba a describir la actual escasez de mano de obra y lamentaba la pérdida de tantos alquimistas con talento en el «conflicto» provocado por la Llama Eterna. Presentaba estadísticas que confirmaban que la economía de Paladia seguía cayendo a causa de la desaparición de alquimistas de todas las edades. Según el autor, la solución eran los nacimientos financiados. De repente, el artículo se transformaba en algo parecido a un anuncio. La directora del nuevo departamento de ciencia y alquimia de la Central, Irmgard Stroud, estaba implementando un programa para apoyar a la nueva generación de alquimistas, utilizando nuevos métodos científicos de selección para ofrecerles un mejor comienzo.

Se buscaban voluntarias. Las participantes recibirían comida y alojamiento y, al terminar el programa, aquellas con antecedentes criminales tendrían un nuevo juicio.

Helena releyó varias veces el artículo, incapaz de creer lo que estaba leyendo. Describía un programa de reproducción como si se tratara de una solución económica, como si los alquimistas fueran perros en celo en busca de habilidades de transmutación que fuesen económicamente rentables.

No era un concepto salido de la nada. «Casarse en resonancia» era una práctica común entre las familias de los gremios, que buscaban parejas con quienes tuvieran la misma resonancia o una complementaria para fortalecer la línea familiar. Aurelia y Ferron eran un claro ejemplo.

Aunque el repertorio de la resonancia alquímica se heredaba, como el color del pelo o de los ojos, la resonancia era impredecible y podía aparecer o desvanecerse sin motivo.

Ninguno de los padres de Helena había sido alquimista. Su padre poseía una resonancia menor al acero y al cobre, pero no la suficiente para formarse o para entrar en un gremio. Hasta donde recordaba, su madre no tenía ningún tipo de resonancia. De hecho, la tía abuela de Luc, Ilva Holdfast, era conocida por ser un lapsus, una hija de alquimistas que no manifestaba resonancia.

Al parecer, Stroud pretendía analizar cuántas probabilidades había de heredar o no la resonancia, y pensaba usar a las prisioneras del Reducto para hacerlo. Al fin y al cabo, ¿quién si no se prestaría voluntaria para un programa de reproducción a cambio de comida, alojamiento y revisiones judiciales?

Se acordó de Grace, muerta de hambre y desesperada, con hermanos demasiado jóvenes para trabajar, dispuesta a vender un ojo. Helena se imaginó cuántas más habría como ella.

Recordó todos esos documentos que Stroud repasaba sin parar. Esto debía de ser en lo que trabajaba: estaba identificando a las candidatas más ejemplares de entre los registros de la Resistencia.

Helena escondió el periódico en el armario y decidió que lo dejaría en cualquier parte la próxima vez que saliera de su habitación. Le dolían las articulaciones por el frío, así que decidió tomar una ducha y se quitó la ropa mojada.

Se quedó debajo del agua caliente hasta que volvió a sentir el cuerpo y desapareció el frío que le calaba los huesos. Después se limpió lentamente, sin prisa por volver a su habitación helada.

Al bajar la vista, descubrió cicatrices de las que no tenía recuerdos.

La más grande estaba en mitad del torso y se extendía entre sus pechos. La cicatriz era como una cuerda, pronunciada y levemente arrugada, como si le hubieran abierto el esternón en canal para luego volver a unirlo.

La tocó con la yema de los dedos y encontró una hendidura en el hueso, y tuvo la vaga sensación de que le habían seccionado algunos nervios.

No parecía que hubiesen empleado la sanación, pues podrían haber hecho crecer el hueso. Ella misma habría cosido los nervios para evitar la pérdida de sensibilidad y, más adelante, habría dibujado los sellos adecuados para que la cicatriz fuera menos visible.

Pero no habían hecho nada de eso. Habían dejado que la herida se curara sin usar la vivemancia.

Tal vez fuera esta la herida grave que mencionó Stroud.

No, con una herida de este calibre no la habrían metido en el tanque de suspensión. Empezó a examinarse el cuerpo con cuidado y encontró más cicatrices.

Parecía como si hubieran adiestrado su mente para pasarlas por alto, pero se obligó a concentrarse y tomar nota de todas ellas.

Encontró vestigios de una herida grande y redondeada que le atravesaba la pantorrilla. También tenía cicatrices finas: una en el estómago y otra entre dos costillas. En esas sí que se había usado la vivemancia para sanarlas, sin duda.

En la mano derecha había más cicatrices: unas fisuras en la palma y en los dedos, como si hubiera agarrado la hoja de un cuchillo con fuerza. Y, lo más extraño, siete puntos de sutura. Estaban perfectamente espaciados y conformaban un círculo en la palma de su mano. No era grande, pero llamaba la atención por cómo le afeaba la piel. La miró fijamente: su forma le resultaba familiar.

Bajó la mano, inquieta, y, por último, descubrió la única cicatriz de la que sí se acordaba.

Apenas se veía, ya que estaba escondida bajo su propia mandíbula. Era larga y fina; le recorría la parte izquierda del cuello y se detenía justo antes de la garganta.

———————

AL DÍA SIGUIENTE, FERRON LE trajo a Helena una capa seca y limpia. Se la tiró a la cabeza sin decir nada.

Helena lo siguió y, disimuladamente, dejó el periódico por el camino. En el porche, Ferron sacó otro. La noticia de la portada trataba sobre un monumento que el gobernador, Fabian Greenfinch, estaba construyendo en honor a Morrough, el libertador de Nueva Paladia. Se inauguraría el año siguiente.

Estaba lloviendo otra vez. Helena echó un vistazo a su alrededor sin saber muy bien qué hacer; no le apetecía caminar en círculos bajo la supervisión de Ferron.

Aunque, con un poco de suerte, igual encontraba un palo bien afilado con el que apuñalarlo.

Paseó por el porche hasta que se aburrió y, después, se sentó a contemplar la quietud de la casa e intentó adivinar cuántas habitaciones habría en un lugar tan inmenso.

En su día, había pensado que la casa de los Bayard, Solis Splendor, era enorme. Se trataba de una de las pocas casas independientes de la ciudad, un vestigio de tiempos pasados, pero Puntaférreo era mucho más grande.

Cuando Ferron se puso en pie y se marchó, Helena dio por sentado que era su señal para volver adentro. Miró de reojo y sintió decepción al ver que esta vez no se había olvidado el periódico.

Se dirigió hacia la puerta. La luz invernal se derramaba como mercurio por los suelos oscuros, pero el pasillo que se extendía más allá desaparecía en la penumbra como unas fauces abiertas. Las cortinas de invierno tapaban la luz del sol y conferían al ambiente una sensación polvorienta y asfixiante, como en una tumba. Las luces estaban apagadas.

Helena tanteó la pared en busca de un botón o interruptor.

El viento recorrió la oscuridad del pasillo, y el olor a polvo y descomposición la sobresaltó como si sintiera cerca de ella un aliento frío. Después, un gemido grave y cambiante hizo vibrar toda la casa.

Helena trastabilló hacia el exterior con el corazón golpeándole en la garganta.

Si se levantaban las nubes, habría más luz. Se acurrucó en el porche y aguardó. A través de la oscuridad que traía la lluvia, la casa que la rodeaba se le antojó una criatura descomunal en hibernación, enroscada sobre sí misma; incluso los pináculos parecían púas.

La lluvia no cesó. Al llegar el atardecer, el cielo se oscureció aún más. En ese momento de los ciclos lunares, hasta Lumitia, la luna más brillante, había menguado demasiado como para que su resplandor pudiera atravesar las nubes.

La luz que se escapaba por la puerta era más débil todavía.

Helena respiró hondo; ya había recorrido ese camino antes. Había unos escalones nada más entrar en la zona de sombras, y, si los encontraba, sabría cómo volver.

Solo eran sombras. No era el tanque, no era la nada. Solo sombras.

Vaciló bajo el marco de la puerta, y todo se tornó más oscuro. La poca luz exterior que quedaba empezó a extinguirse.

Helena sintió que ella también desaparecía a la misma velocidad que la luz. La atenazaba un terror agudo, como garras, pero se obligó a andar. Tropezó con una mesa, pero apenas sintió el dolor en la espinilla.

«Encuentra las escaleras».

«No es más que una casa».

Pero sentía que la oscuridad se la tragaba y la absorbía, que la eternidad la acechaba. Se agarró a la mesa con la que había tropezado, pero le temblaban tanto las manos que la madera empezó a crujir. Entonces algo cayó y se estrelló en el suelo.

«Respira. Solo respira».

Intentó respirar, pero el dolor le atravesó el pecho. El corazón le latía como desbocado, como un pájaro enjaulado, intentando liberarse de sus costillas.

Dio unos cuantos pasos más antes de que le fallaran las piernas. Se dejó caer y se acurrucó en el suelo; el parquet era duro como un hueso. Estaba desapareciendo en la nada otra vez. En aquella nada donde no podía moverse... ni gritar... y nunca venía nadie...

Alguien la agarró por los brazos y la levantó del suelo.

—¿Qué estás haciendo?

Helena parpadeó al verse cegada por una luz repentina. Frente a ella estaba Ferron, con una expresión furibunda.

Había encendido una lámpara de pared, un halo en la oscuridad que solo los iluminaba a ellos.

Helena lo miró a los ojos para olvidarse del océano negro que la rodeaba.

—Estaba... oscuro —consiguió decir.

—¿Qué?

Respiraba a tal velocidad que comenzó a marearse.

—¿Te da miedo la oscuridad? —Sus ojos plateados ardían, su voz estaba cargada de incredulidad.

Helena intentó zafarse. Prefería ahogarse en el pasillo que estar cerca de Ferron, pero él no la soltó, sino que la condujo escaleras arriba, que estaban a apenas unos pasos, y la arrastró hasta su habitación, sin dejar que volviera a caer al suelo.

—Tranquilízate —le espetó en cuanto estuvieron en aquella habitación reconocible para Helena.

Cerró la puerta de un portazo.

Helena se desplomó en la silla, se dobló sobre sí misma y acarició la tela. Los dedos aún le temblaban, el dolor le punzaba en los brazos, pero le daba igual. Necesitaba aferrarse a esas sensaciones tan reales y tangibles, no al abismo vacío donde solo existía su cuerpo.

Respiró aliviada y el aire penetró hasta el interior de sus pulmones.

Estaba en su habitación. La casa no la había engullido, porque en realidad las casas no engullían a las personas. Su mente empezó a despejarse, y el terror asfixiante se fue diluyendo poco a poco dejando espacio a la razón.

Casi era peor volver a pensar racionalmente y saber que sus miedos no tenían sentido. Pero no importaba. A la parte de sí misma que tenía miedo no le importaba ser racional.

—¿Qué es lo que te pasa?

Helena dio un respingo y levantó la vista.

Ferron seguía en la habitación. Al parecer se había quedado para interrogarla una vez que se le hubiera pasado la panofobia.

Ella esquivó su mirada.

—Si no me lo dices, te arrancaré la respuesta de la cabeza.

Helena se encogió. Solo de pensar en su resonancia le entraba pavor. Había zonas de su mente que todavía parecían magulladas, como si se hubieran derrumbado tras el paso de la transferencia.

Abrió la boca y notó que tenía la garganta seca.

—No me gustan los lugares en los que no veo nada.

—¿Desde cuándo? No he visto que aquí tengas siempre la luz encendida. ¿O es que estas sombras son diferentes?

Sintió cómo le subía el rubor por la nuca. Bajó la vista hacia los barrotes de hierro del suelo.

—Conozco esta habitación. Lo que me aterra son los lugares que no conozco, aquellos que no puedo ver dónde acaban. En el tanque de suspensión, por más que intentaba mirar más allá, solo había oscuridad y no podía sentir nada a mi alrededor, solo mi cuerpo, que flotaba, inmóvil. Era un sensación… interminable. Como si no estuviera en ningún lugar. Estuve… estuve allí mucho tiempo. Siempre pensando que alguien vendría, pero… —Sacudió la cabeza—. Cuando veo un lugar oscuro y no sé dónde acaba, siento como si fuera a desaparecer en su interior, pero que esta vez nunca me encontrarán.

Sonaba irracional. Era irracional, pero no podía evitarlo; había una

grieta entre su razón y su mente, una falla que las separaba irremediable-
mente. A su mente no le importaba si el miedo que sentía tenía sentido o
no; simplemente no quería volver a pasar por eso jamás.

Ferron estuvo en silencio tanto tiempo que, al final, fue Helena la
que levantó la vista con una curiosidad morbosa. Sin embargo, él se
mostraba impasible, como una estatua.

Era la primera vez que Helena se dignaba a mirarlo, a verlo tal como
era y no por quién era.

La ropa que llevaba puesta lo ocultaba muy bien, pero estaba extrañamente delgado. Su complexión habitual no era la de un alquimista de
hierro. Ni siquiera tenía el aspecto o la presencia de un alquimista de combate. No lograba imaginarlo con un arma pesada en la mano.

A excepción del brillo depredador en los ojos, sus rasgos eran demasiado delicados, como una estatua que se ha tallado en exceso.

Todo en él era esbelto y afilado.

—¿Sabes qué? —dijo Ferron, sacándola de sus pensamientos—.
Cuando me dijeron que te traerían aquí, estaba deseando quebrar tu voluntad. —Negó con la cabeza—. Pero creo que será imposible superar lo
que te has hecho a ti misma.

CAPÍTULO 7

FERRON LA ACOMPAÑABA AL JARDÍN todos los días. Después del incidente, estaba de mal humor e iba señalando con burla dónde se encontraban los interruptores de luz que ella era «demasiado torpe» para encontrar por sí misma.

La trataba con tal condescendencia que Helena sentía ganas de tirarle una piedra, pero se sintió decepcionada cuando no encontró más que guijarros de gravilla blanca muy refinada.

El jardín le resultaba aburrido. Era una tarea tediosa y hacía un frío amargo. La nieve invernal comenzaba a acumularse en las nubes, aunque nunca había más que polvo en el suelo, lo suficiente para que se le entumecieran los pies con el frío.

Cuando estaba sola, se aventuraba a salir de su habitación, empeñada en encontrar algún arma aceptable; se habría conformado hasta con el clavo de un mueble. Si Ferron no la mataba accidentalmente, se suicidaría antes de que llevara a cabo otra sesión de transferencia.

En las horas en las que la luz del sol penetraba por las ventanas orientadas al este, si se mantenía pegada a la pared y se concentraba en la respiración, conseguía hacer esas breves excursiones.

Sin embargo, cuando pasaba demasiado tiempo fuera de su habitación, los necrómatas empezaban a aparecer como fantasmas. No intentaban detenerla ni la llevaban de vuelta a su cuarto; solo la vigilaban y se cernían sobre ella como una sombra que acecha en silencio.

Trató de ignorarlos, tal como hacía con los crujidos y los gemidos de la casa, o con las sombras en movimiento, pero le impedían encontrar algo con lo que suicidarse. Insistió igualmente, obstinada, pero la mayo-

113

ría de las habitaciones estaban cerradas a cal y canto, y en las pocas que estaban abiertas no había nada, salvo muebles viejos y aparatos inútiles.

En una habitación anticuada, encontró un cuadro escondido tras la estructura desmontada de una cama. Estaba cubierto con una sábana. Tiró de la tela para descubrirlo; sentía curiosidad.

Al retirar la tela, vio que se trataba de un retrato de la familia Ferron. No era de Ferron y Aurelia, sino de Ferron de niño junto a sus padres.

Atreus Ferron, el patriarca anterior, era un hombre enorme que Helena recordaba vagamente de haberlo visto en la Academia. Sus rasgos eran semejantes a los de un halcón: rostro afilado y cejas castañas muy pobladas que ensombrecían unos ojos azul claro. Iba vestido con elegancia, pero la sangre de herreros y ferreteros corría por sus venas, y tenía unos hombros anchos y unas manos enormes adornadas con pesados anillos de hierro.

Kaine Ferron aparecía retratado de pie junto a su padre. Era tal como lo recordaba en la Academia, totalmente distinto al hombre en que se había convertido con los años. Su rostro era más redondeado y, aunque fuese casi de la misma altura que su padre, carecía de la imponente complexión de Atreus. Ferron parecía desgarbado, como un potro. Todo en su apariencia era una clara imitación del hombre que estaba a su lado. Tenía el cabello castaño más claro que el de su padre, pero lo llevaba peinado de la misma forma, y también imitaba la expresión y la postura de Atreus. Pero, en su caso, sus cejas castañas caían sobre unos ojos color avellana.

En el centro del cuadro había una mujer con un vestido gris claro. Llevaba un anillo de hierro en el dedo anular, pero tenía unas manos tan finas que resultaba desproporcionado. Era delgada como un sauce, con un rostro en forma de corazón, ojos grises y mentón pequeño, todo enmarcado por un cabello rubio ceniza. Si Helena hubiera visto un retrato en el que la mujer apareciera sola, jamás habría adivinado que era la madre de Ferron, pero, al verlos juntos, se percató del parecido en la complexión. Los rasgos de la madre suavizaban los de Ferron, mitigando el semblante afilado y halconado, y también la corpulencia que habría heredado de su padre. No obstante, por encima de todo, era en la boca y en el brillo y la forma de los ojos donde se parecía a ella.

Helena analizó los rostros durante largo rato, hasta que se dio cuenta de que el cuadro no estaba terminado. La ropa carecía de detalles y el trasfondo no tenía los motivos que solían incluirse en este tipo de retratos, como si algo hubiera interrumpido su creación y por eso estuviese allí abandonado.

Deslizó la sábana entre sus dedos y volvió a dejar el cuadro en su escondite. Su mente oscilaba entre el Ferron de cabellos oscuros del retrato y su doble de platino de ahora.

———

—La inflamación ha desaparecido casi por completo —anunció Stroud dos semanas después. Había vuelto con Mandl y estaba introduciendo su resonancia a la fuerza en el cerebro de Helena, que de nuevo lo veía todo rojo—. Tendremos que conformarnos con hacer una sesión al mes. Aunque… —cogió la muñeca de Helena e inspeccionó con desaprobación la tonificación de sus músculos— no te estás recuperando tal como esperaba. ¿Estás saliendo todos los días?

—Sí. El Sumo Inquisidor se asegura de ello.

—¿Y haces ejercicio? Cuanto más fuerte estés, más probable será que soportes la transferencia sin que vuelvas a sufrir convulsiones febriles.

Helena fijó la mirada en Stroud, atónita e incrédula al escuchar esa revelación que nadie se había molestado en contarle. ¿Había sufrido convulsiones febriles?

Stroud le devolvió la mirada expectante, y Helena tardó un instante en recordar que la mujer pensaba que las caminatas podían prevenirlas.

—Sí —respondió Helena.

—Bien. Ya está anotado que tienes un trastorno nervioso.

Helena tensó la mandíbula. Por supuesto que Ferron se lo había contado a Stroud.

—Sí. No me gustan… los sitios oscuros que no reconozco.

Oyó que Mandl soltaba un resoplido burlón.

—Bueno, no podemos hacer mucho al respecto —comentó Stroud mientras seguía examinando a Helena—. La verdad, es una lástima que no pueda usarte como sujeto de prueba en mi programa. Estuve releyendo tu solicitud de admisión y tienes un repertorio extraordinario.

A Helena se le cerró la garganta.

—A los Holdfast les encantaba coleccionar alquimistas con poderes extraños —dijo Mandl.

Helena se mordió la lengua hasta que saboreó la sangre.

Stroud asintió.

—Cuando el Sumo Inquisidor haya acabado contigo, creo que pediré que te traigan a mi lado.

Helena levantó la barbilla.

—Pues no tendrás mucha suerte conmigo, me esterilizaron.

Torció el gesto de dolor cuando la resonancia de Stroud se clavó de repente en su bajo vientre. Un instante después, se vio reflejada en su rostro la decepción y la rabia.

—¿Cuándo sucedió eso?

Helena apartó la mirada y fijó la vista en un punto al otro lado de la habitación que se le nubló.

—Fue una de las condiciones que me impuso el falcón para dejarme entrar en la ciudad. Como la vivemancia es una corrupción del alma que comienza en el útero, podía… podía transmitírsela a mis hijos. Yo ya había pronunciado mis votos como sanadora y no podía casarme ni tener hijos, pero él… —Tragó saliva—. Él quiso asegurarse.

—Y, cómo no, tú accediste —dijo Stroud apartando la mano—. Porque pensaste que, si te hacías lo bastante pequeña, ellos te aceptarían.

Un rubor se le extendió por la mandíbula.

—No tenía sentido que me negara. Como he dicho, yo ya había pronunciado los votos.

Stroud rio entre dientes.

—Normalmente eran los niños los que se tragaban esa mentira.

Helena la miró con los ojos entrecerrados.

Stroud arqueó una ceja y lanzó una mirada de reojo a Mandl.

—¿No lo sabías? A tu Llama Eterna se le daba de maravilla identificar a los posibles vivemantes antes de que nacieran. Por eso, hace unos… ¿Cuántos? Hace treinta años que el principado Helios ordenó que los hospitales de la Fe se encargaran de gestionar todos los embarazos. Los médicos devotos estaban entrenados para saber qué buscar y qué soluciones ofrecer. ¿Qué padres querrían quedarse con un monstruo una vez que les advirtieran del peligro?

A Helena se le encogió el estómago.

—A Mandl la abandonaron al nacer y se crio en un orfanato de una de las casas colgantes. A los niños como ella les decían que tenían que purificar la corrupción de su alma, pero que, si hacían lo que se les pedía, tal vez alguien los querría algún día. —Stroud se encogió de hombros—. Evidentemente, ni la Fe ni Paladia los quiso nunca para nada más que para obligarlos a trabajar. Y veo que a ti te trataron igual.

—No —replicó Helena negando con la cabeza—. Luc no era así. Ni siquiera sabía las condiciones que me impusieron para ser sanadora. O cómo funcionaba la sanación. No me lo habría permitido de haberlo sabido. La gente como el falcón Matias tenía opiniones muy fuertes, pero Luc se pasó la vida controlando a la gente como él. Cuando lo hicieron, quiso...

—Si no lo sabía, entonces es que era una marioneta y un incompetente. Y tú sigues siéndolo —replicó Mandl, con el rostro rezumando odio. Se giró hacia Stroud—. Deberías contarle lo que hizo Su Eminencia con Holdfast después de matarlo.

Helena sintió un vuelco en el estómago. Las miró a ambas fijamente, pero Stroud negó con la cabeza.

—Recuerda cuál es tu sitio, Mandl.

Cuando se marcharon, Helena se incorporó, paralizada, preguntándose qué le habría pasado a Luc.

Por supuesto, no le sorprendía que no lo hubiesen cremado tal como debían, pero... ¿qué le habían hecho para que Mandl quisiera torturar a Helena contándoselo?

Luc no se merecía la crueldad y el odio que había sufrido.

Helena era consciente de que Luc no lo había sabido todo, pero eso no lo convertía en una marioneta. La posición del principado era compleja. Ser líder religioso y gobernante a la vez era una tarea difícil, sobre todo durante la guerra, donde se esperaba que luchara y gobernara al mismo tiempo. No podía permitir que lo frenaran las decisiones personales de los demás.

Hubo que tomar decisiones sin él, sacrificios que lo habrían dejado perplejo incluso si no los hubiera sabido, pero eso no lo convertía en una marioneta, sino que lo hacía humano.

Helena lo había amado por la persona que era. No le importaba que fuera el principado ni el favorito de los dioses. Había sido bueno tal como era.

FERRON APARECIÓ COMO SIEMPRE DESPUÉS del almuerzo incomible de Helena. Esta fue de mala gana a coger su capa.

—Hoy no será necesario —dijo él. Helena se detuvo y lo miró con cautela.

La puerta se cerró a su espalda con un leve chasquido.

Giró los dedos y la capturó mediante resonancia, obligándola a acercarse. Cuando estuvo junto a la cama, movió la mano y la dejó caer sobre el colchón.

Ferron se echó encima con gesto aburrido. La única emoción que sentía se reflejaba en el brillo de sus ojos.

Helena se mordió el labio para permanecer callada y se obligó a respirar con normalidad mientras se resistía a su resonancia.

Él la miró con esos ojos sombríos.

A Helena esa situación ni siquiera se le había pasado por la cabeza, pero debería haberlo pensando. Sabía que Ferron era un monstruo, pero jamás había mostrado interés en ella.

Como si el interés tuviera algo que ver… Empezó a pensar a toda velocidad. ¿Por qué ahora? ¿Y por qué hoy? ¿Le había mencionado Stroud que Helena era estéril y lo había visto como una oportunidad? ¿Algo que explotar sin consecuencias?

Se le escapó un sollozo contenido. Deseó poder hundirse en el colchón y desaparecer, deseó poder gritar. Consiguió doblar los dedos, pero en el lugar donde debería haber aparecido su resonancia solo quedaba una herida abierta.

Con la mano derecha clavada en el colchón junto a la cabeza de Helena, Ferron le hizo girar la barbilla hasta que se miraron a los ojos.

Se le encogió el corazón.

Tenía las pupilas contraídas; el gris de su iris parecía una tormenta a punto de estallar.

Sus dedos fríos siguieron la curva de la mandíbula hasta la sien. Helena yació inmóvil, siendo consciente del peso de su cuerpo, y su resonancia le atravesó la mente.

La mente de Helena era como un globo de nieve del revés; todos los pensamientos se arremolinaban como copos de nieve suspendidos por su consciencia.

No estaba realizando la transferencia, pero sí que sentía vagamente la mente de Ferron a través de la conexión. Soportó cómo él se divertía al descubrir las ideas que tenía de matarlo, que se habían convertido en toda una constelación de fantasías oscuras. Las ojeó sin preocuparse y, acto seguido, se hundió más en su propia mente y observó cómo había explorado con cautela la casa, el jardín, los necrómatas, el periódico que había robado y a Stroud. Solo pareció reaccionar mínimamente cuando repasó sus pensamientos constantes sobre Luc y el profundo dolor que le causaba su muerte.

Entonces se vio en la habitación cogiendo la capa, y a él cerrando la puerta, y Helena supo lo que iba a pasar.

El recuerdo se evaporó como la niebla bajo el sol directo, y se descubrió a sí misma tumbada en la cama y a Ferron contemplándola con desdén. Apartó la mano.

—No tengo intención de tocarte —dijo con asco—. Tu presencia aquí ya me resulta ofensiva.

—Menudo consuelo —replicó Helena con sequedad. No era una réplica muy ingeniosa, pero volvía a palpitarle la cabeza, como si la costra de una herida se hubiera desprendido dejando la piel aún sensible.

Ferron se estiró, y Helena pensó que se marcharía ofendido, así que se apresuró a hacer la pregunta que la atormentaba:

—¿Fuiste tú quien mató al principado Apollo?

Ferron se detuvo y se apoyó contra el poste de la cama, donde se cruzó de brazos y ladeó la cabeza.

—Oficialmente... no.

—Pero sí que fuiste tú, ¿verdad? —Cuantas más vueltas le daba al tema, más sentido tenía.

—¿No te acuerdas? —Negó con la cabeza—. ¿Es que no hiciste nada durante la guerra? Por cómo te paseaban los Holdfast, cualquiera diría que habrías tratado de ser útil, pero tienes el expediente más mediocre que he visto. —Resopló—. ¿Cuántos años estuviste en ese hospital? ¿Y para qué? Salvaste a personas que hubieran preferido que las dejaras morir. Pero no, tú los recomponías y los mandabas de vuelta a la guerra para que siguieran sufriendo. —Sonrió lentamente—. Tal vez Stroud se equivoca y sí que apoyabas nuestra causa.

Si le hubiese pegado, no le habría hecho tanto daño como le hacía diciendo esto.

Todos esos años. Toda la gente a la que había sanado, a la que había regenerado para que pudieran seguir luchando, ¿y para qué? Para que los torturaran hasta la muerte, los esclavizaran o... incluso tuvieran un destino peor.

Hasta ese momento, la sanación era lo único por lo que no se había sentido culpable. Aunque Luc estuviera muerto, ella había realizado buenas acciones. Sin embargo, Ferron había destrozado ese mínimo consuelo y lo había convertido en algo atroz.

Se llevó las manos a la boca hasta que sintió el contorno de los dientes y rodó de lado.

Ferron se rio.

—Los luchadores de la Resistencia sois muy fáciles de romper.

Se giró para marcharse.

Aunque la pena se le clavaba en los pulmones, la mantuvo a raya.

—No me has respondido a la pregunta —dijo con los dientes apretados.

Ferron se detuvo.

—Cierto… Bueno, supongo que no hago mal en contártelo. Fue el Sumo Nigromante quien me pidió que asesinara al principado. Ya llevaba un tiempo en Paladia ganando adeptos, pero, mientras Apollo siguiera en el poder, el Concejo de Gremios no lograría el apoyo popular necesario. Había que desestabilizar el país, hacer que el futuro pareciera incierto. Era imposible atacar al principado en público con los paladines, los guardias y todos sus seguidores alrededor, adorando su resplandor. Pero los Holdfast siempre bajaban la guardia en la Academia, convencidos de que cualquiera que atravesara esas puertas quedaría demasiado fascinado por su magnificencia como para hacerles daño.

Lo miró de reojo y vio que Ferron tenía la mano izquierda en alto, como si la examinara.

—Seguro que sabes lo fascinante que es la resonancia de los vivemantes. Hundir la mano en su caja torácica fue como atravesar la superficie del agua. Me deslicé sin más. —Curvó los dedos—. Luego saqué su corazón; todavía latía. Deberías haber visto la sorpresa en su rostro. No caí en la cuenta de que seguiría vivo un instante más, así que vivió lo suficiente como para saber perfectamente quién lo había matado.

El principado Apollo había sido un hombre amable y generoso, con una sonrisa fácil, siempre dispuesto a bromear con cualquier alumno inquieto que se le acercara. Luc se parecía mucho a él: la misma sonrisa ladeada. Estar junto a él era como permanecer bajo el cálido sol de verano.

—Supongo que tu amo quedó muy satisfecho contigo —dijo Helena con voz sombría. No quería darle la satisfacción de que presenciara el horror que sentía.

—Lo cierto es que sí. Todos me estaban esperando cuando regresé. Celebramos una cena con él y con mi madre. Me declaró un prodigio…

Helena levantó la vista. Ferron estaba mirando fijamente por la ventana, como si tuviera la mente en otra parte.

Despertó del ensimismamiento y bajó la mirada.

—¿Alguna pregunta más? —Arqueó una ceja como si la retara a hacerlo.

—No —repuso Helena de inmediato, apartando la vista—. Ya has hecho bastante.

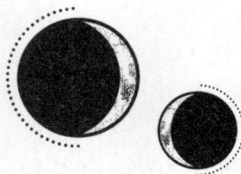

CAPÍTULO 8

*L*UC HOLDFAST ESTABA SENTADO EN *el tejado de la Torre de Alqui-*
mia, encorvado en contra de la pendiente de las tejas. Entre los dedos hacía
girar distraídamente una pipa de opio. El chapitel de la Torre, coronado con
la Llama Eterna, ardía por encima de su cabeza como un faro de luz blanca.

Se estaba poniendo el sol. El mundo se iba tiñendo de tonalidades bron-
ceadas cuando Helena subió para hacerle compañía.

Estaba tan demacrado que incluso parecía mayor que su padre. La gue-
rra lo había carcomido hasta los huesos. Al tragar saliva, los tendones del
cuello se le marcaron como cuerdas. Luc le dedicó una mirada de soslayo y
volvió la vista al frente.

—¿Qué nos ha pasado, Hel? —preguntó cuando la chica se agachó a su
lado.

Helena contempló el horizonte, más allá de las torres, hacia el sur.

—Una guerra.

—Antes creías en mí. ¿Qué he hecho para que dejes de hacerlo? —Su voz
sonaba distante.

—Sigo creyendo en ti, Luc —replicó Helena—. Pero tenemos que ganar
esta guerra; no podemos tomar decisiones basándonos en la historia que
queremos contar luego. Hay demasiado en juego.

—No —replicó Luc—. Así ganaremos. Así hemos ganado siempre. Así
ganaron mi padre, mi abuelo y todos los principados hasta el mismísimo
Orion. Todos ganaron confiando en que el bien siempre vence sobre el mal, y
yo tengo que hacer lo mismo.

Chasqueó el índice con el pulgar y los anillos de ignición soltaron una
chispa. Unas llamas pálidas brotaron al instante, devorándole la palma de la

mano con una luz que era como un sol en miniatura. Luc cerró los dedos alrededor del fuego y solo dejó encendida una única lengua ardiente. La usó para prender la pipa de opio que se llevó a los labios.

Helena apartó la mirada y escuchó cómo fumaba.

—Pero ¿qué pasará si no es así de simple? —insistió—. Todos los que ganan dicen que ellos fueron los buenos, pero en realidad son los que cuentan la historia. Ellos deciden cómo recordarla. ¿Y si nunca fue tan simple?

Luc negó con la cabeza.

—Orion fue bendecido por el sol porque se negó a renunciar a su fe.

Helena suspiró con exasperación y enterró la cara entre las manos.

Oyó el chasquido de nuevas chispas y el siseo de la pipa al evaporarse el opio.

—Luc..., por favor, déjame ayudarte —dijo haciendo amago de acercarse.

Luc se apartó.

—No... me toques.

Estaba acercándose peligrosamente al borde de lo que podía ser una caída descomunal, como si lo estuviera llamando el Abismo. Helena ya no sabía cómo hacerle entrar en razón ni qué decir para que la escuchara.

—¿Te acuerdas de lo que te prometí la noche que viniste aquí, Luc? —le preguntó en tono suplicante.

Luc no respondió. Tenía la mirada perdida y el atardecer delineaba sus rasgos demacrados como si los cubriera de oro.

—Te prometí que haría lo que fuera por ti. —Cerró los dedos en un puño—. Tal vez no entendiste hasta dónde estaba dispuesta a llegar.

———

EL RECUERDO DE LUC AÚN sobrevolaba la mente de Helena cuando despertó por la mañana.

Se quedó en la cama un rato, reviviéndolo. Era un recuerdo olvidado y, aunque eso debería haberla asustado, no parecía contener ninguna información que a Ferron pudiera serle útil. Además, echaba tanto de menos a Luc que no le importó que el recuerdo fuera amargo como el agua salada.

Estaba fumando opio. ¿Cómo era eso posible? Debía de haber sufrido una herida terrible para que le permitieran tomar ese tipo de droga. Su tía abuela Ilva, la mano derecha del principado cuando Luc estaba en el frente, siempre se mostró reacia a que consumiera drogas. Prefería que Helena empleara sus habilidades para no correr el riesgo de que se volviera adicto.

Pero Luc ni siquiera había dejado que Helena lo tocara.

Permaneció en la cama, repasando el recuerdo una y otra vez, y tomó nota de todos los detalles. La luz del atardecer, cómo bronceaba sus rasgos e iluminaba sus ojos. La forma nerviosa y compulsiva en la que movía los dedos para encender los anillos y crear las llamas.

A Helena le fascinaba esa forma de piromancia. Le parecía más magia que alquimia el hecho de que el fuego fuera una extensión de sí mismo con esas llamas brillantes como el sol.

A los Holdfast siempre se les representaba coronados con fuego. La creación de fuego sagrado y la alquimización del oro eran los dos talentos excepcionales que Sol les había concedido a los Holdfast.

La alquimización, es decir, transformar un metal en otro, era la práctica más compleja de la alquimia. Antes de que Orion Holdfast fundara la Academia, los primeros escritos alquímicos la vinculaban más con la mitología que con la ciencia.

El mítico Cetus, a quien solían considerar el primer alquimista del Norte, fue el autor de cientos, quizá miles, de los primeros escritos sobre alquimia, a lo largo de siglos. Los académicos no tenían claro si Cetus era el nombre de una academia o de una secta alquimista. Con el tiempo, se descubrió que el misterio tenía su origen en la superstición. Los primeros alquimistas se vieron obligados a escribir bajo seudónimo para evitar la persecución, mientras que los alquimistas posteriores emplearon los nombres de esos alquimistas más famosos para así darle legitimidad a sus teorías y descubrimientos. Como consecuencia, «Cetus» había escrito casi todos los textos sobre alquimia que habían sobrevivido hasta hoy.

Aunque las obras de Cetus tenían un trasfondo histórico considerable, también eran poco precisas, y lo más probable era que no hubiera existido ningún alquimista con ese nombre, pero, al no haber nadie a quien otorgarle el reconocimiento, casi todas las teorías y descubrimientos anteriores a la fundación de Paladia seguían atribuyéndosele a él.

Fue en uno de esos textos iniciales de Cetus donde se formuló por primera vez el principio alquímico que afirmaba que un metal solo podía transformarse en otro menos noble, siguiendo en muchos casos la jerarquía planetaria.

Posteriormente, sería Orion Holdfast quien descubriría los principios modernos de la alquimización, desbancando las afirmaciones de Cetus y estableciendo tanto los métodos como la disposición de los sellos que se necesitaban para transformar los metales innobles en otros menos corrompibles.

En sus escritos, Orion sostenía que la alquimización se basaba en la pureza espiritual, es decir, solo un alquimista cuya alma fuera tan pura como el elemento que deseaba crear podía lograr la transmutación. Era esa luz y pureza que el mismísimo Sol les había otorgado a los Holdfast lo que les confería la habilidad divina de convertir el plomo en oro puro.

Sin embargo, Luc siempre prefirió la piromancia. La familia debía respetar normas estrictas a la hora de alquimizar oro. No se podía abusar del metal celestial ni emplearlo con fines egoístas; al fin y al cabo, era necesario mantener la armonía con los países vecinos y preservar la propia moneda de Paladia. También existían reglas respecto al fuego, aunque no eran tan rigurosas como las relacionadas con la producción de oro.

Helena recordaba la primera vez que Luc le mostró su fuego. Estaba convencida de que las llamas lo quemarían, pero se limitaron a bailar sobre las yemas de sus dedos, brillantes como estrellas.

Incluso sin las llamas, Helena siempre había sentido calidez cuando estaba con Luc; hasta los inviernos paladinos palidecían en su presencia. Ahora que estaba sola, lo echaba tanto de menos que le dolían los huesos y la piel, anhelando el tacto y el consuelo que solo su abrazo podía ofrecer.

HELENA TERMINÓ DE EXPLORAR EL ala del segundo piso y decidió continuar por la planta baja.

Se plantó delante de las escaleras y observó la curva oscura que dibujaban, mientras los cristales de las ventanas crujían como dientes rechinando y el viento gemía a lo largo del pasillo.

Envolvió los dedos alrededor de la barandilla, suave como un hueso, y la apretó hasta que notó las vetas de la madera. El grillete se le clavó en la muñeca.

No permitió que sus ojos se hundieran en las sombras cuando dio un paso al frente.

Pensó en los acantilados de Etras, en el rugido eterno del océano. En sus recuerdos, volvía a ser una niña, abriéndose paso entre las pozas de marea durante el verano de Latencia, cuando Lumitia menguaba y las aguas se retiraban, dejando a la vista el fondo lleno de tesoros. El resplandeciente sol estival irradiaba sobre toda su piel.

Helena iría al sur. Escaparía y seguiría el río de las montañas hasta llegar al mar, y allí zarparía hasta su hogar.

Llegó al final de las escaleras, donde un necrómata la esperaba. Las luces ambarinas ya estaban encendidas, era el recordatorio silencioso de Ferron: no podía hacer nada ni ir a ninguna parte sin su consentimiento.

Helena tragó saliva con dificultad y dejó atrás su fantasía. Moriría en Puntaférreo.

Las habitaciones de la planta baja se sucedían una tras otra. Puntaférreo parecía tener tantas habitaciones que los Ferron no sabían qué hacer con ellas.

—Vuelve aquí, no he terminado contigo. —Una voz áspera la hizo detenerse, pero entonces comprendió que no le hablaba a ella.

—No hay nada más que decir —escuchó que decía Ferron—. No me interesa.

—¡Ni se te ocurra marcharte! Si me desobedeces, te desheredaré. ¡Borraré tu nombre del gremio!

Helena se asomó al pasillo y vio a Ferron enfrentarse al liche que había visto con Stroud en la Central, el que usaba el cuerpo de Crowther.

—Estás muerto, padre. Es posible que se te haya olvidado. Este cadáver no tiene derecho sobre mi mansión ni sobre mi herencia. Además —la voz de Ferron adquirió un tono más mordaz—, careces de resonancia férrea en ese cuerpo. Por muchos títulos que te conceda el gremio, no tienes ningún poder. Tardaron casi un año en recordar quién eras, y más aún en querer que volvieras. El único motivo por el que te dejo ser maese gremial es porque tengo mejores cosas que hacer que lidiar con la gestión de la fábrica.

La cara del liche se oscureció hasta tornarse casi morada de la rabia. Helena jamás habría dicho que ese ser era Atreus Ferron. Crowther tenía una complexión totalmente distinta, tan esbelta que parecía una aguja, y era una cabeza más bajo que Ferron.

—Debería haberme negado a las súplicas de tu madre y haberte matado cuando estabas en su vientre —dijo Atreus con el rostro contraído por la rabia—. No te mereces el sufrimiento que hemos soportado por ti.

Ferron no se inmutó, incluso parecía aburrido.

—Es una lástima que no lo hicieras. Me habrías ahorrado esta tediosa conversación. —Se dio la vuelta con los ojos grises cargados de desprecio—. Vete de esta casa, padre, antes de que te eche yo mismo.

Helena se encogió para que no la vieran, temiendo que la descubriesen. El necrómata que la acompañaba parpadeó con calma.

—Te arrepentirás de esto. El Sumo Nigromante recordará que no te ofreciste voluntario.

—El Sumo Nigromante sabe perfectamente dónde estoy y lo que estoy haciendo. Si quisiera algo de mí, no me lo comunicaría a través de alguien como tú. Al fin y al cabo, ¿cuántas veces le fallaste para que te negaran un cadáver con resonancia de hierro? ¿Fueron dos o tres?

Helena oyó un rugido, seguido de un golpe metálico y un sonido sordo. Se asomó de nuevo. Atreus yacía en el suelo; alrededor de una pierna tenía enroscada una de las vigas de hierro del piso, que lo arrastraba al ala principal de la casa.

Atreus se aferraba al suelo, arañándolo en su intento desesperado de escapar, pero lo único que logró fue casi arrancarse los dedos. Gritaba con rabia, echando espumarajos por la boca, con un sonido más de bestia que de humano.

Ferron lo siguió como si nada.

—Yo, en tu lugar, tendría cuidado con ese cuerpo. La piromancia es una habilidad poco habitual, ¿sabes? Date unos meses más y, con suerte, seguro que consigues generar una chispa.

En cuanto desaparecieron, Helena se escabulló de vuelta a su habitación. Solo con ver la casa en acción se había vuelto más precavida. Ya sabía que, en teoría, debía ser maleable, pero verlo con sus propios ojos hacía que cada una de las filigranas de hierro forjado adquiriera un significado más profundo.

No eran imaginaciones suyas: la casa era prácticamente un ente vivo.

Igual que Atreus…, que había sido reanimado. Helena hubiera jurado que lo ejecutaron antes de que aparecieran los inmarcesibles.

Seguía intentando recomponer algún que otro fragmento de los recuerdos que había perdido, aunque le costaba saber si los había olvidado o si simplemente no la habían avisado de ello. Al fin y al cabo, a las sanadoras no se les hacía partícipes de la información confidencial. Lo único que conocía de las batallas y la estrategia militar era cómo contener el mar de sangre que venía después.

Aunque sabía que era peligroso, intentaba desenmarañar el misterio de lo que había olvidado. Su mente carecía de contexto. De momento estaba jugando al gato y al ratón con Ferron y su ignorancia era lo único que la protegía. Sin embargo, no lo sentía como una protección, sino como si caminara a ciegas, con la piel despellejada.

Su mente no se cansaba de moverse en círculos. Cada detalle nuevo que descubría lo consideraba una posible pista, y lo observaba desde todos los ángulos, para ver si encajaba en alguno de los huecos de su memoria. ¿Qué podía saber para que fuese necesario ocultarlo así?

«Deja de pensar», se dijo a sí misma. Colocó los pies debajo del armario y empezó a hacer abdominales hasta que le ardieron los músculos. Lila solía hacerlo en la habitación que compartían cuando se sentía nerviosa y estaba fuera de servicio.

Helena debía centrarse en Ferron, encontrar la forma de provocarlo lo suficiente para que la matara.

Debía de tener alguna debilidad de la que pudiera aprovecharse.

«Kaine Ferron, ¿cuál es la grieta de tu armadura perfecta?».

Como si lo hubiera invocado con el pensamiento, la puerta se abrió y Ferron entró en la habitación.

Sus ojos descendieron hasta ver que Helena tenía los pies metidos bajo el armario y estaba tumbada, jadeando del esfuerzo.

—Veo que has encontrado algo que hacer.

Se obligó a rodar sobre un costado y ponerse en pie, aunque tuvo que morderse el labio al sentir el tirón del dolor cuando se impulsó.

Había llegado antes de la hora habitual de paseo, y este cambio en la rutina diaria la hizo sospechar.

—Acércate —le instó y sacó un frasco que contenía varias pastillas pequeñas de color blanco. Observó atentamente su reacción.

—¿Qué son? —preguntó Helena cuando él quitó la tapa del frasco y sacó una.

Ferron arqueó una ceja.

—Te lo diré si te la tragas como una buena chica.

Helena frunció los labios.

Aunque las sanadoras no tenían formación médica tradicional, Helena poseía amplios conocimientos de medicina. Sabía del poder y del peligro que contenía algo tan inocuo como una pastilla blanca.

Helena no esperó a que la empujaran. Se giró y se marchó.

—He visto a esa chica en alguna parte —oyó que comentaba Atreus cuando llegó al pasillo.

—Era la única sureña de la Academia, así que yo diría que le resultaba difícil pasar desapercibida —replicó Ferron, aparentemente despreocupado.

La oleada de adrenalina empezó a disiparse en el cuerpo de Helena. Al llegar a las escaleras, le temblaban tanto las piernas que casi se le doblaron. Buscó la pared más cercana y apoyó en ella las yemas de los dedos, torciendo el gesto en cuanto la tocó. Manchó el papel pintado con su sangre.

Debería haberse rajado la garganta en cuanto cogió el cuchillo.

Era mediados de invierno cuando el gobernador Fabian Greenfinch estuvo a punto de ser asesinado.

Ocurrió durante la ceremonia de inauguración de la nueva estatua en honor a Morrough. El gobernador pronunciaba un discurso sobre la liberación de Nueva Paladia, mientras Mandl, custodio del centro de reeducación del Reducto, cuyos «miembros» habían construido la estatua, estaba a su lado en el estrado. Cuando el gobernador se dispuso a cortar la cinta, una flecha de ballesta surgió de entre los edificios cercanos. Rozó al gobernador, pero alcanzó de lleno a Mandl.

Mandl falleció en el acto.

Delante de una multitud de periodistas y turistas internacionales, ciudadanos y dignatarios extranjeros, una de las inmarcesibles de aspecto claramente inmortal murió.

La muerte conmocionó a toda Paladia e incluso más allá. Los titulares de los periódicos sonaban casi histéricos. Los terroristas que creían haber erradicado habían reaparecido de forma espectacular, ante una audiencia imposible de silenciar mediante amenazas, como solía ocurrir con la prensa nacional.

Las visitas de Lancaster a Puntaférreo se interrumpieron de repente. Aurelia deambulaba por la casa demacrada y paranoica, sobresaltándose con cualquier ruido, como si creyera que los luchadores de la Resistencia pudieran emerger de las paredes para asesinarla. En varias ocasiones, Helena escuchó que interrogaba a Ferron sobre las protecciones de la mansión y le exigía más necrómatas.

Ferron, en las pocas ocasiones en que Helena lo había visto, ya no vestía abrigos, ni capas, ni camisas blancas inmaculadas, ni tampoco usaba armadura, sino lo que parecía una mezcla de equipamiento ligero de combate y ropa de caza. Era habitual que regresase a la casa lleno de barro, empapado por la lluvia y lívido de rabia.

Helena estaba encantada.

Leyó la cobertura mediática de forma compulsiva y con el corazón en el puño. La Resistencia seguía viva.

Los periódicos insistían una y otra vez en que había sido un intento fallido de asesinato; estaban desesperados por maquillar el hecho de que alguien aparentemente inmortal había fallecido por accidente.

Helena sabía que todo el continente estaría especulando sobre cómo lo habían hecho y de qué manera podían replicarlo.

Había una forma de matar a los inmarcesibles.

Helena estuvo de buen humor durante días.

Stroud volvió a visitarla. A diferencia de Ferron y Aurelia, a ella no parecía importarle la insurrección ni el nuevo peligro.

La acompañaba el mayordomo, quien cargaba con una camilla plegable que colocó en mitad de la habitación antes de marcharse.

—Desnúdate y siéntate —le ordenó Stroud señalando la camilla. Luego se giró para revisar un documento.

Helena apretó los dientes, pero obedeció.

—Creía que tendrías asuntos más urgentes que atender en vez de venir aquí —dijo Helena con la esperanza de sonsacarle información.

Stroud la miró de soslayo. Pronunció una negativa con naturalidad, como si no se le ocurriera nada más que decir.

—¿No te preocupa que vayan a por ti?

—Yo no soy una inmarcesible —respondió Stroud encogiéndose de hombros.

—¿Ah, no? —Helena no podía creerlo. Había dado por sentado que alguien tan cercano a Morrough lo sería.

—No. Puede que algún día, pero por ahora no me interesa. El Sumo Nigromante me concede poder para seguir investigando sin debilitarme ni agotarme, siempre y cuando le sea leal.

—No sabía que eso fuera posible. —Le dolían los dedos, todavía tenía la mano izquierda escayolada tras su intento de acabar con Ferron.

—Hay muchas cosas que desconoces. Con los conocimientos adecuados, el desgaste que provoca el uso continuado de la vivemancia es reversible. —Stroud miró a Helena con cierta sorna. La chica le devolvió la mirada con curiosidad.

—¿Pero no es mejor convertirse en inmarcesible?

Stroud negó con la cabeza.

—Los inmarcesibles tienen sus propias... limitaciones. Bennet fue uno de los primeros en ascender. Utilizó el vasto conocimiento del Sumo Nigromante para experimentar más allá de lo que se creía posible. Dedicó varias décadas de su vida a desentrañar los secretos de la transferencia. Todos los que lo conocían admiraban su inteligencia. Yo fui una de las pocas que trabajó mano a mano con él...

El semblante de Stroud se mostró visiblemente afectado, y se aclaró la garganta.

—Pero ni siquiera yo pude negar que, cerca del final, empezó a cometer errores. Consumía una cantidad ingente de recursos para hacer sus experimentos, incluida su propia vitalidad, y, cuanto más lo hacía, más se obsesionaba. Los inmarcesibles suelen desarrollar cierta tendencia al sadismo con el paso del tiempo. Algunos la manifiestan antes que otros. No quiero que mi trabajo se vea afectado por algo así. Tal vez pida la ascensión cuando perfeccione la transferencia. Pero, mientras tanto, el Sumo Nigromante me otorga lo que necesito. Sabe que eso me hace más leal que cualquier otro.

Los inmarcesibles siempre le parecieron psicópatas, pero Helena no había imaginado que la inmortalidad tuviera efectos secundarios.

Stroud palpó a Helena con unas manos fuertes y ásperas por el uso del jabón, y masculló para sí que ya mostraba signos de mantener una alimentación adecuada.

—Tómate esto. —Le dio varias pastillas.

—¿Para qué son?

La impaciencia se hizo visible en el gesto de Stroud.

—El Sumo Nigromante desea verte.

Helena se encogió.

—¿Por qué?

Stroud ignoró la pregunta.

—Si no te las tomas, tengo aquí una sonda —dijo, sacándola de su botiquín médico—. Puedo paralizarte y metértela por la garganta hasta el estómago para suministrarte así las pastillas. Lo he hecho muchísimas veces. Te dañará el esófago y tardarás varios días en poder hablar. Tú decides.

Helena se metió las pastillas en la boca y las tragó sin ayuda de agua, pasando por alto que se le quedaban pegadas a la garganta. Cuando se disolvieron, notó la quemazón en el tejido.

Stroud se dio la vuelta y se puso a rebuscar de nuevo en el botiquín. Había traído muchas más cosas que en las visitas anteriores. Helena entrecerró los ojos para distinguir qué eran, pero de repente se dio cuenta de que se le enturbiaba la vista.

—Espera…

Stroud sacó varios frascos y jeringuillas grandes, y fue colocándolos en fila.

—¿Qué estás…? —Se le estaba adormeciendo la cara.

Pestañeó. Stroud había rellenado una jeringuilla y la estaba agitando para quitarle las burbujas de aire.

Helena intentó leer las palabras del frasco. Se le emborronaron las letras.

—No… —consiguió decir.

—Ya te lo he dicho: todo esto es para prepararte —dijo Stroud al clavarle la jeringuilla en el brazo.

Helena apenas la notó.

La cabeza se le fue hacia atrás y se tambaleó. Estuvo a punto de caerse de la camilla cuando intentó apartarse.

—Túmbate. —Las palabras de Stroud resonaron a su alrededor.

Con un ligero toque, Helena se desplomó hacia un lado. Sintió el frío de la camilla rozando su sien y, acto seguido, el pinchazo de otra jeringuilla clavándose en su brazo. La habitación se sumió en la oscuridad.

Oyó el tintineo de otra jeringuilla.

Después de eso, no recordaba nada más.

———

CUANDO ABRIÓ LOS OJOS, TODO estaba oscuro. Yacía en la cama, con los brazos y las piernas doloridos por los moratones que le habían provocado las inyecciones. Ya no tenía la mano escayolada.

Se sentía como si alguien le hubiera propinado patadas en el bajo vientre y después la hubiera apuñalado para asegurarse de que no podía moverse más. Notaba el cuerpo tenso e hinchado, como si la piel estuviera demasiado estirada. Quiso encogerse sobre sí misma, pero le dolía demasiado apoyarse en los brazos.

En el espejo del baño descubrió que tenía los ojos exageradamente dilatados e inyectados en sangre. Su boca estaba seca y, aunque intentó beber agua, le hacía daño en el estómago. Estuvo a punto de desmayarse en el suelo.

Ferron apareció al día siguiente, o tal vez dos días después. Helena había perdido la noción del tiempo.

—El Sumo Nigromante desea verte —anunció—. ¿Qué te ocurre?

Helena no tenía ni idea de qué le pasaba, lo único que sabía era que le habían suministrado algo horrible.

—Stroud —masculló.

Ferron soltó un improperio y se marchó, para luego volver indignado.

Ordenó que la llevaran en volandas hasta un vehículo que aguardaba en el jardín. La envolvieron en mantas y la acomodaron en el asiento trasero. El aire fresco le proporcionó un alivio momentáneo, lo suficiente para incorporarse y mirar por la ventanilla, aunque todavía le palpitaban los brazos ahí donde se le habían formado moratones.

En vez de dirigirse a la Central, tomaron un puente que se adentraba en las zonas más bajas de la ciudad y atravesaron un túnel. El vehículo siguió avanzando, sin salir a la superficie. De hecho, se detuvo en algún punto indeterminado de la penumbra. Por el suelo se extendía una especie de neblina vaporosa y la oscuridad acechaba desde todas direcciones, apenas interrumpida por unas luces tenues de color ámbar.

El aire era rancio y húmedo. Helena olía el río que amenazaba con filtrarse.

Ferron salió del vehículo y abrió la puerta de atrás con gesto tenso.

—¿Puedes andar?

Las pocas figuras que Helena distinguía eran necrómatas viejos y podridos, así que tragó saliva y asintió.

«No mires las sombras».

—Pues adelante. —La tomó del brazo. No apretó demasiado, pero, aun así, sintió los moratones.

Helena no tuvo más remedio que seguirlo, aunque se iba quedando sin aliento. El cabello plateado de Ferron se convirtió en lo único que veía en la oscuridad. Estiró una mano para buscar un punto de apoyo en alguna pared cercana.

Tocó una superficie húmeda y resbaladiza. Quitó la mano de golpe.

El túnel por fin desembocó en una habitación enorme iluminada por lámparas de cristal verdoso; una decena de pasadizos desembocaban allí, como si fuera el centro de una guarida. Las paredes estaban cubiertas de murales llenos de detalles que empezaban a desvanecerse. Parecía un templo abandonado.

Helena jamás había estado en ese lugar. Sabía que Paladia se había levantado hacía mucho tiempo sobre las ruinas de una ciudad que había sido devastada por la plaga. Caudalón, donde se había producido la Primera Guerra Nigromántica. Siempre creyó que había desaparecido por completo.

El ambiente estaba cargado de un hedor a descomposición, una miasma repugnante que emanaba desde lo más profundo de la estancia.

Todos sus instintos le gritaban que huyera, pero Ferron la empujó hacia delante. Avanzó arrastrando los pies hasta que alcanzaron la pared del fondo.

—Su Eminencia. —Ferron se arrodilló y obligó a Helena a hacer lo mismo—. He traído a la prisionera. Mis más sinceras disculpas por la tardanza.

Hubo un largo silencio, tan prolongado que Helena empezó a dudar que hubiera alguien allí.

—Acércala. —Las palabras flotaban, imprecisas, susurradas desde la oscuridad.

Ferron levantó a Helena y la llevó a rastras por un tramo de escalones que apenas podía distinguir. Luego la obligó a arrodillarse de nuevo.

Helena contempló horrorizada lo que tenía delante. Apenas podía reconocer la forma grotesca que veía.

Morrough estaba sentado en un trono de cadáveres, de necrómatas, retorcidos y enredados, cuyas extremidades se habían transmutado para dar forma a un asiento que se movía a la par, que subía y bajaba como si respiraran al unísono, contrayéndose y expandiéndose a su alrededor. Por algún motivo, Morrough ya no tenía el cuerpo descomunal que Helena había visto en la Central, sino que era más pequeño.

Era como si la piel se le estuviera descomponiendo.

Una de las caras del trono fue levemente iluminada bajo la tenue luz, le pareció la de Mandl, pero no pudo asegurarlo, porque el trono avanzó llevando a Morrough hacia ella.

El Sumo Nigromante ladeó la cabeza; las cuencas de sus ojos no eran más que agujeros negros.

—¿Te he sobrestimado, Sumo Inquisidor? Quería esos recuerdos, pero solo me has traído sobras.

A la lengua de Morrough le pasaba algo: las palabras se le escapaban como si tuviera en la boca un objeto de gran tamaño.

—Os pido disculpas. Intentaré hacerlo mejor.

—Sí, siempre estás intentándolo, ¿verdad? —Las palabras no sonaron amables—. Yo mismo inspeccionaré esos recuerdos. Sujétala.

Se produjo una pausa, donde lo único que se oía era el jadeo de los cuerpos en descomposición. Apareció otra cara medio podrida, pero esta vez Helena reconoció la cicatriz ancha que le surcaba el rostro a Titus Bayard.

Antes de que pudiera encogerse, Ferron le colocó la rodilla entre los omóplatos y le sujetó la mandíbula con ambas manos.

Morrough extendió la mano derecha, decrépita, con unos dedos alargados que parecían las patas de una araña. Los huesos asomaban por la punta de los dedos, excepto en dos de ellos, que colgaban inertes, como colgajos de carne.

La resonancia que golpeó a Helena fue ulcerante y poderosa. La atravesó como la corriente de un cable pelado, abrasándola por dentro. Ella gritó entre dientes mientras la resonancia se abría paso en su cráneo.

Cuando Morrough se dispuso a analizar sus recuerdos, no sintió que los estuviera reviviendo una forma confusa; más bien era como si estuviera desollando su consciencia. El Sumo Nigromante la estaba despellejando mentalmente, arrancándole los recuerdos que encontraba.

Aunque había dicho que quería ver los recuerdos perdidos, no parecía tener prisa por encontrarlos. De hecho, se centró en sus días de encierro en Puntaférreo: la monotonía claustrofóbica, el aislamiento perpetuo, interrumpido ocasionalmente cuando Ferron le revisaba sus recuerdos o realizaba las transferencias.

Morrough mostró un interés particular en las sesiones de transferencia y las pesadillas y las fiebres que las seguían.

Sus miedos le parecían divertidos, y la agonía de la transferencia, una novedad, que se repetía una y otra vez: Ferron aplastándola y consumiéndola hasta que no hubo principio ni fin de ninguno de los dos. Cuando Helena dejó de gritar y quedó inerte, sin resistirse de ninguna manera, él finalmente se volvió hacia los destellos de su memoria, pero también los distorsionó a su antojo.

Luc estaba en el tejado, pero despojado de todos los detalles que hacían que el recuerdo fuese bonito: el fuego blanco, la luz de sus ojos, el resplandor de la ciudad al atardecer, todo eso había desaparecido y solo quedó la distancia entre ellos, cómo Luc se apartó de ella, el reproche de su voz y la droga que lo calmaba.

Morrough repasó varias veces el recuerdo en el que Lila preguntaba sobre las aprendizas, con un deje de curiosidad, pero lo que más le interesó fue aquel recuerdo en el que Lila tenía la cicatriz y lloraba.

Cuando se cansó de ese recuerdo, Helena deseó que hubiera acabado, pero no fue así. Volvió a sumergirse en la última sesión de transferencia.

Helena no logró reunir el poder que había tenido durante un breve momento para expulsar a Ferron de su mente. Morrough prolongó el recuerdo, alargó cada instante insoportable de la violación mental de Ferron y el dolor que sintió al resistirse, hasta que ni siquiera se percató de que se había detenido.

El dolor en su cabeza era tan intenso que borraba todo lo demás; solo era consciente de que respiraba con dificultad. No era capaz de enfocar la vista. No supo dónde estaba hasta que sintió que le latía el pulso en el punto donde Ferron la sujetaba y en la espalda, donde le había clavado la rodilla.

—Bueno… —La voz de Morrough sonó en algún punto de la oscuridad—. Por lo que veo, la animante de la Llama Eterna no está muerta.

—¿Creéis que Boyle sigue viva? —Ferron sonó sorprendido.

—¿Quién?

Ferron soltó a Helena, que se desplomó contra él en la oscuridad asfixiante.

—Stroud la mencionó. Según los registros de la Resistencia, parece ser que fue Elain Boyle la que…

—Boyle no era nadie. ¿No te has fijado en que la transferencia fue distinta a la de los demás?

Helena frunció el entrecejo. ¿Los demás?

—Me dijeron que las transmutaciones de su mente me supondrían una dificultad —admitió Ferron.

—Esa dificultad se debe a que se está resistiendo, porque la chica es capaz de resistirse. Esta… Ella es la animante.

Hubo un silencio que solo se vio interrumpido por el movimiento constante de los necrómatas. Ferron parecía paralizado de la impresión.

—¿No te diste cuenta ni sospechaste nada? —Morrough habló con tal virulencia que tuvo que pararse a recobrar el aliento—. Me extrañó que avanzaras tan poco, que la chica sufriera unas fiebres muy intensas que no se dieron en nuestros sujetos de prueba. ¿Cómo es posible que tenga tantos recuerdos escondidos si solo penetrar su mente resulta tan complicado?

Morrough hablaba despacio, impregnando de temor todas sus palabras. Ferron permaneció callado.

—Solo hay una respuesta: ella es la animante. Incluso ahora, con la resonancia anulada, sigue resistiéndose. Ha borrado de su memoria lo que es para escapar de mí.

A Helena se le nubló la vista del agobio que sentía.

—No es posible —oyó decir a Ferron—. Stroud dijo que era imposible que alguien pudiese borrar sus propios…

—¿Y qué sabrá Stroud? No es capaz de imaginar que alguien tenga más talento que ella. Esta chica es la animante. He notado cómo se resistía a mí. —De nuevo, los cadáveres acercaron a Morrough hacia Helena; las cuencas de los ojos estaban vacías, la resonancia calaba en sus huesos como una vibración afilada.

—Os pido perdón por mi fracaso —se disculpó Ferron con una voz ronca de la conmoción—. No se me pasó por la cabeza.

Morrough estuvo un buen rato en silencio. Helena percibía su rostro esquelético entre borrones.

—Tu padre estuvo aquí hace poco, suplicando una audiencia, tal como ahora tú suplicas el perdón. Afirma que intentó contarte lo que recordaba, pero que no le prestaste atención.

Ferron agarró con más fuerza a Helena.

—Su memoria no es de fiar, Su Eminencia. Me pareció una imprudencia consentir sus arranques de paranoia. No sabía que os molestaría con sus protestas. Sin embargo, sí que empecé a investigar después de oír sus comentarios.

—Y…

—Al parecer, la arrestaron cerca del puerto Oeste, poco después del bombardeo.

—¿Quiso rescatar a la paladina Bayard?

—Un bombardeo me parece un método negligente para rescatar a alguien. Puede que la paladina huyera al mismo tiempo. Como recordaréis, Bayard estaba medio muerta cuando la capturé.

—Fue debido a Bayard. Estoy seguro.

A Helena le palpitaba la mente al tratar de entender lo que estaban diciendo.

Un suspiro áspero y sibilante emanó de los cuerpos, de todos a la vez.

—Todo este tiempo pensábamos que Hevgoss… Y finalmente resulta que fue la Llama Eterna. Debieron de ser ellos quienes lo apresaron.

—Pero, si lo hubieran sabido, no habrían permitido que tomáramos el Cuartel General con tanta facilidad.

—Es posible… —Morrough no sonaba convencido—. Pero eso no lo decides tú. Yo determino qué información nos es útil. Esto demuestra que la Llama Eterna fue más astuta de lo que pensábamos. Sospecho que nuestra prisionera animante sabe mucho más de lo que creemos.

—Entonces seguiré quebrándola —afirmó Ferron, haciendo el amago de levantar a Helena para llevársela.

—¿Te he dado permiso para marcharte? —De repente, Morrough se puso en pie; su cuerpo enorme y distorsionado se cernía sobre ambos. Apenas llevaba ropa, y tenía la piel tan hundida y putrefacta que Helena veía palpitar los órganos que había debajo, brillantes bajo la carne podrida. Los contempló mareada.

Había demasiados huesos: algunos grisáceos y descompuestos, otros aún blancos.

La mano decrépita de Morrough se posó en el hombro de Ferron.

—Te estás volviendo presuntuoso, Sumo Inquisidor.

Ferron soltó a Helena de inmediato, que cayó a sus pies. El suelo estaba caliente, y algo pegajoso se adhirió a su piel y le empapó la ropa. El olor a vísceras y sangre oxidada le inundó las fosas nasales. Sumida en la oscuridad, sintió que unos dedos fríos tironeaban de su vestido justo cuando el trono se transformaba, emitiendo otro suspiro áspero y putrefacto.

—¿Cómo voy a confiar en alguien que da las cosas por sentado y pasa por alto tantos detalles como tú últimamente?

Ferron aspiró profundamente, soltando una bocanada de aire.

—Parece que tus errores se multiplican: pasas por alto los signos de animancia de tu prisionera, ignoras los consejos de tu padre… ¿Y dónde están los asesinos que te ordené buscar?

El hedor a cobre y descomposición del ambiente se volvía asfixiante. La oscuridad se cerraba sobre Helena, y unos dedos muertos la palpaban, aferrándola, como si quisieran arrastrarla al fondo. Todos sus miedos se hicieron realidad.

—Soy vuestro más leal sirviente. No os fallaré. Si fue culpa de la Llama Eterna, lo descubriré.

—Fue culpa de la Llama Eterna. ¿De quién si no? ¿Quién se atrevería a matar a los inmarcesibles? El arma era de obsidiana. Crowther es ahora uno de los nuestros, pero debió de compartir información con alguien que escapó durante la Purga de la Victoria. Puede que su identidad sea uno de los secretos que nuestra prisionera animante está intentando ocultar por todos los medios.

Mientras hablaba, la resonancia de Morrough ocupó el espacio como una masa sólida y pesada que la sofocaba. Las costillas de Helena se hundieron bajo la presión; notaba como si estuvieran a punto de romperse y perforarle los pulmones.

—La muerte de Mandl fue una humillación. Siendo alguien tan ilustre, deberías haberla previsto.

De repente, la presión se relajó lo suficiente como para que Helena pudiera inhalar aire con desesperación, pero la miasma le entró en la garganta y sintió que se asfixiaba.

—Estaba investigando todas las posibilidades —respondió Ferron respirando con dificultad—. Los registros indican que Crowther colaboró con un metalúrgico que murió en la batalla final. He contratado a criptólogos para que reevalúen su investigación y busquen otros posibles colaboradores.

—Eso no es ninguna novedad —le espetó Morrough—. ¿Cuántas semanas llevas investigando las muertes sin obtener resultados? ¿Se te ha olvidado lo que pasa cuando alguien me decepciona?

—Yo...

La vibración que generaba la resonancia de Morrough se concentró en un punto y desapareció. Se oyó un crujido seco, fuerte y repentino, como el de una rama al partirse. Ferron emitió un grito ahogado y cayó como una piedra. En vez de desplomarse en el suelo, se quedó colgando por encima de Helena. Uno de sus brazos se balanceaba sobre la cabeza de ella.

Helena no alcanzaba a ver su rostro. Sus ojos plateados aún brillaban, pero estaba escupiendo sangre por la boca, una sangre que se derramaba de sus labios y caía al suelo. Tenía el gesto contraído, el cuerpo contorsionado y las pupilas tan dilatadas que su iris no era más que una estrecha banda de color plata.

Acto seguido gritó y quedó inerte. Entonces sí, cayó sobre Helena.

El peso de su cuerpo y la protrusión de los huesos rotos la aplastaban. Sin embargo, no notaba el latido de su corazón.

Ni tampoco la respiración. Estaba completamente inmóvil.

Unos segundos después, se estremeció, dio una bocanada de aire y volvió a latirle el pecho. Aunque sufría convulsiones, como si estuviera ahogándose y seguía tosiendo sangre, se apartó de Helena.

—N-no os f-fallaré, lo juro. —Le temblaba la voz, apenas era un susurro, pero consiguió ponerse en pie a duras penas.

—Asegúrate de que así sea —fue lo único que dijo Morrough.

Ferron se agachó y, con dedos temblorosos, volvió a levantar a Helena del suelo. A la chica se le cayó la cabeza hacia atrás.

—Vigílala de cerca. La Llama Eterna irá a por ella dentro de poco, estoy convencido.

—Moriría antes que perderla —afirmó Ferron sujetándola con más fuerza.

—Esta vez quiero vivas a estas últimas ascuas que se han atrevido a burlarse de mí, Sumo Inquisidor. Tráemelos para que pueda matarlos a gusto.

—Los tendréis. Tal como os he entregado a los demás. —La voz de Ferron cobró firmeza. Hizo una reverencia.

Helena dobló el cuello y vislumbró entre borrones las caras verdes y podridas que se aparecían en el trono. Le dio pavor pensar a cuántos reconocería si las viera claramente.

Intentó zafarse de Ferron, pero no podía escapar. La mantuvo sujeta mientras la sacaba a rastras de la sala, a través de túneles enrevesados, sin detenerse ni una sola vez. Ni siquiera la soltó cuando le fallaron las piernas y tropezó consigo misma.

Finalmente, Ferron se detuvo y, sin soltarla aún, dejó que Helena cayera al suelo. La chica se desplomó, boqueando, ya que todavía le costaba respirar. Allí el aire era más limpio, húmedo y pantanoso, pero ya no había rastro del olor a sangre. Las piedras del túnel estaban secas.

Le dolía tanto la cabeza que pensar era como hurgar en una herida abierta, pero tenía demasiadas preguntas.

—Yo… —Se le cerró la garganta, conmocionada—. ¿Yo ataqué una prisión?

—Fue después de la batalla final —replicó Ferron, que sonaba muy distante—. Al parecer, te arrestaron después de que estallara más de la mitad del laboratorio del puerto Oeste. Ibas vestida como una hevgotiana durante el asalto y después desapareciste en aquel tanque, por lo que hay informes contradictorios. La investigación se dio por inconclusa hasta que mi padre recordó dónde te había visto. Estuvo ahí esa noche.

Helena negó con la cabeza.

—Yo era sanadora —dijo—. Es imposible que… No me dejaron luchar.

Ferron no dijo nada.

Ella seguía sin entenderlo.

—¿Y Lila estaba allí?

—Sí.

—Pero estaba muriéndose cuando la… atrapaste.

—Bennet hacía sus experimentos en el laboratorio del puerto Oeste.

A Helena se le escapó un grito de horror. Le dieron arcadas y se dobló sobre sí misma. Ferron tuvo que sostenerla.

—Bébete esto —ordenó dándole un frasco—. Te ayudará.

Le temblaban las manos, pero se lo tomó sin preguntar. Nada de lo que le diera podía empeorar las cosas. Era un calmante tan amargo que le adormeció la lengua. Se sentó, respirando entrecortadamente, y esperó a que le hiciera efecto.

Intentó concentrarse, pero sentía como si tuviera una conmoción cerebral. Cuando se sufrían heridas cerebrales, era importante mantenerse despierto. La conversación ayudaba, porque obligaba a los pacientes a seguir hablando. Se esforzó por hacerlo.

—¿Te ha pasado alguna vez? —le preguntó con voz pastosa. Supo que Ferron la estaba mirando; sus ojos pálidos relucieron brevemente en la oscuridad.

—Más de una vez… —respondió él tras un largo silencio—. Tuve un entrenamiento muy riguroso.

—¿Por qué?

Ferron se removió y dejó escapar un leve gruñido.

—Porque necesitaban comprobar si era mejor que mi padre o si, como él, corría el riesgo de derrumbarme en caso de enfrentarme a un interrogatorio.

Helena frunció el ceño.

—Y eso fue… ¿antes o después de asesinar al principado Apollo?

Su captor soltó un resoplido, como una risa contenida.

—¿Quieres una confesión? —preguntó después en tono seco—. Ya que nos ponemos, puedo contarte todo lo que he hecho hasta ahora.

Helena apenas distinguía el contorno difuso de su cuerpo; estaba agachado delante de ella. Seguía respirando con dificultad mientras la sostenía erguida.

Se preguntó entonces si se habían detenido para que ella recobrara fuerzas o para que él pudiera recuperarse. La dosis de láudano había conseguido aliviar un poco el dolor que le astillaba la cabeza.

Una pregunta asomó a sus labios, como si formularla fuera de vital importancia. Se inclinó hacia delante, intentando verle mejor el rostro.

—¿Tú quieres contármelo?

Ferron se quedó callado un buen rato y, después, se levantó sin pronunciar palabra y la puso en pie. Helena sentía el cuerpo medio entumecido, y él tuvo prácticamente que llevarla en brazos hasta el vehículo.

A la luz, descubrió que estaba cubierta de restos putrefactos, de sangre podrida y vísceras que le manchaban la ropa y las manos. Todos los necrómatas se mantuvieron al margen mientras Ferron la arrastraba hasta el vehículo. Se la entregó a una de las criadas, que se encargó de quitarle el vestido y la envolvió en una tela de lana. Helena se desplomó en el asiento trasero.

Ferron se sentó delante. Cuando el vehículo salió del túnel, el blanco brillante del cielo encapotado la cegó por un instante, pero logró verlo de perfil. Estaba inclinado hacia delante con los ojos cerrados, pálido como si estuviera muerto.

———

Helena tardó dos días en recuperar completamente la vista y tres en sentarse sin que se mareara. Intentó leer, pero las letras se movían ante sus ojos, dejándola sin otra ocupación que sus propios pensamientos.

Al tercer día, una de las criadas le trajo una bandeja con gachas a la cama. La miró fijamente a los ojos, azules y nublados.

—Ferron, ¿puedes venir?

La criada la observó fijamente y, después, apartó la vista sin decir nada. Sin embargo, esa misma noche, cuando estaba cenando con calma, se abrió la puerta. Era Ferron.

—¿Me has hecho llamar? —preguntó con tono irónico.

—Quería hacerte una pregunta —respondió Helena, intentando incorporarse, aunque con ello solo consiguió que le palpitara aún más la cabeza, como si se le fueran a salir los ojos de las órbitas.

Respiró hondo, despacio, y recopiló toda la información que había ido descubriendo en los últimos meses. Casi sin darse cuenta, había tejido un tapiz, y ahora podía distinguir la imagen que se escondía bajo la punta de sus dedos.

—Mandl no fue la primera de los inmarcesibles que murió asesinada —dijo ella al fin—. Llevan semanas desapareciendo. Hasta ahora, no había reparado en qué tenían en común las desapariciones. Pensé que podría tratarse de censura o que tal vez fueran disidentes, pero eran los inmarcesibles. Están desapareciendo porque los están asesinando, y tú eres el que lo está encubriendo todo.

Ferron no dijo nada. Se esforzó por mantener el rostro impasible.

Helena tragó saliva.

—Verás, para mí, la existencia de los inmarcesibles nunca tuvo mucho sentido. Ni desde el punto de vista científico ni desde el lógico. La inmortalidad me parece un regalo demasiado peligroso como para concederlo así, sin más, y no creo que Morrough sea especialmente altruista. Sé cómo funciona la vivemancia. Las regeneraciones complejas tienen un precio y alguien tiene que pagarlo. Es algo inevitable. Para que los inmarcesibles puedan regenerarse como lo hacen, alguien debe asumir ese coste.

—Creía que tenías una pregunta —dijo Ferron.

—A eso voy —replicó Helena con calma, tratando de ignorar la pulsación que sentía en la nuca—. Cuando los inmarcesibles ocupan el cuerpo de un cadáver, pierden la resonancia que tenían antes y adquieren la resonancia del cuerpo nuevo. Igual que tu padre. Él era alquimista férreo, pero no sabe nada de piromancia. Así que, si alguien como tú, un animante, perdiera su cuerpo, perdería también esa habilidad, y, si pensara que ser un liche es un castigo, algo con lo que enseñar una lección, se aferraría a ese cuerpo, aunque estuviera en mal estado, y querría desesperadamente descubrir cómo funcionan las transferencias. Sin embargo, pese a que lo lograra, seguiría necesitando un animante. Pero alguien así se resistiría a la transferencia.

Helena torció el gesto y se llevó la mano a la frente, como intentando despejar la presión que sentía.

—Y ahí... ahí es donde entra el programa de repoblación —dijo con inquietud—. A Morrough no le importa la economía o qué tipo de alquimistas haya en Nueva Paladia. La razón verdadera por la que Stroud está estudiando la reproducción selectiva es para encontrar una forma de controlar con qué resonancia nacen los niños. Por eso trajeron de vuelta a tu padre, y por eso lo vi en la Central. Está intentando producir un animante para Morrough. Si domina el arte de la transferencia para entonces, tendrá tanto los medios como el recipiente perfecto, pero… se le está acabando el tiempo.

Ferron entrecerró los ojos.

Helena respiró hondo.

—Le pasa algo. Es demasiado viejo, y eso suele afectar a la resonancia, pero a él no. Obtiene su poder de otra fuente, lo extrae de algún otro sitio. Y, aun así, se está deteriorando. Lo vi hace unos meses y no estaba así. Es ese trono lo que lo mantiene con vida. Sigo sin saber qué podría hacerle daño a alguien así. Tampoco es que nadie pueda acercársele. Y entonces pensé… Tal vez la fuente de su poder está delante de nosotros, pero oculta, para que nadie la reconozca. Tal vez se presenta como un regalo, algo que la gente ansía ganar, a pesar de que sea él quien la necesite.

A Helena empezó a dolerle la cabeza. Su visión se tornó roja. Emitió un grito ahogado de dolor y se hundió hacia un lado. Ferron se estaba acercando.

La chica levantó la vista y se obligó a hacer la pregunta.

—Los inmarcesibles. Vosotros sois la fuente del poder de Morrough, y la Resistencia… Nosotros lo descubrimos, ¿verdad? Descubrimos cómo matarlo, cómo mataros a todos.

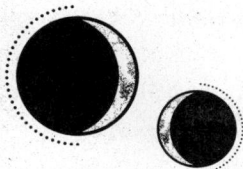

CAPÍTULO 14

Helena estaba sentada en un *taburete del laboratorio. Sobre la mesa frente a ella había metales y compuestos transmutados colocados en fila. Algunos tenían la forma de esferas vacías, mientras que otros todavía estaban almacenados en pequeños frascos, esperando a que los probaran.*

Enfrente se encontraba Shiseo, que estudiaba una esfera que tenía entre los dedos y anotaba observaciones en un papel.

—Tienes un repertorio de lo más interesante —comentó en voz baja. Cogió un frasco de la tercera fila—. Muy inusual. Y una buena atención al detalle. Me sorprende que no seas metalúrgica.

—No estaba segura de qué camino escoger —confesó Helena, entregándole otra esfera para examinarla—. Tenía la sensación de que, independientemente de la decisión que tomase, terminaría decepcionando a alguien. Todos... —Comenzó a gesticular con los dedos, pero se contuvo y cruzó las manos sobre su regazo—. Todos esperaban mucho de mí, y creo que yo nunca tuve claro qué quería. —Se encogió de hombros—. Seguramente fue mejor así. Al final, no importó.

Shiseo no respondió; estaba releyendo sus notas. Después de un rato, miró impasible las manos que Helena había entrelazado sobre el regazo.

—Creo que no te viene bien un arma de acero.

—¿Cómo?

—Tu manejo del titanio es excepcional. Hace tiempo, conocí al maese gremial del titanio, y ni siquiera sus obras eran tan perfectas como las tuyas. —Escogió una pieza de níquel que Helena había transformado y la examinó detenidamente—. ¿Alguna vez has probado a utilizar una aleación de níquel y titanio?

La chica negó con la cabeza.

—Sería la mejor opción para ti. Muy ligera. Con el acero malgastarías tu energía.

—Pero yo no he hablado de armas —repuso Helena rápidamente—. Lo de la prueba era una mera... curiosidad.

Shiseo chasqueó la lengua.

—Bueno..., en caso de que quisieras una, te aconsejo que sea de níquel y titanio. No te límites a seguir los pasos de los paladinos.

———————

HELENA SENTÍA TODO EL CUERPO levemente dolorido y notaba la lengua especialmente sensible, como si el tejido acabara de regenerarse. Se obligó a abrir los ojos.

Desconcertada, contempló el dosel que tenía encima y trató de recordar lo que había sucedido.

Ferron... Había estado hablando con Ferron. Lo buscó con la mirada, pero no se encontraba allí.

Le había dicho que Morrough se estaba muriendo, que el asesinato de los inmarcesibles le afectaba, que por fin lo había resuelto todo y entonces...

Nada después de eso.

Se incorporó lentamente. Debía de haber sufrido otra convulsión. Movió los hombros y abrió la boca con cautela, como si esperara que los músculos le dolieran o que alguna tensión residual fuera a limitar sus movimientos. No fue así.

Se miró de arriba abajo. La habían tratado.

En el hospital militar, Helena no había visto muchos casos de convulsiones, pero Titus Bayard las sufrió después de la lesión cerebral.

La tensión muscular no era algo que se pudiera curar con un simple toque de vivemancia. La resonancia podía aflojar los nudos musculares, pero la tensión había que masajearla manualmente para que las extremidades recuperaran movilidad y elasticidad.

Eso implicaba que alguien le había tocado, al menos, la parte derecha del cuerpo. Se estremeció y rezó para que no hubiera sido ninguno de los necromantes, pero luego se detuvo al darse cuenta de cuál era la alternativa.

Se dio una larga ducha hasta que desaparecieron los últimos restos de dolor en su cuerpo. Echó la cabeza hacia atrás para dejar que el agua le corriera por el pelo mientras revivía aquel recuerdo.

Shiseo. Así que lo había conocido. No quería creerlo, pero ahora estaba ahí, en su mente.

No debían de haberse relacionado mucho. Probablemente hacía los exámenes de resonancia a mucha gente. Tal vez incluso los hiciera para espiar a la Resistencia.

Entonces ¿por qué había ocultado ese recuerdo? Le fascinaba lo mucho que abarcaba la pérdida de su memoria.

¿Por qué los inmarcesibles confiaban en Shiseo si había trabajado y vivido entre la Resistencia durante toda la guerra? Muchos paladinos habían sido asesinados o encarcelados por menos, pero a él lo habían enviado al extranjero.

No tenía sentido.

Después de su fundación, Paladia recibió extranjeros de todo el mundo. Los Holdfast querían que la Academia se convirtiera en la capital alquímica del mundo, donde los alquimistas de todas partes pudieran reunirse para compartir sus técnicas y métodos. Pero Paladia no tardó en olvidarse de ese sueño.

Sobre todo, una vez que la Academia alcanzó su máxima capacidad y el sentimiento de acogida empezó a agriarse.

Tras la muerte del principado Apollo, cuando comenzó a hablarse de guerra, el padre de Helena quiso regresar al sur. Para él, aquella lucha no era la suya y su responsabilidad se limitaba a mantenerla a salvo. Sin embargo, Helena ya le había prometido a Luc que se quedaría, así que su padre decidió hacerlo también por ella.

Y murió por su culpa.

Inhaló con angustia y trazó con los dedos el contorno de la cicatriz que tenía en la garganta mientras salía de la ducha.

Cuando se quitó la toalla, se sintió paralizada al verse en el espejo.

Desde que mejoraron las comidas, había evitado mirar su reflejo; odiaba los cambios que veía en él, como si la versión que conocía de sí misma se hubiera desvanecido.

En sus recuerdos, era una joven demacrada por el estrés: la piel hundida por la falta de luz solar; el cabello casi negro recogido cuidadosamente en dos trenzas apretadas enroscadas en la nuca; huesuda y de extremidades delgadas; los ojos grandes y oscuros, pero con fuego en la mirada.

Cuando llegó a Puntaférreo, aún quedaba algo de esa chica.

Ahora, su rostro ya no estaba demacrado; no tenía las mejillas hundidas, ni los ojos marcados por el cansancio; mostraba mejor color, y, sin peine ni gomas, el pelo le caía suelto como cascada, hasta más allá de los codos. Además, apenas se le notaban los huesos.

Parecía sana.

Guapa, incluso.

Una Helena de una vida diferente.

Pero los ojos…

Los ojos estaban muertos. No había fuego en ellos.

La chispa que antes consideraba una parte esencial de quien era había desaparecido.

Era un cadáver viviente. No se diferenciaba mucho de los necrómatas que hostigaban Puntaférreo.

FERRON VOLVIÓ A APARECER UN día después, mientras Helena cenaba.

Llevaba su ropa de «caza», pero estaba limpia, así que Helena supuso que estaba a punto de salir, no de regreso. Lo observó con cautela mientras entraba. Sin el abrigo y las capas que solía usar, se le notaba mucho más delgado.

Cuando se acercó, Helena lo miró con los ojos entrecerrados. La ropa que vestía era gris oscura, para camuflarse en las sombras de la ciudad, pero en algunos puntos había destellos metálicos. Los más obvios se encontraban en los antebrazos, el pecho y las piernas.

Una armadura reforzada. Por eso no había podido apuñalarlo.

Ferron se detuvo delante de ella, impasible, con las manos cruzadas detrás de la espalda.

—¿Qué te hizo darte cuenta?

Las puntas del tenedor chirriaron contra el plato.

—¿Darme cuenta? ¿De que Morrough se está muriendo o de que ha estado creando inmarcesibles para asegurarse una extraña fuente de poder?

Ferron sonrió.

—Empecemos por lo último.

Helena miró la ventana.

—Todo el mundo se comportaba como si la guerra fuera inevitable,

212

como si fuese parte de un ciclo eterno entre el bien y el mal, pero yo… nunca lo entendí. ¿Por qué Morrough quería controlar Paladia? El Concejo pensaba que Hevgoss estaba involucrado, que buscaban un pretexto para intervenir militarmente y así incluir a Paladia dentro de sus fronteras. ¿Pero qué ganaba Morrough con eso? A nadie pareció importarle. Solo se trataba de un nigromante malvado al que la Llama Eterna necesitaba eliminar. Nadie se preguntaba por qué, qué motivos podía tener alguien para hacer algo así. —Sacudió la cabeza—. No creo que la inmortalidad sea un regalo, sobre todo si Morrough te lo da sin más, a menos que él le saque más partido que quienes la reciben. Las cosas que parecen demasiado buenas para ser verdad suelen tener un precio oculto, que solo se descubre cuando ya es demasiado tarde.

Ferron no dijo nada.

—¿Tengo razón? —preguntó Helena.

La expresión y la postura de su captor no delataban nada.

—¿Acaso importa?

La chica apartó la mirada.

—Bueno, te lo diré… si tú me dices qué acabó siendo demasiado bueno para ser verdad para ti.

Helena tragó saliva y contempló las montañas.

—Paladia. —Respiró hondo y lo miró—. ¿Y bien?

Ferron clavó los ojos en ella, unos ojos que relucían con cierto atisbo de satisfacción.

—Sí, se está muriendo.

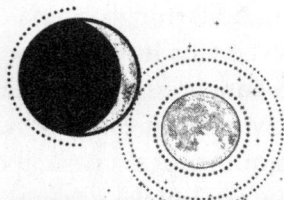

CAPÍTULO 15

EL CAUTIVERIO DE HELENA VOLVIÓ a caer en la monotonía.

Solo vio a Ferron cuando vino a revisar su memoria y, de nuevo, unos días después, cuando le hizo la transferencia.

Helena no se resistió. Todavía notaba la mente débil como una tela de araña. Temía que, si se desmoronaba, Ferron tendría vía libre.

El Sumo Inquisidor no trató de abrirse paso por lugares ocultos, sino que se plantó en medio de su mente y se quedó allí. Cuando él pestañeaba, los ojos de Helena temblaban. Levantó la mano izquierda; ella observó cómo se abría y se cerraba. Su consciencia estaba dividida entre ambos, pero, a cada segundo que pasaba, se sentía más como él y menos como ella misma. La estaba devorando lentamente.

Saboreó la sangre. Le estaba cayendo de los ojos y la nariz.

Cuando terminó, Helena permaneció inerte donde estaba, con la cabeza reclinada hacia atrás, contemplando el techo, hasta que llegaron las necrómatas y la llevaron a la cama.

Como no se resistió, solo tuvo unas décimas de fiebre durante unos días. Al parecer, sí que era ella la animante.

Aquella revelación le oprimía el pecho como una losa. Antes estaba segura de que su pérdida de memoria se debía a una estrategia de la Resistencia para proteger algún secreto importante sobre Luc. Que se trataba de un sacrificio enorme al que había accedido para después confiarle su mente y sus recuerdos a esa misteriosa Elain Boyle.

¿Había sido ella misma la que había tratado de esconderse todo este tiempo? ¿Eso era lo que había pasado? Seguramente había algo más, pero no recordaba nada que tuviera la más mínima relevancia. Ninguno de los recuerdos fragmentados que había recuperado parecía ser muy importante.

Ferron siempre estaba ocupado. Dedicaba la mayor parte de su tiempo a cazar a los últimos miembros que quedaban de la Llama Eterna. Cuando conseguía verlo desde las ventanas que daban al jardín, se notaba que estaba hecho polvo. A veces volvía cubierto de sangre.

Helena se percató de las ojeras que tenía y de la rigidez con la que se movía, y empezó a sospechar que Morrough lo estaba torturando con frecuencia. Como Ferron no podía morir, Morrough se deleitaba asesinándolo una y otra vez.

No volvía a casa lívido de furia, sino conmocionado por la tortura. Cuanto más lo observaba, más evidentes le parecían los síntomas. Era como si, a pesar de recuperarse físicamente, su mente se estuviera erosionando poco a poco.

Intentó no pensar en ello, pero no lo logró, así que decidió procurar que no le importara.

Ferron quería darle caza a la Resistencia. Cada vez que lo torturaban era una señal de que había fracasado. ¿Acaso Helena no había deseado que lo castigaran? Al fin y al cabo, él mismo se lo había buscado. Morrough se estaba muriendo, y Ferron lo sabía y, sin embargo, aún elegía servirlo, haciendo todo lo que el Sumo Nigromante no tenía fuerzas para hacer por sí mismo.

Se merecía sufrir.

CUANDO ENCONTRÓ MANCHAS DE SANGRE entre las piernas, se quedó mirándolas fijamente, sin comprender nada, hasta que cayó en la cuenta de que estaba menstruando. Incluso antes de la guerra, el estrés de la beca hacía que la regla le viniera de forma irregular. Después de los asesinatos, desapareció por completo.

Se había olvidado de que su cuerpo funcionaba así.

Cuando la esterilizaron, Matias quiso que le extirparan el útero, pero Ilva insistió en que el procedimiento debía ser lo menos invasivo posible. Una ligadura de trompas. Por eso aún podía sangrar.

Se colocó un paño entre las piernas y, cuando le llevaron el almuerzo, le preguntó a la criada si podía traerle algo para la regla. Si le hubiera pasado antes, tal vez habría disfrutado al pensar lo incómodo que se sentiría Ferron de lidiar con las vicisitudes de tener una prisionera, pero ahora la incomodidad de Ferron era algo en lo que Helena prefería no pensar.

Diez días después de la transferencia, cuando Ferron acudió a su habitación para revisar de nuevo sus recuerdos, parecía menos alterado. Cuando descubrió que Helena se preocupaba por él, de mala gana, pero de forma compulsiva, rompió la conexión.

Al abrir los ojos, lo encontró mirándola fijamente.

—¿Te preocupas por mí? —Su rostro se retorció en una sonrisa de suficiencia—. Nunca pensé que fuera posible.

A Helena le ardió la cara.

—No te lo tomes como un cumplido. Odio la tortura.

—Menuda santa —dijo con sequedad, y se llevó una mano al pecho—. Estoy seguro de que el generoso de Luc se habría emocionado de ver que tienes tan buen corazón.

—No pronuncies su nombre —replicó Helena con virulencia—. Nunca fuiste amigo suyo.

La chica se incorporó, aunque todavía se sentía mareada.

Ferron se apoyó en el poste de la cama.

—¿Sabes qué? A veces me preguntó quién ha causado más muertes en la Resistencia, si los Holdfast con sus principios o yo. ¿Tú qué crees?

—No es lo mismo.

Al Sumo Inquisidor le temblaron los dedos. Se cruzó de brazos para que Helena no se percatara de ello, y estuvo a punto de conseguirlo.

—¿De verdad hay diferencia entre obligar a alguien a morir por ti y asesinarlos?

Helena sintió que la rabia se extendía por su pecho.

—Sí, estoy segura de que te encantaría pensar que no la hay para así acallar tu conciencia, pero no te pareces en nada a él.

Su captor se limitó a sonreír.

—No creo que tenga conciencia, pero, dime, ¿preferirías que los hubiera mantenido con vida? —Hizo la pregunta con cautela—. ¿Que mantuviera con vida a los miembros de la Llama Eterna para que albergaran esperanzas? ¿Eso te parecería más compasivo?

—Deberían albergar esperanzas, porque sigue habiendo alguien ahí fuera. Un miembro de la Llama Eterna al que no habéis capturado.

—No por mucho tiempo.

Helena palideció.

—¿Lo has…? —Le tembló la voz.

Ferron negó con la cabeza.

—Todavía no, pero te garantizo que lo haré. —Había rabia en su sonrisa—. Pase lo que pase con Morrough, el asesino acabará muerto y enterrado.

—Eso no lo sabes —repuso Helena con fiereza.

—Claro que sí —dijo él, con una expresión tan dura como si estuviera hecha de granito—. Esta historia solo tiene un final. Si la Resistencia quería otro resultado, debería haber tomado distintas decisiones: unas decisiones duras y realistas, y haber renunciado a la idea fantasiosa de que la superioridad moral de su causa les concedería la victoria. Eran unos idiotas, todos ellos. —Resopló—. Si los dioses existieran, habrían hecho que Apollo Holdfast fuese más difícil de matar.

Helena lo miró fijamente y observó cómo se le retorcía el gesto; le brillaban los ojos de la rabia.

—¿A quién odias tanto? —Hasta entonces, no se había percatado de lo enraizado que estaba su odio, como un océano que se extendía hasta el infinito y lo único que prometía era la muerte.

Al principio, la pregunta pareció pillarlo desprevenido, pero luego sus emociones se esfumaron, como si cerrara una caja con cuidado.

—A mucha gente —dijo encogiéndose de hombros con insolencia. Sonrió y su boca se curvó como una guadaña—. Aunque la mayoría ya están muertos.

LANCASTER VOLVIÓ A PUNTAFÉRREO CUANDO el invierno ya había pasado. Helena no le prestó atención. Si fuera miembro de la Resistencia, Ferron ya le habría dado caza.

Al oír el ruido de numerosos pasos, supo que los Ferron estaban preparando alguna celebración. El ala principal de la casa bullía de actividad. Habían traído más necrómatas, y los cadáveres en descomposición que hacían guardia en la puerta principal fueron desplazados a otro lugar.

Había cajas de flores desperdigadas por todo el vestíbulo, listas para adornar la casa. Las habrían enviado desde algún lugar del sur o se habrían cultivado en interiores, porque los parterres de Puntaférreo seguían desiertos.

Helena calculó la fecha y comprendió que era el equinoccio de primavera.

Aurelia iba a dar una fiesta.

Cuando comenzaron a llegar los vehículos, encendieron grandes estufas en el jardín. Desde una ventana del piso superior, Helena observaba cómo llegaban los invitados. Parecía una fiesta más comedida que la del solsticio de invierno. Los solsticios eran las fiestas más importantes de Paladia, al contrario que los equinoccios, que se festejaban más en las zonas dedicadas a la agricultura. Se decía que en Novis celebraban grandes desfiles en primavera en honor a Tellus, la diosa de la tierra.

Una vez que todos los invitados entraron, Helena esperó media hora antes de escabullirse hacia el ala principal. Los necrómatas estaban demasiado ocupados atendiendo a los invitados como para prestarle atención, así que solo la vigilaban los ojos ocultos en las paredes.

Helena oyó las voces antes de acercarse al comedor. Parecía que estaban borrachos. Se deslizó en la habitación contigua. Aunque las voces llegaban amortiguadas a través de las paredes, si acercaba el oído, escuchaba claramente lo que decían.

—Es un fantasma, ya te lo digo yo. Holdfast ha vuelto para vengarse. No hay otra explicación —decía una voz estruendosa que arrastraba las palabras—. Va atravesando las putas paredes.

—Cállate, anda —le espetó alguien—. Los fantasmas no existen, capullo.

—No dirías lo mismo si hubieses visto a Vidkun. Tapió toda la casa y se encerró dentro, solo con los necrómatas que lo acompañaban. Ni una rata podría haberse colado. ¿Cómo es posible que lo mataran?

—Que tú no sepas transmutar nada que no contenga cobre no significa que el resto del mundo no pueda. Todos saben que los Holdfast reunían alquimistas de todo tipo. Seguramente sería uno de esos raritos. Además, Vidkun era idiota. Se quedó en casa, solo. Si no quieres morir, vete a follarte a alguien en su cama en vez de en la tuya.

Un rebuzno de carcajadas estalló entre ellos.

—Hablando de follar —intervino una voz taimada—, ¿cuántos habéis ido últimamente a la Central? ¿Stroud os ha enseñado los avances?

Helena oyó las risillas y se quedó petrificada, incapaz de respirar.

—Siempre es un placer cumplir con mi deber. Paladia necesita más alquimistas —replicó una voz lasciva.

—¿Stroud te deja elegir a la que quieras?

—Bueno —respondió la voz taimada—, seguramente dependa de tu repertorio. Te dará una lista de habitaciones para que elijas. Hay una chica preciosa que no tiene muchas cicatrices. La muy puta me mordió, pero se mostró más dispuesta a cooperar cuando le rompí la mandíbula. Le dije a Stroud que la dejara curarse a la antigua. —Soltó un suspiro dramático—. Voy a volver esta semana para ver si está preñada y, si no, supongo que lo intentaré de nuevo. Casi prefiero que no lo esté; creo que me gustará más si tiene la boca inmovilizada.

Helena sintió como si alguien la apuñalara. El dolor le atravesó el pecho y el estómago.

—¿Eso es todo? Por lo que había leído en el periódico, pensaba que sería algo más burocrático. Tendré que pasarme a ver qué me toca.

Hubo más carcajadas.

—¿Tú has estado, Ferron? Con el repertorio que tienes, seguro que te dejan entrar en todas las habitaciones.

A Helena se le secó la boca.

—No —respondió la voz fría de Ferron—. Tengo mejores cosas que hacer.

—Claro, para qué ir hasta la ciudad cuando tienes a una aquí.

—La prisionera no es para eso —intervino Aurelia—. Además, pronto acabaremos con ella. Y, sinceramente, no es un regalo para los ojos. Lo único que hace es merodear como una rata. Tuve que amenazarla para conseguir que se bañara.

—Vi la foto en el periódico. Tiene una pinta un poco salvaje, pero yo no le haría ascos —afirmó la voz taimada.

Entonces se oyeron unas risas escandalosas.

—¿Os habéis fijado en las flores? —preguntó Aurelia en voz alta.

Respondió una voz de mujer, mucho más suave que la de los hombres, y Aurelia también bajó el tono. Helena agudizó el oído, pero solo distinguió algunas palabras sobre impuestos de importación.

La conversación volvió al asesinato más reciente.

—Espantoso. No pude ni dormir después de verlo. Lo cortaron en trozos tan finos que se transparentaban a la luz. Y se los metieron todos por la garganta.

—Pero después, ¿no? —preguntó una voz nueva, teñida de nerviosismo—. Ya estaba muerto cuando...

—No, lo hicieron antes. Tenía la aleación en la sangre que le impedía regenerarse. El que hemos dejado escapar debe de ser un psicópata.

—Te has dado cuenta de que sigue un patrón, ¿no?

Se hizo un tenso silencio, al que le siguieron unos murmullos de inquietud.

—La Purga de la Victoria —dijo Ferron cuando nadie se atrevió a hablar—. El asesino está imitando las ejecuciones de aquel día. A Vidkun lo mataron de la misma forma que a Bayard y su mujer.

—¿Entonces no es más que venganza? —De nuevo la voz nerviosa—. Durant, Vidkun y los demás son los inmarcesibles que estuvieron allí esa noche. El resto estamos a salvo.

Hubo murmullos de alivio.

—Mierda… —soltó la voz taimada—. Eso significa que no vendrán a por esa putilla frígida. Esperaba que fuera la siguiente.

—Bueno, yo no pienso arriesgarme —intervino otra voz—. Me he construido un búnker. Con paredes, techo y suelos de hierro inerte y plomo sólido. Soy el único con esa combinación. Nada podrá atravesarlo.

Pasaron un buen rato describiendo las distintas precauciones que habían tomado: escalones trampa y defensas escondidas en sus propias casas, todo en función de sus repertorios.

Helena intentó prestar atención, pero la conversación se dividió en varias charlas superpuestas que se fundieron en un murmullo ininteligible. Al cabo de un tiempo, oyó que se movían las sillas y que Aurelia decía algo sobre las flores del invernadero. Después de eso, las voces se dispersaron a otra habitación.

Helena se separó de la pared, incapaz de hacer nada más que permanecer sentada, paralizada por el horror al imaginar lo que les esperaba a las mujeres que se encontraban en la Central.

La Resistencia había contado con muchas mujeres no solo en combate, sino en todos los aspectos: eran las que trabajaban en el hospital, las que acudían al frente como médicos militares y las que arrastraban a los heridos para ponerlos a salvo; las que operaban las radios y enviaban mensajes, que lavaban y reparaban la ropa y los uniformes, y las que hacían las comidas. Todas las tareas mundanas que nunca terminaban, ni siquiera cuando empezaba una guerra. Eran mujeres las que se encargaban de todos esos trabajos. Seguramente las capturaron en el Cuartel General y no las consideraron lo bastante importantes para ejecutarlas.

Durante todo ese tiempo, Helena había considerado que su encarcelamiento era algo terrible. Ahora se sentía culpable por lo poco que tenía que soportar.

La casa estaba en silencio; la conversación se escuchaba como un zumbido lejano, proveniente de varias habitaciones más allá. Poco a poco, emprendió el regreso hacia el ala oeste, aunque todavía se sentía mareada por aquellas noticias tan terribles.

Estaba a punto de doblar la esquina cuando escuchó unos pasos a su espalda.

Se giró a tiempo para ver un borrón. Algo la golpeó.

Al caer al suelo, el aire se le escapó de los pulmones y se dio un fuerte golpe en la cabeza contra el parquet. El mundo se volvió del revés; los techos abovedados se convirtieron en fauces cavernosas que se cernían sobre ella.

Estando tirada en el suelo medio mareada, tratando de recobrar el aliento, vio que algo se le echaba encima. Era Lancaster.

—Te pillé —dijo jadeando, aplastándola con su propio peso. Rio por lo bajo—. ¿Quién hubiera dicho que tendría tanta suerte al salir a mear? Ferron siempre tiene tu ala de la casa llena de necrómatas. No sabía si te encontraría algún día. Hemos tenido que montar una buena fiesta para que estén todos ocupados.

Le pasó el pulgar por la barbilla y la mejilla. Su aliento era cálido y espeso, propio del vino.

—Joder. Mírate. Has ganado peso desde la última vez.

Helena estaba aturdida. «Haz algo», se repetía en su mente.

—Si yo fuera Ferron, te tendría atada a mi cama. —Una mano se deslizó hasta sus pechos y apretó con fuerza. Después, apretó más—. Deberías ser mía. Fui yo quien te atrapó cuando estabas destripando a Atreus. Cuando te vi en las ruinas del laboratorio, rodeada de llamas bajo el cielo abrasador y con todos esos necrómatas a tu alrededor, pensé que eras Lumitia, nacida del fuego.

Helena intentó zafarse, pero no podía mover bien los brazos. Quiso gritar, aunque sabía que él acallaría el sonido de inmediato. Tenía que esperar al momento oportuno.

—Deberían haberme hecho inmarcesible entonces; no te habrían capturado de no ser por mí —susurró Lancaster, con la cara a centímetros de la suya—. Pero desapareciste. Esta vez no pienso perder el tiempo. Por fin vamos a divertirnos juntos.

El corazón de Helena latía con fuerza; se mordió la lengua para ganar tiempo.

Una oportunidad.

—Ya me has escuchado gritar en muchas ocasiones —dijo Lancaster con voz bronca—. Me pregunto cómo será cuando lo hagas tú. —Se rio por lo bajo—. Aunque supongo que tendremos que hacerlo en silencio. No quiero que Ferron nos vuelva a interrumpir.

Rebuscó algo en su bolsillo.

Helena levantó las caderas y le hizo perder el equilibrio. Sin titubear, le clavó el codo en la mandíbula. Aunque logró ponerse en pie, le dolían las muñecas; el núcleo de los grilletes se le clavaba entre el músculo y el hueso, como si un fuego ardiente la quemara por dentro.

Echó a correr hacia el fondo del pasillo, pero la puerta estaba cerrada. Las manos le ardían y apenas sintió el pomo; le temblaban los dedos, aunque solo quería agarrarlo.

Notó que la cabeza se le iba hacia atrás; Lancaster la había agarrado por el pelo. Vio las estrellas, y un brazo le cubrió la boca cuando quiso gritar, una cobertura gruesa que sofocó su terror.

—Qué zorra más lista. —La arrastró hacia atrás un poco más y le echó la cabeza hacia un lado. Entonces le clavó una aguja en el cuello.

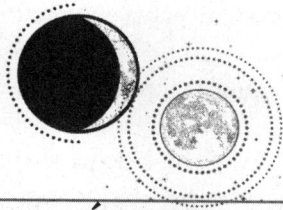

CAPÍTULO 16

ALGO NO IBA BIEN.

Helena no pensaba con claridad, le costaba ordenar los pensamientos y alguien la estaba arrastrando por el suelo. Sintió que la empujaban hacia una esquina oscura.

—No hagas ruido —dijo alguien.

Una figura se acercó entre sombras. Después, una boca presionó la suya, carnosa y húmeda, y una lengua se abrió paso entre sus dientes hasta que se atragantó. Sintió un dolor agudo en el labio y la sangre caliente y salada le corrió por la boca.

—Tengo que abrir la puerta. Espera aquí —dijo, pero pareció pensárselo mejor y se acercó hacia su garganta.

Los dedos de Helena se estremecieron, como un espasmo nervioso. Notó un dolor intenso, como el de una herida abierta, extendiéndosele por sus brazos, cuando unos dientes se clavaron en su cuello. Dio un respingo, pero una mano le tapó la boca y amortiguó el chillido.

Luego, quien la tenía atrapada la soltó.

—Espera aquí. No hagas ruido.

Helena se sentó. Notaba dolor en el cuello y en los hombros. Cuando intentó masajearlos, palpó algo pegajoso y húmedo.

Mientras esperaba sentada en la oscuridad, un pensamiento flotaba en el borde de su mente. La figura regresó. Helena intentó hablar, pero le cubrieron la boca con la mano y la arrastraron al exterior. Las dos lunas estaban casi llenas, colgaban como dos discos luminosos en la negrura.

Alguien tironeaba de su muñeca para instarla a andar. Trastabilló y sintió un dolor que se extendía por todo el brazo.

La estaban arrastrando por la gravilla cuando a alguien se le escapó un grito estrangulado. Unas fauces abiertas se cernían sobre ella.

La verja. Estaba abierta.

—Ya casi hemos llegado. Dios, te voy a despellejar viva.

Otra vez tenía encima el rostro que asomaba entre las sombras. Lo veía a la luz de la luna. Unos labios rojos y dientes. Era Lancaster, con una sonrisa de chacal.

Helena intentó hablar. Sentía la necesidad de decir algo, pero las palabras se negaban a formarse, estaban atrapadas, palpitando contra su garganta. Sintió un tirón brusco y Lancaster desapareció de su lado, mientras a ella le fallaron las piernas.

Entonces oyó un golpe seco.

Se giró, con la mirada nublada, y descubrió a Lancaster estampado contra la pared. Ferron le estaba propinando patadas con tal violencia que se escuchaba el crujido de sus huesos partiéndose.

El Sumo Inquisidor agarró a Lancaster del cuello hasta que quedaron cara a cara. La luz de la luna los iluminaba a ambos, como si estuviesen tallados en plata.

—¿Vas a alguna parte, Lancaster?

Lancaster tosió sangre.

—Como haces la vista gorda con las aventuras de Aurelia, supuse que no te importaría que me la llevase. Fui yo el que la atrapó. Debería ser mía.

—Nunca será tuya.

Sin soltarlo, Ferron hundió la mano en la cavidad abdominal de Lancaster, con la misma facilidad con la que la hubiera sumergido en el agua. Después, sacó sus órganos y los hizo girar lentamente.

Lancaster gritó y pataleó.

Ferron le extrajo los intestinos hasta tal punto que empezaron a contraerse, brillantes bajo la luz de la luna.

—Si vuelvo a verte, te estrangularé con ellos —amenazó Ferron en una voz tan tranquila como letal—. Es una pena que aún no seas inmortal. Si lo fueras, lo haría lentamente.

Dejó caer los intestinos para que quedaran colgando delante de Lancaster, como si fueran la cadena de un reloj. Acto seguido, sacó un pañuelo y se limpió las manos. Lancaster aprovechó para cruzar la verja. Iba gimoteando e intentando meterse de nuevo los órganos dentro del cuerpo.

Cuando desapareció, Ferron se giró hacia Helena. Tenía la cara lívida de la rabia.

—Idiota… ¿Por qué has salido esta noche?

Helena se limitó a mirarlo.

Pensó que debía decir algo, lo que había intentado decirle a Lancaster.

—Ferron siempre viene a buscarme —susurró.

El Sumo Inquisidor se quedó paralizado. No dijo nada durante unos instantes; mantuvo la mandíbula en tensión y los puños apretados. Luego tragó saliva y suspiró.

—¿Qué te ha hecho? —preguntó en voz baja, arrodillándose a su lado.

Helena se miró a sí misma. Tenía el vestido hecho jirones y las medias desgarradas. Todo estaba roto, había sangre y gravilla blanca por todos lados.

Ferron estiró la mano para rozarle con suavidad el hombro, y Helena sintió una oleada de calidez. Se acurrucó contra su mano, pero él se apartó.

—Te ha drogado —afirmó—. ¿Te obligó a tragar algo?

Helena negó con la cabeza.

—Entonces te lo inyectó. Vamos a tu habitación. —Por un instante, se le desenfocó la mirada, pero después la ayudó a levantarse. Helena profirió un grito ahogado al sentir el dolor que se extendía por sus brazos.

Ferron no dijo nada, pero le cubrió los hombros con el abrigo para tapar su vestido destrozado.

La necrómata esperaba en el cuarto de Helena con un barreño y un trapo en la mano.

—Lávala —ordenó, y se fue a la ventana, donde permaneció quieto como una estatua mientras la necrómata llevaba a Helena al borde de la cama y empezaba a limpiar la gravilla y la sangre.

Los dedos de la necrómata estaban fríos, y Helena olió vagamente a carne cruda que se ha dejado a la intemperie demasiado tiempo. Se apartó, pero, cada vez que se encogía, la mujer continuaba, hasta que Helena acabó atrapada contra el poste de la cama. Se echó a temblar.

—Para —le bramó Ferron, tenso.

Helena se quedó quieta, al igual que la necrómata, que se retiró cuando Ferron acudió a verla.

La chica le miró los zapatos. Estaban tan lustrosos que brillaban.

—¿Qué sucede? —preguntó.

Sucedían muchas cosas, más de las que el cerebro de Helena podía recordar en esos instantes.

—No me gusta que me toquen los muertos —respondió en un susurro.

Ferron suspiró y se sentó a su lado. Cogió el trapo de la necrómata.

—No voy a hacerte daño —afirmó con voz tensa. La sujetó por los hombros y la giró hacia él.

Helena sabía que no lo haría. Solo le hacía daño unos días concretos, y ese no era uno de ellos, así que se mantuvo quieta.

Con cuidado, Ferron empezó a limpiarle los hombros, retirando los restos de gravilla blanca y lavando las heridas, hasta que sus dedos le acariciaron la piel. Helena sintió un cosquilleo cálido cuando la piel volvió a unirse, regenerándose y creando un tejido nuevo y delicado. Su captor le sanó los hombros y siguió con el cuello. Finalmente, se detuvo en el labio roto.

Ferron mantenía los labios fruncidos y una expresión profesional y concentrada.

Cuando terminó, se centró en las manos de Helena. Ella notaba que le palpitaban las muñecas y la piel estaba ardiendo y tersa.

Ferron le dio la vuelta a una mano. Estaba llena de arañazos y la gravilla se le había clavado en la palma. Tardó más en sanar las manos y la muñeca y, aunque los cortes desaparecieron, siguieron doliéndole. Las repasó una y otra vez, y luego la obligó a mover los dedos.

Al final, apoyó la espalda con la mirada perdida.

—¿Te ha… te ha hecho algo más?

Helena negó con la cabeza.

El Sumo Inquisidor dejó escapar el aire lentamente, sin apartar la vista del fondo de la habitación.

—Tengo que pasar varios días en la ciudad. Será mejor que te quedes en tu habitación hasta que vuelva.

Helena se quedó mirando la pared, sin saber qué sentir. Su mente solo parecía funcionar a ratos.

Estaba sucia.

Se levantó y se metió bajo el agua. Dejó que los chorros de agua caliente le cayeran por la cara y los hombros.

Todavía sentía los dientes clavándose en su carne, cómo se le había desgarrado la piel bajo su presión. Había zonas que aún estaban demasiado sensibles, y le entraron ganas de meter los dedos dentro y arrancarlo todo.

Encontró un trapo y se frotó la piel de forma compulsiva hasta que se le quedó la piel tan en carne viva que le dolía el contacto con el agua.

Sobre la silla le habían dejado un camisón blanco de franela y también una taza de tisana junto a la cama. Reconoció el olor a camomila, pero, cuando le dio un sorbo, estaba tan amarga que torció el gesto.

Láudano.

Se lo bebió todo y se sumergió en un sueño profundo y vacío.

———————

La niebla mental desapareció a la mañana siguiente.

Después de lo que había estado a punto de suceder, y su incapacidad de asimilarlo en ese instante, sintió que se le contraían los pulmones y su corazón se encogía.

Si Lancaster la hubiera sacado de Puntaférreo, ¿qué hubiese hecho con ella? ¿Se hubiera quedado quieta y le habría permitido hacerlo?

Se encogió sobre sí misma y no se levantó hasta que alguien llamó a la puerta. Entró la criada, que dejó la bandeja en la mesita de noche.

Era el desayuno, y había una tetera de tisana con ese olor tan reconocible a camomila. La criada le sirvió una taza y sacó un frasco que contenía unas gotas de líquido rojo.

Helena negó con la cabeza, pero se arrepintió en cuanto la criada se fue y la dejó a solas con sus pensamientos.

No dejaba de pensar en las chicas del programa de repoblación, engañadas con la promesa de comida y perdón.

Si a Helena no la hubieran esterilizado y no hubiese perdido sus recuerdos, también estaría allí.

En comparación con lo que sufrían el resto de los supervivientes, podría decirse que Ferron la estaba tratando bien. Y ese pensamiento le producía pavor.

¿Cómo era posible que el Sumo Inquisidor fuera uno de los inmarcesibles menos monstruosos? No, eso no era cierto. Había sido testigo de sus matanzas, le había visto extirparle los órganos a Lancaster con sus propias manos, como si nada. Ferron era un monstruo de los pies a la cabeza, aunque lo ocultara detrás de una fría fachada.

Le dolía la cabeza, así que cerró los ojos.

Cada vez que las criadas se marchaban, cerraban la puerta con pestillo, así que Helena no se molestó en salir de la cama. Se quedó encogida bajo las mantas, asfixiada por la desesperación, hasta que el silencio fue roto por el chirrido repentino del metal. La puerta se abrió de par en par.

Helena se levantó corriendo y vio que entraba Aurelia con un periódico en la mano y el bastoncillo de hierro en la otra. Había varios necrómatas esperándola en el pasillo, moviéndose al unísono con ella.

La mujer de Ferron frenó en seco, se dio la vuelta e hizo girar el bastoncillo entre los barrotes de hierro del suelo. La puerta se cerró tan repentinamente que estuvo a punto de amputarle un brazo a la criada. Helena oyó un chirrido metálico mientras el marco de la puerta se cerró para sellar la habitación.

Aurelia se volvió hacia Helena.

—Ven aquí —le ordenó furibunda.

Helena se bajó de la cama con el corazón en un puño y se acercó en silencio.

Aurelia estaba lívida, frágil como un tallo de hierba en pleno invierno. Iba vestida y arreglada con la misma pulcritud de siempre, pero emanaba un profundo desasosiego. Sus pendientes, unos pequeños candelabros adornados con perlitas, temblaron al pronunciar sus primeras palabras.

—¿Sabías que fui la tercera hija que tuvo mi madre?

Helena no sabía nada de Aurelia.

—Mi familia posee una resonancia férrea pura desde hace casi un siglo, y hemos tenido al menos un miembro en el gremio en todas las generaciones, pero nunca llegamos muy lejos. Es difícil competir con una familia como los Ferron. Mi padre siempre decía que en Paladia había que contentarse con la chatarra hasta que consiguieras sacar algo de ella. Y nosotros intentamos sacar algo de la chatarra.

Aurelia respiró hondo y continuó:

—La gente pensaba que a Kaine le pasaba algo cuando nació. Que tal vez era un lapsus, o que no tenía resonancia férrea. Nadie lo supo con certeza, pero sí sabíamos que la familia se mostraba muy reservada al respecto. Mi padre lo vio como una oportunidad. Mi madre y mi padre eran primos, y mi padre pensó que no les costaría demasiado tener una niña con resonancia de hierro pura. Así los Ferron querrían casarla con Kaine y seguirían controlando el gremio.

Aurelia empezó a respirar con rapidez.

—Mi madre decía que las dos primeras niñas que nacieron eran muy pequeñas: «Unas cositas diminutas». —Le brillaron los ojos azules—. Mi padre pagó a un vivemante para que comprobara durante el embarazo si eran niñas, pero, cuando no mostraron indicios de resonancia férrea en el útero, no las dejó nacer. Mi padre afirmaba que, si hubieran sobrevivido, otra familia del gremio habría intentado arrebatarnos el contrato conyugal. Yo fui la tercera. Mi madre siempre dijo que los dos primeros bebés eran suyos y que yo era… de Kaine Ferron. Las quemó en la chimenea y enterró las cenizas en el jardín. Se pasó la vida ahí fuera, junto a ellas.

Helena le dedicó a Aurelia una mirada que oscilaba entre el asombro y la empatía, pero eso solo consiguió enfurecerla más.

—Sabía que meterías las narices donde no te incumbe. ¿Has visto esta noticia? —Aurelia levantó el periódico para que Helena leyera la portada.

Era una foto horrible, incluso en blanco y negro. Arrodillado y con el rostro descubierto, Ferron destripaba a Lancaster como si nada, en la sala de espera del Hospital Central.

Solo pudo ver la foto un instante, porque Aurelia apretó la mano y dobló el periódico; tenía los nudillos blancos de sujetar con fuerza el bastoncillo. La casa rugió y tembló.

—He de admitir —siguió Aurelia con una calma forzada— que, cuando me enteré de que Kaine había matado a Erik, me alegré. Pensé: «Por fin se ha dado cuenta».

Los pendientes con forma de candelabro empezaron a temblar más.

—Traté de ser la esposa perfecta. Sabía que entre nosotros no había amor, pero pensé que entendería que yo estaba hecha para ser su mujer. ¿Cuántos hombres pueden decir eso? Lo he hecho todo tal como debía hacerse.

Apartó la mano sin soltar el periódico. Sus anillos de alquimia brillaron débilmente bajo la luz.

—La gente no lo sabe, pero Kaine no vivía aquí. Me abandonó en el vestíbulo de esta casa el día de nuestra boda. Desapareció un mes entero, hasta que me enteré de que había vuelto a la ciudad. Creía que me estaba poniendo a prueba. Decoré la casa, organicé fiestas, pero él nunca venía. Entonces pensé que llamaría su atención si lo ponía celoso, pero le dio igual. Supuse que prefería estar con hombres o incluso con nadie, y que no podía hacer más que aceptarlo.

El semblante amargo de Aurelia se tornó aún más duro.

—Lo tenía aceptado. —Le temblaba la voz por el resentimiento—. Hasta que llegaste tú y, de repente, se mudó a la casa y puso toda la mansión patas arriba por ti, te sacaba a pasear y te enseñaba cada rincón… a ti.

Helena abrió la boca para explicarle que Ferron lo había hecho porque así se lo habían ordenado.

—¡Cállate! ¡No quiero oír lo que tengas que decir! —El periódico se arrugó en su puño—. Entonces Erik Lancaster empezó a prestarme atención. —Aurelia parecía estar a punto de llorar—. Era muy simpático, me acompañaba a todos los eventos a los que Kaine nunca asistía. Quería saberlo todo sobre mí y se fijaba en cada detalle de lo que hacía para impresionar a Kaine. Quiso ver la casa, cómo la había decorado. Fue el único que me dijo que debería volver a hacer fiestas, para que todos vieran lo maravillosa que era, aunque Kaine no pensase lo mismo. La celebración del solsticio de invierno fue idea suya, esa enorme lista de invitados y todas las cenas… Hasta la fiesta del equinoccio.

Aurelia dejó de hablar y miró por la ventana unos instantes.

—Cuando me enteré de que Kaine había matado a Erik, pensé: «Por fin se ha dado cuenta. Simplemente estaba ocupado. Sí que le importo». Pero entonces… —Aurelia se estremeció—. Entonces caí en la cuenta de que Erik se me había acercado la semana después de que publicaran ese maldito artículo que contaba que estabas aquí. Siempre quería venir a la casa, hasta en invierno, que hace un frío espantoso. Luego pensé por qué desaparecía. En la fiesta del solsticio y en las cenas, también en el equinoccio. Y que siempre estaba alterado cuando volvía y me encontraba.

Se produjo un silencio terrible.

—Todo era por ti —admitió Aurelia al fin—. Erik venía por ti. Kaine lo mató por ti. ¡Erik me estaba utilizando! ¡Me usaba para llegar a ti!

Lanzó el periódico al suelo; las páginas quedaron desplegadas, dejando a la vista a Ferron y su cabello y piel claros, sus manos negras, manchadas de sangre, y a Lancaster, que tenía la mirada perdida y la expresión desencajada.

Kaine Ferron asesina a un iniciado en público.

—¿Por qué se interesan tanto por ti? —exigió saber Aurelia, acercándose a Helena—. ¿Qué tienes de especial para que Kaine se mude aquí, a esta casa que odia con toda su alma? ¿Para que viva con todos estos sirvientes que no soporta pero de los que nunca se deshace? ¿Por qué Erik pasó meses utilizándome para llegar hasta ti? ¿Por qué todo el mundo se interesa por ti?

—Yo…

Aurelia le cruzó la cara de un bofetón; los anillos de hierro se estamparon contra su mandíbula.

—¡No quiero escucharte!

Se oyó un golpe sonoro al otro lado de la puerta, como si alguien quisiera tirarla abajo. Aurelia dio un respingo.

Otro golpe.

Aurelia sonrió.

—Creo que se ha enterado de que estoy aquí —dijo—. Pero no abrirán esa puerta a tiempo, no cuando tengo esto.

Aurelia clavó el bastoncillo entre los barrotes de hierro del suelo y estos se retorcieron como vides envolviendo las muñecas de Helena. La empujaron hacia abajo, y la chica cayó de rodillas con un impacto seco que le sacudió toda la columna vertebral.

Aurelia se plantó delante de ella.

—Te dije que no me causaras problemas.

Los golpes en la puerta empezaron a sonar con más fuerza. Aurelia ladeó la cabeza.

—¿Sabes? Comprarle algo a Kaine es una pesadilla. Nunca encuentro nada que le guste, pero ahora ha empezado a coleccionar algo… ¿Sabes qué es?

Helena sintió que el corazón le latía más deprisa. Negó con la cabeza.

Aurelia señaló la esquina superior de la habitación.

—Ojos. Hay uno ahí mismo. Seguro que nos está viendo. Creo que no tiene ninguno de color marrón.

—No, por favor —suplicó Helena, tratando de zafarse, pero el hierro que la mantenía amarrada no cedió ni un milímetro.

—No te preocupes —le aseguró Aurelia—, así Kaine tendrá algo de ti cuando te devuelva.

Helena trató de liberarse, pero Aurelia hizo que el hierro tirara con más fuerza hacia abajo, hasta que sus hombros amenazaron con dislocarse.

«Ferron vendrá. Ferron vendrá».

Las palabras giraban en su mente como un rezo desesperado. Lo haría; tenía que saber lo que estaba pasando. No permitiría que Aurelia…

Pero estaba en la ciudad. Helena sabía que se encontraba muy lejos.

Aurelia agarró a Helena por la barbilla. Los anillos se habían alargado hasta conformar una punta afilada.

—Abre bien los ojos.

Helena se echó a temblar.

—Por favor...

—Cállate —la interrumpió Aurelia, soltando el bastoncillo para agarrar mejor la mandíbula de Helena. La punta de los anillos se le clavó en la mejilla.

Al otro lado de la puerta, los golpes sonaron con más fuerza.

Aurelia metió la punta de uno de sus anillos afilados en el rabillo del ojo izquierdo de Helena y empezó a hacer palanca apoyándose en el hueso. Sonrió, y los ojos le brillaron con malicia.

—Espero estar presente cuando Kaine te vea. Si me mata, la satisfacción de presenciar su reacción habrá valido la pena.

Helena echó la cabeza hacia atrás cuando el anillo de Aurelia le rozó la mejilla.

—¡Aurelia!

El grito resonó por todas partes. No era una voz, sino varias a la vez. Al unísono.

—¡Aurelia!

Los necrómatas chillaban al otro lado de la puerta. No eran voces humanas, pero estaban desgarradas y llenas de rabia.

Aurelia dio un respingo y soltó una carcajada histérica al mirar hacia la puerta por encima del hombro.

—No sabía que podían hacer eso. Supongo que tú te mereces todo el trato especial.

Se volvió de nuevo hacia Helena y enterró los dedos en su cabello para sujetarla mientras volvía a clavarle la punta afilada en el rabillo del ojo.

Helena notó inmediatamente el dolor y la presión ejercida, parecía que el ojo estaba a punto de salírsele de la órbita. Los necrómatas seguían gritando, pero apenas los escuchaba por encima del latido de su propio corazón. Sintió espanto al saber que el rostro de Aurelia Ferron sería lo último que vería en su vida.

Iba a sumirse para siempre en la oscuridad.

El ojo cedió, y su visión se volvió unilateral.

Entonces, toda la casa tembló, incluido el suelo, como una criatura que cobra vida.

Aurelia la soltó y se giró, desconcertada. Antes de que pudiera hacer nada, los barrotes de hierro se desprendieron del suelo y de las paredes y se lanzaron hacia ella como una víbora al ataque. La capturaron y la apartaron de Helena.

Aurelia chilló cuando sintió que se elevaba del suelo y luchó para liberarse con su propia resonancia. No obstante, los barrotes de hierro apretaron más y más, hasta que Helena oyó cómo se le partían los huesos. Aurelia quedó inerte; se había resistido con tanto ahínco que las púas de los dedos estaban retorcidas.

El tiempo se detuvo.

Tan rápido como había cobrado vida, la casa regresó al silencio.

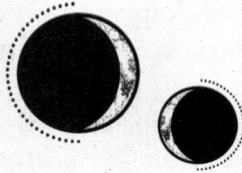

CAPÍTULO 17

HELENA FORCEJEÓ CONTRA EL HIERRO que la aprisionaba, los bordes le arañaban la piel. Sin embargo, por mucho que se retorció, solo consiguió que le ardieran los hombros. Solo alcanzaba a ver la mitad de la habitación que la rodeaba, y todo estaba destrozado. Lo único que oía era su propia respiración aterrorizada. La casa estaba sumida en un silencio inquietante.

Pasó lo que pareció una eternidad y, entonces, oyó unos pasos distantes por el pasillo. La puerta cambió de forma para abrirse y, al instante, Ferron estaba arrodillado delante de ella, tapando la espantosa imagen de Aurelia. Cuando el hierro que le sujetaba las muñecas se derritió, Helena se derrumbó sobre Ferron.

Empezó a respirar con el pecho sacudido por el miedo acumulado.

Cuando Ferron le levantó la cabeza, vio el horror en su rostro. Le tocó con cuidado la mejilla y le sostuvo la cara. Tomó aire antes de hablar.

—Te ha sacado el ojo de la cuenca y tienes una incisión profunda en la esclerótica —dijo con voz trémula—. ¿Cómo lo arreglo?

Helena lo miró desconcertada, temblando. Las lágrimas le surcaban la cara y le manchaban los dedos a Ferron. Cada vez respiraba más acelerada.

Debería saber la respuesta a la pregunta, pero su memoria le fallaba. Lo único que sentía con claridad era el dolor donde la garra de Aurelia le había perforado el ojo.

Ferron la sujetó por los hombros con firmeza.

—Mírame. Necesito que mantengas la calma y me digas cómo arreglarlo. Tú sabes cómo arreglarlo.

Helena se atragantó con un sollozo.

«Piensa, Helena». Ella era sanadora. Alguien tenía una herida en el ojo. Tenía que proceder con eficiencia si no quería que perdiese la vista. «Concéntrate».

—Cuando se perfora una esclerótica… —comenzó con voz temblorosa, devanándose los sesos para recordar el procedimiento. No tenía ni idea de cómo explicárselo a un vivemante novato; nunca le había enseñado a nadie a sanar.

Además, era inútil. Ferron podría reparar el tejido dañado, pero no le devolvería la visión. Seguiría estando tuerta. Se vino abajo al pensarlo.

Ferron la sujetó con más fuerza para mantenerla erguida.

—Vamos. Sabes cómo hacerlo. Dímelo.

Helena tragó saliva con dificultad.

—La resonancia debe establecerse mediante el contacto —explicó, apenas en un susurro—. Empieza en la parte más profunda y replica el tejido con la forma del tejido que lo rodea; no se reproducirá como la piel, que lo hace por sí sola. Tienes que regenerar la estructura por completo, capa a capa.

Esa sencilla respuesta habría desanimado a cualquier sanador con experiencia. La regeneración era un concepto básico, pero recomponer el tejido podía ser una tarea extenuante que entumecía la mente. Era como ver a alguien rascándose: provocaba picor en el cerebro, pero había que mantener la concentración en todo momento.

Ferron no entendía el procedimiento. Aun así, colocó las manos sobre las suyas, dedo sobre dedo, y Helena se percató de que sentía levemente su resonancia a través de las yemas de los dedos, aunque la sensación se cortaba al llegar a las muñecas.

—Enséñamelo.

Tenía las muñecas llenas de moratones. Sintió dolor en los huesos cuando movió los dedos, pero lo ignoró. Se centró en esa intuición que había estado ausente durante tanto tiempo y sintió el ojo mediante la resonancia de Ferron, que fluía por las yemas de sus dedos.

La transmutación siempre empezaba con un roce inicial que forjaba la conexión. Una vez establecida, el alquimista cedía espacio a sus dedos para manipular el canal.

Helena movió los dedos con cautela, guiando los de Ferron, y fue entretejiendo filamentos invisibles de energía hasta conformar un entramado de tejido frágil.

Los ojos plateados de Ferron parecieron iluminarse al imitar sus movimientos.

Sintió un tirón en el centro del ojo.

Gimió, pero se mantuvo firme.

Era como si le metieran una aguja en la incisión y pasaran un hilo una y otra vez.

Necesitó toda su fuerza de voluntad para no apartarse, para concentrarse en el débil rastro de la resonancia y continuar creando la compleja estructura regenerativa.

A pesar de lo pequeña que era la herida, le llevó una eternidad arreglarla. Ferron no se detuvo, ni siquiera cuando Helena sintió calambres en los dedos y dejó caer la mano. Aquello le provocó un dolor que le dio ganas de gritar.

—¿Y ahora? —preguntó Ferron en cuanto terminó, sin darle un segundo de respiro.

Helena respiró hondo.

—En… en caso de… de dislocación ocular —dijo en un tono mucho más tranquilo de como se sentía—, hay que recolocarlo con cuidado, para no dañar el nervio óptico… más todavía.

Fue como hacer girar un botón. Ferron tuvo que apretar para meterle el ojo, que encajó en su sitio con un sonido nauseabundo.

Helena parpadeó lentamente. Le dolía el ojo; estaba seco y pegajoso después de haberlo tenido fuera tanto tiempo.

—¿C-cuánto puedes ver? —preguntó Ferron levantándole la cara para que lo mirase. Le rozó la mandíbula con las yemas de los dedos y, con el pulgar, recorrió el tajo que Aurelia le había hecho en la mejilla.

Helena lo miró fijamente y se tapó el ojo derecho con la mano. Tenía el rostro de Ferron a unos centímetros, pero solo veía un borrón oscuro.

—Nada… —Se le rompió la voz y se le encogió el pecho. Luego, se tapó la boca con la mano para camuflar un sollozo.

—¿Qué más tengo que hacer? ¿Cómo lo arreglo? —La sujetó por los hombros, sin permitir que se viniera abajo.

Helena negó con la cabeza y se llevó las manos a las sienes.

—Seguramente haya dañado el nervio óptico. Pero… no puedo… ayudarte, sería demasiado…

Ferron presionó los dedos contra su ojo, y Helena sintió que su resonancia se desplazaba por el nervio hasta el cerebro. Su cuerpo reaccionó de forma violenta ante aquella presencia, pero el Sumo Inquisidor la mantuvo quieta. Un calor se extendió por su cuerpo. Ferron estaba llevando a cabo el mismo proceso de regeneración para sanar la lesión que tenía entre el ojo y el cerebro. Se le escapó un gemido gutural entre dientes.

Ferron apartó la mano y la miró fijamente. Ahora lo veía con más claridad, como si se asomara a una ventana en un día muy nublado.

—¿Ves algo? —preguntó con brusquedad.

—Tienes el pelo claro. Creo que… distingo un poco tus ojos y tu boca…

—Bien, estamos avanzando. ¿Ahora qué?

¿Quería hacer más?

—Hum… Gotas de atropina, de belladona. Dilatará la pupila y evitará que se tense mientras se recupera el tejido.

—Traed el botiquín —le ordenó Ferron a los sirvientes. Todos estaban inmóviles; como el Sumo Inquisidor le estaba dedicando toda su atención a Helena, se habían quedado inanimados. Uno de ellos cobró vida y salió corriendo por el pasillo—. Tengo que encargarme de Aurelia —añadió—. Espera aquí.

Helena asintió y se dejó caer.

Observó con ojos vidriosos que Ferron se giraba hacia su mujer.

No tuvo ni que tocar el metal retorcido que la envolvía. Con un ademán, la maraña de hierro se apartó y regresó al suelo y las paredes.

Ferron se arrodilló y colocó dos dedos en el cuello de Aurelia.

La visión desequilibrada de Helena le impedía determinar la gravedad de las heridas de Aurelia, pero Ferron comenzó a colocar huesos y arreglar articulaciones dislocadas con la misma calma con la que resolvería un puzle.

Posó una mano sobre el pecho de Aurelia, y Helena pensó que Ferron iba a crear a una nueva necrómata. Sin embargo, Aurelia gritó y se levantó del suelo con los ojos abiertos, absolutamente aterrorizados.

—¿Qué? ¿Cómo has…? —masculló Aurelia. Se llevó las manos al pecho, a los costados, y se palpó todo el cuerpo, desconcertada—. ¿Cómo? ¿Cómo es posible que estés aquí?

—Esta es mi casa. —Ferron imprimía rabia en cada palabra que pronunciaba.

—Pero… ¡estabas en la ciudad! —Aurelia parecía más histérica por eso que por todo lo demás.

¿Acaso no recordaba lo que Ferron le había hecho? ¿O era demasiado para que pudiera asimilarlo por completo?

—Sí, así es. Me causaste un gran inconveniente al obligarme a marcharme en mitad de una ceremonia.

—Pero… ¿cómo has conseguido…? —Aurelia contempló el destrozo de la habitación.

—¿Crees que los necrómatas son lo único que puedo controlar a distancia? Esta es mi casa, y el elemento de mi familia.

Helena lo miró, atónita. Lo que decía le parecía imposible.

No había forma de que alguien pudiera transmutar el hierro desde la distancia, sobre todo de esa manera.

Aunque la resonancia de Ferron superaba todo lo que Helena había visto, no podía creer que pudiera extender su poder desde la ciudad y controlar el entramado de Puntaférreo con tanta precisión. Tendría que hacerlo a ciegas, sin saber lo que estaba sucediendo, a menos que…

Miró hacia el ojo del rincón.

No. Ni siquiera así sería posible. Cuanto más lejos se estaba del objeto a transmutar, mayor esfuerzo había que hacer. Si lo hubiera hecho desde un ala distinta de la casa, ya debería estar muerto, disuelto en la nada como una estrella que emplea demasiada energía al colapsar.

Había sucedido en alguna ocasión en las fábricas, cuando la disposición de los sellos de transmutación había resultado ser demasiado poderosa. Los alquimistas se desintegraban.

—Eso es imposible —replicó Aurelia, reflejando los pensamientos de Helena.

—¿Vas a subestimar a tu marido dos veces en el mismo día? No es propio de una esposa.

—Ah, ¿has venido por mí? No, claro que no, has venido por ella. —Señaló a Helena con un dedo acusador—. Has estado a punto de matarme, y mataste a Erik Lancaster, ¡por ella!

—Sí, es cierto. ¿Sabes por qué? Porque es la última miembro de la Orden de la Llama Eterna, lo que significa que es importante. Muchísimo más importante de lo que tú serás jamás. Más importante de lo que Lancaster habría soñado. Mi trabajo es mantener su mente intacta. Cuando tu padre te educó, ¿no te mencionó nunca que los ojos tienen un nervio que conecta directamente con el cerebro? ¿Qué crees que pasa si le arrancas uno?

Aurelia miró a Helena horrorizada.

Ferron siguió hablando con su tono frío y desprovisto de emoción.

—He intentado ser paciente contigo, Aurelia. He pasado por alto tu comportamiento indecente y tus intromisiones mezquinas, pero recuérdalo bien: para mí no eres más que un elemento decorativo. Si vuelves a acercarte a ella o a dirigirle la palabra, si tan siquiera pones un pie en esta ala de la casa, te mataré, y lo haré lentamente, tal vez en el transcurso de un par de noches. No es una amenaza, sino una promesa. Ahora lárgate de mi vista.

Aurelia se puso en pie con torpeza, con el gesto compungido de miedo y dolor, y huyó cojeando de la habitación.

Ferron se incorporó y respiró hondo para luego girarse hacia Helena. Todavía le ardían los ojos de color plata.

Se acercó a ella lentamente y se arrodilló. Volvió a moverle la cabeza hacia arriba y estudió sus ojos.

—Las pupilas son de tamaños distintos —comentó—. Voy a llamar a un experto. A ver si podemos hacer algo más.

Helena lo miró fijamente. Estaba ojeroso y tenía la piel de un color gris pálido, lo que hacía que sus ojos resaltaran aún más, aunque tal vez se debiera a lo nublada que estaba su propia vista.

—¿Te encontrabas en la casa cuando…? —Helena señaló cómo había quedado la habitación. Ferron miró a su alrededor.

—No. De ser así, lo habría manejado con más sutileza. Estaba entrando en la finca.

—¿Cómo…?

Ferron compuso una mueca de cansancio.

—Es una habilidad que me otorgó Artemon Bennet, aunque por aquel entonces él no tenía ni idea de lo que estaba haciendo. Se suponía que era un castigo.

Helena frunció el ceño, incrédula. No sabía cómo era posible concederle tanto poder a la resonancia de una persona como para que pudiera controlar el hierro desde la distancia.

—¿Cómo es que…?

—No quiero hablar del tema ahora —la interrumpió.

Se hizo el silencio. Helena seguía sintiendo la necesidad de decir algo más.

—¿Cómo sabías que podría curarme el ojo?

—Eras sanadora.

—Sí, pero… —Su voz se desvaneció. No alcanzaba a explicar por qué se sentía tan decepcionada con esa respuesta—. ¿Dónde aprendiste a sanar? —insistió Helena. No solo le había resultado fácil seguir sus instrucciones, sino que también había curado a Aurelia y había reparado el daño del nervio óptico. Todo por sí mismo.

—Bueno, verás, hubo una guerra y, en aquel entonces, era general. Aprendí unas cuantas cosas.

Helena empezó a notar que le dolía la cabeza a causa de su visión desigual.

—Pues tienes… Tienes un talento natural. En otras circunstancias, podrías haber sido sanador.

—Una de las grandes ironías de la vida —masculló mirando hacia la puerta.

La criada había vuelto con un morral, similar a los que llevaban los médicos en el campo de batalla. Lo traía colgado del hombro y sujeto a la cintura. Ferron lo cogió y empezó a rebuscar entre los compartimentos. Helena oyó el tintineo de los frascos de cristal.

—¿Solo atropina? —preguntó con un frasco en la mano.

Helena negó con la cabeza.

—Cinco gotas de atropina disueltas en una cucharilla de solución salina.

Se oyeron más tintineos, el sonido de los tapones al desenroscarse y líquidos vertiéndose. Luego Ferron se metió algo en el bolsillo y cerró el morral. La criada se lo llevó.

Helena quiso ponerse en pie.

—Debería… tumbarme, para que la solución entre en el ojo —afirmó. Perdió el equilibrio; le temblaban las manos y los brazos, incapaces de sostener su propio peso. Se desplomó en el suelo. Tal vez era mejor quedarse ahí.

Una mano firme la sujetó del codo y la obligó a incorporarse.

—No voy a echarme sobre ti en el suelo —dijo Ferron con irritación. En vez de llevarla a la cama, la sacó de la habitación y recorrieron el pasillo hasta llegar a otra estancia.

El aire olía a rancio, y la cama estaba sin hacer. Ferron arrancó la sábana que cubría un sofá y Helena se tumbó allí.

El Sumo Inquisidor se inclinó sobre ella con el frasco en la mano. Cada vez que parpadeaba, la vista se le volvía más borrosa: oscuridad, luz, oscuridad, luz.

—¿Cuántas gotas?

—Un par de ellas, dos veces al día, durante dos días. Y compresas de eufrasia durante una semana.

Ferron se inclinó más y le dejó caer dos gotas de atropina de belladona en el ojo. Helena lo cerró para evitar que se derramaran.

Sintió que le rozaba la mejilla con los dedos, y el corte desapareció.

—Las criadas te prepararán esta habitación.

Helena contó los pasos que se alejaban y se cubrió el ojo izquierdo para verlo antes de que se marchara. Ferron se tambaleaba y tuvo que agarrarse al marco de la puerta para recobrar la compostura, como si hubiera perdido el equilibrio.

Cerró los ojos de nuevo y se sumió en el silencio atronador de la casa.

«No llores, no llores», se dijo a sí misma.

Oyó entonces que llegaban las criadas; le dieron la vuelta al colchón e hicieron la cama con sábanas limpias. Encendieron los radiadores, que empezaron a sisear mientras iba calentándose la habitación. También trajeron las pocas pertenencias de Helena y las guardaron en el armario nuevo. Las cortinas las dejaron cerradas, por lo que solo entraba un rayo de luz.

Cuando se marcharon, Helena se metió en la cama y trató de dormir.

Ferron regresó unas horas después, acompañado de un anciano que portaba un maletín lleno de artilugios.

—Os lo advierto, las perforaciones en la esclerótica son heridas muy desagradables —resolló entre jadeos mientras miraba a Helena de reojo—. No se puede hacer mucho más. Tendremos suerte si no pierde el ojo. He traído unos parches y, si estáis dispuesto a gastaros el dinero, también tengo ojos de cristal que le quedarán mejor.

Se dejó caer en una silla que había traído el mayordomo.

—¿Fue ella la que os enseñó cómo emplear la vivemancia para repararlo? —le preguntó a Ferron, que estaba apoyado contra la pared con la mirada apagada.

Él asintió sin decir nada.

El oculista se acercó a Helena y le abrió el ojo. Usó varios artilugios mecánicos y le retiró el párpado para examinar la herida. Permaneció en silencio un buen rato.

—Es un... trabajo absolutamente excepcional —admitió al fin con voz sorprendida—. ¿Vivemancia, decís? Vaya.

Volvió a dejarse caer en la silla y contempló a Helena, frotándose el mentón.

—¿Dónde aprendiste ese truco?

—Fui sanadora —respondió Helena.

El médico soltó un resoplido de incredulidad.

—Pero has… —La señaló sin terminar la frase—. ¿Cómo conoces este tipo de procedimientos médicos?

—Mi padre era cirujano. Se formó en Khem. Después se mudó a Etras.

—¿Khem? No me digas. ¿Allí hay médicos?

Helena se limitó a asentir.

—Increíble. Nunca he conocido a ninguno de Khem. ¿Y recorrió todo el camino desde el continente Sur? No quiero ni imaginarlo. El mar es… —Se estremeció—. ¿Olas del tamaño de montañas? No, gracias. Dicen que es un pasaje traicionero hasta en la latencia de verano. No quiero ni imaginar cómo será vivir en las regiones costeras. Debes de estar agradecida de vivir ahora tierra adentro, lejos de todo eso.

Helena lo miró fijamente.

El oculista la examinó a través de distintas lentes, mascullando para sí y retorciendo diversos tornillos. Por último, le enfocó la cara con una linterna y volvió a sentarse.

—Creo que te recuperarás por completo.

Miró a Ferron.

—Que no se acerque a la luz y que tome belladona dos veces al día. Es muy probable que solo le quede cierta deficiencia visual.

Helena observó con un ojo cómo se ponía en pie y recogía sus instrumentos. Acto seguido, con un gesto teatral, se giró hacia Ferron y se estiró el abrigo con pomposidad.

—Debo decir que tenéis aquí a una sanadora excepcional. Cuando me contasteis lo que había pasado, pensé que acabaría perdiendo el ojo. Tenemos unos cuantos vivemantes en el hospital, y causan más problemas que soluciones. Siempre creen que saben más que los médicos, pero lo único que hacen es tratar los síntomas, sin molestarse en entender cómo funciona lo demás. Una pandilla de inútiles.

El médico volvió a mirar a Helena. Su mirada se posó en los grilletes que tenía en las muñecas.

—Una pena —masculló para sí—. Qué pérdida de talento.

Ferron emitió un gruñido que no decía nada. El médico se giró hacia él, ruborizado.

—Y vos, señor, es increíble que hayáis hecho una sanación tan delicada imitando sus movimientos. Me parece impresionante. Deberíais trabajar en el hospital.

—Eso me han dicho —replicó Ferron con una sonrisa falsa—. ¿Crees que me contratarían después de que asesinara a alguien en la sala de espera?

El hombre palideció.

—Bueno... Me refería a...

—Si no hay nada más, te acompaño —dijo Ferron marchándose.

<hr />

Helena tuvo que llevar durante un tiempo un parche en el ojo izquierdo. Ferron venía puntualmente para suministrarle las gotas de atropina; era evidente que no se fiaba de que los sirvientes manejaran belladona cerca de Helena. Cuando dejó de necesitar las gotas en los ojos, le trajeron compresas frías de eufrasia.

Acababa de dejar de usar el parche cuando Stroud regresó.

—Por lo que me han contado, has tenido un mes de lo más desafortunado —dijo, mientras Helena empezaba a desnudarse para el examen habitual.

Seguía viendo de forma desigual, no era capaz de enfocar la vista del todo, pero Stroud empezó a examinarla igualmente. La vivemante apuntó algo en su ficha y le pidió a Helena que se tumbara. Luego se pasó más de un minuto tocándole el estómago y la zona baja del vientre.

—Perfecto —pronunció al fin. Dio un paso atrás para tomar más notas—. Por fin estás lista.

Helena tenía la mirada perdida en el techo y se debatió internamente sobre si debía darle o no a Stroud la satisfacción de preguntarle a qué se refería. Stroud esperó hasta que cedió.

—¿Lista para qué?

—Para participar en el programa de repoblación.

Helena la miró desconcertada.

—¿No te lo había contado? —Stroud inclinó la cabeza con altanería—. Se me habrá pasado.

Helena parpadeó lentamente. La visión desigual le hacía verlo todo torcido, como si la realidad estuviera desarticulada.

—Me esterilizaron.

—Sí, lo sé —asintió Stroud—. Creo que soy la primera vivemante que ha conseguido revertir una ligadura de trompas.

La habitación comenzó a darle vueltas.

—No. Me dijeron que sería…

—Bueno, me lo pusieron difícil. Tuve que practicar con varias chicas que teníamos en el programa. Ninguna de ellas ha muerto, no te preocupes. No todas las resonancias merecen reproducirse, y está bien tener algunas como consuelo. A ciertos señores no les gusta oír que no hay nada disponible para sus repertorios.

A Helena se le cerró la garganta.

—¿Qué?

—En fin, no quería decir nada hasta que no estuviera segura. Pensé que te darías cuenta tú sola. Supongo que no eres tan lista como afirma todo el mundo.

Helena intentó ponerse en pie y escapar, pero Stroud le paralizó las extremidades con un ademán poco cuidadoso.

—El Sumo Nigromante está convencido de que eres una animante. Si tiene razón, no podemos permitirnos desperdiciar a una chica como tú. ¿Te haces una idea de lo escasos que son? Y aquí estás tú, en un momento crítico, cuando más lo necesitamos.

Helena empezó a temblar.

—Creía que… la transferencia…

—Ah, ¿ahora estás dispuesta a cooperar con la transferencia? —Stroud se rio—. No te preocupes, seguiremos intentando recuperar tus recuerdos después. Por ahora, vamos a priorizar otra cosa.

Stroud se acercó a la puerta, donde aguardaba una criada.

—Sumo Inquisidor, tenemos que hablar.

Helena permaneció tendida, incapaz de moverse. Ferron no permitiría que aquello sucediera. Llevaba meses practicando la transferencia; Stroud no podía venir y deshacer todo su trabajo.

Intentó respirar con calma. Si empezaba a hiperventilar, Stroud acabaría sedándola o dejándola inconsciente. ¿Y si se despertaba en la Central, esperando a que alguien cruzara la puerta para…?

La vista se le nubló; el miedo le recorrió el cuerpo como si fuera un insecto.

¿Qué iba a hacer? ¿Argumentar que sus recuerdos eran más valiosos que un embarazo?

Si tuviera que elegir entre una cosa y la otra, ¿qué sería peor? ¿Cooperar con Ferron para que extrajera los secretos de la Llama Eterna o dejar que la violaran para producir el niño que Morrough necesitaba para su propia transferencia?

Pero, incluso si dejaba de resistirse a la transferencia y cooperaba con Ferron, ¿no la forzarían a quedarse embarazada después?

—Me has hecho llamar —dijo Ferron al entrar con un deje irritado.

—Sumo Inquisidor, sí, quería informaros de que he conseguido revertir la esterilización de Marino. El Sumo Nigromante quiere que la incluyamos en el programa de repoblación —contó Stroud.

Ferron no se inmutó, pero guardó un silencio espeluznante.

—¿Que has hecho qué? —dijo al fin.

Stroud posó una mano en el vientre de Helena, como si estuviera orgullosa.

—Ya sabéis que los animantes son muy escasos. Si de verdad ella lo es, sería un desperdicio no aprovecharla. He pasado los últimos meses experimentando con la reversión de la ligadura de trompas, y por fin lo he conseguido. Los de la Resistencia fueron unos incompetentes, la verdad; deberían haberle extirpado el útero, aunque en ese caso le habría hecho un trasplante. Tengo muchos sujetos sanos donde elegir. Ha sido un proceso relativamente menor en comparación con lo que Bennet y yo hicimos con las quimeras.

—No mencionaste nada de esto. —La voz de Ferron estaba adquiriendo un tono peligroso.

—Como el programa no forma parte de vuestro ámbito, y habéis insistido en tantas ocasiones en lo frágil que es, pensé que era mejor esperar a estar segura. Sin embargo, el Sumo Nigromante quiere que comencemos de inmediato. Podréis seguir con la transferencia cuando tengamos al niño. Sospecho que entonces se mostrará mucho más cooperativa. —Bajó la vista hacia Helena—. ¿Verdad?

Ferron no dijo nada.

—Bien, podría llevarla de vuelta a la Central. Tenemos una larga lista de señores prometedores, y Marino tiene un repertorio tan inusual que podríamos emparejarla con cualquiera. —Stroud miró a Ferron fijamente—. No obstante... —Hablaba con banalidad, como quien bordea el cauce de un río—. Cuando hablamos de resonancia, hay un candidato que destaca sobre los demás.

—Ve al grano. —Ferron empleaba un tono monótono, pero Helena se percató del instinto asesino que ocultaba.

Stroud se irguió cuan alta era.

—Es hora de que tengáis hijos. Sé que vuestra familia desea que tengan resonancia de hierro, pero para eso tenéis una esposa. Como sois el único animante que tenemos, el Sumo Nigromante os ha elegido para que seáis el primero en intentarlo con Marino. Si ella se queda embarazada, buscaremos cualquier indicio de animancia. Vuestro padre nos ha sido de gran ayuda a la hora de darnos detalles sobre el embarazo de vuestra madre, así que sabemos qué síntomas son relevantes. Sin embargo, dado que el tiempo apremia, el Sumo Nigromante considera que es mejor no cerrarse puertas. Tenéis dos meses para obtener resultados. Si no conseguimos nada, la trasladaremos a la Central para ver si tenemos más suerte con otros candidatos.

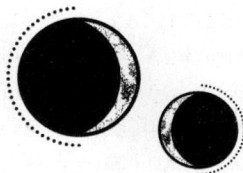

CAPÍTULO 18

TODO SE NUBLÓ A SU ALREDEDOR. Stroud dejó de tenerla paralizada cuando Ferron se excusó, pero Helena permaneció inmóvil.

El sonido áspero y chirriante del bolígrafo de Stroud al rozar el papel era lo único que se oía en la habitación.

A Helena se le había secado la boca, pero consiguió tragar saliva, mientras pensaba alguna forma de revertir lo que acababa de pasar.

Flexionó los dedos y acarició las sábanas de lino para concentrarse en las sensaciones externas. Se le escapó un gemido.

Pensó en gritar, en gritar y gritar sin parar.

—¿Qué sucede? —preguntó Stroud, levantando la vista del expediente médico de Helena.

La chica la miró fijamente.

—Pensé que estarías contenta de que te diéramos un respiro de la transferencia. Con la resistencia que estás mostrando, lo más probable es que tu hígado falle antes de que termine el año. —Stroud tamborileó los dedos sobre el expediente de Helena—. Soy muy exigente con los alquimistas en mi programa. La guerra nos privó de unos linajes muy valiosos. Deberías estar agradecida de que te dejemos participar en algo de tanta relevancia.

—Vas a hacer que me violen ¿y esperas que esté agradecida? —La voz de Helena sonaba apagada, como si llegara desde muy lejos.

La expresión de Stroud se endureció.

—Te estoy dando la oportunidad de que tu vida tenga algún sentido.

La rabia que sentía Helena era lo único que le impedía perder la cabeza.

—Si es algo tan maravilloso, me extraña que no te presentes voluntaria.

Stroud permaneció inmóvil; la rabia se extendió como un rayo por todo su rostro, oscureciendo todas las arrugas. Helena se preparó para el golpe, pero Stroud se limitó a fruncir los labios en una sonrisa tensa y se inclinó sobre Helena con un gesto casi tierno.

—El Sumo Inquisidor lleva casado más de un año y no ha producido ningún hijo. Su Eminencia insiste en que Ferron sea el primer candidato, pero dudo que eso dé resultado. Después de todo lo que le hizo Bennet, no entra dentro de lo que yo calificaría como humano. Cuando lo haya intentado, volverás a la Central, y seré yo quien decida cuál será el siguiente. Durante el tiempo que haga falta.

A Helena se le heló la sangre. Stroud le tocó la frente con la punta de un dedo.

—Con eso en mente, creo que harías bien en vigilar esa lengua que tienes. No vaya a ser que la pierdas.

Helena no emitió sonido alguno hasta que Stroud se marchó. El terror se extendió por su cuerpo como si fuera un veneno, devorando sus órganos, quemándole los pulmones. Deambuló por toda la casa, comprobó si todas las puertas estaban cerradas, desesperada por encontrar algo, cualquier resquicio de esperanza. Tenía que haber algo.

Ferron no apareció hasta la noche siguiente. Mantuvo el gesto impertérrito, pero parecía que sus ojos se desviaban, incapaz de sostenerle la mirada.

A Helena empezaron a temblarle las manos, como si sufriera un ataque nervioso.

—No es esta noche —le comunicó sin más—. Según me han dicho —seguía sin mirarla—, no serás fértil hasta dentro de tres días.

No le sorprendió. Ferron era un asesino y un nigromante. ¿Por qué pensó que estaría por encima de esto?

Pero, aun así, de una forma irracional, pensaba que estaría a salvo... con él.

Estúpida.

—Acércate —le ordenó.

Helena caminó en modo automático, con la vista fija en los botones de su abrigo y su camisa. Ferron estiró la mano y le sujetó la barbilla. Sintió el roce del cuero de sus guantes cuando le levantó la cara para mirarla a los ojos.

—¿Cuánto ves? —preguntó, pasando la vista de un ojo a otro para compararlos.

Helena se echó a reír.

No recordaba cuándo había reído por última vez. Hacía casi una vida. Pero la pregunta era graciosa. Desternillante, incluso.

Todo lo bueno que había tenido en la vida estaba destruido, le habían arrancado cualquier atisbo de consuelo, y ya no quedaba nada de ella, salvo sufrimiento. La habían encarcelado y violado de casi todas las formas imaginables, y ahora iba a infligirle esta última atrocidad, pero él se preocupaba por su visión.

Rio y rio, y, cuando dejó de reír, se echó a llorar. Estuvo llorando hasta que empezó a temblar, meciéndose hacia delante y hacia atrás, casi gritando. Ferron se limitó a esperar.

Helena no paró hasta que se sintió vacía, como si hubiera expulsado todo lo que tenía dentro y lo único que quedase fuera un cascarón hueco. Estaba harta de existir.

—¿Te sientes mejor?

La chica tragó saliva; le dolía la garganta.

—No.

Se percató de que a Ferron le temblaban los dedos, que los cerraba en un puño y los escondía detrás de la espalda. Reconocía ese gesto.

Levantó la vista para mirarlo y se fijó en la palidez de su piel y en su rostro macilento. Bueno, al menos los dos estaban sufriendo.

—¿Por qué te han torturado esta vez? —preguntó con aparente indiferencia, aliviada de pensar en algo, en cualquier otra cosa.

Ferron suspiró.

—Por varias razones. Como suelen recordarme, soy una decepción constante. Además, la gente, en su habitual perspicacia, ha deducido que soy el Sumo Inquisidor.

Esa noticia despertó su curiosidad.

—¿Fue porque mataste a Lancaster?

—Supongo que tuvo que ver. Tampoco ayudó demasiado la pataleta de Aurelia. Tuve que marcharme sin previo aviso, y el Sumo Inquisidor debía estar presente. Los periódicos internacionales no se lo piensan demasiado antes de publicar ese tipo de teorías, así que se ha extendido la noticia. Pronto me nombrarán sucesor del Sumo Nigromante. —Compuso una sonrisa de dolor—. El anonimato del que gozaba era para protegerme, ¿sabes?

—Por supuesto —replicó Helena—. Entonces solo te han torturado un poquito.

—No ha sido nada —dijo Ferron, pero tenía ambas manos detrás de la espalda.

Se movió, como si estuviera a punto de marcharse. Aunque Helena no quería estar cerca de él, la alternativa de quedarse a solas con sus pensamientos le parecía aún peor.

—¿Por qué mataste a Lancaster? —preguntó.

—Puso en peligro mi misión. Lo habría ejecutado de forma oficial, pero estaba ocupado y quería quitarlo de en medio.

—¿Y por eso lo mataste en el hospital a la vista de todos? —insistió Helena con escepticismo.

—Pensaba matarlo en su habitación del hospital, pero intentó huir. —Ferron se encogió de hombros—. Improvisé.

La imagen de Lancaster abierto en canal mientras Ferron lo destripaba estaba grabada a fuego en la mente de Helena.

El Sumo Inquisidor ladeó la cabeza.

—Si no tienes más preguntas, deberíamos acabar con esto. ¿En el sofá o en la cama?

Las palabras la golpearon como una barra de acero en plena espalda, y tardó un instante en comprender que se refería a revisar sus recuerdos.

Había dado por hecho que eso se habría acabado.

—Pensé...

¿Qué pensaba? ¿Que no seguía siendo una prisionera y que, a cambio de su cuerpo, dejarían su mente en paz? Se tragó las palabras y fue hacia el sofá.

Ferron la siguió, impasible, y extendió la mano. Apenas le había rozado la frente con los dedos cuando su resonancia penetró en su cráneo.

Para cuando terminó, Helena sintió que iba a desfallecer. Revivir los últimos días le hizo apretar la mandíbula con tanta fuerza que parecía que se le iban a romper los dientes.

Se derrumbó en el sofá; la amenaza de Stroud seguía resonando en su cabeza.

Hundió la cara en la tela del sofá, que olía a viejo y a polvo, e intentó camuflar el sonido del mundo exterior. Ferron se marchó sin decir una palabra.

EL OJO DE HELENA SE había recuperado lo suficiente para soportar la luz, así que retiró las cortinas; desde su nueva habitación se veía más el jardín que las montañas. En una semana, el mundo había cambiado, y ya se apreciaban los primeros signos de la primavera. El gris apagado al que estaba acostumbrada comenzaba a mostrar pinceladas de color entre la hierba tumbada y las ramas de los árboles.

Una semana antes, eso le habría proporcionado algo de consuelo, pero ahora había un pozo en su interior que transformaba toda belleza en horror.

Dos días. Sus pensamientos se repetían en un bucle infinito, como un animal enjaulado dispuesto a arrancarse las extremidades a bocados para intentar escapar.

Durante la guerra, el riesgo de ser violada siempre estuvo presente. Circulaban historias sobre las prisioneras de los laboratorios, advertencias sobre lo que podría pasarles a las mujeres que capturaban en territorio de la Resistencia. Pero, aun así, violarlas con el propósito de dejarlas embarazadas añadía una crueldad que no era capaz de asimilar.

Sus experiencias con los embarazos no habían sido agradables.

Las medidas anticonceptivas escaseaban durante la guerra. De vez en cuando aparecían chicas en el hospital que pedían, nerviosas, hablar con la enfermera Pace. Normalmente ahí acababa la cosa, pero a veces tenían que volver una y otra vez.

Helena había sido hija única. Su madre, boticaria, se dedicaba a prevenir embarazos, mientras que las matronas del pueblo se encargaban de todo lo demás. Solo cuando las cosas se torcían, las madres acudían a un cirujano como su padre. La mayoría de los bebés que Helena vio cuando era niña nacían deformes, gravemente enfermos o mortinatos.

Y así continuó durante la guerra. Al ser sanadora, a Helena solo la llamaban cuando un bebé nacía prematuramente o cuando se atascaba en una posición indebida, o también cuando la madre no producía leche porque no había comida suficiente. Le preguntaban siempre si había algo que pudiera hacer. En la mayoría de los casos, no podía ayudar. Los bebés eran demasiado pequeños y frágiles, y ni siquiera la vivemancia podía arreglarlo todo.

Tuvo que ser testigo de cómo las madres se desmoronaban, como si un seísmo las partiera por dentro. A veces gritaban, otras se sumían en el silencio y, en ocasiones, eso era aún peor.

Helena siempre agradeció no haber tenido que pasar por eso. No podía casarse ni tener hijos, así que nunca tendría que soportar una pérdida así.

Era lo único de lo que estaba a salvo, o eso pensaba.

Se tumbó en la cama, pero no lograba conciliar el sueño. Lumitia se estaba acercando a su sublimación semestral, y resplandecía con tal intensidad que cubría toda la noche de plata, una luz que contrastaba con la negrura. Hasta el aire vibraba con una resonancia constante.

Helena flexionó los dedos y deseó poder introducir la mano en su cuerpo con la misma facilidad que Ferron había atravesado el estómago de Lancaster. Si pudiera, se arrancaría ahí mismo las entrañas.

Solo de pensar que su cuerpo no tenía más opción que obedecer le provocaba náuseas. Sin embargo, la idea de no quedarse embarazada la paralizaba de miedo. La amenaza de Stroud aún resonaba en su mente.

Se sintió culpable al pensar si debía resistirse o si era mejor cooperar para que todo fuera menos terrible. Estaba a punto de perder la cabeza. Si el destino era inevitable, solo podía prepararse para lo horrible que sería el viaje.

La noche se alargó como una lija raspándole la piel, hasta dejarla en carne viva.

Cuando Ferron entró en la habitación, se le escapó un grito ahogado y estuvo a punto de echarse a llorar.

Al verla, el Sumo Inquisidor pareció querer darse la vuelta y marcharse.

Helena hizo amago de extender la mano, pero la apartó de inmediato y apretó los dedos en un puño. Ese movimiento bastó para retenerlo.

Ferron la miraba a ella y luego a la puerta, dudando, como si todavía estuviera decidiendo. ¿Y si se negaba y permitía que Stroud se la llevara?

La habitación comenzó a dar vueltas. Ya no sentía las manos.

Si Ferron quería marcharse, lo permitiría. Se iría a la Central. No sería tan cómplice como para suplicarle que se quedara.

No lograba descifrar las emociones de su rostro. Era imperturbable, como si no estuviera del todo presente.

Al final, se dio la vuelta. Helena no sabía si llorar o reír ante el hecho de que esto fuera lo único a lo que no estaba dispuesto a acceder. La única orden que se negaría a cumplir. Al fin y al cabo, ahora que todos sabían que era el Sumo Inquisidor, Morrough no podría matarlo.

Ferron sacó una cajita de estaño del bolsillo y se puso algo bajo la lengua.

—Cama —espetó sin mirarla.

Helena no se movió.

Él le dedicó una mirada apagada.

—Espera. —Extendió las manos, como si pudiera mantenerlo alejado—. ¿Y si me matas? —preguntó con voz temblorosa—. Ahora puedes hacerlo. Me dijiste que todo el mundo sabe que eres el Sumo Inquisidor. Morrough no podría justificar tu asesinato por mi culpa. Yo no soy nadie.

Ferron le prestó entonces más atención. Por un instante, se lo planteó. Helena se fijó en sus ojos calculadores y en ese momento se le aceleró el pulso.

—Puedo hacerlo yo misma, si quieres, para que Morrough no se dé cuenta —se ofreció—. Dame algo. No tiene que ser fácil ni rápido, puede ser algo pequeño. Podrías decir que te lo dejaste por ahí y…

Helena supo de inmediato que se había equivocado. La expresión de Ferron se endureció, sus ojos se apagaron, y volvió a apartar la mirada.

—Cama —repitió, esta vez con los dientes apretados.

La chica dejó caer las manos a los costados. Se dio la vuelta lentamente y se acercó a la cama, sintiendo una terrible desconexión de su cuerpo. Se mordió el labio inferior, más y más fuerte, para sentir algo. Notó la sangre en la lengua cuando se tumbó, pero su cuerpo permaneció entumecido.

Poco después, Ferron se acercó y simplemente se quitó el abrigo.

Helena se puso en tensión en cuanto se acercó, tratando de no rechinar los dientes.

El Sumo Inquisidor mantenía una expresión dura como el granito, pero se colocó a los pies de la cama con la vista clavada en el cabecero.

—Cierra los ojos —le ordenó.

Helena se obligó a obedecer e intentó centrarse en respirar. «No pienses». Percibía su olor en la habitación, el aroma a enebro, metal y a descomposición de la casa.

El colchón se hundió a su derecha. Se le encogió el pecho y empezó a respirar más rápido.

—No… no abras los ojos.

Los mantuvo cerrados con fuerza. Se hizo un silencio mientras él le levantaba la falda hasta las caderas y le quitaba la ropa interior. Helena creyó que se le paraba el corazón.

Oyó que Ferron tomaba aire. Sentía su cuerpo cerca.

—Respira —le dijo al oído izquierdo.

Notó algo entre las piernas, húmedo y resbaladizo. Se encogió instintivamente, pero pronto se dio cuenta de que era lubricante.

Helena dio una bocanada de aire y apretó tanto los ojos que le dolieron. Entonces sintió el peso de Ferron contra sus caderas.

Se atragantó con un sollozo incoherente.

Cerró los ojos con más fuerza. Su mente se desperdigó, como si buscara una escapatoria. En el tanque de suspensión, había aprendido a evadirse justo cuando estaba a punto de perder la cabeza.

Así había sobrevivido, ella sola había aprendido a resistir.

Pero ahora no lograba escapar de la misma forma.

Estaba atrapada en su propio cuerpo, como si alguien hubiera atado su consciencia.

«Esto es mejor que la Central», se recordó a sí misma, esforzándose para no hiperventilar, para no arañar, gritar y quitárselo de encima.

Se le contrajo el pecho. Las lágrimas le caían por el rabillo del ojo.

«Es mejor que la Central».

¿Y si esto no salía bien? ¿Y si Stroud tenía razón sobre él y ni siquiera era posible, pero Helena hubiera cooperado igualmente? ¿Y si todo esto no servía de nada?

Se le escapó un grito ahogado de pánico; no pudo evitar encogerse cuando Ferron la embistió por última vez.

Desapareció tan rápido que fue como si se esfumara.

Helena abrió los ojos y él ya no estaba. El violento sonido de alguien vomitando proveniente el baño.

Al cabo de un rato, oyó la cisterna del váter y el agua del grifo, que corrió durante unos minutos.

Tuvo fuerzas para bajarse la falda, pero no consiguió moverse más allá de eso. Tenía el cuerpo dormido.

«Se ha acabado», se repetía una y otra vez para intentar tranquilizarse, pero su cuerpo no cesaba de temblar. Las uñas habían dejado surcos con forma de medialuna en la palma de las manos.

Cuando Ferron salió del baño, ya no mantenía un semblante tenso, como si no pudiera seguir fingiendo. Tenía el rostro hundido y los ojos hinchados y enrojecidos.

Parecía extrañamente mortal, y Helena deseó con toda su alma que no lo fuera.

Apartó la mirada.

Ferron cruzó la habitación en silencio, recogió el abrigo y se marchó.

Helena se sentó en la cama poco a poco, tratando de no sentir su cuerpo.

Fue al baño, abrió el grifo de la ducha y se acurrucó bajo el chorro de agua con la ropa puesta. Cuando el agua comenzó a enfriarse, permaneció inmóvil, sin apenas moverse.

CAPÍTULO 19

AL DÍA SIGUIENTE, HELENA SE obligó a salir al jardín. Necesitaba desesperadamente sentir algo de aire fresco, escapar del peso opresivo de la casa, pero, al abrir la puerta, la golpeó una brisa cálida de primavera que le inundó los pulmones con el aroma a tierra mojada y flores. Vio ramilletes de azafrán y campanillas de invierno asomándose entre la hierba muerta. Las parras negras que cubrían la casa estaban salpicadas de brotes verdes, y había bandadas de pájaros que piaban al surcar los cielos.

Era un paisaje precioso, pero ella lo sintió como una traición.

El mundo no debía seguir siendo bello. Debía estar muerto y frío, como un reflejo perenne de la vida miserable de Helena. Pero el mundo había seguido su curso, dando paso a una nueva estación, mientras ella no podía hacer lo mismo. Estaba atrapada eternamente en el invierno, en la estación de la muerte.

Se recluyó en la casa.

Cuando se abrió la puerta de su habitación por la tarde, sintió alivio al ver que era Stroud, y no Ferron, quien entraba.

Esta parecía de buen humor.

—Pensé que era mejor pasarme por aquí para ver si ha habido algún daño esta primera vez. No queremos que una infección se interponga en nuestro camino. ¿Has sangrado?

Helena no lo había comprobado, pero negó con la cabeza lentamente.

Stroud la miró de arriba abajo con curiosidad.

—Bueno, tienes más de veinte años. No siempre ocurre.

Helena intentó no reaccionar cuando Stroud le posó la mano en la

pelvis, pero, al sentir cómo su resonancia se deslizaba por las partes más íntimas de su cuerpo, se puso a temblar descontroladamente.

—Lo más probable es que no comprobemos si estás embarazada hasta dentro de unas semanas, pero lo sabremos pronto. Se me da bastante bien detectarlo antes de tiempo. —Notó una sensación inquietante en el bajo vientre, como si se ajustara, y profirió un grito ahogado—. Sí, sin duda es el momento adecuado. Te he dejado lo más preparada posible.

A Helena se le erizó todo el vello hasta que Stroud se detuvo.

—Bueno, ¿cómo fue?

—Horrible —respondió Helena, apartando la mirada.

Stroud emitió un ruidito de compasión fingida.

—No me sorprende. Eres muy sensible.

Helena contempló la ventana con la mandíbula temblorosa.

Los labios de Stroud se estiraron como si fueran de plastilina. Dejó el expediente sobre la mesa y recorrió con los dedos el nombre de Helena y los números de otras dos prisioneras que figuraban en la portada.

—¿Sabes? Yo también estudié en la Torre de Alquimia. Fue años antes que tú, por supuesto. No tenía el repertorio ni el nivel de resonancia para seguir ascendiendo, pero me permitieron trasladarme al departamento de ciencia, donde me formé para ser auxiliar médica. Ahí fue la primera vez que escuché hablar de la vivemancia, aunque tardé años en darme cuenta del poder que tenía y en empezar a dominarla. Jamás me imaginé que sería una de las pocas vivemantes que lograrían sobrevivir a la guerra.

Helena no entendía por qué le estaba contando todo eso.

Stroud rebuscó en su maletín y sacó un frasco con pastillas. Partió una por la mitad.

—Abre la boca.

—¿Por qué? —preguntó Helena con los dientes apretados.

Stroud no respondió; se acercó y, usando los dedos y la resonancia para abrir la boca de Helena a la fuerza, le introdujo el trozo desmenuzado de pastilla y la obligó a tragárselo mientras se disolvía. Helena reconoció el sabor cuando le bajó por la garganta.

—Artemon Bennet salvó a gente como yo. Nos dio la oportunidad de poner a prueba nuestras habilidades, sin escondernos, y a estar orgullosos de ellas. —Stroud mantenía aún la mandíbula de Helena entre sus dedos, clavados firmes en la piel.

Helena sintió cómo Stroud estaba manipulando su fisiología, alterándola. Era algo totalmente distinto a lo que Ferron había hecho para aclimatarla a la casa. En lugar de experimentar desapego psicológico, notó un calor que ascendía lentamente, desde la superficie de la piel hasta lo más hondo.

Stroud siguió hablando:

—No digo que fuera perfecto. Bennet creía que los demás vivemantes eran demasiado idiotas para apreciar su inteligencia. —Arqueó unas cejas rubias—. Pero yo le serví sin dudarlo y aparté mis ambiciones personales para permanecer a su lado. Por eso sigo aquí, aunque todos siempre me hayan subestimado.

Helena intentó apartarse, pero la resonancia de Stroud estaba estrangulándole los nervios motores. Una tensión palpitante se encendió en su bajo vientre, y notaba la piel tan sensible que le dolía.

—Ya está. —Stroud la soltó, y Helena cayó de costado sobre la cama—. Ahora lo disfrutarás mucho más.

La chica se quedó inmóvil, incapaz de resistirse o de gritar mientras Stroud la colocaba en la cama, tumbada de espaldas y con las piernas abiertas.

«No, no, no».

—Le diré al Sumo Inquisidor que ya estás lista —dijo Stroud cuando se fue.

Helena esperó lo que le parecieron horas, mientras el deseo le calaba hasta los huesos. El cuerpo le pedía movimiento, caricias, fricción; era un ansia que se le metía bajo la piel.

Cuando Ferron llegó al fin, si hubiera podido moverse, se habría echado a temblar solo con la vibración de la puerta al cerrarse. Sin embargo, lo único que podía hacer era quedarse tumbada, mirándolo fijamente, suplicándole en silencio que se diera cuenta de que le pasaba algo.

Pero él no la miró. Tenía la vista perdida más allá, como si fuera transparente, mientras se quitó el abrigo y lo dejó en el sofá.

Helena lo observó moverse. De repente, su atención se volvió voraz y no podía apartar los ojos de todos los detalles del cuerpo del Sumo Inquisidor. La espera la había vaciado por dentro, dejándole un pozo de deseo insoportable que no dejaba de crecer.

Sabía que sus manos estarían calientes.

Se estremeció por dentro.

«Deja de pensar».

Cerró los ojos, pero el ansia que sentía le minaba su fuerza de voluntad.

La cama se movió. Sintió un escalofrío por la espalda. Ferron le subió la falda y el roce de la tela contra los muslos la hizo respirar con fuerza. Fue la única reacción que tuvo el valor de expresar.

—Respira —dijo Ferron, tal como había hecho la noche anterior.

Helena era plenamente consciente de su presencia, mucho más que el día anterior, pero ahora deseaba lo contrario. Apenas sintió su peso. Quería arquear la espalda, rozarse contra él, a pesar del grito incesante que escuchaba en su cabeza. Abrió los ojos y lo miró fijamente.

Era como si jamás lo hubiera mirado de verdad.

Siempre había existido una distancia clara y cautelosa entre ellos. Cuando lo observaba, lo hacía buscando indicios, debilidades. Nunca lo había contemplado como si fuera un ser humano o una criatura de sangre caliente.

Ahora se le antojaba muy humano. Quería que la tocara. Recordaba el tacto de sus manos, las yemas de sus dedos recorriéndole la mandíbula. Lo deseaba tanto que le ardía la piel. El peso del que tan desesperadamente había querido escapar la noche anterior... ahora lo deseaba.

Unas lágrimas ardientes le surcaron las sienes.

Por un instante fugaz, Ferron la observó de reojo antes de apartar la vista. Se quedó quieto y volvió a mirarla.

—¿Qué sucede? —preguntó.

Ella lo miró fijamente, implorando que la entendiera.

Ferron se apartó y se quitó un guante. Aún los llevaba puestos, incluso ahora.

Apenas la rozó, pero eso fue suficiente para deshacer la parálisis.

El cuerpo de Helena se estremeció y, acto seguido, se encogió sobre sí misma y emitió un sollozo ahogado. Juntó las piernas con fuerza, pero seguía notando una palpitación que le recorría todo el cuerpo. Empezó a respirar con dificultad, y hasta el aire le quemaba los pulmones.

—¿Qué te ha hecho?

No podía mirarlo a la cara.

—Me dijo que era para que fuese m-mejor. —Le temblaba la voz sin control—. Porque me... me quejé. ¿C-cuánto duran las pastillas que me diste la última vez?

—Ocho horas.

—Me ha dado media. —Dio una bocanada de aire—. ¿P-puedes cambiarlo?

—Cuando ya ha hecho efecto, no —respondió—. Tiene que pasarse solo.

Helena asintió. Lo había supuesto, pero tenía la esperanza de estar equivocada. Respiró hondo de nuevo.

—¿Podemos… podemos esperar hasta… después? —dijo con voz estrangulada.

Se produjo un silencio.

—Tengo que marcharme justo después de esto. No volveré hasta mañana por la noche.

Se tumbó, intentando ordenar sus pensamientos. Ya no confiaba en su propia razón.

Era eso o arriesgarse a no quedarse embarazada. A pesar de los embarazos no deseados que había tratado, sabía que los niños no llegaban simplemente así. Sus padres tardaron años en lograrlo; ella nació cuando ya se habían rendido. Un milagro, decían.

Dos meses, y después iría a la Central, con Stroud y…

Se estaba volviendo loca. No podía hacerlo. Una decisión así… No era justo que la obligaran a elegir entre esas opciones. Ninguna de ellas era buena; simplemente estaba eligiendo de qué forma quería odiarse para siempre.

Era lo más cruel que Stroud podría haberle hecho.

—Pues… hazlo ya —cedió, tumbándose de espaldas sin mirarlo.

Contempló el dosel de la cama y se obligó a pensar en otra cosa. La cama tardó en volver a moverse.

Helena jamás creyó que la segunda vez pudiera ser peor, pero fue mil veces peor. Ahora su cuerpo lo ansiaba.

Intentó cerrar los ojos, aunque se sentía inquieta y no conseguía mantenerlos cerrados. Se abrían de nuevo y volvía a mirar a Ferron, descubriendo detalles en los que nunca se había fijado. Sus mejillas y los ojos marcados, sus labios finos, la línea recta de su mandíbula, y cómo desaparecía su garganta pálida en el cuello de la camisa. Quiso que se acercara para poder aspirar su piel, para sentir el calor de otro cuerpo.

—Date prisa —dijo con los dientes apretados, obligándose a permanecer quieta.

No necesitaba lubricante, pero él lo aplicó igualmente. Helena arqueó la espalda hasta que se quedó mirando el cabecero, no dejaba de estremecerse. Enterró el rostro entre las manos y se mordió las palmas con violencia, a punto de venirse abajo.

Un gemido se ahogó en su garganta cuando Ferron se movió. Flexionó los dedos aferrándose al edredón con tanta fuerza que estuvo a punto de romperlo.

Sintió náuseas por el horror que la invadía. Odió cada fibra de su ser, por no poder controlar su propio cuerpo, por sentirse siempre asustada, débil y, ahora, anhelante. Pero no podía escapar. Tal vez Matias siempre tuvo razón: estaba en su naturaleza ser frágil.

Deseó poder escapar de su propio cuerpo, partirlo en pedazos y ver cómo ardían hasta dejar de ser humana.

Pero su cuerpo se contrajo en contra de su voluntad. Ferron emitió un jadeo desgarrador, y sintió que se incendiaba al oírlo. Notaba tanto su peso sobre ella que se le escapó un sollozo desesperado.

Ferron la penetró unas cuantas veces más y acabó con un gruñido torturado.

Al segundo, había desaparecido, retrocediendo, como si estuviera deseando huir de allí.

Helena abrió los ojos justo cuando él salía de la habitación.

Solo lo vio de soslayo, poco antes de que cerrara la puerta de un portazo, pálido y gris, como si estuviera a punto de desmayarse.

Se había ido. La habitación estaba vacía y ella se encontraba sola.

Se encogió de lado y sollozó, escondiendo el rostro entre las manos. La desesperación que ardía bajo su piel desapareció un poco al verse superada por el horror de lo que había ocurrido. Se arrastró al baño y vomitó hasta vaciarse por completo.

Helena siempre supo lo que era el sexo. En Etras, formaba parte de la vida, al igual que nacer y morir, pero en el Norte se vivía de otra forma. Era un tema que solía quedarse de puertas para dentro.

Los chicos podían meterse en problemas si iban a los distritos del placer, pero el deseo se consideraba una parte irreprimible de su naturaleza y un signo de su vitalidad, así que los castigos eran leves, más enfocados en que los hubieran pillado que en el acto en sí. Sin embargo, para las chicas había otra vara de medir, incluso para aquellas que vivían al margen de la sociedad tradicional de Paladia. Lumitia era una diosa virgen, pura y deslumbrante, y a las mujeres que se asociaban con su culto y las oportunidades que este brindaba se les exigía lo mismo.

La vida de Helena en la Academia giraba en torno a una beca que no solo dependía de su rendimiento académico, sino que incluía una estricta cláusula de moralidad. Helena se adhirió a ella con una devoción que superaba al sentimiento religioso, ya que le daban más miedo las consecuencias terrenales que las amenazas divinas. El miedo apagó cualquier tipo de deseo que pudiera sentir por alguien.

En ocasiones, pensaba que algún día, cuando hubiera saldado sus deudas y cumplido todas sus expectativas, cuando alcanzara sus metas, querría ser amada, y conocer qué significaba sentirse deseada.

Ahora lo único que conocía era esta vergüenza nauseabunda.

———— ✦ ————

Cuando por fin se le pasó el efecto de la medicación, Helena se tumbó e intentó pensar en algo, cualquier cosa, pero no tenía mucho en lo que centrarse. Lo único que le quedaba por responder era por qué parecía ser una pieza en una conspiración laberíntica.

En el fondo, sí que entendía los motivos de Morrough y Stroud, por qué la consideraban útil, pero, por muchas vueltas que le diera, Helena no comprendía qué papel tenía Ferron en todo ello, aunque fuera la última persona en la que quería pensar. Al menos, replantearse sus razones políticas le impedía verlo como un ser humano.

Helena estaba convencida de que, de alguna manera, Ferron se había asegurado de que todo el mundo supiera que él era el Sumo Inquisidor. Quizá existieran circunstancias atenuantes, pero, si no hubiera deseado que el rumor se propagara, lo habría contenido. Quería que Paladia y los países de alrededor supieran que era Kaine Ferron.

¿Por qué? ¿Sería un intento de eludir los castigos de Morrough? ¿De convertirse en alguien más difícil de reemplazar? No. Debía haber algún motivo más importante.

Actualmente, Nueva Paladia estaba rodeada de enemigos.

La monarquía Novis, que se encontraba al este del río, tenía parentesco con los Holdfast; la madre de Luc era prima lejana de la reina. Parecía poco probable que Novis legitimara el Concejo de Gremios. Por otro lado, el país de Hevgoss, que se cernía sobre Paladia desde el oeste, tenía la costumbre de interferir de forma clandestina en los países cercanos para provocar crisis y tener una excusa para justificar su «intervención». Las intervenciones solían terminar con gobiernos gestionados por ellos.

Desde el principio, la Llama Eterna sospechó que Morrough era una marioneta de Hevgoss, pero parecía que algo, tal vez Helena, había agriado esa relación.

La economía y la legitimidad de Paladia dependían por completo de la alquimia, y la guerra había diezmado tanto a la población como la industria. Los recursos naturales y los siglos de investigación alquímica seguían existiendo, pero el país era débil y los lobos lo estaban cercando. Lo único que mantenía a raya las garras de los vecinos era el temor a los inmarcesibles, pero ese mito se había hecho añicos. Morrough había desaparecido de la esfera pública y el Sumo Inquisidor era la única autoridad visible.

Quizá Ferron estaba negociando en secreto con Hevgoss para derrocar a Morrough.

Por muy aterrador que fuese el Sumo Inquisidor, los Ferron eran una familia antigua que formaba parte de la historia de Paladia, incluso antes de que amasaran su gran fortuna. Los inmarcesibles gobernaban mediante el miedo, y los pocos ciudadanos de Paladia que seguían beneficiándose de ello cabrían en el salón de baile de Puntaférreo. La ilusión estaba llegando al clímax. Cuando se desmoronara, la gente buscaría a alguien que les resultara familiar, alguien con poder de quien pudieran enorgullecerse.

Y todo el mundo conocía el poder revolucionario del acero. Los Ferron habían forjado la era industrial.

A estas alturas, si Ferron usurpaba el trono de Morrough, los paladinos lo verían como un salvador. Podrían culparlo de la mayoría de las atrocidades que había cometido y asumir la responsabilidad de aquellas que les resultaran convenientes.

Hasta donde sabía Helena, Ferron no tenía rivales. Greenfinch era poco más que una marioneta, y el Concejo de Gremios, un simple chiste. Ferron era el único apoyo real de Morrough.

Eso explicaría por qué el Sumo Nigromante lo torturaba sin descanso: le guardaba rencor porque, al fin y al cabo, le estaba fallando hasta su propia inmortalidad. Dependía totalmente de Ferron, y no tenía a nadie más a quien acudir.

Aun así, Helena tenía la sensación de que se le escapaba algo.

¿Qué pintaba ella en los planes de Ferron?

Fueran cuales fuesen sus maquinaciones, ella sabía que debía tener un papel en ellas. Estaba demasiado obsesionado con su bienestar. Ferron dedicaba unos esfuerzos considerables a asegurarse de que ella se encontrase bien, aunque siempre intentaba disimularlo.

Recordó cómo dudó cuando le pidió que la matara. Se lo había pensado. ¿Por qué? Si era una parte esencial de su plan, ¿por qué consideraba la opción de matarla? Pero, si no lo era, ¿por qué entonces se esforzaba tanto?

ERA DE NOCHE CUANDO FERRON regresó. Al entrar en la habitación, ambos se miraron fijamente, pero ninguno de ellos habló.

No había nada que decir.

Él se dio la vuelta, se colocó una pastilla bajo la lengua y, al girarse de nuevo, tenía la mirada perdida.

Helena se tumbó con los ojos clavados en el dosel de la cama.

No se inmutó cuando sintió que la cama se hundía bajo su peso. No emitió ningún ruido cuando le levantó la falda hasta la cintura. Le tocó la entrepierna, y Helena siguió mirando hacia arriba con tanta concentración que se le nubló la vista.

Cuando la penetró, profirió un grito ahogado y giró la cabeza hacia la pared, retorciéndose de angustia.

Su cuerpo se había anticipado. Al igual que la medicación la había aclimatado a la casa, también la había habituado a esto.

Era una traición en lo más profundo de su ser.

Pensó en empujarlo. Si la forzaba físicamente, si la sujetaba o la paralizaba, tal vez se odiaría menos a sí misma.

Pero estaba harta de sufrir, así que no se movió.

Cuando hubo terminado, Ferron se marchó sin decir nada. Ella no se atrevió a mirarlo a la cara.

Tras cinco días, la puerta permaneció cerrada y la casa se sumió en el silencio. Por fin se había acabado, pero Helena apenas sintió alivio.

Se estaba volviendo loca. La ansiedad la estaba quebrando, se desmoronaba, consumida por la jaula que la mantenía con vida.

¿Y si funcionaba? ¿Y si no?

No sabía qué le aterraba más.

CONFORME EL DÍA SE ALARGABA hasta la noche, Helena empezó a sentirse más inquieta. No comprendió el motivo hasta que la oscuridad cayó solo durante un instante, para luego dar paso a una luz abrasadora.

Lumitia había llegado a la sublimación plena. El mundo exterior estaba bañado por una luz plateada, casi tan brillante como el día, que se extendía sobre el cielo negro. No había estrellas ni planetas. Luna, suspendida a media altura, parecía un trozo de cerámica rota en comparación.

La lenta órbita de Lumitia hacía que solo alcanzara la plenitud dos veces al año, en primavera y en otoño, para luego entrar en fase de latencia durante el verano y el invierno.

Las fases de sublimación ejercían un gran efecto sobre los alquimistas.

Para quienes tenían poca resonancia, el punto álgido de la sublimación era el único momento del año en el que podían transmutar, mientras que los alquimistas más poderosos solían desorientarse bajo su fulgor, un estado que la gente llamaba borrachera de luna.

La sublimación ejercía una influencia aún mayor en los paladines. Según la Fe, se debía a su conexión más profunda con los dioses. Luc y Lila alcanzaban un grado de ebriedad tal que les costaba caminar en línea recta, mientras que Helena (como extranjera infiel que era) solo sentía un poco de ansiedad, un temor pesado que la hundía.

Aquella noche, la cena no apareció.

Era la primera vez en todos los meses de cautiverio que no recibía comida.

Algo iba mal. Aunque hubiera Ascendencia, los necrómatas debían estar presentes, activos de algún modo. Se asomó al jardín y vio a los dos que custodiaban las puertas, inmóviles como estatuas. Pero no se oían pasos al otro lado de la puerta y, cuando salió de su habitación, no apareció nadie.

Helena se dirigió al vestíbulo y siguió el rastro de plata que dejaba Lumitia, esperando a cruzarse con alguno en cualquier momento. Las sombras eran negras como la tinta y contrastaban con la luz brillante y blanca.

El vestíbulo estaba vacío; el mármol blanco parecía resplandeciente bajo la luz de la luna. El dragón uróboro del suelo brillaba como si tuviera escamas; su cuerpo oscuro relucía entre el mármol blanco.

El peso de Lumitia era opresivo. Sentía la resonancia correteando por sus venas, como si quisiera destruir la anulación, como si estuviera en una jaula demasiado estrecha incluso para moverse.

Estudió la casa en busca de algún signo de movimiento. Los necrómatas no requerían un mantenimiento constante. Según los estudios, una vez que recibían órdenes, las ejecutaban en bucle hasta el infinito. Incluso si Ferron estaba ebrio por la sublimación, deberían funcionar como siempre.

A menos que estuviera muerto…

Helena se detuvo en seco. ¿Y si la Llama Eterna había aprovechado el punto álgido de la sublimación para matarlo? Los inmarcesibles de la fiesta decían que el asesino era como un fantasma, que entraba y salía sin dejar más rastro a su paso que un cadáver.

Escudriñó a su alrededor con más atención. La combinación del intenso resplandor plateado y el negro que la rodeaba la marearon de camino a la puerta principal.

Le temblaban los dedos al alcanzar el pomo. No se podía abrir. Movió el pestillo que había debajo del pomo, pero no se movió nada. Tiró con fuerza, ignorando el dolor que se extendió por sus brazos, y trató de abrir la puerta, aunque no lo consiguió. La habían cerrado a cal y canto.

Se le encogió el pecho, y se obligó a ir hacia la otra puerta que daba al exterior. Tampoco estaba abierta.

Recorrió la casa, respirando con más rapidez con cada puerta que encontraba cerrada.

¿Estaría Ferron muerto en alguna parte de Puntaférreo? ¿Iba a encontrar su cadáver? Se preparaba mentalmente antes de entrar en una habitación, convencida de que descubriría sangre entre las sombras.

Pero la Llama Eterna no la habría abandonado. Si hubieran venido, habrían dejado una puerta o una ventana abierta. Le concederían esa ventaja, al menos.

Solo tenía que encontrarla.

Probó con otra puerta. Tiró y tiró hasta que un dolor punzante le recorrió el brazo y le dejó la mano dormida.

Cuanto más buscaba, más convencida estaba de ello: Ferron estaba muerto. La habían dejado atrapada y sola en esta casa.

Stroud no tardaría en venir a por ella. La llevarían a la Central y, si no estaba embarazada, encontraría a alguien que la violara.

Se le estaban durmiendo los brazos, cada vez sentía la cabeza más mareada. Subió al segundo piso y recorrió el pasillo. Siempre había evitado esa parte de la casa porque era donde estaban las habitaciones de Ferron y de Aurelia.

Si Ferron estaba muerto, tenía que verlo con sus propios ojos. Debía averiguarlo o la incertidumbre la atormentaría.

Llegó a la primera puerta a mano izquierda y respiró hondo para tranquilizarse lo suficiente antes de agarrar el pomo.

La abrió en silencio.

La habitación estaba sumida en la oscuridad. La luz de la luna se derramaba como un río de plata a través de las ventanas. Miró la cama: estaba vacía.

En cuanto cruzó el umbral, el aire cambió.

Se giró rápidamente hacia el escritorio. La habitación estaba en penumbra y en el borde solo había unas botellas. Entonces, una sombra se movió y la luz de la luna iluminó la cara de Ferron, reflejándose en su cabello y su piel pálida, como si centelleara.

—Helena —susurró.

Ella se quedó paralizada, no sabía si debía sentir alivio o miedo.

Jamás la había llamado de ninguna forma. En todos los meses que llevaba en Puntaférreo, solo se había referido a ella como «la prisionera». Stroud la llamaba Marino, pero Ferron jamás la había nombrado. Hacía mucho tiempo que no escuchaba a nadie decir su nombre.

—Yo... —Se sintió estúpida—. Creí que estabas muerto.

Debió dar la vuelta y marcharse, pero Ferron parecía tan fantasmal que no consiguió apartar los ojos de él. La expresión de su rostro era de una desesperación absoluta, pero, cuando la miró, los ojos revelaban un sentimiento voraz.

Se levantó lentamente. Parecía moverse con una soltura que no era propia de él. Helena miró el escritorio que había dejado atrás y lo comprendió.

Estaba borracho, demasiado ebrio, tanto por la influencia de Lumitia como por la ingesta de alcohol. Al regenerarse tan rápido, probablemente necesitaba de ambos estímulos.

Cuando se acercó, Helena intentó retroceder, pero entonces chocó con la pared y no tuvo adónde ir. Ya no había espacio que los separara.

Ferron levantó una mano pálida y le envolvió la garganta con los dedos.

Tenía los ojos negros, aunque aún se distinguía la plata por el borde. Se le desbocó el pulso cuando la miró a los ojos.

No le extrañaba que los sirvientes hubieran desaparecido. Tal vez todo el mundo sabía que era mejor esconderse de él en noches como esa, todos menos ella.

—Ah, Marino. —Le pasó el pulgar por el cuello, recorriendo la cicatriz que tenía bajo la mandíbula—. Si hubiera sabido el dolor que me ibas a causar, jamás te habría dejado venir.

Suspiró, y Helena percibió el olor a licor en su aliento cuando Ferron inclinó la cabeza hacia ella. No tenía ni idea de qué quería decir o si debía disculparse.

—Pero, a estas alturas, supongo que merezco arder. Me pregunto si tú arderás también conmigo.

Su rostro estaba tan cerca que sus palabras rozaron los labios de Helena, y su boca se estampó contra la suya.

CAPÍTULO 20

FUE UN BESO ARREBATADOR.

En cuanto sus labios se tocaron, Ferron la aplastó contra su cuerpo. La mano que tenía en su garganta se deslizó hacia su cabello, enredándose entre los rizos, sujetándolos con firmeza mientras el beso se intensificaba. Helena echó la cabeza hacia atrás, entregándose a ese fuego que la consumía. El Sumo Inquisidor siguió besándola con una pasión que dolía, pero sin llegar a romperla, como una tormenta bajando por su garganta.

Cuando jadeó, Ferron se apartó de sus labios y empezó a recorrer a besos su mandíbula y su cuello. Con la otra mano le rodeó la cintura.

Helena se quedó paralizada, sorprendida y a la vez rendida en las manos posesivas de Ferron.

Él le tiró del vestido con determinación hasta que arrancó los botones. Helena tenía la espalda contra la pared y su rodilla entre las piernas, sujetándola por la falda. Mientras tanto, Ferron movía las manos con rapidez; le rasgó la tela y la dejó desnuda hasta la cintura.

Al principio, el aire frío recorrió su piel, pero esa sensación desapareció en cuanto sintió el calor de sus manos y su boca. Se estremeció de anhelo. Ferron tenía la cabeza enterrada en la garganta de Helena y los labios junto a su oreja, sin dejar de darle besos desde el cuello hasta la clavícula. Cuando le pegó un mordisco, Helena... gimió.

El sonido rompió el silencio como un cristal hecho añicos.

Los dos se quedaron inmóviles y entonces Ferron se apartó con violencia.

Helena lo miró fijamente, demasiado desconcertada para moverse. La luz de la luna se colaba por la ventana; un sendero claro y de un plateado impresionante que iluminaba el punto donde ella estaba contra la pared, medio desnuda y... excitada.

Ferron abrió los ojos, conmocionado, mientras su cabello rubio caía desordenado sobre su rostro. Cuando se detuvo a mirarla, sus ojos adquirieron un brillo inquietante que parecía iluminarlo desde dentro. Se pasó una mano por la cara y se peinó hacia atrás. Helena vio que le palpitaba la mandíbula. Sin mediar palabra, hizo un gesto de burla.

Sin embargo, antes de que Ferron dijera nada, un sollozo horrorizado escapó de Helena. Intentó desesperadamente subirse el vestido, pero le temblaban los dedos. Estaba desgarrado, sin botones, así que se aferró a la tela y se cubrió con los brazos. Retrocedió tambaleante hasta que encontró la puerta.

Salió corriendo y huyó. Aceptar lo que había sucedido estuvo a punto de hacerla caer.

Se había mostrado receptiva a Ferron.

Él se había acercado para besarla y ella se lo había permitido. En ese momento, ni se le había pasado por la cabeza alejarlo. De hecho, se había derretido al sentir esa calidez de sentirse sujeta.

Atrapada en Puntaférreo, se aferraba a cualquier atisbo de amabilidad, a todo lo que se pareciera a la ternura.

Pero no era amabilidad. Ferron no era amable; simplemente no era cruel. No era tan horrendo como podría haber sido.

Y, para la mente rota de Helena, la ausencia de crueldad era un consuelo. Para su corazón hambriento, eso era suficiente.

Huyó a su habitación, tiró el vestido desgarrado al suelo bajo la maldita luz plateada y se puso otra ropa, como si así pudiera esconder lo que había hecho.

Helena valía más que aquello. Se llevó la mano al pecho; las uñas se le clavaron en la piel, como si con los arañazos pudiera entrar en razón.

—Lo... lo siento mucho, Luc —dijo con una voz estrangulada por la culpa.

No podía hacer esto. No podía.

No iba a permitir que su mente la engañara, incitándola a anhelar la atención de la persona responsable de que empezara la guerra. Ferron había causado un daño incalculable. Todo, todo lo que había pasado, todo era culpa suya, pero Helena sabía que se estaba consumiendo por dentro, que estaba desesperada por sentir algo que no fuera dolor, que no fuera muerte y vacío.

Pero ya no podía hacerlo más.

Podía soportar el horror de que la traicionara su cuerpo, pero no iba a permitir que la traicionara su mente.

Si era así, entonces prefería perder la cabeza.

Desde la ventana, contempló el jardín vallado, su prisión sin salida. Apoyó la mano temblorosa contra el cristal frío y el entramado de hierro, buscando el poder que ya no le pertenecía, pero no encontró nada.

Había desaparecido, como todo lo demás.

Se le escapó un sollozo quebrado y abatido y, acto seguido, echó la cabeza hacia atrás y la estampó contra el cristal y el hierro con todas sus fuerzas.

Lo volvió a hacer.

Y otra vez.

Sentía que la sangre le caía en los ojos, pero siguió haciéndolo.

Un brazo la rodeó por la cintura, y una mano firme le atrapó las dos muñecas y la apartó de la ventana. Un líquido rojo empañaba el cristal.

Helena se resistió con todas sus fuerzas, intentando liberarse a pesar del dolor que le provocaba, y clavó los dedos de los pies entre los barrotes de hierro para coger impulso.

—No. No. —La voz de Ferron sonó junto su oreja.

La sangre le cubría la cara y lo veía todo rojo. No dejaba de gritar. Toda la culpa y la angustia que había reprimido la estaba devorando por dentro. Gritó como si pudiera hacer trizas el mundo con ello.

Quería terminar.

No podía traicionar a todos: Luc, Lila, Soren, la enfermera Pace, su padre…

—No puedo… —Se liberó de nuevo y arañó con las manos el aire. Quería volver a estamparse contra la ventana.

Ferron le soltó las muñecas, pero solo para posar la palma de sus manos en su frente.

—¡No…!

Demasiado tarde. La resonancia del Sumo Inquisidor le recorrió todo el cuerpo, como si fuera un tapiz. Ferron encontró los hilos conductores de las emociones y los arrancó.

No la sedó ni la paralizó. Fue peor, algo más invasor todavía: le arrebató todo lo que sentía y la dejó aturdida, intentando reconciliarse con la disonancia.

Era el mismo efecto que le hacían las pastillas, pero esta vez estaba empleando la resonancia para que Helena permaneciera así todo el tiempo necesario, hasta que su cuerpo perdiera el ímpetu que le provocaban las emociones ahora desvanecidas.

Dejó de luchar y se desplomó en sus brazos. La sangre le corría por la cara como un reguero, goteando desde la barbilla. Ferron tenía las manos manchadas con su sangre, pero usó la yema de los dedos para curarle los arañazos y las heridas de la frente. Helena también notó su resonancia en el cráneo.

—Una fractura leve —le dijo Ferron, y la mayor parte del dolor desapareció antes de que la soltara.

Helena se quedó paralizada, vacía y perdida. Ferron le había arrancado sus emociones con tanto ahínco que era como intentar llegar al fondo de un pozo.

Miró la ventana manchada de sangre y se planteó volverlo a hacer, pero no serviría de nada. Ferron volvería a impedírselo, hasta que quedara hueca y complaciente: una estatua erosionada y sin rasgos marcados.

El Sumo Inquisidor le hizo girar el rostro para que lo mirara. Sus ojos seguían brillando.

—¿Por qué?

Helena le devolvió la mirada con hastío; todavía le dolía la cabeza. Al menos le dolía algo.

—¿Por qué qué?

—¿Por qué este repentino deseo ahora?

Un movimiento a su espalda llamó su atención. Una de las necrómatas entró en la habitación con las manos ocupadas y dejó la puerta abierta a su paso. Era la anciana, pero por un instante sintió que percibió en ella un aire extrañamente vivo.

No se movía de la forma antinatural que Helena estaba acostumbrada, sino más como un liche.

Como si se percatara del escrutinio de Helena, la mujer disminuyó la velocidad y se movió de forma más mecánica. Traía una palangana y un trapo, y empezó a limpiarle la cara a Helena.

—¿Por qué no? —dijo la chica con voz inerte—. He querido suicidarme desde el principio. Ya lo sabes.

Ferron entrecerró los ojos.

—Y tú sabes tan bien como yo que no te habrías matado haciendo eso.

Helena no respondió.

—Si no me lo dices, buscaré la respuesta yo mismo —añadió cuando se negó a responder.

Helena se encogió y apartó la cara para que la necrómata no pudiera seguir limpiándole la sangre que le quedaba en el rabillo de los ojos.

Abrió la boca varias veces antes de hablar.

—Creo que me pasa algo —dijo al final.

Ferron la miró de soslayo, como si fuera algo evidente.

—Es un instinto de supervivencia o... —Le parecía tan humillante hablar de ello que su cuerpo se puso en tensión y las palabras se le atragantaron—. Puede que sea un mecanismo de defensa. —Apartó la mirada—. Una vez, en la Academia, leí sobre una propuesta de investigación. El autor quería demostrar que sus sujetos podían llegar a desarrollar emociones hacia su... superior. —Estaba a punto de fallarle la voz—. Creía que, mediante sus métodos, conseguiría que sus sujetos fueran más complacientes. Que, si se les condicionaba para que fuesen lo bastante dependientes, acabarían racionalizando y justificando cualquier... cualquier daño que sufrieran, y hasta tratarían de crear una conexión emocional o sentimientos hacia la persona que los controlaba, como una especie de instinto de supervivencia.

Helena creyó que se desmayaba. Notaba sobre ella el peso de la mirada de Ferron.

—Solo era una propuesta, no sé si tendría algo de verdad, pero últimamente no dejo de pensar en eso —dijo con voz ahogada.

Se quedó mirando la ventana manchada de sangre.

—Preferiría pasar el resto de mi vida sufriendo violaciones en la Central que vivir un minuto teniendo sentimientos hacia ti.

El aire de la habitación pareció congelarse.

—Bueno —intervino Ferron tras un largo silencio—, con suerte estarás embarazada y no tendrás que elegir ninguna de las dos opciones. Así te quedarás tranquila.

Al darse la vuelta, la fuerza de voluntad de Helena se desvaneció. Extendió la mano y lo cogió del abrigo para que no se marchara.

Le temblaba todo el cuerpo, pero no podía soltarlo. Lo agarró con más fuerza. No quería estar sola, no lo soportaba.

Ferron levantó la mano y la posó sobre su hombro, y con eso fue suficiente. Helena se desmoronó y cayó en sus brazos. Apenas notaba el tacto de sus dedos en el brazo, pero dejó de sentir la quemazón en los pulmones al respirar. Apoyó la cabeza contra su pecho.

Estaba harta de que todo lo que la rodeaba fuera siempre frío, vacío e infinito.

De repente, Ferron echó la cabeza hacia atrás y la apartó de un empujón. Helena trastabilló hacia atrás y cayó sobre la cama. El Sumo Inquisidor abrió los ojos de par en par y Helena notó que su expresión era tensa. Miró a su alrededor y, después, a la puerta abierta.

Entonces soltó una carcajada suave y amarga.

—Eres patética, ¿eh? —dijo—. ¿Supervivencia? ¿En serio?

Helena no supo a qué se refería.

Ferron volvió a reír.

—¿De verdad esperas que me crea que, de repente, te importa sobrevivir? ¿Después de que todos los miembros de la Resistencia se mostraran dispuestos a morir por su causa? ¿Y tú eres distinta, aunque lleves meses imaginando cómo asesinarme y suicidarte?

Se agachó delante de ella. Nunca había visto tanta crueldad en su semblante. Había una maldad descarnada en su mirada.

—No, lo que te está carcomiendo por dentro no es un instinto de supervivencia ni un deseo inconsciente de calmarme. Lo que no soportas es el aislamiento. La pobre sanadora de la Llama Eterna, sin nadie a quien salvar. Nadie te necesita y nadie te quiere.

Le dedicó una sonrisa que dejaba sus colmillos al descubierto.

—No hay nada más. No soportas estar sola. Harás lo que sea por la gente a la que te permites querer. —Arqueó una ceja—. ¿No fue así en la guerra? Tú querías luchar, pero, cuando descubrieron lo que eras, Ilva Holdfast decidió que serías más útil siendo el chivo expiatorio de Holdfast. Te metieron en el corredor de la muerte antes de que Holdfast pisara el campo de batalla.

—No… fue… eso… lo… que… pasó. —Helena tenía las manos apretadas, clavándose las uñas en las palmas de las manos.

—Fue exactamente eso lo que pasó. Verás, el falcón Matias dejó sus aposentos prácticamente intactos. Mantuvo un montón de correspondencia con Ilva en la época en la que tú estabas de prácticas. Ella sabía que lo único que tenía que hacer era poner la vida de Holdfast en peligro para que hicieras todo lo que te pidieran. —Echó la cabeza hacia atrás—. Hubieras hecho cualquier cosa por tus amigos: tomar decisiones difíciles, pagar el precio sin quejarte, prostituirte si hacía falta, todo por el bien de la guerra. Pero dime…, porque siento verdadera curiosidad, ¿qué hizo Holdfast por ti para que tú lo merecieras?

Helena lo fulminó con la mirada.

—Luc era mi amigo. Era mi mejor amigo.

—¿Y qué?

Helena respiró entrecortadamente y apartó los ojos.

—Mi padre lo dejó todo para que estudiara en la Academia, pero... fue... fue duro. Yo... yo no quería que mi padre supiera lo difícil que estaba siendo. —Sintió como si tuviera una piedra atascada en la garganta—. Pero a mí... me daba mucho miedo estropearlo todo y no... no conocía a nadie. Luc podría haberse hecho amigo de cualquiera, pero me eligió a mí. No hubiera tenido a nadie de no ser por él.

—¿Y ahora qué? —dijo Ferron, alisándose el abrigo para eliminar las marcas que los dedos de Helena habían dejado en la tela—. ¿Soy el sustituto de Holdfast? ¿No puedes evitar cogerle cariño a cualquiera que cometa el error de hablar contigo?

Helena se encogió, pero Ferron no había terminado.

—Entonces te lo dejaré bien claro. No te quiero en mi vida. Nunca te he querido. No soy tu amigo. No hay nada que desee más que el momento en que por fin me libre de ti.

Se dio la vuelta y se fue.

———————

CUANDO STROUD REGRESÓ DOS SEMANAS después, Helena se sometió al examen médico sin pronunciar palabra. Había pasado ese tiempo en una neblina de desconcierto, apenas consciente del paso de los días. Como si fuera un fantasma, dejó que el mundo se deslizara a su alrededor mientras ella permanecía congelada en el tiempo.

—Tienes muy mala cara —comentó Stroud con una mueca de desagrado—. ¿Cómo van los intentos del Sumo Inquisidor?

A Helena se le cerró la garganta y no dijo nada. Se quedó mirándose el regazo, arrugando la fina tela de sus braguitas entre los dedos.

—Túmbate —le ordenó Stroud, dejando el bolso en la mesita de noche.

Stroud le retiró las braguitas y colocó una mano fría en la parte baja del abdomen.

—Creo que es demasiado pronto para saberlo, pero a veces lo noto. En tu caso, cuanto antes lo sepamos, mejor.

Helena sintió que le latía el corazón en las sienes.

Stroud frunció el ceño y, con ello, se acentuaron todas sus arrugas. Hizo que su resonancia se adentrara más, hasta que esbozó un gesto de sorpresa.

—Estás embarazada.

Al principio, Helena no sintió nada. Eran palabras abstractas, conceptuales.

Entonces la atravesaron como una espada.

Sin embargo, no sintió que se le desbordaran las emociones; Ferron se las había arrancado todas. Estaba vacía.

Así que se vino abajo.

Fue como intentar respirar bajo el hielo; no había aire, solo una presión infinita que la aplastaba por todos lados. Su corazón se le aceleró tanto que lo único que percibía era el rugido de su torrente sanguíneo.

Stroud seguía hablando, pero Helena no escuchaba las palabras.

«No».

«No, por favor».

«No, no, no».

Era culpa suya. Se había dejado llevar, no se había resistido.

Stroud continuaba hablándole, cada vez más fuerte. Las palabras sonaban amortiguadas; eran un ruido envolvente e indescifrable.

La habitación le dio vueltas, como si fuera a desaparecer. Helena notó que se le cerraba la garganta, que se asfixiaba. Sintió un dolor punzante en el pecho, como si algo quisiera abrirla en canal desde dentro.

«No. No, por favor».

Stroud extendió la mano y colocó los dedos en el cuello de Helena, pero la chica empezó a gritar.

No era un grito de angustia como le ocurrió con Ferron, sino gritos desgarradores, como los de un conejo moribundo. Agudos, rápidos, repetitivos. Se le escapaban uno tras otro.

Stroud estaba perpleja y le dio un bofetón en la cara.

Helena no podía dejar de gritar.

Todo fue perdiendo color y la visión se le estrechó como si estuviera en un túnel.

Ferron estaba delante de ella, con las manos apoyadas en sus hombros.

—Cálmate —le dijo con firmeza, aunque le temblaban las manos. La acercó para acortar el espacio que los separaba—. Respira.

Le apretó tanto los hombros que la sacó del entumecimiento.

—Vamos. Tienes que respirar.

Helena consiguió tragar una bocanada de aire y se echó a llorar.

—No... —dijo tartamudeando—. No, no, no. Por favor. ¡No!

—Sigue respirando, eso es lo único que tienes que hacer. Respira —le instó Ferron con un gesto cansado. Tenía la mandíbula en tensión.

Se giró para fulminar a Stroud con la mirada, pero no soltó a Helena.

—Sabes que es propensa a los ataques de ansiedad. No puedes soltarle algo así de repente —masculló entre dientes.

Stroud se enderezó.

—Me dijisteis que le daban miedo las sombras. Si va a seguir añadiendo problemas, deberíais hacer una lista y ponerla en la pared. —Puso los ojos en blanco y se cruzó de brazos—. ¿No debería alegrarse de que ya no tiene que esforzarse por concebir?

—No. Y deberías haberlo sabido. Empiezo a pensar que la estás torturando a propósito. ¿Por qué?

—Eso no es cierto —repuso Stroud demasiado rápido.

Ferron entrecerró los ojos.

—Sé sincera. No disfrutarás de que te sonsaque las respuestas.

Stroud palideció y miró hacia la puerta, como calculando la distancia.

—El Sumo Nigromante me contó que fue ella la que bombardeó el laboratorio del puerto Este. Habíamos ganado. Estábamos celebrando la victoria y ella... ¡mató a Bennet! Todos sus años de trabajo. Mi trabajo. Todos nuestros experimentos. ¡Lo destruyó todo!

Se hizo un largo silencio, y los ojos de Ferron se convirtieron en ranuras.

—Entiendo que eres una devota fanática de su recuerdo, pero torturar psicológicamente a una prisionera no sirve de mucho cuando ni siquiera recuerda lo que pasó. Ni tu programa ni tu rango te dan autoridad para vengarte de mi prisionera.

Ferron soltó a Helena y se volvió hacia Stroud. Después, se quitó los guantes.

—Parece que se te ha olvidado que no me gusta que los imbéciles interfieran con ella. He invertido mucho dinero y esfuerzo para mantener su entorno, así que me da igual lo importante que te creas por haber estado a las puertas del laboratorio cuando explotó. El único motivo por el que sigues manteniendo tu puesto es porque todos los que eran más aptos para la tarea están muertos. En todo caso, deberías agradecérselo. Si los demás hubieran sobrevivido, no serías nadie.

Stroud palideció y se le dilataron las fosas nasales.

—Trabajé codo con codo con Bennet. Mi programa de repoblación es…

—Una farsa. Una tapadera perfecta para que el Sumo Nigromante consiga lo que quiere y sacie el apetito infinito de sus seguidores —le espetó Ferron—. Solo sobreviviste porque eras una auxiliar de laboratorio venida a más a la que enviaron a buscar más sujetos. Si no fuera por Shiseo, no tendrías nada que justifique el tiempo que llevas gestionando la Central. ¿Crees que no se nota lo poco que has producido desde que se marchó? No me extraña que tuvieras tantas ganas de empezar con el programa de repoblación.

Ferron la estaba encarando con el mismo tono implacable y despreciativo con el que había tratado a Aurelia.

—Después de que pusieras en riesgo mi misión, investigué tu proyecto. Le diste tanto bombo en los periódicos que tuve curiosidad por ver los datos tan reseñables que sustentaban tus teorías. Yo también me dediqué a la investigación durante un tiempo. ¿Podrías decirme qué controles has establecido? ¿O mostrarme estadísticas o datos históricos? Por mucho que busco, solo encuentro información anecdótica en artículos periodísticos sin base.

—Todavía… estamos en las p-primeras fases de… —tartamudeó Stroud. Ahora su rostro cambiaba de color entre el blanco y el rojo de las mejillas—. Soy una científica acreditada…

—Tu «programa» es un chiste. —Ferron le habló en un tono más grave y amenazante—. Tus auxiliares de laboratorio están más cualificados que tú. La única habilidad que tienes es la vivemancia y yo soy más competente que tú.

Ferron le hizo un gesto al mayordomo, que estaba junto a la puerta.

—Acompaña a Stroud a la salida y no vuelvas a dejarla a entrar en esta casa salvo que esté yo presente para escoltarla.

Stroud soltó un bufido y farfulló algo sobre contárselo al Sumo Nigromante, pero no dejaron de temblarle las manos mientras recogía los expedientes. Cuando se cerró la puerta, Ferron se volvió hacia Helena.

Ella supo que la estaba mirando sin tener que levantar la cabeza.

Ferron estiró la mano y Helena permaneció inmóvil. No le tocó la cara, sino que deslizó los dedos por su nuca, hasta la hendidura en la base del cráneo.

Entonces sí que alzó la mirada, pero no encontró ninguna emoción en su rostro, como si fuese de mármol.

—No me fío de que estés consciente en este estado —dijo.

Helena sintió su resonancia, delicada y punzante como el roce de una aguja.

Una pesadez la invadió, como un maremoto oscuro que la hizo desplomarse.

—No… —pronunció, aunque no sabía bien contra qué protestaba, contra todo.

Aun así, el mundo se le escapó de las manos. Fue vagamente consciente de que Ferron la dejaba sobre la cama y la tapaba con el edredón.

—Lo siento mucho.

CAPÍTULO 21

VOLVER A ABRIR LOS OJOS le supuso un gran esfuerzo. Helena se había despertado desorientada en una estancia opresiva, envuelta en sombras, después de haber pasado un largo tiempo inconsciente. Notaba la boca seca.

Al girar la cabeza, vio a Ferron junto a la doncella. Le hablaba entre susurros rápidos, como si intentara explicarle algo complicado.

Los párpados le pesaban y le daba vueltas la cabeza.

Cuando se obligó a abrir los ojos de nuevo, encontró la mirada fija de Ferron, mientras la necrómata estaba al otro lado de la habitación.

Tras superar el sobresalto inicial, comprendió que podría ponerse enferma con tan solo cruzar una mirada con él. Cerró los ojos con fuerza y se hizo un ovillo para protegerse cuando Ferron se acercó a ella.

—Tienes terminantemente prohibido autolesionarte o ponerte en riesgo de sufrir un aborto, ya sea espontáneo o inducido. A partir de ahora estarás vigilada día y noche para evitar que tu renovada desesperación por suicidarte te lleve a buscar formas aún más creativas de morir.

Pese a la aspereza de su tono, sonaba más cansado que amenazante.

Helena no respondió y esperó a que se marchara, después se encogió aún más, abrazándose el vientre. Sabía que la criatura que albergaba en su interior no era más que un cúmulo de células, pero pronto crecería y entonces ya no podría impedirlo.

Tras varios días sin levantarse de la cama, Ferron regresó.

—No puedes pasarte nueve meses ahí lloriqueando sin hacer nada —le dijo al entrar, aunque ella ni siquiera lo miró—. Tienes que comer y salir a tomar el aire.

Helena lo ignoró.

—Te he traído algo —dijo Ferron tras una pausa.

Helena notó que dejaba algo pesado sobre el edredón, así que echó un vistazo rápido y descubrió un libro voluminoso a su lado: *La maternidad. Un estudio exhaustivo sobre la ciencia y la fisiología de la gestación.*

—¿Y esto? —preguntó apartando la vista.

—Te vas a volver loca intentando encontrar las respuestas a todas las preguntas que seguramente te estarás haciendo —concluyó con resignación. Hizo una pausa, esperando una reacción por su parte—. Mañana te quiero fuera de esa cama.

Y, sin más, se marchó.

Cuando sus pisadas dejaron de oírse, Helena cogió el libro con la intención de tirarlo al suelo, pero vaciló y acabó apretándolo contra el pecho.

Al día siguiente, se levantó de la cama y se sentó junto a la ventana para aprovechar mejor la luz que entraba en la habitación. El libro estaba impecable: el lomo encuadernado en piel crujía al levantar la cubierta y las hojas todavía olían a aceite de máquina y tinta.

Era un libro de texto sobre medicina, no una guía pensada para explicarles a las amas de casa los detalles del embarazo de forma sencilla, sin tecnicismos ni términos médicos.

Cuando Ferron regresó, ya había leído unos cuantos capítulos.

Helena se aferró al libro de manera instintiva, pero él se limitó a observarla con atención.

—¿Cuánto hace que no sales?

—Sí que... he salido... —respondió ella bajando la vista.

No sabía durante cuánto tiempo retenían la información los necrómatas o si eran conscientes siquiera del paso de los días. Si le contaba una mentira, ¿tendría forma de saberlo?

—Fue la semana pasada.

—No es verdad. Llevas semanas sin salir.

Helena miró el libro y no se permitió pestañear hasta que el texto comenzó a desdibujarse. No quería salir, no quería ver la primavera ni oler el aroma del mundo lleno de vida.

—Ponte los zapatos. —Cuando la vio levantarse de la cama sin soltar el libro que abrazaba contra el pecho, él suspiró irritado—. No puedes llevártelo contigo. Pesa más de dos kilos.

Helena lo estrechó con más fuerza. Aparte de los zapatos y los guantes, el libro era su única posesión.

Ferron se masajeó las sienes como si tuviera migraña.

—Nadie te lo va a quitar. —Estaba haciendo todo lo posible por no perder la paciencia. Hizo un gesto a su alrededor—. ¿Quién se iba a molestar en robar un libro? Además, si desaparece, siempre puedo comprarte otro. Déjalo ahí.

Lo colocó con cuidado en la mesa y mantuvo la mano apoyada sobre la cubierta hasta que empezó a buscar sus botas.

El patio había renacido con la primavera. La hierba lo cubría todo y los árboles estaban salpicados de pequeños capullos carmesíes. A las enredaderas que trepaban por los muros de la casa les habían salido hojas de un intenso color verde y ya no parecían tan macabras como antes.

Helena no podía negar que era precioso, pero cada detalle del paisaje parecía viciado y venenoso.

Su acompañante dio un par de vueltas al patio con ella, sin decir una sola palabra antes de escoltarla de nuevo a su habitación.

—Ferron. —Se obligó a llamarlo con voz temblorosa cuando él ya se había dado la vuelta para dejarla sola.

Se detuvo en el pasillo y se giró despacio. Su expresión era indescifrable y su mirada precavida.

—Ferron —repitió apenas en un susurro. Le temblaba el mentón descontroladamente y tuvo que agarrarse a uno de los postes de la cama para mantenerse erguida—. J-jamás te volveré a pedir nada... —Al ver que la expresión de él se volvía fría e inexpresiva, algo se rompió en su interior, pero siguió hablando—: Haz conmigo lo que te plazca. No te pido que tengas compasión hacia mí, pero, por favor, no le hagas esto...

Ferron permaneció inmóvil, impasible.

—El... el bebé también será tuyo. No dejes que... —Se le rompió la voz—. Haré lo que me pidas... Te... te prometo que...

Pero ella no tenía nada que ofrecerle. El corazón le latía a toda velocidad y la voz se le entrecortó al quedarse sin aliento. Se arañó el pecho en un intento por tomar aire.

Un destello surcó la mirada de Ferron, que entró en la habitación y cerró la puerta a su espalda antes de acercarse a ella y agarrarla por los hombros. Mientras ella luchaba por respirar, él cargó prácticamente con todo su peso.

—Nadie le hará daño a tu bebé —dijo encontrando su mirada.

Helena soltó un jadeo de alivio. Estaba desesperada y con eso le bastaba.

Dejó caer la cabeza y el cabello le ocultó el rostro.

—¿De verdad? —Su voz estaba llena de desesperación.

—Te doy mi palabra de que no le pasará nada. Ahora, cálmate.

Qué promesa tan vacía. Suplicar no le serviría de nada. Ferron tenía muchos motivos para mentir, para decir lo que fuera necesario con tal de hacer que obedeciera sin rechistar, para inventar palabras tranquilizadoras pero huecas con las que mantenerla tranquila y dócil.

Se zafó de su agarre con una sacudida y dio un paso hacia atrás.

—Me vas a decir todo lo que quiera oír, ¿verdad? —dijo con voz temblorosa—. Supongo que es lo necesario con tal de mantenerme en un «entorno controlado». —Se abrazó a sí misma y se deslizó al suelo—. Te quiero fuera de mi vista. Solo haré ejercicio y comeré mientras no aparezcas por aquí.

<hr/>

AL DÍA SIGUIENTE, SALIÓ AL patio sola con la intención de ingerir la primera planta tóxica que encontrara. La primavera era la época idónea para ello. El jardín estaba tan crecido que seguro que encontraría alguna mata de vedegambre por ahí. Gateó entre los parterres ignorando los calambres en las manos y los brazos, pero, por mucho que buscó, no logró ver ninguna planta capaz de matarla o inducirle un aborto.

Incluso las flores de azafrán y las campanillas que estaba segura de haber visto habían desaparecido. Ni siquiera halló un mísero bulbo en los cúmulos de tierra suelta que habían dejado atrás al arrancarlos.

Salió todos los días, desesperada por encontrar algún brote que se le hubiera pasado por alto mientras los dolores de cabeza y las náuseas se volvían cada vez más frecuentes. Lo que había empezado siendo un dolor constante en la parte trasera del cráneo fue extendiéndose con cada hora que pasaba. Empeoró semana tras semana, hasta que el dolor se extendió a la vista y ya ni siquiera pudo leer.

Llegó un momento en que se vio obligada a mantener las pesadas cortinas de invierno echadas para que no entrara nada de luz en la habitación. Luego, dejó de comer y, tras pasar dos días sin salir de la cama, incapaz de ingerir o beber nada, Ferron volvió a visitarla.

—Me prometiste que comerías.

Ella resopló y un pinchazo le atravesó la cabeza de lado a lado, como si alguien le hubiera clavado una barra metálica, y la vista se le tiñó de rojo sangre. Un gemido de dolor se escapó de sus labios, sin ser capaz apenas de respirar hasta que cesó.

—Dudo que pueda retener algo en el estómago ahora mismo, incluso aunque la comida me resultara apetecible —dijo con voz tensa—. Encontrarse mal es algo normal durante las primeras semanas de embarazo. Ya se me pasará. La probabilidad estadística apunta a que sobreviviré.

Notó un cambio en el ambiente cuando Ferron se puso rígido, como si sus palabras lo hubieran pillado desprevenido.

—Mi madre estuvo a punto de perder la vida en el embarazo —confesó.

Helena sintió que aquel comentario revelaba algo importante sobre él, pero le dolía demasiado la cabeza como para ponerse a pensar en ello.

Ferron no se marchó. Seguía al lado de la cama cuando Helena cayó rendida por el sueño.

Unos días más tarde, regresó junto con Stroud.

—No creo que esté pagando ya el Estrago propio de la animancia —dijo a gritos la mujer al entrar en la habitación—. Lo normal es que no se manifieste hasta los últimos meses, pero, claro, ella era una sanadora. A lo mejor le queda menos vitalidad de la que imaginábamos.

Se detuvo junto a Helena, aunque ni siquiera la miró. Le quitó el edredón de encima y levantó su camisón para dejarle el vientre al descubierto sin molestarse en avisarla de lo que iba a hacer.

Helena se estremeció y Ferron desvió la mirada.

—Bueno, todavía es muy pronto, pero creo…

Stroud rebuscó en su bolsa y sacó una pantalla de resonancia que sostuvo con la mano izquierda mientras apoyaba la derecha sobre la parte baja de su abdomen. La resonancia de Stroud se filtró en su interior y el gas atrapado dentro del vidrio se transformó en una serie de formas nebulosas. En el espacio negativo que dejaban, se apreciaba algo pequeño que palpitaba tan rápido que casi parecía aletear.

Helena se lo quedó mirando, abrumada.

—Ahí está —dijo Stroud, complacida—. Vuestro heredero… No, perdón —se corrigió—, supongo que lo más acertado sería referirnos a la criatura como vuestra «progenie».

Ferron se había quedado blanco.

—Todo parece ir bien —añadió apartando la mano del vientre de Helena—. No detecto ninguna irregularidad. ¿Habéis comprobado el estado de su cerebro últimamente?

Él negó con la cabeza y Stroud chasqueó la lengua, pero asintió.

—Dadas las convulsiones que ha sufrido, lo mejor será no alterar su situación en este momento tan delicado. —Posó una mano sobre la cabeza de Helena para enviar una ola de resonancia mínima y esta se estremeció de dolor—. Si de verdad es una animante, sospecho que los dolores de cabeza son autoprovocados, así que no hay mucho que podamos hacer al respecto. Viendo el lado positivo, también cabe la posibilidad de que estimulen su cerebro y le devuelvan la memoria.

—¿Qué quieres decir con eso? —preguntó Ferron con suspicacia.

Stroud volvió a cubrir a Helena con el edredón.

—Si el Sumo Nigromante está en lo cierto, ella internaliza su resonancia para bloquear sus recuerdos, y todo apunta a que dedica una buena parte de su energía a mantener la barrera en pie, lo cual no es muy eficiente y explicaría lo aletargada que está siempre. Ahora que está embarazada, no tiene la fuerza suficiente para sustentarse, sobre todo si el embrión es también un animante. El Sumo Nigromante afirma que nació con un poder tan desmedido que consumió hasta la última gota de vida de su madre mientras todavía estaba en su útero y que nació cuando se disponían a quemar su cadáver en la pira funeraria. Tendremos que asegurarnos de mantenerla con vida. Con un poco de suerte, conseguiremos tanto al bebé como sus recuerdos antes de que sucumba al Estrago.

—¿Y por qué no me habías contado nada de esto hasta ahora? —La voz de Ferron era tan afilada como una cuchilla.

Stroud se encogió de hombros con incomodidad.

—Tampoco tengo mucha información al respecto. —Le lanzó una mirada maliciosa—. Deberíais preguntárselo a vuestro padre. Ya sabéis que aquí el experto es él.

Una expresión indescifrable surcó el rostro de Ferron.

—En este caso concreto, no creo que esté dispuesto a cooperar.

—Bueno, ahora mismo lo único que puedo hacer es ponerle una vía intravenosa.

Cuando Stroud se marchó, Ferron permaneció en la habitación.

Helena cerró los ojos. Por fin lo entendía: todos sabían que ella acabaría muriendo. Por eso, su única esperanza era perder la vida antes de que el embarazo fuera viable.

Pensó en el movimiento que había visto en el espacio negativo de la pantalla de resonancia y se le formó un nudo en el pecho. El corazón le latía como si llevara un rato corriendo.

Notó un peso en el colchón y unos dedos fríos que le rozaron la mejilla y le apartaron el pelo de la cara para tocarle la frente.

Unos días más tarde, un médico fue a visitarla y le colocó una vía en el brazo izquierdo. El paso de las horas quedó sujeto al incansable goteo de la solución salina y las medicinas que le administraban a través del frasquito de cristal.

Aunque las náuseas de la mañana parecieron mitigarse, los dolores de cabeza persistieron e, incluso, se volvieron más intensos. Helena apenas podía moverse. Una infinidad de médicos pasaron por su habitación para hacerle todo tipo de pruebas, pero ninguno fue capaz de darle algún consejo útil.

Cada vez que terminaban de examinarla y la dejaban sola, Ferron se sentaba al borde de la cama y le acariciaba el pelo. A veces le cogía la mano y movía los dedos distraídamente sobre los suyos. Después de que repitiera aquella rutina en un par de ocasiones, comprendió que se los estaba masajeando.

Siempre empezaba tocándole la palma de las manos, con cuidado de no doblarle las muñecas o moverle los grilletes, y, luego, iba subiendo hasta alcanzar la punta de cada dedo, nudillo a nudillo. Los masajes hacían que le temblaran menos las manos, así que no opuso resistencia, pero se convenció a sí misma de que no era algo que le resultara agradable.

Perdió peso, tanto que los grilletes quedaron lo bastante sueltos como para que pudiera ver dónde le perforaban la piel los conductos. La doncella que solía vigilarla empezó a mostrarse tan preocupada por ella que ni siquiera parecía una necrómata.

Revoloteaba a su alrededor todo el tiempo y, sin pronunciar palabra, le ofrecía tisanas de menta y jengibre, tazones de caldo y tostadas; también limpiaba su cuerpo con esponjas y le peinaba el cabello en una meticulosa trenza suelta para que no se le enredara. Para ser una doncella, resultaba extraño que fuera una cuidadora tan experimentada.

Ferron también empezó a orbitar a su alrededor. Todavía tenía que ausentarse para salir a cazar y encargarse de las tareas que Morrough le asignaba, pero pasaba mucho más tiempo en su habitación que antes. En más de una ocasión había ido a verla cubierto de suciedad, pues prefería asegurarse de que estaba viva antes de asearse.

Nunca hablaba ni se encontraba con su mirada, pero permanecía a su lado constantemente. A veces la acompañaba durante horas, sujetando una de sus manos entre las suyas, como si eso fuera a impedir que la joven se desvaneciera.

Stroud volvió a visitarla en un momento en que Helena apenas estaba consciente. Le oyó decir que no había esperado que sufriera el desgaste de la vivemancia tan temprano y que la culpa era de las barreras que la transmutación había creado en su cerebro. Además, se quejó de que era demasiado pronto para asegurar cierta viabilidad al embarazo.

Mencionaron a Atreus de nuevo.

Helena soñó que la luna iluminaba la estancia, pero en realidad su luz manaba de Ferron en vez de entrar por la ventana. Estaba sentado a su lado y sus ojos desprendían un misterioso brillo plateado. Había vuelto a cogerle la mano, pero, en aquella ocasión, se la había llevado hasta su pecho para que ella sintiera su pulso.

No podía evitar pensar que algo iba a suceder, pero finalmente nada cambió. La sensación de vacío que se le había abierto en las muñecas era un pozo sin fondo.

Se sentía como un reloj de arena cuyos últimos granos estaban a punto de caer. Casi se le había agotado el tiempo y notaba cómo la vida se le escapaba de entre los dedos.

La realidad dio un vuelco cuando alguien tiró de ella y la estrechó con fuerza.

—Quédate conmigo…, por favor…, quédate conmigo.

La luz se hizo más intensa y una sensación de lo más extraña se adueñó de Helena. Fue como si una chispa prendiera en su interior, una chispa que le resultaba familiar, pese a que estaba segura de no haber experimentado nada igual antes. Esa constante tirantez que notaba en el pecho, como si de una cuerda a punto de romperse se tratara, desapareció poco a poco.

Cerró los ojos, tomó con esfuerzo una bocanada de aire y el sueño se disipó por completo.

Helena se despertó sobresaltada, presa del pánico. Se incorporó sobre la cama y se tambaleó cuando la estancia comenzó a dar vueltas a su alrededor. Haciendo de tripas corazón, se arrancó la vía del brazo y se bajó de la cama con torpeza.

Tenía que hacer algo importante…

Las piernas estuvieron a punto de ceder al tocar el suelo, pero consiguió mantener el equilibrio. También ignoró el latigazo de dolor que le recorrió los brazos.

Sentía que tenía que hacer algo.

Pero ¿qué era?

No lograba recordarlo.

Estaba esperando. Debía estar preparada para...

Pese a que estaba segura de que las respuestas que buscaba se hallaban en la punta de la lengua, todavía se le escapaban.

«No te desmorones».

Había prometido...

¿Qué? ¿Qué había prometido? «Piensa, Helena».

Había llegado el momento de recordar. Se llevó las manos a las sienes.

Unos puntitos rojos le salpicaban la visión mientras el dolor crecía y crecía hasta ser más grande incluso que ella.

De pronto, tenía a Ferron delante.

—¿Qué estás...?

—Estoy esperando... —Clavó la mirada desencajada en él—. Prometí que esperaría...

El dolor le atravesó el cerebro de un extremo a otro y el mundo se partió en dos.

Cuando se le despejó la vista, Ferron seguía a su lado, pero el gris de sus ojos se había vuelto opaco y las sombras que envolvían la estancia le oscurecieron el pelo cuando se lanzó a por ella.

Helena retrocedió instintivamente y buscó a tientas algo que...

Pero Ferron se desvaneció.

La habitación se fragmentó.

Ilva Holdfast estaba de pronto sentada ante ella y la miraba con expresión tensa.

«Estamos perdiendo la guerra».

Antes de que tuviera oportunidad de contestar, Ilva había vuelto a esfumarse. Helena caía.

No..., no caía.

Ferron la sujetaba por el cuello y la golpeaba contra el suelo. La miraba con los ojos entornados.

Un torrente de agua fría le llenaba la boca.

Todo se volvió oscuro, gélido. Estaba sumergida. Veía a Luc, que se arañaba la garganta y al hacerlo provocaba unos surcos sanguinolentos en la piel.

«He cometido un error». Lila, que llevaba el pelo muy corto, lloraba hecha un ovillo contra la pared.

«¿No crees que merezco una recompensa? ¿Algo con lo que calentar este frío corazón?».

Un beso brusco durante el que se vio presionada contra una pared.

«Pareces satisfecha de haberte vendido como una puta barata».

La enfermera Pace la miraba por encima del hombro.

«La pérdida de Lila Bayard no será la única que sacudirá los cimientos de la Llama Eterna. Lo sabes, ¿verdad?».

«Eres mía. Juraste serlo». Alguien le había gruñido esas palabras al oído.

«Si consigues lo que te propones, me temo que acabarás destruyendo la Llama Eterna en lugar de salvarla». Jan Crowther, vivo de nuevo, la miraba con los ojos entornados por la rabia.

«Lo siento. Lo siento. Siento haberte hecho esto». Helena lloraba.

Cuando Ferron reapareció con el rostro rojo por completo de ira y ese sobrenatural brillo plateado iluminándole los ojos, el entorno de Helena se fragmentó.

«Te lo he advertido. Como te pase algo malo, me encargaré personalmente de reducir la Llama Eterna a cenizas. Y es una promesa, no una amenaza. Ten en cuenta que tu supervivencia es tan indispensable como la de Holdfast. Si tú mueres, mataré a todos los miembros de la Resistencia».

Fue como si estuviera cayendo. El pasado quedó libre, inundó su mente y se la tragó entera.

PARTE II

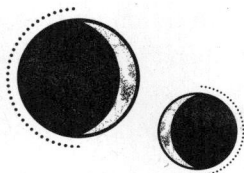

CAPÍTULO 22

Cuatro años antes
Víspera del solsticio, 1785 PD

En la meseta más alta de la isla Este, cerca de la Academia de Alquimia, se alzaba una de las pocas casas independientes de las islas paladinas.

Solis Splendor, la vieja mansión de la familia Bayard, era una de las últimas supervivientes del gran crecimiento arquitectónico de la ciudad. Mientras que la mayor parte de la urbe había cedido ante las inmensas torres interconectadas y cada vez crecía más alto, los Bayard habían decidido mantener su hogar intacto en el lugar en que se construyó. Las nuevas familias adineradas habían conquistado los cielos, pero, en Solis Splendor, jamás intentaron seguir sus pasos. Los Bayard se conformaban con vivir a la sombra de la Academia de Alquimia y la Torre.

Los Bayard estaban tan presentes en la Academia que Helena a veces olvidaba que no vivían allí y que poseían una gran fortuna.

Pese a que la guerra no les permitía cuidar de la casa tanto como merecía, la Solis Splendor, convertida en un asilo para los convalecientes, seguía siendo un edificio hermoso e imponente. Sus espaciosas estancias estaban repletas de camas reservadas para aquellos que habían resultado heridos y no podían volver al campo de batalla. Así, el Cuartel General no se saturaba. Rhea Bayard ya llevaba un tiempo cuidando de los heridos cuando su propio marido se convirtió en un residente más.

Helena se había detenido al pie de la escalera que conducía a la puerta principal para armarse de valor. Hacía tanto frío que no sentía la nariz, y los dedos se le habían entumecido pese a usar guantes de piel de cabritillo. Era el primer día de invierno, pero llevaba meses haciendo un frío terrible.

Se suponía que la celebración del solsticio de invierno giraba en torno a la esperanza, aunque, por mucho que los días se hicieran más largos o cálidos, confiar en que vendrían tiempos mejores resultaba difícil tras cinco años en guerra.

Cuando Helena ya no pudo soportar más el frío, subió los escalones y llamó con timidez a la puerta.

Sebastian Bayard, el tío de Lila y de Soren, abrió de inmediato. Era un hombre alto y esbelto, con la tez y el cabello tan blancos que casi era imposible distinguir uno de otro. El único color que contrastaba con su palidez era el azul claro de sus ojos, que siempre parecían buscar algo que no estaba ahí.

Entre otros méritos, destacaba por haber servido al principado Apollo como su paladín primero, pero, desde que estaba en la reserva, permanecía siempre en un trágico estado de alerta, como si fuera un perro esperando el regreso de su amo.

—Helena —dijo invitándola a pasar—, nos alegramos de que hayas podido venir. Sé que Rhea tenía la esperanza de verte.

La chica entró en la cálida casa sintiendo un nudo en el pecho y, aunque se quitó el abrigo, se dejó los guantes puestos.

Había varios niños repartidos por la estancia, silenciosos y macilentos, pero con la mirada llena de vida. Algunos eran tan pequeños que no habían conocido un mundo sin guerra y, pese a que estaban acostumbrados a no molestar a los adultos y tener cuidado, el solsticio no había dejado de ser un momento mágico para ellos.

Las estancias principales seguían siendo funcionales y estaban abarrotadas de personas. Algunas iban en silla de ruedas, caminaban con muletas o tenían alguna parte del cuerpo vendada, mientras que otras, si bien gozaban de buena salud, no mantenían así su estado de ánimo. El ambiente de la fiesta nada tenía que ver con el que la acogedora luz y calidez de la estancia o la música alegre del gramófono intentaban crear, pues todos charlaban en voz baja y sombría.

—Por fin has llegado. —Lila se hizo oír de repente por encima del murmullo cuando se levantó del extremo opuesto del salón.

Llevaba el pelo rubio recogido, como siempre, en una corona trenzada alrededor de la cabeza, un peinado que le hacía parecer todavía más alta de lo que ya era. Aunque los distintos grupos repartidos por el salón se fueron apartando para que pasase, esquivó sillas, piernas extendidas y mesas dando ágiles saltitos con su resplandeciente pierna protésica en una exhibición ostentosa y nada propia de ella; era evidente que Lila se desesperaba por demostrar que ya estaba recuperada y lista para regresar al campo de batalla.

Faltaban tres días para que el Consejo tomara una decisión. Se celebraría una sesión plenaria durante la cual se dictaminaría si Lila estaba preparada ya para retomar sus tareas como paladina primera. Dado que Helena era sanadora y una de las alquimistas que habían participado en la creación de la base de titanio de su prótesis, ella era una de las personas encargadas de decidir sobre el asunto.

Lila valoró la expresión de Helena en un abrir y cerrar de ojos.

—Pareces estar a punto de morir congelada. Ven conmigo. Luc ha encendido un fuego y te ayudará a calentarte.

Se detuvieron ante el grupo reunido frente a la chimenea con el que Lila había estado hasta hacía un momento. Todos formaban parte del mismo batallón. En el centro, como un colegial que jugueteaba con el fuego, se encontraba Luc, el principado bendecido por Dios. Chasqueó los dedos y las llamas se transformaron en pequeños acróbatas que bailaban por los leños mientras iluminaban su rostro.

Luc era mucho más esbelto y bajito que la mayoría de los miembros de su grupo, a excepción de un par de chicas. Incluso el gemelo de Lila, Soren, le sacaba un par de centímetros; y eso que todo el mundo lo consideraba demasiado bajo para ser paladín.

Siempre se había dicho que la estatura de los piromantes era menor que la de la media, pero las malas lenguas aseguraban que el motivo por el que los principados iban menguando con cada generación se debía a que la tradición dictaba que se casaran con alguien todavía más bajito que ellos.

Helena no sabía nada de la madre de Luc, su estatura era un misterio. Había muerto después de sufrir una larga y devastadora enfermedad cuando el chico todavía era demasiado joven, así que apenas se acordaba de ella.

—Hacedle un hueco —les pidió Lila antes de animarla a entrar en el círculo—. Ahora mismo te traigo un poco de vino caliente para que entres en calor.

—Creo que nunca la había visto mostrarse tan servicial —dijo uno de los chicos con una sonrisilla cuando volvió a desaparecer.

Helena no estaba segura de saber cómo se llamaba. Era uno de los nuevos, un experto en defensa. Su predecesor había muerto en la batalla contra Blackthorne, la misma que le había costado la pierna a Lila.

—Cierra el pico, Alister —dijeron Luc y Soren al unísono.

Un destello rabioso surcó los ojos de Luc, mientras que Soren pareció crecer como una sombra siniestra justo a su espalda. El grupo entero miró a Alister con censura.

—Estaba de broma —dijo el chico, que se movió incómodo y esbozó una sonrisa forzada—. Además, todos actuaríamos igual que ella en caso de necesitar convencer al Consejo de que nos dejaran volver al combate. Lo que no entiendo es por qué está tan preocupada. Podría haber perdido también un brazo y seguiría luchando mucho mejor que la mayoría de nosotros.

Soren se relajó y puso los ojos en blanco, pero Luc mantuvo la mirada clavada con firmeza en el fuego.

Penny Fabien encogió las piernas hacia un lado y, tras encontrarse con la mirada de Helena, dio unas palmaditas en el espacio que dejó junto a Luc. Helena vaciló.

Si se sentaba con ellos, en unos pocos días Ilva Holdfast la llamaría para «charlar un rato». Entonces, durante la conversación, la mujer acabaría hablando de lo delicada que era la situación en aquellos momentos. Le recordaría que, a veces, había que hacer sacrificios. Que también, a veces, la forma de demostrar que alguien te importa consiste en mantener las distancias. Luego, hablaría sobre la lealtad, sobre los miembros de la Llama Eterna que habían apoyado a los Holdfast durante generaciones. El principado tenía que cumplir con ciertos estándares y sería terrible para la causa que la fe que depositaban en Luc se tambaleara si este ponía a ciertas personas por delante de otras.

Helena negó con la cabeza y dio un paso hacia atrás mientras se excusaba en voz baja para ir a buscar a Lila.

La siguiente estancia en la que entró estaba más tranquila. Los heridos que allí descansaban no le prestaron ninguna atención.

Entre ellos, estaba el antiguo general Titus Bayard. Aunque nunca había llegado a ser paladín, era mucho más alto y robusto que su hermano y tenía la amplia frente surcada de arrugas. Había servido para la Llama Eterna como jefe militar durante la mayor parte de la vida de Luc, entrenando y aprobando la incorporación de nuevos miembros, incluidos sus propios hijos, asignándoles sus respectivos puestos de combate.

En ese momento, estaba enrollando una madeja de lana entre sus enormes manazas, despacio, con la misma meticulosidad y atención que les había dedicado a sus anteriores obligaciones.

—Hola, Titus —lo saludó Helena en voz baja y tranquila mientras se arrodillaba a su lado—. Soy la sanadora Marino, ¿te acuerdas de mí?

No dio señales de haberla oído. Ya solo respondía ante Rhea.

—¿Te importa si le echo un vistazo a tu cerebro? Será un toquecito de nada y te prometo que no te dolerá.

Tras recibir un gruñido quedo, la chica se quitó un guante y trazó la amplia cicatriz que le nacía en la sien y le desaparecía bajo el cabello. Entonces dejó que la resonancia brotara de la yema de sus dedos para desplegar una red de energía con la que examinar los tejidos, el cráneo y el cerebro de Titus, desesperada por encontrar algún cambio.

Pero todo seguía igual.

Físicamente, Titus no tenía ni un rasguño. De hecho, salvo por su inactividad, ni siquiera su cerebro presentaba problema alguno. Helena había pasado días regenerándole los tejidos con sumo cuidado y atención a cada detalle para salvarle la vida. El problema era que lo había dejado atrapado dentro de su propia mente y no sabía cómo sacarlo de ahí. Si es que todavía quedaba algo del hombre que una vez fue.

—Eres un ejemplo de fortaleza —comentó con tono cordial mientras le colocaba el pelo para volver a disimularle la cicatriz.

Apartó la vista por un momento de la madeja de lana para ofrecerle un amago de sonrisa y, cuando sus miradas se encontraron, otra punzada de remordimiento atravesó el pecho de Helena. Se moría por decirle que lo sentía, que había intentado salvarlo, que no quiso dejarlo en ese estado.

—Helena.

El estómago le dio un vuelco cuando se giró y vio a Rhea Bayard. La mujer de Titus era alta, de rasgos largos y afilados como los de un cuervo. Soren tenía los mismos ojos verdes y encapotados que ella. Según se decía, había sido una de las mejores alquimistas de la Academia, pero se había retirado para casarse y tener hijos.

—Has entrado tan silenciosa que ni siquiera te había visto. ¿Has hablado ya con Titus? —Rhea sonreía, pero su expresión era tensa.

Helena ya sabía que ese era el motivo por el que la habían invitado. En su desesperación, Rhea confiaba en que Helena encontrara la manera de curar a Titus. Solía llevarlo al hospital casi todos los días, incluso después de que los demás se dieran por vencidos, pues estaba convencida de que el tiempo y los avances científicos acabarían permitiendo que alguien con las habilidades de Helena diera con la clave para devolverlo a su ser.

Helena había temido que Rhea le echara la culpa por no haber conseguido curarlo, pero su inquebrantable fe en ella a veces conseguía hacerla sentir incluso peor.

—Sí, ahora mismo —dijo, aunque sabía que eso no era lo que le había preguntado—. Lo estás cuidando de maravilla.

La mujer perdió la sonrisa cuando Helena no dijo nada más, bajó la vista y se retorció los dedos.

—Bien. Bien. Sí, me alegra oír eso. —Rhea carraspeó y se acercó a una estantería para coger un paquete y ofrecérselo a la chica—. Es un placer verte por aquí. Te has perdido el inicio de las festividades, pero esto es para ti.

Helena contempló el regalo que le ofrecía mientras se le calentaban las mejillas.

—Ay, no sabía... No esperaba que fuerais a intercambiar... regalos. No he traído...

—Has protegido a mis hijos, así que estamos en paz.

Helena se sentó y tiró del cordel para abrir el paquete. Dentro, había un jersey de lana verde, tejido con unos intrincados diseños en relieve que imitaban los símbolos alquímicos.

—Vaya, es precioso. Pero es demasiado, no puedo aceptarlo.

Rhea parecía satisfecha por haberla dejado sin palabras.

—No sabía cuáles eran tus colores o tus elementos aparte del titanio, pero Lila me comentó que te gusta salir a la ciénaga, así que pensé que el verde encajaría contigo.

—Has tenido que pasar horas tejiendo.

—Me viene bien tener las manos ocupadas —suspiró Rhea—. Mis padres provienen de las llanuras de Novis, donde hay muchas ovejas, y mi madre siempre me manda alguna que otra madeja con sus cartas para convencerme de que me lleve a Titus a vivir con ellos. —Apretó los labios—. Estoy segura de que le encantaría estar rodeado de animales, pero tenemos a los gemelos aquí. Además, si nos vamos, ¿cómo encontraremos una cura para su dolencia?

Helena acarició los diseños del jersey con nerviosismo.

—Intentaré seguir investigando para ver si encuentro algo nuevo.

—Gracias... —empezó Rhea, aunque enseguida se interrumpió—: ¡Titus, no! Eso no se hace.

La mujer corrió a quitarle a Titus la muleta que le había robado a otro de los convalecientes.

—¿Te importaría ir a buscar a Sebastian? —le pidió a Helena en un tono alegre algo forzado mientras se peleaba con su marido.

Aunque Titus solía ser cuidadoso con los demás, era el doble de grande que ella y a veces se dejaba llevar por sus rabietas.

Helena buscó a Sebastian por todas las habitaciones hasta que lo encontró en el estrecho vestíbulo que comunicaba con la puerta principal, donde fingía actuar como anfitrión para evitar a los demás.

—¿Vienes por Titus? —le preguntó el hombre, que había adivinado por qué lo buscaba sin que ella hubiera tenido siquiera que abrir la boca.

Desapareció en un instante, y Helena se quedó allí parada, agarrando el jersey de lana. Su oportunidad para escapar estaba clara ante ella; nadie repararía en su ausencia si se marchaba en ese momento.

—¿Ya te vas?

Miró a su alrededor en actitud culpable y encontró a Luc detrás de ella, con dos tazas de vino caliente en las manos.

—Pronto empiezo otro turno —dijo, agradecida por no tener que mentir. Luc siempre se había burlado de ella por ser una pésima mentirosa. Su expresión, según le había dicho una vez, era como un libro abierto.

—¿Cómo es que estás trabajando en un día como hoy? —preguntó desconcertado.

—No es lo normal, pero todo el mundo quería tener el solsticio libre y, como saben que la tradición no está tan extendida en el sur, dieron por hecho que yo no tendría planes, y… acertaron. Al fin y al cabo, no tengo a nadie con quien celebrarlo.

—¿Y yo no cuento? —dijo él arqueando las cejas.

—Por supuesto que cuentas, pero estás ocupado. —Se obligó a sonreír—. Y todos quieren pasar el día contigo.

El chico se sentó sobre el estrecho banco que había junto a la puerta y le ofreció una de las tazas.

—Quédate un poco más. No llevas ni diez minutos aquí.

Lanzó una mirada rápida hacia el resto de las habitaciones para ver si alguien había reparado en ellos, aunque estaba segura de que la ausencia de Luc no tardaría en notarse. Si Soren y Lila no habían salido ya en su busca, seguro que era porque sabían dónde estaba. Luc había debido de pedirles algo de espacio.

Helena oía a Lila en la habitación contigua, pues había levantado la voz para contar con teatralidad la historia de Orion y la gran batalla que había librado contra el Nigromante durante la Primera Guerra Nigromántica. Los niños se habían acercado desde todos los rincones de la casa para escucharla.

Lila ejercía una misteriosa atracción sobre ellos. Podría llevar una armadura de cuerpo entero cubierta de sangre y aun así los pequeños seguirían pidiéndole que los cogiera en brazos. Ella accedería con gusto, por supuesto, e incluso se pondría a jugar con ellos fingiendo que no los veía cada vez que se bajara el visor del yelmo.

Soren estaba cerca de la entrada, escuchando a su hermana con sumo interés pese a que ya había oído esa historia miles de veces. Helena lo pilló mirándolos por el rabillo del ojo, pero enseguida simuló no haberlos visto.

Aquel asalto había estado calculado meticulosamente.

—Te echo de menos —le dijo Luc cuando ella aceptó la taza, resignada a tener que aguantar una reprimenda de Ilva. El chico le dio un suave codazo cuando se sentó junto a él—. Siempre que intento hablar contigo, estás ocupada o te diriges a alguna parte.

—Bueno, piensa que mi trabajo empieza cuando el tuyo termina. Estoy segura de que es por eso —se defendió agarrándose con fuerza a la taza—. En cualquier caso, ya sabes que siempre voy a estar aquí cuando me necesites.

Dio un trago de vino caliente, que sabía amargo y apenas llevaba especias; el desabastecimiento estaba dejando las alacenas vacías.

—Lo mismo te digo. Que seas sanadora no significa que no merezcas descansar un poco. Si te están asignando demasiados turnos, dímelo y me aseguraré de que lo arreglen.

Helena negó con la cabeza.

—No te preocupes, Ilva siempre cuida de mí.

Al fin y al cabo, Ilva la consideraba una pieza clave en la guerra. Era la única sanadora de la Llama Eterna, y, aunque no podían permitirse perderla, tenían que sacar el máximo partido a sus habilidades. Todas las manos con las que contaban eran imprescindibles.

—Me alegra saber que existe una persona en el mundo por la que no me tengo que preocupar —dijo Luc cerrando los ojos por un instante en un gesto de puro agotamiento.

Lila levantó la voz para darle aún más teatralidad a la historia:

—Los muertos los habían rodeado. Orion y sus fieles paladines permanecían espalda contra espalda, envueltos en la más negra oscuridad salvo por el fuego que manaba de las manos de Orion...

—Vas a dejar que Lila vuelva al campo de batalla, ¿no? —le preguntó Luc con un suspiro.

—Ya está lista —respondió Helena sin levantar la vista de la taza—. No hay motivos para impedirle luchar. Además, es la mejor en lo suyo. En mantenerte con vida, quiero decir.

Los niños jadearon al unísono en la habitación contigua cuando Lila pasó a describir cómo los paladines se habían enfrentado a una horda tras otra de necrómatas mientras Orion le plantaba cara al Nigromante en solitario.

—¿Y si te digo que ese es precisamente el motivo por el que no quiero que la dejéis luchar? —confesó Luc con un hilo de voz.

Helena lo miró y se dio cuenta de que ahora era él quien evitaba su mirada con un gesto obstinado.

—Cuando juró sus votos, pensé que hacer lo mismo por ella era lo mínimo si iba a estar ahí para protegerme siempre. —Rozó el borde de la taza con el anillo de ignición que llevaba en el dedo—. Pero no siempre puedo… velar por su seguridad. Ella actúa como si terminar destrozada por mí fuera parte de su trabajo. Me ha salvado la vida tantas veces que ya he perdido la cuenta, pero tengo que aceptarlo porque se supone que eso es lo que se espera de ella —frunció el ceño—, porque es lo que me permitirá ganar la guerra, y entonces todo el sufrimiento habrá merecido la pena. Justo como pasó con Orion. El problema es que yo no soy capaz de pensar así. No soporto que Lila tenga que seguir llevándose todos los golpes por mí.

Tragó saliva con fuerza.

Cargaba con demasiadas personas y demasiadas vidas sobre los hombros. El mundo solo tenía ojos para él, a la espera de que la intuición lo llevara a obrar un milagro, igual que había hecho Orion en el detallado relato con el que Lila no dejaba de arrancarles gritos de asombro y vítores a sus oyentes.

La sensación de estar fracasando atravesaba a Luc como una falla geológica a punto de romperse. Cada muerte, cada cicatriz que marcaba a Lila y a Soren, lo empujaba más y más hacia el borde del precipicio.

—Todo el mundo me dice lo mismo —continuó—. «Ya casi está hecho», «Todo suele empeorar antes de mejorar» o «Esta es la prueba de fuego», así que tengo que demostrarles que puedo con ello…, pero ¿y si me supera? ¿Y si hemos acabado así por mi culpa?

Luc la miró con una expresión afligida que reflejaba con total claridad la culpa que lo reconcomía, así como las dudas que, como principado, no debería sentir. Se suponía que debía ser una figura imperturbable, la viva imagen de la Fe, la divinidad de Sol reencarnada.

Dudar de sí mismo no era algo que pudiera permitirse, porque supondría traicionar la confianza de la gente que estaba dispuesta a morir por él sin pensárselo dos veces.

—¡Un divino infierno de llamas blancas estalló a su alrededor y consumió a todos y cada uno de los necrómatas que los atacaban! —bramó Lila.

Allí sentado junto a Helena, Luc no era más que un huérfano que cargaba con el peso de un legado centenario sobre los hombros y que no tenía la menor idea de cómo ponerle fin a la guerra solo.

—Si yo creo en ti no es porque alguien más me haya dicho que debo hacerlo —dijo Helena negando con la cabeza—. Decidí apoyarte porque jamás he conocido a una persona más valiente o amable que tú, Luc. Eres un modelo a seguir para todos nosotros. Y si estamos contigo no es porque nos hayas engañado para ganártelo. —Le tocó fugazmente la muñeca con la mano enguantada—. La razón por la que tenemos fe en ti es porque no hay nadie más capacitado para encabezar esta lucha que tú.

Él negó con la cabeza.

—Orion lo estaba, al igual que el resto de mis antepasados. A ninguno le tocó enfrentarse a una situación como la nuestra. Cuando un nigromante aparecía, ellos se encargaban de él sin apenas despeinarse, pero yo lo he intentado todo y no soy capaz de…

—Sus guerras fueron más simples que esta —lo interrumpió ella sin miramientos—. Ninguno tuvo que afrontar algo como esto. Puede que Orion estuviera en una situación parecida, pero ¡incluso él lo tuvo más fácil! Mira lo que Lila acaba de decir. Prendió un valle entero con sus llamas y no se detuvo hasta llegar a la cima de las montañas. Aunque tuvieras el poder de hacer algo así, todavía tendrías que contar con que te encuentras en una ciudad en la que hay miles y miles de habitantes. Orion solo tuvo que luchar contra un nigromante. No tienes forma de saber cómo habrían reaccionado tus antepasados ante una guerra como esta. Estás haciéndolo lo mejor que puedes, y, si los dioses están tan ciegos como para no verlo, pues…

—No digas esas cosas —replicó él sin dejarle terminar—. No ayuda nada.

Helena cerró la boca de golpe. No sabía qué más decir, nada parecía servir.

—Allí donde puso las zarpas el Nigromante, no dejaba más que cenizas —concluyó Lila al llegar al punto álgido de la historia.

—¿Cómo se llamaba el Nigromante? —preguntó una vocecilla.

—Nadie lo sabe —respondió la chica con aire misterioso—. A quienes lo sabían los mató. Bueno, ¿por dónde iba? Ah, sí, Orion, envuelto todavía en aquellas sagradas llamaradas solares, recurrió a su piromancia para avivarlas todavía más.

—Pero ¿no habías dicho que las oleadas de fuego lo habían arrasado todo salvo a Orion y sus paladines? —la volvió a interrumpir la vocecilla.

Los demás oyentes rieron y chistaron a partes iguales.

—Bueno, pero resultó que un brasero de hierro había conseguido resistir su azote —dijo Lila con fingida solemnidad—, así que Orion depositó el fuego sagrado en su interior e hizo un juramento solemne ante sus paladines bajo el sol naciente. Juró que, mientras su linaje permaneciera vivo, los Holdfast no permitirían que el fuego se extinguiera jamás y que utilizarían sus llamas para acabar con la corrupción de la nigromancia allí donde apareciera y…

—Yo pensaba que había una piedra —intervino la vocecilla por tercera vez. Según parecía, se negaba a tolerar que la mandaran callar—. En la versión que nos cuenta mi papá, siempre habla de una.

—Ya, bueno, en esta versión no hay piedras —se apresuró a decir Lila para tratar de terminar la historia—. En fin, que…

—Pues a mí me gusta más la versión de la piedra —apuntó otra voz infantil.

Helena dejó la taza sobre el banco y miró a Luc, que se había quedado absorto escuchando a Lila discutir sobre la historia de su familia con un grupito de niños.

—Tengo que irme ya, Luc —le dijo Helena—, pero no pierdas la esperanza. Siempre estaremos aquí para ti. Vendrán tiempos mejores.

—Lo sé —respondió él tras ofrecerle una sonrisa débil y un asentimiento desganado.

Cuando Helena salió de la casa, las estrellas del invierno salpicaban el cielo casi desprovisto de lunas, pero estas quedaron ocultas tras la neblina que salió de sus labios al dejar escapar un profundo suspiro.

Desvió la mirada hacia la Torre de Alquimia, que seguía y seguiría estando siempre iluminada por la Llama Eterna de Orion.

Luc era el único Holdfast que quedaba con vida para cumplir la promesa de mantener viva su luz, pero, tras cinco años, la guerra contra el cada vez más numeroso ejército de necrómatas se había convertido en una batalla de desgaste que no iban a poder ganar ni con todos los sanadores, fuegos sagrados o paladines del mundo.

Helena observó aquel faro de luz con el corazón en un puño mientras contemplaba la posibilidad de que un día se apagara, de que Luc fuera el último Holdfast si nadie encontraba la forma de salvarlo de su destino.

Se miró las manos enguantadas mientras abría y cerraba los dedos lentamente. Luego, inspiró hondo.

—Prometiste que harías lo que fuera por él.

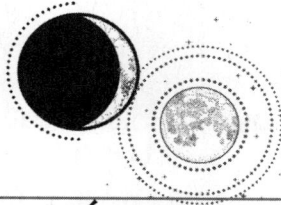

CAPÍTULO 23

HELENA RECHINABA LOS DIENTES MIENTRAS retorcía los dedos en el aire, enfrascada en un tira y afloja con el delicado vínculo que amenazaba con escapar de su control.

Empezaba a notar calambres en la mano derecha, un dolor agudo que se le extendía desde el tendón hasta el codo, pero, si se permitía romper la conexión, si se permitía descansar por un instante, su paciente moriría.

—Venga —masculló para sus adentros sin dejar de agitar los dedos. Se negaba a tirar la toalla—. ¿Dónde está?

Entonces, como si solo hubiera necesitado verbalizar su desesperación, por fin consiguió dar con el punto de presión donde se acumulaba la hemorragia interna.

—Te tengo, te tengo —dijo con un quedo jadeo de alivio.

Aceleró el ritmo y se dispuso a manipular los tejidos, reparar la arteria y alejar la sangre de la herida para poder centrarse en la tarea que tenía entre manos: sanar una caja torácica partida en dos.

Cuando se había dado cuenta de que algo más iba mal, estaba transmutando tejido pulmonar regenerativo con una mano y manteniendo el pulso del paciente estable con la otra, pero su resonancia por fin había dejado de gritarle que estaba a punto de morir.

Helena se permitió abrir y cerrar la mano derecha un par de veces antes de colocar los huesos rotos sobre los nuevos pulmones, fusionar las fracturas y regenerar el tejido óseo perdido. Luego, unió las dos capas de piel desgarrada que cubrían la caja torácica y las remendó tan bien como pudo. Por último, apoyó ambas manos sobre el pecho recién sanado y, con un suspiro, lo obligó a llenarse de aire para que su paciente volviera a respirar.

Le esperaban aún unas semanas de recuperación y tendría que pasar un mes de convalecencia como mínimo en Solis Splendor. Aunque el tejido pulmonar nuevo era sumamente delicado y los huesos regenerados, frágiles, viviría para volver a la batalla.

Sabiendo que no iba a morir, Helena se permitió mirarlo a la cara antes de comprobar que tenía la vía intravenosa bien colocada y de indicarles con un gesto a las médicas que ya podían retomar su trabajo.

El chico era joven y no lo había visto nunca, pese a que Helena conocía a muchos de los combatientes. Debía de ser un nuevo recluta; a lo mejor acababa de cumplir la mayoría de edad. No, eso era imposible: no parecía tener más de catorce años.

Sin tiempo de pensarlo demasiado, se lavó las manos, se las empapó de antiséptico y se dirigió a la siguiente cama marcada con un lazo para indicar que se requería la intervención de una sanadora.

«No compruebes quién es», se recordó cuando las médicas y enfermeras se apartaron para dejarle espacio.

Había perdido la cuenta de las horas que llevaba trabajando sin parar. ¿Cuánto tiempo había pasado? ¿Un día o dos? Era difícil saberlo.

Las primeras heridas que había tenido que curar habían sido todo cortes y perforaciones, puñaladas y huesos rotos. Luego, había pasado a las quemaduras, los miembros calcinados, los pulmones abrasados y la piel ennegrecida que se resquebrajaba y rezumaba sangre.

El hedor de la carne quemada, la sangre y las entrañas se mezclaba con el aroma del aceite de lavanda que utilizaban para desinfectar el hospital.

A Helena solía gustarle el olor a lavanda.

No consiguió salvar a su última paciente. Sus órganos fallaron mucho antes de que tuviera oportunidad de regenerarlos. Estaba tan cansada que, cada vez que retorcía los dedos para recurrir a la resonancia, las manos le temblaban sin control. No fue lo bastante rápida.

La resonancia rebotó contra ella y un pulso de energía le atravesó el pecho con la fuerza de un disparo a quemarropa. Una espectral ola de frío la recorrió de pies a cabeza, pero desapareció tan rápido como había llegado.

Se había ido.

Helena dejó caer los hombros con la respiración entrecortada y unas irrefrenables ganas de gritar. Un minuto más y habría podido...

Se incorporó y dio un paso hacia atrás. Todavía le temblaban las manos. Sin poder contenerse, levantó la mirada y contempló el rostro sin vida de la persona que acababa de perder.

El cadáver estaba tan achicharrado que no habría sabido decir si era un chico o una chica, pero sí era terriblemente joven. Helena miró a su alrededor en busca de otro lazo identificativo, pero no encontró ninguno, así que se acercó tensa a la pared más cercana y se derrumbó contra ella. Tenía la boca seca y todavía le temblaban las manos cuando una camillera dejó lo que estaba haciendo para ofrecerle un vaso de agua.

Era una de las más jóvenes, con los ojos azules y brillantes. Al llevar poco tiempo en el hospital, todavía trabajaba con entusiasmo.

Helena agarró con fuerza el vaso de agua y dejó vagar la vista sin emoción por la sala de urgencias. Recorrió las hileras de camas, las pilas de ropa ensangrentada y los vendajes y sábanas que había tirados por el suelo. Tenía sangre pegada a la cara y el pelo. Solo sus manos permanecían relativamente limpias. Era lo único que había tenido oportunidad de limpiarse en al menos un día.

Se tocó el pecho y encontró el amuleto de heliolita que escondía bajo el uniforme sucio. La sangre había dejado la tela tan rígida que casi crujió cuando se aferró al collar en un intento por tranquilizarse.

—Deberías haberte tomado un descanso hace horas.

Cuando levantó la vista, encontró a la enfermera Pace a su lado, limpiándose la frente con un paño algo sucio. En una mano sostenía un vaso mellado.

La mujer llevaba el delantal tan empapado de sangre como Helena, y también tenía unos cuantos mechones grises manchados y pegados al rostro enrojecido e hinchado.

—Yo tampoco te he visto descansar a ti. —A la chica incluso le temblaba la voz de cansancio.

Pace ya trabajaba en el campo de la medicina mucho antes de que se construyera el Hospital Central Paladino y, por lo que había oído, había sido matrona antes de que la ley nacional de licencias médicas entrara en vigor. Las mujeres necesitaban contar con un título en alquimia para poder ejercer, y, dado que Pace no era alquimista, había decidido convertirse en enfermera.

Helena permaneció allí sentada, con las articulaciones de los dedos doloridas por haberlos flexionado repetidamente sin parar. También notaba un nudo tenso en el pecho y temía el momento en que volviera a sentir los pies.

—Ve a descansar —le ordenó la enfermera.

Helena negó con la cabeza y mantuvo la vista clavada en la puerta por donde entraban los heridos.

—Debería quedarme por si llega alguna emergencia. ¿Maier sigue operando?

Maier era uno de los mejores cirujanos alquímicos de Paladia. Había dejado atrás su trabajo en un hospital de Novis para unirse a la Resistencia y ayudarla a salir adelante después de que los inmarcesibles arrasaran los hospitales de campaña y los centros de atención primaria.

Maier era un genio de la cirugía y se desvivía por su trabajo, pero también se trataba de un hombre de mucho temperamento y no sentía especial cariño por las mujeres. Para su desgracia, en el equipo y la dirección del hospital ellas predominaban, así que el cirujano se limitaba a trabajar con los hombres que había traído consigo desde Novis y le dejaba a Pace la responsabilidad de dirigir el hospital y tratar con las médicas, enfermeras y camilleras.

—La plantilla de este hospital está más que cualificada, Marino. Has trabajado más de lo debido, ve a descansar.

Helena vio pasar una camilla con un cuerpo envuelto en sábanas que se dirigía al crematorio.

—Lo último que quiero hacer ahora es dormir, porque voy a soñar que sigo estando aquí.

Pace suspiró.

—No sé si debería contarte esto, pero el Consejo nos ha pedido que le enviemos un informe. La reunión ya está en marcha por si quieres unirte.

El agotamiento le había embotado tanto la cabeza que a la chica le costó descifrar las palabras de la enfermera jefe, pero la mera idea de tener que ir al salón de mando a dar parte de la situación la paralizaba.

Odiaba aquella sala. Allí todo se reducía a cálculos y zonas de interés, y los muertos no eran más que números.

—¿Tenemos ya las cifras? —preguntó.

—Tan solo las preliminares. —Pace sacó un dosier y se lo ofreció.

―――――――

LA REUNIÓN YA HABÍA COMENZADO cuando Helena entró en el salón de mando. La Resistencia había asentado su base de operaciones en lo que antaño había sido la Academia Holdfast de Ciencia y Alquimia. Al principio, habían ubicado el salón de mando en la sala de profesores, pero habían acabado pasándolo a la sala de audiencias, donde una de las paredes estaba cubierta de extremo a extremo por un mapa escalonado de la ciudad Estado al completo. En él se apreciaban las dos islas principales, el continente contiguo a las montañas, los distintos niveles de la ciudad y el sistema de alcantarillado.

Casi todo estaba señalado con marcas negras o rojas, como un torrente de sangre que rodeaba el área azul que se concentraba en la mitad superior de la isla Este. La Academia era un destello dorado en un mar de marcas azules.

El Consejo de los Cinco se encontraba reunido sobre una tarima ante una mesa larga de mármol, aunque dos sillas estaban vacías. El falcón Matias estaba sentado en el extremo derecho, con Ilva Holdfast a su lado. La mano derecha del principado era una mujer adusta y de cabello gris que llevaba un broche de heliolita prendido sobre el corazón.

En el asiento de honor, el central, no había nadie. Helena llevaba semanas sin ver a Luc. ¿Seguiría luchando en el frente?

El cuarto asiento también estaba vacío, ya que su ocupante, el general Althorne, estaba de pie junto al mapa. Sostenía un largo báculo en la mano con el que iba tocando el mapa para teñir de rojo las zonas previamente marcadas en negro y así identificar las nuevas zonas de combate activas.

En el extremo izquierdo de la plataforma, se hallaba Jan Crowther, que recorría la sala con la mirada y analizaba a los asistentes en vez de prestarle atención a Althorne.

El resto de los presentes se había repartido entre los dos bloques de sillas separados por un pasillo central que ocupaban la mayor parte de la sala. Helena se quedó apartada, pues, a diferencia de los demás, ella estaba cubierta de sangre y otros fluidos.

—Si continuamos plantándoles cara en la zona alta del distrito comercial, deberíamos poder aprovechar la ventaja de... —estaba diciendo Althorne mientras señalaba una serie de edificios cerca de la zona portuaria.

—Un momento, Althorne —intervino Ilva—. Ya tenemos el informe del hospital.

Todas las miradas se posaron en Helena, y muchos se mostraron sorprendidos al verla. Debería haberse aseado un poco antes de entrar, pero, de camino al salón de mando, la situación le había parecido urgente.

—Te cedemos la palabra, Marino.

Helena tragó saliva, bajó la vista al dosier que sostenía y, con un nudo en el pecho, caminó hasta el centro de la estancia, donde había un amplio mosaico con la forma de un sol del que brotaban rayos de luz. Allí era donde los participantes de las audiencias debían intervenir.

—De momento, solo disponemos de las estimaciones iniciales —admitió.

Aunque no habló en un tono lo bastante alto como para hacerse oír, la extraña bóveda que se abría sobre el punto en el que se había detenido estaba diseñada para capturar cualquier sonido y amplificarlo.

—Una estimación nos vale —dijo Ilva.

Helena abrió el dosier. Los números le resultaban tan incomprensibles que amenazaban con distorsionarse mientras los iba leyendo. Representaban a las víctimas, a las personas retiradas de forma permanente del campo de batalla, a los combatientes que aún podían reincorporarse a la lucha. Salvo por la última, las cifras eran demasiado altas.

Cuando acabó de hablar, se hizo un largo silencio.

Althorne carraspeó.

—¿Esas estimaciones variarán en el informe final?

—Podrían incrementarse —respondió ella con voz apagada—. El hospital ha establecido un triaje según el protocolo y les ha dado prioridad a los pacientes con más opciones de sobrevivir, pero los informes preliminares siempre tienden a la baja.

Se oyó un coro de murmullos preocupados.

—Gracias, Marino —concluyó Ilva con cierta tirantez antes de señalar el mapa con la cabeza—. Prosigue, Althorne.

—Un momento —intervino de nuevo Helena. Notaba el corazón a punto de salírsele del pecho cuando levantó la mirada del informe y la clavó en la silla vacía que debería estar ocupando Luc. Haría lo que fuera. Lo que fuera. Lo que fuera—. Presenté una propuesta ante el Consejo hace una semana junto con el informe sobre el inventario del hospital. Y otra unas cuantas semanas antes, pero no obtuve respuesta en ninguno de los dos casos.

Tras un silencio tenso, la chica continuó:

—Sé que… es un tema delicado, pero creo que deberíamos ofrecerles a los miembros de la Resistencia la opción de donar su cuerpo a la causa en caso de morir en combate. En vez de cremar los cuerpos, podríamos… —dudó por un momento, consciente de que no podría retractarse de lo que estaba a punto de decir— reanimarlos y organizar un regimiento de infantería con el que proteger a los soldados vivos. Solo lo haríamos con aquellas personas que nos dieran su consentimiento por escrito y...

—Ni hablar —la interrumpió Ilva.

—¡Sería un acto de traición! —exclamó alguno de los asistentes.

Helena reparó en que el falcón Matias la fulminaba con una mirada encolerizada.

—¿Cómo tienes la desfachatez de proponer que mancillemos el ciclo natural de la vida? Esta es la razón por la que no se puede depositar ni una gota de confianza en los vivemantes. ¡Son criaturas corruptas desde su mismísima concepción! Por eso es por lo que incluso ahora este país se enfrenta a una guerra. Basta con darles la mano para que su naturaleza inmoral los empuje a mordernos el brazo y contaminarnos con sus ideas. —Se giró hacia los miembros del Consejo con la cabeza ladeada—. Me avergüenza que mi oblata haya sido capaz de pronunciar semejante perjurio. Ruego que me disculpéis, miembros del Consejo. Me ocuparé personalmente de que encadenen a esta criatura y la despojen de todo...

—Estamos librando una guerra contra los muertos y los inmarcesibles —dijo Helena. Había sacado el tema a propósito, sabiendo que se negarían a escucharla, pero estaba segura de que eran conscientes de que la Llama Eterna nunca ganaría si la situación no cambiaba—. Jamás reanimaríamos a nadie sin su consentimiento. Si nuestros soldados están dispuestos a morir por la causa, ¿por qué no podemos al menos darles la oportunidad de seguir luchando por los vivos?

—¿Y qué sabes tú de lo que supone luchar? —preguntó alguien a su espalda.

Cuando echó la vista atrás, se enfrentó a tantas malas miradas que no habría sabido decir quién había hablado.

—Tu propuesta va en contra de todo cuanto la Llama Eterna ha defendido desde el momento de su creación —dijo Ilva con voz gélida—. ¿Nos estás pidiendo que accedamos a la condenación de las almas de nuestros soldados? Hiciste un juramento, Marino. ¿Es que acaso te juzgué mal? ¿Han hecho tus habilidades que olvides tu propia humanidad?

—¡No! —exclamó Helena en un arrebato de frustración. Se aferró con tanta fuerza al dosier que sostenía que terminó arrugándolo—. Yo me mantengo fiel a la causa. Juré proteger la vida y luchar contra la nigromancia, cueste lo que cueste. Ese es el objetivo de mi propuesta. Sacrificaría mi alma por la Llama Eterna y puede que haya otros dispuestos a hacer lo mismo. ¿No podemos siquiera someterlo a votación?

El falcón Matias se incorporó. Era un hombre bajito y enjuto, pero parecía estar listo para lanzarse desde la tarima a por Helena para estrangularla.

—La Orden de la Llama Eterna fue fundada por el mismísimo Orion Holdfast con las leyes del ciclo de la vida y la muerte de Sol por bandera. Fueron su valentía y sacrificio los que hicieron que Orion recibiera la bendición de los cielos y saliera victorioso. El uso de la nigromancia transgrede la palabra de Sol, así que tus convicciones y propuestas son una lacra para la Llama Eterna y la historia misma.

—¿A quién estamos salvando ahora mismo? —preguntó Helena, que cada vez hablaba en voz más alta—. ¿A cuántos más vamos a tener que perder antes de que…?

Alguien dio un manotazo sobre la mesa de mármol y el techo cambió de forma sin previo aviso, de manera que la amplitud de la sala engulló las palabras de Helena. Se hizo un silencio sepulcral.

Jan Crowther levantó la mano y la estudió con los ojos entornados.

—A partir de este momento, no volverás a tener voz ante el Consejo, Marino —dijo Ilva tras una pausa con tono frío y decidido—. Sin embargo, como es más que evidente que estás… algo agitada, por no estar en pleno uso de tus facultades mentales, nos comprometemos a no expulsarte de la Llama Eterna. —Mientras hablaba, Ilva se apresuró a mirar a Matias para que no protestara—. Como muestra de agradecimiento por tus años de servicio, omitiremos tu desliz en el acta de esta reunión. —Cerró los ojos por un instante, como si estuviera rezando—. Es una suerte que el principado Lucien no haya estado aquí para ser testigo de semejante acto de traición a la Fe. Dile a la enfermera Pace que, de ahora en adelante, deberá encargarse siempre ella de traer los informes del hospital. Puedes retirarte.

Ilva se giró hacia el mapa de nuevo sin molestarse en mirarla por última vez y apoyó una mano en el brazo de Matias para apaciguarlo.

—Pasemos página. Continúa, Althorne.

La voz del hombre quedó reducida a un murmullo lejano para Helena cuando se dio la vuelta y abandonó el salón de mando.

En el pasillo, comprobó el estado en que se encontraba. Salvo por los guantes limpios que se había puesto al salir del hospital, estaba cubierta de sangre de pies a cabeza.

Después de que el dosier se le escurriera de entre los dedos y cayera al suelo, a Helena se le empezó a acelerar la respiración y tuvo que cubrirse la boca para reprimir un jadeo.

—Aquí no. —Una manaza aterrizó sobre su hombro—. Por la llama bendita, pero ¿cómo has podido ser tan inconsciente?

Se dejó guiar a ciegas por el vestíbulo hasta el pasillo contiguo, donde se apoyó contra la pared, se deslizó hasta el suelo y escondió el rostro entre las rodillas para llorar desconsoladamente hasta dejar la mente en blanco.

Cuando levantó la vista, vio a Soren, que la observaba con esos ojos hundidos tan característicos suyos, recostado contra la pared a unos pasos de distancia.

Si él había vuelto, Luc también estaría cerca. Debía de haber caído rendido de cansancio nada más llegar si habían decidido celebrar la reunión sin esperarlo.

—Te habría venido bien haber soltado alguna lagrimita antes de entrar a dar el informe —dijo negando con la cabeza—. Aunque a lo mejor pensabas que Ilva achacaría tu comportamiento a un brote psicótico.

—Cierra el pico —le dijo ella antes de encogerse un poco más con un hipido.

—También podías haberte aseado un poco si querías que te tomaran en serio.

—Cierra... el pico —repitió.

—Ya sabías que no iba a funcionar. —Se cruzó de brazos—. Lo sabías, ¿verdad? Es imposible. Sería más fácil conseguir que las ranas críen pelo que convencerlos de acceder a utilizar la nigromancia con nuestros soldados. Y no, antes de que digas nada, no lo van a permitir ni con los soldados ni con nadie.

Helena se abrazó las rodillas contra el pecho.

—No te haces una idea de lo que estamos viviendo en el hospital.

—Lo sé —confesó Soren con voz apagada—. Ni yo ni ninguno de los que están ahí dentro. Por eso no entiendo en qué momento se te ocurrió que ponerte a gritar con esas pintas sería una buena idea.

La chica estaba demasiado cansada como para discutir.

—¿Sabes cuál es tu problema? —continuó. Helena no respondió, porque sabía que Soren se lo iba a explicar lo quisiera o no. A diferencia de Luc, él no tenía pelos en la lengua ni se andaba con tonterías—. Tu problema es que no tienes fe en los dioses.

—Sí que la tengo —se apresuró a defenderse.

—Mentira. Crees que la tienes porque supones que existen, pero eso no es tener fe. No confías en ellos.

—¿Y por qué habría de depositar mi confianza en ellos? No han hecho nada para ganársela —dijo con un nudo en la garganta—. Lo he intentado todo, Soren. Intento creer pero nunca es suficiente. Y, aunque lo fuera, renunciar a mi alma me parece un precio irrisorio. Si eso supone salvarte, salvaros a todos —se atragantó—, lo haría sin pestañear.

Soren se acuclilló ante ella para que sus miradas quedaran a la misma altura.

—Pero eso da igual. No te van a dejar hacerlo. Nadie accederá a reanimar a nuestros muertos. Así solo vas a sufrir en vano.

—Entonces vamos a perder esta guerra —murmuró Helena bajando la cabeza—. Y yo voy a tener que recomponeros una y otra vez hasta que llegue el momento de veros morir por nada.

Soren dejó escapar un profundo suspiro.

—Supongo que nadie te lo ha dicho, pero creo que esta última batalla ha sido una pequeña victoria.

Debería haber sentido algo al oír aquella noticia, pero se sentía hueca por dentro.

—A mí ya me da igual que ganéis o perdáis, no soy capaz de ver más allá de las vidas que nos está costando.

—Pensé que querrías saberlo, Porque Luc cree que es una señal de que las cosas por fin empiezan a mejorar. —Helena tuvo la sensación de que se le abría un agujero en el pecho. Un instante más tarde, Soren añadió—: Te pido que no le quites esa ilusión.

La chica asintió en silencio y Soren le tocó el hombro. Aunque era evidente que quería decir algo más, al final prefirió ponerse de pie.

—Vamos a estar por aquí unos días, así que seguro que volvemos a vernos. Deberías ir a lavarte y a echarte un rato. Te vendrá bien.

Entonces se alejó de ella.

Helena permaneció agazapada contra la pared, incapaz de moverse bajo el asfixiante peso del desconsuelo.

—Marino.

Una voz fría la despertó. Tras abrir los ojos de golpe, encontró a Ilva Holdfast ante ella, con ambas manos apoyadas sobre la empuñadura de su bastón. Helena seguía acurrucada contra la pared donde Soren la había dejado.

—¿Te importaría venir a hablar conmigo en privado? —le pidió sin demostrar emoción alguna.

A la chica le dio un vuelco el corazón, pero se puso de pie con rigidez y la siguió hasta su despacho, en el piso de arriba. Al llegar a la puerta, la mujer sacó una llavecita del bolsillo y la metió en la cerradura.

Siempre había admirado a Ilva por no esconder su falta de resonancia, así como por no mostrarse avergonzada por ello. Aunque eran pocos los que contaban con una resonancia lo bastante fuerte como para aprovecharla, desde que Helena se había adentrado en el mundo de la alquimia, a veces olvidaba que también existían personas desprovistas de ella. El futuro y la fortuna de los gremios dependían de que las habilidades alquímicas de sus integrantes pasaran de generación en generación. Por eso, muchos rozaban la superstición en lo que concernía a la resonancia de sus hijos e interpretaban la llegada de uno de los llamados «lapsus» a la familia como una prueba de que el linaje se estaba diluyendo.

Sin embargo, los Holdfast jamás escondieron a Ilva. La Fe mantenía desde tiempo atrás que la resonancia no era una muestra de superioridad, pues era Sol quien bendecía con su poder a quienes considerara oportuno.

Los Holdfast le habían dado las mismas oportunidades que a cualquier otro miembro de la familia. Ilva había sido una de las primeras mujeres en estudiar en el departamento de ciencia antes de decantarse por seguir otro camino y convertirse también en la primera mujer no alquímica en unirse a la Llama Eterna cuando su hermano Helios, el abuelo de Luc, fue nombrado principado.

Como era la única familia que a Luc le quedaba con vida, él la había nombrado su mano derecha para que actuara en su nombre cuando se ausentaba.

Helena se detuvo en seco en cuanto entró en el despacho.

Jan Crowther estaba sentado en una de las dos sillas dispuestas ante el escritorio de Ilva.

Era un hombre delgadísimo, de ropas discretas y cabello castaño peinado hacia atrás. El piromante de llama roja había tomado parte en las cruzadas que la Llama Eterna había librado contra los nigromantes en los países colindantes hasta que había sufrido una parálisis en el brazo derecho.

Pocas eran las veces en que intervenía en público, pues prefería encargarse de los aspectos más logísticos, como la gestión de las provisiones, el racionamiento y los civiles vinculados a la Resistencia. Helena no sabía qué hacía en aquel despacho. Si iban a amonestarla, habría tenido más sentido para ella haberse encontrado al falcón Matias esperándola.

—Siéntate —le pidió Ilva mientras tomaba asiento tras el escritorio cubierto de papeles.

Cuando se acomodó junto a Crowther, el agotamiento estuvo a punto de hacer que se desplomara sobre la silla.

—Según parece, tú y yo estamos condenadas a mantener conversaciones difíciles —continuó la mujer. Helena no dijo nada, así que se hizo una larga pausa mientras Ilva trataba de decidir por dónde empezar—. Estamos perdiendo la guerra.

Helena parpadeó y la estancia cobró una repentina nitidez. Miró a Ilva y a Crowther alternativamente, aunque ambos permanecieron callados, a la espera de su reacción.

No sabía qué decir. Casi todo el mundo creía que la Resistencia estaba predestinada a ganar, que terminaría saliendo victoriosa tarde o temprano. La Llama Eterna no podía perder. En la batalla entre el bien y el mal, el bien siempre prevalecía.

—Lo sé —dijo por fin.

Ilva ladeó la cabeza y pareció atravesar a la chica con la mirada.

—Luc es… un joven excepcional. Yo siempre he dicho que es el mejor Holdfast que ha existido nunca. Cuando una lleva tanto tiempo en este mundo como yo, descubre que es difícil encontrar a alguien con un gran potencial que a la vez tenga un buen corazón. Luc es una de esas pocas personas. Intentar proteger a alguien como él es una responsabilidad abrumadora. —Ilva cerró los ojos durante un instante, y su edad se reflejó en todas y cada una de sus líneas de expresión—. Yo jamás imaginé que acabaría convirtiéndome en la mano derecha del principado. He pasado mucho tiempo preguntándome qué habrían hecho Apollo, mi hermano o mi padre, pero es inútil. Ninguno se compara con Luc. Me duele en el alma que sea tan vehemente. —Se llevó una mano al corazón y la miró a los ojos—. Me alegro de que al menos no estuviera presente para oír tu propuesta.

316

Helena se limitó a apretar los labios, ya que sabía que a Ilva no le preocupaba que hubiera podido hacerle daño con sus palabras, sino que Luc hubiese estado de acuerdo. Porque el chico confiaba en ella y valoraba su punto de vista incluso cuando no coincidían en algo.

De haber estado Luc presente, y si él la hubiese escuchado, todos los demás la habrían acusado de envenenar la mente de su adorado heredero.

—Me reafirmo en lo que he dicho.

Crowther exhaló en un siseo. Al ver que se le crispaban los dedos, Helena se fijó en sus anillos de ignición.

—Ya sabes que es imposible —le recordó Ilva.

—¿Incluso cuando vamos perdiendo? —preguntó Helena encogiéndose de hombros.

—Por supuesto —intervino Crowther con los dientes apretados.

—Sé que solo intentas ayudar —dijo Ilva—, pero tienes que recordar que no luchamos por nosotros, sino por el alma de Paladia. Como principado, Luc no puede permitir que violemos las bases de sus antepasados. —Se miró las manos, que descansaban entrelazadas sobre el escritorio—. Sin embargo, es cierto que nuestros conciudadanos están hartos de esta guerra. La indignación que la nigromancia despertó en su momento ha ido mitigándose con el tiempo, y muchos coinciden con tu punto de vista en la ciudad, pues preferirían que los necrómatas reemplazaran a sus hijos en el campo de batalla. Los inmarcesibles no necesitan comida ni soldados y tampoco les piden a los civiles que aprendan a prescindir de ambos. Eso es lo que ha legitimado al Concejo de Gremios y lo que les ha permitido autoproclamarse los defensores del pueblo.

—¿Y qué hacemos entonces? —preguntó Helena.

Ilva hizo un mohín e inspiró hondo.

—¿Te acuerdas de Kaine Ferron?

La chica ahogó una carcajada incrédula. Todo el mundo recordaba a Kaine Ferron. Había asesinado al padre de Luc cuando todavía era un estudiante de dieciséis años como otro cualquiera. Al arrancarle el corazón al pie de la Torre de Alquimia en un ataque inesperado, había cometido el crimen más terrible jamás registrado en la historia de Paladia.

Aunque varios testigos lo habían identificado como su asesino, como Ferron se había esfumado de la faz de la tierra, nunca llegaron a arrestarlo o a juzgarlo por su crimen.

En los últimos años, algunos informes lo habían identificado como uno de los inmarcesibles, pero poco más se sabía desde entonces de él.

—Sí, lo recuerdo —dijo cuando se dio cuenta de que Ilva esperaba una respuesta.

—Kaine Ferron se ha ofrecido a trabajar como espía para la Resistencia —intervino Crowther.

Helena se giró para mirarlo con brusquedad.

—¿Qué?

—Dice que quiere vengar la muerte de su madre —explicó con una mueca en los labios y la cabeza ladeada—. Lo cual resulta de lo más extraño, ya que, por lo que sabemos, Enid Ferron murió plácidamente en su residencia familiar hará más o menos un año. Cuando le recordamos ese pequeño detalle, admitió que sus servicios están sujetos a una serie de... condiciones.

Helena lo miró expectante, pero fue Ilva quien continuó:

—Quiere que lo absolvamos por todos los crímenes que ha cometido durante la guerra.

Si bien era una exigencia que resultaba obvia, quedaba totalmente descartada. Luc jamás perdonaría al asesino de su padre. Sin embargo, algo en el tono de voz de Ilva le decía que aquella no era la única condición de Ferron.

—¿Qué más quiere?

—Te quiere a ti, Marino —dijo Crowther—. Ahora y para siempre, sin importar cuándo acabe la guerra.

Aunque él habló con total indiferencia, Ilva apretó los labios hasta que se le pusieron blancos. La chica los miró alternativamente, segura de haberlos entendido mal, pero ambos guardaron silencio.

—Ferron cuenta con una información de un valor incalculable para la Resistencia —apuntó Ilva evitando su mirada.

Helena meneó la cabeza despacio; no estaba preparada para discutir los pros y los contras de semejante propuesta.

Crowther e Ilva estaban demasiado separados como para poder estudiarlos a ambos a la vez, por lo que tenía que dividir su atención entre ellos. Ella seguía negándose a mirarla a la cara, mientras que él la observaba con una curiosidad impasible.

A Helena le falló la voz un par de veces antes de ser capaz de hablar:

—Pero... ¿Por qué iba a...? No creo que Ferron sepa siquiera quién soy.

Crowther parpadeó despacio, igual que un reptil.

—Los dos destacabais académicamente, ¿no es así?

—B-bueno, en teoría sí, pero... solo competíamos por entrar en la lista de los alumnos con mejores notas del país. Nunca... nunca llegamos a hablar. Él formaba parte del gremio y ya sabéis cómo eran... Además, yo... Yo era...

El turno de treinta y seis horas que había pasado en el hospital le había dejado el cerebro tan entumecido que no se había dado cuenta hasta ese momento de que Ilva no la había llevado a su despacho para amonestarla.

Volvió a mirar a cada uno de sus interlocutores.

—¿Me estáis pidiendo que...?

—La información que nos ofrece podría cambiarlo todo —dijo Crowther—. Ya tenemos algunos infiltrados, pero ninguno se compara con Ferron y la ventaja que nos daría. Tendríamos acceso directo a una información que, en otras circunstancias, tardaríamos meses en obtener. —Ladeó la cabeza para observarla—. Dada la vehemencia con la que has defendido hoy que la Resistencia debería estar dispuesta a hacer todos los sacrificios individuales necesarios para ganar esta guerra... —sonrió—, pensamos que tal vez estarías interesada en ayudar.

Helena notaba la boca tan seca que apenas podía tragar. Las palabras se le quedaron atascadas en la garganta.

—No vamos a obligarte a nada —intervino Ilva rápidamente—. Seguiremos adelante solo si tú estás dispuesta a ello. Estás en todo tu derecho a decir que no.

—Exacto —dijo Crowther, que le ofreció otra sonrisilla vacía—. Ferron ha dejado muy claro que ha de ser una decisión libre por tu parte.

Debían de estar poniéndola a prueba. No los creía capaces de proponerle algo así después de todo lo que habían vivido...

Ilva jamás la vendería como si fuera un trozo de carne.

—Te concederemos un día de margen para que lo pienses —dijo la mujer.

—Pero, si puedes darnos una respuesta ahora, nos harías un favor a todos —apuntó Crowther sin andarse con rodeos.

—Debería poder pensárselo, Jan —dijo Ilva apretando los puños.

Aquel último intercambio hizo que Helena se diera cuenta de que la situación era real.

Era la primera vez que Ilva le daba tiempo para pensar antes de tomar una decisión irreversible. Casi pudo sentir la cicatriz ya apenas visible bajo el ombligo. Ilva, que siempre había sido una mujer templada, que siempre hacía lo que consideraba mejor para Luc sin pensar en las consecuencias, por fin se había topado con una encrucijada que le removía la conciencia incluso a ella.

No la estaban poniendo a prueba.

—No necesito pensármelo. Si decís que estamos perdiendo la guerra y esta es nuestra única esperanza…, lo haré. —Mientras hablaba, notaba que el color le abandonaba el rostro y que la cabeza y el cuerpo se le entumecían.

Ilva la estudió por un momento y miró a Crowther antes de ofrecerles un brusco asentimiento.

—Muy bien.

En algún momento durante la conversación, Helena había perdido la sensibilidad en los dedos.

—¿Qué le diréis al resto… cuando me vaya? —se obligó a preguntar después de tragar saliva.

Ilva carraspeó.

—Ah, no te irás. Al menos, no por el momento. Empezarás siendo el contacto entre Ferron y la Resistencia. Os veréis… ¿Qué frecuencia habíamos acordado?

—Dos veces a la semana —indicó Crowther.

—Eso es. Te reunirás con él cada cuatro días y le pasarás a Crowther toda la información que te transmita. Él se asegurará de hacérsela llegar a los miembros del Consejo que estemos al tanto de la operación, así como a los comandantes. El resto del tiempo, permanecerás aquí, siguiendo el procedimiento habitual.

—Ah —fue lo único que Helena pudo decir.

Debería haber sentido cierto alivio, pero se sentía hueca por dentro. El despacho pareció estirarse, como si Crowther e Ilva estuvieran al otro lado de un gran telescopio. Incluso sus voces sonaban lejanas.

—Dada su confidencialidad, no dejaremos constancia alguna de esta operación. No figurará en los informes oficiales —estaba diciendo Crowther—. Por supuesto, en ningún caso podrás hablar de esto ni con Luc ni con tus amigos o conocidos. ¿Ha quedado claro, Marino?

—Sí.

A Helena le pitaban los oídos, así que apenas pudo entender a Crowther cuando este le dijo que tendría que curarse ella sola cualquier posible herida para evitar levantar sospechas.

Se limitó a asentir con la cabeza y a decir de nuevo que sí.

CAPÍTULO 24

Febre 1786

PARA CUANDO HELENA LLEGÓ A lo alto de la Torre de Alquimia, ya estaba amaneciendo. Lo que antaño había sido el hogar de la familia Holdfast en la ciudad ahora había pasado a ser la residencia de Luc, los paladines y unos cuantos alquimistas.

Cuando Helena dio la vuelta a la esquina del pasillo, la puerta que había al otro extremo se abrió de par en par y Luc salió a recibirla.

—¡Hel! —Se le iluminó el rostro por un instante, pero luego se detuvo en seco—. ¿Qué ha pasado?

La chica lo miró, sorprendida ante lo rápido que había conseguido interpretar la expresión de su rostro. Luego, se dio cuenta de que estaba observando su ropa.

Bajó la vista: su vestimenta todavía estaba cubierta de sangre seca.

Soren y Lila salieron también de la habitación, vestidos de pies a cabeza con armadura. Aunque se encontraban en un lugar seguro, los paladines jamás cometerían el error de bajar la guardia después de lo que le había pasado a Apollo.

—No es sangre mía —explicó Helena—. Acabo de salir del hospital.

—¡Qué alivio! —dijo Luc, claramente distraído, antes de agarrarla por los hombros—. ¿Te has enterado ya?

Sonaba emocionado y le brillaban los ojos; Helena no recordaba la última vez que lo había visto tan feliz.

—Hemos recuperado el distrito comercial en nuestra última batalla, así que estamos un paso más cerca de liberar la zona portuaria para el verano.

—¿De verdad? —preguntó obligándose a transmitir cierta emoción.

Si Soren no le hubiera dicho antes que consideraban la batalla como un éxito, se habría mostrado escéptica ante la noticia. Sabía que el distrito era importante desde un punto de vista estratégico. Sabía también que las guerras urbanas estaban plagadas de peligros y complejos problemas logísticos. Todos los niveles, distritos y zonas de la ciudad tenían puntos ciegos, de manera que los ataques podían llegar desde cualquier dirección. Haber recuperado un área tan amplia era todo un logro.

Pero ¿cómo podían considerar aquella batalla como una victoria después de haber perdido a tantos compañeros?

La respuesta era sencilla: la zona portuaria garantizaba el acceso a comida, recursos y suministros médicos. Llevaban meses racionándose y las provisiones que conseguían colar de contrabando desde Novis no bastaban para luchar contra el desabastecimiento. Si conseguían liberar los muelles antes del verano, por fin obtendrían la cantidad de suministros que tan desesperadamente necesitaban.

—Hemos descubierto un nuevo truco. —Luc le ofreció otra sonrisa—. ¿Te acuerdas de esos pedazos de lumitio que encontramos de vez en cuando al quemar a los liches y los inmarcesibles? Pues resulta que, si se los arrancas del cuerpo, mueren al instante. Y lo mismo pasa con los necrómatas.

Helena lo miró sorprendida.

—¿Cómo lo habéis descubierto?

La única forma que tenían de asegurarse de dejar fuera de combate a sus enemigos consistía en quemarlos con un fuego lo bastante ardiente y rápido como para que no les diera tiempo a regenerarse. El problema era que, una vez que los prendían, los inmarcesibles y necrómatas se lanzaban rápidamente a por el grupo más cercano de soldados de la Resistencia que encontraran para llevárselos consigo a la tumba.

Por eso tenían que curar tantas heridas por quemadura en el hospital.

—Nos llegaron algunos rumores y decidimos probar suerte. Lila fue la primera en conseguirlo. —Luc sonrió orgulloso y la señaló por encima del hombro con un gesto de la cabeza—. Vamos a salir a celebrarlo. Solo seremos unos pocos, pero ¿te apetece venir después de limpiarte?

La negativa que debería haberle dado se le quedó atascada en la garganta. No quería quedarse a solas con sus pensamientos y le encantaba ver a Luc tan feliz.

—Pues...

Se interrumpió al ver la expresión de Soren, que negaba casi imperceptiblemente con un leve movimiento. La voz de Helena murió en sus labios. Acompañarlos no era una opción, claro. ¿Cómo había podido olvidar el espectáculo que acababa de dar ante el Consejo? Aunque los asistentes se hubieran comprometido a olvidar lo que habían presenciado, no se quedarían de brazos cruzados si la veían con Luc.

—No puedo —dijo al final.

El chico perdió la sonrisa.

—¿Ni un rato? —insistió intentando ofrecerle esa expresión cómplice que solía poner cuando quería convencerla de que dejara a un lado los deberes por un rato—. No tienes que quedarte hasta tarde.

—Es mejor que vaya a descansar, Luc —intervino Soren—. Seguro que ha pasado más tiempo metida en el hospital del que nosotros hemos estado luchando.

Luc lo ignoró.

—Ven a desayunar al menos —le pidió con un mohín terco—. No te pido más. Nunca coincidimos en la cantina. Te esperamos aquí, ve a darte una ducha.

—De verdad que no puedo, Luc. Necesito dormir un rato. Lo intentamos más adelante, ¿vale? —dijo ella con voz temblorosa.

El rostro del chico volvió a ensombrecerse.

—Está bien. Si no te apetece, no te apetece. —Dio un paso atrás y se obligó a sonreír—. Pero te tomo la palabra. Lo dejamos para la próxima.

***

LA HABITACIÓN DE HELENA, QUE por lo general permanecía ordenada, parecía haber sufrido los estragos de un huracán. Lila había regresado con toda la intención de volver a dejar su huella allí, así que había esparcido pilas de ropa sucia, protectores ignífugos de amianto y almohadillas en un rincón. Además, había todo tipo de piezas de armadura, armas, vainas y arneses tirados sobre la cama deshecha, como si hubiera vaciado todo su arcón cuando se vestía.

Uniformada de paladina, Lila daba la sensación de ser una joven templada y eficaz, pero, en la intimidad, era la viva imagen del caos. Cuando estaba fuera de servicio, era una chica nerviosa, incapaz de estarse quieta o de prestar atención a las tareas que no le interesaban. Además, se dejaba sus pertenencias por todas partes. Semanas después de que Lila partiera en una misión, Helena siempre acababa encontrándolas en los lugares más insospechados. Solía tratarse casi siempre de sus almohadillas, partes de cota de escamas o pequeñas piezas del arnés de escalada que Helena esperaba no fueran indispensables en la batalla.

Se quedó allí de pie contemplando el desastre hasta que vio su reflejo en el espejo del tocador de Lila y se estremeció.

Llevaba el uniforme cubierto de tanta sangre seca que no creía que fuera a ser capaz de devolverlo a su color original. Era una pena que solo la tela de amianto pudiera blanquearse con fuego.

Se obligó a sentarse ante el tocador para quitarse las horquillas que le sujetaban las trenzas antes de desnudarse y dirigirse a la ducha. El amuleto de heliolita que llevaba escondido bajo el uniforme estaba caliente por haber estado en contacto con su piel. Cuando se lo quitó, acunó la piedra en la palma de la mano con un nudo en la garganta mientras estudiaba sus rayos de sol dorados y su resplandeciente superficie central roja.

El blasón solar de los Holdfast, que contaba con siete puntas en vez de ocho, representaba cada uno de los siete planetas, excepto el Sol, en el centro de todo.

Ilva se lo había regalado a Helena cuando esta había regresado a la ciudad y había tomado oficialmente los votos de sanadora. La ceremonia, privada y distendida, había tenido lugar bajo la luz de la Llama Eterna, con solo Ilva y el falcón como testigos, pues la mano derecha del principado no quería que Luc oyera las promesas que Helena había hecho en su nombre. Bastante había protestado ya contra los votos tradicionales que sus paladines habían tenido que recitar cuando habían jurado protegerlo. A Luc no le gustaba que nadie muriera por él y mucho menos que prometieran sacrificarse con tal de asegurar su supervivencia.

Y Helena había repetido esos mismos votos.

La mayoría de las sanadoras podían ejercer su oficio durante décadas sin que tuviera consecuencias para ellas, pero ayudar a los heridos a esquivar a la muerte tenía un precio: el Estrago.

Curar heridas mortales y reanimar a los muertos dependía de la vitalidad, de la mismísima esencia vital de la sanadora. Cuanto más compleja fuese la tarea, mayor era su precio. La sanación era el trabajo más sacrificado de todos y por eso la Fe lo consideraba un acto purificador, a diferencia de cualquier otra forma de vivemancia, que estaba estrictamente prohibida.

Convertirse en sanadora significaba que su esperanza de vida iría menguando poco a poco, como si fuera una vela consumiéndose por ambos extremos. Algún día, no sabía bien cuándo, su resonancia empezaría a apagarse y Helena se marchitaría con ella. En ciertos momentos, ya empezaba a notar ese desgaste. Su cuerpo era como un reloj de arena y su esencia vital se iba vertiendo grano a grano desde la yema de sus dedos al cuerpo de sus pacientes.

No tenía forma de saber cuánta arena le quedaba, solo que esta se iba gastando.

Tras la ceremonia, cuando Matias ya se había ido, Ilva había parado a Helena, le había colgado el amuleto del cuello y se lo había escondido bajo el uniforme.

—La tradición dice que las sanadoras deben llevar consigo un amuleto sagrado —le había dicho—. Solo los Holdfast y sus paladines portan este blasón, pero creo que tú también mereces tenerlo.

En ese momento, Helena contemplaba el amuleto sintiéndose fría y hueca por dentro. Los rayos de sol que sobresalían de la piedra se le clavaban en la palma de la mano y le dibujaban un círculo de marcas que estaban a punto de convertirse en heridas. Cerró el puño hasta que se clavó las uñas en la piel y la sangre bañó los detalles dorados del amuleto.

HELENA SE DESPERTÓ AL NOTAR un profundo dolor en las manos que se le extendía desde la palma hasta la yema de los dedos. Las lesiones causadas por los esfuerzos repetitivos eran muy comunes entre los alquimistas. Se masajeó la palma derecha en un intento por relajar los músculos, pero se encogió de dolor. El círculo de cortes que se había hecho con el amuleto volvió a abrirse y la sangre le corrió por la muñeca. Aunque sabía que debería curárselo, pues en el hospital corría un alto riesgo de contraer septicemia, terminó por quedarse mirando las heridas hasta que estas dejaron de sangrar.

Finalmente se vistió, se trenzó el pelo y regresó al hospital, donde le informaron de que tenía los próximos dos días libres. Si bien aquella noticia debería haber sido un alivio, quedarse a solas con sus pensamientos era lo último que necesitaba en esos momentos.

Helena salió del hospital a regañadientes mientras hacía una lista mental de todas las tareas que había estado posponiendo. Lo primero que haría sería revisar el inventario de los suministros del hospital y luego...

Al doblar la esquina, se encontró a Crowther estudiando el mural de Orion Holdfast que decoraba el pasillo.

Cada rincón de la Academia estaba decorado con hermosas obras de arte alquímicas, pero aquel mural era el favorito de Helena, que siempre acababa acercándose hasta él para admirarlo. Sobre todo, cuando se había enfrentado a un turno duro en el hospital o cuando Luc tardaba en regresar del campo de batalla.

En la mayoría de los casos, los artistas representaban a los principados Holdfast con una expresión indiferente para que tuviesen un aire regio o divino. En aquel mural en concreto, sin embargo, en el rostro de Orion se atisbaba el fantasma de una sonrisa que destilaba cierta ternura.

Hacía que se pareciera a Luc.

Los rayos del sol dibujaban una aureola tras el principado, que llevaba una radiante corona en la cabeza y sostenía entre las manos un amplio orbe brillante. A su lado, descansaba una espada envuelta en llamas, enterrada en el cráneo del Nigromante.

Cada vez que Helena se detenía ante él, la chica se recordaba que, algún día, también retratarían así a Luc.

—Ya entiendo por qué te gusta tanto este mural —comentó Crowther al tiempo que le lanzaba una mirada de reojo.

Pese a que se había unido al profesorado de la Academia cuando Helena tenía quince años, la chica apenas sabía nada acerca de Jan Crowther.

Había sido un estudiante becado, igual que ella, que había llegado a Paladia después de que un nigromante lo hubiera dejado huérfano en el lejano territorio al nordeste del continente. Tras completar sus estudios, se había unido a la Llama Eterna y había luchado en las cruzadas hasta que acabó herido. Cuando se unió al profesorado de la Academia, todo el alumnado creyó que se centraría en entrenar a Luc, pues los piromantes eran difíciles de encontrar, pero finalmente resultó que el pequeño de los Holdfast no había tenido nada que ver con su incorporación. Menos de un año más tarde, Crowther volvió a marcharse solo para regresar casi de inmediato, tras el asesinato del principado Apollo.

Cuando se giró para mirarla, Helena reparó en que llevaba el brazo derecho firmemente sujeto contra el torso en cabestrillo. Aunque nunca se quitaba los anillos de ignición de la mano izquierda, jamás le había visto usarlos.

—¿Vienes a mi despacho? —le pidió señalando el pasillo que conducía a la Torre de Alquimia.

Helena no dijo nada, pero subió con él en el ascensor que conducía al piso de los profesores y dejó que la condujera hasta una puerta con una placa en la que se leía su nombre.

Tras pasar la mano por un panel metálico, la cerradura se abrió con un chasquido.

Era evidente que Crowther pasaba bastante tiempo en su despacho. Una de las paredes estaba cubierta de mapas no solo de Paladia, sino también de los países y continentes colindantes. Además, había un sofá viejo que parecía haber sido colocado casi a presión en un rincón. Apenas había espacio para moverse.

—Siéntate —le pidió el hombre mientras él también se acomodaba tras el escritorio. La única ventana de la estancia estaba justo a su espalda, de manera que su rostro quedó ensombrecido—. ¿Qué conoces acerca de la familia Ferron?

Helena se sentó y bajó la vista a su regazo, pues sabía que no iba a poder descifrar las expresiones de Crowther.

—Solo lo típico. Sé que es una de las primeras familias que formó parte de los gremios y que su resonancia funciona principalmente con las aleaciones del acero. También sé que tienen minas de hierro y que desarrollaron nuevos métodos para producir acero industrial desde hace un par de generaciones. La mayor parte de las infraestructuras de Paladia están hechas con su material.

La silueta de Crowther asintió.

—Se podría decir que la familia Ferron es más antigua que Paladia. Ya se dedicaban a la alquimia férrea cuando la cuenca del río no era más que una llanura aluvial. De hecho, empezaron a desarrollar su resonancia buscando depósitos de hierro en los pantanos.

Helena no sabía de qué iba a servirle esa información, pero supuso que cualquier detalle sobre los Ferron era bienvenido.

—Yo fui el tutor de Kaine Ferron.

—¿Lo conociste? —La chica lo miró—. ¿Crees que su ofrecimiento es sincero?

Crowther suspiró y apoyó los dedos sobre el escritorio hasta que sus articulaciones alcanzaron su máxima curvatura.

—El Ferron que conocí en la Academia era un mentiroso, un chico desapegado. Creo que odiaba esta institución, aunque nuestras conversaciones rara vez pasaban de la mínima cordialidad.

—¿Por qué?

—¿Cómo que por qué? ¿No es evidente? Los Ferron son ambiciosos. Jamás se esfuerzan en ocultar lo engreídos que son. ¿Alguna vez has visto el blasón que compraron con su fortuna?

Helena trató de hacer memoria.

—¿Es el de la lagartija?

—No.

Crowther le pasó una hoja de papel. En ella, Helena encontró un dragón de largos colmillos que dibujaba un círculo perfecto al morderse su propia cola. En el extremo superior derecho, un par de alas terminadas en garras trazaban un arco sobre la curva de su cuerpo.

—Es un uróboro —dijo la chica, que no sabía qué debía revelarle acerca de la familia Ferron aquel blasón. Crowther permaneció en silencio, así que se arriesgó a adivinarlo—: En la tradición alquímica de Khem, el uróboro representa el infinito o el renacimiento. A lo mejor eso es lo que vieron los Ferron en su nueva fortuna. No obstante, según Cetus, también se emplea para representar la avaricia y la autodestrucción. A lo mejor ese es el motivo por el que escogieron un dragón en vez de una serpiente. De todas formas, una criatura mitológica es una elección muy poco común.

—Fíjate mejor en el diseño —le dijo Crowther mientras ella trataba de devolverle la hoja. Cuando la chica suspiró sin saber muy bien qué quería que viera, añadió—: Prueba a entrecerrar los ojos.

Hizo lo que le pedía y dejó que la imagen se desdibujara en su mente.

—Vaya. —Se sentía una idiota—. Escogieron el dragón porque las alas hacen que se asemeje al símbolo del hierro.

—Así es. —Helena apretó los dientes ante el tono paternalista del hombre—. Eso dice mucho de la imagen que tienen de sí mismos en esa familia. Los círculos carecen de jerarquía y, sin embargo, su blasón está regido por el hierro. —Crowther dio unos golpecitos en el escritorio con los dedos—. El hierro jamás será un metal noble, pero nadie puede negar que los cimientos de Paladia le deben tanto al acero de los Ferron como al oro de los Holdfast. Los Holdfast gobernaron durante casi quinientos años celestiales por derecho divino, pero el resto del mundo no se ha quedado atrás y sus revelaciones tecnológicas casi están a la par con las nuestras. La tensión entre los ideales de antaño y la realidad que vivimos ahora es lo que ha dado pie a esta guerra.

—¿Qué quieres decir?

La mirada de Crowther resplandeció entre las sombras.

—Que el paso de los años ha permitido que este país se cuestione qué se puede considerar divino y si lo divino tiene importancia alguna siquiera. Nuestro principado cuenta con dos dones excepcionales: el de alquimizar el oro y el de blandir el fuego eterno. Hubo un tiempo que ya solo eso se consideraba un milagro. Pero el mundo ha cambiado y el principado ha ido perdiendo relevancia. Morrough es capaz de revivir a los muertos y de conceder la vida eterna. Los Ferron han encontrado la manera de transformar un material tan humilde como el hierro en una fortuna que parece no tener fin. En semejantes condiciones, ¿de qué sirven el fuego o el oro ilimitados?

Helena se quedó muda al oír a un miembro del Consejo pronunciar aquellas palabras tan críticas.

—Si de verdad piensas eso, ¿por qué estás aquí?

—Porque quiero borrar a los nigromantes de la faz de la tierra. Ese es el objetivo de la Llama Eterna y el motivo por el que el principado hace gala de su corona. Preferiría ver esta ciudad arder antes que permitir que los nigromantes la conviertan en su bastión —dijo enseñando los dientes—. Mientras la Llama Eterna se mantenga fiel a su compromiso de erradicar a los nigromantes del mundo, yo apoyaré la causa.

A la chica se le pusieron los pelos de punta.

—Entonces, aceptar la oferta de Ferron, colaborar con un nigromante para parar al resto, supone una transigencia.

—Sí, pero porque no nos queda otra opción —se defendió Crowther agitando la mano.

Helena no se molestó en recordarle su alternativa.

—De todas formas, me gustaría saber si este plan tiene algún propósito tangible. Soy la única sanadora de la Resistencia y si Ferron… —No fue capaz de decir en voz alta lo que podría hacerle—. Según lo que has dicho, Ferron no tiene motivos para ayudar a la Llama Eterna. No entiendo cómo podría valer la pena confiar en él.

Crowther resopló.

—Estoy seguro de que Ilva te ha llenado la cabeza de bonitas ideas sobre tu importancia para la causa, pero eres reemplazable. De hecho, ya tenemos unas cuantas candidatas en mente.

A Helena se le desenfocó la vista por un momento y sintió como si le hubiera dado una patada en el estómago. Las facciones de Crowther eran lo bastante visibles como para que la chica pudiera verlo esbozar una sonrisa.

—En cuanto al motivo por el que confío en la legitimidad de la oferta de Kaine, te diré que, aunque soy consciente de que no siente ninguna lealtad ni interés por nuestra causa, también sé que habla en serio. Los Ferron han pasado el último siglo rebuscando en su linaje y autoconvenciéndose de que en algún momento los Holdfast les arrebataron el derecho a gobernar. Ellos nunca quisieron ponerse al servicio de otra persona. Cuando Morrough apareció, lo vieron como un simple medio para alcanzar su objetivo, como un forastero con los recursos necesarios para plantarle cara al principado y quitárselo de en medio. Pero ahora Morrough tiene demasiado poder y Ferron está dispuesto a correr el riesgo de ayudarnos a sabotear a los inmarcesibles con tal de equilibrar la balanza.

—Porque, si los inmarcesibles y la Llama Eterna se destruyen entre sí…

—¿Qué mejor para una ciudad en ruinas que quedar en manos de la familia con el acero necesario para reconstruirla?

Helena se irguió en su silla al entender la estrategia.

—Así que acabará traicionándonos, pero no hasta que supongamos una mayor amenaza que los inmarcesibles.

—Eso es —dijo Crowther, y Helena asintió despacio, haciendo caso omiso del nudo que se le había empezado a formar en el estómago—. No será fiel a nuestra causa, pero estoy seguro de que su vanidad hará de él un espía excelente. Ya ha hecho más por nosotros en un día que la Resistencia en este último año.

—¿Qué quieres decir?

Crowther chasqueó los dedos; eran tan largos que a Helena le recordaban a un par de opiliones.

—Cuando nos hizo su oferta y puso sus condiciones, como muestra de su… buena voluntad, nos dijo cómo matar a los liches y a los inmarcesibles sin tener que recurrir al fuego.

—El lumitio —dijo Helena al recordar lo que había comentado Luc acerca del «rumor» que habían oído.

—Exacto. El punto débil de sus «talismanes», que es como los llamó Ferron, fue una prueba de la información que puede procurarnos. Todo apunta a que este acuerdo no tardará en dar sus frutos.

¿Y qué le pasaría a ella cuando ocurriese eso?

—No obstante…, no tengo la más mínima intención de aceptar las migajas de Ferron. Sacaremos el máximo partido de todo esto.

—¿Cómo? —preguntó Helena inclinándose hacia delante.

Crowther enarcó las cejas mientras una sonrisa enigmática bailaba en sus labios.

—Cometió un error al incluirte entre sus condiciones.

A la chica le dio un vuelco el corazón.

—Quiso hacernos creer que su madre es el motivo por el que se ha ofrecido a espiar para nosotros, pero, cuando caí en la cuenta de que mentía y le impedí salirse con la suya, se vio obligado a improvisar. Ahí fue cuando se inventó la excusa de quererte con él. Fue una buena metedura de pata, en mi opinión.

Helena apretó el puño; notó que las heridas que se había hecho antes volvían a sangrar y que se le estaba pegando el guante a la piel.

—¿Por qué?

Crowther se inclinó también hacia ella y sus delgadas facciones emergieron de entre las sombras.

—¿No te parece una petición de lo más extraña? ¿Por qué se iba a interesar Kaine Ferron, el heredero del gremio del hierro, por alguien como Helena Marino? —Ella negó con la cabeza y el hombre siguió hablando—: Podría haber pedido cualquier cosa; podría haber dicho que había tenido una crisis de conciencia o haber exigido una montaña de oro. Sin embargo, solo se le ocurrió pedir… contar contigo. Es una decisión completamente irracional. —Dio unos golpecitos en la mesa mientras pensaba—. Tal vez sea el indicio de una obsesión.

La estudió con un brillo evaluador en la mirada.

—De ser así, dispondríamos de una debilidad de la que aprovecharnos. Como ya hemos establecido, te reunirás con él dos veces por semana y, luego, te asegurarás de hacerme llegar sus misivas de forma segura a mí. Durante esos encuentros, tendrás que hacer todo lo que te pida.

—Lo sé.

—También te encargarás de evaluarlo. Deberás permanecer atenta e identificar sus puntos débiles y sus deseos más secretos. Tendrás que poner en práctica esa mente tan brillante de la que todos hablan. Deja que piense que tiene el control de la situación y, luego, haz que sueñe con conseguir todo lo que no puede exigirte. Quiero que conviertas ese interés pasajero que lo llevó a hacernos semejante exigencia en una obsesión que lo consuma por completo.

—No tengo ni la menor idea de cómo hacer eso —admitió con incredulidad.

—Entonces es una suerte que juegues con ventaja. —Helena lo miró sin entender nada—. Ferron ya había abandonado la Academia cuando descubrimos tu vivemancia. No sabe lo que eres. Con tus habilidades, puedes hacer que sienta lo que tú quieras. Tendrás que cautivarlo.

—Nunca he usado mi vivemancia para… —empezó a decir atónita.

—Pero podrías, ¿no es así? —Crowther entornó la mirada y su expresión se endureció. Por eso había ido a buscarla para hablar; ese era el asunto al que había querido llegar desde el principio—. Tu misión, Marino, será hacer que Ferron caiga rendido ante ti, cueste lo que cueste. Tendrás que utilizar ese maldito don tuyo para hacer que solo tenga ojos para ti, y para nada más.

Helena no podía respirar. Le ardía la cara.

—No creo que eso sea posible…

—Pues haz que lo sea. ¿O es que acaso Ilva no se equivoca al considerarte un corderito obediente? —Helena se estremeció—. Si prefieres conformarte con ser una víctima más, adelante, pero considera la posibilidad de hacer las cosas a mi manera. Kaine Ferron no será tu dueño, sino tu objetivo. Tu trabajo consistirá en sacarle tanta información como puedas hasta que ya no lo necesitemos más. —Le ofreció una sonrisa tirante—. La decisión es tuya.

CUANDO CROWTHER POR FIN LA dejó marchar, Helena estaba agotada, como si acabara de salir de otro turno de tres días en el hospital. Le había dicho que le haría llegar «un aviso» cuando supiera la fecha y la hora de su primer encuentro con Ferron y que, hasta entonces, tendría que hacer como si nada hubiera cambiado.

Así que acudió al archivo de la biblioteca, donde encontró copias de los periódicos que se habían publicado tras el asesinato del principado Apollo. Todos ellos incluían una fotografía de Ferron tomada tan solo una semana antes de lo ocurrido.

Contempló al chico que aparecía en la fotografía en blanco y negro.

Llevaba el uniforme de la Academia, que consistía en una camisa blanca de cuello almidonado, que les obligaba a mantener la cabeza alta, y una chaqueta decorada con las insignias de su gremio: el hierro y el acero. Los estudiantes gremiales solo tenían permitido llevar sus elementos, mientras que Helena usaba una banda donde se recogían las insignias de todos los metales en cuyo manejo sobresalía, como si no destacara ya lo suficiente.

El chico, que tenía el cabello oscuro pero la piel y los ojos pálidos característicos de los norteños, mostraba una expresión tensa en la que se atisbaba el destello de una arrogancia desafiante, como si hubiera sabido de antemano para qué iban a utilizar aquella fotografía.

Estudió su imagen con atención, memorizó cada detalle, e intentó imaginar qué aspecto tendría ahora, cinco años después.

Cuando terminó de leer los periódicos disponibles, Helena consultó varios libros de texto médicos, así como un par de estudios y propuestas sobre el comportamiento humano y la mente.

No sabía explicar por qué no se veía emocional o físicamente capaz de cautivar al chico mediante su vivemancia como Crowther le había pedido, pero que fuera posible desde un punto de vista teórico no tenía por qué significar que fuera viable.

Para ello tendría que provocarle una respuesta fisiológica que pasara inadvertida, empleando técnicas lo bastante sutiles, como acelerarle el pulso, empujarlo a segregar ciertas hormonas o hacer que reaccionara a estímulos concretos. Sería como llevar a cabo uno de esos antiguos experimentos conductuales con la vivemancia como atajo.

Los años de experiencia en el campo de la sanación le habían enseñado que, en pequeñas dosis, el uso de la resonancia le pasaba desapercibido a la mayor parte de la gente. Esa era una de las razones por las que muchos recelaban de los vivemantes: porque temían que los manipularan sin que se dieran cuenta.

El problema era que Ferron la mataría en el acto si en algún momento se percataba de que utilizaba su poder con él.

Y eso significaba que tendría que actuar poco a poco. Necesitaría tomarse su tiempo para conocerlo y comprender cómo funcionaban su cuerpo y sus emociones. Los sentimientos que le inculcara deberían parecer naturales, tan sutiles como un veneno para el que, llegado el momento, ya no encontraría cura.

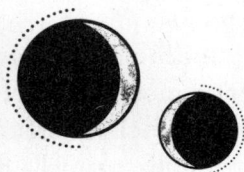

CAPÍTULO 25

Febre 1786

S<small>E DECIDIÓ QUE EL PUNTO</small> elegido para sus encuentros sería el Reducto, un complejo situado en el río, justo debajo de la presa, al norte del Cuartel General. La enorme estructura estaba construida sobre unos descomunales pilares que evitaban que sufriera daños en caso de inundación, pero que le permitían estar lo bastante cerca del agua como para beneficiarse de la hidroelectricidad generada por la presa.

Las fábricas de la zona habían cerrado a causa de la guerra, pero el Reducto había sido asediado por ambos bandos durante los primeros meses de conflicto, cuando intentaron hacerse con el control del complejo y así asegurar un posible puesto de fabricación de armas. Sin embargo, los daños causados fueron tales que el complejo acabó declarándose inservible. Una vez en ruinas, dejó de considerarse un punto lo bastante estratégico como para que supusiera una prioridad y, dado que continuar disputándose el territorio podía poner en riesgo la integridad de la presa, ambos bandos decidieron abandonarlo.

Al fin y al cabo, no le convenía a nadie que Paladia se quedara sin electricidad o que los ciudadanos acabaran con el agua hasta la cintura.

Para Helena, incluso antes de la guerra, el Reducto había sido uno de los lugares más horrendos que había visto nunca, pues era como una brutal mancha negra que alteraba el equilibrio del paisaje. Por si fuera poco, cuando todavía estaba en funcionamiento, el complejo contaminó los cielos con su humo negro y, además, envenenó las aguas y salpicó con una desagradable sustancia viscosa el humedal que se inundaba junto a los suburbios sumergidos y los distritos bajos durante la fase de sublimación.

Por eso siempre había evitado la zona.

A última hora de la tarde del día en que se encontraría con Ferron por primera vez, se quitó el uniforme y dejó todas sus posesiones guardadas con mimo en su arcón, incluido el amuleto de heliolita. No había vuelto a ponérselo desde la reunión que había tenido con Ilva y Crowther, pues se le revolvía el estómago solo de verlo.

Se vistió con las ropas de civil menos llamativas que fue capaz de encontrar, de manera que nadie se fijara en ella, y se tapó la cabeza con la capucha para ocultar lo oscura que era su melena. Sería una ciudadana cualquiera intentando mantenerse alejada del conflicto. Los inmarcesibles no solían molestar a los civiles, dado que preferían convertir en necrómatas a los soldados de la Resistencia para no tener que tomarse la molestia de entrenarlos y armarlos.

El paseo hasta el Reducto era relativamente sencillo. Solo tenía que caminar en dirección norte desde el Cuartel General y cruzar el puente que comunicaba con el continente. Además, como el extremo norte de la isla estaba asentado sobre una meseta, no se vería obligada a moverse entre los distintos niveles de la ciudad. El portón de entrada estaba cerrado, y los guardas que vigilaban la puerta peatonal comprobaron los permisos y la identificación que Crowther le había preparado antes de dejarla pasar.

El río arrastraba el agua que las tormentas habían descargado sobre las montañas, aunque no bajaba tan revuelto como durante la época de las crecidas.

Una vez que hubo salido de la isla, siguió la carretera que conducía hasta la presa y cruzó un segundo puente para llegar al Reducto, donde, para su sorpresa, había un buen puñado de gente. Dado que los edificios estaban abandonados, muchos de los ciudadanos más pobres y sin poderes alquímicos habían huido hasta allí por miedo a verse obligados a unirse a cualquiera de los bandos combatientes. El Reducto era el único lugar excluido del campo de batalla donde podían pasar el invierno sin enfrentarse al frío inclemente de las montañas.

El complejo era una mezcla entre un laberinto y una ciudad, pero sus altísimos muros de metal y cemento hacían que resultara claustrofóbico. Las fábricas habían sufrido todo tipo de sabotajes que solo habían sido posibles gracias a la alquimia, como extrañas transmutaciones y alquimizaciones pensadas para destruir la maquinaria más compleja. Sin embargo, el edificio de apartamentos donde vivía la mayor parte de los desplazados se mantenía en mejores condiciones. Según le habían dicho, lo identificaría gracias al símbolo alquímico del hierro que había en el mosaico decorativo de la entrada.

Helena entró tratando de simular que sabía adónde iba.

El tragaluz que antaño había decorado el techo ahora estaba hecho añicos en el suelo y solo unos pocos módulos tenían puertas todavía. Segundo piso, cuarta puerta a la izquierda. Habían raspado el número que identificaba el módulo hasta dejarlo ilegible.

La chica se quitó los guantes y llamó con firmeza, pero intentando no hacer demasiado ruido.

Como no obtuvo respuesta, hizo una pausa y volvió a comprobar el mapa. Quizá había llegado demasiado pronto.

Tendría que esperar. Se quedó allí de pie esforzándose por parecer tranquila mientras el corazón amenazaba con salírsele del pecho.

Entonces la puerta se abrió sin previo aviso y la luz de un farol eléctrico iluminó el pasillo. Kaine Ferron apareció ante el umbral con el mismo aspecto que en el retrato del periódico, como si para él no hubiera pasado el tiempo. Como si no hubiese envejecido nada en aquellos cinco años.

Ni siquiera aparentaba tener diecisiete años. Todavía mostraba ese aire desgarbado que caracterizaba a los chicos después de pegar el estirón, pero antes de que su figura se transformara en la de un hombre adulto. Incluso iba peinado igual que cuando estudiaba, como si hubiera emergido del pasado.

Llevaba un traje de color gris piedra que casi hacía juego con el tono gris verdoso de sus ojos. Era el uniforme de los miembros de rango medio alto de los inmarcesibles. Cuanto más alto era su rango, más oscuro era su atuendo. Por eso los generales iban siempre vestidos de negro.

El chico de rostro extrañamente aniñado la miró con languidez.

Las circunstancias ya eran de por sí terribles, pero, por algún motivo, nada la había impactado tanto como descubrir que Ferron conservaba una apariencia tan juvenil.

Se lo quedó mirando hasta que este por fin se hizo a un lado y abrió la puerta a modo de invitación, aunque dejó el espacio justo para que Helena tuviera que pasar rozándolo.

El corazón estaba a punto de salírsele por la boca cuando entró. Al cruzar el umbral, se debatió entre estudiar cada rincón del módulo o dejarse llevar por el miedo que le impedía apartar la vista de Ferron.

Al final, aprovechó el breve instante que tardó en darse la vuelta para recorrer la estancia con la mirada, intentando fijarse en el mayor número de detalles. El módulo era sencillo y estaba prácticamente vacío: se trataba de una habitación con las paredes sucias y las baldosas del suelo agrietadas, que contaba solo con una mesa de madera y dos sillas. Al ver que no había ni una cama ni un sofá, no supo si debería sentirse aliviada o aterrorizada.

Su cuerpo amenazaba con echarse a temblar descontroladamente. El movimiento de la sangre le llegaba con tanta violencia a los oídos que apenas registró el sonido de la puerta al cerrarse.

Al encontrarse frente a él, trató de imitar la lánguida indiferencia de Ferron para no denotar lo asustada que estaba en realidad. El chico apenas rozó la superficie de la puerta, pero Helena supo que acababa de encerrarla cuando captó el leve ruido de un mecanismo, seguido del chasquido de la cerradura.

—Según tengo entendido, quieres ayudar a la Resistencia —le dijo cuando se volvió para mirarla.

Oía su propia voz como si viniera de muy lejos. Su mente trabajaba a toda velocidad, anticipándose a lo que pudiera pasar.

¿A cuántas personas había matado? Estaba claro que formaba parte de los inmarcesibles desde hacía años. ¿Cuántos necrómatas tenía bajo su mando? ¿Por qué había pedido verla a ella? ¿Por qué la querría? Si le hacía daño, ¿le daría tiempo a curarse antes de que dieran el toque de queda o tendría que pasar la noche atrapada en el Reducto?

Las preguntas se le agolpaban en la cabeza mientras el miedo correteaba por sus venas como un parásito. Lo notaba en los huesos, buscando la más mínima brecha en su determinación para hacerse un hueco en su interior.

—¿Estás al tanto de mis condiciones? —le preguntó mientras la estudiaba con la cabeza ladeada.

Helena encontró su mirada y se dio cuenta de que, si bien su rostro mostraba un engañoso aire juvenil, sus ojos lo delataban.

—A cambio de recabar información para la Llama Eterna, quieres un indulto. Me quieres a mí.

—Ahora y para siempre, sin importar cuándo acabe la guerra —dijo con un brillo intenso en la mirada.

Helena no se permitió mostrar reacción alguna. Después de pasar años en el hospital, había aprendido a dejar sus sentimientos a un lado para cumplir con su deber.

—Sí —dijo impasible—. Soy tuya.

Aunque Ferron fuera dueño de su cuerpo, ella seguía teniendo el control de su mente y sus sentimientos. Si quería acceder también a ellos, tendría que esforzarse mucho más.

«Acércate, Ferron. Quiero que te obsesiones tanto con mis puntos débiles que no te percates de los que yo voy a introducir en tu interior».

Entonces el chico sonrió y, al hacerlo, su verdadera edad se reflejó de pronto en su rostro. No porque sus facciones envejecieran de un momento a otro, sino porque una malicia enconada, indudablemente por el paso del tiempo, borró por un instante esa fachada de juventud tras la que se escondía.

—¿Me lo prometes? —preguntó.

—Si eso es lo que quieres.

Otra rápida sonrisa cruzó su rostro como una guadaña que buscaba más hacer daño que demostrar una emoción sincera.

—Entonces, júramelo. En voz alta.

Helena se llevó una mano al corazón sin darse la oportunidad de pensárselo.

—Lo juro por mi alma y por el espíritu de los cinco dioses, Kaine Ferron. Seré tuya hasta que exhale mi último aliento.

No fue hasta que hubo pronunciado aquellas palabras en voz alta que recordó todo lo que había jurado en su vida. Todas las promesas contradictorias que había hecho. Tendría que encontrar una manera de reconciliarlas.

Satisfecho, Ferron se acercó a ella.

Un brillo de curiosidad iluminaba sus ojos, como si fuera un lobo acechando a su presa.

—Hasta que no hayamos ganado la guerra, no podrás hacerme nada que interfiera con... con el resto de mis responsabilidades en la Resistencia —farfulló antes de que pudiera tocarla—. Tengo que poder volver sin... sin llamar la atención.

Ferron se detuvo y enarcó una ceja.

—Ya..., pues tendré que mantenerte con vida hasta que todo esto acabe —suspiró—. Supongo que nos servirá de aliciente para seguir adelante. —Se inclinó hacia ella y acercó su rostro al suyo—. Nos guardaremos lo mejor para el final.

—Quiero que tú también lo jures —insistió ella con voz temblorosa.

Ferron se apoyó la mano sobre el lugar que debería ocupar su corazón, aunque la chica no estaba segura de que los inmarcesibles tuvieran uno.

—Lo juro —empezó utilizando un exagerado tono reverencial y haciéndole cosquillas en el cuello a Helena con su aliento—. Por los dioses y por mi alma —continuó con una risita—, juro que no interferiré.

La chica echó la cabeza hacia atrás y lo miró con suspicacia por lo fácil que había resultado hacer que cooperara. Sabía que le acababa de ofrecer una promesa vacía, pero ¿por qué le seguía el juego? Ferron dominaba la situación y, en vez de aprovechar esa ventaja, actuaba como si el acuerdo al que habían llegado fuera mutuo.

Al ver cómo lo escudriñaba, Ferron cuadró los hombros y dio una vuelta alrededor de la joven, chasqueando la lengua cuando ella hizo todo lo posible por mantenerlo en su campo de visión. Un brillo divertido le iluminaba la mirada.

—Vaya, vaya, no te fías de mí, ¿eh? Deja que adivine lo que estás pensando. Crees que os estoy tendiendo una trampa y que cambiaré de opinión en cuanto haya conseguido lo que quiero.

Helena se quedó helada.

—Sí, eso es exactamente lo que piensas. —Se detuvo en seco—. ¿Y si hacemos algo? Como muestra de mi… buena voluntad, te prometo que no te tocaré. De momento. —Le recorrió el cuerpo con una mirada perezosa—. Al fin y al cabo, dejé muy claro que quería que accedieras a ser mía libremente. Y, ahora mismo, no pareces muy contenta de estar aquí.

Aunque sus palabras deberían haberla tranquilizado, se sintió horrorizada ante la propuesta. Aquello no era lo que ella quería. Se suponía que la misión debía comenzar de inmediato y, cuanto más tardaran en ponerla en marcha, más probabilidades había de que Ferron perdiera el interés antes de que ella tuviese oportunidad de manipularlo. La cuestión era que no sabía cómo responder sin dejar claras sus intenciones.

Consciente, al parecer, de la incomodidad que le había causado la oferta, Ferron le ofreció un lento asentimiento y una sonrisa voraz.

—Voy a seguir dándote la información que tu querida Llama Eterna precisa, solo que, por el momento, encontraré otras formas de disfrutar de tu compañía.

Si ya era mala la idea de permitir que hiciera con ella lo que le viniera en gana, el miedo que la embargaba al verse obligada a permanecer en vilo era mucho peor.

Escondió una mano detrás de la espalda y apretó el puño con fuerza para clavarse las uñas en la palma. Los cortes ya casi curados empezaron a dolerle y amenazaron con volver a abrirse.

—Qué… generoso por tu parte —dijo con la esperanza de mostrar docilidad.

—Sí, muy generoso. Sin embargo, creo que lo mínimo es que tú también me des algo a cambio. —De pronto, adoptó una expresión calculadora, acompañada de una sonrisa viperina—. Al fin y al cabo, yo ya he tenido que ofrecerle a la Llama Eterna una información muy valiosa para ganarme tu colaboración. ¿No crees que merezco una recompensa? ¿Algo con lo que calentar este frío corazón?

A Helena se le cayó el alma a los pies y sintió que perdía el equilibrio.

—¿Qué… qué quieres? —preguntó tensa.

Trató de averiguar qué le pediría, aunque acabó hundida metalmente bajo toda una avalancha de posibilidades. Odiaba pensar en el concepto que los hombres tenían de un favor.

—No parece que la idea te entusiasme mucho.

Ferron esbozó una fingida expresión de lástima e hizo un mohín que le dio un aspecto tan aniñado que Helena se sintió tentada de dar un paso atrás.

—¿Qué quieres que haga? —insistió apretando los dientes—. Dímelo y lo haré.

—Por Dios, Marino. —Profirió una seca carcajada—. Sí que estás desesperada.

—Estoy aquí, ¿no? Creo que eso ya lo había dejado muy claro —le espetó con tono apagado, incapaz de mirarlo ya a la cara.

—Bueno, como se ve que tu creatividad a la hora de mostrar gratitud es nula, propongo que me des un beso bien cargado de sentimiento —sentenció. Luego, como si se lo hubiera pensado mejor, añadió—: Decidiré cuánta información proporcionarte dependiendo de lo bien que lo hagas.

¿Un beso? ¿Solo quería un beso? La situación era menos desagradable de lo que había esperado, pero la verdad era que prefería mantener las distancias.

Estaba claro que intentaba provocarla. Desde que la chica había llamado a la puerta, no había hecho más que mantenerla en vilo.

Lo del beso era solo la guinda del pastel. Quería ponerla completamente en evidencia, reforzar el rencor que Helena le guardaba y hacerle creer que le estaba ahorrando una mayor humillación al mostrarle clemencia. Ferron esperaba que lo odiara, esperaba que sus sentimientos la mantuvieran distraída para que le resultara más fácil manipularla y hacerla sentir desgraciada.

Se trataba de un juego, nada era real. Helena no pasaba de ser una distracción para él, algo que incluir en su lista de condiciones para confundir a la Llama Eterna. No formaba parte de su verdadero plan.

Más le valía tenerlo en mente.

Dio un paso hacia él.

Las uñas perfectas, el rostro eternamente joven, cada detalle que conformaba la fachada de meticulosa serenidad de Ferron estaba pensado para esconder el monstruo que acechaba bajo su piel.

Se le contrajeron las pupilas. Un opaco desinterés se adueñó de su mirada.

Helena concentró su resonancia hasta que la notó vibrar en la yema de los dedos y la volvió maleable como los hilos de una telaraña.

Era demasiado pronto para manipularlo, pero un beso le daría la oportunidad de tocarlo, de descubrir cómo era y, ante todo, qué sentía por ella. Le proporcionaría un punto de partida.

No se permitió tocarlo con las manos desnudas nada más rodearle el cuello con los brazos, sino que pasó los dedos por la delgada lana oscura de su chaqueta para atraerlo hacia sí.

Ferron sonrió como si estuviera disfrutando de la situación.

Cuando sus labios estaban a punto de entrar en contacto, Helena vaciló. Una parte de ella esperaba que le arrancara el corazón de cuajo como había hecho con el padre de Luc.

Un escalofrío le recorrió el cuerpo y supo que él también lo había sentido.

El aliento le olía a enebro: fresco, intenso y recién cortado.

La languidez había vuelto a adueñarse de sus ojos entrecerrados al encontrar su mirada. La chica se preguntó qué vería Ferron en ella.

Se dijo que los asesinos también eran personas y él no era más que un muchacho, así que lo besó despacio, con dulzura, tal y como se había imaginado besando a alguien que le gustara. En vez de tratar de seducirlo, se permitió mostrarse vacilante, como si estuviera dando su primer beso. Porque en realidad así era.

Mientras lo besaba, le acarició la nuca y enterró los dedos en su pelo siguiendo la curvatura de su cráneo para colarle una pizca de resonancia bajo la piel.

Ferron no era humano.

Sabía que los inmarcesibles iban en contra de la naturaleza, pero no había estado preparada para lo que se encontraría.

Podía sentirlo, trazar un mapa de su ser como con cualquier otro paciente. Notaba los latidos de su corazón, sus nervios, sus venas, su energía y todos los sistemas interconectados de su organismo, pero había algo que no encajaba. Tenía la sensación de estar tocando el reflejo de Ferron en un espejo.

Aunque él estaba allí presente y, técnicamente, vivo, transmitía una cualidad inmutable que la mente de Helena simplemente se negaba a comprender.

Y ella no podía permitirse centrar toda su atención en aquel aspecto. Tenía que concentrarse también en besarlo, que era lo que se suponía que debía estar haciendo. El problema era que su organismo le parecía mucho más interesante que su boca.

Bajó una de las manos y le apoyó la palma en la mejilla para tener un contacto directo y atraerlo más hacia ella. Cada vez estaba más distraída, pero su cuerpo le resultaba fascinante.

¿Cómo era posible? No pudo evitar presionarse más contra él.

El ritmo de los latidos de Ferron cambió y de nuevo volvió a cambiar.

De pronto, Helena fue consciente de lo que su cuerpo estaba haciendo: tenía un brazo enroscado en torno a su cuello, una mano en su mejilla y la espalda arqueada para salvar la diferencia de altura entre ellos.

El chico se apartó con una sacudida.

Dejó caer las manos de inmediato, estupefacta, intentando no respirar demasiado rápido ni dejar ver lo desorientada que se sentía. ¿Se habría dado cuenta de que había utilizado su resonancia? Escudriñó su rostro en busca de algún indicio de rabia o desconfianza.

Se le había ensombrecido la mirada y parecía mucho menos sosegado. Además, tenía el cabello revuelto y un par de mechones sueltos sobre la frente.

—Vaya. —Parpadeó y meneó la cabeza—. Qué… interesante. —Se pasó el pulgar por los labios sin quitarse el guante. Luego, tras una pausa, añadió en voz más baja—: Eres toda una caja de sorpresas.

Helena no sabía muy bien cómo responder, así que dijo lo primero que se le vino a la cabeza:

—¿Eso es lo que les dices a todas?

Él resopló divertido y se pasó la mano por el pelo para apartárselo de la cara.

—Pues la verdad es que no.

Guardaron silencio por un momento.

Seguro que había esperado que lo mordiera.

Helena se puso colorada y deseó haberlo hecho. Pero jamás se había topado con un organismo tan interesante como el suyo, así que no fue capaz de pasarlo por alto.

Ferron carraspeó.

—Te he traído una cosa —dijo metiéndose la mano en el bolsillo y lanzándole algo.

La chica lo atrapó en un acto reflejo y bajó la vista para estudiar lo que resultó ser un anillo deslustrado. Enseguida supo que estaba hecho de plata. Aunque su resonancia argéntea era mínima y no lo bastante avanzada como para que su repertorio se considerara noble, tanto lo que le transmitía su poder como la apariencia del anillo no dejaban lugar a dudas. No obstante, no parecía producto de la transmutación, sino que había sido forjado a mano. Aún se distinguían las marcas del martillo con el que le habían dado forma hasta trazar un patrón escamado, casi geométrico, sobre su superficie.

Era extraño que un alquimista del hierro tuviera algo así.

—Acéptalo como un símbolo de nuestra relación —dijo Ferron levantando la mano derecha para demostrarle que llevaba un anillo a juego en el índice cuando Helena lo miró sorprendida—. Están vinculados por medio de un enlace espejo. Notarás en tu anillo todo lo que yo haga en el mío. Le aplicaré una transmutación térmica cuando necesite reunirme contigo. Se calentará dos veces si es urgente. Te recomiendo que vengas enseguida en ese caso.

Helena inspeccionó el anillo. El brazalete del hospital también funcionaba mediante un enlace espejo. Se trataba de una técnica de transmutación increíblemente rara que solo unos pocos alquimistas eran capaces de aplicar. Por ese motivo, los objetos enlazados eran muy valiosos, aunque solo si se disponía de las dos piezas. La Llama Eterna llevaba un estricto control de quienes tenían alguno.

Helena intentó ponérselo en el índice de la mano izquierda, la no dominante a la hora de transmutar, pero le quedaba pequeño, así que tuvo que resignarse a colocárselo en el anular.

—Mi resonancia argéntea no es fuerte, pero creo que me las arreglaré con un cambio de temperatura. ¿Tengo que hacer lo mismo para llamarte yo a ti?

—No —le espetó él con una inesperada intensidad—. No te atrevas a llamarme. Como se te ocurra quemarme una sola vez, se cancela el trato. No seré tu puto perro faldero. Si quieres reunirte conmigo, puedes venir aquí a esperarme o dejar un mensaje, y yo acudiré cuando tenga tiempo.

Aquel arrebato resultó totalmente inesperado tras haber mantenido el resto del tiempo una apariencia tan tranquila. Crowther tenía razón: Ferron no quería estar al servicio de nadie. Lo que deseaba más que nada era tener poder.

—Bueno, yo tampoco voy a poder responder siempre de inmediato —le dijo ella—. Si salgo de improviso, podría levantar sospechas. Salvo emergencias, creo que lo mejor será fijar un horario.

—Está bien.

—Los saturnis y los martis suelo salir a buscar suministros médicos justo antes de que salga el sol. Nadie se dará cuenta si regreso un poco más tarde. ¿Te parece bien? Si lo prefieres, podemos cambiar de días.

—De acuerdo. —Asintió despacio—. Pero, si por algún motivo no puedo venir, tendrás que volver a última hora de la tarde.

—¿Y si no me viene bien? —preguntó Helena, que no entendía por qué se mostraba tan reacio a utilizar los anillos para algo más que un par de señales básicas. El camino hasta el Reducto no era tan corto como para que valiera la pena recorrerlo en vano.

—Estoy seguro de que te las arreglarás. —La miró durante un momento antes de meter la mano en su capa, sacar dos sobres y decantarse por uno de ellos—. Aquí tienes mi primera entrega.

Cuando lo aceptó, Helena vio que estaba dirigido a Aurelia Ingram.

—Crowther sabe ya cómo descodificarlo —le indicó Ferron cuando se percató de que ella miraba atentamente la dirección—. Confío en que sea sensato y no utilice toda la información de golpe.

—Tu colaboración es uno de los secretos mejor guardados de la Resistencia. No haremos nada que ponga en peligro nuestro acuerdo.

Ferron le ofreció un vago asentimiento.

—Pues nos vemos el martis. Ahora márchate de aquí y asegúrate de regresar por otro camino.

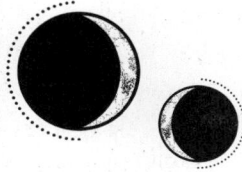

—¿CÓMO QUE NOTASTE ALGO RARO en la resonancia? ¿Qué quieres decir? —preguntó Crowther cuando Helena terminó de contarle todo lo que había pasado. Le había pedido que acudiera a su despacho en cuanto cruzó el portón del Cuartel General.

Helena se cruzó de brazos.

—Supongo que se debe a que es un inmarcesible. Ha sido una experiencia distinta. No sé si podré transmutarlo. Sigue teniendo el mismo aspecto que en su foto de estudiante, así que a lo mejor no se le puede cambiar. No me ha dado la sensación de que sea posible manipularlo e, incluso si lo es, no sé si seré capaz de hacerlo con la suficiente sutileza.

—¿Te ayudaría contar con un sujeto con el que experimentar?

—¿Qué? —Lo miró horrorizada—. ¡No!

—Pero podría serte útil, ¿no te parece?

—No —insistió—. Soy sanadora y he jurado…

—No, no lo eres —la interrumpió Crowther, cuya voz sonó como el chasquido de unas tijeras al cerrarse—. No en lo que respecta al contexto de esta misión. Tu papel como sanadora no nos sirve de nada. Necesito que seas una vivemante dispuesta a hacer lo que sea por la causa. El heroísmo es algo que debemos dejarles a quienes se exponen a la opinión pública. El trabajo de inteligencia, el que hacemos nosotros, consiste en meternos en la cabeza de nuestros enemigos para robarles sus secretos, sin importar lo que cueste. Y ahora tú formas parte de este mundo.

Helena puso mala cara.

—Sé de sobra cómo lidiar con los aspectos fisiológicos. Lo que me preocupa es la regeneración. A no ser que tengáis un inmarcesible a mano, los experimentos no me van a servir de nada.

Crowther torció el gesto y se reclinó contra el respaldo de la silla.

—Ahora mismo no tenemos ninguno, pero podríamos conseguírtelo en caso de necesitarlo. —Entornó los ojos—. ¿Ese anillo te lo ha dado él?

La chica se lo quitó y lo deslizó por la mesa.

—Está enlazado. Su intención es utilizarlo para llamarme en caso de emergencia, pero dejó muy claro que cancelará nuestro trato de inmediato si nosotros lo utilizamos para llamarlo a él. Tenías razón al decir que es arrogante hasta la médula. Estuvo a punto de entrar en cólera solo por contemplar esa posibilidad.

Crowther estudió el anillo con atención mientras le daba vueltas entre los dedos.

—¿Es de plata?

—Sí.

Él asintió.

—Debe de haberlo heredado de su madre. Era una alquimista de la plata aquí en la Academia. Provenía de una familia de la baja nobleza, pero tenía un talento aceptable. Atreus estuvo prendado de ella durante un tiempo.

—¿Los conocías? —preguntó Helena con curiosidad.

—Solo de oídas. La opinión que los miembros de los gremios tenían de los estudiantes becados por aquel entonces no era distinta de la de ahora. Todo el mundo daba por hecho que lo suyo con Atreus no sería más que un enamoramiento pasajero. Un Ferron jamás dejaría a un lado su resonancia. Fue toda una sorpresa que se casara con ella en secreto, aunque es obvio que lo hizo por obligación. No me cabe en la cabeza cómo un hombre tan ambicioso como Atreus acabó metido en semejante embrollo, pero difícilmente habría podido enfrentarse al escarnio social y religioso que se hubiera desatado en caso de darle la espalda a la chica.

Quienes estudiaban el arte de la metalurgia sabían que la plata y el hierro eran elementos incompatibles. No se podían obtener aleaciones de ellos. Pero la plata era un metal noble y la madre de Ferron seguramente estaba por encima de su marido en la escala social, pese a que él dispusiese de mayor fortuna.

—Entonces ¿concibieron a Kaine sin estar casados? —preguntó vacilante.

Crowther negó con la cabeza.

—No, el chico nació un tiempo después. Enid tuvo… dificultades para concebir. Sufrió algunos abortos por culpa de una desafortunada conjunción con la resonancia. Cuando Enid llegó embarazada al hospital, los médicos concluyeron que el feto mostraba claros indicios de vivemancia. Aunque les advirtieron de los peligros de que el niño naciera, Atreus estaba desesperado por tener un heredero, así que se retiraron a su casa de campo. Meses más tarde, descubrieron que Atreus había estado recurriendo a la ayuda de vivemantes para manejar el embarazo de su esposa, un delito por el que lo encerraron durante varias semanas. Para cuando lo liberaron, Kaine ya había nacido.

El hombre dejó el anillo sobre el escritorio.

—Después de aquello, continuaron viviendo en el campo para no llamar la atención. Se decía que el parto había sido tan traumático para Enid que nunca volvió a dejarse ver en público. Atreus rara vez hablaba de ella. Luego, entre los gremios empezó a correr el rumor de que Kaine era un lapsus y que por eso la familia estaba haciendo todo lo posible por mantenerlo escondido. Llegó un momento en que la teoría estuvo tan extendida que Atreus no tuvo más remedio que presentar al niño en sociedad, aunque nunca le quitó el ojo de encima. El pobre diablo era como un perro atado a una correa. Atreus sabía que la Llama Eterna intervendría si el niño mostraba indicios de ser un vivemante. Con el precio tan alto que había pagado por tener un heredero, no podía permitirse perderlo. Nadie esperaba que matriculara al chico en la Academia, pero ¿qué otra cosa podía hacer? Si Kaine no desmentía los rumores acerca de sus habilidades ni obtenía su título, la familia perdería el control de los gremios.

—¿Cómo sabes todo esto? —preguntó Helena mientras volvía a ponerse el anillo.

Crowther enarcó una ceja.

—¿Por qué crees que entré a formar parte del profesorado y acabé siendo su tutor?

Helena lo miró estupefacta.

—Lo vigilabas para ver si resultaba ser un vivemante.

—Así es —respondió con un breve asentimiento—. Él era uno de los estudiantes a los que me pidieron supervisar. Por desgracia, al poco tiempo me reubicaron para investigar ciertos rumores que se habían expandido por la ciudad. De haber estado ahí, habría notado que algo iba mal cuando regresó a la Academia tras la ejecución de su padre. El curso de la historia habría sido muy diferente.

Cuando Helena regresó al módulo una semana más tarde, se quitó los guantes e hizo una pausa para apoyar una mano sobre la puerta con la intención de percibir el mecanismo de la cerradura con su resonancia. Aunque, tanto por dentro como por fuera, su punto de encuentro tenía el aspecto de estar abandonado, la puerta disponía de una intrincada cerradura.

Los mejores cerrojos se fabricaban con una mezcla de metales y elementos raros, adaptada a la resonancia particular del propietario y combinada generalmente con otros elementos inertes para crear puntos ciegos. Para abrirlos, el alquimista tenía que reconocer la sensación de los mecanismos que los componían, así como saber qué partes debía manipular.

Dejó los dedos apoyados sobre la puerta después de llamar. Se quedó tan absorta trazando el movimiento de la cerradura que la mano pálida que salió del interior la pilló totalmente desprevenida cuando la agarró de la muñeca y tiró de ella.

La puerta se cerró a su espalda y Ferron la arrinconó contra la pared.

Y eso que había prometido no tocarla.

Se acercó a ella, le apoyó una mano en el lateral del cuello y le rozó las vértebras con la punta de los dedos. Helena se obligó a levantar la cabeza cuando él bajó la suya.

Le dio un vuelco el corazón al tratar de tomar aire y no ser capaz de hacerlo.

Ferron se apartó y la estudió con una mirada vacía, carente de emoción.

Los pulmones empezaban a arderle mientras trataba de averiguar qué era exactamente lo que le estaba haciendo. Pese a su extensa experiencia como sanadora, aquella era la primera vez que usaban la vivemancia con ella.

Ferron ladeó la cabeza y la mantuvo erguida contra la pared agarrándola de un hombro.

—¿Dónde está tu instinto de supervivencia? Podría haberte matado cincuenta veces desde que has entrado en el edificio.

Helena no pudo responder. Los ojos empezaban a salírsele de las órbitas y su corazón, aunque seguía latiendo, trabajaba a toda velocidad. Debía de tener el rostro desencajado por el miedo, porque el chico se rio entre dientes.

—No te preocupes, que no voy a aprovecharme de ti —le susurró al oído.

Movió los dedos de forma casi imperceptible y por fin le devolvió a Helena el control de su respiración, si bien no del resto del cuerpo. Ella tomó una entrecortada bocanada de aire, en un siseo, lo más próximo a un grito que era capaz de proferir.

No conseguía zafarse de él. Ni siquiera podía encontrar su propia resonancia. La había pillado con la guardia baja al hacerle pensar que iba a besarla.

—Voy a mostrarte algo interesante. Según me han dicho, es uno de mis muchos talentos especiales.

Presionó la mano libre contra la frente de la chica y le oscureció la visión. Luego, sin previo aviso, se coló en su mente, como si le clavara una aguja en el cráneo.

Helena sufrió una sacudida.

Lo sentía en su interior. La resonancia de Ferron había impactado contra la superficie de su subconsciente con la fuerza de un rayo y ahora todos sus recuerdos pasaban por delante de sus ojos como si su mente se hubiera convertido en un zoótropo.

Fue como si estuviera retrocediendo en el tiempo: se vio chocando con la pared y levantando la cabeza para mirar a Ferron, que se cernía sobre ella. Luego se vio apoyando la mano contra la puerta y caminando por los pasillos del edificio y los claustrofóbicos callejones del complejo.

Ferron se adentró más en su mente y Helena se vio entonces cruzándose la bolsa de sanadora para salir a la calle.

Le estaba leyendo la mente.

No podía permitírselo.

Se debatió en un intento por liberarse, por arrancar su consciencia de las garras de Ferron.

Pero él ahondó todavía más en ella.

Ahora estaba en un laboratorio de química vacío, transmutando varios compuestos de gran rareza para elaborar un elixir. Cubrió el anillo que el chico le había dado con él, con cuidado de no alterar el enlace espejo.

Entonces la soltó sin previo aviso y Helena recuperó el control de su cuerpo, pero le cedieron las rodillas y tuvo que dejarse caer hasta el suelo. La cabeza le dolía tanto que incluso veía borroso.

—¿Qué le has hecho a mi anillo? —exigió saber el chico cerniéndose sobre ella.

—¿Qué me has hecho tú a mí? —replicó Helena con la voz temblorosa.

—Es un truco que me enseñó Artemon Bennet. —Ferron se alejó un paso de ella—. Lo llama animancia. Cuando capturamos a los soldados de la Resistencia con vida, solemos examinar sus recuerdos. Si alguna vez te capturan, es muy probable que contigo hagan lo mismo. Por eso supones un riesgo para mí.

Helena cerró los ojos esforzándose por recomponerse. En la Llama Eterna no tenían ni idea de que eso fuera posible. ¿Cómo iban a defenderse de un poder así?

—Te lo preguntaré una vez más. —La voz de Ferron sonaba implacable—. ¿Qué le has hecho a mi anillo? ¿Dónde está?

Helena tragó saliva.

—Es un elixir que se adhiere a las superficies y crea una capa que distorsiona las ondas de luz para que a quienes no saben que está ahí les resulte más difícil ver el anillo.

Ferron se agachó, le levantó la mano izquierda y le pasó el pulgar por los dedos para encontrar el anillo. Entornó la mirada y estudió la mano de la chica desde distintos ángulos.

Cuando arqueó las cejas, asombrado, Helena supo que por fin había conseguido verlo de nuevo.

—Nunca había oído hablar de algo así —admitió tras una larga pausa.

—Todavía está en fase experimental.

—¿Lo has inventado tú? —inquirió buscando su mirada con una ceja enarcada.

Ella asintió a regañadientes.

—Era uno de mis proyectos académicos, pero nunca conseguí que funcionara en superficies grandes. La refracción se vuelve irregular.

Ferron se incorporó y, cuando la ayudó a ponerse de pie, Helena reprimió un estremecimiento al ser consciente de lo que sería capaz de hacer con tan solo tocarla.

—No pienso tolerar que tu incompetencia me pueda afectar de ninguna manera.

Jamás nadie en su vida la había tachado de incompetente, así que se puso a la defensiva.

—¿Y cómo íbamos a saber que querías que tu pequeño trofeo de guerra fuera inmune a la telepatía?

—No es telepatía —la corrigió él con tono burlón—. Solo te he manipulado mínimamente el cerebro. Aunque sientas que me he metido en tu cabeza y que he visto tus recuerdos como si los estuviera viviendo a través de ti, a no ser que haga un barrido exhaustivo y los reproduzca varias veces, lo único que alcanzo a ver son destellos. Una buena parte de la información se pierde entre todo el ruido mental. Los momentos más nítidos y fáciles de descifrar son aquellos en los que tú misma pusiste más atención. Si alguna vez te cogen, no dejes que te engañen. Jamás verán más de lo que tú has visto.

—Entonces ¿qué has descubierto ahora? —le preguntó tratando de entenderlo.

—Que estás aterrorizada. —Sonrió—. Al desorientarte, el miedo te ha hecho vulnerable y te ha impedido pensar con la claridad necesaria para resistirte. Luego, he visto un borrón. Los dos momentos más claros han sido el de la puerta y el del anillo. Como en esos casos no pensabas en nada más que en la tarea que tenías entre manos, tu mente no ha emborronado los recuerdos. Al cerebro se le da de maravilla mostrar las prioridades de cada persona.

Entonces, si los inmarcesibles la interrogaban, no lo verían todo, sino solo aquello que era importante para ella. Magnífico.

—¿Y cómo me protejo? —Odiaba tener que preguntárselo a él, pero lo hizo—. ¿Cómo esperas que me defienda?

—Los interrogadores no se detendrán hasta que les des lo que quieren y no podrás impedir que se cuelen en tu mente, pero, si los convences de que eres débil, no se molestarán en escudriñar tus recuerdos a fondo. Tendrás que darles algún recuerdo lo bastante valioso como para que se crean que te lo han arrebatado. De ese modo, evitarás que accedan a tus verdaderos secretos.

La chica lo consideró por un momento. Todavía estaba apoyada contra la pared, porque no se fiaba de que sus piernas fueran a soportar su peso.

—Piénsalo. Escoge un recuerdo. Si yo estuviera buscando información sobre la Llama Eterna o los Holdfast, ¿qué podrías mostrarme para hacerme creer que he robado uno de tus mayores secretos? Al utilizar la resonancia en la mente de otra persona, se desata en ella la misma reacción que tendría al ver su casa envuelta en llamas. Lo primero que hará su cerebro será ir a buscar lo que considera más importante. Tendrás que aprender a hacer lo contrario. Céntrate en las minucias y recuerda que, mientras tú no llames la atención o ellos no analicen tu mente a fondo, lo único que obtendrán son destellos. No importa lo que tú creas que hayan visto.

—Está bien —dijo ella asintiendo despacio.

—La próxima semana, volveremos a intentarlo. Estate preparada.

CAPÍTULO 27

Febre 1786

Cuando Helena le contó a Crowther lo que Ferron era capaz de hacer, este pidió que la dejaran fuera de todas las reuniones de la Llama Eterna y prohibió que la informaran acerca de las idas y venidas de Luc.

Todo el mundo creía que el cambio se debía a la misteriosa «crisis nerviosa» que, según se rumoreaba, Helena había sufrido. Y, aunque para Crowther resultaba de lo más conveniente, ella se quedó aún más aislada de lo que ya estaba.

La siguiente vez que Ferron y ella se vieron, fue todo un alivio que la invitara tranquilamente a pasar en vez de asaltarla antes de que tuviera oportunidad siquiera de cruzar la puerta.

El edificio le parecía muy deprimente. Estaba claro que nadie se había preocupado demasiado por proporcionarles a los trabajadores un lugar agradable para vivir cuando las fábricas todavía estaban en funcionamiento.

—¿Estás lista? —le preguntó dando un paso hacia ella y quitándose uno de los guantes de piel que llevaba.

Helena, que también se había desprendido de los guantes, apretó los puños y asintió mientras notaba las cicatrices que le surcaban la palma.

Ferron no la paralizó esa vez, sino que se limitó a apoyarle la mano en la frente, pero ella no alcanzó a reprimir un jadeo. Se le pusieron los ojos en blanco tan repentinamente que casi fue capaz de sentir la tensión a la que estaban sometidos sus nervios ópticos.

Aunque ya sabía lo que le esperaba, su mente se resistió, presa del pánico, y voló instintivamente hasta los recuerdos en los que Helena no quería centrarse.

El despacho de Crowther, su cara envuelta en sombras.

Se obligó a pensar en otra cosa.

Luc.

Crowther le había dado luz verde para utilizar la última reunión de la Llama Eterna a la que había asistido como distracción. Habían estado hablando del nuevo método que habían descubierto para acabar con los liches y los inmarcesibles. También habían acordado qué hacer con los talismanes que habían requisado, pues la unidad de Luc había regresado con varios.

La resonancia que se había adueñado de su mente la liberó de manera abrupta y Helena se tambaleó mientras trataba de enfocar la vista y poner en orden sus pensamientos.

—Ha ido mejor de lo que esperaba —le oyó decir a Ferron a lo lejos—. Por desgracia, si te cogen, no te van a interrogar una sola vez.

Cuando volvió a entrar en su mente, fue como si le hubieran abierto una herida recién cerrada y se la abrieran aún más. Pensar le exigía el doble de esfuerzo.

Al fin, Ferron la dejó libre, y Helena tuvo la sensación de que su cráneo se iba a resquebrajar de un momento a otro.

Se mordió el labio con fuerza mientras sus ojos se le llenaban de lágrimas y el pecho se le estremecía en busca de aire. La estancia le daba vueltas y amenazaba con desdibujarse. Al notar que se tambaleaba, buscó la pared a tientas.

—Bébete esto. —Ferron le puso un frasquito en la mano—. Si no lo haces, te vas a desmayar.

Lo aceptó y se lo bebió de un trago, pues no creía que tuviera intención de envenenarla. Y en realidad ya no estaba tan segura de que le importara si la mataba. La cabeza le palpitaba como si tuviera un tambor retumbando en su interior.

El intenso sabor amargo del analgésico le entumeció la lengua y Helena estuvo a punto de escupirlo al darse cuenta de que le había dado láudano para el dolor de cabeza. ¿Es que acaso no era consciente de lo escasas que eran las provisiones de opiáceos en el Norte?

Aun así, como ya lo tenía en la boca, se lo terminó tragando.

Cuando volvió a abrir los ojos, todo parecía tener una suave luminosidad. Parpadeó y los bordes de la estancia, al igual que la silueta de Ferron, se desdibujaron.

—¿Te ha pasado alguna vez? —le preguntó con voz pastosa.

Desconocía si los inmarcesibles sufrían también dolores de cabeza, o si dormían siquiera.

—Más de una vez... Tuve un entrenamiento muy riguroso.

Helena asintió. Resultaba extraño, porque no parecía que la guerra lo hubiera alcanzado. Sin embargo, al margen de su aspecto físico, percibía en él una quietud inquietante, cargada de peligro.

—¿Por qué?

La miró con altanería y su expresión se endureció.

—Porque necesitaban comprobar si era mejor que mi padre o si, como él, corría el riesgo de derrumbarme en caso de enfrentarme a un interrogatorio.

Nunca se había parado a pensar en lo que le había ocurrido a Atreus Ferron después de haber sido arrestado. Todo el mundo sabía que había acabado confesando, pero ella había dado por hecho que había sido una decisión propia.

—Y eso fue... ¿antes o después de asesinar al principado Apollo?

Ferron guardó silencio mientras se le retorcía la boca en una mueca.

—¿Quieres una confesión? Ya que nos ponemos, puedo contarte todo lo que he hecho hasta ahora.

—Pues cuéntamelo —dijo sin ceder ante su mirada burlona.

Un destello de sorpresa le suavizó las facciones durante un breve instante. Era evidente que se sentía solo.

Helena llevaba ya unos días sospechándolo. Desde que Crowther le había hablado de las circunstancias en que sus padres se habían casado, había repasado los vagos recuerdos que guardaba del tiempo que coincidieron en la Academia. Si la memoria no le fallaba, nunca había tenido amigos. Se relacionaba con los otros estudiantes de los gremios, pero no pasaba demasiado tiempo con nadie en concreto. De lo contrario, las personas cercanas a él habrían sido las primeras en verse bombardeadas a preguntas y acusaciones tras el asesinato. Los estudiantes de su curso habían hecho comentarios como «Compartí habitación con él el año pasado, pero apenas hablaba» o «Fuimos compañeros en clase de Aleaciones, pero siempre hacía las tareas solo».

Como se había criado en el seno de una familia centrada casi en exclusiva en su ambición ancestral y, además, lo habían tenido controlado por si mostraba cualquier indicio de debilidad o vivemancia, seguro que jamás se había arriesgado a confiar en nadie. Y la situación no había hecho más que empeorar tras la guerra.

Vivía entre inmortales consumidos por sus propias ansias de poder y venganza. Ella tampoco se fiaría de nadie estando en su posición.

—¿Por qué iba a querer contarte nada? —escupió Ferron antes de alejarse.

Helena no insistió. Tampoco necesitaba saberlo.

Su único objetivo era hacer que se diera cuenta de que quería hablar con alguien…

… de que quería hablar con ella.

Así Helena adquiriría un valor emocional para él. Y así Ferron empezaría a considerarla una persona lo bastante interesante como para bajar la guardia.

—¿Quieres que volvamos a intentarlo? —preguntó con la esperanza de impresionarlo al cabo de un instante.

Pero él se puso de pie.

—Solían torturarme mientras Bennet se colaba en mi mente. Decían que necesitaba practicar… en caso de que me atraparan. —Retorció la boca en una muestra de desprecio—. Pero no era más que una excusa. Ese malnacido disfruta haciéndole daño a la gente, sintiendo el dolor en la mente de su víctima mientras esta grita. Si te capturan, eso es lo que hará contigo.

Antes de que Helena tuviera oportunidad de responder, Ferron le lanzó un sobre con un movimiento tan inesperado que no llegó a atraparlo a tiempo. Para cuando este tocó el suelo, él ya se había marchado.

HELENA ESTABA TRABAJANDO CUANDO ILVA Holdfast y el falcón Matias aparecieron en la sala de urgencias acompañados por cuatro chicas.

—Sanadora Marino, hemos llegado a la conclusión de que, al ser nuestra única sanadora, te hemos sometido a una presión desmedida —empezó Ilva con una expresión indescifrable mientras Matias hablaba acerca de su deber sagrado y pronunciaba una invocación antes de colgarle del cuello un amuleto de heliolita a cada una de ellas—. El poder divino ha guiado a estas cuatro jóvenes hasta el falcón Matias, quien las ha evaluado a fondo para comprobar que su fe es sincera y que su alma es pura de intenciones. A partir de ahora, tu deber sagrado consistirá en guiarlas mientras aprenden a brindar a los pacientes de este hospital la intercesión de Sol.

La mujer hizo una pausa y, cuando el silencio se volvió incómodo, Helena asintió sin saber qué decir. Crowther le había dejado muy claro que contaban con gente capaz de ocupar su puesto como sanadora, pero nunca esperó que fueran a poner a cuatro personas en su lugar.

Matias siempre había rechazado la idea de incorporar nuevas sanadoras, pero parecía que la intervención de Helena en la sala de mandos le había hecho cambiar de opinión: cualquier sanadora sería mejor que ella.

Aunque las chicas serían sus aprendizas, la responsabilidad de formarlas no recaería solo en Helena, sino que la enfermera Pace también tendría que encargarse de enseñarles unas nociones básicas de medicina. Ella decidió morderse la lengua y no comentar que aquel proceso se basaba en la misma combinación de medicina y sanación que Matias tantas veces le había impedido a Helena utilizar abiertamente.

La enfermera Pace ya estaba explicándoles los protocolos de seguridad del hospital a las nuevas incorporaciones, haciendo hincapié en que debían comprobar si los pacientes habían sido reanimados antes de tratarlos. Si la víctima había muerto poco tiempo antes, a veces era difícil de verificar, pero todos y cada uno de los ingresados debían pasar un doble examen: el primero lo llevaban a cabo los guardias en el momento de la admisión y el segundo era responsabilidad del equipo médico. Había que tener una precaución extrema con los pacientes que no hubieran recibido la doble validación, pues podían ser necrómatas o, lo que era peor, liches.

Helena dejó de prestar atención a las explicaciones de la enfermera Pace y reprimió el impulso de llevarse la mano a la cicatriz que tenía en el lateral del cuello. Había perdido la cuenta de la cantidad de veces que había oído esa advertencia, pero, cada vez que se lo repetían, le entraban ganas de meter la cabeza en un cubo de agua helada y ponerse a gritar.

Sabía que debería alegrarse de que hubieran reclutado a más sanadoras, pero se le formó un nudo en el estómago al contemplar a esas chicas.

Iban a ser sus sustitutas porque su trabajo en el hospital había pasado a un segundo plano frente a las nuevas obligaciones que había adquirido al convertirse en el juguete de Ferron.

Esa certeza le abrasaba las entrañas como un ascua encendida.

Una de las aprendizas dio un paso adelante y le ofreció una mano, pero optó por hacer una torpe reverencia cuando vio que Helena no se había quitado los guantes.

—Nosotras ya te conocemos, pero estas son Marta Rumly, Claire Reibeck y Anne Stoffle. Yo soy Elaine Boyle.

HELENA TARDÓ MENOS DE UNA semana en hartarse de las aprendizas. Cuando empezaron a darse cuenta de que la sanación no era el trabajo que esperaban, dejaron de intentar adaptarse a sus nuevas responsabilidades.

Claire y Anne ni siquiera se molestaban en crear un canal de resonancia y a Marta no le gustaba ensuciarse las manos. Elain Boyle era la única que se mostraba dispuesta a aprender, pero no dejaba de intentar curar a pacientes muertos.

Las cuatro solían pensar que solo les bastaba con «sentir» lo que tenían que hacer para que todo saliese bien a la primera. Cuando Helena las corregía, en vez de preguntar, la miraban con la boca abierta, en actitud pasiva, a la espera de que ella acudiera corriendo en su ayuda para proporcionarles toda la información que necesitaban. En ningún momento se les ocurrió actuar con iniciativa o buscar respuestas por sí mismas. Se limitaron a acatar órdenes y aprender lo que se les dijera.

Regresó al Reducto sin haber sido capaz de dejar de pensar en ellas con cierto resentimiento. Ferron pareció darse cuenta de lo distraída que estaba, porque la agarró de la barbilla y le levantó la cabeza para encontrar su mirada.

Esperó con agitación a que invadiera su mente, pero lo único que notó fue su resonancia, tan insustancial como una tela de araña, titilando entre sus nervios. ¿Qué estaba…?

Entonces le apoyó la mano en la frente y Helena no tuvo tiempo de volver a concentrarse antes de que le abriera el cerebro en dos, así que hizo todo cuanto estuvo en su mano para mantener sus pensamientos alejados de las aprendizas y desviar su atención hacia las partes más repetitivas de su vida, aquellas que no tendrían ningún interés para Ferron. Hasta donde el chico sabía, Helena se pasaba los días haciendo inventarios, revisando informes médicos y lavándose las manos.

Cuando finalizó su escrutinio, Ferron la estudió con una expresión que no supo identificar y, en vez de alejarse, dio un paso hacia ella.

Al verlo, Helena se puso tensa, pero se obligó a mirarlo a la cara para que su contacto físico no la distrajera. El chico le rozó el mentón con los dedos desnudos y le levantó la cabeza para dejarle el cuello expuesto.

Helena volvió a sentir su resonancia.

¿La estaba poniendo a prueba para ver si podía sentirla?

—Recuérdame qué incluye tu repertorio —le pidió Ferron en un susurro.

—Es bastante completo —admitió, pues sabía que no le convenía mentir. Era posible que el Concejo de Gremios tuviera acceso a los registros de inmigración—. Por eso me aceptaron en la Academia. Aunque hay algunos compuestos poco comunes que no controlo, por lo general, mi resonancia es de amplio espectro.

Ferron, que todavía permanecía peligrosamente cerca de ella, ladeó la cabeza.

—¿Qué especialidad tenías pensado escoger?

—No llegué a decidirlo.

—Llevabas ya dos años con los estudios superiores. —La agarró de la barbilla—. ¿Cómo es que todavía no habías tomado una decisión?

—Luc quería que lo acompañara en sus viajes. Mi idea era pensármelo a la vuelta.

Ferron dejó caer la mano y su resonancia se desvaneció.

—Ya imagino. Debías de creerte muy especial siendo el perrito faldero de Holdfast —le espetó lanzándole una mirada de reojo antes de sacar un sobre y ofrecérselo con una sonrisilla burlona—. Y mírate ahora.

Helena notó que le molestaban un poco las cicatrices de la palma de la mano cuando aceptó el sobre, que iba dirigido a la misma destinataria que los anteriores.

—¿Quién es Aurelia Ingram?

—Nadie. —Meneó la cabeza en actitud despectiva. Luego, se rio—. Alguien con quien mi padre acordó casarme cuando yo tenía… nueve años. Pero el gremio sigue insistiendo en ello. Temen qué podría pasar si el fuego me consume antes de lo esperado.

—Pero eres… —Helena vaciló. Se le hacía raro usar la palabra en la que estaba pensando— inmortal.

—Hasta cierto punto, sí. —Puso los ojos en blanco—. Sin embargo, mi cuerpo sigue siendo mortal y por eso quieren que engendre un heredero. Mi prometida acaba de cumplir la mayoría de edad. Solo nos hemos visto una vez y no tengo intención de que se repita nuestro encuentro de nuevo. He intentado mandarle algunas cartas, pero, por algún motivo —sonrió burlón—, siempre acaban perdiéndose por el camino.

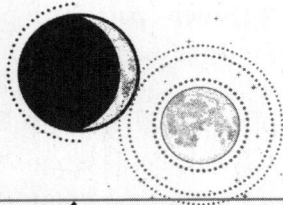

CAPÍTULO 28

Marzus 1786

POR MUCHO QUE LO DETESTARA, Helena tenía que admitir que el entrenamiento con Ferron estaba empezando a dar sus frutos, aunque tal vez no como él esperaba.

Con sus constantes incursiones mentales, había permitido que Helena descubriera una nueva manera de entender el paisaje de su cerebro. De hecho, la situación le recordaba al momento en que había descubierto que era una vivemante. Se había dado cuenta de que su resonancia tenía el potencial de alcanzar niveles totalmente desconocidos para ella hasta entonces.

Sentir la resonancia de Ferron en la cabeza le permitió comprender que manipular la energía que albergaba en su mente también estaba al alcance de sus posibilidades. Le habría gustado consultarle sus dudas, preguntarle si esa era una habilidad innata que había permanecido oculta en su interior o si se trataba de la «animancia» que había mencionado anteriormente, pero sabía que no podía hablar de ello con él. Para Ferron, Helena solo estaba aprendiendo a concentrarse. Nada más.

Sin embargo, había descubierto que podía reforzar su concentración recurriendo a la resonancia, dejando a un lado sus pensamientos y reconduciendo su mente en la dirección que más le conviniese. Al principio, Helena se había limitado a ejercitar aquella técnica durante sus encuentros, pero había acabado utilizándola todo el tiempo para dejar la mente en blanco en el Cuartel General y librarse de las emociones que la consumían por dentro.

Tras ponerla a prueba otra vez, Ferron se alejó de ella para mirar por una de las ventanas sucias del módulo. El Reducto estaba tan abarrotado de edificios que apenas se veía nada desde allí, pero se atisbaba una franja de cielo en dirección a las islas. Allí era donde Ferron tenía clavada la vista, en el cielo blanco, nublado y sucio.

—Siempre sale humo de vuestro Cuartel General —comentó cuando volvió a posar la atención en Helena—. Es del crematorio, ¿no es así?

Ella no respondió, pero había acertado. Siempre había algún cadáver que quemar.

—¿Cuántos soldados os quedan?

A la chica se le secó la boca. Aquella era una de las mayores preocupaciones de la Llama Eterna: temían que los inmarcesibles se dieran cuenta de lo debilitadas que estaban las filas de la Resistencia. Un empujón más y les darían el golpe de gracia.

Así que guardó silencio.

—¿Cuánto tiempo más crees que aguantaréis? —insistió Ferron, cuya silueta quedaba recortada por la pálida luz de la ventana.

Esa pregunta sí que podía responderla.

—Hasta que caiga el último soldado. No vamos a rendirnos.

—Está bien saberlo —susurró él mientras volvía a clavar la vista en el humo.

HACÍA MESES QUE EL HOSPITAL se encontraba en una situación crítica. Les quedaban pocas provisiones y todo lo que conseguían introducir de contrabando desde Novis parecía evaporarse casi al instante.

—Nos hemos quedado sin gasas y la resina de opio se acabó la semana pasada —le decía Pace a Helena en el cuarto de suministros, casi vacío—. El Consejo quiere emplear a más sanadoras para compensar la falta de materiales, pero no podemos fiarnos de ellas.

Incluso en tiempos de paz, la escasez de opiáceos era bastante frecuente. Las mareas duales limitaban el comercio marítimo con las regiones de Ortus durante la mayor parte del año. El único momento en que los viajes por mar eran viables era cuando Lumitia entraba en fase de latencia. Entonces la marea bajaba y las aguas que separaban los continentes se calmaban un poco. El resto del tiempo, las caravanas de suministros rodeaban el mar en un viaje que solía durar casi medio año, por lo que los precios se disparaban.

La Llama Eterna necesitaba muchos más productos aparte de opio:

comida, medicinas, ropa y vendas. Había escasez de prácticamente cualquier suministro que no estuviera hecho de metal o de algún material transmutable. Si la Resistencia no conseguía hacerse con el control de la zona portuaria antes de la llegada de los barcos mercantes en verano, el hambre los obligaría a rendirse cuando llegara el invierno.

—Todavía queda tiempo para que las inundaciones supongan un obstáculo —dijo Helena—. Puedo salir en busca de musgo con el que suplir al menos la falta de gasas. Además, en esta época los sauces están más crecidos.

Pace caminó de un lado para otro sin dejar de mirar las estanterías vacías.

—Algo es algo, supongo.

Sin gasas y vendas limpias y estériles, las heridas de los combatientes se infectarían y su recuperación sería mucho más lenta, lo que aumentaría el riesgo de enfermedades e infecciones contagiosas. Aunque ahora que contaban con cinco sanadoras había manos de sobra para manejar el dolor de los pacientes, la falta de recursos les impediría atender las dolencias más serias.

Cuando Helena se disponía a partir hacia el humedal a primera hora de la mañana, vio a Luc y a Lila entrenando en los jardines, armados hasta los dientes. Ni siquiera se había enterado de que habían vuelto.

Había dormido en un catre en el despacho de Pace, puesto que los pacientes solían pasarlo peor durante la noche.

Se detuvo un momento a observarlos.

Luc prefería luchar siguiendo el estilo tradicional de los Holdfast, que consistía en utilizar una enorme espada envuelta en llamas que dividía a su antojo por medio de la transmutación en un par de hojas más pequeñas. La alquimia ígnea se le daba de maravilla. En aquel momento, unas llamas blancas y brillantes como el sol lo rodeaban como si fueran un par de alas y hacían que sus ojos azules resplandecieran como zafiros. La extrema delgadez de sus facciones le daba un cierto aire más etéreo.

No le sorprendía que su poder se considerara divino.

Aunque Helena sabía que no lo era. De hecho, seguro que ella entendía cómo funcionaba casi mejor que él mismo. Si bien Luc tenía un talento natural para la piromancia, carecía de la paciencia y el interés necesarios para estudiar la ciencia en la que esta se cimentaba. Cuando todavía estudiaban, solía confiar en Helena para que le ayudara a entender las partes teóricas de los trabajos.

La piromancia era mucho más compleja que la transmutación de los metales. En combate, los piromantes tenían que ser capaces de improvisar sin vacilar ni cometer errores. Además, debían realizar una infinidad de cálculos que se basaban en todo tipo de variables, como el viento, las dimensiones de los espacios cerrados, la distancia a la que se encontrara el objetivo o los niveles de oxígeno.

Helena siguió los movimientos de los dedos de Luc y calculó mentalmente qué técnicas o sellos estaba usando para canalizar su poder. Era tan rápido que apenas lograba seguirle el ritmo.

Dado que los proyectiles básicos no servían de nada contra los necrómatas o los inmarcesibles, casi siempre se enfrentaban a ellos con fuego o en combate a corta distancia.

—¡Hel! —La voz de Luc perturbó la tranquilidad del alba cuando se detuvo en seco y la saludó con la mano.

Sonreía de oreja a oreja mientras veía que la chica se acercaba. Iba vestido de blanco de pies a cabeza, ya que se había cubierto la ropa con la protección de amianto que solía llevar bajo la armadura para no quemársela. Tenía el rostro empapado de sudor.

—¿Qué tal lo he hecho? —Helena frunció los labios y él se rio—. Sé sincera.

—Abusas del oxígeno —le explicó con el ceño fruncido—. Es una manía que te podría dar problemas en espacios cerrados.

Luc se rascó la frente.

—Lo sé. Estoy intentando afinar mi alcance, pero no consigo mantener las llamas estables sin perder el control del aire que consumen.

Helena se mordisqueó el interior del labio.

—¿Qué fórmula estás utilizando?

—No sé —admitió él con una mueca avergonzada—. Hace tiempo que no dibujo un sello. Lo trazo en mi cabeza rápidamente, lo improviso, ya sabes...

—Si lo dibujaras en un papel, seguro que darías enseguida con el problema —le dijo ella dedicándole una mirada cargada de significado.

Un brillo astuto le surcó la mirada a Luc.

—Te haré caso si me prometes echarle un vistazo. Estábamos a punto de tomarnos un descanso y he oído que te han asignado cuatro aprendizas, así que ya no te quedan excusas. La última vez que nos vimos me prometiste que a la próxima sacarías un rato para charlar. Como intentes escaquearte de nuevo, te juro que le prendo fuego a algo.

Helena exhaló.

—La verdad es que iba de camino a…

El cielo se encendió sobre sus cabezas con un rugido ensordecedor que ahogó sus palabras.

—Perdona, ¿qué decías? —preguntó Luc.

—Deberías venir, Hel —le dijo Lila, que se limpiaba la cara con una toalla—. Luc lleva un tiempo insistiéndonos con algo que ha estado probando, pero ninguno entendemos de lo que habla.

A Helena se le aceleró el corazón y se atrevió a sonreír.

—Entonces, supongo que tendré que echaros una mano.

—Supones bien —refunfuñó Luc, que le rodeó los hombros con un brazo y tiró de ella para que los acompañara—. Deberías estar entusiasmada. Yo lo estoy.

Helena rio.

No sabía qué lo había puesto de tan buen humor, pero se alegraba de verlo tan contento. Lidiar con Kaine Ferron era un precio que estaba más que dispuesta a pagar a cambio de disfrutar de momentos como ese.

—Marino.

La voz de Crowther se enterró en su espalda como un cuchillo y la hizo detenerse en seco con un escalofrío.

El hombre se había materializado de la nada detrás de ellos en medio del pasillo.

—Tengo que hablar contigo sobre el inventario que entregaste anoche —le pidió señalando en la dirección opuesta a la que caminaban.

—Estoy seguro de que puede esperar, Jan —se adelantó a decir Luc con una frialdad nada propia de él—. Necesito que Hel me ayude un momento.

—Lo siento, principado, pero me temo que es un asunto de cierta urgencia —apuntó Crowther con tono tranquilo, aunque taladrando a Helena con la mirada.

Ella se dispuso a decir algo, pero Luc le dio un apretón en el hombro y le mostró los dientes en una amplia sonrisa.

—Pues yo también lo siento, pero la necesito.

—¿Estáis herido? —preguntó Crowther arqueando las cejas.

—No. —Luc se había puesto rígido—. Necesito que me ayude con mi piromancia.

Crowther se puso en guardia, como un gato sacando las uñas, pero inclinó la cabeza en señal de respeto.

—En ese caso, será un honor para mí ofreceros mis servicios. Vuestra familia se encargó de entrenarme personalmente.

—Lo tendré en cuenta, no lo dudes —dijo Luc en un fingido tono cortés.

—Lo que sea por el principado —dijo Crowther agachando la cabeza—. Sin embargo, me temo que he de insistir en que Marino venga conmigo. Puede que el asunto del inventario os resulte trivial, pero es de suma importancia que el hospital permanezca abastecido como es debido. Se podría considerar un tema de vida o muerte para nuestros soldados.

Miró a Lila y, luego, desvió su atención hacia Soren, Alister y los demás, como si le estuviera dando a entender a Luc que, al quedarse con Helena, estaba poniendo su compañía por encima de la integridad de sus compañeros.

Luc guardó silencio. Helena notaba su creciente desagrado como una presión cada vez más intensa en el aire.

Un enfrentamiento comprometería en gran medida la situación de la Resistencia. El trabajo de espionaje que Ferron estaba llevando a cabo caería en saco roto si Luc desestimaba la información que Crowther le procurara solo porque le causaba rechazo.

—Tiene razón, Luc, debería irme. Lo siento —intervino Helena, que se apartó de él y, echándole un último vistazo, añadió—: Hablamos la próxima vez.

Lila la miraba confundida, pero no dijo nada. Como paladina, no le correspondía intervenir en un momento como ese. Soren parecía resignado, aunque no sorprendido, y, cuando Lila reparó en la actitud de su hermano, le lanzó una mirada inquisitiva.

—Está bien. —Luc se obligó a sonreír—. Te tomo la palabra.

EN CUANTO SE MARCHARON Y dejaron a Helena a solas con Crowther, la expresión afable del hombre desapareció de golpe.

—Te recuerdo que, como defensora confesa de la nigromancia, el Consejo tiene la potestad de expulsarte de la Resistencia si no cooperas. No sé qué privilegios te habrá concedido Ilva en el pasado, pero considéralos anulados hasta que obtengas resultados en tu misión y valoremos si merece la pena el esfuerzo de rehabilitarte.

Las palabras de Crowther seguían resonándole en los oídos cuando partió hacia el humedal. Una espesa capa de niebla cubría la superficie del río y arrastraba consigo un frío que calaba hasta los huesos, pero, por suerte, no olía a sangre o a miasma y tampoco se le llenaron los pulmones de humo. Incluso antes de que estallara la guerra, nunca se había sentido como si estuviera verdaderamente al aire libre al salir de los límites de la ciudad.

El nivel del agua había crecido tanto que no se podía cruzar el humedal en línea recta, así que se vio obligada a avanzar campo a través por la orilla para llegar hasta la arboleda de sauces que crecía justo bajo la presa.

La mejor época para recolectar corteza de sauce era antes de que empezara a empaparse de savia. Aunque su eficacia era mínima en comparación con la del láudano, la corteza tenía propiedades analgésicas y ayudaba a reducir la inflamación y la fiebre. Además, era un buen desinfectante para las heridas y en el hospital estaban a punto de quedarse sin antisépticos.

Recolectó la corteza de manera mecánica, fría, sin preocuparse por dejar a los árboles con las ramas desnudas.

No tenía la menor idea de qué esperaba Crowther de ella y tampoco sabía cómo avanzar con Ferron. En un principio había esperado que la misión, aunque fuese desagradable, resultara sencilla y directa, pero el chico no le daba ningún margen para actuar.

Abrió un grueso brote de sauce por la mitad con la punta del cuchillo y, después, retiró la corteza con un rápido movimiento del brazo y dejó al descubierto la madera blanca.

El sonido de una de las compuertas de la presa al abrirse estuvo a punto de quedar ahogado por el rumor del agua, pero una de sus bisagras chirrió y asustó a las aves que correteaban por la hierba.

Helena se tiró al suelo instintivamente y escudriñó la superficie del agua mientras el barro frío le empapaba la ropa. La niebla empezaba a disiparse, por lo que ya alcanzaba a ver el extremo norte de la isla Oeste al otro lado del humedal inundado y los canales del río. Aunque no creía correr peligro, sabía que no debía arriesgarse a que la vieran.

Las compuertas estaban conectadas a un intrincado sistema de túneles que conducía a los cavernosos tanques de inundación construidos bajo la isla. De la boca de la compuerta abierta, salieron un puñado de necrómatas arrastrando con cadenas una caja grande, seguidos de un grupo de personas ataviadas con uniformes negros y de color gris oscuro.

Un hombre agitó una mano y, cuando los necrómatas sacaron al unísono unos largos pernos de la parte superior de la caja, uno de sus laterales cayó al suelo.

Helena contempló con una mezcla de horror y fascinación que una criatura salía reptando del interior.

Era más grande que un perro, rosada como un cerdo, pero su forma no era normal. Tenía las patas similares a las de un gato y un cuerpo largo y plano, aunque lo peor de todo era su cabeza: reptiliana, plana, con un hocico tan largo que la criatura no paraba de tropezarse con él. Por si fuera poco, un par de colmillos sobresalían tanto de su mandíbula superior como de la inferior.

Helena se quedó helada. Pese a que sospechaba de lo que se trataba, no se lo podía creer. Las quimeras, al igual que los homúnculos, no eran más que uno de los mitos alquímicos precientíficos de Cetus, si bien no había forma de negar lo que estaba viendo con sus propios ojos.

Con un gesto de la mano, uno de los hombres vestidos de negro hizo que un necrómata se pusiera en medio del camino de la criatura.

La criatura se movió a una velocidad pasmosa y el necrómata quedó atrapado bajo su cuerpo mutado mientras, con un destello de colmillos, esta le arrancaba a tiras la piel grisácea de las extremidades. El no-muerto siguió intentando ponerse de pie hasta que la quimera lo decapitó de un mordisco con sus enormes mandíbulas.

En cuanto Helena cerró las correas de su bolsa con dedos temblorosos, comenzó a alejarse despacio, arrastrándose para permanecer oculta entre la hierba.

Los hombres de la otra orilla se quedaron charlando mientras el monstruo devoraba al necrómata, pero no tardaron en darse la vuelta y regresar por el túnel de la compuerta, dejando atrás a la criatura como un centinela pálido y monstruoso.

Vio que la criatura caminaba junto a la orilla dando pasitos cortos y desproporcionados. Le costaba caminar y se mantenía alejada del agua.

Helena retomó la huida sin detenerse a comprobar si la quimera sabía nadar. El frío le había teñido las manos de un tono gris violáceo, así que se las frotó rápidamente, intentando recurrir con torpeza a la resonancia para recuperar la sensibilidad en los dedos.

Justo cuando cruzaba el puente y estaba a punto de llegar al puesto de control del portón, un calor abrasador le envolvió la mano. Fue tan intenso que tuvo que reprimir un grito, pero la sensación desapareció tan pronto como había llegado.

Bajó la vista al darse cuenta de lo que acababa de pasar. Tenía la piel del anular izquierdo enrojecida y, cuando ladeó la mano, alcanzó a captar un atisbo del anillo.

La quemazón regresó.

Estuvo a punto de arrancarse la joya. Con las manos heladas, el calor era insoportable.

Maldito desgraciado. El único motivo que justificaría calentar tanto el anillo sería que Ferron pensara que sufría alguna alteración nerviosa.

Seguro que la había llamado para contarle lo de la quimera y ella ahora tendría que perder el tiempo yendo al Reducto para eso. Helena estaba helada, llevaba la bolsa cargada y habría dado lo que fuera por regresar al Cuartel General.

Pero Ferron no tenía forma de saber que ella ya estaba al tanto de todo, así que se dio la vuelta a regañadientes y partió en su busca.

***

AL FINAL, LLEGÓ AL REDUCTO antes que Ferron. Sabía que lo haría, pero aun así era irritante tener tanto frío y verse obligada a esperar. Apenas pudo abrir la puerta con los dedos entumecidos.

Una vez dentro del módulo, se quitó la capa y la chaqueta para retorcer las mangas e intentar sacarle toda el agua que pudiera. Luego, hizo lo mismo con la tela sobrante de las mangas de la camisa. Tenía las botas tan empapadas que un chapoteo acompañaba cada uno de sus pasos, y casi no notaba los dedos de los pies.

Cuando Ferron por fin entró en la estancia, lo primero que hizo fue evaluar su aspecto con suspicacia.

—¿Qué haces? —le preguntó siguiendo con la mirada el reguero de agua sucia que caía de la tela que Helena estaba retorciendo.

—Me he mojado.

Un destello de irritación le surcó las facciones, pero a Helena no le importaba nada lo que pensara de ella. Sacudió la chaqueta una última vez.

—Bueno, vayamos al tema de las quimeras. ¿Sabes si hay más de una?

Cuando no obtuvo respuesta, levantó la vista. Ferron la miraba confuso.

—¿Ya lo sabías? —Sonaba claramente molesto.

—He visto una —explicó ella con un asentimiento.

Una emoción imposible de describir se adueñó de su rostro.

—¿Cómo que has visto una? ¿Dónde?

—Estaba en el humedal cuando la soltaron.

—¿Y qué hacías en la ciénaga?

Helena odiaba que llamaran al humedal de esa manera.

—Voy allí a buscar suministros médicos. Hay mucho que recolectar... —vaciló—. El humedal nos ha sacado de un apuro en más de una ocasión. ¿Solo hay una quimera?

Ferron se negó a cambiar de tema.

—¿Eso es algo que haces a menudo?

—Depende de la temporada. Cuando el humedal se inunda no hay mucho que recolectar, pero... —Helena se interrumpió al reparar en la expresión atónita del chico. Suspiró con impaciencia—. Ya te he dicho que voy todos los saturnis y los martis. Hoy he tenido que salir a buscar más suministros.

—No... —dijo Ferron despacio, con un filo peligroso en la voz. Aunque seguía teniendo una postura despreocupada, su tono lo delataba—. Has dicho que sales a buscar suministros. Pensaba que te referías a que te citabas con algún contrabandista en la ciudad.

—¿Por qué iban a enviarme a reunirme con un contrabandista? Voy al humedal a recolectar plantas medicinales, para que los medicamentos nos duren más tiempo.

Ferron sacudió la mano en su dirección.

—¿Y vas sola?

—Claro, por eso puedo venir aquí cuando termino. ¿Cómo es que no te has dado cuenta hasta ahora? Te pasas el rato revisando mis recuerdos.

—Tu mente es mucho menos interesante de lo que imaginas. ¿Por qué iba a molestarme en prestar atención a los asuntos a los que te dedicas antes de reunirte conmigo?

Estaba tan ciego que casi resultaba cómico.

—Dile a Crowther que te busque una excusa para no salir de la ciudad —le dijo por fin—. Tienes que ir y venir sin hacer ninguna parada. No pienso permitir que me descubran solo porque tú te dedicas a arrastrarte por el humedal para recoger malas hierbas.

Helena se incorporó, indignada.

—No... No puedes hacer eso.

La expresión del chico se endureció antes de que por fin cruzara la habitación para plantarse frente a ella.

—En realidad, sí que puedo. Te recuerdo que ahora eres mía.

—Sí —replicó ella, que se negaba a amedrentarse. Ya estaba harta de ceder ante la voluntad de otros—. Pero también me diste tu palabra de que no interferirías con el resto de mis responsabilidades con la Llama Eterna. Salir a recolectar forma parte de mi trabajo. Y llevo años haciéndolo. Si quieres controlar lo que hago, tendrás que esperar a que ganemos la guerra.

Ferron se la quedó mirando con mala cara durante unos instantes y Helena temió que la ignorara y hablara con Crowther directamente para obligar a la Llama Eterna a ofrecerle una alternativa.

Crowther se encargaría de solucionarlo. Estaba segura de ello. Haría lo que fuera necesario por tener a Ferron contento.

Helena notaba el corazón latiéndole con fiereza en el pecho y rezó para que el chico no se diera cuenta de que solo estaba fingiendo.

—Está bien —dijo dando un paso hacia atrás. Su mirada era fría como el acero—. Entonces, dime qué haces para protegerte cuando sales de la ciudad. ¿Qué armas te permiten llevar? Quiero comprobar si te servirán para defenderte de las quimeras.

Extendió una mano enguantada y Helena se la quedó mirando. Pese a que todavía no sentía las manos, notó un calorcillo subiéndole por la nuca y un nudo en la garganta.

Tragó saliva.

—Es que no… no funciona así —concluyó en un incómodo intento por esquivar su pregunta.

—¿Así cómo?

—No tengo un… arma reglamentaria. Me retiraron del combate antes de estar cualificada para portar armas. Las personas que solo trabajamos en el Cuartel General no… —Se señaló la ropa—. Yo salgo a recolectar sin armas.

Ferron enarcó las cejas, sorprendido.

—¿Te mueves por la ciudad y sales a la ciénaga sola y desarmada?

Helena se estremeció; sonaba mucho peor de lo que era en realidad. No podía decirle que era una vivemante o que sus incursiones no contaban con la aprobación oficial del Consejo.

Pace estaba al tanto, al igual que Crowther, pero Matias, su verdadero superior, no sabía nada. Helena no había querido darle razones para que le prohibiera preparar medicinas.

—Si saliese con un arma, correría un mayor riesgo en caso de que me capturaran —dijo intentando que su situación sonara más razonable.

—¿Me lo estás diciendo en serio? —preguntó estupefacto.

—Siempre puedo valerme del cuchillo que uso para recolectar.

Ferron parpadeó despacio.

—¿Y qué se supone que vas a hacer con eso?

—En la Academia nos enseñaron nociones básicas de combate —dijo con la cabeza bien alta—. Todavía me acuerdo de lo esencial y se trata de técnicas que funcionan tanto con el apoyo de la transmutación como sin él.

El chico la estudió de arriba abajo.

—¿Y cuándo fue la última vez que practicaste?

—No lo sé —admitió ella evitando su mirada—. La verdad es que no es algo a lo que le preste especial atención. —Se guardó el cuchillo de nuevo en la bolsa, aunque no soltó el mango, tan desgastado que ya no quedaba nada del barniz que protegía la madera suave—. Bastante ocupada estoy ya como para preocuparme por asuntos como ese.

—Bueno, pues ya sabes a qué nos dedicaremos en nuestra próxima cita —dijo Ferron con un suspiro—. Pensaba que nada me pondría más en peligro que tu mente, pero resulta que tú misma sigues siendo un punto débil. Si algo te ocurriese, no voy a molestarme en entrenar a un nuevo contacto después de todo el tiempo que he perdido contigo.

—No será necesario que me entrenes —exhaló ella—. Nunca me he metido en problemas.

Ferron enarcó una ceja.

—¿Te crees que se van a limitar a soltar una sola quimera? Bennet lleva años trabajando en este proyecto. Ahora que ha conseguido dar con la clave para crearlas, se asegurará de repartirlas por toda la ciénaga y los distritos inferiores. La que has visto no es más que uno de los primeros prototipos.

—Entonces, dinos cómo matarlas —replicó ella—. No vamos a dejar de buscar comida y medicamentos solo porque seáis unos psicópatas y hayáis decidido llenar toda la ciudad de monstruos.

Tenía tantas cosas de las que encargarse que no le apetecía tener que añadir el entrenamiento de combate a su lista de tareas.

—Obviamente, ya lo estoy investigando —dijo apretando los dientes—. Por eso te he llamado, para que estéis alerta. Si vas a salir del Cuartel General, tienes que saber defenderte.

Helena resopló exasperada y se giró hacia la puerta.

—Pues entonces practicaré allí.

—¿No quieres que te entrene yo? —preguntó cuando la chica ya se disponía a salir. La voz de Ferron se había vuelto peligrosa—. ¿Por qué? Teniendo en cuenta todo lo que te podría exigir mientras estamos aquí, pensé que preferirías dedicar el tiempo a entrenar.

Helena se detuvo en seco y echó la vista atrás. Ferron la estaba arrinconando.

Aunque no sabía que era una vivemante, debía de haberse dado cuenta de que el propósito de Helena era seducirlo. Maldición.

—Está bien. Pues entréname —escupió.

Ya tenía asumido que el entrenamiento físico que acabara escogiendo para ella seguramente sería mucho peor que el ejercicio mental al que la había estado sometiendo. Desde luego, en un contexto como aquel, hacer que cayera rendido a sus pies iba a resultar bastante complicado.

Lo único que conseguiría sería alimentar sus tendencias violentas.

Notaba un dolor sordo en la cabeza. Luc estaba cada vez más lejos de su alcance. Su vida empezaba a sumirse en las tinieblas.

—Cambia esa cara de decepción. —El tono burlón de Ferron la devolvió a la realidad. Le brillaban los ojos—. Ni que te hubiera pedido que nos acostemos. ¿Acaso preferías eso?

Un lánguido torrente de rabia se fue adueñando de ella.

—¿Eres de los que se dedica a comprar compañía?

No era más que una suposición, pero Ferron parecía de esa clase de tipos. Las familias de los gremios, con la costumbre de celebrar matrimonios concertados por su resonancia, tenían fama de meterse en camas ajenas. Las uniones entre los gremios eran un negocio igual que las casas de seda en el distrito del placer de la isla Oeste.

Otro destello iluminó la mirada de Ferron.

—He de admitir que disfruto de la profesionalidad de esos encuentros —dijo encogiéndose de hombros—. Los límites bien definidos, la ausencia total de expectativas. Y lo mejor es que no tengo que fingir que siento nada por la otra persona.

Retorció la boca con desdén ante esa última frase, como si tener sentimientos fuera el concepto más ofensivo que pudiera imaginar.

—¡Vaya! No me sorprende viniendo de ti.

—No podía ser de otro modo —coincidió con una sonrisa tensa.

A Helena le habría gustado darle donde más le doliera.

Ferron le hacía daño a ella constantemente, sin siquiera proponérselo, y eso que apenas la conocía. Le bastó con incluir su nombre entre las condiciones que le había presentado a la Llama Eterna y con tratarla como si no fuese más que un objeto de su propiedad. Convertirse en un capricho para él era igual que llevar una cadena de hierro al cuello.

—¿Y también hablas con las trabajadoras? ¿Les cuentas lo trágica que ha sido tu vida? ¿O te limitas a entrar y salir de su cama lo más rápido posible? —le preguntó con un tono burlón y divertido.

Los ojos de Ferron refulgieron.

—¿Quieres que te lo demuestre? —Su voz sonaba tan gélida y afilada como una esquirla de hielo.

—No te atreverás —replicó ella encontrando su mirada en actitud desafiante.

El rostro del chico se endureció. Sabía que conseguiría provocarlo si seguía así.

Por fin se lo quitaría de en medio. Crowther e Ilva no la analizarían en cada reunión preguntándose si Ferron la habría forzado ya. Ella misma dejaría de pasar las noches en vela muerta de miedo, preguntándose cuándo ocurriría. Estaba harta de esperar, de darle vueltas al asunto. Era como si tuviera una espada a punto de caerle sobre el cuello.

Siguió hablando:

—Hacerlo con alguien a quien conoces sería demasiado real, ¿no? Yo creo que por eso no me has forzado todavía. Te da miedo que sobrepase esos límites tan bien definidos de los que hablas, así que estás usando lo del entrenamiento como excusa.

Se le crispó un músculo de la mandíbula.

—¿Intentas ponerme a prueba, Marino? —Su tono era gélido como el silbido de un cuchillo.

—Me has pillado —admitió sin pestañear.

Premio. Lo había conseguido.

Ferron la obligó a retroceder por aquella estancia sucia y fría, y, para sorpresa de la chica, el corazón se le ralentizó en vez de acelerársele. Cada pesado latido le retumbaba en el pecho con parsimonia cuando Ferron bajó la cabeza para que su mirada quedara a la misma altura que la de ella.

—Desnúdate.

No dijo nada más.

Helena no se veía capaz de moverse.

Sabía que debía hacer lo que él le pidiera. Ese había sido el trato. Pero, aunque quería pasar cuanto antes por esa situación tan incómoda, su cuerpo se negaba a obedecer.

Estaba paralizada. En aquel módulo con el suelo de baldosas rotas no había más que una mesa de madera. La actitud y la expresión de Ferron dejaban claro, sin ninguna duda, que estaba a punto de hacerle algo terriblemente cruel.

—Ahora lo entiendo. —Esbozó una sonrisa lobuna en la que mostró todos sus dientes—. La espera, no saber cuándo sucederá… Eso te está incomodando más que el tener que follar conmigo. Bueno, pues deseo concedido, Marino. Quítate la ropa.

Helena consiguió tragar saliva a duras penas. Un pitido le estalló en los oídos y fue ganando intensidad hasta que ahogó incluso sus propios pensamientos.

Ferron ni siquiera estaba excitado, eso era evidente. Iba a forzarla para darle una lección.

Crowther se equivocaba. Estaba tan desesperado por encontrar el punto débil del chico que se había convencido a sí mismo de que en su interior había germinado algún tipo de obsesión, pero no era así. Ferron simplemente había identificado lo que Crowther quería creer sobre él.

La misión no llegaría a ningún lado.

A Helena empezó a temblarle la mandíbula sin control.

—Ni siquiera te atraigo. ¿Por qué me pediste a mí?

Ferron se rio.

—Tienes razón, no me atraes, pero nunca me cansaré de ser tu dueño. Eres mía hasta que exhales tu «último aliento». Eso sí que es una promesa y lo demás son tonterías. Me pregunto de cuántas maneras podría hacer que te arrepientas. —Volvió a mostrarle los dientes—. Quítate la ropa, Marino. Ha llegado la hora de que me muestres qué es lo que he ganado con este trato.

La chica se llevó las manos al primer botón de la camisa con dedos temblorosos.

—Es el poder lo que te excita, ¿no es así? —Se le entrecortó la voz de rabia cuando pasó al siguiente botón—. La única forma en que eres capaz de sentir algo es haciendo daño a los demás. Sospecho que ya ni siquiera eso te basta. Por eso te has visto obligado a innovar: hacer que tus víctimas se sientan responsables de su dolor. Les haces creer que se lo han buscado solas, que al prometerte algo han accedido a ello. Eso es lo único que te hace sentir vivo. Te aprovechas de aquello que les importa para manipularlas y esclavizarlas sin ensuciarte las manos ejerciendo un daño físico. —Resopló sin disimulo—. Te crees mejor que el resto por ser inmortal, pero hace tiempo que estás muerto por dentro.

Dijo todo aquello a pesar de que sabía que Ferron disfrutaría viéndola intentar hacerse la valiente, pero necesitaba desahogarse, aunque solamente fuera una vez. Sin embargo, el chico no se rio, sino que la expresión maliciosa que se había adueñado de sus facciones desapareció de inmediato.

Se quedó mirándola, inmóvil, mientras palidecía cada vez más.

Entonces algo metálico emitió un quejido en las paredes del módulo y el aire se estremeció. Helena notaba la resonancia de Ferron en la estancia, como una corriente de energía descontrolada que lo distorsionaba todo. Aquel era uno de los muchos motivos por los que los alquimistas eran peligrosos. Cuando perdían el control, su poder corría el riesgo de expandirse más allá de su cuerpo. Era una técnica de combate que, sin la estabilidad o el control necesarios, podía llegar a destruir cualquiera de los materiales incluidos en el repertorio del alquimista.

Dado que Ferron era un vivemante, Helena entraba dentro de ese repertorio. Ya notaba su resonancia en los huesos.

Le vibraba la piel y un tamborileo le sacudió el corazón.

El rostro de Ferron se retorció en una mueca de pura rabia.

—¡Lárgate!

Helena no se movió por miedo a que la desintegrara de repente.

El chico le dio la espalda con un fuerte gruñido y la puerta se retorció como si estuviera viva, deformándose, doblándose sobre sí misma y partiéndose entre los estruendosos sonidos del metal y los mecanismos al romperse.

—¡Lárgate ahora mismo!

No tuvo que insistir más. Helena salió huyendo. Esquivó de un salto la puerta destrozada y bajó por la escalera tan deprisa que se estrelló contra la pared del rellano, pero enseguida volvió a incorporarse y no se detuvo hasta dejar atrás el Reducto.

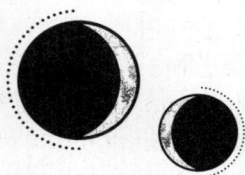

CAPÍTULO 29

Marzus 1786

CUANDO LA CONDUJERON AL DESPACHO de Ilva para que la informara acerca de lo que había visto en el humedal, Helena todavía respiraba con dificultad y notaba un dolor punzante en el costado.

La mujer permaneció tras su escritorio con una pluma en la mano mientras la chica le contaba todo entre jadeos.

—Yo pensaba que las quimeras eran un proyecto transmutacional imposible de conseguir —comentó con tranquilidad cuando Helena terminó de hablar.

—Eso es lo que enseñaban en la Academia —coincidió ella.

—¿Y dices que Ferron asegura que habrá más?

La expresión de Ilva era inescrutable. Helena reprimió un estremecimiento al oír el nombre del chico y asintió.

—Según él, la que yo he visto solo es la primera de muchas.

Un quedo sonido reflexivo escapó de entre los labios de Ilva y sus ojos pálidos vagaban sin rumbo fijo.

Mientras Luc estaba en el frente, le había cedido sus responsabilidades como principado a Ilva sin ser consciente de lo implacables que podían ser sus decisiones con tal de proteger a su sobrino.

A Helena le gustaba en ese aspecto. Cuando Ilva había mostrado interés en ella por primera vez, se había sentido halagada al pensar que las dos luchaban por una misma causa, puesto que ambas habrían estado dispuestas a tomar todo tipo de decisiones difíciles por el bien de Luc.

Siempre había pensado que eran compañeras.

—¿Cómo avanza la situación con Ferron? —le preguntó Ilva cuando se disponía a marcharse.

Helena se detuvo, volvió a hundirse en la silla y se clavó las uñas en las cicatrices de la palma de la mano.

—Es un joven… imprevisible.

Ilva dejó escapar un pequeño sonido reflexivo. La expresión tensa que había dominado su rostro cuando Crowther y ella le habían presentado su propuesta había desaparecido. Ahora Ilva parecía estar conforme con la decisión.

—Con un poco de suerte, la ayuda de las nuevas sanadoras te permitirá centrarte más en la misión que se te ha encomendado.

A Helena se le formó un nudo en la garganta. Apretó tanto los puños al oírle insinuar que habían reclutado a aquellas sanadoras para ayudarla que se le pusieron los nudillos blancos.

—Estoy segura de que nos serán de gran ayuda —coincidió fingiendo una sonrisa—. Aunque… el esfuerzo de formarlas se lleva una buena parte de nuestro tiempo.

La tensión marcó las finas arrugas de expresión que rodeaban los ojos de la mujer.

—Ya te habrás enterado del problema de desabastecimiento al que nos estamos enfrentando en el hospital —continuó—. Por lo general, cuando tengo algún rato libre, intento suplir algunas de las carencias con…

—Ah, sí. Pace lo ha mencionado alguna vez… —dijo Ilva con calma—. Tu padre tenía una… pequeña botica en uno de los distritos inferiores, ¿no?

Helena asintió, sorprendida. Como su padre no había conseguido que le homologaran la licencia médica en Paladia, la botica que había regentado no había sido estrictamente legal. La medicina, como todo allí antes de la guerra, se había industrializado, modernizado y sometido a estrictas autorizaciones. Esto ayudaba a frenar la proliferación de estafadores, pero tendía a disparar los precios. Y el problema era que cualquier suma de dinero considerada insignificante en los distritos superiores equivalía a un mes o un año de sueldo en los suburbios sumergidos.

Una tintura no autorizada tal vez no fuera ni la mitad de efectiva que aquellas que sí lo estaban, pero, para los enfermos y las familias, era un riesgo que estaban dispuestos a correr con tal de no endeudarse y acabar en prisión.

—Era médico, ¿verdad? —preguntó Ilva, cuya curiosidad sonaba sincera.

—Sí, estudió cirugía manual y medicina en Khem. Mi madre y él regentaban juntos una consulta y una botica en el pueblo donde nací.

Ilva ladeó la cabeza.

—¿Por eso decidiste centrar tus estudios en la química? Yo formaba parte de la comisión que aprobaba tu beca cada año. Era algo que nos causaba mucha curiosidad cuando revisábamos tu expediente. Con un repertorio como el tuyo, resultaba de lo más extraño. ¿Lo hacías para poder ayudarlo durante el verano?

Helena se quedó callada. Trabajar siendo menor de edad como quimiatra sin licencia en una botica ilegal no era algo que entrara dentro del código de conducta de los estudiantes de la Academia.

—Lo pasado pasado está, Marino —le dijo Ilva agitando una mano para quitarle hierro al asunto—. No vamos a deportarte por haber cometido una infracción laboral hace seis años. La verdad es que contar con tus habilidades es una muestra de la divina providencia de Sol.

La chica se miró las manos; notaba un sabor amargo en la boca.

—Gracias. —Tragó saliva—. Con el desabastecimiento, intento ayudar todo lo que puedo. He estado extrayendo salicina de la corteza de sauce, que podrá servirnos como recurso provisional hasta que lleguen más medicamentos desde Novis —explicó con voz entrecortada—. La cuestión es que esta es la mejor época para la recolección. En un par de semanas, con el deshielo y con Lumitia en fase de sublimación, el humedal se inundará, así que tengo que procesar la mayor cantidad de corteza posible. Pero, si... el resto de mis deberes me obligan a interrumpir el proceso, toda la remesa podría echarse a perder. Sería un derroche de suministros. Por eso me preguntaba si habría alguien con los conocimientos necesarios que estuviera dispuesto a ayudarme y tomar el relevo si yo tengo que ausentarme. También podría prepararle los materiales necesarios para que se encargara de todo el proceso.

Ilva ladeó la cabeza en un gesto casi mecánico mientras su expresión se tensaba y una sonrisa reticente se dibujaba en sus labios.

—Helena...

—Es nuestra única opción ahora mismo. Dejar pasar la oportunidad sería todo un desperdicio de recursos —añadió apresuradamente.

Ilva hizo una pausa para medir sus palabras.

—Hace unas semanas, esta conversación habría sido muy distinta, pero ahora mismo no puedo permitirme pedirle a nadie que haga semejante esfuerzo. Todos nuestros quimiatras tienen una buena cantidad de tareas con las que lidiar y sospecho que el falcón Matias no sabe nada acerca del reaprovisionamiento que has estado llevando a cabo. Tendríamos que informarle de esto si te asignamos a alguien de manera oficial.

—Lo entiendo.

—Pensándolo bien… —Ilva se cernió sobre el escritorio—. Retiro lo dicho. Acabo de caer en que tal vez haya alguien interesado: Shiseo. Me encontré con él el otro día.

Helena levantó la mirada con expresión confundida.

—¿Quién?

—Ah, es un hombre de Oriente. Del Lejano Oriente, para ser más exactos, del Imperio. Vino a Paladia buscando asilo político después de que el nuevo emperador tomara el poder. —Ilva se dio un toquecito en la barbilla—. Creo que es una especie de metalúrgico. Apollo estaba encantado de tenerlo entre nosotros, porque adoraba aprender sobre el uso de la alquimia en otros países y decía que a Luc le vendría bien descubrir nuevos puntos de vista. Todavía sigue aquí. En mi opinión, es un hombre muy sabio. A lo mejor le interesa disponer de la oportunidad de descubrir la quimiatría paladina.

—¿No trabaja en la fragua? —preguntó Helena, confundida. Al fin y al cabo, el papel de los metalúrgicos era vital para la Resistencia.

Un brillo divertido surcó el rostro de Ilva.

—No, los hombres del Este no tienen permitido entrar en el Horno de Athanor, Marino. —Asintió para sus adentros—. Sí, no creo que le importe echar una mano. Me parece que trabajaríais bien juntos.

Un metalúrgico del Lejano Oriente no era la persona que tenía en mente. No le apetecía cargar con otro aprendiz. Lo que necesitaba era que su vida fuera un poco más fácil.

—Bueno, si está dispuesto a ayudar, supongo que podemos proponérselo.

—Perfecto —murmuró Ilva distraída—. Entonces, puedes irte, Marino. Me parece que voy a tener que enviar a unos cuantos de nuestros soldados a reconocer el terreno y reunir al Consejo para informar sobre las quimeras.

Helena se retiró a su laboratorio y sacó todo lo que guardaba en su bolsa para lavar y secar la corteza de sauce y el musgo. Cuando regresó a su habitación en la Torre con intención de asearse, Lila había vuelto a dejarlo todo tirado como para anunciar que había regresado.

Se preparó un baño y se sumergió en el agua hasta que le llegó al cuello. Estando sola, por fin podía permitirse pensar en Ferron, así como en la estupidez que había cometido y la forma en que él había reaccionado.

Al final no le había hecho daño.

No se había percatado hasta ese momento de lo convencida que había estado de que le haría algo malo. Había dado por hecho que, al provocarlo, ya fuera a propósito o sin querer, acabaría muerta o herida de gravedad.

Todo el mundo sabía que los inmarcesibles eran criaturas violentas y sádicas. Había oído infinidad de historias acerca de la crueldad innecesaria que mostraban en el campo de batalla. Al ser invulnerables, se regodeaban en las atrocidades que cometían.

Helena había esperado que Ferron fuera igual que el resto.

Pero, después de aquel incidente, ya no estaba tan segura de que fuese así.

Había entrado en cólera. Helena jamás había visto a nadie tan enfadado en toda su vida, pero le había pedido que se marchara. No la había tocado en absoluto.

Se hundió en la bañera hasta que el agua le cubrió el rostro.

¿Por qué no le había hecho nada? Al fin y al cabo, a él no le importaba la Llama Eterna. ¿Qué lo había frenado? Era evidente que Ferron no rehuía la violencia. Le había arrancado el corazón de cuajo a un hombre con sus propias manos.

Helena repitió mentalmente lo que le había dicho.

Recordó lo conmocionado que se había mostrado, como si no hubiera sido consciente de su comportamiento hasta que ella le abrió los ojos.

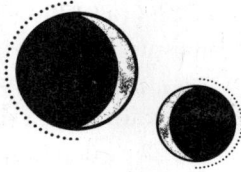

CAPÍTULO 30

ANTES DE QUE LLEGARA EL siguiente martis, Helena solicitó y recibió un cuchillo alquímico reglamentario. Debido a las quimeras, tuvo que ir directa al Reducto, sin detenerse a recolectar materiales, pero contempló con añoranza el humedal de camino a la presa.

Habían detectado más de diez quimeras distintas fuera de la ciudad, merodeando en su mayoría por las orillas de la isla Oeste. Todavía no había noticias de que hubieran causado ninguna baja en la población, pero muchas de las personas atrapadas en la ciudad y el Reducto dependían del río para conseguir comida, así que solo era cuestión de tiempo que acabaran con la vida de alguien.

Varias unidades se estaban organizando para salir a darles caza y, como era de esperar, Luc no había dudado en presentar voluntario a su batallón.

En los apartamentos, la puerta del módulo que Ferron había destrozado ya había sido sustituida. Con la esperanza de que fuera una buena señal, Helena entró sin llamar.

La capa y la chaqueta que había dejado atrás en su huida estaban dobladas con cuidado sobre la mesa.

Pero Ferron todavía no estaba allí.

Recorrió la estancia para inspeccionarla. Había restos de una cocina y una puerta daba paso a un cuarto de baño sucio con un lavabo roto y manchado, como si alguien hubiera vertido algún compuesto químico sobre él. Al menos tenía cuarto de baño. Algunas de las viviendas que había en los distritos inferiores eran tan antiguas que ni siquiera disponían de uno.

Cuando regresó a la habitación principal, Helena se sentó, cerró los puños y recurrió a su resonancia para tranquilizarse y evitar que sus pensamientos se sumieran en una espiral de nerviosismo. Todo iba bien. Ferron solo llegaba tarde.

Los minutos pasaron.

No le había contado ni a Crowther ni a Ilva lo que había ocurrido la última vez que se vieron. Les había dicho que el encuentro había sido breve, que Ferron le contó lo de las quimeras y ella había vuelto corriendo al Cuartel General, pero no había añadido nada más.

No obstante, si el chico no aparecía, tendría que explicarle a Crowther por qué se había torcido el acuerdo. Se le estaba formando un nudo tan grande en el pecho que apenas podía respirar.

Pasados diez minutos, cuando ya se había hecho a la idea de que él no iba a presentarse y se estaba colgando la bolsa del hombro, la puerta se abrió con un chasquido.

Ferron no parecía sorprendido de que Helena lo hubiera esperado.

Cerró la puerta con una expresión indescifrable y se quedó tan inmóvil ante ella que se le erizó todo el vello del cuerpo. Había algo extraño en lo vacía que era su postura.

Desde que Helena se había mudado a Paladia, sus relaciones dependían en gran medida del lenguaje corporal de los demás. Etras era un país muy expresivo: las palabras, las expresiones y los gestos formaban una parte esencial de la comunicación. Pero los norteños eran cautelosos y tendían a favorecer el mensaje implícito de sus palabras frente a lo que en verdad decían.

Por eso había sentido una conexión tan intensa con Luc. A diferencia de los demás, él siempre era sincero. Con el resto, Helena había tenido que aprender a interpretar su lenguaje corporal para descifrar lo que querían decir.

El problema era que el cuerpo de Ferron apenas comunicaba nada, como si fuera el de un jugador que jamás revelaba sus cartas. No había el menor indicio en él que dejara entrever cómo se sentía.

—Lo siento —dijo Helena para romper el silencio tenso—. No debería haberte dicho aquello la semana pasada. Perdí los papeles. Haré… lo que haga falta para compensártelo.

Ferron no mostró reacción alguna, salvo por el destello fugaz que le iluminó la mirada.

—No pasa nada —dijo sin emoción tras una pausa—. Pedí que accedieras a este acuerdo libremente y eso significa que puedes poner los límites que consideres convenientes. Te recomiendo que, en vez de provocarme, la próxima vez te decantes por esa opción.

Helena lo miró estupefacta. Cuando Ilva y Crowther le habían explicado las condiciones del acuerdo, había dado por hecho que, una vez que accediera a ser suya, ya no habría vuelta atrás.

Que le habría dado permiso para hacer lo que quisiera con ella.

No terminaba de creérselo. Le había dicho que esperaba conseguir que se arrepintiera de su decisión. Y en ningún momento le dio a entender que tuviera la posibilidad de cambiar de opinión o de negarle nada. No, estaba modificando las condiciones del acuerdo por lo que Helena dijo.

Lo observó con los ojos entornados en una mirada inquisitiva.

A Ferron pareció molestarle que sospechara de él, porque un destello de irritación le atravesó la mirada.

Helena bajó la vista, consciente de que no le convenía volver a provocarlo. Con el tiempo, estaba segura de que cambiaría de idea, de que redefiniría el acuerdo según le conviniera, pero, en ese momento, Ferron quería creer que tenía ciertos valores y que había límites que jamás se permitiría cruzar.

Asintió como si hubiera decidido creerlo.

—Me han dado un cuchillo alquímico —dijo con la esperanza de distraerlo al cambiar de tema.

—Déjame verlo —le pidió extendiendo una mano enguantada.

Lo aceptó con cuidado, sin que los guantes rozaran siquiera la piel de ella. Desde lo ocurrido, mostraba una preocupación excesiva por respetar su espacio personal.

Inspeccionó el arma y comprobó que estuviera equilibrada. Pese a que no se había quitado los guantes, la hoja cambió y el filo trazó una espiral en torno a su núcleo.

La idea era atacar con la hoja plana y transmutarla una vez dentro del cuerpo del enemigo para que el daño fuera mucho mayor. Cuanto más graves eran sus heridas, más les costaba recuperarse a los inmarcesibles y menos tiempo tardaban los necrómatas en quedar paralizados. La hoja también se podía alargar o acortar a voluntad, pero eso suponía un mayor esfuerzo y requería cierta familiaridad con las particularidades de la aleación para que el cuchillo no se rompiera.

Dado que se trataba de un arma reglamentaria, el cuchillo de Helena estaba forjado con emanaciones de lumitio para incrementar su resonancia. De esa forma, los alquimistas cuyo poder estuviera poco ligado al acero también podían transmutarlo. Aquella característica no solo era innecesaria para Helena, sino que hacía que su resonancia natural percibiera la aleación de forma irregular, pero no le preocupaba demasiado porque le habían dicho que acabaría acostumbrándose a la sensación.

—¿Alguna vez has practicado con cuchillos?

Helena tenía la esperanza de que no se lo preguntara.

—No —admitió.

—Entonces, te defenderás mejor con una hoja más larga. —Lanzó el cuchillo al aire y su superficie metálica se curvó antes de que Ferron volviera a atraparlo con soltura—. Si algo se te acerca lo suficiente como para poder usar este cuchillo, puedes darte por muerta.

La Resistencia jamás le entregaría un arma más avanzada de lo habitual a una persona que no fuera combatiente.

—Pero… algo más grande llamaría demasiado la atención. Será más probable que me paren.

—Hum.

Esa fue la única respuesta que obtuvo mientras Ferron transmutaba el arma para devolverla a su forma original.

—¿Alguna novedad sobre las quimeras?

—Cuatro ya han muerto —dijo devolviéndole el cuchillo—. No toleran el frío. —Se le retorció la boca en una mueca divertida—. Bennet está que echa humo.

—¿De dónde saca a los animales? —preguntó tal y como Crowther le había pedido.

—De donde puede. Los más fáciles de cazar son los animales domésticos, pero prefiere recurrir a depredadores grandes. Creo que han salido de caza a las montañas un par de veces. Y también han recurrido al zoológico.

—Demasiado trabajo para que acaben muriendo en el humedal.

Ferron se encogió de hombros distraídamente y dejó que su mirada volara por toda la estancia para no tener que posarla en Helena.

—Tampoco sirven para mucho más, porque son imposibles de manejar. Se rumorea que el Sumo Nigromante se siente engañado sobre el potencial del proyecto y los recursos involucrados.

Sacó un sobre, pero, en vez de entregárselo en mano, lo dejó sobre la mesa y se marchó sin mediar palabra.

Y lo mismo ocurrió las semanas siguientes. Ferron llegaba, a veces hacía alguna que otra pregunta, y luego se marchaba. Algunos de los encuentros no duraron ni cinco minutos.

Tampoco volvió a comentar nada acerca del entrenamiento. En todas esas ocasiones, Helena tuvo que confesarle a Crowther que no había hecho ningún progreso con Ferron y, si bien la información que les proporcionaba seguía siendo valiosa, ella había pasado a ser una simple mensajera.

Mientras tanto, siguió formando a las otras sanadoras y trabajando en el laboratorio, donde ya le habían asignado un asistente de manera extraoficial. Shiseo era un hombrecillo de cabello ralo y ojos oscuros bastante parco en palabras, pese a que entendía bien el dialecto norteño.

Aprendió rápidamente las técnicas de quimiatría, aunque era muy reservado y prefería limitarse a seguir a Helena por el laboratorio como una sombra, manteniendo las distancias. Helena sabía que debería estar agradecida por contar con él, puesto que había sido ella quien había pedido ayuda, pero, entre las aprendizas y el nuevo asistente, vivía acompañada de un constante recordatorio: si la Resistencia se había amoldado a sus necesidades era porque su prioridad debía ser centrarse en Ferron.

Su vida era una farsa, una tapadera con la que encubrir una misión que no se creía capaz de cumplir.

———————

FERRON LLEGABA TARDE OTRA VEZ. Ya no solía ser casi nunca puntual, pero era la primera vez que la hacía esperar tanto. Aunque temía volver con las manos vacías, al menos el paseo no había sido completamente inútil.

Había vuelto a salir a recolectar. Casi todas las quimeras habían muerto y desperdiciar esos días de primavera le parecía un sacrilegio. El río cada vez bajaba más cargado y las compuertas de la presa se utilizaban para llevar un registro del nivel del agua, que subía despacio con Lumitia en fase de sublimación. Además, el viento de las montañas ya no soplaba tan gélido como en invierno, por lo que el deshielo pronto llegaría a la cuenca e inundaría el humedal hasta el verano.

Helena abrió su bolsa y se dispuso a organizar lo que había recolectado. Parpadeó varias veces para concentrarse. Estaba agotada. Los turnos en el hospital la dejaban tan cansada que hasta le costaba llegar a su habitación cuando terminaba.

Sabía que era una señal de que sanar a los heridos la consumía, pero no estaba gastando más energía que en otros momentos. Nunca se había visto tan afectada y no entendía por qué se sentía así. El Estrago no debería aparecer de un momento a otro, pero era la única explicación que encontraba para lo que le ocurría.

Se quedó despistada contemplando los manojos de hierbas, pero acabó inclinándose hacia delante y apoyando la cabeza sobre los brazos. Al poco tiempo se le cerraron los ojos.

El mecanismo de la puerta la despertó con un sobresalto que la hizo incorporarse de golpe. ¿Cuánto había dormido?

Uno de los engranajes giró, pero ni la cerradura ni la puerta se abrieron. Se hizo el silencio.

Helena se puso de pie en cuanto la persona que había al otro lado empezó de nuevo a manipular los engranajes muy despacio, como si estuvieran tratando de forzar la cerradura.

Entonces se puso a rebuscar con torpeza en su bolsa hasta que encontró el cuchillo y, justo cuando cerró el puño en torno al mango, la puerta se abrió de un bandazo. En medio del panel había un surco rojo terminado en una huella carmesí.

Ferron se tambaleaba en el umbral, con el rostro pálido como un cadáver y la mirada perdida. A Helena se le escurrió el arma de entre los dedos al verlo.

—¿Qué te ha pasado?

El chico la miró como si no hubiera esperado encontrarla allí.

—No... es nada.

Agitó la mano derecha al entrar en la estancia y salpicó todo el suelo de sangre. También había un reguero por el pasillo.

—¿Estás... estás herido?

La pregunta se le quedaba corta: no sabía que podía resultar herido. ¿No se suponía que los inmarcesibles se regeneraban al instante? ¿Cómo es que estaba sangrando tanto?

Intentó desabrocharle la capa para comprobar la gravedad de la herida, pero él la apartó de un empujón y retrocedió.

—¿Qué es... estás haciendo?

La actitud orgullosa que siempre había mostrado desapareció; en su lugar, se movía como un perrillo abandonado a la espera de recibir una paliza. Su mirada estaba tan desencajada que el blanco de sus ojos resplandecía.

Helena se dio cuenta de que tenía la mano con la que lo había tocado manchada de sangre.

—Estás herido.

Ferron dejó caer los hombros y se recorrió el cuerpo con la mirada lentamente.

—Me pondré bien… —balbuceó—. Necesito… un minuto…

Se apoyó contra la pared. La sangre manaba del interior de su manga izquierda y formaba un charco en el suelo. Helena estuvo a punto de entrar en pánico al verlo.

Las hemorragias eran un riesgo muy importante y la principal causa de muerte entre los miembros de la Resistencia. Por eso, todo el mundo estaba entrenado para enfrentarse a ellas con la máxima eficiencia. Como perdiera más sangre de la cuenta, ni el expansor de plasma ni la solución salina servirían de nada.

¿Cuánto aguantaría? Fuera o no inmortal, seguro que su cuerpo no disponía de un suministro infinito de sangre.

—Soy… sanitaria, Ferron —le dijo con un tono de voz tranquilizador mientras levantaba las manos para demostrarle que no quería hacerle daño—. Déjame ayudar.

El chico la miró aturdido, como si necesitara tomarse un momento para procesar lo que le acababa de decir.

—¿Qué ha pasado? —volvió a preguntar al tiempo que se arriesgaba a dar un paso hacia él.

La sangre seguía manando de su herida a una velocidad vertiginosa.

—He perdido el brazo —admitió Ferron por fin, negando con la cabeza.

Se desabrochó la capa como para demostrárselo y, cuando esta cayó junto a su abrigo gris, Helena vio que debajo no había más que retales de tela quemada y una hemorragia imparable allí donde debería haber tenido el brazo izquierdo.

—Volverá a crecer. —Se tambaleó y se le desenfocó la vista—. Pero… está tardando un poco.

Helena nunca había visto con sus propios ojos el proceso de regeneración de un inmarcesible. Los soldados contaban que era rápido y desagradable: los huesos salían disparados del cuerpo; los músculos y los tendones se enroscaban a su alrededor, y, por último, una pálida capa de piel brotaba del tejido desnudo como si fuera moho.

Después de haber pasado tiempo en el hospital tanteando los límites de la regeneración de tejidos, le resultaba difícil creer que alguien fuera capaz de generar una extremidad entera de la nada.

Ella misma había intentado una vez devolverle los dedos a una paciente, pero la cantidad de regeneración espontánea que el proceso requería era abrumadora. La sanación tenía unos límites muy marcados, que, como era evidente, no significaban nada para los inmarcesibles.

A juzgar por la herida, parecía que a Ferron le habían arrancado el brazo de cuajo. El chico se tensó cuando intentó acercarse a él, por lo que Helena se detuvo mientras su cabeza trabajaba a toda velocidad. Quizá debería intentar hablar con él primero. Por el momento, había respondido a todas sus preguntas.

—Yo pensaba que la regeneración era inmediata.

—A veces… requiere más tiempo —admitió caminando hasta la mesa con los dientes apretados y dejándose caer en una silla. La cabeza se le tambaleó hacia atrás—. Demasiadas heridas…

—¿Tienes más?

Le ofreció una sonrisa tensa pese a tener la cara contraída por el dolor.

—Me han asignado un nuevo distrito… —No llegó a terminar la frase. Se incorporó como si tuviera intención de ponerse de pie y parpadeó un par de veces—. El anterior comandante… se había encariñado demasiado con él. —Se encogió débilmente de hombros—. Insulté a su madre… varias veces. Insinué algo bastante feo sobre lo que hacía su mujer con cierto caballo. —Se le volvió a caer la cabeza hacia atrás—. No le hizo gracia. Nos batimos a muerte. O… tan a muerte como las circunstancias nos lo permiten. Como gané yo, ahora me encargo de su puesto de mando.

Helena no alcanzó a entender sus últimas palabras. Hablaba para sus adentros.

Entonces, sin previo aviso, soltó una seca carcajada que la sobresaltó.

—El problema es que era un piromante. Lo del brazo no es nada comparado con las quemaduras. Esas han sido… mucho peores. Pero ya están curadas. Lo normal es que… —Se señaló el cuerpo—. Hoy estoy…

Se interrumpió antes de terminar de explicarse.

A Helena jamás se le habría ocurrido pensar que la clave para soltarle la lengua a Ferron sería recurrir al dolor y la pérdida de sangre, pero había encadenado más palabras en aquel rato que en todas las reuniones de las últimas semanas.

Se le volvió a desenfocar la vista. Su respiración cada vez era más débil, casi entrecortada. Estaba a punto de derrumbarse.

—¿Qué estás haciendo aquí? No tenías por qué haber venido.

Dio un paso vacilante hacia él, preparada para que volviera a apartarla con otro empujón. Pero Ferron parpadeó despacio. La observaba con atención, con las pupilas tan dilatadas que casi se tragaban por completo sus iris.

—Marino… —suspiró como si la respuesta fuera obvia. Seguía farfullando, sin apenas mover los labios—. En cuanto hayamos terminado, pienso pasarme los próximos tres días tan borracho que no recuerde ni mi nombre. Hay un mapa… por aquí. —Helena no se dio cuenta de que su ropa había quedado prácticamente reducida a cenizas hasta que el chico empezó a palparse el cuerpo con la mano que le quedaba—. Joder…

—Tengo experiencia médica —insistió la chica con voz amable pero firme tras dar otro paso hacia él—. Voy a explorarte para ver si puedo ayudar.

Él no pareció oírla. Tampoco se resistió cuando, con la excusa de tomarle el pulso, Helena le presionó dos dedos contra el lateral del cuello para comprobar qué le pasaba mediante la resonancia. Si la primera vez que lo había tocado, su cuerpo le había resultado antinatural, en ese momento era mil veces más extraño. Había perdido tanta sangre que debería haber muerto hacía rato, pero su pecho irradiaba un poder cegador que lo estaba regenerando mucho más rápido de lo que habría tardado en exhalar su último aliento.

Debía de ser efecto del talismán de lumitio, la fuente de poder de los inmarcesibles.

Aun así, su cuerpo estaba empeñado en morir igualmente.

Helena notaba el tejido nuevo que le salpicaba todo el cuerpo. La mayor parte se le concentraba en el torso y la cara, y le llegaba hasta los huesos. Unos cuantos órganos también parecían nuevos.

De todas formas, la hemorragia seguía siendo un problema. El cuerpo no estaba preparado para producir sangre tan rápido, ni siquiera a una mínima parte de la velocidad a la que la estaba perdiendo. Se estaba quedando sin recursos y, además, la poca sangre que regenerara acabaría de igual manera en el suelo. Era un círculo vicioso: su cuerpo estaba tan centrado en producir más sangre que no conseguía regenerar el brazo que le faltaba y así ponerle fin a la hemorragia.

Según parecía, el concepto de la coagulación era ajeno a sus anómalas habilidades de regeneración.

Helena inspiró hondo y habló con tanta firmeza como fue capaz:

—He de admitir que eres el primer inmortal al que trato, pero tenemos que encontrar una manera de hacer que dejes de sangrar. —Cuando le apartó los jirones que le quedaban de la camisa, la tela se desintegró—. Será mejor que te pongamos en la mesa.

Se pasó el brazo de Ferron por los hombros y tiró de él para incorporarlo. Era una suerte que fuera todo hueso, porque de lo contrario no habría conseguido cargar con su peso muerto para tumbarlo de espaldas. En cuanto se le cerraron los ojos, dejó de responder a los estímulos y su respiración se volvió todavía más superficial.

Helena no creía que estuviera consciente, pero siguió adelante con la farsa del examen solo para asegurarse. Le presionó el hombro con la base de ambas manos para ocultar su resonancia mientras le oprimía las venas y las arterias del brazo.

Para su sorpresa, eso bastó para estabilizarlo.

En cuanto la hemorragia cesó, su brazo comenzó a regenerarse de inmediato. Contempló fascinada cómo el hueso brotaba del muñón y los músculos se ceñían a su alrededor para dar lugar al bíceps, al codo, al cúbito y al radio.

Sin poder contenerse, liberó otra ola de resonancia para intentar percibir lo que fuera que… estuviera ocurriendo en su interior. Quería entender cómo funcionaba. Su cuerpo ya ni siquiera transmitía la sensación de estar al borde de la muerte.

Se le desplegaron las falanges y, de inmediato, quedaron cubiertas por un entramado de venas y tejido muscular. Para cuando terminó de regenerarse, era imposible notar que había perdido un brazo.

Le liberó el hombro, así como las arterias y las venas, para permitir que su flujo sanguíneo pudiera circular por el nuevo tejido. Los músculos de Ferron no tardaron en estabilizarse.

Para Helena, la regeneración siempre había girado en torno al tejido nuevo. Sin embargo, al notar que el brazo del chico no solo se había regenerado, sino que ya había regresado a su estado anterior, se preguntó si debería explorar nuevas perspectivas. No tenía por qué limitarse a la regeneración básica.

El poder que el pecho de Ferron irradiaba se fue apagando hasta que se convirtió en un difuso nudo de energía y lumitio apenas imperceptible. Era diminuto en comparación con la cantidad de poder que generaba.

Aunque no se atrevió a tentar a la suerte y seguir explorándolo, no apartó las manos de su cuerpo. De todos los contextos en los que había esperado ver a un Ferron semidesnudo, el de sanarlo u ofrecerle atención médica jamás había estado entre ellos. Y eso que era un escenario infinitamente más llevadero que el de besarlo.

Aquella forma de contacto físico no la incomodaba.

Lo estudió con atención mientras el pulso del chico retomaba un ritmo constante y su cuerpo recuperaba el color que la pérdida de sangre le había robado.

La palabra más amable que podía utilizar para describir su constitución era «esmirriado». Apenas tenía una gota de grasa. Se le marcaban las costillas, el esternón y los huesos de los hombros. Sus brazos y piernas eran largos y los codos puntiagudos. Sin ropa, parecía todavía más joven. No le sorprendía que Ferron llevara tres capas de uniforme para aparentar más edad.

Le pasó los dedos distraídamente por la piel nueva e impoluta.

No alcanzaba a imaginar lo que debía de sentir al haberse quedado atrapado en el cuerpo de un muchacho de dieciséis años para toda la eternidad.

—¿Acostumbras a ser una mirona y a manosear a tus pacientes mientras están inconscientes o yo soy una excepción?

La voz de Ferron cayó sobre ella como un jarro de agua fría, así que apartó las manos de él con el corazón a punto de salírsele del pecho y el rostro sonrojado.

—No es lo que piensas —se defendió con voz tensa y chillona, aunque no tenía excusa. No debería haberlo tocado de esa manera—. Estaba pensando en la proporción de grasa corporal que tendrás con relación a tu peso.

—Y yo que me lo creo —dijo él antes de incorporarse y ofrecerle una sonrisa provocadora.

A Helena le ardían tanto las mejillas que podría haber calentado todo el edificio solo con el calor que emanaba de ellas.

—¡No te estaba mirando de esa manera! —insistió—. A mí no me gustan los chicos de aspecto aniñado y me temo que tú ni siquiera pareces haber dado el estirón.

La sonrisa de Ferron se esfumó. La miró durante un largo y agónico momento antes de incorporarse.

—Si no recuerdo mal, yo no te he pedido que me examinaras —señaló al final en tono seco.

Recogió su capa, que era la única prenda que no había quedado reducida a cenizas, y, al cubrirse con ella, se manchó todo el torso de sangre.

—Lo siento, no era mi intención…

—Tu intención ha quedado clara como el agua —la interrumpió con la voz gélida y los dientes apretados.

—Ferron… —Había caído en la cuenta de algo y no sabía cómo no se le había ocurrido preguntárselo antes—. ¿Te convirtieron en un inmarcesible… como castigo?

Él le lanzó una mirada carente de emoción.

—La inmortalidad es algo que todo el mundo ansía. ¿Quién la vería como un castigo?

Cuando Helena regresó al Cuartel General, se vio asolada por el recuerdo de Ferron. No solo por su última respuesta, sino por toda la conversación.

Durante meses, el chico se había comportado como una criatura sin alma ni sangre en las venas. Había sido una carga que debía soportar, un obstáculo que sortear, no una persona de carne y hueso. Al verlo herido, despojado de la coraza que era el uniforme tras el que se ocultaba, la percepción que tenía de él había cambiado.

No estaba preparada para la fragilidad que había mostrado.

Ferron le había parecido demasiado humano, y Helena no se sentía cómoda viéndolo como tal.

Era un inmarcesible, un asesino, un espía, un objetivo, un peón para la Llama Eterna. Así era como debía verlo, no como una persona capaz de sentir dolor. No como una persona que no entendía las hemorragias o que se ponía a divagar mientras intentaba explicar algo. No como una persona que daba por hecho que, si le tendían la mano, era solo para hacerle daño.

Había pasado mucho tiempo expuesta a su orgullo y su rabia, pero, después de aquella última conversación, no podía evitar pensar que ocultaba algo trágico y terrible en su interior.

Sintió la necesidad de reprimir aquella emoción con urgencia.

Kaine Ferron era un enemigo. La guerra había estallado por su culpa: había matado al padre de Luc.

Helena se lavó la sangre de las manos y empezó a prepararse para un nuevo turno en el hospital antes de recordar que tenía el día libre. Se sentó en la cama y contempló las notas que había tomado mientras trataba de desenredar la maraña de emociones contradictorias que bullían en su interior.

Entonces, Lila entró en la habitación, vestida con la armadura que utilizaba para practicar. Se detuvo en seco al ver a Helena.

—Estás aquí.

Helena cerró el cuaderno.

—Pace le ha pedido a una de mis aprendizas que cubra mi turno para ver cómo les va sin mí. —Lila frunció los labios—. No me dejan supervisarlas porque, según dicen, las controlo demasiado y se ponen nerviosas.

La otra chica asintió, apoyó el arma que portaba en la pared y se colocó la trenza antes de hacer crujir su cuello en ambas direcciones. Helena se estremeció.

—Es verdad que a veces tienes un poco cara de perro —coincidió mientras se quitaba la armadura—. Te van a salir un montón de arrugas justo aquí —añadió tocándole el punto entre las cejas.

Helena puso los ojos en blanco y, al dejar el cuaderno en el arcón con actitud despreocupada, rozó el amuleto de heliolita. Era extraño, pero estaba caliente. Seguía ofreciéndole ese consuelo que conocía tan bien. Estuvo a punto de volver a ponérselo, pero se decantó por colocar la mano boca arriba y mirarse las cicatrices que se había hecho con él.

—No es algo que me preocupe —musitó.

—Hel…, ¿te encuentras bien?

—Sí. —Levantó la cabeza para mirarla—. ¿Por qué?

Lila cambió el peso de su cuerpo de un pie a otro y la armadura desabrochada repiqueteó. Nunca se la quitaba. De hecho, dormía incluso con un ligero traje de cota de malla. Decía que era porque se sentía desnuda sin sus protecciones, pero Helena sabía que temía cometer el mismo error de su tío Sebastian, el paladín del principado Apollo. Se negaba a dar por hecho que había un lugar seguro en el mundo para Luc.

—Te noto rara últimamente. Pensé que te alegraría contar con nuevas sanadoras, que te ayudaría a relajarte un poco, pero pareces… —Lila vaciló— más encerrada en ti misma que nunca. Nunca estás con nosotros, siempre desapareces, y Luc se ha dado cuenta.

—Es que estoy preocupada por la situación, nada más. ¿Habéis tenido suerte con las quimeras?

—No. Ayer salimos a darles caza, pero son endiabladamente rápidas. Tuve a una arrinconada, pero olía a muerto. Mucho peor que los necrómatas. Podría haberla matado, pero te juro por los dioses que el hedor hasta me mareó y luego... —Sacudió la cabeza—. ¿Por qué estamos hablando de quimeras?

Helena evitó su mirada y Lila resopló exasperada.

—Vete a la mierda. No intentes distraerme cambiando de tema. No quiero hablar de las quimeras. —Se acercó a Helena y el sonido metálico de su pierna derecha marcaba cada uno de sus pasos—. Estás muy rara y, en las últimas semanas, no has venido ni a una sola reunión. Ayer conseguí que Soren me contara lo que ha pasado. Así que buen trabajo. Menuda cantidad de secretos os habéis estado guardando.

—¿Lo sabe Luc? —preguntó Helena con tirantez.

—No.

—No quiero hablar de ello —exhaló.

Lila hizo una pausa.

—Me resulta curioso que eligieras dar tu discurso en una reunión en la que justo Luc y yo no estábamos presentes.

—Lo habría dado con vosotros delante también —dijo Helena mientras se tiraba de las pequeñas pieles de las cutículas. Tenía los dedos agrietados de tanto lavarse las manos y restos de la sangre de Ferron incrustados en las uñas—. Pero me alegro de que Luc no estuviera allí. No quería ponerlo entre la espada y la pared. Sabía que el Consejo rechazaría mi propuesta, pero... necesitaba intentarlo. Soren me dijo que la batalla había ido bien, pero en el hospital... Nos habíamos quedado sin suministros. No teníamos camas, vendas, láudano ni antisépticos. Y no dejaban de entrar heridos. Tenía... Tenía la sensación de que nada de lo que hiciera sería suficiente.

Lila se sentó al borde de la cama de Helena.

—¿Es que no...? —La chica no se veía capaz de mirarla y parecía estar midiendo sus palabras con cuidado—. ¿Ya no te encuentras bien? ¿Por eso decidiste hablar con ellos? ¿Por eso han traído a las aprendizas?

Se hizo un silencio. Helena miró a su amiga, pero ella estaba demasiado ocupada desabrochándose una de las cinchas de la armadura como para encontrar su mirada. No esperaba que Lila supiera lo del Estrago.

Estaba demasiado abrumada como para pensar en eso.

—No, estoy bien. Lo de las aprendizas es porque Matias quiere quitarme de en medio.

—Ah, bien. Bueno, bien no, pero tiene sentido —replicó Lila, y carraspeó—. Ahora entiendo por qué no te hace tanta gracia tener ayuda.

Helena se obligó a reír, pero la tensión que se había creado entre ellas no se disipó. Lila continuó:

—Oye, ya sabes que puedes hablar conmigo… siempre que lo necesites.

—No, no necesito hablar. No… va a servir de nada, ya que, como me han recordado, yo no soy una combatiente. No sé nada acerca de la guerra. Así que… ¿qué voy a decir?

Lila se giró hacia ella con un tintineo de la prótesis de la pierna.

—Pues yo creo que trabajar en el hospital es mucho peor que el campo de batalla. —Helena se quedó muy quieta—. Lo comprendí cuando estuve allí por lo de mi pierna. —La chica tenía la mirada ausente y había fruncido el ceño—. En el frente… todo tiene sentido, ¿sabes? Las reglas son claras. A veces ganamos, a veces perdemos. Te golpean y devuelves el golpe. Y te permiten unos días de descanso para que te recuperes. Pero… —bajó la vista mientras se daba golpecitos distraídamente en el punto donde la prótesis encajaba con su muslo— en el hospital, todas las batallas parecen perdidas desde el principio. No me quiero imaginar lo que debe de ser estar ahí todo el tiempo. —Miró a Helena—. Lo único que ves allí es la peor parte de la guerra.

Helena no dijo nada.

Lila suspiró, se quitó un par de piezas más de la armadura y las dejó sobre la cama.

—Cuando Soren me contó lo que dijiste… Quiero que sepas que lo entiendo, aunque no comparta tu opinión. —Helena continuó en silencio, así que Lila le dio un suave codazo y se puso de pie—. Puede que lo de las aprendizas sea un tejemaneje de Matias, pero me alegro de que tengas un poco más de tiempo libre. Creo que te va a venir bien. Necesitas alejarte un poco de todo esto.

CAPÍTULO 31

Abrilis 1786

FERRON YA LA ESTABA ESPERANDO cuando Helena llegó al Reducto. El suelo, la mesa y las sillas de la estancia estaban impolutos, sin rastro de sangre.

Tenía los labios apretados en una fina línea cuando la vio cruzar el umbral y se quitó la capa tan pronto como ella cerró la puerta.

—Veamos qué tal luchas, Marino.

Se lanzó a por ella tan rápido que su silueta se convirtió en un borrón.

A Helena ni siquiera le dio tiempo a sacar el cuchillo, así que tomó la decisión de atizarlo con la bolsa en la cabeza. Aunque consiguió ganar un segundo de margen, Ferron atrapó la bolsa al vuelo y le arrancó la correa de entre los dedos antes de lanzarla al otro lado de la habitación. Helena oyó que los frasquitos de cristal que guardaba en ella se rompían.

Por mucho que intentara huir de él, no tenía adónde ir y no podía permitirse perder el tiempo en abrir la compleja cerradura de la puerta.

Se las arregló para ponerse al otro lado de la mesa y utilizarla de barrera, pero Ferron le dio una patada y la hizo volar hacia ella. Las patas emitieron un chirrido al deslizarse por el suelo de baldosas. Helena se agachó y la mesa impactó con tanta fuerza con la pared que el tablero se astilló.

Cuando la chica cayó al suelo, se retorció la mano izquierda y una ola de dolor le recorrió el brazo al partirse uno de los huesos de la muñeca.

Se la acunó contra el pecho mientras intentaba ponerse de pie con torpeza.

—¡Para, Ferron!

No le hizo caso. Al agarrarla del cuello con fuerza y empujarla contra la pared, en la expresión del chico no había ni rastro de emoción.

Helena forcejeó pese a tener la mano herida; le dejó surcos en la piel con las uñas, e intentó darle un rodillazo en la entrepierna, pero él le hizo la zancadilla y la tiró al suelo.

El impacto la dejó sin aliento y se le nubló la vista.

Entonces Ferron le apoyó la rodilla en el centro del pecho depositando el peso suficiente sobre ella para que notara la presión en los huesos.

—¿No te defiendes?

Helena no podía respirar; los pulmones se le contraían en busca de oxígeno. Se retorció para liberarse, arañando cada centímetro de piel que lograba encontrar, pero Ferron le agarró ambas manos con un extraño brillo en la mirada. Cuando Helena intentó soltarse, se las apretó hasta que un nuevo estallido de dolor se adueñó de su mano derecha y sus metacarpianos rechinaron unos contra otros.

—¡No me rompas la mano! ¡Por favor…, las manos no! —aulló presa del pánico.

—Pues defiéndete —le dijo cerniéndose sobre ella.

Le ardían los brazos. Apenas podía respirar. Ferron estaba a punto de hundirle el pecho. Como intentara zafarse de nuevo, seguro que le rompería todos los huesos de la mano derecha.

Se quedó inerte.

Ferron la sujetó durante unos cuantos segundos más, como si esperara que la chica actuara sin previo aviso. Un destello desconcertado le surcó la mirada, pero dejó escapar un suspiro y su expresión volvió a endurecerse.

—Eres patética —le dijo a la vez que depositaba más peso sobre su pecho. A Helena se le llenaron los ojos de lágrimas, pero no profirió sonido alguno—. Podría hacer lo que me diera la gana contigo, herirte de formas que ni te imaginas, y tú no harías nada para impedírmelo. Ni siquiera me haría falta recurrir a la resonancia. Eres tan débil que me bastaría con usar las manos.

La soltó tras dedicarle una última mirada de desprecio. Tenía las manos manchadas de sangre, pero las heridas que Helena le había abierto en la piel ya se habían cerrado. Ferron se puso de pie, sacó un pañuelo para limpiarse la sangre y se colocó la ropa.

Ella se quedó en el suelo jadeando. Le palpitaban la espalda y la parte de atrás de la cabeza. Cuando trató de incorporarse apoyándose en la mano derecha, estuvo a punto de gritar.

Ambas manos le dolían muchísimo. Sus dedos estaban manchados de sangre y con restos de piel bajo las uñas.

La muñeca izquierda ya había empezado a inflamársele y la derecha no estaba mucho mejor: cuando intentaba cerrar el puño, el dolor se le extendía hasta el codo.

—Esto cuenta como interferir en mi trabajo —dijo esforzándose por mantener la voz firme—, para que lo sepas. La próxima vez que quieras hacerme daño —la mandíbula le temblaba descontroladamente—, mis manos tienen que quedar al margen.

Menos mal que la había animado a ponerle los límites que considerara oportunos.

Ferron no respondió, sino que se acercó a la mesa y se puso la capa sin dirigirle una sola mirada.

Helena se quedó donde estaba. Pese a que la posibilidad de que decidiera hacerle daño siempre había estado ahí, se había permitido bajar la guardia ante la falsa sensación de seguridad que le había hecho sentir.

Que la hubiera engañado de esa manera era mucho más cruel que maltratarla desde el principio.

—¿Me puedes decir al menos por qué lo has hecho? —le preguntó con la vista clavada en el suelo. Le dolían las costillas al respirar—. ¿He hecho... he h-hecho algo que te haya molestado?

—Existir, Marino. ¿No te parece razón suficiente?

Helena no supo qué responder ante eso, así que se puso de pie despacio.

—¿Necesitas que le entregue algún mensaje a la Llama Eterna?

—No —dijo con una débil sonrisa—. Esto ha sido todo.

La chica recogió su bolsa sin mediar palabra y pasó un brazo cuidadosamente por la correa, incapaz siquiera de colgársela al hombro. Cada movimiento suyo iba acompañado del tintineo de los frasquitos rotos.

La semana anterior había preparado un kit de emergencia para estar preparada por si Ferron volvía a llegar herido a uno de sus encuentros. El derroche de suministros hizo que el corazón le doliera casi tanto como las costillas. Por si fuera poco, los fragmentos de cristal y el contenido de los frasquitos habría echado a perder todo lo que había recolectado aquel día. Tantas horas de trabajo desperdiciadas.

Helena se dirigió hacia la puerta e intentó flexionar los dedos para abrirla, pero el dolor se lo impidió.

—¿Te importaría…? —La voz le tembló y terminó por delatarla—. ¿Te importaría dejarme salir?

SI LE HUBIERA LASTIMADO CUALQUIER otra parte del cuerpo, seguir las instrucciones de Crowther y curarse los moratones antes de regresar al Cuartel General habría sido fácil, pero no habían elaborado ningún plan para una emergencia como aquella.

Cuando salió del Reducto, Helena deambuló un rato por la presa. No podía hacer nada sin sus manos. Si volvía tan maltrecha como estaba, le harían preguntas para las que no podría ofrecer respuesta.

Al final, ya desesperada, bajó por el terraplén en dirección al humedal. Sin contar con sus manos, se movía con torpeza, así que no tardó en acabar con la ropa toda manchada. Para cuando volvió arrastrándose a tierra firme, estaba empapada y se había cubierto la cara y el cuello de barro para disimular los moratones.

Al verla, los guardias del puesto de control se apiadaron de ella y no le hicieron demasiadas preguntas. Pero, una vez en el Cuartel General, no poder utilizar el ascensor la obligó a acudir al hospital.

—¿Qué te ha pasado? —le preguntó la enfermera Pace en cuanto la vio entrar por la puerta.

—Me he caído recolectando —dijo evitando su mirada— y me he retorcido las muñecas.

—¿Las dos? —Helena asintió sin levantar la cabeza y Pace la estudió en silencio durante un momento antes de recomponerse—. Vamos a quitarte esa ropa sucia y a ver qué hacemos.

La condujo a una de las salas privadas que solían dejar reservadas para los miembros de alto rango de la Llama Eterna mientras alejaba a todas las personas que se acercaron a ellas.

Helena siempre había valorado mucho la profesionalidad de Pace. Mantenía la cabeza fría en todo momento, sin importar las circunstancias. Helena tenía las manos demasiado frías e inflamadas como para soltarse los botones y las hebillas de la ropa, así que Pace la ayudó a desnudarse sin quejarse de que le manchara de barro el delantal, las mangas y las manos.

—Me viene bien para variar después de tanta sangre —dijo para quitarle importancia cuando Helena trató de disculparse. Escurrió un paño mojado—. Limpiemos la zona y veamos qué te ha pasado. Creo que Elain será la más indicada para el trabajo.

Helena se puso tensa, pero tampoco había nada que hacer. En cuanto Pace viera los moratones, se daría cuenta de que no se había torcido las muñecas al caerse. Por si fuera poco, aunque Elain era la más competente entre sus aprendizas, también era bastante cotilla.

Pace hizo una pausa después de limpiarle el cuello, pues el círculo de moratones que le coloreaba la piel era muy llamativo. Antes de que Helena tuviera oportunidad de inventarse una excusa, alguien llamó a la puerta.

La enfermera apretó los labios y abrió la puerta usando su propio cuerpo como pantalla para que la gente que había en el pabellón principal no viera a Helena.

—¿Qué ocurre, Purnell? —preguntó.

—Tengo un mensaje —susurró una voz—. Me han dicho que es urgente.

Pace aceptó lo que la otra persona le ofrecía y cerró la puerta. Mientras regresaba junto a Helena, desdobló la nota, la leyó y la rompió.

—Me han pedido que te envíe directa a tu habitación —le explicó la enfermera con las mejillas ruborizadas de ira—, pero creo que me dará tiempo a terminar de limpiarte primero.

En cuanto le quitó todo el barro, Pace la envolvió en mantas como si Helena sufriera hipotermia y la acompañó hasta la Torre de Alquimia. Crowther ya las estaba esperando cuando cruzaron el puente colgante y Pace se puso tensa al verlo.

—¿Algún problema? —preguntó el hombre.

Las mejillas de Pace estaban salpicadas de capilares rotos.

—He venido a asegurarme de que Marino se queda en buenas manos.

A Crowther le tembló un ojo.

—Por supuesto. —Miró a Helena—. Entiendo que necesitas atención médica.

Helena había estado considerándolo por el camino.

—Me basta con que me curen la mano izquierda. Luego, me las arreglaré sola.

—Te enviaré a alguien, pero asegúrate de que no te vea nadie hasta entonces. Puede retirarse, enfermera.

Con eso, se dio la vuelta y se alejó de ellas.

Pace, por su parte, no regresó al hospital de inmediato, sino que acompañó a Helena hasta su habitación y se quedó con ella incluso cuando ya se había metido en la cama.

—¿Sabes? Yo conocí a unas cuantas sanadoras en mis años como matrona. —Se sentó a los pies de la cama y dejó vagar la mirada por la habitación—. Los médicos que habían estudiado en la ciudad no tenían ningún interés en desplazarse a los pueblos de la montaña, así que allí los equipos estaban conformados casi en su totalidad por mujeres mayores que no siempre se identificaban como sanadoras. Para muchas, su don consistía en conocer muy bien su cuerpo y recurrir a la intuición. Por eso, cuando me dijeron que nos iban a traer a alguien de las montañas, esperaba encontrarme a una mujer de mi edad. —Miró a Helena—. Eras tan joven... No te haces una idea. Desde entonces no has dejado de sacrificarte sin ser consciente de lo valiosos que son esos aspectos de tu vida a los que renuncias.

Helena se sentía abrumada por la maraña en que se habían convertido sus emociones.

—Nadie me está obligando a hacer nada... sin mi consentimiento.

—Pero, Helena, si no sabes decir que no —le dijo Pace. Y, sin dejarla contestar, añadió—: ¿Te crees que un hombre como Crowther no se aprovecharía de ello?

Parecía que iba a continuar, pero este abrió la puerta y entró con una chica joven.

—Ya puede regresar al hospital, enfermera.

Crowther le lanzó una mirada cargada de significado mientras sostenía la puerta, así que Pace le dio unas palmaditas a Helena en la rodilla, se puso de pie y estudió a Crowther con mala cara al salir de la habitación. Una vez solos, el hombre cerró la puerta y se giró hacia Helena.

—Esta es Ivy. Se encargará de curarte la mano según tus indicaciones.

La chica dio un paso adelante. Se movía con actitud vacilante, como un cervatillo, pero tenía la mirada astuta de un zorro. Aparentaba tener unos quince años, pero Helena no creía que hubiera llegado siquiera a cumplirlos. Nunca había conocido a una vivemante tan joven, pues, como Pace bien había dicho, su poder no se manifestaba hasta más adelante.

En muchos aspectos, la guerra había envejecido a todo el mundo.

Ivy no pronunció ni una sola palabra cuando Helena se señaló la muñeca izquierda y le explicó de la forma más sencilla posible qué le ocurría, qué tendría que hacer para curarla y con qué debería tener cuidado. Siempre se había encargado ella misma de curarse, así que le lanzó varias miradas de pánico a Crowther cuando Ivy le tocó el brazo.

Para su sorpresa, la chica se las apañaba bien con la vivemancia, aunque su resonancia era de todo menos sutil. El dolor y la hinchazón que Helena tenía en la muñeca y los dedos desapareció al instante y, apenas unos minutos después de que Ivy localizara la fractura, Helena volvía a sentir su resonancia y a mover los dedos sin demasiado dolor.

—Gracias —le dijo a la chica antes de apartar la mano lo más rápido que pudo.

Ivy dejó caer también las manos y contempló a Helena con un siniestro brillo de curiosidad en los ojos.

—A mi hermana le caes bien.

—¿Ah, sí? ¿Trabaja en el hospital?

—Lárgate, Ivy —intervino Crowther sin miramientos—. Y no le digas ni una palabra de esto a nadie.

Ella asintió despreocupadamente y salió de la habitación.

Crowther volvió a cerrar la puerta. Helena quería preguntarle por la chica, pero la conversación que se avecinaba la aterrorizaba, así que se concentró en su mano derecha. Se inutilizó los nervios hasta el codo y se examinó la muñeca con sumo cuidado.

—¿Qué ha pasado?

—Creo que Ferron está molesto por lo de la semana pasada. —Se alegraba de tener algo que hacer para no mirar directamente a Crowther a los ojos—. Ya sabes lo orgulloso que es. Me temo que no le hizo mucha gracia que lo ayudara porque me dijo que quería verme pelear en cuanto entré por la puerta.

Levantó la mirada justo cuando Crowther apretaba los labios hasta casi hacerlos desaparecer.

—¿Sabe que eres vivemante?

—No.

—¿Estás segura?

—Lo estoy.

Crowther asintió, aunque parecía escéptico.

—¿Quién era esa chica? —le preguntó Helena.

—Una huérfana que encontramos en los suburbios. —Crowther dejó escapar un ruidito molesto—. Les diremos a los demás que te has cogido unos días de descanso por un resfriado, no podemos dejar que te vean así. Tenemos un punto de encuentro a cierta distancia de aquí, abastecido con ropa y provisiones básicas. De ahora en adelante, cuando pase algo así, tendrás que ir allí directamente. Si en algún momento no regresas al Cuartel General, sabremos dónde encontrarte.

Helena asintió con desgana. La inflamación de su mano derecha ya se había reducido lo bastante como para permitirse evaluar el trabajo que Ivy había hecho con la izquierda.

No podía hacer mucho mientras sus manos terminaban de recuperarse y, aunque lo de tomarse unos días libres le parecía un poco excesivo, era mejor estar segura. Si se forzaba y acababa con una neuropatía en las manos, entonces ya no podría ayudar.

Se mantuvo ocupada ordenando su arcón, pese a que tampoco contenía mucho más que los viejos cuadernos que había utilizado en clase. Las habitaciones pequeñas y el código de vestimenta estricto la habían obligado a dejar casi todas sus posesiones atrás cuando se marchó de Etras. Dentro de una cajita guardaba un ferrotipo de su padre y ella justo antes de que hubiera comenzado los estudios. Tenía diez años, iba vestida de uniforme y parecía emocionada. Aunque no tenía permitido ejercer en Paladia, su padre se había puesto su bata blanca de médico con la intención de dar una imagen profesional.

Helena cerró la caja, sacó el amuleto de heliolita y lo sostuvo de manera que sus rayos se alinearan con las cicatrices que le había dejado en la mano. Luego, se acercó con él a la ventana y salió al tejadillo inclinado que había bajo el faro de la Torre. Había sido Luc quien le había enseñado a trepar por la ventana.

La Llama Eterna brillaba sobre ella, sola en aquel tejado donde lo único que la separaba de una caída mortal era una barandilla de hierro no muy alta.

Helena deseó poder dejar la mente en blanco durante un tiempo. Redirigir sus pensamientos como Ferron le había enseñado le daba algo de margen, pero la tristeza se colaba en cada recoveco.

Contempló el blasón solar mientras las llamas blancas que rutilaban en lo alto iluminaban su superficie. Estuvo tentada de soltar el amuleto para verlo caer hasta desaparecer.

Cada vez que lo miraba se sentía avergonzada por el inmenso significado que ella misma le había dado. Dejó que la cadena se le escurriera entre los dedos, pero la sujetó en el último momento.

No. Este amuleto no representaba a Ilva, sino a Luc. La mujer se había aprovechado de ella, pero su amigo no tenía culpa de nada. Helena estaba haciendo todo aquello por Luc, porque lo merecía.

Volvió a colgarse la cadena del cuello, se lo escondió bajo las ropas y se sentó a contemplar la ciudad mientras la piedra se calentaba contra su corazón.

Cuando regresó al Reducto una semana más tarde, Crowther y ella ya habían acordado cómo solucionar cualquier nuevo imprevisto. El punto de encuentro, que resultó ser un sótano abandonado, les serviría de piso franco. Si Ferron la hería y Helena no estaba en condiciones de curarse sola, tendría que ir allí, donde le esperarían unos cuantos suministros médicos básicos y una radio de onda corta. Bastaría con que enviara un mensaje en clave para que Ivy acudiera en su ayuda.

Ferron llegaba tarde otra vez. Casi nunca aparecía a la hora acordada, pero, en aquella ocasión, Helena estaba demasiado nerviosa como para quedarse a esperarlo. Estaba colgándose la bolsa del hombro justo cuando la puerta se abrió.

Ella se estremeció cuando entró en la habitación y cerró la puerta tras él. Su corazón dio un vuelco al oírla cerrarse con un clic.

—Llego tarde —anunció Ferron.

Helena tuvo que concentrarse en respirar un par de veces antes de ser capaz de hablar.

—¿Vamos a… r-repetir lo del entrenamiento esta semana?

—No —se apresuró a decir él—. No volveré a hacerte algo así.

Ella asintió, pero ahora sabía que era mejor no creerle. Ferron modificaba las condiciones del acuerdo cada vez que le convenía.

Lo estudió con cautela. El chico parecía estar a punto de decir algo, pero se lo pensó mejor y apretó los puños.

—¿Qué pasa? —le espetó Helena con mala cara.

Estaba harta de no saber qué esperar de él.

—No tenía intención de hacerte daño —admitió con la vista clavada en el suelo para no mirarla a los ojos.

—Bueno, imaginaba que ese momento iba a llegar tarde o temprano —respondió ella con una risa crispada.

Un destello de rabia surcó la mirada de Ferron al levantar la cabeza.

Estaba empezando a entenderlo. Se creía mejor que el resto de los inmarcesibles y odiaba que lo consideraran igual que los demás. Por eso había cambiado de idea y quiso hacerle creer que era ella la que controlaba la situación en aquel acuerdo. Sin embargo, por mucho que Ferron intentara convencerse de lo contrario, estaban todos cortados por el mismo patrón, incluido él.

Le lanzó una mirada asesina.

—Si alguien hubiera muerto la semana pasada en el hospital por haberme dejado incapacitada, toda la culpa habría sido tuya.

—¿Y se supone que eso tiene que importarme? —resopló.

—Si fueras humano, te importaría.

Ferron apretó los dientes.

—Bueno, pues ya que nos estamos sincerando, que sepas que eres una negada para la autodefensa. Se te da peor de lo que esperaba. Y eso ya es decir, porque la opinión que tenía de ti no era precisamente buena. Yo pensaba que en la Resistencia entrenaban a su equipo médico para que pudiera defenderse en caso de emergencia.

—El hospital está protegido, y eso es mucho más práctico que esperar que el personal esté entrenado para combatir.

Era evidente que Ferron no pensaba igual.

—Ya, bueno, pero ahora no te encuentras en el hospital. —Caminó alrededor de Helena despacio—. Estás demasiado delgada y no tienes nada de músculo, así que no creo que podamos conseguir algo en estas condiciones. Vas a tener que hacer ejercicios de musculación antes de que pueda enseñarte siquiera a defenderte.

La asignatura que a Helena menos le gustaba en la Academia era la de Calistenia.

—Aunque haga ejercicio, tienes que prometerme que no me harás daño en las manos.

Ferron hizo una pausa.

—Si te haces daño, yo te curaré.

A Helena le daba vueltas la cabeza. Nunca se había parado a pensar que podría herirla, curarla y volverla a herir a su antojo. Y todo sin dejar ni rastro de su crueldad.

Sacó un sobre y se lo ofreció, pero, cuando ella intentó cogerlo, él no lo soltó. La observó durante un instante.

—¿Tenéis escasez de alimentos?

Helena no dijo nada. Se limitó a sostener el sobre a la espera de que

Ferron lo soltara. Crowther le había dejado muy claro que no debía contarle nada acerca de la situación de la Resistencia.

El chico apretó los labios.

—Todo apunta a que la entrega que se llevará a cabo en el cuadrante del sur será de comida. Si os las arregláis para interceptarla, dile a Crowther que te aumente las raciones diarias.

UNA SEMANA MÁS TARDE, UNO de los grupos de avanzadilla se las arregló para capturar y matar a una quimera, aunque la verdad era que ya estaba al borde de la muerte cuando consiguieron arrinconarla.

Después de que llevaran el cadáver al Cuartel General para que lo analizaran, decidieron tras un largo debate que Helena se encargaría de diseccionarlo. Las quimeras habían sido creadas por medio de la vivemancia, así que iban a necesitar a una vivemante para que les explicara el proceso que habían seguido. El deber de la Llama Eterna era estudiar las prácticas de sus enemigos.

Los restos de la criatura apestaban, como si hubiera muerto estando ya en proceso de descomposición. Para crear la quimera, primero la habían descuartizado y despellejado, y, luego, le habían cortado los músculos para combinarlos con los de otros animales. También le habían sustituido varios órganos. Tenía el cráneo de un reptil, pero le habían ampliado la cavidad craneal para que en su interior cupiera el cerebro de un mamífero mucho más grande.

Sabía que no le habían dado vida por medio de la nigromancia, pues muchos habían intentado sin éxito reanimar animales en el pasado. La quimera debía de haber estado viva mientras la creaban, pero Helena no tenía ni la menor idea de cómo consiguieron que la criatura no muriera durante el proceso.

Shiseo se mantenía cerca mientras ella trabajaba para pasarle los utensilios que fuera necesitando. Todavía no entendía por qué había accedido a ser su asistente, ya que su formación era demasiado extensa y sus conocimientos metalúrgicos habrían dejado en evidencia a muchos maeses gremiales. Que Ilva le hubiera pedido que colaborara con Helena era prácticamente una ofensa.

Mientras ella redactaba el informe pertinente, Shiseo se puso a bocetar los sellos compuestos necesarios para desarrollar las tinturas infusionadas con metales de las que habían estado hablando. La plata, el cobre y el hierro tenían propiedades medicinales y podrían ayudar a incrementar la eficacia de ciertos extractos.

—¿No tienes un área de trabajo propia, Shiseo? —le preguntó levantando la vista.

El hombre hizo una pausa.

—No. La idea era que impartiera clases en la Academia, pero… —Negó con la cabeza.

Ella cambió el peso del cuerpo de un pie a otro; se sentía incómoda por haber tardado tanto en comprender por qué había accedido a ser su asistente.

—Debería haberte dicho esto antes, pero, si quieres trabajar en tus propios proyectos, siéntete libre de utilizar este laboratorio.

Shiseo le ofreció una vaga sonrisa y ladeó la cabeza, pero Helena supo de inmediato que no le tomaría la palabra.

A lo mejor se había equivocado. ¿Y si Ilva lo había manipulado para que aceptara la posición? Podría ser… Había llegado a Paladia buscando asilo político y ahora Ilva le estaba haciendo devolver el favor. Eso explicaría por qué se tomaba tantas molestias en mantenerse fuera del camino de todo el mundo. Helena se sentía culpable, pero no iba a negar que su ayuda le venía bien.

—Eso sí, he de advertirte de que el laboratorio es técnicamente robado —le dijo encontrando su mirada—. Como nadie lo usaba, me traje mis herramientas y empecé a trabajar sin pedir permiso. —Se encogió de hombros—. Todos han dado por hecho que alguien le dio luz verde a mi proyecto, así que te prometo que puedes usar este espacio para lo que quieras. Aunque… entenderé que rechaces mi oferta si no te gustan los laboratorios usurpados.

Él la miró impasible, con cautela, pero, entonces, le aparecieron unas arruguitas en las comisuras de los ojos.

—Puede que tenga un par de asuntos que atender.

———————————

Los encuentros con Ferron se volvieron más esporádicos. Helena hacía ejercicio con diligencia, según le había indicado, pero él cada vez se dejaba ver menos. En ocasiones, Helena se encontraba un sobre en la mesa al llegar y, otras, se quedaba esperándolo hasta que no tenía más remedio que marcharse con las manos vacías. También había días en que el anillo se calentaba a horas intempestivas y se veía obligada a acercarse al Reducto para descubrir una carta o un mapa, sin rastro de Ferron.

La información parecía ser de utilidad, pero notaba que Crowther empezaba a darse por vencido y la trataba como si no fuera a conseguir nada más.

Aquel día, se sorprendió al abrir la puerta del módulo y encontrar a Ferron esperándola, sentado a la mesa. Le daba vueltas perezosamente a una moneda de plata entre los dedos.

Ninguno de los dos dijo nada, pero, al cabo de un rato, Ferron habló sin mirarla.

—El Sumo Nigromante va a pasar la próxima semana fuera del país. Se marcha a Hevgoss. Casi un tercio de los inmarcesibles lo acompañarán, por lo que se están volcando en los preparativos. Aun así, el viaje se ha mantenido en secreto y solo unos pocos estamos al tanto de ello. —Hizo una pausa y se guardó la moneda—. Es una situación sin precedentes. Esta es la oportunidad que la Resistencia ha estado esperando. Es muy poco probable que los inmarcesibles se coordinen bien porque todos querrán llevarse el mérito y la gloria.

—Supongo que tú habrás sido uno de los elegidos para acompañarlo —dijo Helena.

No le sorprendería nada que se marchara para que la ciudad quedara reducida a cenizas sin correr el riesgo de que la culpa recayera en él. Así, obtendría la recompensa a su esfuerzo sin importar el desenlace.

Ese había sido su objetivo desde el principio. Su plan era una carrera de fondo y la Resistencia se lo estaba poniendo todo en bandeja, pero Helena estaba atada de pies y manos. Al fin y al cabo, como no aprovecharan una oportunidad así, bien podían darse por vencidos, porque no aguantarían hasta el final de año.

—¿Algo más? —preguntó al ver que Ferron no respondía.

El chico negó con la cabeza, se puso de pie y se acercó a la puerta, pero se detuvo justo antes de abrirla.

—Me parece que lo mejor será cancelar los encuentros de las próximas semanas. No creo que vaya a poder venir.

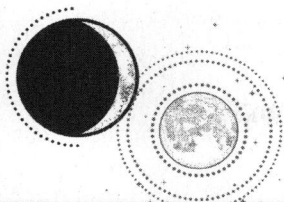

CAPÍTULO 32

Mayus 1786

QUE MORROUGH FUERA A SALIR del país llevándose a tantos inmarcesibles consigo era la oportunidad que la Llama Eterna había estado esperando, así que, como una máquina bien engrasada, la Resistencia enseguida comenzó a preparar el ataque.

Crowther había estado diseminando la información que Ferron les había hecho llegar a lo largo de los últimos meses como si los mapas, los datos sobre las patrullas y sus rotaciones, las cadenas de mando, las jerarquías y los contraataques en caso de enfrentamiento con la Resistencia provinieran de distintas fuentes.

Los batallones estaban ansiosos por actuar.

Sin embargo, Helena sentía bajo la piel un implacable pavor que no dejaba de crecer. ¿Y si estaba todo preparado? ¿Y si Ferron había mentido y la información que les había dado era una trampa? No dejaba de pensar en lo extraño que se había comportado durante su último encuentro.

El personal médico aguardaba el regreso de los combatientes en vilo, atrapado entre la esperanza y el miedo. Entonces las sirenas que anunciaban la llegada de los camiones empezaron a sonar y cada rincón del hospital quedó abarrotado de heridos. No había espacio para tanta gente.

Helena ni siquiera pudo asimilar la angustiosa sensación de culpa que se adueñó de ella al ver las secuelas de la batalla antes de ponerse manos a la obra.

«Es todo culpa tuya. Deberías haberlo sabido. Ferron es un monstruo. Un traidor nato, igual que su padre».

Jamás había sanado a tantas personas en un periodo tan breve de tiempo. El frenesí de la tarea hizo que el amuleto que colgaba del cuello de Helena acabara ardiendo contra su piel y que dos de las aprendizas consumieran toda su resistencia y se desmayaran de agotamiento.

Pasó más de un día antes de que les informaran de que no habían perdido. El ataque no había sido un fracaso, sino un éxito rotundo. La Resistencia había recuperado la zona portuaria y una buena parte de la isla Este. Aunque el combate aún seguía en el extremo sudoeste de la isla, todo apuntaba a que la victoria sería inminente.

Pese a esa confirmación, Helena no terminaba de creérselo. No dejaban de llegar heridos. La Resistencia había encontrado prisiones llenas de disidentes y había descubierto que uno de los edificios más grandes junto a la zona portuaria se había estado usando como laboratorio, así que regresaron con camiones llenos de suministros médicos y utensilios que Helena llevaba años sin ver. Encontraron sedantes y antisépticos de verdad, cajas y cajas de resina de opio, gasas y vendas limpias.

Pero su alegría duró poco, pues, junto a los suministros, llegaron también las víctimas de los experimentos realizados allí. Incluso los miembros del personal, quienes durante años habían mostrado una entereza inquebrantable, se derrumbaron al ver el estado en que aquellas personas se encontraban. Muchos de ellos tuvieron que retirarse.

Resultaba que no solo habían estado desarrollando quimeras a partir de animales. Aquellas personas habían quedado casi irreconocibles después de haber sido sometidas a todo tipo de experimentos que escapaban a su comprensión. Las habían desmembrado para luego reensamblarlas, y eran muchas las que habían llegado en ese estado.

La responsabilidad de tratarlas cayó sobre Helena. Los cirujanos no sabían qué hacer y las aprendizas se veían sobrepasadas por la situación. Aunque ella tampoco tuvo demasiado éxito. Por mucho que lo intentó, no consiguió salvar a ninguna de las víctimas del laboratorio.

Para los combatientes, la reconquista fue rápida. Habían recuperado lo que los inmarcesibles habían tardado años en ocupar con un único ataque bien coordinado. Se trataba de un triunfo militar que pasaría a la historia.

En cambio, para el hospital fue una pesadilla interminable.

La noticia del regreso de Morrough estaba envuelta en rumores que aseguraban que se había desatado una intensa agitación entre las filas de los inmarcesibles mientras buscaban culpables. Luego, llegaron los contrataques y los intentos de recuperar la zona portuaria.

Pasaron semanas antes de que la situación se estabilizara y el personal médico pudiera retomar sus turnos normales. Crowther e Ilva reclutaron a nuevas aprendizas. De alguna manera, sabían exactamente quién contaba con una resonancia latente en su interior, incluso si las propias chicas lo desconocían.

Para cuando todo terminó, Helena estaba tan agotada que pasó unos cuantos días sin poder hablar apenas, casi como si hubiera olvidado cómo se hacía.

Cuando Pace la encontró en el cuarto de suministros haciendo un inventario por pura inercia, le dijo que se fuera del hospital y que, salvo en caso de emergencia, no le permitiría regresar hasta que hubiera descansado cuatro días como mínimo.

Helena quiso retomar sus obligaciones habituales, así que, cuando llegó el martis, se levantó al amanecer, cogió su bolsa y salió de la ciudad. Pasadas las inundaciones de la primavera, la vida había regresado al humedal.

La luz se reflejaba en las alas de los insectos que danzaban en el aire, mientras el sol lamía la cordillera que se extendía por el este y bañaba sus cumbres de oro, y el viento, que por fin había amainado y ya no sacudía los juncos secos, susurraba entre la hierba. Los gorjeos de los pájaros lo inundaban todo. El humedal estaba exuberante, lleno de vida. Helena podría haberse pasado horas recolectando y todavía quedarían hierbas y recursos suficientes. Pero se limitó a coger lo que consideró más valioso antes de lavarse las manos en una charca de color verde alga y, después, se encaminó hacia el Reducto.

Casi no había tenido tiempo de pensar en Ferron, pero decidió que lo mejor sería comprobar si le había dejado algún mensaje. No había recibido órdenes de Crowther desde el ataque.

Lo vio en cuanto abrió la puerta del módulo. Estaba encorvado, con una cadera apoyada contra la mesa, y le colgaban los brazos sin fuerza a ambos lados del cuerpo.

—Tienes una pinta horrible —le dijo en cuanto la vio entrar.

—Pues tú no te quedas atrás —replicó ella parándose en seco.

Ferron se rio con tirantez.

—No me digas.

Al verlo, Helena se sintió demasiado conmocionada como para contestar. El chico estaba demacrado, como si hubiera perdido aún más peso, y tenía todos los huesos del cráneo marcados.

Parecía…

… un cadáver.

Le dio un vuelco el corazón.

Su piel estaba gris y apergaminada, y el pelo, de color más oscuro, sucio y despeinado, le caía sin vida alrededor del rostro. Era como si se hubiera pasado esas últimas semanas sin comer, dormir o bañarse.

—¿Eres…? ¿Eres un…? ¿Estás muerto? —se obligó a preguntar.

No sabía si lo podían matar y luego convertirlo en un liche dentro de su propio cuerpo. ¿Era siquiera eso posible?

Ferron le ofreció una sonrisa que hizo que se le partiera el labio inferior. Un hilillo de sangre le cayó por la barbilla, pero la herida se le curó enseguida.

—Es lo que parece, ¿no? Pero no, sigo… vivo.

—¿Qué te ha pasado?

Se acercó a él, aunque le daba miedo tocarlo por si se desintegraba.

—Bueno —dijo Ferron tras respirar entrecortadamente—, como ya habrás oído, al Sumo Nigromante no le ha hecho ninguna gracia lo de la zona portuaria. —Se quedó sin fuerza para continuar hablando y se le cayó la cabeza hacia delante, pero entonces se irguió de golpe, con el rostro retorcido en una mueca de dolor—. Una faena… para el comandante a cargo de la zona.

Helena se sintió desfallecer. No…, era imposible. Ferron había ido con Morrough y los demás a Hevgoss.

—Pero esa zona no es responsabilidad tuya. —Negó con la cabeza—. Está… El comandante es… es…

No recordaba su nombre, pero no era él. De haber estado Ferron al mando, Helena lo habría sabido. Su rango no era lo bastante alto como para tener una zona tan importante a su cargo.

—Hace poco hubo un cambio de líder —dijo él con voz algo ronca—. Pero da igual. ¿Ha salido bien lo del ataque? Imagino que sí, porque habéis recuperado la isla, pero… —Tragó saliva antes de continuar—: ¿Crees que podréis conservarla? ¿Os quedan suficientes soldados?

Se suponía que no debía contarle nada, pero era tan evidente que estaba sufriendo que no pudo morderse la lengua.

—Más de los que esperábamos —admitió.

Ferron volvió a tragar saliva e hizo un leve asentimiento.

—Bien. —Se le cerraron los ojos por un momento—. Algo es algo, supongo. —Tomó aire con dificultad—. Debería irme. Solo… quería saber… No volveremos a vernos.

Trató de erguirse, pero entonces se desplomó. Tuvo que agarrarse a la silla y dejarse caer sobre ella, incapaz de reprimir un jadeo suave, casi agonizante. Cuando volvió a intentar ponerse de pie, fue como si los brazos no le respondieran. Cada vez le costaba más respirar.

—¿Qué te ha pasado, Ferron? ¿Qué te han hecho? —le preguntó la chica con la voz aguda por los nervios mientras revoloteaba a su alrededor sin saber muy bien qué podía hacer.

Él cerró los ojos e inspiró entrecortadamente.

—N-no te metas donde no te llaman, Marino.

Helena se acercó a él como si fuera un animalillo herido, con las manos en alto y las palmas a la vista.

—Sé que estás herido, pero a lo mejor yo te puedo ayudar —le dijo con la mayor delicadeza.

—No hay nada que puedas hacer —replicó él con una carcajada ronca.

—Déjame intentarlo. —Estaba ya lo bastante cerca como para ver que las venas que le corrían por el cuello no eran azules, sino negras como el veneno—. No voy a hacerte daño.

Ferron abrió los ojos de golpe y la rabia le iluminó el rostro.

—No finjas que te importo —le escupió—. Y no te hagas la tonta. Seguro que sabías que pasaría esto.

Ella negó con la cabeza.

—De haber sabido que te harían daño, habría venido antes.

A juzgar por su apariencia, su salud había ido deteriorándose poco a poco a lo largo de las semanas. Aquel desgaste no era algo que surgiera de un día para otro.

Si era verdad que había estado al cargo de la zona portuaria durante los ataques, entonces le había pasado toda aquella información a la Llama Eterna siendo consciente de las consecuencias que eso tendría para él mismo.

—Por favor —extendió una mano—, déjame ayudarte.

—Esos hierbajos del humedal no van a servir de nada. —Se le retorció el rostro de dolor al intentar incorporarse de nuevo—. ¿Qué vas a hacer tú? Si no eres más que una jodida médica.

Helena tragó saliva con fuerza.

—Te daría la razón, pero no soy una simple médica.

Le tocó la mejilla con la yema de los dedos sin ocultar su resonancia.

Sabía que estaba poniendo en peligro la misión, pero, si Ferron moría, todo estaría perdido. Helena estuvo tentada de apartar la mano en cuanto su poder entró en contacto con el cuerpo del chico, porque el talismán que residía en su pecho irradiaba tal cantidad de poder que estuvo a punto de quemarle las terminaciones nerviosas. Sintió cómo se abrasaban todas las células de su cuerpo.

Se estaba muriendo, una y otra vez. Estaba tan al límite que su organismo dejaba de responder, solo para regenerarse al instante y volver a fallar. Era como si estuviese vivo y muerto a la vez, atrapado en una especie de bucle regenerativo sin salida.

Ferron se apartó como si fuera ella quien lo había quemado y no al revés.

—Puta manipuladora. Sabía que había notado tu resonancia cuando perdí el brazo.

Ella dejó caer la mano y evitó su mirada acusadora.

—Me ordenaron que no te lo dijera.

—¿Y por qué me lo dices ahora? —preguntó entornando los ojos.

—Porque ya da igual. Si no te ayudo, morirás.

—No creo que tenga tanta suerte —dijo en tono sombrío.

Helena extendió la mano para rozarle el brazo.

—¿Qué te ha pasado en la espalda?

Ferron cerró los ojos como si estuviera demasiado cansado para mantener aquella conversación. Las mismas venas negras del cuello también le surcaban los párpados.

—Ya que estás tan decidida a ayudarme, te animo a que lo veas por ti misma.

Muy despacio, con sumo cuidado, Helena le soltó la capa y, al quitársela, Ferron se encogió de dolor, pero no dejó escapar sonido alguno. El pestilente olor de los efluvios de las heridas de varias semanas inundó el aire cuando le desabrochó la camisa y se colocó detrás de él para bajársela por los hombros con cuidado.

No llevaba vendas. Su espalda entera, desde los hombros hasta más abajo de las costillas, era una herida abierta y supurante, como si hubiera sido creada quirúrgicamente.

Le habían grabado un sello alquímico en la piel.

Cuando Ferron tomó aire, Helena vio que incluso el blanco de sus costillas estaba salpicado de marcas. Sin embargo, las incisiones de los hombros eran las peores: no solo alcanzaban el hueso, sino que también lo habían perforado. En los omóplatos le habían soldado unas piezas de aleación de lumitio para mantener el sello intacto y activo.

Ni siquiera las habilidades regenerativas de Ferron eran suficientes para contrarrestar una lesión de tal magnitud.

Los sellos podían tener una finalidad meramente ilustrativa, utilizados para dejar constancia de un proceso o calcularlo de forma visual. Sin embargo, también se utilizaban para llevar a cabo transmutaciones o alquimizaciones complejas cuando la simple manipulación resonántica no era suficiente, así como para trabajar con compuestos de origen orgánico, que tendían a ser más volátiles. Solían dibujarse con tiza o carboncillo, o grabarse sobre una superficie con un estilete. Pero Helena jamás había visto uno inscrito en la piel de una persona.

—¿Por qué...? —Le falló la voz—. ¿Por qué te harían algo así?

—Bueno... —Ferron habló despacio, con voz distante—. Se barajaron muchas ideas y toda clase de castigos para hacerme pagar por mi... error. Bennet estaba indignado por haber perdido su laboratorio, a sus víctimas y sus experimentos. Y, como llevaba un tiempo queriendo hacer pruebas en un inmarcesible, propuso que le permitieran encargarse de mi castigo, argumentando que él había sido quien se había llevado la peor parte tras perder la zona portuaria. —Guardó silencio durante un momento y añadió—: El Sumo Nigromante ha dicho que me perdonará si sobrevivo.

Helena se sentía incapaz de apartar la mirada de la herida. Alrededor de las incisiones, la piel de Ferron presentaba claros signos de septicemia; la infección se había extendido hasta la sangre.

Le posó una mano en el brazo, con miedo de rozar el sello, y Ferron se encogió ante su contacto. Su cuerpo seguía intentando regenerarse, reparando las heridas que conformaban el sello, pero, al tener intacto su sistema nervioso, debía de estar sufriendo un dolor inimaginable.

Helena no sabía por dónde empezar, pero no podía quedarse simplemente mirándolo. Intentó insensibilizar la zona de fuera hacia dentro, aunque el efecto no duró mucho. El poder regenerativo de Ferron anulaba sus esfuerzos siempre que encontraba tejido vivo para trabajar. Ni siquiera podía aliviarle el dolor.

Al aproximarse a la herida tanto como pudo, notó que el metal que le habían soldado en los hombros era una aleación de lumitio y titanio, cuya resonancia era tan intensa que Helena la sentía vibrar hasta en los dientes. Le parecía un milagro que Ferron no hubiera perdido la cabeza con aquel material adherido al cuerpo.

Aquella situación la sobrepasaba por completo. Jamás se había enfrentado a una lesión semejante.

—Lo siento, pero no voy a poder curarte.

Ferron soltó una risotada.

—Ya lo sabía.

—Pero… —Helena tragó saliva mientras pensaba— creo que sé cómo ayudarte a contenerla y reducir el daño que te está causando. Tal vez así puedas… sobrevivir. Esa es la condición que te han puesto, ¿no? Que, si sobrevives, no te harán nada más.

Él no respondió.

Tomando su hombro izquierdo como punto de partida, Helena siguió el recorrido de sus venas mediante resonancia, con los dedos a apenas unos milímetros de su piel, guiando la infección hacia una de las incisiones. Cuando una mezcla de pus y sangre casi negra comenzó a brotar de la herida y a deslizarse por la espalda, utilizó la esquina de un pañuelo de tela para limpiarlo con sumo cuidado, evitando que el fluido se filtrara en las demás heridas.

Ferron se estremeció de pies a cabeza y dejó escapar un jadeo ronco, aunque silencioso.

—¿Qué estás haciendo? —preguntó entre dientes.

—Estás sufriendo una sepsis. Te estás muriendo y tu cuerpo ha estado sacando energía de donde puede para regenerarse y mantenerte vivo, pero ya casi no le quedan reservas. La situación es la misma que cuando perdiste el brazo: no podías regenerarte hasta que dejaste de sangrar, así que, para que te recuperes, primero tendremos que combatir la infección.

El chico dejó caer la cabeza y soltó un suspiro entrecortado.

—Menuda suerte que me examinaras a fondo mientras estaba inconsciente, ¿eh?

—Pues sí —replicó ella con tono seco mientras seguía extrayendo la infección.

Cuando volvió a pasarle el pañuelo por la espalda, Ferron gimió entre dientes y sus manos empezaron a temblarle. Con lo del brazo, no había emitido ningún sonido.

Helena se detuvo, pero no dejó caer las manos.

—¿Los calmantes te funcionan?

—No —dijo él con desgana—. El efecto se me pasa enseguida. Ni siquiera puedo emborracharme en condiciones.

—Yo prefiero bloquear el dolor a nivel local, pero también podría estimular un punto concreto en tu cerebro que te hará perder el conocimiento —comentó Helena, tocándole la base del cráneo con gesto vacilante—. No notarás nada y tu cuerpo seguirá funcionando con normalidad, así que no lo interpretará como una amenaza. ¿Quieres que lo intente?

—¿Podrías…? —Se le quebró la voz—. ¿Podrías hacer eso?

—Sí, creo que sí.

Ferron se lo pensó en silencio, mientras se le estremecían las costillas con cada respiración entrecortada.

—Pues inténtalo, supongo. Si no me has matado ya, no creo que lo hagas ahora.

Helena ignoró su comentario.

—Deberías tumbarte.

La mesa estaba algo rota por el centro, pero seguía siendo lo suficientemente estable para soportar su peso. Helena la cubrió con su capa y la convirtió en una camilla improvisada. Al chico le temblaban las manos cuando se agarró a sus hombros para levantarse con un gruñido. Para cuando se dejó caer sobre la mesa, los temblores se habían extendido por todo su cuerpo.

Helena le pasó los dedos por el cabello para encontrar la curva de la base de su cráneo, justo bajo la protuberancia occipital externa. Con un pequeño cambio de energía, sintió que Ferron se relajaba hasta perder el conocimiento.

Trabajaría mucho más rápido sin que este se encogiera de dolor cada vez que lo tocaba. Mientras drenaba la infección y le limpiaba las heridas, no pudo dejar de pensar en cuánto tiempo podrían tener esas lesiones.

Debería haber vuelto antes. Todo era culpa suya. Dio por sentado que Ferron había decidido marcharse y abandonar la ciudad a su suerte, así que se olvidó de él por completo. Le daba tanto miedo que los traicionara que ni siquiera se había detenido a pensar en qué le pasaría si se mantenía fiel a la causa.

Helena dejó las manos temblorosas a escasos centímetros de las heridas limpias mientras decidía qué hacer. Le habría gustado poder arrancarle el metal que le habían incrustado en los huesos, pero el titanio estaba firmemente adherido al tejido.

Se aferró a su amuleto, desesperada por encontrar algo de consuelo.

Aun así, las incisiones y los metales transmutados eran un problema menor en comparación con el sello. Podía sentir la vibración de la resonancia fluyendo por él. Alterar un sello activo siempre implicaba un riesgo, como la pérdida de alguna extremidad, por ejemplo.

De hecho, intentar romperlo podría matarlos a los dos.

Tenía que encontrar la manera de salvar a Ferron, pero el sello había echado raíces en su cuerpo y, al alimentarse de la energía que manaba del talismán, desviaba el poder que debería estar ayudándolo a regenerarse para que circulara por los trazos que lo componían.

Además, no presentaba un círculo de contención que lo limitara, así que permanecía activo todo el tiempo y, a diferencia de lo que ocurriría en un laboratorio, sus símbolos no actuaban sobre un objetivo externo, sino sobre el propio Ferron. El sello desviaba el poder de su talismán, lo transformaba y luego cerraba el ciclo, devolviéndolo a su interior.

Eso habría acabado con cualquier humano normal, pero Ferron no era tan fácil de matar. Aunque tampoco podía cambiar. Helena empezaba a entender cómo se las arreglaban los inmarcesibles para hacerse «inmortales». Ferron no había dejado de envejecer, sino que su cuerpo estaba congelado en el tiempo desde que comenzó a regenerarse. El proceso no solo lo mantenía con vida, sino que impedía que el paso del tiempo o las heridas alteraran su estado físico. Sin embargo, el sello, así como su poder mutado, estaban diseñados con un único propósito: transformarlo, y esa contradicción lo estaba destruyendo a un nivel mucho más profundo que su espalda mutilada.

Había quedado atrapado en un crisol: el crisol de su propio cuerpo. Y sus únicas opciones eran morir consumido por un sufrimiento atroz o someterse a una alquimización que lo transformara en algo capaz de sobrevivir a semejante paradoja.

Helena estudió los símbolos de su espalda, intentando descifrar la función de cada uno. Nunca había visto un sello diseñado para actuar directamente sobre una persona, pero estaba bastante familiarizada con la notación alquímica.

El diseño central era la estrella celestial clásica, correspondiente a los ocho planetas. A las gentes de Paladia les fascinaban los grupos de cinco u ocho. Hasta donde ella sabía, la única excepción era la estrella de siete puntas de la piromancia, que también aparecía en el blasón solar de los Holdfast.

Quienquiera que hubiera grabado aquellos símbolos en la piel de Ferron los había empleado igual que si hubiera usado una fórmula alquímica para expresar un concepto literario. Era habitual que los alquimistas utilizaran la simbología alquímica al escribir, sobre todo en los libros de texto, para asegurarse de que la información solo pudiera ser comprendida por quienes de verdad fueran capaces de interpretarla, pero Helena nunca había visto ese método aplicado a un sello funcional. Cada una de las ocho puntas de la estrella representaba un concepto concreto, mediante la combinación de los símbolos que la componían. Helena analizó meticulosamente su significado: calculador, astuto, devoto, tenaz, implacable, eficaz, resuelto y severo.

Tenía sentido que el sello no incluyera la fórmula típica de transmutación al estar inscrito en una persona, pero la idea de grabar rasgos de personalidad en un ser humano le resultaba espantosa. Si surtía efecto, la combinación de esas ocho cualidades acabaría por imponerse a la personalidad de Ferron, tal vez hasta borrar cualquier otro rasgo que lo definiera.

Probablemente, le habían realizado curas hasta que el metal se había soldado por completo a sus huesos. Las laceraciones estaban interconectadas para que el sello no se interrumpiera en ningún punto y, por la forma en que Ferron había reaccionado cuando ella se ofreció a dejarlo inconsciente, lo más seguro es que lo hubieran mantenido despierto durante todo el proceso.

Cuando puso una mano sobre la de él, a Helena le temblaban los dedos. Ferron tenía la piel fría y delgada como el papel. Pese a que le habría gustado cerrarle las heridas, la interferencia canalizada por las incisiones era tan intensa que destruiría de inmediato cualquier tejido nuevo que intentara crear.

Si lograba estabilizarlo lo suficiente, cabía la posibilidad de que el poder regenerativo de su cuerpo la ayudara a cerrar las heridas, pero eso llevaría tiempo. Tanto como el que habían necesitado para dejarlo en ese estado.

Helena recurrió a su vivemancia para retirar el tejido muerto de su espalda y, luego, rebuscó en su bolsa hasta encontrar el modesto botiquín que había reabastecido poco antes. Consideró la idea de volver corriendo al Cuartel General a buscar más medicinas, pero tardaría demasiado.

Al final, decidió revisar lo que había recolectado aquella mañana, por si algo podía resultarle útil.

Sabía que los calmantes no servirían de nada ante la interferencia transmutacional, pero un tratamiento tópico tal vez funcionara. Al menos, evitaría que las heridas volvieran a infectarse. Usaría un ungüento percutáneo de acción prolongada y, más adelante, hablaría con Shiseo para ver si a él se le ocurría alguna alternativa.

Helena se mordisqueó los labios, sacó una de las pomadas que había preparado con corteza de sauce y dio unos golpecitos en la tapa mientras pensaba en lo útil que habría sido incluir algún opiáceo entre sus ingredientes. Por el momento, tendría que servir para mantener las heridas limpias hasta su próximo encuentro.

Le extendió todo el bote de ungüento analgésico sobre las incisiones y cubrió las heridas con gasas. Luego, le espolvoreó musgo seco para crear un entorno ácido que evitara nuevas infecciones y le vendó toda la espalda.

Debería haberlo despertado en cuanto acabó, pero se le veía tan agotado que Helena decidió dejarlo descansar un poco más.

Le apartó con timidez un mechón de pelo oscuro del rostro. Estaba demacrado; tenía las mejillas, las sienes y los ojos hundidos, y ya no quedaba ni rastro de ese espeluznante aire juvenil que lo había acompañado cuando se habían conocido.

Ahora solo parecía un muchacho roto.

Helena jugueteaba con sus propias uñas mientras se lamentaba por no poder hacer nada más y luchaba contra la tormenta de emociones que se arremolinaba en su pecho. Estaba acostumbrada a detestarlo, a verlo como una amenaza, tanto para ella como para los demás.

Se acordó de él dándole vueltas a aquella moneda de plata, insistiendo en que la Llama Eterna tenía que atacar. Ya entonces sabía que lo castigarían.

Recordó también los comentarios que había hecho estando apenas consciente, cuando había empezado a divagar sobre que provocó a otro comandante para hacerse con el control de una nueva zona. En su momento, Helena no le dio importancia y pensó que era solo orgullo e inconsciencia, pero ahora lo veía con claridad: Ferron había estado preparándolo todo desde el principio para que la Resistencia pudiera ganar.

Podría haberles tendido una trampa fácilmente, podría haberse dedicado a pasarles información falsa y así llevar a cabo el sabotaje perfecto. En cambio, consciente de que tendría que cargar con las consecuencias, Ferron les había dado una ventaja que no habrían podido obtener ni con un año entero de preparativos.

Y todo dando por hecho desde el principio que Helena conocía sus intenciones. Pensar que él había soportado aquella tortura creyendo que ella sabía lo que le esperaba le partía el alma.

Le tocó la sien y se acercó a él para observarlo con detenimiento.

—¿Por qué estás haciendo esto?

Cuando ya no pudo justificar mantenerlo inconsciente por más tiempo, volvió a pasarle los dedos por el cabello y lo despertó con la mayor delicadeza posible para que el dolor no lo golpeara de repente. Mientras recuperaba el conocimiento, Helena le tomó la mano que tenía más cerca, con cuidado de no moverle el hombro, y se la empezó a masajear despacio, desde la palma, nudillo a nudillo, hasta alcanzar la yema de cada dedo. Utilizaba la resonancia para detectar cada músculo agarrotado por la tensión.

Su padre solía darle esos masajes todas las noches, incluso antes de mudarse a Paladia. Decía que las manos de una alquimista eran tan valiosas como las de cualquier cirujano, y por eso había que cuidarlas mucho.

Helena sabía que Ferron no lo necesitaba. Se trataba de un pequeño gesto que solo ella valoraba, pero era todo lo que podía ofrecerle en ese instante.

Supo cuándo recuperó el conocimiento porque la tensión se extendió por todo su cuerpo. Ferron abrió los ojos de golpe y las pupilas se le contrajeron de dolor. Sus dedos se crisparon entre los de Helena, pero permaneció tumbado sin moverse, así que ella continuó masajeándoselos.

Todavía tenía la mirada algo vidriosa.

—¿Qué me has hecho? —preguntó por fin.

—He drenado la sangre infectada y he retirado todo el tejido muerto —explicó tras humedecerse los labios—. Luego, te apliqué un ungüento analgésico y te vendé las heridas. No es el tratamiento más eficaz, pero te aliviará hasta que pueda prepararte algo mejor en el Cuartel General. T-todavía no puedo cerrarte las heridas, pero, cuando hayas recuperado las fuerzas, creo que lo lograremos. Primero debes mejorar un poco.

Ferron apartó su mano de las de Helena y se incorporó despacio mientras ella hablaba. Cada movimiento debía de ser un suplicio, pero no emitió ni un solo sonido. Se tambaleó como si estuviera a punto de desmayarse cuando se bajó de la mesa.

—Da igual —dijo antes de coger su camisa—. No es tu trabajo curarme.

—Hay que vigilar la evolución de las heridas para evitar que se infecten de nuevo o empeoren. Y tendrás que cambiarte los vendajes al menos una vez al día —apuntó ella dando un paso adelante para bloquearle el paso.

—Pues mala suerte.

—Ferron. —Le quitó la camisa de las manos—. Sé que no estás acostumbrado a que cuiden de ti, pero necesitas atención médica. Si no tienes cuidado, esas heridas podrían matarte… o dejarte en un estado aún peor.

El chico soltó una carcajada ronca.

—Esa es la idea, Marino. ¿Te crees que Bennet me hizo esto esperando que saliera bien?

—Pero yo puedo ayudarte —insistió ella, desesperada, mientras le colocaba la camisa para demostrarle lo útil que podía llegar a ser—. Mira, tengo un laboratorio y se me da bien la quimiatría. Te prepararé un ungüento tópico para las heridas y vendré aquí una vez al día a cambiarte las vendas y asegurarme de que no empeores.

—¿Y vas a tener tiempo para todo eso? —preguntó él con aspereza.

—Ya me organizaré como sea. Te prometo que vendré todos los días. Por favor.

—Está bien —dijo, aparentemente desconcertado. Apartó la mirada de ella—. Nos reuniremos aquí a las ocho en punto de la tarde. Pero, si me haces venir y no apareces, se acabó.

—Estaré aquí cada tarde a las ocho —prometió.

Necesitaría un permiso especial para que la dejaran salir, pero convencería a Crowther de que le preparara uno. Y, si no, ya se encargaría ella misma de falsificarlo.

Helena le abotonó la camisa, pero se detuvo cuando llegó al hueco de su garganta. Se le marcaban los huesos a través de la piel, surcada todavía por venas oscuras.

—Lo siento mucho, Kaine.

El agotamiento le había dejado la expresión casi en blanco, pero el chico enarcó una ceja con esfuerzo, lo que disminuyó un poco su efecto.

—De haber sabido que te tomarías tantas confianzas después de curarme, te habría pedido que me dejaras morir. —Casi sonaba como el de siempre.

Helena se encogió de hombros y tomó la capa para ponérsela sobre los hombros, aunque no estaba segura de que fuera buena idea que cargara con ese peso adicional.

—¿Te molesta que te llame por tu nombre? Me resulta raro que sigamos usando nuestros apellidos. Al fin y al cabo, vamos a pasar el resto de nuestra vida juntos, ¿no?

Él levantó la vista al techo y suspiró.

—Me da igual cómo me llames, pero yo voy a seguir tratándote como siempre.

—Bien. Entonces te llamaré Kaine a partir de ahora.

Tenía que encontrar la manera de pensar en él de otra forma. Lo había juzgado mal en demasiadas ocasiones viéndolo solo como «Ferron».

—Por el momento, me están dejando al margen de las decisiones importantes, pero sé dónde está el nuevo laboratorio de Bennet. —Le dedicó una sonrisa contenida—. Le gusta estar cerca del agua, así que ha elegido una de las naves que hay junto al astillero de la isla Oeste. Te traeré un mapa la próxima vez que venga.

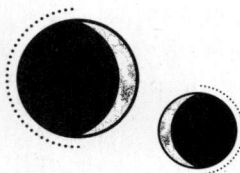

CAPÍTULO 33

Helena salió con tiempo para asegurarse de no llegar tarde. Ahora tenía una nueva autorización para salir con la excusa de que iba al Reducto a prestar ayuda médica.

Una parte de ella se sentía culpable, pues le habría gustado que ese fuera el verdadero motivo de sus salidas. El Reducto cada vez estaba más abarrotado, pero la Resistencia no podía permitirse distribuir sus limitadas provisiones.

Cuando llegó a los apartamentos, había decenas de personas reunidas alrededor de una fogata.

Se detuvo en seco sin saber qué hacer. Con lo mal que estaba Ferron, era imposible que llegara hasta el módulo sin que alguien lo reconociera. Y, en realidad, tampoco sabía cómo se las arreglaba para pasar desapercibido cuando estaba bien.

Mientras Helena buscaba una forma de llegar a la escalera sin llamar la atención del grupo de refugiados, una figura agazapada junto a una pared se incorporó lentamente. La capucha que le cubría el rostro se le deslizó un poco, lo justo para revelar las facciones pálidas de un necrómata.

Helena dio un respingo.

Aquella criatura había sido un hombre en otra vida. La mitad de su rostro estaba cubierta por una barba desaliñada y sus ojos blanquecinos se ocultaban tras unas tupidas cejas. Habían hecho un trabajo de reanimación impecable con él. No presentaba signos de descomposición y lo único que demostraba que estaba muerto era la piel cerosa y los ojos lechosos.

Había escuchado cientos de veces que los necrómatas eran agresivos, pero nunca se le había ocurrido pensar que pudieran pasar desapercibidos, aguardando pacientemente.

Cuando el necrómata avanzó hacia ella, Helena estuvo a punto de sufrir un infarto. Las sienes le palpitaban con fuerza, le martilleaban como un tambor, y un dolor abrasador se le extendió por el lateral del cuello.

«No pienses en ello».

El necrómata se detuvo y se subió una manga. En el brazo llevaba dibujado el mismo símbolo estilizado del hierro que había visto en la entrada de los apartamentos. La criatura estaba al mando de Ferron. Helena había estado a punto de olvidar que el chico era un nigromante. Entonces el necrómata se bajó la manga al tiempo que señalaba a la izquierda.

Saber que trabajaba para Ferron no hizo que perderse voluntariamente con él por el Reducto fuera más sencillo.

El corazón le latía a toda velocidad mientras avanzaban hacia una puerta que se confundía con la pared. El necrómata sacó una pequeña llave y, al abrirla, reveló una escalera de metal que bajaba hacia el corazón de una de las fábricas.

Las tenues luces eléctricas parpadeaban sobre su cabeza. Entraron en una sala de calderas y cruzaron un estrecho pasillo hasta llegar a uno mucho más amplio, donde había una enorme puerta que se abrió de golpe desde el interior. Era más gruesa que el antebrazo de Helena, así que supuso que se trataba de una cámara acorazada.

Al otro lado, en una habitación espaciosa, repleta de muebles caros y lámparas de araña de las que colgaban prismas que refractaban la luz, estaba Ferron… sosteniendo una copa en la mano.

La estancia era tan ostentosa que resultaba grotesca.

Las paredes estaban decoradas con cortinas y murales lujosos, incluso en una de ellas había hileras de decantadores y botellas. Uno de los rincones de la sala contaba con una zona para sentarse, con recargadas mesitas auxiliares, un amplio sofá y un par de butacas. En el extremo opuesto, había un escritorio de caoba y un diván. Todos los muebles tenían una cantidad tan excesiva de detalles que debían de haber costado una fortuna.

—Aquí estás —dijo Ferron, atrayendo la atención de Helena. Vestía solo unos pantalones y una camisa blanca con la mitad de los botones desabrochados.

Helena estaba acostumbrada a que estuviese completamente cubierto, con las capas del uniforme como si fueran una coraza, y, aunque ya lo había visto desnudo de cintura para arriba en dos ocasiones, entonces había sido por razones médicas.

La estancia en la que se encontraban no tenía nada de profesional. A pesar de su aspecto maciento, Ferron —o Kaine, como se corrigió para sus adentros— desprendía un extraño atractivo, como si nunca lo hubiera visto en el escenario que de verdad le correspondía.

—¿Qué es este sitio? —preguntó Helena, avanzando con cautela.

El necrómata no la siguió, sino que dio un paso atrás y cerró la puerta con un golpe pesado y sordo.

—Una habitación del pánico —explicó él—. Mi abuelo la mandó construir en caso de emergencia, tras enfrentarse a una huelga hace un par de décadas.

—No me imagino por qué querrían hacerle daño a tu abuelo cuando claramente gastó su dinero en cosas tan razonables —dijo mientras recorría con los ojos las tres lámparas de araña que colgaban del techo.

—Desde luego, todo un misterio.

Todavía quedaban unos cuantos dedos de líquido en su copa, pero se la acabó de un solo trago.

—Si lo que buscas bebiendo así es perder la sensibilidad, te recomiendo que tomes mejor analgésicos en la misma cantidad —comentó mirándolo de reojo.

—Pero eso no tiene gracia. —Se sirvió otra copa con dedos temblorosos—. El entumecimiento del alcohol solo dura unos minutos. Para colocarme de verdad, prefiero el veneno. Por lo general, dura más, y algunos tienen unos efectos secundarios bastante curiosos. Aunque supuse que eso no te haría mucha gracia —suspiró—. Dada la situación actual del Reducto y que no me apetece volver a tumbarme sobre una mesa de cocina nunca más, se me ocurrió que este lugar sería más apropiado.

Helena asintió, sin saber si debería sentirse ofendida o agradecida al descubrir que Ferron había escogido el módulo y no aquella cámara como su punto de encuentro habitual. Seguramente habría entrado en pánico si lo hubiera visto allí por primera vez.

Arrastró con cuidado una de las mesitas auxiliares de patas largas y delgadas hasta donde estaban, obligándose a no sufrir por si arañaba su delicada superficie al sacar sus materiales.

Ferron se bebió la segunda copa de un trago, se sentó a horcajadas sobre una silla colocada con el respaldo hacia delante y se desabrochó la camisa. Antes de que Helena tuviera oportunidad de ayudarlo, retorció los hombros para quitarse la prenda y ahogó un jadeo de dolor.

—¿Te encuentras algo mejor?

Cuando le tocó el brazo con la mano desnuda, él retiró el suyo de inmediato. Su piel estaba helada, pero Helena tenía la esperanza de que la ausencia de fiebre fuera una buena señal.

Al ver que no respondía a su pregunta, se desinfectó las manos con una disolución de ácido carbólico y comenzó a quitarle los vendajes con la mayor delicadeza posible. Luego, empapó las gasas que le cubrían las heridas en solución salina para intentar retirárselas con cuidado, pero estaban pegadas a la piel. Kaine se apartó con un brusco movimiento, temblando de pies a cabeza.

—¡Joder! ¡No…!

Se estaba agarrando con tanta fuerza al respaldo de la silla que tenía los nudillos blancos.

—Tengo que quitarte las gasas —se disculpó Helena tras apartar la mano a toda prisa de su espalda.

—¿En serio? —preguntó apoyando la frente sobre el respaldo con la respiración entrecortada. La chica no contestó, pues la respuesta era evidente. Él se estremeció de nuevo—. Me cago en la puta.

—Lo siento.

—¡Cállate!

Helena se quedó allí de pie, en silencio, mientras esperaba a que recuperase el aliento.

—Vale —escupió él tras una pausa—. Hazlo.

—¿Quieres que te deje inconsciente otra vez? —le preguntó ella.

Kaine levantó la cabeza y la miró. En sus ojos no quedaba ni rastro de emoción y su rostro estaba marcado por el cansancio y las magulladuras.

—¿De verdad merece la pena todo esto?

Helena sostuvo su mirada con firmeza, decidida a curarlo. No estaba dispuesta a permitir que muriera sufriendo después de haber hecho algo bueno en la vida.

—Déjame intentarlo, por favor.

Un brillo de incredulidad le surcó la expresión. Abrió la boca para decir algo, pero finalmente giró la cabeza y presionó la frente contra el respaldo de la silla.

—Está bien —aceptó con resignación.

Después de pasarle los dedos por la base del cráneo, Ferron perdió el conocimiento en cuestión de segundos. Helena retiró las gasas y limpió las heridas con la solución salina y la disolución carbólica. Al menos, ahora la Resistencia disponía de suministros esenciales para que ella pudiera curarlo adecuadamente.

Lo examinó con su resonancia, sin prisa, para entender mejor qué era lo que el sello le estaba haciendo exactamente. Tras pasar por el laboratorio, había ido a la biblioteca en busca de información sobre los sellos, pero no encontró nada. Nadie había grabado un sello activo en un humano.

Sabía que se estaba muriendo, en su resonancia percibía pequeños destellos helados que se extendían por su cuerpo de manera incesante. El sello no solo consumía la energía del talismán, sino que estaba dejando a su organismo sin recursos.

Ferron no tenía la capacidad de contrarrestar ese deterioro, por lo que su estado empeoraba con cada minuto que pasaba. Helena posó una mano en su brazo para intentar transmitirle algo de calor con su resonancia. Si lo hubiera sabido antes, si Ferron la hubiera llamado a tiempo, a lo mejor podría haber hecho algo más…

Pero ahora era ya demasiado tarde.

Lo estudió por un instante, con un nudo en la garganta que le impedía tragar saliva. Había informado a Crowther sobre su situación, pero a este no parecía importarle ni que Kaine estuviera herido ni que Helena le hubiese confesado que era una vivemante. Se limitó a prepararle el permiso correspondiente y a ordenar que hiciera lo que estuviese en su mano para seguir sacándole información al chico. Además, le dio instrucciones de robar su talismán si no conseguía recuperarse. Ferron no les serviría de nada si se convertía en un liche.

Salvarlo o matarlo, no tenía más opciones.

Helena se puso de pie, contemplando el sello mientras se aferraba a su propio amuleto, oculto bajo la camisa, y sintió las puntas de la estrella clavándosele en las cicatrices de la mano.

No podía matarlo, no después de haber conseguido que confiara en ella. No después de que él lo hubiera dado todo por ayudar.

Unos meses antes, tal vez hubiera contemplado esa opción, pero ya no.

La Resistencia lo necesitaba. Todos los avances que habían hecho, todo el territorio recuperado, todo había sido gracias a él. Tenía que salvarlo.

Se quitó el amuleto del cuello y deslizó los pulgares por su superficie.

Después de volver a ponérselo, notó que ya no estaba tan cansada, que su vivemancia no la agotaba físicamente.

Sabía que los amuletos de heliolita eran especiales, que contenían una parte de la luz y la fuerza de Sol en su interior, pero no había sido consciente hasta ese momento de la diferencia que aquel amuleto había marcado en su vida durante años. La había ayudado a ganar tiempo. La había conducido hasta ese preciso instante.

Si conseguía transmitirle su poder, tal vez pudiera salvar a Kaine. Quizá podría inclinar la balanza a su favor y darle una oportunidad.

Si él moría, poco importaría lo que le ocurriera a ella. Ahora la Resistencia contaba con otras sanadoras y, tras haber recuperado la zona portuaria, las medicinas que preparaba también habían dejado de ser tan necesarias.

Helena era reemplazable, pero Ferron no.

Pese a que su resonancia áurea nunca había sido demasiado potente, intentó recurrir a ella para intensificar los rayos dorados del amuleto. Kaine jamás aceptaría llevar el blasón de los Holdfast, pero, si lograba darle una forma más común…

Al hacerlo, el engaste cedió y la heliolita cayó al suelo. El impacto la rompió. Helena contempló horrorizada que los fragmentos rojos salpicaban la estancia, mientras una sustancia blanca plateada se extendía en el lugar donde había caído la gema.

Se agachó y rozó con los dedos aquel charco de metal líquido. Le recordaba al mercurio, aunque tenía un brillo irisado que casi parecía resplandecer por sí mismo. Al tocarlo, el material se volvía frío y sólido, pero cuando lo cogió volvió a fundirse.

Sintió la cálida energía que desprendía y se filtraba por su piel sin necesidad de recurrir a su resonancia, si bien la sensación desapareció tan pronto como recuperó la solidez de una gema.

Helena estudió fascinada aquella sustancia. Su vibración parecía intensificarse como si estuviera en un sueño: era casi tangible, pero los detalles se desvanecían cuando intentaba fijar la mirada en ellos.

La energía en bruto que desprendía quemaba casi tanto como el talismán que Ferron llevaba colgado en el pecho, aunque, al mismo tiempo, resultaba más agradable, como si fuera una vieja amistad. Helena nunca había dado demasiado crédito a quienes aseguraban que la sanación dependía de una intuición especial o que la vivemancia ofrecía una comprensión casi divina o intuitiva del cuerpo humano, pero estaba segura de que aquel objeto podía curar a Ferron. Sin duda alguna.

Se acercó y tiró de él hacia atrás, evitando presionar sus heridas. Luego, inclinó la mano donde llevaba el líquido, y la gema, de nuevo sólida, rodó suavemente hasta su pecho, cerca de donde tenía el talismán. Al tocar su piel, la sustancia mantuvo su forma en vez de volver a licuarse, aunque Helena la notaba caliente y líquida contra la palma.

Cuando presionó la mano sobre el corazón de Kaine para usar su resonancia, un calor abrasador se adueñó de sus nervios y Helena se sintió como si hubiera sumergido los dedos en agua hirviendo.

La gema se mantenía en estado sólido, pero se calentó rápidamente y se volatilizó en cuanto la resonancia empezó a expandirse por el cuerpo de Kaine.

Helena retiró la mano justo cuando el brillo plateado desaparecía bajo la piel de él.

Por un instante, Kaine se iluminó desde dentro y ella vio las sombras de sus huesos, sus venas y su corazón antes de que el resplandor desapareciera por completo. Helena parpadeó como si acabara de despertar de un sueño profundo. El zumbido de energía se había desvanecido, y el silencio había vuelto a apoderarse de la estancia. Lo único que quedaba del amuleto de Ilva era el engaste con el blasón solar deformado y los fragmentos de cristal rojo repartidos por el suelo.

Tocó el pecho de Ferron con cuidado mientras se preguntaba si todo fueron imaginaciones suyas. Era como si lo que había ocurrido en los últimos minutos no hubiera sido real.

Lo examinó con su resonancia sin saber muy bien lo que acababa de hacer. El chico seguía transmitiéndole la misma sensación disonante, muerta y llena de energía al mismo tiempo. No parecía haber sufrido ningún cambio, salvo quizá un ligero aumento en su temperatura corporal.

Helena se inclinó hacia delante y miró a su alrededor con manos temblorosas. Recogió los fragmentos de heliolita con una calma que en realidad no sentía y los guardó en un frasco vacío que metió en su bolsa mientras su mente se debatía entre creer lo que había pasado o no. Ninguna de las dos opciones se le antojaba del todo verosímil.

Regresó junto a Ferron y lo examinó como si fuera uno más de sus pacientes. Según su resonancia, no parecía haber ningún cambio notable, salvo que las oleadas de frío que la habían sacudido antes ya no eran tan intensas como la primera vez que lo tocó. Sin embargo, en su interior no percibía nada más aparte del talismán que ardía junto a su corazón y la aleación de lumitio que tenía en la espalda.

Cerró los ojos por un instante y levantó la mano para buscar el amuleto que siempre pendía de su cuello, pero recordó que ya no lo tenía. Solo le quedaba esperar y ver qué pasaba.

Le aplicó el ungüento que había preparado junto con Shiseo. Habían utilizado morfina como agente anestésico y la habían combinado con varios tipos de vaselina y cera de abeja para prolongar su efecto, así como con cobre y miel para potenciar sus propiedades antisépticas.

Cuando terminó, le vendó la espalda, se colgó el amuleto vacío del cuello e intentó disimular lo deformado que había quedado el engaste antes de guardarlo bajo la camisa. La pieza de oro estaba helada al tacto.

Mientras despertaba a Kaine gradualmente, Helena tomó su mano rígida por la tensión y se la masajeó suavemente para relajarle los músculos. Percibió que Ferron iba volviendo en sí, pero no se movió ni pronunció palabra durante varios minutos. Finalmente, retiró la mano, se levantó y recogió su camisa en silencio.

Helena lo ayudó a abrochársela mientras notaba sus ojos clavados en ella. Procuró no fijarse demasiado en el punto donde la gema había desaparecido y no levantó la vista hasta que le cerró el último botón del cuello. Ferron tenía la mirada más despejada, alerta, aunque sospechaba que se debía a que ya estaba sobrio.

—Volveré mañana por la noche —le dijo ella.

Para entonces, la piel de Ferron ya no mostraba aquel tono grisáceo tan marcado. Seguía estando en los huesos y todavía tenía el rostro tenso de dolor, pero había recuperado el color y también algo de calor. Se negó a permitir que volviera a dormirlo. Era evidente que no se fiaba de ella y por eso quería saber qué era lo que le había hecho la vez anterior, pero Kaine no lo preguntaría directamente y ella de todas formas tampoco pensaba contárselo.

En vez de curarse o regenerarse, su cuerpo solo había pasado a morirse de una forma menos agresiva. Todavía les quedaba un largo camino por recorrer, uno que dependía de que su organismo encontrara el modo de adaptarse al sello.

Helena intentó limpiarle las heridas con toda la delicadeza del mundo, pero él se estremecía y se aferraba al respaldo de la silla con tanta fuerza que los nudillos se le pusieron blancos. Lo curó con rapidez, avisándole cada vez que se disponía a tocarlo y explicándole cada paso del proceso para ayudarlo a no perder de vista el momento en que dejaría de sufrir.

Sin embargo, él siguió encogiéndose de dolor cada vez que lo rozaba.

Helena regresó al Reducto y siguió la misma rutina noche tras noche. La mayoría de las veces, Kaine ni siquiera le dirigía la palabra. Siempre llegaba algo borracho y, por algún motivo, ver que Helena insistía en curarlo lo ponía de mal humor. Sin embargo, tras cinco días de curas, el talismán que llevaba en el pecho dejó de irradiar energía, como si se tratara de una batería agotada y el deterioro agresivo que sufría a causa del sobreesfuerzo comenzó, por fin, a ralentizarse.

Después de casi una semana curándolo sin que intercambiaran una sola palabra, Ferron habló de pronto mientras Helena se lavaba las manos.

—El Sumo Nigromante está buscando a alguien.

—¿A quién? —preguntó ella tras una pausa.

—A un guardia de uno de los complejos de prisiones de Hevgoss.

—¿Por qué?

—Todavía me consideran una *persona non grata*, así que no me informan con detalle de lo que pasa. Según parece, en algún momento, Morrough le prometió a los estratócratas hevgotianos compartir con ellos la clave para la inmortalidad. Han pasado décadas desde entonces y todavía no ha sido capaz de ofrecérsela como ellos quieren. Si apoyan al Concejo de Gremios es porque el Sumo Nigromante se las ha arreglado para convencerlos de que encontrará la manera de desarrollar una forma de inmortalidad a su medida una vez que se haga con Paladia. Sin embargo, la alianza ha perdido fuerza con los últimos contratiempos y, ahora, Morrough tiene prisa por capturar a ese guardia sin que se enteren en Hevgoss. Hay un puñado de aspirantes que está tratando de localizarlo sin llamar la atención. Si la Llama Eterna quiere saber más, debería enviar a alguien para que los siga.

—¿Por qué no le ha encargado ese trabajo a los inmarcesibles?

—Sería más complicado. Requeriría preparativos muy concretos y, además, tampoco podemos alejarnos mucho.

Helena hizo una pausa.

—¿Por qué?

—Porque estamos ligados a Morrough —confesó el chico, molesto.

Ella se detuvo en seco.

—¿Quieres decir que… —no había forma de preguntárselo con delicadeza— sois como… los necrómatas?

Ferron la fulminó por el rabillo del ojo.

Todo el mundo sabía que los necrómatas no podían alejarse demasiado de quien los había devuelto a la vida sin «morir» de nuevo. La máxima distancia que la mayoría podía alejarse de su dueño no era superior a un par de kilómetros como mucho. Pero los inmarcesibles eran más poderosos que un nigromante común. Los necrómatas que reanimaban se movían por Paladia con tal libertad que nadie había conseguido poner a prueba sus límites, aunque se sospechaba que podían llegar hasta las mismas fronteras del país.

Que los inmarcesibles estuvieran sujetos a unas limitaciones similares dejaba claro que existía cierto paralelismo entre ellos y los necrómatas.

—Así es —dijo Kaine a regañadientes.

—Pero Morrough no se llevó a nadie consigo cuando se marchó y tú sigues aquí. ¿Cómo es posible? —preguntó al tiempo que le aplicaba el ungüento sobre las heridas recientes y en carne viva.

—No siempre estamos ligados a él —suspiró—. Estamos… Morrough utiliza sus propios huesos, fragmentos de ellos, cuando nos concede la inmortalidad. Para crearme a mí, utilizó un segmento del brazo. Las filacterias, que es como las llama, son la base de los talismanes y las causantes de nuestra inmutabilidad física. —Se señaló el pecho—. A veces nos las saca y las sustituye por un hueso nuevo o uno de necrómata para dejarnos atrás cuando viaja. No le gusta recurrir a quitárnoslas a menudo, pero, si se marchase sin retirar las filacterias, la conexión se rompería y nosotros… moriríamos.

—¿Sus huesos? —Helena se había quedado bloqueada con ese detalle.

Ferron asintió.

—Así es. Morrough comparte un fragmento de su ser con nosotros y, a cambio, nos entregamos por completo a él.

Se quedó callado mientras Helena seguía trabajando, asimilando lo que acababa de contarle. Luego, volvió a hablar:

—Algunos de los nuestros trataron de huir después de que estallara la guerra y se dieran cuenta de que tendrían que ensuciarse las manos para deponer a los Holdfast. El Sumo Nigromante los mató, luego reanimó a los cadáveres, preparó nuevos talismanes con las filacterias y se los metió dentro. Creo que vosotros los llamaríais liches en ese caso. Ahí fue cuando comprendimos de verdad lo que significaba ser un «inmarcesible».

—¿Qué pasaría si robases tu filacteria?

El chico se rio entre dientes.

—Si ves eso posible es porque nunca has conocido a Morrough. Puede llenar estancias enteras con su resonancia. En cualquier caso, las filacterias se descomponen después de un tiempo y, aunque su deterioro no nos mata…, nos hace perder la cabeza poco a poco.

Bueno, eso explicaba por qué Ferron necesitaba a la Llama Eterna: dependía de ella para que derrotara a Morrough por él.

—Se lo comunicaré a Crowther —dijo Helena cuando terminó.

SE DETUVO EN MITAD DEL puente de la isla Este para observar la presa y las montañas. Aunque Lumitia estaba en cuarto menguante, pues el verano se acercaba y, con él, su fase de latencia, su luz lo bañaba todo.

En tan solo unas semanas, la marea estival descendería por completo, el mar volvería a ser navegable y, durante un mes, una oleada de comerciantes llegaría al continente. La Resistencia había conseguido recuperar el control de la zona portuaria justo a tiempo para la temporada de intercambio comercial.

Helena contempló el austero mundo que la rodeaba, coloreado en tonos de blanco y negro.

Se sentía perdida. La lesión de Kaine estaba acabando con su desapego hacia él. Sabía que estaba dejando a un lado su objetivo y, ahora que el chico empezaba a recuperarse, no podía permitirse olvidar cuál era su misión.

Tenía que llamar su atención, ganarse su lealtad o convertirse en su obsesión. Lo que fuera más fácil. Por muy valiosa que fuera la información que les ofrecía, Kaine seguía siendo un riesgo si sus servicios dependían únicamente de su buena voluntad.

Inmarcesible. Asesino. Espía. Objetivo. Peón.

Se repitió aquellas palabras para sus adentros, pero ahora le sonaban huecas.

Cada vez estaba más segura de que las intenciones que Crowther le atribuía no eran más que una fachada tras la que Kaine se ocultaba. Helena era una alquimista, así que no tenía la costumbre de manipular o alterar algo antes de asegurarse de haber entendido bien su naturaleza.

Cruzó el puente y, de camino al Cuartel General, un jardín de infiltración le llamó la atención. Había pasado junto a él infinidad de veces, pero nunca se había detenido a admirarlo. Aquella noche, algo la empujó a acercarse. Aunque estaba descuidado, en su día seguramente habría sido precioso. En medio del riachuelo que lo atravesaba había un pequeño santuario consagrado a la diosa Luna.

Pocos eran los devotos que la veneraban en Paladia. Darle por completo la espalda a alguno de los dioses era algo que se consideraba peligroso, pero la mayoría de los paladinos apenas la reconocía como parte de la Quintaesencia.

Consideraban a Luna voluble, vanidosa y tan traicionera como las mareas. Según la Fe, fue la naturaleza cambiante de la diosa la que empujó a Sol a engendrar a Lumitia a partir de su propio corazón, para colocarla en el cielo nocturno y así librar a la humanidad del temor a la oscuridad. Pero Luna, envidiosa de su luminosidad, decidió cobrarse su venganza inundando el mundo. Lumitia se enfrentó a ella en una batalla celestial tan devastadora que una lluvia de fuego descendió sobre la tierra y, tras su enfrentamiento, se hizo un hueco en el cielo y compartió el don de la alquimia con la humanidad para compensar la destrucción causada durante el Gran Desastre. Mientras tanto, implacable incluso tras su derrota, Luna siguió agitando los mares y océanos para expresar su rabia. Lo único que la calmaba era reinar sola sobre los cielos.

Miles de años más tarde, Luna todavía era una deidad repudiada, pequeña e insignificante en comparación con la belleza y el poder de la brillante Lumitia.

La estatua de Luna no era más que una figura abandonada; estaba tan desgastada que ya no se distinguían sus rasgos. Helena se sintió muy conmocionada al descubrir la forma en que los paladinos trataban a la diosa. Era consciente de la devoción que profesaban por Sol y Lumitia, pero su modo de entender la religión era totalmente opuesto al suyo.

En las islas de Etras apenas había metales que manipular mediante alquimia y, al estar tan cerca del mar, los etrasianos consideraban a Lumitia como la responsable de las bruscas mareas que regían su vida. Para ellos, Lumitia era una intrusa agresiva que buscaba destruir el mundo, y Luna, su salvadora. Las leyendas etrasianas decían que Luna había quedado tan malherida tras la pelea que había estado a punto de caer del cielo, que los mares habían intentado levantarse para cogerla al vuelo y que, ante su sacrificio, la avergonzada Lumitia había depuesto la violencia y, desde entonces, ambas compartían la vigilia del cielo nocturno. Sin embargo, los mares no olvidaron lo sucedido: crecían de rabia cada vez que Lumitia aparecía llena en el cielo y no se tranquilizaban hasta que entraba en fase de latencia.

Por eso, en Etras, Luna no solo era la dueña de los mares, sino también la patrona de la protección. Se la veneraba como una mediadora, como una figura materna.

Helena se agachó y cogió un guijarro plano del riachuelo.

En su país natal, para rezar a Luna, apilaban piedras en la playa. Cada una de ellas representaba una plegaria que la marea llevaba hasta la diosa.

Aunque no se encontraba junto al mar, Helena siempre había disfrutado de la concentración que requería el ritual, así que preparó una pequeña pila: colocó una primera piedra por Luc, seguida de otras para Lila, Soren, la enfermera Pace, el equipo médico del hospital, las aprendizas, Shiseo, Ilva (aunque a regañadientes), la Llama Eterna y la Resistencia.

A medida que la pila crecía, esta empezó a tambalearse peligrosamente.

Helena cogió una piedra más y vaciló.

Sabía que, si la construcción se caía sin estar terminada, su esfuerzo habría sido en vano. Por un instante, estuvo a punto de dejarla como estaba.

Pero, finalmente, decidió añadir una última plegaria.

«No permitas que Kaine Ferron muera por mi culpa».

La pila se bamboleó y amenazó con derrumbarse, pero consiguió mantenerse de pie.

A Helena se le formó un nudo en la garganta y el peso que le oprimía el pecho desapareció de repente. Era como si el universo le estuviera diciendo que lo que pedía era posible.

Ese ritual sureño no tenía cabida en las creencias del Norte, pero Helena lo había dado todo por la guerra y ni siquiera eso había sido suficiente.

Ya solo le quedaba rezar.

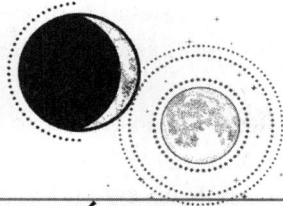

CAPÍTULO 34

Julius 1786

HELENA REPARÓ EN LAS HEBRAS plateadas que asomaban entre las sienes de Kaine mientras le curaba la espalda. Apenas se distinguían, eran solo destellos de un blanco plateado que se entremezclaban con su cabello oscuro.

Se detuvo para observarlas con atención.

—¿Te acaban de salir?

—No me había dado cuenta hasta esta mañana —dijo él pasándose los dedos por la zona.

—Pensaba que no podías cambiar.

—Bueno, ahora soy un sujeto de prueba —dijo cortante—. Nadie sabe qué va a pasar conmigo. En eso consisten los experimentos.

Helena se acercó a él aún más intentando convencerse de que solo eran canas, de que su pelo no estaba adoptando el tono exacto de la gema que había utilizado para sanarlo.

Kaine giró la cabeza para mirarla y su rostro quedó a escasos centímetros del de ella.

—¿Te importa?

—Lo siento —se disculpó avergonzada mientras retrocedía con rapidez.

—Según parece, me van a regalar una quimera —comentó Kaine mientras Helena le vendaba las heridas.

—¿Cómo que te la van a regalar?

Había hablado con tanta despreocupación que sonaba como si le fueran a dar una mascota, no un monstruo rabioso que se iba descomponiendo mientras seguía vivo.

—Hasta ahora no han conseguido domar a ninguna, pero sería lo ideal. —Se puso de pie—. Nos van a «regalar» una quimera a quienes tenemos «recursos» para criarlas e intentar adiestrarlas. Es otra prueba más, por supuesto.

Helena lo rodeó para ayudarlo a ponerse la camisa. Las ojeras macilentas que tenía antes casi habían desaparecido por completo.

—Pero estás herido. No es justo que te pidan domar a una criatura así cuando apenas puedes regenerarte o levantar los brazos.

Kaine la miró con condescendencia.

—Quizá esto te sorprenda, Marino, pero al Sumo Nigromante no le importa demasiado la justicia. Para él, todas aquellas personas sin cerebro y sin instinto de supervivencia merecen sufrir una muerte dolorosa. A ser posible, con él como testigo para disfrutar del espectáculo.

Era evidente que intentaba provocarla.

—¿Sabes ya qué tipo de quimera te van a dar?

—Dado que utilizó la palabra «adiestrar», imagino que tendrá parte de perro. Pero, como Bennet no me tiene especial cariño, estoy seguro de que me tocará la peor de todas.

A Helena le resultaba aterrador que estuvieran creando quimeras capaces de ser adiestradas. Cada vez aparecían más y, aunque no eran difíciles de matar, el número de soldados que se llevaban por delante no dejaba de crecer.

—¿Podrías… matarla?

—¿Crees que debería matar a la criatura que me van a regalar para ponerme a prueba? —preguntó él enarcando una ceja.

Helena sintió un nudo en la garganta, no sabía qué responder.

Kaine ya estaba herido. Si la quimera que le asignaban moría, sin duda lo castigarían, pero…

De repente, él le agarró de la barbilla y le levantó la cabeza para que sostuviera su mirada. Había un ligero brillo plateado en sus ojos.

—¿Qué harías tú en mi lugar?

—Pues… —balbuceó— intentaría ganarme su lealtad.

—¿Y en caso de no conseguirlo? ¿Qué harías ante un monstruo incapaz de ser fiel?

Estaban muy cerca el uno del otro. A Helena se le entrecortó la respiración y sintió que se aceleraba su corazón.

—Buscaría defectos en la transmutación. No las ensamblan bien, así que podrías empeorar su estado para acelerar el deterioro de la criatura.

De esa forma, no la estarías matando, solo… adelantando su inevitable final.

Kaine se inclinó hacia delante, acercando tanto su rostro al de ella que Helena sintió su aliento en la piel. Por un instante, pensó que la iba a besar.

—Qué pragmática eres.

Esas palabras le rozaron los labios antes de que Kaine soltara su barbilla de golpe y diera un paso hacia atrás, con un brillo intenso en los ojos. Helena todavía sentía calor en las mejillas cuando se puso a recoger sus pertenencias sin atreverse a mirarlo a la cara.

—No mueras, Marino —dijo justo cuando la chica se marchaba—. Podría echarte de menos.

Vanya Gettlich era una mujer soltera de baja estatura, con los ojillos diminutos, la nariz larga y redonda y las orejas puntiagudas. Siempre había dicho que aquella extraña combinación explicaba por qué era una de las mejores exploradoras de la Resistencia: nadie se fijaba nunca en una mujer tan poco agraciada.

Por lo general, los exploradores no solían sobrevivir durante mucho tiempo y durar unos cuantos meses de trabajo se consideraba toda una hazaña. La mayoría ni siquiera llegaba tan lejos. Vanya llevaba años formando parte del equipo, entrando y saliendo del territorio enemigo para reunir la información que nadie más se atrevía a buscar.

Pero, cuando desapareció, todos tuvieron claro desde el principio que no iba a regresar. Se la declaró desaparecida durante dos semanas antes de darla por muerta.

Por eso, cuando a Helena le pidieron que acudiera de inmediato al puesto de control después de que una patrulla avisara por radio de que la habían encontrado, se quedó de piedra. Gettlich había aparecido gravemente herida y ya habían confirmado que no era una necrómata. Sin embargo, asegurarse de que no fuera un liche intentando infiltrarse en el Cuartel General a través de su cadáver maltrecho resultaba mucho más complicado.

Al examinarla en busca de un talismán, encontraron restos anómalos de metal distribuidos por todo su cuerpo, incluyendo una cantidad evidente de lumitio. En ese caso no había excepciones: para entrar en el

Cuartel General con lumitio en el cuerpo, la persona debía ser inmovilizada.

Redujeron a Gettlich mientras pedía a gritos que no la ataran y juraba que seguía siendo ella, pero Helena no tenía permitido tratarla si antes no tomaban esa medida de protección.

Justo cuando Helena dio un paso adelante, las puertas se abrieron de par en par y Luc irrumpió amenazando con derribar a su propia guardia si alguien se atrevía a interponerse en su camino.

Lila, que lo acompañaba con las armas en ristre, esbozó una expresión indecisa al verlo acercarse a Gettlich sin miedo al riesgo evidente.

—Lo siento muchísimo —le dijo con voz ronca.

Ante aquello, la mujer se calmó; Luc siempre había tenido ese efecto en los demás. Ella lo mandó callar para que no se disculpara y le advirtió que no fuera tonto. Mientras Helena trabajaba en silencio, Vanya compartió su último informe.

La habían capturado mientras investigaba el nuevo laboratorio del puerto Oeste. Los inmarcesibles la habían utilizado como conejillo de Indias para intentar reprimir su poder. Le habían inyectado todo tipo de metales a lo largo de varios días, pero dieron el experimento por fallido cuando sus órganos comenzaron a fallar.

Los guardias a quienes les habían ordenado que se deshicieran de ella cuando estaba al borde de la muerte habían decidido aprovecharse de su vulnerabilidad. La sacaron del edificio para tener algo más de privacidad y, una vez satisfechos, la dejaron tirada allí mismo, abandonada a su suerte.

Mientras Gettlich le contaba todo aquello a Luc, Helena había ido verificando su testimonio. El metal que circulaba por su sangre interfería con su resonancia y la desdibujaba hasta convertirla en una especie de estática. Tenía los brazos y las piernas cubiertos de moratones, resultado de las ataduras que la habían mantenido prisionera, y estaba empapada de sangre de cintura hacia abajo. Aunque debería haber muerto a causa de las sustancias que le envenenaban el torrente sanguíneo, las lesiones internas acabarían con ella primero.

Las interferencias del metal eran demasiado intensas para que la vivemancia de Helena pudiera salvarla. Tuvo que negar con la cabeza una y otra vez mientras Luc le suplicaba que hiciera algo.

Lo único que podía ofrecerle era láudano, un remedio para aliviar su dolor hasta que todo hubiera terminado.

El corazón de Gettlich se aceleraba cada vez que Luc le prometía que la Llama Eterna jamás la olvidaría, que encontraría a quienes le habían hecho daño. Se aseguraría de hacérselo pagar a todos.

El Consejo tuvo que confinar a Luc en sus dependencias para impedirle que reuniera a su equipo y saliera con ellos a buscar el laboratorio. Los Gettlich eran una familia con raíces profundas en Paladia, y Luc conocía a Vanya desde siempre.

Debido a las circunstancias de su muerte, no se siguió el protocolo habitual. En vez de velarla e incinerarla, llevaron su cuerpo a una habitación protegida, donde la dejaron atada a la camilla, cubierta con una sábana.

El falcón Matias pidió hablar con Helena en su despacho, una estancia gris y desprovista de decoración alguna, salvo por un cuadro enorme que inmortalizaba el sol. La chica siempre se quedaba helada en presencia de Matias.

—El Consejo ha decidido que será necesario hacerle una autopsia a Gettlich —anunció el falcón sin andarse por las ramas. Adoptó una expresión de desagrado al mirarla—. Has sido elegida para encargarte de la tarea.

—Pero yo no estoy entrenada…

—Hay libros que tratan del tema. Puedes pedírselos al cirujano Maier —la interrumpió él agitando la mano.

—¿Y no debería ser él quien…?

—Según me han dicho, el cadáver de la mujer se encuentra en un estado perturbador y, como tú ya la has visto, no te afectará tanto como a otros —dijo volviendo a interrumpirla—. Trabajarás vigilada en todo momento para evitar cualquier imprudencia. —Entornó los ojos azules y acuosos—. Ante la más mínima sospecha de infracción, mandaré que te corten las manos y haré que tu alma sea condenada a hundirse en las oscuras llamas de la tierra. ¿Ha quedado claro?

Matias la fulminó con la mirada. La saliva pegajosa se le acumulaba en los labios mientras hablaba, pues defendía la necesidad de superar las exigencias de la carne y bebía apenas el agua justa para sobrevivir. Aquella era una creencia muy común entre los hombres de fe, pero el falcón la llevaba mucho más al extremo que cualquiera que Helena hubiera conocido.

Ella se puso de pie con el cuerpo agarrotado por el miedo. Nunca había hecho una autopsia.

Además, Gettlich había sido una de las primeras profesoras que había tenido en la Academia con la asignatura de Introducción a la Alquimia. Helena la conocía demasiado bien.

Pero Matias nunca pedía las cosas por favor. Para Helena, su palabra era ley.

Asintió despacio.

—El procedimiento tendrá lugar mañana, cuando Sol esté en su cenit —dijo Matias chasqueando la lengua—. Ve a purificarte antes.

Helena se retiró sintiendo un vacío en el pecho. Sabía que no había nada que hacer y no podía involucrar a Luc en aquello. La muerte de Vanya lo había sacudido hasta lo más profundo, así que no querría que le hicieran una autopsia. Pero el Consejo tenía razón: necesitaban saber qué le habían hecho.

Se pasó la tarde investigando sobre los métodos que se empleaban en las autopsias hasta que llegó el momento de regresar al Reducto. El miedo la tenía prácticamente paralizada, así que agradecía tener una rutina que le permitiera escapar de sus pensamientos.

Ferron la esperaba en el mismo sitio de siempre, con una copa en la mano. Había movido todo el mobiliario para apilarlo junto a las paredes de la estancia. Parecía cansado, con los ojos entrecerrados, pero un brillo intenso y casi plateado destellaba entre sus pestañas.

Helena no hizo preguntas. Tenía demasiadas cosas en las que pensar.

Era evidente que se encontraba de mal humor. Su cuerpo estaba tenso y había algo extraño en su mirada cuando la vio llegar, aunque no era el resentimiento habitual que mostraba en su presencia.

Helena fingió no haberse dado cuenta y, sin decir una palabra, le retiró los vendajes antes de examinarle las heridas. Su piel ya casi había recuperado el color normal y no presentaba signos de descomposición ni infección. Solo quedaban pequeños parches de tejido necrosado alrededor de los símbolos del sello.

Se dio una semana de plazo para intentar cerrar las incisiones. Tener una herida abierta como aquella no era sostenible, independientemente de que sobreviviera o no. Por mucho que Kaine se refugiara en sus rutinas, Helena sabía que apenas podía moverse sin sentir un dolor intenso. Además, no creía que la compasión que Crowther e Ilva le mostraban durase mucho más si no retomaba pronto sus misiones de espionaje.

Le tocó el hombro brevemente, y, aunque Kaine reaccionó al contacto, no se estremeció como en otras ocasiones.

—Ya hemos acabado —musitó después de vendarle las heridas y ayudarle a ponerse la camisa.

Kaine se puso de pie y se sirvió otra copa sin molestarse en responder, así que Helena se dispuso a recoger sus cosas y marcharse, pero la puerta no se abrió. Lo normal era que el necrómata que vigilaba la abriera en cuanto ella se acercaba.

Esperó un instante y luego se giró hacia Kaine, que seguía de pie junto al mueble de las bebidas.

—Al final no tuve tiempo de entrenarte, Marino.

A Helena se le secó la boca. De pronto, era muy consciente del lugar en el que se encontraba. Ya había imaginado que, cuando Kaine comenzara a notarse mejor, sentiría la necesidad de recordarle quién estaba al mando. Era más que evidente que odiaba ser vulnerable, de ahí su impulso por ponerla en su sitio.

Helena había imaginado que reaccionaría de esa manera y, aun así, había decidido considerarlo un problema al que se enfrentaría más adelante.

De repente, retrocedió.

—Ven aquí.

—Tengo… Tengo una tarea muy importante mañana —dijo negando con la cabeza—. Esta noche n-no puedes hacerme daño.

Kaine se quedó quieto, sujetando la copa con determinación, hasta que le palidecieron un poco los nudillos y se le ensombreció la expresión.

—Sé que me consideras un monstruo —espetó—, pero, por lo general, suelo mantener mi palabra. Voy a hacerte daño, así que ven aquí. Quiero que intentes atacarme para ver qué eres capaz de hacer.

—¿Cómo? —Lo miró incrédula.

—Sales del territorio de la Resistencia cuando ya ha anochecido —insistió apretando los dientes—. Y creo que ya ha quedado bastante claro que no sabes defenderte. Quiero comprobar cuáles son tus técnicas ofensivas. Ven. Aquí.

Helena recorrió la estancia despejada con una mirada de incredulidad.

—No pienso atacarte estando herido.

Él la miró confundido.

—Te recuerdo que no puedo morir.

Aunque le hubiera gustado decirle que estaba loco, intentó abordar el tema con tacto.

—Mira, Ferron…, es decir, Kaine, te agradezco la preocupación, pero soy una vivemante. No me va a pasar nada.

—¿Estás segura?

—Por supuesto —dijo con un rápido asentimiento—. Puede que no se me dé muy bien defenderme, pero siempre puedo recurrir a mi poder, así que mis aptitudes para el combate no tienen importancia. De todas maneras… —inspiró hondo—, aprecio mucho tu oferta.

—Supongo que tienes razón —concedió despacio, con la mirada desenfocada.

Entonces Helena oyó que la puerta se abría a su espalda y se despidió con un último asentimiento antes de darse la vuelta para marcharse.

Pero pronto descubrió que no había un único necrómata esperándola, sino cerca de una docena. Entre ellos había cadáveres viejos y grises y otros con heridas recientes y la piel enrojecida.

Helena palideció al verlos.

—No te preocupes, son todos míos —oyó decir a Ferron—. Ahora enséñame cómo usas la vivemancia para luchar.

Añadió algo más, pero Helena había dejado de prestarle atención. No conseguía apartar la mirada de los necrómatas que avanzaban hacia ella, con sus rostros inexpresivos.

Eran demasiados y la rodeaban por todos lados.

Estaba atrapada, atrapada con ellos. Sin escapatoria posible.

Y cada vez se acercaban más.

—Dices que eres una vivemante. Pues demuéstramelo.

Helena apenas lo oyó.

«Esto no es el hospital. No estás en el hospital», pensaba para intentar tranquilizarse, aunque el pecho le dolía y se le cerraba cada vez que intentaba tomar aire. Consiguió dar un paso atrás e intentó extender un brazo para defenderse, pero las violentas sacudidas que la retenían se lo impidieron.

—Marino —la llamó Kaine con tono molesto—, no me digas que les tienes más miedo a los necrómatas que a mí. Me ofende muchísimo.

—D-diles que se retiren —pidió ella con la voz temblorosa, mientras no lograba apartar la mirada de las criaturas.

—No, quiero verte pelear.

—Pero yo no quiero hacerlo. —Retrocedió un poco más, subiendo el volumen de su voz—. Para ya. Me dijiste que podía decirte que no, y eso es justo lo que estoy haciendo ahora mismo.

—No les vas a hacer daño porque ya están muertos. Me has dicho que sabes protegerte. ¡Demuéstramelo!

A Helena le dio un vuelco el estómago y las piernas le flaquearon.

—Deja que me marche —suplicó con voz temblorosa.

—Quemaré a todos los que incapacites —le prometió él, burlón, como si disfrutara del espectáculo—. Venga, muéstrame lo valiente que eres.

Los necrómatas se desplegaron a su alrededor y la arrinconaron hasta que sus hombros tocaron la pared.

—¡Ferron! —aulló ella histérica—. Diles que se retiren. ¡No quiero hacer esto!

—Estamos en guerra. —Su voz le llegaba a Helena desde detrás de la marea de cuerpos que la rodeaban—. No está en tu mano elegir lo que quieres o no. Solo tienes dos opciones: vivir o morir.

Helena se encogió, intentando hacerse lo más pequeña posible. No podía respirar y se sentía como si tuviera unos dedos apretándole la garganta. Los necrómatas iban a despedazarla.

Con un alarido, extendió los brazos.

Todo se volvió rojo.

Todo.

Parpadeó, pero no logró ver nada; la sangre oscura y coagulada le caía por el rostro, le cubría la piel y se le pegaba a las pestañas. Lo único que quedaba de los necrómatas eran pequeños trozos esparcidos por la habitación.

Helena se deslizó hasta el suelo, sin apartar la espalda de la pared ni soltar la correa de su bolsa, cuando le cedieron las piernas.

La boca le sabía a sangre y un espeso hedor a descomposición flotaba en el aire. Seguía ahogándose; la sangre y las vísceras le impedían respirar con normalidad.

Entonces alguien la agarró por los hombros.

Helena liberó su resonancia con un estallido, pero recibió una respuesta aún más violenta, tan brutal que sintió como si alguien hubiera disparado un cañón en el interior de su cabeza.

Se le nubló la vista y, cuando todo volvió a aclararse, encontró a Ferron ante ella, resplandeciente. Sus iris brillaban con un intenso tono plateado.

—¿Qué cojones acabas de hacer, Marino?

Le pitaban los oídos y no conseguía articular palabra, así que se quedó allí arrodillada, contemplando el rostro lleno de vida de él.

—Te he dicho… que no quería hacerlo —consiguió farfullar antes de echarse a llorar.

Se hizo un silencio.

—Creo que te he subestimado —admitió Ferron, sacando un pañuelo de tela para limpiarle la sangre que le apelmazaba las pestañas.

Helena permaneció inmóvil, entumecida, hasta que Ferron la alzó del suelo y la arrastró hasta el cuarto de baño, aunque estuvieron a punto de cederle los brazos por el esfuerzo. Después de meterla dentro de un empujón, abrió el agua de la ducha y sacó unas cuantas toallas y ropa limpia de uno de los armarios.

—Límpiate.

Helena se quedó mirando su cuerpo cubierto de vísceras putrefactas. Ni siquiera en el hospital había olido nada tan nauseabundo. Le sobrevino una arcada.

Se metió en la ducha con la ropa puesta, pero terminó obligándose a desprenderse de aquellas capas de tela empapada, como si fueran una segunda piel.

Se sentía como si Ferron le hubiera descubierto una herida infectada y le clavara los dedos en ella. Apenas logró reunir fuerzas para salir de la ducha.

Sabía que solo estaba retrasando lo inevitable, pero se secó con cuidado y trenzó su cabello despacio, sujetándoselo con mimo, antes de examinar los pantalones y la camisa que Ferron le había preparado. Eran suyos.

¿Acaso vivía allí?, se preguntó. Se vistió sin prisa.

A medida que se abrochaba los botones que ya tan bien conocía, la conmoción fue disipándose y su mente recuperó el pleno uso de sus facultades con una rabia incontenible.

Cuando salió del cuarto de baño, esperaba encontrarse con un escenario de pesadilla, salpicado de sangre y vísceras, pero, por el contrario, la estancia estaba limpia. Debía de haber pasado más tiempo en la ducha de lo que pensaba.

El suelo relucía tras haber sido fregado y todo el mobiliario estaba de nuevo en su sitio; no quedaba rastro de lo ocurrido, si bien el aire seguía impregnado del hedor de la putrefacción.

Ferron estaba sentado, con la silla al revés y los dedos de una mano presionando la frente, como si estuviera sufriendo una migraña.

Esperaba que así fuera.

Cuando levantó la vista, dejó caer la mano con languidez.

—Bueno —dijo despacio, pronunciando cada palabra con calma. Todavía tenía un extraño brillo plateado en sus ojos—. Se confirma que eres toda una caja de sorpresas.

Su falta de arrepentimiento no hizo más que avivar la cólera de Helena, que se acercó al mueble bar, cogió una botella de aspecto caro y se sirvió una generosa copa.

Dio un trago. El líquido tenía un sabor intenso y amargo que le hizo desear haber elegido otra cosa. Siempre había preferido el vino, pero Ferron no parecía tener ninguna botella. Seguro que no era una bebida alcohólica lo bastante fuerte para su gusto.

Hizo de tripas corazón y se lo bebió de golpe, sin reparar en el amargor que se le extendió por la lengua y le quemó la garganta mientras descendía hasta el vacío de su estómago.

Apretó los ojos con fuerza, se sirvió otro trago y se lo bebió casi tan rápido como el primero. Quería emborracharse cuanto antes. Movió los dedos en círculos, manipulando su propio sistema digestivo con la resonancia para acelerar la absorción del líquido. Así, el alcohol entraría en su torrente sanguíneo antes de que hiciera algo de lo que luego se arrepintiera, como lanzarle a Ferron todas las botellas a la cabeza.

Cerró los ojos de nuevo y se dejó llevar por el cálido y placentero entumecimiento del alcohol.

No tardó en recordar por qué no solía beber: acostumbrada a vivir con los nervios siempre a flor de piel, la embriaguez le resultaba peligrosamente cómoda.

Se aferró a la copa mientras se la volvía a llenar.

—Ya vale —dijo Ferron a su espalda—. No creo que tu hígado tenga la capacidad de regenerarse.

Aunque solo había pensado servirse un poco más, las palabras del chico la empujaron a volcar la botella para terminarla. El líquido se desbordó de la copa y se derramó por la alfombra.

—Vete a la mierda —le dijo.

—No te tenía por una malhablada —respondió, divertido.

Helena apretó los dientes, se volvió hacia él y lo mandó a la mierda en otros tres idiomas.

—¿Y ahora se supone que tengo que tomarte más en serio? —preguntó arqueando una ceja.

—Te odio —le espetó ella.

—Lo sé —replicó él, dejando escapar una risa forzada.

Helena bajó la vista hacia la copa. Quería irse, estaba agotada, nerviosa y al borde del colapso, pero la puerta seguía cerrada. Estaba claro que Ferron no pensaba dejarla ir. Se acercó al sofá y se acurrucó en el extremo más alejado de él.

—Te odio —repitió.

—Y yo a ti.

—Esta guerra es culpa tuya. —El alcohol le estaba soltando la lengua—. Tienes las manos manchadas de la sangre de los combatientes. Y ahora, por tu culpa, yo me quedaré sin nada, incluso cuando todo acabe.

—¿Y se supone que debo sentirme mal por ello? ¿Crees que arruinarte la vida es lo peor que he hecho? —Helena desvió la mirada y Ferron aprovechó para preguntar—: ¿Cuándo te enteraste de que eras una vivemante?

No estaba lo suficientemente borracha como para mantener esa conversación. Bebió un poco más, sabiendo que a la mañana siguiente la resaca sería brutal.

—Debería haberlo visto antes, ¿no? —Como Helena no respondió, él siguió hablando—: La vivemancia es una habilidad que se desarrolla tarde, a mediados o finales de la edad adulta. Las personas jóvenes suelen manifestarla a raíz de haber vivido un evento traumático. Lo que les has hecho a esos necrómatas no te ha sorprendido, así que imagino que no es la primera vez que te pasa. ¿Cuál es tu historia? ¿Qué desencadenó tu poder?

Helena echó la cabeza hacia atrás y clavó la vista en el techo. La embriaguez la debilitaba por completo.

—Al principio, pensábamos que la guerra sería como cualquier otra. Por eso organizamos hospitales de campaña, para que la gente no tuviera que desplazarse de una zona de combate a otra en busca de ayuda.

—Las masacres.

Helena asintió con lentitud. Aquellos ataques fueron el primer gran golpe de la guerra. Aunque el asesinato de Apollo había sido devastador, fueron las masacres en los hospitales las que hicieron evidente que el conflicto era real y definitivo.

Los inmarcesibles no tenían escrúpulos; la guerra no sería justa. Morrough quería que la gente tuviera miedo o muriese.

El Concejo de Gremios justificó los ataques asegurando que los hospitales de campaña servían como tapadera para las bases militares de la

Llama Eterna. Los países vecinos aceptaron aquella mentira, porque les resultaba más sencillo que involucrarse en el conflicto paladino.

—Mi padre era un cirujano khemiata. Aquí en Paladia, las cirugías manuales se consideraban un procedimiento anticuado, así que le costó mucho encontrar trabajo. —Helena tragó saliva, con la vista fija en el extremo opuesto de la estancia—. Cuando estalló la guerra, él quiso regresar a Etras, pero yo ya le había prometido a Luc que permanecería a su lado. Mi padre se negó a marcharse sin mí. La Resistencia empezó a montar los primeros hospitales de campaña y yo le sugerí… que colaborara con la causa. Fue idea mía. Pensaba que estaría a salvo. Pensaba que, si la gente veía lo bueno que era, encontraría trabajo… cuando todo acabara.

Bebió otra vez. La cabeza le daba vueltas.

—Yo iba a formar parte del equipo médico de combate, así que me presenté voluntaria para colaborar en el hospital mientras me formaban para salir al campo de batalla. Aquel día…, pensamos que los habían envenenado. Mucha gente acudió a nosotros con una fiebre imposible de bajar. A uno de nuestros pacientes le siguió subiendo la temperatura hasta que empezó a gritar y a ponerse violento. «Sacádmelo de dentro», repetía una y otra vez. Mi padre me envió a buscar ayuda, pero, cuando regresé, el paciente ya había muerto. Mientras intentaban determinar la causa de la muerte, el hombre se levantó. —Se le escapó un hipido—. Sabíamos que los inmarcesibles eran capaces de regenerarse, pero no lo de sus habilidades como liches.

Su voz había quedado reducida a un leve susurro.

—Bloquearon todas las salidas y empezaron a matar y reanimar a todo el mundo. Los necrómatas los ayudaron a acabar el trabajo más rápido. —Tragó saliva—. El hospital no estaba preparado para un ataque. Mi padre… Él nunca… Nunca había visto un necrómata en persona. Eran sus compañeros, sus pacientes. Le recordé que ya no eran las personas que él había conocido, pero se negó a defenderse cuando lo atraparon. —Se llevó una mano al cuello y trazó con los dedos la delgada cicatriz que le cruzaba desde justo debajo de la oreja izquierda hasta la garganta—. Era un hombre tan bueno… Tenía una voz grave que te retumbaba en el pecho cuando te abrazaba. Él jamás me habría hecho daño…

—Los informes confirmaron que no hubo supervivientes —señaló Ferron, cuya voz parecía provenir de muy lejos.

—Tardaron en encontrarme —explicó ella con voz sombría, apretando la copa entre las manos—. Arrasaron todos los hospitales de campaña en un día. No dejaron a nadie con vida. Enfermeros, médicos, cirujanos, pacientes…, todos murieron. Ese día, descubrimos lo de los liches. Y lo de mi poder.

—Según he oído, los liches que se infiltraron en los hospitales fueron un experimento fallido —murmuró Ferron—. Morrough y Bennet trataban de comprobar si era posible controlar un cuerpo vivo implantándole un talismán para que los inmarcesibles no tuvieran que conformarse con cadáveres. Pero los huéspedes siempre acababan colapsando.

—Ah. —Helena apenas pudo articular más palabras. El alcohol empezaba a hacer efecto y cada vez le costaba más encadenar frases, pero se esforzó en continuar. Pensó en Gettlich—. ¿Sabes si están trabajando en algo más ahora?

—Todo lo que sé son rumores. —La miró con suspicacia—. ¿Por qué lo preguntas?

—Por nada —dijo ella evitando su mirada.

—¿Por qué te hicieron sanadora?

Helena lo miró confundida.

—Por pura eficiencia. Con la vivemancia, en apenas unos minutos u horas puedo sanar dolencias que, en condiciones normales, requerirían semanas o incluso meses en hacerlo. Necesitaban a alguien capaz de salvar a la gente. —Ferron resopló como si lo que acababa de decir fuera una tontería, lo cual avivó su rabia—. No tienes ni la menor idea de lo difícil que es revertir todas las formas en que a las personas como tú os gusta destrozar a los demás. —Lo fulminó con la mirada—. Espero que algún día te veas en la obligación de intentar salvar a alguien. A ver si subestimas tanto nuestro trabajo como lo estás haciendo ahora.

Ferron desvió la mirada, y Helena sintió una extraña chispa de satisfacción.

Se hizo un largo silencio. Él parecía perdido en sus pensamientos y ella estaba tan borracha que apenas podía mantenerse en pie, así que cerró los ojos y se dejó llevar. Cuando los volvió a abrir, Ferron la estaba observando.

Al devolverle la mirada, no pudo evitar fijarse en que tenía un aspecto distinto, como más maduro, aunque tal vez se debiera al alcohol.

—¿Puedo hacerte una pregunta? —dijo luchando contra el mareo—. ¿Notas el sello? ¿Sientes si te está afectando de alguna manera?

—Sí —confesó él con un leve asentimiento—. No creía que fuera capaz de cambiar tanto, pero es como si me estuvieran forjando en frío. Como si me estuviesen moldeando a golpes para transformarme en una nueva versión de mí mismo. No contradice quién soy ahora, pero siento ciertas emociones con menos intensidad que antes. Me resulta más fácil ser implacable y no perder de vista mi objetivo. Aunque también me cuesta más controlar los impulsos que me empujan a conseguir lo que quiero.

—¿Cuál es el propósito de este diseño? —preguntó Helena entornando los ojos—. ¿En qué trataba de convertirte Bennet?

—Lo diseñé yo mismo —susurró.

Aquella revelación fue tan impactante que a Helena se le pasó la embriaguez de golpe. Se incorporó en el sillón.

—Era mi castigo. Aunque imaginaba que me mataría, no quise dejar que eligieran en qué me convertiría en caso de sobrevivir. Por eso, como muestra de arrepentimiento por haber fallado al Sumo Nigromante, les pedí que me permitieran diseñarlo.

Helena se inclinó hacia delante para observarlo mejor. No habían sido imaginaciones suyas; Ferron había cambiado. Estaba siendo testigo de una lenta metamorfosis. Todo indicaba que su recuperación estaba amplificando la influencia del sello. El deterioro físico y mental lo hacía más maleable.

Su rostro seguía demacrado, pero sus facciones habían ganado definición y el aire aniñado que había tenido hasta entonces había desaparecido, de manera que por fin empezaba a parecer un hombre adulto.

Helena ladeó la cabeza, consciente de que lo encontraría muy atractivo si lograra apartar de su mente quién era. Ese simple pensamiento la hizo parpadear tan rápido que la habitación pareció desdibujarse ante sus ojos.

—Tengo que volver —dijo poniéndose de pie con rapidez—. Los puestos de control cerrarán pronto.

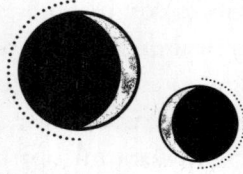

CAPÍTULO 35

Julius 1786

HELENA SE DESPERTÓ A LA mañana siguiente con una resaca infernal que le impidió salir de la cama. El estómago le daba vueltas y ni siquiera se sintió culpable por no levantarse hasta que vino alguien para avisarle de que tenía que llevar a cabo la autopsia.

Estuvo a punto de vomitar al recordarlo, pero el procedimiento no podía esperar. Pasó varios minutos transmutando su propio cuerpo para no marearse al ponerse de pie.

La autopsia se realizaría en el quirófano de la Torre de Alquimia para que el falcón Matias y algunos de los Guardianes de la Llama que dirigían el crematorio pudieran supervisar a Helena y asegurarse de que no profanaba el cadáver.

Con un gesto mecánico, retiró la sábana que cubría el cuerpo, sintiéndose desconectada de sí misma.

—¿Puedo empezar? —le preguntó a la oscuridad.

—Adelante —dijo Matias.

Le resultaba especialmente difícil tener que abrir el cuerpo de alguien a quien conocía para sacarle todos los órganos y examinarlos como si fueran las piezas de un rompecabezas. Y todo ello mientras detallaba los abusos que había sufrido y lo iba registrando por medio de su resonancia.

Deseó poder cubrirse el rostro para no tener que ver lo que hacía, pero sabía que los muertos merecían respeto.

Cuando terminó, dos de los Guardianes de la Llama emergieron de entre las sombras y retiraron el cuerpo con cuidado. Era importante que lo quemaran entero para asegurarse de que sus restos mortales no impedían que su alma ascendiera.

Ya en el centro de mando, Helena escuchó con atención el informe de la guardia que había encontrado a Gettlich y había hablado con ella antes de morir. Luego, Luc repitió todo lo que le había dicho con voz vacía, desprovista de emoción.

El general Althorne señaló la ubicación exacta del laboratorio del puerto Oeste. Habían obtenido esa información de Ferron, que les había dado su paradero exacto. El laboratorio estaba mejor protegido que el anterior, pues habían reforzado la seguridad del edificio para defenderlo de cualquier posible ataque. Sería difícil llegar hasta él y tendrían que poner en riesgo la vida de muchos soldados si se adentraban tanto en territorio enemigo.

—El Consejo requiere la intervención de la sanadora Marino —anunció Matias.

Era la primera vez que Helena hablaba ante la Llama Eterna desde su «arrebato». No esperaba que la hicieran intervenir. Matias podría haber informado él mismo de la autopsia a los demás.

Ilva miró fugazmente a Crowther cuando Helena dio un paso adelante y se humedeció los labios para hablar.

—Según el… examen, la información que Gettlich compartió con Luc…, es decir, con el principado, parece ser cierta. Todo apunta a que intentaron anular su resonancia. Presentaba marcas de inyección por todo el cuerpo; algunas cerca del cerebro, pero la mayoría en los brazos. Le inocularon todo tipo de metales reducidos a micropartículas y mezclados con un fluido portador en los músculos. Me temo que no he podido analizarlos con precisión mediante la resonancia, puesto que algunos de ellos escapaban a mi repertorio. Sin embargo, me he asegurado de enviarles muestras a los metalúrgicos. Tampoco hay forma de determinar con seguridad si neutralizaron con éxito sus habilidades alquímicas, pero, antes de su muerte, debo señalar que no fui capaz de curarla ni de ofrecerle alivio alguno.

—¿Cómo se explica algo así? —preguntó Ilva, que dibujaba círculos distraídamente sobre la mesa.

Helena tomó aire, temiendo que la culparan por lo que estaba a punto de decir.

—Mi teoría es que buscaban crear una interferencia interna con la resonancia de Gettlich. Al introducirle micropartículas cerca del cerebro y las manos, querían nublar su habilidad para percibir el metal fuera del cuerpo. Por el número de inyecciones, creo que le administraron pequeñas dosis hasta que su poder resonántico comenzó a fallar, pero la cantidad de metal acumulado en su cuerpo acabó siendo tan elevada que se volvió tóxico.

—¿Qué probabilidad tienen de conseguir lo que quieren? —preguntó Althorne con su grave voz.

—No sabría decir.

—Lo que yo quiero que me expliques —intervino el falcón Matias, que se había sentado junto a Ilva— es el objetivo del experimento. ¿De qué les serviría anular la resonancia?

—No lo sé —dijo Helena.

—Eres una vivemante —señaló sin andarse con rodeos—. Estoy seguro de que tú más que nadie sabrás para qué les podría servir algo así a los de tu clase.

Luc, que había permanecido arrellanado en su silla desde que Althorne había descartado la idea de atacar el laboratorio, de pronto se irguió.

—¿Qué has querido decir con eso?

Matias chasqueó la lengua y se pasó un pañuelo de tela bajo las estrechas fosas nasales.

—Considero que es una pregunta de lo más pertinente. La sanadora Marino —dijo pronunciando su cargo como si fuera un insulto— tiene el mismo poder que los responsables de la muerte de Gettlich. Por eso creo que podría aportar un punto de vista distinto al de los demás que estamos aquí presentes.

Un brillo peligroso cruzó la mirada de Luc.

—Helena es una sanadora que ha consagrado su vida a la causa. Es tan leal como cualquiera de nosotros y no tiene nada en común con los inmarcesibles.

En vez de responder a lo que Luc acababa de decir, el falcón Matias posó su atención en Helena.

—Sanadora Marino, antes de esta autopsia, ya habías llevado a cabo una disección transmutacional, ¿me equivoco?

Helena asintió y flexionó los dedos.

—A petición del Consejo…

—La respuesta es un sí o un no —la interrumpió Matias con brusquedad.

—Sí.

—Y, en ese caso, examinaste una quimera y analizaste su proceso de creación recurriendo a tus habilidades transmutacionales, algo que está fuera del alcance del resto del equipo médico, ¿verdad?

—Se me ordenó que…

—¿Sí o no?

—Sí.

Matias se volvió hacia Luc con una expresión triunfal.

—Entonces, mantengo la pregunta. Sanadora Marino, en calidad de vivemante, ¿qué clase de uso crees que le darían a la supresión alquímica?

La estancia se desdibujó ante Helena, que solo veía a Gettlich abierta en canal, con la piel agujereada, amoratada y gris por los múltiples pinchazos. Pensó en cómo su propio subconsciente había intentado descifrar la metodología que habían seguido sus atacantes, de entender sus motivos, sin ser capaz de ignorar el margen de mejora del procedimiento. Porque estaba entrenada para percibir el poder alquímico en todas sus formas de expresión, y eso también incluía las torturas.

Si admitía todo aquello, quedaría expuesta ante el Consejo. Pero, si se negaba a responder, podría poner en peligro a la Llama Eterna por ocultar información vital.

—Permitiría controlar mejor a los prisioneros —intervino Crowther antes de que ella tuviera oportunidad de responder—, aunque cabe la posibilidad de que lo utilicen como un arma o para hacer que los sujetos con los que experimentan sean más manejables. La lista es larga, falcón.

Matias le lanzó una mirada mordaz mientras se escuchaban murmullos entre los asistentes. Crowther casi nunca intervenía.

Helena asintió con rigidez.

—Pese al amplio abanico de posibles aplicaciones, no tenemos pruebas de que hayan logrado encontrar una forma eficaz de suprimir el poder alquímico. Solo están intentándolo.

—Deberemos trazar un plan previo en caso de que lo consigan, pero será mejor mantenerlo en secreto —dijo Ilva—. No hay motivo para alarmar a los civiles con algo que tal vez nunca llegue a ocurrir. Y, Matias —la mujer posó su imperiosa mirada en el falcón—, ¿he de recordar ante este Consejo que la sanadora Marino obtuvo su cargo con la bendición de la Fe y el principado?

Matias asintió con mala cara y Helena regresó a su asiento.

No le sorprendía que el falcón quisiera expulsarla de la Llama Eterna y, posiblemente, también de la Resistencia. Con todas las aprendizas que le habían asignado, Helena ya no era tan indispensable como antes. Tal vez Luc fuera el único obstáculo que le impedía a Matias salirse con la suya.

Se suponía que la voz de cada uno de los cinco miembros del Consejo tenía el mismo peso que la de los demás, pero la influencia de Luc superaba con creces la de los otros cuatro juntos. Aunque podrían unirse para superarlo en una votación, jamás se atreverían a vetarlo tan abiertamente.

Preferían dejarlo al margen de sus decisiones.

Luc tenía una inquebrantable noción del bien y siempre se dejaba guiar por su conciencia para tomar decisiones. Pero eso hacía que los demás miembros del Consejo evitaran contar con él en las deliberaciones y lo animaran a pasar todo el tiempo posible en el frente, donde la toma de decisiones no era tan delicada.

Sentado allí junto al Consejo, con Ilva y Matias a un lado y Althorne y Crowther al otro, Luc era como una marioneta ajena a hilos que lo controlaban.

A Helena le habría gustado salvarlo de aquella situación, pero sabía bien que, sin supervisión, su amigo se sacrificaría por la causa sin pensárselo dos veces.

CROWTHER LE PIDIÓ A HELENA que lo siguiera con un gesto de la mano cuando la reunión terminó.

—¿Me va a suponer Matias un problema? —le preguntó la chica en cuanto se quedaron solos.

—Me temo que sí —dijo él mientras cruzaban el puente colgante que comunicaba con la Torre de Alquimia.

Entraron en el ascensor, pero, en vez de pulsar el botón que los llevaría a su despacho, Crowther giró una llave que los hizo descender.

—No te quiere aquí y ya ha empezado a tomar medidas para echarte.

Helena tragó saliva.

—¿Y se lo vais a permitir?

Él le lanzó una mirada de soslayo.

—¿Estás haciendo algo que justifique que me esfuerce en interferir? Porque, hasta donde yo sé, lo único que has logrado en estas últimas semanas es malgastar nuestros escasos suministros de opiáceos con Ferron.

El ascensor seguía bajando pisos, dejando atrás la planta principal de la Torre, y Helena sintió cómo su alma caía con ellos.

—¿Adónde me llevas?

—A un lugar donde comprobaremos lo útil que realmente puedes ser —se limitó a decir Crowther cuando el ascensor se detuvo y las puertas se abrieron para dar paso a un corredor oscuro.

Helena sabía que había instalaciones subterráneas. Había bajado allí en un par de ocasiones hasta los almacenes en busca de materiales. La meseta sobre la que se alzaba la Torre estaba formada por piedra maciza y, a lo largo de los siglos, se habían realizado numerosas excavaciones. Sin embargo, no tenía la menor idea de por qué la había llevado hasta allí.

Crowther salió primero, tomó una linterna de una repisa y, tras encenderla, se la colocó entre el torso y el brazo que tenía paralizado, sujeto con un cabestrillo, para abrir la pesada puerta que se alzaba ante ellos. En vez de conducir a una sala, daba paso a una escalera que descendía hacia una oscuridad absoluta. Todo olía a moho a su alrededor.

—¿Adónde vamos? —preguntó Helena, que se había quedado paralizada.

—De vez en cuando me llegan… prisioneros especiales que requieren atención médica. Ivy no siempre tiene la mano que hace falta. Ven, es hora de que demuestres cuánto esfuerzo mereces, Marino.

HELENA NO SABÍA MUY BIEN qué hacía la Resistencia con los prisioneros, pero dudaba que los encerraran habitualmente en un agujero subterráneo como aquel. Bajo la Torre se extendía un entramado de túneles y salas en ruinas demasiado complejo como para que se hubiera creado solo para servir de almacenaje. La mayor parte de las habitaciones se habían transformado en celdas llenas de prisioneros que Helena no reconocía.

Sabía que las quemaduras eran heridas comunes en tiempos de guerra. La piromancia de combate se basaba en la fuerza bruta y dejaba quemaduras por todo el cuerpo. Para focalizarlas en los puntos donde había una mayor concentración de terminaciones nerviosas, la víctima debía estar atada, y el atacante, ser un piromante muy experimentado.

Helena perdió la noción del tiempo en esa oscuridad, forzando la vista cuando la inestable linterna de Crowther le permitía captar destellos de aquellos prisioneros, con el cuerpo sucio y la piel quemada.

Fue terrible. ¿Para qué iba a proporcionarles alivio si, tarde o temprano, volverían a sufrir todo tipo de atrocidades?

Aun así, limpió heridas, regeneró tejidos, cerró lesiones y curó fracturas; además, se encontró con manos que tenían todos los huesos rotos con una precisión quirúrgica.

¿Haberla hecho bajar allí era una amenaza velada?

—Haré que… Ferron esté curado para la semana que viene —le dijo a Crowther intentando controlar la voz cuando ya estaban de vuelta en el ascensor.

Se había quedado helada y la luz del sol le hacía daño después de haber pasado tanto rato a oscuras. «Cómplice, cómplice, cómplice». La palabra se repetía en su cabeza una y otra vez.

—Me aseguraré de ello —insistió la chica. Crowther, que se daba golpecitos en el antebrazo paralizado con sus dedos delgados como patas de araña, no se molestó en responder. Helena continuó a toda prisa—: Está… Creo que su habilidad para regenerarse por fin está volviendo a la normalidad. Trabajar con el sello no será una tarea sencilla, pero sé que puedo hacerlo. Estoy segura de que supondrá una ventaja para nosotros a la larga. La lesión lo está haciendo más vulnerable a nivel emocional. Está mostrando aspectos de sí mismo que no habrían salido a la luz en otras circunstancias.

—No confundas esa vulnerabilidad con lealtad —le advirtió Crowther, deteniendo por fin el movimiento de sus dedos.

Una ola de terror le estremeció los pulmones.

—No lo haré. Sé que todavía no nos da una ventaja real, pero… el sello lo está afectando. Ha mencionado que ahora le cuesta más ignorar sus propios impulsos. Tal vez pueda aprovecharme de eso.

—Eres una ilusa.

¿Por qué estaba tan escéptico si la misión había sido idea suya?

Crowther posó la vista en ella.

—Kaine Ferron sigue siendo el recluta más joven entre las filas de los inmarcesibles. Hasta el momento, no ha habido nadie que le haya arrebatado ese mérito. —Estaba tan cerca de Helena que esta casi alcanzaba a ver los empastes metálicos en sus muelas traseras—. Los demás deberían haberse aprovechado de él hace tiempo… Al fin y al cabo, era un huérfano con una fortuna inmensa que ni siquiera había alcanzado la mayoría de edad cuando estalló la guerra. Sin embargo, no ha parado de ascender. No tiene amigos ni amantes. Tampoco una puta de confianza. Es joven, calculador y volátil, y corre riesgos que cualquier persona con un mínimo de juicio evitaría a toda costa.

—Ya lo s...

—No, no lo sabes. Si lo supieras, ya te habrías dado cuenta de que estás cometiendo un error con tu estrategia. Ese chico no es una persona, no es humano, así que no conseguirás que confíe en ti. Es un animal.

Helena lo miró, estupefacta. En cuanto el ascensor se detuvo y las puertas se abrieron, salió de allí con un traspié.

—Pero me dijiste que...

—Te pedí que utilizaras la vivemancia —gruñó Crowther—, pero tú no has hecho más que poner excusas: que si encontrar el momento perfecto, que si no apresurarte por miedo a que descubriera tus intenciones... Y, ahora, crees que el sello y las heridas que este le ha provocado bastarán para arreglar todos tus errores.

—Dijiste que debía convertirme en su máxima prioridad para que olvidara su objetivo inicial, y eso es lo que estoy haciendo.

Crowther frunció el ceño con severidad y la agarró del codo, arrastrándola hasta su despacho. No dijo una palabra hasta que cerró la puerta y se aseguró de que nadie pudiera oírlos.

—Te pedí que lo controlaras con la vivemancia. —Su voz se había vuelto gélida—. Lo que estás haciendo ahora es muy distinto: has logrado que dependa de ti, que te considere alguien indispensable. ¿Te crees capaz de inhabilitar el sello? ¿De controlar la intensidad de sus efectos? No, claro que no. No te pedí que hicieras algo irreversible, sino que provocaras en él una obsesión que pudieras manipular mediante tu poder.

—Pues me temo que la vivemancia no funciona así —replicó ella—. Las emociones humanas no se pueden encender y apagar a voluntad, al menos no de la forma que tú esperas. No estamos hablando de magia.

Crowther le lanzó una mirada asesina antes de sentarse tras su escritorio.

—De nada me sirve tener un peón al que no puedo controlar. Si consigues lo que te propones, me temo que acabarás destruyendo la Llama Eterna en lugar de salvarla. La familia Ferron se alimenta de su ambición. Siempre han despreciado a las familias nobles y, ahora que Paladia está construida con su acero, creen que la ciudad les pertenece. Que pueden dominarla o destruirla a su antojo. Por si fuera poco, jamás comparten. Se obsesionan con todo aquello que consideran suyo. Si sigues por este camino, Kaine Ferron no te dejará ir y no tolerará que antepongas a nadie por delante de él.

El miedo atravesó a Helena como un cuchillo, pero cuadró los hombros y le sostuvo la mirada. A pesar de sentirse acorralada, se negaba a retroceder. Crowther se había encargado de dejarla sin opciones.

—Fuiste tú quien me entregó a él —dijo con la voz cargada de rabia—. Seré suya incluso cuando la guerra haya terminado. Esas fueron las condiciones del acuerdo. Dijiste que sin Ferron la batalla estaba perdida, así que he escogido salvarlo. ¿Esperabais acaso que me dejara marchar? —Tomó una bocanada de aire entrecortada—. Me pedisteis que me convirtiera en su misión. Ahora mismo es más influenciable que nunca y puede que esta sea mi única oportunidad. Si consideras que lo que estoy haciendo es demasiado peligroso, dame una alternativa, porque yo no veo otra forma de conseguir lo que me has pedido.

A Crowther le brillaban los ojos de rabia, pero no respondió.

¿Qué esperaba que hiciera? ¿De verdad creía que la vivemancia bastaría para convertirla en la obsesión de Ferron, así sin más? ¿Que las emociones eran como un grifo que podía abrirse y cerrarse a voluntad? ¿Es que acaso nadie entendía la naturaleza de su poder?

Crowther la observaba en silencio y Helena casi pudo ver las piezas de su plan recolocándose mientras decidía qué paso dar a continuación. Al cabo de varios minutos sin hablar, Helena salió del despacho.

Los pasillos de la Torre resultaban asfixiantes durante el verano. El calor era tan intenso que a Helena le costaba respirar.

Salió al puente colgante.

Abajo, Luc y Lila estaban entrenando contra el resto de su equipo mientras Soren corregía sus técnicas de combate. Un pequeño grupo de personas se había congregado a su alrededor para verlos practicar.

Conociendo a Ilva, seguro que le había pedido a Soren o a Lila que mantuvieran a Luc ocupado para que no se obsesionara con lo del laboratorio del puerto Oeste.

La alquimia de combate no debería ser tan atractiva, porque era fácil olvidar la violencia de su objetivo y lo terribles que eran sus consecuencias.

Helena los observó con el corazón en un puño mientras escuchaba a la gente animarlos.

Siempre había creído que era capaz de hacer lo que fuera necesario por sus amigos, pero el pragmatismo le había robado al heroísmo todo su encanto. Y, aunque no dejaba de repetirse que no había nada malo en cambiar de parecer…

Se sentía terriblemente sola.

Agarró el amuleto hueco que llevaba al cuello y dejó que las puntas del engaste se le clavaran en la palma de la mano. Sentía un vacío sordo que ya nunca la abandonaba, una herida silenciosa que se extendía lentamente por su interior y que permanecería abierta durante el resto de sus días.

Helena ya no creía que hubiera salvación para ella, pero nadie parecía haberse dado cuenta de que se estaba desmoronando.

«Estás sola y lo seguirás estando cuando la guerra acabe».

Parpadeó y las siluetas que se movían abajo se desdibujaron hasta transformarse en aureolas doradas y plateadas.

<hr />

Aquella noche, estudió el sello de Ferron con renovada urgencia. Lo conocía como la palma de su mano, pero, cuando se detuvo a observarlo con atención, comprendió que era aterradoramente bello. Un diseño meticuloso, la obra de un alquimista excepcional.

Y Ferron lo había sido antes de convertirse en un asesino.

No lograba entender cómo había sido capaz de crear un sello tan intrincado sabiendo que cada una de sus líneas acabarían siendo una incisión en su propia piel.

—Creo que pronto podré curarte las heridas —le dijo.

—¿En serio? —preguntó el chico tras un silencio tan largo que a Helena le pareció extraño. Aun así, la impasibilidad de su voz le impidió saber qué pensaba realmente.

—El procedimiento tendrá que ser experimental —explicó mientras le aplicaba un bálsamo—, pero ahora comprendo mejor cómo funciona tu poder de regeneración y cómo interactúa con mi resonancia. Lo único que...

Se puso tenso de repente y un ligero escalofrío hizo que las heridas de la espalda se le abrieran.

—¿Qué?

—La latencia. La resonancia estará en su punto más débil y eso me facilitará trabajar con el lumitio de la aleación de tus hombros. Sin embargo, no sé si completar el sello con sus efectos al mínimo será seguro.

—No debería importar, pero durante la latencia me regenero más despacio.

—No pasa nada. De hecho, nos vendrá bien.

Ferron no volvió a hablar hasta que Helena alcanzó la puerta.

—Marino.

Ella se dio la vuelta.

—Se rumorea que Bennet está experimentando con la supresión alquímica.

—¿Por qué? —le preguntó con la esperanza de que supiera algo y poder llevarle esa información a Crowther para demostrarle que Kaine seguía siendo útil.

Aunque no se encogió de hombros, la expresión del chico dejó claro que, si lo supiera, se lo habría dicho ya.

—Quién sabe.

Helena se apartó de la puerta.

—Hace un tiempo me comentaste que Morrough cree que Paladia es la clave para darle a Hevgoss la inmortalidad que buscan. ¿Y si quiere la Gema de los Cielos?

Kaine dejó a un lado la bebida que se estaba sirviendo.

—¿Crees que el Sumo Nigromante ha venido hasta aquí para hacerse con una esfera mágica que no existe?

Ella se sonrojó ligeramente. La gema era solo una leyenda. Una mala interpretación de las primeras representaciones de Orion Holdfast había dado pie a la creencia de que la bendición de Sol era un objeto físico. Mucho tiempo atrás, cuando la región aún estaba en una época precientífica y gran parte de la población era analfabeta, la iconografía había servido para transmitir las enseñanzas sobre la Fe.

Aunque las fuentes históricas ya habían corregido esos errores, los mitos persistieron. Si no fuera porque Luc le explicó la verdad en una incómoda conversación, Helena habría seguido creyendo que la gema era real.

—No —se apresuró a decir—, ya sé que no existe, pero se me ha ocurrido que tal vez Morrough haya venido a buscarla pensando que sí. Que Sol convirtiera su bendición en una gema tampoco suena tan descabellado.

—¿Crees en Sol? —resopló Ferron.

Ella cambió el peso de su cuerpo de un pie a otro, aferrándose a la correa de la bolsa.

—Sí, bueno, no creo en él como la mayoría, pero… ¿tú no? ¿Ni… ni un poquito?

—Ni un poquito —confirmó con un gesto.

462

CAPÍTULO 36

CONSCIENTE DE QUE SUS ENCUENTROS diarios para curar a Kaine estaban a punto de concluir, Helena descubrió que se sentía orgullosa de su trabajo. No estaba segura de poder garantizar una total recuperación, pero la versión demacrada y esquelética de Kaine había desaparecido por completo. Vestido, era imposible adivinar que alguna vez había estado herido.

Cuando la fase de latencia comenzó, Crowther todavía no se había puesto en contacto con ella ni le había dado nuevas órdenes. La decisión de curar a Kaine, así como las posibles consecuencias que esto tuviera, recaían enteramente en ella.

Helena ya había preparado su bolsa con todo lo necesario y le estaba dando los últimos toques al que esperaba que fuera el último lote de ungüento cuando alguien llamó a la puerta.

Se dio la vuelta y se encontró con Luc.

—No sabía que te habían asignado un laboratorio —comentó él echando un vistazo a su alrededor.

Lo que había empezado siendo un destartalado cuartucho se había transformado en un auténtico taller de alquimia, repleto de crisoles, matraces y estanterías abarrotadas de alambiques y retortas.

—Quería ayudar a combatir la escasez de suministros del hospital —explicó ella mientras se aseguraba de que no hubiera nadie más con él.

Había soñado muchas veces con que Luc la visitara, que la viera trabajar y comprendiera todo lo que hacía por él, pero la preocupación le impidió disfrutar del momento.

No podía retrasarse.

Luc le dedicó una de esas sonrisas amplias que ofrecía cuando adoptaba su papel de principado.

—Sol siempre hace su voluntad, ¿eh? ¿Por qué no me lo habías dicho?

—Pues… supongo que nunca ha salido el tema —se disculpó ella dándole vueltas a un tarro de bálsamo entre las manos.

La sonrisa del chico se desvaneció.

—Me temo que hay mucho que no sé, ¿verdad? —Helena se puso rígida y Luc continuó sin mirarla—. Fui a ver al falcón Matias. Quería reprocharle la forma en que te había hablado durante la reunión, porque tú solo estás haciendo lo que te piden. Y él me dijo que tuviste un encontronazo con el Consejo hace meses y que por eso no se fía de ti. Que por eso hay nuevas sanadoras. Me contó que propusiste usar la nigromancia con los soldados caídos en combate. —Soltó una carcajada seca—. Y parece que todo el mundo lo sabía menos yo.

Helena notó que se le secaba la boca.

—No te enfades con Lila. Ella tampoco estaba presente cuando ocurrió.

—Lo sé —dijo apretando los dientes—, pero Soren se lo contó. A mí no me lo dijo nadie. Podrías habérmelo dicho tú misma.

—Me daba miedo que pensaras que había dejado de creer en ti —se defendió ella parpadeando con fuerza—, porque sigo haciéndolo. Es solo que… necesito que todo esto termine.

—Hel… —Luc bajó la vista y se puso a juguetear con sus anillos de ignición—, esta no es tu guerra.

—¿Cómo que no? —replicó ella, encogiéndose como si sus palabras le hubieran golpeado—. He estado aquí desde el principio. Te prometí… —Negó con la cabeza—. Eso a Lila no se lo dirías jamás. Ni a ella ni a nadie.

Él negó también con expresión compungida.

—No, no lo haría, porque los demás saben que, en la batalla entre el bien y el mal, todo empeora antes de mejorar. Nuestra obligación es seguir adelante sin caer en la tentación de tomar el camino fácil.

A Helena se le cerró la garganta y dio un paso hacia atrás. El dolor le ardía en los ojos. ¿Qué era eso del camino fácil?

—Sé que tu intención era buena y que solo querías ayudar. También entiendo que, desde tu perspectiva, puede parecer que estamos desperdiciando una oportunidad para mejorar nuestra situación, pero no…

Conmigo se utiliza una vara de medir distinta. Sol espera mucho más de mí. Y…, si quieres formar parte de la Resistencia, necesito que creas en nosotros.

Helena, por fin, entendía el plan de Matias. Estaba intentando convencer a Luc de que lo mejor y más compasivo sería apartarla de la lucha. Quería que creyese que ella no encajaba allí, que alguien como ella jamás comprendería la Fe y las costumbres norteñas. Así, si algún día decidían enviarla lejos, Luc no lo vería como un castigo.

—Lo siento —le dijo—. Ahora soy consciente de que me equivoqué. Te prometo que no volverá a pasar.

—No —suspiró él—, soy yo quien lo siente. Todo esto es culpa mía. Te he dejado sola todo este tiempo dando por hecho que estarías bien. No es justo y pienso arreglarlo esta misma noche. —Asintió—. El equipo está de descanso aprovechando la fase de latencia, así que ¿qué te parece si te enseño ese sello del que hablábamos? Nos pondremos al día de todo y haremos… lo que quieras. También podrías enseñarme tu laboratorio de científica loca. —Le ofreció una sonrisa torcida—. ¿Qué me dices?

Luego, le tendió la mano.

—Esta noche tengo que trabajar —se disculpó Helena con una voz tan débil que dolía escucharla—. La latencia es importante para… todo lo alquímico.

—Ah, ya…, bueno. —Luc se obligó a sonreír—. Para la próxima, entonces.

Helena logró asentir y le devolvió una sonrisa tensa antes de mirar el reloj, haciendo cálculos sobre cuánto tardaría en recorrer la distancia que la separaba del Reducto. Aunque corriera hasta allí, aunque no hubiese cola en el puesto de control, no iba a llegar a tiempo.

Luc, con la esperanza evidente de que cambiara de idea, permaneció quieto donde estaba, así que ella se dio la vuelta con torpeza y empezó a medir componentes, fingiendo haber olvidado que su amigo estaba allí. Tras un minuto de silencio que se hizo insoportable, se marchó sin hacer ruido.

—Lo siento, Luc —le oyó decir a Lila antes de que se cerrara del todo la puerta.

Helena dejó lo que estaba haciendo y esperó a que bajaran por la escalera o se metieran en el ascensor. Quería darse margen y asegurarse de poder salir sin que la vieran. Mientras esperaba, envió la conversación que acababan de tener a lo más profundo de su mente, intentando evitar que se le rompiera el corazón en mil pedazos.

—————

Echó a correr en cuanto llegó al puente. Ya iba diez minutos tarde.

Kaine enarcó una ceja cuando irrumpió en el módulo, doblándose por la mitad, sin apenas poder respirar.

—Pensaba que por fin ibas a darme plantón.

Helena apoyó las manos en las rodillas mientras trataba de recuperar el aliento.

—Alguien... quería hablar conmigo. No podía... dejarlo con la palabra en la boca.

Notaba un dolor intenso en el costado, así que se llevó una mano a la zona intentando aliviar la tensión de los ligamentos. También le ardían los pulmones. Sin esperar a recuperarse del todo, se puso manos a la obra y empezó a sacar todo lo que necesitaba de la bolsa que llevaba cruzada al hombro, bien ceñida a la cintura.

—¿Vas siempre tan cargada a todos lados? —preguntó Kaine.

—Suelo salir con ella vacía para guardar todo lo que encuentro en el humedal. —Lo observó con atención—. ¿Cómo te encuentras?

Él ladeó la cabeza mientras lo pensaba.

—Me estoy regenerando más despacio y ya no noto el sello clavado en el cerebro como un tornillo, así que me siento de maravilla.

Al dar un trago de un líquido ambarino, se tambaleó un poco, y Helena comprendió que estaba algo borracho y que no mentía sobre la regeneración lenta.

—Me alegro, porque será mejor que estés consciente durante el proceso. Voy a necesitar que te muevas a medida que trabajo para asegurarme de que el tejido nuevo no se desgarre ni quede demasiado tirante. De lo contrario, podría no regenerarse bien nunca más. —Inspiró hondo—. Me temo que te va a doler bastante.

—Ni te imaginas la cantidad de gente que me ha dicho eso antes.

—Hablo en serio. —Se desinfectó las manos—. El alcohol te vendrá bien.

Empezó por el hombro izquierdo, presionando con dos dedos cerca de una de las incisiones. Aunque Kaine se tensó, hacía ya tiempo que no se estremecía ante el contacto de Helena.

La herida tenía el mismo aspecto de una lesión reciente, ya que la latencia disminuía los efectos del lumitio.

Recordando cómo se había regenerado cuando perdió el brazo, Helena estaba segura de que podría reconducir las habilidades regenerativas de Kaine con la vivemancia para que volvieran a la normalidad. No obstante, debería tener mucho cuidado: un mínimo fallo bastaría para que él se quedara para siempre en el estado en que se encontraba en aquel momento.

Le aplicó una generosa capa de ungüento preparado con opio por toda la zona sobre la que no estaba trabajando.

—¿Estás listo?

Cuando Kaine asintió, Helena se concentró en una pequeña sección donde la aleación de titanio y lumitio se había fusionado con el hueso. Cerró la herida sobre el metal con la cantidad justa de tejido cicatrizado.

Una vez regenerada, la piel permaneció viva. El poder regenerativo de Ferron, por fin, era lo suficientemente fuerte como para tolerar la energía del sello.

Le movió el hombro para que lo rotara, lo arqueara y lo estirara en todas las direcciones posibles. Cuando el resto de las incisiones empezaron a sangrar, Helena se estremeció.

El tejido cicatrizado estaba tirante y amenazaba con desgarrarse, así que intentó alterar su composición para hacerlo más elástico, pero la regeneración de Ferron se mantuvo inflexible.

Con un bisturí, abrió de nuevo la incisión y, como temía, esta empezó a cerrarse de inmediato. Tuvo que recurrir a la resonancia para inhabilitar la regeneración mientras retiraba el tejido cicatrizado y comenzaba de nuevo. Kaine no dijo nada, pero respiraba con dificultad y su propia resonancia vibraba en el aire.

Después de terminar con la primera punta del sello, Helena ya no notaba el lumitio bajo la piel de Kaine, parecía haberse integrado por completo.

Logró sanar una segunda punta antes de que Kaine finalmente se derrumbara.

—Dame un minuto —le pidió con voz temblorosa antes de dirigirse al mueble bar, donde cogió la primera botella que encontró y le dio un buen trago.

Helena aprovechó para limpiarse la frente con un pañuelo. No se había dado cuenta hasta entonces de lo rápido que le latía el corazón.

Kaine regresó con la botella que había abierto en una mano y un par de ellas más sujetas entre los dedos de la otra mano. Después, se dejó caer sobre la silla y apoyó la frente contra el respaldo.

Se pasó el resto de la noche bebiendo a un ritmo constante, de manera que el suelo a su alrededor quedó cubierto de botellas vacías. Cualquier persona normal habría muerto ante semejante dosis de alcohol. Cada vez que a Helena le comenzaban a dar calambres en las manos, se detenía a masajeárselas y obligar a sus dedos a cooperar, y Kaine aprovechaba para levantarse a por otra botella.

Cuando por fin terminó, le limpió la sangre de la espalda y le aplicó un ungüento elaborado a base de cobre. Las cicatrices estaban rojas e irritadas, pero había conseguido cerrar todas las heridas.

—Listo.

Helena se sentía un poco mareada, como si hubiera subido hasta la cima de una montaña, donde el oxígeno es escaso y cuesta respirar. Kaine, por su parte, se terminó la botella que sostenía sin pronunciar palabra.

Tras limpiar sus utensilios y guardarlo todo de nuevo en la bolsa, se dio la vuelta y descubrió que él se había incorporado. Comenzó moviendo los hombros poco a poco hasta que levantó los brazos por encima de la cabeza y arqueó la espalda como un arco listo para disparar una flecha. Entonces profirió un gemido casi indecente y su rostro se relajó por completo.

Bajó los brazos a ambos lados del cuerpo, respiró profundamente mientras seguía rotando los hombros y exhaló un suspiro tembloroso que Helena sintió en los huesos.

—Bueno, creo que ya es hora de que me vaya —dijo colgándose la bolsa al hombro, un poco mareada por el cansancio y el alivio.

Kaine se volvió al instante. Aunque seguía teniendo los ojos de una tonalidad oscura, el brillo plateado que había visto en ellos un par de veces era más evidente que nunca.

Se movía con la misma agilidad y languidez que cuando se conocieron, pero ya no había ni rastro del muchacho que había sido meses atrás. Y no era solo por las hebras de cabello plateado que le salpicaban las sienes, ni porque el dolor le hubiera endurecido la expresión, sino porque tenía un aspecto más maduro, como si su cuerpo hubiera dado un salto repentino en el tiempo.

—¿A qué vienen esas prisas? —le preguntó.

Helena se sentía como un animalillo acorralado. No había sido consciente de cuánto se había acostumbrado a la versión herida de Kaine, esa que reservaba gran parte de su energía para soportar el dolor.

Ahora que le dedicaba toda su atención, su mirada era abrasadora.

—¿Te está esperando alguien? —insistió cuando Helena trató de escabullirse hacia la puerta.

—No —respondió ella, parpadeando sorprendida y con un nudo en la garganta.

—A mí tampoco —dijo él con una sonrisa—. Brindemos por este éxito. ¿Qué te apetece?

Se acercó al mueble bar y rebuscó entre las bebidas que quedaban.

—Creo que ya has bebido suficiente...

Kaine escogió un decantador, lo olisqueó y lo levantó para verlo a contraluz.

—Este está bien.

Se acercó a Helena con la botella en la mano y ella sintió un impulso irrefrenable de huir. El chico se movía como una de las panteras que había visto una vez en el zoológico. Sin vendajes ni camisa, tenía demasiada piel expuesta, y, ahora que Helena ya no lo estaba curando, no tenía un motivo de peso para que permaneciera tan descubierto.

—No creo que... —dijo ella retrocediendo hasta chocar con la pared.

—Quédate un rato más —le pidió con suavidad, mientras agachaba la cabeza lo suficiente como para que Helena sintiera su aliento rozándole el cabello—. ¿Sabes qué? Hay algo en ti que me empuja a tomar malas decisiones, Marino. Y, aunque no debería, no soy capaz de...

Se interrumpió al colocarle un rizo suelto detrás de la oreja y acariciarle la mandíbula con un dedo.

Helena comprendió que estaba ebrio. La combinación del alcohol con la euforia de haberse curado lo había dejado borracho como una cuba. De ahí que se estuviera comportando... así.

Debería quedarse. Un momento como aquel era crucial para su misión, formaba parte de su trabajo. Si lo había curado, era para llegar hasta allí. Pero, con lo impredecible que solía ser Kaine, no tenía forma de saber cuánto tiempo le duraría aquella racha de buen humor.

¿Qué clase de persona sería el Kaine Ferron desinhibido?

A Helena se le cerró la garganta hasta que creyó que estaba a punto de asfixiarse.

Kaine le levantó la barbilla con el pulgar y la miró mientras sus ojos se le ensombrecían.

—Tienes una mente fascinante. A pesar de no estar dentro de ella, la veo bullir en tu mirada.

A Helena se le aceleró el corazón. Kaine le pasó el decantador y, cuando ella bajó la vista y quiso devolvérselo, él le acunó el rostro entre ambas manos y lo levantó suavemente para obligarla a encontrar su mirada.

Aquel brillo plateado había reemplazado por completo el tono entre gris y avellana de sus ojos.

Lo que le sucedía no era una simple transmutación. Kaine Ferron estaba convirtiéndose en algo totalmente nuevo. Helena había realizado el experimento sin ayuda; había completado un sello cuyo propósito solo él parecía comprender.

—Quédate un rato —le pidió de nuevo con un tono persuasivo y acercando su rostro a escasos centímetros del de ella—. Tómate una copa conmigo.

Despojado de su habitual frialdad y su actitud defensiva, Kaine le resultaba casi intoxicante.

—Solo una —concedió con un leve estremecimiento en la voz.

El chico sonrió. Aquella era la primera sonrisa genuina que esbozaba desde que se conocían.

—Solo una —dijo.

Apoyó los dedos bajo el decantador que Helena sostenía y, sin apartar la mirada ni un instante, le dio un suave empujón para que se lo llevara a los labios.

CAPÍTULO 37

Julius 1786

EL SABOR INTENSO Y SEDOSO del alcohol le quemó la garganta y le dejó un regusto como a humo de leña en la lengua.

Le ofreció el decantador a Kaine sin saber muy bien por qué estaban compartiendo un objeto tan incómodo de manejar.

Con un solo trago, la bebida ya había empezado a entumecerle las entrañas. Cuando él la animó a sentarse en el sofá, ella se recogió con nerviosismo en uno de los extremos. Kaine le devolvió el recipiente y, al ver que Helena intentó rechazarlo, se deslizó por el sofá hasta quedar pegado a ella. Notaba el corazón a punto de salírsele del pecho.

—Vas a tener que alcanzarme.

—Te recuerdo que mi hígado no tiene la capacidad de regenerarse —protestó, mirando con recelo el decantador y dándose cuenta de que todo el líquido que contenía equivalía a la «copa» que había aceptado tomar.

Aunque el sofá era amplio y Kaine no tenía ninguna razón para haberse sentado tan cerca, apenas los separaban unos pocos centímetros. Helena dio otro trago e intentó devolverle la bebida, pero él se negó a aceptarla. La miraba como si fuera un gato curioso a punto de saltar sobre su presa.

—Como acabe llorando, te vas a arrepentir. —Ya notaba el entumecimiento en la cara—. Me pongo sensible cuando bebo.

Él frunció el ceño.

—¿Tienes motivos para llorar?

Helena bajó la vista y deslizó el pulgar por el vidrio tallado del decantador.

—Siempre hay alguno.

Kaine cambió de posición y restregó los hombros contra el sofá, como si fuera un animal marcando su territorio. Cerró los ojos y dejó escapar un gemido.

—No me había dado cuenta hasta ahora de lo mucho que me gusta apoyar la espalda.

—¿Quieres que te deje a solas con el sofá para que tengáis un momento de intimidad? —le preguntó mientras intentaba apartarse un poco.

Al oír aquello, Kaine se quedó quieto, abrió los ojos de golpe y extendió una mano hacia ella.

—No te vayas.

El rubor le subió a Helena por las mejillas y le trepó por el rostro hasta alcanzarle el nacimiento del pelo. Apartó la mirada y bebió un poco más.

—Sé que ya te encuentras mucho mejor, pero deberás tener cuidado durante unos días —le dijo entre trago y trago—. Creo que he conseguido que el tejido cicatrizado sea lo bastante resistente como para no desgarrarse, pero eso podría cambiar tras la fase de latencia. Si notas algo raro, lo que sea, llámame. Vendré todos los días para asegurarme de que está todo en orden.

—¿Existe alguien en este mundo del que no te sientas responsable? —preguntó Kaine meneando la cabeza con incredulidad.

Ella volvió a bajar la mirada e intentó ahogar el recuerdo de la voz de Luc diciéndole que sus decisiones eran el camino fácil.

—Es mi trabajo —murmuró.

—Gracias, Marino.

La chica tragó saliva y levantó la cabeza.

—¿Sigues negándote a llamarme Helena?

Kaine exhaló y rehuyó su mirada.

—Helena —dijo despacio, extendiendo cada sílaba como si estuviera probando cómo sonaba.

—¿Ves? —Le ofreció una sonrisa—. ¿A que no ha sido tan difícil?

Entonces clavó los ojos en los de ella con una expresión seria. Helena se esforzó por no dejar que su cercanía y su torso todavía desnudo la distrajeran, pero la vista se le desvió sin querer. Por mucho que intentara evitarlo, la situación era extraña; la gente a la que estaba acostumbrada a ver sin ropa solía estar herida o muriéndose.

Y él estaba… muy vivo.

Se le entrecortó la respiración y apartó la vista, temiendo que volviera a acusarla de ser una mirona, aunque él no pareció percatarse de su dilema. Seguía observándola con atención.

No sabía si Kaine estaría muy borracho o no, pero ella ya empezaba a notar los efectos del alcohol: le pesaba la cabeza y sentía un impulso absurdo de reír y llorar al mismo tiempo.

—Deberías ponerte la camisa —le dijo con la voz más aguda de lo normal—. Te vas a congelar.

En un parpadeo, Kaine le cogió una mano y se la llevó al pecho.

—¿Te parece a ti que tenga frío?

Ella negó con la cabeza, muda de asombro, al notar lo cálida que tenía la piel. En vez de estremecerse ante su contacto, como había hecho Kaine en los últimos meses, se inclinó aún más hacia ella.

—Usa la resonancia si no me crees —insistió.

—Supongo que tienes razón —dijo Helena mientras le rozaba el pecho y un escalofrío le recorría la columna.

Sintió cómo él se estremecía bajo sus dedos tras tomar una bocanada entrecortada de aire. Todavía le sujetaba la mano, pero ya no ejercía fuerza para que la presionara contra su piel.

Helena levantó la vista y se dio cuenta de pronto de que lo encontraba atractivo.

Cuando se conocieron, tenía un aspecto demasiado joven y cruel, como una víbora recién salida del cascarón, dispuesta a atacar todo lo que se cruzara en su camino. Luego, al borde de la muerte, su rostro se volvió demacrado y furioso. Pero ahora irradiaba una calma inesperada. Sus facciones ya no estaban hundidas y el cabello oscuro, salpicado de hebras plateadas, lo hacía parecer mayor.

La frialdad que siempre había asociado con su persona se había desvanecido. Kaine tenía la piel cálida, al igual que el aliento que le hacía cosquillas en la mejilla. En ese estado de embriaguez, con su pulso latiéndole bajo los dedos, Helena no recordaba el momento en que había dejado de tenerle miedo.

Kaine habló en voz baja, como si estuviera haciéndole una confesión:

—He de admitir que jamás me habría acercado a ti de haber sabido que te convertirías en una chica tan hermosa. Verte de nuevo fue toda una sorpresa.

Helena lo miró confundida.

—Eres como la rosa que crece en mitad de un cementerio —añadió con una sonrisa amarga en los labios—. Me pregunto qué habría sido de ti en un mundo sin guerra.

—Pues… nunca me lo había planteado.

Él asintió lentamente.

—No me sorprende. —Extendió una mano y atrapó el rizo suelto que antes le había colocado detrás de la oreja—. Me acuerdo de tu pelo. ¿Sigue igual que cuando estudiábamos en la Academia?

Helena se sonrojó; no había otra cosa que recordara con tanto detalle.

—Por desgracia, sí.

—Entonces, vive igual de atrapado que tú —dijo enroscándose el rizo en el dedo—. Pero, de algún modo, se las ha arreglado para permanecer inmutable en su prisión.

La chica lo miró, sorprendida por su comentario, y los ojos se le humedecieron. Al ver que las lágrimas le corrían por las mejillas, a Kaine se le desencajó la expresión.

—Por Dios, Marino, no llores —le pidió con urgencia.

—Lo siento —se disculpó ella, apartando la mano de su pecho y secándose las lágrimas—. Es que… estoy muy borracha.

El momento se desvaneció como niebla bajo la luz del sol. Helena se frotó los ojos un par de veces, con los sentimientos a flor de piel.

Cuando levantó la mirada, él desvió la suya y frunció el ceño.

Nunca lo había visto mostrar tantas expresiones seguidas. Tenía la sensación de estar contemplando por fin al auténtico Kaine. Al principio, le pareció que sentía una profunda tristeza, pero, a medida que lo observaba, un brillo vacío y amargo se adueñó de sus ojos y ensombreció su rostro.

Helena extendió una mano hacia él sin ser plenamente consciente de lo que hacía, pero impulsada por el deseo de sacarlo del agujero negro al que su mente lo estaba arrastrando. Le tomó la mano izquierda entre las suyas y, al no encontrar resistencia, le presionó la palma con los pulgares hasta que la abrió del todo y empezó a masajeársela desde la muñeca hasta la punta de los dedos.

—¿Por qué haces eso? —preguntó al cabo de un minuto.

—Mi padre solía darme estos masajes —explicó ella sin levantar la mirada—. Decía que los alquimistas somos como los cirujanos y que por eso debemos cuidar mucho las manos.

—Pero ¿por qué me lo haces a mí?

Helena se detuvo un instante, con la mirada fija en las líneas de su mano.

—Mi madre murió cuando tenía siete años, después de una larga enfermedad. En realidad, estuvo enferma toda mi vida. Un día, fui a despertarla y estaba... helada. Nos había dejado durante la noche, sin avisar ni despedirse. Después de aquello, empecé a temer el momento de quedarme dormida. No me daba miedo perder la vida, sino que mi padre o yo muriéramos de repente, y que el otro se quedara completamente solo en el mundo. Hace un momento sentí que tú también estabas solo, así que pensé... —Negó con la cabeza y le soltó la mano—. No sé, no importa. Lo siento.

Se puso a juguetear con los dedos, incómoda. Si no se marchaba pronto, el puesto de control cerraría y se quedaría atrapada fuera de los límites de la ciudad durante la noche.

—¿Me harías un favor? —susurró Kaine cuando ella ya se disponía a decir que se iba.

Helena levantó la vista. Él parecía estar relajado de nuevo y el cabello que le caía sobre la frente suavizaba sus facciones. Lo observó un instante.

—¿Qué necesitas?

—¿Te importaría soltarte el pelo? —le pidió ladeando la cabeza—. Me gustaría verlo.

—¿En serio? —preguntó ella parpadeando sorprendida.

Kaine asintió brevemente sin apartar la mirada, así que Helena se quitó las horquillas con torpeza. Las dos trenzas le cayeron sobre los hombros y, tras soltarse también las gomas, pasó los dedos por los mechones para desenredarlos. Sintió alivio en el cuero cabelludo cuando puso sus manos sobre el regazo. No quería ver cómo reaccionaba, ya le ardían bastante el rostro y el cuello por la vergüenza.

—Ahí la tienes. La melena indomable.

Kaine la observó en silencio, como si necesitara tiempo para procesar lo que veía.

—No pensaba que tuvieras el pelo tan largo.

—El peso me ayuda a domarlo —explicó ella, estrechando las horquillas entre los dedos y atreviéndose a echarle un rápido vistazo.

Al ver que él la miraba embelesado, sin decir nada, Helena se sonrojó aún más. Con el pelo suelto, se sentía como si le estuviera mostrando una parte muy íntima de su ser, algo que siempre se esforzaba por mantener escondido, porque casi todo el mundo lo consideraba un defecto, casi como si fuera una debilidad. No estaba preparada para una reacción como la de Kaine.

Él se inclinó hacia delante y, con una mezcla de curiosidad y delicadeza, le pasó los dedos por el cabello desde la sien. Ella se estremeció ante su contacto, sintiendo la calidez de su cercanía.

—Es mucho más suave de lo que esperaba —comentó fascinado.

Helena no supo qué responder.

Kaine le deslizó la mano por el cuello y se la enterró en los rizos que le nacían a la altura de la nuca, con la respiración acelerada. Pero su melena había quedado olvidada; ahora tenía la vista clavada en el rostro de Helena, en sus labios. Un destello plateado iluminó sus ojos cuando se acercó un poco más hacia ella.

—Si no quieres que te bese, más vale que lo digas ahora.

Estaba tan cerca que Helena podía saborear el ardor del alcohol en su aliento.

Todo se había vuelto borroso e irreal, salvo él.

Sentía el peso de su vida como un lastre que la oprimía casi a diario, un lastre que requería más energía de la que podía permitirse gastar. Sin embargo, ahora también sentía la presencia de Kaine, su calidez, la caricia de sus dedos entrelazados en su cabello.

No pensaba que pudiera ser tan delicado. La miraba como si estuviera viendo su auténtico yo.

Y le estaba pidiendo permiso.

Así que lo besó.

Lo besó de verdad, no como la primera vez.

En cuanto sus labios se rozaron, Kaine tomó el control del beso. Fue como si algo se hubiera desatado en su interior. Le rodeó la cintura con un brazo y la atrajo hacia sí, hasta quedar pegados, y ella se sentó a horcajadas sobre su regazo.

Helena apoyó las manos en sus hombros y, con la yema de los dedos, le rozó el borde exterior del sello mientras él profundizaba el beso, como si quisiera devorarla. Cuando finalmente se separó, tiró de la cabeza de Helena hacia atrás y dejó que su aliento y su lengua cálida bailaran sobre la piel desnuda de su cuello.

Era como si con sus dedos trazara un mapa de su cuerpo, un topógrafo explorando la trayectoria de sus clavículas, cada curva y recoveco de su carne y sus huesos.

La pegó con tanta fuerza contra su cuerpo que Helena percibía la barrera que la ropa creaba entre ellos, así como la tela de la falda recogida alrededor de sus caderas. Kaine la rodeó con las manos por la cintura y le acarició las costillas con los pulgares.

Helena deslizó los dedos por su mandíbula y, al rozarle la mejilla, él apoyó el rostro contra la palma de su mano, cerrando los ojos con un suspiro, como si llevara mucho tiempo sin sentir ningún contacto físico.

Kaine le recorrió la espalda con las manos, siguiendo la línea de su columna, y Helena se arqueó como un gato, presionándose más contra él. Su contacto le resultaba embriagador, y sentía la cabeza dando vueltas como si estuviera atrapada en el oleaje.

Nunca se había detenido a pensar en cuánto había anhelado que alguien la tocara. Ella también llevaba demasiado tiempo sin el contacto de otra persona.

Mientras el corazón le latía con intensidad en los oídos, Helena rodeó los hombros de Kaine con ambos brazos, aferrándose a él, y un intenso placer hizo que se estremeciera ante el roce de sus dedos. Se le formó un nudo en el pecho. Kaine empezó a desabrocharle la camisa, botón a botón, hasta que las capas de ropa que los separaban se deslizaron y cayeron.

Nunca se había detenido a pensar en el gran impacto que la falta de intimidad había tenido en su vida. Pero, en cuanto el deseo despertó en ella, aquello que hasta entonces había percibido como una mera ausencia emergió de las profundidades de su piel con uñas y dientes.

Aunque sabía que la gente disfrutaba del sexo, ella siempre lo había considerado una indulgencia. Jamás habría imaginado que pudiera ser un hambre tan voraz.

Ni que ella estuviera tan hambrienta.

Se presionó contra Kaine, desesperada por reducir al máximo el espacio que los separaba, harta de estar siempre sola. De ser una figura aislada y reducida a lo que sabía hacer, su trabajo: sanadora, quimiatra, contacto, peón.

Puta.

Los ojos le ardían, así que los cerró con fuerza e intentó huir de sí misma, escapar a un lugar donde sus pensamientos no pudieran alcanzarla. Pero estos siguieron persiguiéndola, insinuándose bajo su piel allí donde los dedos de Kaine no llegaban a tocarla. Se arremolinaban como un susurro en el interior de su cráneo, como un coro de voces que la juzgaba y se reía de ella.

Aquella era su misión, el trabajo que le habían encomendado hacer. ¿En qué lugar la dejaba a ella responder a sus besos con tanto fervor? ¿O estar tan desesperada por sentirse querida o deseada?

Kaine le rozó la curva de la mandíbula con los dientes y desató en ella un deseo que sintió que la iba a partir en dos.

Helena le clavó los dedos en la piel, estremeciéndose y dejando escapar un gemido sin aliento, cuando Kaine le mordió el lateral del cuello, la tumbó en el sofá y se colocó sobre ella, envolviéndola con su peso y su calor.

Iban demasiado rápido. ¿Por qué había cambiado de actitud con tanta brusquedad?

Un golpe de realidad le sacudió el pecho: no se sentía atraído por ella.

Ya no tenía dolor. Y estaba ebrio.

Desesperado por volver a dejarse llevar por el placer tras meses de sufrimiento.

Ella estaba allí: borracha y dócil, dispuesta a dejarse consumir.

Y él era como un lobo hambriento que se conformaría con devorar cualquier animalillo indefenso.

Helena lo miró. Las costillas le oprimieron los pulmones hasta dejarla casi sin aliento y las sienes le ardieron de vergüenza al apartarse de él.

Kaine se quedó inmóvil, levantó la cabeza y, tras observarla durante un breve instante, apartó las manos de ella y se incorporó.

—Será mejor que te vayas —dijo.

CAPÍTULO 38

Helena también se incorporó, pero no se movió del sofá. Se quedó junto a él, temblando y luchando por contener las lágrimas. Miró el reloj y una ola de desaliento la golpeó de lleno.

—Los puestos de control ya habrán cerrado. No puedo volver a la ciudad hasta mañana temprano.

Kaine suspiró, se estiró de espaldas y desvió la mirada.

Ella se abrazó el torso, se cerró la camisa con manos temblorosas y forcejeó con los botones mientras el pecho se le agitaba, tratando de contener el llanto.

—¿Por qué lloras?

Helena se secó las mejillas con el dorso de la mano.

—Porque me siento sola y te he besado, pero ni siquiera te gusto.

Kaine la observó en silencio, luego echó la cabeza hacia atrás y se quedó contemplando el techo durante un largo minuto.

—¿Por qué crees que te he besado? —le preguntó al fin, con la voz tensa.

—Porque estoy aquí.

—¿Y tú por qué me has besado? —dijo mirándola de nuevo.

Helena fijó la vista en la pared que había al otro lado de la habitación, donde un tapiz representaba el momento en que Tellus había puesto a girar el mundo.

—Porque me has hecho sentir que esa parte de mí que no resulta útil para la guerra también merece existir. Que no soy solo lo que puedo hacer.

Recogió el decantador que habían dejado abandonado en el suelo.

Estaba casi vacío, pero tenía la esperanza de que un último trago la empujara a un punto de embriaguez tal que dejara a un lado sus sentimientos.

Kaine la observó mientras bebía y, luego, se recostó en el sofá y se cubrió los ojos con el brazo. Cuando Helena volvió a mirarlo, ya se había quedado dormido y el brazo con el que se había tapado había resbalado por su propio peso.

Estudió sus facciones durante un largo rato, intentando identificar los cambios que se habían producido en él, pero a ella también comenzaban a pesarle los párpados.

Pensó en levantarse y tumbarse en el diván que había junto al escritorio, pero entonces empezó a ver borroso. Cerró los ojos para descansar durante un instante y se dejó llevar…

* * *

AL DESPERTAR SEGUÍAN EN EL sofá, pero, de alguna manera, se habían enredado sin darse cuenta. Helena tenía la cabeza apoyada contra el pecho de Kaine, con el codo y la barbilla de él clavados respectivamente en sus costillas y la parte superior de su cabeza.

Era un milagro que ninguno de los dos se hubiera caído del sofá.

Como tenía la cabeza a punto de estallar, no se apartó de inmediato. Algo le decía que un movimiento brusco bastaría para que el whisky ahumado y extremadamente caro que había ingerido saliera por donde había entrado.

Con esfuerzo, se tocó la cara para mitigar las náuseas que le revolvían el estómago con la vivemancia antes de separarse de Kaine con sumo cuidado.

El chico, que estaba sumido en un profundo sueño, ni siquiera se inmutó. Seguro que no descansaba en condiciones desde la primavera.

Helena cogió su bolsa, se dirigió a la pesada puerta blindada, la abrió despacio y con esfuerzo y escapó sin mirar atrás.

Tuvo que pararse a vomitar junto a la presa y en el río, justo después de cruzar el puente, pero al final solo se sintió peor.

Regresó sin prisa al Cuartel General, atormentada por lo que había ocurrido la noche anterior. Había besado a Kaine Ferron. Y no había sido una decisión estratégica, sino que lo había besado de verdad y él había respondido de la misma manera. Por si fuera poco, había desperdiciado la oportunidad perfecta para pasar a la siguiente fase de su plan.

Kaine se lo había puesto en bandeja, la misión avanzaba mucho mejor de lo que Crowther o Ilva podrían haber imaginado, pero Helena se había saboteado a sí misma, porque habría deseado que el beso hubiera sido real en vez de una farsa.

Se había dejado llevar por sus sentimientos después de que Kaine la hubiera comparado con una rosa, después de que le dijera que era hermosa y de que aquellos aspectos de su ser que nadie jamás había considerado atractivos se convirtieran en una fuente de deseo para él.

Al parecer, a Ferron no le había hecho falta más para seducirla.

Solo con pensar en ello se estremecía y sintió que el nauseabundo vacío de la vergüenza la asfixiaba.

—Hel.

La voz de Soren la sacó de su ensimismamiento cuando cruzó el puesto de control y entró en el Cuartel General. Estaba sentado con un grupo de guardias.

Helena lo miró, desorientada por el torbellino de pensamientos que la asolaba y demasiado resacosa para articular palabra.

—¿Estás bien? ¿Qué te ha pasado en el pelo?

No entendió la pregunta hasta que se tocó la melena y se dio cuenta de que le caía suelta y enredada sobre los hombros.

—Zarzas —mintió sin pensar.

Soren clavó sus ojos profundos en ella y la observó desconcertado.

—Deberías tener más cuidado, sobre todo durante la fase de latencia.

—He salido al amanecer —explicó mientras intentaba continuar su camino—. Quería recolectar un par de ingredientes, pero voy con prisa, porque necesito preparar algo con ellos.

Soren no le quitaba la mirada de encima.

—¿Te puedes creer que se me había olvidado cómo es tu cabello? Las trenzas que te haces ahora te quedan muy bien.

—Ya. —Se obligó a sonreír, aunque le ardían los ojos—. Me sienta mejor llevarlo trenzado. Apenas soy capaz de domarlo cuando lo tengo suelto.

Se fue directa a su habitación para darse una ducha. Se frotó el cuerpo con violencia en un intento por borrar el recuerdo de las manos de Kaine. El agua ya salía caliente, pero subió la temperatura hasta abrasarse y se quedó bajo el chorro hasta que la piel se le puso casi en carne viva.

Lo que le mojaba las mejillas no eran lágrimas, sino las salpicaduras de la ducha, el agua que caía.

Apenas se molestó en secarse antes de peinarse el cabello en dos trenzas tan tirantes que sintió la tensión en el rostro. Luego, se las enrolló a la altura de la nuca sin preocuparse de que las horquillas no le arañaran el cuero cabelludo al ponérselas.

No se permitió mirarse al espejo hasta que no terminó de peinarse, hasta que no quedó ni un solo rizo suelto a la vista.

<hr />

ESTABA REABASTECIENDO EL INVENTARIO DEL hospital cuando una camillera apareció ante ella y dejó unas botellas de expansor de plasma en una caja.

—Crowther quiere que te reúnas con él en los ascensores, ahora mismo —le dijo la chica sin mirarla siquiera.

Helena se volvió bruscamente. Estaba segura de haberla visto antes, pero la camillera, de rasgos suaves y mirada expresiva, pasaba tan desapercibida que no era más que un destello en la memoria de Helena.

No le sorprendía que Crowther tuviera ojos en todas partes, incluso en el hospital, pero aquel descubrimiento la puso nerviosa.

—¿Quién eres? —le preguntó justo cuando la chica estaba a punto de marcharse.

—Nadie importante.

—¿Cómo te llamas? —Helena quería saber a quién tenía que buscar en la lista de turnos.

La chica levantó la vista, como si se sintiera halagada por su interés.

—Purnell.

Purnell. Tenía la sensación de haber oído ese apellido antes.

—Está bien, puedes irte —dijo Helena, asintiendo distraídamente.

La camillera se retiró con rapidez y Helena terminó lo que había estado haciendo antes de dirigirse a regañadientes a la Torre.

Crowther la estaba esperando allí. El ascensor descendió lentamente.

En los túneles, un chico estaba agazapado junto a una puerta. Helena entrecerró los ojos y reconoció que era Ivy, la otra vivemante de Crowther, con el pelo recogido bajo una gorra. Parecía uno de esos chicos que vivían en la calle.

Ivy se incorporó y abrió la puerta, que daba acceso a una sala donde había una persona atada a una silla. La cabeza le caía hacia delante y respiraba con dificultad.

—¿Quién es? —preguntó Helena, que habría dado lo que fuera en ese momento por salir corriendo de allí.

El olor a sangre seca y humedad le revolvía el estómago.

—Es uno de los aspirantes enviados a Hevgoss —explicó Crowther—. Lo interceptamos de camino y lo trajimos hasta aquí, pero está demostrando ser un hueso duro de roer. Está desesperado por hincarle el diente a la vida eterna y vamos a tener que persuadirlo con métodos que, en su situación actual, no sería capaz de soportar.

Helena esperaba curar quemaduras graves, pero lo que encontró fueron lesiones causadas por la vivemancia.

El prisionero no presentaba marcas visibles de tortura, tampoco cortes o heridas externas. Sin embargo, Helena reconoció enseguida el daño que se le había infligido: le habían pinzado el tracto corticoespinal para dejarlo paralizado sin comprometer los nervios sensitivos.

De esa manera, sentiría todo lo que le hicieran.

Ivy había utilizado su poder para separarle las distintas capas de la piel sin arrancarle la epidermis, provocando una hemorragia interna. En algunas zonas, le había arrancado incluso partes del músculo.

Si curar a los heridos tras una batalla era una experiencia traumática, utilizar la vivemancia como un instrumento de tortura iba a ser una auténtica pesadilla.

Pero Crowther no parecía opinar lo mismo que ella. Ningún sufrimiento físico quedaba fuera de los límites en la guerra contra la nigromancia, siempre y cuando el alma de la víctima permaneciera intacta. Para la Fe y la Llama Eterna, no había nada de malo en torturar a los nigromantes y sus aspirantes; al fin y al cabo, la carne era una sustancia imperfecta que, antes o después, acababa consumida por las llamas. Lo que aquellos individuos estaban dispuestos a hacerles a los civiles y a los miembros de la Resistencia era algo mucho peor que las torturas de Crowther.

El prisionero recuperó el conocimiento mientras le curaba los pies.

—Te conozco —le dijo cuando levantó la cabeza. Su marcado acento norteño hacía que las consonantes salieran forzadas de sus labios. Helena lo miró: tenía el cabello color trigo y una barba ya incipiente—. Eres la putilla extranjera de Holdfast.

Ella desvió la vista, decidida a ignorarlo y terminar su tarea sin pronunciar palabra. Ante aquel comentario, sentía un poco menos de lástima por él.

—Te voy a contar un secreto —farfulló cuando Helena estaba a punto de terminar de curarle las manos—. Vais a perder la guerra. Los inmarcesibles son imparables. Han venido a sustituir a vuestros dioses y, algún día, yo seré uno de ellos. El mundo conocerá a la familia Lancaster.

Helena alzó la mirada. Ya se acordaba de él: había estudiado en la Academia y se había marchado en cuanto obtuvo su título. Pertenecía a una de las familias gremiales, especializada en el níquel, si no recordaba mal.

—Cuando forme parte de los inmarcesibles, voy a torturar a esa zorra tan lentamente que me acabará suplicando que la mate. Le haré sentir todo el dolor que me inflija multiplicado por diez. Y, cuando haya acabado, la devolveré a la vida —dijo enseñando los dientes en una mueca desagradable.

Helena tensó la mandíbula y se esforzó por seguir trabajando concentrada. Crowther le había pedido que mantuviera a sus pacientes conscientes. No quería que se despertaran y descubrieran que estaban sanos, sino que temieran el momento en que Helena terminara su trabajo y la tortura comenzase de nuevo.

Una vez que finalizó, se puso en pie y se marchó sin decir una sola palabra.

Ivy y Crowther entraron juntos en la celda. Apenas se cerró la puerta, los gritos del prisionero hicieron vibrar la madera y resonaron por todo el pasadizo.

Helena se alejó, intentando escapar de sus alaridos, pero fue en vano.

Avanzó sin prestar atención al camino, sin importarle perderse. Bajo la Academia se escondía un auténtico laberinto con decenas y decenas de pasadizos que conducían a una misma estancia: un recinto amplio e iluminado por apliques de vidrio verde, cuyas paredes estaban decoradas con unos intrincados murales desgastados por el paso del tiempo. Recordaba a una iglesia abandonada.

Jamás había oído hablar de la existencia de aquel lugar oculto bajo la Academia.

Los gritos del prisionero que se dispersaban por los túneles parecían intensificarse y concentrarse en aquella estancia. Oírlos le erizaba la piel.

Helena avanzó por otro pasadizo para tratar de encontrar una salida, pero no importaba qué rumbo tomara: todos los túneles parecían conducir a la misma sala. Era como si se burlaran de ella, recordándole que no podía escapar de sí misma ni de la persona en que se había convertido. Aquella era la versión de Helena que la guerra había moldeado.

Al final, cansada de escapar, se volvió despacio y siguió el eco de los gritos del prisionero.

Pasaría por encima de los torturados, vendería su propio cuerpo y le rompería el corazón a Kaine Ferron si eso era lo que hacía falta para ganar la guerra.

SOLO TUVO QUE CURAR A Lancaster dos veces más para que se derrumbara por completo. Cuando le pidieron entrar por tercera vez, ni siquiera parecía que el hombre estuviera cuerdo.

Mientras esperaba en aquellos túneles, cubriéndose los oídos para tratar de ahogar los sonidos que escapaban de la celda contigua, Helena había tenido tiempo de reevaluar lo ocurrido entre Ferron y ella la noche anterior.

Con el recuerdo ya asentado en su mente, los errores que había cometido le parecían menos catastróficos.

Kaine sentía algo por ella. Al fin y al cabo, le había pedido que se quedara con él. Sin embargo, la chispa de deseo o afecto que había despertado en su interior apenas comenzaba a brillar. Si intentaba avivarla demasiado rápido, la apagaría. Lo mejor que podía hacer era detenerse, así él se quedaría pensando en lo que podría haber sucedido.

Empezaba a sospechar que los sentimientos de Kaine eran mucho más intensos de lo que mostraba. Por eso, la clave estaba en alimentar esa llama que ardía en su interior hasta que se convirtiera en un incendio incontrolable.

Kaine era demasiado meticuloso para que cualquier otro plan funcionara. Se trataba de elegir entre todo o nada, así que solo le quedaban dos opciones: o dejar que Kaine siguiera siendo una amenaza para la Resistencia, ahora con mucho más apoyo para cumplir sus deseos, o redirigir su ambición y su naturaleza obsesiva para que se centraran en ella.

La gente siempre decía que no había nada más tentador que lo prohibido.

Y, en cuanto al tema de su propio deseo…, de su propia disposición a estar con él…

Se mordisqueó con nerviosismo la uña del pulgar.

Era lo mejor. Siempre le habían dicho que era una pésima mentirosa.

Ivy salió de la celda.

—¿Otra vez? —le preguntó Helena cuando posó la vista en ella.

Ivy negó con la cabeza y cerró la puerta.

—Crowther sigue trabajando.

La chica se sentó junto a Helena y comenzó a dibujar distraídamente con los dedos en la suciedad del suelo. Helena la observó en silencio mientras intentaba ignorar el olor a carne quemada que comenzaba a flotar en el aire.

—¿Sabes que hay otras formas de sacarle información a la gente? —preguntó, incapaz de contenerse—. No tenéis por qué torturarlos.

Ivy clavó en ella su mirada inteligente con un destello.

—A mí me gusta hacerles daño. Es la mejor parte del trabajo. Lo demás es muy aburrido.

—Ah.

Se hizo un largo silencio entre ellas.

—¿Sabes si la vivemancia puede usarse para borrar la memoria? —preguntó Ivy—. Para hacer que alguien olvide algo concreto y que nunca vuelva a pensar en ello, quiero decir.

Helena la miró con curiosidad.

—¿Hay algo que quieras olvidar?

La otra chica negó con la cabeza, pero su mirada se perdió por el túnel, y una extraña tensión se dibujó en su rostro.

—Mi hermana no recuerda algunas cosas. La enfermera Pace dice que es una fuga disociativa, pero que puede llegar el día en que recupere la memoria.

—¿Y tú quieres que la recupere?

—No —confesó Ivy negando con un gesto antes de mirar a Helena y soltar una carcajada—. Sé que estás pensando que soy una mala persona, pero mi hermana perdería la cabeza si recordara lo que ha olvidado.

La puerta de la celda se abrió y un hedor a carne quemada emergió como una ola del interior.

—Ya hemos acabado, Marino.

Crowther había drogado a Lancaster con una sustancia sintética, dejándolo en un intenso estado alucinatorio. Había estado a punto de partirse la lengua en dos, así que Helena tuvo que paralizarlo para unir ambos pedazos. Además, su piel estaba abrasada de pies a cabeza, aunque Crowther se había asegurado de que las quemaduras no fueran lo suficientemente profundas como para dejarlo sin sensibilidad.

Lancaster no paraba de farfullar. Parecía que Helena e Ivy se habían convertido en una misma figura en su cabeza. A ratos se debatía violentamente contra sus ataduras, intentando morderle las manos o amenazándola con introducirle metal fundido en las venas hasta que los ojos le estallaran como un par de uvas. En otras ocasiones, buscaba su contacto mientras respiraba con dificultad susurrándole que era preciosa y que, cuando se convirtiera en un inmarcesible, le pondría un collar alrededor del cuello y la convertiría en su zorrita, igual que había hecho Holdfast.

Luego, volvía a confundirla con Ivy y amenazaba con comérsela viva, con cortarla en pedazos para recomponerla mal y con violarla de todas las formas imaginables.

Cuando terminó de curarlo, a Helena le hubiera gustado arrancarse la piel allí donde la había tocado.

—¿Por qué no lo matáis? —le preguntó a Crowther cuando salió de la celda, todavía con los pelos de punta.

—¿Por qué lo dices? —respondió él divertido.

—Ya tienes lo que querías. De ahora en adelante estaréis desperdiciando nuestras raciones de comida y medicinas con él.

Crowther negó con la cabeza.

—Se quedará aquí hasta que encontremos al guardia que busca. El interés de Morrough por localizar a ese tal Wagner en Hevgoss nos da a entender que será una pieza clave para nosotros. Lancaster es un aspirante especialmente fiel. Su testimonio podría resultarnos útil si tenemos que ponernos en contacto con Hevgoss en algún momento. No te preocupes por él. Jamás he perdido a un prisionero.

—Entonces ¿puedo irme ya? —preguntó con un hilo de voz. Tenía la ropa empapada con la sangre de Lancaster.

—Sí, te acompañaré hasta el ascensor. ¿Has conseguido curar a Ferron?

Ella asintió distraídamente, sin mirarlo. Ya no le quedaban fuerzas para preocuparse por si Crowther se mostraba complacido o decepcionado.

—Sí, el procedimiento ha sido un éxito.

Se hizo una pausa mientras subían la escalera y, cuando alcanzaron la salida, el hombre le bloqueó el paso, observándola con atención.

—Según he oído, has pasado la noche fuera y has vuelto con un aspecto... algo desaliñado.

Le dio un vuelco el corazón.

—Tardé más tiempo del esperado en curarlo y, para cuando acabé, el toque de queda ya había pasado y los puestos de control estaban cerrados. Tuve que pasar la noche en el Reducto.

Crowther esperó por si le contaba algo más, pero ella guardó silencio y entrecerró los ojos.

—Pues sigue adelante con el plan.

CAPÍTULO 39

Julius 1786

Helena regresó al Reducto aquella tarde, pero la pared de la fábrica que daba acceso a la habitación del pánico de Ferron estaba cerrada y tampoco había rastro del necrómata que solía aparecer con la llave.

El gélido módulo en el que solían reunirse se encontraba vacío, aunque lo esperó allí un rato, por si acaso.

Al día siguiente, ocurrió lo mismo.

Se dijo que era una buena señal, que el procedimiento había sido un éxito, pero le resultaba extraño volver a tener las tardes libres de forma tan repentina.

Helena no se había dado cuenta de cuántas horas había pasado preparando ungüentos y desplazándose de un lado a otro hasta que recuperó de golpe todo ese tiempo.

Cuando llegó el martis, salió a recolectar ingredientes y luego se dirigió hacia los apartamentos.

Ni siquiera había recorrido la mitad del camino cuando una necrómata emergió de entre las sombras y la interceptó. A Helena le dio un vuelco el corazón. No era el hombre de siempre, sino una mujer. Tras enseñarle el símbolo del hierro que tenía grabado en la piel pálida de la cara interior de la muñeca, le tendió un sobre.

En cuanto Helena lo aceptó, la necrómata se dio la vuelta y se alejó sin decir palabra.

Aunque no solía abrir las misivas de Ferron, esa vez rompió el sello y revisó el contenido del sobre en busca de instrucciones o de algún mensaje.

Pero lo único que encontró fue un informe en clave.

El saturnis, el chico tampoco apareció.

No se había planteado la posibilidad de que Kaine se comunicara con la Llama Eterna de esa manera, pero, considerando la forma en que les hacía llegar la información, tampoco había razones para que tuvieran que verse en persona.

Helena pasó su inesperado tiempo libre en el laboratorio, trabajando en nuevos experimentos junto a Shiseo, que se había convertido en un agradable compañero para ella.

Como la sanación se consideraba una rama independiente de la medicina y la asistencia médica, ambas disciplinas no siempre se complementaban. Muchos calmantes interferirían con la vivemancia, lo que obligaba a encontrar fórmulas que contrarrestaran ese efecto o emplear vías alternativas que complicaban innecesariamente el proceso de sanación. Curar a Kaine sin tener que someterse a la supervisión de Matias le había permitido descubrir las posibilidades que ofrecía la quimiatría aplicada a la vivemancia.

Comenzó elaborando tónicos que ayudaran a la regeneración sanguínea o a la reparación ósea, entre otras funciones. Sin embargo, su verdadero interés era encontrar una forma de prolongar los efectos de la vivemancia mediante el control de la propia química del cuerpo. Shiseo y ella trabajaron sin descanso para sintetizar un glucósido a partir de dedalera y extraer alcaloides de varias plantas pertenecientes a la familia de las solanáceas.

Encontrar un hueco dentro de la Resistencia le suponía un gran alivio, puesto que Elain Boyle estaba empezando a convertirse en la favorita de todos. Helena trató de convencerse de que les venía bien contar con una sanadora tan fácil de querer. Le tenían tal aprecio que nadie se inmutaba ni decía una palabra cuando a Elain se le olvidaba ponerse los guantes. Sin embargo, sus habilidades sociales también jugaban en su contra: era demasiado complaciente y eso afectaba a su forma de trabajar. Tenía la costumbre —difícil de corregir— de dejarse llevar por la intuición antes que por su formación, y solía centrarse en aliviar cualquier síntoma lo más rápido posible en vez de detenerse a buscar cuál era su causa.

Una fiebre beneficiosa para el paciente jamás conseguía cumplir su cometido cuando Elain estaba de guardia. Los heridos se sentían mejor, sí, pero sufrían infecciones con mayor frecuencia y tardaban más en recuperarse.

A finales de augustus, Basilius Blackthorne, uno de los inmarcesibles más temidos, intentó recuperar el extremo sur de la isla Este. A diferencia de sus compañeros, él casi nunca llevaba casco y no se molestaba en ocultar su identidad. Ganara o perdiera, la devastación que dejaba a su paso era terrible. Se decía que devoraba a sus víctimas en pleno campo de batalla.

Días después del ataque, cuando quedó claro que su intento había fracasado, Blackthorne prendió fuego a su propio batallón y los obligó a adentrarse lo máximo posible en territorio de la Resistencia. Como la temporada de lluvias no había empezado todavía, el paisaje estaba inusualmente seco y las llamas se propagaron con rapidez. El fuego saltó el afluente que separaba las dos islas y devoró una gran parte de la ciudad. Hacia el sur, el cielo ardía con un resplandor rojo como las ascuas.

El hospital se llenó de soldados y civiles con quemaduras y lesiones pulmonares. Las sanadoras trabajaron sin descanso durante tanto tiempo que Helena perdió la cuenta de los días que habían pasado allí dentro. No fue plenamente consciente de lo agotada que estaba hasta que no acudió al puesto de mando para entregar sus informes y escuchó a Ilva comentar que probablemente no supieran cuántas bajas habían sufrido sus enemigos hasta el día siguiente.

Había perdido más de una semana. Tenía que irse.

Cuando se despertó a la mañana siguiente, la cabeza le daba vueltas. Lila seguía dormida como un tronco, envuelta en una montaña de mantas. Los miembros de su unidad habían regresado todos cubiertos de hollín y con olor a humo. Luc había evitado que el fuego alcanzara el Cuartel General, pero ni siquiera él, con sus habilidades piroímanticas, había sido capaz de contener un incendio de semejante magnitud.

Helena se vistió con la mente embotada por el cansancio, como si no lograra pensar con claridad.

Al salir de su dormitorio, notó que había un silencio sepulcral: incluso los pájaros parecían tener miedo de cantar. El humo pendía sobre la ciudad como una mortaja.

En el Reducto tampoco se oía ningún sonido, aunque Helena no reparó en ese detalle, pues estaba demasiado concentrada buscando a la necrómata que debía entregarle la información que Kaine había preparado para la Resistencia.

Al doblar una esquina, se encontró con cuatro de ellos. Se sentía tan agotada que se detuvo y se los quedó mirando, perpleja, mientras intentaba entender por qué Kaine le habría enviado tantos necrómatas.

Al cabo de unos instantes, comprendió que no eran suyos, sino combatientes.

Helena empezó a retroceder de inmediato, y fue entonces cuando se dio cuenta de que los campamentos, antes desperdigados por el Reducto, estaban reducidos a escombros. Los inmarcesibles habían tomado la zona, y ella se había metido de lleno en la boca del lobo.

Al darse la vuelta para escapar, se encontró con más necrómatas, así que se vio obligada a sumergirse en las laberínticas callejuelas entre los edificios y las fábricas. En una de ellas, tropezó con un cadáver que nadie se había molestado en reanimar.

En cuanto conseguía darle esquinazo a un grupo de necrómatas, aparecía otro distinto.

No solían moverse rápido, pero tampoco lo necesitaban. En aquel momento, su intención era clara: alejarla del puente de entrada, la única vía de escape del Reducto.

Helena se quitó los guantes mientras retrocedía hasta darse contra un muro al haberse quedado arrinconada en un callejón. Por suerte, el espacio era lo bastante angosto como para que los necrómatas solo pudieran atacarla de uno en uno.

Se lanzaron a por ella.

Algunos portaban armas, aunque no habría sabido decir si eran más peligrosos que los demás. En cuanto estuvieron lo bastante cerca, Helena extendió los brazos frente a sí, cerró los ojos por puro instinto y liberó una descarga de resonancia.

Su poder estalló por un segundo, pero se consumió como el filamento de una bombilla.

Al abrir los ojos, estaba tan dolorida que apenas alcanzaba a distinguir a los necrómatas que se le acercaban. Se sentía como si se hubiera arrancado una vena de cuajo.

El agotamiento era normal en los alquimistas de combate, pues solían llevar su poder al límite, pero tampoco resultaba extraño en las sanadoras. El problema era que, una vez que empezaban a sufrir aquellos brotes con frecuencia...

Se obligó a concentrarse.

Había sangre por todos lados, pero aún quedaban dos necrómatas avanzando hacia ella.

Buscó desesperada el cuchillo que siempre llevaba en su bolsa y, con esfuerzo, lo encontró en el fondo en el último momento. Apuntó al necrómata más cercano en el cuello y le atravesó la médula espinal. Al haber llevado su resonancia al límite, no podía transmutar la hoja, pero la retorció y tiró de ella hacia la izquierda para que la cabeza de la criatura cayera con un grotesco sonido húmedo, seguida del cuerpo. Un dolor cegador le estalló en la pierna.

Cuando se lanzó a atacar, el otro necrómata aprovechó para intentar clavarle una punta de hierro, pero falló por poco y acabó enterrándosela en la pantorrilla.

Helena estuvo a punto de derrumbarse mientras lanzaba tajos al aire hasta que, a duras penas, logró cortarle los dedos suficientes a su atacante para impedir que recuperase el arma.

Su cerebro le pedía a gritos que se sacara la punta de hierro que le desgarraba los músculos de la pantorrilla, pero sabía que hacerlo provocaría que se desangrara. El arma se movió ligeramente y Helena tuvo que morderse la manga de la camisa para ahogar un grito.

Todavía tenía que librarse del necrómata. Casi había conseguido dejarlo sin dedos en una mano, pero aún podía matarla a golpes. Además, sabía que lo más peligroso en ellos solían ser los dientes.

Apretó el cuchillo con más fuerza y se obligó a esperar a que la criatura la atacara. Tan pronto como estuvo a su alcance, lo agarró por la muñeca sintiendo la ausencia de su resonancia como un vacío en su interior. Cuando el necrómata se lanzó a morderle la cara, Helena le clavó el cuchillo justo debajo de la mandíbula.

Pero entonces algo la golpeó en el lateral de la cabeza, haciéndole perder el equilibrio.

Su atacante se zafó de su agarre y la arañó con las uñas rotas.

A Helena se le metió su sangre espesa y podrida en los ojos, pero se lanzó hacia delante y, aunque le falló la pierna izquierda, logró tomar el suficiente impulso como para clavarle el cuchillo en lo alto del cráneo. La criatura se derrumbó.

Ella se incorporó, tambaleante, respirando con dificultad, y se limpió la sangre espesa, de un color entre marrón y morado, que le había salpicado el rostro. Su olor era abrumador.

Trató de ubicarse, tomando las torres de la ciudad como referencia. El puente estaba en el otro extremo de donde se encontraba, pero los apartamentos no quedaban lejos.

Primero se escondería allí y, luego, trazaría un plan. Se apoyó en la pared y trató de no cargar demasiado peso sobre la pierna izquierda. Incluso arrastrarla era un suplicio.

Llegó al edificio de apartamentos y trepó por la escalera con manos y pies, pero, al alcanzar el rellano, recordó que la puerta del módulo donde solía encontrarse con Kaine tenía un cerrojo resonántico. No iba a poder entrar.

Aun así, gateó hasta allí y puso la mano sobre la puerta, como si su resonancia fuera un pozo y aún pudiera extraer unas últimas gotas de agua de sus profundidades, aunque sabía que tardaría varios días en recuperarse del agotamiento.

Se quedó allí sentada, maldiciéndose a sí misma por acostumbrarse tanto a la rutina y haber bajado la guardia. Le daba vueltas la cabeza, aunque no sabía si era por el cansancio o por la pérdida de sangre.

Buscó la parte más limpia del pasillo y se obligó a examinarse la herida de la pierna. Tenía la pantorrilla y el pie empapados de sangre, por lo que había dejado tras de sí un reguero evidente. Por suerte, los necrómatas rara vez se fijaban en algo que no se moviera.

La visión se le desdibujó y el dolor comenzó a impedirle pensar con claridad.

No creía que la punta de hierro le hubiera perforado la arteria, así que contempló la posibilidad de extraérsela. El problema era que no disponía de los materiales necesarios para cerrar una herida tan grande.

Sabía que nadie iría a buscarla al Reducto, pero, si conseguía llegar al puesto de control, los guardias la llevarían hasta el Cuartel General.

Rebuscó en su bolsa.

Lo más urgente era estabilizar la punta de hierro y aplicar presión en la herida para reducir el sangrado. Luego ya pensaría en un plan.

Masticó un ramito de milenrama abandonado mientras se envolvía la pierna con vendas, aunque la sangre empapó la tela antes de que pudiera terminar. Le costaba pensar.

Se esforzó por mantener la concentración, pero la cabeza le pesaba demasiado y cada vez le resultaba más difícil permanecer alerta.

«No te duermas. Tienes que permanecer consciente».

Su vista se le volvió tubular, como si estuviese en un túnel; sus piernas parecían estar a metros de distancia de ella, al final del túnel. Todo se desdibujó.

—¿Qué estás haciendo?

Helena se sobresaltó y la pierna reaccionó por reflejo, por lo que un estallido de dolor la atravesó de pies a cabeza.

Kaine se había materializado ante ella, como surgido de la nada.

Al menos, creía que era Kaine. No veía bien y su silueta parecía absorber todo el espacio que se abría ante ella. Cuando su rostro cobró nitidez, Helena notó que la estaba mirando con una expresión gélida.

Le dio un vuelco el corazón al verlo.

—Es martis —consiguió decir.

—¿Qué te ha pasado?

Señaló casi sin fuerzas la punta de metal que aún le atravesaba la pantorrilla, pero él apenas le prestó atención.

—Ya, eso ya lo había visto. He de admitir que me impresiona lo dispuesta que estás a seguir con la farsa. No esperaba que fueras a llegar tan lejos. —Ella lo miró sin entender nada—. Dile a Crowther que no tengo tiempo para sus jueguecitos y que puede dar el acuerdo por terminado si vuelve a hacer algo así.

Al ver que se giraba y se alejaba de ella, Helena comprendió que Kaine pensaba que se había hecho daño a propósito en un intento desesperado por llamar la atención.

Kaine se detuvo antes de bajar la escalera, observó el rastro de sangre que había dejado y luego volvió a posar la vista en ella.

—Levántate —escupió con los dientes apretados.

Ella negó con la cabeza.

—Estoy esperando a que vuelva mi resonancia.

Kaine dio un respingo.

—¿Cómo dices?

—Los incendios… —Bajó la mirada—. Nos hemos visto superadas… y hoy me he levantado muerta de cansancio. No sabía que… Nunca había llegado al extremo de quedarme sin resonancia. Así que… estoy esperando.

Kaine regresó a su lado y se puso en cuclillas ante ella con expresión suspicaz. Ahora tenía muchas más hebras plateadas en el pelo.

—¿Qué clase de vivemancia os están haciendo practicar en el hospital, Marino?

—Depende de quién sea el herido.

Le daba vueltas la cabeza y su consciencia amenazaba con alejarse flotando de ella.

Kaine chasqueó los dedos justo ante su rostro, sin previo aviso.

—Céntrate. Explícame qué proceso sueles seguir. ¿Transmutas las heridas físicas para que desaparezcan o utilizas tu vitalidad para mantener a la gente con vida?

—Depende… —respondió, sin lograr enfocar la mirada. Se quedó ensimismada mirando los ojos de Kaine—. Seguimos un triaje. No podemos permitirnos perder soldados, y menos aún si son alquimistas.

—Yo pensaba que se reservarían eso para Holdfast —comentó Kaine, apretando los dientes.

El pasillo había vuelto a estirarse ante Helena hasta convertirse en un túnel.

—Luc no va a poder ganar solo.

Ferron se acercó a ella para ayudarla a levantarse del suelo, pero una descarga cegadora de dolor recorrió su cuerpo, y un alarido escapó de sus labios antes de perder el conocimiento.

Cuando abrió los ojos, estaba en el módulo, tumbada boca arriba y con la pierna herida apoyada sobre una silla. Tenía la sensación de haber empeorado y mejorado a la vez.

Y estaba muerta de sed.

Kaine examinaba detenidamente la herida de su pantorrilla.

—¿Cómo te curo?

Helena parpadeó lentamente mientras el techo daba vueltas sobre su cabeza.

«Piensa, Helena. No es la primera vez que le enseñas a alguien a sanar».

—Lo primero es adormecer la zona en la que se va a trabajar, pero no me queda sangre para...

Se le trabó la lengua. No lograba encadenar las palabras para explicar que no tenían solución salina ni expansor de plasma a mano. ¿Sabría Kaine siquiera cómo entumecer la zona? Con sus aprendizas, había utilizado la resonancia al mismo tiempo que ellas para guiarlas y mostrarles así qué tenían que buscar.

Tenía muchísima sed.

—No creo... —Negó con la cabeza—. El sistema nervioso... es complicado... para novatos.

Un destello de irritación cruzó el rostro de Kaine.

—Te recuerdo que ya te paralicé una vez. Sabré manejarlo. —Le colocó la mano desnuda justo bajo la rodilla—. ¿Aquí?

Ella asintió, apenas percibiendo la resonancia antes de que se le adormeciera la pierna. Respiró hondo un par de veces al sentirse más estable ahora que el dolor no la distraía.

—Veamos. —Tragó saliva—. Deberás evaluar la gravedad de la lesión antes de sacar la punta. Tengo nervios y venas afectados y, aunque no creo que me haya atravesado la arteria, será mejor que lo compruebes por si acaso. Cabe la posibilidad de que me haya fracturado el hueso también. Lo más fácil de detectar es el flujo sanguíneo. Bloquea las venas y las arterias temporalmente, pero ten cuidado de no tardar mucho.

Kaine no respondió ni apartó los dedos de su pantorrilla cuando su mirada se desenfocó. Helena no pudo discernir qué estaba haciendo exactamente y, aunque en otras circunstancias le habría molestado, en aquel momento no tenía la lucidez suficiente para detenerse a pensar.

Pese a que sentía la pierna dormida, se puso tensa al ver que Kaine agarraba la punta de hierro, preparada para oír el rechinar del metal contra los tejidos. Sin embargo, en vez de arrancársela, el chico transmutó el hierro, que se onduló entre sus dedos y se encogió. De esa forma, pudo sacársela sin forzarle ni desgarrarle la herida, y solo un poco de sangre cayó al suelo. Kaine soltó la punta y examinó el orificio que le había quedado en la pantorrilla a Helena con ojo crítico.

—No percibo ningún resto de metal en la herida. ¿Quieres que te la limpie?

Ella asintió y empezó a temblar pese a que ya le había sacado la punta y no notaba ningún dolor.

—Me queda un poco de disolución carbólica en la bolsa.

Kaine rebuscó entre los materiales que guardaba y encontró el frasquito que le había pedido.

—Es una suerte que te haya curado yo a ti primero —comentó Helena mientras él destapaba el recipiente en silencio y vertía el líquido sobre la herida.

El líquido parecía agua al caer por su pierna, mezclándose con el charco de sangre que se había formado en el suelo.

Cuando la herida quedó limpia, Kaine se dispuso a cerrarla. Helena le había pedido que llevara a cabo una regeneración básica, porque no creía que su cuerpo pudiera tolerar nada más avanzado.

Pasados unos minutos, cuando el agujero había sido reemplazado por una capa de tejido delicado y visiblemente inflamado, Kaine reactivó las terminaciones nerviosas de la zona. El dolor la embistió como una ola. Tendría que hacerse alguna que otra cura más, pero el procedimiento sería suficiente por ahora.

Trató de mover el pie, pero los músculos aún no estaban lo bastante reparados como para que pudiera caminar sin cojear.

—Gracias.

Kaine no dijo nada. Se limpió las manos con un pañuelo de tela y volvió a ponerse los guantes. Cuando Helena se incorporó, apoyando todo el peso del cuerpo en la pierna izquierda, el chico mostraba una impaciencia contenida, una nueva severidad.

Aunque todavía estaba algo mareada, Helena se sentía menos inestable.

Probó a abrir la puerta, pero su resonancia seguía ausente, como si se le hubiera caído un diente y notara el hueco en la boca. Deslizó los dedos por la superficie y, antes de poder reaccionar, oyó que el mecanismo del cerrojo se movía y la puerta se abría con un chasquido.

Miró por encima del hombro, esperando ver a Ferron detrás de ella, pero seguía al otro lado de la habitación.

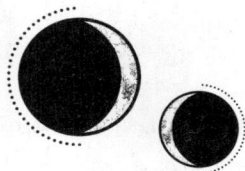

CAPÍTULO 40

Septiembris 1786

AUNQUE LOS INMARCESIBLES SE HABÍAN hecho con el control del Reducto, Helena acudió a su cita la semana siguiente. Era el mejor punto de encuentro, incluso con los necrómatas patrullando la zona. El resto de la ciudad estaba lleno de puntos de control donde los guardias, vivos y con buena memoria, comprobaban sus papeles cada vez que salía. Al ser extranjera, Helena resultaba demasiado fácil de recordar como para moverse de un lado a otro sin que llamara la atención.

A pesar de estar en territorio enemigo, había pocos necrómatas vigilando la zona. Helena lo habría sabido si no hubiera estado una buena parte de la reunión de la Resistencia medio dormida.

Al tener que esperar a que su resonancia regresara, había pasado varios días sin poder curarse y, como resultado, todavía le dolía la pierna cuando apoyaba demasiado peso sobre ella. El músculo regenerado necesitaba tiempo para reintegrarse del todo, pero la lesión no le dejaría secuelas permanentes.

Helena avanzaba por el Reducto con cautela y sin soltar su cuchillo, pero tan solo vio un par de necrómatas en la distancia. Dado que no se le acercó ninguno de los esbirros de Kaine para entregarle el sobre correspondiente, se preguntó si él sabría que, pese a todo, iban a seguir viéndose allí.

Justo cuando estaba a punto de marcharse, el anillo se calentó, así que se dirigió hacia los apartamentos.

Kaine estaba sentado a la mesa esperándola cuando llegó. Se había acostumbrado tanto a verlo encaramado a la silla, con esta dada la vuelta, que le sorprendió encontrarlo en una posición normal.

Le recorrió todo el cuerpo con la mirada, como si esperara verla sangrando de nuevo.

—Creo que ya es hora de que te entrene —dijo en cuanto la puerta se cerró tras ella.

Helena no respondió. Se sentía demasiado abrumada como para enfrentarse a todos sus sentimientos de golpe.

Kaine había decidido volver sin dar ninguna explicación sobre el mes que había pasado desaparecido. Mientras tanto, a ella la habían tratado como una fracasada y la habían sancionado por desperdiciar recursos esenciales de la Resistencia al arriesgarse en vano.

Crowther pasó esas semanas echando humo porque, aunque la información seguía llegando cada cuatro días, Kaine solo compartía lo que él consideraba oportuno. Como no podían exigirle nada, creían que habían perdido el control y no tenían forma de saber cuánto tiempo más estaría dispuesto a cooperar.

Depender de Kaine Ferron era como caminar sobre una placa de hielo que podría romperse en cualquier momento.

Helena apretó los puños y se concentró en sentir las cicatrices que tenía en la palma de la mano, ya que no quería decir algo de lo que después se arrepintiera.

Kaine echó la cabeza hacia atrás, su cabello oscuro estaba tan salpicado de hebras plateadas que casi resplandecía con luz propia.

—¿Cuánto tiempo llevas ejerciendo como sanadora?

—Un poco más de cinco años —respondió ella, tras una breve pausa para calcularlo.

La miró con tal intensidad que casi resultaba abrasadora.

—Imagino que estás al tanto de lo del Estrago. —Helena asintió y Kaine continuó hablando—: ¿Alguna vez habías agotado tu resonancia antes?

Ella negó con la cabeza.

—No, el otro día fue la primera vez —respondió Helena mientras se llevaba los dedos al pecho buscando distraídamente el amuleto que colgaba vacío bajo sus ropas—. Antes solía… aguantar mejor el cansancio.

—Bueno, eso es algo —dijo él poniéndose en pie—. ¿Cómo te explicaron el asunto? Imagino que fueron el falcón o los Holdfast quienes te hablaron de ello.

Helena desvió la vista hacia la ventana.

—La vivemancia es una versión corrupta de la resonancia que bebe tanto de la vitalidad de la persona como de la energía de la propia resonancia. Se produce cuando un alma inviable le roba la vida a otra. Las almas como las nuestras solo pueden purificarse si su existencia gira en torno a la abnegación. El Estrago es... nuestra penitencia. Nos obliga a devolver lo que robamos.

—Ya. —Kaine retorció la boca en una sonrisa burlona—. Recuerdo que me dijiste que tu madre murió cuando eras pequeña.

Helena se quedó fría y asintió sin decir nada. Todavía estaba conmocionada por la muerte de su padre cuando Ilva la había mandado a ver a Matias, que por aquel entonces aún era un alcaudón.

Había sido él quien le había explicado que sus padres habían fallecido por su culpa.

Aunque los médicos creían que la causa era un tipo de tuberculosis, según Matias, la misteriosa enfermedad de su madre había sido resultado del Estrago. Y no porque ella fuera una vivemante, sino porque el alma defectuosa y corrupta de Helena había estado en su útero, desde el mismísimo momento de su concepción, drenando la energía a su madre hasta dejarla con apenas siete años más de vida. Los vivemantes eran parásitos por naturaleza y estaban destinados a arder en las entrañas de la tierra para el resto de la eternidad si no se arrepentían de sus pecados y se purificaban, cediéndoles a otros toda la vitalidad que habían robado.

A Helena se le partía el corazón solo de pensarlo. Después de pasar tantos años junto a su madre, mientras su padre se desvivía tratando de encontrar una cura, hundido bajo una montaña de deudas por comprar ingredientes caros, al final resultaba que todo había sido culpa suya.

—Entonces... —empezó a decir Ferron despacio, acercándose con sigilo—, ¿utilizas tu propia vitalidad para salvar a... quienes tus superiores te ordenan, como si fuera una penitencia?

Helena deseó que callara.

—Quiero enseñarte algo. —Se detuvo ante ella—. Dame la mano.

Ella le ofreció la izquierda a regañadientes y, cuando él se la tomó, apenas tuvo tiempo de reaccionar antes de que una descarga de resonancia le recorriera el brazo y le diera un fuerte tirón.

Se sentía como si él hubiera intentado arrancarla de su propio cuerpo, a un nivel celular. Toda ella se sacudió como si la resonancia de él le hubiera enganchado las entrañas, intentando extraerle el alma de cuajo. Sin embargo, antes de que lograra su propósito, la energía de Helena reaccionó y repelió la resonancia de Ferron con tanta rapidez que le abrasó las entrañas.

A él también le ardían los dedos cuando la soltó. Ella estuvo a punto de caer hacia atrás.

—¿Qué has…? —intentó preguntar, pero su lengua se negaba a obedecerla.

Se dobló por la cintura y estuvo a punto de vomitar. Ferron, por su parte, sacudió la mano como si se hubiera quemado.

—Acabo de intentar arrancarte tu vitalidad a la fuerza. ¿Te ha llamado algo la atención?

Helena se presionó una mano contra el pecho e intentó olvidar la sensación que le había dejado aquel desagradable tirón al recorrer todo su cuerpo.

—Que me ha… dolido.

—Que no ha funcionado —la corrigió—. Es imposible arrebatarle la vitalidad a una persona de esa manera. Si fuera tan sencillo… —resopló—, Morrough no se estaría tomando tantas molestias. Ahora inténtalo tú.

Helena se alejó de la mano que le ofrecía.

—No, gracias. Creo que ya lo he captado.

A Kaine se le endureció la expresión.

—No necesito que lo captes, sino que lo creas. Te estás dejando llevar por la culpabilidad que te hace sentir un crimen que ni siquiera has cometido. Crees que te mereces sufrir por ello, y eso te convierte en un riesgo para mí.

A Helena no le sorprendía que estuviera hablando por su propio interés, eso no era ninguna novedad.

—Dame la mano. —Ella obedeció sin demasiadas ganas—. Sabes reconocer la vitalidad cuando la usas, así que busca la mía.

Le lanzó un vistazo rápido.

—Pero tú no es que seas normal que digamos.

Helena lo tanteó con su resonancia, pero no para evaluar el estado de su organismo, sino para localizar esa chispa de vida que brillaba en su interior. Sin embargo, para su sorpresa, lo que encontró estaba mucho más cerca de ser un sol diminuto que una chispa.

Se sentía como si hubiera aterrizado de cabeza en Lumitia estando en plena sublimación. Una gélida quemazón atravesó sus dientes y sus huesos, pero intentó ignorarla. Tenía que tirar de aquella energía, y no sabía cómo hacerlo. Cuando usaba su vitalidad para sanar, el proceso era totalmente opuesto: consistía en ofrecérsela a la otra persona, en introducirla en otro cuerpo, pero trató de replicar la sensación que Ferron le había hecho experimentar durante su demostración.

Extendió su resonancia hacia aquel ardor indescriptible e intentó tirar de él, pero sintió un retroceso inmediato. Su resonancia rebotó como una goma elástica y le golpeó la yema de los dedos. Una curiosa expresión, casi divertida, cruzó el rostro de Kaine cuando Helena lo soltó.

Tragó saliva y parpadeó rápidamente.

—Pero si... si lo que dices es cierto, entonces ¿por qué murió mi madre?

Kaine exhaló.

—Mi padre buscó un tratamiento para mi madre antes de que yo naciera. Una vivemante a la que habían contratado le explicó que ella probablemente disponía de un cierto grado de vivemancia latente y que, sin darse cuenta, consumía todo el tiempo su vitalidad —explicó sin mirarla—. A lo mejor a la tuya le ocurrió lo mismo.

Al oír aquellas palabras, Helena sintió que el tremendo peso con el que había estado cargando hasta ese momento desaparecía. Aunque la muerte de su madre estuviera relacionada con ella, no había sido por su culpa. Tomó una bocanada de aire temblorosa sin atreverse a creérselo del todo. ¿Por qué le había contado eso Kaine? ¿Qué le importaba a él que se sintiera culpable?

—La vitalidad es una energía curiosa —concluyó dando un paso hacia atrás—. No hace falta mucha para manejar la nigromancia o la sanación. De lo contrario, los nigromantes no seríamos una amenaza real y tú habrías muerto a las pocas semanas de ejercer como sanadora. Pero te contaré algo interesante. Si hubieras probado ese truco en un necrómata, habrías tenido éxito. La reanimación no logra que la vitalidad se vincule del todo con otros cuerpos; solo permite reactivar el cadáver. Bennet daría lo que fuera por ser capaz de transferir el alma de un cuerpo a otro, pero siempre acaba matando a ambas personas. —Arqueó una ceja—. ¿Ves por dónde voy?

—No.

Kaine agitó una mano y, pese a estar en medio de la estancia, abrió el cerrojo y, con él, la puerta del módulo. Para espanto de Helena, un necrómata apareció ante ellos.

—¡Ferron! —exclamó, retrocediendo hasta toparse con algo firme.

El chico se había colocado justo a su espalda y, cuando ella trató de apartarse del necrómata que se acercaba, la agarró por los hombros para impedir que se moviera.

Helena intentó darle una patada con el corazón a punto de salírsele del pecho.

—¡Suéltame! ¡Te digo que me sueltes!

—No lo ataques ni lo hagas estallar en pedazos. Cuanto esté a tu alcance, le arrebatarás la vitalidad que lo ha reanimado.

—¿Has perdido la cabeza?

Volvió a retorcerse para escapar, pero Kaine le atrapó una muñeca y, con firmeza, le extendió el brazo hacia delante para que tocara el pecho del necrómata con la mano abierta.

Era un hombre que parecía rondar los cuarenta años y debía de haber estado varios días muerto antes de ser reanimado. Su aspecto no revelaba la causa de su fallecimiento, pero olía a sangre. Seguramente, ocultaba alguna herida bajo la ropa. Su mirada estaba vacía, con la esclerótica amarillenta y la piel tirante.

—Siente su energía —le susurró Ferron.

Notaba la calidez de sus manos en los hombros, inmovilizándola y dándole apoyo al mismo tiempo. Nunca había tocado a un necrómata con su resonancia de esa manera. Jamás había experimentado la discordancia que se creaba cuando la vida y la muerte se entrelazaban. Al hombre le latía el corazón con languidez y su sangre, desprovista de oxígeno, le fluía despacio por las venas. No había en él ni rastro de vida, solo energía.

El necrómata estaba muerto, así que carecía del dinamismo propio de los vivos. Era como una carcasa animal sometida a una descarga eléctrica constante, necesaria solo para mantener su sistema en funcionamiento.

—¿La notas? —preguntó Ferron, y ella asintió con brusquedad—. Pues cógela.

Helena cerró los ojos con fuerza y tiró. Fue tan fácil como arrancar una planta de la tierra suelta. La energía quedó libre de inmediato y una descarga de poder recorrió su brazo.

Todo a su alrededor se volvió de un tono blanco plateado, como si hubiera explotado y alguien la hubiese recompuesto en el acto.

Oyó el sonido amortiguado del necrómata al caer al suelo y, cuando abrió los ojos, encontró a Kaine arrodillado junto al cadáver. Le tocó la mano por un instante y el muerto se incorporó, se puso en pie y salió de la estancia.

Kaine se volvió para mirarla.

—Si te toca enfrentarte a algún otro necrómata, no desperdicies tu energía explotándolos. Arrebátales la energía que los reanima. —Apartó la mirada—. Puede que también te ayude a mantener el Estrago bajo control.

Helena no dijo nada. Tenía los nervios a flor de piel.

—No sabía que los vivemantes podíamos hacer eso —comentó mientras trataba de ordenar sus pensamientos.

—No es algo que esté al alcance de todos —explicó Kaine levantándose del suelo—. Solo los animantes pueden hacerlo.

Habló con un tono tan despreocupado que Helena tardó un momento en asimilar sus palabras. Clavó la mirada en él.

—¿Cómo lo has sabido?

Esbozó una leve sonrisa.

—Fue una corazonada. —Helena se sonrojó y Kaine siguió hablando—: Aunque me llamó la atención lo rápido que aprendiste el truco de la memoria que te enseñé. —Estiró la espalda—. Ahora que no corres el riesgo de desmayarte por hacer una simple transmutación, quiero verte combatir.

A Helena se le cayó el alma a los pies. Ya sospechaba lo duro que iba a ser con ella.

—Hace tiempo que no practico —se disculpó mientras sacaba el cuchillo de su bolsa. Había vuelto a caer al fondo, así que tuvo que rebuscar entre varios manojos de hierbas y musgo para encontrarlo—. Nunca llegaron a enseñarme técnicas más avanzadas. Ya sabes, por el programa académico que había elegido y todo eso.

—A mí me pasó lo mismo —coincidió él, observándola con los ojos entrecerrados en expresión insolente, aunque aún brillaba un destello plateado entre sus pestañas—. Deberías llevar siempre encima el cuchillo. No puedes permitirte perder tiempo peleándote con esa bolsa. De hecho, lo mejor sería que tuvieras dos.

—Entonces no podría utilizar la vivemancia.

Kaine enarcó las cejas.

—Pero tu poder solo resultará útil con los necrómatas, no con los inmarcesibles o las quimeras.

—¿Por qué? —preguntó Helena levantando la mirada.

—Porque, si te acercas lo suficiente como para tocarlos, puedes darte por muerta. Tú no te regeneras, así que tendrás que mantener las distancias para sobrevivir.

La chica contempló el cuchillo que sostenía. Era pesado y difícil de manejar, como todas las armas reglamentarias.

—No creo que un cuchillo me sirva para mantener mucha más distancia. Además, si voy armada, llamaré más la atención. Estaré más segura si me confunden con una chica cualquiera. Los necrómatas no suelen atacar a la población civil.

—Me temo que eso ha cambiado. Con todas las bajas que hemos sufrido este año y con la Llama Eterna controlando toda la isla Este, ya no hay civiles que valgan. Cualquier persona sin la identificación adecuada será considerada enemiga y tratada como tal.

A Helena se le secó la garganta.

—¿Sin distinciones?

—Se aplica a todo hombre, mujer o niño. Cuando la Llama Eterna no dejaba de perder terreno, los inmarcesibles podían permitirse ser magnánimos. Pero ahora el objetivo es erradicar a los disidentes.

Helena tenía ciertas nociones de combate, académicamente hablando, claro. También había practicado algunos movimientos, pero de eso ya hacía mucho tiempo.

Kaine parecía considerarla la persona más torpe que había visto jamás. Tras observarla durante un rato, empezaron a practicar los movimientos que les habían enseñado el primer año de sus estudios y la obligó a repetirlos una y otra vez hasta que los tuvo dominados.

Dado que Kaine había reaccionado de una forma relativamente civilizada al descubrir que era una animante, Helena no esperaba que adoptara una actitud tan implacable con el entrenamiento. Y, aunque se volvió despiadado, prefería eso a que la persiguiera por la habitación tirándole muebles a la cabeza.

—No creo que esto me vaya a salvar de nadie —dijo tras una semana de entrenamiento.

Se sentía incómoda por sudar tanto y, además, le temblaba el brazo al levantar el cuchillo por encima de la cabeza por centésima vez, mientras canalizaba su resonancia y modificaba la largura y la curvatura de la hoja.

—Si no consigues dominar los movimientos más básicos, puedes darte por muerta.

Una bota impactó contra la parte baja de su espalda y Helena dejó escapar un gritito de sorpresa, pero evitó estamparse contra la pared en el último segundo al apoyar un pie contra ella. Tras darse impulso, orientó el cuchillo hacia Kaine por puro instinto.

El dolor de espalda la estaba matando. Si el golpe hubiera sido más fuerte, podría haberle partido la columna.

—Pero ¿a ti qué coño te pasa, Ferron?

—Vaya, veo que volvemos a los apellidos —dijo él con frialdad.

—Me has hecho daño —se quejó apretando los dientes.

Se tocó la espalda con cuidado para prevenir la hinchazón con la resonancia.

—Pues no bajes la guardia. —Le lanzó una mirada fulminante—. No te estoy entrenando para que superes un examen. ¿Te crees que tus enemigos se van a quedar quietos para ver a quién se le da mejor la transmutación? En el campo de batalla, no sabrás de dónde vendrá el siguiente golpe. Utiliza la resonancia para predecir mis ataques, porque pienso golpearte todas las veces que me dejes acercarme a ti lo suficiente. Sigamos.

Helena meneó la cabeza y se negó a moverse. A Ferron se le ensombreció el rostro.

—He dicho que sigamos.

—Yo no soy como tú —le espetó ella con la voz cargada de veneno—. Si tu intención es que aprenda a base de golpes, vas a tener que darme tiempo para recuperarme. Además, cuanto más cansada estoy, más errores cometo. No pienso quedarme a comprobar cuánto dolor eres capaz de infligirme antes de recordar que una lesión sin importancia puede dejarme paralizada. Es una suerte que con ese último golpe no lo hayas hecho.

Ferron apretó tanto los labios que se le pusieron blancos. Helena se dio la vuelta, envainó el cuchillo y se lo guardó en la bolsa.

—Esto no es un simple entrenamiento —le recordó cuando ella ya estaba en la puerta—. Si no aprendes a defenderte, acabarás muerta. No tienes otra opción si quieres sobrevivir.

—Me da igual lo que sea. Eres un instructor pésimo —sentenció antes de abrir la puerta y cerrarla a su espalda de un portazo.

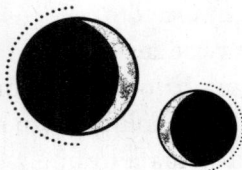

CAPÍTULO 41

LA GUERRA SIEMPRE HABÍA AVANZADO despacio, pero al llegar el otoño su ritmo pareció ralentizarse todavía más. Ambos bandos controlaban casi la misma extensión de territorio. Hacerse con el control de la zona portuaria le había dado un impulso considerable a la Llama Eterna, pero el camino hacia la victoria seguía siendo incierto. La disposición de la isla Oeste era aún más vertical que la de la Este, y las múltiples intersecciones entre torres y edificios convertían la ciudad en un laberinto casi imposible de recuperar sin arriesgarse a tener numerosas bajas.

Kaine era el responsable de que la Resistencia y los inmarcesibles estuvieran casi en igualdad de condiciones, aunque la situación era delicada: no sabían si llegaría algún día en que dejaría de colaborar o, lo que era aún peor, los acabaría traicionando.

En cuanto reapareció, la presión que Ilva y Crowther habían estado ejerciendo sobre Helena se multiplicó por diez, aunque ella no sabía cómo seguir avanzando. Kaine estaba siempre de mal humor y a la defensiva con ella. Además, aunque Helena se había dado cuenta de que ahora tenía mucho más cuidado de no hacerle daño, su método de entrenamiento no daba pie a interactuar de otra forma que no fuera peleando.

Bajo su mirada implacable, Helena aprendió a amplificar su resonancia hasta inundar el espacio a su alrededor para anticipar cualquier ataque con tiempo para reaccionar.

—¡Ya era hora! —exclamó cuando ella consiguió no solo bloquear uno de sus rapidísimos golpes sin perder la posición de ataque, sino devolvérselo.

Aquello fue lo más parecido a un elogio que había salido de sus labios desde que empezaron a practicar.

Helena se derrumbó contra la pared mientras recuperaba el aliento. Le ardían todos los músculos de los brazos por haber pasado tanto tiempo transmutando metales. También le dolían los nervios por abusar de la resonancia, y su cerebro, que iba a mil por hora, emitía una vibración que hacía que le hormiguearan los dientes.

Ahora entendía por qué Lila siempre regresaba alterada del campo de batalla.

Apretó los puños.

—Vas a necesitar un arma mejor. La aleación de la hoja te está ralentizando.

Helena apartó la mirada. Fuera estaba lloviendo y el agua resbalaba por el cristal de las ventanas. Sentía tanto calor que le habría gustado salir y dejar que la lluvia fresca del otoño la empapara.

—Mi rango no me permite solicitar nada mejor.

Los metalúrgicos de la Resistencia contaban con un extenso historial de trabajos realizados, desde herramientas, armas básicas y piezas de arnés hasta armaduras y prótesis. Además, se esperaba que fueran desarrollando nuevas armas a medida que la guerra avanzaba. Dado que la Academia no podría formar nuevos metalúrgicos, los especialistas con los que contaban eran un recurso vital para la causa. La generación que debería estar aprendiendo el oficio para relevarlos estaba combatiendo o había muerto, así que los miembros de la Resistencia tenían que conformarse con las armas reglamentarias disponibles. Si no eran capaces de luchar con ellas, tampoco podrían hacerlo como alquimistas.

Todos los alquimistas de combate soñaban con tener un arma a medida, forjada para ajustarse a sus habilidades resonánticas y a su estilo de combate. Esas armas eran versátiles, ligeras como una pluma y muy fáciles de transmutar, por lo que al enemigo le resultaba mucho más complicado defenderse.

—¿Cómo que no? ¿Acaso no eres miembro de la Llama Eterna?

—Sí —respondió ella en un susurro.

—Pensaba que las armas formaban parte del paquete completo, que os entregaban un arma valiosa en compensación por comprometeros de por vida a seguir esos ideales religiosos tan estúpidos que profesáis.

Helena clavó la vista en sus zapatos.

No se equivocaba. La tradición dictaba que, al concluir la ceremonia de los votos, la Orden de la Llama Eterna debía entregar un arma a cada iniciado para defender los ideales que había jurado seguir. Era un gesto cargado de simbolismo.

Sin embargo, Helena se unió a la Orden justo después del asesinato del principado Apollo, y muchas otras personas hicieron lo mismo. Tenía dieciséis años y apenas había empezado a formarse. Los nuevos miembros, que pronto partirían al campo de batalla, las habían necesitado más que ella. De hecho, Helena ni siquiera sabía qué tipo de arma se adaptaría mejor a sus habilidades.

Cuando pasó a trabajar como sanadora, ese asunto había quedado olvidado. Las armas eran para los combatientes y ella ni lo era ni lo sería jamás.

—Forjar un arma especial que apenas iba a usar no era una de nuestras prioridades.

—Pues ahora tendrá que serlo. Creo que han tenido tiempo suficiente en estos seis años. ¿Cuántas espadas y armaduras tiene Holdfast?

Helena se puso a la defensiva.

—Te recuerdo que Luc lucha en el frente.

—Sí, con fuego —resopló Kaine con evidente desagrado—. Haz el favor de conseguir un cuchillo decente.

HELENA REGRESÓ CON EL MISMO cuchillo.

Kaine estaba al otro lado de la estancia cuando sacó el cuchillo de la bolsa, pero se movió a una velocidad vertiginosa y se detuvo ante ella para arrancárselo de la mano.

—¿Por qué sigues trayéndolo? —siseó—. Te dije que consiguieras uno nuevo.

—No pueden ponerme la primera en la lista, así sin más —explicó ella tratando de recuperarlo—. La gente sabe que hay que esperar semanas antes de que te hagan las pruebas. Llamaría demasiado la atención que me dieran prioridad de repente. —Echó la cabeza hacia atrás para observarlo fijamente y repitió, palabra por palabra, lo que le habían dicho cuando solicitó el arma—: «No podemos aceptar tu petición. Suscitaría demasiadas preguntas».

Ferron la miró como si quisiera estrangularla y levantó el brazo con la intención de tirar el cuchillo por la ventana, pero, finalmente, respiró hondo para calmarse.

—Entonces, dime cuál es tu aleación resonántica —le pidió, dejando el arma sobre la mesa con un golpetazo.

—¿Qué?

Su expresión se volvió gélida.

—¿Ni eso vas a poder hacer?

—Sí..., pero...

La había dejado muda.

—¿Qué pasa?

Las armas hechas a medida tenían un precio prohibitivo fuera de la Llama Eterna, por eso suponía un gran honor recibir una al tomar los votos. Y más cuando, a raíz de la guerra, la mayor parte de los metalúrgicos que no se habían unido a uno u otro bando habían huido de Paladia, llevándose consigo su valioso talento a países más seguros.

Helena se quedó mirándolo sin decir nada hasta que él rompió el contacto visual.

—Considéralo mi forma de darte las gracias por haberme curado la espalda.

—¿Se te ha... se te ha asentado bien el tejido cicatrizado? —le preguntó aprovechando la oportunidad—. Después de haberte curado, volví a comprobar cómo estabas..., pero no...

—Está bien —la interrumpió con la voz y la postura tensas. Había girado el rostro, así que Helena solo le veía la mandíbula—. Apenas lo noto.

—Bien —suspiró ella—. Temía que hubieras dejado de venir porque algo había salido mal...

Kaine se volvió hacia ella.

—Lo que haga o deje de hacer no es de tu puta incumbencia.

Helena dio un respingo.

—Lo que quería decir es que...

—Vete a la mierda, Marino —le espetó con voz mortífera—. No soy tu perrito faldero y no te necesito.

Antes de que Helena pudiera contestar, sacó un sobre del bolsillo interior de la chaqueta, lo dejó junto al cuchillo y salió pisando con fuerza.

Helena se lo guardó en el bolsillo exterior de la bolsa y regresó al Cuartel General sin bajar la guardia hasta que llegó al primer puesto de control. Entonces aminoró el paso sin que le importara mojarse por la lluvia.

¿Qué le había contado sobre el sello? Que, en vez de ir en contra de su personalidad, le añadía nuevos rasgos. Que le resultaba más fácil ser implacable, pero que también le impedía resistirse a sus impulsos y deseos.

Había pasado tantas tardes observándolo que podría dibujarlo con los ojos cerrados.

Calculador, astuto, devoto, tenaz, implacable, eficaz, resuelto y severo.

Lo que Kaine debía hacer no aparecía en el sello, así que quedaba a su elección. Estaba segura de que se creía muy listo por haberse dejado esa laguna como vía de escape.

Pero Helena también se había aprovechado de ella.

Ilva y Crowther habían decidido correr el riesgo de rechazar la petición de Kaine para ver cómo reaccionaba ante una negativa. La excusa que habían puesto para no darle un nuevo cuchillo era legítima, aunque la verdadera intención era ponerlo a prueba para obligarlo a mostrar sus cartas. Y eso era exactamente lo que había hecho.

Helena estaba avanzando.

Pero, en vez de sentirse orgullosa, lo único en lo que podía pensar era en lo mentirosa que estaba siendo y en el peligro al que se exponía.

Al salir de su ensimismamiento, se dio cuenta de que había llegado al jardín de infiltración. El riachuelo bajaba tan crecido que anegaba las riberas y fluía alrededor del pedestal de Luna. Sin embargo, la torre de guijarros que había construido seguía en pie meses después, como si todas sus plegarias hubieran sido ignoradas. Decidió tirar la piedra que estaba en lo alto por su propia mano.

Alzó la vista para admirar los edificios que se erguían sobre ella y dejó que la lluvia le salpicara el rostro. A veces, todavía se sorprendía al recordar lo hermosa que podía llegar a ser la ciudad.

Incluso con el aguacero, los edificios resplandecían.

Contempló el santuario abandonado de nuevo.

«Sobrevive», le había repetido Kaine sin descanso. Ese era su único objetivo. Si Helena estaba aprendiendo a luchar no era para vencer, sino para escapar, como si fuera un animal de presa.

Era muy consciente de que, si en algún momento se veía obligada a enfrentarse a Kaine, ella moriría. Por muy igualadas que estuvieran sus habilidades alquímicas, el asesinato era una competencia exclusiva de él.

Sonrió con amargura al constatar la diferencia.

La cifra de muertes que le manchaba las manos no era sino la representación numérica de sus fracasos, de todas las vidas que no había conseguido salvar, de todos los momentos en que no había estado a la altura.

Para Kaine, en cambio, era una muestra de su poder. Sus víctimas, incluso el principado Apollo, representaban aquello que lo hacía valioso.

Eran dos caras de una misma moneda.

Una sanadora y un asesino, acechándose, atrapados en un inevitable tira y afloja.

DESDE QUE LA RESISTENCIA SE había hecho con el control de la isla, su base de operaciones se había ampliado. El Cuartel General seguía siendo el emplazamiento más protegido, pero obligar a las unidades de combate y a las expediciones de abastecimiento a desplazarse de un extremo a otro del territorio era una pérdida de tiempo y recursos. Por eso, habían establecido una segunda base de mando cerca de la zona portuaria, junto a un hospital secundario. Por el momento, habían destinado a la enfermera Pace allí para que lo pusiera todo en marcha.

Luc ya casi nunca regresaba al Cuartel General e incluso Crowther permanecía ausente la mayor parte del tiempo.

Helena le llevó el informe directamente a Ilva, que no abandonaba nunca la base principal.

—¿Y bien? —le preguntó la mujer al verla entrar en su despacho.

—Me ha preguntado por mi aleación —dijo Helena mientras tomaba asiento ante el escritorio y le tendía el sobre—. Dice que se encargará de conseguirme un arma.

Ilva levantó la mirada y la luz del sol le iluminó los ojos de color azul pálido.

—Ah, ¿sí?

Helena se examinó las uñas, aún manchadas de tierra. La piel de alrededor se había teñido de verde por recolectar ingredientes.

—Me ha dicho que es su forma de darme las gracias por curarlo.

—Seguro —coincidió Ilva con un tono cantarín lleno de sarcasmo.

Helena se mordió el labio. Odiaba tener que informarles de todas sus conversaciones e interacciones con Kaine, desgranar cada palabra, cada gesto, silencio. Odiaba que Ilva o Crowther lo sometieran a una especie de disección emocional para identificar sus puntos débiles y que así Helena pudiera aprovecharlos en su siguiente encuentro.

—¿Algo más?

Helena reparó en que Ilva la observaba con atención. Desde que Kaine había retomado el entrenamiento, la mujer ya no se mostraba tan distante con ella. Ahora que Helena volvía a resultarle útil, Ilva consideraba que merecía unos minutos de su valioso tiempo.

—Tal como avanza la situación, no descartaría que Ferron acabara matándome.

Ilva estiró la espalda y apretó los labios hasta hacerlos desaparecer.

—¿Estás pidiendo que te retiremos de la misión, Marino? —preguntó con una repentina intensidad en la voz.

A Helena se le hizo un nudo en el pecho y negó con la cabeza.

—No. Necesitamos la información. Es solo que... quiero saber cuál es mi prioridad. Elain es la sanadora que mejor preparada está para sustituirme, pero todavía le queda mucho por aprender en cuanto a conocimientos médicos básicos. Y ni siquiera eso sin contar las técnicas de sanación más complejas, que se niega a practicar por miedo. El trabajo no la motiva tanto como debería, pero creo que lo más adecuado sería que el Consejo la nombrara mi sustituta para que yo tenga algo con lo que presionarla.

—Hablaré con Jan y revisaré los informes del hospital. Nos vendría bien que prepararas una lista con las áreas en las que menos os solapáis.

—Me encargaré de ello —respondió Helena con tono seco y mecánico. Entonces se le ocurrió algo—. Shiseo... es metalúrgico. ¿Podrías pedirle que me haga una prueba para determinar cuál es mi aleación?

Ilva carraspeó.

—Como quieras.

Helena se levantó, pero la mujer la llamó con suavidad cuando estaba a punto de alcanzar la puerta, así que se detuvo y se volvió para mirarla. La expresión de Ilva era indescifrable.

—Dime, ¿qué estrategia tienes pensado seguir con Ferron ahora?

Ella lo meditó un momento. Estaba agotada. Ya ni siquiera recordaba cuándo había sido la última vez que se sintió descansada. Se apoyó en la puerta para sostenerse.

—Creo... que me desea. Desde que lo curé, las cosas entre nosotros han cambiado, pero se ha dado cuenta de lo que estoy haciendo. —Tragó saliva—. Se obsesiona mucho con todo. Me parece que siempre ha sido así, pero el sello solo lo intensifica. Si todo sale según lo previsto, eso nos proporcionará una ventaja, porque ya no le dará la espalda a la Llama Eterna. Según parece, para él es fundamental que los demás actúen libremente, y sabe que mi cooperación depende de la supervivencia de la Llama Eterna. Sin embargo..., teniendo en cuenta lo lejos que ha estado dispuesto a llegar por salirse con la suya, diría que hay una posibilidad de que destruya todo lo que se interponga en su camino. Y eso tal vez me incluya a mí.

Ilva la observó en silencio.

Helena se sentía desnuda, como si la estuvieran examinando después de haberle arrancado la piel.

—A lo mejor le estoy dando demasiadas vueltas al asunto.

Ilva bajó la mirada hacia el escritorio, cogió un pisapapeles de cristal y comenzó a darle vueltas entre las manos.

—Has llegado mucho más lejos de lo que esperaba.

¿Se suponía que con eso debía sentirse mejor?

Aunque sabía que debería estar sintiendo algo, Helena tenía la impresión de que su corazón se le estaba compactando en el pecho, que se hacía más duro y pequeño cada día que pasaba. Solía pensar que tenía tanto que ofrecer al mundo que su chispa jamás se apagaría. Pero en ese momento se sentía como una jarra volcada sobre un vaso, impaciente por aprovechar hasta la última gota.

—Yo no... —Se interrumpió y se puso a girar el anillo que llevaba en el dedo—. Creo que se siente solo.

Ilva se enderezó hasta quedar un par de centímetros más alta.

—Espero que no te estés encariñando de él, Helena. La Llama Eterna depende de tu misión. Si te ves en una situación comprometida, debes decírnoslo.

Helena negó con la cabeza. Tendría que haberse mordido la lengua.

—Eso nunca pasará. Siempre le seré fiel a la Llama Eterna.

Pero sus palabras no parecieron tranquilizar a Ilva.

—La única manera que tengo de mantener a Luc y su unidad alejados de las batallas más duras es saber de antemano cuáles van a ser —dijo despacio.

A Helena le dio un vuelco el corazón.

—Lo sé —dijo Helena notando un nudo en la garganta—. Estoy haciéndolo lo mejor que puedo. Jamás pondría en riesgo a Luc.

—Está bien —dijo Ilva, más relajada—. Ya puedes irte.

Agitó la mano con un gesto que la invitaba a salir y volvió a centrar su atención en los documentos que tenía ante ella.

Helena se dio la vuelta y dejó escapar una carcajada rota.

—Acabo de darme cuenta de que, si todo sale bien, controlarás a Ferron del mismo modo que me controlas a mí con Luc. Siento bastante lástima por él.

Ilva no la miró.

—Bueno, piensa que Ferron se lo merecerá mucho más que tú.

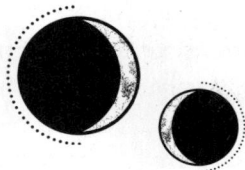

CAPÍTULO 42

SHISEO SE QUEDÓ SORPRENDIDO CUANDO Helena le pidió que la ayudara a comprobar cuál era la aleación mejor para su resonancia.

—¿No lo sabes? —le preguntó mientras ajustaba la temperatura del hornillo del alambique con el que estaba trabajando.

—Nunca tuve oportunidad de hacerme la prueba —respondió intentando sonar despreocupada.

Shiseo era un compañero de laboratorio excelente, pero también era una persona muy reservada. No hablaba de su vida privada ni del Imperio Oriental a no ser que fuera relevante para el proyecto en el que estuvieran trabajando.

—Si no tienes tiempo, no pasa nada. Es solo por curiosidad.

El hombrecillo parpadeó despacio. Sus expresiones eran incluso más impenetrables que las de Kaine.

—Recuérdame de dónde eres.

Helena exhaló y dejó que sus dedos bailaran por el libro de medicina que estaba leyendo. Se le había ocurrido crear un medicamento inyectable para situaciones extremas en las que el corazón requiriera una estimulación más intensa de lo normal, pero no confiaba del todo en la composición que había ideado.

—De Etras. Está en el sur, en medio del mar. Es una de las islas que forman parte del archipiélago entre los dos continentes. Allí apenas hay alquimistas, porque no disponemos de mucho metal. Y no tenemos nada de lumitio.

—¿Por eso viniste a Paladia?

Ella asintió sin levantar la vista.

—Según mi padre, mi repertorio era demasiado especial como para… desaprovecharlo.

Shiseo emitió un ruidito misterioso y asintió.

—Traeré mis herramientas para hacerte la prueba, pero me gustaría pedirte un favor, si no te importa.

Helena se enderezó, ahora era ella quien miraba a su compañero con curiosidad.

—Por supuesto.

—Os escuché hablar de los metales que le extrajeron a aquella mujer de la sangre hace unos meses. ¿Me permitirías identificarlos?

La chica se quedó helada al oírlo mencionar a Gettlich con tanta naturalidad. No había esperado que Shiseo supiera lo ocurrido y mucho menos que se hubiera enterado de que habían encontrado restos extraños en el cadáver. Varios metalúrgicos habían intentado identificar sin éxito los metales y los componentes que habían aparecido en las muestras de sangre.

Shiseo se mantuvo impasible, con la misma expresión plácida que siempre mostraba.

—He oído que no consiguieron identificar algunos de los metales.

—Pediré que nos envíen una muestra.

Cuando Shiseo regresó al laboratorio, traía consigo un pequeño maletín lleno de frasquitos de compuestos puros y metales. Cada uno estaba identificado con una etiqueta que Helena no sabía leer.

Colocó todo en filas ordenadas.

—Estos de aquí son metales típicos de Paladia —dijo señalando los que tenía más cerca—. Y esos —indicó los frasquitos de la segunda y tercera fila— son un poco más especiales. Veamos.

Los fue sacando uno a uno y Helena utilizó su resonancia para darle a cada metal la forma de una esfera hueca mientras Shiseo la cronometraba. Luego, el metalúrgico utilizó su propio repertorio, que era increíblemente amplio, y dividió cada esfera en cuatro partes para examinar la uniformidad de su distribución o la simetría de su estructura, a la vez que iba cotejando cada resultado con una tabla de valores.

Si obtenía alguna nota más baja que otra, disponía de una fórmula matemática para calcular el nivel de emanaciones lumíticas necesario para darle estabilidad a la resonancia de cada posible aleación, ajustándola así a su nivel alquímico básico.

—Tienes un repertorio de lo más interesante —comentó en voz baja mientras pasaba a la tercera fila de frasquitos—. Muy inusual. Y una excelente atención al detalle. Me sorprende que no seas metalúrgica.

—No estaba segura de qué camino escoger —dijo ella ofreciéndole otra esfera—. Tenía la sensación de que, independientemente de la decisión que tomase, acabaría decepcionando a alguien. Todos… —Agitó los dedos, pero, al darse cuenta de que estaba gesticulando más de la cuenta, entrelazó las manos en el regazo—. Todos esperaban mucho de mí y creo que yo nunca tuve claro qué quería. —Se encogió de hombros—. Seguramente fue mejor así. Al final, no importó.

Shiseo no respondió. Examinó las notas que había ido tomando y, cuando levantó la vista, se fijó en las manos entrelazadas de la chica.

—Creo que no te viene bien un arma de acero.

—¿Cómo?

Su resonancia funcionaba de maravilla con el acero y el hierro. Una aleación de cualquiera de esos metales debería ser perfecta para ella. Era la especialidad de la mayoría de los metalúrgicos. En Paladia, casi todas las armas se forjaban con acero.

—Tu manejo del titanio es excepcional. Hace tiempo conocí al maese gremial del titanio, y ni siquiera sus obras eran tan perfectas como las tuyas. —Cogió uno de los pedazos de la esfera de níquel que Helena había creado y la estudió con atención—. ¿Alguna vez has probado a utilizar una aleación de níquel y titanio?

Ella negó con la cabeza.

—Sería la mejor opción para ti. Muy ligera. Con el acero malgastarías tu energía.

—Pero yo no he hablado de armas —repuso Helena rápidamente—. Lo de la prueba era mera… curiosidad.

Shiseo chasqueó la lengua.

—Bueno…, en caso de que quisieras una, te aconsejo que sea de níquel y titanio. No te limites a seguir los pasos de los paladinos.

La idea de darle a Kaine Ferron, el heredero del gremio del hierro, una aleación resonántica sin su elemento le parecía impensable. A lo mejor el titanio y el níquel ni siquiera formaban parte de su repertorio. Le tendría que pedir un arma que no podría sentir o transmutar, y estaba segura de que se lo tomaría como una amenaza.

Tras insistir un poco, Shiseo por fin accedió a incluir el acero aleado en la lista.

Helena estuvo a punto de quitar la aleación de titanio, pero Crowther le ordenó que la dejara. Quería comprobar antes cómo reaccionaría Kaine.

———⁓———

Elain no recibió más formación.

Cuando Helena intentó coordinar con ella más sesiones de prácticas y una salida semanal para recolectar juntas, la chica presentó una queja formal ante el falcón Matias, asegurando que la estaban sobrecargando de trabajo y que nunca había accedido a ser boticaria. Por supuesto, Matias no solo tomó partido por ella, sino que exigió saber por qué Helena estaba ejerciendo como boticaria y quién le había dado permiso para preparar sus remedios.

A Helena le retiraron el permiso para usar el laboratorio. Lo siguiente que supo fue que Ilva había dicho que el laboratorio era de Shiseo y que Helena no era más que su asistente, que se limitaba a hacer recados y recolectar materiales en el humedal para él.

Pese a que no eran más que tecnicismos y que sabía que, en el fondo, era preferible a que le prohibieran ejercer la quimiatría, para Helena fue como recibir un puñetazo en el estómago.

Su único consuelo era esperar que Kaine, que había aceptado su lista de aleaciones sin decir una palabra, le consiguiera un cuchillo a medida.

Le costaba mucho mantener sus expectativas bajo control. Siempre que había utilizado cualquier arma o herramienta, se había preguntado cómo sería sostener un utensilio diseñado para resonar con ella. Lila trataba sus armas como si fueran sus propios hijos: les daba nombre, las cuidaba con esmero y pasaba horas afilándolas para asegurarse de que permanecían en perfectas condiciones. Y lo mismo hacía con su prótesis y su armadura, ambas estaban tan perfectamente adaptadas a ella que eran una extensión más de su cuerpo.

Sin embargo, las semanas pasaron y Kaine no volvió a sacar el tema del cuchillo, así que Helena se obligó a dejarlo a un lado para no sentir una punzada de decepción cada vez que se veían.

Cuando él consideró que sus posturas ya eran «pasables», empezaron a practicar ataques y técnicas adaptadas a sus habilidades.

—Sigues haciéndolo mal —le dijo poniéndose de pie y acercándose a ella—. La idea es ir a por los tendones. Empieza desde abajo, por el talón de Aquiles izquierdo. Luego, pasa a la cara interna del muslo derecho. Cuando tu enemigo caiga, le clavas el arma en el cuello y la cabeza. Entonces le entierras la mano en el pecho y le arrancas el talismán.

Volvió a demostrarle cómo se hacía, pero a Helena se le caía siempre el cuchillo. Aunque el ataque no era complicado, tenía que manejar el arma con la mano izquierda para llevar a cabo la transmutación humana con la derecha al final.

Estaba poniendo a prueba los límites de su coordinación al tener que hacer tres movimientos transmutacionales en apenas unos segundos con la mano no dominante.

Kaine se colocó detrás de ella. No poder verlo hacía que Helena fuera muy consciente de la cercanía entre ambos. Al cabo de un instante, el chico se pegó a su espalda y rodeó sus manos con las suyas mientras le rozaba la cara interna de la muñeca con la punta de los dedos.

Helena notaba su presencia a través de la resonancia. Aunque no lo estaba tocando directamente, el constante flujo de su propio poder le había dejado los nervios a flor de piel y creaba un campo de energía a su alrededor que le impedía ignorar su presencia y concentrarse en el cuchillo que sostenía.

Kaine pegó los brazos a los de ella y la guio para que lanzara una estocada baja con la mano izquierda, orientada de tal manera que alcanzara el tendón de su oponente imaginario mientras curvaba el filo de su arma. Luego, con un rápido giro de muñeca hacia arriba, volvió a transmutar el cuchillo para darle un borde recto con el que cortar el ligamento de la pierna contraria. En ese mismo movimiento, Kaine ensanchó el filo una última vez para convertirlo en una punta diseñada para causar el máximo daño cerebral posible.

Por último, guio la otra mano de Helena para asestar un violento puñetazo al aire. Si utilizara la resonancia, atravesaría el esternón de su oponente y alcanzaría su talismán.

—Como si fuera un solo movimiento —le susurró al oído. A Helena le dio un vuelco el corazón; apenas lograba oírlo por encima del rugido de sus propios latidos—. Tienes que moverte deprisa y golpear tantos puntos como puedas. La mejor forma de ralentizar a tu enemigo es atacar los tendones. Si le clavas tu arma en el cerebro, lo dejarás inconsciente durante unos segundos y desorientado un buen rato. Incluso si no consigues arrebatarle el talismán, al menos no se recuperará rápido: su poder de regeneración se centrará en sanar el cerebro. Sin embargo, como falles ese golpe, puedes darte por muerta.

Volvió a explicarle la maniobra dos veces más; primero despacio y luego más rápido, para demostrarle que la idea de lanzar una cuchillada hacia arriba era conseguir que el contrataque fuera fluido y tan rápido como el rayo.

—¿Lo notas ya? —preguntó en voz baja.

Helena sentía el calor de su aliento en la oreja, revolviéndole el cabello, y eso hacía que le resultara imposible concentrarse. Kaine no estaba ayudando en absoluto. Una presión intensa crecía en su interior cada vez que lo tenía cerca, desesperada y frenética, como si estuviera nadando hacia la superficie, sin llegar jamás a alcanzarla.

Asintió temblorosa y Kaine le soltó las muñecas.

—Inténtalo otra vez.

LA CAMPANA DE LA TORRE hizo vibrar el aire. Era un aviso de ataque o una llamada a las armas, para que los combatientes acudieran al frente y el hospital se preparara.

El aullido estridente de las sirenas por los pasillos retumbaba en la cabeza de Helena cuando iba de camino al hospital.

—¿Qué sabemos? —preguntó mientras se ponía el delantal y se quitaba los guantes para lavarse y desinfectarse las manos.

Fuera lo que fuese lo que había ocurrido, había sido algo imprevisto. Lo normal era que, en caso de ataque, enviaran un mensaje al Cuartel General para que el hospital pudiera prepararse con antelación. Pero, en esa ocasión, las sirenas habían dado la voz de alarma sin previo aviso.

—Todavía nada —dijo Pace, que estaba organizando al equipo médico.

Acababa de regresar del otro hospital hacía solo unos días y, pese al agotamiento, no había dejado de trabajar ni un solo momento.

Las camilleras y enfermeras corrían de un lado a otro, asegurándose de que todo estuviera listo.

La campana de la Torre no había dejado de sonar.

—Voy a acercarme al portón de entrada para ver qué está pasando —decidió Helena al fin.

En el patio, sin las paredes del edificio haciendo de barrera, notaba la cadencia grave de la campana de la Torre vibrando en los dientes y en el estómago.

El estruendo cesó justo cuando llegaba al portón. Había decenas de soldados y guardias esperando órdenes. Crowther también estaba merodeando por allí, tan intrigado por ver qué había ocurrido como los demás.

—¿Sabes qué ha pasado? —le preguntó Helena a un guardia.

—Una emboscada —explicó él sin apartar la vista de la calle—. No tenemos muchos más detalles. Lo único que sé es que no hemos vuelto a saber nada de las dos unidades que han salido hace un rato.

Se produjo un revuelo al otro lado del portón.

Y entonces Helena oyó la voz de Luc, cargada de rabia.

—Soltadme. ¡He dicho que me soltéis!

A continuación, se alzaron otras voces que gritaban «¡Cuidado!» y «¡Sujetadlo!» entre los abrasadores silbidos del fuego.

—¡Que me soltéis!

Helena avanzó por instinto y, con ella, se movieron también otras tantas personas.

Justo cuando Helena cruzaba el puesto de control, se produjo una explosión y, después, se encontró con casi una docena de personas forcejeando con Luc para arrastrarlo al Cuartel General. Soren, Sebastian, Althorne y otros miembros de su unidad lo sujetaban por los brazos y las piernas e intentaban inmovilizarlo contra el suelo.

Aunque habían conseguido desarmarlo, no lograron quitarle los anillos de ignición. Luc intentó soltar una llamarada, pero Crowther se abalanzó contra él y la apagó de inmediato. Trazó un arco con la mano izquierda extendida y, al cerrar el puño, las llamas que los rodeaban se extinguieron al instante.

—¡Marino, déjalo inconsciente! —ladró Crowther.

—¡La habéis abandonado! ¡Soltadme!

Un estallido de fuego blanco brotó del cuerpo de Luc en todas direcciones, violento, descontrolado y alimentado por la rabia. Se puso de pie de un salto y una lengua de metal salió despedida hacia él. Althorne echó el brazo hacia atrás y, en cuanto Luc se desplomó, varios se lanzaron a rodearlo de nuevo. El fuego seguía estallando y apagándose casi al instante.

—¡Marino! —bramó Crowther.

Luc dio una violenta sacudida y, al lograr liberar una mano, una barrera de fuego se alzó de repente a su alrededor, arrollando a Crowther, que chocó contra un muro con un crujido seco y desagradable.

Todos, incluido Luc, se quedaron de piedra.

—No tenía intención de… —Luc todavía seguía forcejeando—. Soltadme de una vez…

Helena le ofreció una mano y él la aceptó sin dudarlo.

—Han capturado a Lila.

Al oír aquello, le estrechó la mano con tanta fuerza que una descarga de resonancia le recorrió el brazo. La miró como si lo hubiera traicionado antes de perder el conocimiento.

Los hombres que lo inmovilizaban lo soltaron con cautela. Helena se arrodilló al lado de su amigo y le pasó los dedos por la base del cráneo, justo bajo la protuberancia occipital externa, para asegurarse de que no se despertara.

Estaba magullado y cubierto de sangre. Además, le faltaban la mitad de las uñas.

Soren, que se había desplomado junto a Helena, no se levantó. Tenía un ojo morado.

—Metedlo dentro y mantenedlo inconsciente —ordenó Althorne—. No quiero que se despierte hasta que sepamos qué le ha pasado a Bayard. Y que alguien lleve a Crowther al hospital.

El hombre tenía un lado de la cara amoratado y una herida profunda en la mejilla, como si algo lo hubiera arañado. Un grupo de soldados levantó a Luc con cuidado y lo trasladó al Cuartel General.

Helena permaneció arrodillada en el suelo.

Habían capturado a Lila. No importaba cómo se mirase, lo que aquello suponía era aterrador. Podrían convertirla en una necrómata y aprovechar su destreza en el combate para atacar a la Llama Eterna y a Luc. O, peor aún, podrían encerrarla en un laboratorio y someterla a todo tipo de experimentos.

—¿Me puedo retirar? —preguntó Soren con la voz apagada pero temblorosa por las emociones que lo embargaban.

Miraba a Althorne como si le hubieran arrancado algo desde dentro. El otro puso una de sus enormes manos sobre el hombro estrecho de Soren.

—Tendrás que ser el paladín primero hasta que rescatemos a Lila. No podemos permitirnos perderte a ti también.

—Se han llevado a mi hermana —dijo Soren, cuya mirada se perdió en la lejanía—. Tengo que recuperar su cuerpo.

—Ya hemos mandado tres equipos en su busca. Haremos todo lo

posible por recuperarla, pero tenemos que dar parte de lo ocurrido y prepararnos. Además, tú debes proteger al principado. Es lo que querría tu hermana.

Tumbaron a Crowther en una camilla y Helena los acompañó hasta el hospital. Allí, Elain ya estaba examinando a Luc y curándole las heridas leves. Cuando preguntó si podía despertarlo, le dejaron claro que lo tenía estrictamente prohibido.

Helena centró su atención en Crowther y la camillera de cara amable, Purnell, se apresuró a ayudarla. El hombre tenía una herida en el rostro, pero lo peor lo había sufrido su brazo paralizado: se había roto el codo.

Cuando Helena se dispuso a inhabilitarle las terminaciones nerviosas, como siempre hacía con sus pacientes, encontró la causa de su parálisis. Tenía una antigua fractura en el húmero que debía de haberle seccionado el nervio radial. La lesión era diminuta; cualquier sanadora que se preciara podría haberla curado.

Por desgracia, la conexión neuromuscular debía de haberse apagado hacía ya tiempo y Helena no sabía si podría ayudarlo a recuperar la movilidad por completo, pero no perdía nada por intentarlo. Si aquel día había aprendido algo era que la Resistencia necesitaba desesperadamente tener más alquimistas del fuego entre sus filas.

Así que le curó el nervio seccionado junto con la fractura del codo.

Justo cuando terminó, oyó un alboroto.

—¡La han encontrado! ¡Han encontrado a Bayard! ¡La están trayendo para acá!

Un grupo de combatientes irrumpió corriendo en el hospital cargando con una camilla. Helena vio el fugaz atisbo de una melena rubia manchada de sangre. Pace alzó la voz para hacerse oír por encima del caos.

Pero Helena apenas escuchaba nada. Se acercó a Lila por instinto mientras el equipo médico la pasaba de la camilla a una de las camas del hospital. Alguien presionaba con firmeza una gasa contra el lateral del cuello de la chica.

«Otras lesiones».

«Prioridad».

«Marino, cúrala cueste lo que cueste».

No habría sabido decir quién le había dado esa última orden, pero tampoco le importaba. Ni siquiera habría hecho falta que se lo hubieran pedido.

Lila estaba cubierta de sangre; sin tocarla siquiera, Helena enseguida supo que tenía varios huesos rotos. El lado derecho del torso estaba salpicado de profundas perforaciones que atravesaban la armadura.

En cuanto la tocó con su resonancia, lo notó.

Lila iba a necesitar un milagro para sobrevivir. Y rápido.

Algo la había mordido hasta perforarle el pulmón derecho, y la cavidad torácica se le estaba llenando de sangre. Además, el hígado y los riñones estaban comprometidos, y las costillas, destrozadas. Había perdido muchísima sangre.

Era una suerte que siguiera viva.

Ante aquella avalancha de fallos internos, Helena no podía andarse con delicadezas. Todo estaba ocurriendo demasiado deprisa y tenía que estar atenta a una infinidad de detalles a la vez. El equipo médico le estaba quitando la armadura lo más rápido que podía, trabajando al unísono, sin entorpecerse los unos a los otros.

El equipo de rescate también había llegado malherido.

—Fueron órdenes del puto psicópata de Blackthorne —dijo alguien.

Helena oía el alboroto a su espalda, pero no podía permitirse preocuparse por nadie que no fuera Lila.

Si su amiga moría, Luc no tardaría en seguir sus pasos. Quizá no de inmediato, pues, si no volvía al campo de batalla, viviría físicamente. Pero, con el paso del tiempo, el remordimiento y la pena acabarían con él también.

—No se te ocurra morirte —le advirtió infundiéndole su vitalidad a la resonancia en un intento desesperado por evitar que Lila se desvaneciera. Obligó a su débil corazón a seguir latiendo—. ¡Ni se te ocurra! Elain. ¡Necesito a Elain! Y a una de nuestras médicas. ¿Dónde está todo el mundo?

Elain apareció a su lado con las manos manchadas de sangre.

—Estoy ocup…

—Me da igual —la interrumpió—. Colócate junto a su cabeza. Necesito que te asegures de que siga respirando. ¡Y no dejes que se le pare el corazón! ¿Me has entendido? Voy a necesitar las dos manos para curarla y tengo que contar con que sus pulmones y su corazón sigan funcionando mientras trabajo.

Esperó hasta que notó la vacilante resonancia de Elain tomando el control de los latidos de Lila, así como del aire que entraba y salía con dificultad de sus pulmones. Todo ocurrió justo cuando el equipo médico logró quitarle la armadura a Lila para que Helena pudiera trabajar mejor.

Una médica se detuvo a su lado, y Helena la saludó con un breve asentimiento.

—Voy a necesitar cuatro dosis del tónico para suplementar la circulación que hay en ese armario. Tendrás que administrárselo con cuidado de que no se atragante.

—Nos han dicho que no...

—¡Necesito más sangre! Si no le repongo un par de litros, la intervención la matará. Y, si no lo hago con la ayuda de los tónicos, otra parte de su cuerpo fallará. No me quedan manos libres. ¡Hazlo ya!

La intervención fue intensa y delicada. Mientras luchaba por estabilizar a Lila, a Helena se le nubló la vista y la resonancia le abrasó los huesos. Oyó a Elain quejarse de que tenía un calambre en la mano, pero le ordenó que cerrara el pico.

Cuando por fin estuvo segura de que Lila había quedado fuera de peligro, Helena estuvo a punto de echarse a llorar de alivio. Habían estado muy cerca de perderla, pero se llevaría ese secreto a la tumba.

Se cernió sobre su amiga, con las manos manchadas de sangre, y le tocó la mejilla por un instante.

—Ya puedes parar —dijo cuando se acordó de Elain.

Había cerrado las heridas del pecho de Lila con piel transmutada, de manera algo tosca. Quedarían cicatrices, pero el cuerpo de Lila tenía lesiones más graves de las que preocuparse, y sobreviviría. Elain desapareció para dejar que las enfermeras y camilleras hicieran su trabajo.

A Helena le temblaban los dedos descontroladamente cuando estrechó la mano de su amiga.

—Ya sabes que no tienes permitido morir, tontorrona.

Entonces le cedieron las piernas, se dejó caer al suelo y apoyó la cabeza contra el colchón de la cama de Lila. Todavía tenía que recomponerle, como mínimo, una veintena de huesos entre las fracturas de ambas piernas y las falanges destrozadas, pero a Helena le latía el pecho con tanta fuerza que no lograba pensar con claridad.

—Marino, ¿te importaría...? —dijo Pace, que se encontraba al otro lado de la cama.

La chica intentó levantar la cabeza, pero no consiguió moverse. Le pesaba todo el cuerpo, pero ¿por qué le pesaba tanto?

—Pace, ayuda a Marino.

¿Era Crowther quien había hablado?

Volvió a intentar incorporarse, pero todo le daba vueltas. Veía los pies del personal moviéndose entre las numerosas hileras de camas, veía el suelo manchado de sangre…

Alguien tiró de ella hacia arriba.

—Venga, Marino, este no es lugar para echarse una cabezadita —dijo Pace cuando la ayudó a ponerse de pie.

Alguien más se posó en su otro costado y, cuando a Helena se le cayó la cabeza hacia un lado por su propio peso, vio a Crowther observándola desde una de las camas.

En cuanto cruzaron la puerta, se dirigieron al cuarto de los informes que Pace utilizaba a modo de despacho.

—Aquí mismo, Sofia, gracias. Ya me ocupo yo.

Dejaron a Helena recostada sobre un catre.

En el fondo, ella sabía que había ido demasiado lejos.

Solía trabajar con cuidado, pero en aquella ocasión no había tenido más opción que tensar la cuerda para salvar a Lila.

Sentía mucho frío y estaba agotada. Alguien la cubrió con mantas y las ajustó a su alrededor. Oyó a Pace decir que era una insensata.

Pero lo único que quería en ese momento era dormir durante un par de años.

Notó un pinchazo en el brazo seguido de un escozor y, cuando intentó aliviarlo usando la transmutación, recibió un manotazo en los dedos.

—Eres la peor paciente que he tenido nunca.

Una espesa y aterciopelada oscuridad se la tragó.

CAPÍTULO 43

Octobris 1786

CUANDO HELENA DESPERTÓ, EL HOSPITAL estaba sumido en un silencio absoluto. Se sentía débil como un gatito, así que permaneció quieta hasta que entró Pace.

—¿Cómo está Lila? —preguntó con un hilo de voz.

—Se está recuperando —respondió Pace en tono cortante—. Es un milagro que haya sobrevivido, y todo gracias a la rápida intervención y al rescate del equipo de salvamento. —Se aclaró la garganta—. Recibirán una medalla por su valentía, y también se han convocado varias misas de ascuas para que los fieles devotos le den las gracias a Sol... por haberla salvado.

Helena siguió mirando el techo.

—¿Cuánto tiempo llevo durmiendo?

—Tres días. —Pace se acercó a su escritorio y rebuscó ruidosamente en un cajón, pero no sacó nada—. He dicho que estabas en cuarentena por haber estado demasiado a la intemperie cada vez que salías a recolectar hierbas.

Helena notó que los párpados volvían a pesarle.

—Gracias.

—Hago lo que puedo. Crowther quiere verte cuando vuelvas a estar operativa —le informó Pace. Hizo ademán de marcharse, pero se lo pensó mejor—. La pérdida de Lila Bayard no sería la única capaz de sacudir los cimientos de la Llama Eterna. Se lo he repetido hasta la saciedad a Ilva, a Crowther y a Matias. Nunca me han hecho caso, pero puede que tal vez tú sí lo hagas. No deberíamos desperdiciar las habilidades únicas de nadie, aunque no les demos el reconocimiento que merecen.

Cuando Helena salió, Luc estaba sentado al lado de Lila, que estaba tan quieta que apenas parecía respirar. Lila era más alta que la mayoría de la gente, pero sin su armadura se veía frágil y pequeña. La habían envuelto en vendas limpias, impregnadas de bálsamos que ayudaban a calmar el dolor y aliviaban la sensibilidad del tejido nuevo. Respiraba lentamente y con esfuerzo, pero a Helena le bastó con rozarle la mano con los dedos para comprobar que seguía estable.

Se quedó junto a la cama, acariciando con cuidado a Lila.

Luc contemplaba el rostro de la paladina y le sostenía una de sus manos entre las suyas. Tenía los ojos desorbitados y unas profundas ojeras amoratadas bajo ellos. Al otro lado del hospital, Soren montaba guardia junto a las puertas.

Los paladines y los Holdfast habían caminado juntos desde los albores de la nación. De hecho, el país les debía su nombre a ellos, como reconocimiento al papel decisivo que jugaron en la Primera Guerra Nigromántica. Con el paso de los siglos, ese papel se fue convirtiendo en algo más ceremonial.

Sin embargo, Lila había supuesto un cambio, ya que poseía un talento único. Sus padres se empeñaron en que tuviera la oportunidad de alcanzar la grandeza, aunque la tradición reservaba esos puestos a los varones. Lila solo cursó la modalidad de combate, lo que la llevó a unirse a las cruzadas y participar en combates reales desde los quince años. Soren optó por la modalidad doble, igual que Luc. De no haber sido por su hermana, que le hacía la competencia, Soren habría sido un alquimista de combate excelente. Pero Lila no tenía rival.

Cuando Lila regresó de las cruzadas tras estar un año fuera, se celebró un desfile. Por aquel entonces, Helena apenas la conocía; para ella, solo era la hermana de Soren.

Lila descendió de su caballo de guerra, se quitó el yelmo y se plantó allí, resplandeciente, como si fuera una diosa salida de una leyenda antigua. Llevaba el cabello rubio trenzado alrededor de la cabeza como una corona y le entregó sus armas a Luc, que se quedó paralizado, como si le hubiera caído un rayo. No reaccionó hasta que Soren le dio una patada en el tobillo.

Luc, que siempre se había tomado a broma los entrenamientos de combate y a quien no le entusiasmaba la idea de tener un paladín, cambió por completo de opinión. Empezó a ausentarse de las clases teóricas y de los actos sociales para pasar el tiempo entrenando con Lila.

Su interés era tan evidente que a Helena y a Soren les daba vergüenza presenciarlo, pero, antes de que sucediera nada entre ambos, asesinaron al principado Apollo.

Lila había dedicado toda su vida a entrenar para ser paladina. Soren no estaba preparado ni de lejos y Sebastian Bayard, aunque capacitado para ello, acababa de romper su juramento: no estuvo presente cuando atacaron a Apollo.

Fue Lila quien juró proteger a Luc con su vida, morir por él si era necesario. Luc no tuvo más opción que aceptar. Lo que hubiera existido o no entre ellos quedó sepultado bajo el peso de aquellos votos.

—Lo siento… —susurró Luc—. Perdí la cabeza cuando vi que se la llevaban.

Tenía la mirada perdida, como si sus ojos azules no consiguieran ver con claridad la habitación que lo rodeaba. Helena reconocía esa expresión: estaba atrapado en el pasado, reviviendo aquel momento una y otra vez, repasando cada detalle, tratando de descubrir qué podría haber hecho de otra forma.

—La quimera venía a por mí. No conseguí desenvainar la espada a tiempo. Tendría que haber usado fuego. —Sacudió la cabeza—. No sé por qué no lo hice. Todo ocurrió demasiado rápido. Lila se interpuso entre nosotros y de repente oí cómo la mordía…

Se hizo el silencio.

Era habitual que la gente se confesara así en el hospital; allí, los fracasos se filtraban por la piel como sudor.

—Estaba sangrando por la boca, pero no gritó. Solo le pidió a Soren que me protegiera. La criatura salió corriendo con ella y yo… debería haber usado fuego… —Se atragantó con las palabras—. Soren no me dejó ir a por ella y…

—Se va a poner bien, Luc —le aseguró Helena—. Hemos estabilizado sus constantes vitales y no le quedarán secuelas permanentes.

El principado asintió con la cabeza, distraído, sin apartar la vista del rostro de Lila.

—Cuando era niño —empezó con aspereza—, pensaba que era injusto que las guerras de verdad hubieran sucedido antes de que yo naciera. Me aterraba ser uno de esos principados que nadie recuerda porque no sucedió nada relevante durante su mandato. —Agachó la cabeza; se estaba arrancando las uñas y sus dedos sangraban—. Ahora daría lo que fuera por una vida así. Ya no saboreo nada que no sea sangre y humo, y no siento tampoco nada… a menos que esté ardiendo. En las historias, la guerra suena increíble. Luchar por una causa, ser el héroe. —Negó con la cabeza—. ¿Por qué todo el mundo finge que eso tiene algo de bueno?

Helena le acarició el hombro con los dedos. No sabía qué decir ni cómo consolarlo.

—Tal vez no les quedó otra opción que recordarse eso a sí mismos para poder vivir con ello. Tal vez es lo único que se permitieron recordar —replicó Helena, aunque ella también se preguntaba quién había visto la realidad de la guerra y decidió adornarla.

LA REUNIÓN QUE SE CELEBRÓ cuando Lila despertó y se confirmó que no corría peligro fue tensa. Era la primera vez que Luc salía del hospital.

Matias, Ilva, Althorne y Crowther observaban desde el estrado a Luc, pero el principado les sostuvo la mirada con un brillo desafiante en los ojos. Cualquier atisbo de penitencia parecía haberse desvanecido.

—Lucien —intervino Ilva tras un largo silencio—, Lila Bayard es tu paladina. Juró protegerte, incluso a costa de su vida. Pusiste en peligro a toda tu unidad, heriste a una decena de hombres, entre ellos a Jan Crowther, miembro de este Consejo, e incumpliste tanto tus votos como las órdenes del general Althorne. Esto es una moción de censura.

Luc alzó la barbilla.

—Juré proteger este país y representar los valores de la Llama Eterna, fundada por mis antepasados. No estaría cumpliendo ninguno de esos votos si permito que otros mueran por mí cuando está en mi mano salvarlos.

—Eres el corazón de la Resistencia, un símbolo de esperanza, luz y bondad. No puedes anteponer tu vida a la de otra persona. Has traicionado a quienes te siguen y has traicionado también a tus paladines, sobre todo a Lila, que conocía su juramento y estaba preparada para asumir las consecuencias de sus actos. Su sacrificio ha estado a punto de quedar en nada por tu egoísmo.

—No soy un símbolo —le espetó Luc—, ni tampoco el corazón de nada. Soy el principado. Lideramos con nuestros actos, no con nuestras órdenes.

Toda la discusión tenía algo de pantomima. El Consejo necesitaba intervenir de alguna manera. Y, sin embargo, allí estaba Luc, de pie, como si fuera un personaje mitológico, imperturbable y decidido. Ilva miró con frialdad a su sobrino nieto.

—Eso no lo decides tú. Si no eres capaz de seguir las órdenes y de respetar los protocolos, incluso en presencia de tus amigos —remarcó la palabra con deliberada malicia—, te reasignaremos a otra unidad y se te proporcionarán nuevos paladines. Aunque, por mantener la tradición, te permitiremos conservar a Soren Bayard.

Luc cerró la boca de golpe, como una trampa al activarse, y palideció.

—Tú eliges —insistió Ilva, satisfecha por su silencio—. Elige bien.

Por un momento, Luc permaneció inmóvil, irradiando rabia contenida. Soren, situado un paso por detrás de él, a su derecha, había asumido el rol de paladín primero mientras su hermana se recuperaba. Parecía algo demacrado.

—Cumpliré con mis votos y con aquellos a quienes me comprometí —cedió Luc con la voz hueca y abatida.

—Bien —repuso Ilva, aunque seguía hablando con frialdad para dejar claro que no le gustaba que Luc tardara tanto en responder—. El equipo de salvamento logró matar a la quimera antes de que escapara de la isla Este. Encontraron una brecha en uno de los muros. Se abrirá una investigación para esclarecer lo que sucedió. Teniendo en cuenta el comportamiento de la criatura, debemos asumir que es capaz de hacer más de lo que creíamos. Según los informes, parece que quieren apresar a Luc con vida y que el animal es capaz de cazar de forma selectiva. Althorne, tienes la palabra.

HELENA POSPUSO LA REUNIÓN CON Crowther todo lo que pudo, pero, al final, se quedó sin excusas. Visto en perspectiva, se había dejado llevar por la impulsividad al curarle los nervios del brazo. No era una situación de emergencia y podría haber esperado a que recuperara la consciencia para preguntarle si quería que lo hiciera.

Había sido una decisión impulsiva. Había visto el peligro que Luc suponía para los demás y había actuado en consecuencia. Ahora se arrepentía. Lo más probable era que Crowther empleara ambas manos para torturar, en vez de proteger a Luc de sí mismo.

Crowther estaba guardando un ajedrez cuando Helena entró en su despacho. Con la mano derecha, iba recogiendo cada una de las piezas y depositándolas en una caja.

—Marino.

Helena se quedó de pie, sin saber a qué atenerse. Crowther dejó de hacer lo que estaba haciendo y contempló su mano mientras la abría y cerraba lentamente. No era más que piel y huesos.

—Supongo que debería darte las gracias por esto.

Ella no estaba segura de si era sarcasmo o no.

—Tendría que haberte pedido permiso —replicó Helena—. Pero es que…, después de lo que pasó con Luc, me aterraba pensar qué habría sucedido si no hubieras estado allí.

Helena no sabía qué pensaba en realidad, pero Crowther asintió.

—Tienes una intuición muy interesante. Puede que la haya subestimado —dijo al cabo de un rato—. Lo cierto es que nunca me gustó demasiado la vivemancia. Aun así, tu trabajo hace honor a la Llama Eterna.

EL INVIERNO HABÍA LLEGADO A Paladia. El viento gélido descendía de las montañas por la cuenca del río, mientras la escarcha cubría con su manto los edificios y las ventanas. Ya no había hierbas para recolectar, así que Helena pasaba las horas encerrada en el laboratorio.

Shiseo había logrado lo que nadie antes había conseguido: identificar los compuestos de la aleación que le habían suministrado a Vanya Gettlich hacía tantos meses.

Solo un único compuesto resistía a los análisis.

Shiseo y Helena emplearon técnicas de la química tradicional y determinaron, al igual que los metalúrgicos antes que ellos, que no se trataba de un compuesto natural, sino de una fusión sintética de lumitio con un elemento que Helena jamás había visto.

Shiseo comprobó el resultado una y otra vez, con las manos temblorosas.

—No sé cómo lo han conseguido —dijo al fin—. Esto no debería estar aquí.

—¿Qué es?

Permaneció callado un buen rato.

—En el Este, en lo más profundo de las montañas, existe un elemento peculiar, aún más raro que el oro. El emperador es el único que puede poseerlo. Lo llamamos *mo'lian'shi*. Su propiedad principal es que crea… inercia.

Helena nunca había oído hablar de algo así. Sabía que existían elementos y sustancias inertes en su forma natural, y luego estaba el lumitio, con sus efluvios, que revertían esa inercia y la transformaban en resonancia. Por ejemplo, el hierro era un material inerte, pero, cuando se convertía en acero, desarrollaba cierta resonancia, aunque no se usaran efluvios para ello.

En sus escritos sobre los orígenes de la alquimia, Cetus ya mencionaba la teoría de la irreversibilidad de la resonancia. Era uno de los pocos principios que habían sobrevivido al paso del tiempo y los avances científicos.

No había nada que se pudiese hacer inerte.

—Desconocía que existiera algo así —dijo Helena.

Shiseo negó con la cabeza frunciendo el ceño.

—Es imposible que lo sepas. Forma parte del poder del emperador. Al igual que el lumitio genera resonancia, el *mo'lian'shi* la absorbe. Esto es… —Bajó la vista, visiblemente afectado—. Esto es *mo'lian'shi* fusionado con lumitio. Al juntarlos produce una especie de apagón de la resonancia.

Miró de nuevo sus notas.

—Es inestable. La fusión se está deteriorando, pero no dudo de que lograrán perfeccionarla en el futuro. Seguramente se trate de su primer intento. Aunque… —Perdió el hilo de lo que decía—. No sé cómo han podido conseguir este elemento.

Se sumió en el silencio, sin decir nada durante un largo rato.

—Cuando el nuevo emperador asumió el cargo, comenzaron a surgir dudas. Nadie sabía de dónde había obtenido el dinero para pagar sus ejércitos.

Desde que trabajaba con Shiseo, Helena había escuchado varios rumores sobre qué le había hecho venir a Paladia. Que era un eunuco que había servido al emperador anterior, o que era el hijo ilegítimo de algún cortesano. Lo observó con detenimiento y se preguntó quién sería realmente. Era evidente que había recibido una educación excepcional, pero no entendía cómo podía saber tanto de un metal secreto.

—Quizá los inmarcesibles lo compraron en el mercado negro —propuso Helena, aunque ya sabía cómo interpretarían Crowther e Ilva esa suposición. Si Morrough había sellado una alianza con Hevgoss y mantenía tratos comerciales secretos con el Imperio Oriental, la amenaza que se cernía sobre Paladia era mucho mayor de lo que imaginaban.

Y, si el emperador había logrado sentarse en el trono vendiendo algo de valor para el Imperio, aquello suponía una violación de sus propias leyes comerciales.

Shiseo negó con la cabeza.

—No comprendes cuánto se protege el *mo'lian'shi*. Es un material peculiar y delicado. Cuando se extrae de la mina, debe procesarse con sumo cuidado para conservar sus propiedades. Normalmente se alea con otro elemento para evitar que se degrade. Pero esto… —Tocó el frasco—. Esto está hecho con *mo'lian'shi* puro. Solo alguien de la realeza que cuente con un sello del emperador tiene acceso a algo así.

—Y tú lo sabes —concluyó Helena.

Shiseo la miró a los ojos, pero apartó la vista rápidamente.

—Y yo lo sé.

Fue Helena quien se sumió en el silencio entonces.

—¿Lo sospechabas? —preguntó al cabo de unos instantes—. ¿Por eso pediste permiso para analizarlo?

Shiseo tenía la mirada perdida.

—Cuando me enteré de que a los metalúrgicos les estaba costando analizarlo, pensé que sería una variedad nueva. Pero estoy seguro de que este es el *mo'lian'shi* del emperador. Es imposible que hayan sido capaces de refinarlo igual.

Helena sintió que caminaban sobre un campo de minas político. En sus manos tenían la prueba no solo de que Morrough había hecho un trato con otro país, sino también de que el propio emperador había traicionado a su imperio. Era una información peligrosa que planteaba más preguntas que respuestas. Si el emperador tenía deudas, ¿cómo había conseguido Morrough el dinero para ofrecérselo?

Shiseo era la única persona que podía haberlo descubierto. Cuando sellaron el trato, seguramente dieron por sentado que nadie lo relacionaría nunca con el Imperio Oriental.

—Oficialmente diremos que se trata de un nuevo elemento sintético, elaborado con lumitio y un compuesto desconocido —dijo Helena tras meditarlo un instante. Observó con atención la reacción de Shiseo—. Y, si en el futuro, es necesario revelar la posible implicación del Imperio, lo haremos… en ese momento.

Shiseo asintió lentamente.

—Pero tendremos que contárselo a Ilva y Crowther. Ellos tienen que saberlo.

—KAINE —PRONUNCIÓ HELENA EN VOZ baja. Estaba sentada en el suelo, tratando de aliviar la cruda sensación que le provocaba su resonancia—. ¿Crees que la Llama Eterna puede ganar la guerra?

Él estaba apoyado en la pared.

—¿Qué importa lo que yo piense?

—Convivo con idealistas, pero lo único que veo son cadáveres. Me gustaría escuchar la opinión de alguien que no crea que el optimismo inclina la balanza a su favor.

Kaine la miró de soslayo.

—¿La Llama Eterna está siguiendo alguna estrategia para alcanzar la victoria?

Helena bajó la vista. Hasta donde sabía, el plan era recuperar el terreno perdido, hacer retroceder a los inmarcesibles y quemar todos los cadáveres que les fuera posible. El mismo método que la Llama Eterna había aplicado en todas las guerras nigrománticas del pasado.

Asintió, aunque sin convicción.

—El Sumo Nigromante hará lo que sea necesario para ganar, sin importarle las consecuencias. Quiere Paladia; en principio, con la ciudad intacta, pero, si eso no es posible, la quemará hasta los cimientos. Estáis luchando contra alguien que solo se niega a practicar un genocidio porque sería un despilfarro de recursos, pero que no dudaría en hacerlo porque así tendría material suficiente para crear más necrómatas. ¿Y queréis ganar con qué? ¿Con la intervención de Sol? ¿Tenéis algún plan que no dependa de la supuesta superioridad del bien sobre el mal?

Ella no conocía ninguno.

—Si piensas que no vamos a ganar, ¿por qué nos ayudas? —preguntó.

Kaine adoptó una expresión burlona.

—¿Crees que no lo mereces?

—Ah, sí, soy la rosa que crece en mitad en un cementerio —soltó Helena acompañándolo con un gesto—. ¿El sello de tu espalda también fue por mí?

—¿Por quién si no? —contestó él con un tono desprovisto de emoción y algo irónico.

—¿Por Aurelia, quizá?

Kaine sonrió.

—Cierto, ya me había olvidado de ella.

—¿Por qué nos estás ayudando, Kaine?

Él la miró de arriba abajo. En los últimos meses, sus rasgos se habían endurecido. Había perdido cualquier rastro de la languidez propia de la juventud; ahora tenía unas facciones más marcadas que reflejaban mejor quién era. El cabello se le estaba encaneciendo rápidamente y ya no quedaba nada de sus ojos color avellana. Parecía totalmente distinto al chico moreno e insolente que había conocido cuando se vieron en el Reducto por primera vez. Ahora tenía un aire fantasmal.

Si alguien lo tocaba, ella sangraría y, sin embargo, no podía escapar de la atracción que le provocaba.

Cuando sus ojos se cruzaron, se percató de que tenía una expresión amarga.

—Qué más da —respondió Kaine, desviando la mirada.

Helena abrió la boca para discutir, pero todo lo que dijera sería una mentira. Fueran cuales fuesen sus motivaciones, no se fiaba de que la Llama Eterna no acabara usándolo en su contra. Los dos sabían que a Crowther no le temblaría el pulso.

—Supongo que no —repuso ella, mientras se ponía el jersey grueso de color verde para contener el frío. Cuando llegó a la puerta, echó la vista atrás.

Kaine apartó la mirada en cuanto se dio la vuelta, como si no quisiera verla marchar. Le dio la sensación de que algo lo perturbaba.

—No mueras, Kaine —le dijo. Él estaba caminando por un desfiladero que le daba mucho miedo. Si el sello había sido el castigo por cometer un error, ¿cuál sería el precio por una traición?

Cuando la volvió a mirar, tenía una sonrisa irónica en los labios.

—Hay destinos peores que la muerte, Marino.

—Lo sé —asintió la chica—. Pero ese es el único que no tiene remedio.

Kaine soltó una carcajada amarga.

—Está bien, pero solo porque me lo pides tú.

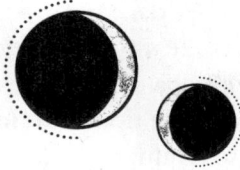

CAPÍTULO 44

Diciembris 1786

LA GUERRA SE CONGELÓ IGUAL que el resto de Paladia. La tensión entre los dos bandos se prolongó de forma interminable. Estaban en un punto de frágil equilibrio que podrían perder en cualquier momento. Todas las batallas eran repentinas y se producían sin aviso previo, dejando tras de sí bajas considerables.

La tensión entre Helena y Kaine era similar.

Él se mostraba más áspero que antes, como si lo estuvieran castigando cual filo de una cuchilla en una piedra de afilar.

A veces aparecía con heridas graves y su recuperación era lenta. Si Helena se ofrecía a ayudarlo, la apartaba con violencia.

Por lo general, cuando ella se marchaba, él ya se había recuperado, pero nunca lograba entender del todo de qué manera le estaban haciendo daño. Como si fuera una consecuencia de haberle pedido que no muriera, se veía obligada a presenciar con tristeza que era incapaz de hacerlo. A Helena le preocupaba que esto se debiera a un fallo del sello.

En una ocasión, mientras él descansaba en una silla viéndola entrenar, de pronto se le pusieron los ojos en blanco y se desplomó.

Cuando Helena logró tumbarlo, descubrió que había un charco de sangre bajo él. Su ropa estaba empapada.

Por debajo del uniforme, estaba completamente vendado, pero la sangre no le coagulaba, por lo que la herida no cerraba. Cuando Helena trató de encontrar la herida, le falló la resonancia.

Horrorizada, retiró las vendas y descubrió una puñalada. No le había atravesado ningún órgano, pero la hoja se había partido y tenía fragmentos incrustados dentro de la herida.

No eran demasiados, pero le impedían regenerarse.

Era Maier quien se encargaba de las heridas de metralla, ya que la vivemancia no servía para tratar ese tipo de lesiones.

Cuando Helena intentó evaluar los daños y calcular cuánto metal quedaba dentro de la herida, su resonancia se disipó.

No tenía instrumental quirúrgico para operar. Se lavó las manos con cuidado e introdujo un dedo en la herida. Alcanzó un fragmento y lo extrajo. Helena notaba que era un objeto físico, tangible, pero, al canalizar su resonancia y dirigirla hacia el metal, no percibió más que estática. Según su resonancia, allí no había nada. El metal empezó a deshacerse entre sus dedos, como si estuviera corroído, y el polvo se mezcló con la sangre de Kaine.

Era una aleación: el lumitio fusionado con *mo'lian'shi*. Habían apuñalado a Kaine con una hoja hecha de ese material y la habían dejado dentro de su cuerpo.

—Serás idiota —le dijo a Kaine, aunque sabía que estaba inconsciente.

Dejó la esquirla sobre una gasa y se limpió los dedos. Si el compuesto se había extendido por el torrente sanguíneo, no sabía qué podría pasarle. El cuerpo de Kaine permanecía inmóvil, pero, teniendo en cuenta que la aleación estaba impidiendo que se regenerara, parecía que los inmarcesibles estaban cada vez más cerca de conseguir una interrupción de la resonancia. Mucho más de lo que podía imaginar la Llama Eterna.

Pasó las manos por la piel de Kaine para hacerse una idea de las lesiones internas que pudiera tener, pero la resonancia le fallaba en algunos puntos, como si estuviese agujereada.

Cogió su bolsa, en ella llevaba todo un botiquín de medicinas y diversos materiales por si algún día Kaine le daba permiso para curarlo. Aplicó un bálsamo alrededor de la herida para frenar la hemorragia y ganar algo de tiempo para pensar. Si tuviera lista la inyección de estimulantes en la que había estado trabajando, podría ser útil, pero aún no había dado con la dosis exacta de epinefrina.

Y, si no podía emplear la resonancia para extraer las esquirlas, solo le quedaba una opción: la cirugía tradicional.

La cirugía alquímica era mucho menos invasiva. De hecho, en la mayoría de los hospitales del Norte únicamente contrataban alquimistas, ya que la cirugía manual se consideraba un método arcaico y brutal que provocaba grandes incisiones y dejaba cicatrices permanentes.

Helena tomó su cuchillo alquímico y masculló una disculpa antes de empezar a deshacer los compuestos. Era difícil volver a ensamblar un arma transmutada. Y sería casi imposible cuando finalizase lo que tenía pensado hacer.

Intentó no pensar en las posibles consecuencias de destruir un arma registrada y transformó el metal en herramientas: pinzas quirúrgicas de mango largo y un bisturí. Rezó para que las pinzas fueran suficiente.

Después, lavó, calentó y enfrió el metal para esterilizar las pinzas.

De niña, solía observar a su padre mientras este operaba y, cuando murió su madre, prefería estar en el quirófano que sola en casa.

Usó su resonancia de forma invertida para ubicar los fragmentos de metralla en el espacio negativo que generaban. Los trozos eran pequeños y se deshacían con facilidad, así que tuvo que trabajar con mucho cuidado. Los fue sacando uno a uno y los depositó en un paño.

Cuando logró extirpar la mayoría, el cuerpo de Kaine pareció recordar cómo se regeneraba y la herida empezó a cerrarse, a pesar de que aún quedaban dentro algunos fragmentos. Helena no tuvo más remedio que usar el bisturí y hacer una incisión tras otra hasta extraer todos los trocitos. Luego limpió la herida todo lo que pudo y comprobó mediante la resonancia que no quedaba nada dentro. Todavía percibía un leve zumbido de interferencia, pero no parecía grave. Con suerte, el cuerpo de Kaine se encargaría de eliminarla.

Se lavó las manos y guardó la mitad de los trozos de metralla en un frasco que escondió en lo más hondo de su bolsa. A continuación, colocó los demás en otro bote que dejó a la vista en caso de que Kaine los quisiera cuando despertase.

La herida dejó una cicatriz que no se desvaneció por completo. Al examinarlo con atención, Helena se dio cuenta de que no era la única.

Posó una mano en mitad del pecho de Kaine y permitió que su resonancia se adentrara en su cuerpo. Todavía estaba débil por la pérdida de sangre y, además, los residuos metálicos ralentizaban la regeneración de los tejidos. Colocó la cabeza de él sobre su regazo y, con mucho cuidado, vertió un elixir por su garganta. Usó la resonancia para asegurarse de que descendía hasta su estómago en vez de hasta sus pulmones. A pesar de estar inconsciente, Kaine mantenía una expresión tensa, como si se estuviera preparando para recibir un golpe.

Ella le apartó el pelo de la frente e intentó suavizar la arruga de tensión que se le marcaba entre las cejas. Se quedó ahí sentada con él durante un buen rato. Cuando sintió que se recuperaba, se inclinó hacia delante y le acarició la nuca con los dedos, instándolo a despertarse.

Kaine abrió los ojos de golpe.

Sin darle tiempo a reaccionar, llevó una mano a la garganta de Helena y la tumbó contra el suelo. Se incorporó de inmediato, con una expresión entre el pánico y la furia.

La reconoció un instante antes de estamparle la cabeza contra el suelo. Helena sintió un crujido en el cuello y todo su campo visual se volvió blanco; un dolor agudo le atravesó el cráneo.

—¿Qué ha pasado? —sonaba algo desconcertado.

Helena notó que Kaine aún tenía las manos alrededor de su cuello y, tras recorrer toda su espina dorsal con resonancia, recuperó la vista. Estaba montado a horcajadas sobre ella, rodeándole el cuello con las manos. Helena sintió el corazón desbocado, latiendo con tanta fuerza que apenas podía respirar.

Kaine también respiraba con dificultad.

—¿Qué cojones has hecho, Marino?

—Te… te desmayaste —consiguió decir.

Él dirigió la vista hacia sí mismo y se percató de que no llevaba puesta la camisa y que la herida había desaparecido. Helena creyó que se relajaría al comprenderlo, pero parecía aún más enfadado.

—He estado a punto de matarte.

—Estabas herido —replicó Helena respirando entrecortadamente—. Herido grave, incluso para tus estándares. —Se incorporó y torció el gesto, tocándose el cuello con cautela—. Tal como te he comentado en otras ocasiones, mi trabajo consiste en mantener con vida a aquellas personas que le son valiosas a la Llama Eterna. Y tú eres una de ellas.

—No iba a morir —dijo Kaine con desdén, aunque se inclinó hacia ella. Helena estuvo a punto de apartarse, pero él se acercó tan despacio que se obligó a quedarse quieta.

Kaine retiró por fin las manos del cuello, pero seguía mirándola fijamente a la garganta. Lentamente, recorrió la piel de Helena con los dedos, y esta reconoció su resonancia como una calidez que le atravesó toda la columna vertebral. Otra grieta en esa fachada de indiferencia que él intentaba mantener.

—¿No se suponía que podías curarte solo? —preguntó Helena, conteniendo un estremecimiento cuando el dedo de Kaine le acarició el cuello—. Puedo… abrirte en canal y meterlo todo dentro otra vez, si es lo que quieres.

El chico se quedó inmóvil y le dedicó una mirada airada.

—No soy uno de tus pacientes.

Tal vez la habría intimidado si no fuera porque estaba sentado en el suelo acariciándole el cuello con las manos y moviéndole la cabeza de un lado a otro. Era evidente que se tomaba muy en serio las lesiones de columna.

A Helena le empezó a latir el corazón con fuerza al recordar cómo le había sujetado el pelo para acercarla hacia sí. Cuando estaba sola, solía regresar a ese momento, preguntándose qué habría pasado.

Respiró entrecortadamente y envolvió su muñeca con los dedos.

—No puedo dejarte morir.

Kaine se quedó inmóvil. Helena sintió su propio pulso vibrando contra los dedos de él. Observó que se le oscurecían los ojos: el círculo negro de sus pupilas se iba expandiendo, como si el calor de sus manos se fusionara con la piel de Helena.

—No me dejan morir —dijo Kaine sacudiendo la cabeza.

Helena le apretó en la muñeca.

—¿Están…? ¿Bennet sigue experimentando contigo? Creía que, si sobrevivías al sello, no te haría más…

Se apartó de su mano.

—Tengo la mala costumbre de sobrevivir contra todo pronóstico. Por lo visto, eso me convierte en algo digno de estudio.

Sin pensarlo dos veces, Helena le acarició la mejilla.

—Lo siento mucho, Kaine.

Este pareció tan desconcertado que, por un instante, su rostro recuperó una expresión joven y asustada, como si aún fuera aquel chico de dieciséis años. Pero enseguida se tensó y se apartó de su caricia. Cuando la volvió a mirar, su gesto mostraba maldad. Negó con la cabeza como si no diera crédito.

—Eres increíble, de verdad. —Helena no sabía a qué se refería. Kaine sacudió de nuevo la cabeza—. Cuando viniste aquí por primera vez, pensé que no tendrías agallas, pero he de admitir que tienes talento.

A Helena se le hizo un nudo en el estómago.

—Harías lo que fuera por esa familia, ¿verdad? Sin embargo, algún día, Holdfast se dará cuenta de que no encajas en su reino dorado de pureza. Me pregunto qué hará contigo entonces.

Sabía que solo quería hacerle daño, pero era algo que ella misma había pensado en tantas ocasiones que ya se le había olvidado lo mucho que le dolía.

—No tendrá que hacer nada; tú te has encargado de eso. —Le dedicó una sonrisa tensa—. Pero, aunque no fuera así, supe que sería prescindible desde el día en que me convertí en sanadora.

Pensó que eso lo dejaría callado, pero Kaine se echó a reír.

—¿De verdad crees que fue entonces cuando empezó? Siempre has sido prescindible. ¿De verdad piensas que esta guerra es por la nigromancia? ¿Que en las guerras anteriores se luchó contra la nigromancia?

Helena negó con la cabeza, recelosa.

—No, siempre se trata del poder, y de lo que la gente está dispuesta a hacer sin reparar en las consecuencias.

Kaine ladeó la cabeza, como si la analizara con atención.

—¿Nunca te has preguntado por qué le resultó tan sencillo al Sumo Nigromante reclutar a las familias de los gremios? Al fin y al cabo, había muchos devotos, y también gente que debía sus grandes fortunas a la Academia.

La chica se encogió de hombros.

—Porque sois envidiosos y crueles, y queréis más de lo que tenéis, que ya es bastante.

Kaine arqueó una ceja mientras se ponía la ropa manchada de sangre.

—Bueno, supongo que en parte sí que fue por eso, pero no del todo. Morrough solo abrió la fisura que los Holdfast llevaban siglos generando. Desde que fundaron esta ciudad, se proclamaron reyes sin reconocerlo abiertamente. No eran de esos que «buscan» el poder; en absoluto, ellos habían sido designados por los dioses. Eran los elegidos.

—Eso es porque nunca quisieron gobernar —replicó Helena con fiereza—. Luc nunca lo quiso, y a Apollo solo le interesaba la Academia. Detestaba la política.

Kaine hizo un gesto indefinible.

—Sí, es graciosa la cantidad de gente con autoridad que detesta la política, como si lo único que quisieran fuese hacer lo que les da la gana y recibir elogios por ello. Y, si no es así, entonces lo consideran algo indigno. A pesar de lo mucho que la detestaban, ninguno estuvo dispuesto a ceder el poder. Los únicos autorizados para encargarse de los asuntos de gobierno eran los cargos religiosos; que fueran los falcones, los cernícalos y los alcaudones quienes perdieran el tiempo con esa tarea tan tediosa. Aunque la Academia se fundara con la intención de alcanzar la excelencia en la alquimia, todo empezó a desmoronarse desde el instante en que la ciencia comenzó a contradecirse con la Fe. Deberías haber visto la crisis que se produjo cuando se descubrieron metales nuevos. La Fe estuvo años insistiendo en que solo podía haber ocho, así que se refería a ellos como compuestos o aleaciones, y se negaba a reconocer de forma oficial a los gremios que los trabajaban porque en la religión, y también en los cielos, el número se limitaba a ocho. Adiós al ideal de unir al mundo mediante el estudio de la alquimia. —Miró a Helena—. Por supuesto, como querían mantener el legado de Orion, no podían romper esa promesa del todo, así que de vez en cuando traían a alguien, algún prodigio de una tierra lejana que usaban como prueba de su magnanimidad, que les servía para su propósito y les ayudaba a mantener el principado.

Helena sintió cómo la rabia le ardía por dentro como un volcán a punto de estallar.

—¡Eso no es lo que hacían!

Kaine la miró de arriba abajo con sorna.

—Eras una alumna becada y desesperada que se echaba a llorar cada vez que publicaban las notas de los exámenes porque así te asegurabas un año más de educación, y tu padre vivía en los suburbios sumergidos porque no le ofrecían trabajo en ninguna parte.

—Sí, pero, si hubieran sido más generosos, los gremios os habríais vuelto locos.

—¿Y qué más daba eso? Nosotros ya te odiábamos. A los Holdfast no les habría costado nada encontrarle un trabajo cualquiera a tu padre. Pero, claro, si tú hubieras dejado de esforzarte, tal vez te habrías dado cuenta de la red en la que te tenían atrapada. Por lo que he oído, Ilva Holdfast tenía un talento especial para engatusar a la gente. Siempre sabía cuánta presión era capaz de soportar cada persona.

A Helena le dieron arcadas, pero negó con la cabeza.

—¿Y los alumnos de los gremios qué hacíais? ¿Seguirles el juego? —espetó con desdén.

Kaine rio.

—No, claro que te odiábamos. Ponte en nuestro lugar: tú eras la línea que los Holdfast dibujaban entre la Llama Eterna y los demás. Eras una chica surgida de la nada y, aun así, recibías toda la atención y los elogios que ningún alumno del gremio conseguiría jamás. Nosotros nos labrábamos nuestro futuro y pagábamos un dineral cada curso para comprarle el título y el lumitio a una familia que generaba riquezas de la nada, y encima esperaban que estuviéramos agradecidos por ello. Cuando pensábamos en lo que queríamos, tú eras lo primero que se interponía en nuestro camino.

Un escalofrío le recorrió la columna a Helena. Kaine paseó la mirada por la habitación.

—Cuando llegó Morrough, ni siquiera tuvo que prometer la inmortalidad o riquezas. Solo se ofreció a eliminar a quienes no nos dejaban avanzar en la vida. Una vez aniquilados los Holdfast, el poder de la Fe empezaría a desmoronarse. Era un traspaso de poderes limpio. La ciudad ni siquiera debería haberse visto afectada. Incluso pensábamos dejar intacta la Academia.

—Pero entonces detuvieron a tu padre.

Kaine asintió con ojos inexpresivos.

—Pero entonces detuvieron a mi padre y, además, todo era mentira. Sin embargo, cuando los que tenían algo que objetar se dieron cuenta, ya fue demasiado tarde.

—¿Hubo inmarcesibles que se opusieron? —Se le aceleró el pulso al pensar que había simpatizantes. Esta información era valiosísima y podría cambiarlo todo, pero Kaine asintió distraído.

—¿Quién? —Helena se inclinó hacia delante—. ¿Quién tuvo algo que objetar?

—¿De verdad quieres saberlo?

Ella asintió con fervor. Su interlocutor le rodeó la garganta con los dedos y la atrajo hacia sí.

—Basilius Blackthorne. ¿Te suena de algo?

Se le congeló la sangre. Sí, claro que lo conocía.

—¿Blackthorne era…?

—Ahora es todo un monstruo, ¿verdad? Ya te hablé de las filacterias, ¿te acuerdas? —Apretó la mano que le rodeaba la garganta, y Helena se limitó a asentir. Su corazón comenzó a latirle más rápido—. Después de que yo asesinara al principado Apollo, Basilius aseguró que él no había accedido a esos métodos ni a ese derramamiento de sangre. Morrough, por aquel entonces todavía se hacía llamar así, fingió pensárselo y, al cabo de un tiempo, nos convocó a todos. Hasta esa noche no sabíamos cuántos éramos. Morrough dijo que nos quería allí para que viéramos cómo hacía cambiar de opinión a Basilius. Traía la filacteria de Basilius en una caja y nos recordó que le habíamos confiado nuestras vidas. Luego empezó a apuñalar la filacteria con un anillo puntiagudo. Basilius empezó a gritar y a arañarse el cuerpo, hasta arrancarse su propia carne, pero no moría, seguía regenerándose. Siguió así, hasta que el suelo se cubrió de su sangre. Según me han contado, cuando Morrough terminó, Basilius volvió a casa y se comió viva a su mujer en la cama matrimonial. Creo que también tenían hijos. Los mató a todos.

Kaine lo contaba sin mostrar expresión alguna y sin apartar los dedos de la garganta de Helena.

—A los ojos de Morrough, todos somos prescindibles, así que, como ves, estoy muy familiarizado con la ilusión del libre albedrío. —Esbozó una sonrisa cruel—. Por eso la reconozco cuando la veo.

Helena negó con la cabeza, pero Kaine apretó con fuerza hasta que notó el pulso latiéndole contra la palma de su mano. El corazón le retumbaba con fuerza en el pecho. Él se inclinó sobre ella, y Helena supo que debía tenerle miedo. Sin embargo, no lo tenía. Ya no.

—Luc no es así —repitió—. Sigo siéndole leal porque sé que él haría lo mismo por mí.

Los ojos de Kaine se oscurecieron.

—¿Tú crees?

Le recorrió la mandíbula con el pulgar. Había recuperado algo de color en las mejillas hundidas. Sus ojos descendieron hasta los labios de Helena, y ella sintió con claridad la atracción que existía entre ambos: como una cuerda, tensa y lista, a punto de vibrar.

Kaine se acercó hasta que sus rostros casi se rozaron, y el resto del mundo desapareció. Helena vio cómo abría los labios, vacilante, tan cerca que podía saborear su aliento. Él respiró hondo.

—¿Y qué diría tu querido Luc si supiera que has dejado que el asesino de su padre te compre como una puta? —Mientras hablaba, la mano que tenía libre se deslizó hasta la cintura de Helena. La atrajo hacia sí y recorrió su cuerpo sin disimulo, manoseándola como si estuviera a punto de lanzarse sobre ella para devorarla ahí mismo, en el suelo.

Pero en su mirada solo había hielo, ni rastro de deseo. Era una pantomima del beso que una vez compartieron; ahora se comportaba con una dura indiferencia, como si solo quisiera recordarle a quién estaba dispuesta a entregarse.

Helena se apartó y retrocedió por el suelo hasta que estuvo fuera de su alcance. Kaine se echó a reír.

Le ardían las mejillas y, al encogerse, sintió frío y calor a la vez. Intentó recobrar la compostura, como si la hubiera tenido en algún momento. Era un ser humano grotesco y patético.

Una propiedad. No, ni eso.

Era una baratija. Algo que él había añadido a su lista de exigencias. Tan insignificante que Ilva y Crowther la miraron y no vieron motivo para negarse.

Por mucho que Kaine intentara convencerla de que los Holdfast tenían la culpa de todo, de que solo le habían ofrecido una educación para mantenerla bajo control, era él quien la había convertido en una puta.

A veces deseaba haber muerto en el hospital junto a su padre, que la recordaran con dolor por lo que podría haber sido, en vez de vivir, día tras día, siendo testigo de cómo esas posibilidades se extinguían una a una. Ahora daba igual que fuera alquimista, sanadora u otra cosa. Para cualquiera que lo descubriera, solo sería algo despreciable. El mundo definía a las mujeres con el adjetivo más rastrero que se le ocurría.

No obstante, lo peor era saber todo eso y, aun así, anhelar los escasos momentos en los que él era amable. Porque eso era lo único que le quedaba.

—Tengo que irme —se obligó a decir—. ¿Tienes… tienes alguna información esta semana?

Era casi irónico preguntar algo así en ese momento, pero Kaine cogió el abrigo que se había quitado y sacó un sobre con los bordes manchados de sangre. Se lo lanzó sin más y cayó en el suelo entre ambos.

Por fuera, Helena aparentaba estar tranquila a su regreso al Cuartel General, pero le temblaron las manos cuando le entregó las esquirlas a Crowther. Este le ordenó dárselas a Shiseo para que las analizara, así que las llevó al laboratorio y se dirigió al hospital para empezar su turno.

Deseó que no fuera un día tan tranquilo. No podía dejar de pensar.

Cuando comenzó el toque de queda, volvió al laboratorio desierto y se quedó allí a solas.

El solsticio de invierno estaba próximo. En el Norte existía la tradición de celebrar un banquete en honor a la costumbre ancestral de sacrificar a los animales que no podrían alimentar durante el invierno, justo antes de que comenzara el año nuevo. Así lograban llenar la despensa y sobrevivir hasta la llegada de la primavera.

En los tiempos modernos, aquella despensa había sido reemplazada por regalos: libros, artesanías, puzles..., todo lo que ayudara a sobrellevar las largas y oscuras horas de los inviernos del Norte.

A Helena nunca se le había dado bien hacer regalos. Solo acertó una vez: cuando le regaló a Luc un mapa en el que había señalado una ruta por todos los sitios a los que viajarían algún día.

El año pasado no regaló nada, pero este año quería hacer botiquines con todo lo básico, para que la gente tuviera algo a mano en caso de que no hubiera cerca ningún médico de combate. Sin embargo, Ilva no la había invitado a unirse a Luc y los demás durante el solsticio, así que descartó la idea.

Unos minutos después, abrió un armario y fue sacando frascos de distintos estantes. Los colocó sobre un trozo de tela encerada y anotó cuidadosamente todo lo que iba tomando. Se obligó a parpadear de vez en cuando.

Tenía un trabajo que hacer. Tenía que hacerlo.

A LA SEMANA SIGUIENTE, ENTRE la lluvia helada y la niebla, Helena cruzó el puente sin distinguir demasiado. Mantuvo cerca el cuchillo que usaba para recolectar y se encaminó al Reducto. Le había devuelto su forma y ya no estaba especialmente afilado, pero seguía siéndole útil.

No volverían a darle un cuchillo alquímico en mucho tiempo.

Si alguien perdía un arma alquímica, debía dar muchas explicaciones para conseguir una nueva. Y si Helena decía que la había perdido, tendría que someterse a un castigo y, además, al no ser combatiente, pasaría a ser la última de la lista. En caso de que atribuyera la pérdida a un ataque, tendría que detallar lo que había sucedido. Hasta que Ilva o Crowther consiguieran un cuchillo alquímico sin dueño, Helena tendría que conformarse.

Aquel día hacía tanto frío en el módulo que su aliento se condensaba en una nube de vapor. Kaine llegó un minuto después, retirándose la capucha de la cara. Helena apartó la mirada, pero no pudo evitar notar que tenía el uniforme negro empapado.

—¿Dónde tienes el cuchillo?

A Helena se le hizo un nudo en el estómago. Había confiado en que no se daría cuenta tan rápido.

—Ah. —Intentó sonar despreocupada—. Bueno… —tragó saliva—, lo he perdido.

—¿Lo… lo has perdido? —repitió lentamente, y Helena casi escuchó la palabra «idiota» que iba implícita en la frase—. ¿Cuándo?

La chica bajó la mirada a sus pies. Kaine se movió sin hacer el más mínimo ruido, como si fuera un gato.

—La semana pasada.

Se quedó inmóvil.

—¿Te atacaron?

Se acercó rápidamente y la miró de arriba abajo con un brillo intenso en los ojos. Helena sacudió la cabeza.

—No, yo, eh… Lo rompí. Cuando caíste inconsciente, necesitaba instrumental para operarte, así que lo creé a partir del cuchillo.

Se atrevió a levantar la mirada y observar su expresión. Sintió cierto placer al verlo desconcertado.

—Ya conseguiré otro —repuso al instante—. Solo hay… una lista de espera. En fin, te he traído un regalo —añadió, forzando una sonrisa alegre.

Rebuscó en la bolsa y sacó una caja envuelta con una tela encerada. Sin más demora, se la entregó.

—Es… es un… Eh… Es un botiquín de emergencia —explicó rápido, antes de que él pudiera rechazarlo—. Lo he llenado con cosas que te ayudarán a regenerarte.

A Kaine pareció pillarlo totalmente desprevenido. Frenó en seco y cogió la caja. Al darse cuenta de que ella aguardaba con impaciencia, suspiró y la abrió.

—¿Sabes que puedo comprarme medicinas y que no soy quien más las necesita, ¿verdad?

—Estas no. Las he creado yo. Están diseñadas para surtir efecto en vivemantes o, en tu caso, acelerar la regeneración.

Helena se acercó con timidez y pasó los dedos por los distintos frascos.

—Están etiquetados y, además, he dejado por escrito en el papel encerado cómo hay que usarlos. Están pensados para aumentar la efectividad de la sanación alquímica. A veces, la medicina tradicional interfiere con la resonancia, así que escogí componentes que complementan la regeneración y la sanación. —Señaló el frasco que tenía más a mano—. Esto es polvo de milenrama infusionado con cobre, sirve para detener hemorragias. Tienes que echártelo sobre la herida antes de vendarla. Sé que estás acostumbrado a dejar que la regeneración haga su trabajo, pero siempre es mejor controlar una hemorragia. —Luego señaló un botecito azul verdoso—. Y esto te ayudará a regenerarte. Tiene una alta concentración de componentes esenciales para tu cuerpo, así que, cuando tu sangre se regenere, no le faltará nada para funcionar como es debido. Este es el bálsamo que te hice para la espalda, muy útil para aliviar el dolor superficial. Si tienes una herida que no se cierra, al menos podrás entumecer la zona hasta…

—¿Hasta qué? —La miró con intensidad.

Helena supo que él esperaba que dijera algo como: «Hasta que nos veamos y me dedique en cuerpo y alma a curarte».

—Esa es la segunda parte del regalo —respondió mirándolo a los ojos—. Creo que te vendría bien aprender algunas técnicas de sanación para que puedas aplicártelas a ti mismo. Sé que normalmente no lo necesitas, pero, si entiendes cómo funciona tu cuerpo y vas guiando la regeneración, te recuperarás más rápido. —Se acercó a Kaine poco a poco—. ¿Puedo?

Obtuvo un breve asentimiento como respuesta. Helena le cogió la mano y la colocó sobre su propio brazo; luego colocó los dedos sobre los suyos e hizo que la resonancia atravesara sus dedos y le recorriera el brazo. Fue como si sintiera un poder intangible bajo la piel.

—Por supuesto, mi cuerpo no es como el tuyo, pero la anatomía es prácticamente igual, y la regeneración sigue las reglas básicas. —Se lo explicaba con la misma precisión que usaba con sus aprendizas. Agradeció la experiencia—. Según me contaste, la regeneración comienza en las partes esenciales del cuerpo: cerebro, órganos, extremidades. Cuando perdiste el brazo, eras incapaz de regenerarte porque te habías desangrado demasiado y todavía te estabas recuperando de las quemaduras graves de la espalda. Que tu cuerpo pueda regenerarse no significa que tenga los recursos físicos necesarios para hacerlo. Esos recursos deben proceder de alguna parte. Si estás gravemente herido, quizá no tengas resonancia suficiente para sanarte a ti mismo, pero sí puedes guiar la regeneración, y el botiquín te da margen para eso.

Le contó toda la información que pudo recordar. Le explicó los distintos sistemas del cuerpo, cómo interactuaban entre sí y los efectos en cadena que se producían cuando había algún fallo. Durante un buen rato, siguió soltando consejos, repasando tantas partes del cuerpo como le fue posible.

—Los ojos son muy complicados. Supongo que, si alguna vez pierdes alguno, te volverá a crecer, pero si no... —Dejó escapar un suspiro—. El tejido no se regenera de la misma manera que la piel. Sanarlos desgasta muchísimo y es algo que saca de quicio a cualquiera. Si te pasa, es mejor... es mejor que vengas a buscarme. Bueno, quiero decir... —empezó a tartamudear.

—El Sumo Nigromante no tiene ojos —la interrumpió Kaine.

Helena se quedó callada y alzó la vista.

—¿Cómo?

Nunca había visto a Morrough, pero, según le habían contado, las pocas veces que se dignaba a aparecer llevaba una máscara dorada con forma de medialuna que le tapaba casi todo el rostro y que se extendía a los lados como si tuviera cuernos. Era como un eclipse de sol.

—Es espantoso verlo, pero a él no parece importarle. —Retiró la mano con evidente cansancio de la lección—. Es como si alguien se los hubiera quemado. Emplea la resonancia para ver.

—No sabía que eso fuera posible. —Se frotó las manos en la falda—. Bueno, ya tienes la información básica. Si quieres añadir algo al botiquín o se te ocurre algo más, puedo intentar fabricarlo.

—¿Eso era solo la información básica? —Sacó un reloj del bolsillo—. Llevas más de una hora hablando.

Helena tanteó en busca de su propio reloj, convencida de que se equivocaba, pero no era así. Si no se iba ya, llegaría tarde al trabajo.

—Bueno... Aun así, solo te he contado lo más básico —repuso a la defensiva. Luego añadió—: Tengo que irme. Feliz solsticio. Espero que tus días se iluminen.

Kaine no le devolvió la felicitación, pero volvió a hablar justo cuando Helena estaba a punto de marcharse.

—Marino.

La chica se puso en tensión, pero se giró. Kaine seguía donde lo había dejado; su mirada delataba cierta irritación. La miró de arriba abajo como si estuviera debatiéndose sobre algo.

—Yo también... tengo algo para ti —dijo un instante después, como si le costara decirlo. Sacó del bolsillo un paquete que estaba envuelto en un paño aceitoso y se lo entregó.

Dentro había un par de dagas preciosas, envainadas en unas fundas de malla. Aunque no las había tocado, Helena sintió cómo su resonancia reaccionaba.

—Ponte la más larga en la espalda y la pequeña en el antebrazo —le ordenó Kaine cuando ella no dijo nada—. Están hechas a medida. El titanio y el níquel conforman una aleación nemotécnica, lo que te permitirá transmutarlas más que el resto de las armas. Siempre volverán a su forma original. Según la resonancia que emplees, pueden adquirir tres formas diferentes, por lo que podrás modificarlas a tu antojo. Por eso, las fundas son extensibles.

Helena escogió la daga más larga.

Después de haber pasado meses entrenando con armas de acero, aquella daga le pareció increíblemente liviana. La sacó de la funda y la sostuvo entre los dedos. Cambiar su forma no le costó esfuerzo alguno: la daga mantuvo el borde afilado, pero cambió de forma y longitud. Se convirtió en un arma larga y flexible como un látigo. Apenas alteró el timbre de su resonancia y, sin necesidad de guiar al metal, la daga recuperó su forma original.

Helena soltó un grito ahogado, incapaz de creer lo fácil que era transmutarla. Le costaba tan poco como mover los dedos, y no pesaba nada. No podía parar de darle vueltas, admirando cada detalle: el peso, la textura, lo afiladas que estaban las hojas. Para un mejor agarre, la empuñadura tenía unos dibujos curvados, como una enredadera.

No sabía qué decir. «Gracias» le parecía insuficiente.

Kaine la observaba con atención, pero, cuando ella alzó la mirada, su anhelo se desvaneció y fue reemplazado por un ceño fruncido.

—No puedes desmontarlas ni convertirlas en instrumental médico. Da igual quién lo necesite.

Helena se ruborizó.

—Pero si acabas de decir que puedo darles forma.

—Sí, pero no puedes deconstruirlas por completo. ¿Está claro, Marino? —insistió con tono gélido.

—Está bien, lo prometo —aseguró ella, poniendo los ojos en blanco. Cómo no, Kaine tenía que arruinar todos los momentos bonitos. Al cabo de unos instantes, volvió a mirarlo—. Gracias. No sé qué decir. Son preciosas.

Kaine no quiso mirarla a los ojos.

—No hay de qué —carraspeó—. Aunque me alegra que te gusten,

porque quiero que las lleves encima siempre que salgas del Cuartel General. De hecho, deberías llevarlas en todo momento. No te las quites salvo para dormir. No puedes guardarlas al fondo de la bolsa. Quiero verlas contigo cada vez que vengas aquí. ¿Entendido?

—Sí, las llevaré encima —dijo como si fuera una concesión cuando, en realidad, no quería soltarlas ni un instante.

—Bien. —Kaine se removió incómodo—. Bueno, ha sido un placer. Ni siquiera recuerdo cuántas veces he deseado que alguien me diera una lección sobre el cuerpo humano.

Helena levantó la vista y vio que estaba fingiendo una sonrisa. Kaine hizo amago de marcharse, pero se detuvo.

—Ahora que tienes un arma decente, creo que es hora de que pasemos a un entrenamiento un poco más intenso. Prepárate para la semana que viene. —Le extendió un sobre—. Mi última entrega.

Cuando la chica fue a cogerlo, Kaine lo sostuvo hasta que sus miradas se encontraron.

—Debo admitir que has resultado ser bastante cara, Marino.

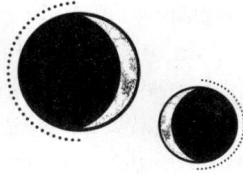

CAPÍTULO 45

Diciembris 1786

CROWTHER TODAVÍA NO HABÍA REGRESADO al Cuartel General, por lo que a Helena no le quedó más remedio que dar parte a Ilva.

Mientras subía los pisos hacia su despacho, ubicado en el edificio principal, Helena no podía dejar de pensar en todo lo que Ilva sabía sobre ella. Durante años había formado parte de la junta que aprobaba la beca de Helena y lo más probable era que también estuviera en la de admisiones.

El interés particular que Ilva le había demostrado desde la muerte de su padre le parecía ahora menos generoso.

Ilva estaba leyendo un informe, jugueteando distraídamente con un bolígrafo en la mano, y no levantó la vista cuando el guardia dejó pasar a Helena.

—Marino —pronunció con tono frío—. Siéntate. Ahora mismo estoy contigo.

Helena aguardó sin parar de abrir y cerrar las manos.

—¿Cómo vais Shiseo y tú con el anulitio? —preguntó Ilva cuando cerró la carpeta y levantó la vista.

Para una mayor comodidad, el Consejo había bautizado como «anulitio» a la aleación de lumitio con *mo'lian'shi*. Aunque no se había extendido la noticia de su existencia, ya había algunos metalúrgicos y quimiatras experimentando con el material.

La pregunta la tomó por sorpresa; esperaba que le preguntara sobre Kaine.

—Bien. Estamos terminando de sintetizar el agente quelante a partir de las muestras que recogí de Ferron. Si alguno de nuestros combatientes resulta herido con anulitio, podremos extraer todas las piezas metálicas de la sangre.

La metralla que Helena había extraído no era suficiente para fabricar un arma robusta, pero la aleación no tenía por qué serlo. La fusión estaba diseñada para ser inestable, para que se hiciera añicos en el impacto y las esquirlas se deterioraran rápidamente al entrar en contacto con el torrente sanguíneo. Allí se disolvían como un veneno, atacando a la resonancia de la víctima. Helena y Shiseo tenían órdenes de investigar posibles tratamientos. Dado que la toxicidad en los metales era algo habitual en ciertos campos de la alquimia, lo más lógico sería empezar con los agentes quelantes.

Ilva asintió.

—¿Qué piensa Shiseo?

—Cree que es imposible que el enemigo consiga suprimir la alquimia por completo mediante el método que están usando. Es cierto que impide la sanación y la cirugía alquímica, pero su uso en batalla suele ser limitado. Aunque eso podría cambiar si aciertan con la ratio y la composición.

Ilva entrecerró los ojos.

—¿Shiseo y tú tenéis algún método alternativo en mente?

Helena tragó saliva e intentó no mostrar debilidad.

—Tenemos una idea, pero por el momento es solo una teoría. No disponemos de anulitio para probarla.

—Y esa teoría se basa en…

A Helena se le formó un nudo en el estómago. Detestaba mantener este tipo de conversaciones.

—Teniendo en cuenta cómo se comporta la aleación y cómo funciona la resonancia, hacer un arma de anulitio o inyectarlo en sangre es menos efectivo que dirigirlo hacia las extremidades. Si centráramos esa interferencia en las manos, los alquimistas perderían la capacidad de percibir su propia resonancia. Shiseo cree que, si combinamos la aleación con un material que tenga una gran sensibilidad a la resonancia, como, por ejemplo, el cobre procesado con una alta concentración de efluvios de lumitio, lograríamos una interferencia capaz de suprimir casi todas las resonancias, independientemente del repertorio del alquimista.

—¿Y cómo contrarrestamos algo así? —preguntó Ilva con interés.

—Bueno, podría hacerlo cualquier metalúrgico, siempre y cuando se sienta cómodo trabajando sin resonancia. Aunque la mayoría de los paladinos nunca han tenido que preocuparse por eso.

—Qué suerte tuvimos de que le sacaras esa metralla a Ferron —dijo Ilva, a pesar de que el tono no reflejó el sentimiento. Helena se limitó a asentir.

—Aquí tienes el informe —dijo dejando el sobre en la mesa. Ilva lo cogió y lo metió en un cajón—. Por cierto… —Helena dudó y sintió que se ruborizaba hasta el nacimiento del cabello y las puntas de las orejas—. Me ha regalado un par de dagas por el solsticio de invierno. Están hechas de titanio y níquel.

Sacó el paño impermeable y lo abrió sobre el escritorio para que Ilva les echara un vistazo. La mujer arqueó una ceja y contempló las dagas un instante para, acto seguido, cubrirlas con la tela, como si mirarlas le pareciera de mal gusto.

A Helena se le cayó el alma a los pies. Envolvió las armas rápidamente, deseando no habérselas enseñado sin preguntar antes.

—Es una buena señal, ¿no?

Ilva la miró con la cabeza ladeada, como si la estuviera analizando.

—Ferron está subiendo de rango —comentó mientras abría un cajón y sacaba otra carpeta. La dejó sobre el escritorio—. ¿Lo sabías?

A ella se le detuvo el corazón. Sí que se había percatado de que su uniforme cada vez era más oscuro.

—Al parecer, ha superado todas las limitaciones que tenía antes de sufrir aquellas lesiones. Tiene controlados varios distritos de gran valor. Hace poco tomó posesión de la fábrica del Reducto, justo donde tú vas a verlo, y está consolidando su poder a una velocidad alarmante. Es evidente que está aprovechando al máximo nuestros últimos éxitos.

Ilva tamborileó los dedos sobre el escritorio y, cuando levantó la vista, le dedicó a Helena una sonrisa gélida.

—No lo sabía —admitió la chica.

Ilva negó con la cabeza lentamente.

—Ya, eso me lo imaginaba. Me preocupa que se te haya olvidado de quién estamos hablando. —Helena contuvo el aliento, pero Ilva continuó con calma, sin dejar de pasar páginas de la carpeta que tenía entre manos—: Hace meses que circulan rumores de que Morrough tiene un arma nueva. Pensábamos que se trataba de las quimeras, como la que estuvo a punto de acabar con Lila, o del anulitio. Pero no es así. No se trata de nada de eso, ¿verdad? —Ilva entrelazó las manos y miró a Helena fijamente—. ¿Cómo es posible que siga vivo?

—Crowther me pidió que hiciera todo lo posible por salvarle la vida.

La mirada de Ilva pasó de la cara de Helena al cuello, donde asomaba la cadena de su collar. Helena se quedó muy quieta.

—Verás, Ferron no es el único espía que tenemos —continuó Ilva—.

Disponemos de varios informantes. Según sus informes, Ferron recibió un castigo cuando recuperamos los puertos. Un castigo brutal. Me aseguraron que estaba muriéndose.

—¿Tú lo sabías? —preguntó Helena con voz trémula—. ¿Sabías lo que le hicieron y no... no me lo dijiste?

Ilva le dedicó una mirada penetrante.

—¿Y por qué habríamos de decírtelo?

Helena no encontraba las palabras.

—¿Por eso el ataque fue tan complejo y necesitó tanta información confidencial? Estabais seguros de que lo matarían por cometer ese error. Porque queríais que lo mataran por ello.

Ilva no respondió, pero Helena empezó a entender por qué Kaine la había mirado con tanto resentimiento y desconfianza cada vez que acudía a las citas.

—¿Por qué no me lo contaste? —Le temblaba la voz de la rabia.

Ilva frunció los labios y miró a Helena con atención.

—Siempre has sido... especialmente sincera. —Esbozó una sonrisa—. Por eso Luc confía tanto en ti. Si te hubiéramos contado el plan, ¿crees que habrías sido capaz de ir allí sabiéndolo todo sin que Ferron se diera cuenta?

Helena empezó a temblar y la visión se le volvió borrosa. Se aferró con fuerza a los reposabrazos de su asiento.

—Dimos por sentado que acabarías dándote cuenta —continuó Ilva—. Cuando se hizo evidente que no había sido así, y que sentías que le debías algo, decidimos que era mejor que intentaras curarlo. Con suerte, comprenderías que no servía de nada y acabarías trayéndonos su talismán. —Ilva se aclaró la garganta—. Así que ya puedes imaginar nuestra sorpresa cuando descubrimos que nuestro espía traicionero no solo había sobrevivido, sino que se había vuelto más peligroso que antes. ¿Cómo lo hiciste?

Helena tragó saliva a duras penas.

—Estábamos perdiendo la guerra, y solo remontamos porque él nos ayudó a retomar los puertos. Lo hizo por nosotros. Tú no lo viste el día que volví. Ferron era consciente de que lo castigarían; había asumido su muerte. —Estaba jadeando del pánico—. Si queríais que muriera, deberíais habérmelo dicho. Crowther me pidió que hiciera todo lo posible.

—¿Qué le hiciste? —El tono de Ilva se había vuelto mucho más tenso—. ¿Usaste...? —Frunció aún más los labios y, de nuevo, buscó con la mirada la cadena que rodeaba el cuello de Helena—. ¿Usaste algo para curarlo?

—Supuse que, si teníais que elegir entre uno u otro, preferiríais que sobreviviera él —respondió Helena apretando el puño. Ilva palideció—. Así que usé el amuleto que me regalaste. Pensé que…

—¿Le diste el amuleto a Ferron? —su voz sonó casi histérica. Helena jamás la había escuchado alzarla.

—No, yo…

—¿Lo sigues teniendo o no?

La chica sintió que se le formaba un nudo en el estómago. Acto seguido, se sacó el amuleto por encima de la cabeza.

—Tengo el amuleto, pero la heliolita ha desaparecido.

Ilva se lo arrebató con tanta ansia que la cadena se rompió contra el guante de cuero que llevaba. Su mano derecha acarició el amuleto, ahí donde debía haber estado la piedra. Parecía completamente horrorizada.

—¿Qué has hecho?

Helena tragó saliva, nerviosa.

—Se rompió y salió una especie de… sustancia. Algo parecido al mercurio. Se… se fusionó con Ferron.

El silencio que siguió fue casi insoportable. Ilva parecía tan perpleja que no dijo nada, solo se quedó mirando el amuleto, como si la piedra vacía fuese a materializarse por arte de magia. Helena esperó unos momentos, pero ya no podía soportarlo más.

—Si no querías que lo sanara, deberías habérmelo dicho.

Ilva no respondió; era incapaz de apartar la mirada del amuleto.

—¿Conoces la historia de la Gema de los Cielos? —dijo finalmente, acariciando el engarce vacío con el pulgar. Helena sintió un miedo que le helaba los huesos.

—No —admitió sacudiendo la cabeza—. Es un mito. Todo el mundo sabe que fue una malinterpretación. Luc me contó que no era verdad.

—Todas las decisiones que he tomado han sido para proteger a Luc —afirmó Ilva. No parecía estar hablando con Helena, sino más bien consigo misma, o tal vez con el amuleto que tenía agarrado—. No me educaron para ser su mano derecha ni para soportar la carga de este legado. Yo estaba satisfecha con mi papel, pero Luc era demasiado joven para asumir la responsabilidad del principado. He intentado tomar buenas decisiones. —Ilva miró a Helena—. Cuando descubrimos que eras una… vivemante, pensé que serías mi salvación, que Sol me había concedido un medio infalible para protegerlo. Por supuesto, tuve que lidiar con los prejuicios políticos, y Matias no me lo puso fácil. Después de todas las exigencias que te impuso, me preocupaba que el Estrago te matara antes de tiempo. Este amuleto llevaba siglos bajo llave, protegido por varias generaciones de Holdfast. Confiaba en que esta guerra lo hiciera despertar de alguna forma.

—¿Qué era? —preguntó Helena.

Ilva se irguió, apoyándose con tanta fuerza en su bastón que los nudillos se le volvieron blancos. Pasó junto a Helena y se asomó a la ventana, desde donde se veía la Torre de Alquimia.

—Mi familia construyó esta institución y esta ciudad para asegurarse de que la nigromancia no volvía a hacerse con el poder. Entregaron sus vidas a esa causa y mantuvieron secretos con el mismo fin. —La mujer se sumió en un silencio profundo durante un buen rato. Helena no se atrevió a interrumpirla—. ¿Has escuchado hablar de Caudalón?

Caudalón era el nombre que tenía Paladia antes de que se produjera la Primera Guerra Nigromántica. La ciudad fue arrasada por una plaga y, cuando el Nigromante se enteró, usó los cadáveres para crear un ejército.

—No hubo ninguna plaga —confesó Ilva sin mirar atrás—. Orion contó que había sido una plaga porque esa era una explicación más amable que la verdad. —Cerró la mano y apretó el amuleto junto a su pecho—. El Nigromante se enteró del poder alquímico de esta zona y vino a Caudalón por la gente que vivía aquí.

—¿Los mató a todos? —La chica no entendía el sentido del secreto. Si el Nigromante había masacrado Caudalón, la historia sería mucho más creíble que la de que había encontrado una ciudad llena de cadáveres cuando más la necesitaba.

Ilva sacudió la cabeza.

—No, siguen vivos. Todavía están vivos.

Helena la miró sin comprender.

—El Nigromante era un vivemante, igual que tú, aunque en aquella época esas habilidades parecían sacadas de un cuento mitológico. Llegó a Caudalón haciendo milagros. La gente pensaba que era un dios. Le erigieron un templo en la meseta, le entregaron todo lo que pidió, y él les prometió la inmortalidad a quienes tuvieran fe. Sin embargo, un día los convocó a todos en una asamblea multitudinaria, en un sitio secreto que había excavado bajo tierra, y declaró que, si confiaban plenamente en él, les concedería la inmortalidad. No sé exactamente qué hizo, pero, cuando terminó, el templo estaba lleno de cadáveres, y las almas de los presentes se habían fusionado. Se habían combinado para formar esta… sustancia. El Nigromante usó el poder que emanaba de esa gema para reanimarlos a todos.

Ilva empezó a caminar de un lado a otro, cojeando; el bastón temblaba constantemente en sus manos. Estaba demasiado nerviosa para quedarse quieta.

—Cuando Orion se enfrentó al Nigromante, las almas todavía conservaban consciencia; sabían que los había traicionado, que el regalo de la «inmortalidad» los condenaba a ser esclavos toda la eternidad. Durante la batalla, el Nigromante perdió el control, y la gema se volvió en su contra. Se produjo un fogonazo tan brillante como el sol, que iluminó todo el valle y aniquiló al Nigromante y a todos los necrómatas en un estallido de fuego. Cuando todo terminó, solo quedaron Orion y sus seguidores. —Ilva negó con la cabeza—. Si alguien hubiera conocido el verdadero origen de la gema, Orion temía que otros intentaran usar el mismo método, así que, cuando los testigos de la batalla dijeron que la gema había sido un regalo de Sol, Orion no tuvo más remedio que permitir que lo creyeran.

Ilva se quedó callada con tristeza.

—¿Todo es una mentira?

La mujer se giró hacia ella y le lanzó una mirada furibunda.

—¿Qué otra cosa podía hacer?

Helena se levantó, exasperada.

—¡Decir la verdad! No podemos inventarnos la historia para que encaje en lo que deseamos creer. ¿Es que no ves adónde nos ha llevado esto? Luc piensa que debe suceder un milagro, que aún no ha ganado la guerra porque no ha sufrido lo suficiente, porque no se parece a Orion, porque no se lo merece… Y que todo es culpa suya. Pero ese milagro nunca llegará. Lo estás torturando con una mentira.

—Por eso soy yo quien le concede milagros —espetó Ilva. También estaba enfurecida, como si Helena fuera una traidora—. ¿Crees que quiero hacerle sufrir? Quisiera contárselo, pero ¿cuándo es el momento adecuado? —Estiró un brazo—. Apollo debía haber sido quien se lo explicara, cuando tuviese edad suficiente y estuviera listo para comprenderlo. Hay que respetar ciertas pautas, pero todo se vino abajo cuando Ferron asesinó a Apollo y desató la guerra. Ahora, lo único que puedo hacer es mantener viva la fe para que Luc no pierda la esperanza.

La historia de la ciudad, del principado, de la Fe, todos los murales y amuletos… Todo era mentira.

—Tienes que contarle la verdad a Luc. No puedes seguir haciéndole esto.

—¿Y qué crees que pasará cuando sepa que no recibirá ayuda de los dioses? ¿Qué le quedará entonces? —Ilva fulminó a Helena con la mirada—. Es un riesgo que no podemos correr y ahora me has dejado sin más opción que tomar decisiones terribles.

Helena apretó la mandíbula. Estaba demasiado enfadada para aceptar la culpa.

—¿Por qué me diste algo así sin explicarme lo que era?

Los ojos de Ilva brillaron con intensidad.

—Porque intentaba salvarte, evitarte sufrimiento. Pensé que este maldito amuleto sería capaz de contener el Estrago, y parece que así ha sido. Pero, cuando Ferron puso sus condiciones, Crowther pensó que no nos quedaba más remedio que aceptarlas. Aquella noche me planteé quitártelo, y lo habría hecho después de lo que le dijiste al Consejo, pero entonces recordé la cara que pusiste cuando te lo entregué. Creí que lo considerarías un tesoro, que lo cuidarías… Pero has cometido la mayor de las estupideces. —Ilva pareció desfallecer y estuvo a punto de desplomarse en el asiento.

—No tienes derecho a mentirme para luego enfadarte porque he cometido el error de creer tus palabras —replicó Helena—. Si la gema es tan especial, ¿por qué no se la diste a Luc?

El semblante de Ilva se contrajo con amargura.

—No responde a los Holdfast. —Apartó la vista de Helena con los dientes apretados—. Ni siquiera en manos de Orion fue más que una piedra dura y fría, jamás mostró su poder a ninguno de sus descendientes. Se volvió cálida para algunas personas, pero siempre se enfriaba con el tiempo. Pero contigo funcionó. Podrías haber hecho lo que fuera con ella, pero decidiste gastarla para curar a Ferron.

—Siento mucho no ser la marioneta que tú querías que fuese —repuso Helena con amargura. Se incorporó con dificultad. Era como si el mundo entero hubiese desaparecido bajo sus pies; no sabía cómo asimilar lo que acababa de descubrir. Después de haber pasado tanto tiempo sintiéndose culpable por su falta de fe, resultaba que todo era un invento. Ya no sabía qué era real y qué no. Todo había sido un engaño enrevesado hasta que la vendieron a Kaine.

Y Luc... Le dolió en el alma pensar en su amigo. ¿Qué haría si se enteraba de la verdad?

¿Debía ser ella quien se lo contara? La religión era un tema del que siempre había evitado hablar, así que ¿por qué iba ahora a sincerarse y destruir todas sus creencias?

No podía hacerlo. Había demasiado en juego, e Ilva lo sabía.

Helena se detuvo bajo el marco de la puerta.

—La próxima vez será mejor que me digas qué quieres en vez de confiar en que fracase cuando tú lo consideres oportuno. Tal vez así evitemos decepcionarnos la una con la otra.

—¿Quieres que te sea sincera? —La voz de Ilva era viperina—. Quiero que mates a Kaine Ferron.

Helena se quedó paralizada y se giró lentamente. Ilva la miró fijamente a los ojos. Había recuperado la compostura y volvía a mostrarse fría como un lago.

—Nuestra intención desde el principio fue que muriera, pero quiero que lo hagas tú. Has creado una nueva amenaza para Luc, así que debes ser tú misma quien le ponga fin.

—Kaine no nos ha traicionado.

—Asesinó a mi sobrino. —La voz de Ilva resonó como un látigo. Helena se percató de la furia y el odio que mantenía ocultos bajo la superficie; ahora estaban emergiendo de lo más hondo como si fuera una bestia—. ¿Qué pretendes hacer? ¿Esperar a que elija a su próxima víctima? ¿Cuántas vidas estás dispuesta a arriesgar?

A Helena se le formó un nudo en la garganta.

—No puedes pedirme que traicione...

—¿Por qué no? ¿Qué ha hecho por ti, Marino, salvo tratarte como la idiota que eres? ¿Te da unas cuantas baratijas y ya estás dispuesta a ofrecerle tu lealtad? —Los ojos de Ilva repararon en la tela impermeable que Helena seguía aferrando entre las manos—. Si Ferron quisiera poseerte, ya lo habría hecho. No eres más que un juguete para él; se dedica a darte cuerda y ver cómo das vueltas.

—No, estoy avanzando. Si me dejas algo más de tiempo, conseguiré lo que Crowther me pidió.

A Ilva se le escapó una carcajada seca y llena de escepticismo.

—Crowther estaba muy equivocado si pensaba que serías capaz de domar a Ferron. Ni siquiera un perro te haría caso. —Sacudió la cabeza con desdén—. Pero adelante, eres libre de negarte a hacerlo. Sinceramente, no importa; tenemos pruebas suficientes para demostrar su traición. Jan ha reunido un buen montón de documentación. No nos costará nada entregársela a los inmarcesibles. Te aseguro que este asunto está más que blindado. ¿Prefieres que hagamos eso? ¿Crees que esta vez lo matarán de una vez por todas?

Helena sintió como si le hubiesen dado un puñetazo en el pecho.

—No podéis hacerle eso.

La mujer ni se inmutó.

—¿Por qué no? A mí me parece lo más adecuado después de todo lo que ha hecho él. De hecho, diría que hasta se lo merece.

Fue entonces cuando Helena cayó en la cuenta de algo de lo que debería haberse percatado desde el principio: Ilva solo buscaba venganza. Mientras que Crowther pensaba en la guerra civil, analizaba los tejemanejes políticos de los países vecinos, la estrategia bélica de Ilva se reducía a un tema personal. Todo giraba en torno a Luc, al legado de su familia y a una sed implacable de venganza.

Crowther era lo suficientemente ambicioso como para querer que Helena se ganara la lealtad de Kaine para usarlo a largo plazo. Sin embargo, Ilva nunca había contemplado ese objetivo.

—Pero lo necesitamos. Sin él no habríamos avanzado tanto. Si lo perdemos, la guerra volverá a torcerse y la gente culpará a Luc.

Ilva sonrió, ladina.

—Afortunadamente, en los últimos meses Ferron se ha convertido en pieza clave entre los inmarcesibles. Cuando desaparezca sin dejar rastro, se generará el caos en sus filas.

—No puedes hacer esto —repitió Helena.

—Estoy intentando salvar a todo el mundo, Marino. —La voz de Ilva se rompió de la emoción—. Y eso te incluye a ti. Por mucho que lo hayas idealizado, Kaine Ferron no es una persona, sino un monstruo. —Ilva se llevó la mano al corazón, un gesto que solía reservar para hablar de Apollo—. Deberíamos haberlo eliminado a él y a su familia hace tiempo, pero a Pol le preocupaba la reacción de los gremios. A pesar de las sospechas que rodearon su nacimiento, dejó que ese chico estudiara en la Academia, y mira cómo le pagó su generosidad. No cometeré el mismo error con Luc.

—Ilva, por favor, puedo conseguir que me sea leal. Solo necesito tiempo.

La mujer la miró fijamente.

—¿Estás eligiendo a Ferron antes que a Luc? ¿Vas a renunciar a los votos que hiciste?

La pregunta la dejó helada.

—No —repuso rápidamente—. No —repitió con la voz quebrada—. Soy leal a la causa, pero... —tragó saliva varias veces—, si tuviera alguna prueba de que me es leal, de que hará todo lo que le pidáis, ¿permitirías que siguiera con vida? Si no lo consigo, te juro que lo... lo mataré yo misma. Porque, si es leal, podría sernos de utilidad. Por favor, Ilva.

La mano derecha de Luc dejó escapar un suspiro; parecía cansada.

—Si eres capaz de poner a Ferron de rodillas, si consigues que se arrastre y esté dispuesto a hacer cualquier cosa, te dejo quedártelo. Te doy un mes. —Luego negó con la cabeza—. Pero sé sincera contigo misma. La gente como él no sabe lo que es la lealtad. Los Ferron son tan corruptos como el hierro que tanto aprecian.

Helena sintió un nudo en la garganta que apenas le dejaba hablar.

—Lo conseguiré, sea como sea. Terminaré el trabajo. Dile a Crowther que no envíe esa documentación.

Ilva apoyó los codos en el escritorio y la cadena del amuleto vacío quedó colgando entre sus dedos.

—Tienes un mes, Marino.

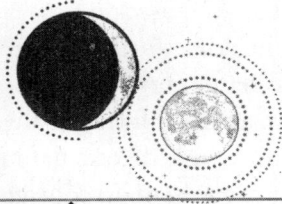

CAPÍTULO 46

Un mes. Fue como si lo hubieran grabado a fuego en los huesos. Aquella noche, Helena no pudo conciliar el sueño. La atormentaba el futuro. Antes del amanecer, asistió a una misa de ascuas en la que el falcón Matias consagró el año nuevo a las manos de Sol y, cuando terminó, se fue a trabajar al hospital.

Se sentía acorralada, como si el mundo se cerrase a su alrededor y no tuviera escapatoria ni a nadie a quien recurrir.

Trató de aplacar sus miedos mediante la animancia, pero aquella práctica le consumía demasiadas fuerzas y acabó sumida en la desesperación.

Cuando terminó su turno, fue a la oficina para ver si podía quedarse durante el siguiente. Lo más probable era que todos prefirieran celebrar el solsticio, y a Helena le convenía mantenerse ocupada.

En el escritorio de la oficina se encontraba Purnell, tras un letrero que rezaba Sofia P. Helena se puso en tensión nada más verla, pero, antes de que pudiese decir algo, Purnell le entregó un folio.

—Ilva Holdfast me pidió que te diera esto al acabar el turno.

Helena dudó un instante antes de leerlo. Solo había unas líneas. Como agradecimiento por su esfuerzo, Ilva le concedía unas horas libres para que acudiera a la fiesta del solsticio de Solis Splendor. Luc estaría allí y deseaba verla. Rhea también quería que asistiera.

Helena contempló el papel sin inmutarse. Ahora veía claramente la manipulación. Ilva estaba perdiendo facultades. O tal vez Helena empezaba a darse cuenta de cómo era en realidad.

Se puso sobre el uniforme el jersey de lana verde que Rhea le había regalado y se encaminó hacia Solis Splendor. Ya era de noche y tanto el año como el sol se estaban preparando para renacer.

En cuatro semanas, Kaine estaría muerto.

Cuando iba a llamar, la puerta se abrió de par en par, derramando calor y luz, música y carcajadas. Helena tuvo que entrecerrar los ojos por la sorpresa. ¿Se había equivocado de casa?

—¿Marino? No sabía que venías. —Se trataba de Alister, uno de los soldados del pelotón de Luc—. Pasa, pasa. Hay un montón de comida.

Nada más entrar, sintió que había escapado de la realidad para adentrarse en una versión de ensueño de Solis Splendor. La casa rebosaba vida, adornada con guirnaldas, serpentinas y ramas de hojas verdes; los niños correteaban por todas partes como una jauría de cachorros salvajes.

Helena sabía quiénes eran, reconocía a cada una de esas personas. Sin embargo, algo se le antojaba extraño, como si estuviera... mal.

¿Por qué estaban todos tan contentos?

En la primera habitación, la música fluía desde un gramófono, acompañada de risas ebrias. Apenas había atravesado la sala cuando alguien le puso una taza de vino especiado en las manos. Le dio un sorbo; estaba caliente y dulce. No se parecía en nada al vino agrio y aguado del racionamiento.

Era evidente que habían recuperado los puertos y que el comercio volvía a surcar el río. Aun así, lo único en lo que Helena podía pensar era: «Kaine os ha conseguido todo esto», y, al mismo tiempo, recordaba las heridas lacerantes de su espalda, el tejido muerto que lo había envenenado. A pesar de estar demacrado, gris y a punto de desfallecer, lo primero que quiso saber era si había funcionado.

La vista se le nubló. Caminó sin fijarse en nada hasta que reconoció a Titus Bayard sentado en el suelo con las piernas cruzadas. Estaba pelando naranjas; debían de haberlas traído de la costa sureña. En la mesa que tenía al lado había toda una montaña de mondas de naranja.

Helena buscó otras caras que le resultaran familiares.

Lila y Soren estaban apretujados en un mismo sillón; este último tenía cara de pocos amigos.

Desde que estuvo en el hospital, Soren dejaba que su hermana se saliera con la suya en todo momento. Lila se había recuperado por completo a gran velocidad y se comportaba como si todos hubieran exagerado lo ocurrido. Cuando se enteró de que Luc había intentado saltarse las órdenes, discutieron acaloradamente. Helena solo lo sabía de oídas, pero el asunto debió de ser grave, porque el pelotón se mantuvo en la reserva durante semanas hasta que se calmaron los ánimos.

Ahora parecía que todo iba mejor, aunque Helena no pudo evitar sentir que el ataque, de alguna forma, había perjudicado a Soren más que a los demás.

Uno de los detalles que se recalcaban siempre que se contaba la historia de los Bayard era que Soren era mayor que Lila. Había nacido veinte minutos antes que ella. En el pasado, esa diferencia de edad fue una cuestión de vital importancia para establecer una jerarquía.

Aunque se comentaba como una broma, Helena sospechaba que Soren se lo tomaba más en serio de lo que parecía. Independientemente de su puesto como paladina primera, Lila no solo era su gemela, sino también su hermana pequeña.

Luc estaba jugando a las cartas con un grupo de soldados convalecientes, mientras que Lila y Soren se limitaban a observar en silencio. Lila no paraba de mover la pierna hacia delante y hacia atrás; los engranajes de la prótesis chasqueaban al mismo ritmo: clic, clic, clic.

Helena se arrodilló junto a Titus. Quería tachar de la lista todo lo que se sentía obligada a hacer antes de marcharse. El ambiente festivo de la casa encajaba tan poco con sus ánimos que le daba náuseas.

—Hola, Titus —lo saludó. Siempre seguía el mismo guion—. ¿Te importa si miro un poco dentro de tu cabeza?

Titus no respondió, pero Helena se quitó un guante y posó los dedos sobre la cicatriz que lucía en la sien. Cerró los ojos para concentrarse en la resonancia. Todo seguía igual, salvo ella misma. Durante el último año había mejorado su técnica y comprendía mejor cómo funcionaba la mente. Había descubierto ciertos patrones de energía que antes desconocía.

Ahora veía en qué se había equivocado. Cuando transmutó el tejido no siguió esas corrientes de energía que impulsaban la consciencia a través del cerebro. Por supuesto, Titus era incapaz de responder y tenía un cerebro limitado; Helena lo había dejado atrapado dentro de su propia consciencia.

La conexión se rompió de repente cuando Titus le apartó la mano. Tenía el rostro compungido y la naranja que sostenía en la mano se había convertido en pulpa entre sus dedos. Agitó la cabeza un par de veces como si quisiera aclarar sus pensamientos.

Helena lo observó, buscando algún indicio de la persona que fue, pero Titus se alejó de ella con expresión inquieta. Volvió a ponerse el guante.

¿Sería capaz de curarlo? La idea le provocaba vértigo. Tenía que estar segura. No podía darle esperanzas a Rhea para acabar rompiéndole el corazón de nuevo.

Un estallido de risas la sobresaltó y la hizo volver a la realidad. Se dirigió a una habitación en la que había menos ruido y también menos gente, y se apoyó en el alféizar de una ventana tratando de recobrar la compostura. Allí hacía más frío, y las cortinas amortiguaban un poco el ruido.

—Helena.

Cuando alzó la vista, vio a Penny Fabien a su lado.

—Sabía que eras tú —dijo—. ¿Te encuentras bien? Tienes mala cara.

Penny era un año mayor que ella. Había sido la responsable de la residencia de Helena cuando estaban en la Academia.

—Hay demasiada gente —respondió, y luego apartó la vista—. ¿Ha pasado algo?

Penny la miró con curiosidad.

—¿A qué te refieres?

—¿Por qué está todo el mundo tan contento?

Penny parpadeó, confundida.

—Estamos contentos porque la guerra está llegando a su fin.

Helena la miró desconcertada.

La guerra no estaba llegando a su fin. Ni siquiera tenían una estrategia para ganar. Llevaban seis años luchando por sobrevivir y esperando un milagro que nunca sucedería.

—¿No has ido a la misa de ascuas? —preguntó Penny—. El falcón Matias nos ha hablado de las fases de la transmutación y cómo cada una se corresponde con un periodo de la guerra. Estamos a punto de sufrir la última transformación, aquella en la que el alma se purifica por completo. Piénsalo. Hace un año, estábamos arrinconados en el Cuartel General, no había suministros y apenas teníamos raciones para seguir luchando. Pero ahora hemos recuperado toda la isla Este y los puertos. Todo porque hemos mantenido la fe.

Helena no había escuchado ni una sola palabra de Matias durante la misa. Lo único que oía era la voz de Ilva repitiendo «un mes» sin cesar.

—¿Qué? —preguntó con un hilo de voz. Penny la miró con pena.

—Supongo que, como no estás en el frente, no tienes ni idea de lo que está pasando, ¿no? Este año nos ha ido de maravilla. —Penny estaba radiante—. Y eso es porque hemos superado la prueba. Nos hemos mantenido firmes y no hemos permitido que el miedo nos corrompiera. Por eso, el dios Sol está remando a nuestro favor. Ahora ya no podemos perder.

Helena se encogió como si hubiera recibido un golpe y miró a Penny con tanto desprecio que la chica perdió la sonrisa y le devolvió la mirada con cierta incomodidad.

—Ah, es cierto… —dijo Penny retorciendo las manos—. Me enteré de lo que pasó en el Consejo. Perdona, no quería decir que tu alma estuviera…

Helena estaba apretando la mandíbula tan fuerte que empezó a temblarle todo el cuerpo. Penny dio un paso hacia ella y le acarició suavemente el brazo.

—No te sientas mal. Estoy segura de que lo hiciste… con buena intención. Todos llegamos a un punto en el que pensamos que lo mejor es rendirse. Pero piensa en lo mucho que todo ha mejorado desde entonces. Tal vez tú fueras… la última prueba que necesitábamos superar.

Helena sintió que perdía el control. Estaba a punto de ponerse a gritar. Jamás había imaginado algo así. ¿De verdad creían que habían tenido éxito el último año, y que estaban a punto de ganar la guerra porque la Resistencia se había negado a su propuesta de usar la nigromancia? ¿Pensaban que habían pasado una especie de prueba espiritual final?

Sin pretenderlo, Helena había alimentado sus fantasías. Ahora ya daba igual lo que sucediera, nadie la escucharía. Siempre sería la que sembró la duda, la que los tentó. De repente, recordó la extraña expresión que adoptaron Ilva y Crowther cuando rechazaron su idea y le pidieron que se marchara. Les había dado una oportunidad de oro.

Por eso Ilva le había revelado la verdad sobre Orion. Porque sabía que nadie creería lo que Helena tuviera que decir.

Y, por si fuera poco, Ilva quería que hiciera algo más: matar a Kaine, enterrar las pruebas, el verdadero motivo por el que habían ganado. Ese era su último milagro.

Helena se obligó a respirar, pero apenas logró emitir un sollozo ahogado. Penny le dio un abrazo con todas sus fuerzas.

—No pasa nada —le decía, como si Helena fuera una niña que necesitase calmarse—. Todos cometemos errores. No tienes por qué sentirte mal. Ya ha pasado. —Penny le dio una palmadita en la espalda—. ¿Sabes qué pasa? El problema es que estás muy aislada. Nosotros estamos en el frente, pero tú siempre estás en el hospital y no ves lo que está pasando en realidad.

—Supongo que debe de ser eso —replicó Helena sin añadir nada más.

Penny la soltó y asintió.

—No te preocupes. Quédate conmigo esta noche. Me aseguraré de que nadie te moleste.

Helena se sentía tan aturdida que no pudo impedir que Penny la apartara de la ventana y la llevara a otra habitación donde Alister estaba tocando el piano. Soren jugaba a las cartas en un rincón, y Lila había desaparecido. Varios del grupo se habían reunido alrededor del piano, cantando, entre ellos Luc. Penny dejó a Helena en el sofá y, tras intentar convencerla de que la acompañara, también se colocó junto al piano.

Helena permaneció en tensión y esperó a que Penny se distrajera lo suficiente para poder escabullirse de allí. Sin embargo, no tuvo ocasión; en cuanto Luc la vio, se acercó y se sentó a su lado.

—Me alegro de que sigas aquí. Temía que ya te hubieras ido.

Ella no dijo nada y se limitó a negar con la cabeza.

—¿Te encuentras bien? —preguntó su amigo.

—Solo estoy cansada.

Luc se acercó un poco más.

—¿Tus aprendizas no son capaces de seguirte el ritmo?

—No, lo hacen bien. Pero… parece que siempre hay algo más que hacer.

—No sé, yo creo que te gusta estar ocupada. —Había cierta ironía en su voz. Helena sintió que se apretaba aún más el nudo que tenía en el estómago.

—Será eso —consiguió responder.

Soren se sentó en el brazo del sofá y luego se dejó caer junto a Helena.

—Tenéis que esconderme. Le han contado a mi madre que estaba apostando.

—Estás muerto —dijo Luc entre risas—. ¿Has ganado al menos?

Soren negó con la cabeza, apesadumbrado.

—Joder, ¿por qué viene Lila para acá?

—Esa boca, por favor… Y encima en la casa de tu madre. —Luc chasqueó la lengua—. Y con tu hermana tan cerca.

—Vete a la mierda.

Lila se dirigía hacia ellos con un rectángulo enorme colgado del cuello. Se paró delante de los tres.

—Mamá me ha obligado a hacer fotos —dijo señalando el aparato. Soren emitió un gruñido—. Poneos derechos y quedaos quietos. Este aparato es muy tiquismiquis —añadió Lila mientras ajustaba la lente, moviéndola hacia delante y hacia atrás—. Soren, ¿es que has perdido la columna vertebral? ¿Cómo es posible que parezcas un saco de patatas con una armadura? Estás arrugado como un fideo pasado. Luc, dale un codazo, ¿quieres?

Luc metió la mano por detrás de la espalda de Helena para complacerla.

—Así está mucho mejor —dijo Lila con una sonrisa de oreja a oreja y, al instante, Luc también iluminó su rostro—. Muy bien, no quiero ver caras largas. Estamos celebrando el solsticio. Alegraos.

Miraron fijamente el aparato y, justo antes de que sonara el chasquido, Luc le pasó el brazo a Helena por encima del hombro y la acercó a él. Helena intentó mantener las comisuras de los labios hacia arriba hasta que el flash los deslumbró a todos.

Luc soltó un gemido y se protegió los ojos.

—Por la luz de Sol, creo que me has dejado ciego.

—Soren, mamá quiere que nos hagamos una foto con papá. —A regañadientes, Soren dejó que su hermana lo levantara del sofá y lo llevase a rastras a otra habitación.

Helena los observó alejarse. Sentía como si le aplastaran el pecho. Tenía las manos tan apretadas que se le estaba clavando el cuero de los guantes en los nudillos.

—¿Estás pensando en tu padre? —preguntó Luc con delicadeza.

Lo cierto era que no, pero tal vez ese era el problema. Debería pensar más en toda la gente que había muerto, en aquellos que lo único que tenían en común era haberse cruzado en su camino. No sabía si la vivemancia se trataba de una maldición, pero cada vez estaba más convencida de que ella sí lo era.

—Hel, ¿qué te pasa? —insistió Luc rozándole el brazo.

Helena lo miró y supo que no tenía más remedio que elegir. ¿Luc o Kaine? Solo podría salvar a uno. Tenía que elegir a Luc, pero eso haría que Kaine muriese.

—Tengo que irme. —Hizo amago de levantarse.

—No es verdad. —Luc la cogió de la mano—. Siempre dices lo mismo, pero esta vez no pienso permitirlo. Quédate con nosotros.

Le dedicó una sonrisa arrebatadora y suplicante. Luc nunca había sido demasiado perseverante. Desde siempre, desde que la encontró llorando al salir de su primera clase porque el profesor tenía un acento norteño muy marcado y hablaba demasiado deprisa para ella.

Luc se armó de paciencia y la hizo entrar en razón en un rincón lleno de polvo de la biblioteca. A la semana siguiente, el profesor habló más despacio y dejó escritos en la pizarra todos los conceptos clave para que Helena pudiera anotarlos y estudiar con calma. Tener a Luc en su vida siempre había sido algo mágico.

No tenía por qué molestarse en hacer todas esas cosas por ella, pero lo hacía, y las seguía haciendo. Desde el primer día que la conoció, decidió que quería que fuese su amiga. Y si eso implicaba estar sentado durante horas en la biblioteca esperando a que Helena terminara los deberes, eso hacía, a pesar de que odiaba los deberes.

Helena no era capaz de imaginar sus años en la Academia sin Luc. Era como imaginar un mundo sin sol.

—Venga, dime, ¿qué pasa? —preguntó, inclinándose hacia delante hasta que quedaron cabeza con cabeza.

Todo iba mal. Todo iba mal y seguiría así, y no era culpa suya, pero eran ellos quienes lo sufrían. No podía decirle eso, claro. Sería demasiado cruel acabar con todo, confesar que toda su vida se había basado en una mentira.

—Están tan contentos que casi me da miedo —respondió al final.

Luc asintió despacio, parecía menos preocupado.

—Lo sé. Cuesta creer que todo vaya a acabar. No parece real. —Le dio un suave empujón con el hombro—. Por eso es importante tener gente que te ponga los pies en la tierra. —Miró a la habitación de al lado, donde Lila y Soren estaban arrodillados junto a su padre. Rhea les estaba haciendo una foto—. Cuando me parece imposible, me ayuda pensar en todo lo que me espera en la vida.

Helena sintió una presión en el pecho y se preguntó a qué fantasía se aferraría Luc para despertarse cada mañana. Como no dijo nada, su amigo le dedicó una sonrisa traviesa.

—Nos iremos de viaje, como dijimos. Cuando la guerra acabe y todo vuelva a su cauce, a Ilva no le importará seguir gestionándolo todo un poco más. No podremos hacer el viaje largo que planeamos, pero, si esperamos a la época de sublimación, podemos visitar Etras y pasar allí una semana antes de que suba la marea. Siempre he querido ver las ciudades perdidas. Todavía tengo en la pared el mapa que me regalaste.

—Eso no va a pasar, Luc —replicó Helena en un susurro. Si él quería creerse esa mentira, estaba bien, pero ella no pensaba hacerlo. No podía participar en sus engaños.

—¿Qué?

Helena miró los guantes que cubrían sus manos, sintiéndose hueca por dentro. Tragó saliva.

—Cuando todo esto acabe, no quiero que pienses que seguiremos siendo amigos. Creo que será lo mejor para los dos.

—¿Por qué? —Parecía horrorizado.

—Porque ya no soy tu amiga. La Helena Marino que conociste murió hace seis años en un hospital de campaña. Ya no existe. Tienes que dejarla marchar.

Pero no lo hizo. De hecho, Luc volvió a tomarla de la mano. Tenía la cara compungida, aunque seguía siendo tan bello como siempre.

Incluso en lo más crudo del invierno, parecía bañado por la luz del sol. Aunque no fueran una extensión de la divinidad, los Holdfast tenían un aspecto que merecía ser inmortalizado en mármol. Habían nacido para pasar a la eternidad, como el sol. Helena no era un planeta ni un ser celestial. Solo era un ser humano atado al presente, a la brevedad de la existencia, y sentía cómo se le agotaba el tiempo.

—No, no pienso dejarte marchar —dijo—. No puedo. Hel, dime qué te pasa. Lo arreglaré. Tú y yo siempre seremos amigos.

Helena se apartó, sacudiendo la cabeza.

Lo único que conocía Luc era Paladia, la alquimia y la Llama Eterna, junto con sus ideales de purificación entre llamas, pruebas y sacrificios, la pureza a través del sufrimiento. Creía que todo merecía la pena con el tiempo, en esta vida o en la otra.

Si Helena hubiera estado en el frente, tal vez también lo habría creído. Sin embargo, llevaba seis años viendo morir a gente cada día. Había presenciado las consecuencias de todas las batallas, había sufrido la devastación hasta sentir que se asfixiaba. Nada ni nadie la convencería nunca de que ese sufrimiento era algo noble o puro. Ninguna recompensa valía algo así.

Engañar a las personas para que pensaran lo contrario era una crueldad. Pero ¿cómo iba a contárselo a Luc? No podía decirle que nada había tenido sentido, que los milagros en los que creía no eran más que trucos de magia, comprados y pagados con traición. No podía hacerlo.

—Si alguna vez fui amiga tuya, déjame marchar. —Se zafó de su mano y salió corriendo de la casa.

Le latía tan fuerte el corazón que le dolía. La sangre le retumbaba en los oídos hasta el punto de que apenas sentía el viento ni el frío que le abofeteaba las mejillas.

Estaba nevando; los copos caían en espiral a la calle.

Alzó la mirada al cielo. Decían que daba buena suerte que nevara el día del solsticio. Algo resplandeciente en la noche más larga del año.

Se quedó mirando la nieve hasta que el frío le entumeció las manos y los pies. Quiso quedarse allí y morir congelada. Una vez leyó que era la forma más apacible de morir, como quedarse dormido.

El faro de la Llama Eterna ardía en lo más alto. Helena le dio la espalda y deambuló sin rumbo. No tenía adónde ir. Su vida era muy limitada, no tenía hogar más allá de la Academia.

Siguió el único camino que conocía de memoria.

En el Reducto se respiraba una calma aterradora. Las nubes cargadas de nieve reflejaban el brillo tenue y plateado de las lunas. Helena siempre había creído que el Reducto era un edificio feo, sobre todo comparado con las líneas orgánicas y elegantes de la arquitectura de la isla. Sin embargo, la brutalidad del acero, los muros de hormigón y las altas chimeneas le parecían mucho más apropiados para las circunstancias actuales. No quería estar en un lugar bonito.

El Reducto carecía de pretensiones y decoraciones que distrajeran la vista; no ocultaba lo que era, y eso no podía decirse de la ciudad ni de la Academia.

Una mentira. Todo había sido una mentira: los emblemas celestiales que engalanaban la ciudad, los murales, los retratos de los Holdfast donde siempre salía el sol… Todo mentira.

Se le entumeció la cara, pero no logró convencerse de dar la vuelta. Fue directa al módulo, donde la puerta se abrió con facilidad a pesar de tener los dedos rígidos. El viento hacía vibrar las ventanas.

Se sentó a la mesa y apoyó la cabeza en el borde. Cerró los ojos.

La puerta se abrió de golpe.

Helena levantó la cabeza al instante y contempló con asombro que Kaine se encontraba bajo el marco de la puerta. Tenía nieve en el pelo, en las pestañas y en las cejas, como si hubiera atravesado una nevisca.

Sus ojos la encontraron de inmediato y la recorrieron de arriba abajo. Ella le devolvió la mirada y sintió que el deseo la consumía por dentro.

—¿Qué sucede? —preguntó en cuanto cerró la puerta—. ¿Ha pasado algo?

—¿Cómo has sabido que estaba aquí?

La miró con dureza.

—Tengo este sitio vigilado.

Cómo no. Que no hubiera visto a los necrómatas no significaba que ellos no la hubiesen visto a ella.

—¿Por qué estás aquí? —repitió mirándola de arriba abajo otra vez—. Y desarmada, además.

Había escondido las dagas en el laboratorio. Si alguien veía que las llevaba encima, le harían preguntas que no sabría cómo responder y, después de la reacción de Ilva, las consideraba demasiado personales como para mostrarlas.

—N-no sabía que iba a venir. No tenía adónde ir.

—Si no es por un asunto de la Resistencia, no deberías haber venido.

La chica se limitó a asentir. Tenía razón, claro. Debería haber ido al puente.

Y saltar desde allí.

No. Parpadeó para alejar ese pensamiento de su mente. El único motivo por el que Ilva y Crowther le habían mentido todo este tiempo era porque sabían que Kaine captaba sus emociones al vuelo. Como si tuviera sus sentimientos escritos en la cara.

—Tienes razón, lo siento —respondió con voz áspera, apenas un susurro—. Ya me voy.

Se movió con lentitud, intentando no mirarlo, pero, al pasar por su lado, Kaine la tomó del brazo y la giró. La dejó con la espalda contra la pared y la miró fijamente a los ojos.

—¿Qué ha pasado?

—Nada. —Se apresuró a bajar la vista. Sentía su mirada como un hierro candente sobre la cabeza—. Solo… solo he venido porque estaba… preocupada por ti.

Kaine soltó un bufido.

—¿Desde cuándo te preocupas por mí?

Sin pensarlo, levantó la cabeza. Kaine la miraba con dureza, a la defensiva. El hielo se había derretido sobre su cabello en gotas que temblaban y brillaban como si tuviera estrellas en el rostro.

—No lo sé —contestó con sinceridad; era algo a lo que se había acostumbrado casi sin darse cuenta. Kaine resopló de nuevo.

—¿Y ahora qué? ¿No puedes evitarlo?

—He venido porque quería verte. —En cuanto lo dijo, se dio cuenta de que era verdad; había venido por eso. El chico tragó saliva.

—¿Por qué?

Sintió un nudo en la garganta.

—Me da miedo venir un día y que ya... que ya no estés.

Kaine se quedó muy quieto y la miró con detenimiento. Se le notaba indeciso, y había un brillo en sus ojos que Helena no logró descifrar.

—¿Te estás despidiendo de mí, Marino? —preguntó con una sonrisa.

La pregunta la hizo sobresaltarse. Lo cogió por la camisa.

—¡No! No.

Un mes.

Tragó saliva.

—Estaba preocupada y no... no tenía adónde ir.

Ya lo había dicho. Se sentía estúpida por haber confiado a ciegas en todo el mundo. Y ahora era demasiado tarde. Había tardado tanto en darse cuenta de que ya no le quedaba tiempo...

Kaine tenía la mano apoyada sobre su hombro, y ella notaba su calor. Helena se mordió el labio y tragó saliva con dificultad.

—Siempre tienes que volver —afirmó—. ¿De acuerdo? No mueras. Prométeme... —le falló la voz.

—Marino, ¿qué ha pasado? —Intentó apartarse, pero Helena no lo permitió.

—¡Nada! Solo es que pasé un montón de tiempo haciendo tu botiquín y estuve casi una hora enseñándote a-a usarlo, así que... creo que serías muy desconsiderado si... si te m-murieras.

A Kaine se le escapó una carcajada seca. Acto seguido, se acercó tanto que le acarició la coronilla con la barbilla. Soltó un suspiro que sonó algo exasperado.

—Está bien —accedió—, pero solo porque me lo pides tú.

Esas palabras la atravesaron como si le hubiera dado una puñalada en el pecho. Durante mucho tiempo, había pensado que podría con todo. Por la guerra. Por Luc. Que tenía el valor de pagar cualquier precio. Pero ahora sabía cuál era su límite.

Kaine no era inocente, pero tampoco se merecía lo que le harían si lo pillaban. No moriría ni aunque ella pudiera arrancarle el talismán para llevárselo. Acabaría en una especie de limbo maldito dentro de Morrough.

Él apartó la mano de su hombro y dio un paso atrás. Se le notaba cansado.

—No deberías haber venido aquí —repitió—. Pensé que era una emergencia. Si vienes sin motivo, pones en peligro mi tapadera. Tendré que decidir si es necesario acudir o no.

Hasta que no mencionó a Blackthorne, Helena ni siquiera se había planteado lo mucho que se estaba arriesgando Kaine. Crowther e Ilva habían insistido tanto en el peligro que él suponía que jamás había pensado en la amenaza que la Resistencia representaba para Kaine.

Sintió que se mareaba. Siempre pensó que él estaba más a salvo que ella, que era ella la que se arriesgaba al adentrarse en territorio enemigo con un cuerpo mortal. Sin embargo, la realidad no era así. Los espías y exploradores que trabajaban para la Resistencia llevaban pastillas de cianuro para evitar ser interrogados si eran capturados. Para Kaine, eso no era una opción.

Tampoco podía huir, porque Morrough tenía la filacteria. Habría estado más seguro enviando a los necrómatas, pero había venido en persona. Y había venido porque Helena estaba allí.

¿Cómo era posible que Ilva no entendiera lo que eso significaba?

—Lo siento —admitió Helena—. No volveré a hacerlo.

Él no pareció creerla.

—Lo juro —insistió—. No volveré a menos que tenga una razón de peso.

Kaine se limitó a asentir.

—Me has dado tu palabra. Espero que la mantengas.

Sintió un nudo en el estómago. «No confíes en mí. No confíes en la Llama Eterna. Somos unos mentirosos».

Helena asintió.

Cuando Kaine se marchó, Helena se quedó sola en el módulo. Las ventanas seguían vibrando por el viento, y cada vez hacía más frío, pero aun así permaneció allí, pensando qué debía hacer.

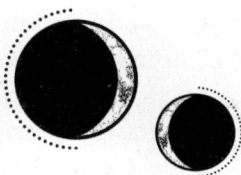

CAPÍTULO 47

Ener 1787

UNA SEMANA DESPUÉS, CUANDO HELENA regresó al Reducto, descubrió una especie de tela gruesa que cubría todo el suelo del módulo, arrugándose a los pies de la puerta.

Ferron ya estaba allí. Se había quitado la capa y el abrigo, vestía con ropa informal y se había arremangado hasta los codos. Helena se quedó inmóvil al verlo.

Los norteños eran tan pálidos que parecían resplandecer en invierno, mientras que la piel de Helena se tornaba macilenta y enfermiza en cuanto escaseaba el sol. Echaba tanto de menos el sol del Sur que, en ocasiones, hasta su piel lo anhelaba.

—No voy a entrenarte para el campo de batalla —afirmó Kaine—. El objetivo de todo esto es asegurarme de que tienes las habilidades mínimas para sobrevivir. A estas alturas, eres capaz de defenderte de los necrómatas, siempre que no sean demasiados, pero, si te encuentras con un inmarcesible, te perseguirá. Y será una suerte si se limita a matarte.

La chica asintió.

—Tus reflejos han mejorado, pero una pelea de verdad es algo distinto. No hay reglas; es contacto físico cercano y sucio. Cada segundo que tardes en atacar o colocarte en posición juega en tu contra. El tiempo nunca estará de tu lado. Tu única ventaja es que van a subestimarte, pero solo la tendrás una vez, en el primer golpe.

¿Por qué siempre que mascullaba algo vagamente parecido a un cumplido venía acompañado de un puñado de críticas?

—De acuerdo.

Kaine la miró de soslayo.

—Careces de complexión de combate o de fuerza, pero puedes usar eso a tu favor. Nadie te considerará una amenaza. Lo más probable es que primero manden a los necrómatas, pero, en cuanto reconozcan tus habilidades, correrás un grave peligro. —La miró de arriba abajo—. Hoy no me apetece recibir una puñalada, así que usaremos dagas de práctica.

Cogió un par de la mesa y se las lanzó. Helena las atrapó a duras penas. Eran ligeras, prácticamente del mismo peso y tamaño que las suyas, pero estaban elaboradas de madera. Apretó la empuñadura y le resultó extraño no poder usar la resonancia.

—Tu objetivo aquí es escapar y dar tres golpes en la pared; si lo logras, lo consideraremos como una huida. O también establecer un canal de resonancia mediante el contacto: eso contará como un golpe. Ya sabes qué hacer si lo consigues.

Parecía demasiado simple, aunque era la primera vez que luchaban en serio, así que quizá solo quería empezar por algo fácil.

—Bien, imagínate que te encuentras en ese lodazal que tanto te gusta. Es un terreno difícil y, cuando estás de rodillas en el barro cogiendo ranas o vete a saber qué, unos necrómatas te descubren. Como no tienes un compañero de combate que te cubra las espaldas, mientras estás luchando con ellos, no te das cuenta de que se acerca un inmarcesible. Él ya sabe que eres una vivemante y está en guardia. Quiere entregarte con vida porque recibirá una recompensa. —Kaine se acercó hasta que sus cuerpos se rozaron—. ¿Qué harías?

Helena apuntó al pecho, pero, en vez de esquivar el golpe o luchar, Kaine le dio en la muñeca con el canto de la mano. Fue un manotazo tan rápido que se le escapó la daga de madera. Él la atrapó antes de que cayera al suelo.

Helena retrocedió e intentó adoptar una mejor posición defensiva, pero la tela del suelo la entorpecía. Un terreno difícil. La mano de Kaine le sujetó la muñeca y la empujó hacia atrás.

Adelantó la mano que empuñaba la daga y puso el arma contra su garganta. Ella intentó bloquearlo con la otra mano, pero Kaine agarró la empuñadura por detrás y se la arrancó de los dedos. La dejó caer al suelo.

—No han pasado ni cinco segundos y ya has perdido las dos dagas —dijo, atrayéndola hacia sí de manera que su aliento le hizo cosquillas en la piel.

Helena intentó darle un empujón. Solo necesitaba establecer un punto de contacto para emplear la resonancia. Al infierno las dagas.

Sin embargo, la mano izquierda de Kaine, que hacía un instante Helena habría jurado que sostenía una daga, de repente estaba vacía y se cerró sobre su muñeca antes de que pudiera rozarlo siquiera. Trató de zafarse, pero él la sujetaba de forma implacable.

—Ahora tienes las dos manos atadas —le explicó como si no se hubiera dado cuenta. Helena se echó hacia atrás para intentar huir.

—Te voy a dar un consejo —comentó con voz tranquila. Ni siquiera parpadeó mientras ella empleaba toda su fuerza y peso para liberarse—. Nunca dejes las muñecas al alcance de nadie. Si te cojo de las muñecas, te tengo totalmente controlada. Me resulta mucho más fácil sujetarte que a ti escapar. Lo mismo ocurre con los pies. No des patadas por encima de la rodilla. Si te atrapan por el tobillo, estarás en el suelo en un abrir y cerrar de ojos. La mayoría de los inmarcesibles pertenecen a los gremios, es decir, pesan el doble que tú. Incluso si consigues matarlos, podrías quedar atrapada. Es mucho más eficaz dar pisotones o rodillazos, sobre todo pisotones, porque ahí empleas todo tu peso, no solo tu fuerza. Da un buen pisotón y apunta con el pie a los tobillos o a las rodillas. Lo importante es dejarlos inutilizados. Si les dislocas una rodilla, tardarán más en regenerarse que con una puñalada. También puedes usar un rodillazo en la entrepierna. —Sonrió de lado—. Hasta los liches detestan eso.

Helena probó a darle un rodillazo, pero Kaine lo esquivó apartándose a un lado.

—¿Ves? Es peligroso perder los brazos.

Helena ya estaba harta de tanto consejo y le dio un pisotón y le propinó una patada en la espinilla. El chico emitió un gruñido.

—Vas mejorando. Aunque, si quisiera capturarte, ya te habría ahogado en la ciénaga para que te desmayaras. O te habría cogido del cuello y te habría metido un rodillazo en la cabeza. Tienes que luchar sucio. Olvídate de todo lo que te hayan contado sobre el honor en la batalla. El honor es sobrevivir.

Kaine la soltó de repente y ella trastabilló hacia atrás. Estaba jadeando, y eso que apenas acababan de empezar. Él la observó con la misma intensidad que un depredador. Helena sintió un escalofrío por la espalda.

—Si te atacan, serán más de uno, y, aunque no fuera así, tú jamás serás tan fuerte ni tan resistente como un inmarcesible. No nos cansamos. Podemos luchar durante horas y, si consigues hacernos daño, nos recuperaremos en minutos, a veces incluso segundos. Pero, si tú resultas herida, perderás velocidad, y entonces estarás peor que muerta.

—Ya lo sé —afirmó Helena con voz cansada.

—Haz lo que tengas que hacer para escapar.

Helena asintió.

—Sé lista. Si tu oponente es más fuerte que tú, aprovecha esa fuerza en su contra. Van a subestimarte, así que se enfadarán si consigues hacerles daño o huir. Eso es un riesgo… y también es una ventaja. Si se enfadan, intentarán ir a por ti, pero también dejarán de pensar con claridad y sus ataques serán más predecibles. En un combate, alguien enfadado actúa como si fuera estúpido.

Le permitió recuperar su daga y se sacó la otra del bolsillo para devolvérsela. Luego la volvió a atacar. Una y otra vez. Siempre ganaba. Aun así, estaba de un humor excelente, algo poco habitual en él. Helena no entendió a qué se debía; normalmente se tomaba sus errores como un insulto personal.

Lo único que ella tenía que hacer para «ganar» un asalto era establecer contacto. En cualquier parte, solo un toque. O, si no, llegar a la pared unos segundos antes de que él la alcanzara.

Sin embargo, ambas cosas le resultaron imposibles. Kaine la desarmaba sin esfuerzo, le arrebataba las dagas de las manos, la derribaba, esquivaba todos sus golpes y se echaba a un lado fácilmente cuando ella lo intentaba atacar. Y, en cuanto ella cometía un error, como, por ejemplo, bajar la guardia, la atrapaba. Kaine no iba armado ni estaba empleando la resonancia; no le hacía falta. Le bastaba con sujetarle del brazo y retorcérselo detrás de la espalda o de cualquier otra forma que la dejara indefensa. Mientras tanto, no paraba de corregirla: le señalaba todo lo que hacía mal, todas las debilidades que podría aprovechar para vencerla.

Helena empezó a enfurecerse cada vez más, algo de lo que Kaine se percató y que pareció divertirle.

—Deberías usar la resonancia —le dijo cuando la atacó por enésima vez y le hizo perder el equilibrio al esquivar un golpe.

Kaine le hizo un barrido con el pie y la derribó. Ella se incorporó con rapidez, pero él la sujetó del tobillo y la arrastró por el suelo. Cuando intentó apuñalarlo, Kaine atrapó ambas muñecas con una sola mano.

La inmovilizó, llevando sus muñecas por encima de la cabeza y la obligó a soltar las dagas. Acto seguido, se montó a horcajadas sobre ella.

—Si fuera Blackthorne, te abriría en canal y me comería tus órganos mientras tu corazón aún late —afirmó inclinándose sobre ella. El peso que ejercía sobre sus brazos la mantenía tan clavada en el suelo que podía notar las frías baldosas a través de la tela.

Entonces Kaine le rozó el vientre con los dedos. Helena sintió un escalofrío interno y un calor que le recorrió todo el cuerpo.

—Se te da fatal el combate cuerpo a cuerpo. Pensaba que las posiciones de combate no eran lo tuyo, pero esto se te da aún peor —dijo, sin apartar la mirada de sus propios dedos.

—Bueno, es algo que no he hecho nunca —repuso Helena sarcástica mientras trataba de liberarse—. Creía que íbamos a luchar con armas.

Kaine soltó una carcajada.

—¿Para qué quiero armas? No puedes vencerme ni con las manos vacías.

Helena lo miró con el ceño fruncido.

—¿Por qué estás de tan buen humor?

El chico arqueó una ceja y se puso en pie. Le extendió una mano para ayudarla a levantarse.

—¿Me prefieres enfadado?

Helena ignoró la pregunta, pero lo observó con atención. A pesar de todas las críticas y advertencias que le había hecho sin parar durante el combate, sobre las formas en que podría haberla matado, seguía extrañamente animado.

Debería haber sentido alivio, porque ya estaba acostumbrada a su rabia, pero en cambio sentía que estaba a punto de derrumbarse solo con mirarlo. Se estaba quedando sin tiempo.

Incluso si lograba manipularlo hasta cierto punto o se aprovechaba de lo obstinado que era, Kaine no era de fiar. Y eso no bastaría para cumplir las exigencias de Ilva.

Recogió las dagas. Sentía una presión constante en el cráneo. Llevaba casi toda la semana sin dormir. En sus sueños, se volvía loca, y se despellejaba viva, como había hecho Basilius, y luego se devoraba a sí misma hasta el infinito, como el dragón del emblema de los Ferron.

La voz de Kaine la sacó de sus pensamientos.

—No temas usar los codos. En un ataque cuerpo a cuerpo, un codazo funciona muy bien. Es más probable que rompas algo con el codo que con el puño.

Se abalanzó sobre ella.

Esta vez, en vez de salir corriendo, Helena fue a su encuentro y, en el último momento, se apartó. Kaine giró, pero la chica había conseguido rozarle la pierna con una de las dagas. De haber sido un cuchillo de verdad, le habría seccionado el tendón y la arteria, lo cual lo habría dejado inutilizado durante unos minutos.

Intentó erguirse para seguir atacando, pero Kaine se impulsó con la otra pierna y la empujó contra el suelo. Ella intentó rodar sobre sí misma, pero estaba atrapada bajo su cuerpo. Pataleó y arañó para liberarse, pero la tenía sujeta por las manos de una forma implacable.

—Si estuviésemos peleando de verdad, ahora mismo estaría muy enfadado —dijo con voz grave mientras se le echaba encima y apretaba sus muñecas contra el suelo. Sus torsos encajaron a la perfección y la boca de Kaine descendió hasta el hueco del cuello de Helena, que notó su aliento cálido sobre la piel.

Ella siguió resistiéndose, arqueando las caderas para liberarse de su agarre. Kaine la soltó de inmediato y se puso en pie entre jadeos. Tenía la mandíbula apretada y los ojos oscurecidos, y estaba algo ruborizado.

—Si alguna vez te sujetan así, no intentes escapar de esa forma —se limitó a decir, y se dio la vuelta como si quisiera recuperar el aliento.

Helena estaba tan cansada que permaneció en el suelo un rato más.

—¿Y cómo lo hago?

—Tal como te he dicho: usa los codos —replicó sin girarse—. Apunta a la nariz o a los ojos. O quédate quieta el tiempo suficiente para que se descuiden y te suelten las muñecas. En cuanto tengas una mano libre, haz lo que quieras, fríeles el cerebro si hace falta. Pero no te… retuerzas.

Ya lo estaba entendiendo. Se incorporó de inmediato.

—De acuerdo.

—Otra vez. —Se dio la vuelta para atacar antes de que le diera tiempo a recuperar las dagas.

Cuando por fin se marchó del Reducto, a Helena le dolía todo el cuerpo. Se detuvo en el puente para curarse los moratones y así caminar con normalidad cuando llegara al puesto de control.

En la biblioteca encontró algunos libros sobre el combate cuerpo a cuerpo y los leyó de principio a fin. Repasó mentalmente todo lo que sabía sobre Kaine, las interacciones que habían tenido, sus palabras, sus gestos, lo que había dicho y lo que no. Quería entenderlo. Después de todo el tiempo que había pasado con Crowther analizando su comportamiento, todavía no tenía ni idea de qué significaba lo que hacía. ¿Qué podría querer Kaine que justificase tantos riesgos? Por mucho que Crowther e Ilva insistieran en que solo era una persona ambiciosa y hambrienta de poder, Helena no lo veía así. Aunque tampoco tenía otra explicación.

En el Cuartel General, quienes habían regresado para el solsticio ya se habían marchado de nuevo. Los héroes tenían que reconquistar más zonas de la ciudad. Nadie se dio cuenta de las horas intempestivas que pasaba Helena yendo del hospital al laboratorio como un fantasma.

Cada vez que volvía al Reducto, retomaban las clases de combate cuerpo a cuerpo. Ella iba armada y él con las manos vacías, como si quisiera enseñarle todas las técnicas para desarmar y matar a los inmarcesibles. Helena deseó que dejara de hacerlo.

—¿Qué sentido tiene que te enseñe si no me estás prestando atención? —exclamó irritado cuando la desarmó sin esforzarse una vez más.

Helena recogió el cuchillo de madera del suelo.

—Es que no le veo la utilidad, sinceramente. Si me ataca un inmarcesible, dudo que vaya a sobrevivir. Y, si lo consigo, seguramente esté tan herida que todo esto carecerá de sentido.

Kaine cambió de postura y la miró con los ojos entornados.

—¿Qué sucede?

—Estoy cansada —confesó Helena con la vista clavada en el suelo—. Estoy cansada de la guerra. Estoy cansada de intentar salvar vidas y no conseguirlo, o de salvarlos para verlos morir más tarde de una forma más sangrienta aún. Es un bucle infinito, lo mismo una y otra vez. No sé cómo salir de él, pero tampoco sé cómo seguir haciéndolo.

—Creía que harías lo que fuera por Holdfast —dijo Kaine mientras caminaba de un lado a otro de la habitación.

—El precio es cada vez más alto —admitió ella en voz baja—. No sé si puedo seguir pagándolo.

Kaine se detuvo en seco.

—Supongo que hasta los mártires tienen un límite.

Helena levantó la cabeza. Por un instante, lo sorprendió mirándola de la forma en que solo lo hacía cuando pensaba que ella no lo veía. No lo había imaginado: estaba ahí, justo bajo la superficie. El deseo que sentía Kaine se le notaba en cómo brillaban sus ojos. Pero no lo dejaba salir. Siempre que ella intentaba acercarse, tentarlo a cruzar esa línea que él mismo había trazado, él respondía con sarcasmo, afilado como una sierra.

Siempre se mostraba más cruel cuando era vulnerable.

Últimamente apenas se había mostrado cruel con ella, lo que le dejaba claro las pocas posibilidades que tenía ahora. Tal vez, si Helena hubiera sido más tenaz, habría encontrado la forma de ignorar el dolor, pero Kaine siempre sabía cómo hacerle daño.

Aun así, tenía que conseguirlo.

Respiró hondo, sacudió la cabeza e intentó concentrarse.

—Solo tengo un mal día —insistió—. Ya estoy bien.

Recuperó el cuchillo y, sin previo aviso, Kaine se abalanzó sobre ella. La chica se hizo a un lado, aprovechando la mano que tenía libre para intentar apartarlo de un empujón, pero Kaine la esquivó con facilidad. En un movimiento rápido, le atrapó la muñeca y le hizo soltar la primera daga. Helena sacó la segunda, le dio un codazo en las costillas y consiguió liberarse.

Adoptó una postura defensiva, recogió la daga larga del suelo y se preparó para seguir luchando. En cuanto se lanzó a apuñalarlo, Kaine la sujetó del brazo y volvió a desarmarla. Helena intentó hacerle una zancadilla, pero él se apartó y le retorció el brazo por detrás de la espalda. Le encantaba hacer eso, se había vuelto casi predecible. Además, siempre relajaba el agarre justo antes de hacer el giro.

Helena arremetió hacia delante y se zafó. Por un momento, disfrutó de la sensación de triunfo, pero enseguida comprendió que él la había soltado.

Aprovechándose del impulso de su arremetida, Kaine la hizo girar, la agarró por la bota y la lanzó contra el suelo. Helena notó que se le escapaba el aire de los pulmones y se quedó jadeando. Kaine se arrodilló a su lado.

—Sigues intentando ganarme en rapidez en vez de con inteligencia. Usa ese cerebro que tienes. Otra vez.

Helena estaba exhausta, pero continuó luchando. Sabía que estaba empezando a entenderlo: veía patrones, oportunidades, se fijaba en las debilidades. Aún no era lo bastante rápida para aprovecharlo, pero lo haría con el tiempo.

Consiguió desestabilizarlo en dos ocasiones, aunque Kaine siempre se recomponía. Cuando trató de sujetarla de nuevo, Helena giró a un lado aprovechando la fuerza residual del movimiento. Al final, cayeron al suelo y Kaine se golpeó contra la pared. Ella aprovechó entonces para arrinconarlo. Aunque su contrincante tenía la mano alrededor de su garganta, Helena sostenía la daga contra la suya y la palma de su mano le sujetaba el pecho: lo estaba atravesando con su resonancia.

Helena sentía el latido de su corazón como si lo tuviera en la mano. Se le escapó una risa por la sorpresa y los dos se quedaron muy quietos. Estaban tan cerca que casi rozaban sus rostros.

—Y ya está —concluyó Kaine respirando con dificultad—. Atraviésame, ahí mismo.

Ella levantó la cabeza y lo miró intensamente. Kaine la observaba en silencio, no iba a hacer nada por detenerla. Estaba a la espera.

La sonrisa de Helena se desvaneció y lo contempló con horror.

Esa amargura en sus ojos… Por fin lo entendía todo. Había estado esperando a que lo traicionara.

Por eso se había contenido.

Siempre lo había sabido, incluso antes de que Helena lo supiera, y aun así la había enseñado a luchar.

No necesitaba a Crowther ni ningún libro para interpretar lo que veía en su rostro. Lo notaba: era calor en el vientre, una presión en el pecho, una palpitación en las venas.

Sentía la calidez de su mano en la garganta y cómo recorría con su pulgar la cicatriz que tenía bajo la mandíbula.

Helena se inclinó y movió la mano del pecho al hombro. Lo atrajo hacia sí y lo besó.

No fue un beso lento ni tierno. No fue un beso impulsado por el alcohol o la inseguridad.

Fue un beso nacido de la rabia, la desesperación y un deseo tan ardiente que amenazaba con convertirlos en cenizas.

Seguramente fuera un beso de despedida.

Quería que Kaine lo supiera, que entendiese que era real. Para ella siempre había sido real.

Kaine se quedó paralizado en cuanto sus labios se encontraron. Helena notó cómo le ponía la mano en el hombro y pensó que la apartaría de un empujón. Aun así, lo besó con más intensidad, aferrándose a su camisa, moviendo los labios con desesperación.

Aunque él vaciló un instante, de repente algo en su interior cedió, como una presa que se rompe, y Helena se ahogó en él.

La abrazó y le devolvió el beso con intensidad.

Compartían una pasión desbordante.

La tensión, la espera. Los meses de anticipación. Después de que le dijeran que había venido para esto, que solo la quería por esto. Era un truco que escondía sus verdaderos motivos. Cuando Kaine exigió que fuera ella quien acudiese, había utilizado el mismo juego de distracción que le había enseñado a ella para proteger sus recuerdos.

Una mentira…, hasta que dejó de serlo.

De algún modo, Helena no había respondido a sus expectativas, y aun así lo había manipulado hasta convertirse en la obsesión que él solo había fingido tener. Kaine le rodeó el cuello con su manos y luego deslizó los dedos entre sus trenzas sin parar de besarla. Al final, terminó colocado encima de ella, sobre el suelo.

Helena introdujo sus dedos por debajo de su camisa, recorriendo el hueco de sus clavículas y la curva de su cuello. Le pasó la mano por el cabello y quiso perderse por completo en esta intimidad. Después, le clavó las uñas en sus hombros mientras sentía las cicatrices de su espalda, percibiendo cómo vibraba la energía en su interior.

Aunque en ocasiones se mostrara frío, un dragón era un símbolo perfecto para los Ferron: levantaba muros de hielo a su alrededor, pero había fuego en su corazón.

Kaine le arrancó la camisa de un tirón. Helena lo atrajo hasta que sus cuerpos se encontraron piel con piel. Lo mordió sin pensar, impulsada por una voracidad insaciable que no conseguía entender, un hambre de sentimiento, de cercanía, de dejar de sentirse vacía. Quería acurrucarse en su cuerpo hasta fundirse con él.

La ropa de Helena fue desapareciendo a medida que las manos de Kaine recorrían sus costillas, su cintura. La besó en los pechos, presionando el cuerpo contra sus piernas, acariciándole el muslo mientras le subía la falda.

Todo ocurrió muy deprisa. Helena nunca había creído que sería tierno o pausado, pero fue como una colisión, como si ambos se estrellaran. Un alud de piel y dientes que la arrasó.

Cuando Kaine se introdujo en su cuerpo, el corazón de Helena se detuvo por un instante. Abrió los ojos de par en par. Se mordió la lengua con tanta fuerza que saboreó la sangre. Los cerró de nuevo, apretándolos. Él se detuvo y la besó con una pasión tan honda que la atravesó hasta los huesos. Helena apoyó el rostro contra el suyo, pero el dolor seguía ahí.

Sabía que, si no se hacía poco a poco, le dolería. Y aun así lo prefirió de esa manera.

Había cosas que, sencillamente, tenían que doler. Había seducido a Kaine sabiendo perfectamente que era una línea que él no quería cruzar. Había insistido una y otra vez hasta lograrlo, porque estaba desesperada.

Se merecía ese dolor.

El cuerpo de Kaine la cubría por completo; sus labios le rozaban el nacimiento de su cabello. Le rodeó los hombros con sus brazos y la sostuvo contra su pecho. Helena abrió los ojos. Quería saber cómo se sentía.

Incluso en ese momento tenía la mandíbula tensa y estaba en guardia. Su boca estaba fruncida en una fina línea.

Pero sus ojos…

En ese momento, Helena lo comprendió.

Era suyo.

Y darse cuenta de ello le rompió el corazón.

Kaine dejó caer la cabeza contra su hombro y gimió sobre su piel, acercándola más, y, de repente, el acto dejó de ser placentero solo para él. Helena sintió el calor extendiéndose en su interior, mientras su autocontrol desaparecía completamente. Pero al mismo tiempo surgieron la vergüenza y la culpa, frías y amargas como el agua del mar, hasta que llegó al borde del desgarro.

Kaine se estremeció. Emitió un gemido grave y se relajó, sin dejar de abrazarla. Su respiración le rozó la piel mientras le dejaba un beso en el hombro desnudo.

Ella permaneció quieta, sintiendo el peso de Kaine encima. De repente era consciente de lo frío que estaba el suelo. La tierra, la gravilla y la tela áspera le arañaban la piel hasta dejársela en carne viva.

Lo único en lo que pensaba era el alivio que sentía de que todo hubiese terminado antes de que pasara algo más.

Ni siquiera las prostitutas caían tan bajo como para deleitarse de su trabajo como ella había estado a punto de hacer.

Intentó mantenerse quieta, sin temblar. El cuerpo de Kaine y sus jadeos eran lo único que le proporcionaba calor en ese lugar tan frío. Pero entonces él se apartó con rigidez. Tenía el rostro desencajado y, sin mirarla siquiera, se puso en pie y comenzó a vestirse.

Helena se incorporó poco a poco, observándolo, sin saber qué tenía que hacer.

Kaine cada vez estaba más pálido, su semblante era de incredulidad.

—Joder… —murmuró pasándose la mano por el pelo. Después se puso la camisa. Empezaba a respirar con dificultad. En cuando tuvo la camisa puesta, intentó abrocharse los botones con torpeza y, cuando descubrió que le faltaba uno, se quedó paralizado.

Se llevó una mano a la boca como si estuviera a punto de vomitar.

Tragó saliva y cerró los ojos. Respiró hondo antes de volverse hacia Helena con un gesto de frialdad. Le dedicó una mirada fugaz, pero no tardó en apartar la mirada. Perdía color a cada segundo.

—¿Eras… eras virgen?

Helena bajó la vista. Tenía una mancha de sangre en la parte superior del muslo. No le extrañaba que le hubiera dolido.

Juntó las rodillas de golpe y se bajó la falda.

—Supuse que lo preferirías así —replicó sin querer pensar en todo lo que esa frase implicaba realmente.

Cuando una chica respetable perdía la virginidad, lo perdía todo: su carrera, su educación, la alquimia. Solo las vírgenes recibían la gracia de Lumitia. Si Helena fuese alguien importante, Kaine se vería obligado a casarse con ella. Una indiscreción así fue lo que motivó el matrimonio de sus padres.

Evidentemente, él jamás la consideraría alguien importante. Sintió una presión en el pecho.

—Yo no… —le falló la voz—. Habría… habría sido más amable… si lo hubiera sabido.

Helena encogió las piernas, como si hacerse más pequeña pudiera protegerla de la vulnerabilidad que sentía.

—No quería que lo fueras —dijo en voz baja. Le temblaron las manos cuando se dispuso a vestirse.

Kaine se quedó en silencio. Helena supo que había cambiado algo entre ellos, pero no entendía por qué había trazado esa línea, por qué justo ahora.

Debía de ser por el sello de la espalda. La había besado justo después de curarse, después de haber interiorizado todos sus efectos. La quería para él. El sello lo había puesto en una encrucijada, por eso se había mostrado tan distante después de aquello. Porque tal vez, si cedía aunque fuera una sola vez, eso bastaría para desequilibrar la balanza. Quizá ya no había vuelta atrás, había tomado su decisión.

Obsesivo y posesivo.

Lo tenía en sus manos, si era lo bastante lista para aprovecharlo.

Lo tenía de rodillas, dispuesto a cualquier cosa, tal como Ilva le había pedido.

Aunque todavía no sabía cómo hacerlo. Era como si Ilva y Crowther consideraran importante que Kaine se hubiese acostado con ella, y por eso esperaban que lo hiciera el primer día.

Helena no sabía si reír o llorar, así que su expresión solo logró quedarse entre el dolor y la sonrisa.

—Vaya, pareces satisfecha de haberte vendido como una puta barata —comentó Kaine con una expresión amarga y despectiva.

Ella se quedó inmóvil y notó que se le nublaba la vista.

—Ese era mi trabajo —repuso en voz baja—. Siempre supiste que esa era mi misión.

—Por supuesto —dijo sin más, mirando a su alrededor como si no pudiera creer que estuviera allí. Los brazos le colgaban inertes a los lados—. Pero... nunca pensé que lo conseguirías. —Se produjo una pausa mientras Helena terminaba de vestirse—. No tenía pensado traicionar a la Resistencia —admitió entonces—. No era mi plan. Ya estabais perdiendo cuando os hice la oferta y, aun así, es probable que acabéis perdiendo igualmente, pero a mí siempre me dio igual. Yo solo quería vengar a mi madre.

Frunció los labios y bajó la mirada al suelo.

—Por desgracia, cuando tuve la oportunidad de ofrecer mis servicios, ya llevaba demasiado tiempo muerta y el informe de un coronel aseguraba que había fallecido por causas naturales. Así que ¿qué había que vengar? —Había amargura en su voz, aunque se mostraba impasible—. Sabía que Crowther solo consideraría mi propuesta si pensaba que era tan valioso como las cuerdas que pudiera mover, por eso le di un cabo suelto al que aferrarse. —Su voz se volvió más seca, más mordaz—. Estuve dándole vueltas a qué podía ofrecerme la Llama Eterna. El perdón, por supuesto, eso era evidente. Pero estabais perdiendo, y todo el mundo lo sabía. Así que entendí que necesitaba un contacto, alguien que se encargara de llevar mensajes y acudir cuando yo lo pidiera. No quería que Crowther eligiera a uno de sus esbirros, así que se me ocurrió que si exigía a alguien concreto me verían como lo que ellos creían que era.

Tragó saliva.

—Pero la Llama Eterna valora demasiado a sus familias de la nobleza. Tenía que encontrar a alguien que consideraran prescindible, y Crowther me observaba, esperando una respuesta. Tenía que improvisar. Y entonces recordé tu nombre de las listas de exámenes. Cuando dije «Helena Marino», a Crowther le brillaron los ojos de tal forma que supe que había mordido el anzuelo. —Puso una mueca de desprecio—. Como si fuera a traicionar al Sumo Nigromante por ti. Sabía que te darían órdenes de someterte a esta supuesta obsesión mía, para asegurarse de que no me aburriera ni cambiase de opinión. Pero a mí eso me daba igual. No eras nadie, solo el perrito faldero de Holdfast. Pensé que sería divertido ver cómo lo intentabas.

Kaine apartó la vista con el rostro sombrío.

—Pero entonces... tú... —Negó con la cabeza—. En realidad, da igual, has superado mis expectativas. O tal vez esté demasiado cansado y triste para alejarte de mí. Tú ganas. —La miró, apenas unos segundos, con gesto amargo y burlón—. Buen trabajo.

Después se apoyó en la pared y cerró los ojos. Helena lo observó en silencio, escéptica. No estaba segura de qué pretendía con esta confesión. Parecía que estaba siendo sincero, y todo encajaba con la forma errática, contradictoria, con la que siempre se había relacionado con ella. Pero no entendía a qué se refería cuando hablaba de vengar a su madre. ¿Vengarla de qué?

—¿Cambiaste de bando solo porque tu madre murió de un infarto? —Se le escapó un bufido. Se puso en pie, ignorando el dolor que sentía—. Su muerte no fue culpa de nadie. Y, aunque lo hubiera sido, ¿asesinaste al principado Apollo arrancándole el corazón sin querer? Saliste corriendo con su corazón en la mano, te uniste a los inmarcesibles, la viste morir, seguiste siendo leal... ¿Y entonces qué? ¿Te deprimiste porque no puedes emborracharte y decidiste jugar a los espías?

Lo estaba provocando. Sabía que así lo enfurecería. Confiaba en que, si lo provocaba lo suficiente, por fin le contaría la verdad.

Kaine abrió los ojos, sorprendido; se habían vuelto plateados. El rubor coloreó sus mejillas hundidas.

—Que te follen.

—Ya lo has hecho tú —replicó con una mueca.

Notaba la espalda llena de moratones, la piel en carne viva por haberse arañado contra el suelo, y le dolía el bajo vientre como si le hubieran dado un puñetazo. Jamás había tenido tanto frío como en ese momento, ahí de pie, pero estaba tan enfadada que lo único que quería era sacarlo todo. Se habían acabado los jueguecitos.

—Eres un monstruo —lo insultó cruzándose de brazos—. ¿De verdad esperas que me olvide de lo que has hecho? ¿Que crea que has subido de rango por la maravillosa persona que eres? ¿Que mencionar la muerte de tu madre borre todo lo demás? Todos hemos perdido a alguien, y muchos han perdido más de lo que tú perderás jamás. Si quieres culpar a Morrough de su muerte, no deberías haber pasado tanto tiempo apoyándolo después de que muriera. Fuiste tú quien dio comienzo a esta guerra. Tú elegiste convertirte en uno de los inmarcesibles.

Kaine estaba tan cabreado que incluso Helena podía sentir la vibración de su resonancia a su alrededor. Le hacía cosquillas en la piel y, si no la hubiera contrarrestado con su propia resonancia, le habría hecho daño.

—¿Quieres saber por qué soy así? —preguntó con lentitud, mostrando los dientes como si fueran colmillos—. Una vez me preguntaste si esto era un castigo y te dije que no. Y no te mentí. Fue el trato que hice.

Se acercó a ella, y la maldad que irradiaba era tan intensa que Helena sintió que la habitación se encogía.

—Después del fracaso de mi padre, después de que revelara los planes de Morrough, ¿crees que el Sumo Nigromante se mostró comprensivo?

La chica lo miró, incapaz de moverse.

—Yo aún estaba en la Academia, acabando el curso. ¿Sabes quién estaba con Morrough cuando llegó la noticia de que habían capturado a mi padre y había confesado su traición? —En el rostro de Kaine se mostraba una expresión de dolor—. Cuando volví a casa, mi madre ya llevaba semanas encerrada en una jaula. Morrough la estaba torturando. —Empezó a respirar de forma entrecortada—. Tú te vendiste para salvar a una persona que te importa. Pues yo hice lo mismo. ¿Qué pretendías que hiciera? ¿Que me negara a matar al principado Apollo sabiendo que entonces me harían sufrir a mí en su lugar? Así —se señaló a sí mismo—, así fue como demostré mi lealtad. Así conseguí que… que dejara de hacerle daño —terminó con el pecho encogido.

Helena estaba empezando a marearse.

—La Resistencia… Yo no lo sabía.

Kaine le dedicó un gesto de desprecio y se dio la vuelta.

—Nunca se recuperó —continuó en voz grave—. Morrough y Bennet andaban escasos de sujetos para experimentar en aquella época. Les gustaba hacerlo juntos. En ocasiones mi madre se pasaba horas gritando. Hacían con ella experimentos que luego revertían para que no le quedaran secuelas. —Se apartó el pelo de la cara y tragó saliva varias veces—. Estuvieron así todo el verano. No pude… hacer nada, salvo decirle que lo sentía. Que asesinaría a Apollo y la rescataría, que no fallaría.

Se apoyó contra la pared como si fuera a caerse. Las palabras, al principio llenas de rabia, se fueron impregnando de la pena que parecía abrirse paso desde su interior.

—Cuando el principado murió y entregué su corazón, el Sumo Nigromante la dejó salir y nos obligó a marcharnos antes de que la Llama Eterna viniera a buscarme. Pero para entonces mi madre… Nunca fue una mujer especialmente fuerte. Cuando estaba embarazada, no hizo caso a los médicos, que le advirtieron de lo mucho que le costaría tenerme. Una vez que dio a luz, se volvió una persona frágil. Mi padre siempre me decía que tenía que cuidar de ella, que yo era el… el responsable. De niño me obligaba a jurarlo una y otra vez, debía prometer que siempre cuidaría de ella. Quise sacarla del país. Lo había preparado todo, pero… ella no quiso hacerlo. No quería irse sin mí. Me dijo que no podía dejarme atrás.

Se llevó el borde de las manos a los ojos.

—Intenté buscar una salida. Los inmarcesibles organizaban fiestas y mi madre me dijo que debía ir yo también, porque pensaba que, si tenía amigos, tal vez me… me protegerían. Aunque no me invitaron por eso. Querían probar hasta dónde se podían provocar lesiones duraderas en alguno de nosotros, y yo era el más joven. Fue la elección más fácil. —Parpadeó como si hubiera dejado de ver lo que lo rodeaba—. Pensé que mi madre estaría dormida cuando regresé, pero me había esperado despierta. Estaba en la puerta y, en cuanto me vio, empezó a gritar. Yo no paraba de decirle que me iba a curar, pero ella insistía en que era culpa suya. Se le paró el corazón y yo… yo no pude…

Entonces, la voz se le rompió y Kaine se dejó caer hasta el suelo, estremeciéndose como si estuviera a punto de partirse en dos. Después volvió a hablar, pero lo hizo con un tono apagado, desprovisto de emociones.

—Cuando murió, empezaron a vigilarme. Morrough sabía que me había unido a la causa por ella. Tuve que ganarme su confianza antes de arriesgarme a hacer nada más. Yo no soy uno de tus amigos idiotas que creen que un solo acto de sacrificio puede cambiarlo todo. Si quería vengarme de verdad, Morrough no podía verlo venir.

Helena permaneció quieta, horrorizada. ¿Por qué nadie sabía todo esto?

—Lo siento mucho —dijo, algo mareada de la impresión.

—No necesito tu compasión fingida, Marino —le escupió Kaine, aunque le temblaba la voz.

Seguramente nunca se lo había contado a nadie. La muerte de su madre había pasado desapercibida. En mitad de una guerra, ¿por qué le iba a importar a alguien un infarto cuando había gente muriendo en el campo de batalla?

Sin embargo, Helena sabía que un vivemante podía llevar a cabo torturas espantosas y arreglarlo después para no dejar rastro. Ya imaginaba el desgaste que eso podía pasarle a un corazón con el paso del tiempo. Kaine había cargado con la culpa durante años y había intentado enmendar sus errores de la mejor manera para vengarla, a pesar de conocer el terrible castigo que le aguardaba.

—No estoy fingiendo —replicó—. Lo siento. Siento mucho lo que le pasó.

Se acercó a Kaine, que parecía absolutamente destrozado, como si estuviera a punto de desmoronarse. Helena posó una mano en su brazo, con cuidado, como si esperara que fuera a darle un empujón. Pero a él solo le temblaban los hombros y dejó caer la cabeza. Ella lo envolvió entre sus brazos, y él la abrazó con fuerza mientras lloraba.

—No puedo… no puedo… —decía una y otra vez.

Helena no sabía qué hacer. Le pasó los dedos por el cabello y siguió abrazándolo.

—No puedo… no puedo volver a hacerlo —consiguió decir entre sollozos—. No puedo volver a preocuparme por nadie. No lo soportaría.

A ciegas, buscó su rostro. Colocó la mano en su mejilla y sintió que las lágrimas recorrían la palma de su mano hasta su muñeca.

—Lo siento. Lo siento mucho, Kaine —repitió una y otra vez.

Se estaba disculpando por todo.

Por primera vez, Kaine Ferron se estaba mostrando como un ser humano. Helena había derribado sus muros, había desmontado todas sus capas defensivas de maldad y crueldad, y había descubierto que tenía el corazón roto.

Podía aprovecharse de eso.

CAPÍTULO 48

Ener 1787

Cuando Kaine dejó de llorar, Helena se apartó para observarlo con detenimiento.

Su expresión se había vuelto cauta y agriada, como si el llanto hubiera borrado toda su ternura y, en su lugar, solo quedara el veneno.

Helena sabía que lo tenía bajo control. Había cumplido con las órdenes que le dieron y, aun así, no estaba segura de cómo demostrarlo, de cómo poner a prueba su lealtad de una forma tangible.

Ilva no le daría crédito a lo que Helena sentía. Que Kaine se preocupara por ella no era lo mismo que tenerlo atado como un perro, y eso era justo lo que Ilva había pedido.

—Si de verdad quieres que gane la Llama Eterna, ¿por qué continúas ascendiendo de rango? ¿Qué pretendes hacer? —preguntó.

Los ojos de Kaine eran como un espejo, en ellos podía verse reflejada hasta la más mínima expresión. Él hizo un gesto burlón. De no ser porque su rostro aún estaba humedecido, jamás habría dicho que había estado llorando.

—Siempre supe que el único motivo por el que aceptasteis mi oferta era porque estabais desesperados. La Llama Eterna afirma ser una organización respetable, pero Crowther es una serpiente. Y da igual lo que prometa Ilva Holdfast, al final no es más que la mano derecha del principado, y encima un lapsus. Sabe perfectamente que, si ganan, la Llama Eterna decidirá cuáles de sus acciones son legítimas y cuáles no, y las que no gusten a los Holdfast desaparecerán en el viento. Di por hecho que, una vez que dejase de ser útil, pondríais en riesgo mi tapadera para aprovecharos de la inestabilidad que causaría la traición. —Enseñó los dientes—. Así que he intentado llegar lo más alto posible, para que las consecuencias sean mucho más devastadoras.

Helena frunció el ceño sin apartar la mirada. Aquello le resultaba demasiado generoso por su parte. Aunque quisiera vengar a su madre, Kaine no sentía ningún aprecio por la Llama Eterna. Para él, no eran más que un medio para conseguir un fin.

—¿Por qué me has besado? —preguntó de repente—. ¿De qué ha servido... todo esto?

Helena bajó la vista, sin estar segura de qué responder.

—Yo no sabía que debías morir una vez que retomaron los puertos. Por lo visto, era algo evidente, pero no caí en la cuenta.

Kaine soltó una carcajada amarga, pero ella no fue capaz de mirarlo a los ojos cuando volvió a hablar.

—Creían que morirías por el sello de la espalda. De hecho, lo estaban... esperando. Cuando supieron que habías subido de rango, dieron por sentado que habías estado enfrentando a un bando contra otro para ser el único que resultara victorioso cuando todo terminara.

—¿Y tú también lo crees? —le preguntó en voz baja. Helena tragó saliva, todavía incapaz de mirarlo a los ojos.

—No, pero da igual lo que yo piense. Justo antes del solsticio, me dijeron que tenía un mes para conseguir que te arrastraras o matarte. Si no, Morrough se encargaría de ello.

Kaine volvió a reírse.

—Me queda una semana, por lo que veo. Entonces ¿esto era un polvo de despedida? ¿El último pago por los servicios prestados?

Helena sintió un escalofrío por todo el cuerpo.

—No. Yo... solo quería... —Sintió que se le formaba un nudo en la garganta. Lo agarró por la camisa, con ganas de sacudirlo. Odiaba la forma en que cambiaba de personalidad. Pasaba de mostrarse vulnerable a tener una actitud cruel en cuestión de segundos—. Solo tengo que demostrar que harás lo que yo te pida. Si lo consigo..., no te matarán.

Lo miró desesperada. Él arqueó las cejas con sorna.

—¿En serio? ¿Eso es todo? Si les sirvo, podré seguir existiendo tan tranquilamente como hasta ahora, siempre que les sea más útil vivo que muerto, ¿no? Qué oferta más generosa. ¿Cómo podría rechazarla?

Helena lo soltó y se rio con algo de amargura.

Kaine no quería que lo salvaran. Ella solo había empeorado las cosas, y solo porque Ilva y Crowther no le habían contado la verdad. Le habían hecho creer que todo era real, pero en el fondo no importaba; nunca importó lo que ella creyera o dejara de creer… porque Kaine siempre lo había sabido.

Respiró hondo para aclarar sus pensamientos, pero su mente se resistía a asimilar la realidad. No podía acabar así. Había hecho lo que le habían pedido. Había cumplido con las órdenes. No debería tener que tomar esta decisión.

—He… he seguido las órdenes. No puedo elegirte a ti. Está en juego la vida de mucha gente —confesó con la voz temblorosa.

—Lo sé.

Helena abrió y cerró la boca, pero no podía añadir nada más.

—De acuerdo —aceptó al cabo de un rato con tono distante. Sentía como si la hubiesen apuñalado; la cruda realidad era como una daga de acero clavada en el corazón—. ¿Quieres…? —Le falló la voz—. ¿Quieres que lo haga yo? ¿O… te da igual?

Sabía que Ilva querría recuperar la gema, si es que eso aún era posible, pero a Helena ya le daba absolutamente igual.

Kaine soltó un bufido.

—Has perdido la oportunidad.

Helena tragó saliva varias veces hasta reunir el valor necesario para hablar.

—Lo siento.

Él no respondió. Sus ojos no mostraban ni una pizca de arrepentimiento, solo una cruel satisfacción.

Helena sentía que el aire desaparecía de la habitación. Por más que tratara de respirar, ya no quedaba oxígeno. Oía un pitido resonando en sus oídos. Buscó a ciegas su bolsa e intentó recordar dónde la había dejado. Con un movimiento titubeante, se puso de rodillas, pero su mente se negaba a funcionar.

—¿Y qué pasará contigo?

La chica parpadeó.

—¿Conmigo?

—Sí. —Kaine se inclinó hacia delante y le sostuvo la barbilla de manera que la luz de la ventana iluminó su rostro con un pálido rayo del sol de invierno—. ¿Qué pasará contigo?

—¿Cuando… tú ya no estés?

Kaine asintió.

—No lo sé —respondió con una carcajada nerviosa, y se apartó—.

Como bien dijiste, siempre he sido prescindible, así que tal vez me ofrezcan al siguiente espía.

—No bromees con eso. Quiero una respuesta sincera —expresó con un deje mordaz en la voz. Helena lo miró a los ojos.

—Te prometí que sería tuya. Me obligaste a prometerlo. No he hecho más planes.

La rabia se dibujó en su rostro.

—Ahora que voy a morir, seguro que tienes ganas de hacer otras cosas.

Helena le acarició con los dedos ahí donde estaba el corazón.

—No, estoy… agotada.

Al ponerse en pie, recordó a Luc en lo alto de la Torre de Alquimia, demasiado cerca del borde. En aquel momento, no entendió por qué estaba allí, cómo era posible que ni ella ni las demás personas que lo necesitaban fueran suficientes para darle ganas de vivir. Ahora, ese mismo abismo parecía llamarla, un abismo que se abriría tan pronto como tomara esta decisión.

Todo le daba vueltas. No podía concentrarse, porque lo único que escuchaba era el latido de su propio corazón.

«Todo el que te toca muere».

—¿Qué es lo que quieren? —preguntó Kaine en un susurro. Helena lo miró.

—¿Cómo?

—¿Lo de… arrastrarse es algo literal o Ilva tiene algo más constructivo en mente?

Helena notó un nudo en la garganta.

—T-tendría que preguntar.

—Descúbrelo. Lo haré. —Parecía exhausto, pero algo ardía en su interior.

—¿Lo dices en serio? —preguntó Helena, aunque estaba segura de que había gato encerrado. Kaine no respondió—. ¿Por qué te estás ofreciendo? —insistió alzando la voz con un matiz de histeria.

Él la miró durante unos instantes.

—Acabo de caer en la cuenta de algo que he pasado por alto. Hasta ahora no había caído en que te he convertido en una baza a mi favor.

Las palabras le golpearon como una patada en el pecho.

—Ah.

Crowther tenía razón desde el principio: los Ferron eran tan posesivos que preferían devorarse a sí mismos antes que renunciar a algo que consideraban suyo.

—Te traeré la respuesta —respondió Helena.

Kaine se limitó a asentir y apartó la mirada. No dijo nada mientras Helena se ponía la capa, cubriendo la ropa hecha jirones, y cogía su bolsa para marcharse.

Cuando llegó a la puerta, se percató de que hacía un movimiento con la mano, pero, al girarse por última vez, Kaine apartó la vista y apoyó su espalda contra la pared. Se quedó con la mirada perdida, tan pálido que podría haber sido un fantasma.

Al salir del módulo, la recibió un chaparrón. Helena se quedó bajo el agua y trató de recobrar la compostura, aunque no respiraba con dificultad. Estaba al borde del abismo; aún sentía la caída que le esperaba si daba un mal paso.

A pesar de tener la capucha puesta cuando pasó por el puesto de control, los guardias la reconocieron rápidamente y no le hicieron el chequeo. Era un fallo de seguridad, pero lo agradeció. Se desvió de su ruta habitual y se dirigió al punto de encuentro. No podía aparecer por el Cuartel General con esas pintas.

Conforme se acercaba, la devastación de la guerra se hacía patente, igual que ocurría en todos los rincones de la ciudad. Los muros estaban calcinados, deformados por el combate.

El piso franco no era más que un almacén en un sótano.

Al cerrar la puerta tras de sí, notó que sus manos estaban rígidas. No podía dejar de temblar, así que, nada más entrar, encendió un fuego en el hornillo portátil empleando un montón de pedazos de leña y periódicos viejos que había por allí.

Se esforzaba por avivar las llamas, deseando que sus conocimientos de piromancia fueran algo más que teoría, cuando se abrió la puerta. Se giró rápidamente con la esperanza de que no fuera Ivy, aunque si se tratase de un desconocido, sería peor.

Era Crowther. Se detuvo con gesto contrariado.

Helena volvió a mirar el fuego.

—¿Estás herida?

La chica negó con la cabeza, y Crowther la apartó de un leve codazo.

Con solo chasquear los dedos, las llamas se avivaron y la madera crujió y prendió con fuerza. Helena extendió las manos sobre las llamas sin decir nada. Crowther se dirigió a la habitación contigua y volvió con una toalla. Helena la aceptó en silencio y se frotó el rostro hasta que dejó de gotearle el pelo. Sentía sus ojos clavados en ella.

—¿Está hecho? —le preguntó en cuanto Helena dejó la toalla sobre su regazo y volvió a extender las manos sobre el fuego.

Notó que se le formaba un nudo en la garganta, pero, tras un instante de duda, asintió.

—Sí, lo he hecho.

Crowther exhaló un suspiro de alivio y le dio una suave palmada en el hombro.

—Dale el talismán a Ilva.

Helena siguió contemplando el fuego.

—Decía la verdad cuando dijo que quería vengar a su madre.

Crowther suspiró, pero Helena continuó hablando:

—Cuando arrestaron a Atreus, Kaine estaba a salvo en la Academia, pero su madre no. Ya sabes que la vivemancia no siempre deja marcas visibles. Kaine mató al principado Apollo porque era la única forma de salvarla, pero ella nunca se recuperó. Cuando se sufre un estrés prolongado, este puede ocasionar daños en el corazón.

Se produjo un silencio tenso, cargado por el escepticismo de Crowther. Helena no apartó la vista del fuego. Sentía un calor abrasador, pero no retiró las manos. Si se quemaba, tal vez dejase de sentir también el resto del cuerpo.

—De niño, Atreus le hizo prometer a Kaine que cuidaría de su madre, ya que lo culpaba por lo enfermiza que se volvió Enid después del parto. Sin embargo, ella se negó a abandonar Paladia y, al final, la tortura acabó con ella. Murió en casa, pero su muerte no tuvo nada de natural.

No se oía más que el crepitar del fuego.

Era posible que Crowther ya supiera todo eso. Helena no era consciente aún de cuánto le habían mentido él e Ilva; habían decidido contarle que la motivación de Kaine se basaba en el poder porque querían que Helena lo percibiera de esa forma.

Cerró los ojos y deseó desplomarse en el suelo.

—Quiere saber qué queréis. Ilva y tú. Qué prueba de lealtad estáis exigiendo.

Hubo un cambio en el ambiente. Crowther apretó el hombro de Helena y la obligó a levantarse y a mirarlo. Sus ojos la recorrieron de arriba abajo y se detuvieron en algunos detalles al hacerlo.

—¿Qué has hecho? —preguntó al fin.

Helena lo miró a los ojos con la barbilla levantada.

—He cumplido mi misión. Ahora me es leal.

Estaba acostumbrada a que Crowther se mostrara siempre impasible, pero ahora parecía que lo había alcanzado un rayo. Sin mediar palabra, la empujó hacia la ventana, donde había más luz, y le retiró la capa para verla mejor.

Sus trenzas estaban deshechas, con mechones sueltos en todas direcciones. Crowther deslizó los dedos por su cuello y acarició un punto que hizo que ella torciera el gesto de dolor. Antes de que pudiera reaccionar, desanudó el cierre de su capa; empapada por la lluvia, esta resbaló de sus hombros y cayó al suelo con un sonido húmedo y denso. Quedaron al descubierto sus ropas hechas jirones y los moratones que le salían en los entrenamientos, que normalmente se curaba antes de volver.

Helena dio un paso hacia atrás y se encogió entre las sombras. Quiso decir que no era lo que parecía, pero dudaba que la fuera a creer.

—Estoy bien —afirmó, aunque le temblaba la voz—. Tan solo he venido a asearme. Me dijiste que no volviera al Cuartel General con este aspecto.

Crowther frunció los labios hasta convertirlos en una línea tensa y, aunque parecía a punto de replicar, volvió a observarla de arriba abajo y decidió soltarla.

Helena se apartó de un tirón y hundió los hombros. La habitación contigua era un baño, y ella se encerró dentro y contempló su reflejo en el espejo: tenía la piel de un gris macilento, pero sus labios estaban rojos e hinchados. El pelo parecía el nido de un pájaro, y la lluvia solo lo había empeorado.

Apartó la vista y buscó un paño, cualquier cosa con la que asearse. Se quitó la ropa interior y la frotó con fuerza, para intentar que quedara limpia. La humedad fría y punzante que sentía entre las piernas estaba empezando a ponerla histérica.

Las manos le temblaban cuando tiró el paño en una papelera que había debajo del lavabo, y así siguieron mientras se deshacía de las horquillas que tenía enredadas en el cabello.

Empezó a trenzarse el pelo, aunque le ardían los ojos y le temblaba el labio. Se le estremecían tanto las manos que no consiguió estabilizar su resonancia, así que dejó los moratones tal como estaban.

«Cálmate. Solo tienes una oportunidad para convencer a Crowther».

Sin embargo, cuanto más lo pensaba, más se alteraba su respiración.

Se acuclilló, cubriéndose el rostro con las manos hasta que recuperó el control.

Al alzar la vista, volvió a mirar su reflejo. Estaba más delgada que la primavera pasada, cuando vio a Kaine por primera vez. Las mejillas se le habían hundido, dos surcos de agotamiento le marcaban la mirada, y se le notaban demasiado las clavículas. El estrés le había dejado rastro, como una corriente de agua atravesando la arena.

Rebuscó en su bolsa y encontró un bálsamo para los moratones que se aplicó en los labios. Para entonces ya había recuperado el pulso suficiente como para eliminar las marcas con una pizca de resonancia, aunque aquello le borró también el leve rubor de su piel.

Se puso una falda limpia y salió del baño. Todo estaba en silencio.

—Crowther —lo llamó con voz hueca. No obtuvo respuesta.

Fue a la habitación principal; el fuego se había reducido a unas ascuas, y Crowther había desaparecido.

Tragó saliva e intentó no romperse. Por supuesto que se había marchado. No pensaba escucharla. Nadie lo haría. Habría cogido aquello que había venido a buscar y se había ido.

Sintió cómo un pozo de desesperación se le abría en el estómago.

«El plan siempre fue que fracasaras».

La habitación pareció estirarse cuando quiso dirigirse hacia la puerta. Le temblaban demasiado las manos para girar el pomo.

Entonces se abrió, y Crowther volvió a entrar. Estaba chorreando, con el pelo fino pegado al cuero cabelludo. Parecía un gato mojado.

—¿Qué estás haciendo? —le espetó cuando cruzó el umbral—. Siéntate.

Llevaba un paquete de papel en las manos, aunque ya se estaba deshaciendo por culpa de la lluvia. Lo abrió y sacó varios frascos.

—No sabía qué necesitarías —explicó.

Helena contempló los frascos. Debía de haber regresado al Cuartel General y pasado por el hospital. En el punto de encuentro solo había suministros médicos básicos, pero nada de valor o que pudiera escasear. Reconoció su propia letra en las etiquetas.

Al leerlas, se planteó tomar láudano, algo que calmara la nitidez de sus emociones, pero tenía que mantener la cabeza fría. Evaluó la siguiente opción: un anticonceptivo.

—Sabes que no lo necesito —afirmó, y lo dejó en su sitio al tiempo que tragaba saliva.

Lo único útil que había traído era una tintura de valeriana, de las que el hospital empleaba para calmar a los pacientes en estado de shock.

—¿Qué ha pasado? —preguntó Crowther mientras Helena abría el frasco y lo bebía de un trago.

—Ya sabes lo que ha pasado —repuso—. Lo que querías que sucediera cuando me mandaste allí. Simplemente voy un poco lenta.

—Marino. —Había empleado un tono cortante, pero pareció arrepentirse, porque enseguida su voz se suavizó—: ¿Qué ha pasado?

Helena tenía pensado presentarse en el Cuartel General y dar parte sin explicaciones sobre por qué o cómo, mostrarse tranquila y decidida, pero Crowther la había pillado antes de tiempo. Empezó a temblarle la mandíbula.

Se sentía usada. Y, en el fondo, entendía que así era como debía ser. La guerra estaba por encima de las personas. Incluso Luc era solo una figura simbólica, una idea más grande que sí mismo, con independencia de la veracidad de su linaje.

Ella lo sabía y estaba dispuesta a cumplir órdenes. Era consciente de las consecuencias y entendía el sacrificio. No necesitaba que le prometieran nada a cambio; ni recompensas, ni reconocimiento, ni la vida eterna. Hacía lo que había que hacer porque era necesario. Sus superiores lo sabían y, aun así, le habían mentido.

—Le dije a Ilva que únicamente necesitaba más tiempo —se limitó a decir—. Solo ha sido algo… abrupto. Estábamos entrenando. De ahí los moratones.

Crowther no dijo nada, pero Helena notaba su mirada fija, como la de un halcón. Le hubiera gustado saber de qué se estaba dando cuenta, qué estaba analizando de su comportamiento mientras la observaba con tanta atención.

Helena se llevó la mano al esternón y extendió el calor desde la palma de la mano por todo el cuerpo, para así poder dirigirse a Crowther con calma. Era la única forma de que la creyese sin considerarla una histérica.

—Cuando me lo confesó todo, estaba muy alterado. Empezó a llorar después de contarme lo de su madre. Siempre supo que lo ibais a traicionar. Era parte de su plan. Por eso ha subido de rango; imaginó que, cuanto más importante fuera, mayor sería el golpe… cuando muriera.

Le siguió un largo silencio, interrumpido por un suspiro grave de Crowther que hizo que a Helena le latiera fuerte el corazón.

—Si es un mártir tan suicida, ¿por qué quiere cooperar ahora?

Notó que se le cerraba la garganta. Retorció la tela suelta de su falda entre los dedos.

—Bueno, ya no puede negar la obsesión que siente. Creo que no sabe cómo dejarme ir. Tenías razón: los Ferron son posesivos de una forma autodestructiva. Y el sello de la espalda ha agravado esa característica. Me considera una... —tragó saliva— posesión. Creo que eso es lo que ha cambiado. No le importa sobrevivir o no, simplemente no sabe cómo dejarme marchar.

Crowther frunció los labios y se los acarició con el pulgar mientras reflexionaba. Helena lo observó mientras sus propios dedos se retorcían y apretaban hasta que los nudillos quedaron alineados.

—¿Puedes... puedes decírselo a Ilva? Sé que los dos pensáis que me he involucrado demasiado, pero he hecho lo que me pedisteis. Kaine dice que hará lo que queráis. Lo he hecho... He logrado que...

La voz se le quebró y empezó a temblar sin control. Se sujetó el brazo y empleó la resonancia para forzar el efecto de la valeriana. Necesitaba calmarse.

—Sí —accedió Crowther—. Hablaré con Ilva. Has... has hecho lo que te pedimos —carraspeó—. Si Ferron está dispuesto a demostrarlo, eso cambia las cosas.

Helena asintió y miró a su alrededor sin ver nada. No sentía alivio.

—Gracias.

Se dirigió hacia la puerta, aunque no sabía adónde ir. Estaba demasiado alterada para regresar al Cuartel General, pero tampoco podía permanecer ahí.

—Marino.

Helena se encogió. Crowther seguía observándola. La miraba de una forma extraña, como si estuviera viendo más de lo que ella habría querido revelar. El hombre tragó saliva un par de veces y juntó las yemas de los dedos.

—Yo tenía la misma edad que tú cuando los Holdfast me trajeron a Paladia.

Ella dio un paso hacia atrás. Sabía que Crowther había sido uno de los alumnos becados por los Holdfast. Había llegado a Paladia siendo huérfano, rescatado por ellos. Helena nunca se había planteado que sus historias pudieran parecerse.

—Mi familia y todo mi pueblo fueron masacrados por un nigromante. Se alzaron del suelo y me dejaron atrás, en la nieve, para que muriera. Cuando llegó la Llama Eterna, ya no había salvación posible, salvo prender fuego a la aberración en la que se habían convertido. Yo me aseguré de distinguirme mostrando que estaba dispuesto a hacer lo que fuera necesario. Nunca quise la gloria ni me interesaba la Fe, simplemente sabía que alguien tenía que detener la putrefacción. Jamás me he arrepentido de mi decisión.

Se miró la mano derecha, la abrió y cerró con lentitud. Era más pequeña que la otra; los músculos se habían atrofiado con el paso de los años. Guardó silencio durante tanto tiempo que Helena acabó por comprender que aquel relato era como una disculpa velada y que, de algún modo, Crowther la veía ahora como una igual. Helena había hecho algo por él y ahora se arrepentía de haberla tratado con tanta condescendencia.

Pero Helena no quería una disculpa.

—¿Estás…? —Parpadeó y volvió a empezar—: ¿Necesitas… que alguien te cure?

Ella se puso en tensión. Lo último que quería era tener a Elain o a Ivy cerca.

—No ha sido violento —puntualizó. Se cruzó de brazos con fuerza. Su voz sonaba tan contenida que se obligó a calmarse—. Solo fue algo… abrupto. Además —permitió que el veneno impregnara su voz—, sanarme sola formaba parte de las instrucciones que me diste desde el principio, ¿no?

Crowther apartó al vista.

—Si necesitas permiso para algo, te lo firmaré.

—Solo he venido a peinarme y a cambiarme de camisa. No estaba herida —replicó Helena, cada vez más enfadada por esa muestra de preocupación repentina tan tardía.

Le habían dejado claro que estaba sola en esto, pero ahora que había descubierto la trampa, ahora que sabía que la habían vendido sin pensárselo dos veces y para toda la vida, ¿creían que necesitaba su preocupación?

Un calor nauseabundo bullía en el fondo de su estómago. Solo de pensar en lo absurdas que sonaban sus palabras, se le escapó un sollozo a medio camino entre la pena y la risa. Crowther pareció enfadarse.

—No tuvimos tiempo de prepararte para la misión. Creímos que lo mejor era dejar que el trato siguiera su curso y… arreglar las consecuencias después. Así resultarías más convincente.

Se le hizo un nudo en la garganta.

—Bueno, Kaine os caló desde el principio. Al final, la única idiota he sido yo. Pero ya tenéis lo que queríais. Supongo que ha sido una suerte.

—Tienes que... —empezó con pesar, pero se calló.

—¿Qué? —insistió Helena. La furia que sentía estaba dando paso al pánico.

¿Acaso no era suficiente? ¿Estaba intentando decirle con delicadeza que Ilva pensaba matar a Kaine igualmente? ¿Que ese último mes también había sido una mentira? ¿Que, por mucho que hiciese, Kaine no podía evitar que lo traicionaran?

Crowther la observó con el entrecejo fruncido.

—He pasado un año intentando encontrar la forma de reemplazarte... Tengo que admitir que eres la integrante más excepcional de la Llama Eterna. Y, por ello, te pido disculpas.

Ahora que conocía el método que usaban los Holdfast a la hora de elegir a sus «prodigios», sí que veía el paralelismo entre ambos: los dos habían venido a Paladia por su talento, sin tener ningún otro sitio al que ir, y habían dedicado su vida a estar solos y ser útiles, porque eso era lo único que conocían.

Tal vez, si ahora la consideraba su sucesora, sí que le parecía una tragedia.

Una semana después, Crowther acompañó a Helena al Reducto.

Tras aquel breve interludio de humanidad, el hombre volvió a retirarse a la sombra y, cuando emergió de nuevo, era el mismo de siempre. Aun así, Helena se percató de que después de los últimos acontecimientos su estatus dentro la estrategia había cambiado.

Durante el trayecto, no le dirigió la palabra. Tomaron un camión hasta la barricada y luego caminaron hasta el Reducto. Era desconcertante lo rápido que se hacía el viaje cuando no iba a pie. Había luz, y caía una llovizna que cubría la ciudad como un sudario. Una neblina espesa lo envolvía todo alrededor de la presa.

Los necrómatas del Reducto se esfumaron entre la lluvia al verlos pasar.

Kaine los esperaba en el módulo, como si no se hubiera marchado nunca. Estaba demacrado, cansado. No la miró a los ojos. De hecho, apenas le dedicó un vistazo. La tela que antes cubría el suelo estaba doblada en un rincón.

Si Crowther tuvo alguna impresión del lugar, no la dejó entrever, aunque Helena advirtió cierta incomodidad cuando sus ojos recorrieron la estancia. Ella ya se habría acostumbrado, pero en ese momento solo vio la suciedad, la pintura descascarillada y los azulejos resquebrajados. Se acordó de lo denigrante que le había parecido aquel lugar la primera vez que entró en él.

Crowther observó todo sin decir nada, y el aire se volvió cada vez más tenso, como un bosque que se sume en el silencio de repente.

Aunque hacía años que no participaba en ninguna batalla, Helena había sanado a suficientes víctimas de sus interrogatorios para saber que Crowther tenía la capacidad de usar la piromancia de forma precisa, y ahora tenía dos manos con las que emplearla. No sabía con certeza hasta dónde llegaban las habilidades de Kaine, pero incluso los inmarcesibles temían enfrentarse con los alquimistas de fuego.

El odio entre Crowther y Kaine era tan denso que hasta el aire parecía vibrar en su presencia. Fue Crowther quien habló primero, y cuando lo hizo le brillaban los ojos.

—Tengo entendido que quieres renegociar tu trato con la Llama Eterna, Ferron. —Había cierta burla en su voz.

Kaine se había quedado sorprendentemente pálido.

—Eso parece.

Helena había supuesto que tendría que mediar entre ellos, pero Kaine la fulminó con la mirada.

—Puedes marcharte, Marino. Estoy seguro de que Crowther sabrá volver solo.

Ella vaciló y miró a ambos hombres alternativamente. A Crowther se le iluminó el rostro con diversión cuando posó la vista en Helena.

—No me apetece volver caminando solo. Espérame fuera, Marino. Estoy convencido de que Ferron no permitirá que te suceda nada en el descansillo.

Kaine apretó los dientes, pero no replicó. Helena les dedicó una última mirada a los dos y se dio la vuelta a regañadientes. Al salir al rellano, antes de cerrar la puerta, oyó una sola palabra de los labios de Crowther:

—Suplícamelo.

Se paseó por el pasillo, inquieta, y se asomó a los módulos que carecían de puerta. Eran todos iguales. Subió a la planta de arriba y volvió a bajar.

La lluvia caía por el tragaluz desprovisto de cristal como una cascada infinita. En la segunda planta, algo escondido entre las sombras le llamó la atención. Se acercó, se puso de puntillas y entrecerró los ojos para ver mejor lo que era. Lo habían colocado de tal forma que apenas se distinguía en la oscuridad.

Era un ojo humano metido en una caja de cristal. La estaba mirando. Cuando ella se movía, giraba y la seguía.

Helena se estremeció. No sabía que se podía reanimar solo una parte del cuerpo, pero era evidente que ese ojo había cobrado vida. Estaba perfectamente conservado y había sido colocado en ángulo para que vigilase todo el rellano desde el rincón.

Así era como Kaine siempre se enteraba de que había llegado.

Estuvo media hora más sentada en los escalones hasta que Crowther salió del módulo. Sabía que probablemente no le contaría los detalles del trato, pero confiaba en que, después de hacerla esperar, al menos le diría algo.

Sin embargo, el hombre se detuvo y la miró de arriba abajo.

—Buen trabajo, Marino.

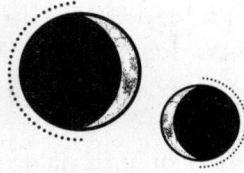

CAPÍTULO 49

Febre 1787

EL AMBIENTE DEL CUARTEL GENERAL se tornó sombrío conforme avanzaba el invierno. Los días eran largos y oscuros, y hacía tanto frío y humedad que hasta dar un breve paseo por los jardines dejaba el cuerpo helado.

Después de meses de avance en la defensa del territorio y la fortificación de las zonas recuperadas, la Resistencia recibió un duro golpe. Una bomba de enorme potencia derrumbó una de las murallas y varios edificios de la isla Este. A continuación, se produjeron más explosiones y, sin disponer de tiempo para evacuar a los supervivientes, aparecieron los necrómatas y las quimeras.

La Resistencia perdió un batallón entero y toda una franja de territorio de la isla Este.

El escuadrón de Luc se quedó atrapado en un edificio y fue perseguido hasta el río, donde acabó acorralado durante más de un día, hasta que la Resistencia reunió una compañía lo bastante numerosa como para rescatarlos. Sufrieron numerosas bajas, la mitad de los integrantes resultaron heridos de gravedad, uno de los médicos fue asesinado en la retirada y otra falleció por las heridas sufridas durante el asalto. Luc logró contener a las quimeras y a los necrómatas levantando un muro de llamas durante horas. A Soren y a varios soldados se les había derrumbado encima un edificio, y él tenía el brazo derecho destrozado. Cuando se produjo el asalto, solo pudo cuidar a los heridos y ver cómo morían uno tras otro.

Se negó a hablar del tema.

ANTES DE QUE HELENA REGRESARA al Reducto, Crowther le informó de que, a partir de entonces, solo vería a Kaine una vez por semana. No le dio explicaciones. Eran los nuevos términos del trato. Cuando llegó el martis, Helena no sabía qué esperar, si todo sería diferente entre ellos, pero, cuando Kaine llegó, desplegó la tela acolchada sobre el suelo sin mediar palabra y se dispuso a entrenar con ella como si nada hubiera sucedido. Aunque ya no parecía el mismo, ya no era capaz de mirarla a los ojos.

—¿Cómo sabes todo esto? —le preguntó ella cuando dejó de atacarla para enseñarle varias formas de romper un brazo de manera que el hueso quedara destrozado o atravesara la piel, porque así se ralentizaba la regeneración.

—Igual que sé todo lo demás —contestó con la mirada perdida—. Cuando uno no puede morir, la gente te hace daño hasta que consigues devolvérselo.

—Lo siento.

La miró con un brillo furioso en los ojos.

—Seguro que sí.

No hubo más conversación. La atacó y Helena no tuvo más remedio que defenderse. En un momento de descuido, consiguió darle un puñetazo, pero apenas tuvo tiempo de celebrarlo porque Kaine le rodeó la garganta con una mano y la atrajo hacia sí.

Los dos se quedaron quietos, mirándose a los ojos, como si el tiempo se hubiera detenido. Kaine apartó la mano y le dedicó una mirada desdeñosa.

—Como no aprendas a pensar más rápido de lo que te mueves, acabarás muerta.

Falló otras dos veces más.

—Ya basta por hoy.

Kaine le dio la espalda, metió la mano en el bolsillo de su capa y sacó un sobre que dejó sobre la mesa. Helena sintió una presión en el pecho cuando se agachó a coger su bolsa y sacó otro sobre. Lo sostuvo, inquieta, antes de darse la vuelta.

—Crowther me pidió que te diera esto.

Cuando la miró, sus ojos carecían de vida.

—Cierto... Mis órdenes de esta semana.

Se lo arrancó de los dedos sin miramientos.

—Kaine...

—Lárgate, Marino. Tengo cosas que hacer.

HELENA FUE LA ENCARGADA DE asegurarse de que Luc se encontraba en condiciones de salir del Cuartel General. El principado seguía tan conmocionado que apenas pareció reparar en que se trataba de ella, lo cual, en realidad, era lo mejor, ya que no habían hablado desde el solsticio.

Luc y Lila se miraban con intensidad y fervor, como si fueran la piedra angular el uno del otro.

De haber podido, Helena habría recomendado que descansaran, que al menos se tomaran unas semanas para recuperarse. Luc estaba tan demacrado que daba miedo verlo, y le preocupaban sus pulmones, pero en ese momento no podían permitirse el lujo de descansar. Ambos regresaron al frente con su armadura recién pulida para insuflar ánimos a los batallones, que cada vez se mostraban más inquietos.

Soren los acompañó unos días después.

Una vez a la semana, Kaine entrenaba con ella durante media hora, le entregaba informes de inteligencia, aceptaba sus órdenes y se marchaba sin mirar atrás. Ya no hablaban. Si Helena preguntaba algo que no tuviera que ver con el combate, él la ignoraba. Era como si se hubiera abierto un desfiladero imposible de salvar entre ellos.

Pero no importaba. Estaba vivo. Cada semana lo veía y sabía que estaba vivo. Sin embargo, a él ya no parecía importarle lo más mínimo. En sus ojos no había más que una desesperación descarnada. Hasta su rabia se había extinguido, como si continuara existiendo por pura inercia.

Al cabo de tres semanas, lo sujetó por la muñeca cuando iba a coger el sobre de Crowther.

—Por favor…, mírame.

Kaine retiró la mano, pero la miró de frente. De nuevo, asomó en sus ojos esa rabia helada.

—¿Es que esto no es suficiente? ¿Quieres más?

—No… —Lo miró sintiéndose impotente—. Lo siento, pensé…

Él soltó una carcajada seca.

—Algún día, cuando vuelva a tener tiempo, te haré una lista de todas las cosas que no se arreglan con una disculpa.

Helena dejó caer las manos.

—Kaine, no…

—No… No me llames por mi nombre. Odio cómo lo pronuncias. —Le arrancó el sobre de los dedos y se marchó.

Poco después, hubo otra avalancha de heridos. Helena apenas conseguía mantenerse al tanto de las batallas y escaramuzas, de las victorias y derrotas. En el hospital, todo se entremezclaba en un grito infinito. El tiempo se convirtió en una monotonía insoportable, interrumpida únicamente por el frío resentimiento de Kaine.

Helena intentó mantenerse ocupada. Con permiso de Rhea, quiso tratar a Titus, pero este no reaccionó como esperaba. Después de sufrir unas fiebres gravísimas, no le quedó más remedio que renunciar a ello.

Se sentía libre, a su aire. Todos los demás iban y venían; muchas sanadoras eran destinadas al sur de la isla para trabajar en el hospital nuevo, pero Helena siempre permanecía en el Cuartel General.

Ilva y Crowther solo le exigían llevar sus órdenes a Kaine. Helena se había convertido en el collar que Kaine llevaba al cuello, y su trabajo era soportarlo.

***

ESTABA VOLVIENDO DEL REDUCTO CUANDO notó que el brazalete del hospital se calentaba. Recorrió el camino que quedaba a la carrera. El suelo de la garita de la entrada estaba lleno de sangre.

Los guardias la estaban esperando.

—¿Dónde te habías metido?

—¿Quién está herido? ¿Qué ha…? —dijo entre jadeos cuando la dejaron pasar.

—Lila —respondió uno de los guardias más jóvenes—. Y Soren.

Sintió que la embargaba el terror.

—¿Dónde está Luc?

Se hizo un silencio que le dejó claro a Helena lo que había pasado.

—Ha desaparecido.

Ella echó a correr, pero su mente se quedó paralizada mientras se dirigía al hospital.

No. Eso no podía estar pasando.

El pabellón de heridos estaba desbordado. Nada más entrar, Elain interceptó a Helena. Tenía las manos empapadas de sangre y la cara lívida de pánico.

—¡No me funciona la resonancia! —exclamó, histérica—. No puedo detener la hemorragia.

Lila yacía sobre una camilla, cubierta de polvo, tierra y sangre. Las partes de la armadura que habían sobrevivido estaban destrozadas y rajadas, y su ropa hecha trizas, como si una explosión la hubiese alcanzado de lleno. Las enfermeras se afanaban por cortar la tela y transmutar la armadura para quitársela. Un tajo profundo le cruzaba la cara, de la sien a la mejilla, y más abajo, justo en la base del cuello, un agujero del que no dejaba de brotar sangre.

—¡No sé qué está pasando! —decía Elain mientras Helena se lavaba las manos con agua hirviendo y las sumergía en una solución carbólica—. Creo que tiene algo dentro, pero la resonancia no me responde. Cuando he intentado sanarla, ha sido como si... como si mis manos no...

—¿A Soren le sucede lo mismo? ¿O solo a Lila?

—No lo sé, no he probado con él. Acaban de llegar. Se está desangrando, ¡y no noto nada!

—Ve a examinar a Soren —le ordenó Helena—. Necesito médicos para Lila. Y avisa a Pace, dile que quiero que venga ahora mismo.

Se acercó a Lila. El cuello era una de las pocas zonas desprotegidas de su armadura. Estaba empapando la cama de sangre. Le habían colocado una sonda intravenosa con expansores de plasma, pero no le serviría para nada si no conseguían cortar la hemorragia.

Lila tenía la cabeza torcida, como si se le hubiese dislocado el cuello. Todavía estaba consciente y no dejaba de mascullar entre dientes:

—... le dije que... corriera. Le... dije que... que corriera.

Helena extendió su resonancia y sintió la perturbación inconfundible del anulitio. Había rezado para estar equivocada, para que Elain se hubiera confundido al estar histérica o, simplemente, exhausta. Cualquier cosa menos eso.

Este anulitio era mucho más potente que la metralla que le había extraído a Kaine. Lo habían alterado de alguna forma para intensificar su efecto.

Intentó hacerse una idea, aunque vaga, de lo que había en la cavidad torácica de Lila. Si iban a aplicar presión en la herida, necesitaba saber si corrían el riesgo de perforar el corazón. Fue como querer ver a través de una niebla espesa. Sentía las manos dormidas, con pinchazos como agujas en los nervios, pero buscó el origen de la disonancia.

Era un objeto largo y fino. Probablemente, le había atravesado un pulmón y estaba cerca del corazón, aunque no podía saberlo con certeza.

—¿Qué tiene? —Pace estaba a su lado.

Helena presionaba una gasa contra la herida para evitar la hemorragia. Lila había perdido el conocimiento.

—Es anulitio. Vamos a tener que operarla manualmente para extraerlo. Maier no sabe hacerlo, pero tú trabajabas en los hospitales cuando todavía se hacía así, ¿verdad?

Pace palideció de pronto.

—De eso hace mucho tiempo, y yo solo era auxiliar.

Helena respiró hondo. No podía explicar la experiencia quirúrgica que tenía con el anulitio.

—Yo solía… ayudar a mi padre. Si tú guías y yo la mantengo estable, podemos conseguirlo. ¿Soren tiene…?

Le daba miedo saber si Soren tenía lesiones provocadas por el anulitio. Si había que elegir a qué gemelo salvar, el protocolo dictaba que debía recibir tratamiento la persona con más probabilidades de sobrevivir, pero al ser Lila paladina primera tenía prioridad.

—Las otras se encargarán —respondió Pace—. Ha recibido un fuerte golpe en la cabeza, pero nada que Elain no pueda arreglar.

Helena cerró los ojos como queriendo obligarse a recuperar la calma y suplicar que Lila sobreviviera, porque esta vez no podría hacerlo todo ella sola.

—Llévala al quirófano —le ordenó a Pace—. Estoy segura de que Maier hará todo lo posible por ayudarnos. Necesitaremos personal de medicina y enfermería. Yo me encargo de ponerlos al día. Tú mantenla estable.

Helena solo había asistido a su padre en algunas operaciones antes de la masacre.

Él siempre le decía que había que ser observadora y mantener la calma en los momentos de crisis, aunque de eso hacía ya mucho tiempo.

Manejar instrumental quirúrgico era muy distinto a operar sin resonancia. Nadie sabía cómo hacerlo. El anulitio que conocían solo interfería si se tocaba directamente, pero este era mucho más difuso.

Una vez que Lila estuvo sedada, la enfermera Pace introdujo un par de pinzas largas en la perforación que tenía en la clavícula y extrajo una especie de lanza alargada y oxidada. Era frágil y, debido a la fusión inestable, estaba empezando a degradarse. Cada vez que se partía, Pace tenía que meter la pinza de nuevo para sacar uno a uno todos los fragmentos.

Usando su resonancia, Helena comprobó que, a pesar de que habían sacado la mayor parte de la lanza, aún quedaban esquirlas disolviéndose en la sangre de Lila. El anulitio se extendía por su cuerpo como una neblina y, a cada segundo que pasaba, se volvía más espesa e impenetrable.

La fragilidad del anulitio era a la vez una bendición y una maldición. Se había abierto paso por donde encontraba menos resistencia. Lila tenía un pulmón levemente perforado, pero el corazón estaba intacto, al igual que el esófago. La lanza solo había afectado a la cavidad torácica, aunque los fragmentos estaban por todas partes, y la aleación era tan inestable que se disolvía rápidamente.

Pace se secó la frente con un paño.

—Vamos a tener que hacerle una toracotomía para sacar todos los fragmentos. ¿Está estable para soportar una operación así?

En circunstancias normales, un cirujano alquímico como Maier habría realizado una toracotomía sin necesidad de abrir al paciente. Las incisiones solo eran necesarias cuando había que introducir instrumental fino, pero, con resonancia y la formación adecuada, el trabajo se limitaba a los dedos y los sentidos.

Helena retiró la resonancia y tocó a Lila para comprobar sus signos vitales; así era más sencillo que tratar de abrirse paso entre toda aquella interferencia.

—Está aguantando.

Le hicieron una incisión entre las costillas y emplearon unos retractores improvisados para apartar los huesos y sacar todas las esquirlas que quedaban. Los fragmentos variaban en tamaño y se deshacían si no se sujetaban con sumo cuidado. Lila tenía pequeños cortes y fisuras en los pulmones y en el corazón, justo donde la habían alcanzado los fragmentos. Eran heridas que Helena podría reparar fácilmente si pudiera usar su resonancia, pero, dadas las circunstancias, tendrían que coserla a mano, un trabajo laborioso y que implicaba mucho riesgo.

La operación superaba todo lo que conocían, y además trabajaban contra reloj. Si el anulitio seguía partiéndose y mezclándose con la sangre de Lila, moriría por la contaminación que provocaba el metal. El cuerpo de Lila estaba llegando al límite y debía resistir sin ayuda de la resonancia.

Helena continuó bombeando sangre de forma manual para que el corazón de Lila no dejara de latir mientras Pace la operaba. Una enfermera llevó los fragmentos más grandes a Shiseo para que los analizara y sintetizara un agente quelante, pero tardaría horas en desarrollar un tratamiento eficaz.

Si no conseguían purgar el metal del torrente sanguíneo de Lila, no podrían sanarla mediante la resonancia.

—Ahora le haremos un lavado torácico —informó Pace, que dejó finalmente el instrumental a un lado. Cuando terminaron, tenía los ojos inyectados en sangre del esfuerzo.

Maier se encargó de la sutura. Los puntos quedaron limpios y perfectos, aunque parecía conmocionado por todo el asunto.

Cuando Helena levantó la cabeza, se dio cuenta de que empezaba a hacerse de noche.

—Voy a ver cómo está Soren.

Se sintió extraña al lavarse las manos. No había usado demasiado la resonancia, pero la tensión de las últimas horas le provocó dolor de cabeza. Salió del quirófano y se encontró a todo el hospital congregado alrededor de una cama.

Soren estaba despierto y sentado. Habían apartado las cortinas que le daban algo de privacidad y, a la cabeza de todos los que lo rodeaban, se encontraba Ilva.

Soren tenía un brazo escayolado y medio rostro cubierto de vendas. No paraba de negar con la cabeza.

—No... no lo recuerdo. Todo sucedió muy rápido.

—¿Reconociste a alguien? ¿Alguna cara, por casualidad? —insistió Ilva, sujetando a Soren de la muñeca.

—No lo sé —repitió Soren con voz cansada—. Hubo... hubo una explosión. Recibí un golpe. No sé si pasaron segundos o minutos. Cuando me levanté, no veía nada. Luc había desaparecido y Lila estaba en el suelo, desangrándose. No paraba de decir: «Le dije que corriera». No sabía dónde buscar, así que regresé aquí.

—¿Nadie os advirtió? —Ilva parecía desbordada de preguntas por hacer, visiblemente afectada—. ¿No visteis ninguna señal? ¿Quién lideraba la unidad?

—No... —Soren frunció el ceño, como si tratara de recordar.

—Siempre mantuve que era un error permitir que una mujer fuese paladina —intervino Matias—. Si hubiese sido falcón en aquella época, jamás habría consentido semejante violación de las tradiciones. Te lo advertí, Ilva. Luc no era imparcial con ella, pero nada. Lila Bayard era demasiado excepcional para separarlos. Y ahora mira lo que ha pasado.

—¡Cállate! —le espetó Ilva por encima del hombro. Todavía tenía los dedos clavados en la muñeca de Soren. Luego se giró y lo zarandeó—. ¿Lila dijo algo sobre que Luc se entregara? ¿Se entregó por culpa de ella?

—No lo sé —respondió Soren en un susurro.

Elain estaba de pie junto a la cama de Soren, demasiado impactada por la presencia de tantos miembros de la Llama Eterna como para atreverse a intervenir.

—Perdonad —dijo Helena en tono cortante, y se abrió paso entre la multitud—. Soren Bayard ha sufrido una contusión cerebral. En estos casos es mejor evitar cualquier tipo de estrés.

Todo el mundo se giró hacia ella.

—¿Lila ha recobrado el conocimiento? ¿Puede responder a mis preguntas? —soltó Ilva poniéndose en pie al instante.

Helena negó con la cabeza, con un gesto algo distante.

—No está en condiciones. Le hemos hecho una operación complicada de forma manual para extraer la lanza de anulitio con la que fue apuñalada. Sin embargo, la aleación se ha deteriorado y distribuido por su torrente sanguíneo, así que no podemos sanarla con resonancia hasta que expulse todo el anulitio.

—¿Cuánto tardará en recuperarse? —preguntó Ilva, con el pánico dibujado en el rostro, pero Helena volvió a negar con la cabeza.

—Ahora mismo está anestesiada, pero estamos trabajando a ciegas. Puede que se levante en unas horas, o tal vez tarde algunos días. Lila es muy fuerte, pero esta lesión es más grave que cualquiera de las anteriores. No podemos dar nada por sentado.

Soren se encogió sobre sí mismo; parecía que estaba a punto de sufrir un ataque de pánico. En cambio, Ilva se envaró como una serpiente.

—Creía que estabais preparados para esto —declaró Ilva—. ¿Qué habéis estado haciendo todo este tiempo?

Helena apretó los dientes. ¿Por qué cuando las cosas se torcían era siempre culpa del hospital? Si Helena hubiera salido diciendo que la operación había sido un éxito y que Lila estaba levantándose de la cama, todos habrían ido corriendo a encender velas en honor a Sol. Sin embargo, las malas noticias eran siempre responsabilidad del hospital.

Qué tranquilos debían de estar los dioses.

—Han hecho cambios en la aleación y la interferencia es mucho más potente. Las operaciones manuales no son simples, sobre todo en un hospital donde solo hay dos personas con algo de experiencia para llevarlas a cabo. Si queréis que el hospital esté preparado para la cirugía manual, el falcón deberá aprobar el uso de cadáveres para practicar, tal como solicitamos hace meses.

Matias tosió con violencia, como si se hubiera atragantado y, de repente, ya no parecía querer estar allí.

Ilva estaba apoyada en su bastón, como si estuviese a punto de desplomarse. Era como si la pérdida de Luc la hubiera dejado totalmente descolocada.

—Adelante, examínalo —cedió Ilva, que se apartó de la cama de Soren con un paso algo inestable—. Nos reuniremos dentro de una hora. Quiero informes completos de los dos Bayard.

Se fueron todos. Cuando la sala quedó despejada, Helena le lanzó una mirada fulminante a Elain para indicarle que volviera a cerrar las cortinas y se sentó junto a Soren. El gemelo estaba apoyado en las almohadas que lo mantenían erguido, cubierto de cortes que ya habían sido tratados. En cuanto lo rozó con su resonancia, supo que había perdido la visión del ojo derecho. El golpe que recibió le había fracturado el hueso del cráneo y aplastado el nervio óptico.

Helena notó que le temblaban las manos.

—No me lo perdonará jamás —masculló Soren en apenas un susurro.

La chica no supo si se refería a Ilva o a Lila. Le apretó la mano.

—Si hubieras ido a por Luc en este estado, ahora los tres estaríais muertos. Eso no le habría servido a nadie de nada. Estoy segura de que hay más gente buscándolo porque has vuelto para contarlo.

Elain lo había sanado bien. Cuando llegó, tenía varios huesos rotos, incluido el mismo brazo que se había fracturado unas semanas antes. Como no había terminado de curarse, probablemente le quedarían secuelas.

—¿Crees que sigue vivo? —preguntó Soren.

A Helena se le paró el corazón. No se imaginaba un motivo por el que los inmarcesibles hubieran querido mantenerlo con vida.

—Hasta que no sepamos que está muerto, sigue vivo. Y vamos a traerlo de vuelta —se obligó a decir Helena con esperanza—. Deja de preocuparte. Tengo que examinarte la cabeza.

Tenía una contusión, pero el ojo y el hueso frontal del cráneo eran lo más preocupante. Después de visitar a Titus en tantas ocasiones, se había familiarizado con la forma del cerebro y creía entenderlo mejor. Al menos, ahora podía diagnosticar con más precisión en lugar de salir corriendo sin saber qué hacer.

Elain no se había atrevido a arreglar el ojo destrozado. Se había limitado a vendarlo y reparar el hueso.

—Soren, el ojo derecho…

—Lo sé —repuso con brusquedad, como si no importara—. Pero puedo seguir luchando, ¿no?

Helena dejó de mover las manos.

—Tienes un brazo roto y has perdido la mitad de tu visión. Necesitas adaptarte a esto. Serás más vulnerable. No verás nada que se acerque por tu lado derecho.

—Pues giraré la cabeza —replicó, seco—. Para eso tengo cuello.

Helena suspiró.

—No vas a volver al frente, al menos hasta dentro de unas semanas.

Soren sacudió la cabeza.

—Lila está inconsciente. Tengo que encontrar a Luc antes de que despierte. No puede abrir los ojos y enterarse de que no lo he traído de vuelta. —Le tembló la barbilla. En los doce años que lo conocía, Helena nunca había visto llorar a Soren. El chico bajó la mirada—. No lo he contado, pero Lila me pidió que la abandonara allí y que fuera a buscar a Luc. No lo hice. Le respondí que iría en cuanto la pusiera a salvo…

Intentó levantarse de la cama, pero no necesitó más que una mano para volverlo a empujar contra el colchón. Apenas tenía fuerzas para sostenerse.

—Soren, tengo que arreglar el tejido desgarrado del ojo —dijo Helena con firmeza.

El chico la ignoró y quiso apartarla de un manotazo, pero Helena ya tenía cierta soltura en combate. Esquivó el gesto con facilidad y deslizó los dedos por detrás de su cabeza. Solo necesitó un cosquilleo de resonancia para dejarlo inconsciente. Soren se desplomó.

Helena le cerró el ojo con cuidado para que no se secara.

—Lo siento —murmuró, y se puso manos a la obra.

Si quedaba algo intacto en la cuenca del ojo, tal vez existía una posibilidad mínima de que recuperara parte de la visión, pero Soren tenía el ojo destrozado. Helena retiró todo el tejido irreparable para evitar que se pudriera y provocara infecciones, y volvió a vendar la zona con cuidado. En unas semanas, podrían conseguirle un buen ojo de cristal o tal vez una gema.

Eso si la Resistencia seguía existiendo dentro de unas semanas.

Rhea llegó justo cuando Helena estaba terminando.

Hacía mucho que ninguno de los gemelos acababa en el hospital.

Su rostro se mantenía sereno, pero sus ojos revelaban un pánico contenido mientras se dirigía hacia Soren. Helena se incorporó.

—Ya he terminado. Puedo despertarlo —afirmó, cubriendo la cuenca del ojo con un paño.

—No, déjalo descansar. —Rhea se sentó lentamente en el borde de la cama y observó el resto de la cara de Soren—. Mi niño… —susurró, como si temiera que Soren pudiese despertarse.

Helena retrocedió un poco; no estaba segura de si necesitaba privacidad o quería respuestas.

—¿Sabes? Cuando nació, era un bebé muy pequeño —contó Rhea, que cogió la mano de Soren en la suya—. Le cabía a Titus en la palma de la mano. Los médicos no creían que sobreviviera. Lila nació gritando, con la cara roja, pero mi pequeño Soren no era más que un suspiro, callado y pálido. No hacía ni un ruido, ni siquiera cuando mamaba. Siempre iba detrás de Lila, jamás causó un problema, pero acababa metido en todos los líos por acompañarla a ella. —A Rhea se le escapó un gemido a medio camino entre el sollozo y la risa—. Cuando nacieron, pensé que había logrado una hazaña. Gemelos, dos bebés para la familia Bayard. Nuestros pequeños paladines. —Rhea temblaba mientras sostenía la mano de Soren—. Y ahora Titus ni siquiera es consciente de lo que están sufriendo nuestros maravillosos hijos… Toda la familia. Solo me quedan los restos.

Se inclinó sobre Soren. Aunque lloraba en silencio, Helena vio cómo su cuerpo se estremecía. Desahogarse así era una rareza: había que aprender a hacerlo.

Ella se retiró con discreción, para que tuviera espacio para llorar.

La reunión del Consejo fue lúgubre. Ilva se sentó a la mesa, aunque parecía que estaba sedada mientras escuchaba todos los informes. El ataque se había producido en los barrios bajos de la isla Este. Luc y Lila encabezaban un batallón hacia el Cuartel General cuando pasaron junto a un edificio en ruinas y, en cuanto lo dejaron atrás, hubo una explosión. El edificio se desplomó.

Soren era el que se encontraba más cerca en el momento del estallido, fue alcanzado de lleno por la onda expansiva y salió despedido por los aires. Solo sobrevivieron dos soldados más, los únicos que se habían quedado atrás. Los encontraron entre los escombros con heridas leves.

En el lugar de los hechos había indicios claros de combate: restos calcinados y un charco de sangre que creían que pertenecía a Lila. También encontraron cadáveres humanos, probablemente de necrómatas, y un liche con el talismán arrancado. Más lejos, como si alguien los hubiera arrojado a propósito, estaban la espada y los anillos de Luc.

Los inmarcesibles no se habían pronunciado aún. No anunciaron la muerte ni la captura de Luc. Se ordenó a los guardias que se prepararan por si Luc aparecía reanimado o por si un liche hubiera poseído su cuerpo. Si Luc reaparecía, había que tomar todas las medidas necesarias. Nadie creería que había escapado de milagro.

El tiempo solo agravó la incertidumbre. ¿Por qué los inmarcesibles lo habían dejado con vida? ¿Por qué no habían anunciado que estaba muerto? ¿O quizá lo tenían encarcelado para negociar una rendición?

Y, si estaba preso, ¿por qué no se habían puesto en contacto con ellos?

—Hasta que sepamos con certeza que Lucien está muerto, daremos por sentado que sigue con vida —declaró Ilva con tono gélido. Se había sentido ofendida cuando uno de los metalúrgicos jefe preguntó cuál era el plan en caso de que sucediera lo peor—. Los inmarcesibles no tienen motivos para ocultar un triunfo como este. Han pasado doce horas y no se han puesto en contacto con nosotros. Puede que esto signifique que no todo es lo que parece.

Cuando la reunión terminó, Matias se levantó y anunció que iba a suplicar a los cielos que Luc regresara sano y salvo. Hubo muchos que lo siguieron.

Ilva permaneció en la mesa conversando con Crowther.

—Marino, no te vayas, tenemos que hablar contigo —dijo Ilva cuando Helena se disponía a volver al hospital.

Ella esperó a que la sala de reuniones estuviera vacía. Con un gesto de Ilva, los guardias cerraron las puertas.

—Tienes que ir al Reducto. Vamos a usar a Ferron —dispuso Ilva con brusquedad—. Quiero saber cualquier información que tenga o que pueda conseguir sobre la posible captura de Luc, y también una explicación de por qué no hemos recibido ninguna advertencia al respecto.

—Por supuesto. —Era lo que esperaba.

—Dile que se trata de una misión de vital importancia —añadió Ilva cuando Helena se giró para marcharse—. Usa esas palabras, Marino. Es una prioridad absoluta. Si él puede traer a Luc de vuelta, nos ahorraríamos las pérdidas que implicaría organizar un rescate.

Querían sacrificar a Kaine para recuperar a Luc. Era la opción más lógica. Un intercambio fácil que cualquier estratega consideraría.

No obstante...

—De acuerdo —asintió Helena sin emoción.

Lumitia pendía del cielo como un enorme disco de plata. Estaba tan cerca de la sublimación absoluta que deslumbraba los planetas y convertía el firmamento nocturno en un abismo negro e infinito. La luz plateada brillante proyectaba sombras por toda la ciudad.

Cuando Helena llegó al rellano del módulo, se detuvo a propósito bajo un rayo de sol que entraba por el tragaluz roto y miró el ojo oculto en el rincón. A continuación, esperó.

Tuvo que aguardar un buen rato.

El viento hacía vibrar los cristales, pero no oyó nada hasta que la puerta se abrió con un chasquido y apareció Kaine. Todo él parecía más... nítido.

—¿Qué ha pasado?

En cuanto formuló la pregunta, Helena supo que no sabía nada. Ilva tenía razón: si los inmarcesibles habían capturado a Luc, lo mantenían en secreto.

—Hoy hubo un ataque, una bomba —explicó con voz temblorosa—. Ha masacrado a casi todo un batallón. Los hermanos Bayard han sobrevivido de milagro, pero Luc... ha desaparecido.

—¿Estás segura?

Helena asintió con rigidez.

—Emplearon un arma fabricada con esa aleación que interfiere con la resonancia. La llamamos anulitio. Apuñalaron a Lila y ha estado a punto de morir. ¿No sabías que estaban desarrollando algo así?

Kaine negó con la cabeza.

—No. Sospechan que hay un espía por culpa de un... sabotaje que se produjo hace poco. Y yo ya no estoy tan presente como antes.

La chica bajó la mirada y respiró hondo antes de hablar:

—Tenemos que recuperar a Luc. Me han pedido que te diga que es de vital importancia, una prioridad absoluta.

—Claro…

—Cualquier información que tengas sobre la captura: quién lo hizo, dónde está, si sigue vivo… El Consejo quiere que… —se le trabó la lengua— que hagas todo lo posible.

—Por supuesto —se limitó a contestar antes de darse la vuelta.

Helena lo observó cuando se alejaba, el movimiento de sus hombros, cómo hundió uno de ellos para alcanzar el pomo de la puerta. No sabía si volvería a verlo.

—Espera —le instó.

Kaine se detuvo, pero no se giró.

—Te llamaré cuando sepa algo —dijo sin más.

—Kaine… Cuando te besé, yo…

El chico se volvió de pronto. En un momento estaba al otro lado de la habitación y, al siguiente, justo delante de ella. Su expresión estaba tan cargada de veneno que le dejaba los dientes a la vista.

—¿De verdad quieres hablar de esto ahora?

Helena sintió un nudo en la garganta. Se sentía culpable y no podía casi ni articular palabra. Pero estaba desesperada por hacerlo.

—¿Puedes mirarme al menos?

Un brillo cruel asomó a sus ojos cuando se miraron cara a cara. Recibir toda su atención fue como si le diese un puñetazo en el estómago.

—¿Quieres que te mire? —Kaine empleó un tono casual, como si pretendiera seducirla, pero por debajo solo había rabia. Se acercó más—. Bien. Te estoy mirando. Y debo decir que es un auténtico placer ver toda esa culpa en tu cara. —Hizo un gesto de desdén y retrocedió un paso—. ¿Sabes? Antes pensaba que estar al servicio del Sumo Nigromante era la peor esclavitud posible, pero, sinceramente, palidece en comparación con la tuya.

Ladeó la cabeza.

—Al menos, antes me consolaba pensando que no era culpa mía. Hacía lo que fuera para mantener a mi madre a salvo. Pero todo cambió cuando ya no quedó nadie a quien culpar salvo a mí mismo.

Levantó la mano y envolvió los dedos alrededor de la garganta de Helena para acercarla hacia él. Ella sintió el roce del cuero de sus guantes.

—Después de todo, fui yo quien te eligió.

Helena lo miró a los ojos y contempló la absoluta desesperanza de su mirada.

—Envidiaba lo ingenua que eras, que quisieras ver mi lado bueno y no te dieras cuenta de que todo fue una argucia desde el principio. Cuando me suplicaste que te dejara curarme, accedí. Y, cuando me tocaste, no me aparté. Pensé: «¿Qué daño puede hacerme? Todo acabará dentro de poco y la vida ya ha sido bastante cruel conmigo».

Helena no se dio cuenta de que estaba llorando hasta que Kaine le acarició la mejilla con el pulgar.

—Cuando comprendí que te había subestimado, ya te habías abierto paso hasta mi corazón. Eres un persona muy predecible, pero eso solo empeoró todo: sabía que me dejarías hacerte cualquier cosa con tal de salvar a los demás, incluso a quienes te vendieron sin pensárselo dos veces. Al menos, cuando yo vendí mi alma, mi madre se puso de rodillas y suplicó ocupar mi lugar. Supongo que, en cierto modo, tengo más suerte que tú.

A Helena se le escapó un sollozo.

—Y, cuando estuviste a punto de morir desangrada aquí, pensé que al menos podía mantenerte con vida. «Se merece tener a alguien que se preocupe lo suficiente como para intentarlo». Creí que, con el tiempo, te rendirías. Pero harás lo que sea por salvar a aquellos de los que te consideras responsable. Por supuesto, después usarás tu culpa para aprovecharte de la mía. —Soltó una carcajada amarga—. Estoy seguro de que todo esto encierra algo poético, pero ahora mismo lo único que veo es un nuevo par de grilletes. —La soltó y se alejó de ella para ir hacia la puerta—. Así que perdóname si no me apetece mirarte. Todavía me estoy acostumbrando a cómo se me clavan.

———————

SOREN ESTABA SENTADO JUNTO A Lila cuando Helena regresó al hospital con el corazón muerto en el pecho.

No había sucedido nada en su ausencia, salvo reuniones y discusiones en las que nadie se había puesto de acuerdo. Helena siempre había sabido que era Luc quien los mantenía unidos, pero resultaba descorazonador ver lo rápido que todo se estaba viniendo abajo.

A Lila le habían cortado el pelo como a un chico, y se lo habían rasurado en la zona donde tenía la herida. Su cara estaba tan hinchada y amoratada que apenas se la reconocía. Maier había intentado cerrar la piel con unos puntos de sutura muy delicados, pero, aun así, la cicatriz la acompañaría el resto de su vida.

—Es más joven que yo —comentó Soren. Helena asintió—. Nadie lo diría.

Se inclinó hacia delante para susurrarle algo a Lila al oído, pero lo hizo tan bajo que Helena no alcanzó a oírlo. Después, se levantó y se fue.

La sanadora lo siguió. Bajo el ojo que le quedaba, se le marcaba un surco que parecía un cráter, y estaba demacrado, se le notaban arrugas de dolor alrededor de la boca y en las comisuras de los ojos. Alguien le había quitado ya la escayola: seguramente, Elain.

—Ven aquí —le dijo, llevándolo a una zona protegida por cortinas donde lo obligó a sentarse.

Primero le atendió el brazo y la mano. El hueso se había soldado sin problema, pero la fractura era tan reciente que corría el riesgo de partírselo de nuevo. Sabía que Soren no tendría cuidado, que volvería al campo de batalla en cuanto le dieran permiso. Lo mejor que podía hacer por él era sanarlo por completo, del mismo modo que lo hacía con Kaine: no se limitaba a «arreglarlo», sino que lo revertía a su estado anterior.

—Necesito tu ayuda —le comentó cuando le estaba poniendo una gasa limpia sobre el ojo. Helena se quedó quieta.

—¿Para qué?

—Necesito una sanadora, y tú eres la mejor.

La chica se apartó y ladeó la cabeza para observar su gesto, aunque siempre se mostraba esquivo.

—Soren, ¿qué has hecho?

Este arqueó una ceja.

—Nada… todavía. —Se le escapó una sonrisa sin remedio, tan leve que apenas le curvó los labios—. Tienes que prometer que me ayudarás antes de que te lo cuente.

Helena se lo pensó. Soren jamás se había metido en problemas, salvo cuando iba acompañado de Luc y Lila. De hecho, Lila una vez bromeó con que Soren era como los gatos que fingían indiferencia, pero al final siempre acababan contigo en la misma habitación.

Soren era un enigma. Helena no tenía ni idea de qué camino elegiría ahora que actuaba por su cuenta.

—De acuerdo, te lo prometo. Cuéntamelo.

—Aquí no —repuso él, poniéndose de pie.

Abandonaron el Cuartel General, recorrieron varios callejones y entraron en una tienda abandonada.

—Traigo una sanadora —dijo en cuanto entró en el almacén. No apartaba la mano de la espalda de Helena, como si temiera que fuese a salir corriendo. Y no era tan descabellado, teniendo en cuenta lo planificada que parecía estar su presencia allí.

Armados hasta los dientes, los esperaban los dos soldados de la unidad de Luc que habían sobrevivido: Alister y Penny, junto a ellos estaban Sebastian y la informante de Crowther del hospital, Purnell, que evitó cruzar la mirada con Helena.

—¿Marino? —preguntó Alister—. Creía que traerías a un médico.

—Un médico no nos sirve —replicó Soren, que se dirigió a la mesa que había en mitad de la habitación. Helena se quedó atrás—. Necesitamos una sanadora. Helena es la mejor que tenemos.

—Es posible… —masculló Alister—, pero nunca ha entrado en combate. Será un peso muerto en una pelea. Igual que esta. —Señaló con desdén a Purnell—. Acabaremos muertos si no hacemos las cosas bien.

—No tiene que luchar, para eso estamos nosotros. Pero, si queremos sacar a Luc de allí con vida, necesitamos a alguien que pueda lograrlo. Hel es la mejor baza que tenemos. No sabemos en qué condiciones lo vamos a encontrar. Ella podrá arreglarlo todo.

Helena no estaba segura de si debía sentirse halagada o presionada por la confianza ciega que Soren estaba depositando en ella.

—¿Has estado en el frente alguna vez? —Alister la miró fijamente.

—No.

—Esto es una locura —insistió Alister—. Te seguiré adonde sea, Soren, pero no es un buen plan. ¿Qué pasa si Luc está herido y solo contamos con ella? ¿Podrá cargar con él?

—¡Yo puedo colaborar! —intervino Purnell de repente—. Después de enseñaros el camino, os ayudaré con Luc. En el hospital soy eficiente.

—Soren —dijo Helena con la voz tensa—, ¿podemos hablar? —Salió con él al exterior—. ¿Qué estás haciendo?

—Vamos a rescatar a Luc —respondió.

—Sí, de eso ya me he dado cuenta —replicó ella zarandeándolo. Le daba igual que estuviera herido, porque estabá a punto de embarcarse en una misión suicida—. Aún no te has recuperado. ¿Qué hace aquí Purnell?

—¿Sofia?

¿Desde cuando trataba Soren con tanta familiaridad a una camillera del hospital?

—Sí, la camillera. ¿Sabes quién es?

—Es quien podría saber dónde esta Luc.

Helena se quedó paralizada cuando comprendió qué hacía allí en realidad Purnell. Se trataba de uno de los tejemanejes de Crowther. No era Soren quien estaba planificando el rescate, sino Crowther, tirando otra vez de los hilos.

Entonces ¿qué pretendía hacer con Kaine? ¿Era solo una distracción? ¿O pretendía asegurarse de que no lo perdía antes de tiempo?

Helena apretó la mandíbula con fuerza.

—¿Y cómo es posible que ella lo sepa? —preguntó Helena para ver si así Soren entendía la locura que estaba cometiendo.

Soren sonrió un poco.

—Crowther la contrató para vigilarnos, pero a ella no le gusta hacerlo. Hace tiempo que se lo confesó todo a Luc. Ha tenido acceso a mapas de una cárcel secreta a la que podemos acceder por el alcantarillado de la isla Oeste.

—Soren… —Helena suspiró y cerró los ojos—. ¿Cómo ha visto esos mapas?

Soren se encogió de hombros. No parecía importarle.

—Crowther la usa como mensajera. Supongo que lo vio por ahí.

Si Crowther era el cerebro detrás de todo eso, lo mínimo que podía hacer era dar la cara y ofrecer instrucciones claras, en vez de basarse en que una camillera había visto un mapa por accidente.

Estaba harta de que Ilva y Crowther manipularan a las personas para conseguir sus «milagros». Como si nadie fuera a prestar sus servicios a menos que los engañaran para hacerlo.

—Si es así, supongo que Crowther conoce esa prisión y tiene mucha más información que un simple mapa. Deberíamos hablar con él.

Soren se negó en el acto.

—No. El Consejo ha dejado claro que nadie moverá un dedo hasta que «sepan» quién tiene a Luc. Ilva cree que puede negociar con los inmarcesibles para que nos lo devuelvan, pero no ha dicho qué está dispuesta a ofrecer a cambio.

Helena sabía perfectamente qué tenía Ilva en mente.

—Yo le debo lealtad a Luc —siguió Soren—, no a la Llama Eterna.

Mientras Lila esté de baja, soy el paladín primero. El Consejo no tiene poder sobre mí, mi deber es para con mis votos y esos votos se los hice a Luc.

Ella había creído que querían que Kaine rescatara a Luc, que arriesgara su tapadera para evitar el envío de tropas. Y, si fracasaba, Ilva lo delataría sin pensárselo dos veces.

Por eso Crowther se había visto obligado a actuar a espaldas de Ilva. Y por eso había usado a Sofia Purnell para filtrar la información a Soren, la única persona que podía actuar por su cuenta.

—De acuerdo —asintió Helena—. Os acompañaré.

Al principio, Soren la miró sorprendido, como si no se esperase que aceptara tan rápido, pero al instante se le escapó el aire en un suspiro de alivio.

—Bien, creo que no podremos hacerlo sin ti.

Helena lo observó con atención.

—¿A qué te refieres?

Soren tenía una expresión conmovedora cuando se ponía pensativo con sus párpados caídos. Aunque ahora solo le quedaba uno, Helena seguía reconociendo el gesto.

—Hel, necesito que hagas lo que consideres oportuno para salvarlo. Cueste lo que cueste. Sé que los miembros de la Resistencia morirían por él, pero yo quiero que tú vayas más allá.

La chica abrió los ojos, incrédula.

—¿Te das cuenta de lo que me estás pidiendo?

Soren mantuvo la cabeza alta.

—Juré proteger al principado con mi vida y mi muerte. Tú eres la única que ha dicho que, si alguien está dispuesto a morir, deberíamos darle la oportunidad de seguir luchando.

Helena notó que dejaba de sentir las manos.

—No puedes obligar a los demás a ofrecerse voluntarios en una misión como esta. ¿Vas a decirles por qué estoy aquí? ¿Que me has elegido porque piensas usar la nigromancia como último recurso? —Había bajado tanto la voz que se había convertido en un susurro lleno de rabia. Dio un paso hacia atrás, pero Soren la agarró del brazo.

—Ese no es el único motivo —insistió—. No mentía cuando dije que eres la mejor. Y no obligaré a nadie, solo me estoy ofreciendo yo. Si todo se tuerce, haz lo que tengas que hacer para sacarlos de allí. Te doy mi permiso.

La chica negó con la cabeza.

—Ni siquiera sé si puedo hacerlo. Nunca...

—Los dos sabemos que quien practica la vivemancia puede practicar la nigromancia. Y, si existe alguien capaz de aprenderla sobre la marcha, esa eres tú. No voy a hacer ninguna estupidez, simplemente... —Tragó saliva—. Esto tiene que salir bien, Hel, no queda otra.

Helena se lo pensó un momento, pero ¿qué alternativa tenía? Todas las decisiones le resultaban insoportables. Y este era el precio que ya había aceptado pagar.

—Está bien —dijo Helena—. Por Luc.

—Por Luc. Vamos.

Tenía pensado hablar con Purnell para que le dijera todo lo que sabía Crowther y averiguar cómo esperaba que se desarrollase la misión, pero la chica no paraba de moverse por la habitación, siempre fuera de su alcance.

—¿Cómo sabes todo esto? —preguntó Helena con un tono mordaz cuando les contó dónde estaba la prisión y que podían acceder a ella a través de unos tanques de inundación.

—Conozco a gente que los usa, exploradores sobre todo. Les sirven para escapar y ponerse a salvo —explicó Purnell.

—¿Por qué no hay patrullas vigilando?

Purnell se encogió de hombros.

—Es un laberinto. Los necrómatas no ven en la oscuridad, o se pierden, y a los inmarcesibles no les gusta reptar por las aguas residuales.

Helena sintió que le daban arcadas solo de pensarlo.

—Entiendo.

—Pero no estará tan mal. Estamos en época de inundaciones —dijo Purnell—. Casi toda el agua proviene de las montañas. Estará fría, pero no será tan asqueroso como en verano.

Menudo consuelo. Helena conocía demasiado bien lo fría que estaba el agua cuando se derretía la nieve e imaginarse que iba a tener que arrastrarse por ahí hizo que le empezaran a doler los huesos.

—¿Y esos túneles están conectados con la prisión donde está Luc?

Purnell esquivó de nuevo la mirada de Helena.

—Se han bloqueado muchos de los puntos de acceso de las alcantarillas, pero se pueden reabrir si tienes los planos originales de construcción. Hace unos meses se hizo una investigación. Es una prisión de máxima seguridad, pero casi siempre está vacía, como si la estuvieran reservando para algo en concreto.

—Si Luc está ahí, eso significa que llevan mucho tiempo planeando todo esto —intervino Sebastian con la voz tomada.

Helena se estremeció de miedo.

—¿Cómo estás tan segura de que Luc se encuentra allí?

—Si lo están ocultando, lo habrán metido en un sitio secreto —se limitó a contestar Purnell.

Helena no pudo evitar pensar que la participación de Purnell echaba por tierra cualquier intento de Crowther por negar su responsabilidad en todo aquello, aunque podría haberlo hecho mucho mejor.

—Si Luc no está allí, nadie sabrá que hemos ido —dijo Soren—. Tenemos que hacerlo esta noche. Mañana habrá sublimación. La marea subirá y no tendremos la cabeza despejada entonces. Tendríamos que esperar dos días más, y Luc no puede permitírselo.

Helena no lo había considerado. Habían capturado a Luc poco antes de la sublimación. ¿Por qué? ¿Para hacer más complicado su rescate? ¿O era una coincidencia?

Tenían un plan que apenas era un esbozo: entrar, encontrar a Luc y salir.

El trabajo de Helena consistía en mantener a Purnell cerca y a la vez lejos de todo peligro. El resto se encargaría de pelear. Cuando encontraran a Luc, lo examinaría para asegurarse de que seguía con vida y, si era necesario, lo sanaría lo más rápido posible. Después lo sacaría de allí. Purnell la ayudaría a cargarlo si no podía salir por su propio pie.

Lo importante era traerlo de vuelta a la isla Este, costara lo que costase. Si tenía que dejar a todos atrás, lo haría. Cuando Luc estuviera a salvo, los demás se dispersarían y se reagruparían más adelante.

—En marcha —concluyó Soren mientras agarraba su armadura. Alister y Penny se cuadraron de hombros.

—¡Esperad! —exclamó Helena, esforzándose por mantener la voz firme, aunque el plan no terminaba de convencerla—. Tengo que ir a por mi botiquín.

Soren le dedicó una mirada cargada de sospecha.

—¿No puedes usar las manos?

Ella negó con la cabeza.

—No. Si Luc está herido de gravedad, hay elixires y bálsamos que le ayudarán a recuperarse más rápido. Si dependemos únicamente de la vivemancia, podría agotarse, pero, si disponemos de medicinas, tendremos más opciones de sacarlo con vida, incluso aunque esté grave.

El paladín se relajó un poco.

—De acuerdo, pero date prisa. Si no has vuelto en quince minutos, nos iremos sin ti.

Salió corriendo por la puerta y se dirigió al Cuartel General, en concreto a la Torre de Alquimia. El ascensor le pareció más lento que nunca mientras ascendía.

—Por favor, Shiseo, espero que estés ahí —rezó mientras se abrían las puertas. Avanzó a paso ligero hasta el laboratorio, dudando de si había tomado la decisión correcta.

Shiseo estaba allí, concentrado en la síntesis de quelantes.

—Necesito tu ayuda —soltó Helena nada más entrar. Cogió su bolsa, abrió el armario de las medicinas y metió en ella todos los frasquitos que encontró. Quería que hubiera dosis doble para todos. Añadió agujas, vendas y kits de sutura manual, y lo introdujo todo en unas fundas enceradas e impermeables para protegerlo de la humedad. La bolsa parecía a punto de estallar.

Acto seguido, abrió el cajón en el que guardaba las dagas y empezó a anudárselas al cuerpo.

—Conseguiste las de titanio y níquel —comentó Shiseo, observando cómo se amoldaban a su piel—. ¿Puedo verlas?

—Ahora mismo no —respondió Helena, que se pasó la bolsa por encima de la cabeza y se la anudó a la cintura para poder correr con ella—. Necesito que hagas algo por mí. No puedo contarte todos los detalles, pero no tengo a nadie más en quien confiar.

Cogió un trozo de papel y escribió con rapidez todo lo que sabía, así como cualquier detalle que le pareciera relevante: ubicación, estrategia, escapatoria…

Cuanto más lo escribía, más evidente le resultaba que el plan era endeble, pero no había otra opción: solo seguir adelante. Alzó la vista.

—¿Sabes llegar a la vieja fábrica del Reducto?

Shiseo asintió.

—Sí. La visité cuando aún estaba operativa.

Helena asintió, temblando.

—Tienes que ir allí lo más rápido que puedas. Es… territorio enemigo, pero, si te cruzas con un necrómata, dile: «Me envía Helena», y te dejará en paz. Sigue este camino. —Trazó a toda prisa un boceto en un papel—. Allí encontrarás unos apartamentos con el símbolo del hierro en la puerta. En el segundo piso verás una entrada. Desliza esto por debajo de la puerta y vuelve. Y, si no quieres hacer nada de lo que te pido, entonces dáselo a Ilva. No puedo… Yo no sé cómo tomar esta decisión.

Le tendió el papel. Shiseo lo miró un momento y luego la observó a ella con un brillo en sus ojos oscuros que Helena no supo interpretar.

—Siempre supe que eras una persona muy interesante.

—Tengo que irme —afirmó Helena.

Shiseo cogió el papel, y ella salió corriendo, sin esperar a ver qué decisión tomaba. Siguió corriendo.

Soren y los demás estaban saliendo de la tienda cuando enfiló el callejón.

—Creía que te habías rajado —comentó Alister lanzándole una sonrisa ladeada. Al parecer, ya había aceptado su presencia.

—No —respondió Helena entre jadeos—. Contad conmigo.

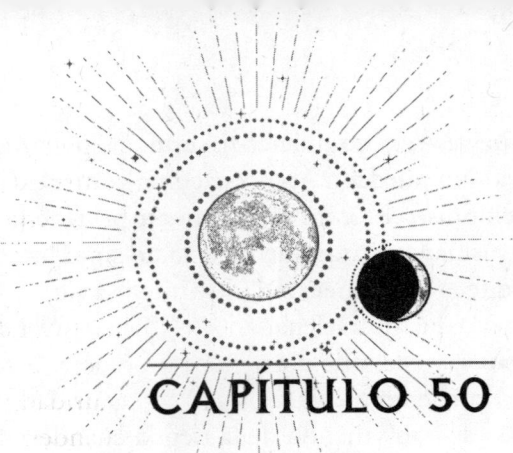

CAPÍTULO 50

Abrilis 1787

LLEGAR A LOS TANQUES DE inundación de la isla Oeste fue casi una misión en sí misma. Tuvieron que esquivar varias patrullas de la Resistencia hasta que, al fin, encontraron un punto débil en el muro, donde Alister se encargó de abrir un boquete. Se adentraron por el hueco y se arrastraron por el agua gélida. Las crecidas de la primavera se habían adelantado y, con Lumitia a punto de alcanzar la sublimación, los afluentes desbordados amenazaban con arrastrarlos a todos río abajo. Tuvieron que agarrarse a la pared de camino a uno de los antiguos puentes anteriores a la guerra. Había sufrido muchos estragos y se mecía peligrosamente. Cuando Helena lo cruzó a cuatro patas, sin atreverse a mirar el abismo de aguas frías y arremolinadas que rugía debajo, el puente parecía a punto de venirse abajo.

Y todo empeoró cuando estuvieron al otro lado. Los tanques de inundación eran huecos de gran envergadura diseñados para contener millones de litros de agua y redirigirla hacia el río, y estaban empezando a llenarse. El agua alcanzaba ya la mitad de la altura de la reja que daba paso a uno de ellos, y estaba fabricada en hierro, por lo que tardaron un buen rato en abrirla. Cuando lo lograron, descubrieron que se asomaba a una caída aterradora: ni siquiera con las antorchas eléctricas veían el fondo. De la oscuridad solo emergía el rugido del agua.

Los demás no se inmutaron. Tenían experiencia en combate y estaban acostumbrados a atravesar el subsuelo de la ciudad, así como a subir y descender varios pisos en rapel. Las armaduras contaban con arneses incorporados y, además, disponían de carretes de cable y ganchos para sujetarse.

Penny, exploradora de reconocimiento, fue la primera en bajar. Se movió con una rapidez asombrosa. Unos segundos después, cuando estuvo anclada a la pared, se zambulló de cabeza en la oscuridad sin volver la vista atrás. No sucedió nada en el primer minuto, pero después los cables se tensaron y se relajaron de nuevo. Era como si vibraran a intervalos. Alister los tocó con los dedos.

—Despejado —anunció, y tensó los cables para enviar la señal a Penny, que esperaba abajo.

Liberaron los anclajes, que se deslizaron en la oscuridad como serpientes metálicas, y los demás comenzaron a descender. Helena y Purnell, sin armadura ni arnés, se convirtieron en un peso muerto en el sentido más literal. Alister descendió con Helena enganchada a él, y Sebastian hizo lo mismo con Purnell. El agua les golpeaba como si estuvieran bajo una catarata, por lo que cuando llegaron al fondo estaban empapados hasta los huesos y totalmente entumecidos. No se oía más que el estruendo del agua al caer, resonando en los muros con una violencia ensordecedora.

Alister estaba temblando de frío, aunque se arrodilló y sumergió las manos en el agua durante unos minutos.

—Hay poca profundidad en los bordes, pero a unos tres metros a la izquierda hay un socavón por donde el agua va mucho más rápido. No toco fondo. —Tenía que gritar para hacerse oír—. Si seguimos recto, no habrá problema, pero será mejor que anclemos un cable antes de cruzar. Yo iré primero; sé por dónde es más seguro.

Cuando llegaron a la pared opuesta, subieron por una escalera que los llevó a una galería superior que discurría por encima de los enormes tanques de inundación. Helena empleó la vivemancia para calentar a todo el equipo, pero no pudo hacer nada con la ropa empapada. Debían seguir moviéndose.

Penny tomó la delantera. Se había aprendido de memoria todos los túneles, cada recodo. Cojeaba levemente a causa de una lesión anterior, y aun así se movía con rapidez y ligereza. Avanzó siguiendo la ruta establecida, asegurándose de que estaba despejada. Después les indicó a los demás que la siguieran con un movimiento de la antorcha.

No se toparon con un solo necrómata.

El miedo de Helena fue en aumento.

Subieron una escalera interminable que conectaba con otro túnel y, después de arrastrarse durante un buen rato, empezó a preguntarse si volvería a ver la luz del día. Pero finalmente desembocaron en un sótano.

—Esperad aquí —ordenó Soren.

Penny se apoyó contra la pared. Respiraba con dificultad, encorvada, con una mano sobre la rodilla.

—Déjame ver —dijo Helena. La chica había sufrido un desgarro en el ligamento y lo habían tratado, pero debería haber reposado en cama unos cuantos días antes de incorporarse paulatinamente al servicio activo.

—Estoy bien. Me lo arreglarán cuando volvamos —replicó Penny, aunque Helena sabía que no era verdad.

Oyeron un grito amortiguado, seguido de un chasquido metálico y un golpe sordo. Un instante después, la cabeza de Soren se asomó a la puerta del sótano donde aguardaban.

—Despejado —anunció en voz baja.

Ascendieron tres plantas. Helena nunca había visto en acción al batallón de Luc, solo durante las prácticas. Eran letales. Apenas distinguía destellos de acero y sangre derramada. Las armas se transformaban en sus manos como si fueran líquidas; retorcían y alteraban las hojas de metal para acabar con todo lo que se les pusiera por delante. Además, usaban los arneses para atacar de maneras que desafiaban a la gravedad.

No cabía duda de que la prisión estaba en funcionamiento. Había demasiados guardias y necrómatas como para considerarla abandonada, pero no tantos como cabría esperar si tenían a Luc prisionero.

Helena no dejaba de repetirse que aquello no era una trampa, pero en realidad así lo creía. Registraron todas las habitaciones; se movían rápido para evitar que alguien descubriera a las víctimas y diera la alarma. No tenía sentido esconder los cadáveres, por lo que Soren iba dejando un reguero de sangre a su paso.

Alister se encargaba de la defensa. Tenía un alcance de resonancia espectacular. Podía hacer volar una pared o derribar a los enemigos con una simple vibración del suelo. Solía quedarse atrás, cubriendo a Sebastian y Soren, mientras estos eliminaban de forma sistemática a sus objetivos en los estrechos túneles.

Cuando Penny terminó su tarea de explorar, se dedicó a cubrirle las espaldas a Alister y a protegerlo de los posibles ataques.

Revisaron todas las habitaciones, todas las celdas. No había ni rastro de Luc ni de otros prisioneros. Parecía que aquel sitio estaba vacío, y sin embargo había guardias.

Al final, encontraron a un prisionero en la última celda del módulo: una persona encogida bajo una manta.

—¿Luc? —La voz de Soren sonaba rota por la desesperación.

La persona que estaba tumbada en el catre se removió. Asomó la cabeza un hombre de cabello canoso. En cuanto los vio, abrió los ojos de par en par y se abalanzó contra los barrotes, farfullando en un dialecto norteño apenas inteligible.

—¿Resistencia?

Eso fue lo único que Helena entendió de todas las palabras que dijo. Parecía del Oeste.

—¿Salvar? —El hombre se señaló a sí mismo.

—No —respondió Soren sacudiendo la cabeza—. Estamos buscando a otra persona.

—Salvar. —Volvió a señalarse a sí mismo.

—Hemos venido a por otra persona —insistió Soren, y se giró para marcharse.

El hombre entornó los ojos.

—¿El chico? —Se tocó el pelo—. ¿Dorado?

Todos se volvieron hacia él.

—¿Está aquí? —preguntó Helena.

El hombre tensó la mandíbula.

—Salvar. —Volvió a señalarse.

—No tenemos tiempo de llevarnos a un prisionero —repuso Soren—. Ya lo encontraremos nosotros.

—¡No! —El hombre parecía aterrorizado.

Helena lo miró atentamente.

—¿Cómo te llamas?

—Vagner —respondió el hombre.

Le sonaba de algo… Vagner.

¿Wagner? Ese era el nombre que le habían sonsacado Crowther e Ivy a Lancaster cuando lo torturaron. Se giró hacia Soren.

—Hemos estado buscando a este hombre.

—Helena. —Soren la miró exasperado—. No podemos cargar con un prisionero.

—Este es importante. Crowther ha contratado a gente para encontrarlo. Si aquí es donde encarcelan a quienes no quieren que nadie encuentre, es porque el prisionero sabe algo.

Soren vaciló.

—Si nos retrasa o pone en riesgo la misión, lo mataré y no me lo impedirás. ¿Está claro?

Helena asintió.

Luc no estaba en esa planta. Subieron un piso más. Cada vez alberga- ban menos esperanza. Tal vez todos esos guardias estuvieran allí por Wagner, que los seguía acobardado detrás de Helena y de Purnell, como si las estuviera usando de escudo humano.

Al doblar una esquina, se toparon con un necrómata alto y macilen- to que estaba plantado delante de una puerta. Sonrió.

Aquello les indicó que no se trataba de un necrómata, sino de un li- che.

—Aquí estáis —ronroneó con voz áspera. Levantó una lanza enorme con una mano y con la otra tamborileó una advertencia sobre la puer- ta—. Me preguntaba si aparecerían los Bayard que aún quedáis. Nos hemos cargado a dos, así que solo nos quedan otros dos. —No le presta- ba atención a Soren mientras hablaba, solamente miraba a Sebastian—. Tu sobrina sonó como una calabaza podrida cuando la apuñalé. Debe- rías haber visto lo rápido que vuestro principado soltó la espada cuando me la cargué.

Sebastian sujetó a Soren.

—¿Quién eres?

El liche volvió a sonreír; los labios hinchados del cadáver se estiraron en una sonrisa putrefacta.

—¿No me reconoces, Sebastian? Pensé que lo harías después de todo el empeño que os pusisteis Apollo y tú en ejecutarme. Me temo que no funcionó. Al contrario que el hacha que le clavé a tu hermano en el crá- neo.

—Atreus —sentenció Sebastian en voz baja, pero agarró el arma con más fuerza.

Helena lo observó horrorizada. ¿El padre de Kaine seguía vivo?

Antes de que pudiera procesar la información, los dos paladines se lanzaron al ataque y Atreus se abalanzó sobre ellos. La pared estalló; bal- dosas y piedras volaron por el aire, levantando una nube de polvo que lo cubrió todo. La galería era estrecha, un espacio de combate reducido donde la velocidad era más valiosa que el tamaño y la fuerza. Si Atreus conseguía acertar un golpe, mataría a Sebastian y a Soren, pero primero debía tenerlos al alcance. Los Bayard eran más rápidos y lo acribillaron a cortes antes de que Atreus pudiera levantar la lanza y coger impulso.

Otra pared estalló cuando Atreus blandió su arma de nuevo.

El aire estaba tan cargado de polvo que apenas se distinguía nada salvo el fulgor del metal. Se oyó un crujido espantoso y algo surcó los escombros y cayó al suelo: era la cabeza del liche.

—Vamos —bramó Soren entre el polvo sofocante. Los demás se pusieron en marcha. Soren empleaba más el brazo derecho y Sebastian estaba sangrando por una herida en la sien, pero ambos estaban ilesos. El enorme cadáver que había albergado el alma de Atreus Ferron yacía a sus pies, cubierto de tajos profundos que habrían matado a cualquiera que no estuviera ya muerto.

—¿No deberíamos sacarle el talismán? —preguntó Helena cuando todos pasaron por encima del cuerpo.

—No tenemos tiempo de hurgar en un cadáver tan grande —respondió Soren, que caminó a trompicones y abrió la puerta de un empujón.

Allí estaba Luc.

Todos se quedaron paralizados.

Estaba atado a una camilla y tenía una mascarilla sobre la nariz y la boca conectada con varios tubos. A su alrededor había un grupo de personas con batas médicas.

Luc estaba abierto en canal, y su torso había sido plegado hacia atrás para dejar a la vista todos los órganos, negros y gangrenosos.

—¡Mierda! —exclamó una mujer en cuanto vio al batallón.

Era evidente que todavía no habían terminado lo que estuvieran haciendo cuando Atreus los alertó.

Dos personas salieron corriendo por una puerta que había al fondo. Dejaron allí a los demás a su suerte, sin tan siquiera mirar atrás.

El quirófano se sumió en la violencia.

Soren se había preparado para este momento. Recorrió la sala y transformó su arma en una hoja larga y curvada. Asesinó a todos los presentes con agresividad. No fueron muertes rápidas ni limpias. Helena notó que le caían chorros de sangre cuando se acercó a Luc.

Además de estar atado, le habían perforado las manos con unas púas de anulitio que Helena reconoció de inmediato por cómo el material se disolvía lentamente en su sangre. Le buscó el pulso con manos temblorosas, aunque no estaba segura de que fuera a funcionarle la resonancia. Colocó dos dedos por debajo de la mandíbula de Luc y se le escapó un sollozo de alivio. Estaba vivo. Anestesiado y abierto en canal, pero vivo.

Le arrancó la mascarilla de la cara y Purnell giró un botón de la bombona para cortar lo que le estuvieran suministrando.

¿Qué le habían hecho?

Helena palpó con las manos, por si le habían metido un talismán, si bien no encontró restos de lumitio ni de ningún otro metal. Tenía los órganos negros, como si lo hubieran envenenado, pero no había tiempo de curarlo de verdad.

Helena cerró las incisiones con todo el cuidado del que fue capaz, dejándolo todo en su sitio. Purnell estaba examinando las púas que tenía clavadas en las manos y no dejaba de jadear entrecortadamente mientras trataba de quitárselas. Su expresión era de un terror absoluto.

Helena se percató de que las venas y las arterias de los brazos de Luc estaban obstruidas y que el corazón le latía demasiado lento por culpa del gas que le habían administrado. Aquello había silenciado su resonancia para que los científicos que acababan de morir pudieran emplear la suya propia. El principado no estaba del todo inconsciente, pero tampoco despierto.

Soren y Alister estaban intentando abrir la puerta por la que habían escapado los dos científicos, pero no lo conseguían.

Helena trabajó lo más rápido que pudo y, cuando Purnell por fin le sacó las púas, aceleró el metabolismo de Luc para obligar a los riñones a ponerse en marcha y al corazón a latir con más fuerza. También le dio un frasco a la chica para que le lavara las heridas y así poder vendarlas luego.

Entonces sintió que su anillo ardía.

Empezó a dolerle la mano izquierda. Se le escapó un grito ahogado, pero siguió trabajando. Apenas había desaparecido el calor cuando volvió a encenderse.

—¿Está vivo? —escuchó que decía Soren con voz trémula.

—Sí, dame un minuto —respondió, tocándole la cara con desesperación—. Vamos, Luc. ¿Me oyes?

El anillo volvió a calentarse.

Entonces sonaron las alarmas, un pitido ensordecedor que lo inundó todo.

—¡Tenemos que irnos! —gritó Soren por encima del escándalo—. Joder, lo llevaremos en brazos.

—Luc, despierta. —La chica lo zarandeó.

Pero Luc pesaba demasiado. No podrían moverlo así. Helena y Purnell no conseguirían sacarlo de allí a rastras si había alguna pelea.

Helena sacó un frasco y una jeringuilla, y la rellenó con manos temblorosas. Nunca había usado esa combinación: epinefrina, calmantes y otras sustancias que activarían su cuerpo. Si era demasiado potente, lo mataría. Y todo habría sido en vano.

—Vamos… —masculló clavándosela en el pecho, junto al corazón.

Al instante, Luc se incorporó y aspiró una bocanada de aire. Su cuerpo recobró la movilidad con una sacudida violenta. Helena vislumbró el azul cielo de sus ojos.

—¿Hel? —gimió con voz áspera. Estiró la mano vendada para tocarle la cara, como si no creyese que fuera real.

—Sí —confirmó ella, conteniendo las lágrimas—. Hemos venido para llevarte a casa.

El principado miró a su alrededor, intentando reconocer a quienes estaban en el quirófano.

—¿Dónde… dónde está Lila?

—En el Cuartel General —respondió Soren con cierta brusquedad—, esperándote.

Luc se puso en tensión.

—¿Pero está…?

—Está viva —se apresuró a decir Helena—. La hemos sanado. Ahora te toca a ti. Tenemos que irnos.

A Luc se le escapó un suspiro de alivio.

—Me dijeron que si los acompañaba… no la matarían. Estaba… sangrando… tanto. No pude detener la hemorragia ni con fuego. ¿Está… está bien?

—Está viva, y recuperándose —respondió Helena—. Venga, coge esto. Tenemos que irnos.

Lo ayudó a incorporarse, pero Luc gimió y se llevó una mano al pecho.

—¿Qué me han hecho?

—No lo sé. Lo arreglaré cuando estemos a salvo —contestó la chica. Partió una pastilla por la mitad y se la introdujo en la boca. Solo podía rezar para que su cuerpo aguantara todo lo que le estaba suministrando—. Estate quieto.

Colocó ambas manos a los lados de su cuello y usó la pastilla para reajustar su fisiología y para asegurarse de que sus órganos funcionaran tal como debían. Cuando se le pasara el efecto, se derrumbaría por completo, pero Helena estaría con él. Lo solucionaría todo en cuanto estuvieran a salvo.

—Levanta —le ordenó. Luc estaba respirando demasiado rápido, y ella se percató de que el corazón le latía a una velocidad peligrosa. Trató de ralentizarlo, pero conforme recobraba el conocimiento era más consciente del peligro.

Helena se pasó uno de sus brazos por encima del hombro y Purnell hizo lo mismo por el otro lado. Tendrían que sacarlo a rastras.

—Has venido… —dijo Luc dejándose caer con pesadez.

—Eres mi mejor amigo —replicó Helena con la vista al frente—. Claro que he venido. Venga, tenemos que salir de aquí.

Luc no paraba de tropezarse con sus propios pies y su cuerpo presionaba con tanta fuerza que sus rodillas casi se doblaron. Agradeció que no llevase armadura, porque de haber sido así no lo habrían conseguido. El suelo resbalaba por la sangre y las vísceras.

—No deberías estar aquí. No tienes… formación —dijo cuando estaban a la mitad de las escaleras.

—Me formaron para ayudarte —repuso Helena.

El anillo no dejaba de arder. Una y otra vez. Lo ignoró.

Temía que, después de todo lo que habían combatido para llegar hasta allí, Soren y los demás estuvieran demasiado agotados para seguir peleando, pero ver a Luc les había dado fuerzas.

Por muy secreta que hubiera sido la prisión, una vez que se activó la alarma empezaron a salir numerosos necrómatas. No se trataba de los necrómatas lamentables y putrefactos que arrastraban los pies y se deterioraban rápidamente; a estos necrómatas los había reanimado una persona experta, y apenas se notaba que estaban muertos, salvo por el hecho de que seguían luchando a pesar de los golpes que recibían de Soren y Sebastian. La estrechez de los pasillos y lo anguloso de su recorrido eran a la vez una ventaja y una trampa.

—Necesito un arma —dijo Luc, e intentó apartar a Helena cuando Soren acabó estampado contra la pared y se derrumbó en el suelo. Un necrómata quiso arrancarle la cabeza, pero Sebastian lo apuñaló. Así ganó algo de tiempo para que Soren se incorporara y lo decapitara.

Estaba luchando con la mano izquierda; el brazo derecho lo mantenía pegado al cuerpo.

La medicación estaba surtiendo efecto. Luc había recuperado la fuerza suficiente como para resistirse a Helena, que pretendía sujetarlo, y también era consciente de que los enemigos los superaban en número. Aun así, Helena trató de detenerlo.

—Luc, estás herido. Ni siquiera estoy segura de cuánto. Simplemente no sientes el dolor.

—No voy a quedarme de brazos cruzados viendo cómo los matan.
—Intentó zafarse de ella y de Purnell, pero Helena le clavó los dedos en los brazos.

—Luc, no tienes resonancia.

—Pues ya me curarás luego —replicó y, al final, se libró de ambas y se lanzó a la batalla. Le propinó una patada a un necrómata con tanta fuerza que le atravesó el pecho. Después, le arrebató la espada.

Soren lo llamó varias veces, pero no pudo más que maldecir, ya que no dejaban de abalanzarse sobre él.

Helena desenvainó una de sus dagas cuando llegaron al sótano. Wagner seguía encogido detrás de Purnell, como si creyera que la chica podría protegerlo. Purnell tenía los ojos desencajados y la mirada perdida por el pánico. No deberían haberla traído. Estaba desmoronándose, no era capaz de resistir la guerra.

Se metieron en el sótano y cerraron la puerta, pero apenas habían girado la llave cuando la pared se hizo trizas. Huyeron por los túneles, arrastrándose uno tras otro por el alcantarillado en dirección a los tanques de inundación. Alister se colocó en la retaguardia y echó abajo los túneles conforme pasaban, paso a paso, para dificultar la persecución.

Cuando llegaron a uno de los túneles principales, se detuvieron a tomar aliento.

—No deberías estar luchando, idiota —le espetó Soren, desplomado contra una pared. A la luz de las antorchas, se le veía muy gris. Tenía la nariz partida y la sangre le corría por la boca y la barbilla.

Purnell estaba encogida en el suelo, meciéndose.

—¿Mami? Mamá, por favor, no lo hagas —musitaba una y otra vez.

—No me digas lo que tengo que hacer —replicó Luc, que respiraba entrecortadamente. Agarró la espada con la otra mano—. Esta espada es una mierda. Podrías haberme traído algún arma. ¿Tenéis mis anillos al menos?

—No tienes resonancia —le espetó Helena.

Luc torció el gesto, pero aferró la espada con más fuerza.

—Me parece increíble que Lila no te haya matado todavía —comentó Soren mientras lograba incorporarse. Se sostenía a duras penas, tambaleante.

—Espera. —Helena se acercó y lo revisó. Tenía el brazo roto otra vez, eran ya tres veces en el mismo año. Lo más probable era que esta vez no se le curara del todo. Le colocó los huesos en su sitio y los soldó.

—¿Tienes algo para el dolor? —preguntó Penny en voz baja—. También me sirve si puedes seccionar algún nervio.

Cuando hubo terminado con Penny, obligó a todo el equipo a tomarse sus tónicos regenerativos. Quería asegurarse de que todos estaban en condiciones de asimilar la sanación si la necesitaban. Había traído dos para cada uno, pero no había contado con un prisionero extra. Wagner se bebió el suyo mientras repartía el resto.

—Tenemos que ponernos en marcha —afirmó Soren. Tuvieron que arrastrar a Purnell con ellos, porque seguía en estado catatónico y tenía la mirada perdida, como si no supiera quién era, y no dejaba de llamar a su madre con una voz infantil y escalofriante.

Regresaron mientras desandaban sus pasos por la maraña de túneles hasta que llegaron al punto por donde habían entrado. Al principio, sintieron alivio al comprobar que nadie los seguía, pero conforme se acercaban les parecía muy extraño.

El anillo de Helena volvió a arder.

—Que Sol nos ampare. ¡Es Blackthorne! —exclamó Penny con la voz estrangulada por el miedo en cuanto doblaron una esquina.

En las partes bajas de los tanques de inundación se extendía una horda de necrómatas, acompañados por un buen número de aspirantes mortales. Permanecían en formación y les bloqueaban el paso por completo.

—¡Atrás! —ordenó Soren al instante, pero nada más pronunciar la palabra se oyó un chirrido de metal a sus espaldas, seguido de un rugido monstruoso.

Quimeras.

Estaban atrapados.

Blackthorne estaba al frente y no llevaba armadura.

—Capturad a Holdfast y matad al resto. ¡Así conseguiréis la inmortalidad!

Los aspirantes rugieron desesperados, mientras que los necrómatas permanecieron inmóviles, a la espera.

—Manteneos cerca —dijo Luc, que se colocó hombro con hombro entre Soren y Sebastian.

—Tenemos que llegar al otro lado —indicó Soren.

El plan, si es que se podía llamar así, había fracasado. No podrían escapar con Luc si el principado se empeñaba en luchar. Los dedos de Helena buscaron las dagas.

Cuando la primera oleada de necrómatas cayó sobre ellos, el grupo se dividió como un barco a la deriva.

Varios necrómatas se lanzaron contra Helena. No tuvo tiempo de pensar. Se movió por puro instinto: esquivó, bloqueó, apuñaló y transformó la daga para que dañara las articulaciones esenciales. Con la mano que le quedaba libre, cercenó la reanimación de los cadáveres.

La energía la golpeó con violencia, fue como una detonación. Perdió el equilibrio, pero los necrómatas que había cerca acabaron pulverizados. En alguna parte había luz, fuego, antorchas que se reflejaban en el agua pútrida que ya les llegaba hasta las rodillas. El sonido era ensordecedor: el rugido y el caos impedían los sentidos. Helena buscó a los demás, pero le resultó imposible distinguirlos en medio de la multitud. Había demasiados cuerpos, vivos y muertos, que se movían en la oscuridad. Kaine la había enseñado a defenderse para escapar, no a luchar en una refriega como esa. Intentó concentrarse en su resonancia, pero había tantos cadáveres, tantos movimientos y tantas armas que empezaba a marearse. Esquivó una porra que venía directa a por ella y respondió con un tajo de su cuchillo. La hoja vibró con resonancia cuando atravesó la piel cerosa y putrefacta, del torso a la garganta hasta hundirse en el cerebro, rajando huesos como si fueran mantequilla.

Con un movimiento de resonancia, la hoja se curvó y cercenó la cabeza del necrómata de forma limpia.

Algo chocó con ella y la hizo tropezar. Una mano caliente impidió que cayera al suelo. «Será un aliado», pensó. Pero entonces vio un guantelete de acero que empuñaba una espada y la dirigía hacia su cabeza. Helena levantó la daga, justo a tiempo para esquivar el golpe con la empuñadura y, acto seguido, la hundió en la clavícula del adversario. Haciendo uso de la resonancia, estrechó la hoja todo lo que pudo hasta que el metal la avisó de que había atravesado la carne. Cuando la tuvo metida hasta la empuñadura, hizo que la hoja se extendiera y la sacó de un tirón. Helena sintió que la sangre cálida y espesa le manchaba la mano y, un segundo después, el guantelete le soltó el hombro. La espada cayó a varios centímetros de su cabeza, y el aspirante se desplomó encima de ella.

Los dos cayeron al agua. Helena sintió el frío como si fuera una patada en las costillas. Intentó incorporarse para librarse del cadáver que estaba a punto de asfixiarla.

Blandió el arma a ciegas: el agua, el ruido y la desorientación le hacían imposible percibir nada más.

Gateó para alejarse del tumulto hasta que encontró una pared y logró ponerse en pie. Trató de recobrar el aliento mientras buscaba a los demás en los intervalos de luz que despejaban las sombras. Se oían unos gritos que no cesaban. Era Purnell, que había superado la congoja y ahora chillaba a pleno pulmón. Los gritos rebotaban en los muros y llamaban la atención. Un grupo de necrómatas avanzaba hacia ella.

Wagner, que estaba al lado de Purnell, la empujó hacia ellos y trató de escapar. Al caer al suelo, la chica pareció recobrar la lucidez, pero entonces comprobó con horror lo que estaba pasando.

No tenía armas, pero reaccionó rápido. Saltó y, de alguna forma, esquivó las manos que se le echaban encima. Corrió hacia el centro del túnel, que estaba inundado de sangre.

Apenas había dado unos pasos cuando desapareció bajo el agua.

Helena lo vio todo y rezó para que volviera a salir a la superficie, para que escapase de la corriente. Sin embargo, justo entonces, algo golpeó a Helena y la hizo caer de costado. Sintió una bota aplastándole su muñeca y se atragantó con el agua al proferir un grito ahogado.

Un dolor abrasador le atravesó las costillas.

Retrocedió a gatas hasta la pared. Tenía la ropa congelada y pegada a la piel. Se giró buscando a sus compañeros, aunque no dejaba de toser agua.

No sabía cómo, pero Wagner había logrado llegar a la pared contraria y ahora blandía una lanza con la que combatía a los necrómatas.

Luc y Sebastian luchaban juntos en el centro de la horda, mientras que Soren se había separado y estaba intentando alcanzar a Alister y Penny, que estaban acorralados, lejos de todo el mundo.

Las luces parpadeaban sin parar sobre el agua, por lo que solo se veían destellos fragmentados de la acción. Las quimeras habían llegado. Helena vio de reojo unos colmillos afilados y unas garras mientras Alister intentaba levantar un muro improvisado. Penny soltó un grito desesperado cuando clavó su arma en el hombro de una quimera y el monstruo la arrastró consigo.

Soren atravesó el agua con gran rapidez, transformando su arma sobre la marcha, tratando de llegar antes de que las quimeras se les echaran encima.

Un hacha surcó el aire y estuvo a punto de clavarse en su pierna.

El joven se detuvo, dando un traspié en el agua, y se giró bruscamente para buscar a su atacante. La guadaña que tenía en la mano esquivó un golpe de milagro, aunque estuvo a punto de perder el equilibrio. Ahora ya sabía a quién se enfrentaba: Blackthorne le impedía el paso.

El inmarcesible, consciente de la desventaja de su contrincante, atacaba siempre a su derecha y dirigía todos los golpes al punto ciego de Soren. Lo estaba agotando.

—¡Soren! —gritó Luc de repente.

Soren se giró en el mismo momento en el que una quimera se lanzaba a por él. La decapitó de un movimiento certero.

Se oyó un sonido terrible, parecido a un crujido húmedo.

Aprovechando que Soren se había vuelto, Blackthorne le había atacado por la derecha. Tenía la cabeza del hacha enterrada entre las costillas y le sobresalía por la espalda.

Blackthorne retiró el hacha y le dio un lametazo a la hoja mientras observaba a Soren caer y desaparecer bajo el agua.

Todo ocurrió muy deprisa.

Luc empezó a chillar, pero el cuerpo de Helena pareció cobrar vida de repente. Se lanzó hacia delante apuñalando todo lo que encontró a su paso, desesperada por llegar hasta donde estaba Soren antes de que la corriente se lo llevara.

Pero Luc fue más rápido. Cuando Helena llegó, él ya estaba de rodillas, sujetando a Soren en sus brazos, bañado en la sangre que escapaba del cuerpo de su amigo. Un instante después, apareció Sebastian, interponiéndose entre ellos y Blackthorne para impedirle el paso, mientras Luc permanecía arrodillado en el agua abrazando a Soren.

Cuando Helena se agachó a su lado, Luc alzó la vista.

—P-puedes curarlo, ¿verdad?

—Luc…

Pero el principado ya estaba entregándole el cuerpo de Soren. El peso hizo que Helena cayera de rodillas en el agua. Agarró al paladín con manos temblorosas, ignorando el dolor punzante que sentía en la muñeca.

—Yo te cubro —aseguró Luc cogiendo la espada. Y, sin más, se marchó.

La batalla no se había detenido por Soren.

Helena trató de aislarse de lo que sucedía a su alrededor y se concentró. Solo necesitaba encontrar un hilo de vida, así lo mantendría a salvo.

Así había mantenido a Lila con vida.

Pero la herida era demasiado profunda. Los soldados con este tipo de heridas no sobrevivían el traslado al hospital. Había recibido un golpe letal. La vida que le quedaba era frágil y se le escapaba de los dedos cada vez que intentaba usar su resonancia.

Unos dedos le acariciaron la mano.

Soren la estaba mirando fijamente.

—Recuerda nuestro trato.

Apenas escaparon esas palabras de sus labios cuando Helena sintió un estallido de energía fría y letal que atravesó su resonancia. Tenía la mente tan sensible del cansancio y estaba tan concentrada en mantenerlo con vida que se le nubló la vista cuando notó que la recorría la descarga de la muerte. Se dobló sobre sí misma y, por un instante, no fue capaz de comprender lo que había pasado. Cuando se le aclaró la vista, se encontró con la mirada vacía e inexpresiva de Soren.

Había muerto.

—No. No. No. ¡Soren!

Lo tenía en brazos; su sangre seguía manchándole la piel. Era el único calor que sentía.

Helena miró a su alrededor. Alister estaba pidiéndole a Penny que emprendiera la retirada. La chica estaba enfrentándose a las quimeras con un simple cuchillo, por lo que debía acercarse peligrosamente a ellas para darles un tajo. Un error y lo perdería todo.

Soren estaba muerto. Purnell estaba muerta.

Sebastian estaba haciendo todo lo posible para contener a Blackthorne y proteger a Luc. Luc seguía luchando, aunque distraído, con la mirada fija en Helena, que seguía arrodillada con Soren en sus brazos. Percibió la desesperación en sus ojos. La certeza de que iba a salvar a Soren porque podía hacerlo. Pero era demasiado tarde.

Ella lo miró a los ojos un instante y, después, consumida por la culpa, le dio la espalda y acercó su cuerpo al de Soren.

—Haré cualquier cosa —dijo posando una mano en su cuello—. Cueste lo que cueste.

Vertió la energía de su cuerpo para devolvérsela a Soren.

Fue demasiado fácil, casi instintivo.

Conocía a Soren, sabía lo que había sentido cuando estaba vivo.

Su resonancia recorrió el cuerpo del paladín como un torrente de agua, cerró la herida de forma limpia, cosió los tajos de los órganos seccionados y recolocó los huesos en su sitio. Sin embargo, no se detuvo ahí.

Helena sintió que la mente de Soren regresaba: una sombra, un leve atisbo de su consciencia, así que centró en eso toda su energía.

«Vuelve. Vuelve. No puedes irte todavía».

Soren parpadeó. Ella notó que había una conexión entre ambos, apenas un hilo. Lo sostuvo, incapaz de dejarlo marchar.

—Todavía no puedes descansar, tienes que proteger a Luc —afirmó, y las palabras resonaron en el interior de Soren.

Soren la reconocía, de eso estaba segura. Sabía que era una amiga. Le resultó horrible sentir aquella vida abominable entre sus brazos. A pesar de lo mucho que se había esforzado, no era más que una sombra. Soren era una marioneta y ella quien tiraba de los hilos.

Después de pasar tantos años sanando, la nigromancia le pareció fácil. No sintió dolor. Se limitó a pedirle al cuerpo de Soren que no muriera, que luchara como siempre lo había hecho. Y Soren los protegería, porque sabía cómo hacerlo.

El paladín se puso en pie y la ayudó a levantarse; ya tenía el arma en la mano.

La memoria muscular no se perdía. Era como si estuviera sonámbulo, a pesar de estar muerto.

Helena podía ver a través de sus ojos. Su consciencia iba y venía mediante la conexión que habían forjado entre ellos. Soren se giró y, al ver a Luc, la chica sintió que deseaba acercarse. Después buscó a Lila.

El principado vio que Soren se ponía en pie y, por un instante, el alivio se hizo patente en su rostro. Sin embargo, no duró mucho.

Luc lo supo. De alguna forma, lo supo nada más mirarlo.

Aun así, Soren se dirigió hacia él. Helena lo detuvo.

—Tienes que proteger a Penny y a Alister —le ordenó, en voz alta y mentalmente. Señaló hacia ellos para que dejara de prestarle atención a Luc—. Sácanos de aquí.

Soren se giró y obedeció. Helena lo observó con la mente confusa; la desorientaba esa segunda consciencia que tenía ahora en su cerebro. La suya propia no sabía adónde ir.

Una quimera se abalanzó sobre ella.

La esquivó, aunque por el rabillo del ojo vio una guadaña.

Soren.

Helena parpadeó intentando hacerse una idea de cómo estaban.

Soren mató a la quimera sin detenerse siquiera en su avance hacia Penny y Alister. Antes de volver, puso a Penny a salvo.

Percibió un movimiento a la izquierda. Helena se encogió para esquivar lo que fuera que se le acercaba, aunque no estaba segura de si estaba viendo a sus atacantes o a los de Soren. Trató de concentrarse un poco en su propia mente y se enfocó en lo que la rodeaba.

Si moría, Soren también lo haría. Tenía que permanecer con vida hasta que Luc estuviera a salvo.

Intentó bloquear los movimientos de Soren, pero estaba demasiado enraizado en su mente. Sintió un gesto a su espalda y se giró un segundo antes de que el impacto la alcanzara de lleno. El golpe le vació los pulmones de aire. Bajó la vista y, al parpadear, intercambió una consciencia con otra.

Soren. Helena. Soren.

Tenía un cuchillo clavado hasta la empuñadura en el lado derecho del pecho.

Helena.

Si se hubiera girado un segundo más tarde, le habría atravesado el corazón, pero entrecerró los ojos concentrándose y comprendió que no había provocado daños en ningún órgano vital.

El dolor fue lo único que hizo que Helena recobrara su propia consciencia.

Actuó de inmediato: le cortó la mano al necrómata que la había apuñalado y así impidió que sacara el cuchillo. Con la mano derecha sostuvo el arma en el sitio para que este no pudiera arrancarla y, acto seguido, le propinó una patada en la rodilla.

Al moverse, se le escapó un gemido de dolor y trastabilló; los bordes de la hoja se le clavaron aún más.

Una quimera cerró los colmillos alrededor de la pierna de Soren y le dejó una herida desgarradora. El paladín la decapitó sin prestar atención a la herida.

Lo estaban destrozando. Helena notaba las heridas, aunque no sintiera el dolor. Esa parte del cerebro no la había logrado reanimar.

Aun así, no dejó de luchar.

«Saca el cuchillo. Cierra la herida».

Helena se dirigió hasta una pared y se acurrucó en el agua congelada. Había otra quimera atacando a Sebastian y a Luc. Por su tamaño, debía de tener algo de oso. A Luc empezaban a fallarle las fuerzas.

La quimera era enorme. Su cuerpo era de mamífero, pero mostraba unas fauces alargadas, propias de algún reptil, y una piel tan gruesa que las armas no eran capaces de penetrarla. Chillaba con voz humana.

Helena intentó concentrarse. Se mordió el labio y se preparó para sacar el cuchillo.

No obstante, unos dedos se enredaron entre sus trenzas y obligaron a Helena a levantarse hasta que apenas rozaba el suelo con los pies.

Basilius Blackthorne le dedicó una sonrisa que dejaba ver todos los dientes. Un reguero de sangre le caía desde la boca hasta la barbilla.

Con esos dientes se había comido a su mujer y a sus hijos...

—Veo que la Llama Eterna cuenta con una nigromante —comentó con voz áspera.

Helena intentó apuñalarle el brazo con el que la agarraba, pero Blackthorne le apartó la mano con tanta fuerza que le entumeció toda la mano izquierda. La daga cayó al agua con un chapoteo.

Intentó agarrarle la muñeca, pero, en cuanto le rozó la piel con los dedos, extendió su resonancia.

Aunque Kaine siempre se lo había advertido: si los inmarcesibles descubrían lo que era, se mostrarían precavidos.

Antes de que pudiera establecer el contacto, Blackthorne se apartó con rapidez y cerró los dedos alrededor de los nudillos de la mano izquierda. No dejó de apretar con todas sus fuerzas, hasta que le partió los dedos como si fueran ramitas.

Helena chilló. El cuchillo que tenía en el pecho se movió y sintió una presión dolorosa en los pulmones.

Blackthorne contempló la mano aplastada de Helena y soltó una carcajada.

—Había olvidado que vosotros no os regeneráis.

Entonces se fijó en la mano derecha y reparó en la extraña manera en la que sujetaba el cuchillo.

—Creo que esta ya está rota, pero vamos a asegurarnos.

Con una suavidad inesperada, el inmarcesible retiró la mano de Helena de la empuñadura del cuchillo y le partió la muñeca. La chica vio puntos negros y empezó a gritar de nuevo.

—Debería mantenerte con vida —dijo mientras le sacaba el cuchillo del pecho muy lentamente, disfrutando del resplandor de la hoja.

A Helena le dolía tanto que su mente no dejaba de intercambiarse con la de Soren en busca de alguna escapatoria.

Los necrómatas lo tenían acorralado. Había acabado con las quimeras, pero eran demasiados necrómatas, decenas de muertos que lo empujaban corriente abajo y lo estaban despedazando. Uno le clavó los dientes en la pierna y le arrancó el tendón a la altura de la rodilla.

Aun así, seguía luchando. Aunque había perdido la guadaña, conservaba todavía un cuchillo. Penny gritaba tras él, pero Alister la retenía. Soren continuaba apuñalando, rompiendo y abriéndose paso a puñetazos; estaba siguiendo la orden de no dejar de luchar, a pesar de que lo estaban destrozando. Unos dedos cadavéricos le tantearon la cara hasta encontrar el ojo que le quedaba. Después, le desencajaron la mandíbula y le dejaron la garganta a la vista.

Helena se estremecía de forma inconsciente cada vez que le arrancaban una parte del cuerpo, pero el dolor no cedía. No sentía los dedos, no eran más que un faro de agonía que se extendía por los brazos.

Notó que le caía un chorro de sangre por el costado.

Creyó que Basilius volvería a apuñalarla, pero el inmarcesible soltó el cuchillo y pasó los dedos por la herida del costado. Helena notó el escozor en la piel sensible.

Entonces recorrió la puñalada que tenía entre las costillas y, sin previo aviso, introdujo dos dedos en la herida. Helena gritó al sentir que abría la piel y le doblaba los huesos desde dentro. Tenía los dedos empapados con su sangre.

—¿Sabes qué? No hay nada que me guste más que una herida —dijo sin aliento—. Están húmedas y calientes, más que cualquier otra cosa.

Helena pataleó y trató de empujarlo con sus manos rotas, y, a pesar de que notó cómo giraban sus huesos destrozados, no sirvió de nada. Gritó y gritó, pero nadie la escuchó, así que le golpeó el pecho con la cabeza hasta que Basilius le agarró la garganta con la mano que tenía libre y presionó el pulgar contra su tráquea para que se callara. Sus pulmones luchaban por encontrar aire.

—Sí, eso es —comentó con un gemido de aprobación—. No te preocupes, no dejaré que mueras. Seguirás viva cuando te entregue. Bennet estará encantado contigo.

Estaba a punto de perder el conocimiento. La vista se le nublaba. Ya no encontraba aire para seguir gritando. Apenas notó que Soren desaparecía de su mente, arrastrado por la corriente; la conexión se disolvió como la sangre en el agua.

—Un grito más. Se te da estupend…

De repente, Blackthorne trastabilló y boqueó como si alguien le hubiera vaciado los pulmones. Sus manos perdieron fuerza y los dedos se resbalaron de su cuello un segundo antes de que él arqueara la espalda.

Helena cayó como una losa. El frío gélido la devolvió a la realidad; de no haber sido así, se habría ahogado. Se acurrucó en el suelo y buscó con la mirada aterrorizada a Blackthorne. Vio que alguien lo arrastraba por el agua con un cable o una soga alrededor del cuello.

Pero la persona que lo estaba arrastrando no era miembro de la Resistencia.

Era un inmarcesible, al que reconoció de inmediato por el yelmo y el uniforme negro.

Cuando los dos estuvieron al alcance el uno del otro, Blackthorne ya se había recuperado y se abalanzó contra su atacante. Había recuperado una espada del agua y la lanzó directa a la cabeza del otro inmarcesible, aunque este consiguió esquivarla.

Blackthorne lo intentó una y otra vez. Atacaba con precisión y se movía con la destreza de un alquimista de combate experto, pero su contrincante siempre lo esquivaba. No llevaba armas, ni tampoco contratacaba. Era rápido y ligero, se deslizaba como si estuviera danzando, hasta que Blackthorne cometió un error. Fue solo un instante, pero el atacante no necesitó más.

El recién llegado evitó un golpe y, empleando sus propias manos, atravesó la armadura y el pecho de Basilius como si estuviera sumergiéndose en el agua. Una mano pálida de largos dedos y manchada de sangre extrajo un fragmento de metal resplandeciente de la caja torácica de Blackthorne.

El hombre se derrumbó en el agua y desapareció.

La pelea no había durado ni un minuto.

En pleno caos, nadie más se había percatado. Helena intentó respirar, pero una presión insoportable en sus pulmones se lo impedía. Pegó el brazo contra la herida para evitar que se le escapara más aire de la caja torácica.

Los necrómatas empezaron a desplomarse. Unos cuantos aspirantes vieron al recién llegado, confundidos, sin entender qué estaba sucediendo. Antes de que pudieran reaccionar, estaban todos muertos. El arma relució tan deprisa que Helena apenas la vio; solo contempló cómo cayeron todos los cuerpos.

Era Kaine.

Nunca lo había visto combatir, porque nunca había querido luchar con ella. Pero lo reconoció al instante. Esa precisión implacable era inconfundible.

Era tan letal como imaginaba.

Helena vio en directo las técnicas que había tratado de enseñarle una y otra vez, la fluidez de la que ella carecía, lo rápido que era. No desperdiciaba ni un solo movimiento. El impulso de un asesinato lo conducía al siguiente.

Los cuerpos caían como estrellas fugaces.

Se abrió paso por el agua en busca de Helena. No dudó ni un momento, se limitó a aniquilar todo lo que se interpuso en su camino.

Cuando se le echó encima una quimera, levantó la mano y, al tocarla, su cuerpo se descompuso. Las extremidades se desprendieron como si le hubiera descosido las suturas invisibles que la mantenían unida. Lo que un segundo antes era un monstruo ahora era un cadáver en el agua.

No era un combate, sino una masacre.

Una cuestión de números: mínimo esfuerzo, máxima eficacia.

Era imposible que alguien lo hubiera visto luchar así antes. Si alguien lo hubiera presenciado, todo el mundo lo sabría.

Metió una mano en el bolsillo y sacó un puñado de fragmentos metálicos. Los lanzó por los aires. Al salir despedidos, Helena sintió cómo expandían la resonancia de Kaine.

La metralla surcó los aires moviéndose como una bandada de pájaros al unísono y acertó como si fuera una descarga de balas. Cada trozo de metal atravesó el cráneo de un necrómata.

En vez de caer, el metal permaneció suspendido en el aire, goteando sangre y vísceras. Kaine hizo un gesto con la mano y todos los trozos se ponían de nuevo en movimiento para atravesar más cuerpos. Cada vez que chasqueaba los dedos, volvían a dispararse.

Cuando Kaine alcanzó a Helena, tenía los ojos ardientes de rabia. Le brillaban como si fuera plata derretida detrás de la máscara.

—Valiente idiota estás hecha —le espetó, pero la sacó del agua sosteniéndola contra su pecho.

Su resonancia espesó el ambiente como una ola que se extendía hacia fuera. Helena contempló cómo atacaba a los necrómatas y a los aspirantes más cercanos. Estos últimos empezaron a retorcerse y convulsionar, hasta que acabaron cayendo al agua. Los necrómatas se desplomaron, mientras que las quimeras y los que quedaban vivos boqueaban como si les faltara el aire, arañándose frenéticamente las gargantas.

Helena aún podía respirar, aunque le costara, pero los demás se estaban ahogando.

Sebastian se derrumbó en el agua antes de llegar a Luc, que se clavaba los dedos en la garganta, con el rostro azulado y los ojos desorbitados.

—Para —jadeó Helena al darse cuenta de que Kaine no distinguía entre los inmarcesibles y la Llama Eterna. Estaba matando a todo el mundo—. ¡Para! ¡No los mates! ¡Detente!

Se removió con esfuerzo para liberarse en cuanto vio que Luc ponía los ojos en blanco y se desplomaba en el agua.

La ola invisible alcanzó los muros. Penny cayó, al igual que Alister.

La lucha había terminado.

—¡Para, para, para! —Volvió a resistirse para que Kaine la soltara—. ¡Para!

—Cállate —le espetó Kaine a través del yelmo, aunque acabó soltándola—. Espera aquí.

Se acercó a ver a Sebastian y Luc, a Penny y a Alister, incluso a Wagner, aunque a Helena le importaba poco si moría o no. Kaine les posó una mano en el pecho y otra en la nuca y, acto seguido, Helena comprobó que se movían y volvían a respirar, aunque no recobraron el conocimiento.

Helena intentó ponerse en pie, pero las piernas le fallaron. Cuando Kaine volvió a su lado, estaba empezando a marearse.

Kaine la arrastró hasta la pared, donde varios túneles se adentraban en la oscuridad.

—No puedes dejarlos aquí —dijo Helena con voz rasposa, intentando zafarse.

—Cállate. —El agua apenas les llegaba a los tobillos, y ante ellos había una escalera que conducía a una pasarela que estaba a la altura del hombro.

—No puedes dejarlos aquí —repitió ella revolviéndose—. Tráelos o no me iré.

Kaine se giró sin pronunciar palabra. Por el camino, empujó a los necrómatas a patadas para que se los llevara la corriente, pero se detuvo junto a unos aspirantes muertos para reanimarlos. Estos se pusieron en pie y lo ayudaron a cargar a Luc y a los demás hasta la pasarela. Con sumo cuidado, Kaine se encargó de llevar a Helena en brazos. Ella se mordía el labio con tanta fuerza que estuvo a punto de hacerse sangre por el dolor intenso que sentía en las costillas. Kaine tenía las manos rojas de la sangre, pero no dijo nada mientras subía la escalera y la dejaba en la parte de arriba.

Los necrómatas se echaron al hombro al resto del equipo y lo siguieron.

En la oscuridad, Helena perdió y recuperó el conocimiento varias veces, y se despertó cuando oyó un chirrido de metal y el rugido estrepitoso del agua que provenía de los tanques de inundación. Siguieron avanzando.

Kaine se detuvo para darle una patada a la pared. Había una puerta prácticamente invisible entre las numerosas pasarelas. Al abrirla, entraron en una sala pequeña.

Había una mesa contra una de las paredes, y Kaine la dejó allí. Luego se giró, cerró la puerta y se quitó el yelmo de un tirón. Tenía el rostro agitado por la rabia.

—Dime que puedes aguantar hasta que encuentre un médico. —Le temblaba la voz. Helena negó con la cabeza.

Kaine estaba jadeando, pero tragó saliva.

—Entonces tendrás que decirme cómo curarte. ¿Puedes hacerlo?

—Sí —respondió con voz trémula, aunque lo único que quería era desmayarse—. Lo primero que hay que arreglar… es el hígado. De ahí proviene la sangre. Creo. Tengo aire… en el pecho, me está colapsando el pulmón. Cuando… cuando arregles… el hígado, podrás… estimular la producción de sangre. No tengo el tónico, pero deberías poder hacerlo con resonancia.

Kaine desanudó las correas de la bolsa y le cortó la ropa empapada para poder acceder directamente a la herida que tenía entre las costillas, que estaba abierta en canal.

Helena se encogió de dolor, pero trató de no moverse mientras Kaine contenía la hemorragia y escuchaba atentamente sus indicaciones para identificar y reparar los conductos colédocos.

No podía usar las manos ni la resonancia, por lo que era como guiar a un ciego.

—Cállate —le espetó cuando se disculpó por no saber exactamente en qué estaba fallando. Metió la mano en el bolsillo de la capa y sacó algo—. Este es para la sangre, ¿no? ¿Te servirá?

Sostuvo en alto un frasquito con algo azul verdoso. Helena lo reconoció al instante. Sintió que se le formaba un nudo en la garganta, pero asintió.

—Sí, me sirve.

Aún más difícil fue el proceso de sacar el aire que estaba haciendo presión sobre el pulmón, porque no tenía material para hacerlo. Tragó saliva con dificultad.

—Hay un tubo en mi bolsa.

Kaine lo encontró, y Helena le indicó con sumo cuidado dónde tenía que anestesiar y hacer la punción. Se le escapó un gemido ahogado cuando hundió el tubo en la piel para introducirlo en la caja torácica.

Helena tragó saliva y contempló el techo que había sobre ellos. Conforme respiraba con más normalidad, su mente empezaba a despejarse.

—Ahora tienes que comprobar si el tejido pulmonar ha sufrido algún daño. Después, hay que lavar la herida y cerrar el músculo del diafragma, y...

Los dedos de Kaine pasaron junto a la herida y Helena se paralizó de inmediato. Acto seguido, se apartó con violencia.

—¡No... no la toques! —pronunció en un grito estrangulado, casi cayéndose de la mesa.

Kaine retiró la mano y se quedó observándola. Helena empezó a jadear, intentando controlar la respiración, aunque a veces se le escapaba algún que otro sollozo.

El corazón le latía tan fuerte que lo sentía retumbar en las sienes.

—Blackthorne iba a... iba a... —Se le trabó la lengua y, siguiendo un instinto protector, intentó cubrirse la herida para que nadie la tocara.

—Está muerto —dijo Kaine, que mantenía un semblante inexpresivo, con una calma deliberada—. No va a volver. ¿Quieres que te tape la herida y te arregle las manos?

Helena negó con la cabeza.

—No, me quedaré quieta. Solo... —Tragó saliva—. Lo siento.

El chico apretó la mandíbula. Al reanudar la sanación, le advirtió cada vez que la tocaba y le explicaba lo que iba a hacer con voz grave y tranquila. Helena cayó en la cuenta de que estaba imitando lo que ella misma hizo cuando trató el sello de su espalda.

Era la parte más sencilla de la sanación, pero Helena solo quería vomitar del miedo que sentía.

—Ya.

El peligro más inmediato había pasado. Kaine también pareció respirar de nuevo.

—¿Por qué has venido? —le preguntó entonces.

Lo miró a los ojos un instante y luego apartó la mirada.

—El Consejo estaba dispuesto a hacer cualquier cosa por recuperar a Luc.

—No tienes experiencia de combate —insistió Kaine. Le temblaban las manos mientras se limpiaba la sangre de la cara—. ¿Por qué te han traído sin asignarte un compañero?

—Tenía una compañera —respondió Helena—. Murió en combate.

—¿Quién?

—Purnell. Era… camillera.

Kaine la fulminó con la mirada.

—Tenía que ser un equipo reducido. Debíamos entrar y salir sin que nadie se diera cuenta. Sofia y yo no íbamos a luchar.

—Sabíais que era una misión suicida. Eso es lo que hacen los Bayard, morir por los Holdfast. No conocen nada más.

—Sí, pero, si Luc muere, será el fin para los demás. Merecía la pena intentarlo.

—¿Y si hubieras muerto tú? —La miró con los ojos brillantes de rabia.

—Otros podrían reemplazarme. Siempre he sido prescindible, ¿recuerdas? —Se apoyó en los codos para incorporarse—. Necesito que me arregles las manos.

El cansancio se hizo evidente en los ojos de Kaine.

—Lo sé.

Helena se obligó a respirar hondo.

—Empieza con la izquierda. Si no queda bien, no será tan grave.

Le durmió el brazo desde el codo, pero le dejó la suficiente sensibilidad para que pudiera advertir si lo estaba haciendo bien o no. Kaine fue avanzando con sumo cuidado. Los huesos rotos rechinaron unos contra otros y, a pesar de tener todo el brazo anestesiado, sintió una punzada de dolor que le llegó hasta el hombro.

—Muy bien —consiguió decir. Dejó caer la cabeza contra su hombro y trató de contener las lágrimas.

Kaine le unió los huesos de la muñeca y, después, pasó a las manos. Tuvo que recolocar manualmente algunos huesos y mover las partes que Blackthorne había destrozado.

Sin la adrenalina del combate, el dolor la estaba consumiendo. Cuando terminó de recolocarle los huesos y empezó a soldarlos, Helena estaba llorando sobre su hombro.

Al acabar, tenía la mano hinchada y amoratada.

Kaine la sostuvo entre las suyas y recorrió con el pulgar toda la palma hasta la muñeca; su resonancia fue como un bálsamo que iba reparando el tejido dañado y las venas partidas. Después pasó a los dedos, siendo muy cuidadoso en todo momento.

Helena reconoció la técnica, aunque no creyó que le hubiera prestado atención.

—Podrías ser sanador —comentó cuando recuperó la sensibilidad en los nervios. Abrió y cerró la mano. Le seguía doliendo; la sentía frágil como si tuviera pequeñas fracturas—. Tienes un talento natural.

—Una de las grandes ironías de la vida —repuso él en voz baja.

Pasó a la otra mano.

—Es mejor que la anestesies por completo —le explicó—. Ya puedo usar mi resonancia.

Trabajaron juntos. Helena se sorprendió de lo rápido que lo hicieron. Cuando terminó, Kaine le masajeó la mano de la misma forma que había hecho con la otra.

—No vuelvas a participar en ninguna misión —ordenó sin levantar la vista, con la mano de Helena entre las suyas.

La chica apartó la mirada y respiró hondo.

—Eso no lo decides tú —replicó. Acto seguido, retiró la mano y se puso en pie. Todo le dio vueltas. Estaba demasiado mareada. No tenía suero fisiológico ni expansores de plasma, como en el hospital. Aunque hubiera tomado el tónico, no contaba con los recursos físicos necesarios para regenerar toda la sangre que había perdido.

Se pasó la bolsa por encima de la cabeza, con cuidado de no dañarse las manos, y se preparó para irse. Nunca se habían despedido, así que no vio motivo para empezar a hacerlo ahora.

Kaine se interpuso delante de la puerta; sus ojos se habían tornado gélidos.

—Recuérdale a Crowther que, si la Llama Eterna quiere que siga cooperando, tienen que mantenerte con vida.

La miró fijamente con ese brillo plateado y frío en los ojos. A Helena le dio un vuelco el corazón, pero después se giró para marcharse. Kaine le había dejado muy claro lo que era para él y lo mucho que la odiaba por tenerlo esclavo de esa forma.

Esta preocupación, esta obsesión por mantenerla con vida, no era por ella. Era por su madre, Enid Ferron, por no haber sido capaz de salvarla. Para él, Helena era la oportunidad de hacer bien las cosas. Un premio de consolación que ni siquiera quería, pero del que no podía prescindir.

No le extrañaba que Crowther se hubiese mostrado tan satisfecho. «Buen trabajo, Marino».

—Todo esto lo estás haciendo por tu madre, Kaine. ¿De verdad vas a rendirte por mí?

Sabía que eso lo enfurecería: insinuar que lo que sentía por ella se parecía, si quiera un poco, a lo que había sentido por su madre. Seguramente le dejaría claro cuánto se equivocaba.

Kaine se quedó totalmente quieto.

Ella lo rodeó para salir por la puerta, pero Kaine la sujetó por los hombros y la hizo girar para mirarla con dureza.

—Mi madre está muerta. Tú no. Mi lealtad residía en quienes no habían sido responsables de su sufrimiento, pero, si la Llama Eterna ha decidido que pueden permitir tu muerte, no seré noble ni comprensivo. Puedo vengarme de ambos bandos. Si te matan, lo pagarán caro.

Helena lo miró sobrecogida. No había tenido esto en cuenta. Sabía que Kaine no era espía por motivos ideológicos; lo hacía por interés propio. Detestaba a los Holdfast y a la Llama Eterna, pero detestaba aún más a Morrough y a los inmarcesibles. Eso no había cambiado, era lo que lo movía a seguir.

Sin embargo, después del comentario inconsciente que había hecho, Kaine parecía estar replanteándose si la Llama Eterna seguía sirviendo a sus intereses.

Helena tragó saliva. Debería mostrarse fría, recordarle que siempre pondría primero los intereses de la Llama Eterna. Si esperaba algo más que eso, ya podía esperar sentado. Y ganárselo.

Lo miró, queriendo dar forma a las palabras en su garganta, pero se le quedaron atascadas. Estaba muy cansada. La vida había sido muy fría durante demasiado tiempo.

«Los demás están heridos. Ni siquiera sabes lo que le han hecho a Luc, y estás aquí perdiendo el tiempo».

Flexionó las manos y sintió los nuevos tejidos. Se centró en eso para ser capaz de alejarse.

—Tengo que irme —afirmó con voz temblorosa.

Pero Kaine no la dejó marchar. De hecho, la sujetó con más fuerza.

—No eres prescindible. No apartes a todo el mundo solo para que les resulte más fácil usarte y dejarte morir.

Helena negó con la cabeza.

—Estamos en guerra —dijo esforzándose por mantener un tono firme—. Ser prescindible no es una tragedia que me autoimponga. Si no lo eres, te conviertes en un lastre para la causa. —Lo miró a los ojos—. Por eso me elegiste, ¿recuerdas? —Se le rompió la voz—. Pues gracias a ti ahora valgo menos. Como tú me necesitabas a tu lado, contrataron a otras sanadoras. He tenido que formar a las chicas que me van a sustituir. —Se le escapó una carcajada amarga—. Tú eres el que me ha convertido en prescindible. Y encima ni siquiera quieres estar conmigo.

Kaine torció el gesto y se relajó apenas lo justo para que Helena intentara marcharse de nuevo. Pero, en cuanto abrió la puerta, él la cerró de golpe.

—No eres prescindible —repitió. Helena notó que le temblaban las manos—. No hagas que tu muerte tenga sentido porque te han convencido de ello. Tienes derecho a ser importante para los demás. Estoy aquí y hago todo esto porque quiero que sigas con vida. Quiero mantenerte a salvo. Ese era el trato. —Buscó en su rostro—. No te lo dijeron, ¿verdad?

Helena sacudió la cabeza y dejó escapar un sollozo. Acto seguido, sin pensarlo dos veces, lo besó.

CAPÍTULO 51

Abrilis 1787

KAINE LE SOSTUVO LA CARA entre las manos para devolverle el beso. La atrajo hacia sí y la rodeó con los brazos.

Helena aún seguía llorando mientras lo besaba, mientras recorría con los dedos el contorno de su rostro y la curva de su mandíbula. Quiso memorizar todos los detalles: su pulso, que latía bajo las yemas de los dedos; sus labios, presionados contra los suyos; su sabor.

Cerró los ojos para asimilarlo todo. Ese momento. Al menos le quedaría esto.

Se lo había ganado.

Entonces, de repente, se obligó a dar un paso atrás y se separó de él.

—Tengo que atender a los demás.

Esta vez no intentó detenerla. Pero al salir no encontró al resto del equipo como esperaba. Los necrómatas los habían trasladado a un rincón más apartado.

A Helena le temblaron los dedos cuando comprobó si tenían pulso. Seguían vivos, aunque Luc ardía de fiebre.

—¿Cómo salimos de aquí? —preguntó mientras revisaba las lesiones. Intentó identificar cuán graves estaban sus compañeros y cuánto le costaría devolverles la consciencia y ponerlos en marcha.

—Por este túnel. Girad a la derecha, luego otra vez a la derecha y después todo recto. Hay unas compuertas en la parte norte.

—¿Donde soltaron a la quimera? —Recordaba ese sitio.

—Tendréis que echarlas abajo, pero podéis salir por ahí.

Helena asintió.

—Tienes que irte antes de que los despierte.

—Lo sé —afirmó, pero no se movió. Se quedó allí, inmóvil, hasta que Helena alzó la vista para mirarlo. Sus ojos brillaban en la oscuridad, como si la luz de la luna se colara bajo la tierra. Le tocó la mejilla, le alzó la barbilla y la besó con suavidad—. Usa el anillo, llámame si me necesitas.

La chica quiso decir que lo haría, pero no consiguió hacerlo.

Kaine era el espía del que dependían. Y ella era...

No era su carcelera. No, ese papel le correspondía a Crowther.

Ella era...

Una prisión.

—Vete —le instó en su lugar. Kaine desapareció por uno de los túneles, seguido por sus necrómatas, silenciosos como espectros.

Primero, despertó a Sebastian, ya que pensó que mantendría la calma y sería más fácil de manejar. También sabría qué hacer. Buscó entre los suministros que les quedaban. Helena había perdido las dos dagas y todo lo que tenía en la bolsa estaba contaminado de aguas residuales. Solo seguía funcionando una de las antorchas, que proyectaba una débil luz en la oscuridad.

Cuando despertó, Sebastian se incorporó en silencio y contempló la cara inerte de Luc mientras ella le recolocaba el hombro y curaba algunas heridas superficiales, que habían dejado de sangrar por el tiempo. Después, la miró.

—¿Qué ha pasado?

Helena negó con la cabeza.

—No lo sé. Perdí el conocimiento y, cuando desperté, todos estabais inconscientes. Me daba miedo que aparecieran más inmarcesibles, así que os traje a todos aquí.

Sebastian le lanzó una mirada acusatoria.

—Helena, sé que usaste la nigromancia. Es imposible que nos trajeras tú sola a todos.

La chica comenzó a negarlo.

—Reanimaste a Soren. Jamás habría sobrevivido a ese hachazo.

Helena se quedó inmóvil. No sabía si decirle que había sido Soren quien se lo pidió o si eso empeoraría las cosas.

—Por eso te trajo, ¿verdad? Ya me lo imaginaba.

Ella no respondió. La muerte de Soren era una herida demasiado reciente para asimilarla aún. No se sentía con fuerzas ni para pronunciar su nombre sin echarse a llorar.

—¿Sigue... por aquí? —La voz de Sebastian sonó esperanzadora.

Helena sintió que se le formaba un nudo en la garganta.

—No, ya... ya no está. Lo siento.

No habría fuego sagrado que liberara el alma de Soren de su cuerpo. En algún punto del río, se descompondría en la tierra, atrapado para siempre. Lila jamás volvería a ver a su hermano. Ni siquiera en la otra vida.

Sebastian permaneció en silencio durante un largo rato.

—A los demás les diremos que los trajimos aquí entre los dos.

Alister tenía sangre seca en las comisuras de los ojos, las orejas y la nariz, por haber abusado de la transmutación. Lo despertó con cuidado, pero, en cuanto recobró la consciencia, se llevó las manos al cuello e intentó arañárselo. Miró a Helena con los ojos desorbitados.

—¿Qué ha pasado? —preguntó entre bocanadas de aire.

—No lo sabemos —respondió Sebastian inclinándose sobre él—. ¿Te encuentras bien? Tenemos que ponernos en marcha antes de que nos quedemos congelados. Luc está muy mal.

—¿Dónde está Soren?

—Murió en combate —se limitó a decir Sebastian—. Marino, ¿puedes despertar a Penny?

Penny tenía la pierna destrozada; le habían arrancado los tendones a mordiscos. No había forma de salvar la extremidad. Helena anestesió los nervios y soldó el hueso para que al menos pudiese apoyarla. Penny ni siquiera gritó cuando despertó. Se limitó a frotarse los ojos y se incorporó con esfuerzo.

Wagner no tenía ni un rasguño. Cómo no, el muy cobarde. Al menos, no tendría que gastar energías curándolo.

Helena intentó despertar a Luc, cuya fiebre no hacía más que subir. Aunque parecía imposible, el calor corporal se incrementaba por momentos. Quiso bajarle la temperatura, pero su cuerpo la rechazaba y la fiebre escalaba, imparable. Lo había medicado en exceso.

Cuando por fin recobró el conocimiento, se puso a gritar, y el sonido de los gritos reverberó por los túneles.

—¡Déjalo inconsciente! —exclamó Sebastian acercándose—. Mantenlo frío. Tendremos que cargar con él.

Por suerte, olieron el aire fresco que llegaba desde más adelante, porque Helena no podría haber explicado cómo sabía por dónde debían salir.

Sebastian tenía un medallón enredado que funcionaba igual que el anillo de Helena. Lo usó para enviar un código al Cuartel General.

De vez en cuando, oían ecos por los túneles: gritos, rugidos, chapoteos en el agua. Avanzaron en silencio. Helena empezó a preocuparse por si Kaine habría logrado salir sin problemas, y luego por si el único motivo por el que no se encontraban con nadie era porque él los estaba protegiendo entre las sombras.

Cuando llegaron a las compuertas cerradas, Alister abrió un boquete en el muro de piedra. Al hacerlo, un torrente de agua helada los inundó, pero consiguieron salir a través de la corriente con cuidado, manteniendo el equilibrio mientras trepaban.

Una niebla densa los recibió al otro lado, que se apartó ante la aparición de un barco de contrabando de poca eslora. Se dirigía hacia ellos en silencio.

Sebastian soltó un suspiro de alivio.

—Althorne.

El general Althorne los contempló con dureza mientras el barco echaba el amarre. Sus hombres descendieron al agua y acudieron al rescate del maltrecho grupo sin hacer ruido ni chapotear lo más mínimo.

—¿Dónde está Soren? —preguntó Althorne con el semblante tenso, vigilando cómo llevaban a Luc al interior del barco.

—Muerto en combate —respondió Sebastian sin añadir más.

Uno de los hombres cargó en brazos a Penny. Alister se subió a bordo por sus propios medios, aunque le temblaban las manos cuando se limpió la sangre fresca de los ojos. Estaba a punto de desplomarse.

Althorne miró a Luc con una expresión que oscilaba entre la preocupación y el alivio.

—Tendremos que mantenerlo atado hasta que lo examinen.

Helena señaló hacia Wagner.

—Lo encontramos en una celda. Creo que Crowther lo estaba buscando. No te fíes de él, mató a Sofia Purnell.

Althorne asintió y dos de sus hombres se acercaron a apresar a Wagner. El hombre gruñó, pero no se resistió. Era evidente que prefería estar cautivo en manos de la Resistencia.

—Estáis todos bajo custodia por haber incumplido órdenes —anunció Althorne en cuanto el barco zarpó. No lo dijo con rencor.

Habían salvado a Luc; cualquier castigo sería solo una formalidad.

Helena se dejó caer sobre la cubierta del barco. El viaje se sucedió casi sin darse cuenta y, al llegar, amarraron en un muelle escondido y los hicieron subir unas escaleras y entrar en la parte trasera de un camión.

Cuando llegaron al Cuartel General, Penny, Alister y Luc fueron llevados directamente al hospital. A Wagner lo metieron en una celda. Helena y Sebastian fueron examinados y, al confirmar que no tenían ninguna herida grave, los escoltaron a sus habitaciones. Allí los encerraron bajo llave y un par de guardias montaron vigilancia en la puerta.

A Helena no le hizo gracia estar confinada en el hospital, aunque allí disponía de suero y expansores de plasma. Con manos temblorosas, se quitó los ropajes mojados y hechos jirones, y se dio una ducha para deshacerse de la suciedad de los túneles y la nieve derretida.

Cuando desapareció todo rastro de lo vivido, se sintió extrañamente desconectada, como si en algún momento de la batalla hubiera abandonado su cuerpo y no fuese capaz de regresar. Ahora que volvía a estar en su habitación, le parecía que todo había sido un sueño.

Soren no estaba muerto. Era imposible.

Cuando saliera de allí, lo vería en el hospital, sentado al lado de Luc.

Al recordarlo muerto en sus brazos, notó cómo se desgarraba la tela de su mente, como si el hilo que le había devuelto a la vida se hubiese roto en cuanto desapareció la conexión entre ambos. La persona que conocía y el cuerpo que había reanimado estaban tan unidos que su partida le había causado un daño físico.

No podía estar muerto.

Había sido una pesadilla.

Se contempló las manos. Por algún motivo, esperaba que estuvieran manchadas o sucias por haber usado la nigromancia.

¿Qué diría Sebastian en el Consejo? Tendría que contar la verdad en su informe. En cuanto saliera a la luz, habría consecuencias.

Habría cometido un delito menor si hubiera asesinado a Soren. El asesinato se consideraba un crimen mortal, mientras que la nigromancia era un crimen en esta vida y también en la siguiente.

Helena guardó todas sus pertenencias en su baúl y esperó sentada.

Entonces escuchó que alguien llamaba a la puerta. Se puso en pie, preparada.

—¡Helena! ¡Helena! ¡A Luc le pasa algo! —Era Elain la que estaba fuera—. ¡Te necesitamos en el hospital!

El temor a que la apresaran se esfumó por completo.

—¿Qué ha pasado? —Helena abrió la puerta y los guardias retrocedieron para dejarla salir. Corrió junto a Elain hacia los ascensores.

—Hemos hecho todas las pruebas pertinentes y nos hemos asegurado de que no lleva ningún talismán. Pero sus órganos... están contaminados. No sé qué le han hecho. Hemos intentado revertir los daños, pero no se regeneran. Estábamos tratando de bajar la fiebre cuando Pace me pidió que lo despertara, pero entonces empezó a gritar. Y ahora no para, ni tampoco deja que nadie se acerque. Se está haciendo daño a sí mismo.

Luc estaba en una sala de cuarentena al fondo del hospital. Lo escuchó antes de llegar.

Tenía los ojos desorbitados, la cara demacrada y las mejillas llenas de arañazos, cubiertas de sangre. Irradiaba calor, como si todo él fuese oro derretido.

Ilva se encontraba en la puerta sin saber qué hacer, junto a Althorne, Maier, Pace y otros médicos. Aunque Ilva no paraba de hablarle, Luc parecía no escuchar nada. Los gritos cesaron cuando se desgarró la garganta hasta dejarla en carne viva. Era como si hubiera olvidado cómo funcionaba su propio cuerpo. Sufrió una convulsión en la que los brazos, las piernas, los dedos y la cabeza se le doblaron en ángulos imposibles y, acto seguido, se lanzó contra la pared.

—He traído a Helena —dijo Elain sin aliento.

Luc giró la cabeza y la miró fijamente. Abrió tanto los ojos que parecía que iban a salírsele de las órbitas. Meneó la cabeza como si fuera una serpiente.

—Hel... —pronunció como un graznido. Estiró la mano hacia ella; parecía que se había roto los dedos, pero no le importaba—. Hel...

—Ten cuidado, se comporta de forma violenta —escuchó que decía Pace. No le prestó atención.

Helena extendió la mano y entrelazó los dedos con los suyos. Luego le acarició el dorso de la cara con los nudillos. Tenía la piel tan caliente que era como si estuviera ardiendo. Aun estando rotos, Luc consiguió doblar los dedos, sin percatarse del dolor. Le agarró la mano y la acercó hacia sí.

—Estoy aquí. Dime qué es lo que sucede —dijo mientras le anestesió la mano y le arregló los dedos en un momento.

Luc tenía la mirada perdida y había empezado a estremecerse.

—Sácalo... —gimió sacudiendo la cabeza—. De dentro...

Helena posó la mano en su frente, ignorando el calor que desprendía su piel, y dejó que la resonancia se introdujera en su cuerpo, buscando el origen del malestar. ¿Qué se le había escapado?

—Hel… —dijo Luc de nuevo.

De repente, un dolor punzante le atravesó el pecho.

El mundo dio vueltas. Todo se tiñó de un rojo sangriento que inundó su cerebro. Un pitido agudo resonaba en sus oídos.

Intentó enfocar la vista, pero no podía respirar.

Se llevó la mano al pecho. Los sonidos se ralentizaban y las caras a su alrededor se deformaban.

Sintió que alguien la sujetaba. Helena soltó un grito de pánico y buscó sus cuchillos, pero no los tenía. Arañó el aire con desesperación para liberarse.

—Tranquila, Marino —le decía la enfermera Pace—. Estás bien, solo fue un susto. Te has quedado sin respiración.

El miedo la embargó por completo. Pero poco a poco la habitación volvió a su forma natural.

Estaba en el suelo, respirando con dificultad. El dolor del pecho la consumía por dentro, pero intentó darle sentido a lo que había pasado.

Luc estaba en la pared opuesta. De repente, su expresión mostraba una lucidez absoluta.

—Tú… —Tenía los ojos claros y ardientes—. Usaste la nigromancia en Soren.

La acusación flotó en el aire como la calma que precede a la tempestad. Todo el mundo se quedó muy quieto.

Helena se puso en pie.

—Lo siento —expresó con voz rasgada; le costaba hablar. Sus pulmones se esforzaban por respirar, pero le dolían las costillas. Cayó de rodillas y estuvo a punto de vomitar sobre el suelo del hospital—. Intenté curarlo. Lo siento.

—Estaba vivo. ¿Por qué no lo curaste? —La voz de Luc sonaba desgarrada por el dolor.

No había respirado lo suficiente para explicarse, para describir lo rápido que murió Soren, que incluso él mismo sabía que moriría y le había pedido que lo hiciera.

—Lo siento, Luc.

—Fuera… —Ya ni siquiera la miraba. Tenía la mirada perdida y se tambaleaba.

—Luc, estás enfermo…

—¡Fuera! —Cerró los ojos con fuerza y, de nuevo, empezó a temblar. Cada vez respiraba más rápido, como si estar en la misma habitación que Helena lo estuviera sacando de quicio—. ¡Fuera! ¡Fuera! ¡Fuera!

Empezó a arañarse el pecho entre alaridos, abriendo surcos en la piel como si quisiera arrancarse el corazón con las manos.

—¿Luc? —interrumpió otra voz.

Lila estaba en la puerta, apoyada en una muleta, y Rhea a su lado para ayudarla a caminar.

En la cara y en el pecho se distinguían perfectamente los puntos de sutura de sus cicatrices. Luc abrió los ojos con asombro al escucharla.

—Lila… —susurró, con la voz rota por el dolor y un alivio profundo, como si hasta ese momento no hubiera creído que ella siguiera viva.

Algunos intentaron detenerla, advirtiéndole en voz baja que tuviera cuidado, pero Lila se separó de su madre y corrió hacia Luc desesperada. En cuanto soltó la muleta, se dejó caer en sus brazos, apoyándose con fuerza en él.

—Te dije que corrieras —le dijo abrazada a él. A Luc le temblaban las manos cuando acarició el corte que le atravesaba a Lila la cara. Lila tocó con suavidad los rasguños que se había provocado él mismo en el pecho—. ¿Qué te han hecho?

Luc negó con la cabeza y la abrazó con más fuerza. Enterró la cabeza en su hombro mientras la rodeaba con los brazos.

Fue un momento tan íntimo que dolía contemplarlo. Si quedaba alguna duda de por qué Luc se había entregado, se disipó en ese instante.

Alguien tocó el codo de Helena. Cuando levantó la vista, vio que Ilva le señalaba la puerta con un gesto.

Ella se puso en pie y se escabulló en silencio antes de que Luc reparara en su presencia de nuevo. Cuando pasó junto a Rhea, la mujer apartó la mirada, evitándola.

Al final, Lila logró que Luc se metiera en la cama y aceptara que Pace y Elain lo examinaran de nuevo. Incluso accedió a que le pusieran una vía intravenosa en el brazo y a tomar la medicina que le bajaría la fiebre.

Helena se sentó en una camilla de la sala principal del hospital con una vía intravenosa en el brazo, mientras Elain le arreglaba una fractura del esternón y extendía un bálsamo sobre el moratón que le ocupaba todo el pecho. Por último, le trató la parte posterior de la cabeza, donde se había golpeado al chocar con la pared.

No era la primera vez que un paciente le causaba alguna lesión, pero esta vez todo era distinto.

Luc jamás la perdonaría por lo que le había hecho a Soren. Lo había dejado destrozado.

La cortina que envolvía la camilla se apartó para dar paso a Ilva. Elain permaneció allí hasta que la mano derecha del principado la fulminó con la mirada; entonces huyó. Helena se cerró la camisa sin levantar la mirada.

—Estamos recibiendo los informes de lo ocurrido —comunicó Ilva sin emoción alguna.

Helena no se inmutó. ¿La llevarían a juicio ahora? ¿O esperarían a que la guerra terminara?

—¿Qué te han contado? —preguntó en voz baja.

Ilva carraspeó.

—Luc ha perdido la razón. No podemos fiarnos de su versión de los hechos, dado que no solo está gravemente herido, sino que además está muy medicado. Alister y Penny han declarado que Soren Bayard murió protegiéndolos. Sebastian Bayard... —se detuvo un momento—. Sebastian Bayard lo ha corroborado, y afirma que fuisteis vosotros dos quienes pusisteis a salvo a los demás cuando la corriente de agua arrastró a la gran mayoría de los atacantes.

—¿Y qué más? —insistió Helena.

—Lucien... ha debido de alucinar con la supuesta reanimación de Soren Bayard. Quizá solo cayó al suelo por un instante. Es imposible saberlo en el caos de una batalla. La cuestión es que habéis llevado a cabo un rescate heroico. Habéis salvado al principado, aunque hemos pagado un precio muy alto. Es la voluntad de Sol.

Helena sabía que debía sentirse agradecida, pero también era consciente de que no estaban mintiendo para protegerla. Todo formaba parte de la historia oficial. Daba igual qué hubiera sucedido en realidad, lo importante era lo que creyese la gente.

—Los juramentos de Soren y Sebastian están por encima de las órdenes del Consejo —prosiguió Ilva—. Alister y Penny solo obedecían a un superior directo. Tú recibirás una amonestación en tu expediente militar, pero, como eres sanadora, no formas parte del ejército. Matias será quien decida qué castigo mereces. Hasta entonces, estarás fuera de servicio. Creo que lo mejor es que te mantengas al margen hasta que hagamos circular la historia oficial.

Helena volvió a su habitación y se dejó caer sobre la cama. El cansancio la envolvió como una ola imparable. Al principio solo hubo oscuridad y olvido, pero después el paisaje de su mente se fue transformando.

Se estaba hundiendo, cada vez más profundo. Unos dientes mordieron su piel, unas manos la arañaban, aferrándose a sus extremidades y destrozándola. Aun así, Helena no dejó de luchar. Unos dedos fríos rasgaron su carne y se clavaron en sus huesos. Intentó resistirse, pero era demasiado.

Sintió cómo se le partían los huesos, cómo los dientes penetraban en la carne. El tendón de la rodilla cedió. En la boca, unas manos húmedas se metieron tan al fondo que no podía cerrarla. La mandíbula se fracturó, dejando la garganta al descubierto. Todavía estaba luchando cuando quedó sumergida bajo el agua.

Helena se despertó de repente, luchando por respirar mientras se arañaba la garganta con las manos.

«Solo ha sido un sueño. Un sueño, eso es todo», trató de decirle a su corazón desbocado.

Pero no había sido un sueño, sino un recuerdo. Los recuerdos *post mortem* de Soren estaban grabados a fuego en su mente como si fueran propios: claros, lúcidos, cargados de detalles.

No sabía que la nigromancia era así, que jamás se libraría de la persona que había reanimado. No le extrañaba que los nigromantes se volvieran locos. ¿Cómo podían mantener la cordura si tenían en su interior la mente de los muertos?

El hueco que había dejado Soren se había convertido en un pozo de culpa infecta. Helena intentó con toda el alma reanimarlo, y ahora solo le quedaba algo muerto y putrefacto. Todo el mundo decía que la nigromancia era una maldición y advertían sobre sus consecuencias, pero en ese momento Helena estaba tan convencida de que la necesitaban, tan absorta en el futuro, que no se había parado a pensar en cuánto le afectaría en el presente.

Permaneció tendida en la cama, aunque aún sentía los dedos fantasmas que la despedazaban y el frío implacable de la nieve derretida. Le robó las mantas a Lila y se acurrucó bajo ellas para intentar dormir y huir de la falta de vida que Soren le hacía sentir en su interior. Cada vez que cerraba los ojos, veía en su mente los últimos recuerdos y sensaciones de Soren.

A pesar de que no había recuperado su capacidad de sentir dolor o emociones, su propia mente se encargaba de llenar esos vacíos con un terror fantasma que la hacía estremecer hasta tal punto que parecía que su mente se rompía, dividida en dos realidades.

Lo único que la anclaba al presente era el dolor, así que empezó a pellizcarse y a arañarse. No era suficiente; necesitaba algo más intenso.

Parpadeó y se descubrió a sí misma sosteniendo uno de los cuchillos de Lila, a unos milímetros de clavárselo en el antebrazo.

Lo dejó caer y salió corriendo de la habitación, aunque apenas veía en los pasillos desiertos de la Torre. Era de noche y reinaba un silencio sepulcral; casi todos ya se habían ido a dormir. La calma le resultó escalofriante, pero a ella la consumía una obsesión implacable.

Salió a trompicones, con la esperanza de que el aire fresco le devolviera la cordura.

Lumitia pendía en el cielo, brillante como un sol blanco en medio de un abismo negro.

A Helena le dolieron los ojos con solo mirarla. La sublimación siempre ponía nervioso a cualquiera, pero Helena ya estaba al borde de la locura. La sublimación solo lo empeoraba.

Cerró los ojos y sintió que se ahogaba de nuevo, que unas uñas le hacían surcos en la piel.

Kaine.

Kaine sabría qué le ocurría. Él lo entendería. Usaba la nigromancia, así que debía de conocer cómo ayudarla.

Sin pensarlo dos veces, se dirigió al Reducto. En realidad, debía llegar allí en tiempo récord, ya que quedaba poco para el toque de queda y todavía tenía que pasar por el puesto de control.

Las calles de la ciudad parecían lazos plateados bajo el brillo de la sublimación plena, pero las sombras eran como colmillos al acecho.

«Un poco más allá», se repetía con cada paso. Hasta que cruzó el puente, donde el río rugía bajo sus pies cargado de agua, y los apartamentos surgieron ante ella.

No se detuvo a pensar hasta que llegó a los escalones.

Le había prometido a Kaine que no volvería al Reducto a menos que hubiera alguna emergencia. Era un espía; su vida corría peligro. Helena le había dado su palabra de que no se acercaría por allí salvo que se lo ordenara la Llama Eterna.

De repente fue consciente de que había puesto en peligro su tapadera, y también a él.

Se dio la vuelta.

Al no tener adónde ir, perdió la concentración.

Soren. Helena. Soren.

Sintió que se le desencajaba la mandíbula, que el aire frío y la sangre entraban en su esófago desgarrado. Unos dedos invisibles se le metieron en los ojos. El agua la estaba sumergiendo. Se estaba ahogando, pero no moría. Seguía ahogándose atrapada en un bucle infinito.

Cuando recobró el conocimiento, estaba tendida en el suelo. El cielo negro, oscuro como la tinta, se cernía sobre ella. Sin embargo, la luz de Lumitia seguía emitiendo un frío punzante que quemaba su resonancia.

—Marino, ¿qué te has hecho a ti misma?

Apenas fue consciente de que la alzaban del suelo. Unas manos cálidas le tocaron la cara y la frente alejando el frío que la asfixiaba. Se acurrucó contra ese calor.

Había perdido la cabeza. Esta vez de verdad, porque Kaine estaba delante de ella acompañado de un enorme perro con alas.

Helena nunca había sufrido alucinaciones, pero, dadas las circunstancias, aquella resultaba extrañamente reconfortante. Kaine era como un horno y, cuando se hundió en sus brazos y posó la cara en su pecho, dejó de sentir los dedos fríos y muertos de sus pesadillas.

—Soren Bayard murió y… y lo traje de vuelta, pero los demás necrómatas lo despedazaron. No dejo de revivir lo que sintió. Creo que se llevó una parte de mí consigo. ¿Cómo lo haces para soportarlo sin volverte loco? ¿Siempre estaré así?

Kaine le levantó la barbilla con una mano para mirarla a los ojos. A la luz de la luna, el color gris resplandecía casi tanto como la propia Lumitia, y su cabello brillaba con el mismo tono plateado.

—¿Habías usado la nigromancia alguna vez? —Ella negó con la cabeza—. Y supongo que nadie te explicó cómo hacerlo, ¿verdad? —Exhaló el aire con lentitud y comprobó la temperatura de su frente con el dorso de la mano—. Tuviste suerte de que fuera alguien conocido. Estás entrando en shock.

A Helena se le escapó una risa nerviosa. Por supuesto que nadie le había contado cómo funcionaba la nigromancia.

Kaine le chistó y la atrajo contra su pecho para evitar que el recuerdo de unos dedos putrefactos clavándose en su piel le erizara todo el vello del cuerpo.

—Intentaste resucitarlo, ¿verdad? Idiota. Estás congelada.

Helena no se resistió cuando la acercó a su perro gigante.

En realidad, ahora que lo veía de cerca, no era un perro, sino un lobo de ojos brillantes y amarillentos, pero tenía el tamaño de un caballo de guerra y las alas de una...

No conocía ningún animal que tuviera unas alas así de grandes.

Kaine la alzó y la sentó sobre la montura, justo detrás de las alas, y luego se aupó para colocarse a su espalda. Helena cerró los ojos y se apoyó en su cuerpo, aunque un escalofrío la hizo encogerse al sentir de nuevo los dedos gélidos desgarrándole la piel. La criatura tomó impulso; sus músculos se le tensaron bajo el espeso pelaje y, de repente, se lanzó hacia delante con su salto que casi hizo que Helena cayera.

Y, sin más, estaban volando.

El viento le azotaba la cara con fuerza. Sintió que los ojos se le volvían hacia atrás. Apenas era consciente de nada más salvo de que Kaine estaba a su espalda y el frío viento rugía en sus oídos.

Entonces empezó a resbalarse, las piernas le flaquearon, y Kaine la sostuvo antes de que cayera. Volaban a tanta altura y la luna emitía una luz tan intensa que se veía incluso más allá de las montañas. Jamás había estado tan alto.

Miró a su alrededor. Estaba en un balcón, a solas con Kaine. Por primera vez en años, sentía una leve distancia de todo lo que la atormentaba. Desde allí, la isla Este se extendía a lo lejos, destrozada tras tantos años de guerra, iluminada bajo la luz de la luna.

El aire era escaso, como si estuvieran en las montañas, y el mundo parecía sumido en un silencio de ensueño.

Helena extendió la mano para que la luz plateada bañara su piel.

—¿Crees que esto es lo que quiere mi subconsciente? —preguntó, y se asomó para ver el faro de la Torre de Alquimia, que brillaba como un sol dorado en miniatura—. ¿Escapar de la guerra contigo?

Kaine mostró una expresión indescifrable cuando la apartó de la barandilla. Detrás de ellos había una puerta oscura, y él la guio para atravesarla y salir al pasillo. Tras el brillo plateado de la ciudad, sus ojos tuvieron que adaptarse a la oscuridad.

—¿Y qué es lo que quieres? —preguntó Kaine.

La voz parecía provenir de la penumbra.

Helena sintió que le ardían los ojos y extendió una mano para palpar la pared con las yemas de los dedos.

—Quiero dejar de estar siempre sola —confesó. Era más fácil ser sincera en la oscuridad—. Quiero amar a alguien sin pensar que, si lo descubrieran, acabaría sufriendo. La gente que me quiere siempre muere. Da igual lo que haga, nunca consigo salvarlos. Tengo que querer a todo el mundo desde la distancia, y me siento muy sola.

La vista se le nubló, pero entonces la oscuridad se desvaneció dando paso a una habitación enorme iluminada por el fuego de una chimenea. Era una casa fastuosa. La residencia de los Holdfast en la ciudad había sido así, repleta de muebles dorados que refulgían bajo las llamas.

Pero, aunque era elegante, carecía de personalidad. No había nada que indicara que alguien vivía en ese sitio.

Miró hacia atrás; Kaine estaba allí. La luz de la chimenea delineaba su figura, tiñendo de tonos dorados y rojizos su ropa oscura. Aún tenía ese brillo etéreo.

—No tienes por qué estar sola —dijo.

Helena bajó la vista y deseó con todo su corazón poder recrearse en esa fantasía, sentirse un instante en calma y convencerse a sí misma de que no le haría daño.

Sin embargo, sabía que era mentira. Su mente nunca se relajaba lo suficiente para disfrutar de algo sin pensar en las consecuencias.

—¿Por qué? ¿Lo dices por ti? —preguntó con amargura. Se dirigió al fuego y se dejó caer de rodillas frente a la chimenea. Allí no podía pensar que se estaba ahogando. Negó con la cabeza—. No puedo preocuparme por ti. —Apretó el puño—. Si me preocupo por ti, no podré usarte. Y eres la única esperanza que tengo para mantener con vida a todos los demás.

Se encogió sobre sí misma y se quedó mirando cómo danzaban las llamas. En algún lugar del Reducto, Helena seguiría tumbaba en el suelo, habría entrado en shock y seguramente se estuviera muriendo de frío.

—Pues úsame —repuso Kaine. Estaba a su lado. Se acercó e intentó besarla, pero Helena se apartó.

—¡No! No, no puedo. —Sacudió la cabeza. «Despierta, Helena»—. No quiero hacerte eso. No…, tú no te lo mereces. Puedo cuidar de mí misma.

Kaine no la soltó.

—No tienes que alejarte de mí para protegerme —afirmó en un tono duro que a ella le resultaba familiar—. Podré soportarlo. Puedes dejar de sentirte sola. No voy a malinterpretar lo que somos. Sé que solo quieres tener a alguien con quien estar.

Helena buscó una puerta, una escapatoria, pero Kaine no la soltaba.

—Helena… —Se quedó petrificada al oír su nombre pronunciado en sus labios—. Yo también me siento solo.

Ella notó que se le formaba un nudo en la garganta; su corazón latía con fuerza.

—Pero no quiero hacerte daño, no te mereces…

La besó y acalló todas sus objeciones. Helena no se resistió cuando la sostuvo en sus brazos. El calor del fuego desapareció al sentir su calidez, sus labios calientes sobre los suyos, sus manos acunándole la cara. Entonces sintió la suavidad de una cama bajo su espalda, almohadas y sábanas, y atrajo a Kaine hacia sí. Buscó con los dedos los botones de su abrigo y los desabrochó, pero él le cogió las manos entre las suyas y las sostuvo cerca del pecho. Se separó de ella y le alzó la cara hacia la luz.

Helena lo contempló desconcertada mientras Kaine le posaba el dorso de la mano en la frente y le remetía las mantas como si estuviera enferma y necesitara cuidados. Cuando intentó levantarse, él se sentó a su lado y la abrazó fuerte, hundiéndole la cara en el pecho.

—La nigromancia no… no resucita a nadie —le explicó—, pero en esos momentos cuesta recordarlo. Cuando se trata de alguien que conoces, cuando sabes lo que te afectará su pérdida, crees que reanimarlo te compensará. A Bayard le diste una parte de ti misma cuando lo reanimaste. En otras circunstancias, podrías haberlo revertido para separarte de él, pero Bayard se lo llevó consigo cuando murió.

Hizo una pausa.

—Te recuperarás, aunque te dejará cicatriz. Tienes que mantenerte cuerda hasta que tu mente comprenda que no puede recrearse en ese momento. Por suerte, la animancia ayuda en estos casos.

—¿A ti te ha pasado alguna vez?

Él se quedó en silencio unos instantes.

—Me pasó algo similar, pero fue hace mucho.

Helena se hizo un ovillo a su lado y escuchó el latido de su corazón.

Estaba vivo. Lo había mantenido con vida. Encontró su mano y se la acercó a la barbilla. La sostuvo con ambas manos y trazó el contorno de sus nudillos. Después entrelazó los dedos con los suyos y se quedó así.

Levantó la cabeza para mirarlo.

Kaine no se movió, ni siquiera cuando Helena le soltó la mano para tocarle la cara. O cuando se giró un poco para rozarle la mejilla con los labios. Después, le acarició la mandíbula y le posó un beso en la sien y otro en la frente. Después, algo vacilante, se acercó un poco más y le dio un beso en la boca.

Estaba ardiendo al tacto.

Helena lo besó lentamente, hasta que Kaine la envolvió con los brazos y le devolvió el beso. No tuvo claro si se estaba aferrando a él o dejándolo marchar.

Lo primero que encontraron los dedos de Kaine fueron las horquillas de su cabello y se las quitó. Las trenzas se desplegaron a su espalda y sus dedos las peinaron hasta que tuvo todo el cabello suelto y enmarañado. La volvió a besar.

Eran besos lentos. No estaban envueltos en desdén, en prisa o en culpa, pero aun así eran desesperados, porque Kaine siempre la hacía sentir así.

Lo estaba besando como siempre había querido hacerlo. Como siempre había deseado en secreto poder hacerlo.

Podía disfrutar de esto.

Al menos por esta vez.

Se le escapó un sollozo. Kaine se detuvo, pero la chica no permitió que se alejara.

—Así... así me habría gustado que fuese —admitió—. Contigo. Me habría gustado que la primera vez hubiese sido parecido.

Kaine se quedó muy quieto.

—Lo siento. Siento que no fuera así —dijo al fin, y la atrajo hacia su cuerpo.

¿Se había comportado de esa manera alguna vez? A veces se preguntaba si era real el recuerdo de cuando lo había besado estando borracha. O si se había imaginado aquella intimidad para sentirla cuando su vida careciera de ternura.

—No importa —repuso apoyando la cabeza en su hombro.

—Claro que importa. Déjame que te lo dé ahora. —Acercó la cara de Helena a la suya y le dio un beso lento e intencionado.

Como si fuera una estrella, Kaine brillaba y se mostraba frío como el hielo cuando estaba lejos, pero, al acortarse las distancias, desprendía un calor infinito.

No despegó los labios de los de Helena mientras buscaba los botones de su camisa y el resto de la ropa; esta vez los desabrochó despacio. La tela emitió un susurro al tiempo que sus dedos recorrían su piel. Con la boca siguió la curva de su clavícula, y le echó la cabeza hacia atrás para saborear la hendidura de su garganta.

Helena le quitó la ropa con torpeza. Le temblaban las manos, pero esta vez no tenía prisa. Consiguió desabrocharle los botones uno a uno.

La trató con una ternura inconmensurable. La tocaba con suavidad y, aun así, hacía que una llama ardiera en su interior, un deseo que le dolía.

No fue demasiado rápido ni brusco, y esperó a que estuviera preparada. Era todo tan lento como ella quería.

Cuando la penetró, la miró fijamente a los ojos.

—¿Está bien? ¿Te gusta?

Helena gimió y asintió. Porque esta vez así era.

—Me gusta. No pares —respondió agarrándolo por los hombros para pegarse aún más a él. Sintió bajo los dedos las cicatrices del sello que tenía en la espalda. No sabía cómo podía mostrarse tan tranquilo con todo el poder que rezumaba bajo su piel.

Kaine colocó los antebrazos a cada lado de su cabeza, como si la encerrara, y entrelazó los dedos en su pelo. Cuando empezó a moverse, presionó la frente con la suya; sus respiraciones se entremezclaron.

Al besarla, fue como si comenzara algo que podía ser eterno.

Sucedió tan despacio que Helena estuvo a punto de olvidar que iba a más. Podrían haberse quedado así, perdidos el uno en el otro, y también habría sido suficiente. Respiró en su cuello y saboreó su piel con la punta de la lengua. Memorizó su aroma y cómo era tenerlo en sus brazos.

El mundo exterior dejó de existir. Kaine sabía cómo acariciarla con los dedos para dejarla sin respiración, besarla de tal forma que apretara las piernas alrededor de sus caderas, y moverse tan lentamente que, al principio, Helena no se percató de la tensión que se acumulaba en sus entrañas. Esa voracidad acechante.

Pero, por supuesto, aquello iba a más, y Kaine quería conseguirlo. Centró toda su atención en observar cuándo se quedaba sin aliento, qué ángulo la hacía arquear la espalda, cuándo se mordía el labio para contener un gemido, en qué momentos se estremecía. Entrelazó los dedos con los suyos y notó que Helena lo abrazaba más fuerte, tanto que le clavaba las uñas en los nudillos. Empezó a jadear más rápido.

Aumentó el ritmo, la fricción y el contacto, hasta generar una sensación más intensa y profunda que la comodidad.

Cuando Kaine deslizó la mano entre sus piernas, Helena se removió. Desapareció esa comodidad. Se quedó helada e intentó retorcerse, deseando escapar. Apartó la mirada.

—No. —No quería sucumbir al pánico, pero eso era un error—. No sigas.

Kaine apartó la mano y le sostuvo la cara para darle un beso.

—Te lo mereces. Esto es para ti.

Helena negó con la cabeza.

—No, no es cierto. —Se encogió sobre sí misma y bajó la barbilla. Empezó a hablar deprisa—: Cuando me hice sanadora, prometí que nunca… Hice un juramento… y… y cuando dijiste… lo de Luc… Si lo supiera. No puedo dejar de pensar en eso. Que… que soy una puta…

Le falló la voz.

—Perdóname. —Kaine aún tenía su mano entrelazada con la suya—. Siento mucho haberte arruinado esta experiencia. Así es como debería haber sido. Déjame que te lo dé ahora.

Helena no se movió; el corazón le retumbaba en las costillas.

—Helena, por favor.

Se limitó a asentir.

—Cierra los ojos —susurró contra su mejilla.

Helena cerró los ojos y permitió que la besara.

Ahora que no veía, podía centrarse en otras sensaciones: el peso de su cuerpo sobre el suyo, cómo se movía el aire sobre su piel. Cuando le rozó con los labios el punto de la garganta donde latía su corazón, se le escapó un gemido. Kaine le acarició los senos y empezó a moverse de nuevo.

La siguió besando mientras deslizaba de nuevo la mano entre sus cuerpos y la besó con más pasión hasta que ella relajó la mandíbula y la boca, y dejó que el placer la embargara de una forma tan intensa que arqueó la espalda. Gimió con aspereza contra sus labios.

Cada vez estaba más excitada; el fuego se encendía, crecía y se extendía por todas sus terminaciones nerviosas, por los brazos y las piernas, hasta que cerró los dedos, enredando las sábanas en el puño. Cuando Kaine se movía, cuando sus labios encontraban algún punto sensible, Helena sentía que se soltaba la tensión, nudo a nudo, hasta que estuvo a punto de deshacerse.

Se le cortó la respiración cuando luchó, tratando de recomponerse y superar el miedo a romperse. No podía hacerlo.

Si se rompía, nadie recogería los pedazos.

—No puedo… —dijo entre jadeos.

—Helena. —Los labios de Kaine le acariciaron la mejilla, la sien;

respiraba de forma entrecortada—. Puedes disfrutar de la vida. Tienes derecho a sentir cosas buenas, a no estar sola. Compártelo conmigo.

Kaine le levantó una pierna para que la penetración fuese más profunda y con un ángulo distinto. La tensión fue en aumento. Apretó su cuerpo contra el suyo y la besó de nuevo.

Helena abrió los ojos de par en par y lo miró mientras su mundo se hacía trizas en esquirlas de color plata.

—Por Dios… —gimió, clavando las uñas en sus brazos—. Ah…, ah…, ah…

Llegó al orgasmo bajo su cuerpo, y él la observó hasta el último segundo.

Helena seguía tumbada, intentando recobrar el aliento, cuando Kaine aumentó la velocidad. La atrajo más hacia sí y vio que se tensaba. Cuando alcanzó el clímax, se le cayó la máscara y, por un instante, la miró a los ojos. Aunque después enterró la cara en su hombro, ella llegó a ver todo el dolor que sentía.

Cuando acabó, la abrazó con fuerza para no dejarla marchar.

Helena alzó la mirada. Kaine la estaba contemplando con expresión distante; estaba ocultando sus sentimientos. Estiró la mano y le pasó un dedo por la mejilla, en busca de algún rastro del chico que la había recibido en el Reducto la primera vez. Sin embargo, ya quedaba poco de él. Hasta su cabello se había tornado plateado.

—Creo que te he memorizado casi por completo —comentó—. Sobre todo, los ojos. Creo que he aprendido a interpretarlos.

Kaine curvó las comisuras de los labios y le cogió la mano para llevársela al pecho.

—Yo también he memorizado los tuyos —dijo al cabo de un rato. Después suspiró y apartó la mirada—. Debería haberlo sabido en cuanto te miré a los ojos. Debería haber sabido que jamás ganaría frente a ti.

La chica esbozó una leve sonrisa; le costaba mantenerse despierta. Le daba miedo que todo se esfumara mientras dormía.

—Siempre pensé que los ojos eran mi mejor atributo.

—Uno de ellos —respondió Kaine en un susurro.

CAPÍTULO 52

Cuando Helena despertó, se descubrió a sí misma en una cama enorme, se encontraba en una gran habitación y, al otro lado de las ventanas, se alzaban las montañas Novis, bañadas por la luz dorada del amanecer.

Estaba envuelta en sábanas con olor a enebro y en los brazos de Kaine. No recordaba cómo había llegado hasta allí.

Volvió a mirar la habitación. Por el ángulo de la ciudad, supo que estaba en la isla Oeste. Seguramente se tratara de una de las torres tan alargadas que desaparecían entre las nubes.

Siempre había dado por sentado que Kaine viviría en una finca en las afueras o en una de esas casas antiguas de la ciudad. ¿Por qué preferiría estar en un sitio como ese?

Él estaba tumbado; sus brazos la envolvían posesivamente, como si así no pudieran robársela, aunque mantenía un semblante plácido mientras dormía. Helena lo observó detenidamente.

¿Qué le había hecho?

Kaine Ferron era un dragón, como todos sus antepasados. Posesivo hasta la autodestrucción. Ermitaño y letal, pero la sostenía entre sus brazos como si fuera de su propiedad. Helena sintió pavor al notar la tentación de ceder, de permitir que la tuviera y de amarlo.

La necesidad de amar a los demás y ese anhelo desesperado por que la correspondieran… Hacía mucho que se había rendido, había guardado ese sentimiento bajo llave y lo había enterrado para dar paso a la frialdad de la lógica, al realismo y a las elecciones prácticas de la guerra. Esto la iba a llevar a la ruina.

Tenía que marcharse antes de que Kaine despertara.

Intentó despegarse tal como había hecho en otras ocasiones, pero esta vez Kaine abrió los ojos. En un primer momento, la atrajo hacia sí, pero entonces vio su expresión temerosa.

Parpadeó un par de veces y la dejó marchar.

Helena se quedó donde estaba.

El miedo y la rabia que él le inspiraba el año anterior se habían desvanecido por completo. Aún percibía el peligro, tal vez incluso con más nitidez, pues sabía lo letal que era. Sin embargo, de alguna manera, saberlo hacía que le diera menos miedo. Ahora sabía además lo mucho que se había contenido. A pesar de todo lo que había conseguido, Kaine Ferron se estaba controlando.

—Esto ha sido un error —dijo Helena—. No debería haber venido aquí.

Kaine tragó saliva y desvió la mirada.

—No te preocupes —repuso con calma—. No te complicaré las cosas. Querías estar con alguien y yo estaba disponible. Sé que no significó nada.

Al oírlo, Helena contuvo la respiración y tragó saliva. Kaine no era alguien sin más. Para ella era...

Ese era el mayor error de todo, lo que la aterraba.

Antes de que pudiera esbozar una mentira para protegerse, algo en su rostro la traicionó. Sus ojos siempre la delataban.

Porque Kaine, cuyo semblante parecía abatido, adoptó una expresión de triunfo. Volvió a atraerla hacia sí con una voracidad y una pasión que atravesó el aire como un relámpago.

Sin posibilidad de huir, Helena regresó a sus brazos, y los labios de Kaine buscaron los suyos. Cualquier rastro de miedo, culpa o decisión se deshizo en el aire. Lo único en lo que pensaba era en lo mucho que deseaba estar allí, en que él la tocara. Kaine era puro fuego, y ella ya se había consumido.

—Eres mía —murmuró contra sus labios. Deslizó los dedos por su garganta y los enredó entre los mechones de cabello, acercándola todavía más.

No fue como la noche anterior. No se trató de un acto de consuelo, sino de dominación.

Helena sintió la boca ardiente de Kaine sobre sus labios, y después sus dientes dándole mordiscos en la mandíbula y en la garganta, también en los hombros. Ella enredó los dedos en su cabello y arqueó la espalda bajo sus manos. Intentó no gemir de lo desesperadamente que lo deseaba, agradecida de no tener que pedirlo. Kaine la acercó a su cuerpo, la envolvió con los brazos y se colocó encima. Cuando se hundió en su interior con una fuerte embestida, Helena sintió su aliento caliente en el cuello.

La poseyó con dureza, como si quisiera demostrarle que ahí era donde debía estar, como si necesitara asegurarle que nunca podría negar cómo la hacía sentir.

Helena sentía su resonancia vibrando en sus propias terminaciones nerviosas. Kaine no se molestó en ocultarlo: estaba sintonizado con ella, y eso le provocaba unas sensaciones y un placer desbordantes.

Cuando Kaine se dejó llevar y su rostro volvió a mostrar sus emociones al desnudo, ya no había un corazón roto, sino una declaración de posesión y triunfo. La atrajo hacia sí, apretándola contra su pecho.

—Eres mía. Juraste serlo. Ahora y después de la guerra. Yo me encargaré de cuidar de ti. No permitiré que nadie te haga daño. No tienes por qué sentirte sola. Porque eres mía.

Helena sabía que debía marcharse, pero se perdió en el momento.

Estaba atrapada en el peligroso abrazo de Kaine Ferron, y se sentía como si estuviera en casa.

Se durmió entre sus brazos, como si el mundo hubiera dejado de existir, y solo despertó un instante al sentir sus dedos acariciándole el hombro. Cuando alzó la vista, lo vio observándola con los ojos oscurecidos.

Helena se acurrucó bajo esa caricia y lo besó ahí donde latía su corazón. Cuando Kaine le tomó la mano, Helena sintió su resonancia en sus propios dedos y volvió a quedarse dormida.

Al despertarse de nuevo, estaba a punto de hacerse de noche y las montañas se habían teñido de un morado y un rojo bruñido que marcaban el descenso de Sol.

Kaine estaba vestido, pero seguía sentado a su lado, mirándola dormir con los dedos entrelazados con los suyos, como si no tuviera nada más que hacer.

—¿Cómo es posible que estés aquí? —preguntó Helena, entre perpleja y exhausta. Por algún motivo, se sentía más cansada que antes, como si su cuerpo, al fin, hubiera recordado cómo se dormía y ahora pretendiera recuperar todos los años de privación.

Kaine arqueó una ceja.

—Vivo aquí. ¿Pensabas que mi residencia habitual era la habitación del pánico del Reducto?

Helena negó con la cabeza y se quedó tumbada de espaldas. Ya no le dolían las manos.

—No, pero ¿cómo es posible que puedas pasar un día entero en la cama conmigo? ¿No eres general o algo así? ¿No tienes reuniones o crímenes que cometer?

En lugar de responder, Kaine se le echó encima hasta dejarla tendida bajo su cuerpo. Con sus brazos alargados, le sostuvo las manos por encima de la cabeza y luego la besó.

—Estoy de descanso —contestó mientras la dejaba sin respiración—. Un concepto que me temo que nadie te ha explicado. —Entonces la soltó y se sentó para admirar las vistas—. A mi madre la torturaron en nuestra casa de las afueras, y también asesinaron allí a nuestros empleados. Después, nos trasladamos a nuestra residencia de la ciudad, y ahí fue donde murió. Quería ir a un sitio distinto, que estuviera alejado de todo eso.

Helena se incorporó.

—Lo siento, no debería haber preguntado. Simplemente jamás te imaginé viviendo a esta altura —comentó. Luego estiró la mano y la posó en su mejilla. Kaine apoyó la cabeza en la palma de su mano y cerró los ojos durante un instante; los mechones de su cabello le rozaron las yemas de los dedos.

Sin embargo, levantó la cabeza de repente.

—Bueno, es lo más práctico. Amaris echa a volar desde la azotea. Ahora se le da mejor, pero le ha costado mucho aprender a hacerlo.

—¿Amaris? —repitió Helena lentamente.

—La quimera. La viste anoche.

Helena parpadeó un par de veces. El recuerdo de un lobo alado, de proporciones imposibles, resurgió en su mente.

—Creía que… estaba alucinando.

Kaine la miró fijamente.

—Te dije que me iban a dar una quimera.

—Bueno, sí, pero di por hecho que sería algo… más pequeño, y, como no volviste a mencionarlo, supuse que habría muerto.

Kaine se encogió de hombros.

—Bueno, al principio era pequeña. Cuando llegó, tenía el tamaño de un potro.

—¿Qué es en realidad?

—Bennet no nos ha dado muchos datos al respecto. Tiene mucha genética de lobo norteño mezclada con algo de caballo de guerra. Aunque no sé de dónde sacó las alas.

—¿Y está... domada?

El chico negó con la cabeza.

—No, simplemente me ha cogido cariño, pero deberías conocerla. Hacía tiempo que quería presentártela, pero nunca encontré el momento oportuno. Ven conmigo.

Helena no se movió, todavía no quería ir a ninguna parte. Algo había cambiado entre ellos: la tensión y la cautela se habían desvanecido por completo.

Nunca se habían tratado con suavidad, ni siquiera cuando eran más jóvenes.

Alejados del resto del mundo, Helena sentía que por fin podía verlo tal como era, y no a través del filtro impuesto por los intereses de la Llama Eterna.

A pesar de estar en una habitación impersonal, a Helena le parecía que era justamente el sitio donde podían existir. No había ni un solo objeto que tuviera un significado especial. Era algo temporal, sin ataduras.

—¿Cuándo te diste cuenta de que no sabía que debías morir? —preguntó en vez de ponerse en pie.

Kaine soltó un largo suspiro.

—El primer día que fuiste al Reducto. Por la cara que pusiste, supe que tú creías que era para siempre.

La chica sintió que se le cerraba la garganta. Kaine apartó la mirada.

—Al principio me pareció... divertido. Estuve esperando a que te dieras cuenta. —Helena sintió que se le ruborizaba el cuello—. Cuando te dije que deberías haber sabido que me castigarían, pensé que comprenderías que todo era una farsa, pero no lo hiciste. Luego supuse que te lo contarían esa misma noche o al día siguiente, pero tú seguiste viniendo. Imaginé que tus superiores querrían algo más, aunque para entonces ya era evidente que no te lo estaban contando todo. Yo estuve a punto de hacerlo un par de veces, pero... —suspiró—. Supongo que estaba disfrutando de que quisieras salvarme.

Helena asintió con pesadez y, con los dedos, acarició la costura de la sábana de lino.

—Crowther hizo mucho hincapié en los objetivos a largo plazo, en que debía asegurarme de que tú no perdieras el interés y en que todo era secreto, que nadie podía saberlo. Pensaba que confiaban en mí. —Se quedó callada unos segundos—. Ilva me lo contó poco antes del solsticio. Supongo que te diste cuenta.

Ella tomó su silencio como una confirmación. Se produjo una pausa en la que recordó algo más.

—Kaine, creo que tu padre no está muerto.

La miró con intensidad.

—¿Cómo?

—Cuando rescatamos a Luc, había un liche. Le dijo a Sebastian que se llamaba Atreus. Estaba custodiando la puerta de la habitación donde lo tenían retenido.

—No —replicó Kaine con voz trémula—. No. Mi padre murió. Si siguiera con vida, habría regresado. Por mi madre.

Las pupilas se le habían contraído hasta formar unos puntos nítidos de color negro. Se negaba a creerlo.

—Era un liche —repitió Helena con todo el tacto posible—. ¿Habría querido verla en ese estado?

Kaine abrió la boca en varias ocasiones, como si quisiera protestar, pero después pareció pensarlo mejor.

—¿Qué sucedió?

—Soren y Sebastian lo mataron. Se interpuso entre nosotros y Luc. Pero no tuvimos tiempo de arrancarle el talismán. ¿No sabías que era un inmarcesible?

Él negó con la cabeza.

—Creía que lo habían arrestado antes de que comenzara la guerra. —Cogió aire con una mueca sarcástica; su expresión se volvió amarga—. Así que, al final, ni siquiera fue capaz de morir por ella.

—¿Por tu madre?

Kaine asintió.

—Lo hizo por ella. Sé lo que la gente decía de ellos, los motivos por los que se casaron, pero en realidad mi padre… la adoraba. Era lo único que le daba sentido a su vida. Cuando nací y ella se puso enferma, se obsesionó con protegerla. No permitía visitas ni nada que alterara su descanso. Morrough le prometió que la curaría y viviría para siempre.

—Entonces no sabrá todo lo que sucedió después de que lo arrestaran —repuso Helena.

Los ojos de Kaine reflejaron un cansancio profundo.

—Probablemente no.

—De haberlo sabido, ¿crees que…?

Kaine negó con la cabeza.

—Estoy seguro de que me culpa a mí. Como siempre. —Se produjo un silencio, y después le lanzó una mirada a Helena—. Hablando de morir, o más bien de lo contrario, ¿podrías explicarme por qué sigo vivo?

De repente, a Helena le pareció fascinante contar los hilos de la sábana.

—El sello era un experimento fallido. Bennet se pasó semanas tratando de arreglarlo, pero no hizo más que empeorar la situación. Cuando finalmente aceptó su derrota, quiso arrancármelo del cuerpo, pero el sello consumía tanta energía del talismán que era incapaz de tocarlo. Dio por hecho que la energía se agotaría en algún momento, o que mi cuerpo acabaría descomponiéndose, y por eso me mandaron a casa, porque no querían que las posibles consecuencias contaminaran el laboratorio recién estrenado.

»Como me he recuperado milagrosamente, Bennet está intentando repetir el experimento. Hasta ahora, todos los sujetos han muerto, de una forma lenta y horrible, y no logra entender por qué soy el único que ha sobrevivido. Tú eres la única persona que nunca ha cuestionado que saliera adelante, y me gustaría saber por qué.

Se hizo un silencio que Helena rompió aclarándose la garganta.

—Tenía un amuleto de los Holdfast. Podríamos decir que era una reliquia sagrada. Ilva me lo regaló cuando me hice sanadora. Y me ayudaba.

—¿Te ayudaba? —La incredulidad era evidente en su voz.

—Me permitía… trabajar más horas —respondió esquivando su mirada—. No me cansaba ni… se desgastaba mi poder cuando lo tenía. Tus heridas eran tan graves que te estabas deteriorando más rápido de lo que tu cuerpo podía sostener. El sello estaba drenando toda tu energía. Como a mí me había funcionado, supuse que a ti también podría ayudarte, que te daría fuerzas para recuperarte.

Kaine elevó las cejas.

—¿Qué reliquia tiene semejante poder?

Helena carraspeó. Debería mentir, puesto que decir la verdad podía considerarse traición. Sin embargo, no se le ocurría ninguna mentira. Además, ya había cometido traición.

—La Gema de los Cielos —contestó—. Yo no sabía lo que era, y en realidad no es… lo que cuentan las historias. Fue el Nigromante quien la creó, pero Orion se la arrebató y la gente asumió que había sido un regalo de los cielos.

—¿Y te la dieron a ti? —Kaine entornó los ojos.

—Por lo visto, me… eligió. No funciona con la mayoría de las personas.

Kaine tenía los brazos cruzados.

—¿Y así me curaste?

Helena se limitó a asentir.

—Así te curé.

El chico quedó en silencio durante un largo rato. Helena no consiguió descifrar su expresión, no tenía forma de saber si la creía o no.

—¿Y dónde está la gema ahora?

—No la tengo —respondió evitando su mirada—. Ya no.

Kaine suspiró.

—Bueno, supongo que tiene sentido que no te dejaran quedártela después de haberla usado conmigo.

La chica forzó una sonrisa culpable. Quizá era mejor que pensase eso.

—Ilva no estaba muy contenta.

—Supongo que no. ¿Sufriste alguna consecuencia?

—Bueno, tenía que m… —tragó saliva— matarte, pero finalmente me libré de hacerlo. Así que al final todo se ha arreglado.

Consiguió esbozar otra sonrisa, pero Kaine no la correspondió. Su expresión se endureció, tornándose distante, vacía.

—¿De verdad crees que lo hemos arreglado?

La cara de Helena se descompuso y, de repente, lo recordó: esa realidad que se interponía entre ambos. Que él habría preferido que ella lo matase, que eso era lo que él había querido. En cambio, estaba sentada en su cama, diciendo con una sonrisa que todo había salido bien porque había conseguido atarlo a la vida.

—No, no quería decir eso. Lo siento.

Se apartó y se giró para buscar su ropa.

—¿Qué estás haciendo? —Kaine se inclinó y la cogió por el tobillo antes de que se levantara de la cama.

—Creo que debería irme ya —masculló Helena con un nudo en la garganta mientras intentaba liberarse de su agarre.

—¿Por qué?

Helena tenía el corazón en un puño.

—Sé que no querías nada de esto. No pretendía fingir que todo iba bien.

La expresión de Kaine se endureció, y la arrastró de nuevo hacia la cama. Helena trató desesperadamente de librarse de su agarre.

—¿Me dejas al menos… ponerme la ropa antes de enfadarte, por favor?

Kaine la miró con intensidad.

—No me refería a mí. Estaba hablando de ti.

—¿De mí? —Le resultó tan desconcertante que dejó de resistirse.

—Sí, de ti. La Resistencia se te ha enganchado como un parásito y tú crees que todo ha salido bien porque son lo bastante generosos de permitirte vivir mientras te devoran por dentro.

—No es así —replicó Helena con dureza.

—Seis años en un hospital de guerra. ¿A cuántas personas has salvado para la causa? Dudo que lo sepas. Pero ¿les parece suficiente? No. En cuanto hubo otra manera de aprovecharse de ti, te vendieron al mejor postor. Incluso a los caballos de tiro se les trata mejor; deberían haberte convertido en pegamento cuando ya no les serviste para nada más. —Soltó un bufido de desdén—. Pero supongo que siempre ha sido así. Los únicos que disfrutan de una jubilación en el campo son los sementales de guerra como los Bayard.

—Cállate —le espetó Helena, y propinó una patada para soltarse. Tenía la cara encendida de rabia—. ¿Crees que no sé que soy prescindible? Tú te has encargado de recordármelo cada vez que has tenido una oportunidad. Pero no tienes ningún derecho a enfadarte por ello, porque has formado parte de todo esto desde el principio. Tú sabías lo que estaba pasando y yo no, y aun así decidiste seguir siendo cruel. Al menos, Ilva y Crowther me manipularon por un motivo. —Apartó la mirada—. ¿Tú cuándo te has mostrado así de generoso?

Kaine se quedó callado. Helena se giró.

—Perdóname —dijo él tras unos instantes. Ella no pudo más que reír, sin alegría.

—Sí, ya te has disculpado, pero no cambias, así que no significa nada.

—Tienes razón.

Se sentó al borde de la cama y se tapó el rostro con las manos.

—También te pido disculpas por eso. Nunca quise que esto llegara tan lejos. Sabía la misión a la que te habían enviado, y yo estaba convencido de que sería inmune, pero al darme cuenta de que para ti era real, cuando vi que estaba funcionando y que estaba cayendo en mi propia trampa, hice todo lo posible para que te alejaras. No se me pasó por la cabeza que tus superiores no te avisarían.

Helena se mordió el labio.

—Creyeron que así sería más convincente.

Kaine asintió con pesar.

—Pensé que, si te trataba con crueldad, te rendirías. Que tendrías un límite y que, cuando lo alcanzaras, dejarías de... abrirte paso por mis emociones. —Se le escapó un suspiro—. Me he pasado tanto tiempo esperando que me traicionaras que no quería que me importase cuando sucediera. Quería hacerte daño, pero siento habértelo hecho.

Helena se quedó contemplando el horizonte y sacudió la cabeza lentamente.

—No sé por qué seguí intentándolo. Hubo momentos en los que vi claramente que toda esa fachada era mentira. Cuando se te olvidaba fingir, siempre parecías sentirte muy solo. Y yo también. —Bajó la vista hacia la cicatriz que tenía en la palma de la mano—. Antes creía que éramos totalmente opuestos. Ahora... —lo miró y extendió una mano—, no puedo evitar pensar que somos prácticamente iguales.

Kaine entrelazó sus dedos con los de ella y la atrajo hacia sí. Esta vez, Helena se dejó caer en sus brazos para que Kaine enterrara su rostro en el hueco de su cuello.

La vida no era fría.

Después, se enderezó para mirarla. Helena observó cómo sus ojos recorrían cada detalle de su cuerpo, como si no quisieran perderse nada. Kaine le envolvió la garganta con la mano en un gesto pasional y posesivo, y luego le acarició la cicatriz que tenía debajo de la mandíbula antes de darle un beso en la frente.

—Tú eres mucho mejor persona que yo. El mundo no te merece.

Helena negó con la cabeza.

—Podría sobrevivir sin llegar tan lejos como tú. Eso no me hace mejor.

—Mantienes con vida a la gente. Nada más tocarlos, tu instinto es salvarlos, sin importar quiénes sean o lo que te hayan hecho. Esa cualidad no la compartimos. Es mucho más compleja que pensar en todas las formas en las que podrías asesinar a alguien. Y te pasa una mayor factura.

Sus frentes se tocaron, y Helena cerró los ojos. Era como si sus almas se estuvieran rozando. Quería quedarse ahí, absorta en ese momento, pero ya había desaparecido un día entero, y nadie sabía dónde estaba. No podía hacerlo.

—Tengo que volver.

Kaine no la soltó.

—Deberías comer algo.

—He de irme —repitió con firmeza e hizo amago de levantarse.

—Date un baño —le pidió tomándola de la muñeca—. Pediré que te suban algo de comer, lo que quieras.

—Kaine —apartó sus manos—, no puedes encerrarme aquí. Tengo que marcharme.

Dudó un instante, lo justo para mostrar un atisbo de instinto posesivo, algo voraz y desesperado. Pero se desvaneció y la dejó ponerse en pie con resignación.

Helena estiró la mano y le apartó unos mechones de la cara.

—No te preocupes. Siempre volveré a ti.

CAPÍTULO 53

Abrilis 1787

UNA VEZ RECUPERADA LA LUCIDEZ, la quimera de Kaine se le antojó aún más grande. Cuando Helena terminó de vestirse y estuvo ya lista para marcharse, en vez de volver a la ciudad de forma discreta, Kaine la llevó a la azotea. Allí estaba la criatura, estirándose y bostezando, dejando a la vista unos colmillos más largos que los dedos de Helena. Las alas se desplegaban de tal modo que ocupaban casi toda la superficie de la azotea.

La quimera fue hasta Kaine al trote y abrió sus escalofriantes ojos amarillentos para observar a Helena; torció el hocico en señal de advertencia.

—Amaris, pórtate bien —la reprendió Kaine al tiempo que le rascaba por detrás de las orejas.

Amaris dejó caer la cabeza, pero siguió enseñando las encías sin apartar la vista de Helena. Fue una bendición que la noche anterior Helena hubiera estado delirando; jamás se habría atrevido a montarse sobre esa criatura de haber sabido que era real.

Kaine acarició al monstruo lobuno y después se arrodilló para masajearle la pata delantera. La chica vio que tenía patas de caballo, pero acababan en unas garras enormes.

Helena dio un paso hacia atrás para darle más espacio. A pesar de que Kaine quería que se hiciesen amigas, era evidente que a Amaris no le caía bien nadie salvo su dueño.

—No está gruñendo por ti —le explicó Kaine antes de que Helena retrocediera un poco más—. Bennet ensambló mal las patas cuando la creó. Cuando crece, se le estiran los nervios y tengo que arreglarlos.

—¿A qué te refieres? —Helena lo observó con atención. Se percató de que estaba usando la resonancia mientras le masajeaba la pata delantera.

—A Bennet solo le interesa la parte estética de las quimeras. Une piezas a la fuerza, sin importarle la funcionalidad. Las quimeras son tan peligrosas porque están rabiando de dolor. Mueren del estrés que sufren. Cuando me dieron a Amaris, me mordió unas cincuenta veces la primera semana. Tal vez recuerdes que por aquel entonces todavía tenía la espalda destrozada. Estuve a punto de partirle el cuello al décimo mordisco, pero pensé: «A mí me duele también tanto que me encantaría morder a alguien. ¿Por qué no va a hacer ella lo mismo?». Por entonces era un cachorro, pero parecía un potro. Se tropezaba y se rompía las alas una y otra vez. —Volvió la vista hacia Helena—. Para entonces ya había aprendido la contención del alivio del dolor, y tú me habías comentado los numerosos defectos que tenían las transmutaciones, así que intenté arreglar todo lo que pude. Cuando Amaris comprendió que no iba a hacerle daño, dejó de morderme.

Se enderezó y acarició a la quimera por debajo de un ala enorme. Las plumas eran del tamaño del brazo de Helena. Kaine frotó los nudillos entre los ojos de Amaris.

—Y, después, me fue cogiendo cariño. Es la única superviviente de toda su camada. Bennet quiso que se la devolviera para ver por qué había salido bien. Estuvo a punto de arrancarle la cabeza, ¿verdad? —Le desordenó el espeso pelaje—. Ven a conocerla, se portará bien.

Le indicó a Helena que se acercara, la cogió de la mano y dejó que Amaris la olfateara. La quimera siguió enseñando los dientes, pero empezó a mover la cola y relajó las alas. Kaine hizo que Helena enterrara los dedos en el espeso pelaje y rascara por detrás de una oreja enorme y puntiaguda.

Helena notó que Kaine no dejaba de mirarla mientras permitía que la resonancia se extendiera hacia el cuerpo de la quimera. Amaris se estremeció, pero no se movió ni gruñó.

Sintió lo mal ensamblada que estaba Amaris; tenía huesos y tejidos que no deberían estar juntos pero que estaban unidos a la fuerza. A diferencia de las quimeras que había examinado en el laboratorio, era evidente que alguien había intentado corregir los fallos más graves: coser bien los músculos, suavizar las articulaciones y los ligamentos cruzados, bloquear los nervios para que no sintiera tanto dolor…

Intentó imaginar a ese monstruo de cachorro, como un potro o un polluelo. Inocente y joven, y entonces...

Dolor y mutilación.

Por supuesto que las quimeras eran salvajes. ¿Cómo iban a soportar tanto dolor sin aprender a morder?

—Has hecho un trabajo excepcional —dijo con la boca seca—. ¿Así es como aprendiste a sanar?

—Supongo que me sirvió de práctica.

Kaine contempló la ciudad, que se extendía como una corona resplandeciente. Lumitia todavía no había salido, por lo que había franjas en la isla Este que permanecían a oscuras. Sin embargo, la Torre de Alquimia se alzaba sobre todo lo demás, con su faro siempre brillante.

—Tenemos que irnos ya. Está tan oscuro que podemos pasar desapercibidos.

UNA COSA ERA ACARICIAR A Amaris y otra muy distinta ir subida sobre su lomo. Helena estaba convencida de que, si quisiera, el lobo podría partirla por la mitad con los dientes. Kaine se quedó junto a la cabeza de Amaris, para rascarle detrás de las orejas, mientras Helena se agarraba al arnés de cuero y se subía a la montura.

Tardó tanto tiempo en hacerlo que empezó a darle vergüenza; era como escalar una montaña peluda. Helena temía darle un rodillazo o un codazo, así que no sabía cómo colocarse. Kaine se montó de un salto a su espalda.

Apenas se había sentado cuando Amaris saltó del tejado.

En un primer momento, se desplomaron hacia el suelo, pero entonces desplegó esas enormes alas para aprovechar una corriente de aire llevándolos hacia los cielos.

Amaris volaba tan alto que el oxígeno comenzó a escasear. Mantuvieron distancia con la ciudad y las torres, y volaron junto a las montañas hasta la presa. La quimera descendió a tal velocidad que el Reducto pasó como un borrón y las ráfagas que provocaron sus alas hicieron vibrar las ventanas del edificio. Aterrizaron en el patio de una de las fábricas.

Cuando se bajó, Helena sintió que las piernas la sostenían a duras penas y agradeció de corazón que hubiera un suelo firme bajo sus pies. Quedó convencida de que los humanos no estaban hechos para volar y que hacerlo era una abominación. Trató de parecer agradecida en vez de a punto de vomitar, pero se alejó de la quimera.

Kaine la siguió. Ahora que le había presentado a Amaris y el viaje había terminado, volvía a haber cierto brillo de resentimiento en sus ojos, como si todavía no tuviera muy claro si debía dejarla regresar al Cuartel General.

Helena fingió no darse cuenta mientras se acercaba a la cancela, pero eso solo consiguió ponerlo de peor humor. Al final se detuvo.

—¿Qué sucede?

—No te vayas —expresó en tono suave.

—Sabes que tengo que irme.

El chico negó con la cabeza.

—No, no es cierto. No les importas.

Las palabras le dolieron como si hubieran tocado un nervio. El dolor resonó por todo su cuerpo. En el pasado lo habría negado, porque tenía a Luc y él jamás le habría dado la espalda, pero ese ya no era el caso.

Sin embargo, no cedió. Negó con firmeza.

—No podemos permitir que ganen los inmarcesibles. Nos jugamos demasiado. Tengo que ir adonde sirva de algo.

La furia se sumó al resentimiento en los ojos de Kaine.

—No, no es cierto. Da igual cuántas veces te rompas, a los dioses no les importa. No habrá recompensa. Esto... —señaló con una mano la ciudad, las montañas y el firmamento negro desde el que refulgía Lumitia—, esto es el Abismo. Ya estamos dentro. Todo lo demás da igual. Al universo le importa un comino el sacrificio y el dolor.

—Te equivocas —replicó Helena.

Kaine abrió la boca para protestar, para enumerar una lista interminable de ejemplos que confirmaban que el mundo era frío y ajeno, pero ella no necesitaba oírlo.

—Te equivocas porque yo formo parte del universo —siguió—. Un trocito de nada, es cierto, tal vez insignificante en términos matemáticos, pero formo parte de igual forma. Tú y yo no somos ajenos a nada. Nadie lo es. A mí me importan las personas que han muerto y las que morirán, y también los que sufren. Me importarán mientras siga con vida. Y eso significa que a esa parte del universo le importa. —Le dedicó una sonrisa—. ¿No te parece un poco más alentador?

Parecía desolado. Aun así, Helena se encogió de hombros.

—Quiero hacer el bien en este mundo. Eso es lo que quería mi padre por encima de todo. —Se miró las manos—. Sé que la mayoría de la gente no lo valorará. He hecho cosas que dudo que me perdonen. Pero me gustaría que me recordaran como alguien que lo intentó, al menos.

Dio un paso hacia atrás, pero Kaine le tomó la mano.

—Helena...

Ella se zafó.

—Ten cuidado, Kaine. No mueras.

—CROWTHER TE ESTÁ BUSCANDO —le dijo el guardia de la entrada al dejarla pasar. Helena asintió y se dirigió hacia la Torre.

Crowther se encontraba en su despacho. Tenía el brazo atado al cuerpo, como si se le hubiera paralizado de nuevo, y miró a Helena con un asco que jamás había visto en él. Le recordó a cómo la miraban los alumnos del gremio, aunque de una manera mucho más intensa.

Los dedos del brazo derecho formaban un puño, lo que significaba que aún le funcionaba, pero que había decidido privarse de ese movimiento. Tardó unos instantes en entenderlo. Lo hacía porque Helena era ahora una nigromante.

—Me han dicho que querías verme —afirmó como si no se hubiera percatado de su expresión.

—Hace horas —respondió Crowther entre dientes.

—Pues aquí estoy.

Crowther chasqueó los anillos de ignición de la mano izquierda y un orbe de llamas relamió sus dedos hasta que los cerró en un puño; la piel centelleó unos segundos antes de que la luz se apagara.

—El prisionero que trajisteis de vuelta se niega a cooperar si no estás presente, e Ilva... —Su expresión se tornó lívida de rabia—. Ilva insiste en que seamos cuidadosos hasta que sepamos quién es. He perdido un día entero esperándote. ¿Dónde estabas?

Helena no lo miró a los ojos.

—Ilva me dijo que me mantuviera al margen hasta que hicierais circular la historia oficial.

—Eso no es lo que te he preguntado.

La chica lo miró a los ojos con la mandíbula en tensión.

—Estaba con Ferron, pero estoy convencida de que eso ya te lo habías imaginado.

El hombre dejó escapar una carcajada de desprecio que le puso el vello de punta. La miraba con tal animosidad que parecía que Helena había dejado de ser humana.

—No fui yo la que quiso usar la nigromancia —explicó, decidida a sonsacarle el origen de su furia—. No había otra opción. Soren no se había recuperado lo suficiente como para embarcarse en una misión así. ¿Qué querías que hiciera? ¿Que dejara morir a Luc?

—¿Que qué quería que hicieras? —repitió lentamente, y se puso en pie—. Tendrías que haberte quedado en el Cuartel General. Solo tenías que hacer una cosa, Marino, y era seguir sana y salva para que Ferron tuviera una prueba de que sigues con vida todas las semanas. Pero se ve que he sobrestimado tus capacidades de deducción, así que te lo voy a dejar claro: a menos que estés mandando algún mensaje, no puedes volver a salir del Cuartel General bajo ningún concepto. El único motivo por el que no te he metido en la cárcel para juzgarte por nigromancia es porque te necesito para mantener a Ferron de nuestra parte.

Helena notó que se le hacía un nudo en la garganta.

—Tú ideaste ese plan. Estaba trabajando con lo que tenía.

A Crowther se le salieron los ojos de las órbitas.

—¿Yo?

—Fue tu informante del hospital la que le dio a Soren toda esa información. ¿De dónde sacó Purnell si no…?

Antes de que Helena pudiera terminar la pregunta, la puerta se abrió de par en par y una chica irrumpió en el despacho.

—¿Dónde está Sofia? He intentado buscarla y nadie me dice nada. ¿Dónde está?

Era Ivy. Su rostro estaba sucio y su cabello recogido en una cofia. Los ojos de Crowther se posaron sobre Helena.

—Marino, ¿quieres decirle a Ivy dónde se encuentra su hermana mayor, Sofia Purnell?

Cuando Ivy se giró, Helena se percató del parecido entre la camillera del hospital y la pequeña protegida de Crowther. Aunque se diferenciaban en unos años y en el color del cabello, los rasgos de Ivy eran más marcados y afilados, mientras que Sofia parecía más amable. Aun así, resultaba evidente que eran hermanas.

—¿Era tu hermana? —dijo Helena con voz estrangulada—. ¿Sofia era tu hermana?

Ivy palideció bajo toda la suciedad del rostro.

—Sofia formaba parte del equipo de rescate que salvó a Luc. Fue ella la que nos mostró la ruta a través de los túneles que llevaban a la prisión, pero, cuando escapamos, la arrastró la corriente. Pensé... pensé... —Helena miró a Crowther— que tú la habías enviado. ¿No fuiste tú?

Ivy miró a Helena fijamente y después se puso a gritar. Helena jamás había escuchado un grito así. Fue como si estallara algo en su interior, tan agudo que pareció que las bombillas a su alrededor iban a estallar. Una rabia lívida recorrió el rostro de Ivy. Helena se preparó para el golpe, pero la chica se giró hacia Crowther.

—¡Me prometiste que la protegerías si hacía todo lo que pedías! Ella no debería haber trabajado para ti. ¡Solo tenías que mantenerla a salvo!

Se abalanzó sobre él por encima del escritorio, como si quisiera arrancarle los ojos, pero, antes de que sus dedos lo rozaran, un estallido de llamas la arrojó contra la pared. Ivy cayó al suelo, y los libros de los estantes se desplomaron encima, incendiándose en su caída.

Crowther se movió con la agilidad de un gato. Sus años de experiencia en combate se notaron cuando se abalanzó sobre Ivy.

—Nunca le hablé de túneles ni alcantarillados, ni tampoco de prisiones —le dijo Crowther. Cerró la mano e hizo desaparecer el fuego—. Si se enteró de todo aquello fue por tu indiscreción. Te advertí que no le contaras nada, pero quisiste impresionarla contándole cómo viajabas por la ciudad sin que nadie te viera. ¿Te sientes ahora orgullosa? Seguro que le mostraste lo fácil que era.

Helena creyó que Ivy se pondría en pie, pero se limitó a quedarse en el suelo.

—Solo quería que supiera salir de la ciudad. Le enseñé el mapa y le hablé de la prisión para que no fuera en esa dirección —replicó Ivy, a quien le sobrevino un sollozo.

—Si me hubieras hecho caso, seguiría viva —repuso Crowther con voz cruel—. Yo he mantenido el trato, y nada de esto es culpa mía. —Le dio una patada—. Quítate de mi vista. Si Lucien Holdfast hubiese muerto en ese rescate absurdo, tú tendrías la culpa.

Ivy se levantó del suelo sin pronunciar palabra, pero, cuando atravesó la puerta, se giró un instante con un brillo asesino en los ojos.

Cuando desapareció, Crowther se dio la vuelta y sacó un transmisor de un cajón de su escritorio. Emitió un estallido de estática al encenderse y, después, Helena reconoció la voz del guardia. Era uno de rango superior.

Crowther musitó una jerga prácticamente ininteligible, pero la chica comprendió algunas palabras: «muy peligrosa» y «neutralizar». Luego guardó el transmisor y miró las quemaduras que había ocasionado en su despacho.

—¿De verdad es necesario? —preguntó Helena.

Crowther levantó la mirada.

—Ya has visto de lo que es capaz. Ahora que no está su hermana para mantenerla a raya, Ivy no me sirve de nada. Recuerda que esa misma regla se aplica a Ferron. —La miró de arriba abajo con repugnancia, como si pudiera ver todos los sitios en los que Kaine la había tocado—. Te aconsejo encarecidamente que te mantengas con vida, Marino.

Cuando Helena vio a Wagner, este le sonrió, pero lo único en lo que pensaba ella era en el rostro aterrorizado de Sofia cuando la empujó hacia los necrómatas.

Habían encontrado un intérprete: un anciano artrítico llamado Hotten que trabajaba en las cocinas. Su hijo era graduado en la Academia de Alquimia y había muerto al comienzo de la guerra.

—Muy bien —dijo Crowther cuando entraron en la celda. Había hecho desaparecer toda su rabia e incluso parecía simpático—, ¿por qué eres tan importante?

Hotten lo tradujo. El hevgotiano era un dialecto del occidente meridional que tenía una cadencia particular y en el que se pronunciaban las palabras con cierto ritmo. Wagner habló sin pausa y Hotten tuvo que resumir después de tratar, sin éxito, de interpretar simultáneamente.

—Conoció a Morrough en Hevgoss. A Morrough se le concedió una unidad de la prisión, los criminales del sector cuatro. Wagner trabajaba allí de guardia —tradujo Hotten con voz pausada.

Hevgoss adoraba, por encima de todo, sus guerras expansionistas y su población encarcelada. Esta última era numerosa, abarcaba varias generaciones y constituía tanto la mano de obra como el grueso de su ejército. Los criminales del sector cuatro solían ser presos políticos, condenados a cuatro generaciones de prisión; una vida tras otra dedicadas a la servidumbre, de la que solo escaparían sus tataranietos.

Las penas de trabajos forzosos se heredaban a la más mínima infracción, y podían prolongarse por días o por generaciones enteras. La mayor parte de los rangos inferiores de su ejército se componía de criminales de los sectores uno y dos, a los que se les prometía el perdón a cambio de una destacada carrera militar. Cada vez que escaseaba la mano de obra o había rumores de inestabilidad política o económica, Hevgoss respondía con la guerra para ampliar sus fronteras y así hacerse con más población que llenara sus prisiones.

En teoría, las cárceles hevgotianas estaban bajo el control estatal, pero eso no evitaba que «alquilaran» presos a quienes quisieran pagar por ellos. La esclavitud era ilegal en el continente Norte, así que Hevgoss la había reinventado.

—Morrough había hecho un trato con los militócratas. Buscaba controlar el poder de la vida. Dijo que dominarlo y recolectarlo era la clave para la inmortalidad. Prometió a los líderes que les enseñaría a hacerlo si le entregaban los materiales para realizar las pruebas, pero los prisioneros —Wagner se encogió de hombros— se resistieron. No querían cooperar. Sabían que morirían.

Wagner sonrió al contarlo, como si reviviera un recuerdo que le parecía reconfortante.

—Mi trabajo consistía en llevar a los prisioneros por la mañana y traerlos de vuelta por la noche, pero, cuando terminaba con ellos, no quedaba ninguno con vida. Morrough me trató con respeto. Me hablaba, me contaba sus frustraciones. Veréis, la energía no se puede otorgar a la fuerza, hay que darla voluntariamente. Ya había descubierto muchos trucos para conseguirla, pero, según decía, cuando los prisioneros morían, la energía lo recordaba, se resistía, atacaba. Por eso le resultaba tan difícil controlarla.

Helena y Crowther compartieron una mirada cómplice. Era evidente que Crowther también conocía la verdadera historia de la victoria de Orion contra el Nigromante.

—Lo resolvió gracias a mi idea. —Wagner hinchó el pecho—. Mi padre fue guardia, al igual que mi abuelo. Los levantamientos en las cárceles son muy peligrosos, algunas prisiones son del tamaño de ciudades. Para mantener el orden, es vital que los guardias no sean vistos como el enemigo, así que convencemos a los prisioneros de que el problema son otros prisioneros, una unidad o un sector distinto. Esos prisioneros son los culpables de que ellos tengan menos; las normas que odian fueron establecidas por culpa de esos prisioneros. Al conceder privilegios a costa de otros, los prisioneros olvidan quién firmó esas normas. A Morrough le gustó esa idea. Para capturar almas, debía hacer que los prisioneros culparan a otra persona. Incluso después de que les arrebatara la energía, la culpa tenía que redirigirse.

Wagner miró a Helena y luego a Crowther, como si esperara que se hubieran quedado sin palabras.

—Entiendo que le salió bien —comentó Crowther.

Wagner asintió.

—Dejó de intentar contener o unir la energía a su cuerpo. En su lugar, empleaba a otro prisionero dentro del sello. —Extendió las manos a ambos lados—. Poseía una alquimia muy rara. A través de su poder, extraía la energía y la ataba al alma de un prisionero. El otro prisionero absorbía toda la rabia y Morrough se quedaba con el poder.

—Pero ¿cómo lo controlaba si las almas…, si la energía estaba atada a otra persona? —preguntó Helena.

—Con sus huesos —respondió Wagner con las cejas arqueadas—. Lo vi con mis propios ojos. Usaba su alquimia para contener las almas dentro de esquirlas de sus propios huesos. Era extraño, pero, si una esquirla estaba en el sello junto al prisionero, este no podía morir ni aunque quisiera. Y, después, Morrough podía quedarse con el poder.

Las filacterias. Era exactamente lo que Kaine había descrito.

—Las almas de los demás… podían percibir esa vida, intentarían resistirse, pero el prisionero no podría morir. Aun así… sus mentes empezaban a… —Wagner se tocó las sienes y tiró de unos hilos invisibles como si desenrollara algo.

—¿Quieres decir que los inmarcesibles solo son una fuente de poder para Morrough? —preguntó Helena.

—¡Sí! Así es como los llamaba: inmarcesibles. Ni vivos ni muertos.

Crowther colocó un papel y un boli delante de Wagner y le ordenó que dibujara el procedimiento y el sello con la mayor exactitud posible.

Quedó claro que Wagner no era ni alquimista ni dibujante, pero había presenciado cómo se realizaba el procedimiento varias veces. Esbozó un sello enorme que Helena jamás había visto. No era ni celestial ni elemental, tenía nueve puntos de referencia y, en el centro, había una plataforma en suspensión desde la que Morrough tenía acceso al cuerpo del prisionero destinado a sobrevivir.

Las víctimas del sacrificio se disponían en las nueve puntas. Morrough abría la cavidad torácica del prisionero elegido como receptor y colocaba una esquirla de alguno de sus huesos en su interior; ese era el último componente del sello. De alguna forma, conseguía canalizar la fuerza vital de los prisioneros en ese hueso y, después, activaba el sello.

El sello creaba una atracción tan poderosa que los sacrificados quedaban como cascarones vacíos, desprovistos de una vida que se introducía en el receptor. Su alma era atrapada bajo las capas y capas de los demás, como un insecto en una telaraña.

Después, Morrough cortaba un fragmento del hueso, lo bañaba en lumitio y lo dejaba en el interior del cuerpo del prisionero. El resto del hueso lo introducía en su propio cuerpo.

Esta información iba en la misma línea de lo que ya conocían, pero la mente de Helena se negaba a creer que algo así fuera posible.

La historia que Ilva le había contado sobre el primer Nigromante ya le había parecido espantosa, pues había manipulado y engañado a muchas personas, pero la magnitud de sus actos hacía que fuese algo impersonal. Sin embargo, este proceso a pequeña escala se le antojó más íntimo e intencionado. La repetición. El alcance. Nueve víctimas, una y otra vez, arrancando esquirlas de hueso una tras otra. En busca del poder. En busca de la inmortalidad.

Así había creado a Kaine.

—¿Cómo es posible que sobrevivieras tanto si sabías todo esto? —le preguntó Crowther a Wagner. Este sonrió.

—Es un hombre egoísta. Para él, las vidas ajenas son un mero recurso. No soy idiota. Cuando vi que tenía éxito, salí huyendo. Sabía que intentaría encontrarme algún día. No querría compartir el reconocimiento por ese gran descubrimiento. Pensé que se había olvidado de mí, hasta que un día desperté en Paladia. Pero ahora el mundo conocerá mi nombre.

Sonrió con astucia. Era evidente que estaba convencido de que la Resistencia lo usaría para rebatir las reivindicaciones de poder y saber científico de Morrough. No obstante, Helena sabía que a nadie le importaría de quién había sido la idea, pues Morrough era quien ostentaba el poder y la habilidad de hacerlo.

—¿Por qué todos los inmarcesibles son capaces de usar la nigromancia? —preguntó.

Hotten tradujo la pregunta.

—Un accidente —respondió Wagner con una carcajada—. Nunca supo por qué.

UNA VEZ FINALIZADO EL INTERROGATORIO, Helena se quedó sin saber qué hacer. La seguridad del Cuartel General se desmoronó cuando los guardias no fueron capaces de apresar a Ivy.

Toda la información que conocía la chica pasó a ser considerada comprometida. Crowther no tardó en trasladar a los prisioneros de los sótanos de la Torre de Alquimia a otra ubicación, algún lugar al sur del Cuartel General, y un equipo de alquimistas bajó al laberinto de túneles y se dedicó a sellarlos para que Ivy no pudiera volver a entrar.

Sin embargo, cuando Ilva y Althorne se reunieron con Crowther para continuar con el interrogatorio, encontraron a Wagner muerto, despedazado, junto a los cadáveres reanimados de los guardias apostados a las puertas de la celda. Los restos estaban dispuestos de forma que se leía: CROWTHER EL SIGUIENTE.

Luc seguía ingresado en el hospital bajo vigilancia constante. Nadie daba detalles concretos de su estado. Según los informes diarios, se estaba recuperando y en unos días lo trasladarían a sus aposentos.

Elain era la única sanadora con permiso para entrar a verlo. Por primera vez en su vida, se mostraba reservada. Iba de un lado a otro con prisa, cogía medicinas de la sala de suministros, hablaba con Pace entre susurros y se apresuraba a volver.

Helena quedó a cargo de los turnos de Elain. Entre esos pacientes se encontraba Penny, cuya pierna había sufrido tantos daños que tuvieron que amputársela a la altura de la rodilla. Cuando Helena descorrió las cortinas, Alister estaba sentado al lado de su cama haciéndole compañía.

Al principio, le sorprendió que tuviera tan pocas visitas, pero entonces recordó que los únicos que quedaban vivos eran Alister, Luc y Lila. Todos los demás seguían enterrados bajo los escombros.

—Tengo que irme —dijo Alister, que se puso en pie—. El tribunal quiere hacernos más preguntas.

Penny asintió sin pronunciar palabra; tenía los dedos cerrados alrededor de las mantas que le cubrían el regazo.

—¿Qué tribunal? —preguntó Helena al sentarse donde había estado Alister—. No os van a castigar por salvar a Luc, ¿no?

Penny negó con la cabeza y enredó con el dedo un hilo de las sábanas de lino.

—No, solo recibiremos una reprimenda. A mí me van a dar incluso dos medallas. El tribunal es por Lila.

Helena levantó la vista de inmediato.

—¿De qué estás hablando?

—Van a nombrar a Sebastian paladín primero en vez de Lila —le contó Penny sin mirarla—. Lo más probable es que degraden a Lila por haber puesto en peligro la seguridad de Luc.

—¿Lo dices en serio? Lila le ha salvado la vida a Luc más veces que…

—Lo sé —intervino Penny—. Todos lo sabemos, pero a Luc no pueden hacerle nada… Es el principado. Así que Lila tiene que asumir la culpa. La gente lleva un tiempo quejándose… Bueno, siempre se han quejado, porque es una chica y los paladines suelen ser hombres, pero con Lila merecía la pena el riesgo. Sin embargo, después de lo que pasó con la quimera y esto…, los jefes consideran que lo vuelve más vulnerable. Creen que, si no hubiera sido por ella, jamás habrían capturado a Luc.

—Pero…

Penny siguió hablando con una mezcla de culpa y resignación.

—Han estado interrogándonos, y el caso es que todos lo sabíamos. Luc intentaba ser discreto, pero se notaba solo con verlos. Sobre todo, en los últimos meses, cuando pensábamos que la guerra estaba a punto de acabar. Creo que Luc pensó que ya no importaba, que no pasaría nada. Después de todo, nunca le reprocharon nada a su padre ni a Sebastian. Pero para las chicas siempre hay más reglas, y nadie que esté bajo juramento puede decir que a Luc no le afecta lo que le ocurra a Lila. ¿Tú podrías?

Helena desvió su mirada.

Pobre Lila. Había sorteado las dificultades de su rango durante años, apenas había cometido un error, pero al final iba a pagar los de Luc.

¿Qué pasaría entonces?

La chica tragó saliva con dificultad y se obligó a centrarse en la tarea que tenía entre manos. No podían hacer nada respecto al tribunal.

—¿Cómo tienes la pierna?

Penny pareció encogerse.

—Bien —respondió demasiado rápido.

Helena se acercó lentamente.

—Verás, a veces las terminaciones nerviosas no se dan cuenta de que ha habido una amputación. Siguen enviando señales como si la pierna aún estuviera ahí, y por eso te duele. Puedo usar la resonancia para bloquearlas y así dejarás de sentir el dolor.

—¿De verdad? —La voz de Penny sonó algo desesperada.

La sanadora empezó a trabajar, pero no pudo dejar de pensar en Lila.

La amputación había sido limpia. Maier había conseguido conservar gran parte de la extremidad y el corte era perfecto, ya que no se había visto presionado por la urgencia propia de una emergencia.

—¿Sabes qué? Tal vez puedas ponerte una prótesis.

—Creo que mi repertorio no es lo suficientemente bueno como para eso —respondió Penny con una sonrisa amarga, pero empezó a aligerarse el cansancio de su rostro—. Aunque quizá pida una básica. Así podría seguir trabajando, tal vez en las transmisiones. No quiero que me despidan.

—Los maestros de las forjas son muy hábiles. Las estructuras de titanio valen para casi todo el mundo, y son mucho más ligeras que los modelos de antes.

—Ya lo iremos viendo —repuso Penny.

Se hizo el silencio mientras Helena trabajaba. Hasta que Penny volvió a hablar:

—¿Es cierto lo que dijo Luc? Cuando Soren vino a salvarnos a Alister y a mí, ¿estaba muerto?

Helena se encogió como si hubiera recibido una patada en la cabeza. El nombre de Soren le cayó encima como un yunque. Empezó a ahogarse de nuevo. La pierna de Penny se volvió borrosa ante sus ojos.

—Cuando oí los rumores, pensé que era una ridiculez. Estaba convencida de que me habría dado cuenta si hubiera estado muerto. Pero, una vez aquí, no paro de pensar en ello, en cómo no dejó de luchar por mucho que le hirieron. No gritó ni una vez, ni siquiera cuando empezaron a hacerlo trizas. —A Penny le temblaba la voz—. Creo que prefiero pensar que ya estaba muerto.

A Helena se le erizó la piel como si esos dedos fríos la acariciaran. Parpadeó, intentando apartar los pensamientos y recuerdos de Soren, y se obligó a concentrarse para esquivar la herida que escocía en su memoria.

Sabía que no convenía confesarlo todo. Se mordió el labio.

—Soren me dijo que teníamos que hacer lo que fuera, costase lo que costase, por salvar a Luc.

Penny guardó silencio un largo rato.

—No sé cómo sentirme al respecto. Sé que estaría muerta si no hubiera venido a ayudarnos, pero… —le temblaron los labios— ¿y si era una prueba? Después de todos estos años luchando por el bien, en el último momento, en vez de permanecer fieles a la verdad, elegimos el camino fácil.

Helena se alegró de estar a punto de terminar con la pierna de Penny, porque la conversación hizo que le temblaran las manos. «Fácil». Detestaba esa palabra. Tragó saliva.

—Si las acciones de una sola persona bastan para condenar a los demás, entonces los dioses son terribles y Sol es el peor de todos.

—No lo dices en serio —respondió Penny al instante. La tomó por la muñeca apretando tanto los dedos que se le clavaron en la piel—. Mírame, Helena. No lo dices en serio. También funciona al revés. Orion pasó la prueba y fíjate en todas las bendiciones que recibieron por eso. —Penny parecía desesperada por convencerla—. Recuerdo el día que llegaste. Estábamos en el mismo dormitorio. Decías que Paladia era el lugar más bonito del mundo, la llamabas «la ciudad resplandeciente». Decías que la gente de Etras no creía mucho en los dioses, pero que aquí en el Norte entendías por qué lo hacíamos, porque ¿cómo si no iba a existir un sitio tan bello? ¿Ya no te acuerdas de eso?

Encontró la mano de Helena y le dio un apretón.

—Eso me dijiste. Creo que, en el fondo, sigues creyéndolo. Simplemente te... te asustaste y... cometiste un error, pero puedes arrepentirte. Si hablas con el falcón, te explicará cómo hacerlo. El viaje, el sufrimiento, eso es lo que necesitamos. ¿Cómo vamos a ser puros si no? Incluso... incluso cuando las cosas se tuercen, tenemos que estar agradecidos, porque eso es lo que nos hace puros.

Penny sonreía a Helena con un fervor que pretendía convencerla.

—Por eso es mejor que todos muramos fieles a nuestras creencias antes que vivir traicionándolas y corrompiéndonos. Sé que tenías buenas intenciones, que querías salvarnos, pero deberías haber confiado en Sol.

Helena apartó su mano.

—Penny, si creyera que simplemente vamos a morir, no me daría tanto miedo perder. Si perdemos, nos harán cosas mucho peores que la muerte. —Sacudió la cabeza—. No habrá nada de pureza en ello.

A PESAR DE RECIBIR UN tratamiento quelante durante días, Lila no recobró su resonancia. El Consejo intentó comunicar esta información con calma, porque no querían alimentar el pánico. En teoría, los quelantes debían haber separado el metal de la sangre de Lila para que su cuerpo pudiera expulsarlo, pero el resultado no fue el que esperaban.

Shiseo no había desvelado el contenido del mensaje que Helena le había pedido que llevara al Reducto sin hacer más preguntas, pero, por primera vez, pareció sentir alivio cuando la vio regresar al laboratorio. Y ese gesto fue más revelador que las palabras.

Pasaron días analizando una y otra vez las esquirlas y nuevas muestras de sangre de Lila para averiguar qué estaban pasando por alto. Cada vez que Helena regresaba de hacer un turno, siempre encontraba a Shiseo trabajando. Al final cayó rendido en la misma mesa.

Helena permaneció sentada en silencio. Estaba observando una llama bajo el alambique de cristal; el vapor subía por la cucurbitácea, se recopilaba en el destilador y descendía por el tubo hasta un frasco que había a un lado.

Ese mismo día, Elain Boyle fue nombrada sanadora jefe de la Resistencia. Había sido Matias quien había creado ese puesto para ella. Elain había llegado al hospital con un amuleto enorme de heliolita colgado alrededor del cuello y, a partir de ese momento, sus tareas consistían en gestionar el horario del resto de las sanadoras y trabajar en atender personalmente a Luc.

Helena se dijo a sí misma que no le importaba.

Su quimiatría se había convertido en algo esencial para las sanadoras. Poco a poco, Pace había ido creando una sección en los almacenes para guardar todos los tónicos y las medicinas. Así, la quimiatría de Helena sostenía buena parte de la carga de la sanación.

Cerró los dedos en un puño. Desde que reconquistaron los puertos, había conseguido numerosos ingredientes, pero, al haberle prohibido Crowther seguir recolectando en el exterior, le preocupaba que se agotasen. Había fórmulas que podía elaborar con materiales importados, pero algunas eran difíciles de conseguir si no las recolectaba ella misma.

Suspiró. En el pasado, disfrutaba de la quietud del laboratorio, que contrastaba de manera brutal con el caos del hospital, pero ahora ese silencio la dejaba a solas con sus pensamientos, y todo lo que se esforzaba por apartar de su mente regresaba para asfixiarla.

Echaba de menos a Kaine.

Cada vez que pensaba en él sentía como si le faltase una parte de sí misma.

La guerra se le había metido hasta los huesos y se había abierto paso por su interior hasta dejar solo lo que la hacía útil: un engranaje perfecto en una maquinaria compleja. Sin embargo, Kaine le había recordado que era humana; que sus dones y cualidades no solo eran válidos porque alguien podía aprovecharlos. Que tenía permiso para respirar de vez en cuando.

Pero, en su ausencia, Helena sentía que se asfixiaba.

CAPÍTULO 54

Abrilis 1787

Cuando Helena se plantó sobre la presa y miró hacia el Reducto que se alzaba al otro lado del puente, dudó.

Había echado de menos a Kaine toda la semana. Sin embargo, ahora que había regresado, sentía miedo. A veces era muy impredecible. Cada momento de ternura que compartían solía ir seguido de todo lo contrario.

Tomó aire un par de veces para calmarse, apretó los dientes y se obligó a cruzar el puente. Un necrómata la esperaba en la puerta del piso. Se le cayó el alma a los pies y tragó saliva con dificultad, pero abrió la bolsa y sacó el sobre junto con los recambios para su botiquín.

Le ardía la cara, aunque hizo todo lo posible para contener su expresión y no mirar al necrómata a los ojos cuando se lo entregó todo.

—Toma. —Lo puso en sus manos y se dio la vuelta.

—Marino.

Estuvo a punto de desmayarse cuando oyó su nombre. Se giró de golpe, pero lo único que había allí era el necrómata.

—¿Puedes… hablar? —Nunca había escuchado hablar a un necrómata. Que usaran sus funciones motoras ya era inquietante, pero reactivar las partes del cerebro encargadas del lenguaje le pareció excesivo. Los necrómatas no hablaban. Nunca lo hacían.

—Entra —pronunció.

Lo siguió con cautela; solo se permitió relajarse cuando se dio cuenta de que se dirigían a la sala del pánico. ¿No podría haberle dicho la semana pasada que fuera allí?

Se sentía indignada cuando llegó, pero se le olvidó en cuanto puso un pie en la puerta, porque Kaine la sostuvo en sus brazos y la besó como si estuviera hambriento.

Helena aferró su capa con sus dedos y cerró los ojos cuando le devolvió el beso. El resto del mundo desapareció. Sintió los dientes de Kaine, voraces contra sus labios y su lengua.

Las manos de él encontraron sus caderas y la empujó hacia atrás. Cuando Helena jadeó, aprovechó para bajar con los labios por su cuello, hasta la hendidura de la garganta, entre sus pechos cubiertos, y él estaba de rodillas, empujándola hacia atrás en el sofá. Se colocó encima y Helena ni siquiera se había quitado todavía la bolsa.

Kaine deslizó las manos por debajo de su ropa; sus labios dejaron un reguero de deseo en cada centímetro de piel que encontró a su paso.

Helena jamás se había sentido tan extasiada.

La resonancia de Kaine vibraba bajo su piel y seguía el recorrido de sus nervios y sus venas, como si la estuviera cartografiando. No era de forma erótica. Se parecía más al pánico que sentía cuando, al atender a un herido, su propia resonancia intentaba localizar la herida. La recorrió entera y, acto seguido, desapareció, aunque sí que se percató de que la lengua de Kaine se deslizaba por la cara interior de su muslo, hasta que notó un placer que la consumió por completo.

Tenía la camisa desabrochada y la falda arrebujada alrededor de la cintura cuando Kaine se hundió entre sus piernas. Helena le rodeó el cuello con los brazos, lo atrajo hacia sí y enterró su rostro en su hombro. El mundo se redujo a una única cosa: Kaine, su respiración, su cuerpo y sus caricias.

Yacer entrelazados en aquel sofá estrecho, con los cuerpos enredados, fue como aquella horrible mañana de resaca, pero totalmente distinto. Esta vez lo estaban haciendo bien. Helena estaba con los ojos cerrados, acariciando su piel con los dedos, pero Kaine se incorporó al poco tiempo.

La miró de arriba abajo, como si la buscara con la mirada. Helena levantó la cabeza; aún le costaba recuperar el aliento.

—¿Qué sucede?

Le tocó la cicatriz de las costillas con el pulgar.

—Estaba preocupado por ti. He tenido mucho tiempo para preguntarme si lo hice todo como es debido cuando te curé.

Helena le tomó la mano.

—Lo hiciste todo perfectamente.

Aún parecía preocupado.

—¿Y no ha pasado nada desde entonces?

—No —respondió la chica—. No he salido del Cuartel General desde que volví. Y no... no volveré a hacerlo, salvo para venir a verte. No puedo... —Se interrumpió al sentir las palabras atascadas en la garganta—. No me lo permiten. Tengo órdenes estrictas al respecto, así que no tienes que seguir preocupándote.

Kaine soltó un suspiro de alivio y, tras besarle la frente, se dejó caer de nuevo a su lado. Helena cerró los ojos y le dejó saborear ese sentimiento, aunque notaba un nudo en el estómago y la mandíbula le temblaba por contener sus emociones.

—¿Qué pasa?

Helena levantó la vista y lo descubrió mirándola de nuevo.

—Me... me gusta recolectar. Solía hacerlo con mi padre en los meses de verano.

Hubo un silencio breve.

—No sabía que era importante para ti.

Helena se quedó callada durante unos instantes. Los recuerdos del humedal se desplegaron ante sus ojos: la naturaleza, las montañas y el brillante cielo azul, el único sitio donde podía respirar sin percibir el olor a sangre.

—Era lo más parecido a la libertad que me quedaba.

Notó que Kaine se ponía en tensión.

—Solo será hasta que termine la guerra —replicó en un tono a medio camino entre la súplica y la promesa. A Helena le sobrevino una carcajada al mirarlo.

—¿Solo hasta entonces? ¿Y cuándo llegará ese momento? ¿Y quién tiene que ganar para que alguno de los dos salgamos bien parados?

Kaine no fue capaz de mirarla a los ojos. Ella también apartó la mirada.

—La Llama Eterna jamás aprobará oficialmente algunas de las cosas que he hecho. No sé qué pasará cuando salga todo a la luz.

Se le formó un nudo en la garganta cuando pensó en todas las celdas subterráneas a las que Crowther la había llevado en tantas ocasiones. La sangre, las quemaduras, las extremidades cercenadas, los nervios destrozados, abiertos y retorcidos de formas horribles y terroríficas. El nombre de Helena figuraba junto a los registros de todos aquellos prisioneros. Era su letra la que describía en términos clínicos las heridas que sanaba, el estado de los prisioneros cuando fallecían o la ubicación exacta en la que se encontraban dentro de aquella terrible cárcel subterránea. Sabía que Crowther lo había hecho a propósito, que quería que apareciera entre el personal médico. Así podría usarlo en su contra.

En el pasado, tal vez se hubiera conformado con una amenaza latente, pero Helena ya no esperaba compasión de él.

Si ganaban la guerra, le quedaban pocos amigos, y ni siquiera Luc estaba ya de su parte.

Kaine le cogió la mano.

—Puedes huir. Dímelo y te sacaré de aquí.

Una parte cobarde y exhausta en su interior se estremeció al oír aquellas palabras. Huir. Libertad. Lejos de la guerra.

No se había dado cuenta de cuánto lo deseaba hasta que lo oyó de labios de alguien que lo decía de verdad. Cuando su padre le propuso volver a Etras, lo rechazó, pero ahora lo deseaba con todo su ser.

Sin embargo, dondequiera que fuese, la guerra continuaría, y Kaine participaría en ella. Él no podría huir. Si se marchaba, Crowther no lo mantendría con vida.

—No —negó mirándolo a los ojos.

—Mantengo la oferta. Te sacaré de aquí si me lo pides.

Helena estiró una mano y le apartó un mechón de pelo rubio de los ojos.

—¿Y tú qué? —preguntó. Kaine torció el gesto.

—Si pudiera huir, lo habría hecho cuando mi madre aún estaba viva.

—¿Te irías ahora si pudieras hacerlo?

Sus ojos se encendieron con pasión.

—Si es contigo, sí.

Helena se obligó a sonreír.

—Entonces nos iremos juntos. Cuando termine la guerra. —Le tomó la mano y se la llevó al pecho para que sintiera el latido de su corazón—. Cuando termine la guerra. Huiremos a un lugar donde nadie nos conozca. Desapareceremos para siempre.

Los ojos de Kaine se humedecieron, pero le devolvió la sonrisa.

—Por supuesto.

Estaba mintiendo.

Ambos mentían. No era más que un sueño.

Helena le apretó la mano hasta que la ilusión se deshizo. Luego tragó saliva; le daba miedo decir lo que venía después.

—La Llama Eterna ha obtenido más información sobre el proceso al que se someten los inmarcesibles para obtener la inmortalidad. Me han pedido que te pregunte por los detalles, para verificar la información.

Kaine le sostuvo la mirada unos instantes. Después, se quedó mirando a la nada.

—Kaine. —Helena lo tocó, y él se sobresaltó.

—Solo veo un borrón —dijo rápidamente—. No lo recuerdo.

—Cualquier cosa servirá. De verdad.

Guardó silencio y respiró profundamente un par de veces antes de volver a hablar:

—¿Qué quieres saber?

—¿Había algún sello en el suelo?

Kaine asintió levemente.

—¿Podrías describírmelo? ¿O dibujarlo?

Negó con la cabeza.

—No llegué a verlo bien. Recuerdo que había nueve puntas y que yo estaba en el centro. Cooperé, pero aun así me drogaron y me ataron para que no pudiera moverme.

Mientras hablaba, miraba la pared del fondo.

—Hicieron pasar al personal de la mansión, a los que todavía no habían asesinado. Yo no sabía cómo funcionaba el proceso, qué iban a… Cuando pregunté qué iban a hacer, me dijeron que tenía suerte de tener tantos sirvientes, porque así no tendrían que usar a mi madre.

—¿Mataron a tus sirvientes?

Kaine asintió distraído.

—En el campo no solíamos tener mucha compañía. Mi madre caía enferma a menudo y, con tantos rumores, mi padre no confiaba en nadie. Él siempre estaba ocupado con el gremio, así que nos encontrábamos allí los dos solos, junto con los sirvientes. Algunos de ellos eran prácticamente de la familia. La doncella de mi madre, Davies, la había acompañado desde que era niña, y vino a Puntaférreo con ella cuando se casó. Cuando nací, cuando mi madre empezó a… Davies fue la que me crio los primeros años.

—Lo siento mucho, Kaine.

Se quedó callado un buen rato, sin atreverse a mirarla.

—Había una plataforma por encima de mí, desde donde se inclinaba Morrough. Tenía algo en la mano. Supongo que sería la esquirla de hueso. Recuerdo que grité. Cuando recobré la consciencia, todavía se escuchaban gritos, pero no era yo quien los profería. No los escuchaba,

simplemente los sentía, como si estuvieran atrapados en mi interior. Todos enredados, pero aún con vida.

Helena lo observó horrorizada.

—¿Sigues… oyéndolos?

Kaine cerró y abrió los ojos lentamente.

—Ahora están más callados.

Helena tragó saliva.

—Según la información que tenemos, los inmarcesibles son el resultado de los intentos de Morrough por hacerse con el poder sin sufrir las
consecuencias adversas.

Kaine guardó silencio unos instantes.

—Entonces, si matamos a los inmarcesibles, lo debilitaremos.

—En teoría, sí. Si destruimos los talismanes, ¿afectará a las filacterias? ¿Así es como mueren los inmarcesibles?

Kaine negó con la cabeza.

—No, puede generar otra filacteria, pero el resultado… Son poco
más inteligentes que un necrómata.

—Pero tiene que haber una forma. La encontraremos.

El chico la miró; sus ojos volvieron a despejarse y a enfocar de nuevo.

—Si los inmarcesibles son la fuente de poder de Morrough, eso significa que la guerra no acabará hasta que estén todos muertos.

Helena supo de inmediato que quería prepararla para lo peor.

—No. Hallaré la forma de revertirlo. Si es posible unir almas, seguro
que también se pueden desunir.

—Helena…

Esta negó con la cabeza.

—Ya creí una vez que no podría salvarte. Deberías confiar un poco
más en mí —carraspeó. No deseaba tener esta conversación, así que se
puso en pie y se vistió con rapidez.

En realidad, le daba igual informar a Crowther. Lo que quería era
revisar el sello que había dibujado Wagner para poder investigarlo.

—Espera. Tengo algo para ti que ojalá no vuelvas a necesitar.

En un paño impermeable se encontraban sus dagas. Helena había
creído que la corriente se las había llevado.

—¿Cómo las has encontrado?

—Hice unas de repuesto. Tardé mucho tiempo en encontrar un metalúrgico que tuviera la resonancia de tu aleación, así que pensé que lo
más sensato era encargar dagas de sobra.

—Gracias —respondió, acariciándolas con cariño y metiéndolas con cuidado en la bolsa. Luego comenzó a trenzarse el cabello.

—Odio que lo lleves así —le espetó Kaine, y aquello la sobresaltó. Alzó la mirada.

—También podría cortármelo. —Él pareció ofenderse de tal manera que tuvo que reírse—. No puedo tenerlo suelto cuando estoy trabajando, y siempre tengo que estar disponible por si hay alguna emergencia. Es práctico.

Kaine no parecía muy convencido.

—Quiero verte más a menudo.

Helena dejó de mover los dedos. Percibió la voracidad de sus ojos, la posesión, el hambre. Si se lo permitía, la alejaría de la guerra y la esconderría. Y ese conflicto se hacía evidente en sus ojos.

Deseo. Deseo. Deseo. Lo sentía igual que el latido de su corazón.

Si no podía esconderla, la acapararía para sí tanto como pudiera. Se había enamorado de un dragón.

—Siempre estaré disponible para ti —replicó—. Si me llamas, vendré en cuanto pueda.

Kaine sacudió la cabeza al oír eso.

—No, no podremos seguir usando el Reducto como punto de encuentro. Hay planes de reconstrucción.

A Helena se le encogió el corazón.

—Ah. ¿Entonces cómo vamos a…?

—La Resistencia no vigila los cielos —afirmó—. Ahora que Amaris ha crecido, podrá volar de noche a la isla Este. Estoy seguro de que hay alguna azotea por allí. Buscaré un sitio para la semana que viene. Si el anillo se activa una sola vez, eso querrá decir que no está relacionado con la Resistencia. Avísame tú cuando llegues e iré a por ti.

Helena levantó la mano izquierda. Había temido que la refracción se desgastara con el paso del tiempo, pero seguía aguantando. Ya no veía el anillo a menos que se esforzara, y era tan ligero que a veces se olvidaba de que lo llevaba puesto.

—Dijiste que si alguna vez te avisaba yo…

Kaine la tomó de la mano y la atrajo hacia sí. La mano que le quedaba libre se deslizó por su garganta hasta que sus dedos echaron la cabeza de Helena hacia atrás. La besó con pasión y, después, la miró fijamente a los ojos.

—Llámame y acudiré.

715

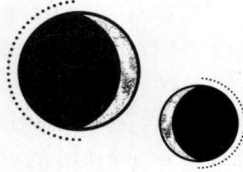

CAPÍTULO 55

KAINE LA LLAMABA CON FRECUENCIA.

A veces terminaba sus obligaciones a última hora de la tarde, pero la mayoría de las veces era ya pasada la medianoche. Si Helena no estaba trabajando en el hospital, se quedaba en el laboratorio hasta que el anillo se activaba.

Había muchos edificios abandonados. Kaine había dado con uno que tenía una azotea grande y despejada, y que además contaba con un ascensor que funcionaba. Helena no tenía que pasar por ningún puesto de control para llegar.

En ocasiones, Amaris ni siquiera necesitaba aterrizar.

Helena esperaba en el centro de la azotea y, silenciosa como un espectro, Amaris caía del firmamento. Kaine se echaba hacia delante y recogía a Helena. Al instante estaban en el aire, surcando el viento, volando por encima de los edificios sin que los vieran.

En cuanto aterrizaban, Kaine bajaba a Helena de la quimera y la examinaba de la cabeza a los pies.

—¿Te encuentras bien? ¿Te ha pasado algo? —preguntaba, a pesar de que Helena había notado la resonancia de Kaine bajo su piel por el camino y sabía que no estaba herida.

Helena jamás hubiera imaginado que se preocuparía hasta ese extremo. Siempre había sido consciente de lo rápido que llegaba al Reducto, de lo cuidadosamente que la observaba, pero no se había dado cuenta de lo profundo que le atravesaba el miedo hasta que dejó de ocultarlo.

Nada más entrar en la casa, Helena le permitía examinarla bajo la luz y extendía los brazos para demostrar que seguía en el mismo estado que la vez anterior.

—Estoy bien. ¿Ves? No tienes que preocuparte.

Aquella afirmación nunca parecía surtir efecto. Lo que le había sucedido a su madre había estado oculto, y Enid Ferron nunca se lo había contado todo, ya fuese porque no podía o porque quería ahorrarle el sufrimiento. Sin embargo, ese secretismo había resultado ser la peor opción. Kaine era igual que ella: se obsesionaba más con lo que desconocía que con cualquier otra cosa.

Helena lo miró a los ojos y le sostuvo la cara entre sus manos.

—Estoy bien. No me ha pasado nada.

Una vez que lo convencía de que no le ocultaba ninguna herida, la tensión de su cuerpo se relajaba. La abrazaba hasta que sentía el latido de su corazón retumbando contra el suyo.

«Tú le has hecho esto —se recordaba a sí misma cuando empezaba a impacientarse con aquel ritual—. Descubriste lo que le hacía vulnerable y te aprovechaste de ello».

Helena le recorría el cuerpo con los dedos para detectar alguna nueva herida antes de que él la volviera a besar. Sin embargo, Kaine solía esconderlas o ignorarlas como si no existieran, a menos que Helena las descubriera.

Las heridas de anulitio habían empezado a aparecer en los soldados heridos en batalla. A veces, Kaine acababa con algo de metralla incrustada en el cuerpo y, aunque a él le afectaba de forma leve, si entraba en su torrente sanguíneo, podía ralentizar su regeneración durante horas, a menos que Helena interviniera.

Nunca había sanado ni nunca sanaría a nadie del modo en que curaba a Kaine: en sus brazos, pegada a su cuerpo. Lo sobornaba para que cooperase dándole besos con los labios separados sobre los hombros, en las manos, en la cara, y, mientras tanto, su resonancia buscaba todos los lugares que estaban heridos y revisaba su cuerpo meticulosamente. Hasta que Kaine se hartaba, le sujetaba las manos, la empujaba sobre la cama y le hacía el amor lentamente. Siempre lo hacían a un ritmo que les hacía perder la cabeza.

Kaine la miraba a los ojos hasta que Helena sentía el roce de sus mentes.

—Eres mía. Eres mía. —Repetía esas palabras una y otra vez—. Dilo. Di que eres mía.

Kaine entrelazaba sus dedos con los de ella, presionaba frente con frente y, en ocasiones, le temblaba todo el cuerpo. Helena lo abrazaba para darle seguridad.

—Te lo prometo, Kaine. Siempre seré tuya.

Había un miedo posesivo en la forma en la que la tocaba, como si creyera que esa sería la última vez que la vería.

Si Kaine no la llamaba, el tiempo se alargaba, y Helena empezaba a sentir un miedo infinito hasta que el anillo volvía a arder.

Entonces era ella quien, desesperada, exigía saber si él se encontraba bien. Las noches que dormía sola, tenía pesadillas en las que alguien lo mataba. A veces desaparecía para siempre; otras, se convertía en un liche, o lo descubrían y lo apresaban. No sabía cuál de esas opciones le daba más miedo.

—Ten cuidado. —Era lo que siempre le decía antes de dejarla en alguna azotea. Le sostenía la cara entre las manos y lo miraba a los ojos—. No mueras.

Kaine inclinaba la cabeza y le besaba el interior de la muñeca o la palma de la mano sin despegar esos ojos plateados de su rostro.

—Eres mía. Siempre volveré a por ti.

Siempre lo hacía.

Sin embargo, con el paso de los días parecía que las probabilidades de éxito se volvían en su contra. Cada vez era más difícil. La guerra estaba al borde de la catástrofe. No estaba segura de hasta dónde la llevaría el sello y su propia determinación antes de que todo se viniera abajo.

Estaba caminando en el filo de una navaja.

Cuando dormía, Helena contemplaba su rostro y rezaba para que sobreviviera. Lo haría posible. Se marcharían lejos, más allá del mar, donde nadie pudiera encontrarlos jamás. Se prometía a sí misma que hallaría la forma de hacerlo, y se lo prometía a él: habría un después de la guerra.

—Yo cuidaré de ti. Te lo juro, Helena, siempre voy a cuidar de ti. —Helena lo escuchaba mascullar esas palabras contra su piel o su cabello. Un susurro apenas audible. Había días en que la compulsión se agravaba.

Aquella noche lo escuchó repetirlo una y otra vez. Normalmente paraba al cabo de un rato, pero esa vez no lo hizo. Helena levantó la cabeza y le sostuvo el rostro entre las manos para obligarlo a que la mirara a los ojos.

—Kaine, estoy bien. No va a pasarme nada.

La contempló con la misma expresión entre la amargura y la resignación, la que había adoptado cuando la entrenaba y cada vez que se daba la vuelta para marcharse, como si se estuviera preparando, esperando lo inevitable.

La guerra era una jaula sin escapatoria.

Aun así, se calmó y descansó la cabeza sobre su pecho, escuchando el latido de su corazón envuelto en sus brazos. Helena le pasó los dedos por el cabello y, aunque estaba callado, notó que seguía repitiendo las palabras.

—Háblame de tu madre, Kaine —le pidió tras un instante de duda—. Cuéntame todo lo que no pudiste decirle a nadie.

Kaine permaneció callado. Ella deslizó los dedos hasta sus hombros y recorrió las cicatrices entrelazadas del sello.

—Puedes contármelo. Te ayudaré a llevar la carga.

Siguió en silencio tanto tiempo que Helena se preguntó si se habría quedado dormido. Pero entonces giró la cabeza, lo justo para que ella pudiera ver su perfil.

—Nunca había visto cómo torturaban a alguien —dijo al fin—. Ella fue… la primera persona que torturaron ante mis ojos. Él… —Le tembló la barbilla mientras buscaba las palabras—. Experimentaron con ella. Aunque ella ni siquiera estaba… No había hecho nada.

A medida que hablaba, fue abriendo los ojos y contempló la habitación con la mirada perdida. Helena también lo vio: él, con dieciséis años volviendo a casa para las vacaciones de verano. Entró sin saber que estaba a punto de enfrentarse a una pesadilla de la que jamás podría escapar.

—Pensé… —Su voz se volvió más joven, más juvenil—. Durante un tiempo, pensé que, si asesinaba al principado rápidamente, ella se recuperaría. Que podría arreglarlo todo. Pero, cuando regresé, no era más que… una sombra de sí misma. Creo que… creo que intentó aguantar el verano, que se mostró valiente mientras estuve presente, pero… No duró ni un mes. —Las palabras sonaron graves, temblorosas.

Helena le pasó los dedos por el cabello. Kaine cerró los ojos y bajó la cabeza; se encogió sobre sí mismo.

—Cuando asesiné al principado, tardé más de un día en regresar, y ellos ya sabían lo que había hecho. Escucharon los rumores, pero no la soltaron hasta que les entregué ese maldito corazón, que todavía latía. Mi madre no paraba de sufrir ataques; se desplomaba en el suelo, dejaba de respirar o se mecía murmurando sin parar. Hice que varios médicos la revisaran, pero todos dijeron que no le pasaba nada, que simplemente era de constitución débil y tenía tendencia a la histeria. Me recomendaron que la ingresara en una clínica o le suministrara tónicos e inyecciones que la dejaban aletargada.

Helena le apretó la mano y siguió recorriendo el sello de la espalda con los dedos. Calculador, astuto, devoto, tenaz, implacable, eficaz, resuelto y severo.

Todo para vengar a su madre. Como castigo por todos los momentos en los que creía haberle fallado.

—Lo siento mucho, Kaine.

Se sumió en el silencio. Después, cerró los ojos y tomó aire con dificultad.

—Entonces... —se le quebró la voz—. Entonces... —le falló de nuevo— se puso mejor. Creí que tal vez se recuperaría, pero yo... yo... Habíamos tomado un nuevo distrito. Había una lista de familias con las que debíamos dar ejemplo. Padre, madre, dos hijas. Cuando asesinamos a los padres, los inmarcesibles reanimaron a la madre y la obligaron a matar a la hija mayor. Se suponía que yo debía hacer algo parecido con el padre y la hija menor. Era muy pequeña, llevaba dos trenzas con lacitos. Había una tarta de cumpleaños. Creo que era el suyo. Durant la arrastró por el pelo y me la puso delante... Sabía lo que querían que hiciera, pero salí corriendo. —Tragó saliva—. Reservé dos pasajes en un barco. Pensé que mi madre y yo podríamos huir por el mar, y que no se daría cuenta de que no podría acompañarla hasta que fuese demasiado tarde. Pero, cuando fui a buscarla, ellos se me habían adelantado. Traían el cadáver de la niña.

—Oh, Kaine... —Helena estaba tan horrorizada que no fue capaz de decir nada más. Él le apretaba la mano tan fuerte que temió que le saldrían moratones ahí donde se entrelazaban sus dedos.

—Traté de buscar una forma de escapar con ella. —Le cambió la voz, fue adquiriendo el tono habitual conforme la historia se adentraba en su vida. Empezó a emplear un tono duro y controlado—. Lo tenía todo preparado, había previsto cada detalle, cada contingencia, pero mi madre no quiso irse sin mí. Me planteé obligarla, drogarla y subirla al barco para alejarla de allí, pero me daba miedo que volviera para buscarme, y no quería que la encerraran. No deseaba ser yo quien volviera a enjaularla. —Su voz se vació de toda emoción—. Si no hubiera vuelto a casa aquella noche..., aún seguiría con vida. No sé por qué lo hice.

Se quedó callado. Helena se removió bajo su cuerpo y se incorporó. No podía mirarlo sin sentir una punzada de dolor en el pecho. Le rozó suavemente la frente.

—Kaine... Yo no soy tu madre.

El chico se encogió y abrió la boca para replicar, pero Helena siguió hablando para que no pudiera interrumpirla.

—La Llama Eterna no me hará daño si fracasas en una misión. No van a torturarme ni a ponerme en peligro para castigarte. No soy el rehén de nadie. Participo en la guerra por decisión propia. No estoy hecha de porcelana y no pienso romperme. Por favor... —Le acarició el pómulo con el pulgar—. Confía en mí, por favor.

Kaine negó con la cabeza.

—Déjame sacarte de aquí. Te juro que no afectará a mi colaboración con la Resistencia. Pero déjame sacarte de aquí.

—No pienso huir mientras los demás siguen luchando. Podemos hacerlo juntos. Permíteme ayudarte. No tienes que cargar con todo tú solo.

La tristeza inundó sus ojos.

—No puedes pedirme que huya de la guerra.

Kaine hizo un gesto amargo.

—¿Por qué no? ¿Es que no has hecho bastante por ellos? Te vendieron. ¿Qué habría sucedido si...? —No terminó la frase, incapaz de mirarla a los ojos—. ¿Qué habría sucedido si hubieran recibido una oferta de alguien que quisiera aprovecharla de verdad? Habrías accedido igualmente... y, si yo no te hubiera entrenado, habrías muerto al rescatar a Holdfast.

—Y yo accedí a hacerlo. A todas esas cosas. Nadie me obligó en ningún momento. No podemos elegir cuándo hemos hecho suficiente y dejar a los demás atrás para que sufran las consecuencias. En una guerra como esta, no hay civiles. Si ellos ganan —extendió las manos—, todos perderemos.

Kaine apretó los dientes, y Helena supo lo que quería decir: que le daba igual. Nunca le había importado que sobreviviera nadie más que ella.

Helena dejó escapar un suspiro de pena y bajó la cabeza hasta enterrarla en su hombro. Él la rodeó con sus brazos.

Casi se había dormido cuando oyó el susurro de su voz:

—Yo cuidaré de ti. Te lo juro, siempre voy a cuidar de ti.

Kaine era el único consuelo de Helena cuando la situación en la Resistencia empezó a deteriorarse.

Cuando por fin Lila recuperó su resonancia, la larga convalecencia parecía haberle arrancado parte de su vitalidad. Ya no era capaz de reponerse de la misma forma que antes, y las cicatrices de la cirugía que habían llevado a cabo en el pecho y en el hombro eran tan profundas que le limitaban el movimiento, por lo que necesitaba de una sanación constante y terapia para recuperar la movilidad.

Helena diseñó un tratamiento para ella, pero se la asignaron a otra de las sanadoras. Luc había exigido que Helena se mantuviera alejada de Lila al igual que de él mismo.

Ella se quedó sentada junto al escritorio de Pace cuando se lo comunicaron.

—Todavía tienes turnos en el hospital —dijo Pace.

—Cierto —repuso Helena sin emoción alguna—. Si está empezando a exigir cosas, supongo que Luc está más lúcido, ¿no?

Desde que trasladaron a Luc a sus aposentos privados, Helena no lo había visto ni había escuchado ni una palabra sobre él ni sobre su estado de salud, aunque el Consejo insistía en que se estaba recuperando.

Los labios de Pace esbozaron una mueca.

—Bueno, podríamos usar la palabra «lúcido», sí —carraspeó—. Estoy segura de que, con el tiempo, volverá a ser quien era. No te preocupes por él; ya tiene gente de sobra para eso. Tú cuida de ti misma, Marino.

Helena se limitó a asentir, aunque a la Llama Eterna no le sobraba el tiempo.

Luc era el pilar de la Resistencia. Sin él, todo se volvía cada vez más incierto. Crowther había empezado a depender más de Kaine, y lo usaba para sembrar información falsa y hacer sabotajes, como si el ejército de inmarcesibles fuera una máquina que había que desarmar pieza a pieza. Los sobres que contenían órdenes eran cada vez más gruesos.

Kaine nunca mencionaba lo que hacía, pero ella notaba que estaba a punto de quebrarse bajo la presión. Cada vez que la veía se comportaba con más desesperación.

A Helena le dolía verlo desgastarse bajo el peso de todo lo que debía mantener y producir para ambos bandos, mientras ella estaba atrapada en el Cuartel General como un animal enjaulado.

Al no poder salir a recolectar, ocupaba su tiempo con una nueva investigación. Con Shiseo como jefe de laboratorio, estaba intentando perfeccionar la anulación de la alquimia. Era algo que había solicitado el Consejo, ya que los inmarcesibles eran prácticamente imposibles de capturar y mantener encerrados, pero con esta anulación podrían conseguirlo. Gracias a Kaine, Helena sabía que el anulitio interfería con las habilidades y la regeneración de los inmarcesibles de la misma forma que lo hacía con cualquier alquimista.

Shiseo había diseñado unos grilletes de anulitio que podían anular la alquimia de forma focalizada. Se cerraban alrededor de la muñeca y hacían que la resonancia se diluyera como si fuese energía estática.

Helena lo puso a prueba: cerró uno alrededor de su muñeca, flexionó los dedos y lo deslizó por el brazo. Cuando le llegó al codo, descubrió que podía vencer la interferencia. Negó con la cabeza.

—No anulan la resonancia completamente.

Se lo quitó e inspeccionó el interior, que Shiseo había recubierto de anulitio.

—Para eliminarla por completo, creo que tendremos que emplear algo interno —explicó—. Si el anulitio estuviera envuelto en cerámica, evitaríamos la corrosión y la biointerferencia. Pero, si lo metemos en un tubito y lo introducimos en la muñeca aquí… —señaló con el dedo el espacio que había entre el radio y el cúbito—, el grillete iría unido a este punzón supresor que quedaría fijo mediante la alquimia. Seguro que así no queda ni rastro de resonancia.

Shiseo parecía tan perturbado que Helena comprendió que lo que estaba proponiendo iba más allá de su función práctica.

Hablaban de diseñar grilletes para los inmarcesibles, que se ocultaban bajo sus yelmos y sus muertos. Y, cuando pensó en Kaine, que probablemente acabaría prisionero en algún momento, sintió que el estómago se le revolvía. Sacudió la cabeza.

—No he dicho nada. Es demasiado enrevesado. No tenemos que anular la resonancia de esa forma.

—Funcionaría.

Helena negó de nuevo.

—No es necesario. Este diseño nos vale.

En ocasiones, el anillo de Helena se activaba dos veces seguidas y, cuando eso sucedía, Amaris llegaba y Kaine prácticamente se derrumbaba de su lomo. Otras veces, Amaris aparecía sola. Helena se subía al lomo de la quimera y se agarraba al arnés, mientras el viento las azuzaba en todas direcciones. Después se dirigían a las entrañas de la ciudad, a algún sótano o edificio destrozado, o también a veces a un callejón, y allí encontraba a Kaine. Solía tener algún trozo de metralla de anulitio en el cuerpo, tan incrustado que no podía extraerlo.

Helena había aprendido a tener siempre llena la bolsa con instrumental médico, vendas y todo tipo de medicinas. Conforme los ataques de anulitio se volvían más eficaces, había que emplear más a menudo la cirugía. Se acostumbró a operar de forma manual con una antorcha eléctrica como única fuente de luz.

Kaine no permitía que lo dejase inconsciente. Quería mantenerse lúcido por si aparecía alguien, aunque lo más habitual era que estuviese desvariando, con los ojos plateados vidriosos, y mascullando entre dientes:

—Estoy bien… Apenas lo noto. No te preocupes. Dentro de poco nos iremos de aquí… Ya lo tengo todo pensado. Solo… solo un poco más.

Helena se sentaba con su cabeza en el regazo, le sostenía las manos y le cantaba en voz baja hasta que lograba estabilizarlo. El anulitio hacía que su recuperación fuese mucho más lenta de lo normal. Cuando perdía demasiada sangre, quedaba flotando al borde de la consciencia o empezaba a temblar hasta que entraba en shock. Entonces ella le pasaba los dedos y la resonancia por las manos, sin dejar de disculparse.

«Tú lo estás matando. Tú lo estás matando. Esto es culpa tuya».

Solo se permitía llorar por él cuando caía inconsciente y no podía verla. Le cogía las manos entre las suyas y trataba de arreglarlo.

—Lo siento. Lo siento. Lo siento —repetía una y otra vez.

Antes de que recobrara la lucidez, se enjugaba las lágrimas y limpiaba la sangre. En cuanto Kaine volvía en sí mismo, Helena notaba cómo se tensaba de inmediato, hasta que la veía y respiraba de nuevo.

En las noches más largas, Amaris se enroscaba detrás de Helena y le daba toquecitos con el morro a las manos inertes de Kaine. Ella se sentaba y le acariciaba la cara, sintiendo todos los latidos de su corazón. Entonces le prometía:

—Yo cuidaré de ti. Te lo prometo, siempre voy a cuidar de ti.

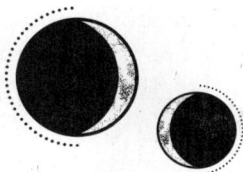

CAPÍTULO 56

LOS INMARCESIBLES LANZARON LA PRIMERA bomba de anulitio a mediados de primavera.

La Resistencia sabía que un ataque así era inminente; desde que los inmarcesibles emplearon el anulitio contra Lila, lo habían estado usando cada vez más. Aunque provocaban heridas graves, las armas de anulitio eran poco útiles, ya que se trataba de una sustancia muy frágil. Sin embargo, las bombas fueron devastadoras.

Para eliminar la resonancia de un alquimista, bastaba con unos pequeños fragmentos de metralla. Si el anulitio se disolvía y se introducía en el torrente sanguíneo, el personal sanitario tenía que coser las heridas de forma manual, suministrar agentes quelantes y esperar a que el paciente recuperara su resonancia.

La medicina alquímica avanzada, junto con la sanación, conseguía que los combatientes de la Resistencia se recuperaran con rapidez; siempre y cuando los soldados no murieran desangrados. Las heridas que en otras partes del mundo tardaban meses en curar se sanaban allí en unos días o semanas.

Sin embargo, con el anulitio, la convalecencia se prolongaba.

El hospital se había preparado lo mejor posible: el personal médico y quirúrgico había aprendido a operar de forma manual y el departamento de quimiatría había producido una gran cantidad de agentes quelantes. Sin embargo, toda esa logística no bastó para subir la moral. La gente estaba aterrorizada. La alquimia y la resonancia lo eran todo; vivir sin ambas era como regresar a la era prealquímica.

Ilva, que siempre había mantenido una fachada de serenidad, desde el secuestro de Luc parecía completamente desorientada, como si no lograra comprender del todo la magnitud del problema ni cómo solucionarlo. Tal vez se debiera a que era un lapsus, pero parecía incapaz de entender la gravedad emocional de la amenaza del anulitio y su impacto en la moral de la gente.

Lo único bueno era que, al parecer, Luc volvía a hacerse cargo de sus responsabilidades. Aunque pasaba la mayor parte del tiempo encerrado en sus aposentos, apareció de repente en una asamblea que había convocado Althorne para calmar los ánimos de la Resistencia. Llegó vestido de blanco y dorado, lívido e indignado. Había adelgazado mucho. A pesar de que la armadura lo disimulaba, se le veía muy demacrado. Aun así, parecía que su cuerpo solo era un cascarón y que era su alma la que brillaba con fuerza. Por muy frágil que pareciese, aún irradiaba vida.

—Morrough, como todos los nigromantes que le precedieron, quiere que la Resistencia tenga miedo y que la luz de la Llama Eterna se extinga —proclamó con los ojos azules centelleantes—. No le daremos esa satisfacción. Paladia nos pertenece. Construimos esta ciudad como un faro, y esa luz ha protegido al mundo de la infamia de la nigromancia durante generaciones. Los dioses están de nuestra parte. Sol es inconquistable. Las leyes de la naturaleza no le concederán la victoria a la corrupción. No fracasaremos; conocemos las recompensas que nuestros ancestros recibieron por su fe y su coraje, ¡y nosotros disfrutaremos de lo mismo!

Había cierta desesperación en su voz y, aun así, resultaba extrañamente deslumbrante, como el sol en su cénit. Helena se dio cuenta de que el ambiente cambiaba: la incertidumbre y el miedo dieron paso a la convicción. A la fe.

Luc continuó hablando. Describió la ciudad con el detalle de quien la conoce como la palma de su mano, y habló de los sueños que su padre y él tenían para el glorioso futuro de Paladia.

Cuando Helena quiso darse cuenta, ya estaban organizando una contraofensiva y preparando escuadrones. El nuevo batallón de Luc, que todavía no había entrado en combate, salió hacia la ciudad junto a cuatro batallones más y lograron recuperar un distrito de la isla Oeste.

Desde un puente colgante, Helena observó cómo regresaban en un desfile de victoria, entre gritos de júbilo. Luc iba de pie en la parte trasera de un camión, acompañado de Sebastian, sin dejar de saludar mientras atravesaban las verjas de la entrada.

Lila no había asistido. En teoría, seguía recuperándose, pero lo cierto era que aún no se había celebrado el juicio y a los líderes les preocupaba cómo iba a reaccionar Luc. Si hacía uso de su poder como principado para oponerse al Consejo y a los comandantes militares, sus órdenes no podían desestimarse sin que se produjera un colapso absoluto de liderazgo, algo que podría destrozar a la Resistencia.

Mientras que él siguiera considerando a Lila su paladina primera, Lila podía ignorar cualquier instrucción del Consejo, ya que sus votos se debían a Luc. Por eso, Lila permanecía en un limbo. Aún no tenía permiso para combatir, pero ya no estaba herida. Se plantó en la puerta de la Torre y aplaudió con todos los demás, aunque la pena era visible en su rostro.

El contrataque había sido tan repentino y descarado que los inmarcesibles no tuvieron tiempo de organizar una defensa. De forma similar, el Consejo se mostró tan desconcertado por el hecho de que Luc asumiera el liderazgo tan rápidamente que no supo cómo reaccionar ante esa determinación. Después del éxito que tuvo en la ofensiva, nadie se atrevía a discutirle nada, especialmente porque había conseguido subir la moral de la Resistencia al tiempo que se consolidaba en el Consejo.

Las batallas empezaron a mezclarse unas con otras. La única diferencia era que ahora había un pabellón médico especializado para los heridos de anulitio, las bajas aumentaban sin cesar y las infecciones y las enfermedades se volvían cada vez más peligrosas. Primero se notó la masificación, luego la escasez de sábanas y vendas limpias y, después, aparecieron las complicaciones médicas.

En ocasiones, Helena trabajaba durante varios días seguidos y tenía que ignorar las llamadas de Kaine, salvo que se tratara de mensajes para Crowther. Al menos, trabajar la mantenía alejada de los pozos de preocupación que acechaban su mente.

Cuando estaba sola, se tumbaba en la cama y miraba fijamente el techo mientras hacía girar una y otra vez el anillo de Kaine en su dedo. No dejaba de pensar en el sello que Wagner había dibujado. Tenía nueve puntas.

La alquimia norteña casi siempre empleaba cinco y ocho puntas, es decir, los números elementales o celestiales. Esas eran las únicas fórmulas que se enseñaban en la Academia, a excepción de la piromancia de los Holdfast, que requería un sello de siete puntas, pero Helena solo lo conocía por haber ayudado a Luc con sus deberes.

Jamás había oído hablar de un sello de nueve puntas. No tenía ni idea de cómo funcionaba, y el único ejemplo del que disponía estaba plagado de errores y lo había dibujado alguien que no sabía nada sobre los principios básicos de la alquimia.

¿Cómo iba a revertir lo que le habían hecho a Kaine si ni siquiera entendía el procedimiento? Movió los dedos para intentar visualizar los canales de energía. Su mente no dejaba de regresar a Soren.

Acalló esos pensamientos mediante la animancia y se obligó a dejar atrás todos sus recuerdos sobre él. Aun así, seguía incordiándola, no tanto por su destrucción sino por el instante en que murió. Siempre intentaba romper la conexión resonántica antes de que los pacientes murieran, pero en aquella ocasión había estado totalmente concentrada en Soren.

La energía la recorrió mientras la sentía como una corriente eléctrica, y no pudo dejar de pensar en ello mientras imaginaba cómo canalizar a través de un múltiplo de tres.

Eso le dio una idea: si Morrough podía atrapar almas vivas en hueso y el primer Nigromante había metido todas las almas de una ciudad en una gema, ¿qué sucedería si se capturaba otro tipo de energía? ¿Alguien lo había intentado?

La siguiente vez que notó que un paciente estaba a punto de fallecer, en vez de romper la conexión, mantuvo el contacto y se aferró a la energía que liberó al morir. Esta atravesó su resonancia y le dejó las manos entumecidas y cosquilleantes durante horas.

Bueno, tenía sentido que no pudiese retener esa energía. Necesitaba algún tipo de recipiente. El amuleto de heliolita estaba hecho de… ¿mercurio? ¿O de vidrio? Tal vez fuese cristal. Probó con distintos materiales que encontró en los almacenes e incluso introdujo de contrabando metales más extraños y otros compuestos en el hospital, para comprobar si la energía se canalizaba en alguno.

Las heliolitas se resquebrajaron, y el metal blanco hizo que su bolsillo se incendiara. En una caja que encontró en un rincón del almacén, había trozos enormes de obsidiana. El cristal volcánico tenía un punto de fundición más alto que el cristal normal.

Se metió un trozo en el bolsillo.

Cuando sintió que la vida de un paciente se extinguía, agarró la obsidiana. Era uno de los pacientes afectados por el anulitio. La metralla le había destrozado los órganos y la infección no había mejorado con el tratamiento. Helena podía obligar a su corazón a que siguiera latiendo, pero solo conseguiría ralentizar su muerte; moriría en cuanto ella se alejara. Tenía la piel ardiendo por la fiebre y ella sostenía su mano con fuerza sin dejar de hablar con alguien que no estaba allí. Sus palabras empezaron a sonar más vagas y escurridizas.

Helena tragó saliva y mantuvo abierto el canal de resonancia cuando sus ojos perdieron la vida. La muerte la atravesó como una descarga eléctrica y fue directa a la obsidiana.

El brazo se le quedó dormido. Cuando recuperó el movimiento, el chico ya estaba muerto y la obsidiana irradiaba calidez entre los dedos de Helena. Podía sentir esa extraña y oscura energía.

Le cerró los ojos y le cubrió el rostro con una sábana, pero entonces notó que le temblaban los dedos. ¿Acababa de atrapar un alma en un cristal volcánico? Lo apretó con fuerza. No. Sabía cómo era esa energía, por el amuleto y por Kaine. Esto era algo distinto.

Aun así, intentó fingir que no estaba en su bolsillo mientras acababa el turno.

Después corrió al laboratorio. Sin embargo, al abrir la puerta, se detuvo en seco, pues allí estaba Lila, encogida en el suelo con la cara hinchada y los ojos rojos.

Helena se quedó petrificada. Por Dios, el tribunal. Debía de haber empezado el juicio.

Apenas había visto a Lila ni había hablado con ella desde que rescataron a Luc. Un día volvió a su habitación y descubrió que todas las pertenencias de Lila habían desaparecido, y se enteró de que habría un funeral privado para Soren cuando ya se había celebrado.

A pesar de lo mucho que le hubiera gustado dar explicaciones, no podía hacerlo, porque la versión oficial mantenía que Soren simplemente había muerto.

No obstante, Luc le habría contado la verdad a Lila.

Helena permaneció donde estaba, no tenía ni idea de qué había llevado a Lila hasta ahí.

—Lila. —Helena dejó la obsidiana sobre la mesa y dio un paso hacia ella con cautela—. Lila, ¿qué sucede? ¿Qué ha pasado?

Lila miró fijamente a Helena y tardó un buen rato en responder:

—He cometido un error —dijo al fin en apenas un susurro—. He cometido un terrible error.

Helena tragó saliva con dificultad.

—No… No pasa nada. Estoy segura de que se arreglará. Da igual lo que hayas hecho, seguro que no es para tanto.

El fantasma de Soren pareció flotar entre las dos.

—No. —Lila sacudió la cabeza—. He estado mintiéndole a todo el mundo. He estado mintiendo toda mi vida. Y ahora… ahora no sé qué hacer… —Su voz sonaba estrangulada. No terminaba las frases—. Soren era la única persona que lo sabía —susurró. Tenía los ojos vidriosos, pero no le cayó ninguna lágrima—. Siempre me guardó el secreto, siempre sabía qué hacer. Decía que su trabajo era… cuidarme.

—¿Qué ha pasado? —Helena se acercó con cautela.

Lila levantó la vista y cogió aire. La barbilla le tembló justo antes de responder:

—Estoy… estoy embarazada.

Helena se quedó inmóvil. Sin palabras. Estaba demasiado perpleja incluso para creer lo que Lila acababa de contarle.

Si sabía que estaba embarazada, entonces debía de estarlo desde hacía dos o tres meses, y eso suponiendo que tuviera un ciclo regular, pero Helena sabía que no era el caso. En aquella época, Lila aún seguía hospitalizada.

—¿Cómo es posible? —Esa fue la única pregunta que a Helena se le ocurrió hacer. Dejó a un lado todo lo que eso implicaba.

Lila tragó saliva y sacudió la cabeza, pero torció el gesto de dolor al sentir que le tiraban las cicatrices del cuello.

—Lo sé. Yo tampoco pensé que fuera posible después de… todo lo que ha pasado. Siempre di por hecho que no podría quedarme embarazada.

—No —la cortó Helena con impaciencia—. Bueno, sí, eso también, pero no estabas embarazada cuando estuviste ingresada. Te dimos el alta hace unos… ¿Cómo sabes que estás embarazada?

Lila bajó la mirada para esquivar los ojos de Helena.

—Ese… ese es el secreto. Sé que estoy embarazada.

Entonces le pareció tan increíblemente obvio que Helena no entendió cómo no se había dado cuenta años atrás.

Lila Bayard, que solía volver de las batallas sin apenas un rasguño, que siempre se recuperaba milagrosamente de sus heridas, quien se había adaptado a una prótesis en la pierna en cuestión de meses cuando todo el mundo decía que tardaría un año. La persona a la que jamás le costaba recuperarse, excepto cuando perdió su resonancia.

—Eres una vivemante —concluyó Helena.

Lila no la miró a los ojos cuando asintió.

—Nunca la he usado con nadie, salvo conmigo misma. Un par de veces en Soren, pero solo cuando él me lo pedía. Me dijo que no podía permitir que nadie lo supiera. Ni siquiera nuestros padres, porque, si alguien se enteraba, no me dejarían ser la paladina de Luc.

—¿Durante todo este tiempo? —preguntó Helena con suavidad, aunque lo cierto era que se sentía traicionada.

—Lo siento. Quería decírtelo, pero… sabía lo que te había pasado a ti. No podía arriesgarme a eso; la vida de Luc estaba en juego. No podía ser como tú… A mí solo se me da bien luchar.

Aquella confesión era más de lo que Helena podía asimilar en ese momento.

—¿Quién es el padre? —preguntó, como si no fuera obvio.

—Sabes que es Luc.

Helena asintió. Quiso enfadarse, pero sus propios secretos eran peores, y que Lila hubiese acudido a ella en ausencia de Soren lo decía todo.

—Seguramente te hayas enterado de que quieren someterme a juicio, a menos que renuncie voluntariamente a ser paladina —le contó con una voz que sonaba hueca y desesperada—. Antes me decía a mí misma que al final todo merecería la pena, pero la guerra ha durado demasiado. Nunca quise… Bueno, él lo intentó en alguna que otra ocasión, pero yo siempre me negué. —Lila sacudió la cabeza—. Aunque ha sido en vano, todo el mundo piensa que hemos estado acostándonos en el frente. No ha servido de nada que no lo hiciéramos. —Bajó la vista—. Cuando regresó después de tomar ese distrito… Sé que no era por mí, pero sentí la frustración de que me hubieran dejado atrás y de saber que ya siempre lo harían. Después vino a buscarme y me dijo que había estado pensando en mí todo el tiempo y… —Se encogió de hombros—. Todos creen que lo estamos haciendo, así que…

Helena posó una mano en su hombro con sumo cuidado.

—No pasa nada. Puedo arreglarlo. Al haberlo detectado tan pronto, podemos usar medicación o la vivemancia, lo que tú prefieras. Nadie se enterará.

—No.

Helena miró fijamente a Lila, convencida de que la había oído mal. La paladina tomó aire sin atreverse a mirarla.

—Sí, vine por eso. Sabía que tú podrías hacerlo, pero… mientras es-

731

peraba no dejaba de pensar. ¿Cuáles eran las probabilidades? —Negó con la cabeza—. No recuerdo la última vez que tuve la regla. Han pasado años. Creía que no podría quedarme embarazada. Siempre pensé que sería Soren el que se casaría y engendraría la nueva generación de Bayard, pero ahora solo quedo yo.

Helena no supo qué responder. Lila bajó la mirada y se encogió un poco más, como si percibiera los prejuicios de la sanadora.

—Lo más probable es que no llegue a término, así que tal vez puedo esperar y… tenerlo durante un tiempo.

—¿Y si llega a término? —preguntó Helena.

Lila no respondió.

Helena sintió una presión en el pecho. Quería decirle a Lila que estaba comportándose como una estúpida por pretender tener un bebé durante la guerra. Lila no sería la primera en hacerlo, pero esas chicas eran diferentes. Lila era alquimista, una guerrera. Ninguna de esas cosas iba de la mano con la maternidad. Las normas eran estrictas.

—No llegará a término —repitió Lila.

—Eso no es una respuesta —insistió Helena—. ¿Qué harás si el embarazo sigue adelante? Vas a tener un bebé durante una guerra cuando ya te estás enfrentando a un tribunal. No volverás a ser paladina. No te dejarán combatir nunca más.

Lila no dejaba de morderse las uñas; le sangraban las cutículas.

—Luc tendrá que dejar de luchar para ser líder. Ilva está demasiado mayor para seguir ejerciendo como su mano derecha, y no confía en nadie más para reemplazarla. Dicen que, si renuncio a ser paladina, no me someterán a juicio. Sebastian aceptará mi cargo y yo podré combatir de nuevo. —Lila respiró hondo—. Seré comandante de mi propia unidad: la primera mujer comandante.

La voz de Lila no mostraba ni orgullo ni emoción por lo que era un logro histórico, porque era imposible que volviese a entrar en combate una vez que le arrebatan su rango y se produjera el escándalo que le seguiría. Tanto su reputación como su legado quedarían manchados para siempre.

—Si dices que estoy enferma, nadie sabrá que estoy embarazada… Y, si el embarazo no sale adelante, volveré al servicio militar como si nunca hubiese pasado.

—O podrías retirarte del combate activo y entrenar a reclutas a los que les vendría muy bien tu experiencia —replicó Helena—. No solo tienes dos opciones.

—No pienso retirarme. Los Bayard no nos retiramos —expresó Lila con los ojos azules brillantes. Después torció el gesto—. Perdóname. La gente no deja de decirme que no es el fin, pero… —Soltó un bufido—. Sé cómo son las cosas. Sé lo que recordarán. No será nada de lo que hice en combate.

Ahí fue cuando Helena lo entendió. El embarazo cambiaba la narrativa. No borraba el escándalo, pero le daba otra forma; en vez de una violación de un juramento que estuvo a punto de ocasionar una catástrofe, se trataba de una historia de amor.

El principado necesitaba un heredero desde hacía mucho tiempo, pero era complicado convertirlo en prioridad cuando la vida de Luc debía estar rodeada de divinidad, y Luc, por razones obvias, siempre se había negado a un matrimonio concertado, que era lo que quería el Consejo.

Un heredero Holdfast podía darle fuerzas a la Resistencia. ¿Cómo iba a ser una guerra perdida si había un símbolo tan tangible del futuro?

Por supuesto que Lila prefería esa versión de su historia en vez de las alternativas a las que se enfrentaba.

Lila siempre le había parecido imparable, pero Helena veía ahora todas las grietas que escondía. Los deseos que nunca se había permitido albergar.

Helena se vio reflejada en ella.

—¿Luc lo sabrá?

La paladina tomó aire y negó con la cabeza.

—No, creo que para él sería una distracción. Ahora mismo está bajo una presión tremenda, y la transición de poderes será complicada. Si lo supiera y después quedara en nada… Le destrozaría haber tenido la esperanza.

—¿Luc… quiere tener hijos? —preguntó Helena con cierta vacilación. No recordaba haber oído a Luc hablar de niños. Lo único que le pedía al futuro era que acabase la guerra y viajar. Aunque también era cierto que el tema de Lila nunca lo habían hablado abiertamente. Helena siempre lo había sabido, pero Luc jamás lo reconoció, ni siquiera delante de ella.

Lila asintió.

—Aquella noche hablamos del tema. Me dijo que él no era como su padre, que no solo quería cumplir con su deber, que deseaba tener una familia para disfrutarla, no únicamente por el bien del principado o porque tuviera que haber un heredero, sino porque amaba tanto a alguien que quería hacerlo. Así es en este caso.

Helena tragó saliva. Seguía sin gustarle todo eso, pero no podía negarle nada a Lila.

—Tendré que hablar con Crowther para barajar nuestras opciones.

A Lila se le descompuso la cara.

—¿Por qué vas a decírselo a él? Es odioso. Luc no lo soporta.

Helena esquivó su mirada.

—Es la opción más útil. No tengo autoridad para poner a alguien en cuarentena. No creo que quieras involucrar a Elain o a Matias. Tus opciones son Crowther o Ilva, e Ilva no se ha mostrado muy digna de confianza últimamente.

—Está bien. —Lila suspiró con un gesto de dolor—. Hablaremos con Crowther.

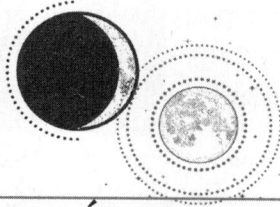

CAPÍTULO 57

Mayus 1787

SEGÚN LOS INFORMES OFICIALES, LILA Bayard sufría un caso grave de tos de los pantanos que había contraído después de ayudar a transportar suministros a los suburbios sumergidos, en el extremo meridional de la isla.

La tos de los pantanos solía aparecer todos los años a principios de verano, después de las inundaciones, cuando el ambiente se tornaba cálido y húmedo, y los niveles más oscuros y escondidos de la ciudad, que estaban apartados de la luz solar, se cubrían de moho negro.

Los síntomas eran una tos expectorante y, en ocasiones, sarpullido. Aunque afectaba sobre todo a los niños y los ancianos, a veces se enquistaba y se volvía tan virulenta que contagiaba a toda la ciudad como si fuera una plaga. Esta era la razón por la que los niveles superiores de la ciudad solían evitar cualquier contacto con los sectores más bajos de la población.

Helena conocía bien los síntomas porque su padre los trataba todos los veranos. La mayoría de la gente que contraía la enfermedad no se podía permitir viajar a los niveles superiores para recibir el tratamiento de un boticario autorizado. Mediante la vivemancia, Helena podía replicar los síntomas a la perfección, así que creó unos sarpullidos morados en las muñecas y ambos lados del cuello de Lila, y cargó sus pulmones de flemas para que tosiera con fuerza cuando vino Pace a examinarla y hacer su diagnóstico.

Al vivir tanta gente en tan poco espacio, el miedo al contagio era constante.

A Lila no tardaron en aislarla en lo alto de la Torre de Alquimia, junto a todos los que habían participado en la entrega de suministros, aunque estos fueron declarados asintomáticos al cabo de tres días.

Una enfermedad tan común no afectó a la moral, especialmente porque se consideraba una dolencia propia de los pobres y de los entornos insalubres. Que Lila se hubiese contagiado solo se interpretó como un signo de que seguía demasiado débil después de tantas heridas. En las habitaciones superiores, bañadas por el sol de la Torre de Alquimia, se recuperaría rápidamente.

Sin embargo, Luc empezó a agobiarse. Exigió verla, pero se le negó rotundamente. Sus propios pulmones seguían deteriorados y dañados, por lo que bajo ninguna circunstancia se le permitía acercarse a Lila hasta que se recuperase por completo.

Helena no sabía por dónde empezar con aquel secreto. Nunca había estudiado los embarazos. Su experiencia con los partos se limitaba a situaciones de emergencia. Buscó en la biblioteca alguna referencia, pero todo lo que encontró le pareció escaso de información, y entonces recordó que la enfermera Pace guardaba muchos libros de medicina en el despacho para tenerlos más a mano.

—Nunca pensé que te interesaría la maternidad. —El comentario de la enfermera Pace hizo que diera un respingo cuando la encontró ojeando uno de los libros. Helena lo cerró de inmediato y lo colocó en su sitio.

—No me interesa, pero el título me ha llamado la atención.

—Puedes llevártelo, si quieres.

—No —negó moviendo la cabeza—, solo era curiosidad.

Se dirigió a la puerta.

—Marino. —La voz de Pace sonó autoritaria.

Helena se volvió. Pace la observaba como un halcón.

—¿Estás embarazada?

—No.

—A veces hay descuidos —replicó Pace apoyándose con calma en su escritorio—. Sobre todo, en tiempos de guerra. No serías la primera a la que le pasa.

A Helena se le escapó un resoplido de frustración.

—No estoy embarazada.

—Solo espero que tu pareja sea responsable…

—No puedo quedarme embarazada. Me esterilizaron —estalló Helena sintiendo una vergüenza tan profunda que no quería seguir escuchándola.

Pace se quedó muy quieta y, después, sacudió la cabeza.

—No. No harían tal cosa. Es imposible que lo consideraran necesario en los tiempos que corren.

A Helena le ardieron las mejillas, pero en el estómago sintió un vacío que se abría cada vez más.

—Pues lo hicieron. Maier, para ser más exactos. Me hizo una ligadura de trompas la semana que volví. Fue... fue una de las condiciones del falcón. Así que, como te digo, no estoy embarazada.

Volvió a girarse hacia la puerta.

—Helena, espera. —La voz de Pace sonó entonces suplicante.

Helena hizo un gesto y se volvió con desgana. Pace tenía una de sus manos rojas y agrietadas sobre el pecho.

—No debería haber insistido. No tenía ni idea. Maier nunca lo mencionó.

—No pasa nada —afirmó Helena con rigidez—. Prefería ser alquimista, y las mujeres no podemos tener ambas cosas. —Levantó la barbilla—. Ahora ya no tengo que preocuparme por decidir entre una u otra. Además —miró a Pace a los ojos—, seguramente muera joven, así que sería una madre horrible.

Pace la observó atentamente.

—¿Tu madre lo fue?

Aquellas palabras le hicieron más daño que si le hubiesen propinado una patada. La habitación le dio vueltas y sintió que se le formaba un nudo en la garganta.

—Cómo te atreves.

—Lo siento, no debería haberlo dicho así —admitió, aunque no parecía arrepentida—. Pero, Helena, no creo que estés siendo honesta contigo misma sobre lo que realmente quieres.

—Era la única forma de hacerme sanadora. Necesitábamos una e Ilva dijo que yo era la única que podría hacerlo. —Le temblaba la mandíbula, así que apretó los dientes para que no se notara—. Me pidieron que decidiera y eso hice. ¿Preferirías que no hubiese elegido ser sanadora?

—No tenías ni diecisiete años. No habías vivido lo suficiente para saber lo que querías.

—Me siento bastante viva ahora mismo —replicó Helena entre dientes—. Y estoy bien.

—Estar viva no es lo mismo que vivir. Espero que algún día tengas la oportunidad de descubrir la diferencia.

Pace se acercó a la estantería y sacó el libro que Helena había estado ojeando. Lo sostuvo con las dos manos y contempló la portada.

—Fui matrona, ¿lo sabías? Hace ya mucho tiempo. —Sacudió la cabeza—. Debería haberme dado cuenta antes. Siempre lo das todo en el momento presente, como si creyeras que solo vas a tener eso. —Se giró hacia Helena—. Si echas un vistazo a la siguiente generación, tal vez percibas el futuro como algo más real.

Extendió el libro hacia Helena. El título —*La maternidad: un estudio exhaustivo sobre la ciencia y la fisiología de la gestación*— resplandeció bajo la luz que entraba por la ventana de arriba.

—Lila Bayard va a necesitar los mejores cuidados posibles.

Helena la miró anonadada.

—¿Cómo…?

La enfermera Pace dejó el libro en sus manos.

—Llevo siendo enfermera el doble de años que tu vida. Tienes una habilidad excepcional para la vivemancia, pero Lila tendría que haberse pasado tres semanas enferma antes de que le aparecieran esos sarpullidos.

CONFORME LUC FUE HACIÉNDOSE CARGO de todo, la salud de Ilva empezó a declinar rápida y repentinamente, como si todos esos años hubiese aguantado para ver el momento en el que su sobrino nieto estuviese preparado. Había días en los que apenas estaba en sus cabales. Crowther, preocupado por el súbito deterioro de Ilva, le pidió a Helena que la examinara. No tenía ninguna enfermedad; simplemente era mayor y estaba cansada.

La guerra seguía siendo un tira y afloja para ambos bandos. Las escaramuzas constantes apenas aportaban ventaja, salvo para causar más destrozos a una ciudad ya devastada.

Luc lideró otro ataque contundente en la isla Oeste, donde lograron tomar un almacén. Lo encontraron lleno de tanques enormes con forma tubular y, en el interior, encontraron cadáveres con tubos en las venas y mascarillas sobre nariz y boca. Eran luchadores de la Resistencia. Todos estaban muertos, pero sus cuerpos aún conservaban calor.

Cuando rompieron el perímetro, las mascarillas suministraron un gas que los asesinó unos minutos antes de que la Resistencia pudiera rescatarlos.

Al Cuartel General llegaron camiones repletos de cadáveres para incinerarlos. Apenas habían hecho un par de prisioneros, pero una era la custodio del almacén, quien se mostró agresiva y se negó a responder a preguntas.

Como la custodio era una prisionera de Luc, no pudieron hacerla desaparecer en uno de los agujeros subterráneos de Crowther ni someterla a tortura para obtener información. Entonces, Crowther recordó que Kaine le había enseñado a Helena un método insólito para extraer información; ella misma lo había mencionado una vez para disuadirlo de seguir torturando.

Helena se horrorizó como los demás al ver esos rostros familiares, sanos e intactos, listos para la cremación, después de haber estado tan cerca de que los rescataran. Accedió sin pensárselo dos veces.

Tras hablar con un par de contactos, Crowther consiguió quedarse un par de horas a solas con la custodio, y llevó consigo a Helena.

La custodio era una mujer de rostro enjuto, cabello corto y boca ancha. Sus ojos azul claro se estrecharon en cuanto vio a Helena, como si la estuviera evaluando. Crowther se quedó en las sombras y dejó que Helena hiciera lo suyo.

—¿Quién eres? —preguntó Helena, que no sabía por dónde empezar.

—¿Y a ti qué te importa? —le espetó la custodio.

—La verdad es que no he conocido a ninguna mujer entre los inmarcesibles ni los aspirantes.

—A los hombres les suele gustar más nuestro cuerpo que nosotras. —La guardia miró el rincón desde donde observaba Crowther—. Supongo que debo de ser especial.

—¿Por qué? —preguntó Helena, aunque ya tenía una idea.

—Seguramente por el mismo motivo que tú. —La custodio se echó hacia atrás y miró a Helena de arriba abajo—. Aunque la diferencia es que yo no soy una traidora a los de mi clase.

—No soy yo la que acaba de asesinar a más de cien personas —afirmó Helena, esforzándose por mantener el temple. No sabía por qué le molestaba tanto que la custodio fuese mujer, pero esa idea la enfadaba.

—Ellos me habrían asesinado a mí si les hubiera dado la oportunidad. Yo los maté primero. —La custodio alzó la barbilla y señaló a Helena con ella—. ¿Qué eres? —La repasó con la mirada—. ¿Sanadora? Seguro que sí. Yo también fui sanadora.

Helena lo dudaba, pero la mujer estaba hablando libremente, así que dejó que siguiera.

—No quería ser sanadora, pero no hay muchas opciones para nosotras. Él quiso que me hiciera monja, que me dedicara a criar a otros mocosos que fueran como yo, que les enseñara a ocultar sus habilidades y los castigara si no lo hacían. ¿Verdad?

Helena se giró para mirar a Crowther, que lo observaba todo sin inmutarse.

—¿La conoces?

—Ah, sí. El cernícalo Jan solía venir a vernos cuando alguien se portaba mal en el orfanato. Siempre traía alguna mascota, alguien atado a quien podíamos admirar, en quien podríamos convertirnos si hacíamos todo lo que nos pedía. Pero me sorprende que seas tú; normalmente eran más jóvenes. —Posó los ojos en Helena.

—Ya basta, Mandl —replicó Crowther con aspereza.

La mujer sonrió de lado.

—¿Ves? Ya sabía yo que te acordabas de mí.

—Sonsácale la información y acabemos con esto —le ordenó Crowther a Helena.

La sanadora tomó aire, aunque Mandl parecía poco impresionada.

—No vas a obligarme a hablar —repuso—. Solía romperme los huesos y abrirme en canal por diversión. Solo para sentir algo en aquel agujero en el que nos criaron. Eres demasiado débil para hacerme daño, traidora.

—Te sorprendería —dijo Helena con el corazón en un puño.

Mandl se limitó a reír.

Los cadáveres del almacén eran una tragedia muy reciente. Todas esas personas, a solo unos minutos de que las rescatasen, habían muerto porque Mandl prefería hacerle daño a la Llama Eterna y a la Resistencia antes que arriesgar su propia libertad.

Helena no se engañaba a sí misma; la Llama Eterna no era el faro de moralidad que pretendían ser, pero ¿cómo podía alguien pensar que los inmarcesibles eran mejores?

—¿Por qué almacenabais a los prisioneros en esos tanques? —preguntó con voz calmada y firme.

Mandl sonrió y su boca ancha pareció estirarse en su rostro. Movió los dedos, a pesar de las esposas de metal inerte que la sujetaban.

—Venga, atrévete a tocarme. A ver quién se rompe primero.

La rabia de Helena cayó como una losa hasta el fondo del estómago. Se acercó a Mandl.

—Estoy segura de que se te da mucho mejor que a mí hacer daño a los demás. No puedo vencerte en tus términos, pero aquí estamos jugando con los míos.

Mandl miró la puerta y después a Crowther, y, por primera vez, sus ojos delataron cierto nerviosismo. Soltó una carcajada forzada.

—¿Qué me vas a hacer?

Helena se colocó detrás de ella.

—Creo que este truco no te lo sabes.

Mandl quiso doblar el cuello para ver qué estaba haciendo Helena, pero se apartó cuando ella apoyó la mano en la base de su nuca y entrelazó los dedos por su cabello corto. La prisionera retorció las manos, forcejeando para intentar liberarse de los grilletes.

—No pasa nada —dijo Helena con una voz tan fría y profesional como la resonancia que usó para bloquearle los nervios de su columna vertebral, evitando que su corazón sufriera un infarto o que algún órgano vital quedara dañado—. Supongo que haberse educado en la Academia tiene sus ventajas.

Helena reguló el ritmo de su corazón para amortiguar el terror que empezaba a apoderarse de la custodio. Como si hubiera abierto una válvula de gas, manipuló el cóctel hormonal que recorría las venas de Mandl y la forzó a calmarse para que no viera a Helena como una amenaza.

—Quieres responder a todas mis preguntas —dijo Helena con suavidad.

Mandl se rebeló con violencia, trató de resistirse moviendo el cuerpo sin cesar. Intentó extender su resonancia para bloquear la de Helena, pero ya era demasiado tarde.

—Puta... puta traicionera... —farfulló mientras Helena se abría paso entre sus emociones desbocadas.

La mirada de Mandl se nubló. Su mente y su cuerpo entraron en conflicto, y fue incapaz de resistirse cuando Helena se coló en sus recuerdos.

Kaine le había explicado el procedimiento de forma sencilla, pero a Helena le pareció mucho más complicado de lo que esperaba. El ruido de otra mente ocasionaba demasiado estrépito y energía en ella, y, unido al pánico de Mandl y sus intentos de zafarse, lo dificultaba todo aún más. Kaine, en cambio, siempre dejaba que los pensamientos de Helena vagaran a su antojo, y los atrapaba al vuelo. Helena no pudo evitar pensar que debía de existir una forma más fácil de hacerlo.

—¿Cómo te llamas?

«Elsbeth».

El nombre resonó desde todos los ángulos de su mente, hasta converger en un solo punto, al frente.

La cara de Mandl estaba inerte y un hilillo de baba le caía por una de las comisuras de la boca. Sin embargo, sus ojos seguían a Helena con una rabia cada vez más intensa. Su mente trataba de resistirse a la manipulación de Helena, pero sin éxito.

—¿Por qué almacenabais a los prisioneros en esos tanques?

Mandl intentó resistirse, pero un recuerdo emergió en su consciencia: un hombre uniformado estaba hablando: «… mantener los mejores especímenes…». La atención de Mandl se desvió por un instante a una mosca que pasaba por allí y el recuerdo se desvaneció.

Helena insistió de nuevo.

—Si recibieras un nuevo prisionero, ¿qué harías con él?

Los fragmentos de memoria eran como imágenes en movimiento, sonidos y sensaciones que se arrastraban como si se los llevase el viento. Helena oía voces, pero eran tan distantes que no distinguía las palabras.

Vio las paredes de un almacén, una luz verdosa que provenía de unas ventanas tintadas. Un chico, que le resultó vagamente familiar, se retorcía de dolor.

La imagen se desdibujó, pero sintió una punzada de anticipación.

El brillo de una aguja hipodérmica bajo la luz tenue. Un dedo golpeándola para explotar una burbuja de aire. De nuevo, el chico.

Desenfoque.

Hileras de cadáveres tendidos sobre camillas junto a los tanques. Un cuerpo hinchado con los ojos amarillentos y la piel gris descolorida. Alguien presionó el brazo del joven y dijo: «Me llevo a este».

Una solicitud que pedía diez sujetos que fueran mujeres, firmada por Artemon Bennet. Las manos de Mandl empujando una camilla en la que yacía un chico, aún con la mascarilla y los tubos enganchados mientras lo trasladaban a una sala vacía.

Cerró la puerta con cuidado. Sintió otro escalofrío en la columna.

Helena rompió el contacto con su mente y apartó las manos. De repente, deseó frotárselas hasta arrancarse la piel.

—¿Por qué lo hacéis? —preguntó. Tenía el vello erizado como escarpias. No quería volver a adentrarse en la mente de Mandl.

La custodio respiraba con dificultad y tenía las pupilas tan dilatadas que apenas se distinguía el iris azul.

—Te lo sacaré a la fuerza si no me respondes —insistió Helena, y la agarró del cabello—. ¿Prefieres eso?

Mandl torció el gesto en una mueca y escupió.

—Los mantiene frescos.

—¿Para qué?

—Para lo que sea. Cuerpos nuevos para los inmarcesibles. Sujetos de prueba. Necrómatas. Los necrómatas duran más si el cadáver es reciente. —Mandl jadeaba con la boca abierta; los labios cada vez se le agrietaban más.

—¿Cuánto tiempo los mantenéis allí?

Mandl sonrió con crueldad.

—Hay mucha demanda, así que no suelen estar más que unos meses. Las descargas eléctricas mantienen los músculos en forma. Ralentizamos sus constantes vitales.

Pasó lo que a Helena se le antojó una eternidad hasta que Crowther consideró suficiente la cantidad de información obtenida. Para entonces, los ojos de Mandl ya estaban tan perdidos que miraban en direcciones opuestas. La fiebre empezó a subirle y se desplomó hacia delante, temblando.

—Bueno —dijo Crowther, bajando la vista hacia Helena—, parece que vas a ser una buena sustituta de Ivy.

Helena no respondió. No quería volver a hacerlo. Se arrepentía de haber accedido a ello.

Se giró sin decir una palabra.

—Traidora —masculló Mandl a su paso.

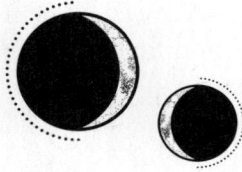

CAPÍTULO 58

Junius 1787

POR MUCHO ÉXITO QUE ESTUVIERAN teniendo los últimos ataques de Luc, el territorio reconquistado estaba dispersando las fuerzas de la Resistencia. A pesar de la admiración que despertaba el liderazgo resuelto y audaz del principado, los altos cargos no compartían ese entusiasmo. Se rumoreaba que Luc había mantenido una acalorada discusión con Althorne y otros miembros del comando militar por actuar sin consultarlos.

Había distritos que estaban rodeados por territorio inmarcesible, por lo que requerían vigilancia y defensa constantes a pesar de que su valor estratégico era escaso. Esos distritos tampoco habían recibido la «liberación» con entusiasmo. Muchos paladinos de la isla Oeste vivían cómodamente bajo la ocupación inmarcesible y temían que los consideraran simpatizantes de la Resistencia si el enemigo recuperaba el control del distrito. Como consecuencia, la Resistencia se vio obligada a defenderse no solo de los ataques del ejército inmarcesible, sino también de las rebeliones civiles.

Se acercaba la latencia de verano, y las tropas se concentraron al sur de la isla para defender los puertos y el paso de los barcos mercantes que pronto arribarían.

El hospital siempre estaba lleno. Ya no se producían avalanchas de pacientes tras una batalla seguidas de un periodo de descanso. Ahora era constante, un goteo incesante que tenía a todo el mundo al límite.

—No sé qué hacer —confesó Helena una noche. Se incorporó porque no podía dormir, ni siquiera en los brazos de Kaine—. No sé cómo vamos a ganar. No veo salida.

—No puedes salvarlos a todos —repuso él con calma.

A Helena empezó a temblarle la mandíbula y apretó los puños.

—Pero es que no estoy intentando salvarlos a todos. No sé cómo salvar a nadie. No consigo entenderlo. Todo lo que se me ocurre es un callejón sin salida. Nos estamos quedando sin tiempo.

Kaine no respondió.

—Es solo que… —Se frotó los ojos—. Estoy muy cansada. Me da la sensación de que todo lo que hago no sirve más que para retrasar lo inevitable, que salvo a alguien hoy para que muera de una forma aún peor al día siguiente. Ojalá no me hubiese hecho sanadora.

Jamás lo había admitido en voz alta. Que lo odiaba.

Entonces se lo contó todo a Kaine. La verdad sobre la gema y su paradero, la historia real sobre los Holdfast, el sello de Wagner y que, por mucho que lo había intentado, no lograba averiguar cómo funcionaba la canalización. También le habló de la obsidiana, que tampoco le había llevado a ninguna parte.

Estaba harta de encontrar posibilidades que no conducían a nada.

—Tráeme un trozo —le pidió Kaine—. Tal vez no la has puesto a prueba como es debido.

Helena negó con la cabeza.

—Tú ya tienes demasiadas cosas encima. No quiero que te preocupes por mis experimentos inútiles. —Se aclaró la garganta—. ¿Te conté que estoy trabajando con mi compañero de laboratorio para revertir la aleación de anulitio y que podamos usar el compuesto en un metal inerte? Se me ocurrió que podríamos transmutarlo para convertirlo en una malla de armadura ligera que fuese resistente y flexible, y que eliminara la resonancia. Los soldados podrían llevarla debajo de la ropa y no interferiría con su propia resonancia, pero el enemigo no podría emplear la suya para atravesarla. —Con un dedo, recorrió la cicatriz plateada del brazo de Kaine—. Creo que ya casi lo tengo. Así no te harían tanto daño.

Kaine le besó la coronilla.

—Yo me curo sin problemas. Tráeme un trozo de la obsidiana. Será más interesante que seguir cumpliendo todas las órdenes absurdas de sabotaje de Crowther. Los inmarcesibles están ya paranoicos, y Morrough está tomando más precauciones que nunca.

HELENA ESTABA REBUSCANDO ENTRE LOS distintos trozos de obsidiana que había ido acumulando cuando estallaron las ventanas. Un rugido atravesó toda la Torre y los instrumentos del laboratorio se hicieron añicos contra el suelo.

Se activaron las alarmas. Todas a la vez.

Otra bomba.

Helena se lanzó escaleras abajo, justo cuando el brazalete comenzó a calentarse, y pisó los cristales rotos que cubrían el suelo.

Los informes de lo que había sucedido comenzaron a llegar, inconexos. Varios edificios se habían derrumbado y los puentes colgantes que unían los rascacielos de la ciudad habían provocado una destrucción sin precedentes en el centro de la isla. El hospital se preparó para la avalancha que sabía que estaba por llegar, pero tras una larga espera solo aparecieron un par de camiones, y todos traían a personas que se encontraban en la zona más alejada del derrumbe.

Helena estaba curando un profundo corte en la frente de una mujer cuando oyó el estrépito de las camillas al moverse por los pasillos. Sin embargo, antes de que entraran al hospital, escuchó los gritos:

—¡Que no entren! Dejadlos fuera. Cerrad las ventanas. Sellad todas las entradas.

Hubo protestas y discusiones ahogadas, y una voz potente se alzó por encima de las demás:

—Hay anulitio en el aire. Están cubiertos de anulitio. ¡Sacadlos de aquí!

Helena se giró, horrorizada, hacia Elain, que parecía desconcertada. El blasón solar temblaba junto a su garganta.

—¿Qué más da que esté en el aire? —preguntó.

—Porque, si lo inhalamos, podríamos perder nuestra resonancia —respondió Helena, y se quedó paralizada cuando empezó a comprender las consecuencias de aquello. La metralla de anulitio había sido devastadora, pero no estaban preparados para una inhalación.

Miró a su alrededor, hacia las altas ventanas del hospital, que permanecían abiertas para que dejaran entrar la brisa de la montaña y aliviar el bochorno del verano. El ambiente estaba neblinoso, cargado de polvo.

Ya lo estaban respirando.

SE PUSIERON MASCARILLAS DE TELA y trasladaron la sala de urgencias a los jardines, donde trataron de mantener apartados a los nuevos pacientes de los que ya estaban ingresados. Sin embargo, era imposible saber a simple vista si el polvo que cubría a una persona contenía anulitio o no.

Los protocolos quedaron relegados en cuanto empezaron a llegar más y más camillas. A medida que rescataban personas de las zonas más afectadas por la explosión, las heridas se volvían cada vez más graves.

Limpiaron todo el polvo que les fue posible para reducir una posible contaminación y separaron a los heridos según la gravedad, identificando a aquellos que ya mostraban signos de haberse expuesto al anulitio.

¿Cuánto tardaría el anulitio suspendido en el aire en penetrar en los pulmones y llegar a la sangre? Una vez que lo hiciera, ¿cuánto tiempo después empezaría a fallarles la resonancia? Nadie lo sabía.

Helena se lanzó a trabajar como nunca lo había hecho antes. Cada segundo importaba. Sanaba sin descanso, con una desesperación inconsciente. Hacía mucho calor, y el polvo en el ambiente se volvió más denso cuando un extraño viento del sur lo arrastró al norte de la isla, donde se encontraba el hospital.

Estaba sudando tanto que la mascarilla se le adhirió a la piel. Las manos se le cubrían de polvo, por lo que tenía que lavárselas después de atender a cada paciente. La mascarilla dejó de funcionar; estaba tan saturada de polvo que apenas podía respirar. La sustituyó con un trapo húmedo, como hacían muchas personas que no tenían mascarilla.

—¡Marino! ¿Dónde está Marino?

Helena levantó la vista del lavabo.

—¿Qué sucede?

Miró al hombre que tenía delante a través de la neblina.

—¿Qué estás haciendo aquí? Deberías estar en el sur de la isla. Te he estado buscando. —Llevaba el uniforme de los conductores de camión y la tomó por el brazo.

Helena lo miró, desconcertada, mientras la empujaba hacia uno de los camiones.

—¿Qué?

—Corremos el riesgo de que la contaminación se extienda si seguimos trasladando a los heridos al norte de la isla. Además, se tarda demasiado. Hay un hospital en el sur, pero están desbordados y no tienen experiencia con el anulitio. Tú estás a cargo del pabellón de anulitio de este hospital, así que gestionarás el del sur. Aquí están las órdenes. —La metió a empujones en el asiento del copiloto del camión y le entregó un documento.

—Yo no estoy a cargo de... —Intentó leer el papel, pero tenía los ojos llenos de polvo—. No me está permitido salir del Cuartel General.

Contempló estupefacta las palabras que afirmaban que Helena Marino estaba al mando del pabellón del anulitio y que debía trasladarse al hospital de campaña para enseñar a los médicos de allí a tratar con los combatientes afectados por el anulitio. El documento estaba firmado por el falcón Matias.

Ni siquiera recordaba la última vez que había recibido órdenes escritas de su parte.

—No puede ser. ¿Ha habido alguna reunión?

El motor rugió bajo sus pies.

—Yo solo cumplo órdenes, Marino. No suelen llevarme a las reuniones del Consejo. Deberías haber llegado hace rato y, como nos cansamos de esperar, vine a buscarte. —El conductor giró la llave, metió una marcha y el camión se abalanzó hacia delante. Sin tiempo para seguir discutiendo, se alejaron a toda velocidad del Cuartel General hacia el sur de la isla.

Helena empezó a ver los edificios que faltaban.

—Tienes que volver y decirle a Crowther adónde me han trasladado. No creo que esto lo haya autorizado el Consejo —le dijo por el camino al conductor.

—Hay un transmisor en el despacho de campaña. Puedes informar tú misma en cuanto llegues.

Se había olvidado de lo rápido que era moverse por las carreteras militares. En cuestión de minutos, el camión se detuvo en un puesto de control improvisado.

A todo el que se dirigía a la zona sur de la isla, ahí donde había estallado la bomba, se le entregaba un mono protector, mascarillas y velos para evitar la exposición. Se detuvieron para cambiarse y luego siguieron avanzando. El polvo flotaba en el aire y el trayecto se volvió más accidentado debido a los escombros que se acumulaban en el asfalto. Era mediodía, pero el cielo estaba tan cubierto de polvo que la luz del sol tenía un sucio color naranja.

A través de la neblina distinguieron dos faroles brillantes que marcaban la entrada del hospital. Dejaron allí el camión. En el interior había médicos, pero ningún sanador, aunque era complicado saber cuál era la función de cada uno.

Todo el personal sanitario llevaba lazos rojos anudados en el brazo. Allí, por fin, Helena vio la devastación que en el Cuartel General habían temido que llegase.

Allí se encontraba lo peor.

Había decenas de cuerpos aplastados. La armadura de los soldados se había astillado con ellos aún dentro. Los médicos que tenían la misma resonancia transmutaban el metal para quitársela, pero, cuando lo lograban, empezaba la hemorragia.

El polvo, el humo, el metal y la sangre se mezclaban en el ambiente. Helena podía saborearlos aunque tuviese la boca cerrada.

No había agua corriente.

Apenas podía ver. Nadie tenía ni idea de dónde estaba el transmisor, o si aún existía. Se estaban ahogando con los heridos.

La mitad de los médicos ya había perdido su resonancia, y no quedaba tiempo para nada que no fuera recurrir a los protocolos tradicionales. Sin agua corriente, era imposible mantener la limpieza básica.

Helena empezaba a notar que le fallaba la resonancia cuando el general Althorne atravesó la puerta empujando una camilla en la que yacían varios cuerpos.

—Creo que siguen con vida —dijo entre jadeos. Estaba cubierto de polvo y no llevaba mascarilla, solo una armadura ligera—. Hay al menos cuarenta más atrapados bajo un muro. Los oímos, pero no sabemos cómo sacarlos de allí sin que todo se les venga encima.

Helena dejó que los demás comprobaran las constantes vitales de los cuerpos y trató de buscarles sitio. El hospital estaba desbordado. Althorne tenía los dedos ensangrentados de excavar entre los escombros. Se dejó caer con pesadez en una silla y empezó a toser con violencia, incapaz de respirar.

—Deberías ponerte una mascarilla —le pidió Helena.

—No puedo respirar con esos trapos —afirmó, y dio un trago de agua—. Qué más da. Ya he perdido mi resonancia. —Entonces parpadeó y la miró de nuevo—. ¿Marino?

—¿Sí? —No sabía que Althorne supiera quién era.

El general se acercó a ella y bajó la voz.

—¿Qué estás haciendo aquí? Vuelve al Cuartel General antes de que Ferron se entere de esto.

Helena se quedó sin palabras. Claro que lo sabía, ¿cómo no iba a saberlo? Lo miró con impotencia.

—Matias ha firmado la orden para enviarme aquí, y no encuentro el transmisor para pedir permiso para volver.

—Vuelve al Cuartel General en el primer camión que salga. Diles que lo he ordenado yo. Lo último que necesitamos es que Ferron se descontrole. —Althorne consiguió ponerse de pie de nuevo.

—Espera. —Helena lo sujetó del brazo y, para su sorpresa, él cayó rendido en la silla. Intentó examinarlo con su resonancia, pero esta era intermitente y solo sintió un borrón—. Althorne, tienes que llevar mascarilla. Si sigues respirando este polvo, sufrirás daños en los pulmones. Eres demasiado valioso para morir —añadió, y siguió buscando la herida que sabía que él le estaba ocultando. Estaba claro que algo no iba bien: estaba tan débil que se quedó ahí sentado, permitiendo que ella lo examinara.

No dijo nada.

—¿Cuándo llegan los refuerzos? —preguntó Helena—. Aquí no hay gente suficiente para gestionar todo esto. Se nos está acabando todo.

—No hay —respondió Althorne en un susurro, como si no quisiera que los demás lo escucharan—. Somos los únicos que quedamos.

A Helena se le paró el corazón.

El general observó cómo unos soldados arrastraban más cuerpos hasta unas literas improvisadas.

—No podemos arriesgarnos a que vengan más combatientes y pierdan también su resonancia. Tenemos que contener este brote —continuó Althorne con voz tensa pero resignada.

Al intentar incorporarse, perdió el equilibrio.

—¿Dónde estás herido? —preguntó Helena interponiéndose en su camino.

Althorne la apartó y se enderezó, pero seguía respirando entrecortadamente.

—Es superficial. Me cayeron encima unos escombros. Todo el mundo está sangrando. Lo superaré.

—Althorne —insistió ella, volviendo a plantarse delante del general—. Estás herido de gravedad. Si tuviera resonancia, te sedaría a la fuerza, porque no estás en condiciones de seguir rescatando soldados. Eres demasiado valioso. Lo sabes. La Resistencia no puede permitirse perderte.

Él le dio una palmadita en el hombro, como si hablara con una niña.

—Mis hombres están bajo los escombros, enterrados, se asfixian. Y fui yo quien los envió ahí.

Un aullido de advertencia se alzó desde la escombrera, al que le siguió otro, más largo y agudo. Eran silbatos. Helena no entendió su significado, pero el semblante de Althorne se endureció. La apartó de un manotazo.

—Cerrad las puertas. Han mandado a los necrómatas; vienen a por los cuerpos.

La dejó atrás y Helena se quedó ahí, inmóvil, sin saber si debía detenerlo o asegurar el hospital. Antes de que pudiera decidirse, Althorne ya había desaparecido entre el polvo. Ella se giró hacia el hospital.

—Hay que mover todos los cuerpos a la parte trasera del edificio —ordenó con voz trémula—. Si no hay espacio suficiente…, apilad a los muertos. Tenemos que cerrar las puertas.

Solo con pensar que iba a encerrarse en un hospital de campaña, se le enturbiaba la vista. Se obligó a mantener la concentración y cerró los dedos hasta que notó las cicatrices en las palmas de las manos.

—¿No podemos avisar al Cuartel General de que nos están atacando? —preguntó un médico. La voz llegó amortiguada a través del traje protector—. Tienen que enviarnos refuerzos.

Helena negó con la cabeza.

—No vendrá nadie. Hay que contener el anulitio.

Todos se quedaron petrificados y la miraron fijamente. Seguramente no debería haberles dicho la verdad.

Helena nunca había sido una líder y no tenía ni idea de cómo convertirse en una de repente. No era la persona más indicada para que la creyeran, y ahí plantada, cubierta de polvo y empapada de sangre y vísceras, no parecía el mejor momento para intentarlo. Se centró en los asuntos prácticos.

—Nuestro trabajo es mantener a salvo a todos. Los trasladaremos al fondo y levantaremos una barricada. Los inmarcesibles no entrarán aquí; a ellos también les afecta el anulitio.

—Pero no hay espacio para mover a nadie, a menos que tiremos abajo los muros, y nadie tiene resonancia para hacerlo. Ya estamos sobrepasados —intervino un médico—. ¿Y cómo vamos a atrancar las puertas?

Helena echó un vistazo a su alrededor. Tenía razón. Si protegían a los supervivientes, tendrían que permitir que se llevaran a los muertos, y eso traería consecuencias aún peores en el futuro.

No había ni espacio ni medios.

Pero ella estaba al mando. Tenía un estúpido trozo de papel que lo decía.

—Hay que evacuar —afirmó. Le importaba un bledo que hubiera que contener el anulitio en la parte sur de la isla. Sería mucho peor si los inmarcesibles se hacían con las víctimas—. No iremos al Cuartel General, pero, si nos acercamos lo suficiente, puede que no nos persigan. Si el Consejo os pone alguna pega, echadme a mí la culpa.

Lo que siguió fue un torbellino de actividad mientras se preparaban para su traslado. Helena se dedicó a coordinar los camiones y utilizó la hoja arrugada de papel que la nombraba jefa del pabellón de anulitio como prueba de legitimidad.

Metieron en los camiones tantos cuerpos como les fue posible: los muertos abajo y los heridos arriba. En cada camión viajaba un miembro del personal sanitario.

La espera hasta que regresaban se le hizo interminable, aunque mientras tanto se dedicaban a preparar un grupo tras otro.

Oían el combate que se estaba produciendo. Veían el fuego brillar a través de la niebla. Los silbatos no dejaban de sonar por todos los rincones, como una señal que indicaba que los lobos se estaban acercando, excepto que no era de noche. El mundo entero se había teñido de rojo.

Helena notó que le ardían los músculos de tanto levantar peso. El número de cuerpos era incesante. Solo quedaban ella y otro médico, aunque todavía faltaban muchos heridos y aún más cadáveres que trasladar.

—Yo me quedo —se ofreció el hombre—. Vete en este camión.

Helena negó con la cabeza.

—Soy la jefa. Me iré la última.

El médico dio un paso atrás y le indicó al camión que avanzara.

—Me quedaré contigo entonces.

Solo le veía los ojos y estaban tan cubiertos de polvo que parecían negros. Le recordó a Luc.

—No —replicó al instante, y apartó la mirada—. Vete, es una orden.

Lo observó subirse a la cabina junto al conductor y el camión se puso en marcha, sorteando los escombros de la carretera. Apenas alcanzaba a distinguir la Torre de Alquimia en la lejanía. La llama de lo alto parecía un sol en miniatura.

El camión se detuvo.

Helena entornó los ojos para ver más allá del polvo y entender qué ocurría. Un camión venía de frente y se movía hacia delante y hacia atrás, bloqueando el paso del vehículo que acababa de salir.

De repente, el camión que avanzaba de frente aceleró. Helena pudo distinguir entre el polvo la cara grisácea e hinchada del conductor.

Las ruedas del camión de la Resistencia chirriaron mientras intentaba dar marcha atrás. Sin embargo, los escombros esparcidos por la carretera no permitieron que se alejara demasiado. El camión del necrómata se estrelló contra el otro.

Hubo un fogonazo de luz.

CAPÍTULO 59

Junius 1787

HELENA YACÍA EN EL SUELO. Entornó los ojos, esforzándose por ver algo más, pero todo era un borrón difuso. Cuando intentó respirar, sintió un dolor tan repentino por todo el cuerpo que recobró la consciencia de golpe. Se llevó una mano al pecho e intentó inhalar, pero apenas lo consiguió.

¿Qué había sucedido? No lo recordaba. Intentó respirar mientras escuchaba un silbido agudo que provenía de alguna parte. Entonces lo vio todo en su mente de nuevo: los camiones, el choque y...

Debía de haber estallado otra bomba.

Trató de ponerse en pie.

Quiso ubicar la explosión, pero el paisaje había cambiado por completo. ¿Dónde estaba la carretera? Solo había fuego y un cráter.

Un dolor agónico la atravesó y su visión se tiñó de rojo.

De alguna parte seguía brotando ese silbido, como si fuera una tetera hirviendo. Cuando intentó localizarlo, se dio cuenta de que provenía de su propia garganta.

Se movió con extremo cuidado. Si se había dañado la columna...

«Cálmate. Concéntrate. Evalúa tu estado y actúa en consecuencia».

Se obligó a mirar hacia abajo y un gemido ahogado se le escapó de sus labios.

Tenía un trozo de metal clavado en medio del pecho, justo en el esternón. No consiguió apartar la mirada; estaba demasiado estupefacta para moverse. Iba a morir. Moriría en un hospital de campaña, igual que su padre. Tanta vivemancia..., para acabar sufriendo el mismo destino.

Cerró los ojos e intentó mantener la calma mientras recuperaba la sensación de su propio cuerpo. Sentía los dedos de las manos. También los de los pies. Al menos, no se había dañado la columna.

Intentó respirar, pero lo único que quería era gritar a todo pulmón. El dolor era peor que una puñalada; irradiaba en todas direcciones, extendiéndose como una fractura por las costillas. Le ocupaba el total de su consciencia.

«Levántate. Tienes que levantarte».

A duras penas logró ponerse en marcha. Volvió a mirar hacia la carretera, aunque ya solo era un agujero. Había desaparecido, pero aún quedaba gente en el hospital.

Consiguió levantar la mano y se arrancó la mascarilla. Pensó que ya daría igual si sufría daños por inhalar el polvo.

El aire era mucho más frío. Inspiró un poco.

No podía morir.

Trató de levantarse y respirar de forma superficial, como si jadeara. Estuvo a punto de desmayarse cuando se incorporó. Cada movimiento era una agonía. La necesidad de respirar peleaba con el dolor insoportable que le causaba mover sus costillas y pulmones. Se mordió el labio y comenzó a andar hacia las puertas, paso a paso.

Notaba en los pulmones las ganas de toser, pero se contuvo. Cada vez que lo intentaba, sentía un dolor tan candente y agudo que se tambaleaba y perdía la visión.

Si tosía, se desmayaría, y estaría muerta antes de que recobrara la consciencia.

No iba a morir. Tenía que esperar. Alguien vendría a buscarla. Maier la operaría. Shiseo trabajaría sin descanso para encontrar el quelante apropiado, y se recuperaría en un abrir y cerrar de ojos.

Le había prometido a Kaine que estaría a salvo, que no le pasaría nada. No podía morir.

Atravesó las puertas y encontró una bandeja con instrumental abandonado y unos cuantos frascos. Rebuscó entre ellos hasta dar con uno de láudano. Nada más descorchar el tapón, dio un trago y el líquido le provocó escozor en la lengua.

No obstante, no tomó demasiado, ya que quería mantenerse lúcida. Buscó entre los demás medicamentos algún estimulante que le permitiera seguir avanzando.

En ese momento hubiera matado por un antitusivo.

Se convenció de volver a mirarse el pecho. Llevaba tantas capas de ropa que no consiguió ver exactamente dónde le penetraba la metralla ni si era anulitio que se disolvería en su sangre o un trozo desperdigado del camión.

Ojalá pudiera arrancárselo, pero sabía que no era buena idea. Si le había perforado el corazón o la aorta, se desangraría y moriría en cuestión de segundos. Tal vez ese trozo de metal la estaba manteniendo con vida.

Alguien vendría. Solo debía esperar a que volviese un camión.

Se obligó a seguir caminando, porque le resultaba más fácil que quedarse sentada sintiendo la herida.

Examinó a los pacientes que quedaban. El más cercano era un chico al que le habían quitado ya la armadura. Le faltaba un brazo. Tenía una vía intravenosa en el otro, pero bajo su cuerpo había un charco con demasiada sangre. Con una mano temblorosa, Helena le comprobó el pulso y, al no encontrarlo, le cerró los ojos y buscó más pacientes.

Había más fallecidos, y otros tantos inconscientes; solo unos pocos seguían despiertos. Los examinó a todos y tomó nota de dónde se encontraban.

El láudano le había calmado el dolor hasta el punto de poder moverse con mayor facilidad.

—¿Mamá…? —gimió uno de los soldados, que cogió la muñeca de Helena cuando esta pasó a su lado.

La sanadora sintió una punzada de dolor en el pecho que se extendió hasta la columna y puso fin al alivio. Estuvieron a punto de flaquearle las piernas y se mordió tan fuerte la lengua que saboreó la sangre en la boca.

El soldado tenía el yelmo aplastado contra el cráneo. En la abertura se asomaba su rostro, con una parte magullada. Una sangre espesa brotaba de su cabeza y empapaba el pallet sobre el que estaba tendido.

—Mamá… —repitió.

—Llegará dentro de poco.

No le soltó la muñeca. Volvió a tirar de ella. La visión de Helena se tornó blanca.

—Mamá… Lo siento. Se me olvidó despedirme. Lo siento.

—No pasa nada, n-no te preocupes —lo tranquilizó Helena.

Sintió que sus dedos se relajaban hasta soltarle la mano. Cuando bajó la vista, comprendió que había muerto.

Dio otro sorbo al láudano. Cada vez le costaba más evitar la tos. No sabía si la sangre que tenía en la boca provenía de sus pulmones o de la lengua.

Aguzó el oído para escuchar si se acercaban más camiones. El sonido de la batalla comenzaba a apagarse. Se acercó con esfuerzo a las puertas.

Conforme pasaban los minutos, estaba más convencida de que su herida era demasiado grave para los medios de los que disponía la Resistencia. Los huesos partidos y la posible perforación en el corazón requeriría una cirugía manual muy precisa que Maier no sería capaz de realizar sin alquimia. Probablemente, también tuviera un pulmón perforado. Necesitaría al menos dos cirujanos, quizá tres.

Si habían activado el protocolo de emergencia que solía aplicarse cuando había heridos en masa, nadie excepto Luc o Sebastian era lo bastante importante como para prescindir de tres cirujanos.

Apoyó la cabeza en la pared.

Incluso si la operaban y todo salía bien, sus probabilidades de vivir eran escasas. Correría un grave riesgo de complicaciones e infección que agotaría los ya limitados suministros. El hospital salvaría a más personas si la dejaban morir. Cualquier análisis médico lo confirmaría.

Independientemente de si llegaban los camiones o no, Helena iba a morir. Miró su mano y deseó tener resonancia para enviar un mensaje pulsado a Kaine, para decirle de algún modo que lo sentía, que lo había intentado.

La visión se le nubló; los bordes comenzaron a difuminarse, como una tela que se encoge lentamente.

Cuando parpadeó, vio a alguien delante de ella. Su mente se tambaleó entre la neblina de dolor hasta que cayó en la cuenta de que se trataba de un necrómata. La miraba con confusión, como si no tuviera claro si estaba viva o muerta.

Notó un espasmo en los pulmones, unas ganas violentas de toser, de expulsar el fluido que inundaba su pecho. Se le escapó un gemido rasgado al intentar contenerlas.

Por el rabillo del ojo percibió movimiento. Había más necrómatas. El sonido de la batalla había cesado. Althorne y sus hombres habían muerto o se habían retirado. Los necrómatas venían al hospital a por los muertos y los supervivientes.

No podía permitir que se llevaran a los supervivientes.

Dio un paso atrás y buscó un bisturí, algo afilado, un instrumento que causara una muerte rápida e indolora. No permitiría que los llevaran al puerto Oeste. Pero solo encontró vendas sucias y frascos vacíos de medicamentos. Necesitaba un bisturí.

Sintió un bulto bajo su ropa. Tardó un instante en recordar qué guardaba en el bolsillo: la obsidiana. La tenía en la mano cuando estalló la bomba y se la habría escondido sin pensar.

Al intentar sacarla, se hizo un corte en el dedo. El fragmento debía de haberse roto en la explosión, pero aún estaba afilado.

Helena iba demasiado lenta. Los necrómatas ya estaban dentro. Había cadáveres junto a la puerta, y algunos necrómatas los apartaban a rastras, pero el resto se adentró en el hospital.

No se movían muy deprisa, pero eran más rápidos que Helena. Alcanzaron a los supervivientes antes que ella.

—¡No! —chilló con una voz rasgada que resonó en su pecho.

Uno de los necrómatas se dirigió hacia Helena, y ella trató de defenderse. Lo único que tenía a mano era la obsidiana. Atacó al necrómata con ella. Su piel suave y en descomposición se rasgó con facilidad y la punta del arma tocó hueso.

Aunque apenas había empleado la fuerza, el movimiento le provocó tanto dolor que le fallaron las piernas. Cuando se le despejó la mente, estaba en el suelo..., al igual que el necrómata.

Sus dedos, cubiertos de sangre, sostenían la obsidiana, cuyos bordes se clavaban en su piel. Aún quedaban muchos otros necrómatas.

Se le echaron encima y sus cuerpos taparon la luz rojiza que se colaba por la puerta. Helena sintió el viento en la cara.

Cerró los ojos.

———

Cuando quiso abrir los ojos de nuevo, los párpados le pesaban, como si las pestañas se le hubieran enredado. Intentó moverse, pero su cuerpo no respondió.

Abrió los ojos de par en par. Había una luz tan deslumbrante que la cegaba y todo lo demás se veía borroso y distorsionado a su alrededor. Se removió en el sitio y entrecerró los ojos.

Kaine estaba a su lado, pálido y con los ojos desencajados; su rostro parecía más demacrado que nunca.

—Tú...

La palabra sonó como un crujido extraño. Notaba la lengua seca y pastosa, como si no hubiese bebido agua en días. No sentía nada del cuello para abajo. Intentó bajar la vista, pero no podía moverse.

Estaba paralizada.

Intentó ver su propio cuerpo, pero lo único que distinguió fue una vía intravenosa en su brazo. Al forzar la vista, vio los frascos suspendidos de suero y otros medicamentos, que volcaban su contenido en la sonda.

—¿Cómo? —preguntó, con la voz quebrada y atascada en su garganta—. ¿Qué has hecho…?

—¿Qué he hecho? —repitió Kaine con calma—. Te he salvado la vida. —Estaba respirando entrecortadamente—. Gracias a las innumerables exigencias de Crowther, el Sumo Nigromante ha tomado una miríada de medidas de precaución. Solo tres personas sabían lo de la bomba antes de que estallara. Y yo no era una de ellas. Cuando me enteré y envié a mis necrómatas, pensé que estaba comportándome como un paranoico. Seguro que entienden que no puedo frenar todas las putas estrategias. Lo hacía por mi bienestar mental, me dije a mí mismo. Para ver lo que había sucedido y saber lo mal que estaban las cosas. Tú no estarías allí, por supuesto. Me dije a mí mismo que no estarías allí, que estarías a salvo en el Cuartel General, porque ese era el trato que habíamos hecho, joder. ¿No fue eso lo que prometiste? ¿Que no te castigarían? Lo sabía… Te dije que esto pasaría…

Se le rompió la voz.

—No fue… Crowther… —Al menos, hablar le humedecía la lengua, pero se moría por un trago de agua. Aún notaba la mente torpe. No entendía cómo había llegado allí.

—¡No los defiendas! —Kaine estaba lívido de rabia—. ¿Te haces una idea de lo cerca que has estado de morir? He tenido que contratar a todo un equipo médico para mantenerte con vida. Si no pretendían matarte, ¿por qué te dejaron sola en ese puto hospital?

—Estábamos… evacuando —respondió Helena poco a poco; su lengua empezaba a obedecer.

—¿Tú sola?

—Yo estaba… al mando. —Sorprendentemente, sintió que recobraba la lucidez—. Los soldados… no se merecían morir solos.

Intentó incorporarse. Creía que sería capaz de pensar con más claridad si podía sentarse un momento para procesar lo que le había sucedido.

—Pues yo no vi a nadie allí mientras tú morías.

No sabía por qué trataba de razonar con él, pero quería tranquilizarlo para poder reorientarse ella misma.

—Estamos en guerra, Kaine. La gente muere. Teniendo en cuenta las muertes que tú has provocado, deberías saberlo mejor que nadie. Sabes que no voy a priorizar mi vida por encima de la de los demás.

La miró fijamente durante unos interminables segundos; su rostro delataba la furia que sentía.

—Pues deberías. —De repente, su voz adquirió un tono gélido y sus ojos brillaron con un plateado que era casi blanco—. Te lo he advertido. Si te pasa algo malo, me encargaré personalmente de reducir la Llama Eterna a cenizas. Y es una promesa, no una amenaza. Ten en cuenta que tu supervivencia es tan indispensable como la de Holdfast. Si tú mueres, mataré a todos los miembros de la Resistencia. Es evidente que ver peligrar sus vidas es lo único que hace que valores la tuya propia.

Helena lo contempló completamente anonadada, aunque ese sentimiento no tardó en convertirse en pura rabia.

—¿Cómo te atreves? ¡Cómo te... atreves! —Había subido tanto el tono que la voz se le quebró.

Si hubiera podido moverse, se habría abalanzado sobre él para darle una paliza con sus propias manos. Quería gritarle.

Sin embargo, más allá de esa rabia, un horror profundo se instaló en ella por todo lo que aquello implicaba. Kaine se había convertido en la amenaza que Crowther siempre temió. En el pasado se había mostrado leal para vengar a su madre, pero Helena ocupaba ahora su lugar, y eso había desatado en él una obsesión y una rabia incontrolables.

Helena cerró los ojos, incapaz de mirarlo a la cara, y en su mente apareció el uróboro como una imagen de autodestrucción infinita: un dragón que se devoraba a sí mismo eternamente.

Se le escapó un sollozo casi roto que le sacudió los pulmones violentamente. Intentó respirar para calmarse y que la habitación dejara de darle vueltas.

La superficie bajo su cuerpo se hundió. Unos dedos metieron un mechón de pelo suelto por detrás de su oreja y le acariciaron la mejilla.

—Conozco tu expresión como la palma de mi mano —suspiró—. Estás pensando que ahora tendrás que matarme, ¿verdad? Que soy una carga demasiado pesada.

Helena no dijo nada y se negó a abrir los ojos.

—¿De verdad lo harías? —Lo miró fijamente—. Ya sabes que... sabes que yo no te elegiría por encima de todos los demás. Sabes lo que pasará si la Resistencia pierde. No puedo elegirte. Ni tampoco te salvaría si lo hiciera.

Entonces Kaine apartó la mirada.

—Y jamás te lo perdonarías.

A ella le tembló la barbilla.

—No, lo cierto es que no… —Se le formó un nudo en la garganta. Le costaba tragar y no podía levantar la cabeza—. Pero no sería lo primero que soy incapaz de perdonarme. ¿Qué más da otra línea en los libros de historia?

Kaine guardó silencio durante un buen rato.

—¿Qué harás cuando yo ya no esté? —le preguntó, como si eso fuera lo único que importase.

—Seguro que te haces una idea.

El techo se distorsionó al imaginar un mundo en el que Kaine ya no estuviera y ella estuviera sola, sin nadie más que ella misma a quien culpar.

Detestaba la guerra. Al principio, pensaba que podría con todo, que era lo suficientemente fuerte, que no habría límite que no estuviera dispuesta a cruzar o soportar. Por lo visto, Kaine se había convertido en ese límite.

No podía imaginar su vida sin él. No creía que pudiese seguir existiendo.

Se le escapó un sollozo estrangulado y sus pulmones se encogieron en busca de oxígeno.

De repente, Kaine estaba sobre ella, sujetándole la cara entre las manos, ladeando su cabeza para que pudiera respirar mejor. Ese era el único abrazo que podía ofrecerle.

—Solo quiero que vivas, Helena. —Le temblaba la voz—. Es lo único que te pido.

Helena soltó un sollozo más grave y oyó cómo le silbaban los pulmones al intentar tomar aire.

—No puedo prometerte eso. Sabes que no puedo. Pero tampoco puedo arriesgarme a que cumplas lo que quieres hacer si muero.

Kaine la besó y ella sintió la súplica en sus labios.

—Lo siento —repitió Helena una, y otra, y otra vez—. Siento haberte hecho esto.

Sonó una fuerte vibración. Kaine se puso en tensión y se alejó mascullando una maldición. Se produjo otra vibración. Dos largas y dos cortas. Cada vez que se oía, la iluminación parpadeaba como un mal presagio.

Kaine miró a su alrededor con los dientes apretados.

—Mierda. Quieren que vuelva a la ciudad. —Dio un paso hacia atrás sin apartar la vista de Helena. Había cálculo en sus ojos, como si estuviera sopesando distintas opciones, aunque finalmente lo que se abrió paso por su rostro fue una expresión desesperada—. Davies, ven aquí —ordenó en voz baja, y sus ojos se desenfocaron durante un instante.

Se abrió la puerta que había detrás de él y entró una mujer. Helena no sabía lo suficiente sobre uniformes del servicio para saber su rango, pero sí reconoció su nombre.

La doncella de Enid Ferron se colocó junto a Kaine y observó a Helena con unos ojos azules y vidriosos. La habitación se inundó de un olor leve, seco pero orgánico. Estaba muerta, pero la habían reanimado con tanta destreza que parecía viva.

Helena miró a su alrededor y luego hacia la ventana. Entonces reparó en que no veía ningún edificio, solo cielo y árboles.

—¿Dónde estamos? —preguntó de repente. Ni siquiera sabía cuánto tiempo llevaba inconsciente.

—En Puntaférreo. La finca familiar de los Ferron —contestó Kaine mientras se ponía el uniforme de abrigo y la capa negra—. Ya te lo explicaré más tarde. Tengo que irme. No temas a Davies. No te hará daño.

Helena observó a la necrómata. Era una de las criadas que habían muerto para que Kaine se convirtiera en inmarcesible, por lo que había dado su vida para que él alcanzara la inmortalidad. ¿La habría reanimado él?

—Lo siento —siguió diciendo—. Pensé que tendría más tiempo para explicaciones. Aquí estarás a salvo. Nadie podrá encontrarte. Volveré tan pronto como me sea posible. Davies, cuídala. —Se inclinó sobre Helena una última vez y le acarició el cabello—. Estás a salvo. Te lo prometo.

Y, sin más, se marchó. Helena oyó un chasquido en las paredes y el suelo, como si algo se moviera, aunque no pudo ver nada. Estaba inmovilizada en manos de una necrómata.

La volvió a mirar. Davies estaba ahí de pie, observándola con una mirada perdida pero imperturbable.

—¿Me das un poco de agua? —preguntó Helena al cabo de un rato.

Davies sirvió un vaso de agua de una jarra que había sobre la mesa y se lo acercó a Helena. Luego la ayudó a beber, aunque solo fuera para mojarse los labios. Estaba amarga, y ella reconoció al instante el sabor del láudano.

No tenía ni idea de que se podía reanimar a necrómatas hasta este punto. Esa mujer parecía viva de verdad.

—Eras la doncella de Enid Ferron, ¿verdad? —preguntó Helena, que luchaba contra el cansancio que el medicamento le estaba provocando.

Davies asintió lentamente, como si comprendiera la pregunta. Helena notó que le costaba enfocar la vista.

—¿Has estado aquí todo este tiempo?

Otro asentimiento. Davies vocalizó una palabra en silencio. «Kaine».

Si era cierto, significaba que la había reanimado hacía casi siete años, pero no mostraba ningún signo de putrefacción. Helena no comprendía cómo podía ser aquello posible.

—¿Por qué? ¿Por qué te haría algo así?

Si la necrómata respondió, Helena ya no estaba consciente para escucharlo.

Perdía y recuperaba la lucidez de forma intermitente y, cada vez que despertaba, el dolor era más profundo. Davies estaba sentada en una silla a su lado, tejiendo lo que parecían unos calcetines. El entumecimiento empezó a desvanecerse. El dolor pasó de ser una impresión distante a una carga que le pesaba cada vez más.

Sentía la garganta hinchada y en carne viva por dentro, como si hubiera tenido un tubo respiratorio en algún momento.

Cuando el dolor se convirtió en tan insoportable que la despertó por completo, descubrió que Kaine había regresado. Estaba de pie a su lado y cambiaba algunos de los frascos que se vertían en la vía intravenosa.

—¿Qué le ha pasado al equipo médico? —preguntó Helena, que volvía a tener la lengua pastosa y seca—. Las personas que me salvaron la vida. ¿Qué les has hecho?

Kaine la miró. La habitación estaba a oscuras y el uniforme negro hacía que se camuflara entre las sombras. Aun así, su cabello rubio y sus ojos brillaban en la oscuridad.

—No hagas preguntas para las que no quieres respuesta.

—¿Los has matado? —Se le agudizó la voz.

El chico encendió un interruptor y toda la habitación se iluminó con un naranja tenue.

—No, no los he matado. Que todo un equipo médico aparezca muerto habría despertado sospechas. Creen que salvaron a una mujer que murió ayer en un interrogatorio. Y les da igual haberse pasado horas salvándote para que al final alguien acabara torturándote hasta la muerte. Están orgullosos de haber servido a la causa. Después de todo, eres una terrorista. Ellos mismos me lo dijeron.

Helena sabía que estaba intentando distraerla.

—Entonces quieres decir que los habrías matado pero no lo hiciste porque sus muertes hubieran despertado preguntas incómodas.

La rabia iluminó los ojos de Kaine.

—Sí, todo esto lo hago por comodidad. Ya sabes que tengo dos amos que me exigen exclusividad.

La culpa hizo que a Helena se le formara un nudo en la garganta.

—No quiero que mates a nadie por mí.

A Kaine se le escapó una carcajada.

—¿Qué es lo que crees que hago todos los días? Mato a gente. Ordeno a otros que maten a gente. Entreno a personas para que maten a gente. Saboteo y socavo a personas que acaban muertas, y todo lo hago por ti. Cada palabra, cada vida. Todo ha sido por ti.

La habitación empezó a darle vueltas, y se le escapó un grito ahogado. Sintió que flotaba, como si la sangre abandonara su cabeza.

La crueldad del semblante de Kaine se desvaneció de golpe.

—Espera, Helena, no pretendía…

—No —lo interrumpió con dureza—. No te atrevas a retirarlo.

—Yo… —Su voz se tornó suave, suplicante.

—No —repitió la chica—. Es cierto. Lo que dices es la pura verdad. Todo lo que haces también es culpa mía. Cada vida…

—Para. —Se sentó al borde de la cama y le sostuvo la mano derecha—. No sigas por ahí. No es culpa tuya. Deja de llevar sobre tus hombros la carga de toda esta condenada guerra.

—Pero esto sí que es culpa mía —repuso—. Yo te hice esto. Yo te convertí en lo que eres. Alguien debería arrepentirse de ello, y tú no puedes. Pero, si lo hago yo…, tal vez eso baste para que algún día dejes de hacerlo.

Kaine apartó la mirada y no respondió. Helena observó cómo le acariciaba los dedos y deseó poder sentirlo.

—¿Qué está pasando en la ciudad? —preguntó.

El chico estuvo callado durante unos segundos.

—Althorne ha muerto. Había varias unidades atrapadas bajo uno de los edificios; consiguieron sacarlos a todos, pero el general murió en la retirada. Según nuestras estimaciones, la Resistencia ha perdido al menos a la mitad de su ejército activo. Retomamos los puertos hace dos días.

No había lugar en su cuerpo que pudiera ya soportar la desesperación que le causó esa información, excepto sentirla como una lanza en la cabeza. No notó un horror que le retorciera las entrañas, no hubo sensación de vacío. No sentía su propio cuerpo, así que solo le quedaba pensar.

—Aun así, ha habido muchas consecuencias después del bombardeo. No imaginaron que el polvo acabaría contaminando las dos islas. La gente ha sucumbido al pánico y a la rabia por haber perdido la resonancia, y los hospitales están llenos de pacientes que necesitan agentes quelantes. Aunque la Resistencia ha sufrido unas bajas considerables, apenas hemos recuperado cuerpos para convertirlos en necrómatas, porque Durant olvidó mencionar que el compuesto anulador interferiría con la reanimación. Tienen que bombear sangre fresca en los cadáveres para poder reanimarlos, así que dudo que vuelva a pasar. Al menos, no a esa escala.

Un consuelo nimio, pero era algo al fin y al cabo.

—No sé qué hacer —expresó Helena al cabo de un rato—. No puedo ignorar una amenaza a la Llama Eterna.

Kaine suspiró y bajó la cabeza.

—Solo estaba enfadado.

—Siempre estás enfadado, pero no puedes soltar ese tipo de amenazas o reducir una guerra a un simple juego de reparto de culpas. Y no puedes tener a la Resistencia de rehén para controlarme.

Kaine bajó los hombros.

—Helena, si mueres, se acabó. No seguiré con esto. Estoy cansado.

Cuando la miró, vio todo el peso de la guerra en sus ojos, la carga que suponía luchar sin ver el final, impulsado únicamente por el miedo de lo que podría pasar si dejaba de cumplir órdenes.

—Lo digo en serio. No los mataré…, pero no volveré a trabajar para ellos. Tú eres mi única condición. Si mueres, el contrato será papel mojado.

Helena consiguió ladear un poco la cabeza.

—Hay vida para ti más allá de esta guerra. Tienes la gema. Si Morrough muere, tal vez sigas con vida y serás libre. Podrías hacer… cualquier cosa. No reduzcas tu mundo a mí.

Kaine hizo un gesto que dejó los dientes a la vista.

—Ah, ¿tú tienes una lista de cosas que hacer después de la guerra y no la has mencionado?

La chica esquivó su mirada.

—Haz lo que te digo, no lo que hago.

Kaine entrelazó los dedos con los suyos y se sumieron en un silencio tan vacío como su futuro.

—Podrías… ser sanador —dijo Helena al cabo de unos instantes. Se estiró para sentir el tacto de su mano contra la suya. El atisbo de una sonrisa asomó a las comisuras de la boca de Kaine.

—No me lo había planteado.

—Pues tienes… Tienes un talento natural… Aunque el trato con el paciente deja mucho que desear.

—Así podría compensar las muertes que llevo a cuestas —replicó sin mirarla a los ojos.

—No debería haber dicho nada. No es culpa tuya.

Kaine sacudió la cabeza y se quedó mirando la pared.

—Puede que eso fuera cierto en el pasado, pero creo que ahora debo asumir la responsabilidad.

Helena tragó saliva. Deseó poder mover los dedos para apretarle la mano.

—Eres mucho más de lo que esta guerra ha hecho contigo. —Lo dijo tan convencida que le tembló la voz, pero Kaine siguió sin mirarla—. Lo digo en serio —repitió con desesperación—. Igual… igual que yo. Somos mucho más… y esa parte aún está ahí, deseando salir. Algún día, dejaremos todo esto atrás. Nos iremos lejos, ya lo verás. Los dos solos… Creo que podremos hacerlo.

Kaine no respondió, pero Helena sintió que le apretaba levemente los dedos.

—Te lo prometo… Ya lo verás… —Empezaron a cerrársele los ojos.

—Duerme. Te queda una larga recuperación por delante.

Helena se resistió y trató de permanecer despierta.

—¿Cuánto tiempo llevo aquí?

—No te preocupes por eso.

—¿Cuánto?

—Han pasado cuatro días desde el bombardeo.

¿Cuatro días? De repente, sintió que el corazón le retumbaba en los oídos y que le dolían los pulmones al intentar respirar.

—Kaine… Tienes que avisar a Crowther de que sigo viva.

—No te preocupes por ellos —dijo con voz grave.

—No, escúchame. Debes decírselo.

Kaine le acarició la mejilla.

—Descansa.

Helena intentó moverse; tenía que hacerle entrar en razón.

—No, prométemelo. Prométeme que lo avisarás. Que te asegurarás de que sepa que voy a volver.

Si Crowther pensaba que estaba muerta, tal vez decidiera que Kaine era un riesgo demasiado alto como para mantenerlo con vida.

—Prométemelo... Prométeme que lo avisarás...

—Está bien. Lo avisaré, lo prometo. Ahora descansa.

Notó cómo se calmaba el bombeo de sangre en su cabeza y se relajó. Kaine le colocó un mechón de pelo detrás de la oreja.

—Vas a estar aquí al menos tres semanas, hasta que no haya restos de anulitio en tu sangre.

—La Llama Eterna ha desarrollado un quelante...

Le dio un toquecito en la nariz.

—Los inmarcesibles tienen quimiatras y conocen perfectamente los agentes quelantes del metal.

Helena puso los ojos en blanco.

—Recuperarás tu resonancia, pero tardarás bastante en recuperarte. Has sufrido varias heridas de metralla y has inhalado una cantidad importante de anulitio. No sé decirte cuánto tardarás en recomponerte. Tendrás que recuperarte con calma, mediante el descanso. Duerme. Por mucho que deteste admitirlo, la guerra seguirá aquí cuando despiertes.

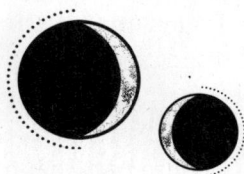

CAPÍTULO 60

Junius 1787

Estar convaleciente era horrible. Helena estaba acostumbrada a que la eficiencia de la sanación resolviera los aspectos más lentos e insoportables de la recuperación, así que verse obligada a aguantar el ritmo natural de su cuerpo le resultó muy molesto.

La mayor parte de la primera semana la pasó aturdida por la medicación, con fiebre por la infección. Cuando recobró la lucidez, encontró a Kaine a su lado. Tenía encima una pila de libros y documentos y los estaba hojeando.

—¿Qué estás haciendo? —le preguntó tras observarlo un rato.

Él levantó la mirada.

—Estudiar anatomía humana para mi futura carrera como sanador —respondió con sequedad.

Helena sabía que la respuesta sincera era que él tendría que convertirse en su sanador cuando el anulitio desapareciese de su sistema. Aun así, le siguió el juego.

—Podemos abrir una consulta los dos juntos, como hicieron mis padres. En lo alto de un acantilado. Así podremos disfrutar de las vistas y ver la marea.

Kaine arqueó una ceja.

—¿Yo tengo algo que decir sobre esa futura vida que tendremos o vas a tomar tú todas las decisiones?

—¿Tienes alguna idea que aportar?

Se hizo el silencio.

—La verdad es que no.

Helena dejó escapar el aire poco a poco. Ya podía mover los dedos. Al flexionarlos, se dio cuenta de que tenía la mano derecha vendada y los dedos escayolados, y recordó los últimos momentos en el hospital de campaña.

—Casi se me olvida —dijo—. Creo que descubrí algo en el hospital.

Kaine levantó la mirada.

—¿Te acuerdas de la obsidiana de la que te hablé? Tenía un trozo en el bolsillo cuando llegaron los necrómatas. Creo que… creo que corté una reanimación con ella.

—¿Estás segura?

Entrecerró los ojos mientras trataba de recordar algo más, pero lo único que se le vino a la cabeza fue la luz roja anaranjada y el dolor.

—No del todo, pero pienso que deberíamos probarla otra vez.

—Bueno, tú no te preocupes por eso ahora. —Cerró el libro de golpe y se acercó a cambiar las vendas.

Cuando retiró la tela, Helena notó que recuperaba un poco de movilidad. Levantó la cabeza con ganas de ver algo más. En el centro del pecho, como una costura serrada, se extendía una profunda incisión cosida con hilo negro y alambre de cerclaje. La piel estaba hinchada, teñida en tonos amarillentos, blancos y rosados.

Helena había visto más heridas de las que podía recordar, había sido testigo de cómo los pacientes lloraban por lo que habían sido y en lo que se habían convertido sus cuerpos. Sabía lo que debía decir, las frases de aliento y confianza, que todo se arreglaría, que todo mejoraría con el tiempo.

Pero, al mirar su propia herida, todo eso se le olvidó.

—Por Dios… —exclamó. Dejó caer la cabeza, sintiendo un nudo en la garganta; le había dado tanto miedo que no quería seguir mirándola.

—Se curará. Dale tiempo —dijo Kaine en voz baja mientras buscaba señales de infección.

Después de haber tratado a Lila, sabía que le quedaría cicatriz. Aunque intentara sanarse a sí misma cuando recuperara la resonancia y reorganizara las matrices, el tiempo para evitar marcas era limitado, y el anulitio parecía tener un efecto queloide sobre los tejidos.

Respiró hondo un par de veces.

Tenía suerte de seguir con vida. Unas cuantas cicatrices no eran nada comparadas con las heridas que algunos miembros de la Resistencia tendrían que soportar de por vida. Aunque conservaba todas las extremidades, los dos ojos, las orejas e incluso todos los dientes.

Lo mirase por donde lo mirase, había tenido suerte. ¿Qué importaba una cicatriz? Todo se arreglaría.

Se dio cuenta de que Kaine la estaba observando y se obligó a decir:

—Creo que tus cicatrices son más bonitas que las mías.

—Yo tuve una sanadora mejor.

———————

EL ANULITIO EN LA SANGRE de Helena tardó tres semanas en reducirse lo suficiente para que Kaine pudiera usar la resonancia y evaluar su recuperación, aunque aún no estaba preparada para sanar de esa manera.

La resonancia de Helena apenas era un murmullo en sus venas.

Cuando Kaine no estaba, era Davies quien le hacía compañía. Helena notó que tenía la mente cada vez más despejada y que ya podía hacer inventario de lo que la rodeaba.

La decoración de la habitación era mínima, casi inexistente. Había una cama, un armario hasta el techo, un escritorio y una silla. El falcón Matias había tenido unos aposentos más confortables, y eso que era un monje asceta.

Cuando se lo comentó en tono de broma a Kaine, este torció el gesto.

—Es mi habitación.

Helena se quedó callada y miró a su alrededor con cierta vergüenza.

—Vaya. Pensaba que en una casa de campo habría habitaciones más grandes.

El chico asintió.

—Las hay más grandes. Me mudé aquí porque estaba más cerca de la habitación de mi madre, y después nunca me fui.

—Siento haberte traído de vuelta —dijo Helena.

Kaine negó con la cabeza.

—No ha sido por ti. Volví para echarles un ojo a los criados.

Helena dudó, pero tenía que saberlo.

—¿Están todos muertos? —Kaine asintió—. ¿Por qué los…?

El chico apartó la vista y tragó saliva mientras se frotaba las manos.

—Fue justo después. No recuerdo nada. Los oía gritar en mi interior. Encontré sus cuerpos amontonados en un rincón, como si fueran alfombras viejas. Todavía estaban calientes. No pretendía… No me di cuenta de lo que estaba haciendo. Solo quería devolverles la vida.

—Entonces son… ¿ellos?

Kaine sacudió la cabeza.

—No sé qué son. Me gusta pensar que fui capaz de devolverles una parte de su esencia, que por eso me resultó más fácil seguir haciéndolo después, pero lo más probable es que se muestren tal como eran porque yo quiero que lo hagan. Simplemente... no soy capaz de dejarlos marchar.

Cuando por fin Helena pudo usar una almohada, Davies le empezó a traer libros para leer durante las horas en que Kaine no estaba presente. Sentía curiosidad por saber qué tipo de biblioteca había en Puntaférreo, pero, por desgracia, Davies resultó ser analfabeta, o al menos lo era como necrómata. Helena recibía libros de temas muy diversos. Un día, le entregó una enciclopedia de especies de mariposas, seguido de una antología de los primeros escritos de Cetus.

Como «Cetus» había escrito miles de textos y cartas alquímicas a lo largo de varios siglos, los académicos solían agrupar sus obras en distintas colecciones según la temática o la historia que consideraran legítima. Según la edición de la antología, Cetus había nacido en diez países distintos. A veces era rey; en ocasiones, sacerdote; y en algunas cartas se afirmaba que había trabajado con el mismísimo Orion.

En la antología que recibió Helena, Cetus se interesaba por una antigua secta khemiata que sostenía que la resonancia humana era la alquimización de la humanidad y que los alquimistas eran seres ascendentes.

—Parece algo que les gustaría creer a los alquimistas —comentó Kaine por la noche, cuando ella le habló del tema. A él le interesaba más el estado de los pulmones de Helena que las antiguas sectas.

Ella se esforzó por no torcer el gesto cuando le retiró las vendas.

—¿Los inmarcesibles tienen religión?

—El Sumo Nigromante es nuestro dios —repuso Kaine, que extendió su resonancia por las costillas de Helena, hasta el punto donde algunas de ellas se habían fracturado—. Nuestras vidas están dedicadas al servicio de su poder infinito.

—Si tan poderoso es, ¿por qué no da la cara y gana la guerra?

Kaine levantó la vista un instante.

—Es un dios. Y, como habrás notado, el *modus operandi* de los dioses suele ser que los humanos mueran en su nombre. Aunque Sol podría destruir a los nigromantes si tanto los odia, por algún motivo, siempre son los Holdfast los que se encargan de ello. Al final, uno se pregunta si le importa de verdad.

Desde que le contó la verdad sobre Orion y por qué los Holdfast se habían convertido en principados, Kaine parecía pensar que, si criticaba lo suficiente a la Llama Eterna, Helena acabaría rindiéndose con la Resistencia.

Ella soltó un suspiro que le provocó dolor en los pulmones, y Kaine pareció olvidarse de la conversación durante unos minutos.

—Desde que Holdfast ha vuelto a la batalla, Morrough se ha mantenido alejado del frente —dijo entonces.

—Pero, si le tiene tanto miedo a Luc, ¿por qué no lo mató cuando lo capturó?

Kaine negó con la cabeza.

—Creo que no quiere matarlo. Las órdenes siempre han sido capturarlo con vida. Antes creía que era porque Morrough temía que alguien más le arrebatara el mérito del golpe final, pero, después de aquella captura, creo que la razón es otra. Holdfast ha combatido en el frente durante los últimos seis años. ¿De verdad crees que, si Morrough lo quisiera muerto, no habría encontrado ya alguna manera de matarlo?

———

Cuatro semanas después del bombardeo, Helena logró levantarse sin sentir que se desmoronaba. Había recuperado apenas un ápice de su resonancia y ya no iba vendada, pero todavía le quedaba el alambre, ya que su esternón seguía muy delicado. Antes de colocarse el corsé en el pecho, se sentó frente al espejo para ver la cicatriz que se extendía entre sus pechos.

No había belleza alguna en esa marca.

Siempre había admirado cómo Lila lucía sus cicatrices con orgullo, cómo bromeaba y les ponía nombre. Ahora comprendía lo difícil que era estar orgullosa de ellas.

Esa herida jamás desaparecería. En un momento íntimo, sería lo único que estuviera a la vista. Tras contemplarla bajo la fría luz del día, Helena no pudo evitar pensar que tal vez llegara el día en que Kaine no querría a alguien con una marca tan pronunciada. Hasta él querría olvidarse de todo en algún momento.

Sin embargo, le resultaría imposible si esa cicatriz permanecía con ella.

Él se encontraba ordenando los frascos de medicina en la mesa, pero Helena sabía que la estaba mirando por el rabillo del ojo.

—Se atenuará —comentó Helena rápidamente.

Le ardía el rostro. Soltó el espejo y se llevó la mano a la cicatriz para taparla. Le ocupaba toda la mano.

—Cuando me ponga mejor, la trataré todos los días para que… se difumine un poco más —añadió.

Tocó con la mano una melladura en el hueso, justo donde se había negado a regenerarse. Podría introducir una placa de titanio para reforzar el hueso, pero, con su repertorio, tal vez aquello interfiriera en su trabajo. Uno de los motivos por los que los alquimistas empleaban el titanio en la medicina era porque había pocos que tuvieran resonancia titánica.

Le tembló la barbilla.

—No será siempre así.

Kaine dejó un frasco sobre la mesa. Sus ojos plateados la miraron con determinación, como si fuera un rayo de luz atravesando una lupa. De repente, solo tenía ojos para ella. Dio un paso al frente y, con suavidad, pero también firmeza, le apartó la mano del pecho.

Helena sabía que él había visto esa cicatriz más veces que ella misma, y en un estado mucho peor que el actual, pero detestaba que la mirase.

—¿Así es como ves tú mis cicatrices? —preguntó al cabo de unos segundos—. Cuando me miras, ¿es lo único en lo que te fijas?

Ella torció el gesto.

—No.

—Bien. —La miró a los ojos—. Porque yo tampoco te veo así. Eres mía. —Le soltó la muñeca y levantó la mano hasta que las yemas de sus dedos dibujaron toda la cicatriz, que quedó oculta bajo la palma de su mano. Helena sintió el calor de su piel, que subió hasta la curva de su cuello—. Lo eres. Da igual lo que te pase, seguirás siendo mía.

HELENA APENAS HABÍA VISTO ALGUNAS partes de la casa, en Puntaférreo. Dieron paseos por los pasillos tenuemente iluminados mientras se acostumbraba al dolor que sentía en el pecho cada vez que se movía. Cuando respiraba hondo, tenía la sensación de que su esternón iba a romperse. La casa estaba decorada en un estilo anticuado y recargado que hacía mucho que ya no se usaba en la ciudad. Había detalles de hierro forjado en todos los rincones, hasta los suelos eran un entramado metálico. Tenía una belleza melancólica.

En el suelo de mármol del vestíbulo había un mosaico de un dragón uróboro, dispuesto de forma meticulosa para mostrar su grandeza y su violencia a partes iguales. Helena lo analizó desde el rellano del piso superior.

Los Ferron debieron de sentirse muy orgullosos al construir esa casa. Debieron de pensar que, de algún modo, habían derrotado a los dioses.

Aquella noche, Kaine durmió con ella en su cama. Él había pasado las noches sentado en una silla a su lado, sosteniéndole la mano y haciendo caso omiso a las veces que le sugirió que habría otras camas en la casa.

Esta vez, él cedió.

Helena se acurrucó en sus brazos; había echado de menos el calor y el consuelo que le brindaba su cuerpo.

En unos días, volvería a la rutina. Ya había reposado más tiempo del que hubiera querido, pero sabía que el viaje de regreso sería duro y que no serviría de nada presentarse en el Cuartel General si no se recuperaba completamente.

Todo sería distinto. El bombardeo había diezmado la Resistencia y había agotado sus suministros. Todo lo que habían ganado en el último año se había perdido, y Morrough sabía que había un espía entre sus filas. Los inmarcesibles estaban buscando a Kaine, querían sacarlo de su escondite, pero eso no frenaría a Ilva o a Crowther cuando decidieran obligarlo a hacer lo que ellos quisieran.

Tenía que volver.

Sostuvo a Kaine contra su pecho y sintió cómo el latido de su corazón vibraba en todo su torso.

Lo atrajo hacia sí, ladeó la cabeza y le dio un beso. Kaine levantó la mano para acariciarle la mejilla, pero se detuvo. Helena sabía lo que iba a decirle: que todavía se estaba recuperando. Sin embargo, estaba harta de estar convaleciente, de tener tan poco tiempo y no dedicarlo a lo que realmente deseaba.

—Si tenemos cuidado, no me pasará nada —le aseguró sin apartarse—. Por favor. Quiero estar contigo antes de marcharme.

Kaine fue muy cuidadoso. Lo hicieron despacio, suave. La acarició como si fuera de cristal. Cuando la penetró, Helena sostuvo su rostro entre las manos hasta que sus frentes se rozaron; los dedos le temblaban.

«Te quiero».

Tenía esas palabras en la punta de la lengua, pero vaciló durante un instante y las contuvo.

Había una parte de ella que creía que, si pronunciaba esas palabras, acabarían condenados. Si quedaba algo importante por decir, siempre habría un mañana.

En lugar de eso, le besó.

«Te quiero». Se lo dijo en la forma en que lo atraía hacia sí, cuando se encontraban sus bocas, en cómo sus manos le acariciaban la piel, cartografiándolo, memorizando cada detalle que componía su ser, recorriendo sus cicatrices con los dedos.

«Te quiero».

«Te quiero».

Se lo dijo en la forma en la que se dejaba llevar para que él la sostuviera. Con cada latido de su corazón. «Te quiero. Siempre te querré. Siempre cuidaré de ti».

ESTABA ANOCHECIENDO CUANDO SE MARCHÓ. Helena salió al exterior por primera vez. Puntaférreo era una mansión enorme que se curvaba hacia dentro y tenía un patio cerrado con un jardín desbordante en el centro.

Allí se encontraba Amaris, impaciente, con las alas desplegadas y en movimiento.

Kaine la llevó en volandas, y el corsé absorbió la presión de su peso. Cuando él se colocó a su espalda, Helena miró la casa. Bajo el resplandor del verano, le parecía un dragón descomunal en hibernación, enroscado hacia dentro, con los chapiteles como si fueran púas. La fachada frontal estaba cubierta casi por completo de rosas trepadoras, y Davies y un criado anciano, que probablemente fuese el mayordomo, observaban todo desde lo alto de un tramo de escalones de piedra.

Cuando Amaris despegó, Helena sintió como si le dieran un puñetazo en las costillas. Se dobló sobre sí misma y se le escapó un grito ahogado de dolor. Kaine se puso en tensión y estuvo a punto de hacer regresar a Amaris, pero ella le agarró la pierna.

—Estoy bien.

Estuvieron volando durante mucho más tiempo del que Helena había volado jamás.

Amaris se dirigía hacia las montañas, intentando vencer la salida de la luna. Estaba tan cerca de la latencia que Lumitia era una medialuna que no alumbraba demasiado. Aterrizaron en la azotea de un edificio que estaba peligrosamente cerca del Cuartel General. Cuando Helena miró hacia al sur, comprendió por qué.

Habían levantado un muro para demarcar el territorio de la Resistencia. Ocupaba más de la mitad de la isla. Al otro lado, vio el tajo que había diseccionado la ciudad, ahí donde había estallado la bomba y los edificios se habían desplomado. El centro de la isla era un cráter.

—¿Tanto hemos perdido?

—No, pero no tenéis ejército para defender más territorio —respondió Kaine con gesto sombrío. Acto seguido, se bajó y la ayudó a desmontar del lomo de Amaris.

El dolor le provocaba náuseas y tenía que esforzarse para respirar; le apretó la mano a Kaine. Aun así, no fue capaz de despedirse. Cada vez le daba más miedo que aquello estuviera llegando a su fin. Sentía que el final estaba cerca.

—Ten cuidado —fue lo único que pudo decir.

—Helena, por favor… —Se le rompió la voz de tal manera que ella se detuvo en seco y se giró. Kaine la tomó por los hombros.

Sabía lo que le iba a pedir, lo leía en sus ojos: «Huye y no vuelvas».

Pero él también sabía que no lo haría, así que tragó saliva, incapaz de mirarla a los ojos.

—No dejes que te hagan daño otra vez —dijo en su lugar—. No…

Helena se puso de puntillas y lo hizo callar con un beso.

—Ten cuidado —susurró—. No mueras.

CUANDO HELENA APARECIÓ EN LA puerta con ropa de chico e incapaz de respirar bien, la recibieron con más cautela que alegría. La tuvieron encerrada en una celda durante una hora, hasta que Crowther apareció para sacarla.

—¿Está seguro? —le preguntó un guardia—. Aparece en la lista de fallecidos de hace un mes.

—Sí, la encontró uno de los grupos disidentes —respondió Crowther—. Sabía que la mandarían de vuelta en algún momento. Dejadla salir.

Helena no sabía si los grupos disidentes dentro de los combatientes de la Resistencia existían realmente, o si era algo que se había inventado Crowther para encubrir todas sus actividades ilícitas. Buena parte de lo que hacía Kaine y también gran parte de la información que obtenía acababa atribuyéndose a esos grupos fantasma.

Crowther parecía no haber dormido en las últimas semanas. Estaba demacrado, tenía los ojos inyectados en sangre y haber tenido que ir para sacar a Helena de la cárcel le resultaba, a todas luces, un incordio.

Helena quería saber todo lo que había pasado desde que desapareció, pero, apenas se abrió la puerta de su celda, Crowther ya se había dado la vuelta.

—Ve al hospital. Pace está de servicio. Mañana hablamos —le espetó por encima del hombro.

La enfermera Pace se echó a llorar en cuanto la vio.

—¡Estás viva! Debería haber ido yo. Cuando me enteré de que te enviaron allí, yo no…

—Me alegro de que no lo hicieras —repuso Helena. Estaba agotada por el vuelo y el regreso. Sentía una punzada de dolor en el pecho. Se llevó la mano contra el esternón para intentar aliviar la presión.

Pace la condujo a un sitio cerrado por cortinas.

—¿Cómo es posible que hayas sobrevivido?

Helena repitió la excusa vaga de Crowther.

—La verdad es que no lo recuerdo. Nos encontrábamos en el hospital cuando se produjo otra explosión. Cuando desperté, no sé muy bien dónde estaba. Me operaron y me dejaron sola para que me recuperara.

—Déjame ver.

De haber sido al revés, Helena habría hecho lo mismo, así que permitió que Pace le retirara la ropa y el corsé poco a poco, dejando al descubierto la cicatriz que le cruzaba el pecho.

—Hala. —A Pace le temblaba la mano, pero inspeccionó la cicatriz con sumo cuidado—. Está… muy bien hecho.

Era evidente que esperaba algún tipo de cirugía más chapucera, con cordel y cuchillos de cocina.

—Sea quien sea tu cirujano, deberíamos pedirle que venga a trabajar aquí.

—No llegué a ver quién era —replicó Helena—. Estoy mejor, pero mi resonancia sigue siendo inestable.

Pace intentó sonreír, pero solo consiguió forzar una mueca.

—Por suerte, los quelantes son de las pocas cosas que todavía nos quedan.

—¿Cómo de mal estamos? —preguntó Helena.

Pace no dejó de moverse mientras seguía examinándola y le preparaba el brazo para colocarle una vía intravenosa.

—Solo sé lo que escucho de pasada.

—¿Cómo dice la gente que estamos?

Pace negó con la cabeza.

—De los soldados que nos quedan, más de un tercio sigue mostrando síntomas de envenenamiento por anulitio. El viento ha cambiado de dirección, así que ya no cae polvo, pero hasta las partes de la isla que están intactas corren peligro. Al menos hasta que llueva.

—Me han dicho que Althorne ha muerto.

—E Ilva.

—¿Qué? —Helena miró a Pace conmocionada.

—Hace poco más de una semana. Su corazón no aguantó el estrés. Luc está desconsolado. Deberías ir a ver a Lila mañana. Se quedó destrozada cuando se enteró de que aparecías entre los fallecidos.

No mencionó la reacción de Luc al enterarse de la presunta muerte de Helena. A ella se le formó un nudo en la garganta.

—¿Cómo se encuentra?

—Todo sigue su curso. Está bastante sana.

EL BOMBARDEO HABÍA DAÑADO LOS cimientos de la isla y los tanques de inundación, y era imposible repararlos debido al riesgo de exposición al anulitio. La Resistencia también había perdido a casi todos sus prisioneros, ya que el edificio en el que estaban confinados se había derrumbado. Entre ellos se encontraban los detenidos de Crowther, a los que había movido para evitar que Ivy los capturara. Los daban por muertos, pero nadie podía verificar lo que sucedía en la zona de impacto.

Incluso la ayuda que recibían de Novis era muy difícil de conseguir, y había tantos heridos de gravedad que resultaba imposible evacuar a los pacientes al país vecino. El entusiasmo de la monarquía por enviar recursos y aceptar heridos de Paladia estaba empezando a decaer.

La guerra había dejado de ser una contienda entre dos bandos: ahora era una caída libre de la Resistencia. Sin Althorne e Ilva, el Consejo se reducía a tres personas: Matias y Crowther, con visiones totalmente opuestas, y Luc, que no se fiaba de ninguno de los dos.

Crowther siempre había operado en la sombra, lo que permitía a Ilva ejercer el liderazgo con su respaldo tácito. Ahora que estaba solo, parecía encogerse y retorcerse bajo la mirada escudriñadora de Luc, como una araña fuera de su red que patalea con unas patas demasiado largas.

Una parte de Helena quería dejarlo a su suerte, pero sabía que, cuanto más impotente se sintiera Crowther, más peligro corría Kaine.

Se sentó y lo observó moverse de un lado a otro del despacho, deteniéndose frente a mapas y diagramas plagados de surcos de tinta negra.

—¿Cuánta comunicación has mantenido con... Ferron? —le preguntó, exhausta tras el paseo desde el hospital hasta la Torre.

—Ninguna, salvo para informarme de que seguías viva y volverías cuando tu vida dejara de correr peligro. ¿Por qué?

Helena respiró hondo con dificultad.

—Creo que he descubierto algo. Desde que Wagner... Estuve estudiando el sello y pensando en las distintas energías resonánticas para entender el proceso que emplea Morrough. —Los ojos de Crowther se iluminaron con cautela—. Verás, normalmente, los sellos son elementales o celestiales, es decir, de cinco u ocho puntas. Sin embargo, la piromancia de Luc emplea siete y Wagner dibujó uno de nueve para el ritual. Kaine confirmó que eran nueve, así que empecé a observar las energías desde otra perspectiva. Cuando traté de visualizar cómo funcionaría, no dejaba de pensar en una sensación que tengo a veces en el hospital...

—Marino, ve al grano.

—Cuando un paciente muere, hay un pico de energía que es la inversa a la que usa Morrough para crear a los inmarcesibles. La vitalidad cambia y, durante un instante, la percibo antes de que se disipe.

—Y...

—Antes del bombardeo, descubrí una forma de canalizar esa vitalidad y atraparla dentro de obsidiana. No creí que sirviera de nada, pero, cuando estuve en el hospital de campaña, corté a un necrómata con ella y se derrumbó, como si le hubiera arrancado la reanimación.

Crowther la miró de arriba abajo con interés.

—¿Estás segura?

Helena se removió en el sitio, torciendo el gesto cuando sintió un dolor que le atravesó el torso.

—Bueno, estaba herida, pero estoy bastante segura. Lo he repasado en mi mente una y otra vez. Deberíamos ponerlo a prueba. —Tragó saliva—. Tengo más fragmentos de obsidiana y, cuando recupere mi resonancia, puedo hacer más.

—Tráelos. Veré a quién puedo pasarle la idea. —Le hizo un gesto para que se fuera de allí.

Pero Helena no se movió. No es que esperara algún reconocimiento; simplemente no pensaba permitir que Crowther siguiera explotándola.

—Debes de estar muy ocupado ahora —comentó.

—Así es.

—Te ayudaré, pero quiero algo a cambio.

Crowther arqueó las cejas.

—No me digas… ¿Y de qué se trata?

Sus ojos inyectados en sangre se iluminaron peligrosamente. Helena no se inmutó.

—Quiero hacer un trato. Estás haciendo cosas ilegales y ya no tienes aliados en el Consejo que te cubran las espaldas. Necesitas a alguien. Me ofrezco para ser tu mano en la sombra. Te daré lo que necesites, igual que hacía Ilva. Pero Kaine es mi condición.

La expresión de Crowther se torció en una mueca de desdén.

—Te tienes en muy alta estima, Marino.

Helena esbozó una sonrisa amarga.

—En realidad, no. ¿No es cierto? Tú mismo lo dijiste. Soy excepcional. ¿Por qué, si no, pasasteis tanto tiempo Ilva y tú manipulándome? Siempre dispuestos a aprovechar lo que podía hacer, pero dejando claro que no servía para nada más. Adelante, sustitúyeme si puedes.

Los dedos de Crowther se cerraron en un puño. Entornó los ojos, pero no respondió. Helena sintió que el corazón le latía con fuerza contra el hueso fracturado.

—Has empleado a Kaine más allá de lo razonable. Si yo fuera una sanadora sin importancia, lo habrías matado diez veces en los últimos meses. Te avisé, pero me ignoraste porque sabes que haré lo que sea para salvarle la vida. —La rabia se hizo patente en su rostro—. Pero que él esté dispuesto a hacer lo que sea no significa que tú puedas seguir exigiendo sin más. He hecho lo impensable por la Llama Eterna y he permitido que él sufriera las consecuencias porque ¿qué otra opción teníamos? Sin embargo, después de lo que hemos conseguido, después de lo que él ha hecho, no tenemos nada que lo demuestre. Todo se ha ido al traste. Y no pienso dejar que sigas obligándole a pagar ese precio mientras tú ganas tiempo.

Crowther se quedó callado unos instantes.

—¿Y quieres hacer un trato? ¿Eso es lo que me estás proponiendo? ¿Tu cooperación a cambio de la seguridad de Ferron?

Helena se limitó a asentir. Si Kaine hubiera sabido que había regresado para esto, se habría arrancado el talismán antes de permitirlo. Era evidente que ella estaba aprendiendo; ya no era tan fácil adivinar sus intenciones.

Se hizo un silencio que se vio interrumpido por una carcajada de Crowther.

—Qué inesperado giro de los acontecimientos. —Se levantó sin dejar de reír por lo bajo—. De acuerdo. Sigue mis órdenes y Ferron continuará con vida. Yo no soy Ilva; no me interesa que Ferron muera antes de tiempo por una venganza personal. ¿Por qué negarle a un arma su utilidad, aunque esa arma sea una abominación?

El hombre rodeó su escritorio con una sonrisa escalofriante.

—¿Sabes? A principios de este año, tuve una conversación prácticamente idéntica con Ferron.

Helena se mantuvo impasible y lo miró a los ojos.

—Mientras me seas útil, permitiré que seas tú quien apruebe las misiones de Ferron. Pero, si me desobedeces o me enfadas, me encargaré de…

—Sí, sé muy bien lo que harás —replicó Helena.

———

HELENA TARDÓ UNA SEMANA MÁS en recuperar por completo su resonancia. En ese tiempo, hizo de conejillo de Indias para Shiseo. Estaban desarrollando un quelante en forma de pastilla, con el objetivo de reducir la demanda exorbitada de suero.

En esa misma semana, un experto en armas le entregó una lanza de obsidiana a un joven ambicioso que quería entrar en la unidad de Luc. Antes de que regresara, los rumores de un arma de efectividad milagrosa habían llegado al Cuartel General.

El experto en armas no reveló sus métodos, aunque tuvo que admitir que había sido Crowther quien le había entregado la obsidiana.

Todo el mundo llegó a la conclusión de que las propiedades de la obsidiana provenían de la piromancia; que la obsidiana debía de estar imbuida de un fuego sagrado y purificador.

La nueva arma aseguró el puesto y la influencia de Crowther, no solo dentro del Consejo, sino también en la Llama Eterna. Cuando por fin Helena estuvo en condiciones de volver al trabajo, le dijeron que, debido a sus heridas, ya no podría incorporarse al pabellón de emergencias, y que quedaba relegada a una tarea menos exigente: cuidados paliativos y ritos de despedida.

Vestía un hábito de tela pesada y negra, lleno de bolsillos ocultos en los que guardaba cristales de obsidiana, y atendía a los pacientes que no tenían salvación. Por mucho que creyera que había visto lo peor del hospital, allí comprendió que siempre había trabajado con los que tenían alguna posibilidad de sobrevivir.

Ahora se sentaba junto a hombres que parecían tener el cuerpo del revés, el corazón fuera, las caras reventadas; a veces quedaba tan poco de ellos que parecía imposible que siguieran con vida. Se aferraban a ella y, a menudo, la confundían con otra persona mientras los atendía como si fuera un ave carroñera.

A pesar de que la obsidiana había sido un descubrimiento sin precedentes, resultaba imposible mantener el ritmo de la demanda, sobre todo entre soldados acostumbrados a entrenar con acero. Aunque el borde era más afilado que una cuchilla, el cristal se partía con facilidad, lo que hacía que las armas fueran poco fiables.

Aun así, descubrieron que la obsidiana no solo funcionaba contra los necrómatas, sino también contra los liches. Cuando un soldado consiguió atravesarle el pecho a un liche, este murió, y todos sus necrómatas cayeron con él.

Recuperaron el talismán y Helena lo examinó. No quedaba en él ni rastro de energía. Lo comparó con los demás y, al cortarlo por la mitad, se deshizo en una arenilla más fina que el polvo.

Kaine la llamó esa noche. Cuando el anillo le ardió un par de veces, Helena salió corriendo del Cuartel General. Subió a la azotea y esperó, con la mano contra el pecho para intentar aplacar el dolor insoportable que sentía.

—¿Qué ha pasado hoy? —le preguntó Kaine en cuanto Amaris aterrizó con pesadez sobre el tejado. No desmontó, lo que significaba que la conversación sería breve. Helena notaba físicamente cada segundo que pasaban separados, lo mucho que le pesaba.

—¿A qué te refieres?

—Nos han ordenado retirarnos del combate con efecto inmediato. Los necrómatas y los aspirantes seguirán luchando, pero los inmarcesibles han sido apartados del frente.

—Un soldado mató a un liche con la obsidiana —respondió Helena—. ¿Crees que es posible que… el liche… haya muerto? ¿Que Morrough no pueda traerlo de vuelta una vez más?

Kaine guardó silencio unos segundos.

—Parece que has encontrado la forma de matarnos —dijo al fin.

No logró descifrar la emoción de su voz, pero ella sintió cómo todo su entusiasmo se desvanecía. Había pasado mucho tiempo temiendo la inmortalidad de Kaine, consciente de que, si lo descubrían o lo apresaban, no podría escapar; lo torturarían eternamente, sin la esperanza de la muerte. Ahora era muy probable que pudiese morir.

Ella lo había hecho posible. No solo no lo había salvado, sino que había creado una nueva forma de perderlo.

—Ten cuidado.

Él la estaba mirando con atención.

—¿Te han dejado recuperarte antes de ponerte a trabajar otra vez?

Helena esbozó una sonrisa.

—Sí, ya no trabajo en el pabellón de emergencias. Me han asignado una tarea menos exigente.

Kaine asintió.

—Al menos es algo.

Se hizo el silencio. Había tantas cosas que quería decirle, tantas que contarle, pero sabía que ya se había entretenido demasiado.

—Si la obsidiana hace lo que creemos, la Llama Eterna se convertirá en una amenaza real para Morrough. Y él reaccionará ante ello —explicó Kaine al cabo de unos instantes—. Deberíais prepararos para eso.

Helena se limitó a asentir mientras él relajaba las riendas. Amaris se dispuso a saltar de inmediato y el viento se levantó alrededor de sus alas.

—No mueras.

Debió de haberlo dicho en voz muy baja, porque Kaine no respondió.

CAPÍTULO 61

Julius 1787

Cuando Helena se quedaba sin ritos de despedida que celebrar, Crowther se aseguraba de mantenerla ocupada.

Teniendo en cuenta lo útil que había sido con Mandl, él no veía motivos para no seguir aprovechándose de ella y así reforzar su posición en el Consejo. Aunque Helena se negaba a emplear la vivemancia como método de tortura, se había mostrado dispuesta a experimentar con la animancia para encontrar una forma eficaz de sonsacarles información a los prisioneros. Y no podía permitirse cometer errores.

La Helena de dos años atrás no habría reconocido a la persona en la que se estaba convirtiendo. Ahora cruzaba límites que jamás se habría creído capaz.

A veces, iba tan lejos que tenía la sensación de estar correteando bajo la piel de los prisioneros, como si su consciencia ocupara por un momento el mismo espacio mental que la de ellos. Cuando eso ocurría, los prisioneros acababan enfermos, con el cerebro ardiendo, como si los hubiera envenenado. Pero el procedimiento era efectivo, así que no prestó atención a las secuelas hasta que Crowther le dijo que dos de sus «sujetos de prueba» habían muerto.

Nunca había matado a nadie antes. No de esa forma. A partir de entonces, se volvió mucho más cuidadosa, pese a que Crowther consideraba su actitud una pérdida de tiempo y compasión. Helena descubrió que las fiebres que sufrían eran menos virulentas cuando las sesiones eran breves pero recurrentes, como si los prisioneros desarrollaran cierta tolerancia a su poder. Una vez alcanzado ese punto, Helena podía extraer la información que deseara con mucha más facilidad.

—Creo que ya sé cómo curar a Titus Bayard —le dijo una noche a Shiseo.

La Llama Eterna había escogido a un nuevo general para el Consejo. Habían perdido a tantos hombres durante el bombardeo que la línea de sucesión se había truncado. Hutchens tenía un buen historial, pero se dejaba llevar demasiado por la admiración que sentía por Luc.

Shiseo dejó a un lado el cuchillo de obsidiana que estaba preparando y Helena respiró hondo antes de continuar:

—Cuando hirieron al general Bayard, yo no entendía qué tenía que hacer. Me equivoqué al tratar la herida como si fuera cualquier otra lesión. A principios de año ya se me había ocurrido una manera de abordar el problema, pero Titus no reaccionó bien cuando intenté ponerla a prueba. Gracias al trabajo de las últimas semanas —bajó la vista—, he caído en la cuenta de que la clave está en avanzar poco a poco para reforzar su tolerancia. Una vez que lo consiga, creo que mi idea funcionará.

Shiseo ladeó la cabeza.

—¿Cómo?

Helena se humedeció los labios.

—Los pensamientos y los recuerdos son como caminos en la mente. Como yo no lo sabía cuando curé a Titus, acabé dejándolo atrapado en su propio cerebro. A lo mejor ya es demasiado tarde, pero tal vez pueda ofrecerle una vía de escape si consigo entrar en su cabeza. —Tragó saliva con incomodidad—. Es algo que pongo en práctica en mi propia mente de vez en cuando. Recurro a la resonancia para alterar mis pensamientos y darle a mi cerebro una nueva ruta.

—Suena complicado —dijo Shiseo tras considerarlo.

Helena agachó la mirada.

—Creo que tengo que intentarlo.

—Haz lo que consideres oportuno —intervino Crowther con cruel interés—. Si matas a Bayard, pues tendremos una boca menos que alimentar.

—Solo intento ayudar —replicó ella tragando saliva con fuerza.

Crowther torció el gesto en un gesto desdeñoso.

—Cuando quiera que hagas algo, Marino, te lo pediré.

Acababan de enterarse de que habían enviado a Kaine a Hevgoss en una misión diplomática sin previo aviso. Él ni siquiera había podido ponerse en contacto con Helena directamente. Solo le había dado tiempo a enviar un mensaje en clave por uno de los canales de radio antes de partir sin despedirse.

———————

Lo único que iba bien era el embarazo de Lila, que estaba aburrida pero sana, mucho más de lo que Helena la había visto en años. No había motivos para temer un riesgo de aborto.

—¿Estás bien? —le preguntó Lila a Helena, que tenía una mano puesta sobre su vientre y había cerrado los ojos para intentar distinguir el latido del bebé del de su madre y comprobar que todo estuviera bien.

La frecuencia cardiaca fetal siempre era mucho más rápida de lo normal, pero percibirla junto a la de otra persona resultaba confuso.

Helena abrió los ojos, secos e irritados por el cansancio.

—Sí, estoy bien —respondió, aunque tenía la sensación de estar muriéndose por dentro.

Había visto muy poco a Kaine en los últimos días y ahora se había marchado y no sabía cuándo volvería. Ya ni siquiera se esforzaba por salvar a la gente, solo pasaba los días esperando a que murieran.

Lila la miró escéptica.

—Pues cualquiera lo diría, porque pareces llevar días sin dormir. Pace me comentó que has estado bastante malherida. ¿Estás ya recuperada del todo? Tú más que nadie sabes lo importante que es sanar bien.

Helena negó con la cabeza.

—No es por eso. Los turnos que me han asignado son más largos, pero no tan duros. Tengo que irme, hay… mucho trabajo que hacer.

—Sé que jamás me lo dirías, pero me consideras una egoísta, ¿verdad? —dijo Lila cuando se puso de pie.

Helena suspiró y se miró las manos.

—Has sufrido mucho, así que no te culpo por querer algo bueno en tu vida. Lo que no entiendo es por qué has tomado esta decisión precisamente ahora. Yo que tú me marcharía a Novis, donde al menos no correrás peligro. —Se encogió de hombros—. Puede que tener al heredero del principado allí sirva para convencerlos de que nos envíen suministros médicos.

Lila se había negado a dejar la «cuarentena» y todavía fingía estar presa de un brote de tos de los pantanos.

—Quiero aguardar un poco más, solo para estar segura.

RHEA LA ESPERABA JUNTO CON Titus en una de las salas privadas. Helena le había enviado un mensaje para decirle que quería hablar con ella sobre un posible tratamiento.

—¿En qué consistiría exactamente? —le preguntó la mujer, sujetando el brazo de su marido para que no se alejara de ella.

—Sería un procedimiento a largo plazo —explicó Helena mientras se secaba las manos contra el hábito negro—, pero similar a lo que intentamos a principios de año. Ahora ya sé cómo controlarlo y, si trabajamos despacio, con intervenciones breves seguidas de periodos de recuperación, creo que Titus podría adaptarse al proceso. La idea es curarlo sin provocar la reacción que tuvo la última vez.

Rhea estrechó la mano de Titus y se inclinó hacia Helena. Le brillaban los ojos.

—Entonces ¿ya lo has puesto en práctica antes? —preguntó con la voz temblorosa de emoción.

Helena carraspeó, porque no quería darle demasiadas esperanzas.

—No exactamente. Era un procedimiento similar. Pero te advierto que conlleva ciertos riesgos. ¿Sabes lo que es el mitridatismo? —Rhea negó con la cabeza—. Es una técnica que consiste en administrar dosis pequeñas de veneno con la idea de desarrollar inmunidad a él. Para curar a Titus, tendré que entrar en su cerebro y el proceso será… similar, porque su sistema inmunitario responderá a mi resonancia con fiebres. Habrá que hacerle un seguimiento para mantener la reacción bajo control y hacer pausas más largas si le sube demasiado la temperatura. La idea es conseguir que tolere mi resonancia en las zonas más delicadas del cerebro.

Aunque había omitido algunos detalles, todo lo que le había dicho era cierto.

Rhea asintió.

—¡Sí! Sí, haz lo que consideres…

La mujer se interrumpió cuando Luc abrió la puerta de la sala y entró seguido de Sebastian.

—¿Qué haces, Rhea? —le preguntó sin aliento.

—Helena ha encontrado la manera de curar a Titus —explicó ella, sorprendida por la intrusión.

Luc miró a Helena con una expresión severa, intensa y febril.

—No me creo que lo estés diciendo en serio. —Helena se dispuso a contestar, pero no le estaba hablando a ella. Se había vuelto a mirar a Rhea—. ¿De verdad confías en ella después de lo que le hizo a Soren?

Helena se estremeció y su mente estuvo a punto de lanzarse de cabeza al interior de esa dolorosa herida que aún estaba abierta en su interior. Tragó saliva con fuerza.

—Soren murió, Luc. Siento en el alma no haber podido salvarlo, pero este procedimiento podría funcionar. Piensa en lo que significaría tener a Titus de vuelta.

Luc la miró de nuevo con desagrado.

—¿Eso es lo que te importa? ¿Cuánto puede valer alguien para la causa? —Miró a Titus, que se había puesto nervioso al percibir la tensión en el ambiente—. ¿Es que acaso solo lo ves como un efectivo militar echado a perder después de lo que le hiciste?

—¿Qué? No, eso no es lo que quería decir.

La mirada de Luc era tan abrasadora como un sol ardiente.

—Como le pongas un solo dedo encima, te juro que…

—No lo hará —intervino Rhea—. Gracias, Helena…, es decir, sanadora Marino, aprecio la oferta, pero creo que será mejor dejarlo.

Luc asintió bruscamente, se giró sobre los talones y se marchó sin mirar atrás. Sebastian les dirigió una última mirada indecisa a Rhea y a Titus antes de salir tras él. En cuanto se retiraron, Rhea se desmoronó con un jadeo y se cubrió el rostro con las manos.

Helena se había quedado sin palabras. Aturdida por la conmoción, vio que Rhea se incorporaba sin mirarla y sacaba a Titus de la sala.

Una vez sola, Helena se puso los guantes y se dirigió hacia la Torre de Alquimia, pero se encontró a Sebastian esperándola dentro del ascensor. Para su sorpresa, había regresado solo y parecía alicaído. Tras una breve pausa, le tocó el hombro a Helena.

—Te honra haberlo intentado.

Helena no fue capaz de mirarlo a la cara, así que clavó la vista en su pecho, en el blasón solar que decoraba su armadura.

—¿Por qué me está haciendo esto? —preguntó—. Todo el mundo lo ha entendido. Incluso quienes consideran que me equivoqué. Luc ni siquiera ha intentado ponerse en mi lugar.

Sebastian suspiró.

—Ya sabes por qué.

No estaba segura de saberlo, pero asintió y entró en el ascensor.

Cuando se acercó a la habitación de Luc, los tres guardias que vigilaban la puerta negaron con la cabeza al unísono en cuanto la vieron, así que Helena regresó a su propio dormitorio, salió por la ventana y recorrió la suave pendiente del tejado para rodear el edificio. El cabello rubio de Luc resplandecía bajo la luz del atardecer. Estaba sentado sobre los talones, encorvado, y le daba vueltas a algo entre los dedos. Se llevó el objeto a los labios y una llamita le iluminó las yemas de los dedos cuando inhaló.

Dejó caer los hombros y todo su cuerpo pareció relajarse.

Mientras lo observaba, Helena pensó en lo dulce y alegre que había sido su rostro. La guerra lo había carcomido hasta los huesos. Allí sentado, sin su armadura, estaba tan consumido que le recordaba al exoesqueleto de un insecto, como las mudas que las libélulas dejaban en los juncos tras la metamorfosis. Ya no quedaba nada de él en su interior.

Luc exhaló lentamente y unas volutas de humo escaparon de entre sus labios.

Era opio.

Fumaba como si llevara haciéndolo toda la vida, con una indiferencia que a Helena le resultó espantosa.

Luc se apartó la pipa de los labios al verla. Su expresión se endureció, se hizo más afilada.

—Vete.

—No —replicó ella acercándose.

Él volvió a darle vueltas a la pipa entre los dedos mientras apretaba los dientes con rabia. Si la golpeaba, era muy probable que Helena cayera de la Torre y muriera.

Se detuvo a unos cuantos pasos de él.

—No pude salvarlo. Ni muriendo yo misma en el intento habría podido hacerlo. ¿Habrías preferido que hubiera sido así?

En vez de responder, Luc tembló como una hoja seca a punto de caer de su rama. Parecía estar tratando de decir algo, pero se llevó la pipa a los labios y la prendió con una débil llamita. Inhaló durante tanto rato que la pipa estuvo a punto de escurrírsele de entre los dedos.

Helena se arrodilló junto a Luc, por miedo a que se cayera del tejado, pero entonces él levantó la vista, encontró su mirada y ya… ya no parecía enfadado, sino agotado.

—¿Qué nos ha pasado, Hel?

Ella lo miró y su corazón, hambriento y falto de cariño, dio un vuelco cuando comprendió lo evidente: no era Luc el que hablaba, sino el opio.

—Una guerra.

Desvió la vista hacia el paisaje en ruinas que se extendía ante ellos. Hubo un tiempo en que la ciudad había sido hermosa.

—Antes creías en mí —dijo con voz distante—. ¿Qué he hecho para que dejes de hacerlo?

—Sigo creyendo en ti, Luc. Pero tenemos que ganar esta guerra; no podemos tomar decisiones basándonos en la historia que queremos contar luego. Hay demasiado en juego.

—No —replicó Luc—. Así ganaremos. Así hemos ganado siempre. Así ganaron mi padre, mi abuelo y todos los principados hasta el mismísimo Orion. Todos ganaron confiando en que el bien siempre vence al mal, y yo he de hacer lo mismo.

Helena lo miró angustiada y él chasqueó los dedos para activar sus anillos de ignición. Dejó que el fuego le lamiera la palma de la mano, que le corriera por los dedos, y lo acunó como si fuera un gatito. Cerró el puño en torno a él y lo convirtió en una única llama antes de llevarse la pipa a los labios para prenderla una vez más.

Helena apretó el puño y reprimió un estremecimiento cuando lo oyó inspirar hondo.

—Pero ¿qué pasará si no es así de simple? —insistió—. Todos los que ganan dicen que ellos fueron los buenos, pero en realidad son los que cuentan la historia. Ellos deciden cómo recordarla. ¿Y si nunca fue tan simple?

Luc negó con la cabeza.

—Orion fue bendecido por el sol porque se negó a renunciar a su fe.

Helena suspiró exasperada y enterró la cara entre las manos.

Oyó un chisporroteo seguido del siseo de la pipa al evaporarse el opio.

—Luc..., por favor, déjame ayudarte. —Ella hizo amago de acercarse.

Él se apartó y un inesperado destello de rabia le surcó el rostro.

—No... me toques.

Estaba acercándose peligrosamente al borde de una caída descomunal, como si lo estuviera llamando el abismo. Helena ya no sabía cómo hacerle entrar en razón ni qué decir para que la escuchara.

—¿Te acuerdas de lo que te prometí la noche que viniste aquí, Luc? —le preguntó en tono suplicante.

Luc no respondió. Tenía la mirada perdida; el atardecer delineaba sus rasgos demacrados como si los cubriera de oro.

—Te prometí que haría lo que fuera por ti. —Cerró el puño—. Tal vez no entendiste hasta dónde estaba dispuesta a llegar.

—No digas eso —le pidió como si hubiera recuperado una repentina lucidez—. No hagas como si toda la culpa fuera mía. Pensaba que podrías curarlo.

Ella cerró los ojos.

—A veces, la gente muere. Ni tú ni yo ni nadie podemos salvar a todo el mundo, pero te pido por favor que me dejes intentar curar a Titus.

—No puedo.

Luc se puso en pie, bajó con torpeza hasta el balcón de su dormitorio y desapareció.

———

LLEVABA DOS SEMANAS SIN TENER noticias de Kaine cuando, al fin, el anillo se calentó.

Helena salió corriendo del Cuartel General sin mirar atrás y, al llegar al tejado y ver a Kaine esperándola allí junto a Amaris, estuvieron a punto de fallarle las piernas. En su uniforme impoluto llevaba una hilera de medallas, como si acabara de participar en algún acto oficial.

—Has vuelto —fue lo único que consiguió decir mientras extendía los brazos antes de haber llegado a su lado siquiera.

Kaine la atrajo hacia sí para abrazarla.

—¿Todo bien estas últimas semanas?

Helena se las arregló para asentir, pero acabó apoyando la cabeza contra su pecho. Estaba tan agotada que cerró los ojos, creyendo por un instante que desfallecería mientras escuchaba los latidos de su corazón. Había vuelto. No podía pedir más. Pero tenía la sensación de que había pasado una eternidad, como si cada minuto de su ausencia le hubiera abierto una herida.

—¿Algo va mal? —preguntó él al cabo de un momento.

Todo.

—Nada —dijo ella—. Es que creo que dejé de respirar cuando te marchaste.

Kaine le pasó los brazos por los hombros de nuevo, aunque con rigidez, como si su mente estuviera en otra parte. El miedo se extendió por las venas de Helena como la sangre por el agua.

Levantó la cabeza.

—¿Qué pasa?

Kaine no la estaba mirando, sino que tenía la vista clavada en la luz cegadora de la Torre de Alquimia.

—Imagino que ya lo sabrás, pero el viaje ha sido una misión diplomática. Nos enviaron a Hevgoss para formalizar una alianza. Llevaremos a cabo una investigación alquímica en su nombre a cambio de que nos apoyen con los mercenarios que luchan entre sus filas.

—Sí, ya lo suponía.

—El nuevo embajador hevgotiano me ha… cogido cariño. Mi principal responsabilidad ahora es mantenerlo entretenido. ¿Queda alguna orden de Crowther pendiente por cumplir?

Helena negó con la cabeza.

—No, estábamos esperando a ver qué ocurría. Querrá un informe, pero eso es todo por el momento.

Kaine la miró con suspicacia.

—¿Nada más? —En su voz se notaba cierta tensión.

—No, nada más. Piensa que acabas de volver.

En vez de mostrarse aliviado, adoptó esa expresión tensa que se adueñaba de su rostro cuando tenía la certeza de que Helena no estaba bien y él no sabía por qué. Dio un paso atrás y la estudió de arriba abajo.

—¿Qué ha pasado?

Ella lo miró desconcertada y negó con la cabeza.

—Nada.

Helena sabía que no la creía, pues el miedo se abrió paso por sus facciones. Le habría gustado tener alguna tarea que encargarle; estaba claro que Kaine pensaba que le daban esa tregua porque a ella le había pasado algo. Finalmente, suspiró y le cogió la mano.

—Después de que Althorne e Ilva murieran, le dije a Crowther que estaban abusando de tu colaboración y le pedí que bajara un poco el ritmo.

—¿Y él accedió sin más? —resopló incrédulo.

—No, hice un trato con él. Lo de la obsidiana y la inestabilidad en el Consejo lo han dejado en una posición vulnerable. Como necesitaba a alguien de su lado, le dije que yo lo apoyaría con la condición de que me deje supervisar tus misiones de ahora en adelante.

En vez de mostrarse aliviado, Kaine se liberó de su agarre.

—¿Por qué has hecho eso? —escupió—. ¿En qué momento pensaste que eso me ayudaría? Es lo último que quiero.

Un pinchazo de dolor, cansancio y rabia la atravesó.

—¿Por qué? ¿Me vas a decir que solo tú tienes el derecho de proteger a las personas que te importan? ¿Se supone que debo quedarme de brazos cruzados mientras ganas la guerra por mí? ¿Es así como ves lo nuestro? —Hizo un gesto furioso señalando el espacio entre los dos.

—Ese era el trato.

—Yo nunca accedí a eso. Además, no estoy haciendo nada peligroso. Ya ni siquiera me dejan salir del Cuartel General.

Kaine la miró furioso.

—Venga…, no seas así —le suplicó Helena.

Pero Kaine no dio su brazo a torcer. Un muro gélido los separaba, como si todos sus fantasmas se hubieran congregado de repente a su alrededor. La muerte los había calado hasta los huesos.

La guerra era un abismo insaciable que se lo tragaba todo. Siempre quería más: otra vida, un poco más de sangre. Los obligaba a ser mejores, más listos, implacables, rápidos y calculadores. A aceptar otra dosis de dolor.

Nada era suficiente.

Pero Helena ya no quería sacrificar más; lo que le quedaba era demasiado valioso como para perderlo. Aun así, de ella se esperaba que fuera dócil, que cooperara, que fuera un trofeo capaz de ofrecer consuelo cuando la realidad era muy distinta.

Tragó saliva con amargura.

—¿Qué esperabas que hiciera?

—¡No quiero que te involucres en esta puta guerra! —exclamó Kaine con la voz rota por la rabia—. Me paso las horas temiendo lo que podría ocurrirte si no cumplo con mi cometido. Si me capturan, no te haces una idea de lo que…

—Lo sé perfectamente —lo interrumpió sin miramientos—. ¿Qué te crees que hago yo todo el tiempo? Yo soy quien se encarga de curar a todas las personas que los inmarcesibles no consiguen matar. Yo traté… traté a los prisioneros que encontraron en el laboratorio del puerto Este y… tuve que verlos a todos morir. A todos. Soy tan consciente de los riesgos que corremos que a veces pienso que van a acabar volviéndome loca. ¿Por qué crees si no que me esfuerzo tanto?

Se le quebró la voz y se dio la vuelta mientras la desesperación la devoraba por dentro. Se había repetido que todo mejoraría cuando Kaine regresara, que podría respirar tranquila de nuevo.

Pero lo único que sentía era un renovado pavor; tenía la sensación de que todo se desmoronaba a su alrededor sin que ella pudiera hacer nada para detenerlo. Acabaría pasando cada segundo de su vida preparándose para lo peor, incapaz de disfrutar siquiera de los momentos que compartiera con Kaine.

—Avisaré a Crowther de tu regreso. —Habló con tono desprovisto de emoción—. Y te diré lo que quiere.

Deseó desaparecer. Estaba harta de todo, de suplicarle que tuviera cuidado de no dejarse atrapar, que no muriera, que regresara con ella. Estaba harta de tratar de convencerse a sí misma de que una promesa significaba algo en una guerra como aquella.

—Ten cuidado.

—Espera. —Kaine la agarró del brazo—. No te vayas.

Helena negó con la cabeza.

—Estoy muy cansada… No quiero que nos peleemos.

—No lo haremos. —Ahora la miraba con más atención—. Ven conmigo. Te has dejado la piel trabajando y no les pasará nada por prescindir una noche de ti. Te prometo que no nos pelearemos.

Helena asintió con esfuerzo. El tiempo se le pasó como un borrón a lomos de Amaris; de hecho, casi ni notó el viento. Estaba medio dormida cuando la quimera aterrizó, así que Kaine la llevó en brazos hasta la cama. Le quitó los zapatos, se sentó en el borde del colchón y le puso una mano entre los omoplatos.

Kaine estaba a salvo. Había vuelto.

Helena se despertó en cuanto apartó la mano.

—Tengo que comer algo y darme una ducha —explicó el chico tras una breve pausa.

Ella le cogió la mano y se la estrechó con tanta fuerza que le clavó las uñas en la piel.

—Tuve miedo de que murieras. Dijiste que no podías marcharte sin una serie de preparativos, pero desapareciste de un momento a otro y pensé… pensé que no volverías. —Tenía la voz pastosa—. Te expones a un peligro tras otro y no puedo pedirte que pares de hacerlo.

—Ya sabes que lo dejaría todo si estuviera en mi mano —dijo acariciándole los nudillos con el pulgar—. Huiría contigo sin mirar atrás.

—Lo sé… —Se le rompió la voz—. No mueras, Kaine. No me dejes.

Kaine se tumbó a su lado y no se movió hasta que Helena dejó de llorar y se quedó dormida.

Cuando el colchón volvió a hundirse, Helena se despertó y lo encontró al otro lado de la cama, con el cabello húmedo pegado a la frente. Se acurrucó entre sus brazos y cerró los ojos mientras deslizaba los dedos por su piel. Lo reconocería incluso a ciegas.

Kaine, por su parte, le cogió la mano, hizo que se tumbara de espaldas y se inclinó sobre ella para observarla con esa tristeza indeleble tan suya, hasta que Helena levantó la cabeza y lo besó. Él subió la mano hasta rodearle el cuello, apoyando su pulgar bajo la mandíbula, y profundizó el beso lentamente. Helena le enterró los dedos entre los mechones plateados.

Nunca había imaginado que llegaría a conocer a una persona de una forma tan íntima. Sabía que Kaine le besaría ese punto del cuello donde su pulso era más visible. Reconocía la forma en que su cuerpo se movía al inclinarse sobre ella, el contacto de sus manos en las caderas, la caricia de sus dientes en la cara interna de los muslos y el calor de su lengua.

—Eres mía. Solo mía —le dijo mientras la besaba.

—Ahora y siempre.

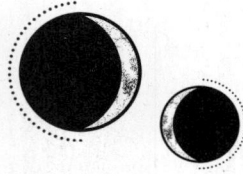

CAPÍTULO 62

Augustus 1787

DESCUBRIR QUE LOS INMARCESIBLES SE habían aliado con Hevgoss no fue ninguna sorpresa.

Se enviaron misivas a los países vecinos para animarlos a oponerse y presionar a Hevgoss para que se retractara, pero apenas obtuvieron respuesta por su parte. Incluso Novis tardó en responder mostrando su repulsa sin mucha convicción.

—Centrémonos en la parte positiva. La alianza con Hevgoss demuestra que recurrir a la obsidiana ha funcionado —dijo el general Hutchens dirigiéndose al resto de los miembros de la Llama Eterna con tono despreocupado.

En teoría, Hutchens tenía un historial intachable: había estado al mando de la zona portuaria y habría conseguido defenderla del bombardeo si la falta de recursos no hubiera obligado a la Resistencia a renunciar a ella para evitar poner en riesgo el Cuartel General. Pese a todo, antes de iniciar la retirada, se había asegurado de sabotear los muelles sin apenas causar bajas. Hicieron bien en contar con él, aunque, como buen devoto de Luc, Sol y la Llama Eterna, tenía una fe ciega en que la victoria estaba asegurada.

Tal era su confianza en que Sol proveería que solía pasar por alto el aprovisionamiento o las tareas más rutinarias.

Crowther no podía ni quería confiar en él, por lo que cada vez había una mayor disonancia entre las circunstancias reales de la guerra y la visión que Hutchens y el resto de los miembros del Consejo tenían del conflicto.

—Lo que debemos hacer es acumular más obsidiana y atacarlos sin piedad antes de que lleguen los mercenarios hevgotianos.

A Helena se le revolvió el estómago solo de pensar en producir más obsidiana. Aunque pudiera, ya había alcanzado el límite de muertes que era capaz de presenciar.

—Perdimos más de la mitad de nuestras fuerzas y de nuestro territorio la última vez que intentamos llevar a cabo una ofensiva similar. —Con la inestabilidad que reinaba en el Consejo, Crowther se estaba viendo obligado a intervenir más de lo acostumbrado y, si bien sus observaciones eran acertadas, carecía del carisma necesario para conseguir convencer a los demás de que se pusieran de su lado—. Aunque confío en el efecto de la obsidiana, hay que tener en cuenta que corremos el riesgo de que la llegada de los mercenarios vaya acompañada de un aumento en el uso de anulitio. Hevgoss no dispone de muchos alquimistas y enviarán a sus tropas desde las prisiones.

Hutchens negó con la cabeza.

—No creo que los inmarcesibles vuelvan a recurrir al anulitio, porque no pueden permitirse perder más territorio. Y recordemos que el polvo residual ha afectado también a la isla Oeste.

—Esta vez nos aseguraremos de pulir nuestra estrategia a fondo —intervino Luc. En las últimas reuniones había adoptado un tono distinto al hablar, más grave y autoritario. A no ser que lo sacaran de sus casillas, antes solía mostrarse mucho más inseguro—. Independientemente de cómo hayamos llegado hasta aquí, creo que estaremos todos de acuerdo en que no podemos permitirnos perder más batallas. Los inmarcesibles nunca habían querido contar con soldados vivos hasta ahora, así que yo interpreto este cambio de estrategia como una prueba indiscutible de que estamos haciendo algo bien. Preguntad a cualquiera que haya estado en el frente últimamente. Hemos conseguido derrotar a inmarcesibles vivos, liches, necrómatas y aspirantes por igual. La obsidiana ha cambiado el rumbo de la guerra. Con esta alianza, están admitiendo que no se ven capaces de ganar solos. Coincido con Hutchens: vayamos con todo a por ellos. Los sacaremos de su escondrijo a la fuerza.

—Aunque fuera posible asegurar nuestra victoria de una manera tan decisiva, hay que tener en cuenta que Hevgoss podría intentar salir ganando sin importar qué bando gane —apuntó Crowther—. Quizá haya llegado el momento de negociar con Novis. Por muy reticentes que se hayan mostrado en estos últimos meses, no creo que a la reina le haga ninguna gracia que Hevgoss se quede con los recursos de Paladia. Con el incentivo adecuado, es posible que vuelva a apoyarnos. Tal vez convenga que el principado les haga una visita diplomática para mostrar nuestro respeto y...

—No pienso salir de Paladia —lo interrumpió Luc sin molestarse en disimular el desprecio que Crowther despertaba en él—. ¿Cómo se supone que voy a inspirar confianza a nuestras tropas si me embarco en una misión diplomática mientras se rumorea que Hevgoss va a apoyar a los inmarcesibles?

Crowther frunció el ceño.

—La negociación sería mucho más efectiva si acudís vos en persona. Ningún recurso o representante que pudiéramos permitirnos enviar a la corte de Novis se entendería como una muestra de respeto tan grande como vuestra presencia, principado. Cualquier otro delegado no...

—No es negociable. Si quieres enviar a alguien a Novis, me parece bien, pero yo no pienso irme de aquí —sentenció Luc con una rabiosa vehemencia.

Helena ya sabía que Crowther tenía intención de presentar aquella propuesta. Había considerado utilizar el embarazo de Lila para coaccionar a Luc y obligarlo a desplazarse hasta Novis con la intención de escoltar a la joven y a su «heredero» a un lugar seguro. Sin embargo, Lila se había negado en redondo a hacer público su embarazo, así que sacarlo a la luz en aquella reunión habría sido una jugada demasiado arriesgada.

Al final, fue Matias quien viajó al reino vecino con un cofre de oro transmutado por Luc. Nadie quedó satisfecho con la decisión, pero, cuando Helena lo vio partir ceremoniosamente hacia Novis, notó que el nudo que llevaba años oprimiéndole el pecho desaparecía.

Apenas había cruzado la frontera cuando la Resistencia se dispuso a prepararse para la batalla.

Era una misión suicida. Aunque no quedaban soldados ni recursos suficientes para afrontar la situación, los exploradores salieron a recorrer las ruinas de la ciudad para intentar recuperar todas las armas y armaduras que pudieran encontrar. También les prohibieron estrictamente traer cadáveres de vuelta al Cuartel General. Quienes murieran en la zona afectada tendrían que permanecer allí hasta que encontraran una forma segura de llevar a cabo una ceremonia fúnebre.

Cualquiera dispuesto a luchar era bienvenido a unirse a las filas de la Resistencia, independientemente de su edad, de su género o de que tuviera poderes alquímicos. Pero no había tiempo para entrenar a nadie. Ni siquiera tenían armas que ofrecer. Allí donde Helena mirara, había niños y niñas practicando con palos o intentando fabricar tirachinas caseros. Y ninguno llevaba armadura, pues no había de su tamaño.

A Helena se le revolvía el estómago.

Eran carne de cañón. Morirían a los pocos minutos de pisar el campo de batalla.

Pero la Resistencia prefería recurrir a ellos que a la nigromancia. Aquel ataque abocado al fracaso dependía de un milagro, de la seguridad de que se verían recompensados por arriesgar todo cuanto tenían. Porque la gloria, la bendición y la eternidad aguardaba a quienes no perdían la fe.

Igual que Orion había recibido la bendición de Sol.

Pero ya no contaban con Ilva para obrar milagros.

—Quiero fabricar una bomba —dijo Helena nada más entrar en el despacho de Crowther.

Había ido a hablar con él en mitad de la noche, pero lo encontró despierto, siempre lo estaba. Su rostro, ya de por sí delgado, cada vez estaba más demacrado. Aunque ni siquiera había cumplido los cincuenta, parecía tener ochenta años.

—No me habías dicho que también eras experta en explosivos —comentó con desdén.

Helena se sentó sin esperar a que le ofreciera asiento, y Crowther suspiró.

Durante un tiempo, ella había pensado que nadie ponía tan a prueba el límite de sus conflictos internos como Kaine, pero lo de Crowther estaba a otro nivel. Jamás había odiado y necesitado a alguien tanto como a él.

Crowther podía permitirle a Helena hacer algo de utilidad, puesto que era el único miembro de la Llama Eterna que se tomaba la molestia de escucharla. El problema era que usaba su obediencia como un arma contra Kaine.

La caza de espías entre los inmarcesibles se había intensificado. El resto de sus informadores habían desaparecido sin dejar rastro, así que recurrir a Kaine o incluso a la información que les proporcionaba suponía correr un riesgo demasiado alto.

—Solía ayudar a Luc a practicar los fundamentos de la piromancia. Además, estoy familiarizada con los procesos técnicos de la combustión, y sus reglas son las mismas con o sin resonancia.

Crowther arqueó una ceja y movió los dedos de la mano derecha para que los anillos de ignición se rozaran unos con otros.

—He estado pensando en ello desde hace tiempo... —Estaba tan nerviosa que incluso le dolía la garganta—. Podríamos utilizar la obsidiana igual que los inmarcesibles usaron el anulitio en su bomba. De hecho, también podríamos combinar ambos materiales.

—¿Y no se fundiría la obsidiana en la explosión?

—No. Shiseo tiene experiencia con la pirotecnia que se utiliza para las celebraciones orientales. Entre los dos sumamos un conocimiento bastante extenso. Si lo hacemos bien, podríamos limitar el calor desprendido por la bomba sin comprometer su fuerza explosiva. No tendría el alcance de su ataque, pero daría igual.

—Confías mucho en tu trabajo para no disponer más que de un certificado básico en alquimia.

Helena apretó los dientes, pero siguió hablando:

—Tenemos una buena cantidad de fragmentos de obsidiana. Durante el proceso de fabricación de las armas, se generan esquirlas y pedacitos demasiado delgados o pequeños como para servir de utilidad. Esos residuos bastarían para la bomba, así que ni siquiera interferiríamos en la producción. —Sacó un montón de papeles doblados—. Lo único que necesitaríamos sería que nos prepararan estos componentes en el Horno de Athanor.

Crowther les echó un vistazo a sus diseños.

—No te prometo nada, pero... —suspiró— supongo que nos vendrá bien.

PENSAR EN LO QUE ESTABA por venir la aterrorizaba y desesperaba a partes iguales. Si la ofensiva salía bien y la bomba debilitaba lo suficiente a Morrough, ¿podría Luc acabar con él?

¿Y qué pasaría con Kaine si lograban derrotarlo?

Cada vez que cerraba los ojos, caía presa de las pesadillas. Soñaba que hurgaba en el cadáver de Morrough a oscuras, con las manos desnudas, y que se manchaba los brazos enteros de sangre buscando desesperada el hueso que albergaba la vida de Kaine. Mientras le arrancaba uno a uno todos los huesos del cuerpo, Luc se acercaba a ella como un sol naciente. Al verlo, ella trataba de explicarse y le suplicaba que la entendiera, pero él nunca la escuchaba. El sueño siempre terminaba con ella envuelta en llamas.

Al despertar, sabía que la realidad sería muy distinta. Cuando Morrough fuera derrotado, ella estaría en el Cuartel General, trabajando en el hospital. No se enteraría de nada hasta que ya fuera demasiado tarde.

Y cada día se preguntaba si su esfuerzo acabaría con su propia perdición o con la destrucción de Kaine.

Después de lo mal que él había reaccionado cuando Helena le contó que había empezado a involucrarse más activamente en la guerra, había decidido no contarle lo de la bomba. Tampoco le costó ocultárselo: su papel como embajador lo mantenía tan ocupado que apenas encontraban tiempo para verse aparte de para intercambiar la información más urgente.

No subió al tejado para llamarlo hasta que Shiseo y ella no tuvieron listos todos los componentes de su proyecto. Tardó un buen rato en aparecer y, cuando lo hizo, iba vestido con un traje formal, sobrio e impecable.

—No voy a poder quedarme mucho rato. ¿Qué sucede?

—Tenemos una nueva arma —se apresuró a decir ella—. ¿Sabes si habrá algún momento en que una gran cantidad de inmarcesibles se reunirán cerca? Lo ideal sería un evento en el que tú no tengas que estar presente. Podríamos colocarla hasta con dos días de antelación.

La expresión de Kaine se endureció.

—¿Habéis fabricado una bomba? —Ante el asentimiento de Helena, preguntó—: ¿De obsidiana?

—Y anulitio, así que tendrás que estar bien lejos de allí.

Kaine asintió y le dedicó una mirada cargada de significado.

—Espero que no la guardéis cerca del Cuartel General.

Ella negó con la cabeza.

—No, está en otro sitio.

—Bueno —exhaló—, al menos la Resistencia se está tomando su última ofensiva en serio. Las fuerzas hevgotianas cruzarán la frontera oeste esta semana, pero unos cuantos estratócratas y oficiales vendrán a Paladia en un día. Se va a celebrar un banquete en su honor la noche siguiente de su llegada. La mayor parte de los inmarcesibles asistirán e incluso puede que Morrough se deje caer por allí.

Helena asintió. Tal vez funcionara.

—¿Podrías colocar la bomba sin levantar sospechas y luego marcharte de allí?

La mirada de Kaine se suavizó.

—Nadie les presta tanta atención como debería a los necrómatas. Dan por hecho que quienes los dirigen están de su lado. Si le arranco la vitalidad al necrómata de otro inmarcesible, puedo dirigirlo para que la coloque y nadie vinculará el ataque conmigo.

—¿Estás seguro de que te dará tiempo a marcharte de allí antes de que explote?

Le daba miedo que estuviera evadiendo la pregunta.

Kaine y ella parecían pertenecer a dos mundos completamente distintos. Él iba vestido con un uniforme hecho a medida limpio y decorado con una hilera de intrincadas medallas, mientras que ella llevaba ropas reglamentarias andrajosas y demasiado grandes.

—¿Cuánto tendré que alejarme?

—Lo suficiente como para que no respires el humo. Habrá micropartículas en el aire y no sabemos qué efecto tendrán. Lo mejor será que estés a la mayor distancia que puedas.

—Me aseguraré de hacer un recado llegado el momento. Al embajador le gusta ser un incordio, así que estoy seguro de que podré convencerlo de pedirme algo absurdo y difícil de conseguir.

Helena asintió.

—Pues que sea un recado largo. Te traeré la bomba mañana.

—No. —La voz de Kaine restalló como un látigo, carente de la dulzura que había destilado hacía un momento—. No toleraré que Crowther te utilice para transportar una bomba.

Helena negó con la cabeza.

—Mientras los componentes no se junten, no se activará. Además, le hemos puesto un temporizador. No me va a explotar en las manos —lo tranquilizó—. No serás capaz de ensamblarla si no te enseño a hacerlo.

—Me da igual. Dile a Crowther que busque otra manera de traerla.

Se había quedado blanco como el papel y su piel empezaba a emitir ese característico brillo inhumano.

—Pero, si no la traigo yo, no volveré a verte hasta… hasta después de la explosión —dijo, dispuesta a recurrir al juego sucio con tal de hacerlo cooperar.

Kaine no cedió.

—Pues nos veremos después. Que se encargue otra persona.

A Helena se le entrecortó la respiración.

—Kaine…

—Recuerda cómo te encontré tras el otro bombardeo —dijo fulminándola con la mirada—. Tuve que ver cómo te abrían en canal para sacarte la metralla. Perdí la cuenta de las veces que estuviste a punto de morir en aquella mesa de operaciones. De haber estado un centímetro más cerca, la metralla te habría atravesado el corazón. Si quieres que coloque una bomba, lo haré encantado, pero no permitiré que te acerques a ella lo más mínimo. ¿Ha quedado claro?

Helena tragó saliva con amargura, agradecida por haberle contado lo justo y no haber mencionado que había sido ella quien la había fabricado.

—Está bien. Como tú quieras.

Se dio la vuelta para marcharse. Todavía tenía muchas tareas pendientes: hacer el inventario, terminar la bomba, ayudar a preparar el hospital. Por si fuera poco, habían vuelto a asignarle un turno en el servicio de urgencias.

Kaine tiró de ella para detenerla.

—Nos vemos aquí en unas horas.

—No creo que sea buen momento —le recordó negando con la cabeza.

Parecía haber olvidado que era él quien tenía prisa, porque se negó a soltarla. Helena deseó que su relación hubiera florecido mucho antes, pues habían perdido un tiempo precioso.

—Está bien —cedió al final—, pero ahora tienes que irte.

Kaine la soltó despacio.

—Te llamaré.

Después de informar a Crowther, Helena regresó al laboratorio externo, donde Shiseo y ella combinaron su resonancia para ensamblar las últimas piezas de la bomba. Se habían asegurado de que fuera lo más compacta posible, pero seguía ocupando casi tanto como el tamaño de un niño pequeño, así que tendrían que colocarla en el centro de una habitación.

Aunque las bombas no eran un invento alquímico como tal, llevaban casi un siglo prohibidas por considerarse armas poco elegantes. Pese a todo, eso no había frenado su desarrollo. De hecho, era bien sabido que Hevgoss sentía predilección por aquel tipo de tecnología, pues consideraba que los ponía en igualdad de condiciones con los alquimistas.

Con la correcta manipulación del aire y las llamas, Luc era capaz de crear bombas incendiarias. Gran parte de sus deberes se centraban en los sellos y los estudios técnicos que diseccionaban las distintas formas de manipular el fuego y convertirlo en un arma. Helena había utilizado muchos de esos conocimientos en la bomba.

La clave había sido diseñar un mecanismo que causara una explosión lo más violenta posible sin llegar a fundir la obsidiana.

Shiseo le había enseñado a fusionar aleaciones para combinarlas mediante un sello transmutacional doble. Era una técnica complicada y peligrosa, e, incluso con todos los sellos que habían dibujado para estabilizar su resonancia, Helena se había abrasado varios dedos casi hasta el hueso.

—¿Estás bien? —le preguntó Shiseo cuando se sentó para regenerarse lo más rápido posible.

Le dolían tanto las manos que casi no sentía la resonancia, pero los años de práctica habían conseguido que curar las terminaciones nerviosas le resultara tan fácil como respirar. Más adelante se regeneraría la dermis para que las cicatrices no fueran tan visibles.

—No ha sido nada —consiguió decir, parpadeando furiosa, mientras contemplaba las líneas que le surcaban los dedos y la palma de la mano.

Se tocó el esternón por la costumbre, buscando la suave hendidura en el hueso. La cicatriz ya no se le notaba tanto, pero el punto donde el hueso se había fracturado todavía le dolía.

—¿Está hecho?

Shiseo dejó dos piezas sobre la mesa y Helena las contempló agotada.

—Terminaremos mañana —le dijo el hombre sin apartar la vista de ella—. Tienes que curarte las manos y descansar un poco.

Ella le ofreció una leve sonrisa.

—Ya descansaré esta noche.

SE MANTUVO OCUPADA REVISANDO EL inventario médico hasta última hora de la noche. Alguien casi había dejado sin existencias las inyecciones de epinefrina, pero quienquiera que se las hubiera llevado no lo había hecho de manera oficial. Helena garabateó una nota cortante. Si Elain iba a tomar las riendas, al menos podía asegurarse de que se cumplieran las normas.

Estaba colocando una pila de vendas esterilizadas cuando el anillo se calentó.

Amaris apenas tuvo tiempo de aterrizar cuando Kaine levantó a Helena en volandas y alzaron el vuelo una vez más. En cuanto estuvieron a resguardo, él la pegó contra la pared y la besó con un hambre feroz.

Helena se aferró a él con fuerza y, aunque se le durmieron los dedos, casi ni lo notó.

Kaine le acunó el rostro entre ambas manos. Apoyó la frente en la suya dejando que sus alientos se entremezclaran antes de besarla de nuevo y guiarla por la casa con paso apresurado. Siempre iban contra reloj.

«Algún día —se prometió—, algún día le daré todo mi amor en un instante que no sea robado».

—¿Te encuentras bien? —le preguntó Kaine una vez que llegaron a una estancia lo bastante iluminada como para distinguir sus facciones.

Extendió una mano y Helena cayó en la cuenta de que, si la tocaba, usaría su resonancia y se daría cuenta de que se había hecho daño hacía poco tiempo, así que se le adelantó. Le estrechó una mano, le cerró los dedos y se la llevó contra el pecho.

—Sí —asintió—. Ahora ya estoy bien.

Kaine la miró. Helena sabía que estaba agotada, que había perdido peso y que estaba pálida por la falta de exposición a la luz natural. El bombardeo había destrozado la mayor parte de las ventanas del Cuartel General, pero habían tapiado incluso las que habían quedado intactas por miedo a que el aire arrastrara el anulitio y se colara en el edificio.

—Debería haberte llamado antes —dijo Kaine mientras le acariciaba la mejilla con el pulgar.

—No habría merecido la pena —replicó ella negando con la cabeza—. No deberías volar tan bajo. Es peligroso y alguien podría dispararte con obsidiana. —Un escalofrío le recorrió el cuerpo con tan solo imaginarlo—. No deberíamos estar haciendo esto. Somos unos necios por correr riesgos.

De pronto le costaba respirar. Kaine desenredó los dedos que tenían entrelazados y acunó el rostro de Helena entre sus manos, como si quisiera acallar sus pensamientos.

—Aquí estamos a salvo.

De momento. Durante un rato.

Pero no duraría. No para siempre.

De todas formas, asintió y se obligó a creerlo. No quería echar a perder el poco tiempo que les quedaba. Se puso de puntillas, lo besó y tiró de sus brazos para que la rodeara con ellos.

«Por favor, que esta no sea nuestra última vez».

No cerró los ojos. Observó todos los movimientos de Kaine en un intento por recordar cada segundo juntos. Quería grabarse a fuego en la memoria la sensación de su cuerpo en las manos, contra la piel, como si pudiera hacer de su secreto algo lo bastante real como para perdurar en el tiempo. Como si pudiese dejarlo escrito en el tejido del universo, de manera que la guerra no lograra borrarlo.

Más tarde, Kaine la estrechó contra su pecho y apoyó la barbilla sobre su cabeza mientras trazaba dibujos en su piel con los dedos.

«Voy a cuidar de ti. Nunca dejaré de hacerlo».

No lo dijo en voz alta, pero Helena percibió sus palabras como un cambio en el aire, y notó que su mandíbula se movía al articular los sonidos.

Había tenido la esperanza de poder dormir, de pasar una última hora en paz, pero estaba demasiado asustada. Cuando se incorporó, los ojos grises como el mercurio de Kaine mostraban una expresión cauta. Helena permaneció en silencio durante un momento, sosteniendo una de sus manos entre las suyas y admirando su rostro, pues esa versión de él era suya y solo suya.

Entrelazó los dedos con los de él mientras intentaba encontrar las palabras adecuadas.

—Existe la posibilidad… —empezó por fin—. Tenemos la esperanza de que esta ofensiva ponga fin a la guerra. No estamos seguros… No sabemos cuánto tiempo más aguantaremos si no sale como esperamos.

Notó que la mano de Kaine se crispaba entre las suyas.

—Si la guerra no termina… —A Helena se le estremeció el pecho y dejó escapar una carcajada estrangulada, al borde del sollozo—, pues imagino que seguiremos luchando. Pero, si ganamos…, n-no sé qué ocurrirá contigo. Lo siento. He intentado encontrar una manera… —Bajó la vista—. No he conseguido…

—No pasa nada.

Ella negó con la cabeza.

—A lo mejor recuperas tu alma si matamos a Morrough. No hay por qué dar por hecho lo contrario. Siempre hay una posibilidad. Quizá la Gema de los Cielos baste para…

Estaba dando palos de ciego y ambos lo sabían.

—Podría bastar —insistió estrechándole la mano—. Lo que intento decir es que, si todo sale bien cuando esto acabe, tienes que escapar, ¿vale? Huye tan rápido como puedas y no dejes que te capturen.

—¿Y qué pasará contigo? —preguntó él mirándola con suspicacia.

Helena bajó la vista y jugueteó con el anillo de Kaine. Hacía mucho tiempo que no veía el que ella llevaba.

—Ya me conoces. Estaré en el hospital. Habrá muchos heridos, así que no podré marcharme enseguida… Tú asegúrate de escapar y yo ya te alcanzaré.

Kaine resopló.

—Si sobrevivo, no pienso ir a ningún lado sin ti.

Helena le puso los dedos en los labios para hacerlo callar.

—No, no puedes arriesgarte a que te atrapen.

Él la apartó, pero Helena no iba a permitir que la interrumpiera. Llevaba días dándole vueltas al asunto y creía que era muy poco probable que Crowther fuera a dejarla ir sin que pagara por haber usado la nigromancia. Con un poco de suerte, se limitarían a expulsarla de la Llama Eterna. Pero, incluso a pesar de ser la decisión más rápida y discreta, podría llevarles semanas o meses.

—Ve al Sur, en dirección al mar. Yo me reuniré contigo en cuanto pueda. Te buscaré y haremos lo que siempre hemos dicho: desapareceremos.

Kaine entornó los ojos todavía más.

—¿Y cuánto tiempo crees que tendré que esperarte?

—No lo sé —admitió Helena bajando la mirada—. Puede que… tarde un poco.

—¿Por qué?

—Porque… habrá mucho que hacer cuando la guerra acabe. Aun así, estoy segura de que preferirán que desaparezca cuando ya no me necesiten, así que iré a buscarte, ¿vale? Creo que hacerlo así será lo mejor para ti. A lo mejor descubres que quieres otra cosa cuando tengas la verdadera posibilidad de elegir…

Kaine la agarró por la nuca y tiró de ella hasta que sus rostros estuvieron a punto de tocarse.

—Eres mía —dijo casi contra sus labios—. Mía. Me lo has prometido. La Resistencia te vendió a mí. No pienso ir a ningún lado sin ti. Mataré a quien se atreva a tocarte, ya sea inmortal o no.

No esperó a que respondiera y la besó como si la estuviera marcando con un hierro al rojo vivo.

Shiseo era la única persona aparte de ella que podía encargarse de entregar la bomba. Helena y él habían cubierto el exterior del artefacto con una delgada capa del *mo'lian'shi* que Shiseo había extraído del polvo de anulitio y con otra del elixir de distorsión que Helena había preparado. Shiseo había conseguido alterar su composición para hacer que funcionara en superficies más amplias. Una vez que la bomba estuviera lista, sería difícil de detectar. Además, su inercia exterior la volvería invisible a la resonancia.

Cuando terminaron, Helena se quitó su anillo y lo estudió con detenimiento. La distorsión ya no era tan efectiva como al principio. Si la arrestaban, la registrarían y le quitarían cualquier metal que llevara encima. Y eso incluía el anillo de Kaine.

—¿Crees que el *mo'lian'shi* interferiría con un enlace espejo? —preguntó.

Shiseo contempló la joya apenas visible.

—Si dejas una pequeña zona sin cubrir, lo más seguro es que puedas seguir usándolo. —La miró con expresión comprensiva—. Salvo que te vieras sometida a un registro exhaustivo, eso lo mantendría oculto en caso de que alguien utilice la resonancia contigo.

No necesitaba saber más. Murmuró una disculpa en silencio, pensando en la quemazón que Kaine estaba a punto de sentir y cubrió casi toda la superficie del anillo con *mo'lian'shi*. Al cabo de un rato, cuando se hubo enfriado, bañó la joya de nuevo con el elixir de distorsión para asegurarse de que quedaba bien escondida y la vio desaparecer.

Mientras Shiseo entregaba la bomba, Helena fue a comprobar cómo estaba Lila. Si el hospital acababa saturado de heridos, no sabía cuándo tendría la oportunidad de verla otra vez.

El bulto que crecía en su vientre ya era imposible de disimular, y Lila, consumida por las dudas, empezaba a preguntarse si había tomado la decisión correcta. Se había mordido las uñas hasta la raíz.

—No me puedo creer que esta sea ya la batalla final —dijo mientras veía a los soldados moverse de un lado a otro por la ventana—. Debería estar ahí con ellos.

—No era algo que hubieras podido prever —le respondió Helena, agotada.

Ya era demasiado tarde para que Lila cambiara de opinión.

—¿Crees que ha llegado el momento? ¿Tenemos opciones de ganar?

—Tantas como la situación lo permite.

Helena estaba aterrorizada, pero, independientemente de que ganaran o perdieran, la guerra tenía que acabar ya. No podían seguir así para siempre.

—Está despierto —dijo Lila, que extendió una mano hacia Helena—. Ven a notar cómo se mueve. Justo aquí.

Lila cogió la mano de Helena y la puso sobre su vientre, por encima del hueso de la cadera. Al cabo de un instante, Helena notó una extraña agitación sin necesidad de recurrir a la resonancia.

—¿Lo has notado? —preguntó Lila.

Helena asintió y recurrió a su don para colarse en su cuerpo y encontrar el latido del bebé, tan rápido como el aleteo de un pajarillo.

Pero ya no dio ninguna patada más.

—Seguro que ya ha vuelto a cerrar los ojos, el muy dormilón —dijo Lila. Helena no sabía por qué estaba tan segura de que el bebé era un niño, pero ya lo llamaba Apollo o, simplemente, Pol, de manera cariñosa—. Deberías ver lo mucho que se mueve por las noches. Yo creo que se pasa las horas dando volteretas, porque te juro que lo noto clavarme los pies en las costillas.

—Vaya, me pregunto de quién habrá heredado los genes de atleta problemático —comentó Helena con aspereza al apartar la mano del vientre de su amiga.

—Podrá disfrutar de todos los buenos momentos que nosotros tuvimos que perdernos. —Lila se bajó la camisa—. Me alegro de que vaya a vivir una infancia en paz, ¿sabes? Estoy segura de que nacerán muchos niños en los próximos años y todos estudiarán juntos en la Academia, igual que nosotros. ¿Te ves teniendo hijos en el futuro?

Helena negó con la cabeza sin decir nada.

—A lo mejor cambias de idea algún día —insistió como si tratara de convencerla—. Solo tienes que encontrar al hombre adecuado. Estoy segura de que serías una madre fantástica.

—Soy sanadora. Ese camino no es para nosotras.

—Pero fue la guerra lo que te obligó a convertirte en sanadora. Nadie espera que sigas ejerciendo cuando todo haya terminado.

Para ser alguien tan consciente de lo excepcional y peligroso que era el cargo que ocupaba, Lila no parecía darse cuenta de que las oportunidades de las que ella había disfrutado, ya fuera por la familia en la que había nacido o por sus propias habilidades, no estaban al alcance de la mayoría. Lila poseía un talento único, una belleza que no se quedaba atrás y un apellido que arrastraba siglos de historia. Ella tenía el privilegio de poder saltarse las normas sin que hubiera consecuencias, pero el resto del mundo no tenía esa suerte. Y mucho menos Helena.

Decidió cambiar de tema:

—Creo que deberías decírselo a Luc. Merece saberlo antes de la batalla. Además, si la cosa se tuerce, la Llama Eterna sabrá que tiene que priorizar tu seguridad.

Para sorpresa de Helena, Lila guardó silencio durante un buen rato.

—Ya lo sabe —admitió en un susurro, sin atreverse a encontrar la mirada de Helena.

—¿Perdón?

—Se coló por la ventana cuando me pusieron en cuarentena y lo vi tan preocupado que tuve que contarle la verdad. Él me dijo que me obligarían a marcharme si alguien se enteraba, que me enviarían a Novis. He insistido en mantenerlo en secreto porque Luc me necesita. Me hizo prometer que no se lo contaría a nadie.

Helena se quedó muda de asombro.

—¿Lo ha sabido desde el principio? ¿Y cómo es que no se ha quejado de que me haya estado encargando yo de tus cuidados si sabía lo del embarazo?

Si Luc había permitido aquello, ¿por qué se había mostrado tan inflexible con lo de Titus? No tenía sentido.

Lila se puso colorada.

—Lo siento. Quería decírtelo, pero sabía que Luc se enfadaría. Todavía no se encuentra muy bien.

—Tengo que irme —dijo Helena poniéndose de pie con torpeza.

Lila se adelantó para intentar detenerla, colocándose delante de la puerta.

—No, está claro que te ha molestado. Por favor, déjame que te lo explique.

Helena la miró. Lila se parecía tanto a su padre que era como una versión femenina de él: igual estatura, el cabello rubio, los ojos azules…, e incluso compartían una cicatriz en el lateral del rostro.

—No eres tú quien debe darme explicaciones. Voy a hablar con Luc.

Lo buscó por todas partes, pero cada vez que preguntaba por él le daban una respuesta distinta: estaba en una reunión, descansando, en el patio, en la sala común… Siempre parecía sacarle un par de minutos de ventaja.

Al final, logró rastrearlo hasta el hospital, pero estaba en una habitación privada y vigilada, sin acceso para visitas.

Helena lo esperó hasta que vio a Elain salir con una bandeja llena de jeringuillas y frasquitos vacíos. Tenía el ceño fruncido en una expresión tensa.

—Necesito ver a Luc —le dijo.

—Está descansando —respondió Elain con un sobresalto al verla.

Helena inspeccionó el contenido de la bandeja, aunque Elain trató de ocultárselo.

—¿Por qué le estás dando todo eso? —le preguntó mientras examinaba cada frasquito—. No deberías mezclar esos medicamentos. Además, Luc es demasiado joven para necesitar muchos de ellos. Y… —cogió una jeringuilla cuya etiqueta estaba escrita con su propia caligrafía—, esto es solo para casos de extrema urgencia. Si se abusa de ello, puede causar una insuficiencia cardiaca. ¿Quién ha aprobado este tratamiento?

Un destello de indignación surcó la mirada de Elain.

—Yo soy su sanadora.

CAPÍTULO 63

Augustus 1787

AL DÍA SIGUIENTE, EL TIEMPO pareció ralentizarse mientras desalojaban el Cuartel General y los soldados se dirigían a sus respectivos puestos de combate. Helena no tuvo ocasión de hablar con Luc antes de que este partiera.

El resto de las sanadoras, el equipo médico y ella misma prepararon el hospital a la espera de recibir las primeras noticias y heridos. Por la hora que marcaban las manecillas del reloj, la bomba ya debería haber estallado. Sin embargo, no se oyó explosión alguna ni sintieron una sacudida.

No había nada que indicara que la batalla hubiese comenzado.

Por supuesto, cabía esperar que la bomba, pequeña y diseñada para estallar en un espacio cerrado, no generara una onda expansiva detectable desde tan lejos. Además, la mayor parte del enfrentamiento tendría lugar en la isla Oeste.

Saber todo aquello no hacía que la espera fuera más llevadera. Helena presentía que la guerra estaba llegando a su fin después de tantos años y ninguno de los posibles desenlaces le resultaba reconfortante.

Tal vez la Resistencia lograba la victoria, a lo mejor todo salía bien, pero entonces Kaine se vería obligado a desaparecer y ella no tendría forma de saber si estaba vivo o muerto, si había quedado atrapado entre los escombros o si había conseguido huir muy lejos.

Tendría que salir a buscarlo para averiguarlo.

El tictac del reloj hacía que se estremeciera. Las camilleras, las médicas y las sanadoras charlaban entre ellas, pero Helena permanecía inmóvil, con las costillas constriñéndole los pulmones.

«Has cometido un error, has fabricado mal la bomba y han capturado a Kaine mientras la colocaba y ahora lo están torturando, pero tú no sabes nada. Todo el mundo va a morir por tu culpa».

Empezó a notar que el hormigueo del entumecimiento se le extendía por los dedos y las manos.

Entonces las puertas del hospital se abrieron de par en par. La estancia pareció desdibujarse. Helena no pudo distinguir quién había entrado, pero oyó los gritos: se había producido una explosión en la isla Oeste. La Resistencia había atacado.

Helena se tambaleó intentando sentir algo, pero todavía seguía vacía por dentro.

Un estallido de calor le recorrió el dedo una única vez.

Se miró la mano, el anillo apenas visible, y le cedieron las piernas.

Se derrumbó y se echó a llorar mientras un estallido de dolor le partía el pecho en dos. Oyó voces a su alrededor, pero no alcanzó a entender lo que decían. Lo único que parecía capaz de hacer era tomar aire, pero sus pulmones se negaban a cooperar.

Una mano cálida la agarró del codo y la ayudó a incorporarse.

—Sentémonos un momento —dijo Pace al tiempo que le pasaba un brazo por los hombros y la guiaba hasta su pequeño despacho, en el cuarto de los informes—. Elain nos avisará si traen a algún herido.

Helena, que se dejó llevar con los ojos cerrados cuando Pace la obligó a sentarse en una silla, se tocó el pecho para notar la cicatriz oculta bajo las ropas e intentar que el ritmo de sus latidos se relajara.

Cuando por fin abrió los ojos de nuevo, encontró a Pace observándola.

—¿Qué te pasa? —le preguntó.

—Nada —dijo negando con la cabeza—. Es solo que estoy cansada.

Pace esbozó una mueca que le arrugó todo el rostro.

—¿Sabías que llega un punto en que los efectos del Estrago se disparan y crecen exponencialmente?

Helena se encogió de hombros.

—Se dicen muchas cosas sobre las sanadoras. Empiezo a sospechar que ni la mitad son ciertas.

—Tal vez, pero no creo que nadie haya llevado su don para la sanación tan lejos como tú. Hace ya un tiempo que no te encuentras bien. ¿Pensabas que no me iba a dar cuenta de que estás complementando tus tratamientos con tónicos e inyecciones? Las aprendizas apenas saben manejarse sin ellos, pero tú has pasado años apoyándote únicamente en tu resonancia. Por lo que sabemos, podrías estar perdiendo años de vida cada vez que…

—No creo que sea eso…

Se llevó distraídamente la mano a la cadena que solía pender de su cuello, pese a que hacía tiempo que ya no la llevaba.

Pace meneó la cabeza con gesto preocupado.

—¿Es por el anulitio? Estamos viendo muchos efectos secundarios desde el bombardeo y tú has sido una de las supervivientes que más expuesta ha estado a la sustancia. Y eso sin contar tu lesión. —Antes de que Helena pudiera negarlo, Pace continuó—: No sabemos qué efectos puede tener a largo plazo. Sospecho que las fiebres que Luc está sufriendo apuntan a que tiene restos de anulitio en el cerebro.

Helena la miró confundida.

—¿Luc está sufriendo episodios febriles?

Pace suspiró.

—Ya viste cómo llegó tras el rescate.

—Pensaba que había sido algo pasajero —apuntó Helena con un asentimiento.

—Intenta disimular para que no nos preocupemos, pero a veces se pone tan mal que delira, se araña la piel y no deja que nadie entre en su habitación. Ni siquiera Sebastian. Y grita cosas como «Sacádmelo de dentro». Elain ha tenido que sedarlo varias veces para que no se haga daño.

Helena tenía la sensación de haber pasado meses mirando un rompecabezas desde el ángulo incorrecto. De pronto lo entendía todo.

—¿Dice «Sacádmelo de dentro»? —Oía su propia voz como si llegara de muy lejos.

—Es lo que más repite.

Le dio un vuelco el corazón.

—¿Podrías… describirme las fiebres que sufre?

Pace frunció el ceño.

—Bueno, yo solo lo he examinado un par de veces. Es Elain quien lleva su caso, porque se muestra más dispuesto a cooperar con ella. Cree que la fiebre se debe a una inflamación del cerebro. Los síntomas que presenta son delirios y taquicardias. Al principio pensábamos que se debía a las lesiones orgánicas, pero ahora creemos que son afecciones separadas.

—¿Y el opio para qué es?

La mujer suspiró y miró hacia otro lado.

—Todo apunta a que lo que le causa las fiebres es alguna afección nerviosa. Mantenerlo calmado impide que le suba la temperatura más de la cuenta. Lo hemos intentado todo, pero inhalar los vapores del opio es lo único que le funciona. Cuando las alucinaciones toman el control de su cuerpo, tarda días en recuperarse y requiere un tratamiento intensivo.

—Pero de esa manera solo se consigue… enmascarar los síntomas. Así no se va a curar. Deberíais haberme contado lo que estaba pasando.

Era imposible.

—Helena —dijo la enfermera Pace con firmeza—, tanto Maier como Elain y yo le hemos hecho mil y una pruebas. Su enfermedad no tiene causa. Está todo en su cabeza. Lo único que nos queda es mantener los síntomas a raya. Luc pidió expresamente que no te involucráramos. Cada vez que alguien menciona tu nombre, se pone peor.

—¿Y nunca os habéis preguntado por qué le pasa eso?

Pace la miró con una expresión compasiva.

—Tú tampoco es que tengas mucha experiencia con este tipo de fiebres.

Helena negó con la cabeza. La mujer se equivocaba. Había aprendido mucho sobre el tema en las últimas semanas y sabía exactamente cuál era su causa: la animancia.

Sin embargo, tampoco era la primera vez que lidiaba con la enfermedad. Ya había visto a alguien sufrir episodios febriles como esos antes, con los mismos síntomas que Pace había descrito: temperaturas altísimas con las que el cerebro parecía querer quemar algo desde dentro; autolesiones, gritos idénticos a los de Luc con eso de «Sacádmelo de dentro»…

Lo había presenciado justo antes de que su padre fuera asesinado: en el hospital de campaña.

La cuestión era que Luc no portaba un talismán como aquellos liches. Lo habían comprobado varias veces. Deberían haber dado con él ya…, a no ser que no lo hubieran cubierto con lumitio y fuera indetectable.

Todos habían dado por hecho que, si Morrough no había matado a Luc, había sido porque no le había dado tiempo a hacerlo.

Pero a lo mejor habían llegado tarde.

Se levantó de un salto y, cuando Pace intentó agarrarla, Helena salió corriendo del despacho para cruzar el hospital e ir directa al salón de mando. Allí no había nadie salvo un cadete, que la estudió con nerviosismo y le dijo que no tenía permiso para estar allí.

Ella lo fulminó con la mirada.

—¿Sabes dónde está Crowther? Necesito hablar con él de inmediato.

El chico negó con la cabeza, molesto por tener que vigilar una estancia vacía.

—No, antes también lo estaban buscando. Por lo que parece, no se le ha vuelto a ver desde anoche.

No tenía sentido.

Helena tenía la sensación de estar metida en una trampa en efecto dominó, de que las piezas iban cayendo a su alrededor y cada vez tenía menos margen de maniobra.

—¿Sabes dónde está la unidad de Luc?

El cadete puso los ojos en blanco y se irguió.

—Eso es información clasificada…

Helena se fijó en que había una banderita dorada en medio de un mar azul en el mapa que descansaba sobre la mesa, así que se dio la vuelta y se marchó dejando al muchacho con la palabra en la boca. Corrió al laboratorio y reunió todo el material que pudo. Primero, guardó su nuevo juego de cuchillos y varias de las armas de obsidiana con las que Shiseo había estado experimentando. Luego, arrasó con los suministros de sanación que quedaban.

Shiseo entró cargando con una caja del laboratorio externo cuando Helena estaba metiendo a presión un último frasco en la bolsa, ya a rebosar. Estaba bastante segura de que su compañero sería la única persona que aceptaría una advertencia por su parte sin cuestionarla.

—Hay que salir de aquí ya. Coge todo lo que puedas y llévatelo al otro laboratorio. Te avisaré cuando las cosas se hayan calmado. No tengo tiempo para explicártelo, pero está a punto de pasar algo terrible.

De allí fue corriendo en dirección al despacho de Crowther, pero lo encontró vacío. ¿Dónde se había metido? No podía permitirse perder tiempo buscándolo, así que desistió y salió del Cuartel General.

Cruzó la isla a pie guiándose por los pasos elevados para saber qué partes de la ciudad seguían intactas y, cuando empezó a oler a humo y a carne quemada, confirmó que iba en la dirección correcta.

Les pidió actualizaciones a todas las unidades de la Resistencia que encontró por el camino. Pese a las múltiples contradicciones, todas coincidieron en que muchos necrómatas se habían desplomado a la vez, lo cual había dejado a los aspirantes solos para defender distritos enteros. La Resistencia estaba apilando los cadáveres y quemándolos para que los inmarcesibles no pudieran recuperarlos y reanimarlos.

Ante esas buenas noticias, Helena empezó a dudar de su corazonada. ¿Acaso estaba dejándose llevar por la paranoia? Todo iba bien. Sin embargo, se negó a darse la vuelta. Tenía que encontrar a Luc.

Un comandante de espaldas anchas a quien Helena reconocía vagamente por formar parte de la unidad de su amigo salió de un edificio.

—¿Marino? —la llamó con voz vacilante.

—Tengo que ver a Luc —le dijo ella aferrándose a uno de los cuchillos de obsidiana con tanta fuerza que se clavó la empuñadura en la palma de la mano.

—Me temo que no está aquí, sino en el frente.

Helena tenía la sensación de parecer enloquecida desde fuera.

—Lo sé, pero es urgente. Me pondré a ayudar al equipo médico hasta que regrese.

El comandante se quedó confundido, pero no opuso resistencia.

Sanar a los soldados en el frente no era una tarea tan organizada como en el hospital. Casi todo su esfuerzo se centró en cortar hemorragias y cerrar heridas, deteniéndose solo para tratar las lesiones más leves. La prioridad era atender las intervenciones más urgentes y enviar a los pacientes al Cuartel General para que allí recibieran el tratamiento adecuado.

Todos creían que la explosión había sido un accidente o un sabotaje. Nadie se había planteado siquiera que la bomba tuviera algo que ver con la Resistencia.

Decían que había sido un milagro, que los dioses estaban de su lado.

Ya habían empezado a llamarlo el Día de la Victoria. Pronto recuperarían el control de la ciudad.

Cada vez fueron llegando menos heridos, dado que, cuanto más se adentraba la unidad en la isla Oeste, menos merecía la pena recorrer todo el camino de vuelta. El comandante al mando estaba preguntando por radio si debían acercarse más al núcleo de la batalla. No les habían dado instrucciones en ese aspecto.

La base de operaciones en la que se encontraban era un edificio viejo del nivel intermedio de la ciudad razonablemente fácil de defender gracias a sus muros resistentes y ventanas pequeñas. Pero el ambiente empezaba a ser irrespirable por el calor que desprendían los soldados hacinados y en constante movimiento. El camión médico había salido en dirección al hospital y todavía no había regresado.

—¡Han atacado el Cuartel General! —gritó alguien cuando Helena estaba cerrando una herida profunda en la cara interna del muslo de un soldado.

Todos levantaron la vista y se miraron confundidos.

El conductor del camión entró tambaleándose y jadeando, con una herida en la cabeza.

—¡Los inmarcesibles han capturado el Cuartel General!

Se hizo un silencio sepulcral mientras la conmoción se extendía por la estancia. En todos los años de conflicto, los inmarcesibles jamás habían llegado a tocar el Cuartel General. Se habían tomado infinidad de precauciones para protegerlo. Era el lugar más seguro de toda la ciudad.

Los soldados reaccionaron de golpe y rodearon al conductor para pedirle información con un clamor de voces furiosas. Helena se abrió camino hasta él para curarle la cabeza. No era más que un rasguño, pero también tenía las manos destrozadas.

—He pasado por todos los puestos de control —explicó el hombre mientras permitía que Helena le ladeara la cabeza para cerrarle la herida—. Comprobaron mis papeles y me dejaron pasar. Todo parecía… en orden. Bajé a los heridos en cuanto paré el camión. —Se pasó una mano por la frente y se la manchó de sangre—. Todo estaba tranquilo, demasiado tranquilo. El puto silencio siempre me pone de los nervios, así que intento llenarlo de alguna manera, ¿sabéis? Le pregunté algo a un guardia, pero no me respondió. Pensaba que la sangre que llevaban encima era de los heridos. Hice otra pregunta y todos vinieron a por mí. Ahí fue cuando entendí lo que pasaba. Eran necrómatas, cadáveres frescos, todavía calientes. Me monté en el camión, atropellé a unos cuantos y no miré atrás. Traté de informar en el primer puesto de control, pero tampoco respondían. Por si fuera poco, habían levantado las barricadas, así que tuve que echar a correr sin saber muy bien adónde ir.

Mientras asimilaban lo que el conductor contaba, el silencio casi se podía cortar con un cuchillo. Era inconcebible.

Para infiltrarse en el Cuartel General, los inmarcesibles habrían necesitado conocer a fondo los protocolos de seguridad, disponer de un espía con una autorización de alto nivel y estar familiarizados con las órdenes de los puestos de control para preparar a los necrómatas. ¿Cómo podía haber pasado? ¿Cómo es que nadie había dado una sola señal de alarma?

El comandante trató de contactar con el Cuartel General por radio, pero no obtuvieron respuesta.

—Tratad de comunicaros con quien podáis sin hacer saltar las alarmas de los inmarcesibles. Tú, tú y tú —dijo el comandante señalando a tres de sus hombres—, id al puesto de control más cercano.

Solo dos regresaron.

—Estaban todos muertos —explicó uno de ellos, que se presionaba el vientre con una mano para detener la hemorragia que le habían causado—. Nos estaban esperando.

El comandante envió a todos los soldados a informar de lo ocurrido, así como a interceptar y ordenar la retirada de cualquier camión o unidad con la que se encontraran por el camino. Mientras tanto, él se sentó ante la radio para repetir un enrevesado mensaje cargado de jerga militar por los distintos canales y discutir con todas las personas que le respondieron, porque nadie quería creerse lo que contaba.

Luc abrió la puerta del edificio de un bandazo y entró seguido de Sebastian, que caminaba unos pasos por detrás e intentaba disimular una evidente cojera, y del resto del batallón.

El chico estaba pálido. Tenía el rostro manchado de sangre y humo, y, aunque se encontraba en los huesos, sus ojos azules desprendían un brillo febril. En vez de dirigirse al comandante a cargo, centró toda su atención en Helena.

—¿Qué haces aquí? —le preguntó.

Ella se puso de pie.

—Tengo que hablar contigo. Es urgente.

Luc la miró estupefacto y luego se dirigió al comandante.

—¿Quién la ha dejado entrar aquí?

—Es por Lila —dijo Helena antes de que cualquiera de los presentes tuviera oportunidad de responder.

El efecto de sus palabras fue instantáneo. Luc se volvió hacia ella y tragó saliva antes de dejar vagar la mirada por la estancia.

—De acuerdo —cedió al cabo de un instante—, hablemos. Prepara a todo el mundo, Sebastian. Vamos a recuperar el control del Cuartel General.

—No, que venga con nosotros. Lo curaré mientras hablamos para ahorrar tiempo.

Luc la miró con desconfianza, aunque asintió. Era el mismo de siempre, pero... era innegable que había algo raro en él.

«Deberías haberlo sabido, deberías haberlo notado».

Luc se volvió hacia el comandante, que parecía perdido.

—Lleva a los combatientes de vuelta al cuartel. Sebastian y yo os seguiremos enseguida.

Mientras se adentraban en la nave, que estaba comunicada con el edificio contiguo, Helena se metió uno de los cuchillos de obsidiana en la parte trasera de la cinturilla de la falda y lo ocultó bajo la chaqueta.

Sebastian tenía unas cuantas costillas rotas y una herida de arma blanca en la pierna, justo en el punto débil de la armadura.

Helena le dio uno de los últimos frasquitos de medicina que le quedaban para regenerar tejidos y facilitar la recuperación de la sangre perdida. Sebastian se quitó el peto antes de que pudiera detenerlo.

—¿Qué pasa con Lila? —preguntó Luc en cuanto cerraron la puerta y los tres se quedaron solos.

—Nada. Está bien. —A Luc se le iluminó el rostro de rabia y Helena encontró su mirada—. Lo que no sabía era que estabas al tanto de lo del bebé.

—¿De qué habla? —intervino Sebastian sorprendido.

Luc se puso tan tenso que el cambio de posición hizo que las piezas de su armadura chocaran entre sí. Sin embargo, mantuvo la expresión controlada. Ni siquiera miró a su compañero.

—¿De qué bebé habla? —insistió el hombre.

—¿Por eso has venido hasta aquí? —preguntó Luc con un brillo gélido en la mirada—. ¿Para pedirme explicaciones?

A Helena le latía tan rápido el corazón que casi le retumbaba en el pecho.

—No, he venido porque no entiendo por qué no me dejas curar a Titus, pero sí cuidar de tu heredero.

—¿Qué has hecho, Luc? —preguntó Sebastian.

El chico, que no le quitaba el ojo de encima a Helena, ignoró a su paladín.

—Lila puede defenderse sola, pero bastante la has liado ya con Titus.

Helena sintió que se le cerraba la garganta, pero enseguida lo tuvo claro: ese no era Luc.

Debería haberse dado cuenta antes, pero había pasado tanto tiempo temiendo que su amigo le diera la espalda, que se abriera un abismo inevitable entre ellos, que no había llegado a cuestionarse lo que estaba pasando.

—¿Sabes una cosa? —preguntó desviando la mirada—. Yo estaba en uno de los hospitales de campaña durante las masacres cuando los liches se infiltraron entre nuestras filas usando cuerpos vivos. Según parece, estos no toleran la presencia de otra alma en su interior y reaccionan a ella como si de una infección se tratara. La temperatura del cerebro afectado sube hasta que enferman, gritan y se autolesionan repitiendo cosas como «Sacádmelo de dentro» hasta morir.

Tomó aire despacio cuando terminó de curar la pierna de Sebastian.

—¿Conoces a alguien que sufra esas fiebres, Luc?

Sebastian se había quedado inmóvil.

—Pues me temo que no —dijo Luc negando con la cabeza.

Habló con tranquilidad, pero la tensión en la habitación crecía a cada instante.

Helena localizó las fracturas en las costillas de Sebastian.

—Te entregaste para salvar a Lila. Sabías que te costaría la vida, pero no dudaste en hacerlo. Una vez me dijiste que la nombraste tu paladina porque querías tenerla siempre a tu lado para protegerla, pese a saber que no debías ponerte en riesgo por ella. Sé lo mucho que sufrías cada vez que Lila se hacía daño. Ni siquiera querías que le diera permiso para volver al campo de batalla después de que perdiera la pierna. —Mientras hablaba, siguió buscando algo que le recordara a la persona que conocía—. Sin embargo, ahora que lleva un hijo tuyo en su vientre, en vez de trasladarla a un lugar seguro, has decidido mantenerla aislada durante meses. Y, por si fuera poco, en estos momentos deberías tener todos los motivos del mundo para creer que la han capturado y que será una de las primeras en morir. Sin embargo, en vez de haber ido a salvarla, te has quedado aquí conmigo. Luc jamás habría actuado así.

—¿Qué has hecho, Luc? —le preguntó Sebastian con una expresión horrorizada.

—¿Quién eres? —le preguntó Helena.

Fue como si alguien hubiera descorrido una cortina. Por un momento, Luc mantuvo la expresión y actitud que lo caracterizaba, pero luego suspiró y pareció desaparecer bajo su propia piel.

—Bueno. —Esbozó una sonrisa que parecía una garganta rajada de lado a lado—. Pensaba que os daríais cuenta hace meses, pero la adoración que sentís por los Holdfast os ciega.

Helena notó que Sebastian temblaba bajo sus dedos mientras los dos contemplaban a la criatura que tenían ante ellos. Buscó a tientas el cuchillo que había ocultado en la parte trasera de la falda.

—¿Quién eres? —volvió a preguntar.

—He tenido tantos nombres que ya no me acuerdo de todos —dijo la persona que vestía el cuerpo de Luc—, pero hubo un tiempo, hace mucho, en que mi hermano me llamaba Cetus.

A Helena se le desencajó la expresión.

—¿Cetus?

Él ladeó la cabeza mientras ella la movía con incredulidad.

Si decía la verdad, era más antiguo que Paladia, más antiguo que el linaje de los Holdfast, más antiguo incluso que la Primera Guerra Nigromántica. Nadie podía vivir tanto tiempo. Cetus era un mito creado a partir de los siglos por alquimistas que escribían bajo un mismo seudónimo. No era una persona real.

Debía de estar mintiendo para distraerla.

—Le hice un reconocimiento y no encontré ningún talismán —dijo Helena tratando de mantener la calma—. ¿Cómo es posible?

El supuesto Cetus ladeó la cabeza de nuevo para crujir el cuello de Luc, como si su cuerpo fuera una armadura que no se ajustaba del todo a sus medidas.

—Mi hermano y yo nacimos vinculados. Llegamos a este mundo como uno solo cuando abandonamos el útero de nuestra madre. La dejamos seca por dentro y las llamas de su pira funeraria nos lamieron la piel y nos marcaron de por vida. Quienes se dignaban reconocer nuestra existencia nos decían que estábamos malditos. La sangre que compartimos lleva siglos fluyendo y, ahora por fin volvemos a ser uno, como siempre debería haber sido —dijo señalándose a sí mismo.

—¿Estás… emparentado con Luc? —preguntó ella con incredulidad.

La misma sonrisa de antes se adueñó de los labios de su amigo.

—Deberías haber visto a Orion. No te haces una idea del efecto que causaba en los demás. La gente besaba el suelo que pisaba. Encandilaba a cualquiera con una sola mirada. Nos consiguió mecenas, alojamiento y financiación para que yo pudiera llevar a cabo el trabajo de mi vida y él encontrara un público que lo adorara. Habría hecho lo que fuera por ganarse la admiración de los demás, así que yo le enseñé trucos para hacerlo. Orion pensaba que lo del oro y el fuego bastaría, que podríamos comprarnos un reino entero. —Cetus esbozó una expresión desdeñosa—. Pero yo aspiraba a más. Los reinos y los reyes acaban desapareciendo con el tiempo, y mi hermano y yo estábamos hechos para la eternidad. Éramos dioses.

»Yo nunca he tenido el carisma natural de mi hermano, pero no se me da mal actuar. Orion llamaba tanto la atención que la mayoría ni siquiera reparaba en mí, así que me hice pasar por él y convencí a algunos de sus seguidores para que cooperaran. Necesitaba esa confianza que le profesaban con tanta facilidad. La necesitaba para mi trabajo, ese del que Orion tanto se había beneficiado siempre. Sin embargo, cuando se enteró de lo que había hecho, cuando descubrió cuál era la fuente de mi nuevo poder, me trató como a un monstruo y me abandonó. Sin embargo, sabía que cambiaría de parecer una vez que desentrañara el verdadero secreto de la inmortalidad. Sabía que me suplicaría el perdón cuando se diera cuenta de que los humanos no son más que marionetas y viera lo que yo podía ofrecerle.

—Tú eras el Nigromante —dijo Helena, que había comenzado a atar cabos—. El mismo que reunió aquel culto en Caudalón. Después de crear la Gema de los Cielos, le pediste a Orion que se uniera a ti, pero intentó matarte cuando vio lo que habías hecho.

Un destello de rabia surcó el rostro de Cetus.

—Esos malditos paladines lo pusieron en mi contra. De haber estado solo, habría atendido a razones…

—¿Por qué has vuelto? Llevabas medio milenio desaparecido. Los Holdfast no quieren tener nada que ver contigo. ¿Por qué ayudas a Morrough?

Helena estudió a su amigo o lo que quedaba de él. Estaba demacrado, empapado de sudor hasta los huesos, y era evidente que se estaba muriendo, aunque de forma más gradual que las víctimas del hospital de campaña.

Luc se rio. Pese a que había oído su risa miles de veces a lo largo de los años, nunca había sonado tan maliciosa y burlona como entonces.

—Yo soy Morrough.

Sebastian se puso de pie de un salto, pero, antes de que tuviera la oportunidad de coger un arma, Luc desenvainó su espada y lo detuvo chasqueando la lengua.

—En realidad, soy una parte de él. Cuando el valiente y joven Luc se entregó a mí, sentí curiosidad por ver si nos parecíamos. Sobre todo, porque yo llevo mucho tiempo en este mundo y él estaba… fresco. Vinculé una parte de mi alma a uno de mis huesos y lo coloqué en su interior. Tenía la esperanza de que su cuerpo me aceptara…, de que nos convirtiéramos en uno, tal y como planeaba hacer con mi hermano. Pero se cree tan moralmente superior como Orion. Por suerte, la sanadora Boyle es una persona tan desesperada por complacer a los demás que no se ha opuesto nunca a mantenerlo sedado para mí.

—Entonces ¿Luc sigue vivo? —preguntó Helena con voz temblorosa.

—Por supuesto. Al fin y al cabo, este es su cuerpo. —Morrough, Cetus o quienquiera que fuera la persona que ocupaba el cuerpo de su amigo se señaló a sí mismo—. Yo no soy más que una sombra en las profundidades de su mente. O lo habría sido si no se hubiera vuelto loco tratando de sacarme de su interior. Al administrarle calmantes, me dieron vía libre para tomar el control.

—¿Lo estás manejando como si fuera un necrómata? ¿Es así como os habéis infiltrado en el Cuartel General?

Una mueca ofendida retorció el rostro de Luc.

—No soy una simple marioneta. He encontrado la manera de alcanzar el objetivo de mi ser primario. Si me matáis, a mí no me pasará nada…, pero Luc no tendrá tanta suerte. En cuanto a lo del Cuartel General… —Negó con la cabeza—. Me temo que el joven principado no es el único traidor entre vuestras filas.

—Pero ¿qué intentas conseguir? —preguntó Helena. Apollo, Luc, Lila… No entendía nada—. ¿Por qué has regresado a Paladia después de tanto tiempo?

—Porque quiero destruir el legado de mi hermano, igual que él destruyó el mío. —La furia brilló en el rostro de Luc—. Trató de borrar mi nombre de la historia, desacreditar todo el trabajo que no pudo robarme o acreditarse. Le atribuyó mis descubrimientos a todo tipo de charlatanes, pero se apropió de mi investigación y la aprovechó para convertirse en un dios. Creo que lo justo es devolverle el favor.

Helena negó con la cabeza. No se lo creía. Morrough había tenido muchas oportunidades de acabar con los Holdfast; incluso Kaine se había dado cuenta de que el Sumo Nigromante le había perdonado la vida a Luc en más de una ocasión.

Recordó la imagen de su amigo abierto en canal sobre aquella mesa de operaciones, con los órganos descomponiéndose en su interior.

—Tu cuerpo se está muriendo —comprendió—. Has venido a Paladia porque ni todo el poder del mundo podrá seguir regenerándote para siempre, porque la inmortalidad tiene un límite y tú lo has alcanzado. Ya no importa cuánta vitalidad acumules o cuántas almas coseches. Te quedaste con el corazón de Apollo cuando hiciste que lo mataran y a Luc no pudimos curarlo porque sus órganos ya te pertenecían por aquel entonces. Estás recolectando a los descendientes de Orion por partes. Y...

—las piezas del rompecabezas fueron encajando poco a poco— por eso... por eso has dejado a Lila embarazada. Te estás preparando otro descendiente. Por eso no has permitido que huya a Novis, porque necesitarás al bebé.

Cetus la contempló con un extraño brillo calculador en los ojos de Luc.

—Chica lista. Los Holdfast nunca han sido conscientes de la joya que importaron al traerte aquí. Una animante a su servicio. Sospecho que Apollo era más inteligente de lo que creía. Supe lo que eras en cuanto sentí tu resonancia. Si no te hubiera lanzado lejos de mí, me habrías descubierto enseguida. Una pena, la verdad. No me dejaste otra opción que enviarte al frente. Matias aceptó la propuesta con gusto, pero tú te las arreglaste para regresar como una cucaracha.

Cetus sonrió y un destello cruel que nunca había visto en Luc cruzó su mirada.

—Pero, bueno, qué más da. Me alegro de poder hacer esto yo mismo. Sebastian —miró al último paladín de Luc—, por fin vas a morir protegiendo a un Holdfast de un nigromante.

Se movió a una gran velocidad. Helena oyó el aullido del metal cuando Sebastian desenvainó su espada y bloqueó el ataque. La estancia era pequeña, así que ella tuvo que apartarse de su camino cuando el paladín empujó a Cetus, sacó otra arma y utilizó su empuñadura para golpearle la mano e impedir que lanzara una llamarada en su dirección.

El cuerpo de Luc estaba débil, exhausto tras la batalla y al borde de la muerte, mientras que Sebastian mostraba un enfado como Helena no había visto antes. En un abrir y cerrar de ojos, derribó todas las defensas de Luc, lo acorraló contra una esquina y levantó la espada para darle el golpe de gracia.

Pero, en cuanto lo atacó, la expresión burlona de Cetus desapareció, reemplazada por la mirada desencajada de su amigo.

—Lo siento —dijo.

Sebastian vaciló un instante y Luc le clavó un cuchillo en la base de la garganta. No llevaba una armadura que detuviera el ataque, así que Cetus empujó el arma hacia abajo, le partió la caja torácica en dos y lo destripó.

Sebastian se derrumbó sin hacer el menor sonido.

Cetus, que ni siquiera se detuvo a verlo morir, se volvió hacia Helena.

—Te toca.

Le había bloqueado el paso y Helena sabía que nadie creería su palabra frente a la de Luc si pedía ayuda a gritos. Cuando Cetus se acercó a ella, repasó mentalmente todo lo que Kaine le había enseñado. Tendría que tocarlo directamente.

Solo necesitaba un instante.

Cetus lanzó un ataque dirigido a su cabeza, pero estaba cansado y Sebastian había conseguido herirle la mano, así que el golpe llegó despacio y con poca fuerza. Helena sacó uno de sus cuchillos de titanio y se las arregló para transmutarlo lo suficientemente rápido para defenderse.

El cuchillo, salpicado de la sangre de Sebastian, destelló; Cetus apuntó directamente a su garganta. Helena le golpeó la muñeca con la empuñadura del arma de obsidiana y, al lograr desviar su atención, soltó el cuchillo de titanio que sostenía en la mano contraria y extendió el brazo para tocarle la frente y sujetarlo por el pelo.

La resonancia de Helena atravesó la cabeza de Cetus como una flecha y lo paralizó igual que Kaine había hecho con ella tiempo atrás.

La espada y el cuchillo de Luc cayeron al suelo con un estruendo antes de que le cedieran las piernas. Helena lo bajó hasta el suelo con cuidado, pero sin apartarle la mano de la frente ni dejar de enviarle un flujo de resonancia a las partes más profundas de su mente.

Helena nunca había entrado en la consciencia de Luc, pero, después de haber pasado tanto tiempo interrogando prisioneros, había comprendido que la mente era como una casa que reflejaba la misma esencia que la persona que la habitaba. Sin embargo, la mente de Luc era como un edificio con las paredes derruidas y manchadas de sangre. Un parásito se había hecho hueco en su interior y se alimentaba de la esencia de la persona a la que había infectado.

Cetus había devorado a Luc y lo vestía como un traje.

Al abandonar su mente, el horror le había dejado tan mal cuerpo que Helena estuvo a punto de doblarse por la mitad. Los ojos de Cetus brillaban pese a que no podía respirar y tenía el rostro retorcido en una mueca.

—Vuelve, Luc —le pidió Helena con voz trémula—. Sé que una parte de ti sigue ahí dentro. Soy Hel. Vuelve conmigo y yo te ayudaré a salir de esto.

Cuando le permitió tomar un poco de aire, Cetus la estudió con interés, sin mostrar el menor atisbo de miedo.

—Tienes mucho talento. Si te unes a mí, me aseguraré de valorar tus habilidades como mereces.

Ella le dedicó una mirada gélida.

—Déjame hablar con Luc.

En la mirada de él se reflejaba una extraña avidez.

—Lo de la obsidiana ha sido cosa tuya, ¿verdad? Debería haberme dado cuenta. Crowther era como una tumba. Dime cómo lo haces.

—Te lo contaré si me dejas hablar con Luc —replicó ella entornando la mirada.

Un destello de rabia cruzó el rostro de Cetus.

—¿Por qué insistes tanto? El joven es débil y tan inútil como Orion. Ha pasado toda su vida conformándose con sus trucos y reprimiendo su verdadero poder, negando su animancia.

—¿Luc es animante? —preguntó estupefacta.

—¿Es que acaso no lo habías notado? —preguntó Cetus con expresión burlona—. ¿Nunca te has parado a pensar en la forma en que el ambiente de una estancia cambia en su presencia o en cómo consigue encandilar a cualquiera que lo escucha?

Helena lo había notado, pero siempre lo había atribuido a su piromancia. La presión del aire aumentaba cada vez que Luc se enfadaba. Helena negó con la cabeza.

—Eso no tiene nada que ver con la animancia.

—Es una de las formas en que se manifiesta. Era la especialidad de Orion. Quería que la gente lo adorara y se aseguró de que así fuera, aunque para lograrlo tuvo que reprimir el resto de su poder y darle caza a cualquiera que mostrara un don similar al suyo.

Helena negó con la cabeza. Era cierto que Luc siempre había desprendido un inexplicable magnetismo. Ella no se había detenido a pensar en ello, y ahora se preguntaba si Luc lo sabría siquiera.

—Déjame hablar con él —insistió— y te diré cómo preparo la obsidiana.

La expresión de Cetus cambió.

—¿Hel? —preguntó con voz temblorosa.

Helena apretó el puño para asfixiarlo.

—Ese no era él —replicó sacudiéndolo—. ¿Te creías que no me iba a dar cuenta? Dame a Luc.

Cetus la fulminó con la mirada y puso los ojos en blanco. En esa ocasión, Helena sintió un cambio en su mente, como si algo emergiera de debajo de varias capas de membrana.

Cetus dejó escapar un gruñido ronco y sus ojos volvieron a enfocarse, esta vez con aire aturdido. El rostro de Luc palideció.

—Corre —susurró con voz áspera—. Corre, Hel. Quiere matarte.

—No, no pienso ir a ningún lado —dijo Helena, que tenía ganas de llorar—. Ahora estoy contigo, y no pienso dejarte solo. Siento haber llegado tan tarde.

Notó que el paisaje mental de Luc volvía a cambiar, que algo lo arrastraba de vuelta a las profundidades. Sin embargo, había prestado atención y ahora sabía diferenciar la forma de Cetus de la de Luc. Después de años trabajando como sanadora, y tras meses de interrogatorios y de la difícil tarea de aprender a percibir la chispa de vida del bebé de Lila oculta dentro de la de su madre, manejaba su resonancia con una precisión quirúrgica. Rodeó a Cetus con su poder y lo asfixió hasta obligarlo a someterse a su voluntad.

Luc logró enfocar la mirada con un jadeo dolorido, aunque temblaba como si estuviera a punto de desmayarse.

—¿Luc? —lo llamó Helena con urgencia—. Céntrate y escúchame. Voy a encontrar la manera de salvarte. Te ayudaré a librarte de él. —Le temblaba la voz. Su atención estaba dividida entre hablar con Luc e intentar mantener a Cetus a raya sin hacerle más daño a su amigo—. Necesito que aguantes un poco más.

—Hel… —dijo él en apenas un susurro—. Intenté… impedírselo…, pero mató a Ilva.

—Lo siento muchísimo. —A Helena se le llenaron los ojos de lágrimas y estas cayeron sobre el rostro de Luc—. Voy a solucionar esto. Te lo prometo.

El chico negó con la cabeza.

—No. Tienes que matarme. Es la única manera de detenerlo.

—¡No! —se apresuró a replicar ella—. Mírame. Voy a salvarte. Por eso me convertí en sanadora, ¿recuerdas? Para poder salvarte si en algún momento me necesitabas.

Luc no pareció oírla. Seguía hablando atropelladamente:

—Lila… Pensaba que era yo…

—Lo siento —repitió Helena sin saber qué más decir.

—No se lo cuentes —le pidió él. Le temblaba la barbilla.

—No vas a morir, Luc.

Contener a Cetus le estaba suponiendo un esfuerzo tan grande que Helena tenía la sensación de que la cabeza se le iba a partir en dos. Apenas podía pensar con claridad.

—Esta es tu oportunidad de matarlo. Nadie más puede...

—No...

Luc empuñaba un cuchillo, pero Helena lo vio demasiado tarde. Estaba tan centrada en mantener a Cetus controlado que había dejado de paralizarlo.

Actuó por instinto.

Bloqueó el ataque siguiendo el movimiento tal y como Kaine le había enseñado en sus entrenamientos: lanzó un tajo rápido que hizo que Luc soltara el cuchillo y, luego, sin detenerse, clavó la hoja de obsidiana hasta la empuñadura en el lateral izquierdo del torso, justo en el punto débil de la armadura.

Un jadeo gutural escapó de su garganta y un temblor incontrolable recorrió su cuerpo. Helena gritó aterrorizada cuando él se derrumbó en sus brazos.

—Lo siento. Lo siento muchísimo —dijo él.

Helena le sacó el cuchillo y le apartó el peto con la resonancia para intentar llegar a la herida.

—¡No! No, no, no me hagas esto. Luc, por favor.

Lo curó tan rápido como pudo. No tardó más de dos segundos en detener la hemorragia y repararle la aorta, pero, entonces, unos dedos se cerraron en torno a su garganta y se le clavaron en la tráquea. Helena se encontró con el rostro de Cetus, retorcido por el odio.

—Niñata... estúpida.

Un rápido pulso de energía muerta acompañó sus palabras, pero el rostro de Luc volvió a despejarse y jadeó aliviado.

—Lo tengo —dijo soltándola y obligándose a sonreír.

Antes de que Helena pudiera contestar, alguien llamó a la puerta.

—¿Os encontráis bien, principado?

Helena esperaba que la puerta se abriera de un bandazo, que los soldados entraran y la encontraran arrodillada junto a Luc con un cuchillo ensangrentado en la mano y el cuerpo sin vida de Sebastian tirado a su lado.

—Estoy bien —respondió él enseguida con voz tensa—. Salgo en un minuto.

Sus hombres se retiraron, pero Luc había mentido.

Aunque Helena le había cerrado la herida y no tenía ningún problema físico, ella percibía que se estaba muriendo. Era un deterioro lento. No había rastro del repentino pulso frío que precedía a la muerte, pero daba la sensación de que se estaba desangrando y que lo que escapaba de su interior era vitalidad en vez de sangre.

No existía una causa, no había una herida que curar, pero lo que la resonancia le decía era que su cuerpo se desmoronaba.

—¿Qué está ocurriendo? —preguntó mientras sus dedos recorrían con urgencia el cuerpo de Luc intentando encontrar una manera de curarlo, pese a que nunca se había enfrentado a una muerte como aquella.

Luc le estrechó la mano lo bastante fuerte como para detener el flujo de su poder.

—No te preocupes.

—¿Cómo no me voy a preocupar? —Intentó soltarse—. Encontraré la manera de curarte. Si me hubieras dado más tiempo…, habría…

—Morí hace meses, Hel… —dijo él respirando con dificultad.

—No. Todavía estás vivo… Podré curarte si…

Intentó liberarse una vez más.

—Para —le dijo con firmeza antes de tirar de ella y obligarla a que lo mirara a la cara demacrada, casi esquelética—. Escúchame. Tienes que salir de aquí antes de que alguien descubra lo que ha ocurrido. Te ayudaré. Creo que puedo aguantar lo suficiente. Ve a buscar a Lila y llévatela lejos para que Cetus, Morrough o quienquiera que sea no pueda encontrarla. No querrá marcharse mientras yo siga con vida.

—Tampoco si mueres. Ven con nosotras. Nos iremos los tres. Entonces, te curaré y luego…

Luc tragó saliva.

—Tiene a otro… a otro Holdfast que proteger. Yo ya no soy… su prioridad.

Helena negó con la cabeza.

—No me hagas esto, Luc.

—Lo siento. No debería cargarte con esta responsabilidad, pero no queda otro remedio.

Trató de tocarlo de nuevo, de devolverle la vida que se le escapaba de entre los dedos.

—Tenemos que irnos ya. —Luc levantó la voz con tono firme y autoritario. La sacudió como si intentara hacer que obedeciera del susto—.

Levanta a Sebastian. Los demás se darán cuenta de que pasa algo si no está conmigo.

Ella lo miró antes de desviar la vista hacia el otro hombre, que yacía en medio de un charco de sangre.

—¿Q-quieres que use la nigromancia?

—Tenemos que salir de aquí juntos —señaló. El poco color que le quedaba en el rostro desapareció cuando se incorporó y empezó a ponerse la armadura—. Levántalo.

Helena notaba el corazón latiéndole en la garganta cuando regeneró a Sebastian lo justo para cerrarle las heridas y hacer que se pusiera de pie. Ya había aprendido la lección con Soren, así que se aseguró de traer de vuelta solo una sombra del paladín.

Sebastian se mantuvo erguido, inexpresivo, vacío. Lo cubrió con su armadura para disimular la sangre, y Helena hizo de tripas corazón antes de volverse hacia Luc.

El chico estaba mirando a su último paladín con una pena que no desapareció cuando posó los ojos en ella.

—Siempre has tenido que hacer cosas terribles por mí.

A Helena, aquellas palabras se le clavaron en el alma. Debería haberlo sabido. Debería haber conocido a Luc lo bastante bien como para entender que jamás le habría dado la espalda. Era un amigo demasiado fiel como para hacer algo así.

Tomó una brusca bocanada de aire.

—Te prometí que haría lo que hiciera falta por ti.

Tras ayudarlo a ponerse de pie, Luc tiró de ella y le dio un fuerte abrazo apoyándole el mentón en la coronilla.

A Helena le ardían los ojos. Luc la estaba estrechando con tanta intensidad que la armadura le dejaría moratones a través del uniforme, pero no le importó. Dejó que su amigo se aferrara a su hombro para recuperar el aliento y abrir la puerta.

Su amigo irguió la espalda en cuanto salieron. La nave había quedado prácticamente desierta. Solo unos pocos soldados indemnes esperaban en posición de firmes. Como estaban igual de cubiertos de sangre que Luc y Sebastian, ninguno se fijó en su aspecto.

Luc avanzó con la cabeza alta y la espalda recta, adoptando la postura que le habían inculcado desde niño.

—Sebastian y yo nos marchamos —anunció—. Vosotros quedaos aquí. Este edificio es un emplazamiento clave y necesitamos mantenerlo bien defendido. Si no conseguimos recuperar el Cuartel General, dependeremos de naves como esta para resguardar a las tropas.

—Pero… —empezó a decir uno de los soldados.

—Es una orden —lo interrumpió Luc.

Tenía las sienes perladas de sudor. Helena notaba que flaqueaba, que se estaba desvaneciendo, y que la energía helada de la muerte lo empapaba todo a su alrededor.

—Sebastian, conmigo. Y tú también, Marino.

Consiguieron recorrer una calle y meterse en el estrecho callejón que se abría entre dos torres antes de que a Luc le fallaran las piernas. Pesaba demasiado como para que Helena pudiera cargar con su peso, así que tuvo que utilizar a Sebastian para cogerlo en brazos, alejándolos de cualquier mirada indiscreta.

Luc se apoyó contra un muro respirando con dificultad y con la vista clavada en los pequeños retazos de cielo que se veían entre los dos imponentes edificios que los flanqueaban.

—¿Ya ha amanecido? —preguntó casi con extrañeza.

—Está en ello —señaló Helena asintiendo.

Luc exhaló.

—Íbamos a… ver el mundo juntos, ¿recuerdas?

Buscó a tientas la mano de Helena sin apartar la mirada del cielo. Helena entrelazó los dedos con los de él y se los estrechó con fuerza, como si aferrándose a él pudiera mantenerlo con vida un instante más.

—Nunca llegué a visitar Etras… —se lamentó con voz débil—. Lo siento. Te prometí… que te llevaría de vuelta.

—No pasa nada.

—¿Cuidarás de Lila y el bebé… por mí? —Cuando Helena asintió, añadió—: No le cuentes nada de esto…

—No lo haré.

Un temblor recorrió la mano de Luc.

—¿Me lo prometes…?

—Te lo prometo —dijo ella tragando con fuerza.

Su amigo no respondió. Cuando Helena levantó la vista, Luc miraba el cielo ya sin ver y el amanecer se reflejaba en el azul vacío de sus iris.

CAPÍTULO 64

Augustus 1787

HELENA LIBERÓ A SEBASTIAN DE la reanimación y lo dejó escondido junto a Luc en el callejón.

Solo pensaba en Lila.

El aire estaba cargado de humo y sangre. El estruendo de la batalla retumbaba a su alrededor mientras avanzaba por la ciudad intentando pasar desapercibida. Sabía que no podría salvar a todo el mundo. De hecho, dudaba de que fuera capaz de poder salvar a nadie.

Debía encontrar a Lila.

Al llegar al último muro que marcaba el límite del territorio de la Resistencia, encontró a un grupo de necrómatas vigilándolo. Eran rostros conocidos. Entre ellos, estaba el comandante de la unidad de Luc. Tenía una herida enorme en la cabeza que le dejaba al descubierto parte del tejido cerebral.

Kaine le había explicado que nadie se molestaba en comprobar a quién pertenecía cada necrómata, pues se daba por sentado que todos formaban parte de un inmarcesible. Si seleccionaba a unos cuantos y les arrancaba la chispa que los reanimaba, podría hacer que la escoltaran hasta el Cuartel General como si fuera una prisionera. El problema era que estaban bien armados.

Necesitaba encontrar objetivos más fáciles, así que dio media vuelta y retomó la huida. Mientras buscaba una manera de regresar al Cuartel General, se escondió en varios edificios, subió y bajó viejas escaleras y escalerillas de evacuación. Los combatientes contaban con arneses para descolgarse por las calles y moverse por los distintos niveles de la ciudad con facilidad, pero ella tuvo que encontrar una ruta a pie.

Los necrómatas la seguían de cerca. Sabía que la estaban llevando adonde ellos querían, que la estaban acechando como una manada de depredadores. Los muertos no se cansaban, así que la suya era una batalla perdida.

Decidió esconderse tras un pilar medio cubierto de escombros para recuperar el aliento.

Oyó unos pasos que se acercaban y su corazón se aceleró. Se puso en pie de un salto con un jadeo y salió de su escondite a toda prisa, pero se topó de bruces con un inmarcesible completamente vestido de negro.

Antes de poder retroceder, una mano la sujetó con fuerza por la cabeza y Helena perdió el conocimiento.

SE DESPERTÓ CON UN GRITO ahogado y encontró a Kaine, cernido sobre ella, tocándole la nuca. Helena se apartó con una sacudida. Su mirada recorrió la estancia, pero no reconocía el lugar. Le daba vueltas la cabeza.

—No pasa nada. Estás a salvo.

Ella lo miró confundida mientras intentaba recordar cómo había llegado hasta allí.

Los recuerdos regresaron de golpe. Luc. Luc estaba muerto.

Lo había matado ella.

Fue como recibir un puñetazo en la garganta.

—¿Qué... qué ha pasado?

Tenía la boca seca. Miró aturdida a su alrededor tratando de localizar dónde se encontraba. Kaine le apartó los dedos de la nuca, pero, aunque parecía calmado, en sus ojos se atisbaba una furia contenida.

—La guerra ha terminado. Los inmarcesibles se han hecho con el control de la ciudad, incluyendo el Cuartel General. Las facciones activas de la Resistencia que quedan están acorraladas. Si no se rinden, acabarán enterrados bajo los escombros antes de que caiga la noche.

Helena se incorporó, pero estaba demasiado mareada como para pensar con claridad. Había estado intentando llegar hasta Lila... ¿Y después? No recordaba nada más.

Kaine empezó a caminar de un lado al otro de la estancia.

—¿Cómo ha pasado esto? ¿A quién se le ocurriría repartirse por toda la ciudad y dejar el Cuartel General desprotegido? ¿Y dónde diablos está Holdfast?

La chica se estremeció.

—Está muerto.

Kaine se detuvo en seco y se volvió hacia ella.

—¿Qué quieres decir?

Helena se miró las manos, incapaz de distinguir la sangre de Luc de la suya propia en su ropa. No encontraba las palabras.

—¿Qué ha pasado? —insistió Kaine.

—Fue… —tragó saliva— un accidente.

Se lo contó todo: lo que había descubierto, la identidad de quien había reemplazado a Luc y todo lo que había sucedido con él en los últimos meses. Le contó que la había engañado, que ella había reaccionado sin pensar y que había llegado demasiado tarde.

—Intenté curarlo… —dijo con voz temblorosa—, pero era como si no quedase lo suficiente de él en su interior. Se estaba desmoronando y no pude… —Se le contrajo el pecho como si estuviera a punto de partírsele en dos—. Mi deber era salvarlo… —susurró. Se le cerró la garganta, se echó a temblar de pies a cabeza y ya no pudo seguir hablando. Kaine permaneció en silencio hasta que logró recomponerse—. Morrough debe de tener cientos de años. Paladia se fundó hace más de cinco siglos.

—¿Toda esta guerra se reduce a un conflicto entre hermanos que se pelean por decidir quién juega a ser dios? —Kaine dejó escapar una carcajada amarga—. Da igual qué puto bando escojamos, porque al final somos caras opuestas de una misma moneda.

Helena no dijo nada. Se aferró a las sábanas que la cubrían con tanta fuerza que se le pusieron los nudillos blancos. Tenía que levantarse, pero se sentía como un jarrón a punto de resquebrajarse.

—Hay que ir a buscar a Lila.

—La guerra ha terminado, Helena.

Ella se estremeció al oír la forma en que pronunció su nombre para decir aquello.

—Lo sé —dijo, presa de un ataque de sudores fríos y calientes al mismo tiempo—. No hace falta que me lo recuerdes. ¡Ya sé que hemos perdido! —Apretó los labios y se frotó los ojos con la base de las manos mientras intentaba controlarse. Continuó con voz aún temblorosa—: No estoy diciendo que no haya acabado. Pero ahora tenemos la obsidiana. Nosotros todavía podemos hacer algo. Si actuamos con precaución, tal vez tengamos la oportunidad de matar a los inmarcesibles y arrebatarle la vitalidad a Morrough.

—Ya no hay ningún «nosotros» —replicó Kaine—. Vas a marcharte de Paladia.

Helena levantó la vista de golpe. Él estaba de pie a su lado, con los brazos cruzados.

—Yo me encargaré de matarlos, pero tu trabajo aquí ha terminado. Holdfast ha muerto y la Llama Eterna está acabada. Debes marcharte.

—No me iré sin ti —dijo ella negando con la cabeza.

Kaine mantuvo una expresión imperturbable.

—Pero yo no quiero que te quedes. Me será más fácil trabajar si Morrough cree que la victoria ha sido aplastante.

Helena apretó los dientes.

—Está bien —concedió con cierta tirantez—. Te ayudaré desde la distancia al principio si crees que eso facilitará las cosas.

—Bien. —Kaine dio un paso atrás y giró sobre los talones—. Voy a prepararlo todo.

Helena lo miró cautelosa, sin saber si debía creerle o no. Por muy razonable que fuera la idea, sabía que Kaine llevaba un tiempo queriendo sacarla de Paladia y tampoco le quedaban más opciones. Tenía que llevar a Lila a un lugar seguro. Hasta entonces, Helena no tendría margen para negociar.

—Solo me marcharé si Lila viene conmigo.

Kaine dio un paso atrás.

—Ni hablar. Si desaparece, os darán caza por todo el continente. No merece la pena correr ese riesgo por ella.

Helena se puso de pie.

—No te estoy pidiendo permiso. Tengo que llevármela conmigo. No pienso marcharme sin ella. Le prometí a Luc que la cuidaría. Ha estado encerrada en lo alto de la Torre de Alquimia, en cuarentena. A lo mejor no la han encontrado todavía. Cuanto antes vayamos a por ella, más posibilidades tenemos de sacarla de allí sin ser descubiertos. Podríamos... podríamos buscar un cadáver y utilizar la vivemancia para hacer que se parezca a ella. Nadie se enterará de que se ha ido.

Algo cambió de pronto en Kaine: la tensión le crispó la boca.

—Llévame hasta allí fingiendo haberme hecho prisionera y úsame como excusa para entrar. Solo han pasado un par de horas...

—Helena...

Kaine pronunció su nombre despacio y en su voz se oyó la mezcla de una advertencia y una súplica. Dejó vagar la mirada por toda la estancia y se detuvo un instante en las cortinas. Helena se quedó muda, se levantó medio aturdida y se acercó a la ventana. Fuera no había luz.

Ya había anochecido.

Pero ¿cómo era posible? Cuando Luc había muerto estaba amaneciendo.

—¿Cuánto... cuánto tiempo me has tenido inconsciente? —Le temblaba la voz—. ¿C-cuánto tiempo ha pasado?

Kaine no respondió.

Helena se dio la vuelta y corrió hacia la puerta, pero él la detuvo, tirando de ella hacia atrás.

—Te lo puedo explicar...

Se debatió contra él forcejeando por liberarse.

—¿Qué has hecho? —preguntó subiendo la voz—. ¿Cuánto tiempo he estado inconsciente?

—Escúchame. —La sacudió con el rostro desencajado—. Después de que estallara la bomba, cuando la Resistencia atacó, Morrough nos ordenó a todos que esperáramos. Estaban al tanto de vuestros números, de la cantidad de combatientes que os quedaban. Era evidente que el Cuartel General quedaría desprotegido. Ya sabían que recibirían un ataque antes de la llegada de las fuerzas hevgotianas... Lo estaban esperando. Tenían a alguien infiltrado entre vuestras filas. Cuando llegué allí, ya no estabas. Nadie sabía qué había sido de ti. Dejé mi puesto para buscarte, así que tuve que regresar en cuanto te puse a salvo.

—Entonces... ¿cuánto me has tenido aquí? ¿Un día? —preguntó ella, con la voz rota, sintiéndose traicionada.

—He vuelto tan pronto como he podido.

Helena se echó a temblar, abrumada por la conmoción.

—Iba a ir a por Lila. Eso era lo que quería hacer, pero no dejaban de cortarme el paso... y... —Se estremeció—. Fuiste tú, ¿verdad? Me dejaste inconsciente. Ni siquiera...

Todos esos necrómatas pisándole los talones. Kaine había matado a esos soldados y los había colocado en posiciones estratégicas para mantenerla vigilada y esperarla. Tenía las manos demasiado manchadas de sangre.

Las mismas manos con las que Kaine le acariciaba el rostro.

—¿Qué esperabas que hiciera? ¿Que te dejara ir directa a la masacre? Nos ordenaron que matáramos a cualquiera que se resistiera.

—¿Están todos...? —Ni siquiera pudo acabar la pregunta. Ya no importaba—. No me marcharé de aquí sin Lila, así que puedes ayudarme o dejarme ir sola, pero no hay más que hablar.

Kaine permaneció impasible.

—Si quieres derrotar a Morrough, no podemos permitirnos rescatar a nadie.

—No habrá forma de acabar con él sin Lila. Está embarazada. Morrough necesita a otro Holdfast y Lila lleva en su seno al último descendiente con vida. Le prometí a Luc que la sacaría de allí. Fue lo último que le dije antes de que muriera. Era lo único que le importaba.

—A mí me da igual lo que quisiera Holdfast —dijo implacable.

No iba a dar su brazo a torcer, ni siquiera por ella.

Helena notó que se le apretaba el pecho y las costillas se le curvaban alrededor del corazón como una jaula.

«Siempre eres tú quien sale perdiendo. Todos tus seres queridos mueren».

—Porque, si me ayudas, lo dejaré... todo. Me marcharé y no volveré jamás. Haré lo que quieras si me ayudas a salvar a Lila Bayard. Haré lo que sea. Lo que me pidas. Te juro que lo haré. —Extendió la mano hacia él con dedos temblorosos—. Por favor.

Kaine se había quedado inmóvil.

—¿Me lo prometes?

Ella asintió.

—Sí... —se le entrecortó la voz—. Sí, te lo prometo.

Él la observó con la mirada entrecerrada, evaluando si podía fiarse de ella o no.

—¿Esa es tu única condición? ¿Harás lo que te pida si te consigo a Bayard?

A Helena se le formó un nudo en la garganta.

—Sí, lo que me pidas. Te lo juro.

Kaine asintió despacio.

—Está bien. Como quieras. Te la traeré.

Helena tomó una temblorosa bocanada de aire, aliviada.

—Gracias.

Él se limitó a asentir distraídamente. Helena esperó a que le explicara cómo iban a hacerlo, pero Kaine solo la observó en silencio.

—¿Qué necesitas que haga? —preguntó al final.

—Que te quedes aquí —replicó él, al tiempo que un destello de irritación le atravesaba la mirada.

—Pero podría ayudar —dijo frunciendo el ceño—. Podría…

—No necesito ayuda.

Cuando Helena abrió la boca para protestar, él se la quedó mirando de arriba abajo.

—Llamas demasiado la atención. Me será más fácil buscarla solo. Si quieres que la saque de allí, tendrás que esperar y resistir la tentación de entrometerte en mis asuntos para dejarme trabajar en paz.

Helena intentó defenderse, pero Kaine levantó un dedo y le apuntó con él a la cara.

—Como salgas de esta habitación mientras no esté, o tenga la más mínima sospecha de que intentas ayudarme de alguna manera, volveré y el trato se anulará. ¿Te ha quedado claro? No te muevas de aquí.

Helena apretó los dientes y asintió mientras se le formaba un nudo en la garganta.

—Tienes comida en la alacena. No abras las cortinas. No tardaré mucho.

—¿Dónde estamos? —preguntó la chica mirando a su alrededor.

—Esta era la habitación del embajador hevgotiano —suspiró—. Murió hace poco en una trágica explosión.

—¿El que estabas…?

Él asintió y se marchó sin añadir nada más.

Helena esperó. Kaine había cogido también su bolsa cuando la había interceptado, así que repasó los suministros que le quedaban. Estaba casi vacía salvo por los medicamentos que reservaba para Kaine. Lo revisó todo con cuidado, rezando para que no necesitaran nada cuando Lila y él regresaran.

Pero lo más seguro era que Lila estuviera herida. No se dejaría atrapar sin oponer resistencia. ¿Cómo iba Kaine a convencerla para cooperar?

Helena se acercó a la puerta, pero se contuvo antes de tocarla. Seguro que Kaine tenía un plan. Siguió revisando lo que guardaba en la bolsa y descubrió que también le había dejado sus cuchillos en el bolsillo exterior.

Trató de mantenerse ocupada, porque sabía que la pena y la culpa la asfixiarían si se paraba a pensar. Luc. Había sido culpa suya. Podría haberlo salvado si se hubiera dado cuenta del cambio que había sufrido. Ahora iba a dejar a todos atrás pese a que sabía el destino que les esperaba.

Sus peores temores se estaban haciendo realidad y no podía hacer nada para evitarlo.

«No puedes salvar a todo el mundo. Nunca estuvo en tus manos hacerlo».

Pero no había otra opción.

En cuanto Lila estuviera a salvo, y si Kaine se las arreglaba para acabar poco a poco con los inmarcesibles desde dentro, la pesadilla terminaría.

El tiempo pareció ralentizarse. Helena se duchó para quitarse la sangre y la suciedad de la ciudad. La sangre de Luc. Y la de Sebastian.

Encontró ropa limpia en un armario: un traje tradicional hevgotiano decorado con un inesperado número de borlas. En la alacena había pan y un pedazo de queso duro de sabor fuerte que se obligó a comer a pesar de que todo le sabía a tierra.

Estaba a punto de ignorar la orden de Kaine y salir a buscarlo cuando la puerta se abrió de golpe y Kaine entró cargando con Lila en brazos. Estaba inconsciente, había perdido la prótesis y llevaba un par de bandas metálicas alrededor de las muñecas.

Helena cruzó la estancia de un salto mientras Kaine tumbaba a su amiga en la cama.

La examinó por si estaba herida, pero no presentaba más que unas cuantas magulladuras. Como su resonancia falló a la altura de las muñecas de Lila, Helena comprendió que los brazaletes estaban diseñados para inhibir los poderes alquímicos.

Por suerte, eran toscos y no necesitó más que un par de utensilios para quitárselos.

—¿Estaba todavía en la Torre? —preguntó al abrirle uno de los ojos para tratar de determinar si la habían dejado inconsciente de un golpe o mediante algún calmante.

—No. Cuando llegué ya se la habían llevado.

La supresión alquímica era externa y su efecto se concentraba en las manos de Lila, así que Helena pudo emplear la resonancia por el resto de su cuerpo.

—¿Dónde estaba?

Comprobó el latido del bebé.

—La habían trasladado al laboratorio de Bennet, pero he conseguido sacarla de allí. Tenemos que actuar rápido y enviaros a las dos fuera de la ciudad antes de que amanezca.

Helena tenía tanto miedo por Lila que tardó un momento en darse cuenta de que había algo en la voz de Kaine que le había puesto los pelos de punta. Levantó la vista y descubrió que en su expresión se asomaba un hambre insaciable; nunca la había mirado de esa forma antes.

Le cogió la mano para asegurarse de que no estaba herido. Había vuelto sano y salvo. Tenía el cabello plateado manchado de humo, pero estaba ileso. Lo inquietante era su expresión.

—¿Qué pasa? —preguntó poniéndose de pie y olvidándose de Lila por un instante.

Kaine curvó una de las comisuras de la boca para dibujar una sonrisa triste y respiró hondo.

—¿Kaine? —Estudió su rostro con atención—. ¿Qué ha pasado?

Él mantuvo la vista clavada en el suelo durante un momento antes de levantarla y encontrar su mirada.

—He echado a perder mi tapadera al rescatar a Bayard.

El mundo dejó de girar. El tiempo se detuvo y el aire se congeló hasta que solo quedaron ellos dos. Nada más existía.

—¿Cómo? —Helena sacudió la cabeza y volvió a intentarlo—. ¿Que has… qué?

Aunque estaba convencida de que no lo había entendido bien, la respuesta estaba clara en su mirada. Se estaba despidiendo de ella.

Negó con la cabeza de nuevo.

—No.

Kaine no respondió. Las protestas de Helena quedaron reemplazadas por una quietud terrible, similar a la pausa que se extiende entre los dos latidos de un corazón que se va ralentizando hasta terminar por detenerse. Era el sonido del fin.

—No —dijo con voz estrangulada negándose a creerlo.

—No había otra manera —explicó él con delicadeza y sujetándola por los hombros cuando ella comenzó a tambalearse.

El corazón de Helena volvía a latir, cada vez más rápido. Se alejó de él sin dejar de negar con la cabeza ni apartar los ojos de la puerta mientras buscaba una salida, una escapatoria. Aquello no podía estar pasando.

Kaine la agarró de nuevo por los hombros.

—Ya sabes que llevaban tiempo tratando de descubrir al espía. Habían instalado medidas de contraespionaje en el laboratorio y no he tenido tiempo de encontrar cómo sortearlas. Para llegar hasta Bayard, tuve que dejar constancia en los registros de entrada porque el laboratorio estaba muy vigilado. No podía quemar el edificio ni abrirme paso a puñetazos mientras cargaba con una embarazada inconsciente. Mañana, cuando el personal de seguridad haga el relevo, verán lo que ha ocurrido en el laboratorio y descubrirán por los registros que fui yo el único que ha salido con vida de allí.

Helena negó con la cabeza y se retorció para zafarse de él.

—No. No, todavía hay tiempo. —Cogió su bolsa—. Seguro que hay una manera de destruir los registros… Puedo…

Kaine tiró de ella con un brillo de determinación en la mirada.

—Te recuerdo que tú te marchas. Ese era el trato, Marino, y yo ya he cumplido con mi parte.

Helena dejó escapar un suave quejido de dolor y se apartó de él.

Los ojos de Kaine resplandecían, como si estuviera tratando de convencerla de que lo entendiera. Su mirada recorrió el rostro de Helena, intentando recordar cada detalle, memorizar todas y cada una de sus facciones, porque aquel era el fin. Era la última vez que la vería.

Helena podría haberle perdonado por ello, pero la adoración que desprendía su mirada quedaba empañada por una afilada expresión triunfal. Estaba encantado de que todo estuviera saliendo como él quería.

—Me prometiste que harías lo que yo quisiera si rescataba a Bayard por ti.

A Helena le habría dolido menos que le hubiera arrancado el corazón de cuajo del pecho.

—Me diste tu palabra —insistió Kaine con más firmeza al ver que se negaba a contestar.

—No… —se le rompió la voz.

La expresión de Kaine se suavizó cuando Helena dejó de forcejear.

—Fue bonito mientras duró, pero lo nuestro no estaba destinado a ser eterno. —Le colocó un mechón suelto detrás de la oreja y bajó la mano para apoyársela un instante en la base del cuello—. Ya lo sabías.

—Kaine, por favor, deja que… —empezó con voz temblorosa.

La expresión de él se tornó gélida una vez más.

—Lo que yo quisiera. Ese fue el trato.

A Helena empezaban a arderle los pulmones. Intentó poner distancia entre Kaine y ella, pero no podía respirar. La silueta de él se desdibujó. Lo veía mover los labios, pero cada vez le costaba distinguir más los sonidos.

Kaine la acercó contra su cuerpo y esa fría determinación que había mostrado se transformó en una expresión preocupada.

—Helena, respira.

Se le nubló la vista; la oscuridad lo engulló todo, salvo a Kaine.

—Helena, no me... —suplicó mientras la zarandeaba—. Venga..., respira, Helena, por favor...

Se agarró a él mientras luchaba por responder.

—No... —insistió con la voz rota—. No me hagas esto.

El dolor se la tragó entera, como una ola, y Kaine se esfumó.

Cuando volvió en sí, Kaine se cernía sobre ella de nuevo. Helena se lo quedó mirando. Le dolía el brazo izquierdo como si tuviera un profundo moratón justo bajo el hombro. Notaba que algo iba mal en su cuerpo; se sentía entumecida y le costaba pensar con claridad. Incluso parpadear le suponía un esfuerzo.

Entonces los recuerdos regresaron, acompañados de una angustia casi violenta.

Aunque no conseguía centrarse, todo indicaba que le habían inyectado algún calmante y por eso le dolía el brazo. Kaine la había medicado, pero también notaba el regusto a sales minerales de las pastillas que había desarrollado. Le debía de haber administrado una para evitar que el susto detonara una descarga de adrenalina en su interior y así mantener sus latidos a un ritmo lento y regular. Eso la había mantenido tranquila, dócil.

Helena lo miró con mala cara mientras intentaba recuperar la voz.

—No voy a perdonarte esto jamás —consiguió decir al final, aunque con la voz pastosa y una cadencia irregular.

Kaine apretó los labios, pero asintió.

—Lo sé, pero me da igual porque estarás a salvo, lejos de la guerra. Esas siempre fueron mis condiciones.

Helena permaneció en silencio, tratando de pensar pese a que la transmutación la tenía al borde de la incoherencia. En su interior bullía un pozo de rabia que no lograba alcanzar, por mucho que lo intentara.

Se obligó a pensar despacio, con gran dificultad, luchando por mantener la concentración. De lo contrario, su mente perdía nitidez. Cerró el puño disimuladamente y presionó los dedos contra la palma para volcar una descarga de resonancia sobre su propio cuerpo. Quería contrarrestar los efectos de las medicinas que Kaine le había administrado, pero llegaba tarde.

—Si mueres, ¿quién detendrá a Morrough? —le preguntó con voz apagada.

La expresión de Kaine se tornó gélida.

—Por mí como si se queda con Paladia para siempre. Si de verdad quería ganar, la Llama Eterna debería haber tomado mejores decisiones. Aunque los riesgos eran evidentes, nunca fueron un incentivo suficiente para hacerlos cambiar de estrategia. Se negaron a pagar el precio de la victoria y estoy harto de verte a ti intentando pagarlo por ellos. —Kaine quiso agarrarle la mano, pero ella retrocedió. Una expresión dolida le surcó las facciones antes de tragar saliva con la mandíbula tensa—. Es hora de irse.

—No.

—Me diste tu palabra —le recordó entornando los ojos hasta que su mirada se volvió implacable.

Helena inspiró hondo sin dejar de apretar los dientes.

—Lo sé. Y me marcharé tal y como me pides, pero primero tengo que hablar con... Shiseo. Si le enseño a utilizar la obsidiana que me queda, él podrá pasarle la información a los supervivientes y así tendrán una mínima esperanza de...

—Me diste tu palabra.

Helena sostuvo su mirada.

—Ya sabes que la Llama Eterna siempre será mi prioridad.

A Kaine se le dilataron los ojos como si lo hubiera golpeado y apretó los labios en una línea tensa mientras bajaba la mirada. Helena lo vio tragar saliva, pero siguió hablando:

—Si me obligas a marcharme sin darme la oportunidad de hablar con Shiseo, lo último que harás será dejarnos en la estacada a todos, incluida a mí. Te recordaré siempre como un traidor. Sin embargo, si me dejas hacer esto, tal vez... pueda llegar a perdonarte algún día.

Él la miró con un brillo dolido en los ojos y una expresión vacía y desesperada, pero Helena no cedió. Estaba demasiado medicada como para dejarse arrastrar por la emoción.

—Está bien —dijo Kaine al final con la voz desgarrada por la amargura.

No volvió a mirarla.

Helena se incorporó con un esfuerzo y dibujó un mapa para llegar al laboratorio en el que habían estado trabajando con la esperanza de que todavía no hubiera sido descubierto por los inmarcesibles. También añadió una lista algo imprecisa con todo lo que necesitaba que Shiseo recuperara.

—Debería estar ahí si no lo han encontrado ya. Necesitaré que me traiga lo que he anotado para explicarle cómo funciona.

Kaine estudió el mapa y la lista con desconfianza.

—¿Quién es exactamente?

—Un hombre del Lejano Oriente. Nos ha estado echando una mano.

—¿Y confías en él?

—Más de lo que puedo permitirme confiar en ti.

Kaine se puso pálido, pero se metió la lista en el bolsillo de mala gana.

—No te muevas de aquí.

Helena le dio la espalda. Lila seguía tumbada ante ella, todavía inconsciente.

En cuanto Kaine se marchó, Helena se levantó y registró toda la habitación, decidida a reunir hasta la última pieza de metal que pudiera encontrar. Lo puso todo patas arriba, sin hacer distinciones, desarmando incluso lo que no estaba a la vista para identificar sus componentes. Luego, fue transmutando su alijo para crear barras compactas de distintas aleaciones y elementos, aunque tuvo que parar cada pocos minutos para combatir el embotamiento que le provocaban los medicamentos.

Estaba segura de que Kaine las llevaría primero a Novis, puesto que era el lugar seguro más cercano. Volarían a lomos de Amaris para cruzar el río sin tener que preocuparse por los puestos de control ni por el papeleo necesario para mover una embarcación. Sin embargo, pese a las dimensiones de la quimera, Helena no creía que pudiera cargar con tres personas a la vez. El cauce del río era demasiado amplio. El peso de dos jinetes bastaría para agotar a Amaris, así que tendría que descansar antes de volver a por quien se quedara atrás.

Después de haber perdido a Luc, Helena no confiaba en que fueran a cuidar de Lila como correspondía. Bajo la influencia del falcón Matias, el hijo de Luc no sería más que un simple peón, un principado al que adoctrinar con las mismas mentiras y tácticas de manipulación que tanto habían atormentado a Luc.

Lila tendría que permanecer escondida.

Kaine debía de tener un escondrijo en mente, pero preparar el viaje llevaría tiempo. Incluso con el dinero necesario, conseguir pasajes seguros y discretos resultaría una tarea casi imposible.

Se acercó a la ventana y echó un vistazo fuera para calcular a qué altura se encontraba, pero descubrió que la calle quedaba apenas un par de pisos más abajo. Estaban en una de las zonas más altas de la ciudad, alejada de la violencia. El edificio se conectaba a los adyacentes mediante puentes colgantes; también se veía una plaza y jardines que se asomaban a las partes bajas de la ciudad. La ventana tenía una salida de emergencia, aunque no era más que un balcón decorativo de hierro forjado, nada funcional.

Al oír unos pasos mucho antes de lo previsto, regresó corriendo a la cama y fingió seguir aturdida cuando Kaine abrió la puerta y entró seguido de Shiseo.

Se incorporó frotándose los ojos.

—Lo has encontrado.

—Dale la información para que pueda irse cuanto antes.

—No es más que un asistente —dijo arrastrando las palabras—. Voy a tener que explicárselo todo con calma.

Shiseo la miró extrañado y Helena agradeció que su expresión fuera siempre tan difícil de leer.

Kaine siseó entre dientes y apretó los puños.

—Está bien.

Helena notaba cómo la impaciencia desesperada de Kaine iba en aumento a medida que se retrasaban sus planes.

—Cruzaremos el río a lomos de Amaris, ¿verdad? —preguntó, y Kaine desvió la mirada hacia Shiseo, pero asintió levemente—. ¿Podrá con todos nosotros?

—Tendremos que hacer dos viajes —respondió él apretando los dientes.

Helena le devolvió un vago asentimiento y se acercó a él, consciente de cómo el cuerpo de Kaine se inclinaba hacia el suyo de forma inconsciente.

—Deberías llevarte a Lila antes de que se despierte —le dijo bajando la voz y deteniéndose a poca distancia.

—¿Quieres que me vaya? —le preguntó él poniéndose recto.

Helena retorció el rostro con una mueca de amargura.

—Bueno, no tiene sentido que te quedes a escuchar mis explicaciones, ¿no? —Se encogió de hombros—. He pensado que…, si te la llevas a ella primero, tal vez tengamos un rato para despedirnos cuando vuelvas a por mí. Pero supongo que da igual.

Se dio la vuelta, agradecida de que el efecto residual de la medicación le permitiera mentir sin esfuerzo. Todavía sentía la mirada de Kaine clavada en ella cuando abrió un cajón del escritorio y encontró una pila de papel grueso, de buena calidad, y se dispuso a buscar un bolígrafo.

Sus latidos marcaban un ritmo fuerte y pausado, guiados por el miedo, cuando se sentó y se puso a escribir despacio, de forma metódica, sin mirarlo en ningún momento.

—Cuando regrese, estés preparada o no, tendrás que venir conmigo.

A Helena se le iba a salir el corazón del pecho. Tardó un instante en poder hablar:

—Está bien —dijo sin atreverse a levantar la cabeza.

Por el rabillo del ojo, vio que Kaine se acercaba a Lila y la cogía en brazos. Cuando llegó a la puerta, se giró para mirarla.

—Volveré en un par de horas. No te muevas de aquí.

Helena notó que se le formaba un nudo en la garganta. Echó la vista atrás y entreabrió los labios para decir…

Para decir…

Volvió a bajar la vista al papel que tenía ante ella.

—Te estaré esperando.

Oyó que la puerta se cerraba, pero no se movió pues esperaba que volviera abrirse de golpe. Solo al cabo de un largo silencio, levantó la cabeza.

—¿Cómo habéis venido hasta aquí? —le preguntó a Shiseo mientras se llevaba la mano al lateral del cuello para tratar de mitigar los efectos de los medicamentos y despejarse un poco.

—Un coche nos llevó por una vía subterránea. Tenía una tarjeta especial con la que nos dejaron pasar. Luego subimos en ascensor.

Helena se dio la vuelta y se puso a revisar la caja de suministros que Shiseo le había traído. Lo sacó todo con rapidez mientras organizaba los materiales en la pequeña cocina de la habitación. Tuvo que aprovechar para trabajar en los fugaces periodos de lucidez en los que lograba sortear el efecto del calmante. Cogió una plancha de metal y empezó a dibujar apresuradamente un sello con el que estabilizar la composición.

—Me ha comentado que me necesitabas para algo —dijo Shiseo tras unos cuantos minutos.

—Lo siento, era mentira —se disculpó ella sin dejar de trabajar en las barras de metal que estaba transformando a toda prisa en una multitud de esferas—. Necesitaba una excusa para que se marchara y me trajera todo esto. Imagino que ya te lo habrá contado, pero hemos perdido la guerra. Luc ha muerto. Deberías huir a Novis. Allí estarás más seguro.

—¿Qué estás haciendo? —le preguntó Shiseo con aparente tranquilidad

Helena se detuvo.

—Voy a construir una bomba. Tengo que volar un laboratorio.

—Ya hemos usado todos los componentes de Athanor —le recordó él tras un largo silencio.

Helena se encogió de hombros mientras calculaba mentalmente de cuántos materiales disponía. No tenía suficientes. Rebuscó entre los armarios de la cocina y encontró una bolsa de harina.

—Esta va a ser una bomba distinta. Contendrá obsidiana, igual que la otra, pero utilizaré un principio distinto. Los libros de texto de Luc siempre advertían del peligro de recurrir a la piromancia en espacios cerrados, puesto que las llamas consumen el oxígeno y crean un vacío. Obviamente, yo no tengo ese poder, pero recuerdo haber visto arder un molino cuando era pequeña. La harina que había en el aire prendió fuego y el edificio quedó reducido a cenizas.

Hizo una pausa y mitigó una vez más los efectos del calmante con su resonancia antes de introducir sulfuro de carbono en las esferas selladas con cuidado de no inhalarlo.

Necesitaba mantener el pulso firme y una máxima concentración.

—¿Vas a quemar un laboratorio?

—El del puerto Oeste —dijo con un asentimiento—. ¿Te acuerdas de Vanya Gettlich, la mujer que tenía anulitio en la sangre? La rescataron de allí. Si lo quemamos, nadie sabrá que ha sido Kaine quien se ha llevado a Lila. Además, si piensan que ha muerto en el incendio, no se molestarán en buscarla. Y también… —tragó saliva— será una muerte más rápida para las personas que sigan encerradas allí dentro. —Se tocó la cabeza de nuevo para despejársela y se despidió de Shiseo con un rápido movimiento—. Deberías irte. No querrás estar aquí cuando Kaine regrese. Además, si meto la pata, es posible que vuele el edificio entero.

—¿No vas a volver?

Helena machacó un puñado de obsidiana en un mortero hasta convertirla en un polvo de esquirlas diminutas.

—Por supuesto que sí. Le he dicho a Kaine que lo esperaría aquí. Es solo que… —Se interrumpió para contener las lágrimas—. Le he jurado que me marcharía de Paladia y tengo que mantener mi promesa. —Tragó saliva con fuerza—. Se quedará… se quedará solo. He de asegurarme de que no le pase nada después de marcharme.

No podía respirar. Un desagradable silbido escapó de sus pulmones, y Helena se dobló por la mitad agarrándose el pecho e intentando meterse los dedos bajo el corsé torácico.

Shiseo le quitó el mortero de la mano.

—Todavía tienes que mejorar el movimiento de muñeca —dijo mientras molía la obsidiana para ella—. Así, ¿ves?

Ella lo estudió. A medida que el efecto del calmante regresaba poco a poco, las convulsiones de su pecho cesaron. Dejó que Shiseo terminara la tarea antes de erguirse con una mueca de dolor.

Cuando la obsidiana estuvo lista, él también la ayudó a moldear las barras de metal que había preparado previamente, pues las transmutaciones complejas se le daban mucho mejor que a ella. Creó unos delicadísimos pasadores que tendrían que retirar para permitir que el sulfuro de carbono se evaporara y prendiera el fósforo blanco.

Helena fabricó tantas bombas como pudo y las guardó en una mochila grande y resistente que había pertenecido al embajador hevgotiano con la esperanza de que no estallaran por el camino. Sacó sus cuchillos de la bolsa y se los metió junto con los pocos suministros que le quedaban del kit de emergencia en los bolsillos de una chaqueta decorada con borlas. Por último, se caló un gorro hasta las cejas para que su rostro y su cabello oscuro pasaran desapercibidos.

Tras un instante de vacilación, dejó uno de los cuchillos de obsidiana sobre la nota que había escrito. Kaine debería tener un arma de obsidiana si no contaba ya con una.

Se colgó la mochila con cuidado de no moverla demasiado, abrió la ventana y se asomó al exterior. Se estaba levantando una neblina roja en el extremo norte de la ciudad, pero no había ni rastro de la luz de la Llama Eterna, que había pasado siglos encendida y se solía ver a kilómetros de distancia. La habían apagado.

—Espera —dijo Shiseo cuando estaba a punto de salir por la ventana. Se volvió a mirarlo—. ¿Volverás?

Helena apretó los labios y asintió mientras pasaba una pierna por encima del alféizar.

—Espera —repitió él respirando hondo—. No suelo encariñarme de… nada. Ni de nadie. —Negó con la cabeza—. Cuando mi padre empezó a dudar de la decisión de haberse casado, yo era todavía muy pequeño. Fui una decepción para todos. La familia de mi madre no estuvo a la altura de sus expectativas, así que mi padre nos apartó y empezó de cero. Al nombrar emperador a mi hermanastro, pasé a ser una amenaza, aunque pensé que me libraría de morir cuando me enviaron a supervisar las minas del Imperio. Pero, al ser acusado de robar elementos imperiales, comprendí que tendría que pasar el resto de mis días vagando por el mundo.

Helena sabía que intentaba decirle algo importante, pero un detalle en particular había captado su atención.

—¿El emperador es tu hermano?

Shiseo, enfrascado en la historia que estaba contando, agitó la mano con desdén, como si no tuviera importancia.

—Siempre creí que lo mejor para mí sería llevar una vida tranquila. Y eso hice durante muchos años.

Helena no sabía si la repentina necesidad de Shiseo de hablarle de su vida le resultaba conmovedora o simplemente exasperante.

—Cuando me dijeron que habías muerto, l-lamenté mucho no haber llegado a conocerte mejor. No me gusta elucubrar ni hacer preguntas, pero… disfruté mucho del tiempo que pasamos en nuestro laboratorio —concluyó con una sonrisa.

Helena suspiró y le devolvió la sonrisa.

—Yo también. Ojalá hubiéramos podido trabajar en otros proyectos.

Salió al balcón de metal.

—Espera.

La chica se puso tensa con una creciente frustración.

Shiseo se acercó a ella.

—Debería ir yo. Si me capturan y les hablo de mi hermano, no me matarán.

Extendió la mano para que Helena le pasara la mochila con una expresión de urgencia. Helena lo miró durante un momento, pero rechazó su ofrecimiento.

—Voy a recurrir a la nigromancia para colocar las bombas. He de ir yo. —El hombre dejó caer la mano—. Cuídate mucho, Shiseo. —Se detuvo cuando estaba a punto de girarse de nuevo—. Si no regreso y vuelves a ver a Kaine, dile… dile que le…

Se limpió rápidamente las mejillas, con un gesto vencido, antes de carraspear y mover la cabeza hacia los lados.

—Da igual, seguro que ya lo sabe.

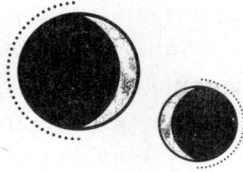

CAPÍTULO 65

Augustus 1787

INCLUSO ANTES DE LA GUERRA, Helena había estado muy pocas veces en la isla Oeste, pero sabía que tenía que dirigirse al sur y descender a los niveles inferiores para llegar a su modesto puerto.

La ciudad estaba oscura y tan en silencio que en la plaza apenas parecía que tuviera lugar una guerra. Utilizar los ascensores, si es que funcionaban siquiera, quedaba descartado, pues tendría que pagar una tarifa e identificarse, pero siempre podía recurrir tanto a las escaleras principales como a las reservadas para el personal de servicios. Serían la ruta más rápida. Cuando se topaba con alguna puerta cerrada, por lo general los cerrojos eran lo bastante sencillos como para poder forzarlos con una rápida transmutación.

No se cruzó con nadie hasta llegar casi a los niveles más bajos. Justo cuando había conseguido abrir un portón, aparecieron dos personas en el último tramo de la escalera. Helena intentó esconderse, pegándose contra la pared para dejarlos pasar sin llamar la atención, pero al final decidió arriesgarse a levantar la vista y tuvo que ahogar una exclamación de sorpresa.

Era Crowther. El hombre la miró con apatía, sin demostrar emoción alguna, pero se detuvo en seco cuando la persona que lo acompañaba se giró y vio a Helena.

Ivy le ofreció una pequeña sonrisa.

—Tú también has conseguido escapar. Tenía la esperanza de que lo hubieras logrado.

Helena la miró horrorizada. Al volver a estudiar el rostro inexpresivo y de mirada vacía de Crowther, comprendió que estaba muerto.

—¿Qué has hecho? —preguntó con voz temblorosa.

La sonrisa de Ivy se desvaneció.

—El Nigromante tiene a Sofia. Me prometió que me la devolvería si lo ayudaba a capturar a Crowther y tomar el Cuartel General. Lo querían vivo, pero me dijeron que no importaba si moría, así que lo he matado.

Evidentemente, creían que Crowther era el cerebro que estaba detrás de la obsidiana. A Helena le daba vueltas la cabeza.

—¿Has sido tú quien les ha estado informando de todo? ¿Tú los dejaste entrar en el Cuartel General?

No había sido Cetus. Ella era la verdadera traidora.

—Tuve que hacerlo. Era la única forma que tenía de recuperar a mi hermana.

—Pero Sofia está muerta, Ivy.

—¡No! —exclamó ella sacudiendo la cabeza—. Está viva. La he visto y me reconoce cuando voy a visitarla. Me la devolverá cuando le entregue a Crowther.

—¿Cómo has podido hacernos esto? —Helena no fue capaz de decir nada más—. Todas esas personas…

—Iban a morir igual —replicó Ivy con un cruel movimiento de la cabeza—. Así ha sido más rápido. Me he asegurado de evitarles una muerte agónica. —Negó de nuevo—. Hubieran muerto igualmente.

Ivy se dio la vuelta y siguió adelante, con el cadáver de Crowther pisándole los talones.

EL LABORATORIO DEL PUERTO OESTE estaba situado en un edificio enorme y sin ventanas que antaño había sido una nave industrial. A principios de año, Kaine le había conseguido a la Llama Eterna un plano del interior del laboratorio, pero nunca habían tenido la oportunidad de utilizarlo.

El sistema de ventilación del edificio se limitaba a unos pocos conductos estrechos, diseñados para proteger el lugar de posibles ataques piromânticos, por lo que el aire solía enrarecerse con facilidad. Y eso era justo lo que Helena necesitaba.

Al avanzar, examinó con desconfianza los edificios más pequeños que había repartidos por las inmediaciones del laboratorio. Mientras evaluaba la nave principal, un necrómata se acercó a investigar, atraído por su presencia, aunque una única persona desarmada no suponía una amenaza. Antes de que la alcanzara, Helena se tocó el cuello para despejarse la mente, extendió la mano y arrancó la energía que animaba al necrómata como si le estuviera quitando una pelusa de una chaqueta.

El cadáver se desplomó contra ella, envolviéndola en el hedor de la descomposición, pero Helena enseguida lo reanimó con su resonancia. No estaba en buenas condiciones: había empezado a hincharse y todos sus tejidos y ligamentos estaban deteriorados.

Se aseguró de usar la mínima energía necesaria.

En cuanto estuvo bajo su control, la criatura se volvió hacia el siguiente necrómata y lo inmovilizó para que Helena repitiera el proceso. En cuanto acabó, tenía más de veinte necrómatas reunidos a su alrededor. Los límites de su consciencia se difuminaron al dividir su atención entre las mentes embotadas de los necrómatas, pero consiguió mantener el control: su mente seguía siendo suya.

—Encontrad todos los accesos al edificio —les ordenó mientras activaba y distribuía las bombas.

El efecto del calmante se había incrementado cada vez que utilizaba la nigromancia. La concentración que exigía la tarea le resultaba agotadora, pero por suerte las instrucciones para los necrómatas eran prácticamente idénticas. Apretó los dientes y completó cada bomba con una transmutación antes de pasárselas a sus nuevos ayudantes para que se alejaran con ellas lo más deprisa posible.

Debía mantenerse en una posición lo bastante alejada como para no quedar dentro del radio de la explosión, pero lo suficientemente cerca como para que el fósforo no prendiera antes de tiempo tras haber sido activado, y eso requería un delicado equilibrio.

Los necrómatas comenzaron a trepar por las paredes en cuanto llegaron a la nave. Helena retrocedió. La vista se le emborronó mientras los seguía con la mirada, cada vez más alto. Por suerte, carecían de centros nerviosos para notar cómo se arrancaban la carne de los dedos al escalar.

Helena cerró los ojos con fuerza y trató de concentrarse en el avance de los necrómatas. Habían alcanzado los conductos de ventilación y las rejillas de la nave. Otros habían escalado hasta el techo y estaban desmontando las cubiertas de los respiraderos. El corazón le latía a toda velocidad cuando uno de los necrómatas, el que aún conservaba una vista algo nítida, sostuvo una de las esferas a la altura de un conducto y confirmó que cabía por la apertura.

A la vez, los necrómatas tiraron de los delicados pasadores que Shiseo había transmutado para ella y dejaron caer las bombas por los conductos de ventilación de la nave reforzada y aislada del exterior.

En cuanto las últimas bombas cayeron, Helena se dio la vuelta y echó a correr.

A sus espaldas se oyó un estallido sordo casi de inmediato cuando las primeras estallaron. Al echar la vista atrás, vio unas diminutas nubes de polvo. Algunas resplandecían, mientras que otras eran de color blanco.

Y entonces el mundo estalló a su alrededor.

El aire se desgarró ante la violencia de la explosión, que le revolvió el cabello a Helena y la persiguió como una ola de calor abrasador.

El fuego trataba de engullirlo todo; se devoraba a sí mismo, ardía desatado y voraz, succionando todo el oxígeno hasta crear un tornado. Helena acababa de cometer todos los pecados piromânticos sobre los que había advertido a Luc.

Las naves industriales no estaban diseñadas para la integridad estructural, sino para albergar la máxima cantidad de mercancía, por lo que los elementos estructurales eran escasos. Los planos de Kaine indicaban con precisión cada rincón. La nave se derrumbó y voló repentinamente por los aires con una segunda explosión. El fuego había encontrado, sin duda, las armas que Bennet desarrollaba o los peligrosos recursos inflamables que almacenaba allí para fabricar sus propias bombas.

El suelo se movió bajo sus pies como si fuera líquido y los adoquines se resquebrajaron.

Helena salió despedida y chocó con uno de los edificios contiguos.

El fuego seguía rugiendo cuando abrió los ojos. El calmante había amortiguado el golpe, pero permaneció tendida en el suelo mientras intentaba recuperar el aliento y un dolor punzante, probablemente insoportable, se le clavaba en el cráneo.

Todo ardía a su alrededor. Sintió cómo subía la temperatura y escuchó nuevas explosiones pese a que un pitido agudo y doloroso amortiguaba el resto de los sonidos. Donde antes se alzaba el laboratorio, solo quedaban escombros y llamas.

Cuando intentó ponerse de pie, las piernas le fallaron y se desplomó, jadeando con dificultad. Le ardían los pulmones, pero la cabeza le daba vueltas con cada bocanada de aire.

Debía de ser por el anulitio.

Se quitó la chaqueta que llevaba y se cubrió la boca y la nariz con ella para intentar respirar despacio.

«Ponte de pie, corre».

Pero estaba agotada y nada parecía real. Estaba atrapada en una pesadilla, una pesadilla interminable. Durante los años que duró el conflicto, se había repetido sin cesar que todo valdría la pena, que todas las mentiras tendrían su recompensa. Pero había matado a Luc, le había atravesado el corazón a la primera persona que debería haber salvado.

Se quedó allí tumbada, dejándose llevar por la pena. Inmovilizada bajo el peso del dolor. ¿Cómo iba a levantarse? ¿Cómo se enfrentaría a esas emociones?

Kaine.

Abrió los ojos de golpe y se arañó el cuello en un nuevo intento por contener los efectos de la medicación mientras el humo del incendio le anegaba los pulmones.

Le había dicho que esperaría.

Si no regresaba, Kaine se encontraría con el desorden de piezas que había dejado al ensamblar las bombas y la nota garabateada que rezaba «Te quiero. Te quiero. Te quiero».

Se obligó a incorporarse. No pensaba morir ni dejar a Kaine atrás. Tenía que volver.

Se las arregló para dar unos pocos pasos antes de derrumbarse otra vez. A través del humo, veía unas siluetas acercándose a ella, pero no conseguía que las piernas la sostuvieran, así que metió la mano en el bolsillo con torpeza y sacó el frasquito y la jeringuilla que se había guardado como último recurso.

Con las manos temblorosas, clavó la aguja en la tapa del frasquito, tiró del émbolo y llenó la jeringuilla. Luego, inspiró hondo para reunir valor y se inyectó el líquido directamente en el corazón. La mezcla de estimulantes había sido idea de Kaine. La descarga de energía fluyó como un torrente por sus venas, arrastrando consigo los restos del calmante y la transmutación que la mantenían adormecida. La energía que vibraba en su interior estaba despejando su mente, dándole nitidez y luminosidad.

Se puso de pie de un salto y corrió más rápido que nunca. Apenas sentía su propio cuerpo. Lo único que sabía era que necesitaba correr.

Algo la derribó. Helena se retorció para coger sus cuchillos, pero notó la caricia del pelaje de un animal, así que se agarró a su atacante y le lanzó una descarga de resonancia buscando los puntos de unión transmutacional que mantenían unidas las distintas partes de la criatura para desconectarlos.

La quimera murió al instante.

Helena se incorporó con torpeza, blandiendo un arma de obsidiana, cuando los necrómatas empezaron a rodearla. Se abrió camino entre ellos a cuchilladas, sin apenas prestarle atención a sus intentos por agarrarla. Se negaba a perder de vista las torres altas de la ciudad. Era allí hacia donde se dirigía. Iba a volver y estaría esperando a Kaine cuando este regresara.

No pensaba morir.

Pero no tuvo tiempo de reanimar a los necrómatas para que la defendieran, así que destruyó todo a su paso con una eficiencia implacable. El poder que fluía por sus venas era tan intenso que su corazón amenazó con partirse en dos si dejaba de moverse. Echó a correr en cuanto se zafó de ellos con la sangre retumbándole en los oídos. Al ver que más siluetas comenzaban a surgir de entre las nubes de humo, Helena se detuvo en seco, horrorizada.

Entre ellas, estaba Althorne.

No tenía ni idea de cómo se las habían arreglado para reanimarlo después de haberlo contaminado con el anulitio. Debían de haber hecho un gran esfuerzo para hacerse con el cuerpo del general. Junto a él, caminaba un hombre joven, de cabello color trigo y rostro cuadrado.

Era Lancaster.

Crowther había comentado que los prisioneros habían muerto en el bombardeo, pero era evidente que se había equivocado. Helena miró a su alrededor, temerosa por descubrir a quién más se encontraría.

—Vaya, vaya, tenías razón —le dijo Lancaster a Althorne—. Sí que había alguien fuera.

—Cogedla —graznó el liche que manejaba el cuerpo de Althorne y la miraba con los ojos entornados a través del humo—. Puede que ella sepa quién ha atacado el laboratorio.

—¿Me la puedo quedar si consigo atraparla? —preguntó Lancaster, que estudiaba a Helena de nuevo con un brillo extraño en la mirada, como si la reconociera.

—Cuando hayan terminado de interrogarla, será toda tuya. Ahora, date prisa.

Al ver que Lancaster avanzaba hacia ella, Helena sustituyó el cuchillo de obsidiana por la daga larga de titanio. Si el liche prefería quedarse atrás y enviarlo a él, debía de ser aún un mero aspirante.

Aunque eso también significaba que el liche era quien controlaba a los necrómatas. Tendría que librarse de él si no quería que acabaran persiguiéndola por toda la ciudad. Pero primero se ocuparía de Lancaster.

Su mayor ventaja era que la querían viva.

—Déjame pasar —le dijo cuando el hombre estuvo casi a su altura.

La silueta del liche empezó a desdibujarse entre el humo, pero Helena trató de no perderlo de vista, de controlar sus movimientos.

Lancaster negó con la cabeza.

—Venga, no te compliques las cosas. Te superamos en número, así que suelta el cuchillo.

Los necrómatas la habían rodeado, todos con armas de largo alcance. Helena miró a izquierda y derecha buscando una ruta de escape mientras evaluaba sus opciones. La sangre le retumbaba en los oídos y la instaba a moverse, a atacar, a correr. Tenía que mantener la mente fría.

Sostuvo la daga durante un instante, notando la textura de la empuñadura y de los delicados detalles que la decoraban, antes de tragar saliva y dejar que se le escurriera de entre los dedos y cayera al suelo con un estrépito. Bajó la cabeza y avanzó en actitud sumisa mientras dejaba caer también la mano para alcanzar otro de sus cuchillos.

—Cogedla —ordenó Lancaster cuando vio que la chica se movía con paso vacilante hacia él.

Los necrómatas obedecieron y bajaron las armas, y, cuando uno de ellos se dispuso a agarrarla del brazo, Helena atacó.

Transmutó la daga en mitad del movimiento y la hizo el doble de larga con un centelleo. Le cortó la mano a la criatura, le atravesó el vientre y le enterró una hoja más corta en el cráneo a otro necrómata.

Luego, esquivó una espada sibilante que dibujó un arco sobre su cabeza y se la clavó al necrómata que se encontraba detrás de ella. Al oírlo gritar, dedujo que no todos sus atacantes eran necrómatas. Serían entonces más fáciles de matar. Aunque, en realidad no intentaba ganar; no estaba librando ninguna batalla. Lo único que quería era escapar. Se mantuvo orientada hacia la dirección en que había desaparecido el liche.

«No vas a morir aquí».

Alguien la agarró con fuerza de la muñeca izquierda y ella se retorció para liberarse, pero un dolor cegador le envolvió el hombro al dislocárselo. Giró sobre los talones y le puso una mano encima a su atacante sin pensárselo dos veces para que la resonancia arrasara con todo lo que tocara. Oyó un grito agónico y, en cuanto su muñeca quedó libre, se arrastró lejos de la persona que la había agarrado mientras intentaba recolocarse el hombro. Apenas podía mover los dedos, pero se negó a detenerse.

«Actúa rápido y con cabeza», le había dicho Kaine. Eso era lo que tenía que hacer para sobrevivir.

Lancaster se interpuso en su camino con una sonrisa triunfal, seguro de su victoria, pero Helena le clavó la daga en el pecho sin dudar y él cayó fulminado.

En cuanto se recompuso, corrió directa hacia el humo y de nuevo pudo ver la ciudad que se extendía al otro lado, resplandeciente y llena de falsas promesas. Los necrómatas todavía le pisaban los talones; los oía pese a no poder verlos. Había llevado su cuerpo tan al límite que su campo de visión empezaba a desdibujarse. La combinación de estimulantes y calmantes estaba haciendo un excelente trabajo enmascarando la verdadera gravedad de sus heridas.

Vislumbró una amplia silueta entre el humo: era Althorne. Cogió la daga de obsidiana y se lamentó por no poder utilizar el brazo izquierdo, pero amplificó su resonancia hasta que vibró a su alrededor como un campo de energía mientras se lanzaba hacia él.

De repente, algo grande y pesado se abalanzó sobre ella. Helena consiguió esquivarlo en el último segundo y su atacante cayó de bruces al suelo.

El liche blandía una guja, igual que Lila, pero con movimientos mucho menos ágiles y elegantes. Helena nunca se había enfrentado a un liche, pero aquel en concreto no parecía estar acostumbrado a manejar su cuerpo. Si conseguía herir a Althorne con la obsidiana, aunque fuera una sola vez, interrumpiría la reanimación. De hecho, si se las arreglaba para clavársela lo bastante cerca del talismán, incluso podría matar al inmarcesible que estuviera moviendo sus hilos.

—Pareces una alquimista de primera —dijo la voz del general. La guja pasó tan cerca de Helena que su estela estuvo a punto de cortarle la mejilla—. ¿Qué eres?

Ella estaba demasiado alterada como para contestar. Toda su atención se centraba en esquivar los movimientos del liche. Por fin pudo ver a Althorne con claridad: tenía el rostro gris y una herida supurante en la cabeza, y aún llevaba puesta la armadura, lo cual suponía un problema para atacarlo.

Al acercarse demasiado a Althorne, este le asestó un revés. Por suerte, consiguió abrirle la piel grisácea de la muñeca con la obsidiana. Helena se dio un golpe tan fuerte contra el suelo que se quedó sin aliento, pero se obligó a levantar la cabeza con un jadeo al ver que el poder de la reanimación escapaba del cadáver de Althorne como si una infección se le extendiera por su brazo.

Se incorporó con torpeza. Aunque los necrómatas todavía la perseguían, ahora se movían más despacio. El liche no se defendió cuando Helena se aproximó a él.

Solo manejaba bien una de sus manos y apenas podía sostener el arma de obsidiana con la izquierda mientras le quitaba la armadura a Althorne con la derecha. Al darse cuenta de lo que estaba haciendo, intentó agarrarla, pero Helena lo sujetó por el cuello, lo agarró con fuerza y le arrancó el esófago de un solo tirón. Althorne cayó como un peso muerto. Helena se tambaleó, apartó la armadura e intentó localizar el talismán de su pecho para saber dónde clavar la obsidiana. Una sangre oscura y putrefacta fluyó del agujero de su garganta y le empapó la ropa, la armadura y la cadena de plata que pendía de su cuello. El colgante manchado de sangre había estado a punto de caer dentro de la herida abierta.

Era un dragón con las alas arqueadas y la cola entre los dientes.

Helena se lo quedó mirando: el liche era Atreus Ferron.

Intentó afianzar su agarre sobre la daga, pero tenía el brazo izquierdo entumecido. ¿Qué era mejor? ¿Matarlo directamente o entregarle el talismán a Kaine para dejar el destino de su padre en sus manos?

No. Tenía que hacerlo ella. Kaine no debería cargar con la responsabilidad de matar a su propio padre. Volvió a explorarlo con la resonancia intentando localizar el talismán.

¡Paf!

Algo le golpeó en la cabeza. Todo se volvió rojo. Cayó sobre el cadáver de Althorne y, al intentar levantarse, el mundo empezó a dar vueltas a su alrededor. Consiguió incorporarse unos segundos antes de desplomarse de nuevo.

Lancaster trastabilló hacia ella, con el torso empapado de sangre y la guja en la mano. Había utilizado un asta para atacarla por detrás.

—Ya puedes darte por muerto —le dijo Helena mientras hacía todo lo posible por ponerse de pie.

—Eso ya lo veremos —respondió él con una carcajada jadeante. La señaló con un gesto de la mano—. Levantadla.

Dos aspirantes tiraron de Helena hacia arriba y le arrebataron el cuchillo de obsidiana de una patada. Las piernas apenas la sostenían. Todo se tambaleaba a su alrededor, pero los medicamentos seguían rugiendo en sus venas y su resonancia vibraba a la máxima potencia. Sin embargo, en vez de enfrentarse a ellos, Helena se apoyó en el aspirante más armado para robarle el primer cuchillo que pudiera sacar con facilidad de la funda.

Eran unos idiotas por caer dos veces en la misma trampa.

Encontró uno mientras la llevaban hacia su líder. Se trataba de un arma de combate reglamentaria, un modelo que conocía muy bien. Lancaster estaba pálido por la hemorragia que sufría, pero no perdió la sonrisa y mantuvo las distancias con ella. Era evidente que prefería arriesgar la vida de sus compañeros que la suya propia.

—Me lo voy a pasar en grande contigo. En cuanto sea uno de los inmarcesibles, me aseguraré de que te despellejen viva.

Helena reunió la poca fuerza que le quedaba y lanzó un último ataque.

Lo habría apuñalado justo en el corazón de no haber sido porque él logró esquivarla en el último segundo. Por desgracia para él, la resonancia de Helena era más amplia que la de la mayoría: atravesó la armadura como si fuera de papel y transmutó el arma con un giro de muñeca para destrozarle los pulmones. Luego, cerró los dedos con fuerza en torno a su cuello.

Lancaster la agarró del pelo y se zafó de Helena antes de que ella tuviera oportunidad de volarle los sesos con su poder. Helena se defendió arañando y clavando las uñas a cualquiera que se le acercara.

—Rompedle la mano. ¡Rompedle la puta mano! —gritaba Lancaster mientras trataba de quitarse el cuchillo que tenía clavado en el pecho sin éxito, pues era consciente de que podría arrancarse los pulmones de cuajo al hacerlo.

Alguien la agarró del antebrazo y le pisó la muñeca derecha con un desagradable crujido. Helena vio, impotente, cómo le destrozaban los huesos contra el suelo empedrado.

Cuando la soltaron, se quedó tumbada en medio de la calle. Lancaster ya se había desplomado. Al cabo de unos segundos, Helena trató de incorporarse apoyándose en el brazo dislocado.

«Corre. Tienes que salir corriendo».

A uno de los aspirantes solo le quedaba una mano, pero desenvainó su espada y le asestó un golpe en la cabeza con la empuñadura.

Helena despertó oyendo gritos.

Estaba tumbada en una superficie fría y dura, y, cuando intentó abrir los ojos, descubrió que los tenía pegados por la suciedad. Al intentar frotárselos, un dolor punzante se extendió ardiendo por su cerebro. Hizo un esfuerzo por abrir los ojos de nuevo, pero sus párpados se resistían a separarse.

—Tranquila. Con cuidado. Tienes sangre seca en las pestañas —le dijo una voz que le resultaba familiar mientras unos dedos suaves le frotaban los párpados—. Prueba ahora.

Helena entreabrió los ojos y, a través de la neblina que enturbiaba su vista, vio a la enfermera Pace mirándola desde arriba. Estaba tumbada con la cabeza apoyada en el regazo de la mujer y se encontraban en un lugar oscuro, iluminado solo por una linterna.

Volvió en sí poco a poco. Aunque el dolor era inmenso, sabía que lo peor estaba aún por llegar. El aire olía a sangre, tanto seca como fresca.

Se oían gritos constantemente.

Y risas también.

Helena trató de incorporarse, pero Pace se lo impidió.

—Ni hablar. Estás muy malherida. He podido colocarte el hombro, pero se han llevado tu corsé ortopédico y tienes la muñeca destrozada.

—¿Dónde estamos? —logró preguntar.

No conseguía enfocar la mirada, pero reconoció a una de las sanadoras, así como a varias médicas y camilleras. Todas estaban agrupadas a su alrededor.

—En el Cuartel General —respondió Pace con una sonrisa tensa—. En el patio.

Helena miró más allá de la enfermera y alzó la vista: había algo sobre sus cabezas. Estaban encerradas en una jaula grande, de las que se usaban para los animales. Había decenas de jaulas repartidas por toda la estancia.

—Déjame levantarme —le pidió incorporándose con esfuerzo.

Su cuerpo empezó a protestar a medida que los efectos de los estimulantes y el calmante iban mitigándose. Sin el corsé, la presión se acumuló en su esternón al intentar mirar más allá de los barrotes de su jaula. Necesitaba saber de dónde venían los gritos.

Era Rhea. La habían colgado de las muñecas. Titus estaba a su lado, cubierto de sangre y con todo tipo de cuchillos, palos y lanzas clavados por el cuerpo. Se sacó uno de los cuchillos de la pierna y empezó a despellejar a su mujer con él.

Luego, se llevó el pedazo de piel a los labios y se lo comió.

Estaba muerto. No podía ser de otra forma, pero eso no hacía que la imagen fuera menos aterradora.

Además, Rhea no estaba muerta.

Junto a ella, había pedazos de carne colgando de distintas cadenas. Helena entornó los ojos en la penumbra para tratar de distinguir mejor qué era lo que estaba viendo.

Brazos amputados.

Un torso.

La cabeza de Alister.

Se le revolvió el estómago y rodó hacia un lado para vomitar con tanta violencia que una descarga de dolor le desgarró la espalda mientras su cuerpo se convulsionaba. Levantó la vista cuando Pace le limpió la boca con un pedazo de tela.

Helena se volvió.

—¿Cuánto tiempo llevan…?

—Todo empezó al atardecer —explicó Pace con voz temblorosa—. En cuanto confirmaron que tenían el control del Cuartel General. Por suerte, no han conseguido atrapar a Luc y a Sebastian, así que todavía hay esperanza.

A Helena se le formó un nudo tan grande en la garganta que por un instante pensó que se asfixiaría. No se veía con fuerzas de decirle a la enfermera que Luc no iba a salvarlas, que ya no podía hacer nada.

Bajó la vista. Le habían quitado toda la ropa y le habían puesto una bata gris. Incluso se habían llevado las horquillas y las gomas con las que se sujetaba su cabello, además del brazalete con el que la llamaban cuando la necesitaban en el hospital. Lo único que le quedaba era el anillo de Kaine, que se desdibujaba ante sus ojos incluso cuando lo miraba directamente. Había funcionado; ni siquiera habían conseguido encontrarlo al revisarla mediante la resonancia.

En la muñeca izquierda llevaba ahora un grillete de supresión como los de Lila. Por lo hinchada que tenía la mano derecha, imaginaba que no habían podido colocarle el grillete que completaba el juego.

Los gritos de Rhea se fueron apagando.

Al oír un rugido de emoción, Helena levantó la vista, aterrorizada ante la posibilidad de descubrir qué ocurriría a continuación.

Un coche largo y bajo cruzó la verja de entrada y a Helena le dio un vuelco el corazón al verlo detenerse ante los escalones que conducían a la Torre. La puerta del vehículo se abrió y Luc salió de su interior con una expresión vacilante, casi avergonzada, como si llegara tarde a una fiesta.

Un susurro recorrió el patio. Todos los prisioneros lo miraron, conmocionados, mientras Luc observaba la escena que se estaba desarrollando ante él.

—No… —dijeron Helena y Pace al unísono.

Luc se volvió e hizo una reverencia profunda y sumisa ante la persona que salió del coche tras él. El hombre era alto, vestía una túnica intrincadamente decorada y una capa azul y dorada, y sobre la cabeza llevaba una corona en forma de medialuna. Era Morrough.

Caminó por delante de Luc y subió los escalones de mármol manchados de sangre. Los restos de los líderes de la Llama Eterna estaban repartidos por el suelo o colgados de las paredes.

Morrough se volvió cuando Luc lo siguió, y Helena pudo ver que llevaba una máscara que recordaba a un sol eclipsado, cubriéndole la mitad superior del rostro. Lo único que se alcanzaba a ver de sus facciones era una boca pálida y sin labios.

Helena nunca había visto al Sumo Nigromante. Había oído rumores acerca de su apariencia durante algunos de los primeros enfrentamientos, pero no tardó en dejar la lucha en manos de los inmarcesibles.

Así que ese era Cetus, el primer alquimista del Norte.

Nadie se atrevió a perturbar el silencio sepulcral mientras Luc subía los escalones detrás de él con obediencia y Morrough estudiaba todo a su alrededor.

—Paladia ha pasado demasiado tiempo al servicio de esta familia de falsos dioses —dijo con una voz rasposa que apenas parecía tener alcance alguno—. Os mostraron sus trucos baratos de fuego y oro, y los considerasteis una muestra de poder divino. —Retorció la boca en una mueca burlona—. Yo he conquistado la muerte. La inmortalidad es mi regalo y, en vez de guardarme este secreto para mí, prefiero compartirlo con quienes considere dignos de recibirlo.

Un coro de vítores estalló. Aunque eso no fue lo peor de todo. Mientras Morrough hablaba, Luc se arrodilló ante él, como suplicándole que le concediera la inmortalidad.

Helena siguió de cerca cada uno de sus movimientos intentando encontrarle el sentido a lo que estaba viendo.

Luc estaba muerto, de eso no cabía duda. Morrough debía de haberlo encontrado y reanimado. Le había devuelto ese aspecto tan vivo para destruirlo de nuevo.

Ante la mirada atenta de todos los presentes, Luc se inclinó aún más y apoyó la frente sobre el suelo de piedra. La sangre que lo cubría le manchó la ropa, la piel y el cabello. Era la misma sangre de aquellos que lo habían apoyado fielmente tanto a él como a su familia.

—¿Me estás suplicando que te conceda la inmortalidad? —le preguntó Morrough.

Luc vaciló, como si le diera vergüenza, pero luego alzó la cabeza, lo miró con un brillo suplicante en sus ojos azules y asintió.

—No eres digno de ella —determinó el Sumo Nigromante, pese a que extendió una de sus manos largas y huesudas como si fuera a ofrecérsela, pero giró su muñeca y dejó la palma orientada hacia la cabeza de Luc.

Helena sintió la oleada de resonancia que surcó el aire incluso desde la distancia. La cabeza de Luc impactó contra el suelo y su cráneo se partió como la cáscara de un huevo. Quedó con el rostro hundido, el cuerpo desmadejado y los sesos esparcidos por el mármol empapado de sangre.

Se alzó un coro de gritos horrorizados.

Morrough le dio la espalda al cadáver.

—Guardadlo a buen recaudo para que su cuerpo no arda jamás.

Dicho aquello, entró en la Torre de Alquimia, el monumento que su hermano había construido para simbolizar la derrota de la nigromancia.

<hr />

EL PASO DEL TIEMPO SE desdibujó. Quienes no habían subido a la Torre con Morrough empezaron a organizar a los prisioneros que quedaban repartiéndolos en distintos grupos y anotando los números inscritos en sus grilletes en una serie de documentos.

Concluida la «celebración», llegaron más coches con miembros condecorados de los inmarcesibles vestidos de uniforme negro; lo que parecían ser oficiales del Gobierno, el Concejo de Gremios al completo y el gobernador Greenfinch.

La mayoría se dirigieron directamente a la Torre de Alquimia, que ya había sido limpiada de sangre.

La puerta de la jaula donde Helena se encontraba se abrió con un chirrido, y varios guardias empezaron a sacar a las prisioneras, distribuyéndolas por distintas zonas del patio.

—¡Con cuidado! —exclamó Pace cuando agarraron a Helena del brazo y la obligaron a levantarse—. Tiene la muñeca rota y necesita atención médica. Estas mujeres son unas profesionales inteligentes y altamente cualificadas. Deberíais...

El guardia la miró con gesto despectivo.

—Ya tenemos prisioneros de todo tipo. —Echó un vistazo a Helena de arriba abajo—. Esta irá con los condenados a muerte. Igual que tú, vejestorio.

El hombre ignoró las súplicas de Pace, aunque no trataba de salvarse a sí misma, sino a Helena. Enumeró sus habilidades excepcionales mientras él copiaba el número de sus grilletes junto a los de la enfermera en una lista. Luego, las empujaron hacia otra jaula y un segundo guardia las metió dentro sin miramientos.

Pace intentó resistirse, protestando, pero se tropezó y cayó tan de improviso que a Helena no le dio tiempo a reaccionar. La mujer se golpeó la cabeza con los barrotes de hierro y ya no volvió a levantarse.

Helena se aferró a los barrotes con su temblorosa mano izquierda y utilizó su cuerpo como escudo para proteger a Pace mientras, desesperada, trataba de encontrarle el pulso. Todos los prisioneros que iban metiendo en la jaula a empujones presentaban heridas graves o eran personas de avanzada edad. El cadete que había estado vigilando el salón de mando yacía a su lado, pálido como un cadáver, y se sujetaba las entrañas, que se le escapaban de entre los dedos.

Helena no podía ayudarlo.

Se dejó caer junto a Pace y colocó su cabeza sobre el regazo con la esperanza de que estuviera muerta, de que no tuviera que presenciar lo que les ocurriría a continuación.

Una sombra se cernió sobre ella.

Levantó la vista, con el corazón a punto de salírsele por la boca, y se quedó helada al ver a Mandl.

—Vaya, vaya —dijo la mujer con una amplia sonrisa—. Ya decía yo que esa melena me sonaba.

Helena estaba demasiado cansada como para que su presencia tuviera algún efecto en ella.

Mandl la señaló con un rápido giro de muñeca.

—Sacadla de ahí.

—Pero es la jaula de los condenados —dijo el guardia que había empujado a Pace lanzándole una mirada de reojo.

Mandl se volvió hacia él.

—Me da igual en qué jaula esté. Sácala de ahí.

Mientras la arrastraban afuera, Helena se golpeó la mano varias veces al pasar entre los cuerpos hacinados y tuvo que reprimir un gemido de dolor. Por si fuera poco, estuvieron a punto de volver a dislocarle el hombro.

—Eres tú de verdad —dijo Mandl estudiándola de cerca cuando la dejaron caer al suelo, a sus pies—. Menuda guerra has dado. ¿Tenías miedo de que te encontrara?

Helena apenas había pensado en Mandl desde el final del interrogatorio.

—Yo me moría de ganas de echarte el guante. —El aliento de la mujer llegó hasta Helena. Tenía un olor intenso y acre, como a formaldehído—. Voy a asegurarme de que Bennet te use para probar uno de sus proyectos especiales. —El guardia carraspeó y Mandl se giró hacia él con brusquedad—. ¿Qué te pasa ahora?

—Dicen que Bennet nos ha dejado.

—¿Cómo?

—Se rumorea que ha sido cosa de Hevgoss —explicó el hombre bajando la voz—. Las bombas son… su especialidad. No se sabe mucho más. Stroud se llevó a un buen puñado de sujetos de prueba y tuvo que traérselos de vuelta a todos. Dice que no queda nada del laboratorio. Que no hay ni rastro de Bennet y los demás. Pero se supone que no debemos correr la voz entre…

Dejó la frase a medias y abarcó el patio con un movimiento de la mano.

Helena sintió un pellizco triunfal en el pecho. Bennet estaba muerto y ya no podría volver a hacerle daño ni a Kaine ni a nadie más.

Mandl se quedó muda.

—Pero ¿qué pasa con la nave de los tanques de suspensión? ¿Nos la cerrarán? —Antes de que el guardia pudiera contestar, ya se estaba respondiendo ella misma—. Por supuesto que no. Aunque Bennet ya no esté aquí para supervisarlo todo, los inmarcesibles todavía necesitarán una reserva de cuerpos en perfecto estado.

Bajó la vista para mirar a Helena, que fingió indiferencia e intentó parecer ajena a la conversación.

—Bueno, sin él aquí, tendré que ser yo quien se encargue del proceso de selección. —Se inclinó hacia delante y agarró a Helena por detrás del brazo—. Me parece que tú vas a ser mi primera opción.

La resonancia de Mandl le atravesó la mano. De pronto, sus terminaciones nerviosas ardían como si se las estuvieran desgarrando. El intenso dolor le subió hasta el hombro y se le extendió por todo el cuerpo hasta clavársele en el cerebro como una estaca.

Gritó y sus músculos comenzaron a estremecerse.

—Ay, madre mía —se lamentó Mandl fingiendo preocupación, pero sin soltar ni por un segundo a Helena—. No quería hacer eso, sino esto otro.

La agarró de la nuca y una renovada descarga de dolor le recorrió su columna, alcanzando todas sus terminaciones nerviosas, y se intensificó hasta que Helena sintió que el corazón le iba a estallar. Habría preferido romperse todos los huesos con tal de escapar de aquella agonía. O arrancarse las extremidades a mordiscos.

Su mente intentaba liberarse de ese sufrimiento pidiéndole desesperadamente que se desmoronara. Que se desmoronara ya.

«No estoy hecha de porcelana y no pienso desmoronarme. Confía en mí, por favor».

Había hecho una promesa. Su cuerpo siguió sufriendo convulsiones, pero acabaron mitigándose al cabo de un rato. Cuando la dejaron tirada en el suelo, sin ningún cuidado, sus músculos aún temblaban. Mandl se arrodilló a su lado y, al intentar tocarla, Helena se apartó encogida de miedo.

Una sonrisa se dibujó en la amplia boca de Mandl.

—¿Ves qué rápido puede aprender una a tener miedo?

Le cogió la mano derecha, le colocó los huesos rotos y le curó las fracturas. Habría sido una excelente sanadora si no estuviera tan perturbada.

Al notar que algo frío entraba en contacto con su muñeca recién curada y se cerraba con un chasquido en torno a ella, bajó la vista, conmocionada y respirando con dificultad. Mandl le había puesto otro grillete. Tenía un número diferente, pero no alcanzaba a leerlo.

La mujer se puso en pie y se sacudió la suciedad de la ropa.

—Metedla en uno de los camiones.

Cuando tiraron de Helena para levantarla del suelo, un joven dio un paso al frente.

—Esperad —balbuceó—. A… a esa tenemos que quedárnosla. Se supone que van a interrogarla. O eso creo. Estoy bastante seguro de que alguien lo ha comentado.

Mandl lo miró parpadeando despacio, como un reptil.

—Estaba en la jaula de los condenados a muerte.

—Son órdenes de arriba —dijo poniéndose colorado y rascándose la cabeza.

—¿De quién?

—Eh…, fue uno de los muertos, pero no recuerdo cuál. Se lo dijo a Lancaster.

—¿Y dónde está?

—Bueno, lo están operando ahora mismo.

Mandl frunció los labios; parecía querer arrancarle la cabeza de un mordisco al aspirante.

—¿Y qué quieres que haga? ¿Que la vuelva a meter en la jaula? ¿Tienes permiso siquiera para hacerte cargo de ella?

El chico titubeó y retrocedió un paso.

—Es que… Es lo que he oído. Puede que otra persona se haya enterado mejor.

Helena no sabía si la estaba salvando o condenando a un destino aún peor. Atreus quería interrogarla para dar con la persona que había orquestado la explosión. Le costaba pensar con claridad y su cuerpo no dejaba de estremecerse. La mezcla de medicamentos que corría por sus venas hacía que le diera vueltas la cabeza pese a que sus efectos ya comenzaban a mitigarse.

Varios liches rodearon a Helena y la arrastraron junto con otro puñado de prisioneros hasta la parte trasera de un camión.

Un interrogatorio suponía un riesgo. Si alguien descubría que había sido ella quien había detonado aquellas bombas, querrían saber cómo lo había hecho. Y por qué.

Después de lo que había vivido, era muy consciente de los peligros de los interrogatorios. Podían hacer que la mente se desmoronara, que el dolor lo asediara todo. Los inmarcesibles recurrirían a todo tipo de torturas con tal de obtener respuestas.

Kaine decía que la animancia era un don especial, único. Si Bennet había muerto, cabía la posibilidad de que Morrough y él fueran los únicos nigromantes vivos con esa habilidad. En ese caso, podrían mandar llamar a Kaine para que la torturaran delante de él u obligarlo a que se encargara él mismo de obtener respuestas. Sus destinos estaban ligados de una manera u otra.

Aunque Helena muriera rápido, el castigo que le impartirían a Kaine por traicionar a los inmarcesibles sería eterno. A lo mejor la utilizaban para hacerle daño igual que habían hecho con su madre.

Los peores temores del chico se harían realidad.

¿Y si encontraban a Kaine en sus recuerdos?

¿Y si...?

Tendría que enterrarlo en las profundidades de su mente, igual que había hecho con...

Soren.

Redirigiría sus pensamientos y transmutaría sus recuerdos hasta que su mente dejara de acudir a él. Era imposible confesar algo olvidado.

Se llevó las manos a las sienes y se estremeció al mover la muñeca derecha, pues Mandl le había curado las fracturas, pero no las lesiones musculares ni los moratones. El anulitio de los grilletes vibraba y distorsionaba su poder, pero no lo suprimía del todo.

Aunque la notaba amortiguada, lo importante era que todavía tenía acceso a su resonancia. Solo necesitaba ser meticulosa y tener paciencia. Cerró los ojos y utilizó ese delicado hilo de poder para alterar su propia consciencia. Después de haber pasado tanto tiempo moviéndose por la mente de otras personas, manipular la suya propia, que ni reaccionaba ni se resistía, era sencillo.

Enterró los últimos dos años de su vida en las profundidades de su cerebro, como si quisiera ahogar los recuerdos. No le quedaba otra opción. Kaine se había convertido en el centro de sus pensamientos.

Sin él, su vida era un vacío, una rutina. Las horas, los días y los años que había pasado en el hospital se difuminaban hasta convertirse en una pesadilla interminable.

Estaba sola. Todo el mundo había muerto. Porque quienes la rodeaban siempre morían. Por mucho que intentara salvarlos, todos acababan sufriendo el mismo destino. Su vida era un cementerio.

Y esos espacios imposibles de disimular los llenó con imágenes de Luc, aunque no de su muerte ni de sus días en la guerra, sino del Luc que había prometido salvar. La versión de sí mismo que él siempre se había esforzado en ser. El Luc que había creído en ella de manera incondicional.

Esa era la forma en la que merecía ser recordado.

Seguía perdida en sus pensamientos cuando el camión se detuvo ante una nave industrial. Debía de haber sido un antiguo matadero, pues había ganchos colgando del techo y mesas de metal repartidas por todo el edificio. El suelo, de cemento, era del tipo que se limpiaba fácilmente

con una manguera. El griterío de los prisioneros la sacó de su ensimismamiento.

—No van a matarnos todavía —dijo con voz ronca—. Nos meterán
en tanques de suspensión para mantenernos frescos.

Los fueron separando uno a uno e inyectándoles una sustancia desconocida.

El proceso estaba tan bien organizado que resultaba aterrador. Era
mecánico. A medida que los prisioneros perdían el conocimiento los colocaron en las mesas, uno junto a otro. Mientras tanto, un guardia iba
quitándoles la ropa.

Algunos intentaron resistirse. Un chico recibió una patada en el
vientre antes de que le clavaran la aguja en el cuello. Llamó a su madre,
se encomendó a Sol y rezó para que Luc acudiera en su ayuda.

La mujer —Mandl, recordó su mente con cierto retraso— se quedó
observando todo lo que sucedía y, cuando le llegó el turno a Helena, señaló el extremo opuesto de la nave.

—Dejadla ahí. Me encargaré de ella personalmente.

La aguja que le clavaron en el cuello era gruesa y la dosis de parali-
zante, exagerada. Se le entumecieron los músculos, pero no los nervios
sensitivos, de manera que lo notaba todo, solo que no se podía mover.

El rostro de Mandl apareció ante ella con una sonrisa satisfecha en
los labios. La recorrió con la mirada de arriba abajo.

—¿Te crees que sabes qué es lo que te va a pasar a continuación?

Helena permaneció inmóvil mientras la mujer le apartaba el pelo y le
adhería algo en la nuca, justo encima del inicio de la columna.

—Esto es para que no se te atrofien los músculos.

Un pulso eléctrico hizo que Helena se estremeciera. Su cuerpo se
contrajo y se relajó varias veces.

Mandl, que deslizó los dedos por la piel fría de Helena, parecía vibrar
de emoción. Le clavó agujas y le introdujo tubos en los brazos.

—Lo de Bennet ha sido una lástima —dijo la mujer—. Sus ideas
siempre me han parecido de lo más edificantes. Si estuviera aquí, te habría mantenido con vida todo lo que yo hubiera querido. Un interrogatorio sería demasiado rápido y dejaría tu cuerpo inservible.

Le cubrió el rostro con una máscara que abarcaba desde las cejas hasta la barbilla y que se sellaba con algún tipo de adhesivo. Era lo bastante
translúcida como para permitir que Helena atisbara la silueta de Mandl
alzando una jeringuilla llena de un líquido azul claro.

—Si te inyectara esto, entrarías en coma. Bennet decía que ayuda a que la carne se conserve tierna, algo así como mantener a los cerdos tranquilos antes de llevarlos al matadero.

Mandl apretó el émbolo y Helena oyó que el líquido caía al suelo. Luego, arrancó una hoja de papel de un portapapeles y la arrugó. Por un instante, Helena alcanzó a distinguir el número que aparecía en la parte superior del documento: 19819.

Sin aquel informe, no había constancia de que Helena estuviera allí. Desaparecería. Se convertiría en un error administrativo.

Mandl le pasó los dedos por el pelo.

—Mientras esperas, quiero que imagines todas las cosas que pienso hacerte cuando regrese —dijo antes de darse la vuelta—. Aquí ya he acabado. Metedla en uno de los tanques.

La montaron en una carretilla y la llevaron hasta una segunda estancia en la que hacía un frío helador. Por el rabillo del ojo, Helena pudo ver hileras y más hileras de tanques individuales. Las imágenes del ataque al primer laboratorio de Bennet acudieron a su mente: cuerpos flotando en el interior de receptáculos idénticos a esos. Y todos habían aparecido muertos.

Los guardias, con guantes de goma que les llegaban hasta los hombros, fueron levantando a los prisioneros uno a uno, metiéndolos en los tanques y conectando los tubos y cables que salían de ellos a las máquinas que había en el extremo opuesto de la sala.

El corazón de Helena se aceleró cuando le llegó el turno y se vio sumergida en el gélido fluido de uno de los tanques.

No podía moverse. Estaba atrapada dentro de su propio cuerpo, como si fuera una jaula que la aislara dentro de su mente. El frío le caló hasta los huesos, le ralentizó el corazón y entumeció su metabolismo. Antes de que la luz también se apagara, tuvo la sensación de que al mismo tiempo pasaba una eternidad… o tal vez un suspiro.

Helena se quedó atrapada en la silenciosa oscuridad.

Su corazón latía con fuerza, movido por el más puro terror. No veía la cubierta del tanque pese a tenerla a centímetros del rostro. La libertad estaba al alcance de su mano, pero también a una distancia inalcanzable.

Trató de respirar despacio en vano. Empezó a jadear y el calor de su aliento empañó la máscara.

También intentó gritar, pero apenas pudo emitir un quejido débil y entrecortado. Cada vez tenía más frío. Sus pulmones se convulsionaban:

el miedo le había hecho consumir el poco oxígeno disponible y un dolor ardiente se expandía por su pecho. Siguió intentando controlar la respiración, pero ya no quedaba aire que respirar.

Desmayarse fue un alivio, era mucho mejor que permanecer consciente.

Un calor ardiente la despertó de golpe.

Había olvidado dónde se encontraba y enseguida le asaltó una nueva oleada de pánico al darse cuenta de que seguía atrapada en un diminuto espacio cerrado, inmersa en la oscuridad. No tenía suficiente oxígeno y no se podía mover.

La quemazón regresó y la distrajo del miedo mientras trataba de averiguar de dónde provenía. Reconocía la sensación.

La mano. Le ardía la mano izquierda. El anillo. Le dio un vuelco el corazón.

Kaine. Había regresado a la habitación del embajador y se la había encontrado vacía. Helena le había dicho que lo estaría esperando, pero había desaparecido. El anillo se calentó una y otra y otra vez.

La estaba buscando. Había regresado a por ella.

Siempre lo hacía.

Pero Helena no podía permitirse pensar en ello.

Tenía que olvidar a Kaine. Si no lo olvidaba y acababan interrogándola, corría el riesgo de que lo descubrieran.

No podía pensar en él. Atrapada, paralizada y sin poder usar las manos, lo único que le quedó fue canalizar su resonancia hacia dentro. Estaba acostumbrada a proyectarla hacia fuera durante el combate, pero, en aquel momento, lo que hizo fue tejer una red de resonancia alrededor de su propia mente.

Sentía esa textura delicada de la manipulación alterándole los pensamientos y dándoles forma para dejar fuera todos aquellos detalles en los que no podía permitirse pensar. Recorrió una y otra vez los nuevos caminos de su mente, dejando nuevas marcas y entrenando su cerebro para que no se saliera de la ruta establecida ni se detuviera más de lo necesario. Contó, trazó rutinas, intentó no recordar.

Si Kaine la encontraba, él comprendería lo que había hecho.

Podría esperar.

«Aguanta. Le prometiste que no te desmoronarías».

PARTE III

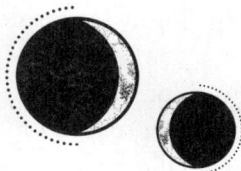

CAPÍTULO 66

Mayus 1789

LA MENTE DE HELENA SE abrió de par en par al recobrar el sentido.

Se incorporó bruscamente, con la cabeza a punto de estallar de dolor. Lo único en lo que podía pensar era en escapar, en correr. La necesidad de huir la estaba consumiendo. Allá donde mirara, no veía más que oscuridad.

Intentó moverse, pero su cuerpo no respondió. Cada movimiento brusco desató una oleada de dolor que recorrió sus muñecas, sus manos y sus brazos al intentar levantarse. Las costillas le constreñían los pulmones y le impedían respirar con normalidad.

Ya no estaba en el tanque, pero todo seguía oscuro y apenas podía moverse.

Una mano le tocó el hombro y Helena dejó escapar un grito ahogado mientras levantaba la vista. Era Kaine. Estaba inclinado sobre ella; su cabello claro y sus resplandecientes ojos plateados eran lo único visible en medio de la negrura. Le temblaban los dedos.

Helena lo contempló, atónita.

Estaba distinto, más mayor. Aunque no solo era por el físico, sino también porque en sus ojos había algo que le hacía pensar que habían pasado décadas desde la última vez que se vieron.

Se estiró hacia él con un sollozo.

—Estás vivo.

Kaine se apartó con una expresión de desconsuelo extendiéndose por su rostro. Helena no comprendió por qué había reaccionado así hasta que la voz temerosa de Grace emergió de las profundidades de su mente.

«Lila Bayard fue la primera a la que trajo de vuelta».

Sus recuerdos resurgieron de golpe: los grilletes, la transferencia, su encierro en Puntaférreo. El Sumo Inquisidor había matado a todo el mundo.

Kaine era el Sumo Inquisidor.

A Helena se le heló la sangre; retiró la mano y se apartó de él, ignorando el intenso dolor que estalló en sus muñecas. Tenía algo enredado en torno al codo y se lo arrancó al retroceder con torpeza. Los brazos y las piernas le temblaban bajo el peso de su propio cuerpo. Estuvo a punto de caerse del borde de la cama, pero se dejó caer hasta el suelo y se quedó arrodillada, contemplando por encima del colchón la habitación oscura de esa casa igual de oscura en la que permanecía encerrada.

Kaine seguía vivo.

Pero eso significaba que no había ido a buscarla, que ella lo había estado esperando en vano.

Aquella disonancia mental le daba ganas de gritar. Helena estaba arrodillada sobre las ruinas de su vida mientras el pasado y el presente colisionaban.

No podía ser él. Ferron le había hecho daño, la había violado y había asesinado a todos.

Kaine jamás sería capaz de algo así.

Le había prometido que siempre…

Una punzada le atravesó el cerebro. La vista se le nubló y un gemido angustiado escapó de entre sus labios. Tuvo que cubrirse la cara con las manos a medida que el dolor crecía y le perforaba la mente hasta volverse tan insoportable que estuvo a punto de perder el conocimiento.

Sentía que le ardía la cabeza, como si le hubieran partido el cráneo, y la presión le estaba derritiendo el cerebro. Gritó para intentar librarse del dolor y no paró hasta quedarse sin aliento. Cuando volvió a levantar la vista, estaba sola.

A lo mejor Kaine nunca estuvo allí con ella. A lo mejor su rostro no había sido más que un producto de su imaginación.

A lo mejor todo fue un sueño. Kaine estaba muerto y ella seguía pudriéndose en aquel tanque de suspensión, olvidada en la oscuridad, donde nadie la encontraría jamás.

Se dejó caer y una mano la agarró del hombro antes de que tocara el suelo. Entonces descubrió con un sobresalto que él volvía a estar a su lado. Cuando sus miradas se encontraron, la expresión de él se desmoronó.

—Estás empezando a recordar, ¿no es así?

Helena se las arregló para asentir y le tocó la muñeca para notar la piel y los huesos bajo los dedos. Era real.

Estaba todavía vivo. Se había convencido de que todo el mundo había muerto, pero Kaine había sobrevivido y, de algún modo, eso hacía que la situación fuera todavía peor.

Giró el rostro y lo escondió en el edredón para ahogar el renovado impulso de ponerse a gritar. Un coro de contradicciones y miedos tronó en su cabeza mientras trataba de poner en orden sus pensamientos. Nada parecía real. Todo era mentira.

Entonces recobró la lucidez y lo agarró más fuerte de la muñeca, tanto que le clavó las uñas en la piel.

—La obsidiana... Mandl y el resto... ¿Fue todo...? ¿Ha sido todo cosa tuya...?

—... Así es.

A Helena le temblaba la barbilla y le ardían los ojos.

—¿Ha sido así... siempre?

—Sí.

Los combatientes de la Resistencia y los miembros de la Llama Eterna que había creído escondidos en algún lado se esfumaron de su mente y quedaron reemplazados por Kaine. Su captor y su mayor pesadilla.

Helena asintió y desvió la mirada, incapaz de reconciliar el alivio y el miedo que sentía al mismo tiempo.

Estaba vivo. Había conseguido salvarlo. Aquello era lo que siempre había querido, pero...

No de esa manera.

—¿Por qué mataste a Lila? —Se le rompió la voz.

—No la he matado. Está viva.

Helena lo miró sin comprender. El dolor de cabeza hacía que Kaine pareciera resplandecer.

—Grace vio su cadáver. Todo el mundo en el Reducto lo vio. Mandl la tenía montando guardia.

—Lila estaba embarazada y era la única superviviente de la familia Bayard. No iban a dejar de buscarla hasta que encontraran su cuerpo, así que les procuré uno. Fue idea tuya.

Helena no se acordaba de eso. Después de tantas mentiras, no se veía capaz de creer nada de lo que le contara.

—Ha tenido un niño. Es excepcionalmente ruidoso y se llama como su abuelo. Lila ha intentado matarme dos veces como mínimo todas las veces que he ido a visitarlos.

Sonaba como algo típico de ella. Helena levantó la cabeza. El deseo irrefrenable de creer en él le había formado un doloroso nudo en la garganta.

—¿Dónde está ahora?

Kaine negó con la cabeza.

—No se encuentra en Paladia, pero la verás pronto. ¿Recuerdas que le prometiste a Holdfast que los protegerías? Te han estado esperando.

El corazón le dio un vuelco, pero entonces se acordó de todo lo que le había contado. Se encogió sobre sí misma.

—No te creo —dijo, incapaz de controlar lo mucho que le temblaba la barbilla.

—Lo sé.

—No lo entiendo. —Negó con la cabeza—. No recuerdo nada... salvo a ti.

Quiso tranquilizarse diciéndose que Kaine era real, pero eso era imposible. La persona que habitaba sus recuerdos no podía existir, porque Kaine Ferron había matado a todo el mundo. Había erradicado a los miembros de la Llama Eterna y les había dado caza a todos aquellos combatientes de la Resistencia que habían osado huir. Tenía las manos manchadas de sangre.

Él tragó saliva.

—¿Qué... recuerdas sobre mí?

Le resultaba una persona familiar y a la vez completamente distinto, como si hubiera sido creado a la imagen y semejanza del Kaine que ella había conocido pero sin ser él.

—E-espiabas para la Llama Eterna —apuntó en apenas un susurro—. Solías llamarme para que me reuniera contigo y te curara... y... y...

Se le trabó la lengua y un dolor carmesí estalló en el interior de su cabeza. El mundo se tambaleó a su alrededor.

Parpadeó deprisa mientras intentaba pensar. Había estado intentando decir algo... algo... Notaba la lengua pastosa. Cuando intentó abrir la boca para hablar, la mandíbula le dio una sacudida y le chasqueó repetidamente.

Luego, las extremidades y los dedos se le curvaron con rigidez hacia dentro, como si fuera una araña muerta, y Kaine la agarró justo a tiempo de impedir que cayera de bruces al suelo.

Helena no podía hablar.

La mandíbula le temblaba sin control y los pulmones se le estremecieron en cada intento de respirar. Notó que la cabeza también empezaba a sacudírsele contra el pecho de Kaine, que le apoyó una mano en la sien para inmovilizarla. El corazón de Helena latía a toda velocidad, aterrorizado.

—Tranquila —le dijo Kaine—. Date un minuto para que se te pase.

Lo sintió respirar hondo mientras ella seguía convulsionando entre sus brazos.

—Le hiciste un buen trabajo a ese cerebro tuyo —añadió con voz calmada—. Las barreras transmutacionales que erigiste están empezando a caer, pero pronto te encontrarás mejor.

A Helena se le contrajo la garganta y todos y cada uno de sus tendones y músculos parecieron replegarse y amenazaron con romperse. Kaine le estaba diciendo que pronto se encontraría mejor, pero ese momento no llegaba.

—Aguanta un poco más.

Cuando los temblores por fin cesaron, su cuerpo se relajó y su mente quedó sumida en una bruma inconexa. Kaine la levantó en volandas. Helena estaba tan delgada que notó los huesos de sus articulaciones al dejarla de nuevo sobre la cama y cubrirla con el edredón. Helena quiso protestar, pero tenía la mandíbula agarrotada y su boca se negaba a moverse con normalidad.

Había un motivo por el que Kaine no debería tocarla. Ella no quería que lo hiciera, pero ya no recordaba por qué. Sin embargo, le aterrorizaba verlo marchar, que desapareciera y la dejara sola en la oscuridad.

Kaine rodeó la cama en silencio, encendió una vela y colocó una bandeja con frasquitos en la mesita de noche. La luz tenue de la vela brillaba entre ellos.

—Has pasado una semana inconsciente —le explicó sin levantar la mirada, como si notara que Helena lo estaba observando—. Sufriste... —se interrumpió y apretó los labios con fuerza mientras tomaba aire—. Sufriste un ataque y no te despertaste. S-según parece, has estado manteniendo esas barreras mentales en pie sin darte cuenta todo este tiempo. Cuando te quedaste embarazada..., el Estrago te ganó la partida. Consumiste toda tu energía.

¿Embarazada? Había olvidado ese detalle. Un jadeo ronco y aterrorizado la sacudió cuando recordó lo que había pasado. Morrough quería

879

un bebé. Helena se había quedado allí tumbada y había dejado que todo sucediera sin…

—¿Por qué…? —fue lo único que pudo decir.

Kaine vaciló y su mirada, que hasta ese momento había permanecido fija en los frasquitos de la bandeja, se dirigió hasta ella. Dejó lo que estaba haciendo y se inclinó hacia delante.

—Escúchame bien. Sé que quieres recordarlo todo ya, pero tu mente necesita estabilizarse. Está pendiendo de un hilo ahora mismo —le dijo con mirada suplicante—. Con el tiempo, todo cobrará sentido.

Kaine no recurrió a la resonancia mientras hablaba. Solo habría conseguido empeorar la situación. Al estar cerca de él, el cuerpo de Helena se calmaba de manera instintiva pese a recordar con todo lujo de detalles las veces en que le había hecho daño mientras había permanecido prisionera en aquella jaula helada que tenía por casa.

Helena se estremeció.

—Aguanta un poco más. Todo terminará pronto.

Pero ella tenía un millar de preguntas. «¿Qué ha pasado? ¿Por qué no viniste a por mí? ¿Por qué me has hecho daño? ¿Por qué me has violado?».

«¿Por qué te convertiste en el Sumo Inquisidor?».

—¿Por qué… —se le quebró la voz— por qué has matado a todas esas personas?

La pregunta pareció sorprenderlo, como si hubiera esperado antes cualquiera de las otras que a Helena se le habían pasado por la cabeza.

—Estaba intentando encontrarte.

A Helena le dio un vuelco el corazón, presa de una reacción visceral tan horrorizada como aliviada.

—¿Fuiste a buscarme? —preguntó con voz rota.

Un destello angustiado surcó la mirada de Kaine.

—Pues claro. Te busqué por todas partes. ¿Creías que te había abandonado?

Intentó recordar qué era lo que había pensado.

—Se suponía que iban a interrogarme. Como aparecías en tantos de mis recuerdos, creí que lo mejor sería olvidar para que no pudieran encontrarte. Sin embargo, nadie vino a por mí. Pensé que todos habían muerto.

Kaine la miró como si acabara de destriparlo, dio un paso atrás y se giró.

—Te busqué sin descanso. Primero fui al edificio que hiciste estallar, luego a la Central y al Reducto, y no había ni rastro de ti. Había un documento que mencionaba el traslado de una sospechosa capturada cerca del puerto Oeste, pero tus heridas eran demasiado graves y te pusieron en la lista de los prisioneros condenados a muerte. Cuando no logré encontrarte entre los cadáveres, revisé cada celda y cada documento que pude localizar, pero habías desaparecido. Por eso me ofrecí voluntario para darles caza a los desaparecidos. Pensé que acabaría encontrando alguna pista que me llevara hasta ti. —Apretó los dientes—. Tuve que entregarles a todos los miembros de la Resistencia que encontré. De lo contrario, le habrían asignado la tarea a otra persona.

Tenía la vista clavada al otro lado de la estancia y se negaba a cruzar la mirada de ella mientras hablaba.

—Fui a Hevgoss unas cuantas veces. Llegué a pensar que tal vez hubieras acabado allí. Estuve incluso en la nave donde te tenían prisionera. Revisé todos los documentos que se guardaban por si encontraba alguna descripción que coincidiera contigo, pero no se me ocurrió abrir los tanques, así que...

Le temblaba el mentón y, en vez de seguir hablando, se limitó a colocar la bandeja.

—¿Por qué no me diste por muerta? —le preguntó.

Kaine dejó las manos quietas.

—Tenía que saber qué te había pasado. —Inspiró hondo—. Esta habitación es segura, pero Morrough tiene ojos por toda la casa. A veces nos vigila desde el pasillo. Ahora que estás embarazada, no creo que pida verte de nuevo, pero, mientras fuera un riesgo, siempre existía la posibilidad de que viera algo que sucediera aquí.

Helena tardó un poco en entender lo que estaba tratando de decirle. Kaine había pasado meses interpretando un papel para Morrough, consciente de que veía a través de los ojos de Helena todo lo que pasara entre ellos.

Entonces ¿qué había sido real? ¿Todo? ¿Nada?

Una ola de agotamiento la embistió. Se sentía como si sus recuerdos hubieran sufrido una sacudida y hubiesen quedado mezclados, revueltos y desorganizados. Ni siquiera se sentía capaz de pensar con claridad.

Quería dormir, sumergirse de nuevo en el abismo, pero tenía miedo de que los recuerdos volvieran a escapársele de entre los dedos. De que Kaine se desvaneciera y se despertara junto al Ferron frío y cruel de nuevo.

Por mucho que lo intentara, no lograba reconciliarlos. Para ella, eran dos personas distintas.

A Kaine lo conocía bien.

Pero Ferron era un monstruo. El miedo y el odio que sentía por él nacían de lo más profundo de su ser. Esa horrible silla de cadáveres, su pila de víctimas. Jamás lograría olvidarlo.

Le dolía la cabeza. El cráneo ejercía tal presión sobre sus ojos que amenazaba con expulsarlos de sus cuencas. Los cerró con fuerza justo cuando sintió que el colchón se hundía a su lado. Kaine la agarró del brazo con suavidad y ella notó cómo la pinchaba con la aguja de una vía intravenosa.

—Intenta no quitártela más —le pidió mientras trabajaba—. Para haber pasado tantos años trabajando en un hospital, eres una paciente terrible.

Le dejó el brazo estirado sobre la cama y volvió a revisar los frasquitos de la bandeja hasta dar con el que buscaba. Luego vertió su contenido por los tubos de la vía, de manera que se mezclara con el suero que le subía por el brazo.

—Deberías descansar. Ya hablaremos mañana.

—¿Y si vuelvo a olvidarlo todo? —preguntó con un hilo de voz, a punto de echarse a temblar de miedo. Kaine no respondió—. ¿Volverás... volverás a comportarte como antes si te olvido?

—Ya casi ha terminado todo —la tranquilizó, aunque no respondió a su pregunta.

Helena notó el medicamento corriéndole por las venas y envolviéndola como un manto pesado. Luchó por mantener los ojos abiertos, por seguir despierta y recordar.

—¿Y luego qué?

La habitación pareció sumirse en la oscuridad.

—Cuidarás de Lila, tal y como prometiste.

Cuando Helena volvió a abrir los ojos, una rendija de luz suave se colaba entre las cortinas, permitiéndole distinguir los detalles de la habitación, de su prisión. Kaine ya no estaba.

A los pocos minutos de despertar, una necrómata abrió la puerta. Helena se la quedó mirando.

—No es la primera vez que te veo… —le dijo cuando dejó una bandeja con un cuenco de sopa en la mesa—. Ya había estado aquí antes.

¿Por qué?

—Shhh…

La necrómata dejó escapar aquel suave siseo entre dientes y negó con la cabeza como para advertirle de que debía guardar silencio. Luego, metió una mano en el bolsillo, sacó un pedacito doblado de papel y se lo tendió.

En él solo había una palabra escrita con letras claras: «Descansa».

La nota se le escapó de entre los dedos, pero la necrómata la atrapó al vuelo y se la guardó en el bolsillo de nuevo antes de ofrecerle la sopa.

Helena se obligó a tomar unas cuantas cucharadas, pero su cuerpo rechazaba la comida y tenía ganas de vomitar. Mientras tanto, se esforzó por no pensar, por dejar de intentar recuperar la memoria, pero era tan inútil como tratar de ignorar a Lumitia en plena sublimación.

Kaine había sabido quién era desde el principio, desde que ella puso un pie en aquella casa.

El proceso de transferencia… había sido idea de la propia Helena. Era lo que había querido utilizar para curar a Titus Bayard.

Y Shiseo…

Se miró las muñecas con renovado pavor.

La transferencia, los grilletes… Era a Shiseo a quien le había hablado de ellos, no a Kaine. La transferencia era lo que había llevado a Morrough a instaurar el programa de repoblación.

Sufrió una arcada y vomitó toda la sopa que había tomado en el suelo, junto a la cama.

Intentó no pensar en ello. Trató de recordar cómo era antes y reconciliarse con la versión de sí misma que había olvidado. Al borrarse la memoria, había perdido una parte de su personalidad; había olvidado lo enfadada que estaba, lo despiadada que podía llegar a ser ella también.

Esa era la persona de la que Kaine se había enamorado, la persona por la que había hecho tantas cosas horribles. Pero esa Helena ya no existía, de ella no quedaba más que una sombra.

Cuando Kaine regresó, ya había caído la noche.

Pese a que el corazón le dio un vuelco de alivio, el miedo se adueñó de ella al verlo en la oscuridad. Era evidente que solo estaba de paso, pues se quedó observándola con frialdad desde la puerta, sin cruzar la estancia.

Helena no sabía qué quería que hiciera. Habría preferido que Kaine no hubiera ido a verla, pero la alternativa era mucho peor. En su ausencia, se veía obligada a lidiar con la posibilidad de que muriera y no regresara jamás. Entonces no volvería a verlo.

—¿Estás enfadado conmigo por algo? —le preguntó.

Kaine, que había permanecido en silencio, apretó los labios en una línea fina, entró en la habitación y cerró la puerta.

—No.

Se acercó a la ventana y descorrió las cortinas lo suficiente como para dejar entrar una suave rendija de luz plateada. Iba vestido de uniforme.

Helena lo estudió, intentando averiguar qué era lo que había cambiado tanto en él.

—Sí que estás enfadado. Siento que lo estás, pero no recuerdo por qué.

—Da igual —dijo sin mirarla—. Ya no importa.

—Pero, si lo que pasó no importa, ¿por qué has estado buscándome?

—¿Recuerdas cómo te capturaron? —preguntó apretando los dientes.

Helena asintió.

—Volé por los aires el laboratorio del puerto Oeste.

Kaine asintió brevemente, sin apartar la mirada de la ventana.

—¿Y recuerdas por qué lo hiciste?

Helena frunció el ceño. Tenía la sensación de que la respuesta era evidente, pero se le escapaba.

—No te fuerces si no consigues acordarte —le dijo Kaine lanzándole una mirada rápida al ver que no respondía.

—Fue por ti, ¿no?

Por algún motivo, pese a no recordar nada más que el fuego, el dolor de oídos y su intento de escapar, estaba segura de estar en lo cierto.

Kaine volvió a desviar la vista, pero asintió.

Helena no alcanzaba a entender por qué se enfadaría por algo así. Cerró los ojos. Ahora que estaba allí con ella, el agotamiento se apoderó de su cuerpo, como si hubiera estado esperando a verlo para descansar.

—Cuando dormías, solía prometerte que cuidaría de ti.

—No —respondió él con brusquedad—. Era al revés. Era yo quien te lo decía.

—Pero yo te respondía lo mismo —apuntó ella abriendo los ojos—. Supongo que nunca llegaste a oírme.

Una expresión conmocionada se adueñó de Kaine antes de que volviera a apartar la mirada y cerrara las cortinas. Entonces su rostro desapareció entre las sombras.

—¿Cuál es el plan? —le preguntó Helena a la oscuridad—. El otro día dijiste que ya casi había acabado todo. ¿Qué querías decir?

Los ojos de él parecieron resplandecer.

—Estamos esperando a que Lumitia entre en plena latencia. Te llevaré al Sur, lo más lejos posible de aquí. Pasarás más desapercibida.

—¿Lila está allí? ¿En el Sur?

—Sí, te está esperando en el continente, cerca de la costa. La dejé a medio camino mientras intentábamos encontrarte.

—¿Por qué hablas en plural?

Una chispa de esperanza floreció en su pecho al pensar que tal vez sí que había supervivientes.

—Shiseo me ha estado ayudando.

Helena retrocedió instintivamente al oír su nombre.

—Se entregó él mismo. —Aunque no podía verlo, a juzgar por el volumen de su voz, Kaine se había acercado a ella—. Enseñó los documentos y el sello que lo identificaban como un miembro de la familia imperial y se ofreció a investigar para los inmarcesibles. Diseñó esos grilletes con la esperanza de que, si alguna vez aparecías, fuera él el encargado de ponértelos.

—Bueno, está claro que la jugada le salió bien —dijo Helena con tirantez—. Todo esto es culpa suya. Si no les hubiera contado lo de la transferencia…

—Morrough te habría diseccionado el cerebro en cuanto te encontraron si Shiseo no hubiera intervenido —la interrumpió Kaine—. Además, era imposible adivinar para qué utilizaría Morrough el procedimiento.

Helena se quedó callada.

—Fue la única estrategia que se le ocurrió para conseguirme acceso a ti y ayudarnos a ganar el tiempo necesario para escapar. Será él quien te lleve hasta Lila.

—¿Y qué pasa con Paladia?

Kaine guardó silencio unos instantes.

—Morrough se está debilitando. Intentó utilizar el cuerpo de Holdfast como recambio, pero no fue suficiente. Ni siquiera introducirse sus huesos en el cuerpo le funcionó. Ha perdido a tantos inmarcesibles que ya no puede moverse ni respirar sin esa monstruosidad que ha creado. Por eso está tan desesperado por conseguir un animante. Cree que le ayudará a empezar de cero.

Los huesos de Luc. Había utilizado los huesos de Luc.

—La clave está en atacar en el momento preciso —siguió diciendo Kaine—. Los actos de Morrough y la gran extensión de la matanza han empezado a tener impacto en el continente. Los países vecinos intervendrán pronto y se rumorea que están formando una alianza. Incluso Hevgoss ha accedido a cooperar. Paladia es una fuente esencial de lumitio y una potencia industrial que no podrán reemplazar así como así con tantos alquimistas muertos. Aunque no quieran verse envueltos en un conflicto civil, harán lo que haga falta para defender sus intereses. Actuarán en cuanto estén seguros de que Morrough es lo bastante débil.

Su tono de voz destilaba una certeza casi absoluta, como si todo estuviera organizado ya al detalle. Aquello despertó el interés de Helena, que trató de recordar lo que había leído en los periódicos.

—¿Y tú cómo…?

—No te preocupes por los detalles —la interrumpió—. Para cuando llegue el momento, tú ya estarás muy lejos de aquí. Si quieres ayudar, asegúrate de comer y recobrar fuerzas para el viaje.

Se marchó sin decir nada más y no regresó hasta varios días después.

Que Kaine ni siquiera se dejara caer por su habitación la puso, tarde tras tarde, cada vez más nerviosa. No pudo evitar hacer el esfuerzo de recordar, de atar cabos y entender por qué estaba enfadado y por qué no volvía con ella. Su memoria regresaba a ráfagas, le teñía la vista de rojo, desordenaba sus pensamientos y la sepultaba bajo una avalancha de estallidos inconexos de emoción y fragmentos de conversaciones.

Estuvo todo el día sufriendo ataques como ese, así que Davies añadió el contenido de varios frasquitos al gotero para dejarla sumida en un estupor que le impedía pensar.

Ya había anochecido cuando el colchón se hundió a su lado y una mano fría le apartó los mechones que tenía pegados a la frente para colocárselos detrás de la oreja. Kaine le cogió la mano. Entrelazó sus dedos largos con los de ella y le acarició los nudillos con el pulgar, pero se detuvo al llegar a su dedo anular y le dio vueltas a algo despacio.

El anillo.

Helena se había olvidado de él.

Cuando los ataques cesaron, Kaine volvió a retirarse, aunque no se marchó. Al principio, Helena pensó que eran imaginaciones suyas, pero era evidente que él estaba intentando poner distancia entre ellos.

Se quedó de pie, con las manos entrelazadas a la espalda, sin mirarla, y respondió a todas sus preguntas en pocas palabras. Ella casi nunca sabía qué decir; todo le resultaba demasiado trivial o abrumador como para expresarlo en voz alta. Ni siquiera sabía por dónde empezar.

«Aguanta —se había dicho una y otra vez estando dentro del tanque—. No te derrumbes». Pensaba que lo había conseguido, pero ahora entendía que lo que quedaba de ella no eran más que retazos.

Permaneció en la cama mirando a Kaine, que seguía con la vista clavada en la ventana. Era de noche, así que no había nada que ver. Lo que no quería era mirarla a ella. Helena sabía que se marcharía en cualquier momento si no decía algo.

—¿Cómo has... estado estos días? —preguntó en un arrebato de desesperación, aunque enseguida se arrepintió de haber dicho semejante tontería.

—Bien.

Helena bajó la vista al regazo.

—Te has casado.

Kaine se puso rígido ante el comentario y respiró hondo.

—Sí, con Aurelia Ingram.

Helena asintió. No entendía por qué le importaba tanto, dadas las circunstancias. Nunca se había planteado la posibilidad de casarse con él. Sin embargo, su mente se negaba a dejar de darle vueltas a ese detalle. Ahora tenía una esposa y, en consecuencia, ella sería...

No sabía lo que sería. Ni lo que había sido.

—Fueron órdenes de Morrough —explicó él, aunque Helena no había dicho nada más—. El Concejo de Gremios quería celebrar un evento de gran repercusión para demostrar que todo había vuelto a la normalidad. No tuve otra opción.

Helena se limitó a asentir, en silencio.

—Yo... —Kaine se volvió para mirarla, pero las palabras murieron en sus labios.

El espacio que los separaba era como un abismo plagado de los pecados que habían cometido contra el otro, pero Helena notaba la rabia de Kaine incluso desde la distancia.

Daba igual lo que dijera. Sabía que estaba enfadado con ella.

—¿Ya puedes viajar? —le preguntó—. Has dicho que has ido a Hevgoss muchas veces.

—Así es.

Helena retorció el borde de la sábana de lino entre los dedos.

—Entonces, cuando todo esto haya acabado, ¿vendrás...? ¿Vendrás al Sur con nosotras?

—Me temo que Lila me sigue odiando tanto como el primer día.

Ella se quedó callada, a la espera de una respuesta de verdad. «Se suponía que íbamos a huir juntos. Me lo prometiste».

Kaine rehuyó su mirada y volvió a fijar la vista en el patio.

—Con un poco de suerte, no me quedaré mucho tiempo en Paladia después de que os vayáis.

—¿Vendrás entonces con nosotras? —insistió con tono esperanzado.

Dentro de los asfixiantes confines de Puntaférreo, le resultaba imposible imaginar un escenario en que se reconciliaran. Sin embargo, si se marchaban lejos de allí, tal vez pudieran empezar de cero. Al fin y al cabo, habían vuelto a encontrarse. Con el tiempo, tal vez podrían intentarlo de nuevo.

Los ojos de Kaine brillaron por un momento.

—Si eso es lo que quieres —susurró tras esbozar el fantasma fugaz de una sonrisa.

Pero no sonó sincero.

CAPÍTULO 67

Mayus 1789

EL TIEMPO NO CURÓ TODAS sus heridas, pero ayudó a que la mente de Helena mejorara. Sus recuerdos parecieron ir asentándose y comenzaron a ordenarse un poco más cada día que pasaba.

Acabó recordando que había engañado a Kaine y comprendió por fin por qué se había mostrado tan paranoico desde que la habían llevado a la casa. Comprendió por qué había revisado sus recuerdos, ansioso por ver incluso sus rutinas más intrascendentes.

La había subestimado una vez y no iba a volver a confiar en ella nunca más. Así que estaba claro que todavía le estaba mintiendo.

Helena ya lo sospechaba, pero le costaba fiarse de su propio juicio o de su capacidad para interpretar lo que le sucedía. Su mente seguía llena de lagunas. Sus pensamientos todavía tendían a quedarse a medias y su cabeza continuaba dejando escapar detalles importantes. Sin embargo, con el paso de los días, cada vez estuvo más segura de que la engañaba.

Su objetivo era mantenerla tranquila, asegurar un «entorno controlado». Incluso entonces trataba de manipularla. Lo que no conseguía entender era por qué. Le había dado mil vueltas al asunto para tratar de encontrar algún vacío en la narrativa que Kaine había construido desde que había recobrado el conocimiento y que con tanto esmero había creado. Necesitaba perspectiva: distinguir mejor lo que era real de lo que no lo era.

Salió de la habitación y miró a ambos lados. Los pasillos, la casa, el recuerdo asfixiante de la muerte y la pena que lo impregnaba todo solían aterrorizarla, pero se quedó ahí, escudriñando el espacio que la rodeaba y se confundía con las sombras. Al final sí que la estaba atormentando un fantasma.

El suyo propio.

Recorrió el pasillo despacio, con los pies descalzos. El frío suelo de hierro la mantenía anclada al presente, la ayudaba a estar segura de lo que era real.

Kaine apareció en el rellano inferior justo cuando ella llegaba a la escalera. Vestía completamente de negro salvo por el prístino cuello blanco y el borde apenas visible de las mangas de la camisa. El contraste era tan intenso que casi parecía un dibujo hecho a tinta: todo líneas rectas en tonos de blanco y negro.

—Pensé que habrías salido —dijo al ver que él permanecía en silencio.

—Sabía que te habías levantado. ¿Te ves con fuerzas para llegar al ala principal?

No, pero asintió movida por la curiosidad de ver adónde la llevaba.

Kaine mantuvo las distancias con ella de forma deliberada y le advirtió en voz baja de todos los puntos desde los que Morrough podría estar observándolos. Helena no dejaba de mirarlo, de estudiar la tensión que lo encorsetaba y la precisión milimétrica de cada uno de sus movimientos. Era tan riguroso que su actitud casi no parecía humana. Cayó en la cuenta, horrorizada, de que todo era resultado del sello. Kaine estaba más destilado que nunca. Su poder lo había transmutado hasta dejarlo reducido a las cualidades que le confería.

En su intento por encontrarla, había permitido que el sello lo consumiera.

Se habían detenido delante de las imponentes puertas que Helena siempre había encontrado cerradas en sus exploraciones por la casa. Resultó que ocultaban una biblioteca.

—Te habría traído aquí antes, pero me daba miedo que Aurelia empezara a sospechar algo si pasabas demasiado tiempo en esta ala —explicó dando un paso a un lado para dejarla pasar—. Estaré fuera hasta última hora de la tarde, pero he pensado que te vendría bien un incentivo para moverte y pasar el tiempo.

Helena no se movió mientras observaba la enorme sala. En la pared opuesta, había unas cuantas ventanas que daban al norte. Pese a estar a finales de primavera, la luz que iluminaba aquella ala de la casa era débil, los pasillos estaban envueltos en sombras y los techos eran tan altos que casi ni se distinguían. La oscuridad parecía a punto de descender sobre ella y engullirla, de hacerla desaparecer sin más.

—También podría sospechar ahora —señaló sin cruzar el umbral.

—No está aquí. —Helena lo miró sorprendida y Kaine continuó—: Ahora mismo permanece en la ciudad. Dudo que vuelva, pero te avisaré si lo hace.

Helena tragó saliva.

—¿Y si…? ¿Y si volvemos en otro momento?

Era evidente que Kaine había esperado que la biblioteca funcionara como un incentivo para sacarla de su habitación. Al fin y al cabo, Helena había pasado la mayor parte de su cautiverio muerta de aburrimiento y él le estaba ofreciendo ahora un mundo de entretenimiento. Le echó una rápida mirada de arriba abajo.

Helena se humedeció los labios y apoyó la mano en la pared para notar la textura del papel bajo los dedos.

—Es que ahí dentro… está un poco oscuro. Es por el techo. No conviene que me dé un ataque… con lo del… lo del bebé.

Se atragantó con la última palabra. Era la primera vez que mencionaba el tema en voz alta desde que había recobrado el conocimiento. Su mente intentaba por todos los medios dejar a un lado aquella realidad, incapaz aún de asumir sus implicaciones.

Kaine también se estremeció.

—Preferiría no entrar, si no te importa.

—Hel…

Kaine avanzó hacia ella, pero, al ver que se ponía tensa, se detuvo en seco. Se la quedó mirando con una mano apenas extendida. A Helena le ardían las mejillas y tuvo que desviar la mirada.

¿Qué sentiría al tener que lidiar con aquella versión deslucida de ella? Helena ni siquiera recordaba del todo lo que habían vivido juntos, y compararse con su yo del pasado le resultaba insoportable. Le tembló la mandíbula.

—Sé que tenerle miedo a la oscuridad es… irracional. Créeme que lo sé —dijo con la voz entrecortada—. Estoy intentando… Sé…

Kaine salió de la biblioteca y cerró la puerta. A Helena se le cayó el alma a los pies al notar que la distancia que los separaba se ampliaba; no quería que la tocara, pero al mismo tiempo se moría por volver a estar entre sus brazos. Su mente y su cuerpo no dejaban de librar una batalla constante.

Era imposible que Kaine pudiera ocupar ese espacio intermedio. No había distancia que fuera lo bastante grande como para ayudarla a olvidar lo que había pasado ni lo bastante corta como para que él siguiera a su alcance.

—No pasa nada —le dijo sin mirarla—. Pensé que te gustaría, pero no estás familiarizada con este espacio y es normal que te dé miedo. Si quieres algún libro, te lo puedo subir yo a tu habitación. —Helena asintió con rigidez—. Te acompaño arriba.

—No, deberías irte —le dijo ella, presionando la mano contra la pared hasta que el grillete se le clavó en la muñeca—. Te voy a retrasar y sé llegar sola.

Un destello fugaz surcó la mirada de él.

—Como quieras…

Se dio la vuelta y Helena lo sujetó de manera instintiva.

—Kaine… —Cuando se detuvo, ella bajó inmediatamente la mano y esbozó una sonrisa tensa—. Ten cuidado y no mueras.

Kaine permaneció quieto durante un momento mientras la observaba, pero luego volvió a girarse.

—Ya.

CUANDO REGRESÓ, HACÍA YA UN rato que había caído la noche. Helena estaba sentada en el sofá de su habitación, trazando el diseño de la alfombra con la mirada mientras esperaba. Había pasado todo el día intentando convencerse de la mentira, encajando una y otra vez las piezas del rompecabezas.

Kaine se detuvo en el umbral, sin entrar, como si quisiera dejar claro que solo estaba de visita y que el encuentro sería rápido e impersonal. Helena lo observó con atención. Siempre había tenido esa tendencia a quedarse totalmente inmóvil. Ese detalle sí que lo recordaba.

—¿Sabes ya qué libros quieres que te traiga? —le preguntó al cabo de un rato.

Ella negó con la cabeza.

—Hoy he estado pensando —le dijo, y Kaine arqueó una ceja—. Tu plan no tiene ningún sentido.

—Bueno, no todos contamos con una mente tan brillante como la tuya —respondió él con ligereza, sin moverse de la puerta.

Helena analizó el espacio que los separaba. Si Morrough los observaba, ¿qué vería? Nada. No había nada que ver salvo el vacío que los separaba.

—Hoy no me has dicho que siempre me encontrarías. Solías decírmelo cuando tenía que marcharme. Cuando… —Parpadeó y una de sus manos sufrió un espasmo—. Era así, ¿verdad?

El rostro de Kaine se oscureció cuando entró en la habitación, cerró la puerta y se apoyó contra ella.

—Me parecía una promesa vacía dadas las circunstancias.

Ella negó con la cabeza.

—No fue culpa tuya. Me buscaste por todas partes. Mandl…

Él profirió una carcajada seca, y a Helena le dio un vuelco el corazón.

—Ya, claro, gracias. —Su voz destilaba sarcasmo—. Por todas partes, sí. Moví cielo y tierra para encontrarte, ¿no?

Ella se lo quedó mirando, y, aunque su tono se volvió pensativo, sus ojos permanecieron impasibles y resplandecientes.

—Entre los escombros, entre las pilas de cadáveres, por las prisiones, las minas y los laboratorios, por todo el maldito continente. Te busqué por todas partes, pero pasé por alto el único lugar que debería haber comprobado. —Se le rompió la voz, pero sonrió—. Te agradezco de corazón que valores el excepcional trabajo que hice.

Había algo en la forma en la que hablaba que a Helena le resultaba familiar. Sintió que se le revolvía el estómago y se le nublaba la vista. El rostro de Kaine de pronto apareció ante ella y ya no estuvo tan segura de saber qué estaba viviendo. ¿Era el pasado? ¿El presente? ¿Una combinación de ambos?

Una nueva carcajada la devolvió a la realidad.

La expresión de Kaine se había torcido.

—¿Cómo que no fue culpa mía? —había seguido diciendo, enseñándole los dientes—. ¿Eso es lo que esperas que me diga a mí mismo? —Se llevó una mano pálida al corazón—. ¿Crees que abrazar un eterno victimismo me hará sentir mejor?

Su rabia era tan intensa que parecía llenarlo todo. Helena bajó la vista mientras intentaba mantener la respiración controlada. Había tantas cosas distintas en su cabeza que se esforzaba por ignorar que le costaba mantenerse a flote. Tenía miedo de hundirse en la ciénaga en que se había convertido su propia mente.

Aun así, sabía que Kaine le estaba mintiendo. Estaba decidido a ocultarle algo, empeñado en mantenerla al margen. Helena estaba segura de que lo sabría si tuviera la memoria intacta.

—Pero no iba por ahí. No quiero hablar de eso ahora. Lo que no entiendo es por qué estás dispuesto a quedarte esperando a que me vaya. Si me escapo, Morrough sospechará que lo has traicionado o pensará que le has fallado.

Kaine respiró hondo para tranquilizarse y adoptar una actitud tan certera y cruel como la trampa de un cazador al accionarse.

—Como ya te he dicho, hemos fijado unos plazos muy concretos, pero eso a ti no te concierne.

Estaba intentando herirla para que dejara de hacer preguntas, pero Helena se negó a ceder.

—Si me voy, Morrough sabrá que eres el traidor —insistió con terquedad—. Y, aunque no lo descubra, te echará la culpa por haberme dejado escapar. Está desesperado y este… este bebé es su última esperanza. Si tuvieras una manera de derrocar su régimen, ya lo habrías hecho. A no ser que algo te esté frenando.

Kaine no respondió, así que Helena tomó aire y continuó hablando:

—Coincido contigo en que se respira cierta inestabilidad, pero hay algo que mantiene el plan de Morrough en pie, algo que impide que se desmorone. Y esa es la figura del Sumo Inquisidor. Todo el mundo lo teme y da por hecho que, si algo le pasara a Morrough, sería él quien asumiría el poder. Y ahora ya se sabe que el Sumo Inquisidor eres tú.

»Teniendo todo esto en cuenta, solo se me ocurre una cosa capaz de hacer que Morrough parezca lo bastante débil como para que los demás países se atrevan por fin a atacar.

Kaine se encogió de hombros despreocupadamente.

—No creo que estés lo bastante familiarizada con el clima político actual como para opinar sobre el tema. Que solo se te ocurra una posible explicación no quita que haya otras.

Helena encontró su mirada.

—Entonces ¿por qué no me explicas tu plan? Así sabremos si estoy pasando algo por alto.

Kaine ladeó la cabeza y una expresión gélida y burlona se adueñó de su rostro.

—¿Qué parte de «eso a ti no te concierne» no has entendido? ¿Es que también has olvidado el significado de esa expresión? ¿Quieres que te traiga un diccionario?

A Helena se le formó un nudo en la garganta y notó cómo se le crispaban los dedos. Kaine siempre se mostraba más cruel cuando se sentía vulnerable.

—Si hubieras encontrado la manera de debilitarlo o matarlo, ya lo habrías hecho —dijo encontrando su mirada—. Habrías... —Se le cerró la garganta—. Yo no estaría... embarazada. Eso significa que hay algo que te impide actuar. Y ese algo soy yo, ¿no es así? Estás esperando a que me vaya, porque para entonces ya estarás muerto y dará igual que Morrough descubra que tú eres el traidor. Porque la única manera de debilitar a Morrough es dejarlo sin su Sumo Inquisidor.

Kaine permaneció inmóvil, pero, al cabo de unos segundos, su fachada se desmoronó y dejó escapar un largo suspiro.

—Tenía la esperanza de que la biblioteca te mantuviera ocupada durante una semana como mínimo —admitió con expresión agotada.

Helena esperó a que se explicara, pero no dijo nada más.

—¿Ese es tu plan? —preguntó con voz aguda y temblorosa por la incredulidad—. Después de todo este tiempo, ¿vas y acabas recurriendo al mismo plan de siempre? ¿De verdad creías que iba a acceder a que me escondieras en algún lado mientras tú te sacrificabas?

Kaine dejó escapar una risita grave, cuya vibración Helena notó en los huesos.

—No me digas que esta vez también tienes una solución mejor —susurró—. Al fin y al cabo, tú no has experimentado todos los horrores que te imaginé sufriendo a lo largo de estos meses. Solo te perdí y pasé catorce meses buscándote sin éxito. Solo te he encontrado rota y torturada. Solo te he mantenido prisionera, te he sometido a la transferencia y te he violado... —La rabia y el dolor le quebraron la voz. Su piel había palidecido, había adoptado un tono blanco resplandeciente y abrasador—. ¿No te parece suficiente? Está claro que nuestra situación aún puede empeorar hasta límites insospechados. ¿Quieres que lo intentemos?

Helena permaneció en silencio. Había tanto que quería decirle que le resultaba imposible decidir por dónde empezar y cómo organizar toda aquella información. Su mente, limitada, no podía contener tantas ideas. Si se forzaba demasiado, se rompería.

Kaine exhaló con brusquedad. Su expresión era ilegible, pero el brillo de antes se había desvanecido y le temblaba la barbilla.

—No puedo hacer más, Helena, lo siento. Ya sé que para ti nunca ha sido suficiente.

—Kaine... —dijo ella con la voz entrecortada.

Él suspiró y apoyó una mano en el marco de la puerta como si lo necesitara para mantenerse en pie.

—Sé que quieres salvar a todo el mundo, como siempre, pero, por desgracia, yo no dispongo de ese talento. Al menos, así verás el fin de la guerra. Eso sí que puedo asegurártelo.

—¡No! —replicó ella con brusquedad.

Kaine la miró y su rostro se endureció.

—Siempre has dicho que jamás me pondrías por delante de la Resistencia y la Llama Eterna. Y yo estoy atado a un barco que se está yendo a pique. No pienso arrastrarte conmigo.

—¡Mentía! —gritó ella—. No… No podía… No iba a… a…

Jadeó en busca de aliento y se agarró el pecho. El ritmo de sus latidos era tan irregular que le impedía respirar. Se presionó el esternón e ignoró el dolor que le subía por el brazo mientras todo a su alrededor daba vueltas.

La rabia en la expresión de Kaine desapareció. Se acercó con cautela y se arrodilló ante ella como si fuera un animalillo asustadizo. La sujetó por los hombros y la mantuvo erguida.

—Helena…, respira. Por favor, tienes que respirar.

Recordaba aquella mirada suplicante. Lo recordaba justo así. En algún momento habían estado exactamente en esa misma situación. Helena se había aferrado a sus hombros y había apoyado la frente contra la suya.

—Por favor, respira —repetía una y otra vez mientras el peso de sus manos sobre los hombros la ayudaba a mantenerse anclada al presente, hasta que su pecho dejó de estremecerse.

—Tiene que haber otra manera —dijo ella cuando logró recuperar la voz—. Dijimos que huiríamos juntos, ¿recuerdas? ¿Por qué no puedes venir conmigo? El otro día me comentaste que habías salido de Paladia. Podríamos marcharnos y buscar una manera de revertir lo que Morrough te hizo. Los países vecinos se encargarán de él si tú desapareces de la ecuación. ¿Por qué no podemos hacerlo así?

—Ya te habría llevado lejos de aquí si hubiera podido. Morrough me permitió llevarme mi filacteria para darles caza a los fugitivos, pero… empezó a sospechar de mí el año pasado. Por eso tiene que ser Shiseo quien se encargue de ayudarte a escapar.

Helena negó con la cabeza.

—No…

Kaine le tomó la mano.

—No sé si te acuerdas, pero me prometiste que harías lo que te pidiera si salvaba a Bayard por ti. Bueno, pues esto es lo que quiero a cambio. Quiero que dejes este maldito país atrás y empieces una nueva vida muy lejos de aquí. Le prometiste a Holdfast que protegerías a Lila y a su heredero. Espero que esa promesa te mantenga ocupada durante mucho tiempo.

—Pero prometí cuidar de ti primero —replicó ella retirando la mano—. Siempre. Te prometí que siempre te cuidaría. Si todo hubiera salido como tenías planeado, me habrías enviado lejos sin que yo me acordara siquiera de ti. No habría entendido nada hasta que fuera demasiado tarde…

—Bueno —dijo él con voz estrangulada—, la última vez que me sinceré contigo, desapareciste para no volver.

Helena se encogió como si la hubiera golpeado y se le volvió a entrecortar la respiración.

—Pero lo intenté. Cuando me atraparon estaba… estaba volviendo a por ti. Intenté…

—Lo sé. Si lo que dicen los informes es cierto, te defendiste con uñas y dientes. Si no te hubieras fijado en mi padre, habrías tenido la oportunidad de escapar. Sé que lo intentaste. —Dio un paso atrás—. Pero no fue suficiente. No pudiste hacer más.

Helena lo agarró para que no se alejara, para que mantuviera su rostro cerca del suyo.

—Pero ¿y si hubiéramos estado ahí juntos? Si hubiésemos trabajado en equipo para salvar a Lila, la situación podría haber sido distinta. ¿Por qué no lo intentamos ahora?

Una expresión que no alcanzó a reconocer cruzó el rostro de Kaine, que se la quedó mirando con el ceño fruncido. Helena comprendió que su pregunta era absurda porque ya no era la misma persona de entonces; de hecho, era poco más que una sombra de quien había sido.

Kaine bajó la vista.

—Nos espera una larga despedida y no quiero pelear contigo, pero no pienso hacer nada que pueda ponerte en peligro.

—Déjame buscar otra solución. Si me pongo a investigar, tal vez encuentre algo que hasta ahora hayamos pasado por alto.

Kaine permaneció callado mientras sopesaba los posibles riesgos, pero al final suspiró.

—Accederé con dos condiciones. Tendrás que parar si el estrés hace que tu salud empeore. Y, cuando Shiseo venga a por ti, te irás con él sin rechistar, independientemente de lo cerca que creas estar de descubrir algo o encontrar una respuesta. No volverás a engañarme o a manipularme. Nos despediremos y te marcharás. —Encontró su mirada—. ¿Te parece bien?

Helena tragó saliva con fuerza.

—Con una condición.

—¿Cuál? —preguntó él apretando los dientes.

—Que no me mientas más. No quiero pasarme los días dándole vueltas a lo que me cuentas sin saber si es verdad o no.

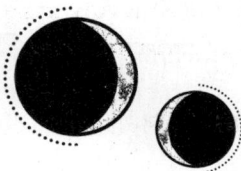

CAPÍTULO 68

Mayus 1789

Tan pronto como accedió, Kaine se puso de pie y la soltó.

—Ya es tarde. Deberías descansar. Mañana iré a ver qué encuentro. Creo que Shiseo preparó un par de cosas para ti.

—Espera —dijo ella apresuradamente, agarrándolo para que no se alejara. El equilibrio que habían alcanzado amenazaba con desmoronarse en cuanto se reabrió el espacio físico entre ellos—. No… no te vayas.

Kaine levantó la vista hacia ella antes de volver a esconderse tras una máscara de fingido desinterés.

—¿Por qué?

Helena apretó los puños.

—Cada vez que te vas, nunca sé qué… qué versión de ti me encontraré la próxima vez que nos veamos. Tengo todos los recuerdos… desordenados y la situación me resulta confusa. La imagen que tengo de ti cuando no estás es la de una persona muy… muy fría.

Kaine escondió una mano detrás de la espalda, pero no logró ocultar a tiempo la crispación de sus dedos.

—¿Qué quieres que haga entonces? —preguntó con una aparente tirantez.

—Quiero que te quedes —dijo ella en un susurro.

Se levantó para ir a la cama y, al pasar al lado de Kaine, sintió que quedaba firmemente anclada a la realidad, si bien no al presente.

«Volvía a la cama mientras él se quitaba el abrigo y lo dejaba sobre el respaldo del sofá. Iba a tumbarse boca arriba, a clavar la mirada en el dosel y a intentar mantenerse quieta…».

Se detuvo en seco. Los pulmones se le constriñeron hasta que se quedó sin aliento y la cabeza empezó a dolerle como si fuera a partírsele en dos.

¿Cómo iban a superar aquello?

La voz de Kaine la sacó de su ensimismamiento. Volvió a mirarlo.

—Será mejor que me vaya —dijo negando con la cabeza—. Regresaré mañana e... intentaré...

—No. —Ella también negó con la cabeza—. Tengo que acostumbrarme a ti de nuevo. Necesito recordar lo nuestro.

Kaine exhaló y se sentó al borde de la cama, como tantas otras veces había hecho antes, entrelazando su mano con la de ella y contemplando la estancia.

Le temblaban los dedos y, pese a lo mucho que se estaba esforzando por dejarlos quietos, la tensión solo empeoraba la situación. Helena no entendía de dónde venían esos espasmos.

—¿Por qué ya no te curas? —le preguntó.

—Quedamos tan pocos inmarcesibles que Morrough bebe mucha más energía de los que estamos vivos —explicó él sin mirarla a los ojos—. Ahora tardo más en regenerarme. Pero... no sé por qué no dejan de temblarme las manos. Supongo que es el precio de la arrogancia.

Durante todos aquellos meses, Helena lo había estado viendo consumirse sin ser consciente de ello. Kaine había estado erradicando a los inmarcesibles pese a saber que, con cada muerte, el castigo al que se vería sometido se intensificaría, al tiempo que su capacidad de regeneración disminuiría.

—Lo siento muchísimo —susurró, y él se encogió como si lo hubiera golpeado al decir eso y estuvo a punto de apartar la mano de la de ella.

—No me pidas perdón —le espetó con una mirada fulminante.

—Pero estás enfadado conmigo, ¿no?

Kaine desvió la mirada y la dejó vagar por la habitación mientras tragaba saliva.

—Eso no significa que tengas motivos para disculparte.

—¿Por qué no?

—Porque... —se le quebró la voz y agachó la cabeza—. Yo debería ser el primero en pedir perdón y n-ni... ni siquiera sé por dónde empezar. Tenía la esperanza de que no recordaras nada de esto. Si te hubiera mentido sobre el rescate de Bayard y te hubiera dejado marchar, nada habría pasado.

Helena se incorporó.

—Me habría matado. Que me hubieras hecho huir y te hubieran descubierto porque yo te había convencido de rescatar a Lila me habría matado. Volvería a pasar por todo aquello sin dudarlo un segundo con tal de salvarte. No cambiaría ni un segundo.

Kaine se volvió para mirarla con una mezcla de sorpresa y enojo surcándole las facciones.

—Pero no me salvaste —dijo al fin cuando consiguió hablar—. Nos sumiste a ambos en un infierno durante dos años.

Una bofetada le habría dolido menos. Helena se quedó helada, perdió todo el color.

—Intenté volver… —insistió con voz temblorosa—. Te lo juro.

La expresión de Kaine se tornó apesadumbrada.

—Lo sé. No quería decir que…

Helena se apartó, tenía la sensación de que le iban a entrar ganas de vomitar si seguía mirándolo.

—No deberías haber dado por hecho que estaría dispuesta a perderte. ¿Creías que me importabas menos porque tenía otras obligaciones? ¿Que mis sentimientos por ti no estaban a la altura de los tuyos por mí? Hice todo, absolutamente todo lo posible por mantenerte a salvo. Ni te imaginas lo que hice por ti.

—Lo que quería decir es que…

—Cada vez que me preguntabas si era tuya, te prometía que sí, que para siempre. Y un «para siempre» no tiene excepciones ni fecha de vencimiento.

***

HELENA SE DESPERTÓ CON UN dolor de cabeza insoportable. Se quedó tumbada en la cama mientras trataba de orientarse en la oscuridad. Notaba los dedos de Kaine entrelazados con los suyos y descubrió que él estaba sentado en el suelo, junto a la cama, con la cabeza caída hacia un lado.

Se acercó a él un poco para contemplarlo en la penumbra.

Su problema eran los espacios vacíos, los momentos en que sus recuerdos giraban como una moneda en la que el pasado y el presente se situaban en caras opuestas. Sin embargo, teniéndolo cerca, pese a las alteraciones del tiempo, Helena sabía que Kaine era suyo. Que lo era igual que antes.

Kaine la había amado. Pese a que había estado convencido de que la suya era una relación imposible, sus sentimientos por ella nunca habían flaqueado.

—Voy a cuidar de ti —articuló en silencio.

Notó enseguida el momento en que él se despertó. La tensión se adueñó de su cuerpo, se le abrieron los ojos de golpe y sus dedos se le crisparon. Sin embargo, toda su rigidez se disipó cuando reparó en Helena. Se puso de pie, se inclinó sobre ella y la observó con atención.

—¿Te encuentras bien?

—Solo es un dolor de cabeza.

Kaine le tocó la frente y alivió la presión que se le acumulaba detrás de los ojos con su resonancia.

—¿Me podrías traer algo para empezar a investigar?

—Creo que deberías descansar —dijo frunciendo el ceño con preocupación.

—No. Pasaré el día nerviosa si no tengo algo con lo que distraerme.

Kaine suspiró y, aunque no le llevó la contraria, Helena sabía que estaba considerando algo mientras la observaba en silencio. Al cabo de unos instantes, respiró hondo y le cogió la mano.

—Voy a confiar en ti. Te pido, por favor, que no hagas que me arrepienta.

Helena no entendió el alcance de sus palabras hasta que le cerró los dedos en torno a su muñeca y la banda de metal que se la rodeaba se soltó de pronto. Contempló, estupefacta, cómo se la quitaba y extraía el tubo de anulitio del interior de la muñeca. La perforación tenía los bordes irregulares, surcados de cicatrices por todas las veces que se había caído o había ejercido demasiada presión sobre la zona.

Le sorprendió ver lo pequeños que eran tanto el conducto como la herida. Siempre había tenido la sensación de que serían más grandes, de que habían ocupado todo el espacio entre los huesecillos de sus muñecas. Extendió los dedos y notó su resonancia por primera vez en mucho tiempo.

—Todavía tendrás que llevar los grilletes —señaló Kaine con voz estrangulada—, pero confío en que tendrás cuidado y no matarás a ningún miembro del servicio ni intentarás huir.

Helena logró asentir, temblorosa y demasiado abrumada como para decir nada.

—Tendré que volver a colocarte el conducto de anulitio cuando Stroud venga por aquí o se dará cuenta de que algo no encaja. Espero que entiendas por qué no he podido hacer esto antes.

Ella volvió a asentir.

Kaine respiró hondo, le cogió la otra muñeca y le quitó el grillete restante. Luego, le dio un momento para que moviera las muñecas y disfrutara de la sensación del poder regresando a sus dedos.

—No era consciente de lo esencial que es la resonancia para mí hasta que la perdí —comentó llevándose las manos a la cabeza para calmar su cerebro inflamado. Su mente era un paisaje extraño, como si dos versiones de sí misma se hubieran solapado y no supiera por cuál decantarse. Levantó la vista—. Creo que ya me veo capaz de comer un poco.

Siguió abriendo y cerrando los puños, deleitándose con la sensación de la resonancia. Kaine la observó, atrapado entre el deseo de mantenerla así, en esa casa donde al menos podía tener el control de todo lo que ocurriera, y el rechazo que le producía tenerla encerrada como si fuera una prisionera.

Tras haberse visto obligado a tomar una decisión, había elegido que fuera libre.

Helena no quería que se arrepintiera de ello.

Llevaba un rato intentando reparar las lesiones que los conductos de anulitio le habían dejado en los músculos y los tendones, pero las cicatrices eran demasiado antiguas y complejas como para desaparecer por completo. El tiempo y el daño habían provocado que sus dedos se movieran con torpeza, que su antigua soltura hubiera desaparecido casi por completo. Al cabo de un rato, se dio por vencida y extendió las muñecas hacia Kaine para que volviera a rodeárselas con la cinta de cobre.

—Te traeré todo lo que encuentre para tu investigación —le dijo guardándose los tubos de anulitio.

Cuando se disponía a levantarse, Helena le cogió la mano. Ahora que por fin se había librado de la debilidad forzada del anulitio, se aferró a él hasta que se volvió para mirarla.

—Ten cuidado —le dijo—. No... —Las palabras se le atragantaron, así que le dio un apretón en la mano—. Vuelve conmigo, ¿vale?

—Por supuesto.

CUANDO DAVIES LE ENTREGÓ LA hoja de papel, ya era mediodía. Helena se sentó a descifrar la variedad de notas escritas con una caligrafía que no supo reconocer. Casi todas utilizaban abreviaturas alquímicas y glosas con las que no estaba familiarizada, pero identificó la letra fluida de Shiseo e incluso la de Kaine.

Había numerosos sellos parciales y fórmulas. Algunos le resultaban extrañamente familiares y los estudió con sumo cuidado, analizándolos hasta que los símbolos se desdibujaron en el papel.

Entonces se hizo un ovillo sobre el costado, se cubrió la cabeza con ambos brazos y se quedó dormida.

Cuando despertó, Kaine estaba sentado a su lado, hojeando una guía sobre embarazos.

Helena se estremeció al verlo. No quería pensar en el bebé. Sabía que estaba ahí, creciendo en su interior, pero su existencia le resultaba abrumadora y tenía asuntos más urgentes en los que centrarse.

Kaine cerró el libro de golpe.

—¿De dónde has sacado las notas que me enviaste? —preguntó con los ojos cerrados para contener el dolor de cabeza.

—Si no me equivoco, algunas de ellas son de Bennet. Shiseo recogió toda la información sobre sellos no metalúrgicos que pudo encontrar. Me dijo que era algo en lo que te había visto trabajando.

Una nueva laguna emergió en su memoria. ¿Había estado investigando sobre ese tema?

—No lo recuerdo.

¿Cuánta información más le faltaba?

—Estoy seguro de que acabarás acordándote.

Pero se les acababa el tiempo. Helena abrió los ojos; su mente trabajaba con dificultad, como una máquina con los engranajes obstruidos.

—Creo que nunca he utilizado sellos para la vivemancia o la animancia. —Frunció el ceño—. Quizá no funcionaban con fórmulas celestiales o elementales. ¿Alguna vez has usado algún otro tipo de numeración con un sello?

Kaine negó con la cabeza.

La conversación sonaba tan forzada que resultaba casi dolorosa. Helena se abría camino a ciegas por su propia memoria para intentar resolver un rompecabezas sin recordar qué piezas tenía en las manos. Mientras expuso sus ideas, Kaine asintió con la expresión atenta que requerían las circunstancias, pero no dejaba de mirar el reloj y se mostró impasible cuando intentó que participase.

Poco a poco, comprendió que todo aquello era una pantomima indulgente. Lo de las notas y lo de quitarle los grilletes no era más que un intento por apaciguarla. Quería hacer lo mismo que con la biblioteca: mantenerla ocupada y motivada para que recuperara fuerzas, pero no confiaba en que la investigación fuera a cambiar su situación. Intentaba tenerla bajo control.

Helena dejó de hablar y Kaine asintió como si coincidiera con lo que se suponía que acababa de decir antes de ponerse de pie.

—Me aseguraré de conseguirte lo que necesitas.

Se dispuso a marcharse, pero se detuvo en seco y se volvió. Miró a Helena y su mirada recorrió la habitación durante un buen rato antes de volver a hablar:

—Sé que… —Se detuvo, cerró el puño y escondió la mano detrás de la espalda. Luego, parpadeó y su mirada se perdió en algún punto detrás de Helena—. Según tengo entendido —comenzó de nuevo con tono distante—, para cuando hayas escapado de Paladia, ya no podrás interrumpir el embarazo por métodos sencillos. Sin embargo, todavía te quedará la opción de la vivemancia o la cirugía. Cuando te vayas, intentaré proporcionarte los materiales necesarios para que puedas encargarte de ello, pero avísame si se te ocurre algo en concreto. Me aseguraré de conseguírtelo.

Antes de que Helena tuviera la oportunidad de responder, Kaine se dio la vuelta y se marchó.

Ella se recostó, dejó el papel a un lado y se obligó a mirarse el cuerpo.

Se tocó la ligera protuberancia que tenía en el vientre con dedos vacilantes, a regañadientes, justo por debajo del ombligo. La mano le temblaba casi con violencia cuando se exploró con su resonancia.

Ya había visto al bebé en la pantalla de resonancia, pero la situación era distinta cuando usaba su propio poder. Se sorprendió al descubrir lo pequeño que era y apartó la mano de inmediato, con el corazón latiéndole de manera irregular.

Helena nunca había pensado en tener hijos. No era algo que estuviera a su alcance, así que lo que quisiera no importaba. Un mes antes, se habría quitado la vida sin dudar para evitar que el bebé, cualquiera que fuera, cayera en manos de Morrough. Para ella, el embarazo solo se reducía a ese contexto.

Sin embargo, si lograba escapar y la decisión fuera solo suya, ¿qué haría?

Cuando Davies subió a llevarle la cena aquella noche, le trajo también una plancha de grabado y un punzón. Helena sostuvo la herramienta, muda de incredulidad. De haber encontrado algo así en sus incursiones, habría intentado atravesarse el corazón sin pensárselo.

Kaine la conocía muy bien.

—¿Está Kaine por aquí? —Davies negó con la cabeza—. Cuando regrese, ¿te importaría decirle que quiero hablar con él?

Ya casi no había luz cuando la puerta se abrió y Kaine se quedó en el umbral, como si no supiera si debía entrar o no.

Helena levantó la vista de la hoja de notas, lamentándose por la distancia que los separaba.

—¿Te había contado que me sometí a una esterilización?

Kaine cerró la puerta a su espalda.

—No, pero me lo imaginaba. Era una práctica habitual entre los fieles de la Fe. Uno de los mayores temores de mi padre era que descubrieran mi vivemancia y me sometieran a la operación, porque eso habría acabado con nuestra familia.

—Vaya.

Le alegraba saber que nunca habían tenido esa conversación.

Kaine apretó los dientes.

—Lo que no esperaba era que Stroud fuera capaz de revertirlo. Pensaba que te salvarías de participar en el programa.

Helena se tocó el vientre distraídamente.

—Quiero hablar de lo que has dicho hace un rato, antes de marcharte.

La expresión de Kaine se volvió indescifrable y a Helena se le formó un nudo en el pecho. La había mirado así en más ocasiones de las que le gustaría recordar, tanto en el pasado como en el presente. Cerró los ojos y trató de dejar a un lado todos esos recuerdos.

—¿Te importaría acercarte? —Notaba la boca seca—. Me cuesta hablar teniéndote tan lejos.

Era evidente que Kaine prefería mantener aquella conversación a distancia, pero Helena lo necesitaba cerca. Se miró las manos.

—No esperaba que pensaras que interrumpiría el embarazo cuando escapara. O sea, entiendo por qué podrías imaginarlo, pero no voy a hacerlo.

Levantó la mirada para intentar descifrar su reacción, pero él no la estaba mirando.

—Puede que cambies de idea una vez que seas libre —dijo sin rastro de emoción en la voz, como si el tema no tuviera nada que ver con él.

—No lo haré —insistió ella negando con la cabeza.

A Kaine se le crispó la mandíbula y la tensión se le acumuló en los ojos.

—No tienes por qué comprometerte a nada por mí. —Le temblaba la voz—. Haz lo que quieras.

—Eso voy a hacer, pero quería que lo supieras. Si no siguiera adelante con el embarazo, me pasaría el resto de mi vida preguntándome cómo habría sido: si el bebé tendría tus ojos o los míos; si sería normal, si nacería con resonancia y cuál sería su poder en ese caso. —Hablaba atropelladamente, porque sentía un nudo en la garganta—. Me preguntaría si tendría el pelo como el mío o si le crecería liso como a ti. Si tengo que seguir adelante sin ti... Si... si mueres..., quiero poder hablarle de ti. —Tragó saliva—. Nunca he tenido oportunidad de hablarle de ti a nadie. Me gustaría que alguien supiera cómo eras.

Kaine la miró.

—¿Cómo soy? —dijo al fin—. ¿Cómo crees que soy exactamente? —Resopló y negó con la cabeza—. Tienes la oportunidad de empezar de cero. No cargues con el peso de mi recuerdo.

Helena sacudió la cabeza y la expresión de él se endureció. Todo en él se tensó.

—¿De verdad quieres pasar el resto de tu vida atada al hijo bastardo de un inmarcesible? Todo el mundo sabe que estás aquí y con quién te han mandado. ¿Crees que no averiguarán quién es el padre y cómo fue concebido? Da igual qué color de ojos tenga o lo mayor que se haga, porque seguirá siendo el descendiente de un asesino que te violó mientras estabas prisionera. Y todo el mundo lo sabrá. Sin excepción.

Estaba furioso. Cerró los puños como si quisiera zarandearla, pero se dio la vuelta con el rostro contraído en una mueca amarga.

—Deja todo esto atrás —dijo tomando una bocanada entrecortada de aire—. ¿Quieres tener hijos? Pues búscate a otra persona con quien tenerlos.

Helena lo miró con incredulidad.

—¿Me ves capaz de hacer algo así? ¿De huir y fingir que fuiste el monstruo del que tuve la suerte de escapar?

Kaine le lanzó una mirada de soslayo. Una resignación vacía se adueñó de sus facciones antes de volver a girarse hacia ella.

—Es la verdad.

Helena notó una presión en el pecho que hizo que se le encogiera el corazón.

—Kaine… —extendió una mano hacia él—, no eres un monstruo. No tuviste otra opción. Ninguno de los dos… Ambos hemos sido violados.

Él se apartó con una sacudida y esquivó sus dedos.

—Para.

Helena dio un paso adelante y le sujetó el rostro con ambas manos.

—Eres mío —le dijo mientras notaba los latidos irregulares de su corazón en el pecho—. ¿De verdad creías que seguiría odiándote cuando recuperara la memoria? —Negó con la cabeza—. Incluso antes de recordar, tú eras la única persona aquí que me hacía sentir segura. Pensaba que me estaba volviendo loca, pero una parte de mí siempre supo quién eras. ¿Leíste la nota que te dejé? Te quiero.

Kaine se estremeció como si sus palabras lo hubieran golpeado. Intentó mover la cabeza, pero ella se lo impidió y lo obligó a mirarla a los ojos.

—Lo digo en serio —insistió con firmeza, aunque la emoción hacía que le temblara la voz—. Te quiero y siempre te querré. Siempre.

Se puso de puntillas, lo atrajo hacia sí y lo besó.

Él se quedó inmóvil cuando sus labios se encontraron.

—Te quiero —repitió Helena contra su boca, como si quisiera hacerle respirar sus palabras.

Kaine permaneció quieto un instante más, pero luego se estremeció. Le sostuvo el rostro entre sus manos, enterró los dedos en su cabello y la atrajo con fuerza para acercarla a su cuerpo y besarla con desesperación.

La besó como si estuviera hambriento, como si estuviera intentando verter su esencia en su interior o consumirla por completo.

«Es mío. Es solo mío», eso era lo único en lo que Helena podía pensar. Le rodeó el cuello con ambos brazos y respondió a todas y cada una de las caricias de sus labios.

Kaine se apartó apenas lo suficiente para hablar, con la frente pegada a la de ella y una mano en torno a su nuca.

—Lo siento… Lo siento tanto… Siento muchísimo todo lo que te he hecho —dijo con la voz ronca y rota—. Te quiero. No tuve oportunidad de decírtelo antes de que te marcharas.

———————

HELENA PASÓ LOS DÍAS ESCRIBIENDO notas, leyendo cada libro y cada texto que caía en sus manos, e intentando dar sentido a los conceptos inconexos que Shiseo había recogido sobre los sellos. Por fin se había acordado de Wagner, del boceto básico que el hombre les había proporcionado y de la infinidad de veces en que ella había intentado comprenderlo sin éxito.

Reconstruir el sello le parecía una tarea imposible, pero no se le ocurría otra opción. Era la única solución viable. A petición suya, Kaine le consiguió la obra completa de Cetus, así como las múltiples cartas, florilegios y textos de atribución dudosa que le habían adjudicado a lo largo de los siglos. Tenía la esperanza de entender mejor sus métodos alquímicos si lograba dar con las fuentes legítimas que documentaran su trabajo.

Sin embargo, por mucho que se esforzó en ignorarlo, una voz en su interior insistía en que estaba perdiendo el tiempo, en que era una ilusa. Si no había encontrado la solución antes, ¿por qué iba a dar con ella ahora? Pero decidió seguir adelante porque no concebía un futuro en el que dejara a Kaine atrás para morir.

Obligó a su mente a escapar del camino estrecho y asfixiante donde se había quedado atrapada y aceptó, en su lugar, el tedioso vacío al que había limitado sus recuerdos. Pero el esfuerzo le causaba tales dolores de cabeza que solo podía trabajar en intervalos cortos de tiempo.

Una mañana, se despertó y encontró a los sirvientes recogiendo todos los libros y las notas que había ido tomando para llevarlos a la habitación contigua a la suya. Hasta ese momento, la puerta que las comunicaba había permanecido cerrada siempre con llave. Kaine estaba de pie junto a la cama.

—Stroud va a hacernos una visita hoy. Tengo que ponerte el anulitio de nuevo.

A Helena se le secó la boca.

—Claro —accedió levantando las manos a regañadientes e intentando no encogerse de dolor cuando los tubos le atravesaron las muñecas y su resonancia volvió a desvanecerse.

Sabía que no era culpa de Kaine, pero una oscura parte de ella no podía evitar sentirse traicionada al bajar la vista para contemplarse sus manos, incapacitadas otra vez.

Se hizo un ovillo en la cama mientras el corazón le latía aterrorizado e intentó aliviar el miedo que sentía frotándose las muñecas mientras Kaine salía en busca de Stroud.

—Vaya, mira quién ha recobrado la consciencia —dijo la mujer cuando entró—. El Sumo Inquisidor estaba muy preocupado por ti.

Creo que ya te daba por muerta. Parece que por fin habéis escuchado a vuestro padre.

Kaine apretó los dientes, sin molestarse en ocultar el rechazo que le causaba Stroud.

—Te recomiendo que te ciñas al motivo de tu visita.

Stroud se mordió los labios con una sonrisa contenida, dejó su bolsa sobre la mesita que había junto a la cama y se inclinó sobre Helena para hacerle una palpación y una exploración resonántica.

—Bueno, parece que lo peor ya ha pasado. Está empezando a ganar peso otra vez. —Presionó varios dedos contra la frente de Helena y aplicó una ínfima descarga de energía. Chasqueó la lengua—. Todavía tiene el cerebro bastante inflamado. Yo no confiaría en que sus recuerdos sobrevivan al resto del embarazo. El Estrago empeorará con el avance de la gestación si el bebé resulta ser como esperamos.

Fue una suerte que Stroud estuviera tan centrada en Helena, porque, de lo contrario, habría visto a Kaine palidecer.

—Ahora que vuelve a comer, tendréis que aseguraros de que sale al patio y hace algo de ejercicio. Cuanto más débil esté, menos probable será que el parto sea viable.

Stroud dejó de tocar a Helena y rebuscó en su bolsa hasta dar con la pantalla de resonancia.

—Veamos qué encontramos por aquí. —Kaine se dio la vuelta en cuanto retiró las mantas que cubrían a la chica y le subió la ropa—. Todo en orden —concluyó con una sonrisa de suficiencia. Señaló con la cabeza la vaga silueta que se veía palpitar en el gas—. Por suerte, no parece que el coma o los ataques hayan afectado al desarrollo del feto. Eso habría sido de lo más desafortunado. Creo que el embarazo está lo bastante avanzado como para poder...

Stroud entornó los ojos y la pantalla cambió: la figura que se veía en ella se expandió. La mujer perdió la sonrisa.

—Es una niña.

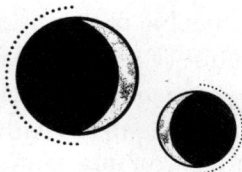

CAPÍTULO 69

Junius 1789

Una niña.

Helena ni siquiera había considerado la posibilidad de comprobar el sexo del bebé. Recordaba que Lila había querido saberlo, pero ella tenía tantos asuntos por los que preocuparse que no se había parado a pensar en ello.

De pronto, su mente pareció adquirir plena consciencia del embarazo, lo cual le resultó abrumador. Hasta ese momento, el bebé no había sido más que un concepto, poco más que una posibilidad, pero ahora era una niña.

Stroud le presionó la parte baja de la zona pélvica con más firmeza y sus facciones se ensombrecieron.

—Vaya decepción. Queríamos un varón —dijo lanzándole una mirada de reproche, como si ella lo hubiera hecho a propósito.

Helena no mostró ninguna emoción y mantuvo la vista fija en el dosel de la cama, como si estuviera demasiado débil para tener una opinión al respecto.

Stroud se volvió hacia Kaine.

—El Sumo Nigromante no va a estar nada contento. Una niña es… inadmisible. Prácticamente impensable.

—Siempre hubo un cincuenta por ciento de probabilidades de que lo fuera —apuntó él con aparente indiferencia—. Según tenía entendido, llegados a este punto, bastará con que presente habilidades animánticas.

—Sí, pero no es un varón —insistió Stroud, como si estuviera hablando de algún experimento fallido—. No le va a hacer ninguna gracia.

—Se llevó una mano a la frente y dejó escapar una sonora exhalación—. Aunque ya es demasiado tarde. No podemos permitirnos volver a empezar y, en las condiciones en que se encuentra, no creo que sobreviva a un segundo intento. Tendremos que seguir adelante. En cuanto perfeccionemos el procedimiento, estoy segura de que conseguiremos un niño. Esto será solo temporal. ¿La tenéis bien vigilada? ¿Os estáis asegurando de que no se altere?

—Sí —respondió Kaine apretando los dientes y señalando la puerta—. ¿Por qué no continuamos la conversación en otro lado?

—Claro, claro —dijo Stroud con impaciencia antes de recoger sus cosas y salir por la puerta, seguida de cerca por Kaine.

Helena se incorporó en cuanto se cerró la puerta, se miró el vientre y se tocó el bultito que crecía entre sus caderas. No notaba nada sin la ayuda de la resonancia; todavía era demasiado pronto para que se moviera.

Una niña.

Kaine apenas mencionaba el embarazo salvo para hablar de sus efectos sobre la salud de ella. Era su embarazo, su bebé. Se negaba a tratarlo como si tuviera algo que ver con él.

Aun así, no podía evitar preguntarse si a él le importaría que fuera una niña. Eran los hijos varones quienes conservaban el apellido familiar y quienes heredaban los gremios. Las niñas con talento para la alquimia solían considerarse un desperdicio, pues solo servían para establecer alianzas matrimoniales. Aunque, siendo una hija ilegítima, tampoco importaba mucho.

Se le formó un nudo tenso en el estómago.

Cuando Kaine regresó, se acercó a ella con cautela y le puso las manos sobre los hombros. Helena notó su resonancia activarse en las terminaciones nerviosas y supo que estaba buscando algo.

—Estoy bien. El bebé no me está haciendo nada si eso es lo que te preocupa.

—Podría empeorar más adelante —dijo mientras la estudiaba con atención—. Y tú…

Le tocó el lateral de la cabeza. Era evidente que estaba calculando los años que Helena había pasado en el hospital y el número de pacientes a los que había atendido para determinar cuánto tiempo le quedaba.

Helena negó con un gesto y lo agarró de la mano.

—Una vez me dijiste que la vitalidad no se puede arrebatar de esa manera. La vivemante que trató a tu madre dijo que el embarazo le había afectado tanto porque había estado abusando de su poder sin darse cuenta. Lila también es una vivemante y Rhea no tuvo problemas durante la gestación.

Kaine la miró como si se le estuviera escapando de entre los dedos sin poder hacer nada para evitarlo.

—Además, me has hecho algo, ¿no? —Helena lo estudió con atención—. Pensaba que había sido un sueño, pero utilizaste la Gema de alguna manera.

—Todavía no estoy seguro de que ayudara mucho. Estabas al límite y entraste en coma. Y lo peor es que yo no estaré ahí cuando salgas de cuentas para...

—Tendré cuidado. Los síntomas del Estrago son fáciles de reconocer y no aparecen de un día para otro.

Kaine asintió despacio, pero Helena sabía que incluso el más mínimo riesgo era demasiado para él.

—Es una niña —dijo al cabo de unos instantes para tratar de distraerlo.

Cuando repitió el mismo movimiento de cabeza distraídamente, a Helena se le cayó el alma a los pies. Si había pasado tanto tiempo preocupada por el bebé cuando apenas existía era porque la pérdida de memoria le había hecho creer que era lo único que le quedaba en el mundo. Kaine no se había equivocado al decir que estaba desesperada por tener a alguien a quien amar. Parecía que ese era su mayor punto débil, el defecto que más comprometía su integridad.

Ahora que tenía tantas preocupaciones en la cabeza, el embarazo había pasado a un segundo plano, convencida de que el asunto podría esperar, pero no era así. Siempre había estado allí y ahora tenía una niñita que nadie, salvo ella, parecía querer.

Frente a la indiferencia de Kaine, Helena sintió crecer en su interior la necesidad de protegerla. Soltó la mano de Kaine y fue hacia el armario para vestirse con tranquilidad.

—¿Qué haces? —le preguntó Kaine mientras ella se abrochaba el vestido.

—Voy a salir a dar un paseo —respondió sin mirarlo—. Le vendrá bien a la niña.

—Te acompaño.

Helena no estaba segura de querer su compañía si iba a seguir mirándola con esa expresión sombría, pero asintió. Kaine le retiró el anulitio de los grilletes y, en vez de conducirla al patio, la llevó hasta la parte trasera de la casa, donde se extendía el laberinto de setos y los jardines abandonados. Había un camino cubierto por un toldo de rosales trepadores.

—¿Y si Morrough nos ve? —preguntó con vacilación.

—Solo vigila el patio.

Caminaron en silencio hasta llegar a un manzano retorcido, de flores pálidas y hojas verdes y frescas. Kaine se detuvo en seco y lo observó con detenimiento.

—Solía trepar a este árbol cuando era pequeño. Lo recordaba más grande.

Nunca había hablado de su pasado sin que ella se lo pidiera. Lo único que sabía sobre su infancia era que había sido un niño muy solitario con un padre ausente, una madre enferma y unos sirvientes cuyos fantasmales recuerdos todavía lo acompañaban.

—Me quedé atascado justo aquí una vez —dijo tocando una rama larga que a Helena apenas le llegaba a la altura de la cintura—. Estaba convencido de que me caería y me abriría la cabeza si me movía, así que me pasé medio día llamando a gritos a mi madre. Se suponía que no debía levantarse de la cama, pero a mí me daba igual. Solo quería que viniera a buscarme y que viera lo alto que había trepado. Al final, acabó haciéndome caso. —Bajó la mano—. Cuando crecí, empecé a sentirme muy culpable por aquello. La de tonterías que uno hace de niño y no entiende lo que sucede a su alrededor.

Helena no conseguía imaginar a Kaine de pequeño.

Él señaló una abertura entre los setos.

—Si vamos por ahí, llegaremos hasta un estanque donde solía haber todo tipo de ranas y salamandras. Siempre pensé que podría llegar a domesticarlas y enseñarles a hacer trucos.

Le contó todo aquello con voz inexpresiva, como si estuviera recitando un texto de memoria. Miró a su alrededor.

—Debería llevarte a ver los pináculos —dijo al cabo de unos instantes—. Creo que me acordaría de muchas más anécdotas allí arriba. Es extraño… No sé por qué me cuesta tanto evocar ciertos momentos.

Emprendió el camino de regreso mirando a su alrededor como si estuviera buscando algo por el jardín. Luego se detuvo y movió los labios unas cuantas veces antes de encontrar la voz.

—Mi madre se llamaba Enid.

Helena asintió. Eso sí lo recordaba.

Kaine contempló el jardín y apretó los puños.

—Ese nombre siempre… me ha gustado.

Helena empezó a entender qué era lo que intentaba hacer. Se estaba esforzando por darle lo que quería. Para él, aceptar que iba a tener un bebé, una niña, implicaba también asumir que no viviría para conocerla. Le estaba contando todo aquello para que Helena pudiera hablarle de él a su hija, para que pudiera contarle cómo era antes de matricularse en la Academia y de que estallara la guerra.

Desvió la mirada hacia la ciudad que se alzaba por encima de los árboles.

—He transferido todo el dinero que he podido a una cuenta extranjera, pero no sé qué pasará con la propiedad y la herencia o si podréis reclamarlas si alguna vez regresáis a Paladia. Puedo intentar informarme si quieres.

A Helena se le cerró la garganta y le empezaron a temblar los hombros. Sus pulmones se negaban a cooperar.

Kaine la miró.

—Nos hemos alejado demasiado.

Ella negó con la cabeza pese a no poder moverse. Tenía tantas cosas que quería decirle que no se veía capaz de hablar sin desmoronarse.

—¿Crees que podrás volver por tu propio pie? —preguntó dando un paso hacia ella.

Cuando consiguió negar con la cabeza, él le rodeó la cintura con cuidado y la alzó en sus brazos. Helena se agarró a su cuello con ambas manos y enterró el rostro en su hombro.

—Enid es un buen nombre —consiguió decir al final con voz ronca—. A mí también me gusta.

Kaine se había tumbado en la cama con Helena, que tenía la cabeza apoyada sobre su pecho y seguía con la vista el movimiento de las manecillas del reloj. Se le agotaba el tiempo. Siempre igual. Nunca tenía tiempo de sobra. Lumitia alcanzaría la plena latencia en menos de un mes.

Kaine también estaba despierto y le dibujaba figuras con las yemas de los dedos por el brazo. Helena se incorporó, se inclinó hacia delante y lo besó despacio para grabarse en la memoria la sensación de sus labios al tocarse y la caricia de su nariz contra la mejilla.

Le enterró los dedos en el pelo para profundizar el beso, ansiosa por perderse en él. Ya se había sentido así antes. Cuando Kaine levantó una mano para cerrarla en torno a su cuello, una oleada de calor la hizo estremecer y le encendió la sangre. Había enterrado los recuerdos de aquellos momentos en las profundidades más recónditas de su mente.

Se pegó más a él y deslizó una mano hacia abajo por su pecho, pero Kaine la agarró de inmediato de la muñeca y la detuvo.

—¿Qué estás haciendo?

Ella se incorporó y respiró hondo.

—Quiero acostarme contigo —dijo, sintiendo cómo le ardían las puntas de las orejas por haberlo admitido en voz alta, pero sin apartar la mirada de él. Quería ver su reacción.

En su mirada había un brillo impertérrito, visible incluso bajo la tenue luz de la luna.

—No.

Helena tiró de su muñeca para que la soltara, y él obedeció. Entonces se abrazó las rodillas contra el pecho. Su corazón latía con fuerza, a un ritmo irregular.

—No quiero que nuestra última vez sea cuando me... —Tragó saliva—. Cuando ambos nos vimos obligados a tener relaciones.

—No —repitió.

A Helena se le crisparon los dedos, pero asintió y se quedó en esa posición mientras observaba cómo las sombras que bailaban por la estancia se intensificaban.

—¿Por qué? —preguntó Kaine al cabo de un instante.

—Te lo acabo de explicar.

—Pero contigo nunca hay una sola explicación.

—No recuerdo cómo era —admitió tras permanecer un rato callada—. Antes de todo esto. Sé que nos acostábamos, pero cuando... cuando intento recordar los detalles siempre acabo volviendo a esta casa. Si nunca recupero esos recuerdos, esto será lo único que me quede.

Se interrumpió al pensar en todas las formas en que la situación podría torcerse, pero no había vuelta atrás. Lo que habían compartido había desaparecido y no era algo que pudiera recrearse así, sin más, porque corrían el riesgo de destruir el frágil refugio que habían conseguido mantener en los brazos del otro.

—Da igual —dijo negando con la cabeza—. Tienes razón, ha sido una mala idea.

Kaine no respondió, pero, cuando volvió a besarla al día siguiente, algo había cambiado.

Había cierta avidez en él.

Cuando regresó después de pasar unos días fuera, la tocó con una pasión abrasadora; le arañó el cuello con los dientes y le enterró el rostro en la piel para inhalar su esencia. Helena de pronto se vio inundada por una ola de calor y dejó escapar un gemido tembloroso mientras se derretía contra él.

—Dime que pare —le pidió moviendo los labios contra su garganta—. Dime que pare.

Ella tiró de él hacia sí.

—Sigue. No quiero que pares.

Kaine le deslizó los dientes por la piel y alcanzó los botones de su vestido para ayudarla a desabrochárselo. Cuando sus dedos encontraron la piel desnuda bajo la tela, Helena se estremeció, desesperada por sentir su contacto.

Solía ser así. Ahora que experimentaba aquella sensación de nuevo, recordaba cómo la había tocado, la manera en que la había sostenido entre sus brazos y la había devorado.

Kaine le besó el cuello hasta que ella dejó caer la cabeza hacia atrás entre jadeos. Helena le acarició la curva de la mandíbula y los hombros, y el recuerdo físico de su cuerpo despertó bajo su piel.

Tiró de su rostro para acercarlo al suyo.

—Te quiero —le dijo entre besos—. Ojalá te lo hubiera dicho mil veces antes.

Encontró los botones de su camisa, se los desabrochó y empezó a desnudarlo acariciándole la piel desnuda, ansiosa por disfrutar de su calidez.

—Dime que pare y lo haré —insistió él con voz ronca.

—No pares.

A Helena le temblaban las manos cuando recorrió con los dedos esas líneas que tan bien conocía grabadas en su espalda. La ropa que los separaba seguía cayendo entre ellos y el deseo tiraba de su cuerpo desde lo más profundo de su ser.

Kaine la tumbó en la cama y se colocó encima de ella para besarle los pechos, pero entonces la situación dio un giro radical. Helena estaba allí tumbada, inmóvil y en silencio, paralizada por el miedo que le daba pensar en lo que ocurriría si reaccionaba. Veía el dosel sobre su cabeza, el cuerpo que se cernía sobre ella, y todo lo que sentía se transformó en una espantosa traición.

Se le helaron las manos, los ojos se le abrieron con violencia y las costillas se le cerraron hasta asfixiarla.

—Para.

Fue como si le hubieran arrancado aquella dolorosa palabra de dentro y, con ella, también sus pulmones.

Kaine se detuvo en seco y se apartó enseguida, pero ella lo abrazó y se negó a soltarlo. Enterró el rostro en su hombro y respiró su aroma para recordar que estaba con él, que Kaine era suyo y no podía dejarlo ir.

Se estremeció y ahogó un sollozo.

Él ni siquiera se atrevía a respirar.

—Ha sido solo un momento —lo tranquilizó con la respiración agitada—. La situación me sobrepasó, pero ahora que sé que puedo pedirte que pares todo irá mejor. Estaba disfrutando. —Siguió abrazada a él—. De verdad, estaba disfrutando. Ha sido un momento, pero… Lo estaba disfrutando.

Sin embargo, Kaine forcejeó hasta que Helena por fin cedió. Se incorporó despacio, con el rostro tenso y las pupilas tan contraídas que sus ojos recordaban al hielo picado. Parecía muy frágil.

Y estaba cubierto de cicatrices. Helena extendió una mano temblorosa y le tocó la que le surcaba prácticamente todo el torso.

—¿Qué te ha hecho?

—Todo lo que ha querido —dijo evitando su mirada.

Helena apoyó la cabeza en su hombro y entrelazó un brazo con uno de los suyos para quedarse allí, en la creciente oscuridad, entre los restos de la relación que una vez habían compartido. Solo necesitaban un poco más de tiempo.

———

Helena había leído todas las obras atribuidas a Cetus y las había organizado en función de su legitimidad. Tenía la sensación de que empezaba a entender los fundamentos de su enfoque alquímico, pero necesitaba encontrar una fuente más reciente, y sabía exactamente dónde hacerlo.

Cuando Kaine se marchó, salió de la habitación y recorrió la casa despacio, evitando las sombras y utilizando las paredes como punto de referencia. Como conocía qué estancias estaban controladas por Morrough, tuvo cuidado de evitar tantas como pudo.

Davies apareció ante ella cuando llegó al vestíbulo, pero Helena siguió adelante por el ala principal. Cuando por fin se detuvo, echó un vistazo por encima del hombro.

—¿Puede verme Morrough ahora?

Davies negó suavemente con la cabeza.

Helena se dirigió a la puerta más alejada de la estancia, cuyo marco estaba combado para mantenerla cerrada. Una persona que no dominara la resonancia férrea nunca podría cruzarla. El poder de Helena vibró entre sus dedos cuando puso la mano sobre el marco y empujó el hierro como si fuera una cortina. Luego, agarró el pomo, que tenía una cerradura sencilla.

Echó una última ojeada a Davies, que había esbozado una expresión aterrorizada, la única, al parecer, que todavía era capaz de expresar.

—Lo siento, pero tengo que verlo.

—No… —dijo la necrómata, con una voz distorsionada, hueca y jadeante.

Helena no supo decir si había sido cosa de Kaine o del fantasma de la mujer que todavía habitaba en su interior.

—Tengo que ver cómo lo hicieron —se disculpó con un movimiento de cabeza.

Davies no la siguió, pero se quedó conmocionada junto a la puerta, repitiendo la palabra «no» en voz baja y desesperada mientras Helena encendía la luz y se acercaba al sello.

Las luces parpadearon sobre su cabeza. Se le retorció el estómago al contemplar aquella jaula tan pequeña sabiendo quién había pasado meses allí encerrada. El corazón cada vez le latía más deprisa, pero se obligó a apartar la mirada para concentrarse.

Se había detenido junto al borde del sello para evaluar el meticuloso esfuerzo que habían hecho por ocultarlo e intentó cotejarlo con el boceto de Wagner y los borradores de Bennet. Si lograba superponer las tres versiones, conseguiría dar con el sello completo.

Trabajó despacio, buscando posibles patrones, pero hacía tiempo que no utilizaba su poder para más que pequeñas tareas relacionadas con la vivemancia.

Se arrodilló y pasó los dedos por cada forma, por cada diseño. Las dos primeras veces que gateó por el suelo siguiendo las líneas e intentando visualizar el flujo de energía, el sello le resultó incomprensible. A la tercera, por fin empezó a tener sentido.

Era un sello animántico. Reconocía su energía y los patrones que seguía. Su resonancia siguió el movimiento de sus dedos mientras los deslizaba por una de las líneas del sello. Sí, esa sensación le resultaba familiar. Otra línea. Esa era falsa. La energía no se retorcía de esa manera.

Volvió a arrastrarse por el suelo, pero moviéndose más despacio, trazando cada línea una y otra vez sin prestar atención a las astillas que se le clavaban en las yemas de los dedos.

El alivio hizo que su corazón latiera con fuerza. Podía resolverlo, iba a encontrar la respuesta. El dolor se extendió por su pecho al ritmo irregular de sus latidos, y lo ignoró, decidida a completar el sello. Pero su corazón bombeaba cada vez más y más rápido, tanto que empezó a notar punzadas en los pulmones. Solo tenía que aguantar un poco más. Necesitaba completar el sello mentalmente para poder dibujarlo más tarde.

El suelo empezó a desdibujarse y Helena parpadeó rápido para intentar concentrarse.

Le sangraban los dedos cuando se los llevó al pecho. Se estaba quedando fría y el corazón le latía descontrolado. Ralentizarlo fue como intentar atrapar un caballo desbocado.

La habitación empezó a darle vueltas. La jaula de hierro y la puerta se mecían de un lado a otro con cadencia y se tambalearon hasta que Helena se derrumbó y se golpeó con fuerza el hombro con el suelo.

Todo se ensombreció y la luz parpadeante del techo se desvaneció.

SE DESPERTÓ DE NUEVO EN su cama, mareada y con un dolor en el pecho, como si tuviera un peso muerto aplastándole la caja torácica. Kaine estaba sentado a su lado y le sostenía una mano.

No recordaba cómo había llegado hasta allí. Le dolían las muñecas y sentía el peso del anulitio en ellas.

—La médica acaba de irse —dijo sin mirarla—. Parece que con la tensión y la angustia del encierro y el embarazo has desarrollado una arritmia. Te la detectaron mientras estabas en coma, pero me dijeron que se curaría sola si te mantenía relajada. Ahora ya no parece que tenga solución. —Helena no sabía qué decir. Kaine apretó los dientes varias veces antes de continuar—: No te haces una idea de lo que he sentido al encontrarte inconsciente en medio del maldito sello de esa cámara de torturas.

—Lo siento. No quería que te vieras obligado a entrar ahí de nuevo.

Kaine exhaló con fuerza y dejó caer la cabeza. Parecía estar furioso, pero se aferraba a su mano como si su vida dependiera de ello.

—No fue un ataque de pánico —dijo ella—. Creo que ya sé cómo utilizó Morrough el sello…, cómo funciona su diseño. Averiguar cómo lo hizo me supuso un alivio tan grande que perdí el control de mis latidos.

Kaine la miró con los ojos encendidos.

—¿Y te crees que eso ayuda? Podría fallarte el corazón en cualquier momento y, si eso ocurre mientras yo no estoy aquí, morirás. Igual que… —Se interrumpió—. No me hagas esto.

Helena sintió la boca seca.

—Pero tengo que salvarte.

—No —replicó con brusquedad—. No tienes por qué. Y tampoco puedes hacerlo. Eres la única que sigue sin entenderlo. —Helena abrió la boca para responder, pero él la interrumpió—: Prometimos decirnos la verdad, y eso es lo que estoy haciendo. No puedes salvarme. No hay esperanza para mí.

Helena se incorporó a duras penas; el pecho le dolía como si el esternón se le hubiera vuelto a partir.

—Eso no puedes saberlo. Déjame intentarlo.

Al ver que Kaine se apartaba de ella con una sacudida y se ponía de pie, Helena pensó que saldría de la habitación, así que se levantó de la cama y fue tras él.

—Kaine…

Él se detuvo a los pies de la cama.

—No puedes tenerlo todo, Helena —le dijo al final—. Llegará un momento en que te des cuenta de que no todo saldrá como tú quieres. Tendrás que elegir y conformarte con ello. Piensa en las personas que tienes a tu alrededor. Le prometiste a Holdfast que cuidarías de Lila y de su hijo. Tú misma tienes un bebé que te necesita y lo sabes.

Helena negó con la cabeza.

—No quiero elegir. Siempre tengo que hacerlo y nunca puedo elegirte a ti. Estoy harta.

—No estás eligiendo nada —dijo él tras volverse a mirarla—. Me prometiste que harías lo que yo quisiera y lo que quiero es que dejes de hacerte daño intentando salvarme. Márchate. Vive tu vida. Cuéntale a nuestra hija que os salvé a las dos. Eso... eso es lo que quiero.

—Pero estoy muy cerca de encontrar una solución. Sé que puedo hacerlo.

—También me prometiste que abandonarías la investigación si afectaba a tu salud —le recordó mientras regresaba a su lado.

—Lo sé, pero...

Kaine dejó escapar una carcajada ahogada que casi sonó como un sollozo.

—¿Sabes que no he conocido nunca a una persona más incapaz de mantener una promesa que tú?

—Solo mantengo las que de verdad importan —dijo ella con un nudo en la garganta.

—No. —Kaine negó con la cabeza—. Lo que pasa es que haces tantas promesas contradictorias que luego puedes elegir las que más te convienen. He reflexionado mucho sobre tu forma de actuar. —Bajó la mirada—. Por eso nunca pareces cumplir las promesas que a mí me importan. —Extendió la mano hacia ella y le acarició la cadera—. Te preocupas por la niña. Has estado pensando en ella constantemente y te has destrozado el corazón temiendo lo que pudiera pasarle. Ahora, estás tan cegada por tu deseo de salvarme que te estás olvidando de que ella depende de ti. No puedo protegerla de tus decisiones, y ponerte en peligro para intentar salvarme es un riesgo para ella.

A Helena se le cerró la garganta y trató de retroceder, pero Kaine la sujetó por los hombros y la obligó a mirarlo.

—Tienes que dejarme ir.

—No puedo —dijo ella negando con la cabeza—. ¿Me ves capaz de mantener la calma si interrumpo la investigación? ¿Si me veo obligada a pasar los días aquí sentada esperando a perderte? Tú no podrías quedarte de brazos cruzados. Nunca harías algo así.

Al final, llegaron a un acuerdo.

Kaine la llevó de vuelta a la habitación de la jaula y permitió que pasara horas arrastrándose por el suelo, copiando cada detalle del sello en planchas de grabado. Además, siempre que él tenía un momento libre, la acompañaba a la biblioteca y dejaba que practicara la animancia con él para que estudiara el talismán que albergaba en su pecho. Por su parte, Helena ya no salía de su habitación sin él.

Una tarde, después de haber estado más de un día fuera, Kaine regresó con una expresión pétrea.

—Mañana tendrás que quedarte aquí encerrada. Aurelia va a regresar para dar una cena y todos los inmarcesibles que aún hay están invitados.

—¿Y cuál es el motivo de la celebración?

—Se supone que tengo que convencerlos de que todo va bien —dijo con una sonrisa tensa.

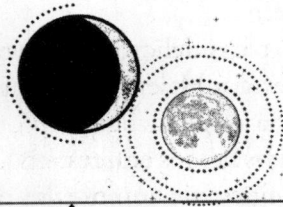

CAPÍTULO 70

Julius 1789

AL ASOMARSE ENTRE LAS CORTINAS, Helena vio que traían más sirvientes de la ciudad, tanto vivos como muertos. Kaine había cerrado con llave la puerta de su dormitorio para asegurarse de que no recibiera ninguna visita indeseada, pero dejó a una de las doncellas dentro con ella.

Helena no se había dado cuenta hasta ese momento de lo pesada que era la puerta ni de lo bien protegida que estaba.

Los primeros vehículos llegaron a última hora de la tarde. Le resultaba gracioso ver entrar a los inmarcesibles en la casa del mismísimo asesino al que tanto temían.

Intentó no preocuparse demasiado. La velada no parecía haber inquietado a Kaine lo más mínimo, pero sabía que era muy buen mentiroso.

Mientras se desarrollaba la celebración, Helena se esforzó por concentrarse en encontrar la manera de revertir la estructura del sello de Morrough. Pero entonces la sirvienta que hasta ese momento había permanecido quieta como una estatua se puso de pie de repente y recogió apresuradamente todos los libros y las notas de Helena para meterlos debajo de la cama.

Alguien se acercaba.

Acababan de esconder los últimos papeles y de asegurarse de que todo había quedado bien oculto bajo el faldón de la cama cuando el sonido del hierro al moverse inundó la estancia. Helena se subió de un salto a la cama y se tumbó sobre el costado, justo antes de que la puerta se abriera y apareciera Stroud seguida de Kaine.

—No entiendo de qué va a servir esto —decía él mientras Helena los miraba fingiendo estar confundida—. Ya sabes lo delicado que es su estado de salud.

—Tenemos muchas cosas delicadas entre manos ahora mismo —replicó Stroud, que se acercó a Helena para sacudirla—. El Sumo Nigromante ha dejado muy claro que debemos proyectar una imagen fuerte. Los asesinatos a los que nos hemos enfrentado han hecho que la sensación de invulnerabilidad de nuestros hombres se tambalee y, si permitimos que el miedo eche por tierra el régimen, todos sufriremos las consecuencias. Debemos demostrar que encontraremos una solución pronto.

—¿Y crees que pasear por la casa a una prisionera embarazada que está aquí claramente para ser interrogada calmará las aguas?

—Creo que explicar el motivo de su embarazo lo hará. La paranoia no les deja confiar en nuestra palabra, pero eso cambiará cuando la vean. La chica fue la última alumna que el principado acogió bajo su protección. —Stroud la miró—. Levántate y ponte algo que muestre la barriga.

Su estado apenas era evidente cuando estaba desnuda, así que Helena dudaba que tuviera alguna prenda que pudiera cumplir con lo que la mujer pedía. Y eso fue más evidente todavía cuando se puso de pie.

—Ay, por todos los cielos. —Stroud se acercó al armario, sacó un camisón y se lo metió a Helena por debajo del vestido para que su vientre pareciera más distendido—. Hala, vamos.

La mujer tiró del brazo de Helena con fuerza y la arrastró hacia la puerta. Ella miró a Kaine, pero no había nada que hacer.

El camino hasta el ala principal de la casa fue más largo y, al mismo tiempo, más corto de lo que Helena recordaba. Se le formó un nudo en el pecho al llegar al amplio vestíbulo principal, pero se esforzó por mantener la respiración controlada cuando la metieron en la amplia estancia donde había visto a Kaine por primera vez en Puntaférreo.

—Ni se te ocurra abrir la boca —le ordenó Stroud clavándole los dedos en el brazo.

Todos los invitados se volvieron cuando Stroud entró con Helena, que se sintió fuera de lugar al instante. Ninguna norteña respetable se dejaría ver en público con el cabello suelto y claros signos de embarazo.

La respuesta ante su apariencia fue un silencio absoluto. Helena recorrió la estancia con la mirada y reconoció un puñado de rostros, entre los que se encontraban Crowther y una malhumorada Aurelia.

«No, es Atreus», se recordó. Su piel grisácea estaba salpicada de manchas en las sienes y ahora llevaba anillos de ignición.

—¿Este es el proyecto secreto? —dijo un hombre con molesta incredulidad. Helena reconocía su voz. Tenía entradas y unas largas patillas—. ¿Este es el proyecto del que hablan todos los periódicos del país?

—Por supuesto que no —dijo Stroud con un ligero tono defensivo—. ¿Cómo iba el Sumo Nigromante a anunciar a bombo y platillo sus verdaderos planes en los periódicos? Esta prisionera fue confinada aquí por otro motivo y tú eres uno de los pocos privilegiados que van a saber por qué. Como seguramente recordaréis, esta es la estudiante extranjera que los Holdfast se tomaron la gran molestia de traer a Paladia para que estudiara en la Academia.

Varios rostros se ensombrecieron ante aquel recordatorio.

—El Sumo Nigromante ha descubierto que la chica posee una manifestación única de la resonancia y ha mostrado un gran interés por cultivarla. Una vez completado el proceso, el poder del Sumo Nigromante alcanzará unos niveles nunca vistos.

—Entonces ¿admites que a nuestro señor le pasa algo? —dijo un liche al otro lado de la estancia.

A Helena se le paró el corazón al ver que era Sebastian Bayard, con los ojos y el cabello claros y la piel de un tono gris.

Stroud frunció el gesto.

—Lo que estoy diciendo es que el Sumo Nigromante ha vencido a la mortalidad, y eso es algo con lo que ninguna otra alma en este mundo había llegado siquiera a soñar. Cuando el proyecto culmine, pues estoy segura de que saldrá adelante, será beneficioso para todos nosotros. Puede que algunos de vosotros recordéis que, durante la guerra, Bennet investigó cómo colocar talismanes en cuerpos vivos. Era uno de nuestros principales objetivos. —Varios liches asintieron—. En aquellos primeros intentos no tuvimos éxito porque las restricciones de la guerra nos obligaron a centrar nuestros recursos en prioridades más urgentes. Sin embargo, hemos dado con un nuevo método en el que el Sumo Inquisidor y yo hemos estado trabajando juntos.

»El estado físico del Sumo Nigromante está... decayendo, pero nadie se atrevería a dudar de su poder. Su intención es transferir su alma a un nuevo cuerpo y así alcanzar un poder inimaginable. Cuando él haya dado ese paso, os concederá el privilegio de hacer lo mismo.

—¿Y cuál será su nuevo cuerpo? —preguntó el primer hombre que había hablado.

Stroud sonrió y empujó a Helena para que todo el mundo la viera.

—El que la prisionera engendrará para él.

Los invitados la estudiaron con atención. El corazón de Helena latía con fuerza; estaba tan concentrada en mantener la calma que ni siquiera alcanzaba a oír lo que estaban diciendo. Notaba la rabia de Kaine vibrando bajo su piel.

Se oyó una carcajada burlona.

La estancia se desdibujó.

—No penséis en el cuerpo como en un bebé —dijo Stroud con tono brusco y en voz lo bastante alta como para que Helena la oyera por encima del estruendo de sus latidos—. No es más que materia humana con la resonancia adecuada fluyendo por sus venas.

La mujer se sonrojó visiblemente. Era evidente que había esperado que su público reaccionara con admiración, no que se rieran de ella. Volvió a tirar de Helena hacia atrás sin ninguna delicadeza.

—He trabajado con Bennet en el proyecto de las quimeras y tengo experiencia con la aceleración del crecimiento. En un par de meses, el feto será viable y tendré los materiales necesarios para diseñarle un nuevo cuerpo a nuestro líder que disponga de la resonancia que necesita. Una vez que haya alcanzado su nueva forma, permitirá que aquellos que le han sido leales reciban también nuevos cuerpos.

Varios de los liches se pusieron alerta con evidente anhelo.

—¿Así que para eso era tu programa entonces?

Helena se estremeció al oír la voz de Crowther emerger desde el fondo de la estancia, donde Atreus estaba todavía junto a Aurelia. Parecía tenerle mucho más aprecio a la nueva señora Ferron que su propio hijo.

—El beneficio económico del procedimiento es legítimo —aseguró Stroud con actitud remilgada—. Aunque admito haber tenido otros motivos.

—Un momento. —La voz de Aurelia surcó la estancia y le recordó a Helena al sonido del cristal al romperse—. ¿Quién es el padre?

—El Sumo Nigromante, por sup... —El inmarcesible que había hablado se interrumpió y, al contemplar a Helena, pareció pensarse mejor su respuesta.

—Sabía que estabas aprovechando para echarte una canita al aire con ella, Ferron —dijo otro hombre, con la cara grasienta y un espeso bigote, que acompañó sus palabras con una seca carcajada.

Las mejillas de Aurelia adoptaron una tonalidad carmesí.

—La decisión se tomó en base a la resonancia. El Sumo Nigromante decidió que sería el candidato ideal —dijo Stroud con tono conciliador—. Os aseguro, señora Ferron, que la cooperación de vuestro esposo no afecta a...

Varias personas rieron.

—¡Fuera de aquí! ¡Marchaos todos! —gritó Aurelia, que se había puesto peligrosamente pálida.

Luego, cogió lo primero que encontró, un jarrón, y se lo lazó a Helena a la cabeza, pero Stroud le tiró con fuerza del brazo y la porcelana pasó volando junto a ella para acabar estrellándose contra la pared.

A Kaine, que se había detenido a su lado, le brillaban tanto los ojos que casi parecían blancos.

—Coincido. —Su voz hizo vibrar el aire como una onda de resonancia—. Si alguien sigue dudando sobre el poder o la estabilidad del régimen, le animo a venir a hablar conmigo en privado.

Tras una pausa, varios de los inmarcesibles farfullaron una disculpa y se dirigieron hacia la puerta. Mientras la estancia se vaciaba, Stroud se encaró con Kaine.

—El Sumo Nigromante dejó muy claro que esta iba a ser una reunión diplomática, no una oportunidad para que vos los obligarais a obedecer a base de amenazas.

Los ojos de Kaine seguían resplandeciendo.

—Lo único que funciona con ellos es el poder y el miedo. No hay forma de razonar con quien ve sus privilegios amenazados. Ahora, si me disculpas, tengo un desagradable conflicto doméstico del que encargarme. Puedes irte y decirle a nuestro amado líder que sus seguidores seguirán cumpliendo órdenes sin rechistar porque saben que es lo único que los mantiene con vida.

Stroud puso mala cara, pero se marchó con la cabeza bien alta.

Helena miró a los rezagados que todavía quedaban en la estancia y se sorprendió al reconocer dos rostros más. Eran las únicas dos mujeres aparte de Stroud y Aurelia. Habían permanecido cerca de las ventanas todo el rato y ambas eran agraciadas, aunque una tenía la piel ligeramente gris y una expresión distante en su rostro de facciones delicadas. La otra tenía un aspecto muy astuto, como de un zorro, y contemplaba a Helena mientras se mordía el labio inferior.

Eran Ivy y Sofia Purnell.

Ivy miró a Kaine con expresión confusa y luego se volvió hacia Helena como si quisiera decir algo, pero terminó bajando la vista y agarrando a Sofía de la mano para sacarla de la estancia.

Por fin, Helena y Kaine se quedaron a solas con Atreus y Aurelia.

—Llevadla a su habitación —ordenó Kaine por encima del hombro mientras pasaba junto a Helena para acercarse a su familia.

Dos sirvientes dieron un paso adelante para obedecer, pero Aurelia los interrumpió:

—¡No! Que se quede. Siempre la tienes escondida para asegurarte de que eres el único que se acerca a ella. Al final ha resultado que mis sospechas eran ciertas.

La expresión de Kaine se tensó.

—Como ya te ha dicho Stroud, tan solo seguía órdenes del Sumo Nigromante. Te aseguro que en absoluto fue placentero ni para la chica ni para mí.

—Pues qué pena —dijo Atreus con la voz grave de Crowther. Arrastró con languidez sus ojos lechosos hasta Helena mientras se acercaba, acompañado de un desagradable olor a químicos astringentes y lavanda—. Tenía la esperanza de que esto al menos te animara a cumplir con el deber hacia tu familia. Sé de buena tinta que frecuentaste con regularidad cierto establecimiento durante la guerra, así que experiencia y habilidad no te falta. La única explicación que me queda es que no estás motivado.

—Tengo mejores asuntos que atender que preocuparme por asegurar tu legado —dijo Kaine con un brillo cruel en la mirada.

Atreus lo estudió con mala cara antes de avanzar sin previo aviso hacia Helena, que se encogió en un acto reflejo orientando el cuerpo hacia Kaine.

—Para ser tu prisionera, no parece tenerte mucho miedo —señaló el hombre desviando la atención rápidamente hacia su hijo.

Kaine agarró a Helena y la apartó de su padre.

—Bueno, eso es gracias a Aurelia. Después de que se pusiera hecha una furia y la atacara, yo terminé convertido en su heroico salvador. —Kaine le dedicó una sonrisa a Helena con una mirada burlona y fría como el hielo—. ¿No es así?

La chica no tuvo que fingir el estremecimiento que le recorrió el cuerpo. El corazón le latía a toda velocidad y la estancia le daba vueltas.

—Es hora de que la devuelva a su habitación. Ya sabéis dónde está la puerta.

Kaine se dio la vuelta para marcharse y tiró de Helena tras él, pero Atreus volvió a hablar:

—Puede que el Sumo Nigromante te haya dado manga ancha antes, pero has sobrestimado tanto tus habilidades y tu papel en la guerra que ahora estás dejando que te use como si fueras su perrito faldero, dejando que te trate como tal. Parece que matar es lo único que se te ha dado bien en la vida. —Kaine mantuvo una expresión impasible, pero Helena lo sintió estremecerse—. Puede que las amenazas te sirvan con los demás, pero yo no te tengo miedo. Has ido demasiado lejos y lo que te espera ahora será una caída inmensa. —A Kaine se le crisparon los dedos contra el brazo de Helena—. Esta es mi casa y, ahora que debo encargarme de las tareas que has sido incapaz de completar, ya no puedes darme órdenes. Cuando haya acabado, dado que esa servil obediencia parece ser la única cualidad que posees, tal vez le pida a nuestro líder que te obligue a engendrar un heredero.

Kaine no lo miró.

—Haz lo que te venga en gana. A mí me da igual.

Salió rápidamente y no se detuvo hasta que llegaron al ala oeste de la casa, donde Atreus y Aurelia quedaban ya muy lejos de ellos. Solo entonces se giró y acunó el rostro de Helena entre ambas manos mientras miraba sus ojos con atención. También notó su resonancia en las terminaciones nerviosas cuando la ayudó a ralentizar los irregulares latidos de su corazón.

—Lo siento —dijo apoyando la frente contra la de ella—. No esperaba que Stroud fuera a hacer algo tan estúpido.

—Da igual. Ya ha pasado. ¿A qué se refería tu padre con lo de que se está teniendo que encargar de las tareas que tú no has sido capaz de completar?

—No es nada. Venga, volvamos a tu habitación.

—¿Qué ha pasado? —insistió Helena.

Kaine exhaló.

—Ahora es mi padre quien se está encargando de dar caza al asesino.

—¿Y eso qué significa?

—Nada. Porque no va a descubrirme. Shiseo regresará en menos de una semana.

Helena recibió aquella noticia como un puñetazo en el estómago. Sabía que se estaba quedando sin tiempo, la oscuridad del cielo se lo recordaba cada noche, pero saber que Shiseo volvería pronto hacía que todo pareciera mucho más definitivo. Permaneció en silencio hasta que llegaron a la habitación.

—¿Conoces a la chica que estaba allí con su hermana?

—Ella fue quien dejó entrar a todo el mundo en la Academia —dijo Kaine entornando los ojos.

—Era una de las chicas de Crowther. Lo mató porque su hermana murió cuando rescatamos a Luc —explicó Helena con un asentimiento—. Está convencida de que la necrómata que la acompaña sigue viva.

—A esa la reanimó el propio Morrough. Casi nunca se toma tantas molestias con los cadáveres, pero eso lo explica todo. La habría matado ya, aunque no me lo ha puesto nada fácil. Esa necrómata es la única que tiene y nunca se separa de ella.

——————⁓——————

PUNTAFÉRREO VOLVÍA A PARECER UN lugar aterrador con la presencia de Atreus y Aurelia.

Como su habitación daba al patio, Helena siempre estaba al tanto de las idas y venidas de todos. Vio a Kaine y a su padre de pie ante la escalera de entrada cuando llegó un camión cargado de prisioneros que fueron conducidos a uno de los cobertizos.

Kaine se dispuso a alejarse, pero Atreus lo llamó con brusquedad y él se dio la vuelta despacio para entrar con su padre en el edificio.

Los gritos que siguieron atravesaron los cristales de las ventanas y flotaron por los sinuosos pasillos de la casa. Y no parecían tener fin. Helena corrió las cortinas y se agazapó en el extremo más alejado de la habitación para tratar de ignorarlos. Tenía demasiados recuerdos relacionados con gritos como aquellos.

Al cabo de un rato, notó el contacto de una mano y se encogió de miedo, pero al levantar la cabeza descubrió a Kaine a su lado. Lo estudió con atención. Tenía el cabello mojado, así que debía de haber salido de la ducha hacía poco.

Los dos se miraron sintiendo el peso de la situación sobre los hombros.

—¿Ha… ha dicho alguien algo que pudiera incriminarte? —preguntó Helena con voz ronca.

Un destello surcó la mirada de Kaine.

—No, ninguno sabía nada.

Helena tragó saliva con fuerza.

«Cada palabra, cada vida. Todo ha sido por ti».

No se veía capaz de hablar.

—Es tarde. ¿Quieres comer algo? —le preguntó Kaine al final.

Ella levantó la vista y vio que había dejado una bandeja en la mesa que había al otro lado de la habitación. Las sombras alargadas que lo bañaban todo le indicaron que debía de haber pasado todo el día agazapada en aquel rincón.

Le temblaba la barbilla y notaba un nudo en la garganta.

—¿Por qué está haciendo eso aquí? —preguntó, como si el lugar donde torturaban a los prisioneros cambiara lo horrible que era el hecho en sí.

—Mi padre cree que hay espías entre los inmarcesibles y que por eso el asesino es tan eficiente. Está convencido de que Puntaférreo es el único lugar verdaderamente seguro que queda. —Bajó la vista—. Deberías comer algo. Yo tengo que cenar con Aurelia y él esta noche.

—¿Volverás después? —le preguntó agarrándolo de la mano cuando ya se disponía a ponerse de pie.

Sus ojos plateados refulgían en la oscuridad.

—Si tú quieres, sí.

Cuando todo estuvo en silencio, sacó los bocetos con los sellos y las notas que había recopilado para analizarlos, modificar algunos de los componentes del diseño que había desarrollado y trazar los patrones con los dedos entrecerrando los ojos, mientras intentaba percibir la energía. Trataba de recordar lo que había sentido al notarla fluir correctamente.

No existían obras ni fuentes de referencia que mencionaran sellos alquímicos diseñados para la animancia, así que dependía por completo de la información suelta que había recopilado y de su propia experiencia.

Se podían tardar años e incluso décadas en perfeccionar un sello.

En el mejor de los casos, ella tendría una única oportunidad para hacerlo bien.

———————

—Shiseo llegará al este de Novis en unos días —le dijo Kaine mientras caminaban por el laberinto de setos para que nadie los viera desde la casa y para que Helena no oyera los gritos repentinos que escapaban del cobertizo donde estaban los prisioneros—. Lo tendremos aquí esta misma semana.

A Helena le dio un vuelco el corazón.

—Ah.

Sabía que se lo había dicho para que empezara a asimilar lo que se avecinaba, pero, en lugar de darle tiempo…, sintió como si le arrojaran un jarro de agua fría.

Tragó saliva varias veces.

—¿Podría acompañarte a la biblioteca? Me gustaría asegurarme de que no he pasado nada por alto.

—Como quieras.

Una vez allí, Helena notó el peso de su mirada sobre ella mientras recorría sin prisa los pasillos entre las estanterías, buscando viejas crónicas sobre las cualidades de la alquimia. Cuando Kaine la observaba, en sus ojos se reflejaba una tristeza tan cristalina que Helena no entendía cómo no la había visto antes.

Sabía que, para él, la investigación no hacía más que robarles un valioso tiempo que podrían estar compartiendo juntos. Si no encontraba nada, habría desperdiciado cada segundo. Pasaría los pocos momentos que les quedaban buscando una solución que quizá nunca había existido.

Aun así, sacó otro libro de una estantería con los dedos temblorosos y lo añadió a la pila.

—Estos también.

—Creo que… he conseguido descifrar el sello y encontrar los materiales que necesitaré para recuperar tu alma —le dijo Helena a Kaine cuando regresó al día siguiente.

Estaba sentada al borde de la cama, con las manos vacías y sin haber tocado la comida que le habían llevado.

Kaine hizo una pausa al entrar y cerró la puerta.

—¿En serio?

Unos espasmos incontrolables se habían adueñado de la mano izquierda de Helena y el corazón le latía con tanta fuerza que sentía cada golpe como si la sacudiera desde dentro.

—Si modificamos la base del sello, podría utilizar sus componentes internos para acumular la energía mientras separo tu alma de la de los demás mediante la animancia.

—¿Pero?

Helena tragó saliva.

—Cuando Luc murió, se fue apagando poco a poco. Cetus..., es decir, Morrough lo había dejado tan maltrecho que su alma se desmoronó tras extraer al nigromante de su interior. No supe cómo... A ti te arrancaron el alma del cuerpo. Si consigo volver a metértela dentro, puede que con el tiempo se reintegre, pero tendremos que encontrar una manera de asegurarla, al menos al principio. Igual... igual que con las filacterias.

—Necesitarías que otra alma se sacrifique.

Ella asintió.

—Y tendría que ser por voluntad propia, porque, de lo contrario, el amarre no resistiría y el plan no funcionaría.

—Entiendo —fue lo único que dijo él.

—Si empiezo de cero, tal vez encuentre otra solución —dijo ella tragando saliva con la mandíbula temblorosa—. Puede que no haya abordado el tema desde el ángulo correcto.

Kaine permaneció en silencio.

Helena notó una sacudida en el pecho.

—También... he estado pensando que podríamos centrarnos en recuperar tu filacteria y marcharnos. Así tendré otro mes para seguir investigando, ¿no? Podría armar una bomba. Lo haríamos juntos, en la vieja fragua. No haría falta que desprendiera demasiado calor o que desatara una gran explosión. Si utilizamos el anulitio, una vez que hiriéramos a Morrough, podríamos quitarle la filacteria y huir. Entonces... entonces tendría tiempo para pensar en algo más.

Kaine se acercó a ella con una expresión impasible salvo por el brillo paciente de su mirada, que molestaba tanto a Helena.

—¿Crees que manejar explosivos estando embarazada es una tarea segura?

A Helena se le cerró la garganta.

—Trabajaríamos juntos. Podría explicarte cómo...

Kaine le cogió una mano y la colocó sobre las suyas para que notara cómo le temblaban los dedos. Por si fuera poco, la mano de Helena sufrió un espasmo.

—¿Quién de los dos tiene el pulso lo bastante firme como para construir una bomba?

Helena se soltó y apretó el puño con tanta fuerza que notó los metacarpianos bajo las yemas de los dedos. La estancia comenzó a dar vueltas y amenazó con tirarla de la cama, así que apoyó la otra mano sobre el colchón para mantener el equilibrio.

—Bueno, puede que si…

—Estoy agotado, Helena.

Ella levantó la vista y vio en su mirada que la guerra lo había consumido. Lo había devorado hasta los huesos y ni siquiera eso había bastado. No era más que una sombra de lo que un día fue.

Ella lo supo desde el momento en que había visto el sello grabado en su espalda. Supo que su poder acabaría empujándolo a focalizar su existencia en un único punto si sobrevivía y que nada lo desviaría de su objetivo. Kaine se lo había dejado muy claro.

No se detendría hasta que Helena estuviera a salvo, y eso lo estaba desgastando casi por completo. Él solo quería tener una meta a la que aferrarse.

A Helena le temblaron los hombros.

—Pero… yo también quiero salvarte.

—Lo sé —dijo él con suavidad—. Y, si alguien hubiera sido capaz de salvarme, esa habrías sido tú. Pero quiero despedirme de ti antes de que te vayas y la investigación te está cegando.

Entonces la estrechó entre sus brazos y apoyó la barbilla sobre su cabeza.

Pero Helena no pudo dejar de pensar. Cuando la dejó sola, retomó el estudio. Empezó de cero. Cada vez que oía que Kaine regresaba a su dormitorio, lo escondía todo y fingía haber dejado el tema apartado. Y, aunque Kaine sabía lo que se traía entre manos, ambos hicieron como si no pasara nada.

Helena lo besó. Lo empujó hasta la cama y se subió a horcajadas a su regazo mientras le enterraba los dedos en el pelo y amoldaba su cuerpo al de él, deseosa por tocar cada centímetro de su piel.

Cuando Kaine se puso a besarle el cuello, ella le soltó los botones y los cierres de la ropa hasta sentir directamente el calor de su piel. Luego, le bajó la camisa por los hombros y guio sus manos hacia la cintura. Kaine se aferró a ella y le presionó los dedos contra las costillas hasta que Helena arqueó la espalda para pegarse más a él.

Helena empezó a desabrocharse el vestido, pero le temblaban tanto las manos que los botones se le escapaban de entre los dedos. Kaine intentó detenerla, pero ella se lo impidió.

—Quiero hacer esto —aseguró con voz trémula—. Quiero hacerlo antes de irme, habiéndolo decidido nosotros. Por favor… —se le rompió la voz—. Esto era algo nuestro… —Tragó saliva y parpadeó con fuerza—. Nos lo arrebataron, pero era nuestro.

Con dificultad, logró soltar el resto de los botones y se bajó el vestido hasta la cintura. Luego, le rodeó el cuello con los brazos y lo atrajo hacia sí para besarlo.

Permaneció encima de él, con los muslos a cada lado de sus caderas, cuando sus cuerpos se unieron. Kaine la agarró de la cintura, pero no la empujó ni la forzó a moverse a otro ritmo que no fuera aquel para el que estaba preparada. Solo la sostuvo. Dejó escapar un leve gruñido cuando Helena movió las caderas hacia delante.

Ella intentó no pensar en el pasado ni comparar aquel momento con otros. Se esforzó por disfrutar del presente, de anclarse a aquel encuentro, pero le resultaba tan familiar…

Recordaba que sus relaciones habían sido de esa manera antes: lentas e íntimas. Recordaba la ardiente reverencia que le transmitía Kaine con su contacto al hacerle el amor.

Eso era lo que habían hecho siempre: el amor. Era lo que siempre habían compartido.

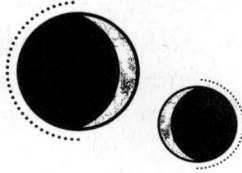

CAPÍTULO 71

Julius 1789

HELENA SE ESTABA CORROYENDO COMO el metal: se disolvía, se descomponía y se partía en pedazos. En su pecho había florecido un dolor constante desde que había empezado a desmoronarse.

Tenía muchas cosas que decirle a Kaine, pero ni siquiera era capaz de pensar en ellas sin que se le cerrara la garganta, el corazón se le desbocara y le entraran ganas de llorar. Nunca había sido una persona de lágrima fácil, pero el embarazo parecía haberla cambiado en ese aspecto. La cuenta atrás la estaba destrozando poco a poco.

Un día, en vez de echarse a llorar, se encaró con Kaine.

Su plan era estúpido y egoísta. No era justo que él muriera y ella se viera obligada a seguir adelante. Si la hubiera dejado participar en el rescate de Lila, no habrían acabado así. Si hubiera confiado en ella, si no hubiera sido tan controlador, si hubiese accedido a colaborar con ella, la situación habría sido muy distinta. Era todo culpa suya.

Él la dejó hablar hasta que se quedó sin aliento y se llevó una mano al pecho tratando de obligar al corazón a recuperar su ritmo. Cuando intentó ayudarla, ella le apartó la mano con brusquedad.

Más tarde, después de que su padre lo llamara y Helena se quedara revolcándose en su rabia, comprendió que Kaine estaba haciendo todo aquello a propósito.

Conocía bien los caminos destructivos por los que la mente de ella tendía a desviarse. Desde que había llegado a Puntaférreo, Kaine se había esforzado por provocarla y llevarle la contraria para hacer que reaccionara. Le había dado un objetivo. Odiarlo la ayudaba a ser menos autodestructiva.

Y, si en ese momento se enfadaba con él, su partida sería mucho más fácil para ambos.

Helena se tragó su rabia, decidida a no dejarse manipular, pero sus emociones le carcomieron las entrañas como si fueran un veneno.

———————

UN CAMIÓN TRAJO UNA NUEVA tanda de prisioneros y Kaine volvió a desaparecer.

Helena no podía evitar preguntarse cómo sería su relación con su padre. Ambos mostraban un evidente desprecio el uno por el otro que ni siquiera intentaban disimular. Atreus parecía encontrar siempre algún motivo para odiar a su hijo, pero tampoco dejaba de buscar razones para necesitarlo. Por otro lado, Kaine culpaba a su padre por la tragedia que había vivido su madre, pero hasta el momento le había perdonado la vida, pese a ser uno de los objetivos más débiles entre los inmarcesibles.

Helena estaba sentada en la cama, entumecida por el desaliento, cuando la puerta se abrió. Se le heló la sangre en las venas al levantar la vista y ver que uno de los guardias uniformados del camión había entrado en su habitación.

El intruso se quitó el gorro que le cubría la cabeza y Helena descubrió que era Ivy.

Se quedó mirándola, sorprendida pero a la vez entumecida, y la otra chica le ofreció una sonrisa vacilante.

—No sabes lo mucho que me ha costado llegar hasta ti.

Helena no se movió.

—¿Qué haces aquí?

—He venido a rescatarte.

Tan pronto como dijo eso, un chirrido metálico voló por la estancia. La puerta se combó y quedó encajada en el marco. Ivy se dio la vuelta e intentó abrirla, pero la estructura no cedió ni un milímetro. Volvió a girarse y avanzó hacia Helena.

—No —se apresuró a decir ella poniéndose de pie—. La última vez que alguien vino y se me acercó demasiado, Kaine le rompió todos los huesos del cuerpo sin siquiera estar presente.

Ivy se quedó inmóvil, mirándola como si fuera un animal enjaulado. Por muy difícil que le hubiera resultado llegar hasta Helena, estaba claro que no se había parado demasiado a trazar un buen plan.

—¿Por qué estás aquí? —le preguntó Helena mientras la estudiaba de cerca. Era muy muy joven, apenas una chiquilla—. Sabes que llevo prisionera en este lugar desde el año pasado. ¿Por qué has venido ahora?

Ivy retrocedió y rodeó a Helena en un arco amplio para acercarse a la ventana y sacudirla con violencia, intentando romper el cristal. Debía de haber perdido su toque, aunque a lo mejor había actuado de forma demasiado impulsiva. Tal vez había calculado mal y esperaba infiltrarse con mucha más facilidad en Puntaférreo.

—Pensaba que estabas aquí para que te interrogaran. No sabía que el Sumo Inquisidor iba a... —sus ojos volaron hasta el vientre de Helena— hacerte eso.

Helena resopló.

—Se lo han hecho a muchas chicas en la Central. ¿Por qué te preocupas por mí?

Ivy se quedó quieta.

—A Sofia le caías bien. Quería que me hiciera amiga tuya. Siempre me decía que debería parecerme más a ti, que debería ayudar a los demás, pero yo nunca la escuché.

—Pues yo no quiero ser tu amiga —dijo Helena con frialdad—. Tu hermana está muerta. Nos traicionaste a todos por un cadáver.

—¡Ya lo sé! —exclamó Ivy con un grito cargado de tristeza mientras se giraba para mirar a Helena con el rostro pálido y los ojos brillantes—. Lo sé, pero no pude..., no fui capaz de lidiar con su muerte. Pensé... —Se le descompuso el rostro—. Me dije que solo estaba herida, que podría volver. Pero no ha mejorado. No puede hacerlo. Y, en caso de que lo hiciera, jamás me perdonaría esto, ¿no crees?

A Helena no le daba ninguna pena.

—Lo hemos perdido todo por tu culpa. Aunque hubiéramos estado destinados a perder, mucha gente podría haber escapado, podría haber huido a tiempo. Pero tú se lo impediste.

Mientras hablaba, la puerta volvió a retorcerse con un chirrido y Kaine entró en la habitación. Las barras de hierro que revestían la puerta se levantaron del suelo y se transformaron en una infinidad de puntas alargadas que apuntaban hacia Ivy. Bastaría con que agitara una mano para que la chica acabara atravesada desde todas direcciones.

Podría intentar escapar, pero no conseguiría dar más de dos pasos antes de que la matara, así que se volvió para enfrentarse a él con una extraña resignación en el rostro.

—Me habría esperado una traición de cualquiera menos de ti —comentó Kaine con un tono que destilaba la más absoluta falta de sinceridad—. He de admitir que no te creía tan tonta como para caer en este tipo de trampa.

Ivy esbozó una amarga sonrisa y negó con la cabeza en un gesto casi apenado.

—No te acuerdas de mí, ¿verdad? Pensaba que acabarías cayendo en la cuenta.

Kaine la estudió con atención.

—Me temo que no.

—Era diferente cuando nos conocimos. Más pequeña. No dejaba de gritar. —Él negó con la cabeza como si aquella descripción pudiese aplicarse a cualquiera e Ivy siguió hablando—: Solía llevar el pelo recogido en dos trenzas con lazos. —Se señaló los hombros con ambas manos—. Después de que los inmarcesibles mataran a mis padres, las utilizaron para arrastrarme por el suelo hasta ti y luego te las pusieron en la mano. Tú también eras más joven.

La expresión de Kaine demostró que empezaba a recordarla.

Ivy apretó los labios y tomó aire.

—Cuando huiste, los demás inmarcesibles fueron a por ti y se olvidaron de mi hermana y de mí. Intenté cortarle la cabeza a mi madre con un cuchillo pastelero para que dejara de hacerle daño a Sofia. Fue entonces cuando me di cuenta de que me habría bastado con utilizar las manos. —Se miró los dedos—. Después de escapar, Sofia seguía viva, pero era… era como si estuviera en trance. Solo se movía o comía si yo la obligaba. Nos escondimos en los suburbios. Cuando por fin volvió en sí, lo último que recordaba fue que había sido mi cumpleaños. Había olvidado todo lo que había pasado. De no haber sido por ti, habríamos muerto.

Kaine esbozó una mueca despectiva.

—Otro motivo más para lamentar las decisiones que tomé aquel día.

Ivy se mostró confundida hasta que Kaine metió la mano en su chaqueta y sacó una daga de obsidiana. Entonces la chica abrió los ojos de par en par en una expresión que, en lugar de miedo, transmitía sorpresa, casi alegría.

—Eres el asesino.

—Sí —admitió él con una sonrisa—, y a ti en concreto tenía muchas ganas de cazarte.

Ivy miró a Helena.

—¿Y tú lo sabías? —Los miró a los dos—. ¿Es esto una farsa?

—Hasta cierto punto —dijo Helena.

No había esperado que ver morir a Ivy la afectara, pero estaba condenada a sentir compasión por cualquier persona cuya forma de actuar entendiera. Crowther había comentado que Ivy venía de los suburbios y que había estado trabajando para él a cambio de protección para su hermana. Si Sofia había estado un tiempo catatónica, no le sorprendía que Ivy se hubiera aferrado a la idea de que su hermana siguiera viva.

—No la mates.

Kaine le lanzó una mirada rápida.

—No puedes esperar que le perdone la vida.

Helena negó con la cabeza.

—Creo que ella misma no espera que se la perdones —dijo. Sospechaba que estaba a punto de cometer un terrible error, pero ya no tenía nada que perder. Miró a Ivy—. Los inmarcesibles están condenados. Lo sabes, ¿verdad?

Ivy asintió. Helena dudaba que se hubiera unido a los inmarcesibles porque estuviera interesada en alcanzar la inmortalidad. Todo apuntaba a que había sido una condición impuesta por Morrough, igual que había hecho con Kaine, para ponerle una correa al cuello a la mortífera vivemante.

—¿Nos ayudarás? —le preguntó Helena.

Ivy los miró alternativamente a ambos con expresión recelosa y calculadora, pero acabó inclinando la cabeza.

—No —intervino Kaine bruscamente—. No podemos fiarnos de ella. —Se volvió hacia Helena. Su resonancia vibró de forma inquietante y el hierro de la estancia emitió un quejido estremecedor—. Te dirá lo que quieras oír con tal de salir de aquí con vida y luego te traicionará igual que ha hecho con el resto.

Helena observó a Ivy y volvió a posar la vista en Kaine.

—Creo que sí que podemos fiarnos. Te lo debe. Te debe años de la vida de su hermana. Nos ayudará por Sofia.

—¿Qué necesitáis? —preguntó la chica con esa mirada brillante, aguda y curiosa que Helena recordaba bien.

—La filacteria de Kaine —dijo sin apartar la vista de ella—. Forma parte del cúbito del brazo derecho de Morrough.

Ivy tembló casi imperceptiblemente. Era evidente que la responsabilidad le parecía mayor de la que había esperado.

—¿Por qué?

Helena la miró y luego desvió la vista hacia Kaine.

—Necesito salvarlo.

Ivy asintió despacio.

—Lo intentaré. Si encuentro la manera de conseguírosla, os prometo que os la traeré.

—No sobrevivirás si lo haces —señaló Helena, que empezaba a dudar de su decisión, pero era incapaz de detenerse. Cualquier oportunidad era mejor que ninguna.

Ivy levantó la barbilla.

—Voy a hacer esto por Sofia. Ya nadie puede hacerle daño y da igual lo que a mí me pase. —Miró a Kaine—. Tú fuiste el motivo por el que pude salvarla una vez, así que esta será mi forma de darte las gracias.

—No quiero tu gratitud —replicó Kaine con una mueca. Cuando Helena lo agarró de la muñeca y lo instó a bajar el brazo, la fulminó con la mirada—. No merece la pena. No está capacitada para hacer algo así.

Helena se puso de pie y recurrió al tono de voz más suave que pudo.

—Dime algo, con la mano en el corazón. ¿Crees que tu situación habría sido distinta si hubieras tenido la oportunidad de salvar a tu madre? Si la respuesta es no, te dejaré matarla.

Kaine apretó los dientes y bajó el cuchillo.

—Lárgate de aquí antes de que cambie de idea.

Ivy vaciló durante un instante y Helena asintió para instarla a marcharse a toda prisa. Cruzó la estancia en un abrir y cerrar de ojos, esquivando los pedazos de hierro, y salió por la puerta. La estancia se reorganizó poco a poco y Kaine estudió a Helena con una mirada acusadora.

—¿De verdad estás dispuesta a arriesgarlo todo después de lo que hemos pasado?

—Si consigo salvarte, merecerá la pena.

—¿Y si no sale bien?

Helena miró a su alrededor. Ni siquiera ella tenía la esperanza o la confianza de que el plan funcionara, pero no se veía capaz de pasar un solo segundo más sufriendo de brazos cruzados.

—Entonces moriré sabiendo que agoté hasta el último recurso, y lo haré feliz, que es mucho más de lo que podré decir si tengo que dejarte atrás y seguir yo sola adelante. Ivy no conseguirá nada si nos traiciona. Ya lo ha perdido todo.

Kaine volvió a guardar el cuchillo de obsidiana en su funda.

—En fin, veremos más pronto que tarde si nos delata.

Se marchó y regresó con otros dos cuchillos y una píldora letal. Una de las armas tenía la hoja de obsidiana y la otra había formado parte de su antiguo juego, el que Kaine había conseguido recuperar tras el estallido de la bomba. Si Ivy los traicionaba y él no lograba alcanzarla a tiempo, Helena tendría una oportunidad de escapar con el bebé.

El día pasó con una implacable intensidad. Cuando cayó la noche, todo siguió igual salvo porque les llegaron noticias de que Shiseo y su séquito estaban cruzando Novis. Solo les quedaban unos pocos días e, independientemente de lo que Ivy hiciera, se les agotaba el tiempo.

Cuando la casa estuvo a oscuras y en silencio, Kaine fue a buscarla. Disfrutaron de cada momento juntos con tranquilidad. No tenían demasiado tiempo y no podían permitirse desperdiciarlo con prisas.

Helena estaba tumbada en brazos de Kaine, escuchando los latidos de su corazón. Siempre que intentaba imaginarse un hogar, lo único que se le venía a la cabeza era lo que sentía en momentos como aquel. Se tumbó sobre la espalda, le cogió la mano y se la apoyó sobre el bulto que le crecía entre las caderas.

—Esta es nuestra niña. Lo más… —se le formó un nudo en la garganta— lo más seguro es que empiece a notar pataditas durante el próximo mes. El libro dice que al principio es como un revoloteo. —Tuvo que tragar saliva para seguir hablando—: Se le llama vivificación… al primer movimiento del bebé, quiero decir. —Respiró hondo—. Si utilizas la resonancia, podrías notarla ya si quieres.

A Kaine se le crispó la mano y vaciló.

—Podemos hacerlo juntos —lo animó—. Deberías conocerla.

***

AL DÍA SIGUIENTE, EN VEZ de salir a caminar por el laberinto de setos, Kaine la llevó al patio.

Helena se quedó helada; el olor a sangre seca y descomposición que pendía en el aire hizo que el corazón le latiera con tanta fuerza que parecía querer salírsele por la garganta y que se le revolviera el estómago.

Desde que Atreus había regresado, habían llevado como mínimo a treinta prisioneros a Puntaférreo. Helena no sabía si la esperanza de que quedara alguno con vida era una idea más reconfortante o desalentadora que darlos a todos por muertos.

—¿Por qué tenemos que caminar por aquí?

Kaine la miró. Corrían el riesgo de que los estuvieran vigilando, así que mantuvo una expresión fría e indiferente. Sin embargo, su tono fue amable.

—Solo será esta vez y no tardaremos mucho.

Helena se obligó a asentir.

El patio era mucho más bonito en verano. Las enredaderas que cubrían la fachada de la casa como venas negras en invierno ahora estaban salpicadas de rosas.

Todavía quedaban dos necrómatas vigilando la puerta de entrada, pero estaban casi consumidos hasta los huesos. Helena los observó recelosa mientras Kaine la guiaba por el jardín.

—No te preocupes por ellos —le dijo en un susurro—. Morrough no puede permitirse desperdiciar su energía en los necrómatas. De hecho, casi han perdido todos los sentidos y todavía no se ha dado cuenta. Ven. Hay un reencuentro que hemos estado postergando durante demasiado tiempo.

Entonces comprendió adónde se dirigían.

—Amaris…

Kaine abrió la puerta de los establos.

—Lo pasó bastante mal cuando llegaste.

Bajo la luz tenue, Helena distinguió una enorme silueta negra que se incorporaba en un rincón y desplegaba las alas. La quimera se acercó a ellos arrastrando una pesada cadena tras ella.

—Me daba miedo que nos delatara si la dejaba acercarse a ti. En estos meses se ha ganado una reputación y tú eres la única persona a la que le ha cogido cariño aparte de mí.

Estaba siendo muy generoso al describir su relación con Amaris de esa forma.

A Helena se le secó la boca. El animal había crecido unos cuantos palmos y sus inmensos ojos amarillos resplandecían en la penumbra. Recordaba lo cuidadosa que la quimera había sido con Kaine cuando estaba herido, cómo se había enroscado en torno a la espalda de Helena para protegerla del frío. Pero la imagen más reciente que tenía de ella era la de haber estado a punto de morir de un mordisco al entrar en los establos.

Dio un paso atrás con nerviosismo.

—No estoy muy segura de que se acuerde de mí.

Kaine levantó una mano y Amaris se detuvo.

—Ah, ¿lo dices por aquello que pasó? No reaccionó así por ti, sino por los necrómatas. Los odia. —Amaris movía la cabeza en actitud impaciente, así que se acercó a ella y le revolvió el pelaje—. Tolera al servicio, pero, si alguno de los reanimados de Morrough se aproxima a ella..., ya sabes lo que pasa. —Miró de reojo a Helena—. Te aseguro que se acuerda de ti. Se pasó medio día aullando cuando llegaste.

Helena dio un paso vacilante hacia la criatura y dejó que la olisqueara y se frotara contra sus dedos. Cuando estuvo segura de que no perdería la mano, se acercó un poco más.

—Shiseo y tú os la llevaréis con vosotros cuando os marchéis —dijo Kaine mientras Helena le acariciaba la cabeza a Amaris—. Lo mejor será que voléis de noche. Tardaréis unos días en llegar hasta Lila, pero de esta forma será más difícil que os rastreen. —Rascó a Amaris en el lomo, justo bajo una de sus inmensas alas—. Tendréis que dejarla atrás cuando subáis al barco.

Helena se detuvo en seco.

—¿Cómo que tendremos que dejarla atrás?

—Estará bien —le aseguró él con voz ronca—. Sabe cazar y no le gustan los humanos, así que se mantendrá alejada de las zonas más pobladas. Con un poco de suerte, volverá a Paladia para venir a buscarme y acabará en las montañas.

—Pero necesita a alguien que... Alguien tendrá que mantener las transmutaciones mientras todavía crece.

Un músculo se tensó en la mandíbula de Kaine.

—Solo queda una quimera viva tras la guerra y todo el mundo sabe quién es su dueño. Basta con que alguien la vea para que cualquier aspirante ambicioso tenga un punto de partida por el que empezar a buscarte. Tendrás que dejarla atrás.

Kaine apoyó la cabeza contra Amaris y la criatura agitó las alas con suavidad. Helena ladeó la cabeza para mirarlo de frente.

—Nos marcharemos juntas, ¿verdad, bonita? Los dos últimos monstruos de Bennet.

El aire del establo hacía que le ardieran los ojos, así que se dio la vuelta y salió de allí.

Cerca de la casa, el ambiente era más fresco. Helena aprovechó para tomar unas cuantas bocanadas jadeantes de aire con la mano presionada contra el pecho, pero entonces oyó unos pasos apresurados y vio a Aurelia bajando los escalones de entrada hacia ella hecha una furia.

Estaba lívida, con la mirada centelleante de rabia. Llevaba un vestido rosa pálido con detalles carmesí, y, cuando estuvo casi a su altura, Helena se fijó en que el dobladillo del vestido y los zapatos eran del mismo rojo intenso.

—¿Dónde está Kaine?

—Aurelia —dijo él desde la oscuridad de los establos—, ¿qué te tengo dicho sobre lo de hablar con mi prisionera?

La chica se volvió hacia el sonido de su voz.

—¡He de hablar contigo! ¿Cómo quieres que la evite si te pasas todo el día con ella?

Kaine salió de los establos y un destello le surcó la mirada.

—¿Qué quieres?

—Necesito que hables con tu padre —dijo Aurelia después de tragar saliva varias veces—. Está destrozando la casa.

Kaine arqueó una ceja con despreocupación.

—Pensaba que te alegraba que se quedara con nosotros.

A Aurelia estuvieron a punto de salírsele los ojos de las órbitas.

—Eso fue antes de que convirtiera la casa en una cámara de tortura. ¡No me importa que se traiga a los prisioneros al cobertizo, pero está empezando a meterlos en casa! Hay pilas de cuerpos desmembrados por todas partes y hoy he pisado un charco de sangre porque ha despellejado a alguien en medio del vestíbulo.

Helena comprendió que el carmesí del vestido de Aurelia no formaba parte del diseño.

—Te dije que era mejor que te quedaras en la ciudad —le recordó Kaine, todavía impasible—, pero te negaste porque mi padre dijo que la dominancia es una fuente de pasión o algo así, y pensaste… ¿Qué? —Se inclinó hacia ella con la boca retorcida en una mueca—. ¿Que eso haría que me fijara en ti?

Aurelia se había puesto blanca, pero dos manchas de un rojo intenso le ardían las mejillas.

—Soy tu esposa.

Kaine ladeó la cabeza.

—Pero no porque yo quisiera.

—¿Qué está pasando aquí? —interrumpió Atreus saliendo del cobertizo.

Estaba manchado de sangre hasta los codos y portaba en la mano un cuchillo largo, de los que se usan para destripar pescado.

Aurelia dio un respingo, se llevó una mano llena de anillos de hierro al cuello y se escondió acobardada detrás de Kaine, pero este se apartó y, con un gesto apenas perceptible, se colocó disimuladamente entre Helena y su padre justo cuando quedaron frente a frente.

—Me temo que a Aurelia no le entusiasma lo que hemos hecho con la casa, padre. Creo que nos considera un tanto… salvajes.

Atreus miró a Kaine durante un momento mientras las estrechas aletas de la nariz de Crowther se agitaban delatando una rabia contenida que Helena reconoció al instante.

—Conque sí, ¿eh? Supongo que me he excedido un poco, pero esperaba que fueras tú quien se opusiera. Pensaba que, en algún momento, el cariño que debes de sentir por la casa te empujaría a actuar. Al fin y al cabo, te criaste aquí… —Dejó la frase a medias y se dio la vuelta para contemplar la inmensa mansión que se alzaba ante ellos—. Esta era la casa de tu madre. Plantó esas rosas el verano en que nos casamos.

Atreus agarró el cuchillo con más fuerza y, por un instante, Helena notó la resonancia de Kaine vibrándole en los dientes.

—Me temo que este edificio nunca ha tenido un valor sentimental para mí —comentó Kaine—. Si hubieras vuelto antes, tal vez podrías haber hecho tú el esfuerzo de conservarlo.

—Por supuesto, pero tengo la sensación de que estás decidido a destruir todo lo que esta familia ha construido —dijo Atreus con el rostro contraído en una mueca tan exagerada que la piel muerta y gris de su rostro parecía estar a punto de desgarrársele mientras fulminaba a Kaine con la mirada—. ¿Qué hizo tu madre para merecer un hijo como tú?

Kaine se inclinó hacia delante mientras una sonrisa afilada se dibujó en sus labios y un destello de puro desprecio le cruzaba los ojos.

—Creo que su mayor pecado fue casarse contigo.

Un fogonazo de rabia atravesó a Atreus, pero Aurelia intercedió:

—¿Ves? ¿Ves? Te lo dije. ¡Ha sido todo culpa suya! Yo he sido la esposa perfecta. Deberías haber visto el estado de este agujero horrendo y mohoso cuando me trajo aquí por primera vez. He hecho todo cuanto ha estado en mi mano para ser una buena esposa. Intenté restaurar la casa, deshacerme de todos esos muebles feos y anticuados que hay por todas partes, y convertirla en el corazón de la sociedad paladina. Si este sitio merece la pena en algo es gracias a mí. Soy igual que tu esposa y…

Atreus se volvió con brusquedad. Se oyó un sonido húmedo seguido de un gorgoteo sofocado. Aurelia dejó de hablar al instante y se llevó las manos al cuello justo cuando un reguero de sangre comenzó a brotarle de la herida que le había hecho Atreus en la garganta. Parpadeó una vez y abrió la boca, pero solo salió un jadeo sanguinolento. Entonces se le fue la cabeza hacia atrás, la herida del cuello se le abrió del todo y su cuerpo se desplomó sobre la gravilla blanca. El vestido rosa se tornó cada vez más rojo.

Helena se tapó la boca con la mano para ahogar el grito que estuvo a punto de escapar de entre sus labios. El lateral del cuello comenzó a arderle al tiempo que el corazón le retumbaba en el pecho, pero no consiguió moverse.

Atreus contemplaba el cadáver de su difunta nuera mientras la hoja curva del cuchillo que le colgaba de entre los dedos goteaba sangre.

—No vuelvas a compararte con mi esposa —dijo sin apartar la vista.

Kaine no reaccionó, pero dio un paso adelante para que Helena no tuviera que ver el cuerpo degollado de Aurelia.

—Dado que nuestro matrimonio fue un acuerdo que tú mismo organizaste, espero que te encargues de lidiar con la familia Ingram.

—¿Qué van a hacernos? —dijo Atreus con una mueca despectiva que Helena conocía bien. Ver las mismas expresiones de Kaine en el rostro muerto de Crowther le ponía los pelos de punta—. Estaba claro que no tenías la menor intención de dejarla embarazada.

Atreus se agachó y levantó el cadáver de Aurelia tirando de uno de sus brazos.

—Me encargaré de resolver este asunto, pero después tendrás que darme el nombre de una mujer con la que estés dispuesto a casarte y engendrar un heredero para el gremio. De lo contrario, una vez que haya localizado al último miembro vivo de la Llama Eterna y se lo haya entregado al Sumo Nigromante, le pediré que te obligue a cooperar y elegiré yo mismo a la candidata.

Atreus se dio la vuelta y entró en la casa arrastrando el cadáver de Aurelia tras de sí. El aroma de las rosas se mezcló con el olor metálico de la sangre fresca.

Helena también se giró, se encaminó hacia el ala más alejada de la casa y no se detuvo hasta que estuvieron dentro, en un pasillo donde no pudieran ser observados. Kaine la había seguido de cerca, y ella sabía que estaba a punto de preguntarle si se encontraba bien, pero decidió adelantarse y hablar primero:

—Lo tenías todo planeado.

Kaine se quedó de piedra.

—¿Qué te hace pensar eso? —preguntó en tono despreocupado.

—Que era un cabo suelto. Si estás dispuesto a dejar morir a Amaris, solo era cuestión de tiempo que te quitaras a Aurelia de en medio.

La expresión de Kaine se endureció.

—¿Y qué esperabas? Intentó arrancarte los ojos de cuajo.

Helena se encogió. Recordaba demasiado bien la sensación de las uñas de Aurelia clavándose en su rostro, el miedo a perder la vista, a quedar atrapada en la oscuridad para siempre.

—No lo he olvidado.

—La habría matado en ese mismo instante, pero tener una esposa atractiva en casa era una buena manera de no levantar sospechas. Vivir solo aquí contigo habría llamado demasiado la atención. Ese fue el único motivo por el que la dejé con vida.

Helena asintió lánguidamente. No le sorprendía, pero tampoco cambiaba nada.

—Odio que mates por mí —murmuró llevándose la mano izquierda a la cicatriz del cuello, mientras pensaba en el rostro de su padre y la horrible cuchillada que le habían dado justo bajo la mandíbula.

Aquella risa burlona era el último recuerdo que tenía de él.

Había presenciado tantas muertes insustanciales que empezaban a desdibujarse. El concepto de «tragedia» se quedaba corto para el número de fallecidos al que se había enfrentado, tan elevado que la cifra empezaba a parecer un concepto abstracto. Helena incluso había dejado de sufrir ante la muerte, y eso que durante años luchó por cada vida que se le ponía por delante, dándolo todo de sí misma por ellas. Ahora, ni siquiera lograba entender qué sentido tenía todo aquello.

Y Kaine y ella estaban en el epicentro de todas esas pérdidas.

—Eres mucho más que las muertes con las que cargas, pero a veces me da la sensación de que no hago más que sacar lo peor de ti. Jamás habrías ido tan lejos de no haber sido por mí. Yo tengo la culpa de que te hayas convertido en esto.

—Supongo que no, así que tienes razón.

—Solía soñar tan a menudo con nuestro futuro… —prosiguió ella con la voz pastosa—. Cuando me preocupaba por ti, cuando tenía que hacer algo que no quería, o cuando el peso de la guerra se volvía insoportable, solía repetirme que algún día huiría contigo a algún lugar tranquilo. No pedía mucho. Me bastaba con tenerte a mi lado. —Se le formó un nudo en la garganta y negó con la cabeza—. No quería nada más que eso. Ver qué nos depararía el futuro tras la guerra era mi único sueño. Pensaba que todo merecería la pena con tal de conseguirlo.

Exhaló y, al apretar el puño derecho, notó las cicatrices que el amuleto de los Holdfast le había dejado en la palma de la mano.

—Pero ni siquiera todo lo que hemos hecho ha sido suficiente. Supongo que al final soy como Luc. Pensaba que, si sufríamos lo suficiente, nos mereceríamos el uno al otro. —Kaine no respondió. Helena estaba harta de que se mostrara resignado—. ¿Por qué estás tan decidido a morir? —le preguntó girándose sobre los talones, pese que se había prometido no volver a enfadarse con él—. Cuando le hiciste tu oferta a Crowther ya te dabas por muerto, como si pensaras que nadie te echaría de menos. Pero ¿por qué sigues actuando igual ahora, cuando sabes con certeza que alguien sí lamentaría tu pérdida?

Kaine suspiró e hizo un gesto resignado mientras presionaba el pulgar contra el anillo que llevaba.

—Por aquel entonces no tenía a nadie, Helena —susurró—. Cuando mi madre murió, me quedé solo. Mi vida se desmoronó al volver a casa a los dieciséis años y, desde entonces, intenté aferrarme a lo que me quedaba. Tras su muerte, todo dejó de importarme… Vengarme era lo único que podía ayudarme a compensar lo sucedido, y a nadie le habría importado que perdiera la vida en el intento… hasta que llegaste tú. —Su tono se volvió amargo—. Nunca he visualizado un futuro después de la guerra porque mi idea siempre fue no tener uno. Siempre supe que Holdfast y la Llama Eterna no ganarían la guerra, y enamorarme de ti, en vez de hacerme cambiar de opinión, solo consiguió… empeorar las cosas.

De repente las luces parpadearon y desde el ala principal llegó un zumbido lejano.

Kaine se puso tenso y miró hacia la derecha.

—Algo va mal. Ya nunca usa ese método para llamarme. Ve a tu habitación y bloquea la puerta.

Se marchó apresuradamente. Desde la ventana de su dormitorio, Helena lo vio salir vestido con su uniforme puesto y el casco que le ocultaba el cabello. Sacó a Amaris de los establos, se subió a su lomo y salieron volando en dirección a la ciudad.

Helena esperó con un cuchillo en la mano. Menos de una hora más tarde, un automóvil se detuvo ante la casa. ¿Habrían capturado a Ivy? A lo mejor los había traicionado. ¿Y si habían llamado a Kaine para mantenerlo alejado de Puntaférreo?

Atreus salió vestido de uniforme, se metió en la parte trasera del coche y se alejó.

¿Qué había hecho Ivy?

No oyó el sonido de la puerta al abrirse hasta bien entrada la noche.

Kaine apareció todavía con el uniforme puesto y el casco en la mano. Su expresión era indescifrable.

—Nos han informado de que el tren en el que viajaba el séquito oriental ha sido atacado en Novis. Todo el mundo ha muerto…, incluido Shiseo.

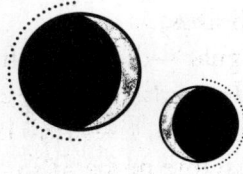

CAPÍTULO 72

SHISEO HABÍA MUERTO.

Su regreso había pendido sobre la cabeza de Helena como una espada, como una certeza inevitable. Él volvería y entonces ella se marcharía. Era una conclusión de la que nunca había creído poder escapar.

Kaine negaba con la cabeza despacio, como si ni siquiera él pudiera creérselo.

—¿Está confirmado?

—Nos han enviado su cabeza. Desde Novis aseguran que no han tenido nada que ver con ello, que han sido los supervivientes de la Llama Eterna, pero… ya no queda nadie capaz de hacer algo así. Ha sido un ataque de prueba. La reina está tanteando el terreno y quiere comprobar si los países aliados se lavarán las manos en caso de verse obligados a escoger bando y si Nueva Paladia tendrá los recursos necesarios para defenderse. —Bajó la vista y el aire se cargó de resonancia, pero aun así dejó escapar una carcajada—. Lo más irónico de todo esto es que este era nuestro plan. Esto era justo lo que teníamos pensado hacer. Pero se suponía que debían esperar hasta que yo hubiera desaparecido del mapa. —Tiró el casco contra la pared—. Ahora han puesto a Morrough sobre aviso y le han dado tiempo para reagrupar fuerzas y sacar a los necrómatas de las minas. Y yo sigo vivo y no puedo negarme a acatar sus órdenes. ¡Joder!

Entonces iban a morir todos. Kaine iba a morir, ella iba a morir, su hija iba a morir. Puntaférreo era una tumba además de una jaula.

Extendió una mano para tocarlo con los dedos al borde del entumecimiento.

952

—No pasa nada. Has hecho todo lo que has podido.

«Prefiero morir en tus brazos».

—Tú te vas a marchar igual —dijo él tras fruncir el ceño brevemente. Helena lo miró sin entender nada mientras él se ponía los guantes. El plan de escape dependía de Shiseo, sí—. Pero hay otras opciones, aunque tienen… más fisuras. Es bastante probable que corras el riesgo de que te sigan si se dan prisa. Morrough hará lo que sea necesario con tal de recuperarte. Si llegas a la costa a tiempo, podrás desaparecer antes de que te alcancen, pero… tendrás que llegar sola hasta Lila. A no ser que te veas con fuerzas para volar en Amaris sin ayuda.

—¿Cómo…? ¿Sola?

Incluso antes, cuando todavía era fuerte y no sufría ataques de pánico sin motivo, montar a lomos de Amaris era algo que solo había tolerado por necesidad. La altura y la velocidad a las que volaba eran aterradoras. Por si fuera poco, la quimera siempre había sabido adónde ir; nunca había necesitado que Helena la guiara.

No concebía volar de noche con Lumitia casi desaparecida en el cielo. El mundo sería un abismo negro bajo sus pies. Se mareaba solo con imaginárselo.

—Te llevaré tan lejos como pueda. Habrá un barco esperándote río abajo para acercarte a la costa. Te enseñaré mis mapas y la ruta que tendrás que seguir por el continente para encontrar a Lila. También podría prepararte algún transporte, pero creo que será más seguro que al menos hagas una parte del trayecto a pie si te ves capaz de ello. Irás a la zona portuaria justo antes de la latencia; allí te he dejado un billete y documentos de identidad falsos para que viajes hasta Etras, donde ya te he preparado un lugar para alojarte.

El corazón de Helena se estremeció y dio un vuelco mientras trataba de asimilarlo.

—No tienes que tomar una decisión ya —la tranquilizó Kaine, apoyando una mano sobre su hombro—. Prepararé ambas opciones para que puedas elegir. Sé que será duro, pero merecerá la pena. Lila lleva ya un tiempo esperándote.

Helena asintió, temblorosa.

Tendrían que actuar deprisa. Lumitia no iba a esperar por ellos y, si estallaba una guerra entre Paladia y los países vecinos, Kaine no quería que Helena estuviera todavía allí para verla.

Después de pasar tantos años con la esperanza de que Novis o cualquiera de los demás países intervinieran en el conflicto, ahora habían decidido hacerlo en el peor momento posible.

—Tengo que irme —dijo Kaine al cabo de un instante—. Vendré a verte en cuanto pueda. Intenta comer y descansar. Y no le abras la puerta a nadie. Por suerte, ahora que Aurelia no está, el cerrojo será mucho más seguro. Crowther no dominaba la resonancia férrea pese a que mi padre se ha esforzado por sacar su poder del fondo de su cadáver decrépito. Mientras la puerta permanezca cerrada, no podrá entrar.

Estaba divagando porque estaba nervioso; la situación empezaba a írsele de las manos. La misma intervención que la Resistencia había estado esperando al ser aniquilada había destrozado también todos sus planes, cuidadosamente trazados.

APENAS VIO A KAINE DESPUÉS de aquello. Pasó varios días fuera y Helena dudaba que estuviera durmiendo en absoluto. Por su parte, ella intentó cumplir con lo que le había prometido: comió e hizo su rutina de ejercicios en la habitación para ganar resistencia y recuperar fuerzas, de manera que el plan de huida no estuviera tan limitado por su condición física.

Atreus regresó a Puntaférreo. Si la noticia del asesinato de Aurelia había salido a la luz, esta no parecía haber tenido el más mínimo efecto sobre su integridad. Sin embargo, por cómo deambulaba por la casa, daba la impresión de haberse quedado sin prisioneros. Helena oyó sus pisadas por el pasillo que conducía hasta su dormitorio y lo vio salir y entrar de la capilla unas cuantas veces.

Cuando las alas de Amaris sacudieron las ventanas, supo que Kaine había regresado, aunque fuera por unas horas. Su plan de huida no era lo único que lo mantenía ocupado. Como Sumo Inquisidor, se esperaba que coordinara la respuesta al ataque que habían sufrido los inmarcesibles.

Por eso, le sorprendió que entrara en su habitación unos minutos más tarde.

Los ojos le brillaban tanto que casi resplandecían, y ese fulgor le hacía parecer menos humano que nunca. Se acercó a ella como si percibiera su presencia, pero sin verla en realidad.

—¿Kaine?

A Helena estaba a punto de salírsele el corazón por la boca, pero él no respondió. Tenía el presentimiento de que algo terrible había sucedido. Un escalofrío le caló hasta los huesos y, aunque todo su cuerpo le pedía que huyera, avanzó hacia él y le tocó el rostro con suavidad.

—¿Qué ha pasado?

Kaine parpadeó y su expresión recuperó un atisbo de humanidad. Helena siguió sosteniéndole la cara y se la bajó con cuidado para que la mirara.

—¿Kaine?

—Nunca había matado a tantos de golpe… —susurró.

—¿Cuántos han sido?

Movió los ojos de un lado a otro, como si intentara calcular el número exacto, pero negó con la cabeza.

—¿Qué ha pasado? —insistió la chica.

Kaine la miraba sin verla, como si no estuviera del todo presente.

—Me pidieron una demostración de fuerza. Que les hiciera una advertencia. —Tragó saliva—. Había hileras e hileras de prisioneros. No sé de dónde consiguieron a tantos.

Mientras hablaba, su expresión se fue descomponiendo hasta volverse dolorosamente juvenil. Con la mirada desencajada, no parecía más que un muchacho. Estaba paralizado por la conmoción y daba la sensación de que estuviera explicándose la situación a sí mismo, más que hablándole a Helena.

—No esperaba que hubiera tantos. Se suponía que la situación no se descontrolaría hasta que yo ya no estuviera aquí.

Helena le rodeó los hombros con los brazos y lo estrechó contra su cuerpo. Pese a que estaban en pleno verano, Kaine tenía la piel fría y húmeda. No parecía que fuera a aguantar mucho más así. Tenía la sensación de que Kaine estaba intentando darle esquinazo a su propio destino. Sin embargo, cada vez que conseguía sacarle algo de ventaja, Morrough le asignaba una nueva tarea.

Y Helena no podía hacer nada para impedirlo. La impotencia la estaba consumiendo.

—¿Has visto a Ivy? ¿Te ha dicho algo? ¿Sabes si sigue con los planes? A lo mejor si…

Kaine pareció volver a la realidad con un parpadeo. Negó con la cabeza y estiró la espalda.

—Para. Estoy bien… Solo me encuentro cansado. Todo irá bien. Esto se acabará pronto.

Aunque trataba de tranquilizarla, sus palabras abrieron un vacío en su interior cuando salió de la habitación.

―――――――

HELENA SE HABÍA QUEDADO CON los nervios tan alterados tras la partida de Kaine que, cuando notó un movimiento en la parte baja del abdomen, su primer impulso fue entrar en pánico.

Se mantuvo quieta como una estatua, con el corazón encogido, y entonces lo volvió a notar. Como un revoloteo. Bajó la mirada y se tiró del vestido para pasar las manos por el bulto que le crecía entre las caderas. A veces, todavía se olvidaba de que estaba encinta.

Aunque el embarazo de Lila había sido toda una sorpresa, a ella siempre le habían gustado los niños. Lila era un imán para ellos: sabía cómo hacerles reír. Helena, sin embargo, nunca tuvo esa cualidad, así que no sabía si sería una buena madre o si la decisión de tener al bebé no era más que el reflejo de su propio egoísmo, de su incapacidad para rendirse.

O de su deseo de querer, de saber que alguien la necesitaba.

La mano le temblaba cuando se presionó el vientre y dejó que la resonancia se sumergiera en su interior tímidamente para percibir los diminutos huesos de la pequeña, todavía más blandos que el cartílago, así como las delicadas venas que surcaban su cuerpecito.

Pronto, su hija sería lo único que le quedara de Kaine en el mundo.

—Voy a cuidar de ti —le susurró—. Es… lo que tu papá y yo siempre hemos hecho el uno por el otro.

Un segundo después de pronunciar aquellas palabras, Kaine entró por la puerta. Había pasado casi un día entero desde el incidente, pero todavía tenía un color perturbador y sus ojos seguían desprendiendo un brillo demasiado intenso.

—Stroud está de camino —dijo con voz tensa—. He venido tan rápido como he podido, pero tengo que…

Tan pronto como llegó a su altura, le quitó los grilletes y le colocó los conductos de anulitio en las muñecas. Helena se estremeció al notar que su resonancia se desvanecía como una luz al apagarse.

Kaine apenas había terminado de hablar cuando se le desenfocó la mirada.

—Ya está aquí. Asegúrate de esconderlo todo.

Cuando Stroud entró en la habitación, Helena supo enseguida que la tensión que se respiraba en el país no le estaba haciendo ningún bien a la mujer. Tenía los ojos hundidos y las mejillas rojas por los capilares rotos.

—La Central está específicamente diseñada para acomodar a las gestantes —estaba diciendo con aquella voz suya tan estridente—. Marino es nuestro sujeto de prueba más importante. Debería estar allí para que yo pueda seguir de cerca el desarrollo del feto y avancemos más deprisa una vez que sea viable.

—¿Y crees que el «entorno gestacional» que has creado le vendrá bien a una persona con una dolencia cardiaca detonada por el estrés? Dejarla allí sería como pedir a gritos un aborto espontáneo —replicó Kaine con una mueca de desprecio—. Marino es mi prisionera. El Sumo Nigromante me la confió para que la vigilara y, que yo sepa, todavía no ha cambiado de idea. No permitiré que te interpongas en mi tarea solo porque ya no cuentas con el trabajo de Shiseo para legitimar tu papel.

El rostro de Stroud adquirió un furioso color rojo, como si una nueva capa de capilares acabara de romperse bajo la superficie de su piel.

—Pienso hablar con el Sumo Nigromante de esto.

—Te animo a que lo intentes, pero ya le he informado de que tus intromisiones han contribuido al estado en que la chica se encuentra ahora. Tal vez no habría desarrollado esa arritmia si tú no hubieras intentado apresurar el interrogatorio al inyectarle una dosis casi letal de estimulantes y amenazarla con cortarle la lengua si no se quedaba embarazada. Ahora céntrate en lo que se supone que has venido a hacer.

El rostro de Stroud permaneció enrojecido de la ira mientras le hacía a Helena el reconocimiento de rigor para comprobar cómo se encontraba su corazón y cómo progresaba el embarazo. Según parecía, su intención había sido colarse en Puntaférreo y llevarse a Helena mientras Kaine estaba ocupado.

En tan solo unos minutos ya había acabado y estaba recogiendo su bolsa hecha una furia. Kaine la acompañó a la salida y Helena se asomó a la ventana para verla subirse a un automóvil y alejarse de la casa. El vehículo apenas había cruzado la verja de entrada cuando las luces parpadearon y se oyó un zumbido lejano proveniente del ala principal. Volvían a llamar a Kaine.

Como no le había dado tiempo a apartarse del cristal, Helena lo vio salir de la casa y subirse a lomos de Amaris, que recorrió la mitad del patio al galope antes de alzar el vuelo. Helena apoyó la mano sobre la ventana y el anulitio hizo presión sobre los tendones de su muñeca.

Le trajeron el periódico del día con la comida. La fotografía de la primera plana bastó para que se le revolviera el estómago.

La habían tomado desde la verja de entrada a la Academia, que se encontraba justo frente a los escalones de la Torre. En esos mismos escalones se veía a Kaine sin el casco, sin nada que ocultara su identidad. Su rostro permanecía al descubierto, pero el intenso brillo de sus ojos había distorsionado la fotografía. Entre la verja y él se alineaban filas y filas de cadáveres.

Esperó durante horas a que Kaine regresara, pero no apareció. No era nada propio de él dejarla sola en la casa con Atreus sin devolverle la resonancia para que bloqueara la puerta.

Cuando la noche cayó, de Lumitia no quedaba más que una delgada franja de luz, como si el cielo nocturno fuera una cortina negra que cubría la luz del sol y alguien la hubiera desgarrado con un cuchillo.

Un aullido grave flotó por los pasillos de la casa. Helena se acercó a la ventana.

Amaris estaba en el patio; la escasa luz de la luna recortaba la silueta de su sombra descomunal. Bajaba la cabeza de vez en cuando para empujar algo con el hocico, luego la ladeaba y profería un aullido suave y entrecortado que recordaba al gemido del viento gracias a esos pulmones de caballo que tenía.

Helena la vio caminar en círculos, arañar el suelo con las zarpas y agitar las alas con nerviosismo. Por un momento, la débil luz de la luna bañó el suelo e iluminó una cabeza de cabello claro.

Helena se apresuró a salir de la habitación y encontró a uno de los miembros del servicio en el pasillo.

—Ve a buscar a Davies y al mayordomo. No sé cómo se llama. Kaine está en el patio.

El hombre se movió muy despacio.

Helena apenas tuvo tiempo de preocuparse por la oscuridad o las sombras mientras bajaba la escalera aferrándose a la pared y tratando de controlar los latidos de su corazón. Flaqueó al llegar a la puerta. La casa estaba completamente a oscuras y no había rastro de Atreus. Trató de tranquilizarse diciéndose que la penumbra era una ventaja, que Morrough no podría ver nada si estaba vigilando la casa.

Tomó una profunda bocanada de aire y cruzó el patio de gravilla para llegar hasta Amaris, que acababa de soltar otro aullido impotente.

La quimera gruñó y se dio la vuelta cuando Helena se acercó a ella.

—Soy yo —le dijo después de detenerse en seco y mostrarle las manos—. ¿Te acuerdas de mí? Déjame ayudarlo.

Amaris paró de gruñir, pero siguió enseñándole los dientes mientras ella se arrodillaba y atravesaba el espacio que la separaba de Kaine a gatas.

Él estaba tumbado boca abajo en el suelo y, cuando le dio la vuelta, Helena se manchó las manos de sangre. Olía a descomposición, igual que aquel horrible laberinto de pasillos subterráneos. Estaba helado y apenas respiraba.

—¿Kaine? ¿Me oyes? ¿Qué te han hecho?

Lo sacudió con cuidado. Ya lo habían herido con anulitio antes, pero nunca lo había visto tan maltrecho como en ese momento y lo peor era que no podía usar la resonancia para ver qué le pasaba. Estaba tan oscuro que ni siquiera alcanzaba a distinguir nada más que su silueta. Notaba su pulso bajo los dedos; era tan irregular que un humano cualquiera no habría tardado en morir. Su corazón se detenía de manera intermitente y luego volvía a bombear un par de veces antes de pararse de nuevo.

El anulitio de las muñecas la dejaba sin fuerza en las manos, así que levantarlo del suelo iba a ser una tarea imposible. Le metió los brazos bajo las axilas para arrastrarlo por el patio, pero pesaba demasiado. Al derrumbarse sobre la gravilla, su cabeza se tambaleó contra el hombro de ella.

—Kaine…

No respondió.

Helena miró a su alrededor en busca de algún sirviente y vio que Davies, el mayordomo y otros cuantos miembros más del servicio salían de la casa portando linternas. Se movían como si no estuvieran del todo anclados al presente.

Amaris gruñó y Helena trató de tranquilizarla acariciándole las orejas y apartándola de Kaine como para que los sirvientes pudieran llegar hasta él.

—Llevadlo a mi habitación —les pidió sin levantar la voz—. Y tened cuidado. No sé qué le habrá pasado.

El mayordomo se echó a Kaine al hombro con cuidado.

Amaris temblaba. Dejó escapar un quejido grave y ronco mientras seguía la trayectoria de Kaine con el hocico, moviendo la cabeza de arriba abajo como si quisiera seguirlo al interior de la casa.

—Yo cuidaré de él y me aseguraré de que no le pase nada. Tú ya has hecho todo lo que podías.

Helena se quedó apoyada contra Amaris unos instantes más, pero luego se obligó a separarse del tranquilizador calor de la quimera para cruzar el patio de gravilla y volver adentro.

«Tranquila. No pierdas la calma —se repitió una y otra vez mientras obligaba a su corazón a latir a un ritmo regular y a su mente, a no dejarse llevar por la oscuridad—. Tienes que subir a ayudar a Kaine».

Llegó a su habitación antes que los sirvientes, así tuvo tiempo para preparar la cama y despejar la mesa, salvo por las medicinas que creía que tendría que utilizar, y comenzó a empapar toallas.

El mayordomo llegó manchado de sangre allí donde el cuerpo de Kaine permanecía en contacto con el suyo.

—Sujetadlo para que pueda quitarle la ropa —les ordenó Helena.

Mientras lo desnudaba, dejó las prendas tiradas por el suelo e intentó encontrar las heridas ahora que tenía luz para examinarlo bien. Pero ya se había curado. No tenía ni un rasguño. ¿Qué le habían hecho? ¿De dónde provenía toda esa sangre?

Al ser incapaz de encontrar la causa de la hemorragia, el miedo empezó a extenderse por su pecho. ¿Y si las heridas eran internas?

—Traedme todo el suministro médico que haya en la casa —les pidió a los dos sirvientes, que esperaban sin moverse, con la mirada más perdida que de costumbre—. Y daos prisa si es posible.

El mayordomo tumbó a Kaine en la cama y Helena se apresuró a limpiarle los últimos restos de sangre. Luego, lo cubrió con las sábanas para tratar de hacerlo entrar en calor y recogió la pila de ropa manchada y maloliente que había dejado en el suelo. Después, hurgó entre los bolsillos del abrigo hasta dar con un objeto que conocía bien: el kit médico. Lo sacó con un jadeo de alivio.

Estaba en perfectas condiciones. Incluso la hoja de papel encerado donde había detallado las instrucciones para utilizarlo seguía intacta. Hacía tiempo que había vaciado algunos de los frascos que le había preparado, pero el que necesitaba en ese momento parecía estar entero aún, junto con su correspondiente jeringuilla. Estaba claro que era algo que él utilizaba con regularidad.

Helena presionó la frente contra el kit, suspiró aliviada y regresó junto a Kaine para comprobarle el pulso. Seguía siendo intermitente: sus latidos se ralentizaban, se interrumpían y luego volvían a arrancar de nuevo.

Le limpió los restos de sangre del pecho.

—Lo siento —murmuró antes de llenar la jeringuilla, darle un par de golpecitos para eliminar las burbujas y clavársela en el pecho, justo encima del corazón, para inyectarle la dosis completa.

Kaine se incorporó de golpe llevándose una mano al pecho antes de que Helena tuviera tiempo de retirarle la jeringuilla. Cuando volvió a caer sobre el colchón, se le quedó el cuerpo sin fuerza, pero permaneció consciente. Sus ojos vagaban por la habitación sin ver nada.

—¿Kaine?

—¿He-elena…? —balbuceó con voz desconcertada.

Dejó la jeringuilla sobre la mesa y se acercó a él, pero sus ojos no seguían sus movimientos, sino que volaban de un lado a otro como si buscara algo en lo que fijarse. Helena se inclinó sobre él y le acarició el cabello.

—Estoy aquí. ¿Qué te ha hecho?

Kaine frunció el ceño.

—¿Dóndessstamos?

A Helena se le formó un nudo en la garganta y miró a su alrededor. Las luces estaban encendidas y la estancia la conocía perfectamente. Su rostro se encontraba a centímetros del de Kaine, pero él miraba a través de ella.

—Estás en mi habitación. Te derrumbaste en el patio e hice que los sirvientes te trajeran dentro. ¿Me ves?

—N-no… —Helena nunca lo había visto tan asustado como en aquel momento, mientras sus labios trabajaban con esfuerzo por formar cada palabra—. No… v-veeeo…

De pronto, su expresión cambió y la buscó a tientas hasta que su mano encontró el brazo de ella.

—¿Estás bien? ¿Y tu corazón? ¿Late… con…?

Helena le agarró la mano y se la llevó primero al pecho y luego a la cara. Los dedos de Kaine se estremecieron contra su mejilla.

—Estoy bien. Mi corazón está perfecto. Soy sanadora, ¿recuerdas? Te he curado infinidad de veces, así que puedes estar tranquilo.

Carraspeó y se sentó al borde de la cama para que sintiera su cercanía mientras volvía a comprobarle el pulso. Ahora el corazón le latía a toda velocidad, pero al menos ya no fallaba.

—He tenido que inyectarte un estimulante para que no se te pare el corazón como hace un rato. ¿Puedes intentar quitarme los grilletes para examinarte con la resonancia?

Le guio las manos hasta sus muñecas y se las colocó sobre los grilletes, pero Kaine se movía de forma descoordinada y tenía un extraño temblor en los dedos. Todavía no sabía qué le habían hecho, pero debían de haberle causado algún tipo de daño neurológico. Nunca le había visto síntomas como aquellos. Tras intentarlo un par de veces más, Helena le sujetó los dedos para obligarlo a detenerse.

—Déjalo —dijo esforzándose por mantener la voz estable—. No te preocupes, trabajaré manualmente. —Tragó saliva—. ¿Recuerdas qué ha pasado? ¿Por qué te han hecho esto? No has incumplido ni una sola de sus órdenes.

Kaine permaneció en silencio durante unos instantes y, cuando por fin habló, lo hizo con más fluidez, con frases completas y bien articuladas.

—Hevgoss ha anunciado esta tarde que va a aliarse con el Frente de Liberación. —Eso debería haber sido una buena noticia—. En su… declaración, han dicho que ha sido mi «brutal matanza» la que los ha empujado a hacerlo. Según parece, yo debería haberlo previsto y haberme negado a acatar órdenes. Me han impuesto un castigo ejemplar… para demostrar el precio del fracaso y la incompetencia.

Se le convulsionó el pecho como si intentara reír.

—¿Qué te ha hecho? —volvió a preguntar Helena con temor al ver que evitaba la pregunta.

Kaine exhaló.

—Primero me ha arrancado la cabeza. Dijo que era… lo m-más apropiado…

Helena se quedó muda. Jamás habría esperado que los inmarcesibles pudieran sobrevivir a algo así.

—Creo que le debo una disculpa al principado… Es una forma horrible de morir —dijo arreglándoselas para esbozar un amago de sonrisa—. Aunque me volviera a crecer, ha sido la peor parte…

Su voz se apagó.

Helena agradeció que no pudiera verla mientras se obligaba a respirar despacio con la mano en el pecho, como si necesitara cerciorarse de que su propio corazón seguía latiendo.

—¿Y luego qué?

A Kaine se le retorció el rostro.

—No… Todavía estaba… —Se señaló el pecho—. Me hizo algo… en la columna, creo. Ya no veía nada. No podía moverme. Ni siquiera recuerdo cuándo dejaron de funcionarme los ojos…

Helena se tragó el nudo que tenía en la garganta para mantener la voz firme.

—Bueno, tu ritmo cardiaco vuelve a ser estable. No sé durante cuánto tiempo tendrás que lidiar con los síntomas neurológicos, pero lo mejor es que descanses y te des tiempo para recuperarte.

Los sirvientes regresaron por fin con varias cajas de madera llenas de suministros médicos.

Helena se quedó sentada junto a Kaine mientras comprobaba lo que le habían traído. Había muchos más estimulantes, pero esperaba no tener que recurrir a ellos otra vez. Kaine se había quedado dormido al cabo de un rato, aunque no dejaba de moverse y sus dedos seguían sufriendo espasmos constantes. En un par de ocasiones, se despertó sobresaltado, todavía ciego, y buscó a Helena a tientas para asegurarse de que su corazón seguía latiendo, pero, en cuanto ella le decía que estaba bien, volvía a caer rendido.

Lo que más le preocupaba era la espasticidad que mostraba. Se tensaba y se estremecía; los músculos se contraían con violencia, y las manos y los dedos se le agarrotaban como si fueran garras.

Sabía que los estimulantes provocaban síndrome de abstinencia, pero temía más lo que pudiera ocurrir si esos síntomas se combinaban con la lesión cerebral o espinal que padecía. ¿Debería permitir que se curara solo? ¿Era posible que desarrollara una neuropatía permanente? Últimamente, le costaba mucho más regenerarse que antes.

Tomó la mano derecha de Kaine entre las suyas y se la masajeó despacio, nudillo a nudillo, hasta que el agarrotamiento desapareció. Notaba los tendones de la muñeca tensándose contra el anulitio cada vez que movía los pulgares, pero no le prestó atención. Siguió masajeándole el brazo hasta el hombro y luego pasó a la otra mano. Un dolor lacerante le subió por el brazo izquierdo, pero no se detuvo.

Era lo único que podía hacer por él, así que no iba a echarse atrás.

Le tomó el pulso de nuevo. Por fin había recuperado un ritmo regular. La expresión de Kaine se relajaba cada vez que oía su voz, así que le habló en un susurro de todo lo que se le pasó por la cabeza. Le dijo todo lo que siempre había querido decirle.

Después de que pasara medio día sin despertarse, le puso una vía con suero, aunque tampoco reaccionó. Oyó a alguien moviéndose por el pasillo un par de veces, pero, si Atreus estaba merodeando por la casa, no se atrevió a acercarse a su dormitorio.

Cuando Kaine por fin abrió los ojos, lo primero que hizo fue buscarla con la mirada.

—¿Me ves? —le preguntó quedándose muy quieta.

—Distingo siluetas, que ya es algo —dijo él entornando los ojos antes de cerrarlos con fuerza y reabrirlos con un estremecimiento—. Creo que voy mejorando.

—Me alegro —respondió Helena temblorosa—. Temía que la ceguera temporal fuera resultado de un coágulo o alguna dolencia nerviosa causados por el fallo cardiaco.

Kaine asintió distraídamente, tampoco eso importaba ya demasiado. Arrastró los dedos por la cama para llegar hasta ella.

—¿Te encuentras bien?

—Por supuesto —dijo ella, agradecida por que todavía viera borroso; estaba demasiado agotada como para que la mentira resultara convincente.

A Kaine empezaron a cerrársele los ojos, pero los abrió de golpe.

—Mi padre está al otro lado de la puerta. —Se incorporó con rigidez y dejó escapar un gruñido—. Tengo que ir a hablar con él. Todavía quedan cosas que no he…

Helena lo sujetó por el hombro.

—No puedes levantarte aún, no estás recuperado del todo.

Él le agarró las manos e intentó darle un apretón, pero sufrió un espasmo en los dedos.

—No nos conviene que mi padre me encuentre aquí. Además, ya no necesito recuperarme. Tienes que marcharte esta misma noche. No voy a poder asegurarte el viaje perfecto, pero bastará con lo que ya está organizado. Te las arreglarás bien.

—¿E-esta noche?

Kaine no respondió. Se levantó de la cama, se quitó la vía del brazo y se vistió apresuradamente. Helena tuvo que ayudarlo a abrocharse los botones.

—Ya veo mucho mejor —comentó con voz ronca—. Lo suficiente como para percatarme de la mirada de desaprobación que me estás lanzando.

Tomó las manos de Helena entre las suyas y, no sin esfuerzo, se las arregló para controlar el pulso lo bastante como para quitarle los grilletes. Ella misma volvió a colocarse las bandas de cobre en torno a las muñecas.

—No abras la puerta. Regresaré cuando caiga la noche.

CAPÍTULO 73

Julius 1789

Helena recorrió la habitación con la mirada. Pese a que era pleno verano, en el interior todavía hacía frío, pues el hierro no se prestaba demasiado a la calidez. Las sábanas estaban manchadas de sangre y el olor de la putrefacción flotaba en el aire, como si la necrosis estuviera corrompiendo cada centímetro de su vida.

Estar encerrada y, al mismo tiempo, temer salir de su prisión era una paradoja de lo más extraña.

Se acercó a la ventana después de oír gritos y vio a Kaine saliendo por la puerta delantera de la casa. Ya se movía con mucha más soltura. Atreus se había quedado en el umbral y estaba tan encolerizado que Helena apenas alcanzaba a distinguir lo que decía.

Kaine, por su parte, se limitó a entrar en los establos para sacar a Amaris y subirse a su lomo con una agilidad de lo más convincente.

Atreus seguía gritando cuando la quimera alzó el vuelo, agitando el puño hacia el cielo. Ver el cadáver de Crowther en movimiento siempre le ponía los pelos de punta a Helena.

Cuando por fin se cansó de vociferar, el hombre se detuvo un momento y levantó la mirada para clavarla directamente en la ventana a la que estaba asomada. Ella retrocedió enseguida, pero ya era demasiado tarde: la había visto. Un inexplicable pavor le caló hasta la médula.

Se acercó a comprobar que la puerta estuviera bien cerrada y que su revestimiento de hierro, al igual que el de las paredes, siguiera intacto. La habitación estaba atrincherada. Atreus no tenía forma de entrar.

Más tranquila, se sentó a estudiar el sello que había diseñado y trazó sus líneas con los dedos. El diseño funcionaba, podía proporcionarle el

965

poder y la estabilidad que necesitaba, pero no servía de nada. Para utilizarlo requería cinco materiales y ella solo tenía tres.

Había perdido demasiado tiempo.

Enterró el rostro entre las manos durante un momento, pero lo alzó de golpe cuando un olor a humo y a carne quemada le inundó las fosas nasales. Un humo negro empezaba a colarse en la habitación; la puerta se estaba carbonizando y el hierro que la revestía ardía con un brillo rojo cada vez más intenso.

—¡Sal de ahí, pequeña prisionera, sal! —dijo la voz de Crowther desde el otro lado—. Solo quiero hablar contigo.

Helena vio horrorizada que la madera se consumía y dejaba al descubierto la silueta de Atreus tras los barrotes de hierro. El resplandor rojizo del fuego le daba un color a su piel gris y muerta que casi le hacía parecer vivo.

Los barrotes que le impedían entrar en la habitación siguieron calentándose y pasaron del color rojo al naranja, mientras que la habitación prendió fuego y el papel de pared empezó a arder de manera espontánea. El recipiente de cristal de la esquina estalló con un chasquido y el ojo que contenía cayó entre las llamas que lamían la pared.

Crowther jamás se habría molestado en recurrir a la piromancia para manipular un material tan inferior, pero Atreus Ferron, el maese del hierro, intentaba hacer que el metal se doblegara a su voluntad una vez más. Si no lo conseguía, lo más seguro era que acabara quemándola viva en aquella habitación.

—¿Qué quieres?

—Tengo que hacerte una pregunta. Acércate. —Al ver que Helena vacilaba, insistió—: No creo que quieras morir asfixiada aquí dentro, ¿verdad? —La alfombra comenzaba a echar humo—. Te digo que te acerques.

Dio un paso hacia él con cuidado, procurando mantenerse lo más alejada posible de las zonas donde el calor era más intenso. Esperaba que Atreus no hubiera aprendido a utilizar la piromancia a distancia como Luc y Crowther.

Una sonrisa aterradora se extendió por el rostro del hombre.

—He habitado muchos cuerpos a lo largo de los años, pero es curioso... Este sufre una reacción violenta cada vez que te ve. Lo conocías, ¿verdad? Al menos, eso creo.

Helena trastabilló. No sabía que los liches retenían los recuerdos de los cadáveres que ocupaban, pero tenía sentido que quedaran ciertos vestigios de sus huéspedes.

—Al principio no me acordaba de ti. Pensaba que no era más que una reacción del cadáver, pero, al verte atacar a mi hijo, me vi transportado a aquella noche. El cuerpo que manejaba entonces llevaba tanto tiempo muerto que apenas tenía recuerdo de él, pero tú quedaste grabada en mi memoria. El Sumo Nigromante estaba encantado de que por fin fuéramos a obtener respuestas sobre la explosión. Como recompensa, compartió conmigo algunas de las técnicas que requiere su resonancia.

Los dedos largos de Crowther se retorcieron y el calor se intensificó.

Helena no dijo nada. El hierro que los separaba brilló más intensamente y la pared empezó a echar humo mientras se abrasaba. Atreus estaba conteniendo el fuego, pero bien podría reducir la habitación a cenizas si se lo proponía.

El calor del hierro al rojo vivo distorsionaba el aire y amenazaba con calcinarle la piel.

—Aquella explosión fue un ataque de lo más curioso. Ese zoquete de Lancaster se volvió loco al verte. Según me dijeron, todo fue culpa tuya, pero estoy al tanto de tu historial. No eres nadie. No estás entrenada ni tienes experiencia en combate. ¿De verdad esperan que me crea que una sanadora de poca monta fue la única responsable de uno de los ataques más devastadores que hemos sufrido nunca?

Stroud también había mencionado la falta de información que había sobre ella. En su momento, no le había dado importancia, puesto que casi siempre habían tendido a considerar su trabajo de sanadora como una intercesión religiosa en vez de una labor médica, pero Crowther había hecho que firmara los documentos de los prisioneros, la había atado a él. Por si fuera poco, también estaban todas las medicinas e inhibidores que había desarrollado con Shiseo. La bomba. Seguro que había registros de todo aquello.

A no ser...

Kaine no habría querido que llamara la atención de los inmarcesibles y, si habían colocado a Shiseo en la Central para interceptarla en caso de que reapareciera..., tampoco podían permitirse que la relacionaran con él.

—Te usaron como señuelo, ¿verdad? —dijo Atreus interrumpiendo el hilo de sus pensamientos—. Todo el mundo sabe cómo trataban a los tuyos. Eras la candidata perfecta que sacrificar a cambio de proteger al último miembro vivo de la Llama Eterna.

Esbozó una sonrisa maniaca y su rostro se iluminó con una expresión triunfal.

Helena había dado por hecho que Atreus había ido a buscarla porque sospechaba de ella después de lo ocurrido con Kaine, pero no, su misión lo cegaba y, como interrogar a todas aquellas víctimas no había dado resultado, había decidido centrarse en ella.

—Te enviaron aquí porque sabes algo de vital importancia. El Sumo Nigromante le confió a mi hijo la tarea de averiguar el qué, pero ahora está tan preocupado por lo que crece en tu interior que ha olvidado que tú conoces la identidad del asesino, de la persona que puso una bomba en el banquete y en el laboratorio del puerto Oeste. Una vez que lo capture, el Sumo Nigromante ya no tendrá nada que temer.

Un resplandor amarillo se extendió por el hierro y los barrotes empezaron a derretirse.

—No me acuerdo —dijo Helena. Su sangre estaba ejerciendo una presión atronadora en sus oídos mientras el calor era cada vez más intenso sobre su piel. Cada vez le costaba más respirar—. No recuerdo nada de lo sucedido. El Sumo Inquisidor intentó sacarme la información, pero se ha perdido, si es que alguna vez lo supe.

—No te creo.

Atreus dio un paso atrás y le asestó una patada a la puerta. Los barrotes de hierro fundido se doblaron sobre sí mismos y cayeron al suelo. Cuando entró en la habitación, Helena alcanzó a ver una masa carbonizada desmadejada en el suelo. Uno de los sirvientes había intentado detenerlo.

El hombre la obligó a retroceder mientras chasqueaba los dedos y hacía que unas llamas rojas y ardientes se materializaran a su alrededor.

—Mi hijo se pasa las horas preocupado por ti y por tu delicado corazón —dijo con voz inquisitiva—, como si fueras una flor exótica. Kaine cree que el camino hacia el éxito consiste en actuar como un esclavo obediente. —Negó con la cabeza—. Siempre le ha tenido demasiado miedo al fracaso como para entender que alcanzar el éxito implica correr riesgos…

La voz de Atreus se apagó y Helena desvió la mirada hacia la ventana, rezando desesperadamente por ver a Amaris de regreso.

—¿Estás esperando que venga a por ti? —De cerca, Atreus resultaba aterrador. La agarró del brazo y la arrastró hasta la ventana, presionándola contra el cristal—. ¿Crees que mi hijo vendrá a salvarte?

A Helena se le cerró la garganta cuando los dedos finos y alargados de Crowther se le enterraron en el brazo y sintió que el enrejado de hierro de la ventana se le clavaba en la piel. No vio ninguna criatura surcando el cielo.

Estaba sola.

Nunca se había enfrentado a un piromante. Si intentaba defenderse usando la resonancia, delataría a Kaine. Atreus sabría de inmediato quién le había quitado el anulitio de los grilletes, así que tendría que matarlo. No podía permitirse vacilar. Tenía el cuchillo de obsidiana escondido bajo el colchón, pero la cama estaba ardiendo, al igual que el resto de la habitación.

Atreus acercó su rostro al de ella y contempló el cielo despejado a través del cristal. El aroma a lavanda que desprendía su piel casi quedaba enterrado bajo el hedor a sangre de su ropa.

—Le has cogido cariño, ¿no es así? Puedes decírmelo. Al fin y al cabo, te saca a pasear y te tiene en esta habitación con todo lujo de comodidades y sirvientes que te protegen y se mantienen a tu entera disposición. Yo creo que le gusta tener a una criaturita como tú, tan ansiosa por complacer a sus amos. Los Holdfast te han adiestrado bien.

Helena apenas logró tomar una bocanada de aire entrecortada.

—Mi hijo disfrutará mucho menos de tu compañía si me obligas a arrancarte las respuestas con fuego —dijo moviendo los labios de Crowther contra su oreja.

Una única oportunidad. Solo tendría una oportunidad para pillarlo desprevenido y arrancarle el talismán.

—No me acuerdo de nada —insistió mientras trataba de calcular lo rápido que tendría que moverse y decidir en qué dirección girar para zafarse de él.

—A lo mejor es que no lo has intentando con suficiente empeño.

Antes de que pudiera reaccionar, Atreus chasqueó los dedos y una ola de dolor se extendió por la espalda de Helena cuando su vestido prendió fuego. Fue como si le hubiera marcado los hombros con un hierro candente. Las piernas le cedieron mientras gritaba.

Entonces oyó un siseo y las llamas que le devoraban la espalda desaparecieron. Sin embargo, ni el dolor ni el calor remitieron. Movió la boca sin emitir ningún sonido. Lo vio todo blanco.

Olía a humo y a pelo quemado.

—Esa será tu única advertencia. No me mientas —le ordenó Atreus, que la alzó de un tirón y la sujetó contra la ventana aplastando sus quemaduras con el peso de su cuerpo y arrancándole un aullido ronco de dolor—. No suelo ser tan directo durante mis interrogatorios, pero no tengo tiempo de infundirte miedo poco a poco —le advirtió al oído—. Dime quién es el asesino o te haré daño de verdad.

—No lo sé… —dijo casi en un sollozo—. Te prometo que no lo sé.

—Kaine se va a llevar una decepción cuando te encuentre —suspiró.

Atreus chasqueó los dedos de nuevo y el fuego estalló contra su espalda como un látigo. Helena se estremeció con tal violencia que se golpeó la cabeza contra el cristal y estuvo a punto de perder el conocimiento. Los oídos le pitaban y todo pareció ralentizarse, pero el pánico dio paso a una lucidez extraña, somnolienta.

Kaine no iba a llegar a tiempo.

Después de sobrevivir durante tantos meses, se había agotado su suerte justo medio día antes de que todo hubiera acabado.

Atreus volvió a incorporarla.

—No soy tonto. Todo el mundo creía que había un espía entre nuestras filas durante el año previo a la derrota de la Llama Eterna, porque la Resistencia sabía demasiado. El Sumo Nigromante sospechaba que el traidor se encontraba entre sus confidentes, pero no lograron identificarlo. Es nuestro único cabo suelto. Las pruebas son irrefutables. Las masacres y los sabotajes nunca fueron propios de la Llama Eterna, así que esa persona también debe de estar detrás de las explosiones, incluyendo la que destrozó el laboratorio del puerto Oeste. Desapareció tras la batalla final y regresó al poco de que tú aparecieras, así que tú sabes quién es.

Helena trató de zafarse de su agarre y arañó el aire intentando alcanzarle la cara. Sabía que le bastaría con tocarlo, pero Atreus depositó todo su peso contra sus hombros abrasados y le arrancó un alarido estrangulado. Unos puntitos negros comenzaron a salpicarle la vista.

—Dime quién es —dijo zarandeándola.

—Kaine morirá… si me haces daño —respondió ella con voz ahogada.

El cuerpo se le estaba entumeciendo. Estaba tan conmocionada que su mente empezaba a disociarse, como si fuera un animalillo al que hubieran dejado colgando del pescuezo.

—El Sumo Nigromante me lo perdonará si con ello consigo atrapar al asesino.

Helena veía su rostro reflejado en el cristal de la ventana. Su mirada albergaba un brillo de pura desesperación. Incluso con el rostro de Crowther, sus expresiones le recordaban tanto a Kaine que le ponían los pelos de punta.

—Kaine sobrevivirá. Ya engendrará más hijos.

Le daba vueltas la cabeza. El humo casi no le dejaba respirar y las llamas estaban a punto de devorar la estancia por completo.

Al comprender que no volvería a ver a Kaine nunca más, no pudo evitar buscarlo en el rostro de Atreus. Sus ojos eran tan esquivos como los de su hijo cuando hablaba. Además, tenían la misma desesperación furiosa que Kaine mostraba cuando se sentía acorralado, cuando creía que no tenía nada que perder.

Pese al desprecio que sentían el uno por el otro, Kaine había heredado los peores defectos de su padre.

Enid lo había sido todo para Atreus, y, ahora que ya no estaba, lo único que le quedaba era aferrarse a su fantasma. ¿Cómo habría sido Kaine si hubiera tenido cerca a alguien que le recordara constantemente a la persona a la que perdió? Tal vez se hubiera parecido más a Atreus, quien no era capaz de mantener las distancias con su hijo pese a no poder soportar su presencia.

Por fin lo entendió todo.

—Si no encuentras al asesino…, va a matar a Kaine, ¿verdad? El castigo que ha recibido no ha sido solo por lo de Hevgoss. También ha sido una advertencia para ti.

La expresión de Atreus se ensombreció por completo. La zarandeó con tal violencia que estuvo a punto de desmayarse.

—¿Quién es el último miembro de la Llama Eterna?

—Se parece a tu esposa, ¿no? Tiene los mismos ojos, la misma boca. Kaine es lo único que te queda de ella, pero, cada vez que lo miras, ves en él el odio que te tenía su madre. —Atreus levantó una mano y sus anillos de ignición centellearon—. Fui yo quien voló el laboratorio del puerto Oeste —se apresuró a decir antes de que prendiera fuego a los anillos—. Solía ayudar a Luc a estudiar piromancia. Se suponía que no debía hacerlo, pero trabajaba mejor en compañía. Apliqué los principios básicos y la teoría que acabé aprendiendo, incluso sin manejar ese tipo de resonancia, para diseñar las bombas, y luego las coloqué en el edificio con la ayuda de unos necrómatas. Porque yo soy el último miembro de la Llama Eterna que queda con vida. —Respiró hondo—. Pero tienes razón…, también había un espía. Yo era su contacto.

Un brillo triunfal surcó la mirada de Atreus. La victoria estaba al alcance de su mano.

—Pero no salvarás a Kaine al encontrarlo. El asesino al que buscas es tu propio hijo.

El hombre la miró estupefacto antes de retorcer el rostro con rabia. Le rodeó el cuello con ambas manos sin molestarse en usar la piromancia.

—Mi hijo jamás se aliaría con la Llama Eterna.

—Pues lo hizo. Odia a Morrough —graznó la chica—. Siempre lo ha odiado. ¿Nunca te has parado a pensar en lo que le pasó a tu familia después de que te arrestaran?

—Nada —resopló con desprecio—. Cuando Kaine mató al principado, mi desliz fue perdonado.

Helena negó con la cabeza.

—Entonces ¿cómo explicas la jaula de hierro inerte y el sello transmutacional que hay grabado en el suelo de esta misma casa? ¿Por qué murieron todos tus sirvientes? ¿De verdad crees que una persona como Morrough iba a mostrarse comprensivo durante los meses que Kaine tardó en regresar a la Academia?

Una sombra de duda surcó el rostro de Atreus.

—Morrough mantuvo a tu esposa encerrada en esa jaula y la torturó. La obligó a ver cómo le arrancaba el alma a tu hijo. Kaine mató a Apollo en un intento por salvarla. Y todo por tu culpa.

—¡Mientes!

Sabía que debería darle el golpe de gracia en ese momento, pero quería hacerlo sufrir.

Le agarró la cabeza con ambas manos, ignorando el dolor de sus hombros abrasados, y le lanzó una onda de resonancia directamente al interior del cráneo aprovechando que el hombre estaba demasiado aturdido como para defenderse.

Nunca había utilizado la animancia con un liche. Fue muy fácil, como hundir los dedos en una calabaza podrida. Su mente era sencilla. Carecía del ruido característico de una criatura viva. Sus pensamientos eran lineales, planos, y todos y cada uno de ellos giraban en torno a Kaine, pues era lo único que le quedaba de Enid.

Cuando Kaine había revisado sus recuerdos, Helena había notado la consciencia de él en su interior, al igual que sus emociones. No había nada que le impidiera a Helena mostrarle sus recuerdos a través de la conexión en vez de arrancárselos a él.

Quería que lo supiera todo, que fuese consciente de las consecuencias de sus actos.

Canalizó toda la rabia que tenía en su mente hacia el cerebro de Atreus.

Kaine estaba arrodillado ante ella y Helena tenía las manos extendidas hacia él.

—¿Ha... ha dicho alguien algo que pudiera incriminarte?

No. Eso no era lo que quería enseñarle. Trató de concentrarse.

Kaine la besaba, acunaba su rostro entre las manos y se cernía sobre ella en la cama presionando su cuerpo contra el suyo.

Sus recuerdos estaban desordenados y se solapaban. Ni siquiera sabía si ese recuerdo era reciente o no.

—*A ti te arrancaron el alma del cuerpo. Si consigo volver a metértela dentro, puede que con el tiempo se reintegre, pero tendremos que encontrar una manera de asegurarla, al menos al principio. Igual... igual que con las filacterias.*

—*Necesitarías que otra alma se sacrifique.*

Ella asintió, incapaz de levantar la mirada.

—*Y tendría que ser por voluntad propia.*

No, eso tampoco. Enid. Necesitaba mostrarle algo sobre Enid.

—*Mi vida se desmoronó cuando volví a casa a los dieciséis años y, desde entonces, intenté aferrarme a lo que me quedaba. Tras su muerte, todo dejó de importarme...*

Percibía la conmoción de Atreus, su indignada incredulidad. Entonces trató de apartarse de ella y Helena estuvo a punto de perder el control. La conexión entre sus mentes se tiñó de rojo.

El rostro encolerizado de Kaine, mucho más joven y con el cabello todavía oscuro, apareció ante ella.

—*¿Sabes quién estaba con Morrough cuando llegó la noticia de que habían capturado a mi padre y había confesado su traición?*

Atreus dejó de forcejear. Por su parte, Helena luchaba por respirar, pero tratar de cristalizar sus recuerdos había hecho que se perdiera en su memoria.

—*En ocasiones mi madre se pasaba horas gritando.*

Un calor abrasador la consumía, pero no podía detenerse.

—*Ella insistía en que era culpa suya y, luego, se le paró el corazón...*

Alguien levantó a Helena de un tirón. La cabeza se le cayó hacia atrás y, allí donde posó la mirada, vio el fuego trepando por las paredes, consumiéndolo todo.

Un rostro pálido apareció ante ella. Le costaba enfocar la mirada.

—Aguanta.

Aunque distorsionada, la voz era inconfundible. Extendió las manos con torpeza y el rostro de Kaine se volvió nítido con un parpadeo.

—Has venido… —Se aferró a él—. Supongo que siempre acabas viniendo.

—Aguanta. Voy a sacarte de aquí —le dijo bajándole las manos y presionándola contra su cuerpo.

Algo dolorosamente pesado se enroscó en torno a ella y Kaine la levantó del suelo. Helena arqueó la espalda por el dolor al sentir su brazo presionándole la piel abrasada, pero él la agarró con fuerza mientras la sacaba de la habitación en llamas. El pasillo estaba cubierto de humo y el fuego había empezado a propagarse por toda la casa, así que Kaine no se detuvo hasta que estuvieron fuera.

Helena respiró el aire limpio y fresco con avidez mientras él la tumbaba en el suelo.

—¿Qué ha pasado? ¿Qué te ha hecho? —preguntó Kaine, a quien le temblaban tanto las manos que ni siquiera era capaz de establecer un canal de resonancia estable.

Entonces, algo negro y enorme se cernió sobre ella y Amaris eclipsó el cielo hasta que su amo le ordenó que retrocediera.

Helena no logró pronunciar palabra. Los pulmones se contraían en busca de oxígeno y la cabeza le daba vueltas. Por si fuera poco, cada bocanada de aire era tan dolorosa que tenía ganas de gritar. Kaine siguió haciéndole preguntas, pero ella era incapaz de concentrarse.

Atreus salió al patio tambaleándose. Tenía el rostro manchado de humo y la expresión incendiada por la rabia.

Al verlo, Helena se aferró al brazo de Kaine.

—Sabe lo de tu madre. Lo siento. He tenido que decírselo.

—Da igual —dijo mientras se ponía de pie.

El humo negro estaba inundando el patio, como si la casa fuera ya un cadáver abrasado.

—¿Por qué no me has contado nunca lo que le pasó a tu madre? —preguntó Atreus con un gruñido.

Kaine se enfrentó a él con los hombros tensos.

—¿Habría cambiado algo?

Atreus se lanzó a por su hijo.

—Deberías habérmelo dicho. ¡Era mía!

Kaine dio un paso hacia un lado, aunque no con la fluidez que lo caracterizaba. Fue un movimiento rígido, acompañado de un espasmo en los dedos. Helena captó un atisbo de su rostro y vio que le brillaban los ojos.

—Ya, y eso le supuso un auténtico martirio, porque se lo contaste a Morrough. Nunca te preocupaste por los rumores que corrían por la ciudad, pero tuviste que hablarle de ella, decirle que lo era todo para ti y que harías cualquier cosa que te pidiera. La convertiste en tu prueba de fidelidad a la causa. —La voz de Kaine destilaba ira—. ¿Crees que a Morrough le importó cuánto tiempo pasaron torturándote? No, la clave fue que acabaste hablando. Y ella, tu más preciada posesión, quedó a su alcance. Tu amor la llevó directa a la tumba.

Los dedos largos y delgados de Atreus se curvaron con un destello de los anillos de ignición.

Kaine profirió una carcajada amarga.

—Debió de parecerles divertidísimo que siguieras siendo fiel a los inmarcesibles después de que te trajeran de vuelta. Y tienes el valor de llamarme a mí perro faldero.

La rabia le confirió un color violáceo a la piel grisácea de Atreus.

—Deberías habérmelo contado.

—¿Para qué? ¿De qué habría servido? ¿Cuál habría sido tu terrible venganza? No creo que hubiera merecido la pena poner en riesgo mi trabajo.

—¿Qué trabajo? ¿Acurrucarte y lloriquear entre las piernas de la zorra de Holdfast? —escupió haciendo entrechocar sus anillos.

La resonancia de Kaine surcó el aire y la chispa que su padre había prendido quedó suspendida en el aire cuando el hombre salió despedido en una dirección y los anillos de ignición en otra. Atreus aterrizó derrapando varios metros por la gravilla. Las llamas se apagaron. Cuando levantó la cabeza, una sangre violácea brotaba de las heridas que le surcaban el lateral del rostro.

—Mira tú por dónde —dijo Kaine, que se quedó de pie junto a él. Su voz destilaba pura maldad—. Parece que has vuelto a perder tu chispa, padre.

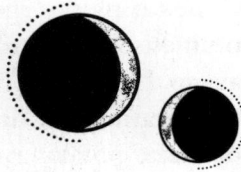

CAPÍTULO 74

LOS DETALLES EN HIERRO FORJADO que decoraban la casa cobraron vida como si fueran serpientes y se enroscaron en torno al cuerpo de Atreus para inmovilizarlo como a un insecto. Su hijo le rompería todos los huesos del cuerpo antes de que tuviera oportunidad de escapar.

Kaine regresó junto a Helena y le tocó el rostro con una mano temblorosa.

—¿Te ha hecho mucho…?

—Solo… solo ha sido la espalda y no es muy… No es una herida muy profunda. Las terminaciones nerviosas siguen intactas.

Eso era bueno, pero también explicaba el dolor insoportable que sentía. Se quedó quieta, con el torso contra las rodillas, mientras Kaine le insensibilizaba la espalda con la resonancia.

—Necesito recuperar el aliento, nada más —lo tranquilizó pese a que estaba temblando descontroladamente.

—Ya casi ha terminado todo. En cuanto estés curada, te irás con Amaris. ¿Te ves capaz de volar?

Helena no sabía si podría permanecer consciente durante mucho más tiempo, pero tampoco iba a decirle que no.

—¿Por eso has montado todo esto? —Oyeron la voz furiosa de Atreus desde donde estaba retorcido en el suelo—. ¿Solo porque intentas salvarla?

Helena pensó que Kaine ignoraría a su padre, pero levantó la vista para mirarlo.

—Según parece, estoy condenado a amar como tú.

—Después de que te haya matado, Morrough moverá cielo y tierra para encontrarla. La chica no tendrá dónde esconderse. Te vas a sacrificar para nada.

Kaine no respondió y sus ojos se desenfocaron un instante.

—El fuego ya se ha apagado. Entremos dentro.

Antes de que Helena pudiera intentar incorporarse, un estruendo desgarró el aire. Por un momento, pensó que era la señal con la que llamaban a Kaine, pero provenía de la dirección equivocada. Al girarse, vieron que un camión se aproximaba rugiendo por la carretera a tal velocidad que estuvo a punto de chocarse con la verja.

—¡Ya vienen! ¡Soltadme! —aulló Atreus—. ¡Soltadme, os digo!

El vehículo frenó en seco y una persona se bajó con torpeza del asiento del conductor. Llevaba algo aferrado al pecho, como si huyera con un bebé en brazos.

—¡La tengo! La tengo. Cogedla rápido.

Era Ivy. Se presionó contra la verja mientras miraba desencajada hacia atrás, como si la estuvieran persiguiendo.

Helena cruzó el patio, trastabillando y con los brazos extendidos hacia ella.

—¿Cómo has…? —preguntó con voz temblorosa por la incredulidad.

Ivy le pasó el fardo húmedo y con olor a gangrena y formaldehído a través de los barrotes. Entonces la tela cayó y reveló un brazo descompuesto arrancado a la altura del codo. Bajo la piel desprendida faltaban varios huesos. De hecho, tan solo le quedaban tres dedos, que se estremecían como si aún tuvieran vida.

—Ha sido Sofia —explicó Ivy, temblorosa y sin aliento. Tenía los ojos enrojecidos y el rostro manchado de lágrimas y carne podrida—. Intenté acercarme a él por todos los medios, pero fui incapaz. —Negó con la cabeza—. Fue ella quien lo logró.

—¿Cómo?

—Morrough no les presta atención a sus necrómatas —admitió con una mueca—, pero Sofia siempre hace lo que yo le digo. Siempre. Cuando se acercó a él, ni siquiera se percató de su presencia. Le arrancó el brazo de cuajo y me lo lanzó. Como la atacó a ella primero…, yo pude escapar. —Se le arrugó el rostro—. ¿Crees que podría perdonarme si lo supiera?

Helena no sabía qué decir.

—Tu hermana te quería.

Ivy se quedó allí temblando. Kaine por fin había llegado hasta ellas y, aunque su expresión era inescrutable, metió una mano dentro de la chaqueta de su uniforme y sacó un cuchillo de obsidiana.

—¿Qué estás...? —empezó a decir Helena, pero entonces el chico le dio la vuelta al arma para ofrecérsela a Ivy, que la aceptó sin vacilar.

—En el pecho, cerca del corazón —le dijo—. Es la manera más fácil.

Ivy asintió, se dio la vuelta y se subió con torpeza de nuevo al camión. Se alejó en un abrir y cerrar de ojos, y el rugido del motor se fue apagando hasta que de su visita no quedó más que el polvo suspendido en la carretera y el fardo al que Helena se aferraba.

—Kaine —le dijo con la voz ronca por el humo—, ahora ya puedes venir conmigo. Escaparemos juntos.

Él negó con la cabeza.

—Entra en casa.

Helena lo miró estupefacta y se negó a moverse cuando intentó arrastrarla de vuelta a Puntaférreo, así que Kaine apretó los dientes y la cogió en brazos.

—¿A qué viene esto? —Helena trató de bajarse sin soltar el fardo, consciente de que las quemaduras de la espalda se le iban a poner en carne viva—. Ya tenemos lo que necesitábamos. Nos dará un mes de margen y nos permitirá buscar la manera de...

—No puedo acompañarte —la interrumpió él sin detenerse—. Mi padre tiene razón. Cuando Morrough se entere de que has escapado, te dará caza, haya guerra o no. Si me fuera contigo podría protegerte durante ese mes, pero luego te quedarías sola, y a Morrough le bastaría con sus rastreadores para encontrarte. Al final acabaría haciéndolo. Si me quedo, ahora que tenemos la filacteria y ya no puede controlarme, puedo asegurarme de que nadie salga de la ciudad hasta que tú estés a salvo.

Helena se aferró a su hombro en un intento por hacer que la escuchara.

—Pero, si revertimos el...

Kaine negó con la cabeza; casi habían llegado a la puerta.

—Necesitarías un alma dispuesta a sacrificarse por mí y los dos sabemos que no vas a encontrar ninguna, porque la única persona que se prestaría a algo así serías tú.

Helena lo miró como si la hubiera golpeado en la garganta.

—¿En serio? ¿Ni siquiera me lo vas a preguntar a mí? —dijo Atreus con tono burlón desde el suelo.

Helena jadeó y se retorció contra el hombro de Kaine para mirar a Atreus. Seguía tirado sobre la gravilla, inmovilizado por el hierro, incapaz siquiera de mover los dedos.

—¿Lo harías?

—Prefiero morir —intervino Kaine antes de que su padre tuviera oportunidad de responder.

—Necesitas un voluntario —dijo Atreus sin quitarle el ojo de encima a Helena—. ¿No es así? Necesitáis un alma dispuesta a sacrificarse. Ahí también tienes mi filacteria. Es la falange media del dedo índice.

La chica bajó la vista al brazo descompuesto. Rezumaba una sustancia negra y espesa en vez de sangre y, en efecto, contaba con esa falange entre los huesos que le quedaban. El corazón le dio un vuelco con incredulidad.

—¿Por qué ibas a prestarte tú voluntario? —preguntó Kaine, que lo miraba con una mueca de asco y los ojos encendidos de rabia—. Me has odiado desde que nací.

—Tu madre habría querido que te salvara —dijo el hombre esquivando la mirada de su hijo.

—Bueno, pues llegas tarde.

Kaine llevó a Helena adentro sin detenerse siquiera cuando ella se lo pidió.

—Me niego a discutir. Lo único que me queda por hacer es sacarte de aquí lo más rápido posible. Es una suerte que los ojos de los necrómatas que montaban guardia en la puerta estén prácticamente licuados, porque de lo contrario nos habrían pillado.

Atravesó los restos calcinados de la puerta del dormitorio de Helena y esquivó el cadáver que yacía allí. Era una de las doncellas. El resto del servicio lanzaba agua por toda la estancia para asegurarse de que el fuego estuviera completamente extinguido. También recogían todo lo que hubiera sobrevivido a las llamas. La ventana estaba abierta y, pese a que el ambiente estaba menos cargado, todavía olía a la alfombra quemada, al hedor amargo de la madera mojada y a la acritud del hierro fundido.

Kaine la dejó en el suelo y abrió el cerrojo de una de las habitaciones que había a un par de puertas de distancia. En su interior había suministros médicos y bolsas de viaje. Sacó una caja.

—¿Cómo…? Las quemaduras. Nunca he…

—Si tu padre…

—No pienso hablar del tema hasta que te haya curado —sentenció con firmeza—. Ahora, dame eso.

Le quitó el brazo de las manos, lo metió en un armario y cerró la puerta para contener el hedor que desprendía.

A Helena no le parecía que tuviera intención de hablar más tarde, pero tendría que curarla antes o después.

—Córtame el vestido. Tendremos que usar suero para despegarme la tela de las quemaduras.

Kaine le echó la melena chamuscada hacia delante y sacó un par de tijeras para cortar la parte trasera de la prenda con cuidado.

—Odio estos vestidos —dijo ella mientras él le limpiaba la piel y empapaba la tela restante para intentar retirársela.

Entonces se tocó el hombro y utilizó la resonancia para hacer un balance de los daños. Las quemaduras eran más graves de lo que pensaba. Sus terminaciones nerviosas estaban intactas, pero, dado el tamaño y la profundidad de las lesiones, tardaría más tiempo del que disponían para curarse por completo. A Kaine le temblaban demasiado las manos para poder llevar a cabo una tarea tan repetitiva como la regeneración de tejidos y Helena no iba a poder contorsionarse lo suficiente para alcanzar todas las heridas. Kaine consiguió curarle las lesiones más superficiales, pero, al cabo de un rato, sus dedos dejaron de cooperar y la resonancia empezó a fallarle. Dio un paso hacia atrás respirando con dificultad.

—No pasa nada —lo tranquilizó ella.

—Claro que pasa.

—Aunque tuvieras el pulso firme, tardarías demasiado en curarme todas las heridas. Con que me dejes la espalda limpia y entumecida, aguantaré.

Kaine asintió despacio y rebuscó en una caja para sacar un tarro de ungüento que Helena reconoció enseguida.

—¿Esto te iría bien?

—Sí, servirá —dijo ella con una suave carcajada.

Kaine se lo aplicó con cuidado y le envolvió la espalda con vendas de seda, porque eran más suaves que las de lino.

—Ojalá hubiera podido darle estos lujos yo también a tu pobre espalda —comentó mientras Kaine la curaba.

Su resonancia bailó por las zonas doloridas que le había dejado el aire abrasador, así como por el pequeño corte que le surcaba la frente y que

Helena ni siquiera había notado. Le curó todas las pequeñas magulladuras con las que pudo lidiar.

—Kaine —le dijo ella cuando terminó—, tengo que hablar con tu padre.

—No nos va a ayudar. Solo ha intentado darte falsas esperanzas para hacerte daño. Y, si hablaba en serio, tampoco quiero tener una parte de su alma en mi interior. Bastante me parezco ya a él.

Helena le giró el rostro para obligarlo a mirarla.

—Eres lo único que le queda de tu madre. Cuando te mira, solo la ve a ella. Era consciente del riesgo que correría al venir a por mí. Me ha atacado porque pensaba que eso te salvaría. —Tomó aire—. Sé que no quieres creerlo porque la esperanza te aterroriza, pero preferiría morir intentando salvarte que vivir sabiendo que tuve la oportunidad de hacerlo y la dejé pasar. —Kaine empezó a ceder—. Me prometiste que huiríamos juntos, ¿recuerdas?

Él agachó la cabeza.

—¿Por qué tengo yo que mantener todas mis promesas? Tú no cumples ni una sola.

Helena negó con la cabeza y alzó el rostro para apoyar la frente en la suya.

—La primera promesa que te hice fue que, mientras estuviera viva, sería tuya. Y esa tengo intención de cumplirla.

***

La habitación de Helena estaba destrozada y toda su ropa había quedado reducida a cenizas. Por suerte, Kaine había preparado ropa resistente y de colores neutros para el viaje. Se vistió con cuidado intentando no rozar las quemaduras de la espalda.

El pasillo estaba empapado y también había quedado completamente carbonizado, pero el hierro que revestía las paredes permanecía intacto, como el esqueleto de una bestia.

Atreus seguía tirado donde Kaine lo había dejado. Tenía los ojos cerrados, pero los abrió al oír sus pisadas. Levantó la cabeza, los miró a ambos y se echó a reír.

Helena agarró a Kaine del brazo antes de que pudiera reaccionar.

—Quiero hablar con él a solas —dijo Helena.

—No —replicó Kaine.

—No va a hacerme nada. Tú espera aquí.

Notó la mirada de Kaine clavada en ella mientras se acercaba a Atreus, quien la estudiaba también con un intenso interés.

—Mi oferta no iba dirigida a ti —le dijo el hombre cuando ella llegó a su altura.

—Sabes de sobra que él no te lo va a pedir —replicó arrodillándose junto a él.

—Pues entonces no hay más que hablar —zanjó Atreus apartando la mirada.

El miedo le formó un nudo en el pecho a Helena. Sintió el impulso de ponerse a suplicar, pero sabía que con Atreus ni la compasión ni la humillación servían de nada.

—Yo voy a escapar independientemente de lo que decidas. Si te niegas a ayudarlo, lo estarás sentenciando a muerte.

Atreus desvió la vista más allá de Helena y la posó en Kaine, que los observaba con atención. Había un anhelo desesperado en los ojos de Atreus cuando miraba a su hijo. Helena quiso decir algo, pero prefirió esperar a que él rompiera por fin el silencio.

—No me di cuenta de lo mucho que se parecía a ella hasta que regresé. Lo pasé por alto incluso cuando era un chiquillo. —Entornó los ojos, como si le costara distinguir las facciones de Kaine en la distancia—. Nunca entendí por qué Enid estaba tan empeñada en tener un hijo. Yo habría estado dispuesto a adoptar un heredero de cualquier familia del gremio del hierro de haber sido necesario. Mi amor debería haberle bastado.

Helena se compadeció de él. Sentía tanta envidia de su hijo que resultaba patético.

—Kaine es lo único que queda de ella en el mundo. —Por fin miró a Helena—. ¿De verdad puedes salvarlo?

—Sí, pero solo si tú colaboras de corazón.

A Helena se le cayó el alma a los pies cuando Atreus no respondió enseguida. El vínculo se desvanecería si no se sacrificaba voluntariamente y Kaine se le escaparía de entre los dedos, igual que le había pasado con Luc.

—Enid lo era todo para mí —dijo al final—. Si ella estuviera aquí, me pediría que lo salvara. Nunca fui capaz de negarle nada.

Helena tocó el hierro para liberarlo y Atreus se incorporó despacio, se dio la vuelta y entró en la casa sin mirar a ninguno de los dos.

CUANDO ENTRARON EN LA SALA de estar, Atreus no despegó los ojos de la jaula. ¿Acaso no la había visto nunca? Quizá no se había parado a pensar cuál había sido su cometido.

—¿Cuánto tiempo estuvo…?

Tocó los barrotes con dedos temblorosos y se dejó caer de rodillas, como si tratara de arrastrarse adentro para ocupar el mismo espacio que su difunta esposa.

—Cuatro meses —dijo Kaine con voz carente de emoción.

Sus ojos vagaron por toda la estancia, como hacía siempre que entraba allí. A Helena le habría gustado reconfortarlo, pero se estaban quedando sin tiempo y aún tenían mucho que hacer, así que se puso a trabajar en el sello del suelo. El que ella había bocetado había ardido con las llamas, pero se sabía cada trazo de memoria. Lo único que necesitaba era la parte central del sello original, la cual habría que reconstruir y modificar. Tenían que contener el alma de Kaine hasta que pudiera fijarla en su interior.

Su intención era dibujar el nuevo sello con hierro, pues era perfecto para lo que se proponían hacer, y de eso en aquella casa había más que suficiente.

Cuando estuvieron listos, Kaine y ella se arrodillaron el uno frente al otro, dejando el diseño entre ellos. Kaine cerró los ojos y, al abrirlos de nuevo, sus iris resplandecían. Pese a lo mucho que le temblaban las manos, su resonancia era mucho más fuerte que la de ella. El aire vibró, la casa emitió un quejido y el hierro empezó a fluir hacia ellos como si fuera agua. Cuando el metal alcanzó el sello, Helena utilizó su propio poder para guiarlo y hacer que siguiera los trazos grabados en el suelo, en dirección al círculo de contención que habían marcado en el centro.

Los sellos industriales de los gremios podían extenderse hasta cubrir la planta entera de un edificio, pero Helena nunca había trabajado con uno que excediera el tamaño de la palma de su mano. El diseño con el que iban a trabajar era tan enorme que ni siquiera alcanzaba a verlo entero de una sola vez y tenía que arrastrarse por el suelo para comprobar que cada trazo y cada símbolo eran correctos. Debía ser perfecto.

El corazón le latía con tanta fuerza que parecía querer salírsele por la boca latiendo a un ritmo irregular.

Tenían una sola oportunidad.

—Está listo —dijo por fin poniéndose de pie y colocándose en el centro del sello—. Comencemos.

Kaine asintió, pero se dirigió a la puerta. Los sirvientes que quedaban se habían reunido en el pasillo, encabezados por Davies.

—¿Está Amaris preparada? —Uno de ellos asintió en silencio, y Kaine hizo una pausa y dijo—: Nunca... nunca os he dicho... que siento mucho no haber podido salvaros.

Davies dio un paso adelante con indecisión, murmuró su nombre, como solía hacer, y le peinó el cabello hacia atrás con gesto maternal antes de tocarle el pecho con ambas manos y empujarlo suavemente. Lo alejó de ellos.

Helena cogió el brazo de Morrough allí donde Kaine lo había dejado. El hedor que desprendía era como una patada en el estómago, así que se apresuró a diseccionarlo. Era repulsivo. Al sostenerlo, percibía todo el poder que contenía, todas las vidas que albergaba en cada hueso. La sección del cúbito más próxima a la mano le resultaba aterradoramente familiar. Ese era el fragmento que había usado para vincular a Kaine. Tras retirarlo, descartó el resto del brazo.

Kaine se había colocado en el centro de la estancia y se había desnudado de cintura para arriba. Pese a tener la piel surcada de cicatrices, la más llamativa de todas era el sello de su espalda, y a Atreus no se le pasó por alto. Como era evidente, no lo había visto antes.

Kaine, por su parte, solo tenía ojos para ella.

No había una plataforma que la elevara por encima del sello, así que había tenido que meterse dentro con él.

—Túmbate sobre la espalda —le pidió antes de arrodillarse a su lado. Luego le colocó las manos en el lugar correspondiente y lo miró a los ojos. Su corazón empezaba a resentirse y su ritmo cardiaco amenazaba con volverse irregular—. Te prometo que va a salir bien. Voy a salvarte.

Tocó el hierro frío del sello con ambas manos y dejó que su resonancia fluyera por él.

La única vez que había volcado su animancia en un sello había sido mientras experimentaba con las planchas de grabado. Requería mucho más poder de lo que había esperado. Al activarse, un resplandor fue extendiéndose poco a poco por el hierro, hasta que el sello empezó a emitir un suave zumbido. Kaine pareció volverse translúcido y Helena tuvo la sensación de ver un entramado de huesos y órganos a través de su piel, así como el talismán enredado junto a su corazón.

Helena preparó la filacteria. El hueso era tan antiguo que amenazaba con desintegrarse de un momento a otro y estaba tan desgastado que tuvo que concentrarse a fondo para percibir la energía que contenía. Era como un paquete atado con un cordel tan anudado y retorcido que resultaba imposible de soltar. Tendría que trabajar con sumo cuidado o, de lo contrario, correría el riesgo de hacerle daño a Kaine. Desenredó y desenredó con su resonancia ese cordel que parecía ser infinito hasta que oyó un repentino golpe sordo. Al levantar la cabeza, descubrió que uno de los sirvientes del pasillo se había derrumbado.

Volvió a centrarse en el sello y siguió adelante, aunque se encogió cuando oyó que otro necrómata caía al suelo. Y otro. Y otro más. Como era de esperar, al haber sido la primera en morir, la última en caer fue Davies. La mujer sostuvo la mirada de Helena un instante antes de desplomarse.

El fragmento de hueso se desintegró y desató una energía convulsa, pero, en lugar de dejar que se transformara en un torrente frío y muerto, Helena tiró de ella para contenerla dentro del sello.

El ambiente se iluminó y el cabello de Helena se le levantó de los hombros.

Entonces Kaine empezó a gritar.

Se le desencajó y desenfocó la mirada; se le arqueó la espalda, y arañó el suelo hasta dejarse las yemas y las uñas en carne viva. Helena se cernió sobre él.

—No, no me hagas esto. Aguanta —le pidió mientras forcejeaba con él para inmovilizarlo y obligarlo a permanecer en el centro del sello.

Le ralentizó el pulso y le paralizó las extremidades para impedir que se moviera, pero Kaine no dejó de gritar.

Buscó a tientas la filacteria de Atreus y, en cuanto desenredó la energía ya fuera de sí, el hueso se desintegró y el sello trató de absorber también el alma del hombre. Helena se aferró a ella con la mano izquierda y se negó a soltarla; no podía permitir que se mezclara con la de Kaine. Con la resonancia al límite, empezó a sufrir calambres en los dedos que pronto se le extendieron por el antebrazo. Presionó el pecho de Kaine con la mano libre y tiró del torrente de energía que fluía por el sello para tratar de sumergirlo en él, pero el dolor estaba haciendo que él proyectara su resonancia hacia fuera, contra ella. Por mucho que Helena se esforzó, no logró contenerla.

Se inclinó hacia delante, hasta que la frente de Kaine tocó la suya.

Había dejado de gritar después de quedarse sin voz y sus ojos seguían desenfocados.

—Te necesito. Ya casi hemos acabado, pero tienes que regresar aquí conmigo. Recuerda que vamos a escaparnos. El bebé, tú y yo. Vamos a ser libres. Voy a salvarte, pero necesito que luches conmigo.

Una repentina descarga de dolor estalló en su mano izquierda y perdió la sensibilidad en dos dedos. Se le quedaron sin fuerza y apenas pudo mantener el control de su resonancia, así que se lanzó hacia delante y besó el rostro de Kaine.

—Vuelve. Quédate conmigo.

Sus ojos por fin parecieron posarse en ella.

Helena volvió a presionarle el pecho y fue como si le insuflara todo el oxígeno de la estancia en un intento por meterle dentro toda la energía acumulada. El brillo que iluminaba los bordes del sello se fue apagando y filtrándose hacia el centro del diseño hasta desaparecer bajo Kaine. La tensión que le agarrotaba la mano izquierda a Helena por fin cesó.

Kaine apenas respiraba y emitía un silbido ronco cada vez que tomaba una bocanada de aire, así que Helena tuvo que actuar deprisa. No permitiría que le pasara lo mismo que a Luc. Esta vez sabía a lo que se enfrentaba.

Manipuló el alma de Atreus por medio de la animancia, la estiró hasta convertirla en un hilo fino y la vinculó a Kaine, igual que hacían con las filacterias, enrollando su energía una y otra vez como una tela de araña en torno a sus costillas y su talismán.

No utilizaría tanta energía como para crear un nuevo parásito como Cetus, pero sí la bastante como para que el cuerpo de Kaine recordara lo que era tener un alma.

Cuando terminó, él permaneció tumbado en el suelo sin moverse, así que le tocó el pecho para comprobar que todo iba bien. Estaba vivo y era mortal.

Ni rastro de la fría sensación de la muerte.

Helena dejó caer los hombros; estaba tan cansada que bien podría haberse derrumbado junto a Kaine, pero todavía no habían acabado. Aquello no había sido más que el principio.

Se puso de pie con torpeza.

El cadáver de Crowther yacía muerto de nuevo junto a la jaula.

Helena todavía tenía la mano izquierda agarrotada en un puño en el que sujetaba los restos maltrechos del alma de Atreus. Apenas le bastó con tocarle el pecho y depositar en él la poca energía que le quedaba a la filacteria para reanimarlo.

Los ojos de Atreus volvieron a enfocarse poco a poco. Allí, arrodillada junto a él, Helena notaba la misma sensación que cuando Luc había muerto gradualmente. Aunque seguía vivo, la energía se le escapaba despacio de entre los dedos.

—¿Está vivo? —preguntó mirando a Kaine, que seguía tumbado en el suelo.

Helena asintió.

—¿Me ayudarías a levantarlo? No voy a poder sola.

Atreus se incorporó y se acercó a su hijo, pero Helena se quedó rezagada mientras intentaba curarse la mano izquierda. Llegó a su lado cuando el hombre estaba incorporando a Kaine y vistiéndolo rápidamente. Cuando lo levantaron entre los dos, la cabeza de Kaine se venció hacia atrás, aún incapaz de sostenerse a sí mismo. Helena volvió a detenerse para reanimar a los sirvientes: necesitaría su ayuda una vez más.

Hacía tiempo ya que había caído la noche. Lumitia apenas era visible, la luna se mostraba en cuarto creciente y el cielo estaba salpicado de estrellas.

Amaris los esperaba fuera y golpeaba el suelo con las zarpas en actitud nerviosa. Le habían dejado colocada una silla de montar equipada con alforjas. Agitó las alas al ver que los sirvientes sacaban a Kaine.

—No pasa nada. Está bien —la tranquilizó Helena, que se acercó a la quimera con paso vacilante haciendo sonidos tranquilizadores para que se agachase. Si se quedaba de pie, sería imposible subir a Kaine a su lomo.

Cuando Helena tiró del cabestro que le rodeaba la cabeza, el animal se agazapó a regañadientes, sin apartar los ojos amarillos de Kaine. Este parecía empezar a recuperar el conocimiento y había entreabierto los ojos cuando lo subieron a la silla de montar. Helena lo aseguró con las cinchas y el arnés que la equipaban, que probablemente estaban pensadas para ella.

Amaris intentaba girarse una y otra vez buscando a su dueño mientras profería suaves gimoteos.

—Tranquila, bonita —le dijo Helena mientras se acomodaba tras él en la silla. Metió la mano en el bolsillo para sacar los anillos de ignición de Atreus y ofrecérselos—. Hay que destruir el sello. Nadie debe enterarse de que sigue vivo.

Amaris se incorporó y extendió las alas, impaciente por alzar el vuelo. Helena estaba a punto de soltar las riendas y dejar que echara a correr cuando Atreus habló:

—Kaine…

Él levantó la cabeza lo justo como para mirar a lo que quedaba de su padre. Su rostro reflejaba el agotamiento y el dolor que sentía, pero no había ni rastro de la crueldad y el odio que solía mostrar al contemplar a Atreus.

—Padre…

El rostro del hombre pareció suavizarse de golpe. Hizo intención de extender una mano hacia su hijo, pero Amaris le lanzó un gruñido de advertencia y él cerró el puño de golpe.

—Tu madre siempre estuvo orgullosa de ti. Decía que eras lo mejor que habíamos traído a este mundo. —Miró a Helena y añadió—: Sálvalo.

En vez de responder, ella se limitó a soltar las riendas de Amaris, que cruzó el patio al galope. Bajo la silla de montar, los músculos de sus alas se tensaron y se agitaron antes de alzar el vuelo de un salto. Batió las alas negras como el ónice para perderse en el cielo nocturno y volar cada vez más alto. El aire silbaba a su alrededor y Helena tuvo que agarrarse al arnés que sujetaba a Kaine a la silla.

La ciudad resplandecía bajo sus pies, pero el continente era como un vacío, un abismo de negrura del que intentaban escapar al volar cada vez más cerca de las estrellas.

Cuando Amaris dejó de ascender, una chispa prendió en el suelo y creció hasta convertirse en un inmenso anillo de fuego que devoró Puntaférreo con sus llamas.

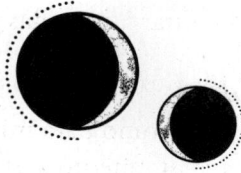

CAPÍTULO 75

Julius 1789

LAS MONTAÑAS DE NOVIS SE recortaban contra un cielo carente de estrellas y Helena hizo que Amaris las dejara atrás para volar en dirección sur.

La última vez que Helena había volado a lomos de la criatura, esta era mucho más pequeña en todos los sentidos. Ahora que había crecido, sus alas se desplegaban fuertes y firmes. En cuanto señaló hacia el sur, Amaris enseguida entendió que tenía que seguir el curso del río.

La oscuridad que se extendía bajo ellos era casi infinita, interrumpida solo por los racimos de luz de los pueblos y las ciudades que iban dejando atrás. Allí donde miraba, Helena únicamente veía una negrura inabarcable. Enterró el rostro en la espalda de Kaine mientras se esforzaba por respirar.

—No mueras —repetía una y otra vez, apoyando la frente contra el hueco entre sus omoplatos, atenta al débil latido de su corazón para asegurarse de que seguía vivo.

No habría sabido decir cuánto tiempo estuvieron volando; la noche parecía no tener fin. Sin previo aviso, Amaris empezó a descender y Helena estuvo a punto de caerse de la silla de montar. Por un instante aterrador, temió que se precipitaría al vacío.

Kaine recuperó la consciencia de una sacudida y echó el brazo hacia atrás para sujetarla con firmeza mientras ella intentaba recuperar el equilibrio y apretaba las piernas alrededor de la criatura. Las tenía tan cansadas que ya casi no alcanzaba a sostenerse.

Amaris aterrizó con rapidez y mordió con fuerza su propia lengua para no maldecir. Miró a su alrededor desesperada por averiguar dónde se encontraban mientras la quimera seguía abriéndose paso al trote por la oscuridad. Llevaban una linterna en una de las alforjas, pero ya no recordaba en cuál exactamente. Amaris se detuvo y esperó a que Helena descendiera. La criatura era varios palmos más alta de lo que recordaba, así que sus pies no tocaron el suelo cuando se bajó de su lomo y acabó cayendo sobre el espeso pasto. Se quedó tumbada contemplando las estrellas, que trazaban un camino resplandeciente por el cielo.

Antes del Desastre, se decía que la gente viajaba utilizando las estrellas para orientarse, pero ese era un conocimiento que se había perdido con el tiempo. Helena se incorporó con esfuerzo.

—Kaine —lo llamó abriéndose paso a tientas por la oscuridad. Primero encontró el pelaje de Amaris y, luego, la pierna y la bota de Kaine, enganchada al estribo—. No sé dónde estamos. ¿Qué hacemos ahora?

Kaine levantó la cabeza despacio. En la oscuridad solo alcanzaba a distinguir su silueta, pero Helena vio que intentaba bajarse de la quimera antes de darse cuenta de que estaba atado a la silla de montar. Buscó a tientas la cabeza de Amaris y la instó a agacharse para encontrar las cinchas y sujeciones, y soltarlas lo mejor que pudo sin ver nada. Kaine apoyó su peso en ella nada más desmontar.

—Hay una cabaña de caza justo... —dijo con voz ronca.

Avanzaron despacio hasta encontrar unos escalones y una puerta de madera. Una vez dentro, Helena encendió la lámpara que vio sobre la estantería de la entrada. Era una choza sencilla y rústica, pensada solo para pasar la noche.

Había dos camas estrechas, pero Kaine y Helena se derrumbaron sobre una de ellas sin molestarse en quitarse las botas ni la capa.

—Lo hemos conseguido, Kaine. Como siempre soñamos.

———————

HELENA SE DESPERTÓ CON LA espalda ardiendo y la muñeca izquierda palpitándole tan violentamente que el dolor casi le nublaba la mente. Abrió los ojos con esfuerzo y miró a su alrededor desconcertada hasta que recordó dónde se encontraban.

Kaine estaba sentado a su lado, despierto pero exhausto. Estaba inclinado hacia delante y tenía una mano apoyada en el pecho, como si se le hubieran partido todas las costillas.

—¿Estás... bien? —le preguntó ella incorporándose con dificultad.

—Sí. —Kaine asintió con brusquedad—. Estoy seguro de que pronto me recuperaré.

Su voz todavía seguía ronca. Se había debido de lesionar gritando durante el ritual y su cuerpo tardaría en curarse por sí solo.

—¿A qué te refieres? —Intentó tocarlo, pero sus dedos solo consiguieron rozarle el abrigo. Se sentía tremendamente débil—. ¿Qué te ocurre?

—No es nada. Es que no estoy acostumbrado a sentirme… humano.

Helena logró acercarse lo suficiente para tocarlo. Tenía razón, todo iba bien, pero ahora su cuerpo era tan delicado como una tela de araña. Bastaba con que uno de sus hilos se rompiera para que todo su esfuerzo se viniera abajo.

Apoyó la cabeza en su hombro y respiró despacio.

—Deberás tener más cuidado de ahora en adelante. Tu alma podría tardar meses o incluso años en reintegrarse completamente. No podrás utilizar ni la vivemancia ni la animancia ni nada que dependa de tu vitalidad. Un error bastaría para matarte. Ya no tienes opción de apoyarte en el sello. No te regenerarás, y eso podría hacer que se te abran las heridas de la espalda de nuevo.

Kaine le colocó un mechón de pelo tras la oreja.

—Eso ya me lo dijiste ayer. ¿Sabes que tengo la costumbre de escucharte cuando hablas?

Helena asintió, pero no pudo evitar insistir:

—Debes tener cuidado.

—Te prometo que lo tendré. ¿Tú estás bien?

—Solo estoy cansada —dijo volviendo a dejarse caer sobre el colchón, aunque el dolor que se le extendió por los hombros la abrasó como si la hubieran vuelto a marcar con un hierro al rojo vivo.

—¿Qué tal la espalda?

Helena se estremeció. Habría preferido no hablar del tema, porque sabía que no le haría ninguna gracia no poder curarla.

—Creo que se me ha pasado el efecto del analgésico y me está empezando a doler un poco. —Kaine hizo ademán de tocarla, pero lo detuvo—. Quieto. Solo necesito un minuto. Aplícame el ungüento y nos vamos.

—Descansaremos hasta que caiga la noche —dijo él mientras se disponía a hacer lo que le había pedido—. Amaris es demasiado reconocible como para viajar a plena luz. Tardaremos un par de días en llegar a la costa.

Cuando Helena volvió a abrir los ojos, ya había anochecido y Kaine estaba guardando sus pertenencias en las alforjas. Levantó la vista en cuanto notó que se había despertado.

—¿Te ves con fuerzas de retomar el viaje?

Se habrían quedado en aquella cabaña si le hubiera dicho que no, pero Helena era consciente de que, cuanto más se alejaran de Paladia, más difíciles resultarían de rastrear. Era una carrera contra reloj y la latencia de Lumitia no iba a esperar por ellos.

—Sí —mintió.

Volaron durante casi toda la noche. Cuando Amaris volvió a descender, el cielo había empezado a teñirse con el color plateado del amanecer. En esa ocasión no contaban con una cabaña, así que Kaine retiró la silla de montar y durmieron contra uno de los flancos peludos de Amaris, con sus alas negras sirviéndoles de pantalla ante la salida del sol.

Cuando Helena abrió los ojos, Kaine seguía a su lado, con el rostro orientado hacia ella, como si se hubiera quedado dormido mirándola. Bajo la tenue luz del amanecer, recorrió con la mirada sus facciones, ahora mortales.

Eran libres.

Se le encogió el corazón. Tenía la sensación de estar viviendo un sueño, como si un solo paso en falso bastase para que todo se desmoronara. No terminaba de creerse que Kaine estuviera realmente allí. Y, si de verdad era real, algo le decía que su felicidad no duraría mucho.

Las cosas buenas de su vida no solían hacerlo.

Kaine permanecía tan quieto que sintió el impulso de tocarlo. Lo rozó con dedos temblorosos y, al instante, él frunció el ceño y abrió los ojos. Se le iluminaron en cuanto la vio.

—Hola —se limitó a decir; estaba demasiado abrumada como para encontrar algo mejor. Carraspeó y se sentó—. Tengo que comprobar cómo estás.

Amaris se puso en pie, se estiró y desapareció entre los árboles mientras Helena le abría la camisa a Kaine y posaba una mano en su pecho para saber cómo se encontraba ahora que había descansado lo suficiente.

Seguía sin irradiar la energía de una persona corriente, eso era innegable, pero ni aun así podía hacer nada más aparte de darle tiempo y rezar para que su cuerpo recuperara un mínimo de normalidad. Su vitalidad era débil, como si el más mínimo roce pudiera desintegrarla.

Y su condición física también le preocupaba. Lo mejor habría sido esperar. Todavía se estaba recuperando de lo que Morrough le había hecho, y era posible que nunca volviera a ser el mismo. Tanto su ritmo cardiaco como sus temblores le parecían preocupantes, y el sello de su espalda amenazaba con carbonizarlo si se dejaba llevar por su poder. Todo ello hacía que a Helena se le formara un nudo en la garganta. Las manos empezaron a temblarle.

—Hay cosas que estás acostumbrado a tratar como ordinarias y que ya no puedes soportar.

—Lo sé —respondió él todavía con voz ronca.

Helena se acercó un poco más a él y le tocó el cuello para curarle el tejido afectado.

—Sé que lo sabes si te paras a pensarlo, pero tendrás que procurar no actuar por instinto. Llevas años adquiriendo malos hábitos de los que ni siquiera eres consciente.

Aquella idea le resultaba aterradora. ¿Y si los atacaban? Kaine se defendía bien en el combate, pero no sabía luchar sin la ayuda que le otorgaba su inmortalidad.

Debería haberlo planeado todo mejor. Kaine le había insistido en que necesitaba recobrar fuerzas, pero ella se había centrado demasiado en su investigación. Y, aunque gracias a ello había conseguido salvarlo, ¿qué pasaría si los atacaban y no era capaz de defenderse? Kaine moriría y todo habría sido en vano.

El miedo le cruzó el pecho como una fisura que se abría entre sus costillas.

Miró a su alrededor tratando de encontrar la alforja donde había guardado sus cuchillos. Los iba a necesitar. Debería llevarlos encima.

Pero la claridad era tan cegadora que…

—Helena. Helena, respira. Mírame. Te prometo que tendré cuidado. No dejaré que nada me aleje de ti.

Ella intentó asentir, pero se le formó un nudo en la garganta.

—Pero ¿y si algo sale mal? —preguntó con la voz estrangulada—. Todo se va a desmoronar. Siempre… pasa igual.

Trató de alejarse de él mientras miraba en todas direcciones a su alrededor. Allí, al descubierto en medio de un bosque que se extendía hasta donde alcanzaba la vista, estaban expuestos a todo tipo de peligros. Y ya no solo estaba pensando en los inmarcesibles, sino en cualquier otra amenaza.

Kaine la obligó a darse la vuelta para que lo mirara a los ojos.

—Mírame. No hemos dejado ningún rastro. Llevo meses dando caza a fugitivos, así que sé perfectamente lo que hace que a uno lo capturen. No nos van a atrapar. Si antes luchaba sin cuidado era porque podía permitírmelo, pero he aprendido a ser más precavido. La regeneración lenta me ha enseñado esa lección. Mírame. Confié en ti y has conseguido traernos hasta aquí. Ahora te toca a ti confiar en mí. —Helena asintió con un estremecimiento y él extendió las manos hacia su regazo—. Ahora, ¿me explicas qué te ha pasado en la mano?

Ella bajó la vista. Tenía el dedo meñique y el anular izquierdos curvados hacia dentro, inmóviles. Cerró el puño para disimularlo.

—El sello tenía mucha fuerza y tuve que forzarme un poco para llevar a cabo el ritual. El nervio cubital se me… desgarró. He intentado curarlo, pero… el daño ha sido demasiado grave y ya no hay nada que hacer.

Kaine le cogió la mano con delicadeza y le estiró los dedos. Cuando le acarició la zona afectada con el pulgar, Helena no sintió nada ni en los propios dedos ni en la parte externa de la palma. La mano se le estremeció.

—No importa —lo tranquilizó—. Ni siquiera es mi mano dominante, así que todavía puedo practicar la alquimia. Seguro que ni lo noto en cuanto me acostumbre.

—Para —dijo él apretando los dientes—. No hagas como si no tuviera importancia.

—Me ha permitido tenerte aquí conmigo, así que ha merecido la pena —replicó ella soltándose y utilizando la comida que guardaban en las alforjas de excusa para buscar sus dagas y escondérselas entre la ropa.

Pasaron las horas. Cuanto más tiempo permanecían libres, más crecía el nerviosismo de Helena. Kaine también parecía inquieto, aunque lo disimulaba mejor. Le habría gustado salir a explorar la zona y comprobar que efectivamente estaban a salvo ahora que había recuperado un poco las fuerzas, pero se quedó con Helena, velando su sueño. Ella seguía durmiendo inquieta, aferrada a su camisa y con el rostro hundido en su pecho.

Después de su siguiente vuelo, llegaron a otra cabaña de caza, tan exhaustos que apenas hablaron. Se limitaron a meterse en la cama y dormir entrelazados hasta última hora de la tarde. Cuando Helena se despertó, Kaine estaba sentado a su lado. Sus ojos desprendían de nuevo un ligero resplandor.

Parecía una pintura al óleo.

Ahora que un brillo posesivo volvía a brillar en su mirada, Helena se dio cuenta de que no lo veía desde que había tomado la determinación de dejarla marchar. Kaine se inclinó sobre ella y la besó.

Helena le rodeó el cuello con ambos brazos, desesperada por sentirlo cerca, por hacerle un hueco bajo la piel, entre las costillas, dentro del corazón. Quería tenerlo tan cerca que nada pudiera separarlos. Quería que el miedo a perderlo por fin desapareciera.

El tiempo había jugado en su contra. Por fin empezaba a notar lo hambrientos que los había dejado el sobrevivir durante años a base de momentos robados.

No se dio cuenta de que ya no le dolía la espalda hasta que estuvo tumbada a su lado, mientras trazaba distraídamente las cicatrices del sello. Las molestias deberían haber vuelto, pero no lo habían hecho. Estiró el brazo hacia atrás y se tocó los hombros. Kaine se incorporó.

—¿Qué has hecho? ¿Me has curado? —Se volvió para mirarlo—. ¿Qué te he dicho? Te advertí que no debes utilizar la vivemancia.

—Estoy bien —dijo él, sin el menor atisbo de remordimiento—. He tenido cuidado y ya sabes que en muchos casos no hace falta recurrir a la vitalidad para sanar. Ya estabas bastante maltrecha para afrontar este viaje como para tener que soportar el dolor que mi padre te grabó a fuego en la espalda.

Helena le tocó el pecho con dedos temblorosos por miedo a lo que fuera a encontrarse, temiendo que Kaine ya se estuviera desvaneciendo. ¿Y si se hubiera despertado y se lo hubiese encontrado muerto a su lado? Tendría que haber averiguado ella sola lo que había pasado. Lo sondeó varias veces con su resonancia.

Tuvo que tragar saliva antes de ser capaz de hablar.

—No deberías haber hecho eso —dijo con voz temblorosa—. No merecía la pena. Muchas personas se recuperan de una quemadura sin necesidad de recurrir a la resonancia. Estaba bien. Te lo prometo.

Kaine le acunó el rostro entre las manos.

—Mírate, Helena. Te has roto mil veces por mi culpa y no pareces darte cuenta de que eso me mata. No tiene sentido seguir viviendo si tú tienes que pagar el precio por ello. Déjame arreglarlo como pueda.

Helena cerró los ojos y apoyó de nuevo la cabeza sobre su pecho, escuchando sus latidos y obligándose a creer que no le había pasado nada por curarla.

—Tenemos que dejar de hacernos daño a nosotros mismos por el bien del otro —dijo al final—. Y eso va por los dos. No llegaremos muy lejos si no aprendemos a demostrarnos nuestro amor de otra forma.

Retomaron el vuelo en cuanto cayó la noche. A Helena se le cortó la respiración al ver que algo inmenso y de un suave tono entre rosado y plateado aparecía ante ellos en medio de la oscuridad.

Era el mar.

Viraron hacia la izquierda y se alejaron del río.

Kaine parecía saber exactamente adónde se dirigían pese a que casi no se veía nada. Sobrevolaron varias masas de agua y un pueblecito, pero no se detuvieron. Siguieron adelante hasta ver el suave destello de una luz que se colaba entre los postigos de una casa.

Amaris descendió directamente hacia ella y el viento que levantaba con sus alas hizo que esos mismos postigos se estremecieran. Helena desmontó, con las piernas doloridas.

La puerta se abrió de repente y la cálida luz que brotó del interior la cegó.

En el umbral, envuelta en un halo de luz, estaba Lila.

CAPÍTULO 76

Julius 1789

LILA JADEÓ, AHOGÓ UN SOLLOZO y bajó los escalones de entrada con torpeza. Llevaba una prótesis algo tosca y se apoyaba en una muleta, pero eso no le impidió tirar de Helena para estrecharla entre sus brazos con ferocidad.

—Hel, Hel, estás viva de verdad.

Lila recorrió a su amiga con las manos. Le tocó la cara y los hombros como si no terminara de creerse que Helena era real.

Pero ella estudió a Lila con la misma incredulidad. Pese a que ya sabía que estaba viva, se había acostumbrado a pensar que todo el mundo había muerto, por lo que le resultaba imposible asimilar la situación.

Lila parecía distinta. Se había teñido el pelo rubio de castaño y estaba demacrada por el cansancio. Todavía tenía esa cicatriz dentada en el lateral del rostro y lloraba mientras abrazaba a Helena.

—Lila…

Tenía la sensación de que le iba a estallar el corazón. No había esperado que su reencuentro la conmovería de una manera tan visceral al recordarle que todos los demás las habían dejado.

—Pensaba que no volvería a verte nunca. Mírate. Estás en los huesos.

Lila recorrió el cuerpo de Helena con la mirada, pero se detuvo al reparar en su vientre.

—Ya lo sabías, ¿verdad? —preguntó Helena con un nudo en el pecho—. Kaine me dijo que se había mantenido en contacto contigo.

Su amiga asintió despacio y, cuando Kaine se bajó del lomo de Amaris tras ellas, levantó la cabeza de golpe, como si no hubiera reparado en su presencia hasta ese momento.

—¿Qué estás haciendo tú aquí?

Se lanzó a por él sin previo aviso y Helena tuvo que interponerse entre ellos, empujando a Lila para que se separara de él.

—Hemos escapado juntos. No le hagas daño, que ya no es un inmarcesible.

Un brillo implacable cruzó los ojos azules de Lila.

—¿En serio?

—No te equivoques, Bayard, que no te va a ser más fácil matarme que antes. Como pierdas alguna extremidad más, no podrás hacer nada para proteger a ese pequeño principadito tuyo.

Lila gruñó como un gato montés, dispuesta a arrancarle los ojos en cualquier momento.

—Parad ya los dos —intervino Helena, furiosa al ver cómo habían conseguido arruinar su reencuentro en menos de un minuto.

Lila no intentó atacar más a Kaine, pero no dejó de fulminarlo con la mirada.

—Supongo que no debería sorprenderme que al final murieras intentando salvarla.

—Cierra el pico, Lila —le espetó Helena—. He sido yo quien lo ha traído hasta aquí. Si quieres enfadarte con alguien porque siga vivo, tendrás que hacerlo conmigo.

Lila se volvió para mirar a Helena con una expresión incrédula que se transformó en una resignación desconsolada. Dio un paso hacia atrás.

—Está bien. No volveré a decir nada, pero aleja a ese bicho de aquí. No quiero que se acerque a Pol.

—Ve tú con ella —le dijo Kaine a Helena— y no te preocupes por mí. Ya sabía que mi reencuentro con Bayard no iba a ser precisamente agradable.

Se dirigió hacia Amaris para meterla en el establo.

Cuando desaparecieron de su vista, Helena se volvió hacia Lila. De pronto, se sentía agotada. Una parte de ella había creído que la felicidad les duraría un poco más, pero el momento ya parecía haber pasado.

Tampoco esperaba que la situación fuese a ser fácil; al fin y al cabo, estaban rodeadas por un océano de pérdidas. Ni siquiera alcanzaba a imaginar lo que Lila debía de sentir al ver a Kaine después de todo lo sucedido. Aunque no esperaba tener que justificar algo tan personal como su relación nada más verse.

—Si le haces daño, no te lo perdonaré nunca —le advirtió a Lila.

—Podrías aspirar a alguien mucho mejor —dijo Lila negando con la cabeza.

—No. Kaine es la persona que necesito y quien me ayudó a salvarte.

En los labios de Lila se acumularon una multitud de protestas, pero acabó apartando la mirada y diciendo:

—Vamos adentro.

Helena no se dio cuenta de que Lila todavía llevaba grilletes hasta que no la vio a la luz. Aunque no eran de supresión completa como los que Helena había tenido que soportar, bastaban para debilitar la resonancia de su amiga.

—¿No te los ha quitado nunca? —le preguntó Helena.

Lila bajó la vista con un gesto incómodo.

—Sí, durante un tiempo, pero entonces intenté arrancarle el talismán. Cuando desperté… —Meneó la muñeca—. Hace ya tiempo de eso.

Helena miró a su alrededor. La casa era pequeña y se notaba que llevaban viviendo allí un tiempo. Contaba con una cocina, una mesa y una cama en la esquina más alejada de la puerta, oculta tras una cortina. Todo era tan mundano que no terminaba de encajar con Lila. No tenía nada que ver con la Academia, con Solis Splendor y su resplandeciente armadura de paladina.

—¿Has estado aquí todo este tiempo? —preguntó confundida.

Lila negó con la cabeza.

—No, cuando Ferron creía que te encontraría pronto, te estuvimos esperando al otro lado del río, en Novis. Luego nos trajo a Pol y a mí hasta aquí. —Esbozó una débil sonrisa—. Está durmiendo, pero ¿quieres verlo?

Helena la siguió tímidamente y ambas se asomaron a la cortina para ver a un niñito pequeño durmiendo en la cama. Tenía los cabellos dorados, las mejillas regordetas, las pestañas oscuras y espesas, y unos brazos y piernas rechonchos extendidos como una estrella de mar.

Lila contempló a su hijo con una intensa adoración.

—Le va a hacer mucha ilusión tener compañía —susurró—. No solemos bajar mucho al pueblo, así que pasamos solos la mayor parte del tiempo.

—¿Nunca has pensado en huir?

—No habría podido —dijo tragando saliva—. Al principio, por el embarazo y, luego, por tener que cuidar del bebé. Y me faltaba la pierna.

Para cuando nos dejó en esta casa…, comprendí que no tenía adónde ir. Ferron me dijo que, si intentaba escapar a algún lugar como la corte de Novis, no verían en mí más que a una paladina deshonrada con un hijo ilegítimo, aunque me hubieran creído al revelarles mi identidad. Y, en caso de que decidieran considerar a Pol como un principado, no permitirían que alguien como yo lo cuidara y lo protegiera. Buscar a la familia de mi madre también habría sido peligroso. Por si fuera poco, cada vez que pensaba en marcharme, me aterraba considerar la posibilidad de que aparecieras y yo ya no estuviese aquí.

Lila corrió la cortina del todo para que la luz no molestara a Pol y se dio la vuelta.

—Ferron le dio dinero a alguien del pueblo para que se asegurara de que no nos morimos de hambre, porque no se me da muy bien trabajar la tierra. Tenemos gallinas y unos patos horribles. Ahora también tejo, igual que mi madre, aunque Pol no para de crecer y toda la ropa se le queda pequeña casi en cuanto la termino.

—Sabes que no vamos a quedarnos aquí, ¿no? Nos marcharemos en barco.

La expresión de Lila se endureció, pero asintió con la cabeza.

—Ya, Ferron me habló de su plan, aunque ha dicho tantas cosas que he aprendido a no esperar mucho de sus palabras. —Exhaló—. ¿De verdad… de verdad va a venir con nosotros? ¿En serio vas a… jugar a las casitas con él?

Helena se tensó.

—Sí. Nosotros siempre tuvimos la intención de huir juntos. Le pedí a Kaine que te incluyera en el plan porque Luc me pidió que me asegurara de poneros a Pol y a ti a salvo.

Lila la miró estupefacta.

—¿Viste a Luc antes de que…?

A Helena le dio un vuelco al corazón al darse cuenta de que tendría que contarle una mentira. ¿Sería capaz de hacerlo? ¿De ocultarle la verdad para siempre? Cuando se disponía a hablar, vio lo desesperada que estaba su amiga por aferrarse a la memoria de Luc, por escuchar sus últimos momentos, y tragó saliva.

—Aquel día estaba preocupada por él, así que salí del Cuartel General. Nos… nos reconciliamos justo antes de que Luc regresara. Creo que, de algún modo, sabía que la guerra iba mal y por eso me pidió que le prometiera que cuidaría de ti. Eso fue lo último que me dijo.

A Lila se le escapó un sonido roto y jadeante.

—¿Sabes cómo lo capturaron? ¿Cómo consiguieron llegar hasta él?

Helena apretó los labios y negó con la cabeza. Hasta donde todo el mundo sabía, Lucien Holdfast había muerto ante los escalones de entrada de la Torre de Alquimia. Eso era lo que figuraría en los anales de la historia y lo que Lila tendría que creer.

Kaine entró en la casa y Lila borró todo rastro de sus emociones de su rostro. La temperatura de la estancia pareció descender de golpe. Sin embargo, Kaine no le prestó atención; solo tenía ojos para Helena. Frunció el ceño.

—¿Le has dado algo de comer? —le preguntó a Lila.

—No... —La chica miró a Helena—. ¿Tienes hambre?

—Está embarazada y hemos tenido que racionar la comida del viaje, por lo que apenas ha comido nada estos días —explicó Kaine con mala cara.

—Podrías habérmelo dicho.

Lila se acercó a un armario y, tras rebuscar en su interior, cogió una jarra de leche, un poco de pan, queso y un racimo de uvas, y lo dejó todo en la mesa. Helena se obligó a comer algo con desgana porque sabía que Kaine la estaba vigilando, pero tenía el estómago todavía revuelto y no sabía si era por el cansancio del viaje o por su nerviosismo general, acrecentado por el reencuentro con Lila y la certeza de que su situación nunca sería fácil.

—Antes de que nos vayamos, tenemos que quitarle los grilletes a Lila. ¿Y hay alguna manera de conseguir materiales con los que prepararle una prótesis?

A Lila se le iluminó el rostro ante aquella pregunta, pero Kaine apretó los dientes y suspiró.

—No va a hacer falta.

Metió la mano en el bolsillo, sacó una llavecilla delgada y se la lanzó a Lila. Sin dar más explicaciones, salió de la casa y regresó poco después con un cofre metálico cubierto de tierra, como si acabara de desenterrarlo. Tras abrir el candado con facilidad, Lila descubrió que lo que guardaba en su interior era su prótesis, envuelta en una tela impermeable pero algo golpeada.

—¿Ha estado aquí todo el tiempo? —le preguntó Lila tras permanecer un buen rato muda de asombro.

—La traje antes de que tú llegaras, pero no confiaba en que no fueras a atraer miradas indeseadas. Mi intención era explicarle a Helena dónde encontrarla. Estaba entre los escombros tras la explosión.

Helena comprobó que todos los componentes de la prótesis de Lila funcionaban como debían antes de volvérsela a colocar.

—Lumitia entrará en plena latencia en tres días —apuntó Kaine—. Las rutas comerciales llevan funcionando quince días, pero ahora el mar estará más calmado, y los barcos, más concurridos. Nos ayudará a pasar desapercibidos.

—¿Adónde vamos exactamente? —preguntó Lila mientras Helena equilibraba la prótesis.

—Hay cientos de islas entre Etras y el continente. Nuestro destino es una de las más pequeñas, cerca de un enclave comercial.

HELENA CONOCIÓ A APOLLO HOLDFAST al día siguiente.

Pol había escondido el rostro contra el cuello de Lila con timidez, pero dejó que sus ojos recorrieran el rostro de Helena cuando su madre se la presentó. Era un niño robusto que había heredado la constitución de los Bayard, así que bastaba un vistazo para saber que sería muy alto cuando creciera.

—Esta es tu madrina, Helena —le dijo Lila enterrando el rostro en su cabello rubio y revuelto—. ¿Te acuerdas de lo que te he contado de ella? Era una de las mejores amigas de tu padre y siempre cuidó de nosotros. Ahora… —Lila tragó saliva—. Ahora me va a ayudar a cuidar de ti. ¿No es genial? Ha venido hasta aquí con Ferron. A lo mejor no te acuerdas de él, pero lo conociste cuando eras más pequeño.

Pol se asomó entre los cabellos de Lila para estudiar a Helena con una mirada llena de vida, igual que la de Luc, y fue como reencontrarse con él, con la versión joven de su amigo que había desaparecido ante sus ojos.

Se le formó un nudo en la garganta que por un instante le impidió hablar.

—Hola, Pol, me alegro de conocerte por fin.

El niño ahogó una risita y se cubrió el rostro con la mano.

—Le cuesta un poquito abrirse, pero todavía no ha conocido una criatura viva de la que no haya querido hacerse amigo.

—Se parece muchísimo a Luc.

A Helena no se le ocurría nada más que decir. Lila había empezado a explicarle algo sobre la dentición, pero el corazón empezó a latirle con tanta fuerza que dejó de oír lo que le estaba diciendo.

—Creo que Helena necesita descansar —la interrumpió Kaine sin andarse con rodeos.

Lila se quedó de piedra, pero observó con atención a su amiga y asintió.

—Claro. Pol y yo tenemos que salir a darles de comer a las gallinas. Vamos, campeón.

Helena los vio salir por la puerta y se fijó en que Lila volvía a moverse con soltura. Cuando miró a Kaine, estuvo a punto de dar un respingo. Tenía el pelo castaño, casi tan oscuro como antes de que se le volviera plateado. El contraste con su piel y sus ojos pálidos hacía que sus rasgos fueran más pronunciados. Se había puesto un atuendo discreto compuesto por unos pantalones marrones y una camisa de tejido áspero, pero aun así nadie lo confundiría con un granjero cualquiera.

—No te gusta —dijo llevándose una mano a la cabeza.

Helena no pudo dejar de mirarlo.

—No estoy acostumbrada a verte así —dijo. Casi sintió el impulso de echarse a reír al tocarle el pelo y recordar el momento en que había empezado a perder el color—. Voy a echar de menos el plateado.

—No es permanente, así que todavía lo verás de vez en cuando.

Pero ya apenas reconocía a Kaine en él. Helena permaneció dentro de la casa, pues la amplitud e inmovilidad del paisaje le ponía los pelos de punta cada vez que salía. Sin embargo, después de haber vivido tanto tiempo en peligro, moviéndose de un lado para otro, la casita de Lila era tan normal que tampoco parecía real. Kaine y Lila se turnaban para hacerle compañía. Cuando Lila se quedaba con Helena, Kaine se marchaba y no volvía a aparecer hasta que Lila salía con Pol.

Helena supuso que él estaba ocupado ultimando los preparativos del viaje hasta que Lila le comentó que estaba en el establo. Siempre se iba al establo. Al oírlo, Helena se apresuró a salir y se detuvo un instante antes de entrar en el sombrío edificio.

Tal y como su amiga había dicho, Kaine estaba sentado en el suelo junto a Amaris, que tenía la enorme cabezota apoyada sobre su regazo. Kaine, que le estaba rascando la parte de atrás de las orejas a la quimera, no levantó la vista cuando entró.

—Debería sacrificarla —dijo con voz queda—. Sería la opción más compasiva, porque no va a entender que la deje atrás.

A Helena se le encogió el corazón al acercarse.

—Dijiste que podía cazar y cuidarse sola.

Él asintió.

—Pero las transmutaciones se irán desgastando con el tiempo y acabarán matándola, igual que le pasó al resto. Y eso sin contar con la posibilidad de que cualquier otra criatura la ataque primero. Además, si la ven merodeando por esta zona, podría conducir a los inmarcesibles hasta nosotros.

—¿Se sabe algo de Morrough?

—No, estamos demasiado lejos y no han llegado noticias todavía.

Helena contempló a Amaris.

—Ya no va a crecer más, ¿no? Si ya no depende de la transmutación, le irá bien.

Kaine guardó silencio durante un rato.

—No merece la pena correr ese riesgo.

—No creo que sea del todo justo no darle una oportunidad de sobrevivir —dijo Helena con un nudo en la garganta—. No estaríamos aquí de no ser por ella.

—Solo es un animal.

Helena no respondió porque no hablaba con ella. Era evidente que llevaba varios días dándole vueltas al tema. Amaris levantó la cabeza, dejó escapar un gimoteo ronco y le lamió toda la cara. Kaine frunció el ceño y le empujó el hocico para apartarla.

Echó la cabeza hacia atrás con un suspiro.

—Después de matar a tantísima gente, no me puedo creer que me estén entrando los remordimientos con un animal.

La mañana en que se marcharon, Kaine se levantó en silencio y fue al establo mientras Lila guardaba las últimas pertenencias que tenía intención de llevarse. Helena se quedó en tensión cuando él desapareció en el interior y el estómago se le retorció hasta formar un doloroso nudo.

Kaine salió un minuto más tarde y se quedó mirando el cielo durante tanto rato que a Helena se le desbocó el corazón. Cuando volvió a entrar en la casa, se detuvo detrás de ella.

—Algún día, tu misericordia nos traerá problemas —susurró apoyándole una mano en el hombro.

—Bastantes muertes llevamos ya a las espaldas como para añadir otra muerte más —le dijo ella posando la mano sobre la suya.

Kaine le dio un apretón en el hombro.

—Es hora de irse, Bayard —dijo un minuto más tarde.

EL MAR PERMANECÍA EMBRAVECIDO, INCLUSO en ese momento de marea baja en que sus aguas solían calmarse. El puerto estaba plagado de recién llegados y viajeros a punto de marcharse. Su documentación falsa les estaba esperando en la oficina postal de la ciudad.

Helena ya había olvidado lo diferente que podía llegar a ser el mundo. La forma de vestir y las costumbres del Norte eran tan uniformes que se había acostumbrado a ellas, pero, una vez al año, durante la latencia, la ciudad portuaria se convertía en un crisol de marineros y viajeros llegados de todas partes del mundo para aprovechar la oportunidad de desplazarse de un continente a otro en unas pocas semanas, en vez de tardar meses.

Había bastantes norteños como para que Kaine y Lila pasaran desapercibidos, mientras que Helena se confundía con sus compatriotas etrasianos. No había visto tantas melenas rizadas y oscuras y pieles oliváceas juntas desde que se había marchado de su país natal. Por si fuera poco, le sorprendió oír a varias personas hablando etrasiano despreocupadamente y descubrir que había pasado tanto tiempo que incluso le costaba entenderlo.

Descendieron desde el acantilado hasta un muelle de embarque y Helena se aferró a la mano de Kaine como si su vida dependiera de ello mientras esperaban a que les revisaran los papeles y los billetes.

La cubierta del barco estaba abarrotada. Lila tenía tanto miedo de que le dieran un empujón y Pol cayera al mar que entraron enseguida para buscar una escotilla junto a la que sentarse en vez de quedarse en la proa.

Helena sentía el corazón a punto de salírsele del pecho: temía que alguien los reconociera, que alguien levantara la vista y pronunciara el nombre de alguno de ellos.

Kaine permaneció tenso y alerta. Helena notaba su resonancia siguiendo el ritmo de sus latidos mientras le dibujaba círculos con el pulgar en la palma de la mano, ayudándola a mantener el contacto con la realidad. Una sonora voz norteña se alzó por encima del clamor en la mesa de al lado.

—Estoy intentando llevar tanto aceite al otro lado del charco como pueda antes de que estalle de nuevo la guerra. Los libertadores pagarán un riñón por él cuando ataquen Paladia.

Lila se volvió hacia el hombre.

—¿De qué guerra habla?

Los dedos de Kaine se crisparon y se cerraron en torno a la muñeca de Helena. Entre los preparativos y el esfuerzo por mantener la paz, ella había decidido no mencionar la situación en que había quedado el país cuando huyeron.

Un norteño con un bigote poblado y patillas miró a Lila.

—¿Es que no ha leído las noticias? El Sumo Inquisidor de Paladia por fin ha muerto. Novis y el resto de los países vecinos deberían atacar en cualquier momento. Ha sido portada en todos los periódicos de los últimos días.

Lila pareció quedarse blanca.

—¿Tendría alguno a mano?

El hombre rebuscó en el bolsillo de su levita y sacó un panfleto.

—¿Ve? Tendrán que recurrir a una buena cantidad de maquinaria para encargarse de todos los cadáveres o lo que sea que los nigromantes hayan estado cocinando, así que necesitarán aceite. Si logro ir a Khem y regresar antes de la sublimación, me haré de oro. En cualquier caso, incluso viajar por tierra me saldría rentable si consigo ser el primero en llegar. Debería haber visto el precio del opio hace unos años. —Se le levantó el bigote al sonreír—. No hay nada como una guerra para ganar un buen dinero.

Los tres estaban demasiado distraídos leyendo el periódico como para responder. No era una publicación al uso compuesta de artículos, sino una especie de boletín, de esos que solían leer los hombres de negocios.

En la parte superior, el titular de la primera noticia rezaba en negrita: «El Sumo Inquisidor ha muerto», seguido de un texto en letra más pequeña: «El mundo entero ha suspirado aliviado ante la noticia de que el magnate del acero y heredero del gremio del hierro, Kaine Ferron, más conocido como el Sumo Inquisidor, ha fallecido en el último ataque de la Resistencia, lo cual ha dejado herido de muerte al régimen de los inmarcesibles».

Helena se aferró a la mano de Kaine al leer el titular de la siguiente noticia: «El estandarte de la Llama Eterna se alza de nuevo: ante la alianza contra Paladia, algunos recuerdan a los combatientes caídos».

—¿Vosotros sabíais esto? —preguntó Lila por fin.

Kaine no respondió a su pregunta, mientras que Helena habló en voz baja y extendió la mano para darle un suave apretón en la muñeca desnuda a su amiga.

—Sabíamos que se estaba buscando una alianza, pero no esperábamos que se alcanzara un acuerdo tan deprisa. Tampoco estábamos seguros de que se fuesen a creer lo de la muerte del Sumo Inquisidor.

Lila se recostó contra el asiento estrechando a Pol entre sus brazos, pero había desviado la mirada hacia la escotilla para contemplar el continente mientras la bocina del barco sonaba, indicando que estaba a punto de zarpar.

—No tenía ni idea —dijo mientras negaba con la cabeza.

Helena pasó mareada la mayor parte del viaje, pues el embarazo empeoraba las náuseas que en cualquier otra ocasión habrían sido tolerables. Cuando llegaron a una de las islas mercantes principales, todavía tenía la sensación de estar a punto de vomitar. Kaine les ofreció la opción de descansar en una posada y terminar el viaje al día siguiente, pero Helena sabía que él prefería dejar el mínimo rastro posible. Cuantas menos paradas hicieran y menos hablaran con desconocidos, más difícil sería rastrear sus movimientos. Se subieron a un autobús para desplazarse al otro lado de la isla, cuyo paisaje era completamente distinto del Norte. La ciudad se extendía a lo ancho en vez de a lo alto como en Paladia y la mampostería no tenía nada que ver con la arquitectura alquímica. Una vez que se bajaron del autobús, se subieron a un carromato que los condujo hasta su destino.

La carretera era amplísima y estaba pavimentada para que se pudiera cruzar a la isla más pequeña cuando la marea bajaba. Dado que la latencia había hecho que el mar se retirara por completo, el fondo marino había quedado al descubierto, unos metros por debajo de la calzada. Había gente caminando por allí, recogiendo los tesoros que el agua hubiera dejado a su paso.

Helena y su padre solían salir cuando la marea bajaba para buscar conchas y tesoros, y estudiar los peces que quedaban atrapados en las balsas de agua que quedaban. Era una práctica muy popular durante la latencia, puesto que el Desastre se había llevado consigo infinidad de ciudades e, incluso un milenio más tarde, los restos de esas civilizaciones todavía descansaban bajo el mar.

Echó la vista atrás para ver cómo reaccionaban Lila y Kaine ante aquel paisaje. Él estudiaba el horizonte impasible, pero Lila parecía más asustada de lo que la había visto nunca. Tardó un instante en recordar que el mar les resultaba aterrador a los norteños. Incluso la costa estaba plagada de peligros para ellos, como si el hecho de preservar un lugar así fuera un acto de temeridad suicida. Para quienes vivían en el interior, la mera idea de habitar las zonas costeras les resultaba demasiado ajena.

—No te preocupes. Le enseñaré a Pol que debe tenerle respeto al mar, pero acabará cogiéndole cariño. Igual que tú.

Lila asintió nerviosa.

El edificio al que llegaron estaba emplazado en lo alto de un acantilado. Era una casa grande de dos pisos hecha de piedra que contaba con un establo y unos cuantos anexos. La isla, según había comentado Kaine sin darle demasiada importancia, era privada y el edificio había sido construido por su anterior dueño. Por eso era mucho más grande que las que conformaban el pueblecito por el que habían pasado de camino.

Estaba prácticamente amueblada. Habían pagado a una de las vecinas del pueblo para que la mantuviera cuidada y desembalara todo lo que hubiera llegado con antelación. Los suelos eran de piedra cálida y los techos de viga descubierta. La luz del sol se colaba por todas las ventanas abiertas, acompañada del intenso aroma del mar.

Kaine fue el primero en entrar, y lo hizo apresuradamente. Helena percibió su resonancia empapando el aire mientras inspeccionaba la casa con desconfianza y se mordió la lengua para reprimir el impulso de recordarle que tuviera cuidado. Pero su paranoia estaba demasiado arraigada. Si le decía algo, Kaine seguiría haciendo lo mismo, solo que a sus espaldas.

—Tengo que asegurarme de que todo está en orden —les dijo antes de salir.

—Bueno, está claro que esta casa es mucho más grande que la otra —señaló Lila acunando el cuerpo dormido de Pol entre sus brazos mientras miraba a su alrededor—. ¿Vamos a buscar las habitaciones? Estoy a punto de quedarme sin brazo.

Subieron al piso de arriba y se asomaron a las distintas habitaciones en busca de alguna cama.

El primer dormitorio que consiguieron encontrar era muy amplio, pero casi parecía más una biblioteca equipada con una cama. Lila echó un vistazo y arrugó la nariz.

—Me imagino que esta está pensada para ti. Deberías descansar. Todavía sigues verde del viaje. Pol y yo encontraremos otro lugar donde dormir. ¿Crees que Ferron me devolverá mi espada si le prometo no usarla contra él?

Tras decir eso, ella se alejó y Helena entró en el dormitorio.

En realidad, no era tan grande como parecía. Los techos encalados y de vigas descubiertas hacían que las estancias no resultaran tan asfixiantes como las oscuras habitaciones de Puntaférreo. En la pared opuesta, justo donde estaba colocada la cama, había un amplio ventanal con vistas al mar.

Helena avanzó con cuidado, pegada a la pared, y recorrió las estanterías con los dedos mientras leía los títulos de los distintos tomos y colecciones. Había libros de alquimia, pero también novelas, crónicas y diarios de viaje.

El dormitorio también contaba con un escritorio, unas sillas, un sofá y una alfombra mullida. Al detenerse ante la mesa, encontró papeles, plumas, planchas de grabado y estiletes en los cajones, como si la hubieran estado esperando.

Había materiales suficientes en esta habitación como para mantenerse ocupada el resto de sus días.

Eso era lo que representaba aquel dormitorio: la vida que Kaine había intentado dejarle preparada. Helena quería valorar el esfuerzo que debía de haber hecho, pero algo le escamaba. Era demasiado perfecta. Como si fuera una trampa pensada específicamente para inculcarle una falsa sensación de seguridad.

Ahora Kaine era más vulnerable que nunca.

Lila no estaba en absoluto en condiciones de luchar y, aunque lo estuviera, su prioridad siempre sería la seguridad de Pol. Si Helena se permitía creerse a salvo, si bajaba la guardia, aunque fuera un instante, ocurriría algo malo. Estaba segura de ello.

Vivía en una constante cuenta atrás, a la espera de la próxima catástrofe que sería incapaz de prever. Se agazapó en la esquina entre la cama y la pared, agarrándose el pecho con la mano derecha para intentar mantener el control de su ritmo cardiaco.

«Tranquilízate. —Cerró los ojos con fuerza—. Respira».

¿Dónde estaba Kaine? Ahora que ya no se encontraban en Puntaférreo, ya no sabría cuándo lo necesitaba…

Abrió los ojos, se tocó el anillo que llevaba en el dedo anular entumecido de la mano izquierda y se aferró a él con todo su ser para enviar un rápido pulso de calor a través de la plata.

Un instante más tarde, Kaine le respondió con otro.

Se quedó allí, con los ojos cerrados y la mano presionada sobre el corazón, hasta que oyó que la puerta se abría.

—¿Helena?

—Estoy aquí —dijo con voz trémula.

—¿Qué te pasa? —preguntó él tras aparecer ante ella en un abrir y cerrar de ojos.

Tuvo que tragar saliva unas cuantas veces antes de poder hablar:

—Pensaba que me alegraría de haber llegado aquí, pero… ¿y si nos encuentran? ¿Y si alguien da con nosotros por haber dejado de huir?

Kaine frunció el ceño y le acarició la mejilla con el pulgar.

—¿Quieres que sigamos huyendo?

A Helena le dio un vuelco el estómago solo con pensar en más barcos, más sitios nuevos, sin detenerse nunca, siempre vigilando por encima del hombro.

—No, pero ¿por qué siento que hay algo que no encaja? Es como si nada de esto fuera real y, sin embargo, es lo que siempre hemos querido.

Kaine la estrechó entre sus brazos e hizo que hundiera la cabeza bajo su barbilla.

—No creo que una vida normal llegue nunca a parecernos real a ninguno de los dos.

Un desaliento se apoderó de ella al comprender, agotada, que tenía razón.

—Creo que el problema está en que, para mí, nuestra meta siempre fue huir. Nunca me he parado a pensar en qué sería de mí cuando llegáramos aquí.

Se quedó quieta, entumecida.

—¿Te gusta la casa? —preguntó Kaine al cabo de un rato.

—Sí —dijo ella mirando alrededor y tratando de animarse un poco—. ¿Cómo la conseguiste?

—Fue casi todo por correspondencia. Recordaba que me habías hablado del mar, así que empecé a buscar un poco antes de que terminara la guerra. Se me ocurrió que todo sería más fácil para ti si acababas en algún lugar que te gustara.

—¿Y tenías pensado dejarme sola en esta casa tan grande?

Aunque habló con tono despreocupado, la idea la horrorizaba.

—Por aquel entonces Lila ya formaba parte del plan. Pasé por aquí el verano pasado. Fue uno de mis últimos viajes —murmuró—. Antes de eso, me dediqué a enviar todo lo que se me ocurrió que pudiera gustarte.

Helena volvió a recorrer la estancia con la mirada. Había preparado todo aquello sin saber siquiera con seguridad si estaba viva.

—Venga, vamos. Seguro que lo ves todo con otros ojos una vez que hayas descansado.

Cerró los postigos y Helena se derrumbó sobre la cama. Las sábanas eran suaves y estaban frescas gracias a la brisa marina, lo cual hizo que se sintiera como si hubiera vuelto a casa. Kaine se sentó a su lado, entrelazó sus dedos y le pasó el pulgar por los nudillos. Como no notaba ni el meñique ni el anular, cada vez que le acariciaba la zona, Helena no sentía más que una extraña pausa de vacío.

Había empezado a quedarse dormida cuando Kaine le soltó la mano y, entre las pestañas, vio que se levantaba y empezó a pasear despacio por la habitación. Se arrodilló, pasó una mano por el suelo y luego recorrió las paredes con la mirada, admirando cada rincón. Cuando se dio por satisfecho, se dispuso a marcharse sin hacer el menor ruido.

—Kaine —lo llamó, y él se detuvo en seco y se dio la vuelta—, ¿estamos a salvo?

Él sufrió un leve espasmo en los dedos y apretó el puño.

—Sí… Hay un par de asuntos que me gustaría mejorar…, pero hemos sido muy cuidadosos. No creo que les haya dado tiempo a salir a buscarnos antes de la subida de la marea. No tienes de qué preocuparte.

—¿Y tú? —La pregunta pareció sorprenderlo. Helena extendió una mano hacia él—. Se supone que por fin ha llegado el momento de descansar. Tanto para mí como para ti. No te he traído hasta aquí para que tengas que seguir al pie del cañón.

Los ojos de Kaine, que de pronto parecía muy joven e inseguro, revolotearon por toda la estancia. Helena lo contempló con tristeza al comprender que lo que los diferenciaba era que él nunca había soñado con lo que haría después de la guerra. Nunca se había permitido considerar siquiera la posibilidad de sobrevivir, así que no tenía ni idea de cómo comportarse si no era como un combatiente.

Kaine abrió la boca para decir algo, pero no emitió sonido alguno.

—Quédate conmigo. Tú también necesitas descansar.

Asintió como si entendiera el concepto de lo que ella le pedía, pero se quedó junto a la puerta. Helena fue a buscarlo y lo agarró de la mano.

Encontró un sorprendente número de armas de lo más inusuales en sus bolsillos y descubrió que llevaba protecciones de cuerpo entero debajo de la ropa de civil. Hasta ese momento ni siquiera había reparado en ellas.

—¿Te has traído algo más? —le preguntó con tono burlón cuando hizo que se sentara al borde de la cama y se topó con una daga de puño escondida en una de sus botas, pero él eludió la pregunta.

Se tumbaron uno frente al otro, aunque Kaine no paraba de desviar la mirada hacia el lugar donde Helena había puesto todas sus armas, así que ella le tocó la barbilla con el dedo índice para recuperar su atención.

—¿Qué querías hacer antes de la guerra? —le preguntó.

—Era el heredero del gremio del hierro…, nunca me dejaron aspirar a nada más. Lo único que quería era seguir en la Academia después de obtener el certificado. Mi padre no lo consideraba necesario, pero mi madre siempre había querido continuar sus estudios cuando estuvo allí. Su familia no pudo permitírselo. Dado que mis notas eran lo bastante buenas como para optar a ello, convenció a mi padre para que me dejara seguir. Sin embargo, cuando regresé a la Academia, Crowther se interesó por mí y quiso saber por qué alguien de mi estatus querría formarse más allá de lo requerido por su oficio. Aquello enfureció a mi padre, así que sospecho que, aunque no lo hubieran arrestado, tampoco me habría permitido seguir estudiando.

—Pues tendremos que buscarte algo —dijo ella, que apoyó la cabeza en su hombro. Kaine le enterró los dedos en el pelo para sentirla más cerca—. ¿De verdad estamos a salvo?

—Sí, de verdad.

Helena inspiró hondo y cerró los ojos.

—Me alegro, porque estoy agotada.

Cuando se despertó, Kaine seguía dormido y, al apartarse de él, ni siquiera se inmutó. Los años de cansancio acumulado lo habían arrastrado al fondo del sueño. Pasó días enteros durmiendo. Ni siquiera reaccionó cuando Helena le apoyó una mano en el pecho para sondearlo con su resonancia. El alma de Kaine por fin parecía estar empezando a reintegrarse.

Durmió junto a él durante la primera semana. No había esperado estar tan cansada como para dormir durante varios días seguidos, pero se sentía como si se hubiera quitado un gran peso de encima y descansara, por primera vez en su vida, de verdad.

Se despertaban solo para comer. Bajo la atenta mirada de Helena,

Kaine salía a recorrer el borde del acantilado, registraba la isla y deambulaba por la casa para terminar quedándose dormido de nuevo.

Pero solo se permitía descansar si Helena permanecía cerca. Cuando ella se levantaba para ojear los libros que colmaban las estanterías, él se despertaba y se incorporaba de golpe.

—Puedo levantarme ya —dijo.

—No te preocupes, yo sigo cansada —mintió ella—. Solo quería leer un rato.

Regresó a la cama con unos cuantos libros y, al poco de entrelazar sus dedos con los de él y ponerse a leer, Kaine había vuelto a caer rendido. Ahora, cuando lo tocaba con su resonancia, ya no sentía su organismo como algo a punto de desmoronarse.

Había pasado casi dos semanas enteras durmiendo cuando Lila abrió la puerta y asomó la cabeza.

—He dejado a Pol echándose una siesta. ¿Te importa si entro?

Helena cerró el libro y la invitó a pasar con un movimiento afirmativo. Apenas se habían visto desde que llegaron. Lila se acercó y contempló a Kaine durante un instante antes de girarse y sentarse al borde de la cama, dándole la espalda.

—Llevo un tiempo queriendo hablar contigo, pero no he encontrado el momento hasta ahora. La gente del pueblo dice que la marea anegará la carretera pronto. —Helena asintió y Lila tomó aire—. Cuando Ferron me contó lo vuestro, yo al principio no lo creí. Me dijo que Luc y los demás habían muerto. Incluso me trajo periódicos para demostrármelo, y me dijo que tú eras la única razón por la que yo no había sufrido el mismo destino. Me lo creí casi todo, salvo lo que me contó de ti. —Lila tenía la mirada clavada en el suelo—. Me parecía increíble que algo así hubiera pasado…, que tú… Pero entonces pensé en lo retraída que te volviste justo cuando las cosas empezaron a mejorar. Luc, Soren y yo solíamos hablar de ello y ninguno de los tres lográbamos entender tu comportamiento. Cuando Ferron me explicó cuándo habíais empezado a veros, enseguida me di cuenta de que las fechas coincidían, pero estaba convencida de que lo estabas engañando para que pensara que te importaba. Me pareció tan patético que se lo creyera…

La mano que Helena tenía entrelazada con la de Kaine se crispó.

—Al principio, venía a verme casi todas las semanas. Fue como estar con alguien muriéndose de hambre mientras te buscaba. De hecho, creo que perdió la cabeza durante un tiempo. Empezó a amenazarme, diciéndome que todo era culpa mía, que, de no haber sido por mí, ya te habría puesto a salvo. También me avisó de que tendría que ser yo, por una vez, quien cuidara de ti cuando te encontrara. Con el tiempo dejó de hablar de lo que pasaría cuando por fin te encontrase. —Apretó los labios—. Cuando me avisó de que te habían localizado, me dijo que no te acordabas de nada. Ni de él ni de lo de mi embarazo. Me explicó que intentarían sacarte de Paladia antes de que Lumitia entrara en plena latencia, pero que tendrían que hacerlo con el tiempo justo para que no pudieran seguirte la pista. Luego empezaron a llegarme rumores sobre el programa de repoblación. No esperaba que te hubieran obligado a participar...

—Kaine no tuvo elección. Si no lo hubiera hecho él, me habrían entregado a otro. Era eso o matarme.

Lila tomó una temblorosa bocanada de aire.

—Bueno, me alegro de que estés viva —dijo al final—, pero todavía odio a Ferron y odio que estés atrapada con él, porque tenías razón y ninguno te hicimos caso. Y, encima, te quedaste a nuestro lado pese a saber lo que ocurriría. No te mereces nada de lo que te ha pasado. No deberías vivir el resto de tus días presa de las promesas que otros te obligaron a hacer.

Helena se puso rígida y, cuando Lila se percató de su cambio de postura, apretó los labios.

—No me refiero solo a Ferron, sino a Pol y a mí también. Luc te hizo prometerle que nos protegerías y sé que te quedarías a nuestro lado para el resto de tu vida sin rechistar, pero quiero que sepas que no tienes por qué hacerlo. Ya nos has ayudado mucho más de lo que cualquiera se atrevería nunca a pedirte. Te mereces pensar también en ti misma. No sigas viviendo una vida atada a viejas promesas. Ni por Luc, ni por mí, ni... por Ferron. Por nadie. —Cerró los ojos y exhaló—. Tenía... tenía que decírtelo al menos una vez antes de que nos quedemos atrapadas en esta isla.

Se puso en pie y salió de la habitación igual que había entrado, sin hacer el menor ruido. Helena se quedó en silencio y, al cabo de un rato, bajó la vista.

—Ya puedes dejar de hacerte el dormido. —Kaine abrió los ojos y la miró con una expresión perfectamente hermética, así que Helena arqueó las cejas—. No creerás que me he tomado la molestia de salvarte solo porque te hice una promesa, ¿verdad?

No respondió, pero tampoco hizo falta. Helena negó con la cabeza notando un nudo en la garganta.

—No es justo que pienses eso de mí. Además, me dijiste que nunca habías conocido a alguien tan incapaz de mantener una promesa como yo. Una cosa no es compatible con la otra.

—Helena… —empezó a decir con suavidad, aunque ella no le dejó hablar.

—Nos prometimos que estaríamos juntos para siempre, ¿no? —preguntó con voz estrangulada—. Para siempre. Bueno, pues si tú ya no quieres que mantenga esa promesa como hasta ahora, lo iré haciendo poco a poco. —Le apretó la mano—. Te elegiré cada día. Así sabrás que sigo queriendo estar a tu lado. —Desvió la mirada hacia el mar, que ya empezaba a subir—. Estoy segura de que tendremos días buenos y días malos. No vamos a poder dejar todo lo que hemos vivido a un lado, pero, si tú eliges estar conmigo y yo elijo estar contigo, creo que seremos lo bastante fuertes como para salir adelante.

ANTES DE QUE LA MAREA separara la isla del resto de Etras, llegó un montón de periódicos viejos provenientes del Norte.

En uno de ellos, encontraron un artículo entero dedicado a la muerte del Sumo Inquisidor. Puntaférreo había acabado reducida a cenizas. De ella no había quedado más que un armazón de hierro fundido y, entre los escombros, habían encontrado una infinidad de cadáveres calcinados, incluidos el de Kaine Ferron, el de su mujer, Aurelia, y el de Atreus Ferron. La culpable había sido Ivy Purnell, que se había suicidado no muy lejos de allí utilizando una de las armas de obsidiana de la Llama Eterna. Purnell formaba parte de los inmarcesibles, pero su familia había estado vinculada a la Llama Eterna antes de la guerra. También se creía que era la responsable de todos los asesinatos que se habían ido sucediendo a lo largo del año.

Otros artículos hablaban del Frente de Liberación, una alianza militar organizada contra Paladia que no tardaría en atacar. Sin embargo, como Etras volvía a estar aislada del continente, todavía no habían declarado la guerra de manera oficial.

En la isla, el tiempo se distorsionaba. Los días se hacían interminables. Salvo por las subidas y las bajadas de la marea, vivían en una nebulosa llena de parsimonia.

La alquimia, Paladia y la guerra prácticamente no existían en Etras.

Helena retomó el hábito de salir a recolectar, y su cocina no tardó en llenarse de hierbas colgadas para secar, decocciones, aceites infusionados, extractos y destilaciones. Y, como preparaba más remedios de lo que cuatro personas necesitarían en toda una vida, Lila, que era más sociable que Kaine o Helena, empezó a llevarlas al pueblo.

A Kaine no le hacía ninguna gracia la idea. No quería que Helena tuviera que responsabilizarse de un pueblo lleno de desconocidos, pero acabó cediendo porque sabía que estar ocupada la ayudaba a mantener los nervios a raya.

Según parecía, no era raro que los norteños de clase alta huyeran al Sur para escapar de los escándalos que hubieran desatado en Paladia. Sin ir más lejos, los anteriores dueños de la casa eran una familia noble pero poco importante de Novis. Por eso, la llegada de una nueva hornada de forasteros dio, como era lógico, bastante que hablar en la isla.

Kaine, Helena y Lila solían debatir sobre los riesgos a los que se enfrentaban, al igual que sobre la manera de encontrar el equilibrio entre llevar una vida reservada y socializar lo suficiente como para no levantar sospechas. Cabía la posibilidad de que incluso los rumores más inocentes escaparan de la isla y bastaran para identificarlos. Sin embargo, como Helena era etrasiana y había demostrado con creces su utilidad, el pueblo se volcó en proteger a sus extraños vecinos.

A Kaine fue a quien más le costó adaptarse. Permanecía todo el tiempo alerta, preparándose para lo peor. Cuando no estaba con Helena, deambulaba por la propiedad y se acercaba al pueblo para reunir cualquier información que llegara desde la isla principal por si alguien de fuera aparecía.

Una tarde, cuando ya era casi de noche, Helena oyó que el viento aullaba y los postigos se estremecían mientras diseñaba una muñequera para su mano izquierda que le permitiera doblar los dos dedos paralizados. Su idea era utilizar un mecanismo transmutacional conectado a los tres dedos restantes. En un principio no le dio importancia al ruido, pero entonces se fijó en que Kaine se había quedado inmóvil como una estatua. Otra racha de viento azotó la casa.

Helena abrió los ojos como platos y ambos corrieron hasta la puerta principal. Correteando de un lado para otro con las alas extendidas y el hocico pegado al suelo estaba Amaris. La quimera levantó la cabeza cuando Kaine salió por la puerta y se dejó caer para arrastrarse hasta él con el vientre pegado al suelo, agitando las alas y gimoteando repetidamente. Él le abrazó la enorme cabezota.

—Pero ¿cómo has llegado hasta aquí, bestia loca?

Apenas pudo pronunciar aquella pregunta, porque Amaris empezó a lamerle la cara una y otra vez mientras levantaba una polvareda con las alas.

—Supongo que no se veía capaz de dejarte ir —intervino Helena.

Le hicieron un hueco a Amaris en el establo y se aseguraron de dejarla salir solo por las noches. Era la mejor solución que se les ocurrió dados el tamaño y las inusuales características de la criatura. Sin embargo, a ella no pareció importarle. Cuando empezaba a oscurecer, la dejaban corretear un rato alrededor de la casa y luego Kaine se la llevaba a volar por encima del mar.

Helena se alegraba de que por fin tuviera algo que hacer. Antes de que Amaris apareciera, se había limitado simplemente a existir. Podía leer y le hacía compañía, pero no parecía saber cómo era desear algo para sí mismo. Al fin y al cabo, había pasado toda una vida con un collar atado al cuello.

A medida que las semanas se convirtieron en meses, su posesividad desmedida regresó con una renovada intensidad. Durante el día, se pasaba las horas mirando a Helena trabajar tan fijamente que ella notaba su mirada clavada en la médula. Aun así, cuando estaban solos, la chica interrumpía lo que estuviera haciendo y dejaba que la devorara, susurrando palabras como «perfecta», «preciosa» o «mía» cada vez que le rozaba la piel con los labios.

—Siempre seré tuya —le prometía ella.

Cada vez era más evidente que el universo de Kaine giraba en torno a Helena y, ahora que por fin la había puesto a salvo, ya no tenía nada con lo que obsesionarse. Lo único que le importaba era ella. Al principio, Helena pensaba que sería algo pasajero, pero, con la llegada del otoño y el paso de la fase de sublimación, empezó a sospechar que Kaine no tenía la menor intención de buscar otros intereses. El rescate de Lila y Pol, los proyectos de alquimia..., todo habían sido formas de complacerla.

Incluso lo del bebé. El embarazo de Helena se estaba convirtiendo en una pieza esencial de su relación, pero sus preocupaciones se limitaban al estado de salud de ella. A su corazón. Al riesgo de que el Estrago volviera a apoderarse de su cuerpo.

Si no era para recordarle que «su hija» necesitaba que Helena respirara o que debía tener cuidado por el bien de «la niña», apenas le prestaba atención.

Una noche, tumbados en la cama, cuando ella intentaba hacerle sentir las constantes pataditas a las que se veía sometida, se dio cuenta de que la atención de Kaine estaba fija en sus muñecas; más concretamente, en las perforaciones que los grilletes le habían hecho.

Helena sabía que temía que lo del nervio cubital solo fuera el principio, que los conductos de anulitio le hubieran dejado más secuelas. Siempre la vigilaba cuando trabajaba y pocas veces le permitía cargar con cualquier peso que supusiera un esfuerzo para sus muñecas.

—Kaine —le susurró y su atención regresó a ella—. Kaine, tienes que preocuparte también por la niña.

Él la miró inexpresivo. A Helena se le secó la boca.

—No puedes ser como tu padre. —Su rostro se endureció y ella le agarró la mano—. Tienes que mostrar interés por ella. Debes elegir hacerlo. Por cómo eres, si no te esfuerzas, si no se lo demuestras..., se dará cuenta enseguida. Igual que te pasó a ti. No puedes hacerle eso. Tiene que ser alguien por quien decidas mostrar interés. —Tragó saliva y bajó la vista—. No sabemos cuánto tiempo tendremos... después de todo. En caso de que me pasara algo, necesito que me prometas que la querrás —se le rompió la voz— como yo la habría querido. Tendrás que convertirla en tu todo. ¿Me lo prometes?

Kaine se puso pálido, pero asintió.

—De acuerdo.

—Prométemelo.

—Te lo prometo.

HELENA GUARDÓ REPOSO DURANTE EL último mes de embarazo porque incluso algo tan sencillo como subir las escaleras empezó a suponer un esfuerzo para su corazón.

Después de que hubiera estado a punto de desmayarse, Kaine la había llevado a la cama sin darle tiempo siquiera a que se le pasara el mareo, y desde entonces no le permitió moverse de allí.

Entonces se marchó a lomos de Amaris a una de las islas más grandes para buscar varios textos médicos sobre el embarazo, se los leyó de principio a fin y se nombró a sí mismo su obstetra particular. Se negaba a dejar que hiciera nada por su cuenta. Cuando ella intentaba protestar, recurría a ciertos pasajes de esos mismos libros para fundamentar su postura.

Varias de las mujeres del pueblo se acercaron a la casa para ayudar a Lila a cocinar y a limpiar. Al no tener nada más que hacer, Helena empezó a escribir un diario con todo lo que se le pasaba por la cabeza. Quería dejar su versión de lo que había vivido por escrito. Quería documentar quién era, qué había escogido hacer y por qué. Respondió a todas las preguntas que le hubiera gustado hacerle a su propia madre.

El solsticio de invierno pasó y, con él, la fecha en que Helena salía de cuentas. Cuando ya pensaba que permanecería embarazada para siempre y nunca dejaría aquella cama, por fin empezaron las contracciones. Estuvo más de un día de parto sin mucho progreso y Kaine se iba poniendo cada vez más y más nervioso. Lila, por algún motivo, fue la que mantuvo mejor la calma de los tres.

—Somos todos vivemantes, así que sacaremos a ese bebé de ahí de una manera u otra —dijo arrodillándose entre las piernas de Helena, que a su vez estaba recostada contra Kaine.

Él tenía la mano puesta sobre su corazón para asegurarse de que su ritmo cardiaco se mantuviera regular mientras las contracciones iban y venían.

—Esto es horrible —dijo Helena al cabo de un rato, pues comenzaba a creer que el sufrimiento no acabaría nunca.

—Lo sé —la tranquilizó Kaine apartándole el pelo húmedo que se le pegaba a la cara.

—Duele.

—Ya.

—Estoy cansada. Llevo horas empujando.

—Lo sé.

—Para de darme la razón como a los tontos.

Kaine dejó de responder después de aquello. Ni siquiera protestó cuando ella estuvo a punto de partirle la mano al apretársela durante una contracción que hizo que todo su cuerpo se crispara violentamente.

—Ya casi está —dijo Lila—. Le veo la cabeza. Un último empujón y los hombros habrán pasado. —Miró a Kaine—. ¿Quieres cogerla tú?

Él negó con la cabeza.

Helena notaba que su corazón intentaba desbocarse. Estaba cerca, muy cerca. Un último esfuerzo y todo habría acabado.

—¡Eso es! ¡Muy bien! Le veo los hombros. Respira, que ya…

Se oyó un lamento confuso. Lila levantó un cuerpecito húmedo que se retorcía y se lo pasó a Helena. La chica ahogó una exclamación de sorpresa al ver la carita diminuta y arrugada de su hija acurrucada contra su cuerpo. Tenía la cabeza cubierta por una mata empapada de rizos oscuros y apelmazados.

Aquello fue todo cuanto le bastó para olvidar el cansancio. Acunó a la pequeña contra su pecho con manos temblorosas, y la niña levantó la cabecita para mirarla antes de abrir la boca diminuta para proferir un rabioso alarido de protesta.

Lila estaba diciéndole algo, pero Helena solo podía mirar al bebé, que frunció el delicadísimo ceño y, por un instante, abrió los ojos de par en par.

Eran del luminoso color plateado de una tormenta eléctrica.

Helena reprimió un sollozo y la estrechó con más fuerza.

—Kaine…, tiene tus ojos.

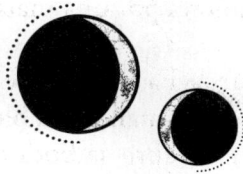

CAPÍTULO 77

Ener 1790

HELENA ESTABA SENTADA EN LA cama contándole los deditos de los pies y de las manos a su hija, estudiando sus diminutas uñas y admirando su perfil achatado. Lila le había limpiado a conciencia el unto sebáceo que la cubría al venir al mundo y la había envuelto en una mantita con una pericia asombrosa antes de devolvérsela a su madre.

El pelo apelmazado empezaba a secársele y lo tenía de punta alrededor de la cabeza.

—Parece que el pelo lo ha heredado de mí —comentó levantando la vista con una sonrisa.

Kaine se había puesto tan lejos de ella como podía sin llegar a salir por la puerta. Helena lo miró confundida. Apenas se había apartado de su lado en las últimas semanas, pero ahora parecía sentirse acorralado.

—Kaine..., ven a verla.

—Helena... —dijo él tragando saliva.

—Es tu hija.

—Sí, lo sé —dijo apretando los dientes—. Recuerdo perfectamente cómo la concebimos.

Helena perdió súbitamente la sonrisa y bajó la vista. El silencio que se hizo en la habitación era tan ensordecedor que creyó que no volvería a oír nada más en toda su vida. Algunas heridas jamás sanaban. A veces tenía la sensación de que entre los dos sumaban una cantidad casi mortal de ellas.

—Creo que debería irme.

—Ven aquí —le dijo Helena con voz firme e inexpresiva, sin darle tiempo a que interpretara su silencio como si coincidiera con él.

Kaine exhaló y la miró desesperado, como si le estuvieran arrancando el corazón del pecho, pero no se movió.

—Kaine…, ven aquí —insistió con decisión, y él se acercó tragando saliva—. No tuvimos otra opción. Ninguno de los dos. Pero eso ya ha quedado atrás. Dijimos que empezaríamos de cero cuando escapáramos y eso es lo que vamos a hacer ahora. Ella nunca conocerá el mundo que nosotros hemos dejado atrás.

La mirada de Kaine vagó por toda la habitación con tal de no posarse en el bebé.

—No te va a hacer daño y tú a ella tampoco.

—Helena —rogó con voz estrangulada—, yo no debería disfrutar de esta vida. Paladia ha quedado manchada de toda la sangre que yo mismo he derramado. ¿Crees que no he matado a niños? Nunca he destacado en nada salvo en el asesinato. ¿De verdad quieres tener a alguien así cerca de tu hija?

Helena se quedó de piedra mientras lo miraba, pero terminó por agachar la cabeza.

—No te dieron otra opción. Además, no solo has matado a gente. Me salvaste. Salvaste a Lila y a Pol. Hicimos… hicimos lo necesario para sobrevivir, pero ahora tenemos la oportunidad de ser mejores. Por ella.

Kaine por fin apartó la vista de la pared.

Su hija dejó volar los ojillos plateados entre ellos. Su cabello por fin se había secado en una aureola de rizos oscuros. Había conseguido sacar las manitas de la manta y las tenía cerca del rostro, todavía achatado por el parto. Se estaba chupando los nudillos de la mano derecha.

Era la criatura más perfecta que Helena había visto nunca.

—Mírala. Es nuestra. Solo nuestra. Y no vas a hacerle daño.

Kaine la contempló petrificado, conteniendo el aliento. Sus dedos temblorosos sufrieron un espasmo cuando por fin se atrevió a acariciar la palma de la mano de la niña de manera casi imperceptible, como si temiera que su contacto fuera a envenenarla o a romperla. La pequeña cerró la manita diminuta en torno a su dedo.

Helena lo estudió con atención y reconoció la expresión que se adueñó poco a poco de sus facciones mientras miraba a la personita que se aferraba con tenacidad a él: una posesiva admiración.

Enid Rose Ferron fue, según Lila, el bebé más fácil de cuidar de la historia. A medida que crecía, más se parecía a Helena, salvo por los ojos, que, tanto en forma como en color, eran iguales a los de Kaine y a los de su abuela, la mujer de quien había heredado el nombre.

La pequeña dormía de maravilla y casi nunca lloraba. Se pasaba horas y horas dormida en brazos de su padre, que se lo consentía todo y más; se acurrucaba contra su pecho mientras él veía a Helena trabajar en la cocina o en el modesto laboratorio que habían preparado en uno de los anexos.

Enid hacía gala de la solemne curiosidad de un búho, pues movía la cabeza de un lado a otro y observaba a cualquiera que tuviera delante. Helena solía llevarla colgada contra su pecho, estrechando su diminuto cuerpo entre sus brazos en actitud protectora cuando las sombras crecían más de la cuenta.

En cuanto fue capaz de mantenerse erguida con seguridad, la pequeña empezó a pasar la mitad del tiempo sentada sobre los hombros de Kaine, que salía a recorrer el perímetro de la casa sin descanso para comprobar todos los edificios. También visitaban a Amaris, que vibraba de emoción al verlos, pero se quedaba quieta como una estatua cuando Enid le tiraba de las orejas y la acariciaba.

Kaine hablaba con Enid más que con cualquier otra persona, incluida Helena. Sus soliloquios no tenían fin: le hablaba de los árboles, del mar, de la marea y las lunas, de las técnicas alquímicas y las teorías sobre los sellos, del tiempo que haría… Y Enid lo escuchaba con atención; incluso se ponía nerviosa si su padre se distraía o se quedaba en silencio durante demasiado rato.

El verano siguiente, el regreso de la fase de latencia trajo consigo noticias del Norte, sobre el asedio que se estaba llevando a cabo. Estaban matando a la ciudad de hambre para que se rindiera, puesto que no había atendido a razones frente a las exigencias de la alianza.

Cuando la latencia pasó, los tres se quedaron aliviados al descubrir que ya no quedaban más incógnitas en el aire; ninguno se preguntaba si podrían o deberían hacer algo más.

Enid habría sido la niña perfecta de no haber sido por la terrible influencia de Apollo Holdfast. En cuanto la pequeña empezó a caminar, la idílica tranquilidad de la isla se esfumó para siempre. Los dos niños corrían por la casa gritando, ajenos a la forma en que sus padres se encogían o se sobresaltaban ante cualquier ruido repentino.

Gracias a Pol, Enid aprendió a trepar colinas y árboles, y a destrozarse la ropa bajando por los acantilados. Preparó tartas de barro, sopas y pociones «curativas» en los tarros que robaban de la cocina. Aprendió a pelear y a utilizar las espadas de juguete que Lila había hecho para enseñarle a su hijo los fundamentos básicos del combate.

El niño tenía intención de convertirse en un guerrero algún día y Enid no iba a ser menos. Ambos mostraban a Lila una gran estima, pues era una guerrera con una pierna metálica, la cual les resultaba mucho más interesante que las suyas de carne y hueso.

Pol también demostró desde bien pequeño una notable habilidad para la piromancia. Y, luego, Enid, para no quedarse atrás, le curó el labio a su amigo cuando se lo abrió al chocarse con una puerta. A Helena le horrorizó que su poder se manifestara tan pronto, pero Lila la tranquilizó diciéndole que su resonancia había empezado a manifestarse de manera intermitente más o menos a su misma edad.

Enid ya había aprendido a leer cuando les llegó la noticia de que Paladia por fin se había rendido. Los aliados habían entrado en la ciudad y se habían encargado de los necrómatas que quedaban, tan delgados y desnutridos que apenas opusieron resistencia. Oyeron rumores acerca de las condiciones en que lo habían encontrado todo. Los civiles estaban tan desmejorados que los soldados los confundieron con necrómatas cuando los rodearon para pedirles comida.

Según se decía, la campaña fue todo un éxito, puesto que los ejércitos aliados casi no habían sufrido bajas. El Frente de Liberación recibió un sinfín de alabanzas por haber derrocado a la tiranía de los inmarcesibles, pero leer aquellas noticias hizo que a Helena se le revolviera el estómago. Se sentía tan traicionada que le resultaba abrumador. La situación habría sido muy distinta si la comunidad internacional hubiera decidido preocuparse por la situación de Paladia antes, aunque le hubieran dedicado una décima parte de la atención que finalmente le brindaron. Pero Hevgoss y Novis habían estado más centrados en decidir quién se quedaría con Paladia cuando la guerra terminara que en ayudar. Todos los países vecinos se habían tomado su tiempo, a la espera de que la situación se volviera intolerable y tuvieran la oportunidad perfecta de conseguir una victoria fácil pero heroica.

Las terribles historias que se contaban en los periódicos, con todo lujo de detalles escabrosos, solo servían para destacar el mérito del rescate de los paladinos, no para criticar la permisividad que los países aliados habían demostrado antes de actuar.

Morrough no se encontraba ni entre los muertos ni entre los prisioneros, pues se las había arreglado para permanecer con vida en el sistema de cuevas que se extendía bajo la Academia. Tras varios intentos fallidos de llegar hasta él, el Frente de Liberación decidió dejarlo allí con la esperanza de que muriera por sí solo.

Una vez superado el capítulo de la «Liberación», los aliados pasaron a centrarse en asuntos mucho más urgentes, como hacer que Paladia volviera a ser económicamente productiva; debatir cómo debería ser en el futuro, y decidir si podía conservar su estatus de nación independiente o se convertiría en un territorio compartido entre Hevgoss y Novis.

Se esperaba que pronto comenzaran a celebrarse los primeros juicios. La comunidad internacional negó tener conocimiento alguno sobre los trabajos forzosos que se habían llevado a cabo en el Reducto ni sobre el lumitio, tan vital para la industria, que los necrómatas habían extraído en los últimos años. Sin embargo, no pudieron fingir que desconocían el programa de repoblación, así que insistieron en que, hasta donde ellos sabían, la participación había sido voluntaria.

Entre el asedio y la toma de la ciudad, Stroud desapareció.

Cuando empezaron a liberar a las mujeres encerradas en la Torre, comenzaron a surgir historias sobre el programa, sobre los abusos y las torturas que Stroud había permitido, así como sobre los niños sometidos a todo tipo de experimentos para estudiar el desarrollo de la resonancia durante la infancia. Sin embargo, los periódicos consideraron aquellas historias demasiado terroríficas como para publicarlas. El foco de atención se puso, en su mayoría, en los trabajos forzosos del Reducto, en las minas y en el hambre que había padecido la población civil.

Se hizo bastante presión para que el asunto del programa de repoblación se solucionara discretamente y se instó a las prisioneras a que pasaran página con la excusa de ahorrarles el mal trago de revivir su trauma ante los tribunales. Además, nadie esperaba que un puñado de madres solteras e histéricas ofrecieran testimonios fiables. Que se hubieran cometido semejantes atrocidades era una mancha para la identidad norteña, así que se trató la reproducción selectiva como si fuera un retorcido invento del régimen de los inmarcesibles y no una práctica asentada desde tiempo atrás en la tradición gremial.

No, a las madres se las acomodaría en conventos y a los niños en orfanatos, donde crecerían para convertirse en miembros productivos de la sociedad. Y así todo quedaría olvidado.

Kaine fue el único a quien no pareció sorprenderle cómo se desarrollaron los acontecimientos. A Helena le afectó tanto que pasó varios días en cama y Lila empezó a desaparecer y a dejar a Pol con Helena y Enid durante largos periodos de tiempo.

Una noche, después de acostar a los niños, Lila bajó a la cocina, donde Helena estaba trabajando en un proyecto de quimiatría con el que esperaba regular su ritmo cardiaco.

—Necesito hablar contigo —le dijo.

Estaba pálida como un fantasma. Desde el fin de la latencia, había pasado unos días muy callada, más retraída de lo normal. Se sentó y contempló el fuego durante un largo rato.

—Tengo que volver —añadió al final.

Helena siempre había sabido que ese día llegaría, pero el corazón le dio un vuelco igualmente. Lila no estaba hecha para una vida tranquila y no podría ser feliz en aquella isla. Si se había quedado allí tanto tiempo había sido por Pol y por Helena. Desde que habían leído aquel boletín en el barco, Helena supo que Lila lo habría dejado todo para unirse al Frente de Liberación sin pensárselo dos veces de no haber tenido que ocuparse de su hijo.

—He estado dándole vueltas durante un tiempo. No voy a permitir que hagan esto. Están llevando a cabo un borrado masivo de lo ocurrido, de todos nosotros. Van a ocultarlo porque lo único que les importa es reactivar la industria. Son como una bandada de buitres que por fin han encontrado la oportunidad de devorarlo todo, después de años viéndonos morir.

Helena suspiró.

—¿Y de qué te va a servir volver?

—Voy a matar a Morrough. Entraré ahí y acabaré con él. Después me aseguraré de que nadie se olvide de la Resistencia. —Lila tragó saliva varias veces y la cicatriz que le surcaba el rostro le retorció las facciones—. Por eso necesito que cuides a Pol por mí. Necesito aprender a luchar utilizando la vivemancia y reunir todas las armas de obsidiana que nos queden. Y también que me enseñes a construir una bomba.

—Morrough podría morir en menos de un año.

—Lo sé, pero no pienso esperar tanto. Voy a ir a por él este mismo invierno, cuando Lumitia entre en fase de latencia.

—Pero el viaje sería peligrosísimo —replicó Helena abruptamente.

—¡Tengo que ir! —exclamó Lila levantando la voz—. Mataron a mi familia, a Luc, a… a todo el mundo. No puedo contarle a Pol lo valiente y maravilloso que fue su padre sabiendo que la persona que lo asesinó sigue ahí fuera. A nadie le importa que Luc luchara y sufriera lo indecible intentando salvarnos —dijo gesticulando furiosa—, y todo porque no ganó la guerra. El mundo se olvidará de él si no regreso.

—Podrías morir y entonces dejarías huérfano a Pol.

Lila mantuvo la mirada clavada en el fuego, con una expresión tan intensa, tan llena de anhelo, que parecía estar dispuesta a meter la mano entre las llamas si eso le permitiese tocar a Luc de nuevo.

—Juré dar mi vida por proteger a Luc, pero él está muerto mientras que yo sigo aquí. He intentado vivir con ello por Pol, pero no puedo seguir así. Ya no.

***

Helena recopiló a regañadientes sus averiguaciones sobre la fabricación de bombas. La técnica que había utilizado para hacer estallar el laboratorio del puerto Oeste era la que más potencial tenía, sobre todo si eran capaces de encontrar las salidas de aire que mantenían las cuevas ventiladas.

Había pasado años pensando en aquel diseño y, aunque había tenido que trabajar contra reloj, improvisando y recurriendo a los materiales que tenía a mano, con tiempo y recursos, podría lograr una que fuera mucho más efectiva.

Mientras tanto, Kaine enseñó a Lila a manejarse en la vivemancia de combate. Para sorpresa de nadie, Lila había estado entrenando en secreto. Desde un punto de vista objetivo, ella era mucho mejor combatiente, pero Kaine no seguía ninguna regla. Pasaba de la vivemancia a la alquimia de combate y al combate sucio constantemente, de manera que, en cuanto Lila empezaba a sacarle ventaja, la pelea daba un giro de ciento ochenta grados. Fue un maestro implacable y demostró una rigurosidad y una impaciencia que pusieron de manifiesto lo blando que había sido con Helena. Con Lila no tuvo la misma consideración y la obligó a curtirse a base de golpes.

Helena no había sido consciente de todo el tiempo y la dedicación que Kaine había invertido en pensar cómo matar a Morrough, en idear una estrategia. Era como si hubiera pasado los años que llevaban en la isla esperando a que Lila sacara el tema. Y a lo mejor así había sido.

Aunque, de haber estado en condiciones de hacerlo, Helena no dudaba de que él mismo habría querido regresar a Paladia para matar al Sumo Nigromante. No había llegado a recuperarse del todo de las torturas que sufrió y, cuando se estresaba, le temblaban las manos incluso más que a Helena.

—Deberías ponerle nombre —dijo Lila cuando Helena por fin le entregó los diseños de la bomba—. Aunque la gente piense que estás muerta, tu trabajo debería recibir el reconocimiento que merece. Luc solía decir que acabarías eclipsándonos a todos.

Helena negó con la cabeza.

—No quiero que se pregunten qué fue de mí o que se pongan a investigar sobre mi vida. No merece la pena correr ese riesgo. Tú di que te llevaste el diseño contigo al escapar y que no sabes quién es el autor o la autora.

Pol fue asimilando poco a poco que su madre se iba a marchar. Para entonces ya tenía cinco años y su cumpleaños estaba muy cerca del de Enid. Como regalo anticipado, Lila y Pol viajaron a una de las islas más grandes y regresaron con un perro pastor blanco y patilargo al que llamaron Cobalto, igual que el caballo de su padre.

—Te hará compañía y te protegerá hasta que yo vuelva —dijo Lila.

Había dejado que el tinte fuera desapareciendo con los lavados para que su pelo recuperara su rubio natural. Lo llevaba recogido en una trenza que se había asegurado con horquillas alrededor de la cabeza, porque así era como quería que Pol la recordara.

—No podré enviarte cartas, pero te mandaré algún mensaje de vez en cuando, ¿vale? Cuando veas a Lumitia en el cielo, será porque me estoy acordando de ti. Y, siempre que el sol brille, sabrás que tu padre está velando por ti mientras yo no esté aquí. —Lila tenía los ojos brillantes por las lágrimas—. Tú cuida de Enid, ¿vale? Es tu mejor amiga y tenéis que estar ahí el uno para el otro. Porque eso es lo que hacen los amigos.

———————

El Sumo Nigromante, Morrough, el hombre que una vez fue conocido como Cetus, el alquimista del Norte, murió un día de primavera.

Según los periódicos, un equipo de élite conformado por fuerzas militares de Novis y Hevgoss, acompañado por Lila Bayard, paladina de Luc Holdfast y último miembro vivo de la Orden de la Llama Eterna, consiguió acceder al bastión subterráneo donde se escondía y utilizó una misteriosa bomba piromántica en su primer ataque.

La explosión había provocado el derrumbe de la afamada Torre de Alquimia y el equipo tuvo que abrirse camino laboriosamente entre los escombros para infiltrarse en los pasadizos subterráneos mientras se veían asolados por un ejército de necrómatas.

Muchos murieron durante el ataque. La propia Lila Bayard había estado a punto de perder la vida. El general que había dirigido el ataque ordenó que todo el mundo retrocediera, pero ella se había negado a obedecer y había entrado sola.

Los periódicos de todo el continente habían publicado una fotografía de Lila Bayard saliendo de entre los cascotes de la Torre de Alquimia, sin casco, con el rostro sucio y la armadura manchada de sangre. La terrible cicatriz que le surcaba el rostro acaparaba todas las miradas y enmarcaba una gélida mirada de triunfo mientras arrastraba los restos mutados del cadáver descompuesto de Morrough tras de sí.

Nadie se atrevió a dudar del heroísmo de Lila Bayard, pues había logrado lo que una decena de países habían sido incapaces de hacer.

Contar con un miembro vivo de la Llama Eterna que había hecho lo imposible dificultaba a las naciones aliadas considerar a Paladia como una nación fallida y necesitada de control externo. A Lila le ofrecieron todo tipo de cargos ceremoniales, pero ella los rechazó. No había regresado para gobernar, sino para asegurarse de que las vidas que habían perdido fueran recordadas. Quería que se le hiciera frente a la guerra para que una tragedia como aquella no volviera a repetirse jamás.

En ausencia de Lila, Pol y Enid se volvieron todavía más inseparables, hasta tal punto que Helena y Kaine empezaron a preocuparse.

—No va a poder soportarlo —dijo Helena mientras los dos niños corrían de una poza a otra junto a la orilla del mar—. Se parecen demasiado a nosotros. No sé si prepararla para su partida será mejor o peor para ella.

Kaine asintió mientras los niños molestaban a un cangrejo, que empezó a corretear de lado tras ellos. Enid y Pol huyeron entre tropiezos aullando de risa e intentaban tirar el uno del otro para escapar de las pinzas del animal, mientras Cobalto ladraba desenfrenadamente.

Les habían llegado noticias de que Lila iba a liderar la reconstrucción de la Academia de Alquimia para que esta volviera a abrir sus puertas. Se erigiría una nueva Torre y un nuevo edificio, pero sus esfuerzos y su limitado número de admisiones no girarían en torno a la alquimia norteña. Se habían perdido siglos de conocimiento durante la guerra y el continente necesitaba desesperadamente más alquimistas, tantos como pudieran formar. Presentarse a la certificación ya no sería un privilegio exclusivo de los alumnos de la Academia, sino que la organización quedaría en manos de organismos externos y cualquiera que hubiera superado las pruebas de nivel resonántico podría acceder a ella.

La Academia volvería a su propósito original: explorar los horizontes de la alquimia y descubrir nuevos avances.

Tras mucho debate, y a petición de Lila, se incluyó la vivemancia como un campo de estudio más. El poder de los sanadores había sido esencial para la Llama Eterna durante la guerra. Y, mientras que se había criticado y desperdiciado el potencial que albergaba su resonancia por culpa de la superstición durante años, la suya no debería ser una habilidad exclusiva de quienes estuvieran dispuestos a abusar de ella. El tratamiento discriminatorio hacia los vivemantes en Paladia les había dado la oportunidad a los inmarcesibles de reclutar a más gente sin esfuerzo. La nación tenía que evolucionar.

Tras un año y medio fuera, Lila regresó, si bien no para quedarse. Se iba a llevar a Pol a casa.

Helena había intentado hacer que cambiara de opinión, pero Lila se mantuvo firme. El hijo de Luc tenía que regresar a Paladia para ver lo que su familia había construido. El único consuelo de Helena era que Pol jamás ostentaría el papel de principado.

El mundo entero había visto a Lucien Holdfast arrastrarse ante Morrough y suplicarle que lo hiciera inmortal antes de ser ejecutado. Incluso aunque algunos defendían que lo habían obligado a hacerlo con la promesa de mostrarle clemencia al resto de la Llama Eterna, el mito que rodeaba a los Holdfast y la idea de una divinidad heredada habían pasado a la historia.

Pol regresaría a Paladia como un Holdfast, y su madre y él reconstruirían lo que siempre había sido más importante para su familia: la Academia de Alquimia.

—Vuelve conmigo, Helena —le dijo Lila a solas cuando Kaine se llevó a los niños a caminar junto a los acantilados—. Podrías encargarte del departamento de vivemancia. Piensa en lo que podrías conseguir: formalizarías las bases de un nuevo campo de estudio para la alquimia. Serías la persona idónea para ello.

—¿Y cómo lo hacemos? —preguntó ella. Era evidente que hasta ese momento Lila no se había parado a pensar en las intrigas políticas y la presión que acarrearían sus decisiones—. ¿Dejo a Enid aquí o me la llevo conmigo para tratar de limpiar el nombre de Kaine?

Lila apartó la mirada y contempló el mar.

—No vas a poder limpiárselo. Es imposible. Sé que tú lo consideras un héroe trágico, atado de pies y manos, pero ha hecho cosas horribles. La gente habla de Morrough y hacen chistes con él, pero ¿sabes de quién no se atreven nunca a bromear? Del Sumo Inquisidor. Se ponen enfermos con solo mencionarlo. Su sello y su firma aparecen en todas partes. Su participación ha sido total. No existe ni una sola actividad del régimen que Kaine no haya supervisado.

A Helena se le formó un nudo en la garganta.

—Bueno, eso es lo que tiene ser un espía cuyo objetivo es desestabilizar el sistema. Tienes que estar al tanto de todo. ¿Cómo si no habría hecho su trabajo?

Lila dejó caer los hombros. Helena entendía por qué no quería que la vieran como la única superviviente, como una heroína solitaria. En Paladia siempre estaba rodeada por una bandada de buitres a la espera de que cometiera un error, dispuestos a despedazarla, igual que le había ocurrido cuando era paladina.

Aunque sabía que Pol estaba a punto de caer también en sus garras, Lila no quería dejar atrás a su familia, pero tampoco podía ignorar su país ni su legado. Nunca había sido una de esas personas que se rinden sin luchar.

—No voy a dejar a Kaine atrás —dijo Helena tras una pausa—. Yo jamás habría sobrevivido a la guerra sin él. Siempre le fui leal a Luc y sé que quieres que Paladia lo recuerde, pero ese país tiene tanta culpa de su muerte como Morrough. No puedo volver.

Lila asintió y se dispuso a marcharse, pero se detuvo.

—Sé que te prometí que no diría nada más, pero tengo que decirte esto antes de dejarte aquí. —Lila tragó saliva y la cicatriz de su rostro se volvió más prominente, como siempre le pasaba cuando se alteraba—. Eres todo lo que me queda aparte de Pol. Sé que quieres a Kaine y que él te quiere a ti, no voy a negarlo. Pero creo que no eres consciente de lo inhumanamente frío que es con cualquiera que no seáis Enid o tú. El resto del mundo podría irse al garete y a él le daría igual. Ni siquiera se daría cuenta. ¿De verdad es eso lo que quieres?

—Ya sé cómo es —le dijo con brusquedad—. Tanto tú como yo seguimos vivas justo por eso. —Un destello de frustración surcó el rostro de Lila, que se dispuso a abrir la boca para protestar—. ¿Qué pensaste al matar a Morrough?

La chica la cerró de golpe y desvió la mirada con una creciente expresión de angustia.

—En Luc. Estaba pensando en todo lo que le hizo a Luc.

Helena se miró la mano izquierda. La capa de distorsión bajo la que había ocultado el anillo se había desgastado con el tiempo, pero ahora la muñequera que llevaba lo escondía casi por completo.

—El amor no es algo tan puro ni tan bonito como a la gente le gusta pensar. A veces es algo retorcido. Kaine y yo nos complementamos. Yo lo convertí en quien es sabiendo lo que el sello le haría si lo salvaba. Si él es un monstruo, yo soy su creadora.

CUANDO ENID DESCUBRIÓ QUE LILA se iba a llevar a Pol, al principio no lo entendió, pero pronto se puso fuera de sí.

—¡No! ¡No puedes llevártelo! Pol es mío. Es mi mejor amigo. ¡No me lo puedes quitar!

En vez de dejar que Kaine o Helena trataran de consolarla, se aferró a Pol y se negó a dejarlo ir. El niño estaba evidentemente dividido, pero no soltó la mano de su madre ni por un segundo.

—Que venga con nosotros —dijo mirando a Helena con rostro serio—. Yo cuidaré de ella.

A Helena se le cerró la garganta.

—No. No, Enid tiene que quedarse aquí hasta que sea mayor —dijo intentando soltar a Enid de su amigo.

—Pero yo quiero irme con ellos —sollozó la niña al tiempo que Helena la obligaba a soltar los pantalones de Pol—. Quiero vivir en Paladia también. ¿Por qué no nos vamos todos allí?

—Lo siento, pero no podemos —se disculpó Helena, que agarró con fuerza a Enid cuando esta trató de tirarse al suelo y arrastrarse hasta Pol—. No es seguro. Por eso vivimos en esta isla, ¿te acuerdas? Porque a mamá se le acelera demasiado el corazón si viajamos demasiado. Mamá no puede ir a sitios donde el corazón le lata más deprisa de la cuenta.

—Pero Pol es mi mejor amigo. Me quedaré sola si se va.

Kaine se volvió hacia la puerta con un ataque de espasmos en las manos y se metió en la habitación de al lado un momento.

Pol soltó la mano de Lila y se acercó a Enid.

—Tienes que quedarte con tus padres, E —le dijo con voz vacilante—. Todavía no puedes venir a Paladia.

—¿Y por qué no? Tú te vas a ir.

—Ya —coincidió el niño despacio, mirándola con los ojos azules muy abiertos y pensativos. Entonces se le retorció el rostro de pena—, pero tienes que cuidar de Cobalto. La ciudad no es un buen sitio para un perro. Además, nunca hace caso cuando lo llamamos, así que podría atropellarlo algún camión.

Enid levantó la cabeza.

—¿En serio? —preguntó con voz trémula.

—Sí, y los barcos también son peligrosos, así que tendrás que cuidar bien de él por mí. Necesita salir a pasear todos los días.

Enid asintió mostrando una ferviente comprensión ante lo importante que era la tarea que le estaba asignando. Pol le pasó su correa.

Cuando Lila y Pol partieron, Enid se sentó al borde del acantilado y lloró agarrada a Cobalto.

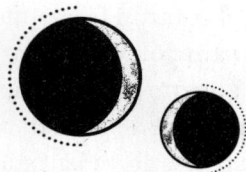

CAPÍTULO 78

Cuatro años más tarde

—Mamá.

Helena levantó la vista de la tintura que estaba preparando, uno de los remedios más demandados en el pueblo. Enid estaba sentada en la cocina viéndola trabajar.

Desde que Pol se había marchado, la niña había perdido buena parte de su carácter juguetón. Kaine y Helena habían intentado devolverle su alegría y encontrarle niños de los que pudiera hacerse amiga, pero Enid siempre se había mostrado reticente a socializar.

Había demasiados obstáculos: no podía hablar de la alquimia, tampoco mencionar el verdadero nombre de Kaine o de Helena, ni revelar adónde se habían ido Pol y Lila. Todas aquellas reglas y barreras la ponían de los nervios y, en consecuencia, había preferido quedarse en casa y salir solo para acompañar a sus padres o sacar a Cobalto a pasear cada día.

En las noches más oscuras, Kaine también aprovechaba para llevarla a dar una vuelta a lomos de Amaris. A veces volaban a otras islas juntos, pero Enid nunca había mostrado interés en hacer amigos, sin importar cuál fuera el destino de su viaje.

Lo único que le daba color a su vida eran las dos semanas que su familia y ella pasaban cada verano en la ciudad portuaria del continente norteño, donde visitaban a Lila y a Pol.

—¿Por qué tienes esos agujeros en las muñecas? —le preguntó—. No he visto a nadie más que los tenga.

A Helena se le encogió el corazón al bajar la mirada. Solía procurar llevarlos cubiertos, pero había estado tan centrada en el trabajo que se había arremangado sin darse cuenta. En cualquier caso, haber conseguido ocultarlos durante ocho años a una niña curiosa había sido todo un logro.

—No, no hay mucha gente que los tenga —murmuró—. Durante la guerra, algunos creyeron que podrían ganar si el bando contrario se quedaba sin resonancia, así que intentaron buscar maneras de anularla. Y… estos agujeros fueron una de esas ideas.

—¿Hicieron que te quedaras sin resonancia? —preguntó la niña acercándose para mirarlos de cerca.

Helena presionó los labios y asintió.

—Así es.

—Pero ya te ha vuelto, ¿no?

—Tu padre me la devolvió —dijo con un asentimiento—. Fue hace mucho tiempo, pero algunas cicatrices nunca curan. Son raras, ¿verdad?

Enid le tocó una con curiosidad.

—¿Te capturaron durante la guerra?

A Helena se le formó un nudo en la garganta. Dio un paso hacia atrás, sacó una pastilla del armario y se la tragó rápidamente con un vaso de agua. Siempre había sabido que tarde o temprano acabarían teniendo aquella conversación. Enid se estaba haciendo mayor y ya no podían evitar sus preguntas, sobre todo porque estaba desesperada por viajar a Paladia y estudiar alquimia como Pol, que acababa de empezar su primer año en la Academia.

—Sí —admitió al final—. Me atraparon durante un tiempo y no fue nada agradable. Por eso decidí huir y tenerte a ti, que era algo mucho más divertido. —Cuando Helena vio a Kaine entrar en la estancia, se puso tensa—. E, ¿te importaría acercarte al pueblo y traer algo de queso para la cena? Se nos ha acabado.

Enid se levantó de un salto y su pelo rizado voló en todas direcciones antes de desaparecer por la puerta.

—¿Qué pasa? —preguntó Kaine en cuanto la niña se hubo marchado.

—Enid se acaba de fijar en las cicatrices de los grilletes —explicó ella sin atreverse a mirarlo a los ojos.

—¿Y qué le has dicho?

Helena inspiró hondo.

—Solo lo que he considerado que estaba preparada para saber. No le he mentido.

Kaine se limitó a arquear una ceja. Helena apretó los dientes, se acercó a una de las estanterías y sacó un periódico.

—Hoy ha llegado una caja llena. Encontré esto mientras les echaba un ojo.

Levantó el papel. «Una criminal de guerra aparece ahogada en Hevgoss».

A Kaine se le iluminó la mirada.

—Era Stroud —apuntó Helena bajando la cabeza para estudiar el artículo—. La han encontrado en un lago. Dicen que sufrió un ataque al corazón mientras nadaba. Están investigando al gobierno de Hevgoss, porque, según parece, le dieron asilo e inmunidad a cambio de que investigara para ellos. Lo cual es irónico teniendo en cuenta que declararon culpables a todos los guardias que pasaron por los juicios que presidieron. Decidieron perdonar en secreto a la peor persona de todas.

Se hizo un breve silencio.

—Es una pena que no fuera asesinada —dijo finalmente Kaine.

—Todo apunta a que lo fue —siseó Helena. Él la miró impasible—. Para. Ni se te ocurra mentirme.

Kaine dejó escapar un suave suspiro y, cuando levantó la vista, la frialdad volvió a instalarse en su rostro como un témpano de hielo. El Kaine que era todo amabilidad, sonrisas y largos monólogos, la versión de sí mismo que mostraba en la isla cuando Enid estaba presente, desapareció y quedó reemplazada una vez más por su verdadero yo, frío y afilado como una hoja de acero.

—¿Por qué lo has hecho? —preguntó Helena, que tenía la sensación de estar desgarrándose por dentro—. ¿No has tenido ya suficiente? ¿Por qué has corrido un riesgo así? ¿Te paraste a pensar en algún momento en lo que habría ocurrido si te hubieran…?

—Tuve cuidado —la interrumpió él, aunque no para justificar sus acciones—. ¿De verdad creías que iba a dejar que viviera?

Helena intentó tragar saliva. Había pasado todo el día tratando de mantener su ritmo cardiaco bajo control, pero aquello había sido la gota que colmó el vaso.

—Me has mentido. Lo hiciste cuando fuimos a la zona portuaria, ¿verdad? Cuando dijiste que tenías que encargarte de un asunto económico. Ahora, cada vez que vayas a… a cualquier lado, me pasaré las horas preguntándome dónde estarás de verdad. Y temiendo que no regreses a mi lado…

Se le rompió la voz.

Kaine trató de abrazarla, pero ella se alejó de él y se llevó una mano al pecho para regular el ritmo de sus latidos y así seguir hablando y demostrarle su enfado. Porque estaba muy muy enfadada con él.

—¿Es que acaso no soy suficiente para ti? ¿Tan insatisfecho estás con esta vida que prefieres correr el riesgo de morir con tal de vengarte? —Le ardían los ojos—. Dentro de unos años tendremos que contarle a Enid quién eres. Pronto empezará el colegio y, aunque sea aquí en Etras, cuando le hablen de la guerra mencionarán tu nombre. Ambos sabemos dónde va a acabar y allí ya no habrá manera de ocultarle nada. Cuando se entere, su mundo se pondrá patas arriba…, incluso si eres tú quien se lo cuenta primero.

Kaine apretó los dientes.

—No…

—Nadie puede tener todo lo que quiere en esta vida, ¿recuerdas? Me lo dijiste tú. Me dijiste que llegaría un momento en que comprendería que no iba a poder tenerlo todo, que tendría que elegir y conformarme. Pensaba que habíamos elegido esto. ¿Me vas a decir ahora que me he estado mintiendo a mí misma durante todos estos años?

Los pulmones se le contrajeron violentamente y un terrible silbido le trepó por la garganta.

—Merecía morir después de lo que te hizo —dijo él, que se negaba a ceder y no mostraba remordimiento alguno—. No iba a permitir que escapara después de averiguar dónde se escondía.

—No deberías haberla buscado. Tendrías que haberlo dejado estar. —Helena habló negando con la cabeza, pero, tras fulminarlo con la mirada un segundo más, acabó echándose a llorar—. No sabes lo que me alegro de que esté muerta.

Kaine dio dos rápidas zancadas y la atrajo hacia sí antes de que Helena tuviera oportunidad de apartarse, así que ella cerró los puños en torno a su camisa y se aferró a él.

—Espero que la hicieras sufrir, aunque habría preferido que no te hubieras encargado tú de ella. ¿Por qué siempre tienes que encargarte tú de estas cosas? —Enterró el rostro en su pecho—. La odiaba. La odiaba con toda mi alma. Me alegro de que esté muerta.

—Lo sé —dijo él rodeándola con los brazos—. Pero ya no está. No queda nadie que pueda hacerte daño.

Permanecieron con las manos entrelazadas mientras las últimas volutas de humo del barco se desvanecían.

—Ya solo quedamos nosotros —dijo Helena con aire pensativo.

Kaine permaneció en silencio, con los ojos plateados clavados en el mar, como si todavía pudiera distinguir la silueta del barco tras la curva del horizonte.

Helena le estrechó la mano.

—Sabes por qué se marcha, ¿verdad?

—Sí… —dijo él con un estremecimiento.

La joven apoyó la cabeza contra su hombro.

—Supongo que era inevitable. En esta familia no estamos hechos para dejar pasar las cosas.

—Yo al menos he tenido mis momentos —resopló divertido—. Pero tú…

Ella se rio y alzó la vista. Todavía le sorprendía lo mucho que echaba de menos el blanco plateado de los cabellos del Kaine joven. Seguía tiñéndose para pasar desapercibido, pero en un par de años podría dejar de hacerlo. Por suerte, sus ojos eran los mismos de siempre. Por mucho tiempo que pasara mirándolos, Helena siempre encontraba nuevos detalles en la forma en que el color cambiaba, en los destellos de emoción que los surcaban de vez en cuando.

Kaine le devolvió la mirada y el mundo se desvaneció a su alrededor.

A Helena le dio un vuelco el corazón.

—¿Y ahora qué hacemos?

—Cualquier cosa. —Kaine curvó una comisura de sus labios para esbozar esa sonrisa que se reservaba siempre para ella—. Lo que tú quieras.

EPÍLOGO

Julius 1808

EL FERRY QUE SURCABA LAS aguas del sinuoso río dobló el último meandro y Paladia apareció ante los ojos de los pasajeros. Aquellos que nunca habían visto la famosa ciudad ahogaron una sonora exclamación.

Resplandecía como una corona gigantesca, colocada en el río y enmarcada por unas imponentes montañas.

En la proa, una joven de grandes ojos plateados contemplaba la ciudad, incapaz de apartar la mirada incluso cuando el barco atracó y los demás pasajeros comenzaron a desembarcar.

Se detuvo en lo alto de la pasarela mientras buscaba un rostro conocido entre la multitud que se había reunido en el muelle.

—¡Enid! —la llamó alguien.

Varias personas se volvieron para mirar a Lila Bayard, la antigua paladina, que corría en dirección al barco, seguida de su hijo Apollo y varios guardias.

Lila llegó hasta ella la primera y la estrechó en un abrazo antes de retroceder.

—¡Mírate! Ha pasado tanto tiempo que temía no reconocerte —bajó la voz—, pero eres la viva imagen de tu madre.

Enid sonrió.

—Lo sé —dijo con un suave acento etrasiano—. Padre siempre me lo dice.

Lila negó con la cabeza.

—No me puedo creer que por fin te hayan dejado venir. Pensaba que te harían seguir estudiando en Khem, pero me alegro mucho de que vayamos a tenerte en el programa.

Enid le ofreció una sonrisa astuta.

—Bueno, sabían que siempre había querido estudiar en la Academia. La formación que se imparte en Khem es muy distinta... y se centra sobre todo en la metalurgia.

Lila echó una mano hacia atrás y tiró de Pol, que se había quedado atrás con timidez, para que se uniera a la conversación. Enid y él cruzaron miradas un brevísimo instante.

—Bueno, ojalá te hubieran permitido venir antes —suspiró Lila—. Tus habilidades nos habrían sido de gran ayuda. Por desgracia, Pol ha heredado los pésimos hábitos de estudio de sus padres y ha tenido que examinarse dos veces de Piromancia.

Pol se puso colorado.

—Pero solo la parte escrita. Además, aprobé la certificación hace años —masculló.

—Serás el director de la Academia algún día. ¿Cómo te van a tomar en serio con un expediente así? Es una suerte que ahora contemos con Enid. Ella nos dará la legitimidad académica que nos falta. —Lila miró a uno de los guardias—. Trasladad su equipaje a Solis Splendor. Tomaremos la ruta panorámica antes de volver a la Academia.

Un coche los llevó por las sinuosas calles que ascendían desde la zona portuaria hasta los niveles superiores de la ciudad, en dirección al norte, y se detuvo en una plaza amplia, abierta al cielo. Allí había una estatua rodeada de unas altas columnas.

Lila vaciló antes de abrir la puerta.

—Deberías ver esto —le dijo saliendo del coche—. La terminaron hace solo unas semanas.

En la plaza había un reducido grupo de personas, aunque la mayoría de la gente se apartó de su camino al ver que Lila se dirigía hacia el centro del área.

La estatua representaba a un soldado de la Resistencia, vestido con una armadura de combate y su correspondiente arnés de escalada. A sus pies, podía leerse: EN RECUERDO DE LOS CAÍDOS.

Las columnas estaban hechas de mármol liso y estaban llenas de nombres: Apollo Holdfast, Lucien Holdfast, Soren Bayard, Sebastian Bayard, Eddard Althorne, Jan Crowther, Titus Bayard... La lista era interminable.

Lila miró a su alrededor.

—Aquí fue donde estalló la bomba de anulitio. Ha sido uno de los últimos lugares en reconstruirse, porque proteger a los trabajadores de la contaminación era una tarea complicada. Yo quería que se erigiera un monumento conmemorativo en recuerdo de las personas que murieron en la guerra y decidieron colocarlo aquí. Creo que me gusta, pero… siento que nada me parecerá del todo suficiente. ¿Qué opinas tú?

Enid se encogió de hombros, pero recorrió las columnas rápidamente con una aguda mirada.

—Nunca había visto un monumento conmemorativo de la guerra. No sé qué debo sentir exactamente al verlo.

—Yo tampoco lo sé —admitió Lila tomando aire—. Tenía la esperanza de que fuera…

Antes de que Lila pudiera terminar de hablar, una mujer agarró a Enid del brazo y tiró de ella.

—¿Helena?

Enid se volvió, sorprendida, para mirar a la desconocida, que tenía el rostro surcado de marcas y una pequeña cicatriz en la muñeca. La mujer retrocedió apartando la mano.

—No. No, qué tontería. Lo siento. Pensaba que te conocía.

Lila se giró. Le temblaron los labios antes de hablar:

—Penny, esta es Enid Romano. Ha venido a participar en el programa de vivemancia. Pol y yo le estamos enseñando la ciudad.

Penny contempló a Enid durante un instante y frunció el ceño.

—Vaya —dijo con voz entrecortada—. Lo siento, seguro que te he dado un buen susto al agarrarte así. De espaldas eres idéntica a alguien a quien conocí hace tiempo. ¿No se parece muchísimo a Helena, Lila?

Enid mantuvo una expresión neutra, pero le lanzó una mirada inquisitiva a Lila, que entrecerró los ojos como si intentara entender a qué se refería la otra mujer.

—Creo que es por el pelo. —Lila miró a Enid—. Helena Marino formó parte de la Resistencia, pero murió antes de la Liberación.

—Mi más sentido pésame —le dijo la chica a Penny.

La mujer se la quedó mirando como si estuviera viendo un fantasma antes de darse la vuelta. Una segunda voz los interrumpió casi tan pronto como se hubieron quedado solos.

—Por fin te encuentro, Lila. No te he visto por aquí desde que inauguramos el monumento.

Lila esbozó una mueca antes de forzarse a sonreír mientras se giraba hacia la mujer que había hablado.

—Señora Forrester, qué sorpresa encontrarla aquí.

La mujer, de mediana edad, respiraba con dificultad.

—¿Me puedes explicar por qué corre el rumor de que los Holdfast están volviendo a traer a estudiantes extranjeros a estudiar en la Academia?

La sonrisa de Lila se desvaneció de inmediato y se enderezó para mostrar lo imponente que era su estatura.

—Enid ha sido una de las mejores estudiantes de Khem y ha presentado una propuesta de lo más prometedora sobre el uso de los sellos vivemánticos para tratar lesiones pulmonares. La Academia la ha invitado a venir para apoyar su investigación, porque varias de las dolencias asociadas al anulitio todavía no tienen una cura efectiva.

El rostro de la señora Forrester enrojeció, y luego ella tosió varias veces contra un pañuelo de tela.

—Vaya, ¿dices que está buscando un tratamiento para los pulmones? Qué interesante.

Enid dejó que Lila se encargara de aceptar la pobre disculpa de la mujer y se alejó para examinar las columnas de cerca. Intentó leer los nombres recogidos en ellas, pero había tantos y estaban tan juntos que era casi imposible hacerlo.

En apenas unos minutos, Lila y Pol habían quedado rodeados de personas. Aunque la figura del principado ya no existiera, el atractivo de los Holdfast seguía intacto. Al otro lado de la plaza había algunas tiendas, así que Enid se encaminó hacia allí echándole un último vistazo a sus acompañantes y cruzando fugazmente una mirada con Pol, que la observaba con expresión desconsolada.

Entró en una librería y lo primero que encontró fue un expositor lleno de libros gruesos.

La historia completa de la Guerra Nigromántica de Paladia, escrito por William Dover.

Enid hizo una pausa y contempló los libros durante un momento antes de coger un ejemplar.

—Acaba de salir a la venta esta semana —dijo el dependiente, que se había acercado a ella y miraba la copia que sostenía.

—Me lo he imaginado al no reconocer el título —comentó Enid, que abrió el libro para ojear el índice, pasó el dedo por el nombre de cada capítulo y se detuvo brevemente en uno.

—Bueno, este libro es una de las mejores opciones para entender Paladia y la guerra. O sea, parece que hablas bastante bien el dialecto, pero, si de verdad quieres descubrir todos los detalles de lo ocurrido…, las explicaciones que encontrarás aquí te dirán todo lo que necesitas saber.

Enid arqueó una ceja y el dependiente pareció tomárselo como una invitación para acercarse un poco más.

—Dover ha pasado más de diez años escribiéndolo. Consiguió un permiso especial de la Asamblea y el Frente de Liberación para acceder a todos los registros, incluso a las transcripciones de los juicios, que ni siquiera se habían hecho públicas. Es bastante impactante. Hay algunos capítulos que te recomiendo que te saltes si no deseas pasarlo mal. En cualquier caso, si quieres saber qué pasó, este libro te lo contará todo, absolutamente todo. El autor se ha asegurado de dejar constancia de lo que la gente necesitaba saber.

—¿Y tú lo sabes? —preguntó Enid y, al ver que el dependiente vacilaba, aclaró—: ¿Conoces todo lo que la gente necesitaría saber sobre la guerra?

El joven carraspeó.

—Bueno…, es difícil no conocerlo. Yo fui uno de los niños que nacieron en la Torre. No sé si has oído hablar de eso, pero se juzgó a bastantes personas y nos llevaron de un sitio a otro sin saber muy bien qué hacer con nosotros.

—Lo siento mucho.

Él volvió a carraspear.

—En fin, lo que quería decir es que leer ese libro… me ha ayudado a ponerlo todo en perspectiva.

Enid bajó la vista para contemplar la cubierta de nuevo.

—Tendré que echarle un ojo entonces. Yo vengo de Etras, pero incluso allí se sigue hablando de la guerra de Paladia.

Sin soltar el libro, Enid rodeó al dependiente y se dispuso a deambular por la tienda. En cuanto encontró un pasillo vacío, se apresuró a abrir el libro por el índice y deslizó el dedo por cada capítulo hasta encontrar el que buscaba.

Pasó las páginas hasta llegar a él.

Kaine Ferron, conocido como el Sumo Inquisidor, es el asesino más importante de la historia. Según las fuentes consultadas, fue el miembro más joven de los inmarcesibles al unirse a Morrough, asesinar al principado Apollo Holdfast y sumir la ciudad Estado de Paladia en una de las guerras más devastadoras de la historia a los dieciséis años. Ferron dedicó su vida a escalar entre las filas de los inmarcesibles y no solo fue uno de los nigromantes más jóvenes en «ascender», sino que también se convirtió en uno de los miembros más jóvenes en alcanzar el rango de general durante la guerra.

La destacada aptitud de Ferron como alquimista y vivemante se consideró algo antinatural y un resultado de la experimentación con humanos, una terrible práctica que acabaría pasando a definir el régimen de los inmarcesibles. Sin embargo, a diferencia de los demás sujetos de prueba de Artemon Bennet, Ferron se ofreció voluntario para que experimentaran con él.

Muchos de los inmarcesibles se retiraron tras la guerra. No obstante, el ascenso de Ferron no fue más que el principio. Encabezó las batidas de búsqueda e interrogó a todos los miembros de la Resistencia que consiguieron atrapar antes de matarlos y utilizarlos en las minas de lumitio. Fue precisamente su gusto por las masacres lo que le aseguró su puesto como Sumo Inquisidor y su eventual nombramiento como sucesor de Morrough.

Muchos creen que, si Ivy Purnell no hubiera acabado con la familia Ferron, el régimen de los inmarcesibles habría perdurado unas cuantas décadas más. El estado de salud de Morrough se había deteriorado tanto que hay quien asegura que habría acabado cediéndole el control de Paladia a Ferron antes de que hubiera terminado el año.

El académico Eustace Sederis, especializado en el campo de la nigromancia, escribió lo siguiente en su libro, *Ferron: la biografía del Sumo Inquisidor*: «Kaine Ferron ya era un monstruo mucho antes de que Morrough llegara a Paladia. Unirse a los inmarcesibles solo permitió que un psicópata nato se regalara en su crueldad y, cuando ni siquiera la inmortalidad ni la inmutabilidad lograron saciar sus impulsos sádicos, se entregó a la experimentación para alcanzar sus metas».

PRIMEROS AÑOS
Kaine Ferron fue el único hijo de…

Enid oyó un ruido a su espalda, cerró el libro de golpe y se dio la vuelta. Pol estaba al otro lado del pasillo y la miraba con una sonrisa ladeada y triunfal.

Apollo Holdfast era la combinación perfecta de sus padres. Mientras que los ojos azules, el cabello rubio y la sonrisa cálida como el sol eran típicos de los Holdfast, tenía la estructura ósea de los Bayard, lo cual había hecho que fuera incluso más alto que su madre.

—Hola.

Una sonrisa jugueteó en los labios de Enid, que arqueó una ceja y lo estudió con frialdad.

—Hola —respondió.

Pol apoyó una mano en la balda que quedaba un poco más arriba de la cabeza de Enid para inclinarse sobre ella. La chica se limitó a levantar el mentón.

—¿Ya te estás escondiendo de nosotros?

Enid perdió la sonrisa y bajó la vista al libro que sostenía.

—No. He visto que han publicado un nuevo libro sobre la guerra y he pensado en leer qué decía la parte del Sumo Inquisidor.

Pol también perdió la sonrisa.

—No hagas eso. Sabes que nunca van a contar la verdad.

—Ya —dijo ella con un asentimiento y encogiéndose de hombros—. Es que… siento que tengo que conocer qué dicen. Todos repiten lo mismo. Y sé que siempre será así, pero no puedo evitarlo. Este además incluye esa cita de Sederis. —Le ofreció otro encogimiento de hombros que casi resultó convincente—. ¿Qué te apuestas a que mamá ni siquiera aparece en el índice?

Pol le tocó la muñeca.

—Para.

Pero Enid no le hizo caso. Se dio la vuelta, apoyó el libro en el borde de una estantería, lo abrió por el índice alfabético y pasó el dedo por la página hasta detenerse.

Exhaló despacio.

—Mira…

Se movió rápidamente por el libro hasta llegar a una fotografía en el capítulo de Lucien Holdfast.

Enid y Pol se quedaron un rato observándola. En ella aparecían Soren Bayard, Helena Marino y Luc Holdfast, sentados juntos en un sillón. Luc tenía un brazo apoyado sobre los hombros de Helena y los tres miraban a la cámara.

Helena se situaba en el centro. Estaba en los huesos e iba vestida con un uniforme médico que le quedaba demasiado grande y un jersey de punto. También llevaba el pelo recogido en dos trenzas tirantes, sujetas en un espeso moño a la altura de la nuca. Sus ojos grandes y tristes traicionaban la sonrisa que se había esforzado por esbozar.

Enid contempló la imagen durante unos instantes antes de tocarla.

—Nunca había visto una foto suya de la guerra. La única que tu madre nos envió es la que aparecía en su expediente académico.

Pol no dijo nada, pero, cuando Enid fue incapaz de dejar de apartar los ojos de la página, le posó una mano vacilante sobre su hombro. Ella levantó la vista y encontró su mirada antes de ofrecerle una sonrisa triste que recordaba a la de la chica de la fotografía.

Luego, volvió a bajar la cabeza y pasó los dedos por las palabras que acompañaban a la imagen, como si quisiera borrarlas.

—Algún día…, alguien debería aclarar las cosas —murmuró.

Pol carraspeó.

—Ya sabes que mi madre se ofreció a hacerlo. Quería contar lo que ocurrió de verdad justo hasta que se produjo el incendio, pero tus padres se negaron.

Enid asintió despacio, sin despegar la vista de la fotografía.

—Lo sé. Sé que fue una decisión suya y lo entiendo. Si yo hubiera vivido todo aquello…, lo único que querría sería dejarlo atrás. Tratar de explicar algo así no tendría ningún sentido, porque nadie lo entendería. Pero… —le tembló la barbilla— mi madre no merece pasar al olvido. No debería haber quedado relegada a una simple nota a pie de página. Esta no debería ser la única parte del libro en la que aparezca. Se merece su propio capítulo. No, se merece un libro entero. —Le tembló la voz—. Y las cosas que dicen sobre papá…, como si hubiera querido hacer todo aquello, como si hubiera pedido que le hicieran… —Se frotó los ojos con el dorso de la mano y respiró hondo—. Lo siento. Siempre me creo capaz de manejar este tema, pero me enfada tanto que se me revuelve el estómago. —Parpadeó rápidamente—. En cualquier caso, me alegro de haber venido. Necesitaba ver la ciudad donde todo pasó.

»Me resulta tan duro no tener a nadie con quien hablar de esto… Mamá dice que puedo hablar con ella o con papá, pero siempre acaba teniendo que tomarse sus pastillas y presionándose los dedos contra el pecho cuando cree que no la veo. No quiero hacerle pasar por eso solo porque yo desee hablar de la guerra. Y sé que papá teme que no vuelva a dirigirle la palabra nunca más cada vez que sale el tema.

Sujetaba el libro con tanta fuerza que se le estaban poniendo los nudillos blancos, así que acabó dejándolo sobre una estantería y soltando todo el aire retenido.

—No sé qué habría hecho sin ti y sin la tía Lila. Creo que eres la única persona que me conoce de verdad.

Pol le ofreció una sonrisa que le iluminó la mirada.

—Siempre puedes contar conmigo.

Enid asintió, apretó los labios y terminó devolviéndole la sonrisa.

Se hizo una pausa y de pronto cayeron en la cuenta de que estaban solos en aquel pasillo vacío. Enid se sonrojó y a Pol se le ensombreció la mirada al inclinarse hacia delante para cerrar el espacio que los separaba.

Pero entonces oyeron la campanilla de la puerta y Pol se incorporó, retiró la mano y se la pasó por el pelo varias veces antes de carraspear.

—Mamá vendrá de un momento a otro. O los guardias. Pero, cuando lleguemos a casa…, deberíamos… hablar un poco más… —movió la cabeza— sobre… —carraspeó de nuevo—. Bueno, si quieres… hablar de… de cualquier cosa.

Enid parpadeó y asintió con un gesto afirmativo.

—¡Sí! Deberíamos. Pero mejor esperar a casa. Allí… hablaremos más tranquilos.

Asintió de nuevo y pasó junto a él para abandonar el pasillo.

Luego se apresuraron a salir de la librería, dejando atrás el libro de historia, abierto por la página de la fotografía. El pie de foto decía así:

SOLSTICIO DE INVIERNO, AÑO SOLAR 1786 PD. El principado Lucien Holdfast con su paladín, Soren Bayard (ver Bayard, Soren; capítulo 12, «El legado de una vida»), y la alquimista extranjera Helena Marino. Marino se marchó de la ciudad cuando estalló la guerra civil paladina para estudiar sanación y, aunque sobrevivió al conflicto, murió prisionera antes de la Liberación. Fue un miembro pasivo de la Orden de la Llama Eterna y no luchó en la guerra.

SOLSTICIO DE INVIERNO, AÑO SOLAR 1786 PD. El principado Lucien Holdfast con su paladín, Soren Bayard (ver Bayard, Soren; capítulo 12, «El legado de una vida»), y la alquimista extranjera Helena Marino. Marino se marchó de la ciudad cuando estalló la guerra civil paladina para estudiar sanación y, aunque sobrevivió al conflicto, murió prisionera antes de la Liberación. Fue un miembro pasivo de la Orden de la Llama Eterna y no luchó en la guerra.

Advertencia de contenido

Alchemised es una obra de fantasía oscura que contiene escenas de violencia, abuso religioso, traumas complejos, impulsos suicidas, autolesión, experimentación en humanos, tortura médica, eugenesia, canibalismo, abuso sexual, violación y alusión a la necrofilia. Por favor, recuerda que ninguno de estos temas cuenta con mi respaldo. Dado que *Alchemised* es una obra escrita en tercera persona con un punto de vista limitado, el relato presenta ciertas distorsiones, omisiones y malas interpretaciones. Algunos pasajes podrían herir la sensibilidad del lector.

Agradecimientos

Este libro es ya de por sí demasiado largo como para añadir la lista infinita de personas a las que me gustaría darles las gracias por haber estado a mi lado durante esta travesía, pero permitidme plasmar aquí mi más sincero agradecimiento a todas y cada una de las personas que, desde que descubrieron mis historias, me han transmitido su entusiasmo en cada paso de este inesperado viaje. No sabéis lo mucho que ha significado para mí que os hayáis alegrado y emocionado tanto por mí.

A Caitlin Mahony y Rikki Bergman, mis agentes. Gracias por brindarme vuestra paciencia, cariño y protección durante este torbellino de emociones y tomaros siempre la molestia de responder por mensaje de texto a las enrevesadas preguntas que debería haberos enviado por correo. Gracias a Suzy Ball por llevar las riendas de todo en el mercado británico y a Frankie Yackel por el trabajo que haces entre bambalinas.

Emily Archbold, mi querida editora, gracias por enviarme esos interminables correos electrónicos que me dieron una excusa para dejar de escribir; por tener en cuenta con tanta consideración esas ideas locas que te comentaba a última hora, y por tus pacientes comentarios y tu fe inquebrantable en mi trabajo. Gracias a Jordan Pace por lidiar con mis ataques de pánico cada vez que he tenido que promocionar mi libro en voz alta en vez de por escrito. Al maravilloso equipo de Del Rey: Scott Shannon, Keith Clayton, Tricia Narwani, Julie Leung, Alex Larned, Marcelle Iten Busto, David Moench, Ashleigh Heaton, Tori Henson, Kay Popple, Maya Fenter y Madi Margolis, gracias a todos por compartir conmigo vuestra visión, apoyo y entusiasmo en cada etapa.

Mi eterno agradecimiento a la encantadora Rebecca Hilsdon y al equipo de Michael Joseph: Stella Newing, Riana Dixon, Sriya Varadharajan, Clare Parker, Jessie Beswick, Jack Hallam, Vicky Photiou, Bronwen

Davis, Kelly Mason, Akua Akowuah, Richard Rowlands, Jessica Meredeen, Helen Eka, Dan Prescott, Jill Cole y Hayley Shepherd.

Gracias a todas las personas que han trabajado en las ediciones internacionales. Que mi historia haya sido traducida a otros idiomas es un verdadero honor.

A Jame, gracias por seguir a mi lado contra viento y marea pese a que sufro de un abuso crónico de las comas; nunca habría llegado hasta aquí sin ti. Rei, gracias por ayudarme con las búsquedas etimológicas y enfrentarte al lore enrevesado que te pasé sin darte ni una gota de contexto.

Avendell, jamás dejará de sorprenderme tu capacidad para sacarme las ideas de la cabeza y arreglártelas para convertirlas en las obras de arte más preciosas que he visto.

A mi familia, gracias por vuestro entusiasmo, apoyo y comprensión cuando me vi obligada a perderme ciertos eventos para poder llegar a la fecha de entrega. Wren, gracias por ofrecerme un sitio donde quedarme cuando tuve que pasarme las noches en vela escribiendo y por asegurarte de que comiera algo, aunque no pudiera permitirme dormir. Kimi, gracias por esperar tan pacientemente durante años a que me animara a hablarle al resto de nuestra familia de mis relatos.

Andrew, gracias por haber adoptado con tanta valentía el rol de figura parental principal sin previo aviso. Y, ante todo, gracias a T y a E por el orgullo que me profesáis y por hacerme compañía entrando silenciosamente y leyendo libros de fantasía en mi cama mientras yo escribía libros de fantasía en mi escritorio. Os quiero más que a nada en el mundo.